LION LIMB:

THE

BOY KING OF THE SOUTH SEA ISLANDS.

𝔄 𝔑𝔬𝔳𝔢𝔩.

ILLUSTRATED WITH NUMEROUS ENGRAVINGS.

LONDON:

GEORGE HOWE, RED LION COURT, FLEET STREET, E.C.

———

MDCCCLXXI.

THE BOY KING
OF THE SOUTH SEA ISLANDS.

THE MUTINY.—*See page* 16.

CHAPTER I.

THE DEATH SENTENCE—THE FATHER CONDEMNS HIS OWN SON—SCENES IN COURT.

THE Central Criminal Court was crowded almost to suffocation the day on which our strange and startling story opens.

Ladies and gentlemen of the highest title and standing were present, and had given almost fabulous sums to gain sitting, or even standing room in the court-room.

Dozens of carriages, containing the brave, beautiful, and gay in the world of fashion, were blocking the main and bye streets leading to the court.

It was almost a matter of impossibility for any one to pass or repass the precincts of the courts.

The dense mass of human beings who were crowding and squeezing in the main halls, staircases, lobbies, and waiting-rooms, were red, perspiring, and impatient to hear the news, and to ascertain the result of an all-important trial, which was then progressing within the court.

What, then, was this trial, and of whom, which had caused such a commotion in the world, and for several months previous had filled the columns of both morning and evening newspapers?

Four youths were then standing in the felon's dock, charged with the awful crime of—

Wilful Murder!

From all accounts the murder and robbery of Alderman Inglis had been wrapped in such profound mystery, that for more than two months the police were unable to trace the perpetrators of the foul deed.

At last suspicion had fallen upon four youths, who had at one time been employed in the office of the worthy alderman and shipowner.

They were brought to trial, and it was rumoured that the evidence of a certain clerk, one of their former companions, would be more than sufficient to convict them.

This, then, was the case which had attracted so much attention in all circles of society, and particularly in the fashionable world, for two of the youths accused were twin brothers, and of such remarkable beauty and similarity in feature, that scarcely any judge could tell them one from the other when apart.

But there was another reason why these twin brothers caused so much stir.

This was from the fact that, when babies in arms, they had been left in a covered basket, one cold winter's night, at the good old alderman's door, and the snow almost covered it from view.

When the children were discovered by a policeman, taken out, and cared for, it was found that they were clothed in the finest linen, on which were traces of some nobleman's coronet, which had been so defaced or worn, that it was not recognizable by the most profound of heraldists.

A note, addressed to the alderman, explained that they were the children of a noble lady, and that if he would rear and educate them, all and every expense would be paid, and he himself most handsomely rewarded.

Alderman Inglis had done as he was desired.

The twins received the names of Edgar and Allan Norman, and were sent to the Bluecoat School until the age of fourteen.

The alderman then placed them both in his extensive shipping offices, where it was hoped they would learn the routine of business, and become useful members and ornaments of society, at least until such time as their parentage was discovered,

as promised when they reached the age of twenty-one.

Edgar and Allan, however, did not like to be cooped up in close offices down a narrow court in the city; and, finding it impossible to tame their wild and roving spirits, the alderman threatened to send them to sea in one of his own ships.

Three nights after this threat the good old man was waylaid, murdered, and his private offices and chests ransacked and robbed of every farthing.

Some few trifling articles which formerly belonged to the murdered man were found on Allan and Edgar Norman.

They were accused of these dreadful crimes by a fellow clerk named Marks; and, at the moment of which we speak, these youths, with two other brothers, named Edward and James Rawlings, were then in the criminal's dock, and awaiting the decision of the jury.

The trial had occupied the whole day, and for a whole day had these four boyish-looking youths stood in that dock without flinching, and they looked as handsome, proud and independent as if that vast assembly of people had come to crown them with laurels, rather than to be witnesses to the course of law in this mysterious case.

The jury had retired to deliberate, and were then absent more than half-an-hour.

All eyes in court, save those of one man, were now turned upon the prisoners.

That one man was the judge himself.

He could not, he *dared* not, look upon Edgar or Allan Norman!

The jury at last returned, walked into their box slowly and quietly, and took their places.

For a moment there was a general buzz of excitement and expectation.

Some ladies, so overcome with the oppressive atmosphere of the court, fainted as they sat.

After a few seconds a death-like silence reigned. Not a syllable was whispered by any one.

The falling of a pin might have been heard as the clerk of the court rose, and said slowly,

"What say you, gentlemen of the jury, are the prisoners at the bar guilty or not guilty?"

The foreman of the jury raised himself up, and, with a trembling voice, replied,

"We find that Edward Rawlings and Edgar Norman are guilty of wilful murder, but neither James Rawlings nor Allan Norman."

Edgar grasped his brother firmly by the hand as he heard it, and prevented him from fainting.

James Rawlings fell in the dock as if shot.

But his brother, like Edgar Norman, stood boldly up and faced the judge unblanched, and with a firm, proud look of innocence.

Every eye was now turned towards the prisoners

Allan Norman and James Rawlings were discharged immediately, and ordered to leave the dock.

James Rawlings left, but Allan Norman refused to do so.

"If I am innocent, my lord and gentlemen of the jury," said Allan, in a firm tone, "so is my brother. If he is to suffer, let me suffer also, or, if you will, let us die together."

The gaoler obeyed the judge's nod.

Young Norman was forcibly removed from the dock, but to the last he clutched his brother's hand, and clasped him round the neck with such a tight embrace that the gaoler had to use force to remove him.

This little episode caused a great impression and commotion in the court.

This lasting affection of the two handsome and

noble youths caused briny tears to flow from the eyes of many then present.

Even the judge averted his face, and hung his head as if the display of brotherly love were too much for him.

After a few seconds, and when silence was again restored, the judge made a few remarks on the enormity of the crime for which they had been found guilty, saying that it would have been impossible for any jury to have returned a different verdict under the circumstances, and in the face of such strong testimony as that given against them by their former fellow clerk and companion, Marks.

While making these observations the judge's voice faltered so much that he was scarcely audible to those nearest to him.

His face turned deadly pale, and he cast his eyes on the ground.

He asked, in a faltering tone, the two young prisoners at the bar what they had to say, why sentence of death should not be pronounced upon them, when Edgar, in a calm voice, and with a steady look, remarked—

"That he had nought to say, but to repeat there again and again that he was innocent, yea, as innocent of the foul crimes laid to his charge as a child unborn."

His companion made some similar remark; and their handsome features, mantled as they were with looks of boyish innocence, was a matter of wonder to all present who gazed upon them with astonishment and doubt.

The jury hung their heads and sighed.

Ladies sobbed.

Lawyers, and dozens of other professional gentlemen, averted their heads.

Even policemen and gaolers, hardened as they were, felt convinced in their hearts that the two youths in the dock were innocent of the crime for which they were to suffer.

An awful pause now ensued.

The judge slowly rose and put on the black cap.

Every one felt horror-stricken at the sacrifice which the law was about to make of these two innocent boys, and, with bated breath, they listened to the judge's awful words as, with stuttering utterance, he pronounced the dreadful sentence of death upon each of them.

He had scarcely uttered the words, "To be hung by the neck until you are dead! dead! dead!" when several females screamed aloud—one, more piercing and harrowing than the rest, who was carried out to her carriage in an insensible condition.

The judge himself, scarcely able to walk from his seat into a private room adjoining, no sooner staggered through the door than he fell like a dead man upon a sofa, muttering, in an agonizing whisper,

"Oh, heavens! it is his very image. *I fear I have pronounced sentence of death on my own son—Edgar Norman!*"

CHAPTER II.

THE CONDEMNED CELL—THE YOUNG CONVICT'S DREAM.

FOR a moment after the awful sentence had been pronounced upon them, young Norman and Edward Rawlings stood in the dock as if stunned at the echoes of the judge's words.

They did not utter a syllable, but remained hand in hand, like two brothers.

The fresh color on their cheeks did not change to ashy paleness, neither did the bright and innocent lustre of their eyes desert them.

They looked around with the air and manner of noble born youths, who were doomed to become martyrs for the crimes of others.

The court, however, was all in confusion.

Loud conversation was heard on every side.

Sighs and sobs were audible on every hand.

Some gazed upon the youths with looks of astonishment, and could not believe that two boys could have passed through such an awful ordeal without a painful display of feeling.

Tears and sobs were looked for as a matter of course by the rabble.

Some expected that the youths might even have cried or wailed and raved.

But no; the expectations of all were blasted.

These two brave, lion-hearted boys smiled upon the sea of upturned faces around them, and appeared the least concerned of all there present.

"Come," said the gaoler, in a kindly tone of voice, "come, my lads, you have heard the sentence, all is over. You must return to your cells."

He led the way from the dock down a short flight of stairs, and they crossed the prison yard in silence.

First one iron door and then another was opened but quickly closed upon them again.

They walked along several cold, damp, dimly-lighted narrow galleries of stone.

Every door was bolted.

Every window was barred with iron.

When they had proceeded some distance, the gaoler stopped in a portion of the building, which was by far stronger than all the rest.

Not a sound was heard, save the awful click of massive locks, and the sliding of heavy bolts and bars.

The turnkeys now opened two of the condemned cells.

A cold shudder passed through the frame of young Norman and his companion as they quickly scanned the poor, cold, comfortless aspect of the place in which they were now doomed to dwell.

But the most painful trial of all was the parting of these two youths.

At first they supposed that the authorities would have placed them together in one cell for companionship's sake.

They were mistaken.

This was a great affliction to both.

Each had to occupy a cell apart; and as they were separated, Norman said in an affectionate tone of voice,

"Well, good-bye, Ted, we shall meet again."

"Good-bye, Edgar," said the other.

They shook hands in silence, and slowly walked into different and distant cells.

"Yes, there ain't no mistake about it," said one gaoler to another, in a half whisper, "they'll meet together again without a doubt; on the gallows, though, eh, mate?"

"I believe you, when old Calcraft joins their hands and necks together, and they dance on nothing to the music of St. Sepulchre's bells, eh?"

"Ah, poor young devils! Do you know, mate, I can't think as how these two boys could be guilty of that 'ere murder."

The other one shook his head as if in grave doubt.

"There's no knowing anything about it; the boys now-a-days ain't what they used to be in my time; they are more hardened and wicked than they used to be."

"That may be; but you can nearly always tell a rogue, thief, or vagabond from their looks, and I'm sure neither o' these boys look like anything o' the kind."

The other gaolor again shook his head in doubt.

"Why, look at that young Norman; see what a brave, handsome, open face the lad's got; such eyes and hair too, why he looks more like a duke's son than anything else."

"T'other don't, then."

"Well I can't say as I take so much to Rawlings as t'other one, although he's got a clear eye, and a merry twinkle in it, and a laughing-looking face altogether."

"Well, no matter, there they is, and it's all over with 'em, say I. I'm a father of a family myself, and knows what boys are; but all I can say I thinks it were a evil day on which they were born, and no mistake. I pities their fathers and their mothers."

"They has none—never had, so I hears."

"Then how did they come to live at all?" said the other, grinning.

"You needn't be so sharp, mate. I knows very well kids can't come into the world without fathers and mothers, as well as you do; but what I means to say is, they is all orphans."

"More's the pity, then, poor little devils. Didn't his lordship seem cut up when he was passing sentence on 'em?"

"So I hear, poor man. Ah! he's a kind-hearted judge, he is; no wonder he felt queer when passing sentence on two mere boys like them."

"There never were a better man than he is."

"That boy Norman looks uncommon like the judge in the face, though, I thought."

"Does he?"

"He does that, and no mistake. If they were put side by side, *one would almost swear they were father and son.*"

"Nonsense, what are yer talking on, man? D'yer think as how he'd——"

"No, I don't mean to say as how he *is* a son of his lordship—how should I, when we all know my lord's his a married man, and has children of his own; but still I say, and I sticks to it, that that young Norman is the dead image of his lordship."

"He may be the *dead* image when Calcraft has done with him," said the other, grinning, "but at present I think he's a good specimen of a live one."

So, thoughtlessly, chaffed and joked the two gaolers when they had locked up Edgar and Ted in their condemned cells.

But there is many a true word spoken in jest; and, as we have said in the preceding chapter, his lordship the judge, without a doubt, had strange misgivings that he had pronounced sentence of death upon his own son, Edgar Norman.

*   *   *   *   *   *

But the day passed quickly, and night came on apace.

By six o'clock every one in the vast prison were a-bed, and supposed to be fast asleep.

Except the chimes of distant church clocks, and the occasional footsteps of prison guards walking along the stone galleries, no sound fell upon the attentive ears of the many poor restless wretches confined in that immense mass of iron-bound granite.

Sleep!

Sleep in a condemned cell!

Ah! few indeed can.

And so thought Edgar Norman, as he lay tossing and turning upon his prison pallet, unable to close his eyes against the four bare white-washed walls of his prison cell.

But neither he nor young Rawlings were alone.

Each was watched by an attendant of the prison.

So careful are the authorities that the victims destined for public slaughter shall not in any way injure themselves, and thus mar the perfectness of the public sacrifice.

But at last, wearied out with reading and writing, or thinking, and conversing with the gaoler in attendance, Edgar Norman fell back upon his pillow, and, with a happy smile upon his handsome face, slept his first sleep in the gloom and unearthly quietness of the condemned cell.

Hours flew by, and yet he soundly slept.

The same happy look sat upon his manly brow, and he murmured in his sleep, while his lips twitched again and again in a half-suppressed smile.

He was dreaming.

Dreaming, truly, but not of mother nor father, friends nor relations.

He had neither one nor the other now.

For who is a friend to a condemned man?

Yet he smiled on unconsciously in his sleep, and dreamed—aye, very pleasant dreams.

And his imagination pictured bright scenes in distant climes.

Islands and seas, rivers and lakes, with bands of warlike soldiers came up in his mind, while troupes of beautiful maidens, with music and song, set a princely diadem upon his brow in far-off lands, unknown to the rest of the world.

Of such things he dreamed, and still the bold, handsome boy, smiling in his sleep, dreamed them over and over again till his face became flushed with a rosy hue of pride and pleasure, as he suddenly shouted out,

"Hurrah, hurrah! I am lord of all I survey, and King of the Pacific on land and sea!"

He suddenly woke from his dream, and looked around him in bewilderment at the cold, comfortless cell.

The bell of St. Sepulchre's tolled the hour of three.

He sighed.

He was in prison, and all that glorious landscape, which moments before had flitted through his mind, had vanished into the air.

It was all a dream.

Only a dream he thought.

Yet would it come to pass?

Would it be realized?

"Ah, how can it ever prove true," he thought, "when here I sit on my humble bed of straw, a convicted murderer in this condemned cell!"

Poor Edgar, he little knew what the future had in store for him.

"Your mind has been rambling at a rare rate, my lad," said his attendant, smiling.

"Has it though?"

"Yes, and no mistake. You have been talking of a dreadful mutiny on board one of Her Majesty's ship's; of a fearful storm and shipwreck. You were then on a raft buffeting about for weeks on the ocean, without sufficient food or water; you landed on some desolate island with your companions; fought battles with the natives, smugglers, free-booters, and the like, and then fancied yourself at the head of an army, who crowned you king, and I know not what all."

"Ah," said Edgar, smiling; "I have often dreamed of such things before; yes, many times before; but they can never prove true *now*, alas!"

"No, my lad, not now; for you know where you are, and why, I suppose? You are in a condemned cell."

"True, sir, true; but I can assure you I am innocent. I know no more of the murder than you do; yet, oh! if my dreams should ever come to pass."

And Edgar reclined on his couch, and, for a moment, was lost in deep thought.

"It was only a dream," he said again and again, sadly; "and will never prove true, I fear."

"How can it? Foolish boys are always dreaming about such nonsense as that. They always fancy they are going to be something very great and grand when they grow up, but in nine cases out of ten, it's all fudge."

"It may be," said Edgar, with a very solemn manner; "but some kind spirit, which visited me in sleep, told me over and over again, that my dream would surely prove true, and that I should not innocently suffer for the dreadful crime for which I and young Rawlings have been falsely accused and condemned."

"And do you believe it?" asked the gaoler with an incredulous smile.

"I do. I *know* it will come true."

"We shall see," was the surly reply.

"So we *shall* see," said Edgar; "and, mark me, if my words do not prove true."

"If they do, I hope you'll send me over a big lump of gold, then," said the gaoler, grinning. "Go to sleep, lad; go to sleep, or else I shall think you are turned crazy."

Whether Edgar's dreams came true or not, or whether he had suddenly turned mad, the reader will quickly see to his very great surprise.

CHAPTER III.

THE SWORN COMPANIONS—THE CONDUCT OF THE SNEAK, MASTER MARKS—PRANKS OF THE FOUR YOUNG CLERKS.

BUT if Edgar Norman could bear up under such a severe trial without flinching, and talk not only reasonably, but amusingly to the attendant in his cell, which he did from day to day, not so with young Ted Rawlings.

While in the company of Edgar he would be brave enough.

But directly he was left to himself, young Ted began to feel the awful position in which he was placed.

The Rawlings and Normans were all orphans.

The two brothers Rawlings, when infants, had been put upon the parish, for their parents had run away and left them, and for several years they had been reared within the four gloomy walls of Marylebone workhouse

Mr. Alderman Inglis, being in want of two errand boys, had applied to several persons, and the young Rawlings were recommended to him as being fitting subjects for his charity and kindness.

He accepted the boys, and after a few years they had grown up to be such good lads that the old alderman raised them step by step from errand boys to be junior clerks in his extensive warehouses down by the docks.

This is how it happened that they became acquainted with the Normans.

The Rawlings boys were of a vastly different disposition to the Normans, however.

The latter seemed to have been born gentlemen; but all the education in the world could not make young gentlemen of the former.

However, Edgar Norman had taken a great liking to Ted Rawlings, and Allan Norman to Jem Rawlings.

Ted and Jem were never happy except in the company of Allan or Edgar.

They would do "any mortal thing," as they were often wont to say, for the alderman's adopted sons.

If Allan went out for a walk, poor little Jem would beg hard to go with him.

If Edgar went to the play, Ted would also go.

Thus the intimacy between the four lads had grown stronger and stronger day by day, and the young Rawlings became so much attached to "their young masters," as they always called Allan and Edgar, that one could not move without the other.

Whatever larks the Normans had, Ted or Jem was sure to be in them also.

If they got into any scrapes the young Rawlings always bore the blame.

And it must be confessed that with two such wild young rogues for masters Ted and Jem got into numerous scrapes, and got many a smack on the head from the senior clerks and managers for pranks which Allan or Edgar had played upon them.

If Allan thought proper to mix up pepper in Mr. Smith's snuff-box, and Jem had a ruler thrown at his head in consequence, he would only grin, but would never "split."

Did Edgar take it into his head to well wax Mr. Brown's office stool, and thus fasten that fat old gentleman to his seat, Master Ted had his ears pulled in consequence.

But, like his brother, he would never "let on" who played this or that trick on Brown, and then from year's end to year's end, these four boys were continually laughing and joking, and playing pranks on every one around them, greatly to their own delight, and the terror of all the old women in the neighbourhood.

As we have said, Ted could be brave enough, and sometimes saucy enough; in Edgar's company he always felt brave, and would not have feared to face the devil himself, because he well knew that Edgar would always take his part, and pull him through any awkward fix he might get into.

For both the young Normans were noble and brave young lads, and could fence and box, or swim or run and jump with any one almost twice their own age.

This Master Ted well knew, and he remembered how more than once Edgar Norman had soundly thrashed a big, bullying clerk in a rival office opposite Mr. Inglis's warehouses, and gave him a pair of black eyes and a swollen nose.

And Master Jem well remembered, how on one occasion, he and Ted were playing peg-top, and when the "bobby" ran after them, Allan Norman tripped him up, and sent him sprawling in the gutter over a poor old apple-woman's stall, knocking over the apples, oranges and nuts, to the great delight of some dirty little urchins close by, who picked them up and scampered off without paying.

These, and a thousand other things Ted now remembered, as he lay upon his prison bed, and he could not forget, how, on a certain day, Edgar had taken his part against that blear-eyed bully, Marks, and given the "sneak" a terrible thrashing, although Marks was six years older than either of them.

This Marks had always had a bitter grudge against the young Normans, but against Edgar in a particular manner.

Why, no one could tell.

Edgar, though much younger, could beat Marks at anything, whether in the office or out of it.

It was said that Marks had been placed in Mr.

Inglis's offices because his father had loaned the alderman a considerable sum of money.

Whether this was true or false will appear during the progress of this story of startling adventure.

Suffice it to say that young Marks "was a regular spy and a sneak," as Edgar often told him to his teeth, and a cat could not sneeze without he hurried off to his father, or Alderman Inglis, to tell him all the particulars.

Marks, as will be already guessed, was what one might truly term "a young scoundrel."

He was not only this, but a great coward, and a deliberate liar also.

He feared the young Normans and hated them intensely; and, in order to gain friends among the senior clerks, and others in the alderman's employ, he resorted to the system of bribing and eaves-dropping.

That is to say, he would give a cigar to one, a fancy pipe to another, a cheap ring or pin to a third, and so on, in hopes that they would take him into their confidence, and tell him all the odds and ends they knew about Alderman Inglis and the two Normans.

Besides this, he had long vowed to ruin the four boys, because they shunned him, and wouldn't let him into any of their secrets.

But whether he had become false witness against these lads, or at least spoken and sworn to more than he actually knew of the murder, will be seen in the course of our narrative.

Suffice it now to say that both Edgar and Ted felt furious against Marks, as did Allan and Jem also; but Master Marks made up his mind to keep out of the way of Allan for a long time to come, but rejoiced in his inmost heart that his old enemy, Edgar, was condemned to death.

Poor Ted Rawlings, however, now that he was separated from Edgar, began to feel his courage oozing away very rapidly, and more than one tear flowed from his eye, as he sat on the edge of his bed thinking of all that had passed.

If Edgar had been there he would have felt all right.

But his "right hand," as he termed young Norman, was far away in another cell, and poor Ted felt disconsolate and wretched.

"They won't hang us, will they?" asked Ted of the gaoler in attendance.

"Of course they will."

"But why? I ain't done anything," said Ted, in surprise. "They won't 'scrag' a chap for that, will they?"

"You have been convicted of murder," said the gaoler, "and are condemned to die."

"But I didn't do it, I tell you."

"Why didn't you prove it, then, upon the trial?"

"'Cause I had no witnesses."

"The proof is too strong against you. All the witnesses in the world could not have got you off after what young Marks swore to."

"Oh, Marks is a liar!" said Ted, getting red. "He can never look any one fairly in the face, and if ever I meet him, I'll punch his head into a jelly, see if I don't."

Ted couldn't imagine it possible that he was condemned to die.

And so he began to growl and whimper by turns, and swore, with tears in his eyes, that neither Calcraft nor any other man living should hang him.

With all Ted's blubbering and restlessness, he was at last forced to be quiet, and for several days afterwards he seemed resigned to his fate.

During the second week after their conviction, both Edgar and Ted were greatly surprised one afternoon to hear that a very distinguished visitor had visited them.

But they knew not that this visitor was none other than a lady of the highest rank and fashion.

CHAPTER IV.

THE JEW, MARKS—HE REJOICES AT THE FATE OF EDGAR NORMAN—SOME ACCOUNT OF THE YOUNG VILLAIN IS GIVEN—PLOTS AGAINST THE NORMANS—THE ALDERMAN'S RUIN IS DETERMINED ON—THE QUARREL OF FATHER AND SON—IMPORTANT DISCLOSURES.

BUT let us return for a moment to the eve of the day on which young Norman and his companion were convicted.

And, as Master Marks is a very important personage in this story, we will say a few words concerning him.

As his name would indicate, young Marks was of Hebrew birth, and his father was a paltry petti-fogging lawyer, who kept two small, dirty, dingy offices in an out-of-the-way alley near the docks.

Mr. Marks, senior, was not so much of a lawyer, however, as a grasping, griping money-lender.

He had been in business many years, and by dint of great care, and much clever knavery, he had accumulated a very large fortune.

Not only did he lend much money to merchants and others, but it was whispered that many persons even of rank and title had patronized him.

Hence, at the time of which we speak, he had in his possession, as security for money lent, deeds and documents which belonged to some of the first nobility in the land.

The more money he made, however, the more he wanted to make, so that he did not care into what speculation he entered, or with whom, so that he got the "lion's" share of the profits.

He had learned, a year or two before our story commences, that Mr. Alderman Inglis was in great difficulties, and in need of money.

Lawyer Marks, with a savage grin, heard of the good old man's distress, and offered to lend him any amount he desired.

But the interest he demanded, and the conditions of the loan, were so binding and severe, that for several days the honest Alderman refused the Jew's offer.

At last, however, the lawyer abated in some small degree his extravagant terms, and the alderman, through stress of circumstances, accepted them.

A week after this transaction, Lawyer Marks called on the alderman, and asked him as a *favour* to take his only son as clerk in his office.

This request the alderman willingly granted.

But the good old man little thought that he was taking a *viper* to his bosom when he admitted the lawyer's son into his offices.

But as the sequel will show, young Marks proved to be worse than a viper.

" Now, my son,' said the cunning old Jew, with a malicious grin, "now that you are in the alderman's confidence, I consider that your fortune is made. Keep your own council, hear everything you can, but mind, do not say a single word which will betray my plans."

" What plans, father?" asked young Marks, with a fox-like grin. "What plans do you mean."

" Why, now that I have got old Inglis in my clutches I'll take good care, in the first place, that he pays me double and treble for what he owes me."

" I see," said young Marks, laughing, "there is

nothing like getting these rich Gentiles under our thumb."

" That's just it, my son ; our people make their fortunes that way—*we live on the necessities and miseries of others*," said the father, showing his large teeth in great glee, " and why not ?"

" Serve 'em right," said the son. "Who cares what people suffer, so that *we* gain by it."

" Exactly so ; and now you must be guided by me in all we do."

" How ?"

" Whatever secrets you can worm out of the firm do so, and inform me immediately ; for if they know how the market is going, what it wants, and what it does not—what's likely to sell well, or what will rise or fall in price—tell me, I repeat, immediately, for I will put on some of *our own people*, who will buy up all that is wanted in the market, and thus be beforehand with Alderman Inglis. By this means, I shall be able, with one or two others in the secret, to out-buy and out-sell all who want his goods, thus make a rapid fortune, ruin Inglis, and still get my own money back again."

" I understand," said young Marks, gleefully.

" Now, my son, you must remember this Inglis is a very extensive merchant, the largest in his particular trade. Wouldn't *you* like to supercede him ?"

" I would ; but how? Those two fellows, the Normans, I understand, will succeed the alderman in the business."

" Who told you ?"

" One of the head clerks. I hate those Normans, Edgar especially, he was the one who gave me that ugly black eye I had a few weeks ago."

" Never mind that, a black eye is nothing ; do you do as I tell you—be guided by me. These two Normans need not, nor *will* they succeed to the business if you will do as I tell you. You can have revenge out of them in a thousand different ways ; but never let them think for a moment what you are aiming at."

Thus father and son often spoke together, and young Marks was too good a disciple not to heed what had been told to him.

Immediately after he had given his evidence, however, before the court in the case for which Edgar Norman and his young friend were convicted, he hurried away from the place, feeling as if he had committed some fearful crime, which in truth he had

Wherever he went, the face of Edgar Norman seemed to haunt him, and a voice said loudly in his ear,

" Rascal, you have perjured yourself ! The blood of two innocent boys is on your head ! You are a murderer in your heart, and, until your dying day, the spirit of the dead shall haunt you !"

Wherever he went he seemed to be followed by some avenging angel, who shouted aloud to all who passed,

" *Behold a murderer ! shun him ! fear him !*"

For several hours after the conclusion of the trial, he went hither and thither, knowing not what to do or where to go. First down one street, and then up another, he aimlessly walked through the rain, but as as he did so, a coarse laugh would escape him, and his blear eyes emitted a strange, wild-looking light.

Marks, however, was a hardened young villain, and did not heed much the voice of conscience constantly shouting in his ears.

" What do I care if even I have told lies ? Who is to find me out ? Why, no one. I have had revenge on Edgar, at all events, and I am deuced sorry the others also were not found guilty. I shall go to the execution, and laugh in Edgar's face."

Now, Marks was a red-headed, sallow-complexioned youth of about nineteen years or so.

His eyes were like those of a cat, and his manner was always very humble and abject.

He had money to lend on all occasions at heavy interest, like his father, and he could rub his bony, hard, clammy hands and smile if even struck in the face, as he had been more than once for his knavery by young Edgar.

Although, as we have said, he had money and more than sufficient for his wants, he lived like a miser ; would feast ravenously on a sausage and a penny roll for dinner, could " never afford " a glass of ale, or a " pickwick," like other young clerks, and was so avaricious in his nature that he would not expend a single shilling to buy a penknife wherewith to pare his nails, but would bite off the ends when angry until he almost made his fingers bleed.

His attire was always shabby.

His walk was shuffling, and not upright.

He always had something to sell at a high price, but would not give a halfpenny away to any beggar if even it were to save the poor wretch from starvation.

Such was young Marks.

He went home to his father full of fiendish glee and told him all about the trial, and seemed happier on that day than he had ever been for many months before.

" Two of them will be hung," said he, rubbing his bony hands. " I would have given half-a-crown if all four of them had been convicted."

" It was on purely circumstantial evidence," said the father.

" I don't care how it was," said young Marks. " They will be hung, and that is all *I* want."

The father looked at his son full in the face as he said, turning deadly pale—

" You have got your revenge at last."

" So I have, and more than I expected."

" Did you not state *more* than you knew about this murder, my son ?"

" No," said the son, with a guilty look.

" But you stated as positive evidence and swore to that which you only imagined ; at least, in some instances you did, for I was there."

" Well, and what of it ?" said the son, grinning. " Ain't you as glad as I am that the Normans are out of our way ? Of course you are. I put the thing as strong as I could against them, and no one can be the wiser—because, after all, the whole murder is wrapt in such mystery that no one can unfathom it."

" Except *you*, perhaps," said the father.

" *Me* ?"

" Yes, you."

" Why, what do you mean ?" said the son, startled and rising from the table. " You'll be for accusing *me* of it next ! You lawyers suspect every one."

" No they don't," the parent replied ; " but if the law knew as much about that affair as *I* do, the verdict would have been far different."

" Indeed ! And what do *you* know about it ?"

" How came your coat to be torn on the night of the murder ?"

" My coat torn ?" said the son, reddening.

" And bloody also ?"

" Oh, that is nothing ; I had a fight in the street, that's all."

" But why did you burn it ?"

" I did not burn it."

"You attempted to do so, but from some strange and mysterious cause you became suddenly alarmed, and fled. Where is your long knife, my son?"

"My bowie knife? Why, I lost it long ago," said the son, stammering.

"Whether you did or not, I found it in your room, and it was covered with blood."

"As I live, this is all a lie!" said the son, in a great passion. "If you found it in my room some one must have placed it there, that's all."

"It is *not* all," said the father, in a whisper, and turning deadly pale.

"Tell me no lies! Revenge has carried you too far, my son, and I never expected you would do such a horrible act. There is an indelible crimson stain upon your heart: it is like the lion's paw!—it is the stamp of crime!"

"I did not do it," said the son, wildly, and with an astonished look; "I defy all the lawyers in the world to prove it."

"If you did not do it, you know those who did the deed, Jerry, and must have had some hand in it yourself. This all comes from your buying or selling with house-breakers to make money fast. I thought they would teach you too much, and this is the end of it. See to the red stain on your heart at once."

"'Tis false: I am not branded!"

"Nay, it is true; but not until it was too late did I discover the facts of which I speak. These two boys are innocent, and you have perjured yourself, my son. Jerry, your hands are stained with blood—the blood of Edgar Norman, whom you have long christened 'Lion Limb.'"

"Liar!" said the son, jumping up fiercely, "liar! I had nothing at all to do with Lion Limb. Curse him!"

And at the same time he rushed at his father with a dirk, and, in his passion, would have plunged it into the old man's heart.

But at that moment a servant hastily entered the room, stammering out,

"I—beg—pardon—Mr.—Marks—but—a—a—a—detective—is—at—the—door—and—asks—for—your—son—Jerry."

"For *me?*" said the enraged youth, looking like a red devil.

"Yes, for you, sir," said the servant. "I told him you were out, sir; but he said he know'd different, and that you were at home, and he must see you at once."

"Must see *me?*" said the son.

And he fell back into a chair, looking as pale as death.

The police-officer entered the room.

"Mr. Marks," said the detective, bowing politely.

"That is my name, sir," the father replied, in a trembling voice.

"This is your son, I believe, Mr. Jeremiah Marks, is it not?"

"It is."

"The very young man I've been looking after," said the officer. "Can I speak to you for a moment privately?" said the stranger, whispering to Jerry.

Jerry trembled in every limb, and his face was as pale as ashes. His jaws rattled like dice in a box.

"M-e-e?" he said.

"Yes, you. Come out in the passage; I want to have a word or two in private."

Jerry very cleverly concealed the dirk in his coat-sleeve, and rose from his seat slowly.

He cast a withering glance at his father, accompanied by a frightful oath, and left the room.

"What do you want?" said Jerry, in a tone of well-assumed indifference when he got in the passage.

"I want you to come with me."

"For what?"

"I will tell you after awhile."

"But, suppose I refuse to go with you?"

"You cannot; you *must* come with me."

"Where is your warrant? Show it."

"Oh," said the officer, smiling, "you are mistaken; no warrant is necessary in a case like this."

"Oh, isn't it, though?"

"No."

"But I protest against such a proceeding. Why should I go at your or any man's bidding without I see your proper warrant? What have I done?"

"You are *wanted*, I tell you," said the officer. "There, is that sufficient proof for you?"

At the words "you are wanted," always fatal from the mouth of a detective, Jerry felt as if he could have sunk through the flooring, as he sighed, "I am undone."

A cab was already at the door.

Into it the officer and Jerry went, and not another word was spoken for some time, as the vehicle rolled on rapidly through the crowded and busy streets.

"Shall I stab him, and thus get free?" thought Jerry, as he felt for the dirk up his sleeve.

This subject occupied his mind as they approached the prison; but, greatly to Jerry's joy and surprise, the cab passed the gloomy gaol at a very fast rate, and, ere long, arrived in a fashionable square in Belgravia.

"Why, what's the meaning of all this?" thought Jerry, as the vehicle stopped at the corner of the square.

In a moment the detective jumped out—for such he had said he was—and a strange, full-whiskered, long-haired gentleman, in a long black cloak, with spectacles, long beard and moustachios took his place inside.

The cabman seemed to know what to do, for directly this had happened he drove off at a desperate rate, and Jerry began to look and feel very uneasy.

Where they were going to he had not the slightest notion.

And who his strange, hairy-looking companion was, with fierce eyes glaring through green spectacles, was equally a mystery to him.

He felt as if he were sitting beside some dumb demon.

Not a word was spoken.

On went this cab through dark, muddy streets, and in heavy rain.

At length, after more than an hour and a half, the cabman pulled up at a small, lonely cottage on a wild heath.

Jerry trembled: he refused to get out of the cab, but the sharp click of the stranger's pistol altered his mind.

He dared not speak, for instinct told him that he was in the hands of an enemy.

He entered the cottage, followed by the stranger. The cab then drove away almost as rapidly as it came.

"What is the meaning of all this?" said Jerry, half aloud. "Have I got into the hands of a band of cut-throats or body-snatchers? I begin to fancy the fellow who called for me was no officer at all."

"He was *not*," the mysterious stranger replied; "he was a friend of mine, but an enemy to you."

Jerry felt very unhappy.

"Come this way," said the stranger, gruffly.

And he showed Jerry into an inner apartment.

It contained nothing but three or four chairs, a deal table, and a small grate without the least fire.

THE DEFENCE OF THE MAGAZINE—(*See page* 18).

At the table sat a woman dressed in deep black.

She not only wore a thick veil, but a mask also under it, which completely hid all her features from the keenest scrutiny.

"Sit down," said the stranger, pointing to a chair.

Jerry did as he was told.

At about three feet sat the woman on his left, and on his right was the stranger, who pulled out his gold watch, and placed it within easy reach on the table.

Yet not a word was spoken.

The blood curdled in the Jew's heart at the awful silence of the two sitting near him.

The small candle flickered and flared with a ghastly light.

The rain fell in torrents on the roof, and the

No. 2.

rumbling of distant thunder, and the flashing of forked lightning across the window panes, made up a scene in that dismal abode which would have harrowed the blood of one even less guilty and braver than the perjurer.

"What is the meaning of all this?" Jerry at last managed to ask. "Am I inveigled by body-snatchers? Where is the cab? Let me return from this place at once; I fear ye both. Where is the cab?"

"It will quickly come," was the reply.

"Then I shall return."

"If you do it will be as a *dead body*," said the fierce man in the long cloak, "not as a living one."

"What is this I hear?" said Jerry. "Am I, then, come hither to be murdered? No, never, impostors!

you are for once deceived," said he, fiercely drawing his dirk and brandishing it.

But at that instant the stranger presented a revolver at his head.

"Sit down," said he, calmly, and with a hollow laugh, "put up your little weapon, and listen to what I have to say."

Jerry sat down meekly.

"Your life is in our hands," the stranger began. "If we were to murder you no one would be the wiser ; you must consent to three things. You must promise to remain here two whole months without attempting to escape, on pain of instant death, and without speaking a syllable to any one ; in the second place, you must swear to a written oath that all you have said against Edgar Norman was basely untrue ; and, in the third place, you must with your own free will state, in your own handwriting, that you have voluntarily committed suicide. Quick ! time is flying !"

For a moment there was a solemn pause.

"I will give you five minutes by this watch to decide, in writing. If you do not do so to a second, I will blow your brains out," said the stranger.

Jerry was not long in deciding what to do.

And so he resolved to remain in the cottage two months without attempting to escape, and without uttering a syllable to any one under pain of death, to write down and swear to his own guilt, and to pretend to have committed suicide.

"For," thought Jerry, "they won't be here all that time, and I shall have plenty of chances to escape."

He signed the agreements in writing, and gave them to the cloaked stranger in double quick time.

The lady and gentleman rose.

Jerry heard the wheels of some distant cab rolling over the heath at a quick pace.

It quickly drove up to the door.

Four men jumped o t and entered the cottage.

They all bowed to e lady and gentleman in a very profound manner, and received the first of the papers which had been written by Jerry.

"If he speaks," said the stranger, "yea, only one word, mind me, despatch the rascal on the instant."

"We will, my lord," was the reply of all.

The lady and gentleman got into the cab and rode away, leaving the perjurer in the hands of four desperate-looking men.

Jerry's head drooped, and he inwardly cursed the unlucky and mysterious fate which had befallen him.

What happened to him after this we shall quickly see.

CHAPTER V.

THE NIGHT BEFORE EXECUTION—AN UNKNOWN LADY VISITS EDGAR—THE PRISONERS PREPARE TO DIE—ALLAN NORMAN'S ARRIVAL—HE STABS HIMSELF THROUGH GRIEF—THE UNEXPECTED NEWS.

TIME rolled on, and the day appointed for the execution of Edgar Norman and his young companion fast approached.

The newspapers had daily accounts of the two prisoners, and the governor of the jail was overwhelmed with letters from hundreds of persons, both rich and poor, begging permission to visit the condemned cells of the two young culprits.

The fame of Edgar's noble bearing, and his bold handsome features, was the theme of general conversation among ladies of fashion.

The print-shops were crammed with portraits of him and Ted Rawlings in all sorts of styles and colours.

Some people said they were two hardened young scoundrels, and deserved to die.

Others thought differently, and signed petitions to the Secretary of State, asking him to use his best endeavours to procure the royal pardon, and have the extreme sentence of the law commuted for penal servitude.

But all these petitions were unavailing.

The Secretary for the Home Department turned a deaf ear to petitions of every sort in their behalf.

He said that the case had been so clearly made out against the two lads, and the indignation of the citizens of London was so great on account of the foul murder of their Alderman Inglis, that any petition appealing for mercy on behalf of the two youths would be looked upon as no better than so much waste paper.

Day after day all sorts of propositions were mooted and spoken of in the daily papers to procure the pardon of that handsome, noble-looking youth, Edgar Norman.

But they came to naught.

Days and nights came and went.

Hours flew swiftly by ; but still the chaplain and gaol authorities held out no hope for the prisoners —not the slightest hope, and they were pressed to confess that which they had not done.

Both felt that they must shortly die, and prepared themselves for that awful moment with becoming gravity.

Edgar was quiet, upright and gentlemanly in his bearing towards all.

His pleasant smile still remained to him, nor did he show the slightest signs of fear.

The chaplain was astonished at his coolness and good temper.

The gaolers looked upon him with admiration.

"What a nerve the lad has got !" said a lady visitor in a whisper, to one of the turnkeys.

"Yes, ma'am, he just has, and no mistake ; and a finer lad in every way you would't find in a long day's walk."

"He has the bravery, nerve, and strength of a young lion," said a second,

"His companions always called him 'Lion Limb,' and so do we here," a third remarked.

"He'd make a splendid soldier, and it is a great pity to hang such a lad as he is."

"You call him Lion Limb, do you?" said the lady, as she kindly advanced towards Edgar, and took him by the hand.

"My dear child," said she, while tears rolled down her face, "believe me it is not idle curiosity which prompted me to come and see you, but a far better motive. I have endeavoured to the utmost of my power to gain your release, and tried all sorts of expedients to mitigate your sentence, but all in vain ; believe me there are thousands in England who as firmly believe in your innocence as I do, but the die is cast, there is no hope, no, not the slightest ray."

And as she spoke, she clasped young Edgar to her heart in a fond embrace ; her tears trickled on his upturned face, she kissed him and pressed him to her heaving bosom, and rushed from the cell, as if her heart would break.

No one was more surprised at this than Edgar himself.

The lady's manner, her look, her emotion, and the elegance of her figure and attire, struck all with wonder.

"Who was that distinguished-looking person ?" asked Edgar, when she had gone.

"She gave the name of Lady Clarence, and said she was the wife of a naval captain of some celebrity," a jailer replied.

No more was said at the moment; but had Edgar been able to look into the future, he would have been much surprised and startled at the influence which this lady was destined to have on his own fortunes and those of many others.

But we are anticipating.

Suffice it to say, that the visits of strangers and their condolings were cold comfort to the two boys under sentence of death.

But these visits became still more frequent as the fatal day approached, until at last both Edgar and young Rawlings begged that they might not be again disturbed; a request which was willingly granted.

At last the eve of their execution arrived, and, strange to say, as yet the prisoners had not been visited by their brothers, a fact which struck all save the condemned themselves as something very singular.

Now both Allan and Tom had frequently written to say that they would not come until every hope for their deliverance had vanished.

They had made up their minds to move heaven and earth in their brother's behalf; and as they had not yet come, Edgar felt certain that something important had kept them away.

It was now near midnight!

On the morrow, at eight o'clock, they were both to expire!

All within the prison was death-like silence, the chaplain had paid his visit and gone to bed weeping over the fate of the two blameless boys.

Edgar sat at the table writing.

"What noise is that?" he said.

His attendant seemed loth to answer.

"What noise is that, I hear? It sounds like a hammer at work."

"Yes, my lad, it is," said the officer.

"What are they doing?"

"Erecting the scaffold."

A sickly smile flitted across Edgar's face, as he said,

"And occasionally I hear a dull roar, like the surging of the ocean, now strong, now weak, and then again rising higher and higher. What is it?"

"There are thousands of people outside the prison, nay, tens of thousands, waiting to see the execution; the noise you occasionally hear is the sound of their swaying, quarrelling, fighting, singing, pushing, and the like," said the officer; "the authorities have been obliged to put down barriers in all directions to keep the mob from suffocating themselves."

"Are they so thirsty for our blood, then?" asked Edgar.

"Nay! they would tear the prison down in your behalf if they could."

"They are friends, then?"

"Yes; if ever any two lads had friends you have, and no mistake; the governor of the prison is so fearful that he sent for several companies of soldiers to guard the place; they are inside the walls now, keeping very quiet, so that if the mob really do intend to attack the place, and tear it down stone from stone, as they threaten, why, then, we are fully prepared."

"I thank them for their sympathies," said Edgar, "but I sincerely hope and trust no blood will be shed on my behalf."

The night passed on.

The last night of life!

What an awful thought!

The sounds of distant hammering in the prison yard went on.

The swaying of the noisy multitude outside was distinctly audible at intervals.

The solemn hour of midnight tolled out from the grey tower of St. Sepulchre.

And yet Edgar slept not.

He was thinking of all that was dear to him on earth, but not a sigh or tear escaped him.

He was musing of his brother Allan.

Why had he not yet come?

Scarcely had the thought occurred to him than the gaoler opened his cell door, and announced his brother's arrival.

Allan rushed towards Edgar.

For a moment they were locked in a tight embrace, and not a syllable was uttered.

"Well, Allan; what news?" said Edgar, calmly.

Allan hung his head, and dashed a tear from his eye.

"None, brother; none."

"No news is good news, so they say," Edgar remarked, smiling. "Come, Allan, don't take on that way; don't weep for me. I am fully prepared to quit the world, and from my heart I fully forgive those who have falsely accused me."

"I don't!" said Allan, fiercely, "and never until my dying day will I cease hunting the rascals down who have caused your ruin and my disgrace."

Of the two brothers Edgar was by far the more composed and calm.

Allan was broken down in spirit.

He had been working night and day getting up petitions and the like.

He could not eat or sleep, and looked the picture of haggardness and misery.

Yet the night passed on.

Hour after hour flew by, and the noise outside increased.

The brothers remained conversing, hand in hand.

All hope was lost!

The clergyman came, and administered consolation.

A cup of tea was all the breakfast that Edgar needed.

One more hour passed even more rapidly than the rest, when, suddenly turning their heads, Allan and Edgar beheld a revolting object in the cell.

It was the common hangman!

He had entered to pinion the arms of Edgar.

Not until now had a shudder passed through young Norman's frame, but the demoniacal look of the common hangman, with his buckles and straps, chilled his blood.

Not from fear of death did this feeling arise, but from pure abhorrence of the wretched man who followed such a horrible inhuman calling.

He could not look upon the noble features of the intended victim without winking and blinking and averting his cat-like eyes.

"Come, are you ready?" said the hangman, in a quick, sharp tone. "It's getting very near the time; besides, I want to make haste this morning, I've another job in the country, and must be away from here before nine."

"Yes, I am ready," said Edgar, perfectly calm. "You can pinion me, your buckles and straps have no terrors for me."

"Hold! rascal, hold! Take off your hateful bloodstained hands!" said Allan, jumping between the hangman and his brother. "Never shall he be polluted by your filthy touch! Here, Edgar, if you must die," said he, brandishing a dirk, "let us die together; death shall never separate us!"

The hangman rushed back in fear.

Three or four officers darted in, and after much trouble secured Allan, and hurried him from the cell.

"Whose blood is that upon the floor?" asked Edgar, in surprise.

No one knew.

Allan had stabbed himself!

"Don't say a word to Lion Limb," one of the officers whispered to another, "but his brother Allan's wound, the surgeon fears, is mortal!"

What a desperate youth was Allan!

His brother's execution had turned him raving mad!

During this time Edgar had been under the hangman's care.

His arms were tied by his side.

His shirt collar was opened, and his white manly breast was bare, revealing one of the most beautiful necks that a human being could boast of.

He stood in the stone gallery outside his cell.

In a moment afterwards Ted Rawlings appeared pinioned in the same manner as Edgar.

He had to be assisted along, for he was too pale and weak to walk.

"I cannot shake you by the hand any more, Edgar," said he in a faint voice, faltering at each word; "but you know I love you, and always did, yes, better than my own brother."

And from sheer weakness he fell upon Edgar's neck and kissed him, while tears flowed continually from his eyes.

The bystanders were silent and sorrowful.

Slowly knelled the passing bell, and in solemn silence the procession moved to the gallows foot.

Two by two they walked, sheriffs, clergyman, and friends.

Another instant and the victims would have ascended the scaffold, when all at once a startling shout was heard behind them.

It echoed through the long stone galleries like a trumpet.

"Stop! stop! stop!" said the messenger, running with all his might. "Stop! pardon! stop! stop!"

And with all speed he ran up to the sheriff, and gave him a despatch from the palace.

He carefully examined the seals, and then read it aloud—

"The sentence on Edgar Norman and Edward Rawlings is commuted to penal servitude for life."

"That is worse than death itself," said Edgar.

He was unbuckled, and returned to his cell.

A terrible yell from the crowd outside saluted the disappointed hangman.

And he was pelted from the scaffold with all manner of filth and missiles, while the densely packed crowds on hearing the good news, again and again gave deafening cheers that shook the very prison walls.

CHAPTER VI.

THE TWO YOUNG CONVICTS EMBARK FOR THE PENAL SETTLEMENT—THE DARING DEEDS OF EDGAR NORMAN—HE IS PROMOTED BY CAPTAIN CLARENCE—THE MUTINY ON BOARD—HEROISM OF EDGAR NORMAN—PLANS OF THE MUTINEERS—THE DESPERATE OUTBREAK ON BOARD—THE BRAVE DOG, DRAGON—THE TERRIFIC FIGHT.

IN less than a week after the exciting events narrated in the previous chapter, Edgar Norman and his young companion were taken from the prison in which they were, and sent to Portsmouth.

The eight-gun sloop of war, "Rattlesnake," under the command of Captain Harry Clarence, was under orders to sail for the Pacific, and was then preparing for the voyage.

The "Rattlesnake," besides her own crew, was to carry out fifty additional sailors for different vessels abroad.

Besides this, about twenty surplus cannon, several cases of rifles, powder, shot, caps, shell, and other stores, such as revolvers, swords, and the like, were stowed away for the use of several vessels, who were short of such warlike articles.

In addition to these things, the "Rattlesnake" was heavily laden with cargo of a peculiar description.

The government were sending out in her several houses, made of wood and iron, as presents to various petty kings and queens in the Pacific islands.

Ploughs, spades, a steam engine, all manner of tools for blacksmiths, masons, carpenters, and other trades, were stowed away, which were destined for certain missionaries on different islands.

A select assortment of poultry and general live stock was also to be carried to various places for breeding purposes, and to furnish barren places with useful animals.

In one word it might be said that the "Rattlesnake" was loaded down to the port-holes with a general cargo.

Instead of carrying only sufficient food for his own crew, Captain Clarence had an endless number of bales and boxes, and sacks and bags on board, each containing something which would prove useful in the foreign climes which he was ordered to visit.

It was generally expected that the "Rattlesnake" would be about two years absent from England, and as the dockyard was in great need of store ships, this sloop had been used as one from pressing necessity.

Captain Clarence was a very kind good-hearted sailor; he had seen much hard service, and wore several medals on his breast.

He was a widower, it must be remembered, and had one only child.

This child was called Emma Clarence.

For it must be explained here in one word, that the lady who had visited Edgar in prison, and had passed under the name of Lady Clarence, was *not* Mrs. Captain Clarence at all.

Who and what she was will appear hereafter.

As little Emma, his only child, was weakly, and extremely delicate, the good captain resolved to take her with him on the present voyage to the Pacific, hoping that a change of air and several months stay in foreign parts, would restore her to perfect health, while at the same time be company for himself.

Captain Clarence had been sent for by the officers of the Admiralty, who explained to him the object of his voyage.

"You have been selected for this present undertaking, Captain Clarence, because the government have every reliance and confidence in your ability to perform with prudence the very delicate, and often-times difficult duties you will have to encounter."

This was not the first time by many that the worthy captain had been praised by his superior officers.

He bowed and stammered out his thanks for the compliments paid him.

And what was more to his liking, government had ordered him to make out a perfect inventory of whatever else he thought might be wanted by the various island settlements, in addition to what they had already provided, and were then stowed away on board the sloop.

Captain Clarence did so, and, as might be expected, from his good nature, he asked for numerous things and necessaries which the government had forgotten, so that people in the dockyard were wont to smile and say jokingly,

"The Rattlesnake is taking out sufficient things to supply all the islands in the vast Pacific."

Captain Clarence didn't care a straw for what they did or did not say.

He knew very well that a vessel going into such outlandish places ought to be well stocked with every article of utility, and as he had full power, he was determined to leave nothing behind which would be of use to the "Island Settlements" in the far south-west.

But there was one thing which Captain Clarence did *not* like.

He was ordered to take on board some fifty convicts, most of them being quite boys.

Among them were Edgar and Ted.

This part of his "cargo," as he termed it, gave him much anxiety and annoyance.

He had never been so employed before, and the idea that a gallant sloop-of-war should be thus degraded by being turned into a convict hulk, greatly vexed him.

These fifty youths were to be landed at the cold, foggy, bleak, and dreary Falkland Islands, one of the severest convict settlements under the crown.

And had any of the poor boys known the sort of place to which they were now about to go, they would have prayed for death instead.

As we have before observed, it particularly annoyed Captain Clarence to be ordered on such a service as carrying convicts to distant settlements.

He would have much preferred to have been sent against an enemy with hopes of distinction, honour, and promotion.

But he was, however, too much of a good sailor to disobey the orders of his superiors, and therefore went down from London to his ship, grumbling and growling.

As he was likely to be a long time away, he obtained permission to take his only child, Emma, with him, and set sail for his destination with the best wishes of all who knew him, and with a fair wind blowing.

The young convicts were placed below, and very harshly treated by many of the men.

Some of the poor lads gave vent to their feelings and were punished severely on several occasions.

Most of the sailors took a very great dislike to the poor boys, and when it got whispered among them that a convicted murderer was on board, they cursed and swore most horribly and growled among themselves, saying, "What ship ever had luck which carried a murderer on board?"

"The sharks will never leave us," said another.

"They will follow in our track for ever until we find out who this young murderer is."

"True, mates," said a fierce, tyrannical, and savage boatswain, with a horrible oath, "true mates, and none of us will ever reach the shore alive again, until we throw the young ragamuffin into the sea, whoever he is."

These sentiments were echoed by most of the crew, and it was secretly resolved to find out who the murderer was, and to trip him over into the sea on some dark night when unperceived by any of their superior officers.

The result of this was, that the fifty convict lads were always treated with the utmost severity on all occasions, but unknown to the captain, who was by far too kind a man to have permitted anything of the sort with his own knowledge.

Yet, strange to say, although Norman behaved himself better than any one else on board, the captain treated him more harshly than the rest.

Why was this?

It is easily explained. Some one had written to Captain Clarence the day before his sailing out of port, giving such a terrible character of Lion Limb and of his evil propensities, that the good-hearted captain began to think that Edgar Norman must truly be a young fiend in human form.

Who this correspondent was the captain did not know.

Yet he looked upon the contents of the anonymous letter as perfectly true, and resolved to keep more than an ordinary watch upon young Norman, and to treat him more strictly than the rest.

Poor Norman soon saw the difference in the captain's behaviour towards himself.

Had he known who and what the unknown person was, who had thus caused his misery on board, it would have surprised him much.

But this he was not destined then to know.

However, he bore his treatment with the utmost coolness, and never complained in any manner.

Whatever he was told to do, he did with promptness, and in a light-hearted manner.

There were only two persons on board who seemed to like him with sincerity.

The first of these, as might be expected, was young Rawlings.

And, strange to say, the second person was no other than the captain's daughter, Emma.

Although the authorities had cut off his hair in the prison fashion, and clothed him in a convict's suit, there was something about young Norman so gentlemanly—his language and behaviour were so manly and polite, that, notwithstanding his unprepossessing exterior, young Emma liked him above all the rest on board.

And when Norman moved about the ship, engaged in any occupation, Emma followed him with her eyes, and in her heart would not believe he was the character her father depicted, but some innocent one suffering for the crime of another.

A strange and secret attachment it was on both sides

No matter how harshly he was treated by Bill Whetherby, the boatswain, on all occasions; no matter, either, how much more work was thrust upon him than the others, Norman bore it all patiently and silently.

A single glance at the bright face of the captain's daughter seemed to banish all memory of punishment from his heart, and illumined his soul with rays of gladness.

Yet what a gulf was between them !

She was a lady by birth and position.

He was a convict—a so-called murderer.

It was because "Lion Limb" would not wince under the cruel strokes of the savage boatswain—it was because he did not murmur at aught that he was commanded to do—and, moreover, it was because he never quailed on any occasion to do the most dangerous duties on board, that most of the crew, led on by Bill Whetherby, hated him.

"I'll get that young imp's neck broke, somehow or other," the boatswain would say. "We ain't all going to Davy Jones's locker on his account."

And acting up to this resolution, Whetherby poisoned the mind of Captain Clarence against Norman, and gave him the most difficult and dangerous jobs on board.

Once, when the wind was blowing a perfect hurricane, and in the middle of a dark night, Norman was thrown out of his hammock in a brutal manner, and sent aloft to the mast-head, to unravel a knot in the signal halyards, a knot which had been purposely made by some one of Whetherby's favourites.

Norman went aloft as nimbly as a monkey.

And, although the fierce winds were howling and screaming through the rigging, and the ship was pitching and rolling from yard-arm to yard-arm, he held on like grim death, and not only accomplished the task, but descended to the deck as nimbly and as gaily as if nothing had happened.

When helping to furl sails on one occasion two of the crew tripped him up, and Norman fell from the yard-arm into the sea.

"He is gone," said Whetherby, to one of his mates, laughing; "it was only an accident, you know, we can't help these things at sea. No matter, we have got rid of him at last, the stiff-necked young villain! I never liked him."

But Norman was *not* thus got rid of.

He was a splendid swimmer, and, clutching a stray rope which hung over the ship's side, he clambered up on deck again, laughing as gaily as ever, and none the worse for his unexpected salt-water bath.

"Shiver my top-lights if he ain't on board again," said one.

"He ain't gone, arter all," said another, with an oath.

"He's got more lives than a cat," said Whetherby; "I've tried all sorts of capers to get rid of him, but it's all no use."

But, although Norman smiled at all the cruel tricks which most of the sailors played upon him, desires for revenge entered into his heart.

"If I could only hope to meet these vagabonds face to face some day on shore," he thought, "I'd soon let them know what I was made of. But what can a few lads do against a ship's crew armed to the teeth, as they are, and big, grown men?"

One day Norman had been sent to perform a variety of menial offices, and Whetherby stood over him with a rope's end in hand, ready to administer punishment at the slightest provocation.

It was towards evening, and yet, although the other convicts had gone to rest below, Whetherby took it into his head to punish Norman still more and more, hoping, perhaps, to drive him mad.

Now there was Captain Clarence's favourite New-foundland dog on board, and his kennel was made, for convenience, on the quarter-deck.

The name of this noble-looking dog was Dragon, and both the captain and his daughter seemed particularly fond of him.

In truth Dragon loved his young mistress, Emma, so much that he gambolled and played with her like a child, and would not receive his food from any other hands but her own.

He was firmly chained to the mizen-mast, and it was the duty of the boy prisoners to clean his kennel out by turns.

But, strange to say, Dragon had taken a great fancy to Norman, and when any one but he approached the kennel he growled and snarled, and showed his teeth in such a ferocious manner that not even the tyrant Whetherby much cared to go near him.

"Go and clean Dragon's kennel," said Whetherby, in a rough tone of voice to Norman, and with a scowling look.

The prisoner did not make any reply, and was about to do as he was told, when the cruel boat-swain raised a thick rope, and made a blow at the youth, which, had it hit him, must have knocked him senseless to the deck.

But a sad accident was the result.

An accident which proved a turning point in the fortunes both of Whetherby and Norman.

For the captain's daughter was on the quarter-deck leaning over the ships's side watching the sport of several sharks.

And the blow which was aimed at Norman missed him, and knocked Emma Clarence overboard.

Here was a terrible situation.

The girl was in the water surrounded by sharks!

Without waiting a second to think of his own danger, Norman snatched up a long knife which lay on deck and plunged headlong overboard after the helpless girl.

"Man overboard! man overboad!" was the cry which rang throughout the length and breadth of the ship.

"Lower the boats! lower the boats!" said Captain Clarence, rushing on deck, looking pale.

"The captain's daughter has fallen overboard!" said one.

"She was knocked over by that young Lion Limb!"

"Yes, Lion Limb, or Devil's Limb, as I call him!" said Whetherby. "And, if we manage to rescue him, we shall have some fun in hanging him, my lads, so bear a hand and man the boats!"

The ship's sails were backed on the instant by many hands who would have been only too much pleased had it been Norman alone who had fallen overboard.

The boats were lowered, however, as quickly as possible, and into one of them the captain jumped.

"Bear away, my men! bear away!" he cried, steering the boat towards the spot where Norman was last seen upon the water.

As they approached the spot a strange and horrible sight appeared to all.

The surface of the sea was all a foam for many yards around, and dyed with blood!

"They are both lost, captain," said several; "the sharks have taken them down."

But the sharks had *not* taken them down.

Norman, the instant he reached the water, perceived Emma sinking, and madly dived after her.

He clasped her in his arms and rose to the surface.

Then it was that the terrible truth was apparent to him.

All around him were voracious sharks with staring eyes and open jaws ready to devour him.

Escape seemed impossible.

Death was certain.

Still with the left hand he supported his lovely burden and bravely swam out with the other, knife in hand.

He kicked and plunged wildly about in the water to terrify the savage monsters around him.

This trick for a moment deceived the sharks.

But they soon rushed at him right and left and on all sides.

With the faithful knife, however, he savagely cut his way through them, and the water was quickly darkened with streams of gore.

For Norman well knew that once a shark is wounded and its blood is tasted by others, they will, from instinct, fall upon and tear it to pieces.

Then, having wounded several, the bleeding sharks were set upon by dozens of others, and, instead of attacking him or the girl any more, they turned their attention upon each other and fought so savagely that the water was not only soon all a foam but also dyed a deep red colour.

It was well, perhaps, that this happened as it did.

For, at that instant, Norman was not only exhausted, but unconscious.

He was sinking.

This world's light was fast closing on him for ever.

But strong, vigorous hands grasped him when about to sink, and drew both him and Emma Clarence safely into the boat.

This noble behaviour caused the captain afterwards to look upon Norman with much admiration and favour.

The truth soon became known, however, and Bill Whetherby was not only deprived of his position as boatswain, but condemned to receive two dozen lashes for his cruelty to the prisoners on board.

He was, moreover, ironed and sent below, and kept under a very strong guard for several weeks.

He bore his punishment in silence, but swore in his heart to raise a mutiny among the men, and to leave the vessel to the mercy of the winds and waves.

By all sorts of whispers and backbiting he poisoned the minds of nearly all the crew.

This went on for more than two months, and at last the captain was told that a conspiracy had been formed against him and the chief officers of the vessel.

The plans of the mutineers were known only to themselves.

Nor did they betray their secret to any one whom they thought would in any way side with the captain.

"See how he favours them young scoundrels, the convicts," Whetherby would snarl, with an eye flashing deadly anger.

"Yes," another would whisper; "ever since that young Devil's Limb rescued his daughter the captain has treated him like a young lord."

"Aye, and the other convicts also," a third remarked.

"Well, never mind," said another, "we have made up our plans, so let us stick to them."

"When we are once in the South Pacific Ocean we'll suddenly rise and seize the vessel."

"That would be the fine way of getting discovered by our own British cruisers, I think."

"Then seize her for a few hours only so as to get all we want out of her, and——"

"Then scuttle her."

"Send the captain, his officers, and the convicts to the bottom, eh? Is that what you mean?"

"Yes," said Whetherby; "we'll take all the boats, arms, and whatever we can carry, and sail away to a group of beautiful islands that I know, not far to the westward, and set up as free-booters there."

"That's just the thing for us," said several at once.

"We can, then, set up little kingdoms for ourselves among the natives, and plunder right and left."

"Won't that be sport, eh?" said several.

"And won't we lay hands on many a fine ship going home to England with gold dust from California, or some rich craft from China or the Indies?"

"Have you made all arrangements, Whetherby?"

"I have; I will be your leader, mates."

"But when shall we refuse to work?"

"Directly we are in the latitude of Valparaiso, we shall then be only two days' sail from Juan Fernandez, the island on which Robinson Crusoe lived."

"Why, I have been told that the islands round about there were once used by the Spanish buccaneers, who have left ship-loads of treasure behind."

"So they have," said Whetherby; "but you don't know as much about those islands as I do."

"How do you mean?" asked several, in a whisper.

"Why, I know more than fifty of my former pals who are living there already."

"The devil!"

"You don't mean that, Whetherby?"

"I do, though, and they are getting along famously."

"Then you came out in the 'Rattlesnake' expressly to cause a mutiny in the ship?"

"Yes, if I could, and seize it, and make a settlement for myself and others in the Southern Seas."

"Why not seize this vessel, then? She's rich, and has a splendid cargo of all sorts of things on board."

"So I would, and so I intended, until a few days ago, when I heard the skipper say as how the Pacific was swarming with British and American cruizers, and to seize a ship under such circumstances as those places all our heads in a noose. We'll try and seize her if you like, though, when no sail is in sight."

"Agreed; but if we can't, why, let us scuttle her beforehand, and put plugs in the holes until the proper moment."

All these plans were agreed upon, and so widespread had the conspiracy become, that it was evident a terrible mutiny might break out at any moment.

The captain and his officers had few friends around them; but from the willingness with which the crew obeyed all orders, it seemed to him impossible any plot whatever could exist among the men at all.

For what had he done to offend them?

He had been, and proved himself to be, on all occasions, the best and most deserving superior officer who had ever commanded a crew.

Why, then, should they rebel?

What occasion had they to do so?

But some men are such villains that nothing whatever will satisfy them.

And so it was with Captain Clarence's crew.

Whetherby and several others had shipped on board this vessel with no other object than to seize her if they could, and from the moment they had left port, he and his companions had been gradually poisoning the minds of the crew.

And the chief reason why the ring-leader, Whetherby, so hated Lion Limb, was because he would not listen to that rascal's hints, and seemed to love both the captain and his officers more than the conspirators liked to see.

"We have a deadly foe in that youth," said several.

"Why didn't you kill him long ago, then?" said the ringleader. "A sly thrust with the knife would have silenced him if you had only thought of it—the proud young villain!"

"It is impossible to do so, now, however, for the captain has taken him into his own cabin to wait at table, and such like."

"Do you think he has any notion of what we are up to?"

"No, not he. What does a mere lad like he know of such things? If he did, we should have heard of it weeks since, for he's a babbler, a sneak, and a tell tale, I can tell you all that."

"Don't talk any more about such poor devils as those boy convicts," said another, with contempt. "What could they do to prevent our designs? Why, nothing."

"I would undertake to cut the throats of every one of them in less than ten minutes," said one red-haired fellow.

The conspirators were over confident of themselves, however.

Lion Limb *did* know of the conspiracy.

With the eye of a young hawk, he narrowly watched all the motions of Whetherby and his gang.

More than this, the captain and his chief officers had been so good and kind to all the young convicts of late, that they really loved Captain Clarence, and would have died for him if need be.

Norman, however, laid his own plans, and very carefully.

He secretly robbed the arms chests, and gave to each of the young convicts a revolver and cutlass, which they hid away very cleverly from all observation.

"When I bid you rise," said Lion Limb to them, "do so, like true English lads. You have elected me your chief, and I will show you, at the proper time that I am worthy of your confidence; but the moment has not yet arrived."

That same night, at midnight, however, and before Lion Limb expected it, the mutiny broke out on board, and in great fury.

The first intimation Lion Limb had of it was made known by loud laughter on deck.

The mutineers, led on by Bill the Boatswain, had suddenly secured and firmly bound all the officers on deck and below.

Some had been killed, and thrown overboard.

This had been done so quietly that not one of the captain's friends below even heard the slightest noise, or dreamed of such a thing.

Having accomplished this cold-blooded feat they broke open the spirit-room, and helped themselves to wine, brandy, rum, gin, and tobacco, and whatever else they could lay their hands on.

And, as might be expected, they were too intent upon plundering the ship to care about anything else.

Lion Limb was the first one to suspect how matters stood.

He rose from his bunk in great haste, and, girding on his revolver and cutlass, suddenly entered the captain's cabin, aroused him, and told him of all he suspected.

For a moment the worthy commander would not believe the startling news.

He hastily rose, however, and armed himself, and, sword in hand, issued from his cabin.

The deck, at that moment, was swarming with armed men.

Some were loading the numerous boats with arms, ammunition, food, rum, and whatever else they could lay hands upon.

Others were dead drunk, and lay prostrate in all directions.

The ship was drifting before the wind.

No one was at the wheel to guide it.

In the distance rose up out of the sea bold outlines of a beautiful group of islands not more than five miles away to the westward.

The mutineers had evidently quarrelled as to what to do, and each company of four or five were providing for themselves, regardless of the curses and wishes of the others.

Some were for seizing the vessel as it stood, and for murdering the captain, and all who favoured him.

Others chose to land on the islands, immediately to sink the ship, and all who remained behind.

On every hand was great confusion and uproar.

Already had Lion Limb sounded the note of alarm, and bravely did the convicts and others answer to his call.

They rushed upon deck, sword and pistol in hand.

Fighting was going on in every direction.

Groans, curses, yells, moans, and the report of fire-arms were heard on every side.

The vessel was a perfect pandemonium, and in every corner of the ship there was deadly strife.

The captain behaved bravely—yea, as bravely as man could do.

He cut down one of the ringleaders at the first stroke.

Several others, maddened, and raving drunk, rushed upon him, yelling like fiends.

He put his back against the mizen-mast, and defended himself heroically; and many had to succumb to his own good sword.

Lion Limb was singled out by many of the mutineers, and terrific combats ensued both to the right and left.

The clash of swords was fearful, and the cracking of pistols almost deafening.

While this was going on, however, Bill Whetherby, the ringleader, was intent on securing the ship for himself, and a few other hardened villains, who refused to put off with the boats.

He put two men at the helm, and one on the look-out aloft.

"If there is no sail in sight," he said, "we'll massacre all these convicts, and sail away to different islands than those the long boats have rowed off to yonder."

But just in the midst of the fight, and when he thought that in five minutes more he would be perfect master of the sloop, his look-out at the mast-head sang out, lustily—

"A sail! a sail, ho!"

This news startled Whetherby and his comrades not a little, but still they fought on with the ferocity of demons, each moment hoping to conquer all who opposed them.

Bill turned deadly pale, but sent a fresh man aloft to take observations with the teluscope.

He did not remain long aloft, but hurried down on the deck again, saying, with a quivering lip—

"It is a man-of-war bearing right down upon us!"

"A British vessel?" asked Whetherby, turning.

"Yes, a frigate; and answering some signal of ours."

"Of ours?" growled Bill, with a savage oath.

As he looked up at the peak, he discovered a signal flying out in the wind.

It had been run up by Lion Limb himself, the moment he rushed on deck, and had not been discovered by any of the mutineers on account of the smoke and confusion of the fight on deck.

"Is she bearing down on us?" asked Bill, grimly.

"Yes; with open ports and shotted guns!"

"Lion Limb, then, is the cause of all this: *he* is the one who ran up the signal," said Bill.

"He shall die, then!" swore many.

"We are lost! we are lost!" said several, dashing towards Lion Limb, to murder him. "Revenge! revenge!"

"Death!" swore Bill, red with anger. "Prepare the boats, my lads; prepare the boats."

"Blow up the magazine," shouted the mutineers.

"Follow *me*, then," said Bill, with a flaming torch in hand. "Death to Lion Limb and his Boy Band!"

But at that dread moment Bill and his party paused, with looks of horror!

Something appalling occurred to all on board!

LION LIMB

THE BOY KING
OF THE SOUTH SEA ISLANDS.

THE SCENE ON THE RAFT.

At that moment the gallant youth, Lion Limb, gained possession of the pivot-gun on the quarter-deck, and had primed it to the muzzle with grape-shot and canister.

With a look of triumph he met the onslaught of the mutineers undismayed.

No. 3.

Just at that precise instant, when Whetherby and his bloodthirsty gang would have rushed upon and massacred the brave and faithful convict lads, Lion Limb touched off the cannon !

The sudden flash, the deafening roar, and the unearthly rattle of the iron hailstorm among the mutineers, caused a frightful spectacle that would have appalled the bravest of the brave.

Heads and legs and arms were strewn about in all directions.

Whetherby, cruel, savage, and hardened as he was by a lifetime of crime, recoiled before the sight with looks of horror.

With recovered breath and courage, Whetherby and his followers looked around them, as if they had just awakened from some horrid dream.

In an instant the combat was renewed with greater fury than ever.

With eyes all on fire with blood-red rage, Whetherby hoarsely shouted out—

"'Twas all a fancy, my men; only fancy; on to the convict brats, and slaughter every one. Let a party go below, and set a slow match to the magazine. We will blow them all into eternity."

But the leader of the mutineers had made a great mistake; he could not, and did *not* blow up the magazine, as intended.

He sent men below to break open the magazine, and to wait for the proper command before applying the slow match.

But when these messengers arrived at the door of the magazine, they were shot dead by young Ted Rawlings, who had been placed on guard there, and told to fire at any or every one who approached it with evil intentions.

And right well did young Ted fulfil Lion Limb's orders.

Several had attempted to enter, and by means of a slow match to set fire to the large quantity of powder stored here.

But young Ted concealed himself behind a large barrel, and, revolver in hand, watched for the rascals as one by one they approached.

Six of the mutineers had paid dearly for their temerity.

Young Ted had taken deliberate aim, and concealed as he was from view, knocked them over very cleverly, one at a time, and remained master of the magazine.

Fear had made Ted braver than usual, but as he was excellently screened from view, he considered himself quite a hero, and popped away right merrily and thought it fine fun to have knocked over so many of the black-looking, half-tipsy crew.

But there was now a very sanguinary scene transpiring on deck.

Bill Whetherby and his few followers, half-maddened by the severe and grievous losses which they had suffered at the hands of Lion Limb and his brave young companions, resolved to cut them limb from limb.

"Forward, men, follow me!" the leader shouted, breathing fearful oaths. "Follow me; let some of you dash into the cabin and secure the captain's daughter; bring her to me, I will slay her before her own father's eyes."

"Never!" said Lion Limb, brandishing his cutlass.

And he dashed into the cabin, and standing in the doorway, beat back all who attempted to pass and lay unholy hands on the young innocent within.

Many a cut did Lion Limb receive in defending his young mistress, but he fought with the fury of a young tiger.

He secured Emma Clarence in an inner cabin, bade her be not afraid, and rushed out upon deck again. He seemed invincible.

Whomsoever encountered him he slew with the ease of a practised and accomplished swordsman.

Every one seemed to be afraid of him and shunned his shining steel as one would the vivid lightning

The fatal words of "a sail, a sail!" struck terror to the hearts of Bill Whetherby and his ferocious gang of mutineers.

Bill thought it impossible that any one could have gone aloft and hoisted a signal unknown to him. But he was greatly mistaken.

Lion Limb at the first moment of the terrible outbreak on board, had clambered up the shrouds with the agility of a cat, and fastened a red shirt at the peak.

"Bloodhoof, Redfin, Gregory," Whetherby cried, "ascend and tear down the signal; do it instantly or the stranger will bear down upon us and blow us all to atoms."

Several of the gang, directed by Bloodhoof and Redfin, ascended to obey their leader's orders, armed to the teeth, and swearing most awfully against the gallant boys led on by Lion Limb.

But the mutineers could not get very far aloft before they were savagely attacked by some of the convict lads, who fought like heroes, and one by one Bloodhoof's men were shot or stabbed in the rigging by the boys aloft, and tumbled on deck bleeding, gasping and dying.

"Death," growled Whetherby, when he saw that he was foiled at all points.

"Rouse, my lads, arouse, and slay every mother's son of the convict brats," said he, and he dashed hither and thither, foaming at the mouth with rage, sword in hand.

Wherever he went, however, he was forestalled and beaten by the brave lads led on by Norman.

Lion Limb seemed to be everywhere where danger threatened, and performed prodigies of valour.

"I'll soon bring old Clarence to his senses," said Whetherby.

And he rushed down below with a furious gang at his heels.

In an instant, by the combined strength of so many, they broke open the cabin door, and seized the captain's daughter by the hair of her head.

They dragged her senseless upon the main deck, laughing and jeering like so many incarnate fiends.

"Surrender! Captain Clarence, surrender!" shouted Bloodhoof.

"Surrender, and we won't harm you!" cried Whetherby. "It is only on those d—d convict lads, led on by young Devil's Limb, that we wish to wreak our vengeance!"

"Surrender, old man, or we'll cut your daughter's throat!" said Gregory, reeling, half drunk.

"Never," said the noble-hearted captain, surrounded by a few of his crew. "Never will I surrender and allow these noble lads to be butchered before my eyes. Do your very worst, demons; but never while I have life will I surrender the command of my ship."

"Hurrah! hurrah!" shouted the convict lads, in wild triumph.

Bloodhoof, with his sheath knife, held the captain's daughter by the hair of her head, and raised his deadly weapon.

It was at this moment that young Lion Limb dashed forward to rescue the girl or die.

With a shout of confidence he leaped upon Bloodhoof, but at the same instant the dog "Dragon," after more than an hour's tugging at his chain, broke it, and with a terrible growl leaped into the midst of the mutineers.

He seized one by the throat, and in an instant strangled him.

A deep purple stream of life blood stained the deck.

A second he seized by the leg, and bit therefrom a large piece of flesh.

ext he leaped towards Bloodhoof.

ut that savage man, terrified by the animal's ocity, loosened his hold of the captain's daughter, d retired a pace, looking pale.

It was at this moment that Lion Limb came to the rescue.

He had fought his way manfully against a dozen foes, and vanquished them.

With a growl of satisfaction Dragon allowed Lion Limb to bear his young mistress away.

With great presence of mind Norman seized the young girl round her slender waist, and bore her from the midst of the combatants, and placed her in a secret hiding-place.

But while he was away Bloodhoof and Whetherby had almost gained possession of the deck.

The fighting had been very fierce in his absence.

When he returned to the scene of strife the captain was hand to hand with Bloodhoof, and engaged in a terrible combat.

In another moment the good old captain would have been killed.

Norman, with the bound of a young lion, jumped in between them, knocked up Bloodhoof's arm, and the next instant felled him to the deck with a single blow of his fist. (See cut in No. 1).

This action was witnessed by nearly all the combatants on both sides.

The boys rent the air with their shouts.

Bill Whetherby and Gregory, now enraged beyond all measure by their signal failure, rushed upon Lion Limb.

They fired their pistols at the brave lad.

But although he was wounded by the shots, he did not quail or fall.

"He scorned to fall and leave the fight while life remained," he said.

With vengeance in his eye, therefore, he met the onslaught of his foes with great coolness and determination, and in less than three minutes he had wounded Whetherby most severely, and disabled Bloodhoof by a cut in the right arm.

"Fight men, fight!" roared Whetherby, foaming with rage.

"Give no quarter!" cried Bloodhoof, his eyes all red with passion.

"Blow up the magazine," shouted Gregory, "blow it up!"

One more, and the last effort they made was desperate in the extreme.

Seeing that nearly all hope was lost, the mutineers who remained on board made a desperate and combined attack upon Lion Limb and his heroic followers.

For a few moments the strife was desperate in the extreme.

Groans, moans, shrieks, and curses were heard on every side.

But they were conquered.

At every point were the mutineers vanquished.

The captain and many of his men were wounded desperately, and they lay on the deck insensible, and bleeding profusely.

"To the boats! to the boats!" shouted the beaten foe, and they swarmed into what boats remained, carrying with them the insensible form of Bloodhoof, Gregory, and Bill Whetherby, leaving many dead companions behind.

But they were not allowed to do this undisturbed.

Lion Limb and his brave lads fought them hard, and did not allow a single moment for reflection.

Several of the boats were capsized, and many of the mutineers were seized and devoured by ravenous sharks, who were playing around the ship.

Their shouts and cries in death agony were most appalling.

Thus for a whole day had the unequal fight continued, and as the sun set upon the scene, Lion Limb was conqueror and master of the ship.

Loud hurrahs hailed the conclusion of the desperate fight, and as the mutineers pulled off to the neighbouring islands in their boats, Lion Limb charged four of the cannon with grape shot, and fired a parting salute after them, killing many and wounding dozens.

CHAPTER VII.

AFTER THE BATTLE—THE STORM—THE RAFT—EXCITING SCENES.

BUT now that the terrible strife was over, worse dangers were about to fall upon Lion Limb and his brave followers.

A storm sprung up.

The vessel which had been signalled was not able to beat up to the captain's assistance, and ere it got within gunshot distance, heavy squalls struck her, and beat her off again.

The night now began to set in apace.

Everything looked dark, cloudy, cheerless, and threatening.

The winds, which at first began to blow gently and softly, suddenly changed into a hurricane, and screamed through the rigging like shrill voices of the dead.

The vessel rolled.

The sea ran high.

Thunder rumbled overhead, and far and wide forked lightning cleft the heavy clouds, and in the far distance they could see the vessel, which had promised assistance in the morning, tossed upon the angry waves, with sails blown into shreds, and apparently ungovernable upon the wild waste of waters.

The captain and all on board the "Rattlesnake" were too much fatigued, and weak from loss of blood, to attempt to guide their vessel aright. They lay in groups here and there fast asleep, with swords and pistols in hand, just as they had squatted down or fallen from faintness.

Some had scars.

Others were profusely bleeding.

The faces of all were begrimed with dirt, powder, or perspiration.

All—all were sound asleep, or immovable, save Lion Limb.

He walked about from place to place, greatly disturbed in mind.

Many of his young companions had been wounded, and some were killed.

He mourned their loss, deeply and sadly.

The noble vessel was now shaken from head to stern.

The rudder was gone!

The craft was now tossed about on the angry waves, like a cork upon the water.

Worse than all, she was leaking!

Lion Limb had heard a peculiar sound below for several minutes, but could not tell what it meant.

But now that he had an opportunity of discovering the state of things on board, he was amazed to see the wanton havoc which the mutineers had made of everything and anything which they were unable to carry away with them in their boats.

Thanks to the vigilance and bravery of young Ted Rawlings and one or two others, Bloodhoof and his men had not been able to set a slow match to the magazine.

But they did quite as much mischief.

They had scuttled the ship!

The noise which Lion Limb had heard below was the rush of water into the hold!

Without waiting a moment to consider, Norman roused up several of his young friends, and they went below with lanterns and bedding.

Up to their necks in water, they worked like young heroes, and for several hours.

But their labour seemed all in vain.

They stopped up several large holes, by stuffing therein bedding, pillows, blankets, and the like.

No doubt, had the weather permitted, they would have succeeded in stopping up all the holes, but the ship began to roll so frightfully that it was found impossible to finish the work.

The storm above had risen to greater and greater fury.

The main-mast was struck by lightning, and shivered into a thousand pieces.

It fell with an awful crash upon the main deck, and thoroughly startled Lion Limb and others below.

What was to be done?

The boats were gone.

To stay in the vessel now was certain death.

The storm was increasing in its fury each instant.

Waves washed over the ship in all directions, and it threatened to fall to pieces.

Many turned deadly pale.

A few trembled.

Some sat down in deep thought, as if buried in despair.

Of them all, Lion Limb was the only one who seemed prepared for the occasion.

"Come, my brave lads; come, it is of no use to sit down thinking and repining. All of us must be up and doing."

"What *can* we do?" asked a dozen at once.

"Why, a great deal. A fellow who can't face and do battle with danger and difficulties is no man at all. What can you do?—why, everything, if you so choose. Am I not your leader — your chosen captain?"

"You are! You are!" they answered, with a shout.

"Then throw off all this despondency. You have soundly thrashed the mutineers; what you have not killed you have driven from the ship, and now remain the conquerors."

"We are sinking," said several; "there is no hope for us."

"Fie, fie!" said Lion Limb, cheerfully, "while there is life, there is hope. See the fire burning on yonder island?"

"We do."

"Well, those are the mutineers. They have landed, and camped there for the night."

"There are several islands."

"I know it," said Lion Limb; "I saw them when the lightning flashed just now, and beautiful places they seem to be."

"What shall we do, then, Lion Limb?" asked many.

"Why, help me to build a good stout raft, my lads, so that if the ship sinks we can float off to some island, and there make a settlement for ourselves."

Bravo, Lion Limb!—Who'll plan the raft?"

"I will," said Lion Limb, gaily. "But before we begin, let every lad have half a gill of rum or brandy; there is plenty yet in the spirit-room. A little drop of something will drive the blue devils away, and cheer you up."

The same lads, who, a few moments before, had been sad and melancholy, were now so much encouraged by young Norman's words, that they set to work like Trojans.

Spare spars, and casks, and barrels, and ropes, were quickly gathered, and lashed firmly together.

Planks in abundance were found below, and all sorts of necessary timber.

Hammers were soon sounding in every direction, and a general racket of carpenter's tools, and saws, and augers, seemed for a time to drown the hissing of the fast increasing storm.

Ted Rawlings and several others packed up a lot of things to carry away with them.

Several bags of biscuits and a large cask of water were got ready.

Some tobacco, a few bottles of spirits, a few swords, two or three rifles, and some ammunition, were also got ready.

In truth, in less than four hours after the lads began to build their raft, it was completed, and ready to launch in case of necessity.

But how were they to do so?

It was much too heavy to haul out of the ship, and, even had they been able to do so, it would have been smashed to atoms in a few moments, by the violence of the waves dashing against the sides of the vessel.

Lion Limb seemed to be in despair at the failure of his project, but he soon rallied again.

"It will float out of the vessel," said he; "all who like to remain in the sinking ship may do so, but I for one will not."

"No, lad, no; you are perfectly right," said the captain, "I am glad you have built yourselves a good strong raft, for I am certain, if this storm continues for an hour or two longer, the 'Rattlesnake,' will go down, and all hands with her."

"But you will come with us, also, Captain Clarence," said several at once.

"No, my lads, I shall remain where I am, and live or die by my ship."

"But it is certain death, captain."

"I know it; but I do not fear it. I have only one regret in dying——"

He did not speak further.

His utterance became smothered.

He was thinking of his daughter.

"Lion Limb," said Captain Clarence, grasping Norman's hand; "you have proved yourself a true hero. I shall not survive this dreadful storm rising on every hand around us, and I have one last favour to ask."

"Captain Clarence, I can guess what you would say. You mean your——"

"I do, my noble lad; I do."

A solemn pause ensued; neither spoke.

The moment, however solemn to both of the speakers and all concerned, was not to be wasted in idle words.

The waves now began to burst in upon the deck, and several persons were washed overboard.

The raft was lifted up from the main deck by the force of the waters, and tilted on the edge of the bulwarks.

The vessel again and again was struck by heavy squalls, and reeled over so much that no one ever imagined she could right herself again.

She came to, however, but the decks were deeply flooded, and all was a scene of confusion and danger.

"Not a moment is to be lost, boys," said the noble-hearted captain; "if you do not go on your raft now, we shall all go down together."

He affectionately, but hastily, kissed his daughter,

Emma, who was, half unconscious and pale, beside him.

"Take her, Lion Limb," said he; "protect and love her. If you *are* saved, remember me. Quick, lad, quick; a squall will strike us in a moment."

With these words, Captain Clarence threw several sealed bottles overboard.

As all hope seemed to be lost, he had written a few particulars of the mutiny, the storm, the brave conduct of Lion Limb, and of the shipwreck, with many other particulars.

He also gave the latitude and longitude of the disaster, and, being well sealed, he cast the bottle into the sea.

His will also he altered, and put in a second bottle, and this likewise was thrown overboard.

"For," said the captain, "all hope is useless now; nothing but death stares us in the face."

Lion Limb also, seeing how affairs were likely to end, also provided himself with a bottle, and placed a short, hurriedly-written note in it, which read:—

"In great haste. The ship 'Rattlesnake,' 8 guns, is a total wreck. Each moment we expect to be our last. Most of the crew have mutinied, and have gone away in all the boats well provisioned. There was a terrible fight on board, which lasted one whole day. The boy convicts defended Captain Clarence and his officers to the very last, and drove off the mutineers. We are now somewhere in the South Pacific; all hope of saving the vessel is lost. We are sinking.
"EDGAR NORMAN.

"Whoever finds this will please send the note to the nearest British consul. Farewell to all. "E. N."

This half-gallon stone jar Lion Limb threw overboard; but neither he nor the captain imagined the influence it would have in their after fortunes.

At that instant, a vivid, blinding flash of lightning lit up the whole ocean.

The thunder crashed in deafening peals.

In a second gigantic waves came rolling towards the doomed ship.

With a sudden bound, several jumped on to the raft, and clung tight to its ropes and spars.

Lion Limb had before this lashed Emma Clarence to a jury mast on the raft.

A moment of blindness and unconsciousness ensued.

And when they turned to look the vessel was far behind them, and the captain stood waving his handkerchief to cheer them on.

But of the many who had determined to go forth on the raft not one half were there.

The other ones Lion Limb could see clinging to the rigging of the doomed ship.

And their lusty shouts were faintly audible through the whistling of the storm like the weird whisperings of the night.

Onward, onward rolled the mighty storm-crested waves.

And on the bosom of the upheaving deep floated the raft of Lion Limb.

Rain poured down in pitiless torrents.

Heavy, inky, impenetrable masses of lightning-laden clouds hovered and lowered over the frail raft, as, beaten about, it rose and fell.

Now, on the top of a mountainous wave, they could get but a glimpse of the sinking vessel as, afar off, it looked but a speck upon the waters.

And then again they were engulphed in a deep abyss between almost perpendicular, watery, foam-crested walls, which each instant threatened to topple over and crush them.

Still bravely did Lion Limb guide his raft.

He hoisted a sail to steady it in the storm, and high above the hissing tide floated his signal of distress.

But little did Lion Limb imagine, as he stood on that tiny structure, encouraging a few disheartened youths, and cheerily singing in the midst of that ocean, boiling around him in tempestuous wrath; little did that fatherless, friendless and half-naked cast-away think of the terrible trial, strange, startling adventures, and the glorious future that were in store for him.

But, we will not anticipate.

Truth *is* stranger than fiction, however wild and startling it may be written, and we beg our young readers to follow us week by week, by which we shall faithfully chronicle the career of one of England's greatest heroes.

CHAPTER VIII.

THE RAFT—A SAIL IN SIGHT—HOPE IS ABANDONED BY ALL SAVE LION LIMB.

THE night which followed the sudden and unlooked-for departure of Lion Limb and his followers from the sinking ship was so dark and tempestuous that they could not see a dozen yards before them.

The winds howled more fiercely than ever.

High waves rolled and dashed against their little barque, tossing it so high that Lion Limb, brave as he was, expected each moment would be their last.

The wild waters seemed to riot in their madness and grandeur, and washed over the raft mercilessly and furiously.

More than once the little mast and its single sail were thrown down and well-nigh carried overboard.

Most of those on the raft would have perished had it not been for young Lion Limb's forethought and wisdom.

His first care was for the safety and comfort of those around him more than his own.

With all the spare rope he could find, he firmly lashed most of his companions to the raft, and so tightly that it caused them pain and their limbs to swell.

Little Emma he was particularly careful of, and made her a safe place wherein to lie; but still the cruel waves washed over her frequently, and even Lion Limb's stout heart felt that perhaps none of them would ever again see the morning's light.

With his own hands he repaired the sail and secured the planks and spars more firmly together, and of all the party his were the only eyes that were not closed; his the only soul which still hoped on.

With a long harpoon, he moved from side to side, beating off and wounding innumerable sharks which played on all sides, hungry and voracious as they were, and ready with their tremendous jaws to snap at any arm or leg of the unconscious sleepers as their limbs carelessly hung and dragged in the sea.

The waters were all alive with monsters of the deep, and their flight to and fro near the surface of the boiling sea, were plain to the eye.

Such sufferings as these boys endured on that dreadful stormy night; such dangers and escapes that occurred to these ocean wanderers, can never be properly narrated.

Yet what of those who had remained on the wreck?

Were they still alive?

Was that ill-fated vessel still floating and buffeted about on the angry sea, or had the noble captain and all hands perished with him?

These were the thoughts that flitted constantly through Norman's mind as he gazed in sadness upon the cold, cheerless, half-naked, and more than half-dead forms which, in all attitudes and in every conceivable posture, lay grouped about him.

But at last the black and angry clouds began to disperse.

The lightning now was no longer visible; but afar off, yea, scores of miles, perhaps, in the impenetrable horizon beyond, a sudden and faint flash would from time to time appear; and the low rumbling, grumbling roll of thunder, told Lion Limb that the winds at last had had compassion on him and were beating off the storm to regions and climes hundreds, if not thousands of miles away.

One by one the dangerous, storm-burdened clouds burst asunder, and one by one the stars appeared.

The winds died away until their whisperings were no more than the soft breathings of an infant sleeping.

The fair round moon came out and sailed majestically through the heavens in all her virgin purity and brightness.

And it gladdened the heart of Lion Limb to think that perhaps the beating of the waves would also shortly cease, and that their many sorrows would have an happy end.

With the morning came still greater hopes.

The sea was comparatively calm, and all on the raft after being refreshed with a little nourishment, were in hopes of meeting with some vessel shortly which would receive them.

All were set to work to do various things, which they gladly performed under Lion Limb's guidance, and the raft was made still stronger and stouter than ever.

Lion Limb slept but little. The care of so many human beings on his shoulders made him restless.

A sharp look-out was kept for any passing ship or sight of land.

But neither one nor the other were visible.

Whither they were now drifting to, no one had the slightest notion.

They had been driven by the storm, Lion Limb and the rest supposed, hundreds of miles from where the "Rattlesnake's" crew had landed on the unknown island and lit their camp fires.

They were in the South Pacific Ocean it is true, but the exact latitude no one could guess.

Ted Rawlings clambered up the pole which served as a mast.

Perched up there, hour by hour, under the blazing, blistering sun, he shaded his eyes and scanned the broad Pacific.

But no sail appeared in sight.

Black despair seemed to sit on the countenances of all save that of the bold young Lion Limb.

He appeared cheerful as ever, and sang songs, and told comic stories, to keep up the flagging spirits of those around him. But all in vain.

That day passed, and then another, and yet there was no sign of hope.

Lion Limb portioned out the amount of biscuit and water which each was to receive.

And little it was, in all truth, and not even sufficient to keep body and soul together.

Most of their provisions had been washed overboard in the storm, and little now remained.

Thirst was the most cruel torture that they had to endure.

The sun was intensely hot, and each one became so blistered and feverish that though Lion Limb did not utter his thoughts, he felt convinced that if no relief came within two or three days, some of his companions would go raving mad.

Four days passed in this manner, and now their little stock of food and water were well-nigh exhausted.

Although he did his utmost to prevent it, some of the silly lads began to drink sea-water, to allay their burning thirst.

The result was, that a few hours' exposure to the hot sun turned their brain.

They cursed and swore most frightfully, and had to be tied down with ropes, to prevent them jumping into the sea.

They prayed for death, but it came not.

One lad bit his arm, and sucked the blood therefrom to quench his thirst, but soon afterwards he fell overboard, and was instantly snapped in twain by huge sharks, which had been following and playing around the raft for two or three days.

Even Lion Limb began to look serious.

Some of his comrades had already died.

Others were slowly dying.

A few were raving maniacs, and of the whole number there were not more than half-a-dozen sane persons on board.

Of these six, Lion Limb, Emma, and Ted Rawlings were three. the fourth was a stout-hearted young sailor, and the other two boy convicts.

Six days had now passed, and yet no sail had appeared in sight.

The last portion of biscuit had been given out to each.

Not a single drop of water remained.

Nor had they had any for two whole days, except what they caught in their caps during a short shower of rain.

They could not live long in this way.

All felt sure, and maybe began to think secretly, about the necessity of casting lots to see who should first be killed and eaten, to keep the rest alive.

These thoughts Lion Limb was aware were in the minds of some, and he felt sure that the maddened lads would pitch upon little Emma first.

But Lion Limb loaded his pistols, and swore he would die himself, rather than any vile hand should be laid on her he had learned so dearly to love.

Seven days had now passed, and the eighth day had dawned.

Every one was so weak that they could scarcely stand, and the poor dog, "Dragon," which had jumped on the raft after his young mistress, closed its eyes, and placing its head in little Emma's lap, seemed so weak and feeble as if about to die.

It looked up into her face so pitifully, and with so much eloquent meaning, that the poor girl watered its face with her tears.

No one was scarcely able to stir from sheer exhaustion, and the raft lazily sailed along on the sunlit waters, aimless and rudderless.

As if inspired, Emma suddenly jumped up from her seat beside Lion Limb, and shading her eyes from the dazzling sunlight, exclaimed aloud,

"A sail! A sail in sight!"

"Where? Where?" was the eager question of all.

And so glad were their hearts, that it renewed their strength, and several jumped to their feet and gazed intently in the direction pointed out by Emma.

"I don't see it."

"Nor I."

"Nor I."

"It is only a cloud, I tell you, girl. I am taller than you, and I can't see it."

"A sail! a sail!" said Emma, clapping her hands. "I know it is—this makes my dream come true. There it is yonder, like a tiny cloud ducking on the edge of the horizon. It is a sail!"

"Hurrah!" said Lion Limb, "make signals to it, Emma, or they may not see us."

On the instant Lion Limb, who jumped on an

empty water barrel, caught Emma up in his arms, and she waved a large white handkerchief towards the ship.

But Lion Limb was too weak to support Emma's weight alone.

Ted Rawlings, and all who were able, lent their aid, and assisted him to uphold her weight.

"Do you see it?"

"Does she answer our signal?"

"Has she changed her tack?"

"Does she come towards us?" asked first one and then another in breathless expectation.

"Yes, yes, she comes this way. Hold me up a little longer, and then they will see our signal of distress more clearly."

All did, to the utmost of their power, and held her aloft as long as they possibly could.

Even "Dragon" seemed animated by the unusual excitement, and hope depicted on every face, and he wagged his tail and feebly barked in joy.

For more than an hour was Emma upheld in her position.

The strange and distant vessel tacked first one way and then another—at one moment giving hopes, and the next one dismal fears, until at last little Emma burst out into bitter tears.

The vessel had caught a fair wind, and sailed out of sight.

CHAPTER IX.

LAND HO!—SUDDEN JOY—SAVED! SAVED!

ALL hope now seemed lost, and most of those who yet survived gave up every thought of ever reaching land once more.

If possible the sun was more terribly hot than ever.

Scarcely anyone could breathe.

Each one dreaded suffocation.

"Water! water!" was the feeble cry, on every hand.

But there was water, water everywhere, yet not a drop to drink.

Lion Limb advised all to bathe their legs and arms to allay their parchedness, a device often resorted to, and successfully, to moderate burning thirst.

Several did so.

Yet "water! water!" was the constant heartrending cry from all.

"Let us cast lots to see who shall die!" raved one. "Better one be made a sacrifice than that all should perish!"

"Yes, yes, let us cast lots."

"Kill the captain's daughter, she is of no use to us," groaned another.

"Silence, fools!" said Lion Limb, pistol in hand, "do I not suffer as well as you? Have I not had the least share of everything, and given my water away to those who needed it more than myself?"

"Water! water!" was still the cry.

"The first one that dares stir to lay a finger on this sinless maid, shall die by my hand," said Lion Limb, fiercely.

"Water! water!" murmured many.

"If some one must die to save the rest, let your lots fall on me," said Lion Limb; "let me die a thousand times ere you shed the blood of this faultless maid."

Lion Limb's brave attitude for a time silenced the grumblers, and as night came on, they dozed off to sleep, and were raving in their dreams.

The night came on very dark and cloudy, and so thick was the atmosphere that no one could discern any object before them beyond half a dozen yards.

No moon nor stars lighted them on their weary way, and Lion Limb sighed to think that perhaps another dreadful storm was about to burst over them.

Many imagined that this was the last night they should ever see on earth.

And so did Lion Limb also.

Yet he kept strict watch over Emma as she slept, nor did he even close his eyes for a single moment.

With revolver ready cocked, he sat beside the beautiful girl, and his eyes flashed fire in the darkness, as he heard two persons whispering together, and planning how to kill the girl for their next day's food.

He ground his teeth in anger as he faintly listened to their fiendish plans, and felt more than half inclined to blow their brains out on the spot, but——

All at once the raft struck something hard, and every plank shivered with the shock.

"We are lost," thought Lion Limb; "we have struck some reef or hidden rock."

And he jumped to his feet ready to clasp Emma in his arms, in order that they might die together, when the raft bumped again and again more heavily than before.

"Merciful heaven! we are saved!" he exclaimed, aloud; "the raft is on the lea shore of a large island!"

Yes, it was true.

Weakness, and the darkness of the night, had so impaired Lion Limb's vision, that what he had mistaken for heavy lowering banks of clouds were nought else but high cliffs and hills.

The raft had drifted into a small bay, and was now forced by the tide upon a sandy shore.

The truth flashed across his mind instantly.

"Quick," thought Lion Limb, or she may drift off again.

And quick he was in all truth.

He seized a spare coil of half-inch rope, and winding most of it round his body, he tied one end to the mast of the raft, and was about to jump into the serf. But he quickly retraced his steps.

A thought, full of dismal forebodings, crossed his mind.

"All who are not asleep are almost raving mad," he thought. "Perhaps, while I am on shore, fastening the line, and hauling the raft higher upon the sand, they may murder little Emma."

To prevent such an act on the part of his raving comrades, he roused Emma, took her in his arms, jumped into the serf with her, followed by the faithful dog Dragon, and soon reached the shore in safety.

Exhausted and nearly fainting, Lion Limb ran up and down the sandy beach, and at last found the stump of an old tree.

"Come, Emma," said he, "cheer up, my bonnie lass; we are saved at last."

And both of them tugged at the rope long and vigorously, almost with the energy of despair.

The tide assisted their more than human efforts.

"When the tide recedes," said Lion Limb, "it will leave the raft high and dry upon the beach. Won't it be a surprise to all on the raft?"

Emma did not reply.

Her young heart was too full for words.

She sank down upon her knees and prayed.

The hot, scalding tears flowed down her pale wan cheeks.

Her large, lustrous, dreamy eyes were upraised to heaven.

For the first time during the whole of her trials, she now gave way to uncontrolled grief, and sobbed almost convulsively, as she murmured,

"My father! oh, my poor brave father!"

And with a heartrending hysterical cry she flung herself upon Edgar's manly breast, fainting.

And Lion Limb, with a look of joy and triumph, pressed the fair one lovingly to his heart, murmuring, half aloud,

"Oh, if after storms and trials such holy calm and joy shall come, then let Boreas blow, and Neptune roll as often as they will."

And on the shore of that wild unknown land, in that dark and cloudy night, Edgar Norman, young Lion Limb, the Boy Convict, kissed the upturned cheek of Emma Clarence, and swore, by the eternal stars, come weal come woe, to love, protect, and cherish her as long as life should last!

CHAPTER X.

FRESH DISCOVERIES—THE FEROCIOUS FOE.

BUT now that they had reached the shore, Lion Limb began to provide for the safety of his companions, who still lay in groups upon the raft, totally unaware of what had occurred to him and the captain's daughter.

From the spot were he stood, Lion Limb could distinctly hear them groaning and moaning, and so weakened that they could not move hand or foot.

"Water—water—water!" were the cries which still reached his ears.

"Poor fellows," sighed Lion Limb; "their trials for the past week have been awful; I much fear if many of them will fully recover their senses again."

In truth, the only ones of the whole party who could be considered really sane, were Ted Rawlings and the gallant young seaman, Harry Woodruff.

But they were at the moment fast asleep, and Lion Limb did not like to wake them.

"Oh, that I could find a spring," said Lion Limb; but all around was total darkness, and as the rocks above shelved over, and formed a place of safety, Lion Limb thought it wise not to venture out far upon the island, for he was very weak, and, except his long knife and revolver, had no other weapons with him in case of any sudden attack from ferocious beasts, or equally savage natives, who might be prowling about the coast.

At this moment, and while praying that he might discover water of some sort, "Dragon," the gallant Newfoundland dog, came bounding towards him in great glee.

Lion Limb, at the moment, thought it indicated the presence of savages close by.

But the faithful animal ran towards his mistress, and began to lick her hands and feet; and the moisture of his lolling tongue was so cold, that Lion Limb immediately felt certain that the good animal had discovered a spring somewhere.

This was the truth.

"Dragon," directly he got on shore, had gone whisking about in all directions.

At one moment he would gallop away and quickly return again, joyfully barking, as if to tell the news.

"Have you found water, 'Dragon'?" asked Lion Limb, with a smile, patting his head.

The dog barked loudly in answer, as if he had perfectly understood the question; and shook himself so vigorously, that a perfect shower of water was thrown off his coat into Lion Limb's face.

This was positive proof of water being near by.

"Thank heaven!" said Lion Limb, and the dog, darting before him, ran along the beach under the cliffs, and, after going about 100 yards over the shingle, Lion Limb was attracted to a small rivulet of water, running into the sea, into which "Dragon" had again plunged, and was swimming about in great glee.

Lion Limb tasted the water, and found it to be excellent, and of almost icy coldness.

"We must all be very careful how much we drink of this water for a day or two, or the lads will do themselves great harm," thought the young chief.

He himself only drank about a gill of it, and then began to think how he could convey some back to Emma.

While attempting to carry some in his cap without succe-s, he stumbled against a hard vegetable substance, and fell over it.

It proved to be an immense water melon, almost dried up to a crisp!

In a moment he slashed it in halves with his knife, scooped out the inside, and then made two portable vessels, each of which would contain half-a-gallon of water.

He filled both of them, and, one under each arm, he hurried down the shingle to the projecting rock, under which Emma lay.

He gave her a small quantity to drink, and this reviving her to a very great degree, she accompanied him to the stream, leaning on him for support all the way.

While "Dragon" jumped about as if he had gone mad with joy; leaping first on one side, and then on the other, endeavouring, in his way, to kiss the hands of his young master and mistress.

As Lion Limb would not allow Emma to drink much water at a time, she followed his advice, and in a degree assuaged her burning thirst by washing her face, head, hands and feet in the water, and then lay down under a tree, guarded by "Dragon."

But during all this time Lion Limb felt convinced that there were wild animals or something of the kind about, and he kept his revolvers cocked ready for immediate use.

Nor was he mistaken.

He heard the distant footfalls of something as it cautiously and slowly approached through the brushwood.

His noble dog raised his ears and growled in a low, ominous manner.

Lion Limb held him firmly by the neck.

Nearer and nearer the unknown object came.

All was darkness.

Lion Limb could not distinctly make out what the object was. Yet he could see the grim, dark, and huge outline of something human.

Two red eyes glared in the darkness like burning coals.

The arms were outstretched like those of a man.

Lion Limb could even hear its heavy breathings near to him.

The moment was one of intense excitement.

What was it that thus grimly confronted the brave lad?

He knew not, nor could he even imagine.

That it was something very gigantic, human-looking, and very ferocious, there could not be a doubt.

But yet he feared not; the gallant lad's nerves were as immovable as brass.

In an instant, and just when he was about to advance and attack this unknown foe, the object bounded away into the dense thickets and was lost to view.

Could it be fancy only, or was it reality?

His eyes, ears, and understanding could not be so deceived.

"It must be some enemy," he thought.

Nor was he wrong, as he boldly plunged forward to confront and do battle with his unknown enemy; but the search was all in vain.

The grim object had fled, whither he could not tell.

LION LIMB

THE BOY KING
OF THE SOUTH SEA ISLANDS.

LION LIMB RESCUES THE CAPTIVES FROM THE STAKE.

"Dragon," too, had been sniffing and growling rather bad-temperedly, which fact put Lion Limb on his guard accordingly.

"If I could only light a fire," said he, after he had recovered from astonishment at the sudden departure of his unknown visitor, "all would go well until morning."

But he had no matches, and to make a fire seemed an impossibility.

He thought for a second.

"I have it!" he said, joyfully. "'Necessity is the mother of invention.' A lad don't know what he can do until he tries. There is a good quantity of wadding in this old jacket of mine," he said, "and plenty of flints upon the beach."

In an instant he took off his old jacket, ripped out some of the wadding lining, selected a good flint, and placed them beside Emma and her faithful guardian, "Dragon."

He next went into a small copse and gathered a large armful of small twigs, dry leaves, and some decayed sunburnt branches.

Almost staggering under his weight of fire-wood, he went back to Emma, who took up the wadding, flint, and several dry branches, and they slowly made their way back to their first resting-place.

Nor was "Dragon" useless in this case.

The faithful dog, perceiving the heavy burdens which Lion Limb and Emma were carrying, picked up a small bunch of a blasted, sun-dried tree, and dragged it along with all his strength.

When they had built up this fire-wood against and under the projecting rock, Lion Limb set to work, and began to knock the flint against the back of his knife.

After ten minutes of hard labour, several sparks flew out upon the cotton, and, to the great joy of both, the fire began to burn brightly and cheerily.

While Lion Limb was doing this, and making Emma comfortable near the fire, Harry Woodruff, the young sailor, and Ted Rawlings, had thoroughly awakened from their long sleep on board the raft.

At first, when they perceived the distant fire, they thought that it must be all a dream, and could scarce believe their senses.

But, straining their eyes, and perceiving the fire to blaze up each moment more and more brightly, Harry Woodruff, with all the strength he could muster, put both hands to his mouth and shouted out—

"A-h-o-o-y! a-h-o-o-y on shore, there!"

The rocks echoed the sound a hundred times, and at last Harry and Ted became convinced that, while asleep, the raft had struck upon a rock or an island.

With all his strength, Lion Limb answered the shout again and again.

In a moment, Lion Limb perceived the rope with which he had fastened the raft to the shore to be jerking violently, and in a short time, greatly to his astonishment, he discerned two figures struggling on the rope, and endeavouring to reach the shore.

These two figures were Harry Woodruff and Ted Rawlings, the former carrying the latter upon his back.

They reached the shore, and were amazed at all Lion Limb told them.

A little water was given to each, and they crept close to the bright fire, and its genial warmth soon changed their shivering into hopes and smiles.

"The tide will soon leave the raft high and dry," said Harry, in a husky voice.

"I know it will; but we must take great care the lads don't get to the water and drink too much. If they do, it will kill them."

"Quite true, Captain Lion; quite true, and I'm glad you've good sense enough to know it. Leave 'em to me, I'll take care every one obeys your orders as they should do."

Leaving Harry and Ted at the fire guarding Emma, Lion Limb went forth towards the rivulet again.

He called "Dragon," who, perceiving that his young mistress was well cared for, bounded along before Lion Limb, barking most merrily.

It had been Lion Limb's intention to have got another load of wood from the forest, and some more water.

But other adventures were in store for him.

"It is of no use trying to look out for anything to eat," he mused, "the night is very dark, I cannot see very far before me, and beside, I have no rifle or anything save my revolver and knife. In the morning I will get the two guns off the raft and go out among the hills and hunt with Harry and Ted. There must be plenty of game somewhere hereabouts."

He had just entered the forest which skirted the rivulet and had begun to gather a large bundle of branches and dead wood—indeed he had put a cord about the sticks with the intention of carrying them away, when a dreadful growl like the echoes of distant thunder reached his ear.

"Dragon" ran back to his master, and for a few moments Lion Limb did not know what to make of the noise.

The dog barked, and the growl became louder and louder until the earth seemed to shake under Lion Limb's feet.

He looked forward into the deep darkness and within a short distance of him he perceived two glaring eyes which shone like balls of phosphorus in the distance.

It was a young lion!

"Dragon" had disturbed it, and enticed him from his lair.

And there the young lion stood with head erect, flowing main, and swishing his tail angrily about from side to side, and pawing the earth.

He was a grand young animal, and looked the very picture of majesty.

Escape was now impossible.

Lion Limb did not dare to turn his head or look on one side for a moment.

He gazed in astonishment at the ferocious young lion, but his nerves were cool and undisturbed.

He knew it was now a case of life or death for himself or the beast.

With great nerve he unsheathed his knife, and with the revolver took deliberate aim at the animal.

At the same instant he fired, the young lion bounded towards him.

The shot had stunned the beast and he reeled again.

With a terrible roar, he rushed at Lion Limb, but the active youth jumped nimbly behind a tree, and fired every load his revolver had into the head and eyes of the huge beast.

And even then it was not conquered or killed.

In its death agonies it proved more ferocious than ever, and, had not one of the shots broken its fore legs, Lion Limb's chance of escape would have been very small indeed.

However, he rushed upon the lion with more than manly daring.

"They have always called me Lion Limb," said he, half aloud, "and now that I have the chance, I will give no one reason to doubt my nerve and courage and title to that name."

Knife in hand, then, he boldly advanced towards the wounded lion.

Thrice he plunged his long knife into the side of the beast, and thrice did the noble animal rear itself up and fight bravely against its fate.

It made one last desperate effort.

With a roar like distant thunder, it leaped upon Norman with open jaws.

The moment was an awful one for the young chief.

He fell crushed by the weight of the young lion, but as he fell he quickly plunged his knife into the animal's heart, and with a last death growl it rolled over and was dead.

Lion Limb was quickly on his feet again, and carefully examined his prize, and beside him stood "Dragon,' panting and barking over his own share in the victory.

The young lion was a noble-looking animal and its coat both soft and silky.

"This will make me a capital mantle," thought Lion Limb, and without hesitation he began to skin the beast, which task he soon accomplished, and with great success.

During this operation, however, "Dragon," for a time, left his young master, and when he returned, Lion Limb found him licking his chops as if he had been enjoying a fine meal somewhere.

To dispel all doubts upon this point, Lion Limb took up his lion's skin and penetrated still deeper into the forest.

Within a short distance he came upon a sort of cave or den, and by the moonlight which now began to break through the clouds and peep through the trees, he discovered the body of a fine young deer, which the lion, no doubt, had been upon the point of devouring when annoyed and discovered by the dog "Dragon."

"This is better and better," thought Lion Limb; "we want food of some kind, and here it is ready for instant use."

He took up the young buck and carried it on his shoulders towards their camp fire, followed by "Dragon," barking and jumping about all the way, and his arrival was hailed with great applause by Harry, Ted and Emma.

It is needless to say that within a few minutes, every one there were very busy in cooking venison steaks, and enjoyed themselves immensely with this their first meal on the unknown island.

CHAPTER XI.

ALONE IN THE FOREST WILDS.

WITHIN a very short time the tide began to fall, and after the little party on shore had partaken of a very slight repast—for Lion Limb was careful that none should over-charge themselves for fear of sickness after their long and painful fasting—all set to work manfully to convey their exhausted companions to the shore.

The sun had now began to gild the eastern skies in ruddy glory.

It was just past twilight, and Harry Woodroff, Ted Rawlings, and the faithful "Dragon," went towards the raft, aided even by Emma, and directed in all their operations by Lion Limb himself.

Harry Woodruff and Lion Limb each took one of the sufferers in their arms, and conveyed them to the overhanging rock.

Emma had collected a lot of grass, dry leaves, and small branches of trees, and thus not only made comfortable beds for the sufferers, but with the leaves and branches formed a sort of shade from the heat of the sun, which every moment became warmer and warmer.

By great exertion Lion Limb and his two companions brought every one on shore, and laid them down near the fire.

Emma cooked some of the venison, and made everything as pleasant as she possibly could.

There were very few articles of value on the raft, but whatever was of use, in the way of planking, old sails, nails, hammers, and cording, were quickly conveyed away, and in less than three hours the raft was broken up piece by piece, and all the lumber conveyed to a spot beyond the reach of the tide.

When all these things were done, Lion Limb began to think of exploring some part of the island on which they had been cast.

He had an old rifle, found among various odds and ends on the raft, and this he set about cleaning immediately, and soon had it ready for use.

His stock of powder and ball, however, was very scarce indeed, and as he was the best shot in the whole party, he took particular charge of the ammunition and fire-arms himself.

Having provided himself with a few slices of roasted meat, and a calabash filled with water from the rivulet near by, he called "Dragon" to his side and prepared to set out on his exploring expedition.

Before he did so, however, he gave directions to Woodruff what to do in regard to the sick boys, and particularly charged him not to allow any of them to partake too freely of food, and more especially of water.

"Because," said he, "they have been so very long without, and have become so prostrated from privation, that if they over indulged themselves for a day or two, death will be the consequence. But above all," said Lion Limb, "don't allow the fire to go out—there is plenty of dry wood around us—because we might have great difficulty in lighting it again. And in case the island may be inhabited by savages, do not allow the smoke to curl up higher than possible, for it would attract them; they might fall upon us unawares, and as we are not numerous would very likely massacre every one."

Promising to return that same evening, Lion Limb, with the lion's skin cast over his shoulder, took up his rifle and went forth, accompanied by "Dragon."

When they had reached the rivulet, Lion Limb thought it wise to indicate the path he had taken in case he was lost, by cutting slips of bark from the tree with his knife.

Thus, when he had waded up to his waist, and crossed the rivulet, he plunged into the dark dense forest, in hopes of soon reaching a very high hill which he saw in the distance.

The dog "Dragon" went before him, and every twenty yards Lion Limb stopped and cut a large slice of bark off various trees, thus marking the way as he went.

For several hours he travelled thus through the forest, ever on his guard against any surprise from strange or ferocious beasts.

From the frequent growlings and barkings of Dragon, and the rush of something through the low brushwood, Lion Limb became convinced that the forest was thickly tenanted with animals and birds of all sorts.

The chattering of monkeys, the grunting of wild hogs, the hissing of serpents, and the low, deep growls which from time to time caught his ears, and the incessant whistling and flight of many-coloured birds, convinced him that the forest, perhaps, had seldom, if ever, been disturbed by the presence of any man before.

Onward he toiled, however, through the entangling wild vines and brushwood, with rifle cocked, and knife ready for instant use.

After several hours of excessive labour he perceived that he was gradually emerging into an open country.

The hill he longed to climb was not more than half-a-mile away, and towards it he hastily bent his steps.

Various four-footed beasts, alarmed at his

presence, stood for a moment and gazed at him—more especially at Dragon, who was dancing about full of life and activity—and then darted away snorting, and howling, and bellowing, into what seemed to be almost impenetrable thickets and jungle.

Once at the base of the hill Lion Limb cut for himself a stout ash limb, and this served him as a mountain staff to climb more easily.

For more than half-an-hour he struggled up the rough, rocky sides of the hill, and at length, fatigued, red in the face, and perspiring at every pore, he reached the top.

He sat beneath a small group of trees he found there, and then began to scan the prospect all around him.

He could distinctly perceive the smoke curling up in a tiny wreath from the boy's encampment, but so well had Harry and Ted obeyed his orders, that there was not the least sign of any living creature in that direction.

Far away in the calm, and shining ocean he perceived several specks, some large and some small.

These he took to be islands.

All around and beneath him were beautiful valleys, small rivers, and dense forests, but two-thirds of the island was hidden from his view by a lofty chain of mountains rising in imposing grandeur to the westward.

"This is a splendid island," thought Lion Limb, as he shaded his eyes from the blazing sunlight, and surveyed the variegated panorama before and beneath him. "It is well wooded and plentifully watered, and no doubt superabundantly stocked with game and animals of all sorts, therefore we shall not starve. What adventures we shall have, too! What grand hunts, and fishing excursions we'll have! I'll make a boat when I return, and sail all round the island, and have a good look at it. I wonder if it is inhabited, though?" thought he, "*that* is the main question."

As thus he mused, Dragon, who had crept down the hillside among the low shrubs in search of game, suddenly returned, and growled warningly.

Lion Limb patted him on the head, and, in a whisper, bade him lie down and be quiet.

But Dragon would not.

He had seen something he did not at all relish.

Lion Limb felt convinced that the faithful dog's uneasiness had a cause.

He therefore hid himself in some bushes, and holding Dragon by the mouth, so that he should not bark or growl, he waited and listened in breathless anxiety.

Presently the bushes began to move, and, greatly to Lion Limb's surprise, four or five athletic, naked, copper-coloured savages emerged from the thicket, and were jabbering away rapidly together in some unknown and barbarous language.

They were all men, and as ugly as could be, with large mouths, glistening fang-like teeth, long, black, wiry hair, dirty in the extreme, and powerfully made.

They carried all manner of rude, warlike implements with them.

One had bows and arrows, a second a long spear, a third an immense club, the head of which was bristling with spikes.

The one with the club appeared to be a chief among them, and wore a bunch of many-coloured feathers in his head, and, in addition, had a girdle of beads and shells round his waist, from which depended a slight apron-sort of garment, painted in various colours, and with all manner of rude devices.

They were all fierce, warlike-looking wretches, and their hands seemed to be stained with blood.

Their eyes were small, cunning, restless, and like black beads.

Each one was talking as rapidly as possible, and gesticulating wildly as if engaged in conversing about a matter of vital importance.

"I thought so," thought Lion Limb, from his place of concealment, and with a sigh. "We haven't been on the island many hours before these savages have discovered us."

He was right.

For the chief, with club in hand, pointed towards the boy's camp, and shook his brawny arm in that direction with a fierce laugh of triumph.

His companions danced around him with wild shouts, and acted like men who had become suddenly deranged.

The chief spoke again, and one of them counted on his fingers the number of persons he had discovered landing from the raft.

For Lion Limb now felt sure that he and his party had been watched, and he sighed to think what a poor resistance he or they could make in case of some sudden attack.

In a moment afterwards the savages disappeared down the mountain side, and Lion, still muzzling Dragon, came forth from his covert.

He was very wary, nor would he have ventured out at all so soon were it not that he could plainly hear the voices of the savages dying away in the distance.

"This day may be the ruin of us," thought the courageous lad, "for if he barks or flies at any of them, I shall be discovered and murdered."

He therefore took off his belt, and formed a sort of muzzle for Dragon, holding the end of it in such wise that in a moment he could loosen it, and allow the animal free use of its jaws again, if necessary.

He stealthily followed the dusky islanders down the mountain side, carefully making his way as before by chipping and slicing strips of bark from the trees.

He had not gone far, however, when loud, fiendish shrieks, cries, and laughter, proceeding from a small valley below, attracted his attention, and arrested his further progress.

It was fortunate that Lion Limb stopped when he did, for had he gone three or four feet further, he would have been precipitated several hundred feet below.

He was standing on a shelving rock, overgrown with trees.

His blood curdled again as he thought of the imminent danger he had run.

He sat down, however, and peering through the dense foliage, looked into the small valley beneath him, anxious to ascertain the cause of the loud shouts, and shrieks, and cries which had for the moment startled him.

He gazed for a moment, and the cause was self-evident.

The sight he then beheld was horrifying.

It was a feast of cannibals!

The savages, numbering over one hundred, and dressed in the wildest and most fantastic manner, were dancing and yelling round some dozen victims who were bound hand and foot.

These victims had evidently been cruelly tortured, and the sands seemed dyed with their blood.

They were evidently prisoners of war, and were doomed to die.

This convinced him that the island was inhabited by more than one tribe of savage men, or that they had been captured on some adjacent islet and brought to this one.

Some of the barbarians, both men and women, were dancing and drinking; even the children seemed to take delight in insulting the victims of their parents.

Large stakes had, in several places, been thrust into the ground, around which were gathered and piled up large quantities of faggots.

To each of these stakes was firmly tied some unhappy wretch who was doomed to be burnt alive.

Several of the executioners, with firebrands in hand, stood ready to apply the fatal torch.

But it seemed to Lion Limb that the proper moment for the cruel sacrifice had not yet arrived.

The savage chief, the one described with the huge spike-headed club, had arrived on the scene, and seemed to be holding a council of war.

He frequently pointed to the hill-top and shouted savagely.

His threats, and shouts, and oaths, were echoed by his followers, and re-echoed by numbers of ravines, caverns, which cut the base of the hill at every side.

Lion Limb heard the sound distinctly.

"It bodes my little colony no good," he thought; "and, after this inhuman sacrifice of their prisoners, they will, no doubt, collect all their forces and attack us in the night. What had I better do? They know our number well enough," mused Lion Limb, "for I saw one of the savages counting on his fingers. They suppose we are all weak things, and would fly at the first approach of danger. They are much mistaken, though! Harry Woodruff is worth any dozen of such dusky rascals as those I see below—so am I—so is Ted Rawlings—aye, even little Emma would not fear death any more than I! The cowards!" thought Lion Limb, "they are going to burn their victims alive! But I'll soon let them see what sort of metal we are made of! I'll attack the rascals this instant—single handed and alone!"

Thus resolving, and with his face flushed with honest, manly indignation at the inhuman ferocity of the savages below, he examined his weapons, and, leading Dragon by his belt, he cautiously picked his way down the mountain's side, bent on rescuing the victims from their cruel fate.

And, as he went, his heart beat wildly with joy, as he said—

"Lion Limb shall be king of the island, and no other, or I will die in the attempt!"

CHAPTER XII

LION LIMB, SINGLE-HANDED, RESCUES SEVERAL VICTIMS FROM THE STAKE—EXCITING MOMENTS.

DOWN the rugged rocks he climbed, the gun in his right hand and leading Dragon by the left.

In his belt were a revolver, a long knife, and an axe.

On his shoulders carelessly hung the skin of the lion which he had but recently so nobly slain.

It was as much as he could very well do to keep the dog from barking or growling as they nearer and nearer approached the cannibals step by step.

But Dragon's instincts told him that danger was at hand, and at his master's whispered commands he obediently and silently followed as intelligently as a human being.

Lion Limb had scarcely reached the base of the hill, and was approaching within full view of the cannibals, when he heard a mysterious rustling among the leaves and high grass of the thicket in which he stood.

Something told him that some deadly foe was near at hand.

But before he could recollect himself a violent blow was aimed at his head by some one, who was unseen but very near.

The stroke just grazed Lion Limb's head, and so violent was it that the heavy spikes in the war-club penetrated the tree beside which he had been standing, and there it remained fast and apparently immoveable.

In an instant Lion Limb turned and confronted a tall, powerful, hideous-looking savage, who, with a loud laugh of triumph, rushed upon him scalping knife in hand.

As quick as thought Lion Limb closed with him, hand to hand.

It was a certain case of life or death for one or both of them.

Not a word was uttered by either one or the other.

Dragon rushed at the huge cannibal, but being muzzled by Lion Limb's strap he could do no harm.

With the grip of a vice Lion Limb seized the upraised hand of the powerful savage and averted the deadly blow which was intended for him.

In another second Lion Limb tripped him up, and his huge opponent fell to the ground with a great shock.

Lion Limb's knife glittered for a second before the eyes of the savage, and next instant was plunged into his breast up to the hilt!

A loud and savage yell broke from the lips of the fallen chief.

It was his death-wail!

What to do next, Lion Limb scarcely knew, for a moment.

He unmuzzled "Dragon," and peeped out through the trees, and there beheld the greatest commotion among the savages round the fires of their roasting captives.

The death-wail of their chief had been heard by them.

With loud shrieks and cries, they rushed about madly, hither and thither, arming themselves with clubs, and bows, and slings, and tomahawks.

"Now, or never!" thought Lion Limb. "It is better to present a bold front to these savages, than to be surrounded and slaughtered by them."

"Here goes, then, for death or glory!" he said.

And with a loud shout, he rushed among the savages, carrying with him the terrible spike-headed war-club, which had belonged to the fallen chief, and which, after much difficulty, he had loosened from the tree.

He first fired his gun right among the dark, dirty, and hideous-looking rascals.

For a moment they seemed petrified at the sound, and the awful destruction which the deadly weapon had made among them.

This was the first fire-arm they had ever seen or heard, and its echoes startled myriads of birds and animals from the woods on every side.

Ere the brave lad had time to reload, however, the savages assailed him in great numbers, and with frightful deafening outcries.

Arrows flew through the air in all directions.

Stones were hurled from slings without number.

It seemed as if the black villains were about to surround Lion Limb and slay him.

With a cheerful voice he spoke to his faithful dog.

"On to 'em 'Dragon!' On to 'em! Bring 'em down! Good dog—'Dragon!'"

The animal did not require to be told twice.

With a good-humoured growl, he rushed among the savages, biting their legs and arms, and all parts of their persons, without much ceremony, and soon caused them to scatter right and left.

Three or four of the ringleaders, however, more determined than the rest, made a bold stand, to prevent the rescue of the poor victims who were then roasting at the several fires.

Perceiving how bravely Lion Limb and his dog were fighting with and vanquishing their tormentors these wretched beings rent the air with their doleful shouts and cries of acute agony.

But the more they kicked and plunged, the more they caused their fires to burn up, with increased volume, around them.

Lion Limb perceiving this, rushed forward, club in hand, and felled several brawny fellows to the earth.

He next jumped amid the blazing faggots, and cut the thongs which bound the victims to their stakes, and then let them free.

One or two were full-grown men, three were women, and one, the last, a sweetly pretty girl, of about fourteen years of age, who had been condemned to die with the rest.

That this girl was of high rank in savage life, could not be for a moment doubted, for the cannibals fought furiously to prevent Lion Limb from rescuing her, and besides, as a sure sign of important station, she wore gold earrings, armlets, and rings about her well-turned ankles and neck.

But the efforts of the obstinate savages to kill their victims were of no avail.

Lion Limb took the maid in his arms, and fought his way with her to a place of safety, and Dragon, his long fangs dripping with human gore, stood watch over the fainting Indian maid, and presented such a fierce and ferocious aspect, that he bade defiance to all comers.

The male victims jumped from among the flaming faggots, and snatching up fire-brands, rushed upon their foes.

The three women were almost suffocated, and one by one had to be carried by Lion Limb to the shelter of an adjacent grove, where they lay gasping for breath, and by far more dead than alive.

Having thus rescued the helpless ones from amid the flames, Lion Limb faced his enemies more boldly than ever.

His young heart bounded with manly joy at the thought of what he had done, and he felt emboldened, and as if he had been miraculously endowed with the strength of half-a-dozen men.

For two whole hours did the brave lad, Lion Limb, contend against the savages, and although he was several times wounded, yet he fought on as if nothing whatever had happened, and unconscious of fatigue.

His escapes from certain death were truly marvellous at times, when it is remembered that in more than one instance, and on several occasions during the combat he was opposed to dozens of savages at once.

The barbarians were astonished at the power of this pale-faced youth.

Their women stood and gazed on him in admiration.

The men were astounded.

Whatever they attempted to do, Lion Limb thwarted, and wherever they appeared, he was before them, and defeated them at every point.

At last, however, after having left more than a dozen killed and wounded on the ground, the savages retired from the scene and were soon lost in the depths of a dense forest, whither Lion Limb deemed it imprudent then to follow.

He collected a few of the savages' warlike weapons which were strewn upon the ground, and retraced his steps to the spot where he had placed the beautiful Indian maid.

He soon reached it and discovered her lying on the grass in the cool shade, guarded by the faithful "Dragon," who blinked his eyes and wagged his tail in joy at the approach of his brave young master.

But the next instant the noble animal turned his head and growled most ominously.

CHAPTER XIII.

TED RAWLINGS AND HARRY ARE LEFT IN CHARGE OF THE CAMP.

HARRY WOODRUFF, as the commandant of the camp, directly Lion Limb had started on his tour of observation in the morning, set about building a temporary hut out of the logs and planks of the raft which yet remained.

In this work he was assisted by Ted Rawlings and little Emma, both of whom worked like Trojans to get the place comfortable for their suffering companions.

Now, if Lion Limb had had the pick of a hundred men he could not have chosen a better or a braver young fellow than Harry Woodruff as second in command.

Harry had been a sailor for several years, and during that time had visited various climates, and got accustomed to the products and peculiarities of different hemispheres and zones.

"Lion Limb's a brave young devil and no mistake," thought Harry, "and as good a boy as ever broke bread. He knows more than I do in book-learning, seeing as how I can only barely read and scrawl; but he don't know everything for all that."

"We must go out, and get something to eat, Ted Rawlings," said Harry, "because this venison which Lion Limb brought us won't last long; besides, it ain't suited for these sick lads here, nor to Miss Emma neither. We must get some fish for 'em, you know—lobsters, crabs, oysters, salmon, and all them sort o' things."

Ted's mouth began to water as he thought of such delicacies.

But he heaved a very big sigh as he said,

"Ah! you're joking, Harry Woodruff. We ain't in London now, you know; we are on a lonely island where there is no Billingsgate market to buy at. I only wish we *could* get some of these things you name, especially oysters or salmon."

"And so you shall, my lad," said Harry, laughing, "and turtle into the bargain."

"Turtle?" said Emma.

"Turtle!" remarked Ted, with eyes of wonder, "Why, that's what the London aldermen eat and get fat on. Oh! only bring some here, that's all, Harry Woodruff, and you will soon see how quickly I'll peg into it."

"You'll have plenty of it by-and-bye, no fear, my lad," said Harry; "but we must catch it first."

"Aye, that's it," said Ted, with a cunning wink. "Jugged hare is all very nice, but first 'catching the hare' is the main point. I suppose it's about the same thing with a turtle?"

Harry laughed, as he said,

"No it ain't, Ted, not quite; but if Miss Emma don't mind us going a little way up the beach, we'll both go out in search of something for dinner."

Emma said she wasn't afraid, and would tend the sick youths until Harry's return.

So young Woodruff and Ted started off on a voyage of discovery.

They had not gone very far up the beach when Harry pointed out a small ridge of rocks, and telling Ted there must be muscles somewhere about, he went on further.

"Muscles, eh?" thought young Ted. "That ain't a bad dish to commence on, at all events."

Regardless whether Harry needed his assistance or not, and only mindful of the cravings of his own stomach, young Ted tucked up his trousers, and began to paddle about in search of shell-fish.

In a moment afterwards, however, Harry Woodruff heard him uttering most alarming cries, and therefore hurried back again to render all the assistance he could.

Ted now began to bawl more loudly than ever, and when Harry arrived upon the spot, he discovered him dancing about in the water, and howling most pitifully.

A large lobster had seized Master Edward by the leg, and resisted all his attempts at release.

It let go its hold, however, when Harry approached, and made off into deep water; but Woodruff followed it, and, by a dexterous stroke with his knife, he killed it, and brought it safe to shore.

And a fine large one it was.

"This ain't a bad beginning, Ted," said Harry, triumphantly holding up the large lobster. "This will make a capital dinner to start on."

"Ain't it a bad beginning, though," said Ted; "I think it is. Just look at my leg!"

And, as Harry perceived, the lobster had left several small wounds in Ted's legs, from which the blood was trickling.

Ted tied a thick rope to the lobster, and slung it over his back, and marched onwards.

They had not proceded far along the shore when Harry perceived and pointed out to Ted some half dozen large objects lying on the sand in the blazing sun.

"There they are, Ted," said he, triumphantly; "I told you we should find some turtle before long."

"And are them 'ere things turtles?" said Ted, in amazement, for he had never seen a turtle before in all his life. "Why, they look like immense crabs."

"Not much unlike, lad."

"But what are they doing, Harry?"

"Laying eggs in the sand."

"You don't mean that them big thing lay eggs, do you?"

"Yes; and nice things they are when properly cooked. What do you say to our boiling half-a-dozen for our supper by the time Lion Limb returns to camp? And suppose we catch a turtle and have a jolly good feed?"

"All right; I'm agreed. Won't it be jolly?"

"Give us that line of yours, Ted," said Harry. "We mustn't get too near 'em or they'll paddle into the sea before we catch one."

Harry, then, with great dexterity, threw the noose of his line right over the head of a turtle and made the other end fast to a tree.

"Come along, Ted," said Harry, "the turtle can't get away. Let's go and turn one or two of 'em on their backs."

This was accomplished after much exertion and dexterity, and Ted felt proud of the deed.

While Harry dragged one of the turtles towards the camp Master Ted discovered large quantities of oysters on some rocks near to the sea, and after much labour he clambered up, and soon succeeded in detaching over a bushel of them from the crags, and piled them up in a heap.

He also found a thick deposit of dry salt between the fissures of the rocks, which, no doubt, arose from the evaporation of sea water by the sun.

When they had conjointly done this much, and prepared viands for supper, both Harry Woodruff and Ted were somewhat weary, for the sun was excessively hot, and the burning sand got through the cracks of their boots and shoes, so that they could not walk with ease.

Towards sunset they began to think about preparing for supper for themselves, for young Lion Limb, and for their invalid companions, who, thanks to the care and exertion of little Emma, were now progressing very favourably indeed.

"We've got the grub, Harry," said Ted; "but how are we to cook it? we have no pots or pans."

"Oh! we'll soon find some," said Harry, good humouredly. "Do you go and gather up all the dry leaves and sticks you can find, and leave the rest to me."

"But," said Ted, "we are all dying for something to eat, and how can we cook without saucepans and such like? You seem to take things very easy, Master Harry; but how you will make soup and such such like things puzzles me. We can't boil things in our caps, you know."

"Never mind, do as I tell you; go and get all the fresh water you can, and leave the rest to me," said Harry, with a good-natured laugh. "Be quick, or perhaps Lion Limb will return before we have prepared anything."

Ted went off for the wood and water, grumbling much at the want of saucepans, and the like; but, nevertheless, he collected and brought to the camps a large quantity of dry wood, and all the water which the gourd and their own canteens would hold.

In the meantime Harry Woodruff also started out, and discovering the heaps of oysters which young Ted had collected, but felt too lazy to carry into camp, he pulled off his old flannel shirt, made a bag of it, and carried several bushels of the bivalves to camp, and after having washed them well in sea water, promised to make a delicious soup for all hands.

He then went forth again to the banks of the little fresh water stream which Lion Limb had discovered during the previous night, and found a large quantity of gourds, some green and others quite dry, and well baked in the sun.

The latter he cut off the vines, and after dividing them into halves scooped out all the vegetable matter until the gourds were nothing but hard dry shells.

He put one half within another, as we might place one bowl within another for the sake of convenience, and when he came to count his gourds he found he had no less than twenty, all of which were beautifully and carefully cleaned and hollowed, thus forming basins, deep dishes, or even wash-bowls, according to size.

As he returned to the camp joyful with his labours, and pleased to think that the island, unknown as it might be, was yet beautiful and fruitful of thing which would restore the health and strength of all his comrades in misfortune, he suddenly stopped in surprise as he neared some dark almost leafless bushes, on which were an immense number of re.. ..ds.

Any one less acquainted with the tropics might have thought that these red pods were poisonous.

Not so, Harry Woodruff.

He was rejoiced, and put down his gourd-bowls in haste.

"Bravo!" said he, half aloud, "bravo! we are lucky, and no mistake. Young Ted has discovered dry sea-salt in the fissures of the rocks, and here are thousands of pods of Chili pepper. Hurrah! we shan't die of starvation, that's very certain, if we go on discovering things in this way."

Without more ado, he plucked a large number of the red pepper pods from off the bushes, and filled his pockets.

Taking up his twenty gourd bowls again he hastened off to camp, and was happy to learn from Emma that several of the lads were rapidly recovering.

"But what are *them* things?" said Ted, pointing with a look of contempt towards the gourd bowls. "What are them things for? to drink out of, or *wh t?*"

"They can be put to a thousand uses," said Harry, with a good humoured smile. "This large one, when dried and hardened a little more in the sun, will do to wash in; these others, next in size, will do for preparing the food, and the smallest of all will do for drinking cups or soup bowls."

"Yes; but where are the pots to make the soup in?"

"You'll soon see. Commence and open some of those oysters."

With a sudden cry of pain, young Ted rose from his seat, and all were startled at the movement.

CHAPTER XIV.

INDIAN CAPTIVES—THE PURSUIT.

THE cause of Dragon's growling was soon explained. Seated under a tree and not far off was one of the young men whom Lion Limb had rescued from the burning stake.

He was a fine young fellow of about twenty years of age, but very different in all respects to the savages he had contended against a short time before.

This youth was not black, but brown; his features were regular and handsome; his teeth were as white as ivory, and around his neck there dangled beads of gold, and at his ankles gingled rudely-made bells of the same precious metal.

Directly he saw Lion Limb approach, he fell upon his knees, and kissed the feet of his brave deliverer, and murmured words which Lion Limb felt were meant for a prayer of heartfelt thankfulness.

Though older, taller, and more powerfully built than Lion Limb, there was something superior in our hero's manner, and the eyes of the suppliant prisoner were cast modestly down to the ground again as they encountered those of his noble champion.

Lion Limb made a gesture to him to remain where he was, and then went immediately to see how the Indian maid was progressing.

He procured water and bathed her temples.

He next gave her a very small quantity of brandy which yet remained in his canteen, and this seemed greatly to revive her.

The handsome girl began to breathe more freely.

Her limbs quivered, her lips moved, and then she opened her dark bright eyes.

Lion Limb was kneeling beside her, and when she saw him, a deep blush suffused her cheeks, and her eyes were dripping with pearl-like tears.

"Poor girl," thought Lion Limb; "she's handsome though, and so is that young fellow under the tree, yonder; much more so than the other man and the three women. Perhaps she's some young Indian princess abducted by the savages, who knows? There is some mystery here, without a doubt, but I question if ever it will be solved."

There *was* a mystery, truly, but it was solved much sooner than Lion Limb ever expected.

But of this anon.

Lion Limb was a youth of forethought and action.

He knew now full well that the island was not only inhabited, but, what was worse, that it was peopled by a savage, barbarous race of cannibals.

Without loss of time, therefore, he made preparation for his return.

With the chopper, therefore, he cut down two stout poles, and gathered a large quantity of wild vine stalks.

These stalks he lashed to the sides of the poles, and thus formed a sort of palanquin, or litter.

He then placed the young girl in the litter, and formed a sort of pillow and mattress for her with thick layers of grass and leaves.

He summoned his five prisoners to his presence, and they immediately obeyed.

They then threw themselves on their faces before him, and did not attempt to stir till, by a sign, he bade them rise.

They did so.

But when they perceived with what ingenuity and care Lion Limb had prepared the litter for the girl, their eyes danced with joy, and they clapped their hands in great glee, as if the sight had cured them of their own sufferings, and more than compensated for all their past trials.

Lion Limb was much pleased at this exhibition of joy, but was greatly surprised when they again and again fell on their knees, and kissed his hands and feet with the greatest reverence, and placed a hand on their hearts in token of devotion and gratitude.

Lion Limb gave the signal for them to lift the litter on their shoulders, which was instantly done.

The youth was not permitted the honour to be one of the bearers, for the others seized the opportunity themselves, so anxious were they to do honour to the suffering maiden.

Lion Limb, however, made use of him, for he packed heavy weights of various trophies upon his back, and thus they started homewards towards the encampment.

Dragon went first, then followed the captive youth with his load of trophies, the litter and its four bearers next came in order, the rear being brought up by Lion Limb, gun in hand, and the war club slung on his back.

Dragon did not need to be told the way his master had come by in the morning.

His scent was so strong he easily discovered it, and went on his way rejoicing, from time to time looking behind to wink and blink at Lion Limb, or else to go smelling round the legs of the four captive litter bearers.

It was well that Lion Limb left the battle ground when he did, for he had scarcely gone when a numerous band of ferocious, tattooed savages rushed out from the forest, brandishing all manner of weapons.

LION LIMB

THE BOY KING
OF THE SOUTH SEA ISLANDS.

FLOTTING THE DESTRUCTION OF LION LIMB.

But when they perceived that Lion Limb and the captives had fled, they gathered up the dead bodies of their comrades, and made the little valley ring again with their shouts, and cries, and oaths of vengeance.

No. 5.

CHAPTER XV.

THE RETURN OF LION LIMB AND HIS CAPTIVES.

THE sudden cry of young Ted, which for a moment had caused astonishment, soon made Harry Woodruff and the other lads laugh when they ascertained the true cause of Master Ted's note of alarm, for, dancing about, he shouted aloud—

"Hang the oysters! *I* can't open them."

"But try again," said Harry, laughing.

"I can't," said Ted; "I've tried, and almost cut my thumb off already."

"Well, all I can say is, you are very thick-headed, Ted," said Harry. "Watch me, and see how soon *I* will open three or four dozen."

So saying, Harry placed about sixty oysters upon the hot coals.

It is needless to say that this soon caused the oyster shells to open, and as fast as they did so Harry shelled them, placing the oysters in a large gourd which was half filled with fresh water.

"Going to wash 'em?" said Ted, very eager for something to eat.

"No, I'm going to boil 'em."

"How can that be? how can you boil anything in a green gourd?" said Ted.

"You will soon see."

By this time Emma had collected all the pieces of sea biscuit she could find, and broken them up very fine.

These were thrown in among the oysters, and when a small quantity of red pepper was added, Harry stirred the whole mess up with his knife.

"We ain't going to eat that mess, are we?" said Ted, ever intent, as usual, upon his stomach.

Harry made no answer; but went and collected about one hundred stones.

These he carefully washed and dried, and placed in the midst of the blazing wood fire.

Emma, knowing that, perhaps, in future, she would have to make herself generally useful, watched Harry intently.

Ted, however, grinned as he said,

"Well, I never see such a go in all my life; the idea of roasting stones, ha! ha! What's the use of 'em? Are you going to play a game at magic?"

"Yes, nothing shorter, as you'll quickly see."

One by one the stones became very hot, and as they did so, Harry plucked them from the fire, and having well dusted them, dipped them into the oyster pot until they were quite cooled.

This process was repeated more than a dozen times, and now the truth began to dawn on Emma and Ted's mind.

Harry had learned this trick from the American Indians, and then by means of his hot stones he soon made a very palateable and savory oyster stew, the former of which seemed to make young Ted more hungry than ever.

When sufficiently cooked, the first portion of it was given to the sick lads lying under the rocks, and so grateful was this rudely-made repast to them that they craved for more.

Harry gave each a second allowance, and then re-commenced to make a fresh supply for himself, Lion Limb, Emma, and Ted.

But as young Ted begged of Harry to let him superintend the cooking of the second edition of oyster soup, there cannot be a doubt that during the process of cooking the artful young rascal tasted it so often to "see if it was done or not," that it is more than likely he had much more than his share, and long before he heard the loud "halloos" from a neighbouring hill, and the barkings of a dog, which told both that Lion Limb was approaching, and not very far away.

The welcome sounds of the dog barking caused a deep blush to suffuse the cheeks of little Emma, who, as young as she was, hourly began to entertain the deepest affection for Lion Limb.

"He was so brave, so manly and so handsome," thought Emma, as she busied herself about the camp-fire to prepare some refreshment for her young champion and deliverer.

"Now, Edward," said she to young Rawlings, "you must open the very best of the oysters for Lion Limb, for I know he must be very hungry after his long journey in the hot sun."

"Please don't call me Edward," said Ted, who felt rather humbled. "Please don't call me Edward any more, for I don't like it. Call me Ted as much as you like, for it sounds more friendly. Lion Limb always calls me Ted."

"Then so will I, also," said Emma, as she bustled about to prepare supper for our young hero.

In order to please Emma, young Ted selected, as the best, the very largest of the oysters, and placed more than a dozen upon the red-hot coals, and in an instant one of them opened its shell.

"Oh, here's a stunner," said Ted, in great glee. "Look at this monster oyster, Miss Emma—look here, Harry Woodruff, ain't this a fine one?"

Just as he spoke, he took the oyster off the coals, and next instant began to dance about like a Merry Andrew, and pulled such ugly faces, as made Harry Woodruff roar again with laughter.

The oyster had closed its shell rather suddenly and unexpectedly on Ted's fingers, and gave them such a tight squeeze that the astonished youth got very red in the face.

While this was going on around the camp fire the dog "Dragon" came bounding towards them in great glee, and in a doggish manner that was full of brute affection, he began to lick Emma's hand and gambolled about in high glee.

In another instant he darted off again to meet his young master, who was not far off.

Ted Rawlings forgot all about his pinched fingers when he knew that Lion Limb was at hand, and started off to meet him.

Judge of his astonishment, however, when he suddenly confronted the procession of Indians carrying the wounded and captive girl.

Lion Limb soon explained every circumstance when he arrived in camp, and no one was more surprised at his adventures than little Emma, who sat beside him, and with her mild, loving eyes, seemed to drink in every word he uttered.

CHAPTER XVI.

LION LIMB ON A VOYAGE OF DISCOVERY— STARTLING INCIDENTS.

"AND so you've been fighting with the Indians, already, eh, Lion Limb," said Harry, with an air of annoyance. "I am very sorry for it. Once blood has been shed between us and the natives, whoever they are, I fear they will give us no peace, and strife will be lasting between us."

"It couldn't be helped, Harry."

"I know that well enough, my bold young captain; but I would much rather we had made friends with them, had it been possible."

"Never fear, Harry," said Lion Limb, cheerfully; "pass along the oysters, for I am amazingly hungry. Never fear, the black rascals can't do us much harm."

"No, not in fair fight, I'll allow," said Harry; "but it is their treachery I fear."

"Then, what would you advise?"

"Why, build a strong log-house as quickly as possible, so as to resist these Indians if they are inclined to attack us."

"A very good thought, Harry; but that job I must leave to you."

"Won't you stay and help us?"

"I can't."

"If you go roaming about the island alone, you will be waylaid and murdered."

"Have no such fears for me, Harry," said Lion Limb, laughing. "I have made great discoveries since I have been away."

"What discoveries?"

"Why, from signs and such like, I understand from these captives of mine that there are or have been white men on the island."

Harry Woodruff for a moment paused in the conversation, and looked troubled.

"What makes you so suddenly silent Harry?" asked Lion Limb, good-humouredly.

"And do you believe these Indian captives?" asked Harry.

"I do. Why not?"

"Well, I don't, captain. I have travelled much further in my time than you have, and seen much more of the world, as you'll allow, and my experience is—"

"What?"

"Why, that your natives, on whatever islands you find them, are the greatest liars and impostors in all creation."

Lion Limb laughed right heartily at Harry's bluntness, and finished his supper.

"You may laugh, my young captain, as much as you please; but if these natives ain't sharp and cunning enough to cheat the very devil himself, why then my name ain't Harry Woodruff, that's all."

"Well, I don't think we shall have much to fear from the prisoners here," said Lion Limb, "for you must know I have rescued them from certain death, and from what I have seen of them on the road home here, I imagine they will serve me as faithfully as dogs would, if I required it."

Harry grunted out something about "ugly devils with large rolling eyes."

"Besides," said Lion Limb, "they have as far as they could given me much and very useful information."

"What about?"

"About certain strange objects on the island."

"How do you mean?"

"Why, as we came along, and just as we had mounted a very lofty hill, one of them began clapping his hands, and pointed to some large black object which seemed to be on the sea-shore."

"Did you make out what it was?"

"No; the sun had just set, and although I strained my eyes, and used my telescope, I could not make out what it was.

"What did it look like, captain?"

"More like a huge whale that had been stranded than anything else."

"It's an old wreck you may depend, captain."

"I don't think so, Harry; for if it were so, the natives, as you say, would have plundered and torn it to pieces long ago."

"Perhaps they couldn't."

"Why not?"

"Who knows but some of the crew may be on board of her still," said Harry.

"If it were to turn out to be the wreck of the 'Rattlesnake!' said young Ted, with wondering eyes.

"Ah, no fear of that," said Harry, shaking his head, "no fear of that, my lad, the 'Rattlesnake' has gone to the bottom long ago—poor devils."

For a moment a solemn pause took place.

At last Harry said,

"How far is it from here where you saw the large black-looking object on the shore, captain?"

"I should judge it was fifteen or twenty miles from here, Harry."

"Is the island so large?" said Ted.

"Yes, much larger than you would imagine, Ted. I got on top of a very high hill, and even then did not get a clear view of the whole island. But it is a beautiful place in every respect—fine forests, rivulets, valleys, lofty mountains, and such like."

"Then, what do you intend to do, captain?" asked Harry.

"Why, at sunrise to-morrow, I intend to start out in search of this unknown object, and find out what it really is, for I begin to imagine there are white people as well as natives on the islands."

Around the camp fire then it was decided that Lion Limb should start out again on the morrow, while Harry and the natives, with whatever assistance he might obtain from his other companions, should begin to construct a strong log-house, out of the remains of the raft.

Lion Limb wished Ted Rawlings to remain behind and help Harry; but young Ted didn't like hard work much, and begged so hard to be allowed to go on the exploring expedition, that Lion Limb and Harry consented.

"Oh, yes, take him with you by all means, captain," said Harry, laughing, "take him with you, for he's of no use here. Hard work and he don't agree, I think."

Ted coincided with Harry's sentiment, and was overjoyed when told he might accompany his young master.

Late as it was Harry was bent upon work.

So that when Lion Limb had retired to rest after his fatiguing journey, Harry gave the male prisoners a hearty meal, and prepared to make them "generally useful," as he said.

Ted Rawlings was inclined to creep off to rest likewise, but just when about to do so Harry Woodruff collared him, and, in a good-humoured manner, said,

"Come here, you young slippery eel, come here, don't you know that Captain Lion Limb has given me command of the camp always during his absence?"

"I know it. Well, what of that?"

"I want you to help me and the natives to haul up all that old timber from the beach before you go to roost."

"But I'm going out with our young captain early in the morning," said Ted, half grinning, "and want rest."

"I dare say you do, and so do I; but pray, what has made you so tired, I wonder? Eating too many oysters, or what? Certainly not hard work, Master Ted, for I'll say this much of you, a lazier, and at the same time a more mischevious young devil never was than you. So come, tuck up your sleeves, and let us go to work, the moon is shining very clear and bright. Follow me."

Young Ted didn't much like it, yet was compelled to "lend a hand," as Harry termed it; and the native prisoners, being told what to do by signs and otherwise, much heavy lumber was got up from the beach, and every preparation made for building the block-house on the morrow.

Harry bade the prisoners lie down by themselves, and he stood guard over the whole, gun in hand, until such time as some one of his companions should awake to relieve him.

The Indian girl, however, was not forced to work in any manner.

The greatest kindness was shown to her, and

Emma became so much attached to her, that she shared part of her humble bed with her.

As good fortune would have it, several of the lads had somewhat recovered from their trying illness, and, on the night in question, two of them rose and stood guard in the place of Harry Woodruff, who warned them to keep a bright look-out.

"If any of those native devils attempt to escape," said Harry, with an oath, "you fire a bullet or two into 'em; that will make 'em luff up in the wind mighty sharp."

Giving directions to be awakened at sunrise, Harry went "to roost," as he termed it, and slept soundly.

Just as the sun rose in the east, and gilded the distant ocean, the little camp was all astir, and making preparations of every kind.

Some were busy in cooking whatever was left from the previous meal.

Others, under Harry's orders, were cutting down trees, and splitting them, as best they could, with a couple of old axes they had found among the remains of the raft.

The natives (the females excepted) were digging up the earth, so as to make a deep foundation for the logs; and, in one word, all who were able were busy at one thing or another for the common good. And right merrily did they work, each and all obeying Harry Woodruff, who, as we have said before, was captain in command during the absence of Lion Limb.

Lion Limb, it must be confessed, had thoroughly equipped himself for his journey, and, with Ted Rawlings, had departed at the break of day.

Little Emma very much regretted the necessity which compelled her gallant champion to go forth so frequently, yet, as he departed on his journey, she ran after him, saying she had forgotten to say something to him.

But, whatever Emma had to say, she found no expression for, but leaned on his arm, with trembling lip and moistened eye, in speechless eloquence, as Lion Limb shyly kissed her unseen by any one, and bade the maiden to cheer up, and have no fears.

Then he and Ted started off together.

They pushed along the shore vigorously for two hours until they came to a very large, dense wood.

Here they rested in the shade near a pleasant little stream, and partook of some slight refreshment.

Birds of rare plumage flew about in all directions.

Young Ted began to think that he had seen some monkeys hopping about in the topmost branches of the tall nut trees.

Nor was he mistaken, for the barking of Dragon confirmed this.

Ted ran off some short distance to confirm himself in his belief, when he tumbled over some large substance hidden in the grass, which proved to be a decayed cocoa-nut.

After half an hour spent in the pleasant shade Lion Limb pursued his journey.

They advanced through the wood with great caution, apprehensive of treading upon serpents or some other venemous reptiles.

Dragon was made to walk in advance to give notice of danger; and each cut a long, thick cane, with which to beat down the high grass in their path.

But Lion Limb was much surprised to find a rich glutinous juice oozing from the cut end of his cane.

He tasted it, and felt convinced he had met with a plantation of sugar canes.

He sucked it more and more, and felt very much refreshed.

He did not tell young Ted of his discovery, however, but resolved that he should find out the thing for himself.

Soon afterwards, however, the juice began to ooze out of his cane, and young Ted almost jumped for joy when he discovered it was real sugar.

So delighted was he that he began to suck so many pieces of the cane that Lion Limb had to stop him for fear of the consequences.

Ted, however, cut a small bundle of canes to take home when they returned, and onwards they trudged through the palm grove.

Suddenly a number of monkeys, alarmed at their approach, and by the barking of Dragon, fled with such rapidity up the trees that they reached the top almost instantly.

Having clambered far out of danger these monkeys began to chatter and grin, and squeel out their anger in the most discordant noises imaginable.

As Lion Limb saw that the trees were cocoa palms, and feeling desirous of having some fruit, he determined to make use of the monkeys to attain his object.

Ted, however, who had become annoyed at their impudent chatter, greatly wished to shoot some of them.

But Lion Limb was more prudent, he would not waste his powder so.

He collected a lot of stones, and began to pelt the monkeys, who, in revenge, tore off dozens of cocoa-nuts, and showered them down upon them.

Ted laughed heartily at this stratagem of his young master, and when the nut-throwing had ceased, he collected as many as he wanted, and they both sat down to enjoy them.

After sucking some of the milk by means of the holes, which they opened with their knives, they broke the nuts open with a hatchet and ate all the kernel with much satisfaction.

They liked best, however, a sort of thick cream which adhered to the shells, which they scraped off with bits of shell, and mixing it with the sugar-cane produced a most delicious dish, which young Ted did not fail to partake of immediately.

"Ain't it fine, though?" said young Ted. "I wish we could take a lot of these nuts home to our camp, the milk would be very refreshing to Miss Clarence and our poor boys."

"I have thought of it," said Lion Limb; "but we can't do everything at once; besides, we must not overburden ourselves with carrying heavy loads, for we have a long way to go."

"When we return, then, we'll carry a few, eh?"

"Yes, when we return; but we shan't carry them for all that."

"Who, then?"

"Ah! you must wait and see; I have a very good plan."

"I should dearly like to catch one of them monkeys," said Ted, looking up into the cocoa-nut palms with an envious eye.

"Why, what use could you make of him?"

"Oh, have him for fun; we'd have such jolly larks."

"I dare say you would; but we have more to feed now than we can find food for, Ted, so the monkeys must remain at large for the present, and manage to feed themselves," said Lion Limb, who even thus early gave tokens that he had great forethought and judgment in the management of affairs.

They had not gone very far through the dense forest—the dog Dragon, as before, always in the advance—when young Ted felt greatly alarmed at the agonizing shrieks of some animal that he could not as yet distinguish, and turned deadly pale.

"Did you hear that noise?" he asked, with a trembling lip.

"I did," answered Lion Limb, with a smile.

"What was it, then?" said Ted. "It made me tremble in every limb."

"I dare say, if you were served in the same manner that the animal is that you heard screaming, you also would bellow loudly enough."

"How do you mean?" said Ted, rather offended than not at the nonchalent and good-humoured manner of the young captain he loved so well.

"You shall presently see and understand all," said Lion Limb.

They went forward in silence for a few hundred yards, when the dog Dragon before them halted and growled very maliciously.

"What does Dragon see, I wonder?" asked Ted. "I wish we had kept on our journey by the sea-shore, and not ventured to enter this dismal, treacherous forest, for there is danger on every hand."

"Courage," said Lion Limb, good-humouredly. "I shall begin to think you are an arrant coward, Ted, if you go on grumbling and trembling in the manner you have done all the morning."

"Coward!" said young Ted, swelling out, and slapping his chest in a very pompous manner. "Nonsense! I am as brave as a lion."

"Yes; a dead one, I imagine," said Lion Limb, laughing; "but, if you are with me long, I'll make you courageous and bold, even against your will. Look yonder," said he, pointing to a tall oak tree, straight in their path, and but fifty yards away; 'do you see anything yonder, Ted?"

"No. What is it?"

"Look again."

Ted looked again, and saw some living animal, which frightened him, for he said, retreating a yard or two,

"Oh, lor! let us get up a tree; let us do something to get out of the way, I don't care what it is."

"Nonsense," said Lion Limb, "don't be so silly; be more of a man. I thought you said just now that you were as brave as a lion?"

"So I am—sometimes," said Ted.

And he began to climb a tree immediately, out of the way of danger.

Lion Limb laughed right heartily, and threatened to discharge his musket into the seat of his companion if he did not descend on the instant.

Fearing the effect of a full load of shot, Ted descended very hastily, for he full well knew that if Lion Limb said a thing he really meant it.

"What do you call that animal I see yonder?" asked Ted; "that big, black, fierce, four-legged thing, with two long tusks?"

"They call that a wild boar," was the answer.

"A wild boar, eh? How ugly and fierce it looks."

"It is much more ugly and fierce than it seems," was the answer. "They are terrible things when fully aroused, and will attack almost anything or anybody."

"Then let us get out of the way."

"Have no fear; it won't trouble us at all."

"But it is coming towards us."

"I know it; but in a moment or two it will be killed."

"Killed?"

"Yes, killed."

"But, how? Surely you are not going to waste powder and shot over it; it isn't worth eating, I've heard you say."

"It is not a very dainty dish, certainly," said Lion Limb, "but in the case of a hungry or starving person, the flesh of a wild hog is not to be despised. But if not very valuable to us," said Lion Limb, "it serves as a very dainty dish for that animal you see yonder quietly waiting for his hog-ship to approach."

"What animal?" said Ted, suddenly stopping, and looking about him very anxiously. "What animal?"

"Why, look up into that tall old tree yonder. Do you observe anything hanging from that out-stretched branch?"

"No, I don't see anything very particular."

"Look again."

Ted did look again, and then saw what he imagined a very thick coil of rope, dangling from and entwined round, a stout limb of the old tree.

"Well, what you think looks like a coil of rope, Ted," said Lion Limb, laughing, "is nothing else than a live boa constrictor."

"A w-h-a-t?" gasped Ted.

"An immense serpent, which is called a boa constrictor, and the thickest part of its body is several feet in circumference."

"You don't mean that?"

"I do though."

"Then let us turn back at once. I've often heard of serpents in shows and fairs, and in the Zoological Gardens, but I never imagined I should ever come so near one alive, and outside a strong cage. Let us go back, let us go back! for I've heard that it swallows a man at one mouthful."

Lion Limb laughed, as he said,

"No, we will not return by any means. Look, watch and see what the boa constrictor does with that wild boar yonder, and then that will account for the frightful screams which you heard a little while ago."

Ted, all anxious and timorous, stood beside Lion Limb, and, from their place of observation, could plainly see all that took place between the two animals.

The boa constrictor was coiled round the stout branch of a wide-spreading tree, and seemed festooned like ivy vines.

It betrayed not the slightest sign of life as far as movement went.

Yet any one, even at the distance our young adventurers were, could plainly discern its bright, sparkling eyes, as, with head at rest on the broad branch, it glared upon its intended victim approaching.

The wild boar, unconscious of the presence of its most deadly and cunning enemy, was picking up chestnuts at the foot of the tree, and munching with a grunting, snorting glee.

When it began to feed at the foot of the tree on which its enemy was perched, the boa constrictor's eyes became brighter, redder, and more deadly in their expression.

Noiselessly its tail is uncoiled from the limb of the tree, and silently descends.

When within a few feet of its victim, the tail falls suddenly, and, instantly encircling the boar, tightens its folds.

The boar makes a sudden plunge to liberate itself, but at the same time the monster serpent tightens more and more its deadly folds, and the boar, hopelessly shrieking and plunging, is borne up in the air!

Louder and louder shrieks the boar, until it makes the deep, dense, dark forest ring again; but tighter and tighter the serpent squeezes it.

At last, when it has ascended a sufficient height, the victim, half dead, is loosened from the torturing folds, and falls to the ground with a dull heavy sound, and is almost smashed into a jelly.

After this the boa constrictor was seen to descend from the tree and coil itself upon the ground near the dead boar.

Now it began to smear it all over with deadly saliva, and having completed this, next began the operation of slowly and gradually swallowing it whole and entire as it was.

The whole process from beginning to end was witnessed by Lion Limb and young Ted.

The latter was horror-stricken at the sight, and proposed to take revenge.

But Lion Limb said, with a laugh,

"Never mind it now, Ted, we'll pay our respects to the boa constrictor when we return from our exploring expedition ; he will be fast asleep, and in profound torper, then there will be no fear to either of us. He will be unwieldy and unable to repel our attack on account of his immense gorging."

Thus at every step in their progress through this immense primeval forest, the young explorers saw things that were now entirely strange or wonderful to them.

But yet their journey was not undertaken merely for purposes of pastime.

They had a far more important object in view, as we have already explained.

They sallied out on this expedition to ascertain whether or not there really was a wreck on the island shores.

And more than that, Lion Limb felt particularly anxious to find out whether there were any white people on the island beside himself and his companions.

From the rude hints and signs of the prisoners he had taken, Lion Limb was inclined to think that there were persons of European origin on the island or on some one adjacent.

Full of hope and expectation, thus the brave youth set out with a solitary companion, who on most occasions was as timid as a hare.

"But how do you know that we are going the right course, captain ?" said Ted.

"Of course I know, stupid. Why do you ask such foolish questions ? March on in advance. Come, no more sitting down and eating cocoa-nuts until our journey is over."

"Why, this morning you said the objects on the shore which you intended to examine were on the north side of the island," Ted remarked, who lost no occasion to sit down and rest.

"So I did."

"But how do you know that you are going right ; you can't see the sun, can you, in the thick forest ?"

"Well, what of that ?"

"How can you tell which way you are going, then ?" said Ted. "We may be going round and round for all I know, and are no nearer than we were two hours ago."

"Get up, and don't be so talkative, Ted."

After a time they came to a small tree, before which Lion Limb stopped,

"In case you may ever lose your way in the woods, Ted," said he, "I'll show you an easy way to correct yourself, and put you on the right track again."

"How ?"

"Very easily. Listen to me, Ted. Examine the bark of that tree all round—do it carefully. Then do you perceive anything on one side of it more than another ?"

"Yes," said Ted. "There is a lot of green, damp moss growing on one side of it and none on the other."

"Exactly so," was the young captain's answer. "On every tree there is a damp side, Ted, and that side is the north side ; the opposite is the south side ; to the right hand, facing north, is east, and on the left is west. There you have a compass to guide you anywhere, like the Indians ; and even if we did not chip the trees as we went we could easily find our way home to camp again."

"I never knew that before," said Ted.

"Perhaps not ; but, for all that, remember it."

Thus conversing, the two companions pursued their journey further and further into the dense forest.

From the oppressive heat and unnatural closeness of the atmosphere, Lion Limb made sure that a violent storm was coming on, and therefore felt very anxious, for young Ted's sake, to get out of the forest.

For he knew full well that of all places in the world a forest is the most dangerous one in a storm of wind, or when lightning flashes in the gale.

That it was so was fully proved on this occasion.

CHAPTER XVII.

TERRIFIC STORM IN THE FOREST—THE UNEXPECTED MEETING—BLOODHOOF AND WHETHERBY BENT ON MISCHIEF.

THEY had not proceeded very far when the storm which had threatened came upon them with full violence.

The forest, which before had been somewhat dark, and to such a degree, on account of the gigantic foliage that the sun's rays could scarcely penetrate, now became perfectly black, as if night had set in.

This sudden change greatly retarded their efforts, and for a time they knew not which way to proceed.

"We had better clamber up this old oak tree," said Lion Limb, "until such times as the storm shall have passed over us."

"But I have heard," said Ted, with a rueful face, "that a tree is the most dangerous thing to be near to in case of lightning."

"Quite true," was the answer ; "but as there are no caverns or places of the kind wherein we can hide, we might as well sit in a tree as any other place."

For some few minutes Ted felt inclined to disregard the advice of his young captain.

But an incident occurred at the moment which very soon changed his notions.

The clouds had gathered in such heavy dense masses that before any one would have imagined it, vivid lightning flashed through the forest with almost blinding brilliancy, and was succeeded a moment afterwards by a terrific and sudden peal of thunder that shook the very earth.

It startled Master Ted considerably.

He had heard thunder in England ; but he knew not nor did he even dream of the awful grandeur of a lightning and rain storm in the South Sea.

The lad looked pale and as if terrified.

Nor did the laughter of Lion Limb in any measure re-assure him ; but, if anything, added to his annoyance and fears.

At that moment, however, and while he stood at the foot of the tree, undecided whether to ascend or not, Master Ted heard a dismal growl close by in the bushes, which soon made him decide what to do.

For while he looked to the right and left alternately, the growling and hard breathing came nearer and nearer.

"That can't be thunder, can it?" he asked.

But he had scarcely so spoken to Lion Limb, when a huge bear appeared within a few yards of him.

"Oh! lor!" said Master Ted.

He jumped to the tree at once.

And if ever a youth climbed a tree in double quick time, young Rawlings did on that occasion.

Not the cleverest monkey in the whole forest could have clutched the branches and swung from one to another with greater skill than did Master Ted.

Lion Limb, perched a little over head, in the tree, laughed so heartily at Ted's haste and excited manner, that he almost fell from his seat.

"Wh-a-a-t are you l-a-u-g-hing at?" said Ted, out of breath. "I-I-I don't see any cause for l-a-u-ghing."

"I do, though," said his good-tempered young captain, who laughed all the more at Ted's pale face, and stuttering utterance.

"And what is there so very funny in it?" asked Ted in a surly tone. "If you are fond of attacking lions and all those sort of things, I ain't, and that's flat."

"It wasn't a lion, Ted."

"Well, whatever it was, it looked to me as big as an elephant."

"When people are afraid, their eyesight magnifies every thing they see; it was only a harmless bear."

"Only a harmless bear, eh!" said Ted. "If it had got hold of me in its arms, it would not have felt very comfortable, I think," said Ted, who shuddered at the thought.

But while the two lads were thus conversing up in the tall oak tree, the storm continued with unabated violence.

In truth, its fury increased each moment to such a pitch that it threatened to destroy the forest and everything in it.

Flash after flash of lightning followed each other rapidly.

Thunder pealed over head, with a sudden crash and almost deafening roar, which shook the very earth.

Trees were struck by forked lightning and split into a thousand splinters.

Old, gigantic trees, which had flourished for centuries and were kings of the forest, were blown down one upon another.

Branches and limbs of trees were flying about in all directions in the whirlwind.

Beasts of all kinds rushed about to and fro in every direction.

Wild hogs, chased by panthers, jumped madly away.

Deer and antelopes galloped off to safe retreats.

Monkeys, hyenas, jaquas, and other kindred animals screamed and yelled out fiercely and wildly.

Parrots, canaries, cockatoos, wild turkeys, fowl, ducks, geese and numerous other denizens of the forest or its many pools, rivulets or ponds, seemed suddenly seized with madness, and flew about, tossed like bits of paper in a sudden hurricane.

"Crash" went old and young trees in all directions as they fell with a heavy sound on the ground.

The winds still howled through the deep, dense forest; yet, above all, could be heard the distant roar of leopards, tigers, and American lions, which kept up a fearful chorus as they went to and fro, among the undergrowth, in cane breaks and in the jungle.

"Is it not a grand and glorious sight?" said Lion Limb, who stood on a lofty limb surveying the storm with a proud look and bright eye, "Isn't it a grand and glorious sight, Ted?" said he.

"I don't think it is; I don't see any beauty about it; there is plenty of danger though on every hand, if that is what you call grand and glorious," Master Ted replied, "for since I have been sitting here, I have seen more wild animals jumping and romping about, than would suffice for a dozen menageries."

"It would be a capital time for hunting them," said Lion Limb; "now that they are aroused and driven from their lairs, we could have splendid sport."

"Sport, eh! no thank you, none of it for me, if it's all the same to you. But come, captain," said Ted, "the storm has abated, let us descend and get out of this forest as soon as possible."

"Stay where you are," said Lion Limb, "the storm is not yet over, it is only a sudden lull, an unnatural calm that always precedes another outbreak here in the tropics."

Ted had imagined that because the rain, thunder and lightning had suddenly ceased, that the hurricane had entirely passed over.

But he was greatly mistaken.

In a few seconds the lightning flashed again and thunder pealed forth with incredible fury and violence.

The two lads were almost shaken out of the tree when on a sudden a stroke of lightning struck the trunk and split it.

The tree toppled over, and fell, throwing the two lads, but not with great severity, upon the ground.

They were more astonished than hurt, for they clung on bravely to the branches, and this saved them.

Lion Limb laughed at the mishap, but Ted looked rueful and annoyed.

"Come," said the bold young leader, "come along, Ted; I think the storm is now over, and judging how far we have come, I have no doubt we are very near the object of our journey.

But while he thus encouraged his companion, Lion Limb seemed astonished at some distant sounds which reached his ears.

He listened, but could not at first conjecture what it was.

At last he felt convinced that the sounds were those of persons speaking.

But their words were unintelligible.

Whether to proceed or hide would be best, he knew not at the moment.

But his course of action was soon decided.

The voices came nearer and nearer.

"Jump up into this tree, Ted, and let us listen; perhaps it may be a band of savages approaching."

The two lads got up into a thickly foliaged tree, and there, concealed from view, remained as silent as mice.

In a few moments the voices were heard again, and coming nearer and nearer.

To his astonishment, Lion Limb thought he could distinguish several words spoken in English.

While he and young Ted intently watched, the sounds of footsteps through the brush-wood were heard distinctly.

"I wonder who or what they can be," thought Lion Limb.

While he spoke, two naked savages appeared, and turned to look for some one that followed, and beckoned them on.

"Aye, aye, ye naked devils, we are coming, never fear," said a rough seaman's voice with an oath.

Filled with astonishment, Lion Limb beheld Bill Whetherby and Bloodhoof!

CHAPTER XVIII.

LION LIMB OVERHEARS THE PLANS OF THE MUTINEER LEADERS—STRANGE AND UNLOOKED-FOR DISCLOSURES.

THE two savages made signs with their hands and feet to Whetherby and Bloodhoof, as if they desired to impart some important information.

The two mutineers had swords and pistols, and in every way seemed well prepared for attack or defence.

One of the savages pointed in a northerly direction through the forest, and then began to count on his fingers, at the same time moving his feet as if in the act of walking.

"What does the ugly brute mean, I wonder," said Whetherby, with an oath; "he has brought us many a good mile this morning, and what's the good of it? What do they mean by those signs I wonder?"

"They mean," said Bloodhoof, who had been intently watching the native counting his fingers, "if they mean anything, that these people with white faces, they gave us to understand were on this island, are not more than a few hundred yards away."

"Oh, if that is what they mean, all right; but we mustn't go too close to the spot. We had better follow the natives as far as we safely can, and then reconnitre, and find out who they are."

"If these white-faced people are not so very far off, why not climb one of these trees, and have a good look-out ahead?"

"Well said, Bloodhoof," Whetherby answered, "I never thought of the masthead look-out before; what say you, shall you or I go up?"

"Oh, I will go," Bloodhoof replied; "do you keep a sharp eye on those two dusky devils, for, after all, they may be leading us into some trap."

"All right, mate, leave 'em to me; they won't run far while I've got a revolver and eight loads."

It was a moment of intense excitement to Ted, when he saw and recognised these ringleaders of the mutineers; for of all the beings in the world, he desired least to meet them.

Yet how did they get there?

How had they made friends with the natives?

These were questions that neither Lion Limb nor Ted could answer.

But when young Ted heard their resolve to climb a tree, he made sure Bloodhoof would select the very one in which they themselves were.

Lion Limb's feelings, however, were quite different.

He was rather pleased than not, that he and his old enemies should have thus met.

"If they climb our tree, Ted," said he in a whisper, "I shall fire; but, if not, leave them alone and be very silent."

As he spoke, Bloodhoof could be heard ascending a tree next to the one in which the lads were.

When he had clambered quickly and cleverly to the top, Bill Whetherby hailed him.

"Messmate, ahoy! what's in sight?"

Bloodhoof did not answer.

He began to descend again very quickly, and, as he did so, gave vent to his feelings in a volley of oaths.

"What cheer?" said Whetherby.

"Bad."

"Why, what did you make out?"

"A wreck."

"You don't mean that. Where abouts does she lay?"

"Why, on the beach, about half a mile from where we are."

"What does she look like?"

"The wreck of some man-of-war."

"Suppose it turns out to be the 'Rattlesnake?'"

"No fear of that. She was too well scuttled, I fancy, for any such hopes."

"Anybody about it?"

"Yes; and that's what gives me most trouble," said Bloodhoof.

"Why?"

"Because, I can see there are at least ten people, big and little, about the wreck. Whether there are any more or not I can't make out."

"What do they look like?"

"They are small chaps, as far as I could see, and haven't any arms."

"No arms?"

"No; none that I saw."

"And what were they doing?"

"Digging a deep ditch and throwing up walls of sand as if to guard against any surprise from the natives."

"Then these ugly devils are right after all," said Whetherby.

But not feeling satisfied with Bloodhoof's account, Whetherby ascended the tree himself, and took a long survey.

When he had descended, he felt very wrath at what he had seen, and gave expression to his thoughts with a round volley of oaths.

"Well, and what can you make out on it?" asked Bloodhoof, in a surly tone.

"Make on it! Why, nothing shorter than that there craft is the very identical 'Rattlesnake.'"

"You don't mean that?"

"I do, though; and more than that, them chaps, as you made out, are for the most part boy convicts which that young Devil's Limb—"

"Lion Limb."

"Yes, that's his name—the very same as he fought us with. If it ain't them, you can hang me," said Whetherby, with an oath.

"Who'd a thought it?" said Bloodhoof. "I can't believe it."

"Ah, who would have thought it, but there it is, high and dry upon the beach, and there are them young devils there also, and one or two of the crew with them, if I'm not blind."

"If, so, then we must have the wreck, and murder every soul of them, if they resist us."

"Just what I was thinking; but we must return to our own island first, and rouse all the men, for these convict lads will fight for their treasure like young demons."

"Suppose we creep nearer towards the beach and have a good long view, so as to report when we set sail for home."

This proposition was acceptable, and, guided by the two natives, the mutineer leaders walked into a dense thicket and were lost to view.

"Come," said Lion Limb, when they had departed, "Come, Ted," said he, "no time is to be lost, not a moment must be wasted; we must arrive at the wreck before them, and warn our friends, if indeed they should prove such. Follow me, and as quietly as possible."

It was a moment of great excitement.

LION LIMB

THE BOY KING
OF THE SOUTH SEA ISLANDS.

THE ATTACK ON LION LIMB'S CAMP BY THE MUTINEERS.

Young Ted could not imagine the reason why his gallant young leader should be in such a hurry to reach the wreck, if there really was one; nor could he see any good reason as he said for running his head among persons he did not know.

No. 6.

The chief reasons why Lion Limb desired to forestal the chiefs of the mutineers, were these—

If the wreck spoken of really were the remains of the ill-fated "Rattlesnake," and the persons living near proved to be his former companions, he wished to put them on their guard against any treacherous designs which might have been formed against them.

With all haste, therefore, and as quietly as he could, Lion Limb and Ted pushed their way through the forest, and by hiding their heads were concealed from observation.

As it happened, the route Lion Limb had selected was much shorter than that chosen by Whetherby and Bloodhoof.

When, therefore, they had reached the edge of the forest, and came within sight of the wreck, Lion Limb felt much relieved.

He was about to rush out upon the beach, when a voice near him suddenly said in a hoarse manner and in English,

"Halt! Who comes there?"

This startled Ted, for he heard the click of a gun.

He therefore fell flat upon his face, each moment expecting a bullet to whistle past his head.

"Halt! Who comes there?" was the repeated challenge, in a low hoarse voice.

"A friend," replied Lion Limb, in a half whisper.

"Advance, then, friend, and give the counter-sign."

Lion Limb advanced as ordered, but for some time could not discover the whereabouts of the sentinel.

At last, when he least expected it, the sentry stepped forth from a hollow tree in which he had been concealed, and confronted Lion Limb with looks of blank astonishment.

"Is it possible!" he gasped, "or do I see the ghost of Edgar Norman?"

"Not a ghost, my brave lad, but Lion Limb himself!"

"We all made sure you were lost, and that the raft had broken up into ten thousand pieces."

"Fortune was more favourable," said Lion Limb. "But, for my part, this meeting seems more like a dream than reality, for how could the old ship have withstood such a terrific and continuous a storm?"

The sentinel was about to explain everything that had occurred as he stood shaking Lion Limb and young Ted cordially by the hand; but Lion Limb said, hurriedly—

"We must leave all such explanations and pleasing details until some other time; each moment is precious."

"You look serious, captain," said the sentinel.

"I am," was the reply. "I come to warn all of you that our enemies have laid a plot to murder every one of you and seize the vessel."

"How can that be?" was the reply. "We have not been here long enough for any one to dis-cover us."

"You are mistaken."

"How, in what manner? If we have any enemies at all to contend against, they are simply natives, and they are not much account."

"You make a very grand mistake; for during the past hour I have discovered that some of the sailors who mutineered on board the 'Rattle-snake' are already on the island."

"Impossible!"

"Nay, 'tis true. Ted Rawlings and myself saw them."

"And who are they, pray?"

"Our worst foes—none other than Whetherby and Bloodhoof."

The boy sentinel seemed astonished at this announcement, and could scarcely believe it.

"'Tis true," said Ted; "we have seen and heard them arranging their plans to destroy us all."

"And who could have so informed the villains of our presence here?"

"Some of the villanous and treacherous natives. But speak low and in whispers. Secrete yourself in this hollow tree again; for Bloodhoof and Whetherby are not far off, I know, for they have come as spies to reconnoitre and arrange for their attack upon you."

In a few words the boy sentinel directed Lion Limb which way to go in order to get on board the wreck unseen.

"Keep to the edge of the wood," said he, "and if you should meet with any of the convict lads on guard, and they halt you, the countersign is 'Emma Clarence,' in memory of the good old captain's daughter, who we all supposed was drowned with you upon the raft."

Lion Limb did not then inform the youth that she still lived, but listened as the boy sentinel con-tinued his instructions thus:—

"In less than five minutes you will arrive at a natural ditch, which is now dry at low water; jump into this and walk on towards the sea; the wreck will soon appear high and dry on the sands."

Without stopping to ask any more questions, Lion Limb and young Ted proceeded on their way as directed, and passed a sentinel who was reclining against a tree, fast asleep.

Lion Limb did not like this, so said to Ted,

"Take up that lad's musket you see against the tree, and keep guard until I or some one else relieves you, for the poor lad is overcome with fatigue and much suffering, no doubt. The place must be well guarded, however, for the treacherous natives might be tempted at any moment to make an assault upon the wreck, and massacre every one on board."

Ted didn't much relish this idea of standing guard and doing the duty of the sleeper, but Lion Limb's look was firm.

And Ted knew well that, when his young chief looked so solemn, he meant all he said, and would have punished any disobedience upon the spot.

With the activity of a noble and gallant youth, the young chief leaped into the deep dry ditch, and hurried along towards the wreck, which was high and dry, far upon the sands, and with not a single soul visible on deck.

The sun was shining with oppressive heat, the sides of the good old ship were all cracked and open from exposure to the sun, and all looked deso-late, with a wilderness of broken spars and remnants of sails lying about in all directions and in inex-tricable confusion.

"What means all this?" thought Lion Limb. "Surely all on board cannot be laid down with sickness."

He ran up the plank which served as a companion way to the shore, and once more stood on the well-known decks.

All was silent.

Not a soul was visible.

He descended below, and, as he did so, his quick ear discerned the well-known sounds of persons snoring in their sleep.

He entered what had once been the captain's and officers' cabin, and there beheld a singular singular sight.

The tables and cabins were strewn with bottles, cans, pots, pans, and the remains of what had been a sumptuous repast.

In all directions lay half a score of sailors and more than twenty of the boy convicts.

They were all fast asleep, and on their faces all

wore the sure and certain signs of poor fellows who had been long suffering from excessive trials and dangers, and were now exhausted with their labours and hardships.

"P. or fellows!" thought the gallant youth, "they have doubtless been toiling much longer than my own companions, and now that they have reached a place of comparative safety, all have indulged in a little pardonable relaxation, and are overcome with sleep."

But this accident saved all from wholesale slaughter, as will be afterwards seen.

It had been Lion Limb's determination that the aspect of all things round and about the wreck should appear desolate and defenceless, in order to deceive the spies, who, he well knew, were looking out of their forest covert, and accurately taking note of all things.

"I will let the lads sleep on," said he, "and thus keep them all on board; the spies will be then deceived, and, when they attack us, if indeed they have so much courage left, they will find out that things on board are very far from their desires."

Lion Limb therefore drank a glass of wine and smoked a cigar in the midst of the sleepers, and, after half-an-hour had passed away, he fired his pistol through the window in order to awaken them all at once.

This had the desired effect.

Every man and boy jumped to his feet, and seized his arms, but, when their gaze fell upon Lion Limb as he sat on the dining table in the midst of all, they started back as if they had suddenly confronted some apparition.

For a moment they looked upon him in doubt.

Some rubbed their eyes as if they believed that what they saw was all a vision.

"Is it?"

"Can it be?"

"It is his ghost!"

Thus said one and another.

But when the brave youth seized a cup of wine and coolly drank to the health and prosperity of all, they rushed towards him and almost pulled him limb from limb, so glad were each and every one at his sudden, and, as it seemed to them, miraculous re-appearance.

Every man would have shouted out aloud for joy, had he not ordered silence among them.

As it was, he was immediately surrounded, and deluged with a multitude of questions on all sides.

In one word he told them that nearly all his companions were saved, and doing well, and were then awaiting his return to "Woodruff Bay," the name which he had given to the beach and cove on and into which his raft had drifted during a dense fog.

But when he explained the real object why he desired them to maintain profound silence—namely, in order to deceive the spies, who were not far off, and upon the watch, arranging plans for the capture of the wreck, and the destruction of every one who was not their friend—the boy convicts and all of the crew gave vent to their feelings against the cowardly mutineers in loud and angry expressions.

"Where are the villains?" asked half-a-dozen, in a breath, and with drawn weapons.

"Let us go forth at once, and hang the rascals," said others.

"Death to Bloodhoof! the worst of tortures for Whetherby!" were words on the lips of one and all.

"No, no," said Lion Limb; "let no one go forth except at my bidding, unless you have thought proper to elect another captain."

"We elected another leader in your absence, captain," said a chorus of voices, "but now we recognize no other chief than you."

"Lion Limb for ever!" they said aloud, and with flushed features.

"And who is your present captain?"

"Here I am," said a bold, handsome young sailor, "here I am, Lion Limb. Dick Hamilton is my name; I don't think you have quite forgotten me, for we fought side by side on the quarter-deck against Whetherby's bloodhounds.

So speaking, Dick doffed his hat and shook hands heartily with Lion Limb, who said,

"No, Dick, I can never forget your bravery or daring, and you more than deserve the confidence which all the brave lads, both men and boys, have reposed in you."

"No, no, Lion Limb; no compliments, sir; Dick isn't near as good a leader as you are, or else all the lads wouldn't have over eaten or drank themselves to sleep as they did to-day. But I know I'm expressing the wishes of every one when I say that you could not pay us a higher compliment than being our leader again through thick and thin as you have already done before."

"Well done, Dick," said many, in chorus, "quite true, every word of it."

"Therefore, captain," continued Dick Hamilton, "if you'll only say you'll be our leader, now and always, I know there ain't a man nor boy but will follow you to death if need be."

"So we will; so we will," was the response from all sides.

"Well, then, my brave lads, as you insist upon it, I will consent to be your captain once more."

"Bravo! bravo!"

"But on one condition," said Lion Limb.

"Name it."

"The only condition I wish to impose on all is this—that each and every one swears to obey me in all things."

"We will! we will!" was the unanimous answer.

And, as they spoke these words, they crowded round Lion Limb and would have carried him in triumph on deck.

But this Lion Limb would not allow.

"For the spies," said he, "have very quick eyes, and would take note of every one we have."

After a pause Dick Hamilton came forward again, and said—

"When we landed here, or rather were driven on shore, I placed guards out in the edge of the woods in order to warn us against the approach of strangers."

"A very good thought, Dick."

"After that I got all the tools I could out of the hold, and we set to work and dug a large trench on three sides of the wreck, so that, if we were attacked night or day by superior numbers of the savage natives, we could offer a better resistance."

"Very wise."

"After that we got all the live stock out of the hold, at least, all that were uninjured by the terible storm we had encountered, and landed them on shore to graze, hobbling them with ropes and chains so that they could not run away into the woods."

"Your arrangements were excellent, and no mistake," said Lion Limb.

"I intended to do a great many more things in a day or two, but as you are now my superior officer, Captain Lion Limb, I give up my command to you and hope that what I have done may meet with your approval."

"It does, Dick" said Lion Limb, grasping and shaking the young sailor's hand with genuine pleasure, "it does, Dick; and, to prove what I say, nothing shall be altered of what you have done."

"Hear, hear!" said several.

"And now, captain," said Dick, "as I wish to be of as much use as possible to all my companions, you must tell me what to do in future, and I'll obey as cheerfully as if I had never been captain."

"Then," said Lion Limb, "with the consent of all present, I hereby name Dick Hamilton one of my trusty lieutenants, and along with him I appoint Harry Woodruff equal in command."

General approbation followed this announcement; and to seal the engagement every one present filled up a goblet of wine and tossed it off, drinking success and long life to Captain Lion Limb and his two trusty lieutenants.

"What name have you given this place, Dick?" asked Lion Limb.

"We call it Clarence Harbour, captain, in memory of our old commander and his lovely daughter, Emma."

"The name, then," said Lion Limb, "shall not be changed, and I hope it may last for ever."

CHAPTER XIX

THE FLEET OF BOATS—REPORTS FROM THE BOY SENTINELS—THE UNEXPECTED GREETING.

THE first thing which the gallant young leader did was to send out two or three guards to relieve those who were already concealed in the outskirts of the forest, for he knew that they must be weary.

When this was done Lion Limb called up the youth who had been concealed in a tree, and questioned him.

"When you left me, captain," said the youth, "I remained concealed in the hollow tree, and was much astonished soon afterwards to hear persons conversing in a low tone near to me. Every word that they uttered I carefully noted, and was not long in recognizing Bill Whetherby and Bloodhoof."

"What did they say?"

"From what they saw they felt convinced that the wreck could be no other than that of the 'Rattlesnake,' for," said Bloodhoof, "any one could tell that from her figure-head."

"And what resolve did they arrive at?"

"Bloodhoof proposed to go boldly on board at once, and see how the land lay, as he termed it.

"Whetherby, however, was averse to this.

"'But I don't see any one to oppose us,' said Bloodhoof. 'Why should we hesitate, for the craft is heavily laden with everything that we require?'

"'True,' said Whetherby; 'we don't see anybody about; but there may be, you know, and if we attack them as we are, and should happen to encounter young Devil's Limb,' as they call you, captain, 'I fear he and his convict lads will prove too many for us, hardy men as we are.'

"'Well, then, I'll tell you what we'll do,' said Bloodhoof, 'from what I can make out from the signs of these two natives, these convict lads must have been mixed up in a fight with the natives, and carried off some prisoners,'

"'So I think,' Whetherby remarked.

"'Well, then, in that case revenge will cause these natives to be sworn friends to us; they will assist us when we attack the young brats,' said Bloodhoof.

"'So they will; but when this affair is to come off we cannot yet say, for you know it is a long way off to our own island, and if we attack these young devils at all it must be by surprise, and at night.'"

"This news you bring is most important," said Lion Limb; "but, take my word for it, while I am in command of the brave boys, the scoundrel mutineers will never take us by surprise."

When this was said Lion Limb called a council of war, and discussed the plan of action which he wished to adopt.

It was decided that Harry Woodruff and his camp should be at once apprized of what had taken place, and directed to escort every one at his own camp, and thus join forces.

But how was this to be done?

"If we only had a horse or a pony now," said Lion Limb, "we could easily send a messenger."

"We *have* got a pony," said Dick. "It was among the live stock sent out for one of the island settlements."

"Where is it?"

"Out grazing in a small valley near by; it cannot run away, for it is securely tethered."

"Then let it be brought in at once."

"Who knows the way, captain?"

"I do; I'll ride the pony," said Ted, in high glee, astonished to be the first to take the glad tidings to his companions.

When one of the lads brought up the pony a rough and temporary saddle and bridle was made, for there was as yet no time to examine into the ship's miscellaneous cargo to discover such articles.

When all was ready young Ted mounted the pony, and being directed by the captain to keep to the sea shore, and not venture into the forest, he started off at a gallop, and in high spirits, bearing a note to Harry Woodruff, which read as follows:—

DEAR COMPANIONS,—After considerable toil through the forest, and much danger, myself and Ted Rawlings arrived at the object of our search, and you will wonder, when I say that we have actually discovered the wreck of the ship, and a great number of boys and a few sailors on board; all well.

By a singular accident we saw Bloodhoof and Whetherby, who, in company of two natives, were exploring the coast, and one of the boys overheard them concocting a scheme for the total destruction of every one of us.

It appears that Whetherby and his gang are in possession of an island some distance away, and that the natives have already informed them of our presence here.

We shall have to defend ourselves right manfully against all attacks of these hardened villains, for I am certain they will not let us rest in peace for many days, perhaps not for twenty-four hours.

When you receive this note, therefore, make all the haste you can, collect everything that is of value, and wait until the boats arrive, which I will send round the island to bring you away. Keep a good look out, for if the wind and tide are favourable you may expect some of the lads to-night.

Yours, in haste,
LION LIMB.

Now it must be stated that Ted Rawling's pony did not depart for Harry Woodruff's camp empty-handed.

Two small panniers or baskets were shaped on behind Master Ted, containing whatever might prove of comfort to Emma and the rest, which baskets Ted did not fail to stop and examine.

He alighted from the pony when he had proceeded about ten miles, and regaled himself with a bottle of brandy, and the heat being intense he sat under a shady rock, with bridle in hand, and before he was aware of it fell into a sound sleep.

This sleep almost proved certain destruction to the rash lad, but we will not anticipate.

As will be seen from Lion Limb's letter, he promised to send boats to bring Harry Woodruff and the party away.

"But where are the boats?" asked several.

"Yes; where are the boats, captain, there ain't

one on board!" said Dick Hamilton. "The mutineers stole all the boats, every one on 'em."

"Never mind, we must make some, Dick."

"Make 'em!" said Dick, in astonishment. "Build half a dozen boats before night, captain!"

"Yes, Dick, we could build fifty, if necessary."

Dick, and several bystanders, scratched their heads in very grave doubt.

"I'll soon show you how to build boats," said Lion Limb. "Let some of the lads go and get axes and follow me."

A dozen axemen were soon provided and ready for orders.

Lion Limb led the way to a cypress grove he perceived close at hand.

"There," said he, pointing to an old cypress tree, of great girth, "let four of you set to work and cut that down as quickly as possible. When it falls, cut the trunk into equal portions."

He directed four lads to do the same with other trees, and in a few minutes the woods resounded with the noise of their heavy blows.

"Get a pitch-pot," said Lion Limb to another youth, "and fill it well; build a fire, and let it boil. Do you stand by and stir it well with a thick stick."

"Knock out the heads of several old water-casks, Dick," said he. "Bring nails, hammers, and such like, with you and all the old tow you can find."

These things being in readiness, the young captain proceeded to the cypress grove, and was glad to find that his industrious lads had cut down there very large trees and severed the trunks into equal portions.

Nor did the lads find it difficult to do this, for cypress trees are hollow, and in no instance is the trunk more than six or eight inches thick, though the trunk itself may be, in some instances, ten feet or more round.

Thus the lads by their labour had procured "six barrels," so to speak, and these again, by Lion Limb's orders, being split up lengthwise, gave twelve shells about four feet broad, by sixteen feet long.

Ropes were attached to each, and a numerous body of men and boys pulled them down towards the beach where the pitch was boiling.

Now came the process of forming them into canoes.

One end of each was sharpened off to a point and covered with planks.

The stern was filled with half the head of a water-barrel, and when all the carpentry work was completed, the cracks and holes were caulked up with pieces of wood and tow, and the outside thickly coated over with pitch.

These were then launched one by one, and found perfectly water-tight, amid the greatest applause of all there assembled.

But all was not yet accomplished.

They were drawn on shore again, one by one, and thick pieces cut off each side, so as to make the bottom sharp.

In addition to this, all hands set to work to make and fit temporary rudders and small sails.

When evening approached, however, six of the boats were ready, and a sailor placed in each, with two of the convict lads to assist in navigating it.

Dick Hamilton was delighted with these light, serviceable canoes, and went sailing about in one of them to test its qualities.

"It's wonderful how soon you thought of these things, captain," said he, "and it's astonishing how soon all hands made them; but between you and me, they won't stand much rough weather, though,

and may capsize, without you have a very careful person to steer."

Lion Limb was perfectly aware of all that.

He did not expect that these frail barks would serve him in rough water, but if they only accomplished his present purpose, he was satisfied.

When night came on, therefore, so many volunteered to serve on board these boats, that Lion Limb felt great difficulty in selecting proper persons.

At last the selection was made, and all was ready.

A light load of provisions was placed in each, and whatever they could conveniently carry.

Dick Hamilton was left in charge of the wreck.

Lion Limb took command of the first boat, and hoisting his pole with the small sail thereon, a light wind took him from the shore, followed in close order by the others.

The night was beautiful and unclouded; nought but the stars illumined the skies, and as the little fairy-like fleet of boats dipped and rolled on the glassy waves, rocked by gently-blowing, perfumed zephyrs, Lion Limb could see afar off red lights twinkling.

"They are the camp-fires of the mutineers on some neighbouring island," he thought, and as he sailed lazily along, he counted twenty such fires.

Towards midnight he altered his course, and turned his vessel to the land again.

For he imagined, from the distance he had sailed, that he must be somewhere near Harry Woodruff's camp.

A small twinkling light on shore confirmed this opinion, and signaling the others to follow carefully, and to lower their sails as they approached the beach, Lion Limb turned on the other tack, and sailed straight for the light.

They had almost reached their intended landing-place when the fire on shore was suddenly extinguished, and several shots were fired into the advancing boats, which rattled about the ears of those on board very unpleasantly.

CHAPTER XX.

TED RAWLINGS—THE LOST MESSENGER—THE NIGHT FIGHT BEGINS.

THIS unlooked-for reception caused great surprise and annoyance to young Lion Limb, who could not understand its meaning.

"Surely the rascally mutineers under Whetherby and Bloodhoof cannot have discovered the whereabouts of the little camp and stormed it during my absence. Yet, it must be so, or why this sudden opposition?"

And, as he thought of the indignities and sufferings to which little Emma and his friends must have been subjected to at the hands of the inhuman ruffians, Lion Limb's colour rose, his heart beat wildly and loudly, and he resolved to take signal revenge whenever a fitting opportunity presented itself.

Again and again did Lion Limb attempt to reach the shore.

But, although he wasted his breath in fruitless shouting, to make Harry Woodruff and all with him fully understand who and what they were who now approached the shore, still shots were fired in rapid succession, and, for a moment, he knew not what to do.

At last he hit upon a successful method of making his arrival known to all on land.

One of his brave lads volunteered to swim

ashore, and ascertain whether the camp was really occupied by friend or foe.

"Let me swim ashore, captain," said young Joe Hawkins. "I can dive like a duck, and you, therefore, need have no fear for my safety."

After a little consideration Lion Limb consented to this proposal of Little Joe, as he was called, and allowed him to do as he pleased.

On the instant Little Joe, who had been an expert swimmer and diver, well known at many of the London swimming baths, leaped over the side, and disappeared under the glassy water.

He rose once or twice to breathe and look around, and then dived again like a duck.

Nor was he perceived at all by those on shore, so intent were all in watching what appeared to them to be the mysterious manœuvres of the fleet of boats.

Contrary to Lion Limb's expectations, the camp was still safe, and when Harry Woodruff and his companions saw the figure of Little Joe emerge from the water, they were almost struck dumb with astonishment.

He presented his revolver, and would have discharged it at the gallant swimmer but Little Joe shouted out as loudly as his exhaustion would allow,

"Don't fire, Harry Woodruff; I am a friend!"

Explanation soon told Harry how matters stood; but, even then, so careful was he of those under his charge, he imagined that perhaps there might be some plot against himself and those who were under his charge.

He directed Joe to swim back again, so suspicious was he, and say, if they were friends, one boat only should be allowed to approach and land.

If he was satisfied, the rest might follow, he said.

Little Joe laughed at Harry's fears, and swam off again to Lion Limb's boat with all haste.

In a few minutes Lion Limb learned how matters stood, and, with a hearty cheer, he sailed towards the shore.

The other boats followed successively, and great was the joy of all at this unexpected meeting.

"But why did you make such an opposition to our landing, Harry?" asked Lion Limb.

"How did I know, captain, but what you might be some of the mutineers, or perhaps a party of natives?"

"But young Ted Rawlings, my messenger, informed you of our coming."

"Ted Rawlings! I have neither seen nor heard anything of him," said Harry, in surprise.

"No! Why, I sent a letter by him, posted him off on a pony which was on the wreck, and sent some refreshments."

"Haven't seen him at all. Which way was he to go?"

"I directed him to keep close to the beach, as being the safest route."

"Then, he is drowned, or been killed by the way."

"How?" said Lion Limb, in surprise.

"You may rely upon it that he has been overtaken by the natives, or else drowned in the tide."

Lion Limb felt sorrowful to hear this; but, when he came to reflect, it seemed to him highly probable that he had fallen a victim to one or the other of those accidents which Harry named.

For the shore rose very abruptly in several parts, and it was possible that the fast-flowing tide had encircled him before he could ride out of danger.

But still the present was no time for condoling.

Action was the word for all.

So that when Lion Limb had explained to all the position of affairs at the wreck, and warned them of the intended attack, Harry Woodruff and every one was incensed at the perfidy and treachery of the vagabond mutineers.

With an unanimous shout, all resolved to gather together all that was of use and value, and sail at once in the boats to the rescue of their brave companions on the wreck.

It did not take them very long to place on board all that they desired to transport, and in less than half-an-hour every one was safely provided for, and the six large canoes, now that they were weighted down, sailed with more ease and swiftness than they did when almost empty.

But when they had embarked, and got fairly out sea, a great danger arose.

The sky, which had been before clear and starlit, became gradually overcast, and threatened a sudden storm.

Lion Limb saw this, but did not communicate his thoughts to any one, least of all little Emma, who was on board with him.

"We had better make short work of it this trip," he thought, "and get into a safe harbour before the storm breaks over us, for our vessels won't stand much knocking about, I imagine."

He therefore hoisted every bit of sail that he could, and this example was followed by those in the boats following.

Little Emma held up her apron to catch every gust of wind; and several old coats and jackets, spare sails, and the like, were spread out in all sorts of ways, until at last the little squadron bowled along the water in gallant style.

For two hours or more were each and all threatened with great danger.

Yet all that time the storm held off, and the wind began to freshen at every gust.

"Keep near the shore. Don't go out too far," shouted Lion Limb, to the canoes following him, "for if we are caught in a gale we must land."

Cautiously sailing along the coast, the six boats hugged the land, and as they did so, looked like so many swans dancing on the tide.

"Bravo! bravo! my lads!" shouted Lion Limb, cheerily. "We shall get into harbour safely, after all, I think. Clap on every stitch of canvas you can."

While speaking thus in encouraging tones, little Emma shouted out,

"Look, Lion Limb, look! What is that floating on the water, near to us?"

And as she spoke, she pointed to some dark object on the waters.

A cold, sickly feeling came over the brave young leader, as he thought of the probable fate of Ted Rawlings.

But instead of it being a human body, when dragged towards the boat, it proved to be only one of the two small baskets which Ted had carried with him.

The contents had gone, and there it was empty, and a sign of some dreadful calamity to Ted.

Lion Limb did not communicate his thoughts, but he could not help musing, half aloud,

"There is no doubt of it now. He has been surprised and swallowed up by the tide."

He felt sorrowful for the fate of his young companion, but resolved that whenever the first occasion offered he and a party of youths should go forth and search for the body to give it decent interment, and not allow it to be disfigured by the savage natives, or by wild beasts.

But as they nearer and nearer approached

Clarence harbour, and the storm held off, all hearts felt light.

When they got within sight of the huge black wreck looming on shore, Lion Limb warned the boats to be on their guard, for he perceived in the distance several suspicious craft floating about.

What these might be he could not then imagine.

But the thing was soon explained.

Dick Hamilton, when Lion Limb had departed with the six canoes, felt uneasy, and thought it possible, perhaps, that the mutineers might make a sudden attack in the darkness.

To be warned in time of this, if any such thing were intended, he launched several of the new canoes that remained, and placing two or three trusty persons in each, he sent them out with orders to keep a sharp look-out eastward, towards the island on which several red lights had been seen glimmering afar off.

From time to time one of these canoes had run into shore again to inform Dick and his little colony of what they had seen.

But nothing that was visible on land or sea gave any token of what was shortly to come.

When Lion Limb, therefore, fell in with several of these look-out canoes, he was puzzled to understand who and for what they were.

When informed, however, of Dick's forethought and vigilance, he highly commended his lieutenant's zeal, and soon afterwards, with all his party—including the Indian princess and his captives—were safely and snugly on board the wreck, engaged in disposing of a plentiful supper.

The only drawback now to the pleasure of all was the absence of Ted Rawlings.

Every one who knew him felt sorry for "poor Ted," as he was called.

Yet Lion Limb did not let the thoughts of the mysterious disappearance of their young companion to interfere with or retard the execution of his plans.

He placed sentinels out in the woods and told them to fire and arouse all on board should any one approach.

He likewise gave orders to the look-out boats to be more vigilant if possible than ever.

He told them that if they saw any black objects approaching from the direction of the island to row into shore at once and give warning.

This being done he loaded two of the cannons on deck with grape and canister shot ready for immediate use.

Arms were stacked and loaded in various places, and every one on board knew his exact position when aroused.

Having made every disposition for the safety of those under his command, Lion Limb called all around him, and said—

"I have made every possible preparation, my brave lads, to meet those villanous mutineers should they dare to approach, but I think they have not courage enough to attempt such an expedition to-night. At all events," said Lion Limb, "if they do come, you must all sally forth quietly to meet them and take the position I have assigned to you behind the breastworks, for we must not allow them to get within a hundred yards of the wreck if possible. But in all things," said Lion Limb, in conclusion, "be obedient to the orders of your several leaders, and let your leaders be guided by me and the circumstances in which they may be placed during the fight."

With these few words the young captain dismissed his followers, and all save those whose duty it was to keep guard lay down upon the deck, armed as they were, to catch a little sleep.

The moon had risen and sunk again below the horizon.

The plaintive songs of night-birds was heard in the forest, while gentle murmuring waves washed the pebbly shore.

All was calm.

The night was far advanced.

No one now even dreamed that any attack was probable.

But when least expected shots were heard in the distant forest.

Bang! bang! bang! in rapid succession went the guns of those on guard.

A faint cheer was now heard.

The enemy had appeared when least expected.

The battle began—the first of many sanguinary ones which subsequently took place between the boy convicts and the barbarous mutineers and cutthroats of adjacent islands.

CHAPTER XXI.

THE ATTACK OF THE MUTINEERS BY NIGHT.

BEFORE the echo of the shots had died away Lion Limb jumped to his feet and made his final arrangements for the combat now beginning.

Harry Woodruff had command of the left, Dick Hamilton superintended the right, while the centre and all the movements were under Lion Limb's chief command.

Without any hurry Lion Limb disposed his little army as best he could into three parts; so near, however, that one could support the other in case of need, and so screened from view that the number could not be counted on account of the sand hills.

He next scanned the ocean to see if any boats were in view that might attack his own.

But none were to be seen.

He therefore signalled to his own boats to return to the shore, and for the men to take part in the combat.

This was most readily done.

When, therefore, all was ready, Lion Limb and his brave young companions waited for the attack, but for a short time no one appeared.

At last, however, a party of natives were seen approaching at a run, and yelling most terrifically, brandishing war-clubs, bows, arrows, and all manner of implements in a frantic manner.

When they came within convenient distance part of Dick Hamilton's and part of Harry Woodruff's lads fired into them point blank, and such a howling as ensued was never heard before.

They scampered off to the woods faster than they came, dragging some of their wounded away with them.

The mutineers now began to imagine that they were not opposed to more than a dozen persons altogether, and, with a loud shout, advanced sword and pistol in hand.

They were very numerous and well armed.

They divided themselves into three parties, and pressed forward in a determined manner.

* * * * *

But before we speak of this sanguinary engagement between the villanous mutineers and the Boy Convicts with their friends, the few noble sailors, who remained true to them, let us for a moment return to Bill Whetherby and his companion, Bloodhoof, and narrate what they said and did when we last left them on their way towards the wreck.

Neither Whetherby nor Bloodhoof ever dreamed

that while in the forest making observations from the tallest of trees, that they were both seen and heard by Lion Limb and his faithful young companion—Ted Rawlings.

When they proceeded towards the camp where the wreck was, led as before by the native guides, they frequently paused, and listened for any sounds which might indicate the number of those who were living around the wreck.

As we have seen, both Lion Limb and Ted Rawlings arrived on the scene much sooner than their enemies, and the result was that the curiosity of the mutineer leader was foiled.

When they reached the edge of the forest, and very near to the sea, Whetherby and Bloodhoof paused, and lay flat on their faces in the high grass.

But unknown to them one of the convict boys, as we have seen, was on guard there, and according to the directions of Lion Limb, he hid himself in the trunk of an old tree, and heard nearly every word that was uttered by the spies and leaders of the mutineers.

"I don't see any one about," said Whetherby, in a tone of joy.

"Nor I," said Bloodhoof. "Yet from the signs of these rascally natives I should have thought there might have been dozens, if not scores, of the convict brats hereabouts. Perhaps half of them may have been killed off, either by the savage natives or by fever and sickness of different kinds."

"That may or may not be," said Whetherby; "but from all appearances I should think there cannot be more than a dozen at most who are on board, if even that number."

Still full of suspicions, they remained where they were for a considerable time, and perceiving no signs of life or activity on board, they arrived at the conclusion that there were very few, if any, persons about the wreck who were able to make any show of stout resistance if suddenly and vigorously attacked.

"I tell you what it is," said Bloodhoof, in a savage tone, "I've a good mind to go forward single-handed and see for myself."

But being dissuaded by Whetherby, he resolved to follow his leader's advice, and return without making himself known, or giving any sign of what they intended hereafter to do.

When, therefore, they had fully satisfied themselves how things stood, they rose from their recumbent posture, and retraced their way through the forest, led and guided as before by the two ugly-looking natives.

When they had reached their boat, which was concealed in a creek, they hoisted sail, and set out on their homeward journey to the island whereon they and the rest of the mutineers had established themselves, and which was fully twenty miles from where they then were.

So far distant was it, in truth, and so low did the land lay on the ocean, that it was scarcely visible, and even then indefinable to the leader of the Boy Convicts, who over and over again had stood gazing in that direction to ascertain the correct distance and its natural strength or weakness.

When Bloodhoof and Whetherby arrived, after rapid sailing, at their island home, they called a council of war, which was numerously attended by their noisy and bloodthirsty followers.

"What," said one, "you don't mean to say that the wreck of the 'Rattlesnake' has drifted to their island westward?"

"Yes I do, though," said Bloodhoof.

"Then the information which we received from the savages of our neighbouring island proved true."

"Quite so."

"And how many brats are there?"

"That we cannot tell; but I should suppose there are not many, for the wreck looked all deserted."

"But I thought that the savage natives reported them at two score or more?"

"They did so, but must have been mistaken, for although we lay watching an hour or more I never saw the least signs of life or activity."

"Then they are all struck down with fever or sickness."

"Very likely: and that is the reason why I should advise an immediate attack. The cargo of the wreck is not to be despised."

"I should think not indeed," several replied.

"She has plenty of powder on board," said one.

"Yes, and arms too."

"There is any quantity of bread-stuffs and liquors on board, things which we much stand in need of," grumbled many.

"But about the live stock which were below?"

"I don't know, nor can I imagine what has become of it all."

"There were several cows and calves," said one.

"Yes, and goats too."

"And a horse."

"A young bull and two donkeys."

"Besides any number of cocks and hens, ducks, geese, and the like."

"So there were, mate, I remember now."

"I ought to know," said one, "for I used to feed and tend 'em every day."

"What has become of all such things I can't say, mate," said Whetherby, "but from distant sounds which Bloodhoof and I heard while watching, we thought that these animals, or such as still lived, might be in some neighbouring valley."

"So much the better then," said many; "we'll have a rare feast when we conquer and destroy these boy convicts."

"What say you about setting out on the expedition at once?" asked several.

"We had better be quick about it," said more than one, "or the natives may get all before we arrive there."

"True," said Bloodhoof, "and for that reason I say let us prepare the boats, and set sail."

"Shall we make the attack from the sea?"

"No; if any are still living they will keep a sharp look out to seaward."

"Then what do you propose, Bloodhoof?"

"Why, this," said the ugly and ferocious mutineer, when appealed to, "I propose that we prepare and man the boats at once."

"It is not necessary to take all our men in this expedition," said Whetherby.

"True," Bloodhoof replied; "thirty will be more than enough for our present purpose; besides, the natives, to the number of a hundred or more, will assist us, and will be assembled ready for action at the place we intend to land."

"And where is that?"

"In a wide inlet south of the island where we landed before," said Bloodhoof; "the distance thence through the woods is not more than a couple of miles."

"That plan fully meets my ideas," said Whetherby, "me and our natives can travel through the woods without noise or confusion, and when all are a-bed and fast asleep on board the wreck, we will make a sudden attack and slay them before they can make any show of resistance. Follow me!"

THE BOY KING
OF THE SOUTH SEA ISLANDS.

LION LIMB CROWNED KING OF THE SOUTH SEA ISLANDS.

" Let the natives be the first to attack," said one, " for the convict brats can then waste their strength on them, and when we commence they will be exhausted."

This plan of action was acceded to by all, and the boats were prepared and armed forthwith.

When they set sail a strong wind was blowing. which drove them somewhat off their course, and then it was that Lion Limb's look-out in the boats did not espy them at all from seaward.

They arrived safely, however, some time after midnight.

No. 7.

They met their Indian friends ready to receive them at the spot indicated.

How they commenced the attack we have already seen.

But return we now to the sanguinary fight.

*   *   *   *   *

When Whetherby saw that the natives ran at the first fire, he and Bloodhoof were greatly enraged.

The shouts of the wounded savages raised their anger to a high pitch.

The sight of bloodshed seemed to whet the appetites of the mutineers.

"Lead on, Whetherby!" cried the followers of that black-looking rascal.

"Move forward, Bloodhoof!" cried others.

At one and the same moment the mutineers raised a loud shout, and ran from the wood, never for a moment thinking that any great opposition would be made to them as they advanced with coveteous eyes towards the wreck.

When they reached the breastworks of sand, however, and found a yawning pit before them, they hesitated.

"Now's the time, my merry merry men!" shouted Lion Limb, cheerily, to his companions. "Aim low and steady."

A withering volley was now delivered by the boy convicts, and with such accuracy that it made the mutineers and their savages yell again with surprise and horror.

Many fell dead headlong into the ditch.

Others leaped across it and fought hand to hand with the brave lads.

"Follow me!" shouted Lion Limb, as he led on the advance.

"Follow me, boys!" said Dick Hamilton, as he led on his wing against the enemy.

"Come on, my brave lads!" shouted Harry Woodruff, as, sword in hand, he dashed out from behind the breastwork, right into the midst of the enemy.

The fight now became terrible in the extreme.

Whetherby and his men were now furiously assailed on three sides.

And yet they fought on with the utmost desperation.

Shouts were heard on all sides.

The clash of steel was deafening.

Cries of the wounded and dying filled the air.

Each and every one fought with the utmost desperation.

The mutineers were all full-grown men.

Yet the boy convicts on all occasions proved a match for them in everything.

The one party was fighting to gain possession of the wreck and its treasures.

The boy convicts were absolutely fighting for life itself.

They well knew that if conquered, scarcely one of them would escape a cruel captivity or death.

With these feelings on either side, augumented by a spirit of terrible hate, revenge, and deadly resolution, the combat became more sanguinary each moment that it lasted.

The chiefs and leaders on both sides behaved as if life or death depended on the issue.

The Indians seemed animated by fresh courage, and took part in the bloody strife with loud shouts and yells.

The conflict now assumed a general character, and was terrific in its intensity.

For some time it required all the judgment and persuasion of Lion Limb to restrain the ardour of his gallant young followers.

They wished to rush forth from their defence of sand and assail the dastardly mutineers hand to hand.

But this action Lion Limb would not allow.

"Remain where you are," said the wise young chief, "and do not sally forth into the open ground until I bid you; they may be much more numerous than we imagine."

Mistaking Lion Limb's coolness for want of courage, Bill Whetherby and Bloodhoof shouted at the top of their voices to their companions to assail and surround the sand defences.

They endeavoured to do so, but for a time they were driven back.

"Give ground, Harry Woodruff, give ground, and let the villains approach nearer the wreck; I have something very nice in store for them!" said Lion Limb, laughing gaily.

This order was passed to Dick Hamilton, and, at a given signal, the boy convicts fell back towards the wreck very suddenly, and pretented to be very much disordered by the onslaught of their enemies.

Bloodhoof and Whetherby perceiving this movement, made sure that the victory was already theirs.

With loud shouts and hurrahs, therefore, they leaped over the sandy breastworks, waving their swords in wild triumph.

The native Indians also with terrific yells and barbarian shouts followed the mutineers.

The onset of these invaders was so loose and unorganized that it proved fatal to them.

For when they approached nearer and nearer to the much coveted wreck, they suddenly paused and seemed struck dumb with astonishment.

Lion Limb had charged two cannons with grape shot.

At a proper moment he took deliberate aim at the mass of fierce invaders and fired.

The wreck trembled again with the concussion.

The rocks and hills resounded with deafening echoes.

Dozens of the Indians and mutineers together were cut down by the terrible shower of iron hail.

They were appalled.

The Indians were struck dumb with astonishment, and stood like as if they were turned to marble.

They would have retreated, and were preparing to do so when Lion Limb, with a loud shout, rushed forth upon the invading robbers and attacked them with redoubled fury.

The fight that now ensued was terrific in the extreme.

Bloodhoof, Whetherby, and their gang of desperadoes, fought like demons more than men.

But the Indians deserted them at a critical moment, and left the field of battle in consternation.

Assailed on three sides by Lion Limb, Harry Woodruff, and Dick Hamilton, the mutineers knew not which way to turn. They continued the fight, it is true, but resistance seemed hopeless.

On every hand, and wherever they dared to make a stand, they were put to the rout by the brave band of boys.

The dog Dragon, also, was not behind in gallantry on this occasion.

He sniffed the scent of battle almost as quickly as any one engaged, and bounded forth into the midst of the combatants, playing sad havoc among the half-naked Indians, and their friends the invading robbers.

Some of them Dragon bit in the leg, and made them hop about in very comical style.

More than once he saved Lion Limb and others from treacherous blows, by seizing their foes by the throat and strangling them.

Dragon, indeed, was the mortal terror of all engaged in the fight that day.

He was everywhere!

Wherever danger was the greatest, and the combat thickest, Dragon was sure to be there.

Time and time again were pistols and guns discharged at him with deadly aim.

But it seemed impossible to hit the noble and brave animal.

Whetherby and Bloodhoof had very good occasion to remember the performance of Dragon on this occasion.

The noble dog had inflicted frightful wounds upon those two ruffians, and well nigh killed Whetherby.

On every hand, then, were the mutineers being driven back, and their losses were considerable.

Several long hours the conflict continued with unabated fury.

Little by little, the invaders were driven from the wreck, and made to fall back again over the sandhills, which they had crossed not long before with such jubilant shouts.

Inch by inch, and yard by yard, Lion Limb and his two brave lieutenants, Harry Woodruff and Dick Hamilton, forced back the mutineers, until they were on the edge of the forest, whence they had originally issued.

Bloodhoof and Whetherby imagined that Lion Limb would not dare to follow them so far.

They were terribly mistaken, however.

Having fairly beaten the rascals in the open ground, Lion Limb exhorted his men by words and deeds to follow up the villains, and allow them no rest.

"Follow them, my brave lads! On to them, my merry, merry men!"

"Wave the flag of old England, in front," said he, "and let us attack them tooth and nail. Forward boys! follow me."

And the brave lads did follow their gallant young leader.

Across the sands they marched in martial array.

Over the hills they went in splendid style.

Their approach towards the forest was perceived by Bloodhoof, who was now in command of the invaders.

Whetherby had been seriously wounded, as we have already said, and carried off the ground.

Bloodhoof, with a great oath, and burning with desires of vengeance, arranged his men in the edge of the forest, and told them to lie down.

"Lie down, men! lie down, and let not a single one of you be seen. These convicts, led on by young Devil's Limb, are pursuing us. See, they are coming close upon us. When I give the word of command, let every one among you, who are able, draw his trigger and bring down one of those rascally brats who are opposed to us, yonder."

"Aim at young Devil's Limb and Harry Woodruff," said several.

"Yes, my men, aim at the boy chief, and be sure of your mark; if we can only succeed in killing him, all will go well with us," said Bloodhoof.

According to his direction, Bloodhoof's men lay down in the edge of the forest, with loaded weapons, ready to cut down all who dared to approach within gun shot.

They even laughed and joked at the sad havoc they were about to commit, and rejoiced over the expected and much-desired death of Lion Limb.

But all their calculations were at fault.

Harry Woodruff, Dick Hamilton, and other prominent leaders of the boy convicts.

They expected that, screened as they were, the boy convicts would all be cut off, and they themselves suffer no hurt.

But, just at the moment when they were taking deadly aim at the boys approaching in gallant array, several shells were fired from the wreck by Emma Clarence, and fell bursting right in the midst of the mutineers.

Had an earthquake occurred at that moment the mutineers could not have felt more surprise.

They were almost petrified.

But, before any of them could recover from their stupefying astonishment, other shells came whizzing and bursting among them, causing loss of life and limb.

With fierce oaths at thus being thwarted and punished still more than ever, Bloodhoof and his gang fired a wild, random volley at their approaching foes, and retreated faster than ever through the forest towards their own boats and landing place.

Thus, after many, many hours of hard fighting, the boy convicts and their few sailor-companions were left masters of the well-fought field.

All were fatigued beyond expression.

Some were seriously wounded, several were dying among the boys.

All were dusty, powder-blackened, and scarred by stray shot or sabre cuts.

The sands were dyed with gore.

Dead Indians dotted the beach around the wreck, some without arms, legs or heads.

It was a ghastly sight to behold!

But the greatest destruction of all was caused by the explosion of those shells which, unknown to Lion Limb, had been so carefully aimed and fired at the foe by Emma Clarence.

With loud and triumphant shouts the enemy were pursued through the woods, but, ere long, Lion Limb recalled his men from the pursuit, and returned on board the wreck in triumph.

Lion Limb felt certain that the mutineers would make another attack upon him at no very distant day, and therefore made every preparation in his power to give them a very warm reception.

He placed double guards out that night, and, having provided for the comfort of all those around him, he sat down upon the noble old wreck to enjoy a cigar or two and a stiff glass of rum and water.

But, while he and his brave companions for the most part were thus regaling themselves after the fatigues and dangers of the day, Lion Limb was suddenly surprised at something he saw in the far-off distance.

His companions rose to their feet in dread alarm.

Far away they perceived an immense fire blazing.

A forest was in a state of conflagration.

It had been set on fire by the mutineers!

At the same moment, and from towards the sea, arose a faint and feeble cry of,

"Help! help! help!"

CHAPTER XXII.

THE COUNTESS OXENFORD AND EDGAR AND ALLAN NORMAN.

BUT while we are thus detailing the varied fortunes of Lion Limb abroad, thousands upon thousands of miles away on the South Sea Islands, let us return to England again, and trace the rascally doings of some knaves who have to do with the current of our story.

That Edgar Norman and his brother were children of parents who wished to remain unknown is very clear.

But who were they?

Why did they thus desire to bury the evidences of their crime?

Two nobler, or handsomer youths than the Normans, could not be found anywhere, and yet they could claim relationship with no living creature.

It was a sad day, however, for the unknown parents of the Brothers Norman when Edgar left England, and, as it was supposed, for ever.

The first intimation which the English public had of the fate of the "Rattlesnake" and all hands, in the South Pacific Ocean, was by means of the bottles which Lion Limb, Captain Clarence, and others had thrown overboard.

One of these bottles was washed on to the Chilian coast, and on being examined was handed over to the English consul.

The consul was pained at the sad news of the wreck, and immediately sent off the message from the sea to London, when the fact was made generally known by the newspapers.

Many of the journals bewailed the loss of brave Captain Clarence and his noble crew in unmeasured terms.

But not one of the newspapers thought proper to express a single word of sorrow for the fate of the boy convicts, who were supposed to have been lost likewise.

Repine for the loss of a shipload of convicts, say many! Why so? It is rather a benefit to society than otherwise; let us, therefore, rejoice.

Such was the language of many who were selfish and thoughtless; but when the news spread far and wide there were many hearts of poor honest parents which were racked with pain for the disaster and awful fate which had overtaken their erring children in that ill-fated ship.

But be this as it may, there was *one* heart which was almost broken at the news.

How it came to pass, and why, we will explain.

On a cloudless afternoon in June a magnificent lady was to be seen riding a thorough-bred along Rotten Row.

Gentlemen of title, as they recognized or passed this beauty, touched their hats and bowed.

"That is the fair Countess Oxenford," said a fashionable spark to a companion; "how splendidly she rides!"

"Yes; and how handsome she still is! I wonder what her age is?"

"Impossible to say; perhaps forty-five."

"No, not so much as that by ten years," the other spark replies.

"How do you know?"

"I heard her husband, Lord Oxenford, say so."

"What a silly old fool he must be, then, to go and marry a woman young enough to be his own daughter. Why, Lord Oxenford must be close upon seventy, if I'm not much mistaken."

"What does that matter? He's got plenty of money, that's all these dashing beauties care for."

"Well, then, if *I* were a young girl, I'd see any rich old fool in Jericho before I'd marry him."

"That may be."

"Has my lord any family?"

"No, nor any likelihood of it."

"Then one of these days we may live to hear that the beautiful countess is a dashing widow?"

"Very likely, and if it turn out to be so, I have

no doubt there will be many hearts broken about her."

Such was the conversation of two young fashionable sparks as they strolled along admiring the display of pretty women in Rotten Row.

But the "dashing handsome lady" they had referred to in such glowing terms, namely, the Countess Oxenford, although exhibiting herself to the best of advantage before the admiring gaze of Rotten Row, and although all her movements were watched with looks of admiration, she was not happy.

Not happy, say you; not happy with wealth and rank?

No, money does not make happiness.

That handsome woman that dashed past but a moment ago is unhappy.

She is, in truth, supremely miserable.

She smiles, it is true, and appears to be among the gayest of the gay.

Light musical laughter escapes her lips as she listens first to the soft nothings of one friend or the encomiums of another.

Yet a worm is eating her life away.

There is a cancer in her heart.

Every cup of happiness is embittered to her.

She lives and moves a hypocrite.

A deep crime is on her soul.

Shame stains her character like a purple dye, but of this the world knows nothing.

The world sees nothing more than outward appearances; but if her heart could speak aloud how the Countess Oxenford could astonish the world!

But no, she laughs and smiles in public, yet often weeps in the privacy of her own chamber.

The opera-box often sees the Countess Oxenford. She is a great dancer also, and in the giddy whirl of the waltz, she glides along noiselessly and happily to the strains of deliciously soft and seductive music.

But in the still small hours of the night, when all is still, when all is darkness, and the church clock tolls the solemn hour, then, when alone, her conscience awakes, her heart flutters, she is almost breathless with excitement, and her thoughts find utterance as she rises from her bed in haste and exclaims in a paroxysm of agony, in a half-suppressed whisper,

"My son, my children; give them back to me; give me Edgar! Oh, my boy, my darling boy; forgive me, oh, God! forgive me," and sinks to the ground almost paralyzed and trembling with intense excitement.

This lady is the mother of the young Normans.

But Lord Oxenford is not their father.

It will be our duty to trace this lady and her extraordinary doings, and of the important part she is called upon to play in the fortunes of brave young Lion Limb and his companions.

CHAPTER XXIII.

UNEXPECTED REVELATIONS — THE ESCAPE OF YOUNG MARKS — BARON TEMPLETON HAS A FIERCE AND DEADLY ENEMY ACTING PRIVATELY AGAINST HIM AND LION LIMB — FALSE NEWS — EYES IN THE DARK.

THE evening of the same day which saw the handsome Countess Oxenford galloping along Rotten Row, proved to be an eventful one in the fortunes of Lion Limb and his young friends.

For while the handsome, pale, proud countess sat languidly lolling at the drawing-room window after dinner, several visitors arrived.

Among them was the judge who had tried and condemned Lion Limb.

His title was that of Baron Templeton.

He was a handsome-looking man of about forty-five years of age, and looked and moved about from place to place more like a gallant soldier than a judge.

He bowed to the countess when introduced in a mostly courtly manner, but with the air of a man who had perhaps never spoken to her before in all his life.

Yet he was the very same person, as we have seen, who accompanied Jerry Marks in that mysterious midnight ride during the dreadful storm.

He was the natural father of the young Normans, but as he bowed profoundly before the beautiful countess his manner was as cold as ice.

Yet she—the smiling, beautiful, heartless countess—spoke in an indifferent and haughty manner to the man who was the father of her two sons.

They met as strangers, spoke as strangers, and the world knew not of the criminal intimacy which had existed between them for years.

Such is life!

Lord Oxenford, the devoted old husband, believed his wife to be as chaste as Diana; and had angles spoken to the contrary he would not have believed them.

He had married one of the greatest beauties London had ever seen, and was happy in his dotage.

She, in her turn, had married one of the most opulent nobles of the day; and, without the least spark of love in her heart, treated him privately with contempt.

But though Baron Templeton seemed an utter stranger to the countess on this occasion, he continued to sidle up to her in a careless manner, and slipped a note into her hands, whispering in her ear—

"Read it at once."

The baron did not long remain in Lord Oxenford's house on this occasion, but took his departure for the opera he said.

But the truth was that he called for a Hansom cab and drove to his own official chambers in Lincoln's Inn.

He hurried up the flight of dusty, rickety old stairs, and entering his room threw himself into an easy chair, deep in thought.

He had not long remained thus pondering when a gentleman was announced.

It was none other than Lawyer Marks, the father of Jerry.

With very low bows, the Jew lawyer sidled into the room, winking and blinking, and showing his white, fang-like teeth.

"Mr. Marks, I believe?" said the baron, waving Jerry's father to a chair.

"Yes, my lord, exactly. Thank you; much obliged."

And old Marks continued bowing mechanically.

"Well, Mr. Marks, and what may be your business, pray?"

"Very important, my lord; very important indeed, I can assure you."

"What is the nature of it?"

"Oh! monstrous, I can assure you."

"Well, what is it?"

"I wish to ask your advice, my lord," said old Marks, very slowly, "about my son Jerry or Jeremiah."

"Your son Jerry, Mr. Marks? Why, what can you mean?" said the baron, in surprise.

"I mean this, my lord," said old Marks, with a cunning look at the judge, "that you may be able to tell me what to do in regard to him."

"Explain yourself, Mr. Marks."

"My son Jerry, then, my good lord, was abducted, snatched away, smuggled, kidnapped—whatever you like to call it."

"Well, and what has this case of abduction got to do with me?" said the baron, with a slight tinge of crimson in his cheeks.

"I don't say, my lord, that it *has* anything to do with you, neither do I say that it *hasn't*," replied old Marks; "but all I know is that I have very strong suspicions that he was spirited away on account of that evidence he gave against the young Normans in the murder case."

"But what motive could any one have in thus entrapping your son, Mr. Marks?"

"That I leave for others to say," the Jew replied; "but all I know is, that my son Jerry proved too clever for his gaolers by half, and has escaped from the cottage in which he was confined."

"Escaped!" said the baron, half-aloud, as if speaking to himself.

"Yes, escaped; and during the time he was confined there by those villains employed for the purpose, he learnt more than he cares to tell about *certain* parties that you know of, my lord."

Old Marks repeated the latter part of the sentence in a very slow, drawling manner, so as to impress the baron.

But the judge took no notice whatever of the Jew's insinuating manner, and rising, said,

"Well, Mr. Marks, if this is the only business you came to consult me upon, I should advise you to call in the aid of some clever detective officer to help you to discover the persons who have wronged you, and thus claim——"

"Damages, I suppose, my lord?"

"Just so, Mr. Marks. I must now say good evening to you," said the baron, rising, and going towards the door.

"I beg your pardon," said old Marks; "but I have heard it whispered, to-day, that you and other kind friends have petitioned the government to have the sentence of Edgar Norman and Edward Rawlings remitted on the strength of a bonâ fide confession made by a third party."

"I have nothing to say in the matter. Those who procured this confession you speak of ought to know sufficient of its genuineness."

"So they ought, my lord, and so they do," old Marks replied, with a sly grin sideways.

"On the strength of this confession, whosever it is, the Government have granted pardon to the two youths you have named, and letters to that effect have gone out to the colonies this very day."

"Well, my lord, did you never hear who this party was that made this strange confession?"

"How should I?"

"Well, it was my only son, Jerry, my lord."

"Impossible, Mr. Marks," said the baron, in tones of surprise. "By-the-bye, now I come to recollect, your son's evidence was what convicted them. Yes, now I come to consider, I have heard it rumoured abroad that your son *has* given a full denial to all his former evidence."

"Yes, but it is not a true denial, my lord. It was made under threats and compulsion."

"You surprise me, Mr. Marks."

"He was obliged to make this denial at the hazard of his life, my lord; but in a lucky moment he has miraculously escaped from his forced confinement, and calls aloud for revenge on those who incarcerated and ill-treated him."

The judge smiled, as he quietly observed,

" Instead of speaking about revenge, and all such nonsense, Mr. Marks, I think your son would do well to leave the country, for if the officers of justice lay hold of him, he will, without a doubt, be transported for life, for swearing away the lives of others."

"Yes, my lord, if that confession was a real one; but it is not; and as to him having revenge, he has had part of it already."

"How do you mean, Mr. Marks?"

"The ship in which the youths sailed has been wrecked, and every soul on board buried in the sea."

"What!" said the baron, hastily rising, looking deadly pale at the smiling Jew.

"Nay, my lord, do not take such trifling news so much to heart," said old Marks, with malice glistening in his eyes. "Nay, do not let such a trifling matter discompose you. Even a *parent* could not show any more sudden or greater concern than you do about this transported lad, Edgar Norman."

The Jew looked fixedly at the judge, who seemed to take no notice of what the lawyer had said, but murmured again and again,

"Poor, poor lad! My heart told me he was innocent, but the evidence of that young demon, Marks, was so conclusive and circumstantial, that there was no possible way of saving him. Poor, poor Edgar," he thought. "I am justly punished."

"Who told you of this news, Mr. Marks?" said the baron, rousing himself, and speaking in his usual calm manner.

"The papers are full of the matter, my lord. Several bottles have been sent to England by various consuls on the South Pacific coast, in which were notes and letters all detailing the one great fact that a mutiny had occurred on board the 'Rattlesnake,' that most of the crew had departed from the ship in all the boats, and that the vessel was leaking very badly, and not expected to float an hour longer."

The baron had not heard this news before, and was stunned.

"Here is the evening paper, my lord," said Marks. "Read for yourself."

The baron seized the paper, and as he read the "message from the sea," his hands shook violently.

"'Tis true, 'tis too true," said he, and he sank into his chair, looking calm and pale, his handsome brow contracted in deep thought, and a slight quivering tremor playing about his mouth.

Old Marks watched him like a cat does a mouse, for a few moments, and a dead silence was maintained by both.

At last the eyes of both met fully and fairly, yet neither spoke a word.

Each was endeavouring to read the secrets of the other's heart.

At last, awakening from apparent reverie, the baron said, with a sickly smile—

"Mr. Marks, will you, for once in your life, answer me one question fairly and with honesty?"

"Your lordship is inclined to be complimentary."

"No I am not, Mr. Marks."

"What, then, may be your lordship's question?"

"Simply this. What did you visit me for this evening? What is your real business, or do you come to squander my time in idle conversation?"

"No, my lord, I came on business of the utmost importance."

"Then what is it?"

"My son, by accident, found two letters in the apartment in which he was confined. He discovered them the same evening on which he was conducted thither by some one unknown."

"Found letters?" mused the baron, walking up and down in deep thought. "I wonder if this cunning Jew is playing upon me, or whether he suspects me. I must be careful. I am dealing with a man who is as cunning and slippery as a serpent."

Then he said aloud.

"Letters, you say, Mr. Marks?"

"Yes, my lord."

"And did he preserve them?"

"Oh, yes, my lord; he hid them in his breast for safety."

"And what were they about? Did they contain any news of importance, or did they throw any light upon who they were who had abducted your son, and so imprisoned him?"

"What they spoke of I know not, my lord; but before my son left my home this very evening, after escaping from his confinement, he placed this note in my hand, begging of me to deliver it to no one but you."

Old Marks handed over the note very humbly, and with many bowings and scrapings.

My lord tore open the note, and read as follows:—

"MY LORD,—I herein enclose the envelopes of two notes which I picked up in my prison house; the contents of the letters I keep for my own purposes.

"Your enemy for life,

"JERRY MARKS."

The two envelopes alluded to were eagerly looked at by the judge.

One was in his own handwriting addressed to the Countess of Oxenford, and the other was addressed to himself by the countess in reply.

For a moment the baron could not believe the evidence of his own senses.

"If the young villain," he mused, "has really got possession of the two letters, I am ruined."

He walked to and fro for a few moments in a hurried manner, and then quickly resumed his old quiet ways again as if nothing had happened.

"I cannot see what object your son, Mr. Marks, could have in sending me these two envelopes, because they are downright forgeries."

"That may be, my lord; but if the letters are not, what then?"

"Have you seen the contents of the letters, then?"

"I have not; but I have heard my son speak regarding them."

"And where is your son now, Mr. Marks?"

"That, my lord, I cannot tell; he may be far away by this time. If you like, however, I will hasten home again and see if he be in any of his old haunts round our neighbourhood."

"Do so, then, friend Marks. And when will you return?"

"In less than an hour, my lord."

"In an hour, then, I may expect you?"

"You may rely on my punctuality, my lord."

With a sly grin old Marks, the lawyer, left the judge's chambers.

But just as he left the apartment a side door from an inner room opened stealthily when the baron's back was turned.

A head was thrust forward, the features of which could not well be made out.

After glancing about the room it glided into the main apartment like a shadow, and soon hid itself beneath a large round table, the covering of which reached to and hung on the ground.

As if startled by some sudden thought that flashed across his mind, the baron turned from the window, and gazed around him in the gloom of the twilight.

He did not know, nor could he tell why he was

so superstitious, but he felt as if some spirit were haunting him from place to place.

His blood began to beat wildly through his veins.

His colour rose to a feverish glow.

He sat down in his easy chair again for some time in deep thought.

The twilight became each moment more gloomy and dull, until at last it changed into complete darkness.

And still Baron Templeton, without light of any kind, sat in that lonely room thinking of all that had happened for many years past, and heavy sighs escaped him.

At last, while he thus pondered, he suddenly raised his head, and stared like a madman.

His gaze was met by the staring eyes of some unknown one who sat within three yards of him.

It was a fearful moment of doubt, anxiety, and terror.

"What was it? who was it?" he thought.

But the stranger spoke not.

The eyes stared as before out of the darkness like two coals aglow.

"Who and what art thou?" the baron at last gasped, with a trembling voice.

"Thy enemy," was the slow, half-whispered reply.

CHAPTER XXIV.

TED RAWLINGS AND THE SHARKS—AN UN-PLEASANT PREDICAMENT—THE RESCUE.

THE faint, feeble, and oft-repeated cries of, "Help! help! help!" which rose out of the dark sea, not far from the wreck, startled the ears of all who heard them.

At first Harry Woodruff would not believe that the sounds were those of a human voice at all, and he scoffed at all who held a contrary opinion.

"I tell you it ain't a voice," said Harry, bluffly, and with a broad grin of humour on his manly, weather-beaten face. "It is only the echoes of the wind among the rocks, Lion Limb."

But the bold young captain listened again more attentively than before, and peered out upon the waves anxiously.

"Help! help! help!" were the cries which again reached them.

But this time the sounds were more faint than ever.

"I see a speck upon the troubled waters," said Emma, clinging to Lion Limb, affectionately.

"Where? Where?" asked several at once.

"Why, yonder," said the pretty maid, with a trembling lip, pointing towards the sea.

"And so do I," said Lion Limb, hurriedly. "Follow me, Harry. Come along, Dick Hamilton. Who knows but what it may be one of our lads?"

"How can that be?" said Harry Woodruff, gruffly. "All our lads are fully accounted for, save Ted Rawlings, and as to that young beggar——"

"It may be Ted, after all," said Lion Limb. "Come, let us jump into one of our boats and save the poor devil, whoever he may prove to be."

"Lead the way, then, captain," said Harry, "we'll follow."

Quicker than can be imagined, Lion Limb and his gallant lieutenants jumped into one of their newly-made canoes, and although the surf beat wildly upon the beach, they launched their frail bark, hoisted their little sail, and were soon far away from the shore.

Little Emma and the boys watched the canoe intently, as it put off in search of those in distress.

Soon, however, the white sail of the canoe disappeared, and the boat was lost to view.

Lion Limb was wrought up to a pitch of great enthusiasm when he thought, perhaps, that the cries of distress might have been raised by young Ted.

He scanned the sea, far and wide, but no object was, as yet, visible.

They had now proceeded more than two miles from the shore, and were about to give up their search, when the eagle eye of young Lion Limb espied some object floating on the waves, not very far from where they then were.

With a joyful shout, Lion Limb steered the canoe still nearer and nearer towards the speck upon the waves, and as he approached it, he perceived the water all afoam with sharks.

"Pull men, pull!" said Lion Limb, in haste. "We may yet be in time."

"What is it?" asked Harry, gruffly.

"A human body," was the reply.

"Can you make it out?"

"Yes, it is the body of a boy, and from where I am it looks like that of poor young Ted Rawlings."

"The devil!" said Dick.

"Pull away my lads, pull away; it seems lashed to the trunk of a tree; the sharks are snapping at his legs, but they are too high out of the water; pull away, quick! quick!"

Harry Woodruff and Dick Hamilton strained every nerve, and after a few moments the canoe was abreast of the floating tree.

In an instant Lion Limb unshipped his boat-hook, and striking the floating tree therewith, drew it towards the canoe.

To the surprise of all it proved to be none other than young Ted Rawlings.

The sharks had been very busy around him and fighting with each other, but by good fortune they were unable to harm the poor lad.

Insensible as he was, and more dead than alive, they cut the rope which bound him to the old tree and lifted him into the canoe.

He was just alive, but only that.

The poor boy was perfectly unconscious, and looked miserably pale, haggard and death-like.

"Let us sail home again now, my lads," said Lion Limb; "we have done our duty and successfully; each lad adds to the security of our island home."

The wind lying in their favor, towards the shore, it was not necessary to row again.

But Harry Woodruff and Dick Hamilton were not idle.

While Lion Limb steered, and the craft shot like an arrow before the wind, his two lieutenants began to operate on young Ted to see what they could do in order to renew almost suspended animation.

For this purpose Harry and Dick held poor Ted up by the legs, and shook him violently.

This caused the lad to eject a large quantity of salt water, and each moment afterwards he began to rally very much.

His limbs were chafed vigorously, and at last, as the canoe approached the wreck, young Ted opened his eyes, and with a faint smile recognized his three friends.

There were great rejoicings among the lads when it was discovered that Ted Rawlings had been rescued from a watery grave, and all felt very anxious to learn the story of his almost miraculous escape.

Many of them, indeed, even then began to question poor Ted; but he was borne off to his bunk in triumph by Harry and Dick and well plied with brandy and water.

While young Ted was thus snugly provided for beneath the blankets, an important council was being privately held by the little colony of boys and seamen unknown to Lion Limb.

This council had for its object the election of a king of the island.

CHAPTER XXV.

LION LIMB IS ELECTED KING OF THE SOUTH SEA ISLANDS.

"I'LL tell you what it is, lads," said Dick Hamilton, when the boys had all assembled around him, "I'll tell you what it is, we had better make Lion Limb king of the island at once."

"Hear, hear," shouted many at once.

"He's brave as a lion," continued Dick.

"Aye, braver."

"Well, and he's got more sound sense than all ours put together, as he has shown in our last battle; and therefore, I say, we want a king for a leader, and a king we'll have."

"Bravo, Dick."

"And he shall be the boy king of the South Sea Islands, my lads."

"Good, yes, king of them all."

"But I'm afraid Lion Limb is too modest by half to be a king—he won't accept the dignity."

"Oh, but he must."

"He shall, he shall."

"We'll make him, eh, my lads," said Harry, laughing.

"Yes, but we want a queen also," shouted several at once.

"Havn't you got one already, stupid heads," said Dick, indignantly; "what is Emma Clarence, but a queen, every inch of her."

"True, true, Dick, we forgot all about that."

"Let Emma Clarence be crowned queen then; we are all agreed."

"One thing at a time, my lads; don't be in any hurry; we must crown Lion Limb king first, and when we have thrashed all the cursed mutineers, and got the island a little quiet with these deceitful natives, we'll crown Emma Clarence with double honors."

"Hear, hear."

"To-morrow morning, then, my lads, we'll raise the banner of old England upon the island, and crown Lion Limb, king, with a salute of twenty one guns."

*   *   *   *   *

The meeting then broke up.

Each and every one was anxious for the dawn of the following day which should usher in the crowning of the Boy King of the South Sea Islands.

But Lion Limb was totally unaware of any such intention on the part of his followers.

He was already their acknowledged captain and leader, but never dreamed of aspiring to any such dignity as that of king of all the Islands.

However, when morning came he was greatly surprised to find that every one of his followers and companions were dressed up in their best attire, and wore happy smiling faces, much more so than common.

Harry Woodruff and Dick Hamilton together with some others had, during the night, descended to the hold of the ship, and broken up large boxes of new clothes and uniforms of various descriptions.

Arms were also procured in a similar manner, and everything that the good old ship contained that might add to the beauty and luxury of the feast.

The lads did not divulge their preparations, but kept on working in a quiet, shady grove, and, when all was completed, Harry Woodruff and Dick Hamilton appeared, followed by all the lads in military order.

When Lion Limb appeared on deck at the break of day he was surprised and pleased at the sight which was presented on the sandy beach.

All the colony were assembled in beautiful order, and for a moment Lion Limb knew not what to make of it.

"What means this, Lion Limb?" asked Emma Clarence, in doubt and fear. "What means this?" she repeated, clinging to her young lover, and knowing not what to do or say. "Have all your late companions thus assembled in arms against you?"

"I cannot believe it," said Lion Limb, fearlessly.

"Why, even the Indian captives are decked out," said little Emma, with a tone indicating jealousy of the beautiful Indian princess, whom she saw among the boy convicts and sailors, attired in the most fanciful manner.

Lion Limb spoke not a word.

In truth he knew not the meaning of all that he saw, for the preparations had been made while he was fast asleep.

"Does it mean treachery?" he thought for a moment. "Has Harry Woodruff or Dick Hamilton formed any base design against me?"

"No," he answered to himself; "I cannot, I will not believe it."

"Yet why this solemn silence, Lion Limb?" asked Emma, slightly trembling. "They do not speak nor cheer, nor greet you, as is their wont when they see you. I cannot make it out."

"Have no fears, Emma," said Lion Limb, proudly; "if the truth should prove to be that they have grown indifferent to me, or that the mutineers and buccaneers have influenced them and formed some foul plot against my life, why then, be it so. I can die, that's all. I am not afraid of death."

So speaking, Lion Limb descended from the ship with a firm step, and approached his companions, all of whom, as we have said, were drawn up in solemn silence, commanded by Harry Woodruff and Dick Hamilton.

"I will go also," said little Emma, running after her noble young lover; "I will go also, Lion Limb," she repeated, "if these your late companions have resolved to do you harm, why then," she added, sobbing, "let us die together."

Lion Limb clasped her affectionately round the waist, as he murmured in loving tones,

"No, Emma, you must not go; stay you here at the wreck; no harm can or shall befal you while I have breath in my body. Let me go first and ascertain the meaning of this unusual parade."

Little Emma wept, and seemed rooted to the spot.

Tears gushed from her eyes, and she sobbed aloud.

With all Lion Limb's persuasion he could not prevail upon the noble young girl to remain behind.

Lion Limb, with a proud step, and with the air of a monarch, walked straight towards the young troops assembled.

When he had approached within twenty yards of them, he halted, and, baring his breast, looked first at one detachment and then another.

But there was no indication in the features of any of all those assembled as to what they thought or intended.

THE BOY KING
OF THE SOUTH SEA ISLANDS.

THE MEETING OF LION LIMB AND THE CANNIBAL KING.

Harry Woodruff, sword in hand, stood silent and thoughtful before his men.

Dick Hamilton, on the left hand, did likewise.

Every one of the boy convicts, and their brave companions, the faithful sailors of the "Rattle-snake," did not by a single feature indicate their true feelings toward the young chief.

"What means this solemn silence?" Lion Limb asked at length, in a firm voice.

There was no response from any one.

"Have I not acted faithfully as your captain in all things?"

Still there was no reply.

"Have I not been the foremost in every danger? Have I not studied your safety and comfort on all occasions?"

No answer.

"Have you, then, grown dissatisfied? or have you leagued with the murderers and buccaneers of the neighbouring islands, and resolved to kill me? If so, I am ready," said Lion Limb, baring his breast still more. "If I have acted treacherously, and you wish to rid yourselves of my leadership by killing me, here I am—fire!"

For a moment there was no response.

Every man and boy in the ranks seemed to be deeply moved at the few words young Lion Limb had uttered.

Yet they spoke not.

"Shoulder arms!" shouted Dick Hamilton and Harry Woodruff to their followers. "Forward, march!"

This order was given at the same moment by both commanders.

Without a word, the orders were obeyed.

The boys advanced within ten paces of Lion Limb, and at the word "halt," they came to a standstill, and almost surrounded Lion Limb and little Emma, who thought each moment that they would fire and kill them both.

But Harry Woodruff and Dick Hamilton stepping forward, bowed to Lion Limb, while the former said, in a firm voice—

"Captain Lion Limb, we have a few words to say to you, and as plain, blunt fellows as we all are, our words will be quickly spoken."

"Speak, then," said Lion Limb, "and quickly. If I am to die, do the deed at once, but spare this innocent girl, for she has harmed no one."

There was another dead pause.

At length Harry said—

"There is one word which you have uttered, Lion Limb, which fully expresses the sentiments of all assembled here."

"Then speak that word," said Lion Limb, boldy.

"You said if we were dissatisfied with you——"

"You might kill me on the spot," said Lion Limb, interrupting the speaker.

"Exactly so," said Dick, "and we *are* dissatisfied with you, every one of us, are we not, boys? Speak boldly."

"We are—we are!" said all, loudly.

"And he shall not be our captain any longer, eh, is that it?" said Harry.

"Quite true, just so, Harry."

"In what manner are you dissatisfied, then?" asked Lion Limb, proudly.

"Because we think you are too modest to do justice to yourself," was the calm reply.

"What!" said Lion Limb, in astonishment. "I know not what you mean. Explain yourself."

"Then, in one word, we have resolved that you shall not be captain over us any longer, but be nothing else than king!"

"King!" said Lion Limb, astounded.

"Yes, king: not only of us but of all the South Sea Islands," said Harry and Dick, all in a breath.

Loud and ringing cheers greeted this announcement, and before Lion Limb, or trembling little Emma, could recover from astonishment, the young convicts and the brave sailors rushed around their chosen king and lifted him on their shoulders, amid deafening shouts.

Some sang.

Others laughed and shouted wildly with joy.

Yet they all quickly re-formed their ranks, and with Lion Limb on high in their midst they marched towards the little shady grove in which they had prepared a banquet to celebrate the great event.

A throne had been erected under a few trees, at the head of a long table.

And on this rudely-constructed royal seat the boys placed young Lion Limb.

Wine flowed freely on all sides, and all went as merry as marriage bells.

Toasts, and songs, and speeches, followed each other in rapid succession.

Jokes and merriment were the order of the day on every hand.

Leaping and jumping, foot-races, sword-play, gymnastics, and all manner of antics were the amusements resorted to.

There were plenty of choice provisions got out of the ship of every sort.

As a matter of course, the young colonists were not slow in paying their respects to everything eatable and drinkable which came to hand, and several hours passed very rapidly and joyfully.

But the chief feature of all was the grand coronation of Lion Limb.

Seated on his rustic throne, with flags and banners on all sides, fluttering in the wind, Lion Limb made a grand speech to his followers, at the conclusion of which Harry Woodruff, Dick Hamilton, and others, stepped forward, and presenting a crown, which they had made over night, placed it on the head of Lion Limb, and declared him king, amid the shouts, cheers, and vollies of musketry of all those surrounding him.

It was a joyful occasion, and for many hours all was a scene of exultation and merriment.

One of the sailors, named Bob Sawyer—of whose pranks and games we shall have occasion to speak on many occasions—produced a fiddle, and played away like a lunatic, and surrounding him were a numerous band of dancers, who clapped their hands, and jigged away as nimbly as if they had all been on the green fields of old England.

Some told stories; a few were absolutely drunk; but the majority were kept in soberness through the exertions of Harry and Dick.

Old Bob Sawyer, however, played away on his fiddle as if for a wager, until at last the grog got the better of him, and he fell from his seat, roaring out an old sea-song at the top of his voice.

The Indian captives for a long time could not make out the meaning of all this unusual display.

But Ted Rawlings, who had almost entirely recovered from his sufferings and exposure, made friends with the Indians, and by signs explained the purpose and intent of the whole ceremony.

When they fully understood what was going on, they joined in the merry scene as best they could, and seemed to enjoy the festivities as much as any there.

There was only one of all then and there assembled who was moody and silent.

This one was the Indian princess, whom Lion Limb, as we have seen in a previous number, had rescued from the stake.

While the Boy King was seated on his throne, and whispering the softest and most loving of words in young Emma's ears, the Indian princess lay under a tree near by.

But neither by word, look, nor sign, did she reveal the thoughts which were passing through her mind.

The truth was, from the first moment she had seen Lion Limb, she loved him!

She never for a moment dreamed that Emma Clarence was Lion Limb's chosen bride.

But now that she saw little Emma blushing, beautiful and bashful, seated by the side of Lion Limb, envy and deadly jealously entered the heart of the Indian maiden.

Perceiving that she did not seem to enjoy or even notice the happiness of others, but lay lonely and thoughtful some distance away, one of the Indians approached her.

He knelt before her, and bowed lowly to the very earth.

"What doth Yokee desire?" murmured the princess, in her own language, with a curl upon her lip, and scarcely glancing at him.

The Indian scarcely dared to raise his eyes to his princess, but he suppressed a deep-drawn sigh, as he murmured.

"My princess is dull; she does not mingle with the pale-faced strangers; she is unhappy; she is sorrowful, our own beautiful princess. You, Marmi, daughter of the king, my master, who rules the hundred islands far away yonder in the sunlight; you, Princess Marmi, are unhappy."

"Yokee," said Princess Marmi, speaking in a choked and sorrowful tone. "Yokee, we were prisoners here on this island, and would have been burnt alive, but for the bravery of that handsome youth, who has just now been crowned king."

"Yes, princess, you speak truly, our worst enemies, at a hapless moment, pounced down upon us, and would have sacrificed us to their gods, but we have escaped that awful fate, and are now safe in the hands of the strange pale-faces; but *that* is not the cause of Marmi's sorrow?"

"It is not," was the soft reply.

"Yesterday you were happy, Princess Marmi; a cloud has come over your sparkling face."

There was no reply given to this.

But the Indian glanced at his princess, and was surprised to see two tear drops glistening in her eyes, which even then were directed towards Lion Limb and Emma Clarence, who, surrounded by friends, were unconscious of the Indian princess sitting apart from them.

"Never until now," thought Yokee, the Indian captive, "never until now have I ever seen Princess Marmi weep. What can be the cause?"

And as he thought thus, he cunningly caught the gaze of Marmi, who, still looking towards Lion Limb, said, half aloud,

"He loves another! The young brave chief of the pale-faced strangers has no fond look for Marmi."

And thus murmuring, as she thought unconsciously to herself, Yokee's eyes flashed with fire, as he thought,

"Marmi loves the young stranger, and scorns me, the one who has adored her secretly for years."

He was about to rise from his humble posture, when Marmi said to him,

"Yokee, I am your princess; my father is your king; if you love me, do my bidding."

Yokee bowed more lowly than ever, as he said,

"Until death."

"Then find out who this pale-faced girl is, and at the earliest moment tell me all."

"Could I not escape from the island in one of their boats, and take the news of all that has happened to us to the king your father, O Princess Marmi!"

"It could be done," was the murmured answer.

"And you, Marmi, escape with me."

"I will think of it, faithful Yokee; but for the present watch the chief and his pale-faced bride. I *hate* her, Yokee! I *hate* her!"

These few words were uttered in a hissing tone, yet, as she spoke, the bright eyes of Marmi flashed, and in her animation she looked more lovely than ever.

Yokee rose.

He left the princess burning with anger and desires of revenge.

"Marmi loves this young chief," he muttered, "and I love Marmi."

He clenched his fist, and ground his teeth as he swore to be revenged on one or both.

From that moment Yokee was the secret yet deadly enemy of Lion Limb.

What this infuriated, disappointed, and revengeful Indian accomplished we shall quickly see.

CHAPTER XXVI.

IN WHICH JERRY MARKS ENCOUNTERS HIS ENEMY, BARON TEMPLE—THE RESULT.

IT will be recollected that in a previous chapter we spoke of the strange interview between Mr. Marks, the lawyer, and the judge, Baron Temple.

The baron, as he sat in his lonely room, had not the remotest idea that there was any second person present; but after a time his eyes confronted those of the wild and savage looking youth, Jerry Marks.

The baron would have started from his seat, but seemed fixed to the spot.

Jerry's glistening eyes fascinated him.

For a moment neither spoke.

At last, after an evident effort, the baron said, repeating Jerry's former words—

"What! my enemy, say you?"

"Yes; you might have made me your friend once, but you have allowed the chance to pass. I am now your enemy."

"And what came you here for, to threaten me?"

"No, not to threaten; but to *do*."

"To do? To do what?"

"Make you my willing and most humble servant."

The baron rose indignantly as he heard these last words, and the colour mantled to his very brow.

"How! knave, how now! Know you to whom you are thus speaking?"

"I do, my lord; I once had the honour of appearing before you in court when I gave evidence against those brothers, the young Normans."

"Which evidence was false," said the baron; "you yourself have written and signed a confession to that effect."

"Quite true," replied Jerry, with a malicious grin; "but it was under compulsion. You made me sign while holding a pistol to my head, or I would never have done so."

The baron did not reply.

The young Jew still continued to speak by fits and starts, thus—

"You cleverly got me into your power, but you never imagined I should ever regain my liberty, eh? Ha! ha! you see you are very wrong in your calculation, my lord, for once."

"I should like to have this rascal hung," muttered the baron, half aloud.

"I dare say you would, my lord; but, you see, instead of having me in your power you are in mine."

"In what manner, ruffian?"

"I will quickly explain, my lord. I am most happy to inform your lordship that Edgar Norman was drowned when the 'Rattlesnake' was wrecked. Now, there have been several bottles picked up, which were cast from the sinking ship, one of which contained the will of Captain Clarence."

"Well, what of that? What have you, such a young villain as you have proved yourself to be, to do with such a noble fellow as Captain Clarence?" said the baron, in disgust.

"Much, my lord, very much, as you shall hear. This will left all the captain's property to Edgar Norman, if he should ever be found; but as that young murderer," said Jerry, with a devilish leer, "has been drowned, this property of Captain Clarence goes to the next-of-kin."

"To Edgar's brother?"

"True, my lord; but it will not."

"Will not?"

"Nay, it *shall* not," said Jerry, hissing out his words.

"Shall not, eh?"

"No, it shall not. But don't turn pale, my lord; I have not done yet."

"Who is to prevent it, pray?"

"*You* will, my lord."

"I?"

"Yes, you."

"But I will not, if even I could."

"Yes, but you *shall*, my lord," said Jerry, with a loud chuckle, "or else——"

"Or else," repeated the baron, "or else. What can this ruffianly intruder mean?"

"He means this, my lord—that before I leave this room, you must write, sign, seal, and deliver to me, on your lordship's oath, that *I* am Edgar Norman's brother."

"You? But you are *not* his brother."

"No one knows that better than you, my lord," said Jerry, grinning. "There is no one else knows that better than you, my lord, except one, whose name is——"

"What?" gasped his lordship, staggered at Jerry's boldness. "What other person do you allude to, villain?"

"The wife of Lord Ox——"

"Stop!" said the baron, rising hastily and turning pale, "stop, villain, stop! mention no one's name but mine in this apartment, for walls have ears."

He sat down in his capacious chair again, and fo a few moments spoke not.

At last he collected himself, and said, with a smile,

"I have listened to all you have had to say, young man, and I find that you are one of a band of impostors who go about extorting money by working on their fears; but in this instance you are caught in a trap."

"Indeed!" said Jerry, with ears cocked. "How so, pray?"

"I can raise an alarm and have you transported for this."

"But you dare not."

"Dare not?"

"No; if you were to place a hand upon that bell-rope to cause any alarm, I should place this knife into your throat," said Jerry, brandishing a long and shining weapon, which flashed in the faint light.

"This fellow is a demon," muttered the baron.

"No, I am a Jew, and in saying that I say all. Once make a Jew your enemy, my lord, and he will hunt you down to the day you die. They are almost as bad as lawyers," said Jerry, chuckling at his triumph.

"And for what reason should I do this base thing you demand of me?" the baron asked. "It is impossible; it cannot be done."

"But it *must* be done, or else Lord Oxenford shall know all," said Jerry, "for I have documents in my possession, my lord, which would cause you transportation, if not more."

"But where is this youth, Norman, living?"

"That remains a secret, my lord. But the question is, will you or will you not make out and sign this deed?"

The baron did not answer, but immediately wrote out the document desired, and sealed it with his own official seal, stating that the bearer was none other than Edgar Norman's brother, and, as such, entitled to Captain Clarence's property.

He handed it across the table to Jerry, who read every word again and again, and felt satisfied.

"Now, my lord," said the young Jew, "if any witnesses are required will you condescend to attest the truth of this document before them?"

The baron scarcely heard what Jerry said, but nodded.

"You will not even mention it to——"

"Silence!" said the baron, furious with passion; "you have the document. Begone! knave."

"Not at this moment," said Jerry, "I have not any witness to this deed."

"Oh! you needn't wait long for that," said a third person, who entered rather unexpectedly.

It was Jerry's father—old Lawyer Marks.

The young Jew recoiled before his father.

The baron was astonished at this unlooked-for intrusion of the greasy-looking lawyer.

"Your business, sir?" said the baron, stammering with rage. "Am I, then, the victim of a base conspiracy?"

"Oh! not at all," said the lawyer; "I only come in the very nick of time to serve my son in this business, that's all," said he, signing Jerry's document. "There, that will do, will it not, my lord? We have soon transformed Jeremiah Marks into Allan Norman, I think."

"Who told you I had business here?" asked the son, eyeing his father like a lynx.

"I guessed it."

"How did you know that *I* was here?"

"I smelt you afar off," said the father, grinning. "Come, my son, let us go; his lordship requires rest. We will retire."

With ironical bows the two Jews left the apartment and were soon in the open air.

"That was a fine stroke of business, Jerry," said the father, chuckling and rubbing his hands; "your fortune is made."

"Well, and if it is, what of that? I didn't want any assistance from you."

"Didn't you though? Ha! ha!" laughed the father, "let me have a good look at the document; here, under the lamp-post, will do."

"Oh, no it wont," said Jerry; "you ain't going to put *your* paws on this deed; *I* know you, old man. Go your way and I'll go mine; I could have got along very well without you."

"No you couldn't, Jerry. Without a witness the deed wouldn't have been worth a penny, and his lordship knew it very well."

"Ah! you are very clever, I dare say," Jerry remarked, keeping a foot or two away from his father out of fear; "but I am not your son, Jerry Marks, now, you know, I am Allan Norman."

"You are more than that," said the old lawyer,

with twinkling eyes; "your are more than that, Jerry."

"How do you mean?"

"I mean to say you are now legal heir to all the property, which I know the baron and Lady Oxenford have put in the hands of trustees for Edgar and Allan Norman."

A new light seemed to dawn on Jerry's mind.

This view of the question had never presented itself to Jerry.

But he saw through the matter clearly enough now, and his hair almost stood on end with astonishment, as he gasped—

"The devil! Why, so I am. Why didn't I think of that before?"

"Because you hadn't brains enough, Jerry," said the old man; "but now that we are both rowing in the same boat——"

"Same boat, eh? Oh, no we ain't, thank you. All I've got, or going to get, is mine, and, more than that, you ain't going to have a penny, don't you think it. Oh, no, Walker," said Jerry, whistling ironically, "you don't come that game on me, old man. You've altered all at once; you called me murderer, villain, and all such names a little time ago, and disowned me; but now that I've got a streak of luck you chime in, and want to go shares, eh? Oh! how kind you are all at once."

And Jerry whistled again more loudly than before.

"You shan't have a farthing of all this without I say so, Jerry," the father remarked.

"What!"

"No, not an iota, Jerry."

"Who's to prevent me?"

"I can."

"How, by turning informer?"

"No."

"Then, how can you or any other man prevent me having all this property?"

"The thing is simple enough, Jerry. You are not twenty-one years of age yet, and, until you are so, I am your guardian in everything—not a farthing can you have before that time unless I say so!"

It was now the old lawyer's turn to whistle or laugh.

But Jerry leaned against a lamp-post, sick at heart and disappointed.

A feather could have knocked him down.

"Hang the luck!" he said, and cast a ferocious look at his father.

"It's no use to curse and swear over it, Jerry," said the father; "law is law all the world over."

"And must I place all my expectations in your hands, and take whatever you like to give me?"

"Yes, until you are twenty-one, Jerry; and if even I were to die—die suddenly, I mean——"

"Die suddenly!" said Jerry, hurriedly. "Well, what then, could I then control the property myself?"

"No," said the old man; "I have already appointed you two guardians in case of my death, Jerry, and they would manage in my stead until you had come of age."

"Hang the luck!" said Jerry, "and hang all the lawyers also, for here am I rich and yet can't get sixpence without you will it!"

"Quite true, Jerry, quite true. But come, let us go home. I must be your father now, and you are compelled to be my son. Let us go; there is yet another very important matter to settle before we do anything else."

"What is that?"

"Why, to put Allan Norman out of our way."

"Out of our way! How do you mean?" said Jerry, looking sideways, and speaking in a whisper.

"Come, and you will soon see how a lawyer can dispose of a troublesome customer."

"Out of the way! Put Allan Norman out of the way!" said Jerry, to himself, in whispers, as he followed his father homeward.

"Does the old man mean to kill him, I wonder?"

And a cold tremour came over Jerry which made him shake from head to foot.

"Kill him! Aye, we will do more than that, Jerry; we have commenced the game, and now that we are fairly in it we must not hesitate even at killing."

And the old man grinned like a very demon.

Even Jerry shuddered.

And then went homewards, bent on other crimes, two of the greatest villains that ever breathed.

Allan Norman's fate was sealed!

CHAPTER XXVII.

THE MEETING OF LION LIMB AND THE CANNIBAL KING.

THE few words which Yokee had heard Marmi utter about Lion Limb, and the tender looks she cast towards him as he sat upon his rustic throne, with Emma Clarence by his side, acted like poison on the Indian's heart.

He sought no more to dance, or join in the noisy festivities of the coronation.

He slunk away, and, beneath the dense shadow of a willow tree, he watched every movement of Lion Limb with an expression of deadly hatred.

"And Marmi loves this pale-faced boy," he muttered again; "Marmi, my princess, whom I have doted on since childhood. How her colour came and went, how the glow of love mantled her brow, and how her eyes glistened as she spoke!

"But must Yokee, the warrior of his tribe, must Yokee, who has rejected the fairest of the fair for Marmi, be thus cast aside?

"No," he muttered, "one of us must die. Revenge, Yokee, revenge! Marmi's heart is given to another. Revenge! blood! blood!"

The Indian's eyes rolled in deadly hate and anger as thus he muttered to himself.

For it must here be explained for the information of the reader that Marmi was the only child of a chieftain called Katamar, who ruled as king on an island far distant to the south-west.

Old Katamar was the terror of many islands near to his own, and by force of arms had made them all pay tribute to him.

His subjects were very numerous and warlike.

The savages on Lion Limb's island had always been at war with him.

But owing to the great distance which was between them old Katamar could not successfully wage war against them by sea or land.

These savages, a few nights before Lion Limb's arrival on the island, had gathered together many rudely-made boats and canoes, and set sail towards Katamar's dominions.

They landed in the dead of night.

Through the agency of a deserter and spy they suddenly made an assault upon Princess Marmi, and a few attendants who were around her tent, Yokee, her Indian lover, among the number, and carried them away in triumph as captives.

It was the intention of the savages to have burnt their prisoners alive, according to custom, out of evernge for all they had suffered at the hands of old Katamar and his Indians in times long past.

For, in the memory of the oldest islander, the savages on Lion Limb's island had always been at deadly war with the brave old chieftain Katamar.

That the savages would have carried out their diabolical intentions towards Princess Marmi cannot be for a moment doubted, had not the timely arrival of the brave young Lion Limb put an unexpected stop to their fiendish designs.

This much explanation is necessary to enable the reader to follow up the stormy adventures and bold exploits of young Lion Limb and his band of youthful followers.

But these facts above mentioned were unknown to young Lion Limb.

As yet he had not time to explore the island thoroughly.

For, from the moment of his arrival on that unknown land until then he had been beset on all sides with dangers of various sorts, as we have already seen.

But now there is another person who suddenly appears upon the scene of action.

This gaunt, savage, tall, powerful, and cross-eyed villain was none other than the king of the savages, and known among his remorseless tribe under the name of Red Wolf, on account of his cunning, sly, and bloodthirsty disposition, and the cat-like manner in which he was wont to creep upon and slay his unwary and perhaps innocent foe.

Of the deeds of this monster in human form we shall have frequent occasion to speak during the progress of this adventurous narrative.

*　　*　　*　　*　　*

While, therefore, all was merriment in Lion Limb's camp, while feastings and songs were the order on every hand, and the boy convicts were drinking health, long life and happiness to their newly-crowned king, and, with bumpers were christening the island on which they were by the name of Lion Island, Red Wolf was making preparations to attack the pale-faced strangers who had thus carried off his highly-prized captives, and taken possession of his dominions.

The Indian guides who had led Bloodhoof and his gang through the forest towards the boy's encampment, and those who had escaped from the battle which took place afterwards, were not long in hurrying to and informing Red Wolf, the savage king, of all that had taken place.

Red Wolf was astounded at the intelligence.

He roared and swore until he almost foamed at the mouth.

His cross eyes rolled most horribly, and he gnashed his teeth like a maniac.

He made a fearful blow with his spike-headed war club at the breathless messenger who had brought the news of Lion Limb's victory, and vowed vengeance against every stranger on the island.

"What!" roared Red Wolf, striding up and down in a fearful passion, "what! My men to be killed or beaten off in battle by a few white-faced, beardless boys!"

And he tore his hair in rage.

"Marmi, Katamar's daughter, rescued also, and Yokee, who killed and scalped my own brother not long ago, he also escaped me!"

So fearful was his rage, and so well did his savage attendants know the fate of all who should dare to further annoy him in such a mood, that they stood at a great distance from him in solemn silence trembling.

For some time Red Wolf remained silent and thoughtful.

His ugly eyes rolled and twinkled like those of a ferret in the dark.

He was planning some devilish scheme to destroy Lion Limb and all his followers.

Suddenly rising from his mat of dry leaves, he called to one of his many attendants, and spoke a few words hurriedly, and in a quick, harsh tone.

When this was done he seized his terrible war-club, and, with knife in his belt, and bow and arrows on his back, he plunged into the dense forest, and whither he went no one knew, and but few would have dared to enquire.

*　　*　　*　　*　　*

Lion Limb, however, and his gallant band were not permitted to end their day's festivity without a sad occurrence, which, for a time, marred all their pleasures.

It was towards evening, and the sun was declining fast when one of the boy convicts, bent upon amusement and adventure, left the camp, and strolled into the forest to kill game for supper.

He had his rifle upon his shoulder, and went forth gaily, but against the express orders of Lion Limb, who had given notice that no one should be allowed to leave the camp alone.

Joe Telford, however—a rash youth indeed he was—sallied forth, unknown to any one; but he had scarcely reached the edge of the forest, when he espied a fine buck grazing.

"If I can only knock him over," thought young Joe, "we can all have some capital venison for supper."

He was about to raise the rifle to his shoulder when he was struck in the arm by an arrow.

The rifle fell from his hands, and he shouted aloud for help.

This cry reached the ears of Lion Limb, who, with a few others, hurried away to learn the cause of the cry.

They soon reached the spot at a run; but as they approached poor Joe, who lay moaning and groaning on the ground, Lion Limb distinctly heard the rustling of something as it rushed through the brushwood.

Lion Limb fired.

The only reply was a loud and savage laugh from some one unseen.

"'Tis one of the savages," he said, while red anger mantled his handsome brow.

Harry would have gone in pursuit on the instant, but Lion Limb would not permit it.

He inquired of poor Joe how the whole affair had happened, but the poor boy was suffering too much pain to make any clear answer.

All that he knew was that he had disobeyed orders in strolling away, and had been shot severely in the arm in consequence.

The poor lad was carried into the camp, and the arrow speedily extracted from his arm.

But all were horror-stricken to perceive that the barb was poisoned.

What to do no one knew.

The wound would not prove fatal if the poison could be extracted.

Yet, who could or who knew how to do it?

The boys were worked up to a terrible rage by this unexpected accident to poor Joe, and it required all the authority and persuasion of Lion Limb to prevent them from sallying forth in pursuit of the unknown assassin.

At this moment, however, Yokee and Marmi approached the spot, and gazed on the wounded boy.

"That is one more the less to kill," thought Yokee, with a strange twinkle in his eyes.

Marmi, however, as soon as she saw the arrow, made signs that she knew who had fired it.

On the instant she ran away towards the woods, and quickly returned with a bunch of herbs.

These she chewed, and then placed the vegetable pasty material on poor Joe's wound so as to extract the poison.

"That's all very well for his outside," said Dick Hamilton, in a dry sort of way; "but I've heard, and Captain Lion Limb and Harry Woodruff will tell you the same, that the lad must be made quite drunk so as to kill whatever poison has got into his blood."

"Quite right, Dick," said Harry.

"Then get all the spirits which remain in those bottles there," said Lion Limb, "and let's see what effect your new method has."

Joe didn't care to drink much, but it was almost forced down his throat; nor did Harry or Dick cease their kind attentions to the wounded lad until they had made him swallow almost a pint of brandy.

"That will kill him," said one.

"Not a bit of it," said Harry, "and if he could only be made to swallow about a pint more he'd be as right as ninepence in the morning."

"How is that?"

"Well, you see, my lads, when the poison hasn't got far into you a half-pint of strong rum would kill it; but in this case it takes more."

"More, I should think so," said Dick, who appeared so very learned on the subject of killing poisons. "More, I should think so," said he, rolling a quid of tobacco in his mouth. "Why, I knowed a shipmate of mine who was bit by a large black snake in the West Indies, and he drank more than three pints of stiff old Jamaica rum before you could make him drunk and kill the poison in him."

"Well, all I hope is, then," said Lion Limb, "that very few of us will get poisoned, for if it takes as much liquor as all that to cure a man I fear our little stock of spirits won't last long."

These words were followed by a general laugh from those around.

At that moment Yokee, who had not given expression to any feeling whatever by look, word, or sign, whispered something to Marmi, which made the maiden blush scarlet with pleasure.

She approached Lion Limb with eyes beaming in joy, and, tapping him on the shoulder affectionately, made signs, the meaning of which was that she would willingly show her young preserver where to gather the valuable herbs which would prove an antidote to all poisons.

Her manner was so simple, child-like, and confiding that Lion Limb could not resist her kind offer, but resolved to go with her to the woods at once, and there learn the spot, and the exact herb which Marmi had so quickly gathered from among the surrounding and poisonous weeds.

His companions were unaware of his intentions, and Lion Limb went forth alone with Marmi to the forest, saying that he would not be many moments absent.

When they entered the dense thicket Marmi left his side for a moment, and went forward alone.

In an instant afterwards, however, she uttered a piercing cry, and running towards Lion Limb, with looks of alarm and horror on her fair countenance, clung to him for protection.

What the meaning of this was the bold youth could not imagine.

But when he was about to speak words of kindness and encouragement to the trembling maid he was surprised to see emerge from behind some tall trees the gaunt and terrible form of Red Wolf, the savage king, with spike-headed club in hand, and looks of vengeance as, with a loud, wild laugh, he grinned at the trembling maid and her fearless young protector (see Cut).

CHAPTER XXVIII.

IN WHICH A TRAP IS LAID FOR ALLAN NORMAN BY OLD MARKS THE LAWYER.

WHEN the two rascals, Marks the Lawyer, and his son Jerry, reached home, they began to converse about the prospect of realizing the estate which Capt. Clarence had left to Edgar Norman, and which, by the course of events, should have been delivered over to his brother Allan.

"We have done a very fine stroke of business, Jerry, my son," said old Marks, in an oily manner, and rubbing his hands; "a very fine stroke of business indeed, thanks to my cleverness."

Jerry shrugged his shoulders, and looked fixedly on the ground.

"If we have I can't touch any of the money, you seem to say, until I am twenty-one years of age."

"Quite true, my son."

"Then how can it be so very fortunate, then?"

"Well, if not fortunate to you, you know, Jerry, it is very much so for me, for I am your father, guardian and everything."

Jerry smiled in a most ghastly manner.

He knew full well that his father had him under his thumb, and perhaps would not allow him anything after all his boldness and knavery.

"But the affair is not yet over," said Jerry to his father, who was writing what appeared to be a note; "we have not settled with Allan Norman."

"I know that," said the old man, grinning like a hyena, "but this note will."

"What is it about?"

"Mind your own business, Jerry, and ask no questions."

Calling in his half-starved servant-girl.

"Take this to my friend, Dr. Killum's, immediately," he said, "and wait for an answer."

"Why, what's the matter with you?" asked Jerry. "What do you want of Dr. Killum?"

"You will shortly see, my son."

And as he spoke the old lawyer rubbed his clammy hands, saying,

"This affair is too important to be slightly dealt with; we must not do things by halves."

Jerry had misgivings that his father meant mischief towards him, and perhaps wanted Dr. Killum to prescribe some deadly drug for him.

However, he did not speak, and in less than half-an-hour, Dr. Killum drove up in a cab.

Old Marks received the doctor in a very obsequious manner.

"Any business of very pressing importance, Mr. Marks?" said the doctor.

"Yes; of the greatest importance."

"And pray, what is it?"

"A gentleman, a client of mine, has a very dear son, a youth of about sixteen, who is rather touched in the brain, and who persists in calling himself Allan Norman—the name of one of those young villains, you will remember, who were concerned in the foul murder of my dear friend, the old alderman."

"Well, what else, Mr. Marks."

"This youth has also an idea—the most insane one you ever heard of—that he has been left or ought to come into possession of a large amount of property bequeathed by a certain Captain Clarence.

"Anything else?"

"No; except this. His father is in Australia, and left this son in my care."

"And you, of course, don't know what to do with the young fellow?"

"Just so, doctor."

"Then I should advise you to have him examined by some of our most eminent surgeons, and, if he really is a lunatic, they will sign a document and place him in an asylum where he will be well treated."

"You are sure it requires more than *one* surgeon's signature, doctor?"

"Yes."

"Ah," said old Marks, "well, then, we must see about it; but you wouldn't mind signing for one, would you, doctor?"

"Well, I should not object if I had seen him."

"Aye, there's the difficulty, you see; this youth is in the country, and I have already got the signature of one surgeon down there," said old Marks, producing a paper which purported to be a proper document.

"Let me see it."

Marks handed over the forged letter, which Dr. Killum read attentively.

He smiled, and whispering to Marks, said—

"I am very short of money, Marks. Couldn't you lend me two or three hundred for a short time?"

"Well—ah—that is to say, Dr. Killum, of course I will if—you understand?"

"I do. What is this youth, then?"

"A witness."

"Oh! only a witness—in some petty case or other?"

"Just so."

Some more conversation took place between the lawyer and doctor, carried on in whispers.

Jerry tried to hear what it was about, but could not.

Whatever was said between them it ended in the doctor receiving a large sum of money in the way of a loan, and he left the house of old Marks radiant with smiles.

When he had gone the old lawyer wrote a note, which read as follows:—

ALLAN NORMAN, ESQ.

DEAR SIR,—Certain valuable documents have come into my possession of the greatest importance to you. By calling on me to-morrow evening between 8 and 9 o'clock, the matter will be fully explained.

Your humble servant, J. MARKS, Solicitor, &c.
14, Folio Chambers, New Inn.

N.B.—Be sure you bring this note with you.

"There," said old Marks, "the trap is ready; the bird will be caught without a doubt."

"What does all this writing and whispering mean?" said Jerry.

"It means that you must have a still tongue if you would be wise. You say you know where Allan Norman lives? Take this letter and leave it with his landlady. Here's a sovereign for you, Jerry."

"Give me another."

"I would give you a hundred if you would only contrive to break your neck on the road."

Jerry knew this very well.

An unnatural hatred had sprung up between father and son.

Were it not that one was interested in the life of the other they would have come to blows, and in likelihood have cut each other's throats.

Jerry, however, took the two sovereigns that lay on the table.

He delivered the note to the landlady at young Norman's lodgings, and said to her in a careless manner—

"What kind of a lad is this Allan Norman, ma'am?"

"One of the best behaved young gentleman whoever lived, sir; so hard working and honest, sir; he is poor, sir; but that's no matter, you know, for he's got goodness and vartue marked on his face, which is a thing can't be said of every one now-a-days, for the world is full of wicked young rascals; and he has living with him a young fellow named Rawlings, which he loves like a brother, and poor young Rawlings is very sick in bed unable to work, and young Master Norman supports him like a lord, sir, and———"

Jerry did not hear more.

He hastened from the door disgusted, and giving vent to oaths against both Allan and Edgar Norman.

In an hour afterwards Jerry was half drunk, and reeling down the Haymarket.

*   *   *   *   *

Poor Allan!

How overjoyed he was when he received the lawyer's note cannot be fully described.

Young Rawlings, his invalid companion, also shared in the joy of Allan.

But after a time, and after considering the subject attentively, Allan said—

"I fear after all that this goodness will not move him."

"Why do you think so?" asked young Rawlings, with a hectic flush upon his pale and fevered brow.

"Why do I think so?"

"Yes. What reasons can you have?"

"Very good ones, indeed," said Allan, biting his lip, "for of all the men in the whole world I fear no one so much as I do old Marks the lawyer."

"True," said young Rawlings, "now that I come to think of it, he is Jerry's father."

"And if he is in any respect like his son," said Allan, "I have cause to fear him, for the dastard Jerry was the sole cause of Edgar and Ted being first condemned to death, and afterwards transported for a foul deed in which they had no part."

For a moment there was a solemn silence.

Both young Rawlings and Allan were thinking each of his brother who was then far away, and perhaps buried deep in the bosom of the sea.

"If you fear anything, then, Allan," said young Rawlings, "do not go."

"Nay, but I will though," Allan replied, with a proud eye. "Nay, but I *will* go, and if they are bent upon any more devilish work, I will go fully prepared for the inhuman, bloodthirsty rascals."

Young Rawlings endeavoured to dissuade Allan from going to the den of old Lawyer Marks; but the brave boy Allan resolved to do so at all hazards.

"For," said he, "if there really is any good news it will be of benefit to you if not to me."

"Nay do not go, Allan, do not go," said young Rawlings, beseechingly. "Do not, I pray you, go. I fear—nay, I tremble at the name of Marks. They are fiends both of them; they mean you ill, they are bent upon the ruin of us both."

"Fear not for me," said Allan. "I will beard the lions in their den. I am bent on revenge for Edgar's sake, and for yours."

"Nay, do not go," still said the pale and trembling youth, clutching Allan by the hands in a feeble manner.

In a twinkling, however, Allan rushed from the house, maddened with rage.

He had fallen into a deadly snare!

LION'S LIMB

THE BOY KING
OF THE SOUTH SEA ISLANDS.

ALLAN NORMAN IN THE LUNATIC ASYLUM.

CHAPTER XXIX.

ALLAN NORMAN FALLS INTO A TRAP.

WHEN young Jem Rawlings found that Allan Norman had really made up his mind to face the enemy and beard the lion in his den, he felt sorrowful and almost disconsolate,

"No good can come of it," he said, over and over again. "No good can come of it, for I feel certain that both old Marks. the lawyer, and his villanous son Jerry, mean no good either to Allan or myself. I hate Jerry Marks with all my heart," said he often to himself, "and if I were not so weak and ill as I am, I would hunt him down to the very death."

It must here be explained that the natural love which these two boys had for one another had been greatly intensified of late. They had undergone the same trials and dangers together, as we have seen.

They had stood in the criminals' dock and been tried for their lives.

Each had a brother who was far, far away in strange, unexplored lands, if indeed they were not dead.

Since the trial Jem Rawlings had been confined to his lodgings through sickness, and had not been able to earn a single penny. But Allan Norman scorned to desert a friend on account of poverty, and resolved, as he often said, to "stick to him while he had a shot in the locker," or, in other words, the brave boy vowed never to leave him while he had a loaf to share, or a halfpenny to spend.

Hence, as may be expected, young Allan Norman had kept to his word, and during the long sickness of his companion, he had bravely supported him, and had done everything in his power to alleviate Jem's sufferings.

But could he always do so?

No.

Poor Allan was not always in work, and then the two lads had to live as best they could upon dry bread and water.

Work, constant work, and plenty of it was what Allan craved for.

" If I can only get constant work, Jem," he used to say, "you shall want for nothing."

" I know that, Allan," Jem would reply, in a feeble, thankful tone, "but you cannot always get it, I know."

This was perfectly true.

Allan could not get constant employment, and this thought almost turned the brain of Norman, for if *his* right hand should fail, what would become of his poor invalid companion?

And why could not Allan get plenty of work?

He was persecuted.

Yes, he was dogged, and tracked, and persecuted until the brave boy almost lost all heart and gave up everything as lost.

When he applied for a situation anywhere, his appearance was so prepossessing, and his manner so frank and manly, that his appeal was listened to with favor by very many old gentlemen and merchants in the city.

Allan might be told to call again next day.

In the meantime, however, a stranger would call at the offices visited by Allan, and say in a bland, smiling manner,

" I beg pardon, sir, but a youth called here this morning for the situation of clerk?"

" He did; why?"

" Oh, nothing!"

" But why do you ask?"

" I have great reasons, sir; but pray let me ask, what name did he give?"

" Allan Norman."

" Allan Norman, eh. Ah, I see he gave the right name then. I thought, perhaps, he had changed his name."

" You seem to know him, then?"

" I should think I do," the stranger would reply, with a dry, cunning smile; "I am an officer, and know that youth well; he was once tried for murdering

his employer; his brother, Edgar, was transported, but this youth was let off, but I am not quite certain that he is innocent for all that, and I am still on the watch, for I have received private information from a lawyer in the city which convinces me that the case is not yet quite done with."

Speaking thus, the stranger, would go his way rejoicing.

Allan would, perhaps, next day apply for the situation and be indignantly refused it.

But who was this stranger who dogged Allan's footsteps?

Who was it that endeavoured on all occasions to prevent the honest lad from earning his living?

Who was this remorseless, bloodthirsty hound that tracked his footsteps day by day, and blasted his character before the world?

" I wish I knew who it was," though poor Allan, on many occasions, when he returned joylessly home again to his poor lodgings without obtaining work; " I wish I could only find out who this heartless villain is."

" And so do I," sighed poor Jem.

Yet it was a long, long time ere either of the poor boys discovered and unearthed the paltry rascal who thus deprived them of daily bread.

Yet let us return to our story, and the exciting events which follow.

*　　　*　　　*　　　*　　　*

Young Allan, with his heart beating high with hopes and misgivings, hurried forward to the lawyer's office, and when he arrived found old Marks at home.

" Who wants me at such an unreasonable hour?" he said, as if much displeased at the call.

" A handsome youth, who calls himself Allan Norman, sir," the servant replied.

" Oh, indeed! And what does he want, pray?"

" I don't know, sir; but he looks a little excited."

" Excited, does he? And how do you know that?" the old lawyer replied, seating himself in his arm-chair, and taking a pinch of snuff. "Excited, eh? How do you know that?"

" He is flushed, sir, and his eyes are very bright."

" Oh, indeed; then show him in. But, by-the-bye," said the lawyer, "stop a moment."

He commenced to write a note in a very hurried manner, and gave it to the servant, saying—

" When you have shown this youth into my office take this note at once to Dr. Killum's, and say he must come immediately."

In a few moments Allan Norman was introduced into the dusty, mouldy office of old Marks, and took a seat near the door.

Old Marks began to write for some time, and took no notice of Allan, who began to think the lawyer had forgotten all about him.

At length the door bell rang, and Dr. Killum arrived, and entered the office also.

When he had done so, and the trap was all prepared, old Marks opened the business.

" Have you brought the note I sent to you, young sir?"

" Yes; here it is."

" All right, give it to me."

Allan handed it over, and old Marks threw it into the fire.

" What is your name?" he asked, still writing very rapidly.

" Allan Norman."

" Your brother was transported?"

" He was."

" For what?"

" For nothing."

"Just so," laughed the lawyer; "that's what all culprits say."

Dr. Killum stroked his chin and looked very seriously and steadfastly at Allan, as he said—

"You have heard of the wreck of the 'Rattle-snake,' I suppose?"

"And of certain papers which were washed up from the sea?" added old Marks.

"I have; and if all be true which I have heard, I am the rightful heir to all which my brother Edgar would have enjoyed had he lived."

"A very clear answer," said the lawyer, with a wink at the doctor.

He added in a whisper—

"I told you so."

The doctor nodded.

"But what is the real business here?" asked Allan, impatiently.

"You shall quickly see, only don't be in so much of a hurry, young man," the lawyer replied.

After a pause old Marks said—

"Did you ever know a youth named Jerry Marks?"

"I did, unfortunately."

"And what do you think of him?"

"He is a scoundrel—a villain who deserves to be hung!"

"Very complimentary, certainly," the doctor remarked, dryly, and with a slight laugh.

"But I am his father, young man," the old lawyer said.

"That is not much to boast of, I think," Allan rejoined, boldly. "I would never own relationship or even acquaintanceship with such an imp of the devil!"

"You are embittered against him, sir."

"I am; and shall never rest satisfied until I have placed him where he placed my brother Edgar!"

"And where was that, pray?"

"In the condemned cell at Newgate!"

"But if I were to recover for you the property left your brother by Captain Clarence, would you not think differently and more kindly of Jerry and myself?"

"You cannot recover what is not yet lost," said Allan. "And, as to you, sir, I have nothing to say, for as yet we are strangers and have had no dealings together."

"Very properly answered," said the lawyer, smiling grimly.

After a pause old Marks wrote something on a piece of paper, which the doctor read and nodded assent to.

"Well, Mr. Allan Norman, if such really be your name——"

"Yes, if such really be his name, you know——" the doctor echoed.

"If it is my name!" said Allan, surprised.

"Yes, we say if, young man, because we do not as yet know whether that is your name or not."

"But all the world knows it!"

"And yet all the world, as you call it, may be wrong, young man," the lawyer replied, smiling.

After a pause he added—

"You never knew who your father was; and how then can you say that Allan Norman really is or is not your name?"

"True, sir," Allan proudly replied. "I do not know who my father was, nor perhaps do you know who yours was; it is a wise person who knows his own father."

Allan thought at first to say that the devil himself was the legitimate father of all lawyers.

But he refrained from doing so.

At length he said—

"Allan Norman is my name, sir, and has been such since my childhood, gentlemen. I have never altered it, or had any other."

"In that case, then," said the doctor, "we had better proceed to business at once, Mr. Marks."

"I quite agree with you. You feel satisfied as to the truth and justice of this case?"

"Oh, quite so."

"Well, then, Mr. Allan Norman," said the lawyer, "as we feel quite convinced of the justice of your claims, we will prepare the necessary papers immediately, and by to-morrow night have all ready for your signature."

"But what is the total amount of the property, sir?" asked Allan.

"Well, at this present moment it would be difficult to say. You are, of course, naturally very anxious to know."

"I am, sir," said Allan. "I am very poor, and can scarcely get a living."

"Oh, as to that, we will provide you an excellent living for years and years to come, won't we?" he said, looking slyly at Dr. Killum.

"Oh, without the shadow of a doubt; if he leaves the matter in our hands we will guarantee to provide a handsome and commodious mansion for him."

"I am delighted," said Allan, in a transport of joy, "for I have a young companion who is very sick and needs great care."

"And who is he, pray?"

"His name is James Rawlings; we have always been constant companions from childhood, but of late he has not been expected to live, and I have had very hard work, very hard work indeed, to get bread for him, without speaking of medicines and the like."

"What a noble youth you are, Mr. Norman," said the lawyer, dryly; "even at the moment when you are about to become wealthy and independent your chief thoughts seem to be of your poor sick friend."

"They are, sir; we have sworn to be fast friends and inseparable companions, even in death," said Allan, proudly.

"What heroism," muttered the doctor, smoking a cigar and drinking brandy.

"Well, then, this friend of yours may partake of your present prospects with all my heart, Mr. Norman; and when you come to sign the deeds to-morrow night, bring him with you."

"Oh, yes, bring Mr. James Rawlings with you by all means," said the doctor, slyly winking at the lawyer.

"Yes, yes, a good thought," the lawyer added; "as this youth James Rawlings is the only friend you have in the wide world, bring him with you by all means."

"Don't forget to do so," said the doctor.

"No, I will not, if he is able to come, gentlemen," said Norman, rising.

"Then at nine o'clock to-morrow night we may expect you to call again?"

"Without fail, sir."

"And bring your friend also?"

"If possible, I will."

"Then do so, and all will be well."

Allan was about to leave the office when old lawyer Marks called him back, saying, with a cunning smile,

"Before you go, Mr. Norman, I have one word to say."

"What is it?"

"Don't mention this transaction to any one, not for the world, for it is a secret as yet, and we are working for your interests, not for love of money, but solely with a desire to serve you."

"You are very kind, indeed."

"And as to what my villain of a son has done to you and your brother, forget it. I despise him as much as you do; and the only object I have in getting this property settled properly upon you is to show you what Christian feelings I entertain towards you, and how utterly I abhor the rascality of my son Jerry."

The doctor sighed like a saint when he heard the lawyer's words, and drowned his feelings with some more brandy.

As Allan departed, old lawyer Marks dropped three sovereigns into his palm, squeezed his hand, and said affectionately and in fatherly tones,

"Good night, Mr. Norman, good night; heaven bless you, call without fail to-morrow night."

"I will," said Allan, jingling the sovereigns as he departed, and hurried homewards at the top of his speed.

On his way he changed one of the coins and bought a bottle of wine, some mutton chops, new rolls, and whatever else he thought his sick companion might like and relish.

He bounded up the stairs joyfully, and dashed into his little back room, exclaiming,

"Hurrah, Jem! hurrah, my boy! Cheer up, our fortune is made."

But in a moment afterwards he turned deadly pale, and looked around the room in astonishment.

Jem Rawlings was not there!

He had crept out of bed, ill as he was, and had fled—gone—none knew whither!

*   *   *   *   *

"Ha, ha!" laughed the doctor, when Allan had gone. "Ha, ha, ha!"

"What are you laughing and grinning at?" asked old Marks, rubbing his hands, and looking very well satisfied with what he had done. "What are you laughing at, doctor?"

"Oh, nothing, nothing at all, Marks; but I must certainly compliment you on the way you do business."

"I don't understand you."

"What I mean is this—you acted towards that boy so kindly and affectionately that a stranger would have taken you to be father and son, or relatives at least."

"Well, what of that?"

"Instead of that, you were preparing a pit for him to fall in."

"Well, and if I did, what matters? I know my own business best."

"Of course you do, and a pretty trade it is, and no mistake."

"We lawyers are forced to be hypocrites occasionally."

"Occasionally—ahem!—always, I think."

"True, when we are deeply interested——"

"For yourselves; don't say for your clients," the doctor remarked, laughing. "Lawyers are birds of prey."

"Well, have it so if you like."

"You wove as pretty a web round that youth as ever a spider did round a fly."

The lawyer grinned, as he thought to himself,

"And I'll weave another round you when I am done with this affair, and so tight and strong shall it be that not all the cart-horses in the kingdom will be able to drag you out of it."

But, after a moment, the lawyer said aloud,

"Well, doctor, neither your trade nor mine is all honesty and fair dealing. If your patients are not sick you make them so; as to my clients, I——"

"Get them into difficulties if they are not already so," laughed the doctor.

"We will say no more about it," the lawyer remarked. "You are well paid for the part you have to take, and so am I if I am successful."

"Not much fear of that after to-morrow night."

"I don't know that; something strikes me both of us will have more trouble than we care about with this young Allan Norman."

"What makes you think so?"

"I can't tell, but I have such a foreboding."

"Well, if you are successful, Marks, I hope you'll not fail to remember me."

"Oh, certainly not," said the lawyer, with a grim smile.

"Where do you intend to take him?"

"Far into the country," said the lawyer.

"The country is far better than the town."

"So it is."

"But, where about?"

"I have not made up my mind as yet."

"But, you will require my presence, Marks, I think."

"No, not at all," said the lawyer, who wanted to baulk the doctor's curiosity, and throw him off the right scent.

"Then, I have no occasion to call to-morrow night?"

"You may come if you like; perhaps it would make things look all the better if you were present."

"Very well, then. What time shall I call?"

"Not before eleven."

"Eleven! That will be too late."

"Oh, no it won't. I shall have a very long talk to the lad, and some business to transact before you come."

"Well, then, let it be eleven o'clock," said the doctor, rising to go home.

"Eleven, without fail; be punctual to a minute."

"I will."

"Good-night."

"Good-night."

"By eleven o'clock to-morrow night all will be accomplished," said the old lawyer, rubbing his hands, "and Dr. Killum for once will be made a fool of. He must not—he shall not know which way or where we go to; that must be a secret to all the world, save my own particular and trusty friends."

After a few moments of profound reverie, the old lawyer rose, rubbed his hands, and sighed,

"The inheritance is *mine*."

At that moment his son Jerry, drunk, mudstained, his clothes all torn, and bleeding from the nose, staggered into the office, cursing like a madman.

*   *   *   *   *   *

For a moment neither the old lawyer nor his son spoke a word.

Yet, for the first time in his whole life, old Marks seemed to stand in terrible awe of his only son.

There was something so wild, revengeful, and yet withal cunning and cowardly in Master Jerry's countenance that made his father quail before him.

There was a remarkable difference both in the father and the son.

Old Marks, up to the present time in his life, had never been drunk.

He was always sober, cool, and designing.

Jerry also had followed his parent's example up to a certain period; yet, since the conviction of young Lion Limb and Ted Rawlings, his whole nature had suddenly changed.

He would not work at anything, and seemed fit for nothing, save to laze about and get drunk.

What he could not beg or borrow, he stole from his father, and squandered it upon the worst of indulgences—drink and women.

There was something on Jerry's mind which seemed to be gnawing his very heart-strings.

He was now cruel, reckless, and abandoned beyond all hope.

"Did you take that note I gave you?" the father asked, after a very long pause.

"Y-e-s-s I—I did," hiccupped Jerry, "but the brat wasn't at home."

"How came you to be so muddy and torn, and with your nose cut?"

Jerry did not answer, but attempted to laugh, and meanwhile grinned like a maniac.

"Have you been ill-used?" the father asked.

Jerry did not answer, but attempted to smile.

But in a moment or two he let out his pent-up rage in a volley of frightful oaths and imprecations and laughed wildly and hysterically, like a hungry hyena.

Jerry did not not tell his father how it came about that he should have returned home in such a sorrowful plight; but the truth was this:

He had gone down to the Haymarket, and mingled among some of the very worst characters that nightly congregate in that great promenade of vice.

He had spent some part of the money which his father had given him, and was robbed of the rest by a gang of pimps and sharpers, who make their living by robbery there.

Maddened with drink and rage, he entered a public-house, and, to his surprise, saw standing at the bar two or three of the late Alderman Inglis's clerks.

He had the impudence to accost and speak to them.

As he deserved, these young gentlemen treated him with silent contempt.

Not satisfied with this, Master Jerry advanced to the bar, and attempted to help himself to what the young clerks were drinking.

This audacious conduct was resented, when Jerry seized hold of a quart pot, and attempted to strike one of them on the head with it.

A blow on the nose was the counter movement of this; and in less than half a minute three or four violent punches in the ribs and on the face soon enlarged Jerry's Jewish nose to the size of a respectable cucumber.

The landlord and potman now interfered, and, as the young Jew was cursing and alarming every one with his violent gestures and beastly language, the broad-shouldered youth who was potman seized Master Marks by the neck and threw him into the gutter among a waggon-load of filth.

This timely bath brought the young villain to his senses.

He picked himself up as soon as possible, and amid the jeers and laughter of those he had been associating with not an hour before, he wended his way homewards, cursing and swearing like a young demon.

"Well, you had better go to bed," said the father, in a mild but sorrowful tone.

"Bed!" gasped Jerry. "Not for me. I want some more money."

"More money?"

"Yes, more money."

"You can't have any."

"But I *will* have some!" spluttered the son shaking his fist in the lawyer's face.

"What do you want with it, for are you not raving drunk already?"

"That's nothing to do with you, is it? I suppose I can do as I like, can't I?"

"No, you cannot—at least you shall not, while I am your father."

"Oh, that's it, eh, guv'nor?" said Jerry. "Well, we'll soon see about that. You'll repent it, old man, if you do *not* give me some more money."

"Why so? How so?"

"You think you have got me under your thumb, don't you, but you haven't. There are more lawyers in the world besides you, and if you don't come down handsomely with some more coin, I'll expose you."

"Expose *me?*"

"Yes, you; and let all the world know what a scheming old scoundrel you are."

"By exposing me you expose yourself, Jerry."

"No I don't. I know as much about law as you do, old man. You say I can't touch any of that property till I am twenty-one years of age, because you are my parent and guardian. Well, then, as a minor I am not responsible for my own deeds, but *you* are for me, so if I expose *your* rascality the law will excuse me."

"You are talking nonsense, Jerry."

"Nonsense, eh? I'll soon let you see whether I am or not if you don't fork out some money."

"More money you shall not have, Jerry," said the father, in an angry manner.

"Won't I though. Take *that*, you old villain!" said the son, striking his father to the ground with a single blow.

The suddeness of the attack completely stunned the old lawyer, who laid upon the ground perfectly insensible.

Jerry laughed like a maniac at the effect of his cowardly act, and grinned at his father like some wild animal.

In a moment afterwards, however, he robbed his father of his gold watch and chain, took the keys of the desk out of the old man's pocket, and began to look for all the spare cash he could find.

He did not discover much, however, for the Jew lawyer had several secret hiding-places which Jerry knew nothing of.

He found about £10, however, and left the house soon afterwards, not knowing or caring whether he had maimed or killed his own father.

This was the real beginning of Jerry's career of crime about town.

What he had done in secret heaven alone knew; but we may conjecture that if the truth was known, this young demon was steeped in crime and iniquity of all sorts.

But of his career, and the just punishments which befel both father and son for their evil deeds, we shall hear more during the progress of this truthful narrative.

But let us again return to Allan Norman, and what befel him through the villany of old Marks, and his accomplice, Dr. Killum.

*   *   *   *   *   *

When Allan discovered that young Jem Rawlings had left the house he acted like one distracted.

No one in the house had seen or heard anything of Jem.

"What had best be done?" thought Allan, as he sat on a rush-bottomed chair, absorbed in thou

"I know the lad has been very, very ill, but he cannot have gone crazy, and left me keepers some sudden fit of madness."

The sudden disappearance of young Jem was a sad blow to poor Allan, for, as we have seen, the two lads loved each other more than brothers.

They had always been inseparable, and now more so than ever, since the cruel sentence had been passed upon their brothers.

Whatever Allan had, or could work for, Jem had shared, and whatever Allan might desire, poor Jem tried to do.

Jem was too weak to work, but while Allan was out in the day-time, Jem would clean up the room, make the bed, prepare their poor scant meals, and, in truth, would often get up from his sick bed, and stagger about the apartment, endeavouring to do whatever, in his judgment, Allan might approve.

When young Norman came home, these two young, faithful friends, would sit round the fire reading, or telling tales, often sighing for the fate of those dear ones which were then (supposed to be) far away, toiling in some distant convict settlement, and encouraging each other with words of consolation and hope.

But now that his only companion had fled, Allan felt somewhat disheartened.

He was not possessed of that lion heart which Edgar had, and he acknowledged it often and often both in words and actions.

Leaving what he had bought for poor Jem untouched upon the three-legged deal table against the wall, Allan buttoned up his coat, and sallied forth into the pouring rain in search of Jem.

It was a frightful night for any one to go forth into.

But love and friendship are strong passions, and Allan resolved to leave nothing undone which might tend to discover poor Jem.

Through one street and down another Allan trudged manfully, and he never passed a poor beggar by without giving a penny.

"I am poor myself," he thought; "yes, very poor, but, if I hope to prosper in this world, I must not forget to help the houseless and hungry ones, who are seeking shelter in door-ways and bye-ways out of the pelting storm."

And as time after time he bestowed a copper upon some child or faint and dripping woman, his heart felt lighter and lighter, and he walked along as if he was carried on springs.

First to one police-station and then to another he went, seeking poor, half-crazy Jem.

But no tidings could he learn.

At some of the stations he was received kindly by the inspectors, and left a full description of his missing companion.

At other stations he was treated harshly and bluntly.

The police officers looked upon him with suspicion, and winked at one another in a sly, cunning manner.

They asked a multitude of questions that had nothing to do with the subject, and then dismissed Allan very curtly and unceremoniously, whispering one to another,

"Some young thief or other on the look-out for a pal who is missing."

"Oh, he can't be up to much if he lives in such a place as Golden Lane," another would remark. "I've had my eye on that youth for many a day; he's not up to much."

These cruel remarks were not needed, but policemen generally are very cunning and suspicious, and will upon every man as a rogue until he is proved

But.

"Wethroughout that stormy night Allan Norman honesty about from one place to another. sick you n

He was wet through three or four times, but not until broad daylight had dawned upon the town did he give up the search.

Yet it was all in vain.

There were no tidings of poor Jem, nor did any one in all the wide world care one iota about the poor lad except the noble-hearted Allan Norman.

Weak and tired, and almost fainting from his long walks, Allan returned to his humble lodgings and sat upon the edge of the bed.

He soon fell fast asleep, and there he remained for many, many hours, unconscious of the flight of time.

When he awoke he was shivering and numbed in every limb, and trembled as if attacked with ague.

He rubbed his eyes, but all was darkness around him.

It was now night again.

The lamps were lighted, and, as he looked out of his windows in Golden Lane, the gin-palaces were all blazing and brilliant with gas, and crowds of drunken idlers around the doors.

"Can it be that I have been dreaming?" he thought.

For a moment he reflected, and then distinctly remembered all that had happened.

He recollected the engagement to meet Mr. Marks, and, doubtful of the right time, he swallowed a little food and drank a little of the wine which, as we have seen, he bought for his sick companion, and hurried from his lodgings post haste.

When he got into the street he looked into a public-house and saw that it was half-past nine o'clock.

The distance to Folio Chambers was considerable, and, shivering as he was from wet and cold, he ran through the streets and soon reached the offices of Mr. Marks, all breathless from hurrying.

Old Marks was alone, and deep in thought.

He sat in his arm-chair playing with his bony hands and twisting his lean, lank fingers until he made the joints crack again.

His small, black, bead-like eyes twinkled again with deadly pleasure when young Allan entered the room.

"Ah, Mr. Norman, I am most happy, most happy indeed, I am, to see you."

Allan bowed, but felt very unwell, and did not answer.

"I am glad to see you so punctual, sir," the old lawyer went on, still rubbing his hands; "there is nothing like punctuality in business."

"I am a little before my time, I think, Mr. Marks," said Allan.

"True, my lad, so you are; but that doesn't matter—in fact, it is all the better. But, you look wet and cold."

"I am both, sir," Allan answered.

"Brandy is a good thing for that," said the old man, who had that moment resolved to drug some if Allan could be got to partake of any.

But young Norman refused to take the lawyer's brandy, and old Marks grinned in disappointment, as he said,

"Did you see a cab at the door as you came in?"

"Yes, sir."

"That's all right, then; we can now proceed to business."

So speaking, old Marks put on his overcoat and hat.

"Are you going out, sir?" Allan asked.

"Yes, and you will come with me."

"Why, sir? Is not the legal business to be done here?"

"Oh, dear, no, my young friend, oh, dear no. A

gentleman—a legal gentleman of my acquaintance—has made the deeds, and he now awaits us some little distance away at his offices; it won't take us long to get there. Come, follow me."

Without the least suspicion of any harm being intended, Allan followed Marks to the cab and got in.

The cabman had received his directions beforehand, and drove off at a rapid rate.

Little conversation took place between Allan and old Marks as they journeyed onwards, and in less than half-an-hour the cab stopped in a rural-looking neighbourhood on the road to Hendon.

"Stop here, cabby," said old Marks. "I will call upon my friend first, and see if he is at home; if he is not you can drive us back again. Don't be impatient," whispered he to Allan; "I shan't be five minutes absent."

In a twinkling old Marks disappeared in the darkness, and, although he was more than twenty minutes away, it did not seem more than five minutes to Allen, who was deeply absorbed in thought.

"Here I am again," said the old lawyer, returning with a smiling face. "You can go, cabby; you need not wait. Here is your fare."

"Can't I drive yer up to the door, guv'nor?" said cabby, with a peculiar smile, which, for a moment, startled the lawyer.

"No, no, no," Marks hastily replied. "My young friend and myself will walk."

Allan followed Marks in the darkness without breathing a word.

As they went away the cabby muttered.

"That's another; poor young devil! Vell, if the old 'un von't let me drive him up to the door, I'll go down the street, and vatch vhere the old bloke goes to, and who he is; so help me tater, I vill!"

And, smoking his short pipe, the cabman turned his horse, and went round the first corner he came to.

Meanwhile the lawyer and Allan proceeded towards a fine, strongly-built mansion, which stood some distance apart from all others.

A porter at the lodge opened a gate, and they walked up to and entered the entrance hall.

There was nothing outside this mansion which indicated it to be anything else or less than a gentleman's private residence; and everything about the gardens indicated the greatest of care and attention.

The lawyer and Allan were met in the entrance hall by a gentleman in black, who looked very solemn, and more like a doctor than a lawyer.

"This way, gentlemen," said he, conducting them, and leading the way up-stairs. "This way, gentlemen, if you please."

Allan followed old Marks, and, in a few seconds, they all entered a large room, which was shut off from another by folding doors.

Allan could not but perceive at a glance that the apartment was very meagrely furnished.

However, he took a seat, and waited for business to commence.

"Oh, this is the young gentleman you spoke of, Mr. Marks, eh?" said the solemn-looking gentleman in black, with a dry smile.

"Yes, this is the person."

"What is his name, Mr. Marks?"

"Ask him," said the lawyer; "he will tell you everything."

"My name is Allan Norman," said the youth.

"Ah, just so, just so."

"And I came here with my lawyer, Mr. Marks, to enquire into a certain property which falls to me by the death of my brother, Edgar, who was drowned when the 'Rattlesnake' was wrecked in the South Seas."

"Just as you told me, Mr. Marks; just as you told me, my dear sir; the case is clear."

"I am glad to hear you say so," said Allan, who thought that the solemn-looking gentleman was referring to his own particular "case" in law.

"How long has this youth been heir presumptive to the estate he speaks of?" asked the solemn gentleman, winking at old Marks.

"Oh, a long, long time now," said the lawyer, who sat in an arm chair winking and blinking like an old owl in noonday; "he is always talking about it."

"Oh, I can perceive that it is a clear case," said the Medico; "his flushed face, wandering, staring, and unnaturally bright eyes, together with his shivering, tells me it's a clear case. The poor lad requires proper care; and in this establishment, Mr. Marks, you may have it. He is rather gentle for a lunatic, though," said the Medico.

"A what!" gasped Allan, jumping to his feet, and for the first time perceiving the true designs of the lawyer. "A what!" he gasped. "A lunatic?"

"Yes, a lunatic; but come, come, my lad, be quiet, you shall be well taken care of here," said the Medico, kindly.

"A lunatic!" repeated Allan, red with rage, and with clenched fists. "So this is a lunatic asylum, eh, Mr. Marks? and the villanous scheme is yours, eh, rascal?"

"He is getting violent, you see," said old Marks, who feared each moment that Allan would rush at him and strangle him.

"Oh, we can soon cure him of that," said the master of the establishment.

At the same moment he touched a small bell.

The door was opened without noise.

Jerry Marks and a keeper came forward without being heard or seen by Allan.

The latter brought in some ropes and a chain, which he noiselessly placed upon the floor, and then retired till called for again.

At a sign from the Medico, however, Jerry, unperceived, advanced towards Allan, and seized him roughly by one arm, while the Medico laid hold of him by the other.

Allan seemed petrified and rooted to the spot with amazement at the sudden and awful change which had taken place in his prospects.

He did not attempt to resist, but stood gazing at old Marks, who sat in his arm-chair triumphant and smiling.

"What!" said Allan, in bitter scorn; "this, then, is a lunatic asylum, and I am your victim, eh, lawyer Marks; but heaven is witness I am not mad" (see Cut), said Allan, in a proud, defiant tone.

At the same instant, and while he spoke, the folding doors behind were pushed ajar, and, unseen by any one, a head was thrust forward, and looked upon all that was passing within.

The intruder's head was that of a boy.

It was no one else but the faithful lad, Jem Rawlings.

With a loud shout of disdain, Allan, by a mighty effort, tore himself from those who held him.

With one blow he knocked Jerry sprawling on the ground.

The next to receive a tremendous thwack was the Medico, who howled out,

"Murder, murder! help, help, help!"

At that instant and while Allan held old Marks by the throat with a deadly clutch, a body of keepers rushed into the room.

CHAPTER XXX.

THE MEETING WITH RED WOLF—THE INDIAN MAID DECLARES HER LOVE FOR LION LIMB—THE SPY—EMMA CLARENCE'S SUSPICIONS ARE AROUSED—YOKEE'S PLANS OF VENGEANCE.

THERE was something so awful and savage in the looks of the cannibal king, that, for a moment, Lion Limb, sword in hand, stood gazing in wonder at his tall, gaunt antagonist, and spoke not a word.

At last, the brave lad, without the slightest fear upon his handsome and noble countenance, approached his grim foe still nearer.

Brandishing his good sword, he would have rushed upon the savage monster, and slain him.

But Marmi touched Lion Limb's arm, as if bidding him to desist for a moment.

Red Wolf perceived the movement, and, with a grim smile, lowered his deadly bludgeon, and said to the Indian maiden, in tones that she well understood—

"Marmi, the daughter of mine enemy, Katamar, has found new friends in the pale-faces; she looks proud and defiant, yet let her fear Red Wolf for ever."

"Nay, I fear ye not, Red Wolf," she replied in her native tongue, and with a deep blush suffusing her pretty features. "I fear ye not, Red Wolf; it was by cunning, and not by honourable warfare, that I became your captive, and the great thunder-rolling God who lives in the skies, and rules all things, directed this brave leader of the pale-faces to the spot where you would have burned me alive."

"Nay, Marmi, the fawn-like daughter of Katamar would never have been tied to the stake had she consented to become the bride of Red Wolf."

"I know it," the maiden boldly replied, still clinging to the side of Lion Limb. "I know it well, Red Wolf; but rather than become the wife of such a bloodthirsty and remorseless man as thou art, I would have willingly suffered ten thousand deaths."

"Ha! what is that I hear?" growled Red Wolf, with rolling eyes; "what is that I hear? Does the weak, timid child of Katamar, dare to speak thus in the presence of Red Wolf, the island king?"

"Island king!" Marmi answered, with scorn upon her curling lips; "island king, ha, ha! Red Wolf, never no more can you or your demon-like followers lay claim to that proud title, for behold!" said Marmi, proudly pointing to Lion Limb, "behold the true king of all these islands! Before this pale, proud, and valiant youth you, and all your followers, shall bow the knee, and accept the yoke of bondage."

"Bow the knee!" gasped Red Wolf, breathing hard in anger. "Accept the yoke of bondage, and be slaves to the pale-faces! Never!"

"Nay, Red Wolf," Marmi replied, "let not your huge breast heave in senseless anger, for the thunder-rolling God above us has so decreed it."

"Then let the pale-faced boy die!" said Red Wolf, with awful passion. "He shall be my slave, not I his."

"Put down your war-club, Red Wolf," Marmi replied; "if you do but approach a yard nearer the weapon of this pale-faced boy will be dyed in your heart's blood. Rather than be your wife, Red Wolf, I would be his slave for ever."

Marmi had scarce uttered these words, when the savage chief, with an awful oath, rushed upon Lion Limb.

He aimed a terrible blow at Lion Limb, but that youth was too nimble to be thus struck down to the earth unawares.

So great was the force of the blow, that it made the infuriated cannibal king whirl round again like a top.

Lion Limb laughed with scorn at the dastardly attempt of his cunning enemy.

But Red Wolf rushed upon him again, and for the second time made a fearful blow at his head with the spike-covered bludgeon.

But this attempt was no better than the first.

Indeed, it was well aimed, but Lion Limb again dodged, and this time the spikes of the deadly weapon struck against a tree near by, and almost buried itself in the soft, pulpy bark.

In an instant Lion Limb rushed upon him full of vengeance.

But Red Wolf was too cunning for the brave boy.

Finding that his weapon was immovable in the tree, the cannibal king retreated several yards, and as Lion Limb pursued him he dashed into the thicket and was lost to view, calling after him several of his followers who that moment had come upon the scene.

For a moment Lion Limb was astonished and annoyed.

He had made up his mind to fight the huge cannibal, and did not for a moment expect that the ruffian would have proved so cowardly as to run away.

But as yet Lion Limb knew but little of the true nature and deep cunning of those who were around him upon the island.

In truth Red Wolf was so much struck with the bold, handsome youth, and at the same time so much astonished at his courage, daring and coolness, that he felt not only nervous in his presence, but felt as if he had stood in the presence of some superior and all-powerful being who had just dropped from the skies.

The flash of Lion Limb's bright fearless eyes had appalled him.

For a moment, then, as we have said, our young hero stood gazing in astonishment at the retreating forms of Red Wolf and his men, not knowing how to account for such extraordinary cowardice.

But he was brought back to consciousness again by Marmi, the Indian maiden.

She ran again to his side and kneeling kissed his hands again and again; but though tears were flowing from her eyes, she looked up to Lion Limb with looks of proud pleasure as if gazing at some young much-loved warrior who had delivered her from certain death.

"Away, away," she said to him, in her native tongue, and with many imploring gestures; "do not follow Red Wolf into the forest. Back, back to your followers; the forest is filled with foes; this is but a trick of the cunning Red Wolf; he saw that you were brave and fearless and wished you to fall into his snare. He thought you would surely follow him."

"And so I will," said Lion Limb, boldly, who was just beginning to understand some little of Marmi's words and gestures, "and so I will follow him."

"Nay, nay, you must not! Do not! pray do not! your life is precious, nay, too precious to hazard it for such a paltry price."

"Hands off, Marmi! hands off," said Lion Limb, endeavouring gently to untwine himself from the maiden's light embrace; "hands off, Marmi; fear not for me. Lion Limb scorns to flee before any score of such cunning, cowardly villains."

He would have cast Marmi aside, but the faithful girl clung to him still closer, and finding her strength failing; she gasped out in soft accents—

THE BOY KING
OF THE SOUTH SEA ISLANDS.

AN ADVENTURE WITH A BUFFALO.

"Do not—do not go; for *my* sake, do not. You know not how much I love you. For *my* sake, noble youth, do not go forth after those ruthless villains."

There was something in her tone of voice which instantly acted like a spell upon Lion Limb.

But then there was an irresistible eloquence and a love-light in her tearful eyes, which told him, plainer and more loudly than words could do, that Marmi, the beautiful Indian princess, was deeply in love with him !

He did not understand all—indeed, but very little—of what she said.

The sword dropped to his side.

He gazed upon the charming girl kneeling suppliantly before him.

He felt, for a moment, unmanned and undecided.

Marmi, scarcely knowing what she did, or why, took the sword from his hands, and smiled upon him with the looks of a fair conqueror.

"She loves me," sighed Lion Limb.

At that moment, and while Lion Limb and Marmi were alone in the forest, Yokee had not been asleep.

He had watched all the motions of the pair, and, hurrying to the camp, by words and gestures intimated to Emma Clarence that he desired her to follow him instantly.

Fearful that something might have happened to Lion Limb, she followed Yokee unperceived by any of those in the camp.

When she arrived at the edge of the forest, Yokee led the way, and in a few moments Emma came in full view of the spot where Marmi was kneeling before Lion Limb.

The colour rushed to her fair cheeks.

Her eyes were brightened with passion before unknown.

Her lips trembled and her hands quivered.

"You see?" said Yokee, in his native tongue, a little of which Emma now understood. "You see?" said Yokee, hiding himself behind a tree out of view.

Emma did not answer.

Yokee's eyes were rolling in savage delight, and he grinned most horribly, as he said, in an undertone,

"Yokee your friend; Yokee your servant—your slave."

And as he spoke, the dusky, cunning rascal bowed himself to the ground in a posture of the most abject and slavish submission.

Emma Clarence for a moment spoke not.

She still stood gazing at Marmi and Lion Limb as calmly as a marble statue.

"See how her eyes are flashing with delight!" thought Emma. "She loves him!"

After a pause, she said, half aloud,

"And *he* loves her. See! she has his sword in her hands. Look how he gazes upon her! 'Tis well; I have seen all. Now I know that his heart is not mine. 'Tis well, Lion Limb, 'tis well. I love you also, but I love you too well to interfere or thwart you in those you love better."

Yokee, in his kneeling position, had been intently watching every change of feature in Emma's face.

When he saw two tear-drops sparkle in her eyes, he trembled for the success of his deadly schemes.

But when afterwards he perceived a red glow mantle her pale cheeks, and her eyes flash, he rejoiced.

"I have sown the seeds of deadly jealousy," thought the crafty Indian. "I must mind how I proceed, else I shall be discovered, and, perhaps, be slain by this bold young leader."

"Your slave, mistress," he murmured again, after a long pause.

Emma turned her eyes upon the prostrate form of the dusky rascal, and looked upon him with a cold hard gaze.

She touched her lips in token of secresy, and then trod upon his neck with her foot, as a sign that she had accepted his servitude.

Yokee rose to his feet, all smiles, and bowed to the ground again and again.

She motioned him to return to the camp.

He did so on the instant.

Soon afterwards she herself returned to the camp also.

There was not the slightest trace of any recent weeping upon her handsome features.

The merriment in the camp still continued, and soon afterwards Lion Limb left the forest, and returned to his followers, looking thoughtful and rather melancholy.

"I might have acted the part of a villain to this poor Indian girl," he thought, "but I would not, I will not. No; I will be to her as a brother, or a friend; but nothing more."

In a few words he told Harry Woodruff and Dick Hamilton all that had happened to him while away as far as his meeting with Red Wolf was concerned.

But he spoke not a word to them of Marmi.

Harry and Dick were surprised and for a moment alarmed at the extreme danger in which their chief had been, and in their anger blamed Marmi for enticing him to stray away.

They immediately placed a party of men and boys to stand guard during the night, and be on the watch for any sudden attack made by Red Wolf and his bloodthirsty followers.

When this was done, and while Lion Limb was seated beside Emma Clarence, full of talk regarding what he intended to do for the future, Emma said, carelessly,

"Lion Limb, I wish to ask you a favour; it is the first I ever asked you."

"Then ask a dozen, Emma," said Lion Limb, with a triumphant smile; "ask a hundred if you will, for even a dozen is not sufficient. Ask anything you please; you, you know, are queen of these islands, and I——"

"You, Captain Lion Limb, are king," said Emma, coldly.

"And what, pray, is the favour our young queen would ask?"

"Not much. I want a trusty servant."

"A servant, Emma! You surprise me. Are we not all your servants? Is there any single one among us all who would ever refuse you anything?"

"That may be," said Emma; "but I have taken a particular fancy to the Indian captive Yokee, and would much like to instruct him so as to make him more useful. I understand much of what he says in his native tongue already, and have an idea that he would soon learn to speak English."

"Well, be it so, then, Emma; we can deny our fair young queen nothing, you know; but I should have thought that one of our own boys would have been much more useful and agreeable to you as a servant than Yokee. Why not have Ted Rawlings?"

"Oh, that would be certain death to him, for Ted Rawlings couldn't live out of *your* sight, Lion Limb," said Emma, with a slight smile.

"Why not have some one better suited than Yokee?" said our hero, again.

Emma did not at the moment answer, but she thought—

"He dislikes Yokee. But why, unless the Indian knows more about Marmi than Lion Limb cares for him to know."

"But still," in her soft mild way, she said, aloud, "you seem to object to Yokee, Lion Limb."

"N-n-o," our hero replied; "not exactly."

"Is he not honest?"

"Oh, yes, I think so, as far as I can see."

"Is he not very much attached to you?"

"Yes, I believe he is."

"And so is the captive, Princess Marmi, I think," said Emma, very slowly.

Lion Limb did not reply.

He was deep in thought.

Yet the bare mention of Marmi's name brought the colour to his cheeks, as he replied—

"Gratitude for saving her life makes her like me perhaps, Emma; nothing more."

A long pause ensued.

At last Emma said—

"Then, it is decided that Yokee shall be my attendant, Lion Limb?"

"Well, as you wish it, Emma, yes; but be on your guard with him at all times. Is this the favour you wished to ask me?"

"It is."

"Then," said Lion Limb, laughing, "you are very easily pleased."

Then, calling Ted Rawlings, he said—

"Call Yokee here."

Ted was off like a shot and found Yokee, who was lying all fours on the grass eyeing Princess Marmi with the intentness of a watch-dog.

He rose at Ted's command, and, as he left the spot where Marmi sat, he clenched his fist and rolled his eyes in deadly passion.

Lion Limb soon made Yokee understand what was wanted of him; and the Indian, with a broad grin on his features, bowed himself to the very earth in token of submission.

"At last," thought Yokee, "at last! My plans succeed. Revenge is sweet! Fear me, Marmi! Fear me, Lion Limb! You may cut out my very heart, but you will never discover my thoughts, desires, or resolutions! This fair-faced maid is *mine!*"

CHAPTER XXXI.

THE BUCCANEER'S HOME—NAT, THE DON—HE VOWS TO EXTERMINATE LION LIMB AND HIS BAND—THE COUNCIL OF WAR.

BUT return we now for a moment to the doings of Bloodhoof and his gang.

As we have before narrated in this story Bloodhoof, Bill Whetherby, and his gang of mutineers, had taken possession of a distant island but a few hours after they left what they then supposed to be a sinking ship.

Although they landed in safety in their numerous boats, and took a large store of food, arms, and ammunition with them, it did not suffice for the wants of the disorderly and riotous company on the the island.

Great to the joy of Bloodhoof and the rest, however, they found the island occupied by a strong party of men who had mutineered and escaped from different ships.

These fellows carried on the trade of buccaneers in the South Seas, and many a good ship, richly laden, and homeward bound, had been boarded and rifled by these island sharks.

These buccaneers were men of almost all nations.

Some were Spanish, French, Portuguese, Italian and German, but the greater number were English, who had formerly been on men-of-war.

When Bloodhoof and Whetherby made this joyful discovery, and found among the island buccaneers, not only a large party of Englishmen, but many former shipmates, their excitement and hilarity knew no bounds.

The buccaneers were equally glad to make the acquaintance of the ragamuffin rascals who had mutined, and the greeting on all sides was cordial and noisy in the extreme.

Nat Jackson, who was chief of the buccaneers, recognised Bloodhoof and Whetherby as old shipmates in years gone by.

"But," said the tall, bushy, red-faced, and double-fisted Nat to Bloodhoof, on the sly, "my name is not Nat Jackson here, mind you; I am called Don Carlos."

"All right," said Whetherby and Bloodhoof with a knowing wink; "all serene, Don Carlos; a wink is enough for old salts like us. Lead the way to your strong vaults, and let us taste of your best."

"I thought I should find you on one of these islands," said Whetherby.

"'Twas lucky you were so fortunate as to land on the right one, then," said the Don; "for the others are peopled by savages. But come, my lads, we have plenty of everything to eat and drink, so for the next week, at least, we shall do nothing but do all honour to your arrival."

For a full week, then, after they had landed, had the mutineers been carousing with the buccaneers, and Bloodhoof was duly elected to be one of the Don's chief officers, and to act under his orders.

Bill Whetherby was much disappointed that he had not been chosen, and swore to himself that, ere long, he would have revenge both on the Don and Bloodhoof.

But he kept this resolution a great secret.

To the surprise of all one morning, the signal was made by a look-out man from a high rock that a wreck was in sight.

Nat Jackson hurried to the spot and with Bloodhoof, telescopes in hand, they had a good view of the wreck.

At night time Whetherby and Bloodhoof set out in sail boats to the distant island, as we have narrated in another place, and were vastly surprised to discover that it was the remains of the Rattlesnake and that is was guarded by a party of the boy convicts and some faithful sailors.

One of Nat's guides, who was friendly with Red Wolf's Indians, planned the order of attack.

But how it fared we have already seen.

When, therefore, Bloodhoof and Whetherby returned to their own abode (which was known to them under the name of Blue Rocks) Nat was astounded at the news of their discomfiture.

He raved and swore like a madman.

"My men routed, beaten, and maimed by a handful of boy convicts—impossible! I never knew there were any white men within hundreds, nay, thousands of miles around me. I am astounded. Bring me brandy somebody," said he, "brandy quick, I say. I say Tonio, bring me a bottle; quick, you black-skinned rascal," said Nat the Don, red with rage.

Bloodhoof and Whetherby had both been wounded in the fight, and their blood-stained features were horrible to look upon.

But neither of them dare speak to Nat while he was in such a rage.

"Who the devil leads these boys? What did they say his name was?"

"They call him Lion Limb," murmured Bill Whetherby.

"Lion Limb or Devil's Limb, it matters little to me," said Nat, gulping down some more brandy. "Lion Limb or Devil's Limb, it matters naught to me; he must be killed, yes every one of them; we can't allow such disagreeable neighbours to live in sight of us. They must all be slaughtered, I say, or else 'Blue Rocks' will be too hot to hold us, ere long. I am king here."

The rage of Nat Jackson, or Don Carlos as he was called, was really something terrible to behold.

He the buccaneer chief of the South Sea Islands to be thwarted by the bravery and prowess of a mere boy like Lion Limb, caused the grim, gaunt, heavy-booted buccaneer to tremble with rage.

His eyes rolled most horribly.

He gnashed his teeth and swore a long string of most frightful oaths.

He drew his cutlass and twirled it above his head, swearing to cut Lion Limb and his followers to pieces whenever they should chance to meet.

"How old is this young villain?" he asked of Bill Whetherby, in tones of contempt and scorn.

"Not more than sixteen, if even he is that age," Bloodhoof replied.

"Sixteen!" said Nat the Don, in tones of contempt, "and could you not conquer such a mere brat as he is then?" he gasped.

"He seems to have a charmed life," replied Bill Whetherby.

"A what!"

"A charmed life."

"What makes you think so?"

"During the fight he was everywhere, and although I and others fired at him continually, we always missed him."

"Did Red Wolf's men run, then?"

"They did, and although the Indians fired dozens and dozens of poisoned arrows at him, the bold boy was unhurt."

"Where did he stand during the battle?"

"In the midst of danger on all occasions."

"And yet every one of you missed him?"

"We did; but the Indians suffered most awfully, and dozens of them bit the dust."

"So much the better," said the buccaneer chief. "I always hated Red Wolf, and it is my hope that this boy you call Lion Limb will exterminate his whole tribe, for then we shall have fewer enemies."

For a moment a dead pause ensued.

At last Nat, the Don, said to Bloodhoof in a whisper.

"You say that this boy chief has a charmed life?"

"We do," replied Bill Whetherby and Bloodhoof, in a breath.

"And your reason for thinking so is, that he seems to, and really does, escape all dangers?"

"Yes, that is our chief reason for thinking so, Don Carlos. Without a man's life was charmed, he could not have escaped the many shots and snares which we have repeatedly laid for him."

Don Carlos, the buccaneer chief, turned pale.

He walked up and down in mental abstraction for some few moments.

At last he said, calling Bloodhoof to him—

"Bloodhoof," he said, "I wish to speak to you in strict confidence."

"About what?"

"Regarding that boy Lion Limb."

"Indeed! then what is it?"

"You will not divulge my secret to any one?"

"I will not."

"Then," said Nat, trembling from some unknown cause, "listen to me."

"I am all attention."

"You know I am king of the buccaneers on the Blue Rocks?"

"I do."

"You also know that I have for many years ruled the seas for hundreds of miles around, and that my very name carries terror to the hearts of all?"

"I have heard it."

"Well, since you and your companions have joined us, the Spaniards, Frenchmen, and others of my old companions have taken such a liking to you that they have made you my second in command."

"I am aware of that fact," said Bloodhoof, proudly, "and feel highly honoured at their choice."

"The choice was a good one, Bloodhoof, and when I am gone I have no doubt you will govern the band well, and prove as brave a man as I have."

"When you are gone, captain!" said Bloodhoof, rather astonished at the despondent and sorrowful tone in which he spoke. "When you are gone!" Bloodhoof repeated, looking at Don Carlos.

"Yes, when I am gone, Bloodhoof, for I shall not live long, I imagine."

"What mean you, captain?"

"What I mean is this, Bloodhoof," said Nat the Don, in a whisper, "and it is a great secret."

"Name it."

"Then, in one word, I *fear* this boy."

"This Lion Limb?"

"Yes, Lion Limb; I fear him."

"Why?"

"His life is charmed, I am certain of it."

"But why think you so?"

"I will tell you," said Nat, standing and looking towards the sinking sun in a calm and sorrowful manner. "I and the buccaneers, not more than three years ago, attacked a trading vessel which was coming from Chili and Peru."

"Well, what of that?"

"We knew that she was heavily laden with gold and silver, for one of my spies had watched her movements and informed me of all facts concerning her."

"Well."

"When the vessel had come into our latitude, we attacked her one dark night and took possession of it, but the scene of bloodshed on board was something horrible."

For a moment Nat was silent, but afterwards continued—

"We gave quarter to no one, for all on board fought like devils, and defended the ship right manfully."

Another pause occurred.

"We slayed every soul on board and spared not a single one."

"Well, what of that?" said Bloodhoof, with a bitter smile; "that is nothing very extraordinary, is it? Why, it is the trade of all true buccaneers who live by slaughter and plunder."

"I know it, Bloodhoof," said Nat the Don, with a dark scowl upon his ugly countenance, "but in this case I regret it."

"Why?"

"My own wife was on board that vessel, Bloodhoof," said Nat the Don, grinning like a fiend.

"Your wife!"

"Yes. I wrote to England telling her what sort of life I was leading here in the South Seas, and she, poor girl, with a baby in her arms, had gone to Peru and Chili in hopes of finding me as I had appointed; but in an evil hour she embarked on board the specie vessel, and in the hurry of the battle in the darkness of night I slew her with my own hand!"

Bloodhoof, with all his ferocity, was appalled.

"Your own wife, eh?"

"Yes, my own wife, Bloodhoof! Cursed hour that I ever entered on the life of a buccaneer."

"Well, and what followed?"

"I did not know what I had done, but when we had transferred all the most valuable part of the cargo to our own vessel, and when about to depart, leaving our prize to sink with all on board, the stray rays of a lantern revealed to me the features of my own wife as in her death agonies she raved."

"And what did she say?"

"In her death agonies, Bloodhoof, she foretold me many, many things."

"It was only raving."

"No, it was not. She seemed to be gifted with prophecy, for she foretold to me at that dreadful moment that our colony on the Blue Rocks would be shortly increased to a great number of men, some of whom would prove to be worse than myself in crime and iniquity, and that one, whose name she mentioned, would be called the 'Scourge of the South Seas.' All that she said has proved true as yet."

"And who was this man she described that should be called the 'Scourge of the South Seas?'"

"The name she mentioned was your own, Bloodhoof?"

"Mine?"

"Yes, yours."

"Impossible, captain; you are raving!"

"I was never more sober and sensible in my whole life," said the gruff chief.

"And you believe all this?"

"I do; for as yet, as I have said, all has come to pass as she foretold."

"Did this dying woman, your wife, captain, say more?"

"Yes; much—very much more."

"What about?"

"I will tell you. Before she died the poor thing recognized me, and, lifting up her eyes, said—

"'Beware of a youth who is called Lion Limb! He will land on an island near to you. He and his little colony of boy convicts and brave young sailors will make their names famous in this part of the world; he will be called the Boy King of the South Sea Islands, and will prove to be the bitterest enemy which ever crossed the path of mutineers and buccaneers!'"

"And do you believe this woman's twaddle, captain?" said Bloodhoof.

"I do; for since that moment, as I have said again and again, all has proved true which she has predicted."

"What else did she say?"

"Why, that I should be slain one day in a hand to hand encounter with this same boy, Lion Limb, and that my body should be hung in chains as a warning to all buccaneers, and serve as a landmark for all passing ships."

"Oh, I cannot believe these ravings of a dying woman, captain," said Bloodhoof. "And, as to this Lion Limb, or Devil's Limb as we call him, who has set up his throne in yonder island, leave him to me. A week shall not pass ere I bring you his head as a trophy."

"If such a thing could come to pass, Bloodhoof, I should imagine that the spell was broken."

"Then, captain, it shall be broken. Whetherby and all of us have the most deadly hatred of this boy leader of the young convicts."

"But then he has the old wreck in his possession, and, from all I have heard you say, it contains arms, ammunition, and lots of provisions."

"It does," said Whetherby, with a wicked smile, "and live stock besides. From all I can see, this youth, Lion Limb, seems determined to found a little kingdom, for already he has the British flag flying from a tall tree; he has put out his cows and other live cattle to graze; he has built earthworks, and mounted them with cannon; all his men are drilled twice a day like soldiers; he has also portioned out parts of the land near the sea-coast for his followers, and built log houses."

"That is all true," said Nat the Don; "but I know more than all that, for I sent out a spy last night who has returned not more than an hour ago, and he tells me that nearly everything of value has been taken from the old ship; the boys, and the sailors with them, under the guidance of two young men named Harry Woodruff and Dick Hamilton, have commenced to break up the old wreck, and are actually engaged in building a fine, fast-sailing schooner."

"They are not idle then, captain."

"No; and that is the reason why I fear them all the more. If these boy convicts under Lion Limb had squandered all their treasures, and not had such a clear, calculating, clever eye to the future, I should not have feared them at all; but you see that all their movements and actions are guided and directed by some master spirit, who seems to know everything that is or should be required."

"And that master spirit is——" said Bloodhoof, with an oath.

"None other than Lion Limb, my deadly enemy," Nat answered; "and, to speak the truth, I fear him more than a whole squadron of British ships."

"Then we must commence at once, and lay plans for Lion Limb's destruction," said Bloodhoof; "we cannot live in peace for many hours, for we are living too close together."

"True," said the Don; "there cannot be two masters here among the islands."

"No; either we must rule, and he shall die, or he be slain, and we remain masters of all we survey."

"I fear him."

"I do not," said Bloodhoof, with a savage oath; "leave it all to me. Lion Limb shall die!"

CHAPTER XXXII.

THE COLONISTS BUILD AND ARM A SCHOONER—
THE BUCCANEERS ARE ATTACKED—CAPTAIN
LION LIMB LEADS THE WAY.

THE intelligence which had been brought to the chief of the buccaneers was perfectly true.

But his spy had not seen all the changes which Lion Limb was making in his little colony.

As the spy informed Nat the Don, Lion Limb had fully employed his men in unpacking the cargo of the vessel, and was doing everything in his power to make the colony as prosperous and happy as possible.

All the agricultural implements, such as ploughs harrows, forks, rollers, scythes, reaping-hooks, and the like, were placed on shore, and ready for immediate use.

"For," said Lion Limb to Harry Woodruff, "our colony will be prosperous one of these days, and, if I am not much mistaken, it will add glory to our name, and to the glorious flag of old England, under which we live."

Hence, to provide sufficient food for his followers, was one of his chief thoughts.

The cows and oxen which had survived the storm and wreck were brought on shore; yokes were placed round their necks, and in a few days a pleasant and fertile valley near which their camp stood was in the hands of half-a-dozen ploughmen, and ready for sowing the seed of wheat, barley, oats, and other grains.

Flower seeds of every sort and variety were also sown in abundance, and a pleasant part of the valley (which was called Riverdale by the boys, on account of a lovely stream which ran through it,) was portioned off as the destined site of a little town.

The spot was excellently chosen as a place of residence, for it commanded a full view of the sea-coast on one side, and on its western side rose a chain of lofty hills, which perfectly guarded the intended village from the attacks of Indians and all others.

Log houses rose quickly on every hand, but they were all of large size, strong, and would serve as forts in case of war.

These strong buildings were arranged on three sides of a large square, in the centre of which was erected a very lofty flag-pole, from which flapped in the breeze the English flag.

Under the orders and guidance of Lion Limb, Harry Woodruff, and Dick Hamilton, things in the little colony were put into "ship shape," as Harry was wont to say.

From sunrise until sunset the lads were always working to plant their little colony.

True, none of them were overworked, but each did a little and did that little well, so that in a few days a great deal was done by them all.

The woods resounded with men and boys plying the axe, and in a short time the intended site of the village was cleared of all unnecessary timber and undergrowth to such an extent that young Ted Rawlings was in ecstacies, and jumped about snapping his fingers, saying that the spot was as clear and level as a cricket field, and wanted the lads to have a game of "rounders" immediately.

Ted was as happy as if he had been at home, and didn't seem to give a thought to the dangers which surrounded them all night and day from the Indians on one side and the buccaneers on the other.

One of the first things which occupied the attention of Lion Limb was the building of a vessel.

They had built boats, it is true, but building a large vessel was quite a different matter, and caused the bold young chief much serious thought, for he had no suitable place to build it.

But Lion Limb was a lad that shrank from no enterprize.

"You can't do it," said Harry, shaking his head.

"The thing is impossible, captain," chimed in Dick.

"You can do almost anything we all know," said several; "but we fear, captain, you will have to give up all thoughts of building a ship."

"And yet if we don't have one of some sort we shall be confined to this island like so many rats," said Ted, "and I want to sail about and go on a voyage of discovery."

"And attack the buccaneers, I suppose," Lion Limb remarked, in a dry manner.

"Buccaneers, eh? Oh, no, thank you, not for me, if you please," said Ted, shaking his head. "I'd rather have ten fights with the Indians than one with those ugly buccaneers."

"Well, then, I suppose we must give up this idea as a bad job, captain, eh?" said Harry.

"No, my lad, not so; a ship I want, and a ship I'll have!"

"True, captain; but how?"

"Leave that to me. But listen. The craft that I want must be of light draft, so as to run up streams and hide in small coves out of sight."

"Quite true, captain; a big ship would be useless and dangerous among these islands and many rocks and shoals."

"She must be able to outsail everything she comes across," said Lion Limb, thoughtfully.

"Yes, one that can fly like a swallow," said young Ted. "I'll be the steersman!"

"Hold your noise," said Harry, gruffly, "or we'll make you the powder-monkey."

"And yet for all she must carry four guns."

"Yes, yes, that's all right enough, the craft that you want must be a beauty, I know," said Dick; "but how the devil are we going to get it?"

"Easily enough," said Lion Limb, laughing.

"How?"

"Why, cut down the old 'Rattlesnake' there; the hull is almost quite sound."

"The devil!" said one and all, in surprise. "Who would ever a thought of such a thing!"

"But you see I did," Lion Limb replied, laughing. "Necessity, you know, is the mother of invention."

"Well, dash me, if ever I should a thought on it!" said Dick. "But it's a capital idea, though; the old hull will do famous for a light draft schooner."

"And a schooner it shall be, Dick," said Lion Limb; "and such a fast sailer as was never seen in these waters before."

Next morning, bright and early, all hand were employed in taking everything out of the vessel.

When the high tide rose all the lads tugged long and hard in pulling the old craft high up a small creek near by.

"There," said Dick, "there she is, high and dry, captain; and now we can commence to cut her down."

And cut her down they did.

Four and twenty willing hands were soon hard at work chopping and sawing and tearing away the upper deck.

In less than twenty-four hours nothing but the lower deck remained.

The old "Rattlesnake" was stripped of everything and looked, as she was, a perfect shell.

But all the cabin fittings and whatever else was useful were taken care of, and housed away on shore.

An immense quantity of powder and ammunition of all sorts were carefully placed in a dry rocky cavern, not far off, and a huge stone rolled to the mouth of it to keep out intruders until such times as a regular powder magazine could be built.

"There, my merry, merry men," said Lion Limb, cheerily, "now who says we shan't have a fast sailing craft? Look at the old ship. Now, all we have got to do is to plug up all the holes, caulk up the sides, shift the rudder, and we can launch our schooner in less than three days."

"Three days," said Harry, "why, it will take three months, captain."

"No it won't, Harry, for we must all work at it night and day until the job is finished."

And work night and day they did.

One gang under Dick Hamilton worked at night and the rest under Lion Limb laboured during the day, cheerfully and with a good will.

The lads knew that the sooner they had a vessel afloat the better it would be for all.

Their safety and very existence depended upon it.

With this thought they hammered away night and day without ceasing, and in less than a week from the commencement of the undertaking, a new craft was made out of the old one.

Not only was it cut down into a rakish-looking schooner, but four guns were mounted on deck, and the various store-rooms provided for powder, provisions, and the like.

"There she is," said Lion Limb, looking in rapture at the change he had made, "there she is my brave lads, and, I warrant me, none of the cursed buccaneers and mutineers, or Indians either, will trouble us much now."

"But, how are we to get this new craft afloat?" said many.

"I'll soon show you," said Lion Limb. "Let all of you get into your small boats and canoes, and pull at this rope as hard and as steadily as you can, for when the tide rises she'll float off beautifully."

When, therefore, the tide rose, the lads in their boats began to pull at a strong rope with a hearty good will, and, amid noisy shouts, cheers, and laughter, the newly-made schooner gracefully floated with the tide, and glided down on to the bosom of the ocean.

Lion Limb was at the helm, while Dick, Harry, and some of the sailors set the sails, and the new craft bent to the evening breeze, and sailed as gracefully as possible.

"I think she'll do, captain," said Dick to Lion Limb, when they had been sailing for about an hour.

"She's a regular clipper, and no mistake," said Harry, in raptures.

"She is rather rough-looking at present, my lads," said Lion Limb, "but we can soon trim her up and make her look prim and smart with plenty of paint. Let us sail towards the land again, and cast anchor for the night."

"All right, captain."

And, steering homewards again, the schooner cast anchor in a safe and roomy harbour; but the sailors were not allowed to land, but ordered to keep watch and watch, just like regular man-of-war's men.

"Now that we have got a good craft, and in fighting order," said Lion Limb, "we must take care of her, and not let any of the buccaneers board and seize her while we are asleep."

When Lion Limb went on shore, young Ted Rawlings came running towards him in great haste.

"What's the matter, Ted?"

"Oh! Lion Limb, while you have been sailing about, I have been watching from yonder tree-top."

"Well, and what did you perceive?"

"With your telescope I could see red rockets flying in the air. The buccaneers are on the move; I shouldn't wonder if they mean to attack us to-night."

"So much the better, then, Ted; I am longing to meet them."

Going down into the centre of the encampment he fired his revolver three times in quick succession.

In an instant he was surrounded by all his followers.

He soon told them how to act in case of any attack.

He then selected twenty volunteers, and started for the schooner.

"Come, my brave lads," he said, "follow me; we will give these villanous buccaneers such a thrashing that they'll never forget it. Follow me."

They all went on board the schooner.

In less than half an hour, the vessel shot out upon the broad ocean like a thing of life.

*　　　*　　　*　　　*　　　*

Gallantly and right nobly did the exquisite craft sail before the wind.

She rushed through the sparkling waters like a sea sprite.

"What do you think of her, my lads?" asked Lion Limb, with a flush of pride upon his manly brow.

"Think of her!" said Harry, "why I think that this ere craft has got human life in her, that's what I think, cap'n."

"See how close she runs to the breeze," said Dick; "I never saw such a pretty creature in the whole course of my life."

"Up she goes," said Ted, in raptures, jumping about the deck like mad! "up she goes and down she goes, bounding and bouncing like a seagull."

"You hold your noise, my young shaver," said Dick; "we shall have plenty for you to do besides talking in less than an hour."

"How is that?"

"Why, we are going to have a fight, that's all," said Harry, grinning at the prospect of giving the buccaneers a good trouncing.

"A fight, eh?" said Ted. "Well, all I know is that fighting never agreed with me in all my life."

"Didn't it, though? then you must make it agree with you, you young skip-jack,"

"Do you see anything yet, Harry?" asked Lion Limb, who was still steering.

"No, cap'n, not yet,"

"A heavy haze and fog seems to have fallen to

the westward," said Dick, "and it may prevent us having a good sight of the cut-throat villains."

"Never mind, my merry lads, if we can't see them, we must feel them."

"Feel 'em!" said Ted. "How's that?"

"Why, with round shot, to be sure," said Dick.

"Clear the decks, my lads," said Lion Limb. "The fog is lifting again, and the moon shines like a silver dollar on a darkie's face. Clear the decks, my boys, and let's have a good look at the island yonder."

"Aye, aye, sir," said all, cheerily.

"Everything is ready for action, sir," said Harry.

"Go aloft, Dick, and keep a sharp look-out. This schooner of ours is dashing through the water at race-horse speed; we shall soon be upon them."

"All right, sir," said Dick; "I'll keep my weather eye open for the rascals, never fear."

And up aloft Dick climbed as nimbly as a monkey.

"What do you see, Dick?"

"Do you make 'em out?" said Harry, in a gruff voice.

"Not much as yet, Captain Lion Limb."

"Don't you see anything at all? We are very close upon the island now."

"There it goes," said Dick; "do you see it, captain?"

"No, what is it?"

"Three red rockets," said Dick, shouting on deck.

"Oh, I see them now, that is their danger signal," said Lion Limb. "Here, Harry Woodruff, you take hold of the tiller; I will also go aloft, and see what these rats on the Blue Rocks are up to."

"There it goes again," said Dick; "three blue rockets this time."

"They are not near the beach, Dick?"

"No, sir; those signals come from a spot at least a mile inland."

"I fear we have made a mistake in our reckoning; we shall have to land, I fear, and fight the devils on foot."

"They are cunning rascals without a doubt, sir," said Dick; "but I wouldn't land for all that."

"Why not?"

"Their gang must be very numerous, sir, and we should stand no chance against them, for we are only twenty-four on board all told."

"I fear nothing on that score," said Lion Limb; "we are a fit match for the villains any day. Coast along, Harry, coast along," said he, in a loud voice; "let every man stand to his gun, and when I give the word, let all be ready for instant action."

"Hullo! there they are! there they are!" said Dick, in high glee. "Don't you see the rascals swarming down to the beach?"

"Yes, yes, Dick, I see them; they are bold villains."

"They are getting into their boats, sir."

"They mistake us for some friendly trader Dick."

"It seems like it, sir."

"Stay where you are, Dick; when I give the word follow me on deck."

In a moment Lion Limb was down the rattlings.

"Let every one of you hide. Lay low; don't let a head be seen."

On the instant every one on deck crouched under the bulwarks.

But the buccaneers could not see a single gun on deck, for as yet the port-holes were not opened, nor were the guns run out.

Meanwhile, the schooner lay lazily in the wind near the shore of the Blue Rocks.

The buccaneers jumped into their numerous boats and pulled towards the strange craft with great vigour.

The villains had, for once in their lives, made a great mistake.

At first their look-out man on a high peak of rocks, looked upon the schooner like as if it were some phantom of the deep.

The gruff, rough rascal had never looked upon such a pretty craft in all his life before.

She lay so close to the wind, and answered her helm so readily, that in the distant moonlight she looked like some sea-sprite or phantom ship.

When, however, the vessel came closer and closer he signalled her approach to Nat the Don and the buccaneers, who at that moment were holding a council of war among themselves as to their intended attack upon Lion Limb and his little colony.

When the startling signal "a sail! a sail!" was made known to them, they rushed up the nearest point of high land.

The unanimous opinion of all was that the strange craft was, perhaps, some trader who had got off her proper course.

What puzzled Nat more than all was that the beautiful schooner approaching displayed no colours of any sort, and that no one could be seen on deck.

"Never mind, my lads; we'll soon make a prize of her. Follow me."

Whetherby, Bloodhoof, and all his bloodthirsty followers hurried to the beach filled with great hopes and expectations.

They jumped into their boats, which were more than ten in number.

Each boat contained eight well-armed men.

They struck out for the strange craft, and the first to approach it, as she now lay lazily on the waters, was Nat the Don in one boat, Bloodhoof in a second, and Whetherby in a third.

"Ship ahoy!" bawled out Nat, in stentorian tones.

The cry was heard on board, but no reply was made.

"Keep low, my merry lads, keep low; let 'em come a little closer first, and then we'll give 'em pepper."

"Ship ahoy!" still bawled Nat and the rest, now not more than a hundred yards off, "if they won't answer, fire into her."

On the instant a small cannon was fired at the schooner.

A terrific shout was the defiant answer of all on board.

The guns were run out in an instant.

"Fire!" said Lion Limb, waving his cap and sword, "fire! sink 'em!"

THE BOY KING
OF THE SOUTH SEA ISLANDS.

THE ATTACK ON LION LIMB'S SCHOONER.

The scene which a few moments before had been one of serenity and beauty, was suddenly changed. The buccaneers' boats, which until now had approached quietly, were totally taken by surprise, though they were thoroughly prepared for the best or the worst that might come.

When Lion Limb, in stentorian tones, gave the signal "fire! fire!" the deck of the gallant little schooner was suddenly all alive with the shouts of his merry men.

The first gun fired was under the immediate direction of Lion Limb himself, who had pointed it with deadly precision at the advancing boats.

The sudden roar, and still more sudden deadly execution of the grape and canister shot, for a moment appalled even the stoutest of the buccaneers.

"That's it, captain," said Harry Woodruff, "that's it, Captain Lion Limb, let the black-hearted cutthroats have another dose."

"Hurrah, boys, hurrah !" shouted Dick Hamilton; "we'll blow the land-sharks clear out of the water before we've done with 'em."

"Steady, my brave lads, steady; don't do anything in too much of a hurry. Don't waste your powder and shot."

"Stand by, my lads, stand by," said Harry Woodruff, with the practical eye of a sailor, "we have sunk one of their boats."

"They are dividing their forces, captain," said Dick.

"I see they are," Lion Limb replied, "but it won't do them much good; they are inclined to board us on both the larboard and starboard sides at once. Stand by, my merry men, stand by," said he, in a cheerful tone; "every one to his post, and be ready to repel boarders."

But the buccaneers also were excited to the very highest pitch of fury.

They never thought that the peaceful-looking and rakish schooner so near them contained so many men and such heavy guns.

At the first discharge one of their boats was smashed into atoms.

Those in it were for the most part killed, wounded, or drowned.

The huge boat itself capsized in an instant, and went down with both the dead and wounded.

When Nat the Don perceived the sudden destruction of one of his boat's crew, he raved and swore like a maniac.

"Fire !" said he. "Fire ! and blow all the young brats to the devil !"

All his boats fired their bow guns at the schooner at almost one and the same moment.

The sudden roar was awful.

Nat the Don look forward anxiously to see the effect of his shots, but he was fearfully amazed when he perceived that most of his shots had taken little or no effect.

"What is the meaning of this ?" he shouted out, with an oath.

"Can't help it, captain," said Bill Whetherby; "no man can lay a gun better than I can, but the sea is rising and our boats begin to pitch."

"Fire away, then, and do the best you can; pull in towards the schooner, and let us board her at once !"

And now the engagement commenced in real earnest.

The buccaneers, filled with desires of vengeance, used their best strength and endeavours to disable the schooner, but most of their shots flew wide of the mark.

The crews pulled away closer and closer towards the schooner, but as they did so numbers of them were slaughtered by the unerring aim of the guns directed under Lion Limb, Dick Hamilton, and Harry Woodruff.

"I think we are peppering the ugly rascals pretty nicely, captain," said Dick.

"Yes, so we are," Lion Limb replied. "But, except those who are actually employed at the guns,

let every one else hide under the bulwarks, and be ready to repel boarders; they are approaching us very fast."

"All right, sir," said Harry. "I find that all our lads obey me pretty willingly except that young Ted Rawlings."

"And don't he also ?" asked Lion Limb, smiling.

"No, sir; he's hopping about from place to place like a parched pea."

"Tell him I say he must keep out of danger."

"I have, sir; but he wants to stand on the bulwarks near to you, for he wants to see what's going on."

"Then, if he disobeys orders, give him a taste of the rope's end, that's all; we must have no disobedience here."

Poor Ted, who, though thoroughly disgusted with warfare in any form, was so much attached to Lion Limb that he insisted upon being near to him.

However, the action now became general on all sides.

The buccaneers signalled for help to their companions on the Blue Rocks.

This signal was soon answered.

Many other boats could be seen leaving the shore filled with armed men.

"What a lot of scoundrels there are there to be sure," said Dick, as he doubly charged his gun with grape and canister.

"The island shore seems to swarm with them, captain," said Harry.

"No matter, my lads; return gun for gun with the villains. I care not how many there are—the more the merrier."

"Aye; true, captain," said Dick; "you and I agree on that point."

"How's that, Dick ?"

"Why, sir, I means to say that we might as well finish 'em all off at once," said Dick, with a knowing grin.

"Just so; but, do you see that ?" said Lion Limb, pointing to the shore. "Why, the rascals have got a battery playing on us from the island."

"Why, so they have, sir," said Harry; "but, with your leave, captain, I'll soon settle them."

"In what manner, Harry ?"

"You'll soon see, sir."

And, without another word, Harry discharged a shell at the guns which were blazing at them on the island.

The shell coursed through the air.

Every one on board the schooner watched its flight with great interest, for Harry had the reputation of being a good marksman.

In a few seconds the shell descended, and was succeeded by a sudden roar.

Cheers went up from the schooner.

The greatest commotion was visible among those on shore.

In a moment afterwards there was a dreadful explosion on the island.

Harry Woodruff's shell had blown up the powder magazine of the buccaneers !

The guns on shore were quickly silenced.

On shore several wooden buildings had taken fire, and the flames rushed up to the skies in great grandeur and fury.

"I think they won't trouble in that quarter for some time," said Harry, who still continued to pour shot and shell into the wooden buildings and dismantled battery on shore.

"Well done, Harry," said Lion Limb. "You have given the rascals a taste of our quality."

"And so has Dick, captain," Harry modestly replied. "He has been sweeping the seas for the last twenty minutes, and several of the enemy's boats have been sunk."

"So I perceive, Harry; but I fear the rascals will not attempt to board us after all," said Lion Limb.

"Not much fear of that, I think sir," said Dick. "They have been reinforced, and, I am sorry to say, that we are running short of ammunition."

"Running short of powder and shot? How can that be?" said Lion Limb, in amazement. "We had plenty on board when we started."

"So we had, sir, but young Rawlings, who has just been down to the magazine brings word that part of the magazine is swamped with water."

"Have we been struck below the water-line by any shot, then?"

"Not that I knows on, sir; but that ugly-looking Indian——"

"Yokee?" said Lion Limb.

"Yes, Yokee; he begged to come along with us, sir, and I put him down below to hand up the powder and shot, and how the deuce the water has got into the magazine without his knowing it before this I don't know."

"It must have been by mere accident," said Lion Limb, "for I cannot for a moment think but the Indian is an honest fellow."

"Honest or not," thought Harry and Dick, "it may cost the lives of every one of us."

"If I had my way, I'd throw the dusky savage overboard."

"So would I, Dick," said Harry; "but you see Captain Lion Limb has taken a great fancy to the ugly brute, because Miss Emma Clarence has selected him as her servant."

"See to the ammunition at once, then, Dick," said Lion Limb. "It may not be so bad, after all. We shall have enough of powder and shot left to finish off these blue devils."

Dick Hamilton went below, and the first person he espied was Yokee, who, full of grimaces and eye-rollings, bowed before him.

Dick, however, gave that dusky hero a sound kick in the posterior, which hurled him headlong among a pile of blacks and iron-work in a dark corner.

Yokee groaned aloud at this indignity.

Yet his eyes rolled and flashed again with deep, dark pleasure, and he grinned like a huge ape at the mischief he had secretly done.

Dick and young Ted Rawlings dragged out a great deal of dry powder, and other munitions of war, which were quickly passed on to the upper decks.

When he had done this, he said to young Ted,

"You are fond of defending powder magazines, I know. It was you who knocked over so many of the mutineers who tried to seize the powder and shot on board the old 'Rattlesnake.'"

"I know all about that, Dick," said Ted, laughing. "I'd rather be below than above when so much business is on hand. It suits me better."

"Well, then, you cock your revolver, and sit down here. If any one dares to approach the magazine without proper orders, brain him."

"All right, Dick."

"And as to that Indian scoundrel you saw me kick just now, don't wait till he comes too near you; if he dares to do so, shoot him between the two eyes, and blow his brains out, if he's got any. I hate that dusky vagabond. He's a hypocrite and a secret enemy, Ted. I'm sure of it, no matter how much Miss Emma Clarence likes him, or Captain Lion Limb either."

"All right, Dick. I hear a dreadful row upon deck, at this moment. Perhaps you had better go and leave me."

What young Ted said was really true.

The booming and explosion of cannon had been regular and almost deafening on both sides.

But now loud cheers were heard from the numerous boats approaching to board the schooner.

Dick was on the main deck in a moment.

One of their guns had been knocked off its carriage and disabled.

Several shells had fallen on the deck and exploded.

Captain Lion Limb and Harry Woodruff were both slightly wounded by pistol-shots, and were bleeding from the left arm and thigh.

It was a momentous moment.

Nat the Don, and his fierce followers, exasperated at the strange misfortunes which had befallen them on sea and shore, were wrought up to a frightful pitch of fury, and burning with revenge.

It was but natural that these ruthless men should be furious.

Their storehouse and powder-magazine had been blown up, and were at that moment burning furiously, fanned by the wind.

Their small battery among the rocks, which had often been deemed impregnable, was destroyed and the guns smashed.

Several of their boats had been sunk.

Many of their men had been killed or drowned.

These, and other losses, exasperated the buccaneers up to a pitch of fiendish fury.

But more than all which angered Nat the Don was this.

The schemer had surprised and deceived him who had never been deceived before.

The dominion of the neighbouring isles and seas were about to pass from the inhabitants of the Blue Rock, unless they conquered and exterminated these intruders.

But that these "intruders," as Nat the Don called them, should be for the most part "boys," and headed by a boy chief, almost drove him mad.

With eyes glaring in madness, with a huge cutlass in the right hand and a black flag in the left, he roared out, again and again, in deafening tones, which could be heard above the roar of the battle,

"On, men, on! pull away, pull away! quick—quick! or every mother's son of us will be cut into pieces by these cursed convict brats, and their sailor friends. Pull away, pull away!"

A drunken cheer was the response to this.

His men used every endeavour, and strained every nerve to get nearer and nearer.

But the schooner slowly drifted away, and for a time kept the boats of the buccaneers at sufficient distance, so that their grape and canister shot should take better effect.

This manoeuvre annoyed Nat more than ever.

"Should these mere boys conquer him?" he thought, gnashing his teeth with rage.

"Should all the islands fall into the hands of Lion Limb," he muttered, "and he, Captain Nat, the Don, be subdued? No, never."

Several of the islands were not only very beautiful, but very productive and fruitful in the extreme.

Several of them contained fruits, flowers, rivulets, and the like.

Others were known to contain silver, gold, pearls, and precious stones in great abundance.

A few were inhabited by warlike natives, who could fight like heroes when necessary.

One island, not very far away, was said to be ruled and governed by Amazons of exceeding beauty.

Wild animals of all kinds roamed at large upon others.

In one word, the dominion of all these islands would fall to those who should conquer in this fierce sea-fight.

"And should Nat the Don, who had ruled long and without dispute, should he, who was called the 'Scourge of the Seas,' be subdued, and bend the knee like a slave to a *mere boy?*"

This was the thought that made Nat the Don feel so furious and demon-like.

"Who is that youth, Bloodhoof, that I see standing on the bulwarks of the schooner, cheering his men, and giving orders?" he asked.

"That is the brat of whom I have often spoken," Bloodhoof replied, in a surly, sour tone.

"Is that Lion Limb?"

"Yes, Nat, that is the lad."

"May I never live to see another day, then, but I'll cleave his skull with my own hands."

"He is flying the British flag, you see," said one.

"That won't do any of them much good if we once get on their decks," said Nat the Don, with an awful oath.

"They are tacking, and seem inclined to run us down," said Bloodhoof.

"So much the better, we can get closer and sooner," said Nat; "pull away, boys, and, when you strike her sides, all clamber up with speed, and spare no living soul on board."

"No quarter, mind, my lads," said Bloodhoof, in high glee. "No quarter, mind, we are fighting under the black flag. No one must rule the Southern Seas but us."

All this time the battle raged fiercer and fiercer than ever.

Hundreds of small shot were fired at Lion Limb, as he stood on the bulwarks of the schooner giving his orders.

But scarcely one touched him.

He was slightly bleeding from a wound in the left arm, however, and his clothes were all rent and torn from the shots which had been poured upon him from all quarters.

Yet he heeded them not.

He stood proudly and calmly, and faced the buccaneers with a pleasant, confident smile upon his manly face.

He felt confident of victory.

When the boats and the schooner got nearer and nearer, the guns and cannon on both sides belched forth death far and near.

"Board her, board!" roared Nat the Don, holding fast to the schooner with a boat-hook.

A wild cheer burst forth from the buccaneers as they now grappled with the schooner.

"Board—board!" shouted Bloodhoof.

"Up you go, men, up you go," said Bill Whetherby; "follow me."

"Follow me," said Bloodhoof, with cutlass in his mouth, climbing up the side.

"No quarter, men, no quarter!" roared Nat, clambering up also.

But, although a moment before scarcely half-a-dozen heads could have been seen on deck, now that the swarm of buccaneers clambered up on all sides, up rose the crew of the gallant schooner from under the bulwarks, where they had been lying according to Lion Limb's orders.

With a loud, wild shout they uprose, sword in hand, and assailed the buccaneers with great fury.

Lion Limb singled out Nat the Don for himself.

Dick Hamilton rushed forward to meet the ferocious Bloodhoof.

Harry Woodruff bounded in another quarter to confront Bill Whetherby, who was leading on his gang on the other side.

Nat the Don fired his pistol point blank in the face of Lion Limb, but our young hero seized his arm, and jerked it up; the ball tore off his cap but nothing more.

With the strength of a young lion, he struck Nat a tremendous blow with the heavy rammer of a gun and knocked the grim chief senseless into one of his own boats.

The fight on deck was now maintained with great fury on all sides.

Dick Hamilton fought hand to hand with Bloodhoof, and a fearful encounter it was. But just at the moment when Dick had run his sword through the body of his grim opponent, a shot struck him on the head, and he fell bleeding and senseless to the deck.

Lion Limb, with his eagle eye, saw how events were turning.

He jumped forward, placed himself over the fallen body of Dick, and cut down more than half-a-dozen of the grim buccaneers.

He used his sword with such precision, and did such frightful execution, that many of the rascals fled before him.

But treachery was at work.

One of the buccaneers, who a moment before had fallen, pretending to be wounded, rose upon his hands and knees.

He levelled his pistol at Lion Limb, who had his face turned away.

Our young and gallant hero might never have survived the villain's treachery but for a singular incident.

The faithful dog Dragon, who had been up to the present moment chained up in his master's cabin now broke loose.

The first thing the good dog did was to rush towards his young master, then fighting against great odds, and nearly surrounded by a band of buccaneers.

As Dragon bounded forward, instinct told him that his master's life was in danger from some treacherous hand.

Before, therefore, the villain could fire his fatal shot, Dragon flew at his throat and in an instant strangled him.

With jaws all gory, Dragon flew to the aid of his young master.

Some he bit by the legs.

Others he seized by the arm.

Not a few were upset, and several were seized by the throat.

"'Tis the devil!" growled some of the buccaneers "it is the devil himself in the shape of a dog fighting against us!"

Everywhere, when anything was to be done, did the good dog Dragon fly.

Numerous shots were fired at him—many a well directed cut missed him.

But in no case did the faithful animal miss his mark, and numerous were the curses which the defeated and wounded buccaneers hurled against him.

The fight on deck had now lasted more than half an-hour.

For a time no one could tell which party would remain masters of the schooner.

But the buccaneers, numerous as they were, were appalled at the immense slaughter which had been made among them, and fought their way back to the boats again as best they could.

Harry Woodruff had conquered Bill Whetherby single-handed.

Harry was not content with giving that villain a fearful blow on the head and then disabling him.

He did more.

He tied Whetherby hand and foot and would have thrown him overboard.

But Lion Limb forbade this.

"Keep him a prisoner, Harry," said he; "we have nearly beaten these buccaneers in fair fight, if they were nearly five to one; but all is not over yet until we capture their stronghold on the Blue Rocks."

"There is a gang of them still on board, sir," said Harry Woodruff, whose arm was bared to the shoulder, and whose cutlass was dripping with gore. "There is a gang of them still on board, sir, as you see yonder in the bows, and they are fighting like fiends."

"We must force them to surrender. Call upon them, Harry, 'tis useless to shed more blood."

"I have called upon them several times, captain, but they have exasperated our men so very much that I fear they will show no mercy to the black-looking villains."

"Is all right below, Harry?"

"I think so, sir; but a few minutes ago I heard some shots fired, and, as I passed the hatchway, I could hear young Rawlings dancing about and shouting like a madman, so I came to the conclusion that some of the rascals had intruded and met their death there."

"All right, then; there is no fear, I hope, for I have no doubt young Ted has been on the watch, and knocked the villains over just as often as they dared showed their heads."

All this time, however, the conflict continued on board.

Those of the buccaneers who were unable to reach their boats still continued to fight on with the fury of despair.

Many a gallant boy lay weltering in his blood, near where the schooner's colours defiantly flew in the breeze.

It had been the darling wish of the buccaneers to tear down the brave old English ensign.

When first they rushed on board, headed by their ferocious chief, they all ran towards the halyards to tear down the colours, and, in hopes of raising their own detested flag, they fought like demons.

But all their efforts were unavailing.

Wherever the villains made a stand they were assailed with such fury that the stoutest-hearted among the invaders stood as if paralyzed at the valour displayed by the youthful followers of Lion Limb.

But now, however, the conflict was nearly over; the buccaneers, for the most part, were only too happy to escape the carnage which had taken place among them.

"Surrender—surrender!" shouted Lion Limb to those who still hopelessly fought on.

"Surrender—surrender!" he cried, "we do not wish to shed blood uselessly."

An ironical and defiant cheer was the only response which this band of buccaneers thought proper to return as an answer to Lion Limb's merciful proposal.

"Surrender? No, never!" roared out one from among the buccaneers. "Surrender? No, never! Surrender to such a bastard brat as Lion Limb!"

"Fight on, men! fight on!" shouted another. "Never give into such vermin as these boy convicts!"

"They are getting frightened; this boy-leader is getting scared!" said another.

"Buccaneers never haul down their flag for mere boys!"

"Well, then," said Lion Limb, reddening up to the very temples, "if you are so insolent, when mercy is offered to you all—why, then, we must teach you better manners, that's all."

"On to them, lads, on to them!" shouted Harry Woodruff. "Their black flag still waves; you know what the skull and cross-bones mean, I suppose? Follow me!" said he, brandishing his blood-red cutlass and rushing into the midst of the fray.

Lion Limb, however, was the first one to lead forward.

His men followed to the attack with loud shouts.

The clash of arms was now more deadly than ever.

Lion Limb seized one huge ruffian, a German, and, at the first stroke, cleaved the head clean from his body.

Another one, who came to his companion's assistance, was run through and through.

Frightful scenes of bloodshed were visible on every hand.

Pistols, guns, knives, swords, and daggers were used on every side.

"Surrender, villains, surrender!" shouted Lion Limb.

This time, however, his proposal was listened to.

Most of the buccaneers were killed or disabled.

A few who still lived cast a longing eye towards their own boats, which were now far away from the schooner, and with bitter imprecations on the heads of those who had thus left them they threw down their weapons and gave themselves up.

All gave up their arms save one.

This one was a noble-looking youth, who, as Lion Limb approached him, said, with a smile—

"I shall not give up my sword."

"You will not, eh?" said Harry Woodruff, brandishing his cutlass with looks of vengeance. "You will not, eh? Well, then, I'll soon make you!"

He was upon the point of dealing the youthful prisoner a deadly blow, but Lion Limb knocked aside his sword.

"You will not deliver up your sword, you say?" said Lion Limb, sternly. "Why not, pray? Do you not know that your companions have all been defeated?"

"I do; and for that reason I will not give up my sword, except on one condition."

"And what is that, pray? A captive demanding conditions—who ever heard of such impudence?" said Harry, hot with rage. "Leave him to me, captain; I'll soon make conditions for him!"

"Throw the impudent fool into the sea!" said one.

"Blow out his brains!" another exclaimed.

"Hold your peace, men," said Lion Limb, as he approached the handsome and bold young buccaneer, saying, "What is your condition, then, young sir?"

"Why, simply this, Captain Lion Limb: I was deceived, grievously deceived in this affair, and shall not deliver up my weapon until you hear me."

"This is no time for talking, captain," said Harry, gruffly. "We can hear his yarn some other time. We must trim our schooner and make sail after those blubbers who have escaped from us in their boats."

"Quite right, Harry," said Lion Limb, with a smile. "Make things all ship-shape, and sail in towards the Blue Rocks; we haven't done with these buccaneers yet. Meanwhile, I will listen to what this young man has to say."

While some were tending to the wounded, therefore, and others clearing the decks and trimming sails under Harry Woodruff's orders, Lion Limb spoke to the young buccaneer thus—

"You acted very rashly in not giving up your sword; it might have cost you your life."

"I had no fear of that," was the calm reply.

"No fear?"

"No, Captain Lion Limb, not while you stood by."

"You reckoned, perhaps, too much upon my power among the crew."

"No, I did not. I watched you all through the engagement, and more than once saved you from an ugly cut aimed at you by some of the buccaneers."

"Indeed! And why so, pray?"

"Because from the first moment I saw you I liked you. As I have said before, I was deceived by Nat the Don, or I would not have joined him in his attack upon you."

"How could you refuse—how could you dare to disobey your chief?"

"He is not my chief," said the young man, smiling.

"Indeed!"

"In truth he is not."

"Are you not then one of his band of sea-robbers and cut-throats?"

"No, I am not."

"You dress as the rest are dressed."

"I know it, but I am nothing more than a captive among them."

"A captive?"

"Yes, nothing else. The ship I was sailing in to England was attacked by Nat Jackson's ferocious band and robbed. Some of the crew were killed, others were induced to join him as buccaneers; but, although he offered me a very high post among his band, I treated all his allurements with scorn."

"It seems very strange, then, that a young man with such high sentiments should have joined the ruffian, Nat Jackson, in any enterprize."

"I can easily explain it," said the young man, whose brow was now mantled with crimson.

"How so?"

"On board the vessel in which I sailed was a young and beautiful damsel, whose heart I had fairly won. I made known my passion and she smiled upon me with favour."

"A love affair, then," said Lion Limb, with a dry sort of smile; "such things seldom or ever trouble me. I have too much to do to find time to fall in love."

"That may be true in your case, Captain Lion Limb, but in *my* case I confess I was hopelessly in love. I had seen her in high society two years ago in England."

"High society!" said Lion Limb, in surprise and momentary doubt.

Yet after a moment's pause he said,

"I beg your pardon for smiling, but I confess your language and manners convince me that you are a gentleman, at least, by education, if not by——"

"By birth, perhaps, you would say," the young man said, with a light laugh.

"Such was my thoughts, I confess."

"Then let me assure you that I am a gentleman both by birth and education; more than that, I am a noble."

"Indeed!"

"Without a doubt; and I can give you every evidence that is necessary to prove it," the young man replied, proudly.

After a pause the young stranger said,

"I met this beautiful maiden, as I have said, in the best and the highest society at a ball given by the Countess Oxenford. My notice was directed towards her by Baron Templeton, who was there."

A crimson blush flushed the cheeks of Lion Limb as he heard the name of the baron mentioned.

Baron Templeton was the very man who had condemned him to die.

He sighed but spoke not a word.

The young stranger continued,

"There was some mystery attached to this young lady; reports were very rife concerning her, for she was the dead image of the countess. And allow me to say," the young man remarked, "I never saw such a striking likeness in my life as——"

"Between the countess and the young lady, I suppose?"

"No, *as between you and* Baron Templeton; an extraordinary likeness indeed."

Lion Limb laughed.

This was not the first time he had been told so, but he said not a word.

The young man continued, "This young lady, whose name was Jenny Lovedale, suddenly disappeared from society, very suddenly. It was said that she was an orphan, and that her only friend, the Countess Oxenford, had sent her away to Chili, to distant relations. I there sought and met her. I was bent upon marrying her, but in an unlucky hour she disappeared again, and whither she had fled I could not learn."

"Giving up all for lost I took passage in a sailing-ship for England.

"I embarked at a port in Peru, and, judge of my astonishment, when I discovered that Jenny Lovedale was also a passenger in the same vessel, and bound for England by the orders of the Countess Oxenford.

"On our way, as I have said, we were attacked by Nat Jackson.

"The maid was spirited away none knew whither, for the buccaneers had had several fights about her.

"Nat the Don said that she was dead; but I did not believe him.

"In his drunken moments he confessed that Jenny was taken to one of the neighbouring islands and given to a buccaneer chief.

"When your vessel came in sight Nat the Don told me that your craft was the one he long expected, for Jenny was on board, and if I liked to prove myself a man they would attack the craft and rescue the maid.

"Under this belief I joined in the attack, and from no other cause, on my oath."

"I fully believe you."

"And now that I have told you all, and the plain truth, let me say that I beg to be taken into your company of colonists; and I resolve to give up this sword, with your permission, to none until I have dyed the blade in the vile blood of Nat the Don or some others of the vile crew he rules over."

"Your face and open-hearted manner is sufficient to recommend you to me," said Lion Limb. "What is your name?"

"My name is Arthur Flaxman; my title, Lord Wraxmore."

"Then, Arthur Flaxman," said Lion Limb, with a smile, "for such I shall call you, since there are no lords here, you are welcome to join my island colony; all I require is obedience in all things. And as to your lost love, Jenny Lovedale, rest assured that if she is still to be found in any one of the numerous islands in these Southern Seas, she shall be discovered speedily and restored to you."

"Enough," said Arthur, with a flush of pride upon his brow, "enough, Lion Limb; you are as generous as you are brave, and in the unfortunate Arthur Flaxman you will find an obedient and willing servant."

Lion Limb shook him cordially by the hand, and told him to go below and change his attire as quickly as possible.

At that moment Harry Woodruff came up with a smiling face.

"Well, Harry, what is the best news?"

"The best news, captain, is that nearly all our wounded men and lads are doing well; and if I'm any judge of surgeon's work, I don't think that any of our lads will go to Davy Jones's locker this time."

"That *is* good news, Harry."

"Ah, sir," said Harry, with a sigh; "our lads are brave fellows, every one; lor! how they did let the ugly rascals have it to be sure. I never see such plucky lads in all my born days."

"But how about the wounded buccaneers, Harry? How do they get along?"

"Rather poorly, I hope; they don't trouble me, not a ha'porth. I wish all the rascals were at the bottom of the sea, that's all the harm I wish 'em."

"And how is Dick?"

"Oh, as lively as a flounder, sir, and takes his grog like a man. But we are close in upon the island shore; now, sir, what are your orders?"

"My orders are these, Harry; sail slowly and gently down the coast, and keep a sharp look-out for rocks and reefs."

"But ain't you going to give the varmint another thrashing, sir."

"Yes, but from what I have learned from one of the prisoners, I am certain that the buccaneers have some prisoners concealed in some out-of-the-way place, and I want to liberate them at once."

"You don't mean that, captain?"

"I feel sure of it, Harry, so therefore sail slowly down the coast, and when the black, hairy ruffians least expect it, we'll land, and attack them in the rear."

"Not a bad idea, sir; I see you are as good a soldier as you are a sailor."

Harry didn't like the idea of sailing away from the buccaneers' landing place, "because," said he to himself, "the devil's will think we're afraid on 'em."

However, he obeyed the orders of Lion Limb, and the schooner hugged the island very close for more than half-an-hour, and sailed a considerable distance from where the buccaneers had landed.

Nat, wounded as he was, fully expected that Lion Limb would follow up his success, and land on the Blue Rocks.

To prepare for this expected event, he ordered up every man he had to their old boat landing, and, after arming them, made every preparation in his power to repel Lion Limb's onslaught.

But when he saw the schooner sail away down the coast, he burst out into loud, derisive laughter.

"I thought we had taught them young ragamuffins a good lesson," said he. "See, they are sailing away quite satisfied with the dressing we gave them, the accursed convict brats."

The schooner disappeared from his view, round a headland, and Nat, followed by his men, repaired to their caves and caverns, bent upon having a deep carouse.

Lion Limb, however, and his trusty lieutenant, Harry Woodruff, were on the watch, and, as they sailed down the coast, they minutely examined with their glasses every object that came in view.

"We had better call up that young man, Arthur Flaxman," said Lion Limb, "he may be able to point out to us many things of interest that escape us."

"Not him, captain," said Harry, in disgust; "*he* can't tell anything if he's been a prisoner among them."

"Perhaps not, Harry; but at all events bring him on deck—nay, stay; send one of the lads for him, I want you here."

After a few moments' pause, Harry said—

"Ain't that smoke I see yonder rising in that little valley? it looks very much like it, captain."

"It *is* smoke, Harry, without a doubt, and where there is smoke there must be fire of some sort."

"Yes, and people also, if I'm not much mistaken."

For a moment, Lion Limb and Harry spoke not. They were intent upon examining the smoking object in the valley.

In the mean time Arthur Flaxman came on deck.

He approached unperceived, and stood close to Lion Limb, and broke the silence by saying—

"That smoke comes from one of the buccaneer's strongholds."

"I thought as much, for I can see no house or hut of any kind," said Lion Limb; "do you know anything of it?"

"No, sir, but I have heard Nat the Don whispering to some of his men about such a place."

"They spoke in Spanish, a language which none of them supposed I understood."

"And what had they to say about it?" said Harry, gruffly.

"Not much at any time, but I suspect there is great wealth of all kinds concealed there."

"Nothing else?"

"Perhaps some unfortunate captives, for all I know."

"Very likely; how far is it from the shore do you think, Harry?"

"About three miles, captain, I should judge."

"Then we will attack it."

"With all my heart," said Harry. "I dare say the ugly mongrels are in no humour to offer much of a resistance to us in that quarter."

"How far is that cavern from their boat-landing, Mr Flaxman?" asked Lion Limb.

"Well, sir, I have often heard them say in whispers that it was a good two hours' walk."

"So much the better, then, for us, Harry; we can land a party of men and attack the place long before the villains can assemble their forces and march to resist us."

"Well, then, sir, I propose that we do so at once."

"You will find it a dangerous experiment, I fear, sir," said Arthur Flaxman, "for it is naturally a very strong place."

"I care not if it were built of iron a foot thick," said Lion Limb; "if there are any prisoners there we will rescue them or die."

"That's the way to say it," said Harry, in high glee, "and particularly if they are Englishmen, eh, sir?"

"Just so, Harry. Englishmen will sacrifice anything to save their countrymen and rescue them from danger, for in this case there may be ladies for all we know."

"What! ladies!" said Harry.

"Yes, there is no knowing."

"Then by all the great gems in England," said Harry, with great earnestness, "I'll fight till I die in the cause of a woman. Yes, I'll shed every drop of blood in my body."

Harry was in great glee at the thought that there might be female captives on shore, and secretly made up his mind if any of them were handsome he would pick out one for a wife and make her Mrs. Woodruff.

"Yonder cave is a splendid place to run the schooner into, captain," said he ; "you couldn't find a better one. It is shut out from all view by tall hills."

"Then shorten sail, and steer for the cave at once."

Harry did not need to be told twice.

He gave the necessary orders instantly.

They were quickly obeyed, and the schooner quietly glided to the selected anchorage, and every one on board made speedy preparations for their expedition on shore.

The anchor was cast about half-a-mile from shore.

Harry Woodruff lowered a boat and took an armed party with him to reconnoitre the shore.

Lion Limb remained on board and during Harry's absence selected fifteen men and boys to go on the errand all had in view.

When the boys were informed of what was about to take place, they were very eager to be of the party.

Even the wounded begged to go, but Lion Limb could not allow such a thing.

Poor Dick crawled from his bunk and begged to accompany his young captain.

But he was too pale and weak from loss of blood.

In a short time, however, Harry Woodruff returned with the boat and in the very highest spirits.

"What news, Harry ?"

"The very best of news, sir ; we have gone on shore, and discovered a stream that leads up to the very spot where we saw the wreaths of smoke curling up."

Lion Limb received this information with a great deal of pleasure, because if his boats could approach the spot they intended to attack much time would be saved and perhaps a great deal of bloodshed prevented.

After some little time consumed in consultation, he decided to delay the intended attack no longer.

"It is true that we thought of returning to the island again," said Lion Limb, "and, therefore, what we have in hand must be done in double-quick time. We must not leave our islanders unprotected much longer, for doubtless Red Wolf, the cannibal chief, will have plenty of spies out, and might make an attempt to storm our camp and in one short hour destroy all we have been attempting to do since our arrival."

"You will find your present undertaking to be filled with dangers, Captain Lion Limb," said Arthur Flaxman.

"Not more so than our former attack."

"Perhaps not, sir ; but from all I could glean the place is heavily fortified, and almost defies any attack from without."

"Never mind, captain ; we can but try, and if we fail——"

"Fail ?" said Lion Limb. "There is no such word as fail ! Follow me ?"

So speaking, he ordered another boat to be lowered, and in a few moments all those who were intended for the expedition made ready and left the schooner and pulled ashore.

Now, there was one little incident with the departure of this expedition up the river which we must not fail to mention.

Young Ted Rawlings earnestly begged to go with the boats.

But this request was stoutly refused both by Lion Limb and Harry Woodruff.

Poor Ted for a time was disconsolate, and so great was his disappointment and grief that he was almost upon the point of blubbering right out.

"Hang Harry Woodruff !" said he, impatiently.

"He's always getting me into hot water, and won't let a fellow have any fun. But I *will* go !" said he, "see if I don't. But I won't let Harry know anything about it."

Having made up his mind young Ted armed himself with a revolver and cutlass like the other lads, and concealed himself beneath an old sail which lay in the bottom of one of the boats.

He kept perfectly still, and did not stir.

But it happened as the boat approached the shore Harry Woodruff stepped upon the sail, and feeling something very soft under his foot he lifted the sail and discovered young Ted.

Ted begged to be allowed to go up the river in piteous tones.

But Harry would not listen to him.

To send him back to the schooner was out of the question, for it would have delayed the expedition.

The only alternative was to leave Master Ted at the mouth of the river.

He was told to stay there and keep watch until the boats returned.

"All right," said Ted, as the two boats started up the river. "All right, Mr. Harry Woodruff, but you'll see if I do stay here until the boats come back. No, not me ; if you won't let me join the boats I'll follow on foot, see if I don't."

And, true to his word, Young Rawlings *did* follow on foot.

The resolve was a bold but a very rash one.

He knew nothing of the country through which he had to pass, and might fall into the hands of the very worst of enemies.

But this young Ted never thought of.

Follow Lion Limb he would, he thought, and nothing in the wide world should prevent him.

With this resolve he clambered to the top of a high rock, and from that elevation he had a good view of the river's windings.

He quickly descended, and began to follow the course of the stream.

In the calmness he could distinctly hear the oars of the boats not far distant from him as they pulled up the stream.

But, as the river was a winding one, young Ted took a straight course, and thus managed to keep up with the boats, whose route was much farther than the one he himself was taking.

Ted had not gone more than a mile when he came across a small, well-used footpath, on which there was but little grass.

"Hullo," he thought, "I must keep my eyes open ; there are people about here, or else this footpath would not be so hard and well defined."

Yet forward he went, revolver in hand ready cocked, and ready for immediate use.

Once or twice he thought he heard distant voices.

He hid among some bushes, and listened.

Could it be that he had been discovered ?

Or were these sounds from the boats ?

He listened again and again, still hiding behind the bushes.

At last, when he least expected it, he heard some one whistle loudly.

The signal was returned, but in a fainter sound, from the direction in which young Ted Rawlings had come.

"I am discovered," thought he.

He did not attempt to leave his hiding-place, however, but crept closer and closer to the ground.

At last the signal was heard again.

It was not answered this time.

But, instead thereof, a man ran up towards the spot where he was hiding, looking wild, haggard and breathless.

THE BOY KING
OF THE SOUTH SEA ISLANDS.

JERRY VISITS HIS VICTIM.

He was met by a second, who now appeared in view.

Young Ted began to feel very uneasy.

Both of the ruffians stopped in the footpath right

No. 12.

opposite to and not more than six feet from where he was crouched down.

Neither of them spoke for a few seconds, but shook hands.

They were breathless from running.

"I saw your signal, Dominic, and hastened to meet you."

"What news?"

"The very worst of news."

"How so? Come, hasten away to the cavern; all speed, or all is lost."

"Hang the luck!" thought Ted. "I shan't hear what they have got to say after all."

Young Ted had scarcely time to lift his head and take a good view of the two ruffians when he gave a sudden shriek of pain.

"All is lost!" he exclaimed, in a loud voice. "I am a dead man."

The sound of his voice grew fainter and fainter.

He uttered a loud groan and fell senseless to the ground.

A sudden grunt, as of some wild beast, was now heard.

The two ruffians for a moment were startled.

Then, with a loud laugh of triumph, they shouted,

"Ha! ha! a spy in the bush! Hang him! kill him!"

With daggers drawn, they dashed into the thicket!

CHAPTER XXXIII.

THE ATTACK ON THE SECRET CAVE — TED RAWLINGS AMONG THE PRISONERS — THE CHALLENGE ACCEPTED.

WITH frightful oaths and flashing weapons, Dominic and his companions rushed into the bush.

A savage growl greeted them.

They stopped for a moment, when, to their surprise, a savage wolf-dog jumped towards them.

"What, Viper," said the two ruffians, instantly recognizing Nat's favourite dog. "What, is that you, Viper?"

And they affectionately played with the huge native animal, who showed his white teeth, and jumped away again.

Dominic followed, and was astonished to find young Ted Rawlings lying on the ground, bleeding.

"'Tis a spy!" said Dominic. "Shall we kill him outright, or what?"

"No, don't kill him," said the other, who was called Lopez, "don't kill him. The dog has made a frightful wound in his shoulder, but he still lives. He is more frightened than hurt. Let us throw some cold water over him, and see who and what he is."

It was true what he said.

Young Ted was more frightened than hurt.

When he was suddenly attacked and seized by the savage dog Viper from behind, he made sure it must have been some panther or lion.

The savage grip had stunned him for a moment.

But recollecting himself, he lay perfectly still upon the ground.

For he had read somewhere in books, when at school, that the best way to escape instant mangling when attacked by wild beasts of any kind is to pretend to be dead.

This young Ted had done.

When the animal had bounded away from him to meet the ruffians, he recovered consciousness to some degree, and prepared to use his revolver, but just as he was about to shoot, the two ruffians ran to the spot.

To fight two men and a dog at one and the same moment was an undertaking that required more nerve and courage than young Ted possessed.

He had more discretion than valour.

He thought of the head-lines in his old copybooks, that—

"He who fights, and runs away,
Lives to fight another day."

This thought consoled him in his pain, and when Dominic threw a gourd-full of water over him, he felt much refreshed, and he lifted up his head, very slowly and cautiously, for he still felt a mortal dread of the glistening fangs of the wolf-dog Viper, and expected that that ferocious beast would each moment fly at his throat, and strangle him upon the spot.

And so Viper would had he not been held back by the strong hand of Dominic, the buccaneer.

"I only wish Lion Limb's dog Dragon was here," sighed Ted. "I should be safe enough; for while he settled this savage, Viper, I would let these two cut-throats have the contents of my revolver."

But the good dog Dragon was not there, and young Ted had to make the best of a bad bargain.

"Who are you?" said Dominic, kicking poor Ted in the ribs with his heavy-heeled boots. "Who are you?"

"Me?" said Ted.

"Yes, you, you young imp," said Lopez; "speak quickly, or the dog here shall complete his work."

"Me! Who am I?" said young Ted, looking very forlorn and pale. "Oh, I'm nobody."

"Ain't you, though?"

"No; upon my life I'm nobody."

"Then what brought you here?"

"My legs, of course," said Ted.

"Come, come, none of your saucy answers here."

"Life or death depends upon what you say, youngster," Dominic remarked.

"Do you know who you are talking to, eh?" said Lopez.

"To gentlemen of course," said Ted.

"I'm glad you think so," said Lopez.

"Don't you know who we are?"

"No, not in the least degree."

"Well, then, we are buccaneers of the renowned Nat Jackson's band."

"You don't say so," said Ted, as coolly as possible; "and who is Nat Jackson, pray? Never heard of him before in all my life. What is he?"

"He is the Scourge of the Southern Sea, a man who was never yet conquered on land or sea."

"But come along," said Dominic; "rise up; you must come with us, and we'll soon let you know who and what Nat Jackson is, won't we, friend Lopez?"

"Not much doubt about that. Come, come along, you ain't much hurt after all."

"I know what he is," said Dominic; "he's one of Lion Limb's gang of young convicts, and sent out to spy into the country; we'll shoot him when we have leisure."

"No, upon my word I'm not a spy," said Ted. "They left me on this island and refused to take me in their boats."

"Where have the boats gone to, then?" asked Lopez.

"Why, this young scoundrel knows as well as I do that they are on the way to our captive cave."

"The devil!" said Lopez; "you don't mean that?"

"I do though," said Dominic.

And then in a language which young Ted knew nothing of, Dominic told Lopez all that had happened, and of the disasters which had befallen the gang in their attack on Lion Limb's schooner.

Lopez was in a terrible rage when he heard this, and would have shot young Ted there and then.

But Dominic restrained him by saying, perhaps their captive might be prevailed upon to turn informer, and then they could gain very valuable information from him, which might help to lead and guide them in another attack which Nat the Don had resolved to make on Lion Limb's stronghold.

"What," said Lopez, in amazement, "is it possible that we have been worsted in a regular sea fight by that young villain, Lion Limb?"

"There is not the slightest doubt about that," said Dominic; "and to speak the truth, they gave us all such a thrashing as we never had before in all our lives."

"Were all our men engaged?"

"No, not all; but we had many more than they had; and it strikes me, Lopez, that this Lion Island on which the boy convicts and their sailor friends have settled will prove the downfall of the Blue Rocks."

"Impossible," said Lopez, twirling his rough moustachios in great anger. "What can mere boys do against such hardy fellows as we've got?"

"Well, you may have the chance of tasting their quality sooner than you expect, Lopez," said Dominic, with a dry laugh; "they fight like young demons."

"How many leaders have they got?"

"Three. Lion Limb is the chief, and his two lieutenants are named Dick Hamilton and Harry Woodruff. Bill Whetherby is a prisoner in their hands."

"Who told you all this?"

"We had a spy among them, an Indian who hates the whole colony; Yokee is the black-looking rascal's name. Lion Limb, I understand, saved him and several others from certain death, and yet Nat the Don has secretly bought him over through the cannibal chief, Red Wolf. Nat the Don has already laid a plan to kill Lion Limb with his own hand, and swears to accomplish his purpose, or die in the attempt."

"I never knew Nat to fail yet," said Lopez; "he is as cunning as a fox and as brave as a tiger."

While the two buccaneers were thus talking together, and hurrying forward to the cave of the captives, they suddenly stopped upon some rising ground and surveyed the windings of the river which were clearly visible.

"There they are," said Dominic, pointing out two boats which, in the distance, looked like small specks upon the dark waters; "there they are. Do you see them, Lopez?"

"I do," was the gruff answer; "but what can such a few as they do against our stronghold?"

"Not much, perhaps."

"Nothing at all."

"They must have some one among them who knows more about us than we expect," said Dominic.

And so in truth Lion Limb had.

For it must not be forgotten that Arthur Flaxman was in Harry Woodruff's boat, and, though the information he gave was not much, it greatly assisted Harry in the leading boat.

"They will be some time ere they reach a proper landing place," said Dominic, "so we needn't be in such a hurry; "if they find the cave, they must attack us at the great gate, for no other entrance is known to them."

"And, if they are foolish enough to do that,"

said Lopez, "half-a-dozen of us can fire at them through our loop-holed wall, and kill every one in less than ten minutes."

Thus congratulating themselves the two buccaneers left the spot, and left the river bank.

They had not gone far before Dominic led the way behind some rocks, and, walking up to an old oak tree of immense size, which was blasted by great age, and quite hollow, he crept through a hole and disappeared.

Lopez blindfolded young Ted, and led him forwards towards the old oak tree.

He thrust him through the large hole, and followed himself.

Ted had not the slightest notion where they were leading him.

But the truth was that a rough sort of staircase had been formed from the roots of the old tree, which led down an intricate winding way far into the earth.

After going a long distance, still led by Lopez and followed by the savage brute "Viper," young Ted thought he heard the gentle trickling of water.

This sound gradually increased until the blindfolded captive made sure that he was very near a stream of water.

He was not deceived.

He was actually walking along a small foot-path which had been formed out of the solid rocks, and beneath was a deep rivulet several yards broad.

In a short time they came to a small bridge which crossed this unknown rivulet, and light began to appear.

At a short distance a harsh, husky, and savage voice challenged those approaching.

Dominic and Lopez gave some secret answer, and advanced.

A large oak door of immense strength was now opened, and in half-a-dozen yards more the bandage was pulled from young Ted's eyes.

He found himself in a spacious stone chamber, which was but dimly lighted from above by several holes not larger than a man's hand.

"There is no escaping from here," thought poor Ted.

And he sat down, weak and wounded as he was, upon a stone bench and sighed.

The oak door he could hear had been shut to and doubly locked.

"I must be in one of the chambers for prisoners," thought Ted.

He looked around.

But the light was so dim that he was some minutes before he became accustomed to it.

He saw no one, yet he frequently heard sighs and groans.

"There must be some one here," thought Ted, "I'm not quite alone, that's one great comfort."

He peered as well as he could in all directions, and at last perceived several dark objects lying in the corners.

They were all gazing at him intently, and their staring eyes for a moment filled young Ted with fear, but as he crept closer he felt compassion for them.

"Unhappy youth," sighed one in English, "unhappy youth, are you also a prisoner here?"

"I am."

"And doomed to die," said another captive in a faint voice. "I heard the two men who brought you here speak together in Spanish, and your death was decided on after they had got all the information they can from you."

"He is a very pleasant speaking fellow," thought

poor Ted, sighing; "he might have kept such dismal news to himself, I think, and no mistake."

"What is the matter with these monsters, our masters, to-day? I have overheard much of their conversation, and they seem to dread an attack from some quarter. Can you explain this, young man?"

Ted could have told them much, but he feared there might be treachery among those who were in the cave with him, and so held his peace.

"If I say much I may be overheard by some of the black-looking villains, and in that case they would shoot me upon the spot. Besides, if I tell these captives here about Lion Limb's expedition, I may raise up hopes in their hearts which will not be realized, so I had better keep my tongue still. If Captain Lion Limb *does* rescue us all, well and good; if he does not, why they we must die like men."

For more than an hour these captives lay whispering to each other, but to all questions Ted Rawlings answered not a word.

The buccaneers who were in the cave numbered more than twenty.

They passed and repassed through this strong cell of the captives in a very hurried and excited manner.

What was apprehended by them no one could guess save Ted, and he pretended to be overwhelmed with grief and hid his face in his hands.

"If Lion Limb's men are successful in beating in this entrance gate, the ruffians will retreat this way and murder every one of us in cold blood," thought Ted sorrowfully.

At last one of the heavy doors opened, and Ted, with the other captives, could faintly hear the report of guns and pistols.

They could have danced for joy at this welcome sound, for it was plain to all that some one was attacking the cave.

But they dared not display the feelings which possessed them, for Lopez dashed into the cave, sword in hand, and looking more furious and ferocious than ever.

He cast a scowling look upon the captives as they crouched down to the ground in fear and trembling.

Then, approaching Ted, he seized that unhappy youth with his left hand, by the hair of his head, and brandished his cutlass with the right.

"Dog!" said he, "answer truly; how many men started up the river in those boats?"

"I do not know; on my oath, I do not."

"How many boats, then?"

"Two, I believe."

"You lie! only one."

"There were two, I say," said Ted.

"Then where is the other, what has become of it?"

"I know not."

"Where is this braggart boy, called Lion Limb, who boasts of having vanquished Nat the Don? Is he afraid of attacking us? ha, ha!"

"What can have happened?" thought Ted; "two boats started, but this villain says that only one has appeared to make the attack."

"The other boat may have met with some disaster," said Ted, "perhaps struck a rock and sunk."

"Good news; but let me tell you, dog," said Lopez, "only one boat's crew landed against us, and we have beaten them back, ha, ha! beaten them back like cowards, as they are. They could not break down our wooden gateway; they have been firing at it for more than an hour and done no harm; we are now going to sally forth and drive these young scamps to their boats again; and when we return let each of you expect the very

worst; every one of you shall be tortured by slow fires; we'll have no more sobbing and sighing."

At that moment Dominic entered, and all could hear the loud cheers of the buccaneers, who were triumphant.

"Do you hear that," said Dominic, to poor Ted, "do you hear that joyful sound?" said he, grinning at the poor captives like a fiend. "We have waited for the assault and repelled it, and now we go forth to exterminate every one."

"I would give ten thousand doubloons to fall across this Lion Limb, chief of the boy convicts," said Lopez, with a savage oath.

"He is afraid to face us this time," said Dominic.

At that moment, and while every one was intent upon looking at the angry features of Lopez and Dominic in dread of instant death or some sudden punishment from their brutal hands, the heavy oak door through which Ted had entered was burst open with a dreadful crash that startled all.

In an instant Lion Limb jumped through the rent woodwork, sword in hand.

He dashed towards Lopez and Dominic with a flushed countenance as he said boldly,

"Villain! I heard your challenge; here I am."

CHAPTER XXXIV.

EXCITING SCENES IN A MAD-HOUSE—JEM TRIES TO RELEASE ALLAN—THE LUNATICS ARE SET FREE.

"WE'VE got him out of the way at last," said Jerry, when he and his father, the old lawyer, left the private lunatic asylum and wended their way homewards together.

"Yes, at last," said the old lawyer, grinning.

"But won't the secret leak out, think you?"

"How should it, without you go and split?"

"Me? there is not much fear of *me* doing such a thing; it is more than my life is worth."

"I'm glad you think so," the old man replied, "and, now that this Allan Norman is out of the way, you must not forget to play his part well."

"No fear of that," said Jerry, laughing.

"But I *have* fears," the father replied, "and very great fears too."

"Why so?"

"You have taken to drinking of late."

"Not to any very great degree. But, suppose I have; don't all young gentlemen get drunk occasionally?"

"Very seldom, indeed," said the father; "from all my experience in life I find that your true gentleman is very temperate; it is only snobs, and those apish fools who think they imitate gentlemen, that get drunk."

"What would you have me do, then? Am I to act the part of heir to these estates in question, and still not spend a penny?" said Jerry, indignantly. "What is the use of money if not to spend it?"

"I did not say that you must not take a glass of wine occasionally."

"Oh, what is wine," Jerry remarked, scoffingly; "that's an old man's drink. I like something stronger; something that will fire you, and——"

"Get you a black eye, eh?" said the father. "You must beware of drink, Jerry; as long as you keep sober I have no doubt you are clever and cunning enough to evade all the enquiries and such-like which will be put on foot about this affair; but if you still persist in getting drunk, as you have of late, you might let the cat out of the bag, as the saying is; for you know the old proverb, 'there is truth in wine,' in other words, when a man's drunk he let's out the truth."

"No fear of me," said Jerry, jauntily placing his hat on three hairs; "no fear of me; I can play the gentleman with any one living. But, now I come to think of it, we ain't going to walk home, are we? I shan't, if you do."

"I don't see any cabs about, Jerry."

"But I do. There is one yonder. Call it."

Jerry called the vehicle, but the driver was so muffled up in his great coat that old Marks did not perceive that it was the same person who had driven himself and Edgar Norman but an hour or so before."

"The werry same parties," thought cabby, as he eyed them when they got in. "Both on 'em Jews; no, they ain't, though, the young 'un ain't the same; he's got too much of a nose for that handsome boy which came up with the old 'un. I wonder what they've done with that ere young party. To White-chapel, sir?" said he to Jerry, touching his hat.

"To Whitechapel? No! Why the devil did you ask us such a question for?"

"Beg pardon, sir, I though that perhaps——"

"You had no business to think, sir. I suppose you take us for Jews—Petticoat-Lane merchants, eh?"

"Beg pardon, sir," said cabby, as he drove off to Oxford Street. "Beg pardon, gents."

But he added to himself,

"If them two parties ain't Jews, why, then, I'm a Dutchman, that's all."

As the cab rolled along the father and son began to speak very loud and angrily.

So vehement were they in their remarks that even cabby could overhear much that was said.

"How much do I want?" said Jerry. "Why, I want one or two hundred."

"Two hundred pounds?" said the father. "Why, the boy must be raving mad."

"No, I'm not," said Jerry. "If I'm to play the gentleman, why, of course, I want money to do it with."

"But, I thought you were going to set up in business of some kind?"

"Business, eh? No, no; no business for me while the money lasts."

"But suppose I refuse?"

"You dare not; I tell you I *will* have it," said Jerry, with an oath. "Besides, I want to go to the races, and enjoy life. I must and will have the money."

The old man sighed and said something in an under tone, which the cabman couldn't hear.

"They is a couple of nice 'uns, I know," thought the driver; "they is quarrelling about the money already. Surely they haven't been cracking some crib up this way? If so, I must keep a sharp eye on 'em."

Cabby drove his fare to the corner of Oxford Street and the Circus, when both father and son alighted.

"Ain't you coming home, Jerry?" asked the father.

"No, the night is young yet," said Jerry. "I'm off to the Haymarket."

And he left his father standing waiting for a Whitechapel omnibus.

"I thought so," said cabby, who had been watching all their manœuvres. "I thought that hooked nose came from somewhere near the Lane. And, so the young party has gone down the Haymarket, eh? Ha! ha! he's a pretty article to go swaggering down there, and no mistake. Well, I think I shall go on the rank there myself. I might fall across the young 'un; he might lush a cove. I'm not up to much business to-night, and I should rare-ly like to find out the bottom of this nice little game."

He drove down Regent Street at a slow pace, thinking—

"If a four-wheeler could only speak, what a many tales it could tell, to be sure, and no mistake. Not long ago a pretty-faced party hailed me, and I took her to London Bridge; she hadn't got out more than three minutes when I heard a scream—it was all over with her, she had jumped into the river. Another time I carried two foreigners a long way into the country; when I got to my journey's end I opend the door—there was only one party inside, and he was dead! T'other night a lady left a large parcel inside. I goes and looks after her, but when I comes back there was sum-mut in the parcel a squalling. It were a fine baby! My old woman is very fond of the kid, through having none of her own; and a fine bouncing boy it is. Ah, if my old four-wheeler could only tell a tale, it would surprise a good many, both rich and poor."

Thus thinking, and feeling very desirous to know more about that "young party," Jerry Marks, cabby placed his cab on the Haymarket rank and went into a public-house to warm his nose with half-a-go of hot rum.

* * * * *

But let us return for a moment to the private asylum in which young Edgar Norman had been so cruelly incarcerated through the villany of lawyer Marks.

It will be recollected that young Jem Rawlings, "faithful Jem," as Allan used to call him, had been missing from his lodgings, and whither he had gone Allan could not tell.

But the truth was this:—

Jem stood in great awe of the very name of Marks.

He looked upon Jerry as the very incarnation of wickedness, and felt positive that neither father nor son meant any good towards Allan.

He therefore stepped from his lodgings, as sick and weak as he was, and watched the house of Lawyer Marks both night and day.

When he saw the cab drive off he jumped upon the springs behind and rode thus every step of the way.

When the asylum door was opened, he, un-perceived by any one, slipped in and hid himself in the room behind that in which the interview had taken place between the victim and the con-spirators.

He heard every word of what was said, but felt more dead than alive when he heard the astound-ing announcement that his friend Allan had been placed there as a lunatic.

He expected treachery from Marks, but he never for a moment dreamed that they could prove such very demons as they did.

To disclose himself would have been madness.

He, therefore, resolved to remain quiet, and if possible assist Allan to escape.

He wept like a child, but suppressed his sobs, and, when Marks and his son had departed, he began to revolve all manner of plans for rescuing his dear companion and friend.

"I'll do it if I die," thought Jem. "I know I'm only a poor, weak boy, but still I can do a great deal, and, before long, I hope to rescue Allan from this horrible place."

The room in which poor Jem had concealed him-self contained a sofa.

Upon this he sat down, and, while he thought of the best manner to carry out his kind intentions towards Allan, a sudden silence was observed in the adjoining room.

"Had he been asleep?" he thought.

In truth he had.

Poor Jem was so weak and ill, that he had fallen fast asleep.

In the meantime he now discovered that Allan had been removed from the apartment, and taken he knew not whither.

All was darkness.

He crept from his hiding-place, and entered the next room.

No one was there.

Thence he wended his way catlike and softly along a long gallery.

On each side of this gallery were numerous rooms.

He stopped at the door of one, listening.

Deep groans issued from the place, as if some poor creature was suffering dreadful agony.

"Could those deep sighs and dismal groans come from Allan?" he thought.

In a moment the person inside dashed furiously against the door, and began to kick and plunge in such a frightful manner, that it made poor Jem's blood curdle in his veins.

He crawled on his hands and knees to another door, and peeped through the key-hole.

It was moonlight, and inside Jem could see a half-naked man dancing and throwing his arms about wildly.

A third room contained a person who was preaching aloud.

A fourth had for its tenant a maniac, who was singing all manner of songs.

Wherever he went to, Jem heard and saw many things which thrilled his very soul.

"And this is the place," said he, half aloud, "to which they have brought poor Allan."

He made up his mind to go on through the whole building in search of his young master; but, just as he was about to descend the stairs, two keepers appeared at the bottom, with lanterns in hand.

They were just upon the point of going their rounds.

"Have you visited No. 4?" said one.

"Yes, and he's tumbling about his room worse than ever."

"I wish he'd break his neck."

"So do I, mate, for he gives us a deal of trouble. Dr. Shorthorn says that one of us should sit up with him all night."

"I daresay he does, but I ain't going to do it."

"Nor me, neither. Let's tell him that we have done so in the morning, and he'll be none the wiser."

"How about that wine which the doctor said should be given to No. 2?"

"Oh, I've got it safe enough. It'll do us a deal more good than No. 2."

"So it will; are you going to have a sleep?"

"Yes, I shall take three hours, and then you shall have three hours; the patients will get along quite well enough without any watching to-night; besides, the doctor won't know anything about what we do, he's in bed and snoring long ago."

"But how about that young fellow who was brought here to-night?"

"Oh, the doctor has made short work of him, I hear."

"How's that?"

"Why he fought and struggled so hard when he was got out of the stranger's reception room, that it took half a dozen to hold him."

"He's a strong 'un then?"

"Strong! I believe you; as strong, mate, as a young ox."

"And only a lad, too."

"Lad or not, he gave the doctor a black eye, and an ugly one it is, I can tell you."

"You don't mean that?"

"I do, though; he tripped one of the old keepers down stairs, punched one or two very hard in the ribs, and at last they were obliged to 'cage' him."

"Serves him right, the young rascal."

"They'll soon take all the pluck out of him in that place, I think."

"Yes, skilly, dry bread and water, and such like, ain't very fattening things."

The two keepers laughed in a suppressed manner and ascended the stairs.

Jem saw them coming, but did not perceive any means of escape.

He therefore crouched down very low in the deep recess of a door-way, and thought to hide there unperceived until the two keepers had passed him.

He had nearly succeeded in deceiving them when one of them said,

"Hillo! what is in that corner yonder?"

He had scarcely uttered these words when Jem rose up, and raised to the utmost pitch of excitement and fear, he darted at the two burly keepers, and so sudden was the attack, that he knocked both of them over and fled down stairs like some spirit swiftly and noiselessly.

Had the devil himself appeared to the two burly keepers they could not have displayed more surprise and alarm.

For a moment they could not breathe.

The breath had been knocked out of them.

They lay sprawling upon the floor like two stranded flounders.

Their lanterns were broken and the lights blown out.

"Did you see him?" asked one.

"I felt, though I didn't notice him," said the other, rubbing his knees.

"That's No. 30 for a sovereign."

"Not that young 'un that came to-night, think you?"

"No, it can't be him, for he's in the cage and safe enough."

"We must follow and capture him, at all events."

"And when I lay hands on him, won't I let him have it," said the other, doubling his fists, and swearing, "for he plunged his head right into my stomach."

Neither of the keepers very much liked the job of chasing the supposed lunatic who had escaped, but they went below armed with staves, and swore they'd break his head.

"He can't escape," said they, "the walls are too high and bristling with spikes and broken bottles."

Down stairs they went, hurriedly, and searched in every hole and corner of the large establishment.

But in no place could they discover the runaway.

The keepers did not desire to alarm the whole house, but went from place to place very quietly and steadily.

Master Jem, however, had given both of them the slip.

He ran down to the bottom of the house and finding the kitchen door open he entered and locked himself in.

He was dreadfully hungry and thirsty also.

So the first thing which Jem did was to go to the cupboard and help himself plentifully to whatever he found.

There was cold meats and vegetables in abundance.

Jem perceived on the table signs which led him to believe that some one had been having supper there not long before.

It was not the cook, for she had been in bed hours before or *should* have been so.

On closer inspection Jem saw a policeman's hat and gloves and truncheon on the table!

"Hillo," thought Jem; "some bobby has been here making love to cookey and the cold mutton without a doubt; but where is Master Bobby, I wonder?"

He did not stop to ask himself many questions but ate and drank as fast as possible.

When he had satisfied his hunger, Master Jem on tip toe went towards the wine cellar.

It was open.

Inside sat a policeman talking to cookey, who was helping him to some of her master's very best wine.

"He's got a good cheek at all events," thought Jem, and without any more ado he locked the loving couple in the wine cellar very quietly, and then began to yell and make all manner of dismal noises, which attracted the attention not only of the two keepers but of a sergeant who was going his round in the vain hope of discovering the missing policeman.

The alarm which Jem gave was of so sudden and startling description, that the sergeant made his way on to the grounds of the establishment, and with the two keepers proceeded towards the wine cellar, from inside which proceeded great knockings and thumpings.

"Some thief has been caught in a trap," said the sergeant, "but we shall soon secure him."

The door was forced open, and by this time Dr. Shorthorn and all his household were alarmed and rose from their beds. They got into the kitchen with another key and went straight to the wine cellar.

The door at that moment had been forced open.

"I give him in charge," said the doctor to the sergeant.

"I am a policeman," said the half-intoxicated captive.

"I don't care who and what you are," said the doctor, furiously. "You are a thief. I give him into custody, sergeant; and you, cook," said he to the weeping woman, "I give a week's notice."

"Come, come along," said the sergeant, "I must take the charge."

"Take *me*?" said the policeman, indignantly.

"Yes, you," said the sergeant; "so come along quietly, it will be all the better for you."

"You may take the charge as much as you please," said the bobby, "but you won't take *me*."

And so speaking he struck the sergeant between the two eyes, and knocked him down.

And now commenced a regular fight.

The sergeant and the policeman went at it hammer and tongs, and had what is generally termed "a slogging match."

Poor cookey, finding her sweetheart getting the worst of it, rushed in to rescue him.

She fought like a wild cat, for, having now lost her character, and being moreover a little the worse for the wine she had been imbibing on the sly, she hit right and left, not being very particular who she did or did not strike.

Dr. Shorthorn had two or three thwacks on the jaw, the sergeant's clothes were torn into ribbons, and still the fight continued.

A large house-dog had been let loose by the doctor, and, no sooner had he rushed upon the scene, than he began to bite and tear without mercy.

Knowing cookey better than any one else present,

on account of the many savoury meals which she daily gave him, he obeyed her readily.

And the first persons that the dog paid his attentions to were the two keepers, who, at that moment, were assisting the sergeant.

These two worthies were each bit in the leg, and went limping away, cursing and swearing most dolefully.

And the serjeant himself would have fared no better, but, at that moment, several other policemen, attracted to the spot by the noise, and thinking that all the lunatics were fighting for their liberty, ran to the assistance of their serjeant, and, in five minutes afterwards, the cook, her lover, and the dog, were taken into custody, and led away to the station-house.

* * * * *

But while all this commotion was going on, young Jem Rawlings had not been idle.

Finding that every one in the house were attracted to the kitchen and wine-cellar by the fight and noise, he made his way up stairs again, and, to his great joy and surprise, found a bunch of keys upon the landing, which had been dropped by one of the two night-keepers.

Without much ado, and with the greatest expedition, he went from place to place, and at last thought he had discovered the strong room in which Allan was confined.

He listened for a moment, and could hear some one within walking up and down and sighing.

He was now breathless with anxiety.

"Allan," he whispered, through the keyhole; "Allan, is that you?"

"Can it be possible?" said a voice within. "Can it be possible that it is you, Jem?"

Jem waited no longer.

He tried one key after another, and at last found one that exactly fitted the door.

He unlocked it hastily.

"Now," said he, "Allan shall be free again."

He entered full of joy and hope.

"Here I am, Allan; 'tis me, Jem Rawlings. Don't be afraid, it's all right, come, fly this instant."

But it was impossible for Allan to fly.

Inside the room, Allan was confined in a large cage!

It was of great strength, and their united strength, with the energy of despair, was insufficient to wrench out a single bar!

"It has a small door," sighed Allan, "but it is doubly locked."

"I have a bunch of keys here," said Jem, joyfully.

"'Tis no use of trying them, Jem," said Allan, with a sigh; "there is but one key which can open this door, and that key is always kept by the doctor himself."

"Oh, the deadly villains!" said Jem. "Then I fear that all hope is lost."

"I fear so, Jem," said Allan; "it is impossible to release me."

"At present, perhaps," said Jem. "But I'll tell you what to do. There is a window behind you."

"Yes, and six iron bars in it."

"No matter if there were six dozen."

"What would you have me do?"

"I'll tell you, Allan. When you are alone take off your shirt, tear it into very small strips, and form a line with it."

"Well?"

"Let one end of your line out of that window; tie your shoe or anything to the end of it, so that it shall fall to the ground."

"I understand."

"Well, I will be here to-morrow night about

midnight, and will place several fine files at the end of your rope. You know what I mean ?"

" I do."

" Well, then, little by little you can cut the bars one by one, each night, and when all is ready throw out your line again and I will attach a strong three-quarter inch rope to the end of it ; draw it up, and then escape is certain."

" I fear I shall be too well watched, Jem, to do all that."

" Never mind, do as much as you can. I shall be on the watch every night ; and when I find that line of yours dangling on the ground, I shall know all is right."

" But if all is not right, Jem, what then ?"

" Why, I'll wait for some dark night and clamber up the iron rain-pipe."

" It might be the death of you, Jem."

" No matter, Allan, I am resolved to set you free or die in the attempt!" said Jem, in a soft but determined tone of voice.

Allan extended his hands through the thick bars, and for a moment these two young and faithful friends were too much overpowered by their feelings to utter a sigle word.

But their mutual silence was far more eloquent than any words they might have uttered.

Poor Jem felt terribly cut up at the situation in which he found Allan, and could have shed tears because he was unable to liberate him.

" Never fear, I will make my escape, Allan, and have lots of revenge also ; good-bye."

" Good-bye," said Allan.

They shook hands again and again.

" I won't lock *your* door, Allan," said he, " for I want you to see the fun."

What this fun was is easily explained.

Jem, out of revenge, went to each door and unlocked it.

He had not made his own escape down to the lower part of the house more than ten minutes, when there arose strange shouts and noises from all parts of the establishment.

All the lunatics were loose !

In all directions they were running about.

Some were dressed, others were half nude.

Some carried chairs or sticks in their hands ; in fact, anything or everything which they could, and the greatest noise and confusion reigned on every side. Doctor Shorthorn was alarmed.

Whichever way he or his keepers and servants went, they were confronted by a little army of infuriated and screaming lunatics.

But Dr. Shorthorn was one of those men who, though they can talk bravely enough, are very careful of their own bodies.

When, therefore, he perceived some of the worst of the mad people approaching him, he fled down stairs and they after him.

The fighting now commenced on every side.

Such yells, and screams, and oaths, and stampings were never heard before in any place.

Allan understood it all.

He could see more than a dozen of the poor wretches dancing about the passage past his own room door. But he was unable to stir, and therefore contented himself with looking on.

Some of the mad people rushed into his room and danced around his iron cage like ghosts.

Some half dozen tried to tear down the bars and set him free. But the cage was too strong.

It resisted their united strength, and they rushed forth in all directions again.

How long this uproar and confusion might have lasted, no one could tell. The neighbourhood far and near was excessively alarmed.

At last a messenger was sent to the nearest police station, and a posse of valiant officers appeared upon the scene, truncheons in hand.

The police were very roughly handled, and more than one got heavy blows on the nose and in the eyes, but one by one the lunatics were secured and placed again in their respective rooms.

When the morning came, and all the establishment was in something like order again, Dr. Shorthorn wrote an account to the newspapers detailing the rascally trick which had been played upon him by some person or persons unknown, and he offered a reward of £100 to any one who should give such information as would lead to the apprehension and conviction of the aforesaid person or persons.

Now two of the most inquisitive readers of newspapers were Marks and Jerry.

When, therefore, Jerry read the account of a " Revolt of the Inmates of a Lunatic Asylum," and saw the name of Dr. Shorthorn affixed to the £100 reward, he became alarmed.

He hurried along homewards, and told his father, the old lawyer, who was dismayed at the news, and after a short consultation they decided to go at once to the asylum.

In due course Marks and Jerry arrived at the asylum, and were received with great politeness and courtesy by Dr. Shorthorn, who explained at great length all he knew of the late revolt.

Dr. Shorthorn led the way, and opened Allan's door. Allan sat within the cage reading a book.

Directly he saw old Marks and Jerry, he rose abruptly, the blood mantled to his brow, and his eyes shone like two burning coals.

The youth, who a moment before was pale and meekly looking, now made the iron bars shake as he clutched them, and trembled with rage.

" Oh, I see he is safe," said Jerry, with a grin, " it is quite a nice place for young silly villains such as he is." (See Cut.)

Allan, without a word, hurled his book through the iron bars, and struck Jerry on the nose.

" Take that, you imposter," said Allan, in tones of disgust ; " if I were only free for five minutes," said he, trembling violently with rage, " I would wrench your vile neck off."

" Take no notice of what he says," Dr. Shorthorn remarked ; " these mad people have strange whims."

" True, so they have," said old Marks, standing in the back ground, and attempting to smile ; " but it will be a long long time before this youth is cured, will it not ?"

" Oh, yes."

" For several years, perhaps," said Jerry, with scowling triumph.

" Perhaps not many hours," thought Allan ; but he said aloud,

" Marks, you and your son Jerry now triumph over me ; but remember, *my* hour will come."

" Raving again," said Dr. Shorthorn. " Oh, it is a clear case."

" Liar !" said Allan, and he shook the iron bars with such vigor that the cage shook again.

Jerry turned deadly pale.

Lawyer Marks started back.

But judge of the horror of all when, in a frightful fit of fury, and as if endowed with the strength of a giant, Allan seized one of the bars, and by main strength jerked it from its place, wrenched it out of its socket, and rushing out of his cage, with a loud shout, he flourished the iron bar in his right hand.

It was a horrible moment of dread and alarm !

LION LIMB

THE BOY KING
OF THE SOUTH SEA ISLANDS.

EMMA CLARENCE SAVES LION LIMB'S LIFE.

CHAPTER XXXV.

LION LIMB LEADS THE WAY TO VICTORY.

THE sudden and warlike appearance of young Lion Limb, as he dashed through the ruins of the broken gate-way, and stood before the startled captives, sword in hand, filled Dominic and Lopez with astonishment and alarm.

"Here I am," said Lion Limb, in a manly voice, and with a glittering eye, that cowed the rough and villanous buccaneers.

"Defend yourselves, villains; I would not slay you in cold blood."

Dominic and Lopez were bursting with rage and shame. The very youth they had been reviling in the presence of the helpless prisoners, now stood before them face to face.

The idea of a mere youth thus challenging them to mortal combat, and in their own stronghold also, was more than they could bear.

"Defend yourself, rash boy," said Dominic, gnashing his teeth, and rolling his large black eyes in deadly hate.

"Defend yourself, rash boy!" said he again, in contemptuous tones, and at that moment he would have rushed upon the bold, youthful intruder.

But just as he raised his heavy weapon, Dick Hamilton, and a party of volunteers at his heels, clambered through the broken gate-way, shouting heartily and fearlessly.

"Stand back, Dick! stand back!" said Lion Limb, never for a moment allowing his eye to stray from the object of his vengeance.

"Stand back, Dick! stand back, I say!" he repeated in an angry manner. "Leave this affair to me. Come, villains, draw; defend yourselves!"

"'Tis well that you crow thus, stupid youth," said Lopez, with a curling lip; "'tis well that you crow thus, when you have many to assist you."

"Would he were alone," growled Dominic.

"I am alone, rascals!" said Lion Limb, trembling with rage. "Not one of these my followers will interfere; they dare not unless I command!"

"Let me engage one, captain," said Dick, tucking up his sleeves, and grinning with delight.

"No, stand back, I say," said Lion Limb; "let not one of you dare approach; this is my affair, my lads, not yours. I heard them vaunting and boasting of what they could do and what they would do, if they only had the happiness to meet me. They were gibing and insulting these poor wretched prisoners here that you see lying upon the floor in chains and manacles, and, now that I stand before them, they quiver in every limb. They are poltroons; they fear the boy king they ridiculed a moment ago. They are not men; they are boasters, braggarts, and base cowards!"

"Liar!" roared Dominic, as he brandished his sword and approached.

"One at a time," said Dick. "If that black rascal Lopez dare interfere, I'll chop him into pieces."

"Stand back, Dick, stand back, all of you, I *command* you! The first one that disobeys me shall fall by my own hand."

These words were spoken in such tones that they could not be misunderstood by any one.

"Come on, rascals, come on, both at once! Come on!"

Without uttering another word, Lion Limb dashed at Lopez and Dominic with such fury and vengeance that astonished his own followers not a little.

The poor captives were almost struck dumb with astonishment at what they supposed was Lion Limb's madness.

The onset was fearful.

Except those engaged in deadly strife, all were pale spectators of the scene.

The clink of swords was quick, sharp, and almost deafening.

Sparks flew from their weapons on every side.

Both Lopez and Dominic, though excellent swordsmen, were baffled by the superior skill of Lion Limb.

They tried to do their very best to disable the intrepid young leader.

But all their plans were in vain.

The buccaneers swore often in a low, growling tone at their want of success.

But not so Lion Limb.

With steady eye and hand he beat back his huge antagonists.

He foiled all their attacks, and smiled with contempt at every attempt they made to take him by surprise.

More than once did he draw blood both from Lopez and Dominic.

But the sight of human gore only added to their rage.

They were too hardened in crime to feel faint hearted at the sight of a wound.

They fought on desperately.

Each moment, however, they were getting weaker and weaker.

Perspiration poured from every pore.

Their long black locks dangled in confused masses over their face and shoulders.

"That's it! that's it! Give it to 'em!" shouted young Ted Rawlings, in ecstacies.

"That's it, captain; let the brutes have it. Don't spare the fiends," he shouted, and clapped his hands with delight when he saw blood flow from the buccaneers.

"Cut the bastard's throat," growled Lopez to Dominic. "He is a spy; we owe this surprise to him. Cut him in two!"

Dominic, finding that he could not hit Lion Limb at all, made a side stroke at poor young Ted, which, had it been well aimed, would have lopped off his head.

But on the instant it was warded off by Lion Limb, and Ted's life was saved.

"Bravo, captain, bravo!" shouted Dick Hamilton, in raptures.

"That was splendid!" said a dozen voices at once, in admiration of the brilliant swordsmanship of their young leader.

But whether it was "splendid" or not, young Ted crawled away out of the reach of Dominic's sword, and contented himself with shaking his fist at the buccaneers as they fought on.

"Surrender!" said Lion Limb.

"Never!" was the gruff response of Lopez. "Nat Jackson's men never surrender to brats of boys!"

"What's that?" said Dick, red with passion. "Brats of boys, eh? I'll soon let you know what we are!"

"Stand back, I say!" repeated Lion Limb. "It is nearly all over now! I'll soon bring both the rascals to their feet!"

With extraordinary skill, and with a sudden bound, Lion Limb jumped in between Lopez and Dominic.

His cutlas flashed a single instant.

With a loud groan Lopez fell to the ground bleeding profusely.

A second blow brought Dominic to the ground, and he fell like an ox over the prostrate body of his companion.

Loud and deafening cheers from Lion Limb's followers made the cavern and its adjacent galleries echo and re-echo again.

"Follow, boys, follow!" said Lion Limb, flourishing his blood-red sword.

Another deafening shout was the response.

With swords, clubs, iron-bars, and axes, the boys followed Lion Limb, cheering.

Door after door was broken and smashed to splinters as they hurried along the dark stone galleries which led to the main entrance of the cave.

Distant cheering could now be heard from without.

"Stop!" said Lion Limb, to his impatient followers.

He listened.

"'Tis the buccaneers, I fear," said Dick; "they may have overpowered Harry Woodruff and his small party."

"There it is again, captain," said another.

"We had better retreat," said a third.

"Retreat!" said Lion Limb, scornfully, "retreat! No, never! Follow me! Let all cowards, if there are any among you, lag behind!"

Another cheer was now heard louder than all the rest.

"I knew it was Harry Woodruff's party," said Lion Limb, with a confident smile. "Follow me, my lads!"

Again the gallant boys, led on by their chosen chief, hastened through the long, broad galleries which had been cut through solid rock by the buccaneers.

Huge, heavy, iron-riveted doors impeded their progress time and time again.

But Dick and the strongest of his followers battered them down one after another.

Not one of the party had time to look and examine the successive caverns and large cells which they passed through.

In many instances not a ray of light was visible from any rent, and what these places contained, or had been used for, no one could tell.

The further they went, however, the more distinct became the shouts of battle going on not far off.

The more Lion Limb heard the cheers, and shouts, and oaths of both friend and foe engaged in deadly strife, the more impatient and fretful he became.

At last, with a torch, which Dick Hamilton had by accident seen and lighted on their way, Lion Limb discovered an iron gate, of immense strength, which retarded their further progress.

"This is the last obstacle, lads," said he. "If we only break through this one, we shall take the villains in the rear."

"Quite true, captain," said Dick, "quite true. I can hear them at it in the next cavern."

And this was true.

The oaths and shouts of the buccaneers could now be plainly heard.

With an immense sledge hammer Dick battered at the door.

He was assisted by others with crow-bars and other heavy implements.

But the noise they made was heard by the combatants within.

They now became aware that they were attacked vigorously on both sides.

Their rage now knew no bounds.

They raised a shout of defiance that was almost deafening.

Still Lion Limb and his followers worked on manfully and without fear.

When least expected, however, by the boys, the heavy door or gate suddenly gave way, as if lifted off its hinges.

With a demon-like yell, those inside rushed upon their assailants.

Guns, pistols, knives, swords, and daggers were now used on all sides.

Both parties fought more like fiends than men.

The buccaneers made sure that they would receive no quarter, and hence they swore to die sword in hand.

To add to the horror of the fight, Dick Hamilton's torch was knocked from his hand, and the place was almost in total darkness.

How the fight may have ended cannot be imagined, had it not been for an accident.

While Lion Limb and his followers stood shoulder to shoulder and back to back, fighting manfully against great odds, the buccaneers rushed hither and thither, and in many cases, struck some friends instead of foes.

For directly Lion Limb perceived the doorway fall, he gave orders to his followers to stand, as we have said, and not to stir.

By doing this they knew very very well that all who might assail them *must be* foes.

This plan saved the brave lads from much loss.

They could not well see what they were about, but had to *feel* for their enemies with their swords, and fire at random.

This mode of fighting completely foiled their furious foes, many of whom singly and in small parties rushed on to the weapons of the lads who thus formed square, and defended the doorway.

But better than all this, when the fight was hottest, Dick Hamilton stumbled and fell on the ground.

He was considered dead by both friend and foe.

He was trampled under foot, but spoke not a word.

He had fallen upon a small bag of powder.

The bag weighed about five pounds, and this Dick held fast.

He crawled through the buccaneers in the darkness, and approached the strong, iron-barred oak gateway, against which Harry Woodruff and his men had been fighting.

Dick placed the small bag of powder under a broken panel, and from thence laid a small train to the immense lock, which he stuffed with loose powder.

Having done this at the peril of his life (for the bullets of Harry Woodruff's party were pelting against the gateway in showers), he picked up a fragment of the torch smouldering on the ground, and threw it upon the powder.

Before he did this, however, he shouted out, "Down, lads, down!" and knowing that an explosion of some kind was about to take place, Lion Limb and the rest instantly obeyed.

In a second afterwards the gateway was rent in a dozen places; the lock was blown off, the doorway flew open, and daylight was admitted.

The explosion was so sudden and unlooked for, that several of the buccaneers were knocked down by fragments of the gate.

The others, who were as yet uninjured, stood as if paralyzed.

But a moment afterwards the destruction was visible to all, and the fight was renewed with increased fury.

Dick Hamilton, directly the gate was destroyed, rushed forth into the open ground, and waved his cap to those outside.

He was immediately recognised by Harry Woodruff's party, who, not knowing Lion Limb's great success inside, for a moment imagined that the buccaneers themselves had met with some disaster, and had accidentally set fire to their powder.

When Dick, however, with stentorian lungs, shouted to them, they rushed forward with all speed, and ran into the great stronghold of their enemies.

Never were men more surprised than the buccaneers were when they found themselves attacked both in front and rear.

With a wild shout, the lads of both parties closed upon the foe, and, in a few moments, their enemies were all killed or made prisoners.

" Three cheers for Lion Limb !" shouted Dick, all powder-blackened and gory.

" Nine times nine !" roared a dozen, waving their swords, and shaking hands with one another.

Cheers and shouts without number were now indulged in by the boys, and the caverns echoed back the noise again and again.

" Where is Tom ?"

" Where is Ralph ?"

" Anybody know where Ted is ?"

Asked one and another, as they hurriedly inquired for their friends, fearful that some accident might have befallen them in battle.

" Where is Ted Rawlings ?" asked Lion Limb ; " I've not seen him for half-an-hour or more ?"

" Nor I either, captain," said Dick. " I think the stroke that Dominic made at him has given the young rascal a headache."

" He's not very fond of fighting if he can get out of it," said Harry, laughing.

" Let Master Ted alone," said Dick ; " no harm will ever befal him, if he can help it."

Thus spoke one and another, as they tapped a barrel of wine which was in the place, and helped themselves after their hard fight.

But where, again let us ask, was young Master Rawlings during all this bloody fray ?

The next chapter will show.

CHAPTER XXXVI.

TED RAWLINGS IN HIS GLORY—HIS REGAL CROWN.

MASTER RAWLINGS, the instant Dominic and Lopez were knocked senseless to the floor, and could not harm him any more, raised himself out of a corner in which he had been hiding, and began to caper about like a half wild monkey just released from a cage.

He thought at first to follow Lion Limb and the other lads.

But on second thoughts he turned back again out of the dark gallery into which he had entered, saying—

" Oh, it's no use of me troubling myself, I've had enough of fighting for some time to come. I shall go back, and look after the captives."

When he re-entered the cell, he found several of the poor prisoners already trying to free themselves from their chains and cords, and assisted them to the best of his ability.

But now and then Master Ted would give a very suspicious side look at Dominic and Lopez, both of whom were bleeding and groaning.

" I daresay there is any amount of gold and diamonds, and them sort of things hid away somewhere hereabouts. I'll help myself before any of our lads return."

With this resolve, Master Ted allowed the captives to shift for themselves as best they could, and set about looking for hidden treasures.

The very first place he tried was the capacious pockets of Dominic.

He approached that prostrate ruffian, however, very cautiously and slowly, much like a mouse when entering a trap.

Once or twice Dominic groaned, and Master Ted took hasty strides away.

But, getting bolder, he creeped up again, and pulled a large gold watch out of Dominic's pocket, and stood looking at it in raptures.

" Oh, ain't this fine, though ?" said Ted. " I'll search again."

He next approached Lopez, and quietly loosened a massive gold chain which hung around his neck.

" This isn't bad either," thought Ted. " I'll dive into their pockets again."

He did so, but found nothing, and was so annoyed at his disappointment that he kicked Lopez.

Lopez opened his eyes, and grumbled out an oath in such a tone that the next moment Master Ted darted out of the cavern like a shot.

" The ugly-looking villains are not dead after all," he said.

But, still he didn't like to look at their revengeful eyes any more, and so groped his way along a gallery, and at last fell down a flight of six steps.

His fall was very sudden and painful.

His watch was broken and his nose came in violent contact with a door at the bottom of the steps, which made Master Ted wince again with pain.

" I didn't know anything about these dark steps," he grumbled. " Why couldn't some one have told me ?"

But Ted was in luck.

His fall had shaken the door very much, and, to the young urchin's delight, it opened at the slightest push.

Ted was astonished.

It was a sort of cellar lighted from above by a small hole in the rock.

On every side were bundles and bales and casks and boxes.

Some rude shelves formed by the inequalities of the rocks, were piled up with jars and bottles and cans, with a thousand other things too numerous to mention.

" Oh, ain't this fine ?" said Ted, rubbing his hands. " This is a store-room, and contains plenty of everything ; its makes a fellow hungry to think of it."

In a trice Ted began to open first one thing and then another, and discovered biscuits, potted meats, preserved fruits, and many pleasant things.

" Oh, ain't this jolly, though ?" said he, knocking off the neck of what appeared to be a wine-bottle. " Here's a bottle of old port wine ; here goes."

And, without much reflection, Master Ted swallowed more than a gill of what the bottle contained before he discovered that it was nothing else but the vilest vinegar.

With a vengeance he dashed the bottle on the ground, and twisted his face into a thousand shapes.

He placed both hands upon his stomach, and was seized with acute pains.

" Why the deuce didn't I smell it first ?" he sputtered, and wriggled and writhed with stomach pains.

However, Ted's patience was fully rewarded.

He at last discovered several bottles of genuine wine, and drank freely.

" Ah ! that's something like," said Ted, smacking his lips. " I can feel this stuff creeping round my toe-nails, and I could slay all the buccaneers that ever were. No wonder those ugly devils fight hard, when they have such wine as this to live on."

What with eating and drinking, Master Ted allowed the time to pass very merrily.

He sang several songs to himself, and drank his own very good health so very often, that ere long he had finished one bottle and commenced to pay his respects to a second.

" This is the way I like to do it," said he, half tipsy. " Let those fight who like it—I don't ; and let those drink good wine who can get it—that's *me*. Brayvo, Ted ! brayvo for you, my boy ! If Captain Lion Limb likes to get his head broke, why, let him, say I ; and if I like to stay here out of the way, why, that's *my* business, and no one else's. These are my sentiments, and I don't care who knows it."

For a full hour did Master Edward Rawlings feed and stuff himself with the good things he found stowed away in this out-of-the-way store-room, until at last the foolish boy became well-nigh intoxicated.

With a swaggering gait he rose, and, greatly to his joy, discovered a bran-new suit of clothes, of a half-Spanish, half-Mexican pattern.

All the articles of attire were much too large for him.

But of this he took no notice.

All the things were richly embroidered with gold lace, and the broad-brimmed sombrero had a large feather.

"Ah!" thought Ted, "this is very lucky indeed. I will dress myself in these clothes, and will then go forth on a voyage of discovery, and see what else I can find."

Master Ted, with much difficulty, dressed himself in the newly found clothes, and put on the sombrero with a great air of gallantry.

The long plume tickled Ted's fancy amazingly.

"What would the English girls think of me now," he sighed, "wouldn't they stare though?"

No doubt if any English girl had seen Master Rawling's that moment, they would not only have stared, but without a doubt must have burst out laughing.

For, if the truth must be told, the clothes were not only too big for him, but his face was smeared with dirt, gun-powder, and blood.

His nose looked very red, and was swollen to thrice its ordinary size.

However, he picked up a rusty old sabre that lay in a corner, and, with a bottle of wine in his left hand, he mounted the steps, chanting the fag end of an old drinking song, thus—

> "With my pipe and my glass,
> And a merry little lass,
>   I'd live contented here, here, here!
> For brandy, rum, or wine,
> I never would repine,
>   But enjoy my English cheer, cheer, cheer—
>   Roast beef and good British beer!"

When Master Ted had delivered himself of this doggrel several times, and repeated again and again the line,

> "Roast beef and good British beer, beer, beer!"

he wended his way towards the cell in which he had left the captives.

The bodies of Dominic and Lopez were no longer there.

What had become of them he knew not, and cared but little.

The captives, however, had for the most part released themselves from their bonds, and were now seated together eating and drinking.

When Master Ted swaggered in towards them no one moved, but went on devouring what was before them.

This want of courtesy on their part greatly annoyed Master Ted, who, as well as he could, staggered to the group, and flourishing his rusty sabre, shouted—

"How now, knaves! What mean you by this behaviour? Know you not who I am? I am king of this island, and no mistake about it! I am king of the Blue Rocks! Down on your knees, slaves, and do homage to your king!"

At first the captives smiled at the grotesque figure before them, and took no notice of him.

But Ted was getting angry, and roared out—

"What, are these dastardly captives to disobey Lion Limb's chosen and favourite lieutenant?

Down on your knees, slaves, and swear allegiance, or, by this good sword, I'll slay every man of you!"

At the bare mention of Lion Limb's name the captives instinctively fell upon their knees and bowed very meekly.

"Ha, ha, knaves, you know me now, do you? You recognise your king at last, eh? Well, then, crown me at once—crown me king of the Blue Rocks, and swear allegiance to me and no one else! Hang Lion Limb and everybody else! I was born to be a king, and a king I'll be, in spite of every one!" said Master Ted, half tipsy.

According to Ted's directions, some of the captives proceeded to the store-room and brought forth several dozen bottles of good wine and spirits of all kinds.

As nothing else was to be had conveniently, one or two of the captives procured some dry sea-weed and rushes.

With these a rough sort of crown was made and placed on Ted's head, who, seated on a stool, was singing snatches of all sorts of songs.

"Now for the oath of allegiance," said he, reeling from the effects of the wine he had taken. "Knock off the necks of your bottles, and, kneeling on one knee, swear to obey me in all things."

"We swear!" said more than half-a-dozen who were almost drunk; "we swear!"

"That's it," said Ted, "swear away until I say stop."

Several times Ted's newly-made subjects swore to serve him as their king and master, and all was progressing very favourably with Master Rawlings, who was in the midst of a song, when a rough voice behind said,

"Seize him."

It was Lion Limb and his followers returning from their combat.

"Seize the stupid youth and bind him hand and foot."

When Ted heard these words he was sobered in a moment.

He fell from his throne to the floor as helpless as a bundle of rags.

"Mercy, mercy, captain!" said poor Ted, "I was only larking, 'pon my word I was."

"Seize him," said Lion Limb.

"Bind him hand and foot, my men," said Dick; "we'll hang him for half-an-hour by way of experiment; out of fun, you know."

"He is creating mutiny," said one, "and deserves punishment."

"He wants to put himself up for king and desert Captain Lion Limb."

"He has been stealing all manner of things from the store-rooms, and been ill-treating the poor captives," chimed in several.

Poor Ted was in great agony.

He knew that he had done wrong, and felt certain that Captain Lion Limb would punish him for disobedience.

It was with much difficulty, therefore, that Dick and others got Master Ted to the boat, for his legs were too weak to carry him; and when he got there, he tumbled into it head first and remained at the bottom moaning and groaning, for he felt certain "that his head would split in two," he said.

Leaving one of the boats behind with a strong guard to bring away everthing that was of value, Lion Limb and the captives went down the stream in his own boat, and made as much haste as possible to reach his gallant little schooner and place the captives in a place of safety.

His arrival on board was hailed with cheers by

his trusty followers, and ere many minutes the poor half-starved captives were properly cared for, and Lion Limb thought of departing again in the boat to assist in bringing on board the plunder which had been taken from the cave.

"He's taking great care of these poor half-famished devils," said Master Ted; "but I suppose Captain Lion Limb has forgotten all about me."

"Oh! no he hasn't," said Harry, ironically.

"Well, if he can give good beds and the best of food to them, I think he oughtn't to forget *me* altogether."

"Never fear," said Harry, grinning. "You will be taken great care of."

"How do you mean?"

"You are a prisoner."

"The deuce I am!"

"Not a doubt about it, and I have already been told what to do with ye."

"And what is that, pray?"

"Put you down below."

"Down below?"

"Yes; and why not, you were guilty of disobeying orders."

"Was I though, and how, pray?"

"Why, instead of fighting or doing your duty like a man, you went off prowling about and getting half tipsy."

"Is that all?"

"And quite enough too. I think you know how strict our young captain is; if one disobeys, all will do so in time."

"And do you mean to say that Captain Lion Limb intends to put me down below, and keep me on bread and water?"

"I do, until such times as the court-martial shall sit and decide your case, my boy."

"That's rather hard," grumbled Ted, who now began to think he had got into a mess. "What's the use of fighting if one doesn't have a lark once in a while?"

Poor Ted was conducted below and placed in the same place as Yokee.

"This is all your fault, Yokee," said Ted, jabbering to the Indian as well as he could, "and I've a jolly good mind to punch your head."

Yokee didn't speak, but rolled his dark eyes about in a sullen, revengeful manner, until at last he could stand Ted's taunts no longer.

He rose and gave young Rawlings a sound spank on the jaw which made that youth howl again.

Neither of them had weapons of any kind, and so they fought hand and foot in the most uproarious manner for some time, until at last the cell door was opened, and Harry Woodruff threw a couple of pails of water over them both.

"That will cool both on ye," said Harry, grinning; "I dare say it's nice and warm in there, so if you don't want any more of my polite attention with these two buckets you'll keep quiet."

The water effectually stopped both Yokee and young Ted in their pugnaciousness, and they sat dripping from head to foot like half-drowned rats.

Meanwhile, however, Dick Hamilton and the other boat party had now returned to the schooner, and ere long the pretty fast-sailing craft was on her way homewards across the blue waters, and left Blue Rocks far behind.

There was much to do on board, however.

The sick and wounded had to be cared for, the booty had to be sorted and divided, and several large holes in the ship's side had to be repaired, and some torn sails replaced with new ones.

In a few hours, however, after they weighed anchor from the Blue Rocks, all on board were happy and merry.

The wounded were carefully provided for, and every one on board felt a just pride in the part they had had in the two desperate engagements with the buccaneers.

"Keep a good look-out, Dick," said Lion Limb, as they bowled along before the wind at a rapid pace. "Keep a good look-out, Dick, for, if I'm not very wrong in my reckoning, we shall soon be in sight of home."

"We are in sight now, sir," said Dick, in a low, tremulous voice.

"What's the matter, Dick," said Lion Limb, as Dick descended to the deck from aloft. "What's the matter? Do you see anything dangerous ahead?"

"I don't know what it is, captain," said Dick, "but if you'll only let me have the helm while you go aloft and see for yourself, captain, I should feel much more satisfied."

There was something in Dick's manner which alarmed Lion Limb.

With wonderful agility he clambered aloft, and, shading his eyes, looked towards their island home, which was just visible on the horizon.

"Can it be the effect of sun-light, or what is it?" thought Lion Limb in doubt. "I never saw such a sight in my life before."

He gazed intently and long, before he could make up his mind as to what the strange and unexpected sight might be.

Directly over their island home hung dense masses of black smoke, which rolled away slowly.

Now and then could be seen a faint light, running like a streak of gold between these heavy black clouds and the tops of the trees.

Now this streak of fire would appear red, then gold, and immediately afterwards a silver colour to the eye, and then quickly change to a dark blood colour.

The schooner was yet a considerable distance away from the island, and this beautiful sight, whatever it might be, was still a mystery to Lion Limb.

"If that beautiful sight frightened you, Dick," said Lion Limb, smiling, when he reached the deck, "I shall say you have no eye to the beauties of nature."

"Nay, captain, I have seen such sights before."

"It is simply the effect of sunlight."

"Nay it isn't, captain," said Dick, moodily.

"What else then?"

Dick seemed to decline any answer.

But at last, with a choking sensation in his throat, he said hoarsely,

"It's all the doings of Red Wolf and his bloodthirsty Indians, captain."

"Red Wolf! what mean you, Dick?"

"I mean this, master; the black scoundrels, because they can't fight us fairly, like men, have taken the notion to burn us out?"

"What!"

"Quite true, sir; what you saw and what I saw, sir, is nothing else but the woods on fire; the villains have made up their minds to force us from this island by burning us out like rats."

This announcement was received with looks of horror by young Lion Limb.

In a moment afterwards, however, he seized his telescope and went aloft once more with Harry Woodruff.

"There ain't any mistake about it, sir," said Harry, "the island is on fire; the winds are blowing the flames towards our camp; all our friends will be burnt alive if we ain't quick."

But what could they do?

"Poor Emma," thought Lion Limb, "it was wrong for me to leave her alone and unprotected," and for the first time in his whole life, Lion Limb turned pale and bit his lip in annoyance if not pain.

Soon the news spread on board the schooner in whispers, "The island is on fire!"

CHAPTER XXXVII.
LION LIMB TO THE RESCUE.

"OH if we only had a fair wind," said Dick, as he looked towards the island, "how I should like to jump ashore and have a turn hand to hand with those ugly devils."

"And I, also," said Harry; "if I only get my foot on dry land, I'll never rest till I kill half a dozen of them."

"Here comes the wind, right abeam, sir," said Dick, as he perceived a change that was favourable. "Who'd a thought the wind would have changed so quickly?"

"Put up every stitch of canvas she can carry, my lads," said Lion Limb; "we must take advantage of this change in our favour and not allow a gust to pass us by."

"Never fear, sir," answered a dozen voices, "never fear, sir, the schooner shall carry every yard of canvas that she can, you may depend, captain."

"This is what I call bowling along, sir," said Harry, with a bright countenance, "our schooner is doing seventeen or eighteen knots, or you may hang me."

"Keep her up to the wind, Dick," said Lion Limb; "don't let her fall off half a point for anything."

"No fear, sir; I'll keep her right up in the wind's eye."

The waves now began to dash against the schooner's sides, and lashed the gallant craft as she sped through the foamy waves, while now and then she shipped a heavy sea, and plunged ahead at a rapid rate.

"This will do very nicely," said Dick, at the helm; "I can scarcely hold her, sir."

"Never mind, stick to her, Dick," said Harry; "if the wind only holds good for another half hour we shall be close in shore, and then devil take Red Wolf and his gang for all I care."

But the wind, which had so suddenly veered round and drove the schooner along at a fearful pace through the boiling waters, was very unfavourable to the fire on the island.

This was perceived by all on board, and they hailed the fortunate change with loud cheers.

"Bravo, bravo! we shall soon cast anchor in a snug harbour," said Harry, "and when we do, lads, let each and every one arm himself, and prepare for a jolly good fight with the bloodhounds under Red Wolf."

This announcement greatly pleased all the crew, who were now incensed and infuriated against the islanders for their base treachery and cowardice.

As the schooner approached nearer and nearer to the shore Lion Limb could plainly perceive signals of distress flying.

With his telescope he saw several small parties of his followers assembled round one of his log houses, and seemed prepared to defend their camp against all who might approach to assail them.

In a conspicuous place he saw Emma Clarence waving a flag, and holding in her hand a small light rifle which she could use with deadly effect.

On every side those on board could perceive the effects of the ravages which the fire had made.

But, strange to say, the camp itself was not touched, and remained almost in the same state of order and cleanliness as it did when the schooner had set sail on its expedition against Nat Jackson's buccaneers on the Blue Rocks.

This was all owing to Lion Limb's prudence.

Although he had never dreamt of the Indians or any others behaving so treacherous towards him and his followers, this wise act and prudent forethought saved the camp from total destruction.

The fire had actually burnt every tree near to them, but having nothing further to feed upon, its ravages were confined within a certain limit, beyond which it could not go.

Faint cheers from those on shore were heard by those on board, and lusty shouts were given in return.

Guns were fired on shore in token of safety, and ere long the schooner, skirting the land as closely as possible, fired several shells into the woods far and near among hordes of savage wretches, who were only too eager to rush upon the defenceless colonists, and massacre them.

The shells were well aimed, however, by Lion Limb.

The savages saw them coming, but had no idea of their deadly effect.

When one or two, however, fell among them, and exploded, some of the half-naked rascals took to their heels with all speed.

Again and again did Lion Limb fire round shot and shell at the savages; but some of them, who were perched up in a distant tree, thought themselves perfectly safe, and would not come down.

"The impudent varmints," said Dick, "I'll soon bring 'em down all of a heap."

He took a long aim at the tall tree in which the savages were perched as thick as bees in a hive, and in an instant afterwards the tree was struck fairly in the trunk, and toppled over.

"I think that did the trick for 'em, sir," said Dick, admiring his own handiwork.

"Without a doubt, for I saw them tumbling out of the tree head first, like so many blackberries shaken off a bush."

"They won't get up another tree in a hurry to make fun of us," said Dick; "that grape shot whistled round their ears in fine style, I know."

But by this time the schooner turned the headland.

"Here we are lads, lower the sails! All together, and cast anchor when I give the word."

CHAPTER XXXVIII.
IN WHICH LION LIMB MEETS WITH AN UNEXPECTED ENEMY.

IN a very short time the gallant little schooner glided into the small and ripless bay which had been discovered and allotted to her by Lion Limb.

"Let go," said the Boy Chief.

"Aye, aye, sir," was the ready answer of those on the forecastle.

Immediately afterwards the schooner's coils dropped as if by magic, the anchor splashed into the water, and the craft swerving round, was safe from the heavy waves which now began to rise and fall upon the angry sea outside the tiny harbour.

"Lower the boats, quickly," was the order now given, and with alacrity all hands prepared to disembark in the boats, not forgetting to arm themselves well in case any necessity should arise for them to engage any of Red Wolf's savages who might be prowling about in the woods.

With a loud cheer the boats put off to shore, and they were hailed with loud expressions of delight by little Emma and the rest of the colonists who had been left behind.

Small parties were immediately organized to go forth and scour the woods in all directions.

One of these gangs was led by Dick Hamilton, a second by Harry Woodruff, and a third, the largest and most powerful of all, being directed and guided by Lion Limb himself.

"Don't go, Lion Limb, don't go," said Emma Clarence, clasping her lover round the neck," don't go, I beg and pray of you."

"Why not?" said Lion Limb, smiling at the maiden's fears, and patting her affectionately on her fair cheek, "why not—wherefore look so pale—why tremble so? What, you, Emma, who have so bravely withstood the attack of these Indians in my absence, fear for me who am a man? Fie, fie, you must think I am chicken-hearted."

"I do not; heaven knows, no one admires your daring and bravery more than I do, Lion Limb; your praises are on every lip; all the boys love you; there is not one among them all who would not risk his life for you willingly."

"Then, if they love their leader so much, Emma, would it be fair, would it be honourable for me to allow them to encounter danger and *I* remain idly at home? No, Emma, I am captain of them all, and crowned king of all these islands, and will always be the first one to go where danger is."

"Nay, do not go, I beg and pray you will not," said Emma, leaning on his shoulder, "for my sake, do not."

"Nay, I must, Emma; I *will* go; I, who have faced Nat Jackson's gang of ruffians and cut-throats, do not fear the weapons of Red Wolf's hounds."

So speaking, Lion Limb tore himself away from Emma, and, waving his hand, was soon out of view.

In a short time the popping of fire-arms could be heard in different parts of the forest.

The shouts of the brave lads led on by Lion Limb, Dick, and Harry, mingled with the shrieks and yells of Red Wolf's savages, some of whom still lingered in sight of the camp, eager at the slightest opportunity to rush in and despoil it of its treasures.

For the ignorant savages, although they had been beaten back several times during the day by the young colonists, led on frequently by Emma Clarence in person, still imagined that the fire would be again fanned by a favourable breeze and destroy them all by suffocation if not by fire.

Gallantly had the young colonists fought that day, and more than one poisoned arrow had penetrated the clothing of Emma Clarence.

The noble girl seemed to court every danger.

Wherever the fight was hottest there she made her way, and by words and actions cheered on the lads to fresh deeds of prowess.

She had been entreated often and often to retire out of danger.

But she would not.

She scorned to hide while others were fighting for their very existence, and for her personal safety.

"No," she said, "no, my brave comrades, I am an English girl, and would despise myself were I not to handle my rifle on such occasions as this. Besides," she would often add, with a flush of pride, "isn't your brave young leader, Lion Limb, away on the ocean with his brave crew fighting the buccaneers, and shall I then sneak like a coward to some place of safety?"

The boys found it useless to argue with her.

She insisted upon having her own way, and, with rifle or flag in hand, she had been foremost all day long, fighting as courageously as any one.

The intense excitement had nerved her throughout the day, but when the savages fell back into the wood on the approach of the schooner, she felt once more a girl again.

She was prostrated with fatigue, and overjoyed at Lion Limb's safe return.

Hence it was that she so suddenly begged that he would not expose himself to new dangers' for she dreaded some treachery would prove fatal to him.

When, therefore, Lion Limb left her side, she sat down and wept.

Her hair in rich masses fell upon her shoulders, and she bent her head in grief.

"He does not love me," she thought, as her tears fell fast. "I am sure of that; and yet I would willingly lay down my life for him."

How long the lass thus remained weeping and absorbed in thought she knew not.

She was awakened from her deep reverie by some one touching her on the shoulder saying,

"Where is Captain Lion Limb?"

She looked up and discovered that it was Harry Woodruff and Dick Hamilton.

She was surprised, and trembled at the question.

The truth was soon told.

All the boys had returned from the woods without their leader.

No one knew where he was.

Without stopping for an instant to ask any further questions, she darted off towards the woods like a deer, greatly to the surprise of all.

They shouted for her to return.

But all in vain.

She heard them not.

With remarkable swiftness she sped away, and soon entered the woods at the spot where she had last seen Lion Limb.

From the looks of certain shrubbery she felt certain that the good dog Dragon had passed that way, for there were small bits of hair here and there upon the prickly bushes.

She followed up this trail for more than half-an-hour, when at last to her great joy she perceived young Lion Limb reposing in a quiet spot, pillowing his head upon Dragon, both dog and master being fast asleep.

She would have rushed towards him, but to her intense horror she perceived the tall, gaunt figure of a ruffian stealthily approaching the sleeper in a noiseless manner.

His intentions were plain.

He was bent upon cold-blooded murder!

He was heavily armed at all points, and the nearer he got towards his intended victim the more his eyes gleamed in fiendish delight as he gloated at the evil thoughts which possessed him.

Still the sleeper remained immovable.

Both dog and master were overcome with excessive fatigue and the noxious fumes of carbon which filled the air.

Emma Clarence was stupefied with apprehension and horror.

She clutched her pistol, and hid herself from view.

With a savage oath the ruffian rushed upon the sleeping form of Lion Limb, brandishing a deadly weapon.

At that instant a pistol report was heard.

Emma screamed and fell senseless.

With a heavy groan the ruffian threw up his hands, and staggered backwards.

THE BOY KING
OF THE SOUTH SEA ISLANDS.

WITH AN UNEARTHLY YELL THE UNKNOWN SPRANG UPON LION LIMB.

CHAPTER XXXIX.

TERRIBLE CONFLAGRATION—DEATH OF NAT JACKSON—HIS DYING CONFESSION.

THE sudden report of the pistol, immediately followed as it was by the deep groan of the ruffian,

No. 14.

and the agonised scream of Emma Clarence, aroused Lion Limb from the state of lethargy into which he had fallen consequent upon his many and hard labours of the previous day.

The dog, Dragon, who had accompanied Lion

Limb in all his wanderings and dangers, was no less overcome than his young master.

But the sudden report, as we have said, proved more than sufficient to thoroughly arouse them both.

With a deadly growl Dragon sprang to his feet.

Lion Limb a second afterwards stood erect.

He looked about him for a second or two in wonder.

He recollected how he had directed his gallant followers to push forward through the woods after the savages, but forgot that he had sat down for a moment.

Nor did he recollect how in that single moment he had rested how sleep had overcome him, and that the noxious fumes of the burning vegetation, and the poisonous effects of charcoal had lulled him to sleep.

For a moment, as we have said, he stood looking first in one direction and then another to ascertain the cause of his sudden awakening, and irresolute as to what he should or ought to do.

He was alone. Not a soul could be seen.

He was in the forest some distance from his camp, and now all was as still as death.

His first impulse prompted him to draw his weapons, and be ready for any sudden attack from unknown enemies.

But when he looked around again he perceived the tall gaunt form of a stranger.

It was no one else but Nat Jackson, the buccaneer chief.

The good dog, Dragon, had been the first to perceive the villain, and dashed towards him with a savage, ominous growl.

Lion Limb now rushed forward, for Dragon had seized the rascal by the throat, and, wounded as he was, Nat Jackson was more than a match for the faithful animal.

"I would not have the dog killed," thought Lion Limb, "for all the world. The animal is brave even to rashness."

He perceived that Nat the Don had drawn a dagger to stab Dragon, and in an instant he rushed forward to save him.

He seized Dragon and pulled him away from Nat's throat, and then he stood face to face with his old enemy.

"What! Is that you, Nat?" asked Lion Limb.

"It is; you need not be surprised. I came to slay you, but I fear that a stray shot, fired by some one unknown, has done for me; it entered my side, and I think that all is over."

"How came you to leave the island? I thought you were on the Blue Rocks."

"So I was; but, hurt as I then was by you in the fight we had, I resolved to meet you fairly hand to hand, and rid the world of my only rival."

"But was it brave, was it manly to assail me when asleep?

Nat smiled grimly as he said—

"All is fair in love or war, you know."

"I am glad you think so," said Lion Limb; "it was some friendly hand that saved me from certain death."

"I know not that," said Nat, sinking to the ground with weakness and loss of blood. "I know not that it might have been from some of my own friends or my own men."

"Your own men!" said Lion Limb, in surprise. "Why, have you any of them on this island, then?"

"I have, and many; but it is all up with me now I feel, so I don't mind telling you all and everything."

"Speak, then!"

"When you had fairly and honourably beaten us

in the sea fight we returned to shore, as you know, the best way we could."

"I am glad you confess your defeat."

"There is no use disguising it, boy; but listen to me further. When we got on shore loud murmurs were raised against me by many in my gang that we should have been beaten by such mere boys as you are, and then I resolved on a bold move."

"And what was that, pray?"

"Our men on the look-out discovered that you had not sailed homewards as soon as we expected, and we were wondering what your next move would be."

"And did you discover our intentions?"

"We did; our look-outs informed us that you had sailed partly round the island, and landed with two boats' crews. Is not that correct?" Nat asked, with a ghastly smile.

"It is. What else?"

"Our own vessel was on the other side of the island looking out for strange craft, and she was too far away for us to signal her to return. We held a council of war, and when we found out that some traitor had informed you of the captives we had in the cave inland, and that you had started to liberate them, all my followers were exasperated to the very highest pitch."

"I suppose," said Lion Limb, "you and your boats' crew were too far away for us to interfere, and try to prevent your expedition? But we resolved on instant revenge, and, as I have said before, I hit upon an excellent plan."

"And what was that?"

"Why, to get together a couple of fast-sailing boats, and attack your settlement in your absence."

"And you did so?"

"We did. I led them, and Bloodhoof was left in command at the Blue Rocks. We landed, and communicated with Red Wolf, who, with his men, hit upon the plan of setting fire to all the woods round your camp, and, while all was in confusion with you, to sally forth from the woods, and destroy every living soul."

"But you did not succeed."

"No, we did not, and I felt that we should not, for something in my mind told me plainly that our plans would not succeed, and that we should be beaten back with disgrace."

For a moment Nat spoke not.

His wound was mortal, and the life-blood was oozing from him.

His countenance gradually became livid pale.

His teeth chattered, and his eyes rolled.

He was evidently in great pain.

But he suppressed every expression of suffering as well as he could, and at length proceeded with what he had to say, in short, and sometimes almost inaudible words.

"We set the woods on fire," said he, "but the wind changed, and blew off the flames from your settlement."

"And then——"

"Seeing that there was no chance of burning you out, I ordered all my men and the savages to make an attack on your camp from all points."

"And did they?"

"Yes, but they were shot down with unerring aim; and chief among the defenders was a pretty girl."

"A girl!" said Lion Limb, in surprise. "Fair or dark?"

"I could not distinctly see, but I think she must have been a European, for no native could have displayed such coolness and courage."

"And so you were beaten back?"

"Yes, I must confess it, we were beaten back again and again. The Indians became alarmed at the numbers of their killed and wounded, and, at last, hid themselves wherever they could out of danger. Some lay flat on the ground, others scampered away all speed, and a great many climbed the trees, and sat chattering like so many apes."

"And not a few were killed by our shells and grape-shot."

"True, boy; quite true, but, finding that your schooner had returned, I made every preparation to return with safety, but, seeing that you were very careless where you went to, and that you rambled about unattended, I watched you."

"In order to fall upon and kill me, I suppose ?"

"No, Lion Limb; my first wish was to capture, not to kill you."

"Then, why that dagger I picked up near where I lay ?"

"My intention was to kill your faithful dog first and make you my prisoner; but if you resisted I swore to have you dead or alive."

Lion Limb did not speak to the dying buccaneer, but looked upon him with pity and contempt.

"Nay, look not so sourly at me, Lion Limb," said Nat, almost gasping for breath, "but listen: I am dying."

"So I perceive."

"And in my last hour I wish to prove your friend."

"My friend ?"

"Yes, that I do, and I will prove it."

"In what manner ?"

"Hear me. You have enemies surrounding you."

"I know it."

"Not the natives, mark me."

"Indeed, who then ?"

"Enemies worse than the natives.'

"Who are they ?"

"Some of your own men."

"Nay, I will not believe it," said Lion Limb, indignantly; "all my followers are faithful and true !"

"You only think so; but I can prove to the contrary."

"And the proof ?"

"Is this. Hear me: I have been informed of all your movements both night and day by one of your own people who has constantly and regularly communicated with me by messages or signs."

"You astonish me."

"These traitors I know not by name, but one of them promised to meet me to-morrow, and bring all the news he can collect."

"And where was he to meet you ?"

"In a cave where I have long deposited my choicest plunders, unknown to any of my gang, for, Lion Limb, although I am now dying, I have been hording up immense quantities of wealth."

"Ill-gotten wealth," said Lion Limb.

"Yes, ill-gotten wealth, truly; for I had resolved to leave all my companions some day and return to Europe a rich man."

"And where's this cave ?"

"You would never discover it unless I tell you the whereabouts."

"Can't you tell me? These riches are worthless to you now."

"I know they are worse than worthless. Every gold coin and every trinket which I have stolen seems to press into my soul like red-hot iron !"

And, as he spoke, Nat writhed in awful agony.

"This enemy of yours was to meet me there; *he* knows the way, and has been there before. But, had I lived, he should never have returned again. I would have served him like I have served many a one—ha, ha ha !"

The last laugh proved more than Nat's declining strength could bear.

The exertion caused the rupture of some blood-vessel.

He fell back suddenly, with a loud groan.
He was dead !

CHAPTER XL.

AGREEABLE DISCOVERIES—THE HAPPY BANQUET.

THE almost miraculous escape of Lion Limb from the wicked and cold-blooded designs of Nat Jackson soon became rumoured abroad among the youths who were in camp.

Many of them proposed to go forth and attack Red Wolf and his savages at once, and take signal revenge on them for the bold treachery.

"No, no," Lion Limb said, "you have all done quite enough of fighting for the present. We must not seek quarrels at all; if the Indians come upon us, then let us fight like brave fellows, but do not go forth to seek useless encounters with the natives. Besides, the natives will not stand and fight like other men; they run away, and, as they know more about the ins and outs of the island than we do as yet, let us be content to rest awhile, and improve our little colony."

Then a council of war was held, at which Lion Limb presided, to decide upon the fate and punishment due to their prisoners, and especially in regard to Bill Whetherby, whom it will be recollected was in their hands.

"Never mind discussing that subject yet," said Lion Limb; "we can put the rascal in heavy irons, and he cannot get away; meanwhile there is a great deal to do in order to enlarge our sphere of operations. In the first place, my lads, we must refit and repair our gallant schooner, for she has suffered a great deal from the shot of the enemy, and her sails want mending."

"Leave that to me, captain," said Dick, "I'll set to work and do all that to-morrow."

"It will take us three days to make all things ship-shape, sir," said Harry.

"Well, in three days, then, if she is quite ready for sea again, we will make another cruise."

"Not against those villains on the Blue Rock's, captain ?"

"No, I will pick a select crew and sail to the south-west, for, from all I can learn, old Katimar, the father of our young captive princess, is a very powerful king; we must make his acquaintance."

"Hear, hear."

"And, if he likes to be friendly with us, all well and good; but if he shows any inclination to be otherwise we shall know how to act."

"Quite right, captain."

"We must cruise about, and let all these islanders know that *we* are the real masters of these seas, and fear no one," said Dick.

"Right, Dick, so we must," said Lion Limb; "from all the information which I can gather, I learn that several of these islands are the most beautiful and fruitful places in the whole world."

"No doubt of it, captain."

"Some of them are reported to be rich in precious metals, and abound in pearls and precious stones. I hear that the Indian natives are decked and adorned with pearls of the greatest value, and that the plumage of the rarest birds are used as ornaments."

"I long to get there," said one.

"And so do I. Won't we make a haul?"

"Some of the islands also abound in all manner of fine fish, and have coral reefs, so that if we are successful and make friends of the islanders each and all of us may make our fortunes, and if we should ever be so lucky as to return to old England we shall not be beggars but rich men."

"Hooray! hooray!" shouted several in delight.

"But until our schooner is ready we have much to do. Our camps must be put in good order and fortified, so that we need not fear Red Wolf's men; besides, we must not forget to plant seeds and prepare for next year's bread. We have plenty as yet, but we must not eat it all without preparing for the time to come."

"Hear, hear, captain, you are wise," said Dick. "Our lads here think perhaps that the ship's stores will last for ever, but they won't, as I have often told them, so that we had better select a gang of our lads to go ploughing; the soil is very rich, and if I'm not greatly mistaken, we shall grow much more than we can well store away."

"So much the better, Dick; but you must recollect that we must sow not only oats and wheat but hops and barley also. When we have nothing better to do, we must turn to and brew our own beer, for the lads are very fond of it."

"So are we, captain. Don't let us forget to sow plenty of hops and barley," said the lads in chorus.

"We have discovered a great many things round about us, captain, while you were away on your expedition to the Blue Rocks," said one of the lads.

"Indeed! and what are they?"

"Miss Clarence went out yesterday and found some splendid vines bending down with grapes."

"That is not bad news. Well, what of them?" said Lion Limb, laughing. "I suppose the first thing you did was to eat of them until you made yourself very ill?"

"No I didn't, captain," said the lad, grinning. "I eat one or two, and they were sour. Miss Clarence ordered us not to touch them."

"Why not?"

"Because they were green; but she went further in her walks and discovered both ripe grapes and plums. We gathered a large number—two baskets full of the grapes, and brought them home. We crushed them with two flat stones, and then Miss Emma put them out to dry in the sun to make raisens."

"Which shows that Miss Clarence is much wiser than you imagined."

"Besides the grapes," said another, "Miss Emma caught a hawk."

"A hawk?"

"Yes."

"How?"

"She found it fluttering about on one leg, and it had hurt its wing and could not fly."

"What can she want with a hawk?"

"She says it will be of great use, for she will go out hawking and tame the bird so as to know her."

"How can she do that, I wonder?"

"Where did the young lady learn to tame hawks?"

"This one is as wicked as anything," said another, "and picked at my hand and made it bleed."

"But it didn't hurt Miss Clarence, though," said the first speaker. "She took all the wildness out of him very soon."

"How?" said Lion Limb.

"One of the lads was smoking a pipe, and she ordered him to puff all the smoke in the bird's face."

"And what good did that do?"

"At first the hawk turned almost mad, but his legs were fastened, and he could not get away; when he had been well smoked for some time, he became quieter and quieter, and at last seemed stupefied and drunk. While we were thus smoking him to train him, Miss Emma made a hood to keep his eyes from the light and took him home. She says she will train him to pursue and kill all manner of winged game."

"Not a bad idea," said several. "I hope Miss Emma may prove successful and supply us plentifully with teal, and duck, and snipe, and every other sort of delicacy."

"You are only thinking of one side of the question," said Lion Limb, "but you must remember that Miss Emma is wiser than you imagine. She knows that this hawk, simple as it is, will save us pounds and pounds of powder."

"So it will."

"So it will."

"I never thought of that," said first one and then another.

"But I did, my lads, for, although we have plenty, yet we may not always have it, therefore we must be very sparing in the future, for if we spend as much as we did the other day with those rascally buccaneers, we should not have much very long."

"Quite right, captain, quite right," said Dick, "we must be very sparing of our powder, and no mistake, and look upon it as more precious than gold."

"Then what say you, my lads, suppose we give up the charge of all our ammunition to Dick Hamilton and let him serve it out, because, up to the present moment, each one of us have had as much as we wanted and as often as we wanted."

"Whatever you say is right, captain," said all in chorus; "let Dick be powder-master."

"What else has Miss Emma discovered since I have been away?" said Lion Limb with a good-natured smile.

"Well, you see, captain, the young lady has been well educated and knows a deal more than any on us, as far as books go, and when we went out towards the woods, she pointed out all sorts of flowers and told us the names on 'em; some of 'em she said would give a great deal of oil besides scent, and others she said could be boiled down to make medicine. But when we went out in the morning, I saw Miss Emma stand a long time looking at a thing which looked very much like a small pumpkin. I was very thirsty at the time and wanted some water badly; the sun was so hot, I was almost parched.'

"'Come along, Miss Emma,' I says; 'that's only a small wild pumpkin.'

"'No, it isn't,' she said, smiling, and showing all her pretty teeth, and shaking her curls all over her back.

"'If it ain't a pumpkin, you may eat me, miss,' says I, very respectfully to the young lady.

"'You are mistaken, Joe Pebbles,' said she. 'This is worth more than a thousand pumpkins.'

"'What is it, miss?' said I, scratching my head, and awful dry at the same time.

"'Lend me your knife, Mr. Pebbles,' said she. 'Are you thirsty?'

"'Yes, miss. I am almost parched.'

"'Then drink some of this,' says she, and Mis Emma cut off this pumpkin-looking thing and bored a hole into it.

"'No, thankee, miss,' said I. 'I don't know what it is. It might be poison, you know.'

"Miss Emma laughed, and drank some of it herself. Then I tried it."

"And was it good?" asked Dick.

"Just for all the world like new milk. It was nice and no mistake."

"'You mustn't drink any of this milk at night, Mr. Pebbles,' said she 'for all this milk turns to rank poison,' says she; 'and don't tell any of the lads where to find this fruit without I tell you, for they may get intoxicated.'

"'Drunk, miss?' says I. 'Why, I could drink a gallon of that milky stuff. It wouldn't hurt a lamb.'

"'Yes it would, Mr. Pebbles,' says she.

"And so we returned to camp.

"About noon the sun was plaguey hot, and I thought I should have fainted almost, carrying a heavy load of grapes on my back.

"'I wish we could make some good wine, miss, out of these grapes,' says I. 'It would be very nice drinking this hot day."

"'If you behave yourself, Mr. Pebbles,' says the young lady, 'I'll give you some when we get into camp.'

"'Thank'ee kindly, miss,' says I, and I trudged along with my heavy basket of grapes.

"As we passed the spot where them pumpkin-looking things were, Miss Emma cut one off and brought it home with her.

"I was awful tired, captain, and no mistake, for Miss Emma always finds plenty of work for the lads whether you are in camp or not.

"So I says to myself, 'I hope the young lady won't forget to give me that wine she promised'.

"I had hardly spoken when up comes Miss Emma with the pumpkin in her hand and a small tin half-pint cup.

"'Here is the wine I promised you, Mr. Pebbles,' says she.

"'What, that is only milk, Miss,' I says; 'the same as I had in the morning.'

"She smiled, and says—

"'Taste it, then.'

"I did so, and it was wine—yes, as good as any champagne as ever was made!"

"You don't mean that?" said Dick. "Wine?"

"Yes, and no mistake. Miss Emma told me the juice of the fruit, the real name of which she couldn't recollect, was like milk in the morning, the heat of the sun turned it into wine at noon, and at night it was real poison."

"You are sure it was wine?" said one.

"Oh, Joe Pebbles is dreaming, captain."

"No, I ain't, for I drank a half-pint and felt as merry as a cricket all the rest of the afternoon, and only felt sorry I hadn't got more to drink."

This announcement of the discovery of so precious a fruit greatly pleased all who had heard the particulars, and it was resolved that some of the "wine-pumpkins," as they were now called, should be gathered at some future day so as to allow all an opportunity of judging for themselves as to its merits.

While light and amusing conversation thus took place among the youths, other matters of greater importance was disposed of.

Sam Stokes, who, from his fondness for cooking, had been unanimously chosen chief cook for the boys, entered the council tent, and, flourishing his cap, respectfully announced the joyful tidings that supper was ready.

This news was received with loud applause, and all entered a large, comfortable log-house, of barn-like appearance, which had been especially erected for a mess-room during the absence of Lion Limb on his expedition against the buccaneers.

"What, a new house, Sam?" said the Boy Chief, clapping his chief cook on the back.

"Yes, captain, Miss Emma proposed that we should surprise you all on your return, and so we set to work, every man Jack of us, Miss Emma and all, and built this place. It is eighty feet long by fifty wide. We can fold up the table when necessary, and have a good place for a dance."

"But you must have had hard work to do all this while I was away."

"So we had, captain, but all the boys love you, and we would do anything to please you."

Lion Limb went into the room, and was astonished to see how nicely it had been prepared.

From the beams and the walls, garlands and evergreens hung.

The long tables were all prettily laid out with wild flowers.

The tables were laden with all manner of good things, including oysters, trout, perch, eels, venison, kid, beef, and a dozen other things.

Emma Clarence sat at the head of the table on the right hand of Lion Limb, Dick Hamilton on the left, Harry Woodruff on the right next to Emma Clarence, and the others in rotation.

"Why, where on earth did you procure such an abundance and variety of things?" asked Lion Limb, in amazement.

"Perhaps Miss Clarence could tell," said one.

"Nay, ask Pebbles and Stokes," said Emma, laughing.

"Well, the truth is, captain, I shot a wild bull and a deer, Sam Stokes snared the wild kid, and Miss Emma caught the fish."

"How was that?"

"We thought of fishing with lines, captain," said Stokes, "but Miss Emma had read of a better mode to capture fresh-water fish."

"In what manner?"

"By fish-traps, sir."

"Fish-traps? I never heard of fish-traps before," said one.

"Nor I either."

"They are very simple when you once see them."

"What sort of things are they then?"

"Small square boxes, with a hole in the bottom

of each, are partly sunk in the water; the fish enter, and nibble the bait, and, directly they touch the bait, a small door falls, and closes the hole. The fish can't get out, and they swim about in the box until we go and take them out."

"An excellent plan. How many fish-traps have you?"

"Over twenty now, sir," said Stokes. "We found lots of biscuit-boxes, and all we had to do was to cut out a square hole at the bottom, and form a little door with leather hinges, and, when the fish enter and nibble, down goes the door, and the fish can't get out, but will remain there alive and kicking until some one goes and takes them out."

With jokes and merriment the meal proceeded. All were happy.

The guards, who had been detailed to mind the camp, were watchful at their posts, and, long after midnight, long after Miss Emma and others had retired to their respective quarters, Lion Limb and his boys were singing and enjoying themselves.

But Lion Limb at that moment, and happy as he was, little thought of the plan which had been formed against his life.

CHAPTER XLI.

THE INDIAN PRINCESS SAVES LION LIMB FROM DEATH.

WHEN the gallant little schooner had been safely anchored in the bay which had been selected, and Lion Limb, with his men, had with one or two exceptions gone ashore to drive off the savages who threatened the camp, Yokee began to think of some plan to escape.

He and Ted Rawlings, it will be remembered, were confined below.

But poor Ted was overcome with grief to think he had fallen into disgrace; and after grumbling and crying he fell fast asleep, and soon became totally oblivious of everything around him.

Not so with Yokee, however.

He was wakeful and watchful.

His dark eyes rolled, and he gnashed his teeth in rage.

When he heard that all was quiet around him, he crawled from his corner and opened one of the lower port holes, which had been left ajar to give the prisoners sufficient air.

With great quietness and caution he looked through the open port hole and resolved upon attempting his escape.

He dared not go on deck, for several of the boys where on guard and would have shot him instantly.

He therefore got through the port hole and slipped into the sea quite unobserved by any one.

The Indian was a splendid swimmer, and could dive for a great length, trusting in his known skill.

With the grace and swiftness of an otter, Yokee dived below the moonlit waters, and except for a moment or two, in order to gain fresh breath, he never appeared upon the surface.

With a knife which he had concealed about his person, he repelled the attacks which several sharks made upon him, and ere long he reached the shore, panting and well nigh exhausted. He hid beneath a cluster of palms, and listened for any sounds which might come from the boys' camp not far off.

He heard the loud laugh of merriment, and could distinguish the sounds of joyous songs borne upon the night air as Lion Limb and his companions enjoyed themselves.

His eyes rolled in fierce and fiery anger, and his bosom heaved as he sighed,

"I cannot be mistaken. I know that voice, and have heard it more than once in the heat and smoke and noise of battle—it is Lion Limb. It is my foe, my enemy—he shall die! Yes, with this shining blade I will do the deed," he said, brandishing his knife. "I care not if I die for it. My rival shall not live. Katimar's daughter shall be mine, or she also shall die!"

For more than three hours Yokee remained in his hiding-place, and when all was silent he crawled along on his hands and feet through the low bushwood unobserved, and approached the tent in which the Indian princess lay fast bound in slumber.

Yokee listened.

He could plainly hear the breathings of the maiden, and more than once he heard her mention Lion Limb's name in her sleep.

Yokee was almost driven mad at the thought that Lion Limb had forestalled him in the maid's affection.

He crawled into the tent and touched her.

"It is I, Yokee; be not afraid," he whispered.

The startled girl was filled with astonishment and horror.

"Speak a single word and you shall die!" he said; "I have sworn it. I have come at the hazard of my life to say once more that I love you; once more I ask you to flee with me from the camps of these pale-faces."

The girl was too much alarmed to speak in reply.

"Speak!" said Yokee, hissing out his words. "Speak! I have come to kill Lion Limb. If you promise to forget him and to love me his life is safe. Speak! one word is enough. I am desperate! I care not for my own life. Tell me that you will forget him."

For some time the girl spoke not.

Indignation at Yokee's villany choked her utterance; at last she gasped out—

"Begone! Yokee; I will promise anything to save the life of Lion Limb."

"'Tis well," said Yokee, and he silently slunk away like a snake.

Prostrate with sorrow and alarm at the imminent danger of one she had so soon and hopelessly learned to love, the pretty sun-tanned, dark-eyed girl, with dishevelled hair and streaming eyes, knelt in silent supplication to the Most High.

"Alas!" she sobbed, "why did I ever behold him? Why did my footsteps stray among them that I should suffer this strange feeling—these unutterable pangs of sorrow and remorse?"

The camp was silent, not a footstep stirred.

The fires flickered and flowed with cheerfulness and warmth.

The pale, twinkling stars shone out from the azure sky like bright, clear, shining silver lamps around the celestial throne of the great Jehovah; and as her soul was convulsed with sorrow, as her young tender and heaving frame swathed in smothered emotions that fain would escape in words from her trembling lips and choking sighs, the night winds swayed the lofty branches of ancient mammoth trees, as if unseen spirits were hovering near her humble tent, speechless witnesses of the great conflict then raging in her soul between a whole life of Self-Sacrifice and newly-awakened new-born Love.

The dusky figures of the boys were curled in sleep.

Grotesque forms huddled here and there before the ruddy glow of expiring fires.

And not a sound disturbed the awful, unearthly quiet that reigned over all save the fitful crackling of unburnt faggots.

"Oh! that I ne'er had seen him, or seeing him had died!" she muttered, half inaudibly. "Why that mine eyes should fall upon a pale-faced stranger! Why that my life and fate should culminate in one short fleeting hour! Never till now have my heart and soul strayed from paths antagonistic to our race. Yokee," she said, "thou hast triumphed o'er a woman's broken heart—nay, heart I have none now," and bending low upon her pallet of humble straw, tears flowed down her sorrow-stricken cheek in bright, pearl-like streams.

"Who sobs thus in the quiet of the night?" said a husky voice without. "Knowest thou not that the pale-faced stranger but for me might now lie in the agonies of death?"

"Death!" cried the girl, rising instantly from her recumbent attitude. "Say not *death!*" and with loose garments flowing in the night winds, with weird, untold beauty, with hair streaming over her bare, exquisitely moulded shoulders, she rushed across the green towards Lion Limb's tent, with the unstudied air and gait of Nature's child.

The act was so unexpected and so sudden that it took Yokee by surprise, and she was far beyond his reach ere he recovered from his astonishment.

"She shall die," he said; "she dare not tell this pale-faced youth of what I intend to do; she will only warn him, and mention no names. She has played false to me," he said, "I also will prove false to her."

He crept on his hands and knees towards the tent of Emma Clarence, and stealthily awakened her.

"Come, lady, to the opening of your tent. Behold yonder," he said, in triumph, pointing to the forms of Lion Limb and the Indian maid, as they stood conversing in the moonlight.

"They meet, you see, fair queen," he said; "they meet by stealth. At the hazard of my life, I have watched them; Yokee is always your faithful slave."

"Without such proof I could never have believed that Lion Limb was so false and heartless," she said, and, turning into her tent again, sat down and wept bitterly.

Yokee, having fulfilled his devilish mission, disappeared like a shadow.

An hour afterwards, however, when Lion Limb went to the vessel, he was astonished to find Yokee just where Dick Hamilton had left him; his clothes were dry, he pretended to be fast asleep, and there was not the slightest sign to make Lion Limb believe the cunning villain had ever left the ship.

"The Indian girl must have been dreaming; those on board have kept constant watch and have seen nothing; here the Indian is fast asleep and not the slightest sign of ever having stirred. She *must* have been dreaming."

Lion Limb was certain that Yokee was safe and harmless, so he left the ship once more and went ashore.

Directly he had gone Yokee also left the ship, and swam ashore.

He got into one of the many canoes that were on the beach, and, being favoured by night, paddled away until far from land, and then, hoisting a small sail, was soon lost to view upon the dark blue ocean.

"I am free," he chuckled; "when I have fully completed all my plans I will return and massacre every one of them. 'Tis useless for me to stay among the pale-faces any longer, for they will watch me both by night and day, perhaps kill me when I least expected it. I am free! Revenge will come; delay will only make it all the sweeter."

When morning came Yokee could not be found anywhere.

Lion Limb did not take any notice for he was too busily engaged in preparing to revisit the Blue Rocks again.

He remembered well the last words of the buccaneer chief Nat Jackson, and resolved at all hazards to visit the treasure cave, and discover, if possible, the spy and traitor who had, up to the present moment, informed the buccaneers of what was going on in the colony.

In secret, therefore, he called Dick Hamilton aside and told him all.

Dick was furious, and for a moment raved like a madman at the bare idea that any one should have proved so base and ungrateful.

"Never mind, Dick, let us keep this affair secret, equip the largest of our boats, and make ready to sail with me to-night, and we'll go on a voyage of discovery, and ferret out the rascal whoever he is, and bring back as much treasure as possible, which Nat the Don has been laying by for many years."

Dick was red with passion, but he did as Lion Limb ordered him, and prepared the largest of the schooner's boats, provided sails, a few gallons of water, and necessary food, and by sunset all was ready.

Harry Woodruff was not informed of this expedition until the last moment. He was left in command of the camps, but grumbled a little because he also could not go.

However, Lion Limb picked out a third party to accompany them, namely, Joe Pebbles, and, unknown to any but Harry Woodruff, they launched the boat, and directed their course straight towards the Blue Rocks.

The night was beautiful and bright when these three adventurous spirits started from the island; but when they had been gone about an hour, the weather changed, and everything gave signs of a coming storm.

But such men as Lion Limb, Dick Hamilton, and Joe Pebbles, cared nothing for danger.

They were by nature hardened, and even liked to encounter difficulties which other men would have been too willing to shun.

The wind now began to blow, and increased in violence each instant.

Many clouds gathered overhead, and the shrill

cry of sea-gulls and other marine fowl as they whirled swiftly overhead, told too plainly that a severe storm was approaching, and not far distant.

"This is what I call jolly, captain," said Joe Pebbles, as the boat pitched and rolled, and was tossed to and fro by the surging waves.

"This is what I call jolly, captain," said he. "Don't our boat ride well?"

"Yes, I believe you, my boy," said Dick, who was at the tiller. "She answers the helm fine, and floats as gracefully as a duck."

"I'm glad you like it," said Lion Limb. "I would not give a fig to be out sailing without I had a good stiff breeze. It blows all the dust and cobwebs off one. What say you, Dick?"

"Just so, captain; but if you'll take my advice we had better make all things taut and ship-shape, for when the 'blow' comes our little craft will careen over, and play us the devil of a dance, for she jumps about just as if she had life, and rollicked in the storm."

"Don't forget to make fast that gallon of rum you've got there beside you, Dick," said Lion Limb, "for I have been taking notice that Joe here has been paying his respects to it rather often."

"Never fear, sir, I'll keep my eye on Joe; he's a good fellow, but rayther fond of a drop of grog when he can get at it."

"It's better than all Miss Emma's pumpkin champagne, I think," said Lion Limb, laughing, "judging how Joe smacks his lips over it."

"Look out, sir, look out; hold fast; here it comes. Be ready to let the sheet go when I give the word, the squall will be upon us in less than a minute," said Dick.

True to his word the squall came, and struck the boat with great fury.

She careened right over, and for a moment she looked as if she would never right herself again.

"That's one, sir," said Dick; "but we shall have another or two before long, see if we don't."

By this time the wind began to howl fearfully.

The waves rose to a great height all around them, and the little craft seemed at times to be engulphed by mountainous waves.

Lightning flashed throughout the darkness, and thunder rolled sullenly overhead.

Not a speck of land could be seen, save at times the glimpse of a small headland which Lion Limb quickly recognized as the bold foreland of the Blue Rocks.

"I think we cannot be very far off the Blue Rocks now, sir," said Dick, "I've been calculating our rate of sailing and feel certain we can't be far off."

"We are not, Dick; I have sighted the island, but according to my calculation we are a good distance away yet from a comfortable and safe anchorage"

"Keep a sharp look out, sir, if you please, for it is a very treacherous coast, and we have been running too much to the south-west to land at our old spot; we may strike on some reef before we know it."

"All right, Dick, let Joe Pebbles go into the bow and keep a good sharp look out while I trim the sails, and be ready for another squall."

Joe did as he was told.

But, though he looked very sharp for any reef, he saw not the slightest indication of land, for the waves and darkness all round were thick and impenetrable.

When least expected, danger came upon them.

"Land, ho! Port the helm, Dick, port the helm, or we are lost!" shouted Joe; but before Dick could obey, the sea dashed the boat with great violence through a narrow channel between some sunken rocks, and before any one could realize the sense of the deadly peril they were in, the boat was washed high and dry ashore on the top of a gigantic wave.

"Safe!" said Lion Limb. "Save we are."

"Yes; but we got a good shake and a thorough ducking," growled Dick, who was angry at Joe.

"Never mind, my lads, never mind, we are lucky after all, for this is the very spot that Nat told me about. His secret treasure cave is not far off, if I am not very much mistaken."

"You take charge of the boat, Joe," said Dick, "and see if you can't manage to break it all to pieces while we are away."

"We shan't be long, Joe, and I don't think that any one can have watched us such a night as this."

Lion Limb and Dick went forth in the darkness; but in about an hour they returned unsuccessful.

They could not discover anything regarding the cave or its whereabouts.

When morning began to dawn, however, they went forth again, and soon had the pleasure of discovering foot prints in the sand.

These marks were tracked for a considerable distance, and led to a small grove of trees.

The two heroes were well armed, and they spoke not a word.

Very carefully and quietly they followed the foot prints, and at last came to a solid rock.

There was a huge loose stone at the spot where the foot prints were last seen.

This Dick and Lion Limb quietly displaced, and then perceived that it had hidden a small passage which evidently led to some place within the interior.

"This must be it, Dick," said Lion Limb in a whisper. "Prepare your weapons, and follow me."

On his hands and knees Lion Limb crawled through the passage without making the slightest noise. Dick followed closely at his heels, carrying one of his weapons between his teeth.

They had not gone more than ten yards, when Lion Limb found himself in a cave (slightly lighted from a hole in the roof), from the walls of which hung several skeletons.

The floor was strewn with boxes, gold trinkets, coin and other valuables in abundance; but though he peered about, he was unable to penetrate the many dark corners and recesses of the cave.

"Come, Dick, come on," said he, sword in hand.

But at that instant, and unknown to him, a deadly enemy was concealed in one of the recesses, whose eyes shone in the darkness like two burning coals (See Cut). He glared like a wolf at young Lion Limb, who, as if from strange instinct, stood still and listened.

A mortal enemy was at his back, who was crawling like a tiger in the darkness, and ready to spring upon him unawares, and armed to the teeth.

With an unearthly yell the unknown sprang upon Lion Limb with the fury of a demon. In an instant Lion Limb was cast to the floor.

It was a fearful struggle for life or death.

"Revenge, revenge!" cried the unknown, holding Lion Limb's throat and brandishing a glittering knife.

THE BOY KING

OF THE SOUTH SEA ISLANDS.

"HE SEIZED THE INTRUDER BY THE THROAT."

CHAPTER XLII.

THE HIDDEN TREASURE.

THE attack was so sudden that Lion Limb was almost senseless from the fall.

Recovering himself, however, he seized the up-

lifted arm of the black-looking villain, and held it with the grip of a vice.

The ruffian's dagger was now useless to him.

So tightly did Lion Limb hold him that the cowardly rascal shouted with pain.

"Don't kill the villain," said the brave Lion

Limb to Dick, who raised his sword and was about to strike a fatal blow; "don't kill the villain, Dick, he's much too precious to dispose of in that way; drag him away."

In an instant Dick seized the rascal by the hair of his head and pulled him off his young leader, who jumped to his feet gaily and laughing.

Dick, however, could not restrain his indignation and anger.

He was purple with rage, and after wrenching the dagger from the villain's hand, he dealt him a terrific blow with his clenched fist right between his eyes, and knocked him sprawling on the ground.

"There," said Dick, "I think I gave him a good one that time, the ugly brute."

"As I live, it is Yokee," said Lion Limb, now recognising the features of the Indian whom he had saved from certain death and dragged from the death fires of Red Wolf's band of savages.

"Why, so it is," said Dick, in astonishment, as he approached closer to obtain a better view of the villain's ugly features; "why, so it is, by all that's lucky. Oh, you ungrateful son of a gun," said Dick, squaring off at him, and ready to administer another rib-roaster on his enemy.

"Don't touch him, Dick," said Lion Limb; "he is now disarmed, and can do no hurt. I will question him. He may have some secret cause for thus attempting to take my life. I will pump him."

"Why, the villain's face was a dirty red colour yesterday, how is it that he is now black?"

"He has been disguising himself."

"If he had the part of devil to play he would suit exactly," said Dick, "for an uglier, more dirty rascal I never saw in all my travels."

"We must take good care he does not escape us," said Lion Limb. "I see a rope on the ground; let us bind his hands behind, and then he can do no harm."

"Right you are, captain," said Dick, who seized the rope, and quickly tied Yokee's hands.

The villain finding himself completely at the mercy of his enemies, uttered not a word, but cast down his eyes, and looked resigned.

He who a few moments before had rushed forth from his hiding-place, bent on taking the life of the very youth who had saved him from the burning faggots of Red Wolf's gang, was now as meek and as humble as any hypocrite that ever breathed.

He sat in a corner of the cave, and held down his head.

"What brought you hither, Yokee?" asked Lion Limb.

The Indian answered not.

"Tell me, I say what made you attempt my life? How came you to escape from my schooner and visit the Blue Rocks?"

Still no answer.

"Oh, I can soon make him speak," said Dick; "if the ugly brute objects to open his mouth when a gentleman speaks to him I'll teach him better manners; I'll soon make him find his tongue."

And as he spoke Dick pulled out his dagger, and would have "tickled" Yokee's ribs with it, as he said, in a laughing mood.

"Put up your dagger, Dick," said Lion Limb.

"But why should you spare the rascal?"

"No matter; put up your dagger."

"He tried to take your life."

"That concers me," said Lion Limb, sternly, "and not you, Dick."

"What! are you going to give the brute another chance of taking your life?" said Dick, in wonder.

"He will never do so any more," said Lion Limb; "if we wish to live in peace among ourselves and to make friends of the natives on these surrounding islands, we must not use measures that are too harsh with them."

"Well, he is a rum 'un," said Dick, who could not understand the meaning of his young captain's mercy. "Well, he is a rum 'un, and no mistake; that ugly beast tries to take the captain's life, and, instead of having satisfaction out on him, he spares him."

"Listen to me, Dick," said Lion Limb. "I am your captain, I believe?"

"That you are, sir, and our lawfully-crowned leader into the bargain, and no mistake," Dick replied, bowing.

"Very well; then, as your leader, I do all things for the best for our little colony. If I thought it would benefit our colony I would burn this rascal alive, as Red Wolf's gang were about to do until I rescued him; had he been a white man, and had acted as he has done towards me," said Lion Limb, getting red with passion, "I would have blown the villain's brains out; but he is a savage, Dick, and, although we have tamed him somewhat, he is not as responsible for his actions as we are. Now, instead of killing the poor wretch, I will tame him by kindness, and he will (as you will hereafter find) prove to me and you all one of the most obedient and obliging slaves that man ever knew; he will love instead of hating us."

"I don't understand them sort of things, captain," said Dick, in a surly tone. "If a dog tries to bite me, you know, I cuts his wizen."

After a moment's pause and reflection, Lion Limb approached Yokee, and then spoke in the language of the Indian, which he had fully learned to speak of late.

"Yokee, your life is in my hands; you are deserving of death; but, on one condition, I will spare it."

Yokee held down his head and sighed.

"What is that condition?" said Yokee, sullenly.

"If you will answer all my questions—honestly, mind—your life shall be spared"

"I promise," the Indian replied.

"Nay, swear it."

"Yes, swear it," said Dick. "Let's have no beating about the bush, you know; swear it on your life."

"I swear it," the Indian answered; "and, if I ever tell an untruth again, or if I ever do that which is wrong again, burn me alive."

"Ah, that's talking like a man, that is," said Dick.

"How came you here, then, Yokee?" said Lion Limb.

"I stole one of your boats, and paddled across to the Blue Rocks to see Nat the buccaneer chief."

"And for what purpose?"

"To fulfil my promise which I made to him."

"To kill me?"

"Yes."

"But, what have I done to you, Yokee, that you should attempt to kill me?"

There was no answer.

"Come, speak up," said Dick; "let's have none of your ugly manners now, you know. You must consider yourself very lucky you haven't got a bullet through you, my fine fellow."

"Did I not rescue you from the hands of Red Wolf's gang?" asked Lion Limb.

"You did."

"Did I not drag you away from the pile of burning faggots by which you were surrounded?"

"You did."

"Have I not since then treated you and the other Indians all alike?"

"Treated them all too well, *I* think," growled Dick.

"And given you to eat and drink in plenty?" said Lion Limb.

"Too much by half," Dick remarked. "He's as fat as butter, and so are all the Indians among us; but, if I had anything to say, I should keep 'em all as lean as greyhounds. Hang all the Indians, *I* say; they are all sly foxes and wolves if they can only get a chance."

"You have treated me well," muttered Yokee.

"Then, why attempt to take my life?"

"Because I hated you," said Yokee, with flashing eyes.

"There, I told you so; I thought the villain would speak the truth for once. Let's blow out his brains," said Dick.

"Hate me, Yokee? And why?" asked Lion Limb.

"Marmi," the Indian sighed.

"Marmi the Indian princess — well, what of her?"

"You love her."

"Me?" said Dick, in surprise, who thought Yokee addressed him. "Me love Marmi? No, by all that's lucky, I don't; she's a nice girl enough, but I don't like redskins; give me an English girl or none at all."

"You were not spoken to, Dick," said Lion Limb, tartly, "and, as for Marmi, although she is *not* white, she is nevertheless a beautiful girl, and worthy of any man's love."

Turning to Yokee, he said.

"Yokee, you are deceived. Now I know all; you love Marmi, and jealousy has caused you to do wrong."

"It has," was the muttered response.

"As for me, Yokee, I have never spoken to Marmi in any way except that of a friend; nor shall I ever."

"But she loves you," said the Indian.

"Me!"

"Yes. I have proof of it."

"It is not returned, then, Yokee; but this much I will say: I love Marmi as I would a sister, but nothing more; and, to prove to you the truth of what I say, I shall sail away in a day or two, and restore the maiden to the arms of King Katamar, her father."

He had scarcely finished speaking, when Yokee fell at his feet and kissed them.

"I am your slave for ever; treat me as you would your dog, I ask nothing more," said the Indian, and tears of gratitude poured down his cheeks.

"See this, Dick," murmured Lion Limb, "this is the effect of love; he loves Marmi, and would die for her."

"Oh, it's all very well," said Dick, "but I don't believe in these Indians, they are all rogues at heart; but if he wishes to be treated like a dog, captain, I should begin at once and give him a sound thrashing to commence on; he'll like you all the better for it."

Lion Limb laughed at Dick's advice, but ordered him to search the cave for Nat's treasure.

There were several boxes strongly bound with iron in the place, and these Lion Limb and Dick soon broke open.

They contained bars of gold and silver, and all marked with the royal crest of Spain.

"Hillo," said Dick, "these bars must be very old, and no doubt come from Spanish men-of-war."

"What's this?" said Lion Limb, reading some faded writing pasted inside the lid of the chest.

"Oh, that's Spanish, captain."

"Why, so it is."

After a little time Lion Limb made out the meaning of the writing, which ran thus:—

"These chests of gold and silver bars were found on the wreck of a Spanish frigate which drifted on to the Blue Rocks in March, 1760. Miguel de Panos, Captain of the gang."

"The devil," said Dick, in surprise, "you don't mean to say the buccaneers have lived on this island all that time."

"There cannot be a doubt but they have visited the place if they have not lived in it for more than a century; for under the name of Miguel de Panos there are several scrawls; the first reads:—

"Miguel de Panos died very suddenly—1765."

"Very suddenly, eh!" said Dick, "no doubt of it by poison."

"And was succeeded by Don Sebastiano as captain by a unanimous vote of the freebooters."

"He was the chap that did it, then," said Dick.

"And under the name of Sebastiano is written a long string of names thus:—

"Don Sebastiano, killed by an accidental shot—1772, and was succeeded by Tomasso, who was drowned in 1780. He was succeeded by Francesco, the Portuguese, whose head was blown off by a cannon shot while engaged in a fight with an English merchant ship. The next captain was an Irishman, judging by his name," said Lion Limb, "Bill Burke, who drank himself to death; and so they go on for a long time," said Lion Limb, glancing over the list of names; "some were Spaniards, French, Portuguese, one or two English, Irish and Scotch are among them, but the greater number appear to have been South American half breeds, but nearly all of them came to violent deaths. Two or three of them were killed in quarrels, others had their heads blown off in sea-fights, others drank themselves to death or were drowned; and so the list goes on down to the last name."

"Is not Jackson's name there, captain."

"I cannot see it, Dick."

"Oh, he musn't be forgotten in the list of 'honorable's'," said Dick, laughing, and with a piece of chalk wrote on the wall, "Nat Jackson, killed by Miss Emma Clarence."

"Who told you that?" said Lion Limb, in surprise.

"Ask that black rascal if it isn't true."

"Nat Jackson dead!" said Yokee, in surprise.

"Yes."

"What makes you turn so pale?" asked Dick. "You might as well tell all. Remember your oath."

"I do," said Yokee. "I laid the trap for Lion Limb, and thought that the buccaneer chief would have killed you. Marmi told me that she had seen the young white lady save you, but did not say that any one was killed."

This greatly surprised Lion Limb, who now, for the first time, learned the truth of his preservation, and in his heart of hearts, although he spoke not, he loved Emma more and more.

"Come, quick!" said he. "We must not spend much time here, for the buccaneers might get wind of our visit to this place, and as there are but two of us, it would be a hard fight."

"All right, captain," said Dick. "There seems to be plenty of gold and silver about, but what use is it? We can't spend any here among the savages."

"True, Dick, but we may not spend all our lives on these islands, and if any of us should ever have a chance of returning to England——"

"England!" said Dick, in ecstasy. "Don't mention it. The very thought drives me almost mad, that it does. Oh, what would I not give to return home again, if only for a week," and then he burst out in a song, which made the cavern ring again, as he shouted,

> " ' There's a land which bears a well-known name,
> It is but a little spot.' "

"Very true, Dick, but don't make so much noise, for remember, we may be overheard, and discovered."

"I forgot all that, captain. I was thinking of my sweetheart, just then—lovely Sal," and then he commenced to sing again louder than ever,

> " ' Of all the girls that I love best
> There's none like pretty Sally,
> She is the darling of my heart
> And she lives in our alley.' "

Lion Limb could not help but laugh at Dick, but after a little time, he said,

"Well, drag out these boxes first, Dick, and return some other time for these other things lying about, and if any of us ever *do* get back to England we shall be rich and as fine gentlemen as any in the land."

"Money makes the mare go, captain, whether the man's got legs or no, so they say, and there ain't a doubt about it. Just fancy you and me, and Harry Woodruff, swelling it up Regent Street, eh, in fine clothes, and plenty of money in our pockets."

"Yes," said Lion Limb; "and there are many more unlikely things than that, Dick, for it strikes me, some ship will call at these islands before long."

"Pull away, then, captain. Let's get these heavy boxes out first."

"No, I have a better plan. Get out the bars, and pass them from one to the other through the hole; that is easier."

"So it is, but I don't see why we should do all the hard work, and let that ugly lubber sit there and do nothing. What say you, captain, shall we unbind him and make him work?"

"We may as well."

"So I think."

And in a trice Dick loosened Yokee's hands, and they all began to pass the treasure through the hole.

It was a difficult and very fatiguing task, but after working for two hours, the three chests were emptied, and then they sat down to rest.

"Now we have got the gold and silver out, captain, I think we might as well give a good look around and see if we can't find something to present to Miss Clarence."

"A good idea, Dick; so we will."

Dick and Lion Limb now began to search and toss things about, and at last discovered a large number of splendid shawls, scarfs, rolls of silk for dresses, and a thousand other valuables.

Some of these were quickly packed up in a large bundle, and by accident a jewel box was found hid away on a ledge of the projecting rock.

Lion Limb soon broke it open, and was delighted at its contents.

There were several large gold chains of fine workmanship, ear and finger rings, brooches and watches.

"These watches will be useful to us, Dick," said Lion Limb. "You can have one, I will have another, Harry must have a third; but the best of all must be reserved for Emma Clarence."

"Just what I was going to say," Dick replied; "but will they go, though?"

"I think so."

Lion Limb wound up the watches, and they went splendidly.

Yokee was struck with amazement as he heard the watches ticking, and started back as if expecting that the watches would hurt him.

"There; I think we will do pretty well this time, captain," said Dick. "Suppose we go down to our boat, and have a look at the state of the weather."

One after another they crept through the hole, and rolled back the large stone which concealed the entrance, and each seizing the bundles, made their way down towards the boat.

"Just to fancy the gold and silver and jewels there is in that place," said Dick. "What thieves these buccaneers must have been in their time."

"No doubt of it. But then you know there used to be more gold ships running from South America than there are now, Dick. You've heard of Captain Kidd?"

"Of course I have."

"Well, I've heard he buried millions and millions of gold and silver dollars, and no one can find any of it to this day."

"This cave of Nat's, though, is much better than Captain Kidd's," said Dick. "Why, captain, there's enough of stuff there to supply half the jewellers in all London."

"Yes; I perceived there was an immense amount of gold and silver ore."

"And not only ore, captain, but stocks of bags filled with Spanish gold ounces and doubloons. I stumbled over a lot of 'em, and almost broke my nose. But," said Dick, "I don't like the looks of them skeletons hanging on the walls; they give a fellow the horrors, and no mistake. How came they there, I wonder?"

"Oh, I dare say some of the dead chiefs, whose names we read, had occasionally a grudge against some one, and after inviting them there, killed them."

"Perhaps so; but then the other buccaneers would find it out."

"I don't think so, for it appears that this cave and its secret treasure is not known to the band at all."

"You don't mean that?"

"I do, though; it seems that one chief always left it as a great secret to the one who should succeed him, and he in his turn to the next."

"But how were they to know it?"

"Nat said that it was always the practice for the chief to leave a note in writing, which none of the band, under pain of death, should open until he was dead, and then it came into the hands of the chief who should follow him."

"Well, all I can say is that the chief who shall take Nat's place will find this secret treasure less bulky than it was before, and if he is at all lazy it will all disappear in less than a week."

While they were thus conversing and carrying their loads down towards the beach, Dick threw down his burden, and burst out into loud laughter.

"Well I never, captain; look yonder," said he.

Lion Limb looked over a rock, and down on the beach he perceived Joe Pebbler smoking his pipe, while around him were twenty or thirty Indians, dancing and capering about like madmen!

CHAPTER XLIII.

THE CAPTIVE'S NARRATIVE.

BUT while Lion Limb, Dick Hamilton, and Joe Pebbles were away at the Blue Rocks, as narrated in a previous chapter, Harry Woodruff was in chief command of the gallant little band at the colony, and, with the assistance of Emma Clarence, did everything in his power to make every one happy and comfortable.

Miss Emma was very desirous of ascertaining the history of each one of the poor prisoners, and the narratives of their trials, sufferings and adventures served not only to amuse but instruct her and the young colonists, who, at sunset, sat round their camp fires, all intent to hear their stories.

"Now, old man," said Harry to a grey-headed person, who had the looks and manners of one who had once been a sea-captain, "let us hear your story; fill up your pipe, and drink a drop of grog, it will cheer you up."

The old man did so, and thus began to speak :—

"You must know that I have been for many years engaged in the South-American trade, and was at Peru when war was declared against that state by Spain, of which, no doubt, you have read full accounts in the English newspapers, and was employed by the Peruvian government to take charge of a very valuable cargo which was sent to England to sell, the proceeds of which were to buy munitions of war.

"The brig which I at that time commanded was called the 'Raven,' as fine a vessel as I ever stepped aboard of.

"On this cruise an immense venture had been confided to me.

"I had shipped a large amount of gold, and the goods I had in were of great value.

"It was, therefore, necessary for me to keep in with the convoy.

"The wind, at the expiration of three days, died quite away, and for nearly the whole of the next day also there was a dead calm.

"Towards the close of the day, the heat, which had been almost unbearable all day, was more oppressive than ever, and a bank of dark clouds collecting in the eastward gave promise of something unpleasant.

"I had long been waiting for a signal for shortening sail from the man-of-war; but not receiving one, I determined now to act without orders.

"I got my top-gallant masts and yards down, furled every stitch of sail, braced the yards sharp up, and battened the hatches down.

"'We shall have a sneezer directly, my lads,' said my mate.

"'What do you think of it, Robinson?' I asked.

"'I think with you, captain,' returned the mate; and a great many of those crafts to leeward will be supplying old Davy Jones's grocer's shop with sugar before to-morrow morning.'

"The prophecy was soon fulfilled.

"My preparations were only just completed when a light air sprang up again from the S.W., and the ships from the convoy ran hard of me.

"But the deceit was fatal to many.

"Some of the ships let fall their courses, and would, if they had had more time, have set their studding-sails.

"But in an instant a cloud, like the darkness of night, came over us, and, bursting from it, flew one of the most terrific hurricanes which could be conceived.

"The sea, which a minute before was like a millpond, was torn up, and flew over us as if it was smoke.

"The wind came from all quarters at once, as though each were contending for the mastery.

"The first decided wind took us on the lee bow, that is, as my yards were braced, and threw the vessel on her beam ends.

"The vessel lay in the same position for a minute, then she righted a little, and gradually fell off before the gale.

"The sea, in about three minutes from its commencement, had been aroused into a boiling surge, which dashed over us without a moment's cessation.

"Notwithstanding, we must have been going at the rate of twelve knots.

"The deck was now completely flooded.

"Night setting in added not a little to the gloominess of the prospect.

"Not a syllable was spoken by anyone for full an hour, and then only in short and hurried sentences.

"'Had we not better keep our wind, captain?' said the mate. 'I think there is a slight lull, and I am afraid of the land.'

"'It will be as well, I think,' he answered.

"'Luff her to them,' said I.

"He did so.

"'Meet her.'

"I had hardly said this, when a green sea came over the gangway, and completely swept the deck, carrying with it the boats, caboose, and everything moveable, and the lee bulwarks, guns, and all.

"The hurricane and the rain continued almost unabated the whole night, during which time we had not a stitch of canvas set.

"As daylight broke, the hurricane subsided, and not a ship of the convoy was to be seen.

"The sea still ran very high, and the vessel having no sail set, rolled heavily.

"As the sun got up the wind went down, and I went to the mast-head to look around.

"With my glass I discovered no less than ten vessels, totally dismasted, ahead, and I made out what I conceived to be the frigate in company with them, giving assistance.

"I soon had the 'Raven' under all sail, and I ran down towards them.

"I had approached within two miles, when I observed that the vessel near and in company with the dismasted ship was not a frigate, but a corvette, which I suspected to be Spanish.

"Accordingly, I hove to, hoisted the Spanish colours, and fired a gun.

"This was immediately answered by the corvette hoisting Spanish colours and throwing out some signals, at once convincing me she was not English.

"It appears they mistook the 'Raven' for a privateer brig cruising in those regions.

"Such being the case, I tacked and made all sail away.

"The corvette made all sail in chase, but hull down, and as she soon was on the lee-quarter I gave myself little or no uneasiness about her.

"By noon it was a perfect calm, which was not at all agreeable, and what made the matter much worse was my fear that the wind would come round from the westward again, which would give my adversary the weather gage.

"She approached us within two miles before we felt the breeze.

"We then crowded all sail, but by sunset she had so far gained on us that we were within range of her long guns.

"Fortune now appeared to have taken her departure from us, and, although I did not suffer a fear to escape m lips, I began to think the 'Raven,' with her valuable cargo, was in a fair way of being lost.

"I called my mate to me, and told him of my design to escape.

"He expressed himself well of the plan.

"I then, without delay, gave orders to the men.

"Darkness had closed around us, and, most providentially, a cloud appeared and screened us from our pursuer's gaze.

"I called the men aft, and addressed them in these few words—

"'My lads, you are now almost in the hands of an enemy, but I think we may slip through their fingers if we mind what we are about. Give me the helm,' I said, to the steersman.

"Without another word of command my orders were obeyed with a celerity which would have done credit to a smart man-of-war.

"I put the helm up, and brought the wind on the other quarter.

"In about ten minutes I distinctly saw lights on the corvette as she passed me, and could hear the noises and confusion on board of her.

"'Now then, my lads, be quiet, but be quick.'

"Sail was now made as if by magic, and, contrary to the general plan, I followed in the wake of my pursuer.

"My contrivance succeeded beautifully.

"The corvette, finding I had got astern of her, hauled to the windward, and for the time I saw no more of her.

"But fortune had not yet done with me.

"The daylight, which warned me I had escaped the corvette, brought to my view a larger and as fearful an enemy.

"A strange sail—apparently a frigate—was bearing down under all sail.

"No time was to be lost.

"I ordered the studding sails to be set, for I would not set them before for fear of coming up with the corvette, and determined to try my rate of sailing.

"My ruthless pursuer gained on me rapidly.

"'I must try the old rig, Robinson,' said I; 'get out the Spanish colours.'

"Accordingly Spanish colours were hoisted.

"I waited impatiently for theirs, and, as I expected, she lowered her fore-royal and hoisted the Spanish flag.

"I accordingly took in the studding sails, hauled up the main-sail, and hove to.

"Upon this the frigate shortened sail, and as I kept the brig forging ahead a little I found the frigate would be obliged to pass under our stern.

"'Get your red caps out,' I said to the men, 'and ease off some of your top-gallant sheets, hang two or three swabs over the side, and make her look as lubberly as possible.'

"As the frigate passed by me she hailed me first in English, which I professed not to understand, then in Spanish, to which one of my men returned answer where we sailed from, and stated we were in great distress, having lost our boat and being much damaged in the hurricane, concluding by asking them to send a boat aboard with water.

"The ruse succeeded.

"The frigate unsuspectingly hove to leeward, lowerd her boat down, and after putting some water and provisions in her she rowed towards us.

"The boat had approached within a hundred yards of the brig when we filled and made all sail to windward with a fine breeze.

"As soon as the frigate saw what I was about, she saluted me with her whole broadside as I expected, which, however, did me not much damage, only one shot striking the main-mast and cutting away two shrouds on the starboard side.

"My object was to delay the frigate as much as possible by making her wait to hoist her boat up, and thus to get a good start.

"In this, however, I was deceived.

"The Spaniard thought a good prize was of more consequence than a boat's crew.

"So, without paying any attention to them, he gave chase after us, leaving them to their fate.

"I found that I had gained considerably, but it was on account of the frigate keeping up an almost constant fire upon me, as long as her shot, which made a few holes in my sails, could reach me.

"The wind freshened, but I dared not shorten sail, and I ordered away my royals a long time after the frigate had taken her's in.

"By three o'clock I was about two miles on the frigate's weather-beam, having taken in my royals, flying jib and fore top-gallant sail.

"The wind still increasing, my prospects were, therefore, anything but pleasing.

"The frigate just held her own, gaining rather than anything else, and there was every chance of its coming on to blow heavy, in which case the frigate, from her size, would have the best of it.

"'She is going through it nicely, now,' I said, looking over the side, 'must be going at least nine knots.'

"'She is a fine craft captain,' said Robinson, 'but the little schooner we belonged to twenty years ago was as fast.'

"'Did you ever hear what became of her?' I asked, 'for I shall never forget the "Raven."'

"'Why, I'll tell you, captain,' answered the mate, 'she was lost in just such a hurricane as we had t'other day and never heard of.'

"'There's her fore-topmast gone' said Robinson, starting up, who had been watching the frigate attentively while he was speaking to me.

"We looked, and to our inexpressible joy saw it was so, and a short but loud cheer burst spontaneously from all.

"My breast heaved with gratitude to the providence which had preserved us from a capture almost inevitable. Each man now took such refreshment as could be had.

"But the sky was threatening us with a gale.

"The night had not closed upon me until I became sensible of fresh danger.

"A strange sail was reported on the larboard beam.

"I went to the mast-head and made out the stranger to be a ship of war under her top-sails running before the wind.

"I watched her for a long time to see if she altered her course, and from her not doing so I conjectured I was either not seen or that the ship was a merchantman.

"I remained at the mast-head until the darkness shut her from my sight, and then descended comparatively easy in my mind.

"Greatly fatigued, I turned in after leaving orders to be called on any change of the weather or anything occurring.

"But I could not get anything like sleep.

"The anxieties I had endured for the last two or three days returned in all their force upon me, nor could I banish from my mind the idea that the sail I had made out was an enemy.

"I was aroused after what appeared to me a very short time, by the report of a gun and a confusion on deck, which convinced me there was something wrong.

"It was now two bells in the middle watch and blowing very hard.

"At this time we had our studding-sails in, but whole top-sails, fore-sails, and maintop-gallant sails set, with the wind on the quarter, and going ten knots.

"The ship that had fired upon us was on the larboard, within gun shot.

"I immediately ordered the mainsails to be set, but the wind blew so hard that we had the greatest difficulty in getting the main-jack aboard.

"When we had done, she tore through it like wildfire, and seemed to leave her pursuer far behind.

"For some time the chase was in doubt, and daylight broke ere our pursuer thought he could fire at us again with effect.

"The wind freshened so much as the sun got up, that he was soon glad to shut up his ports and secure his guns, and I was obliged, reluctantly, to shorten sail.

"My enemy was the corvette which I had doubled the night before, and I soon found I stood no chance of getting away.

"I was, however, obliged to carry sail, to keep the vessel from foundering, and I continued my course under double-reefed topsail and foresail.

"After a few hours our enemy was within musket-shot of us, on our weather-quarter.

"She then hailed, and ordered us to heave to, enforcing the command by a volley of musketry.

"My interpreter, by my desire, said I could not do so with the sea then running.

"He replied by another volley of musketry, which badly wounded one of the men, and slightly wounded another.

"I then told my interpreter to say that I would heave to, but expected to lose my masts in doing so.

"I sent the man aloft to close reef the topsails, in doing which another of the men was wounded.

"The revenge of the cowardly wretches, it seemed, was not satisfied with our propriety, feeling so indignant at the escape I made from them the night before.

"As soon as the topsails were re-hoisted, I accordingly hove to, and watching the seas, did so with safety.

"I shall never forget that ship.

"Her model was extremely beautiful.

"She was more than two hundred tons, and coppered.

"Two thousand pounds, the only two thousand pounds I had in the world, were embarked in this my craft; besides, I loved my little brig, she was a kind of solace for my recent heavy loss.

"As my vessel bounded over the water so my heart seemed also to bound, and the reflection that this was the day when I should no more stand as captain of the 'Raven's' deck caused me unfeigned sorrow.

"At the instant we were repining at our misfortune 'the deed was doing' which was to set us at liberty.

"The corvette, in order to come up with us, had been carrying double-reefed topsails and foresail.

"But, after we rounded to, instead of taking the precaution I had resorted to of close-reefing, she hauled up.

"An immense sea took her amidships, which, adding to an increased gust of wind, sent her foretopmast and mainmast over the side together.

"Here was a deliverance as unexpected as pleasing. I believe I never raised my thanks more devoutly to heaven than at that time.

"I at a great risk, for a tremendous sea was running, put the little 'Raven' again before it, and, in a few days afterwards, reached Chili in safety.

"I was the first to bring the news of the hurricane, and have often related the news of this voyage, which I considered to be as remarkable as to deserve a place among a sailor's reminiscences. I afterwards learned that five of the ships that started out with me were lost, and several others seized by Spanish cruisers.

"This was my most remarkable voyage, for the next time I went to sea I fell into worse hands than the Spaniards; I was seized by the buccaneers."

CHAPTER XLIV.

RED WOLF AND KING KATAMAR MEET.

"WHAT the deuce are they after?" said Dick, who now dropped his burden, and peeped over the rocks

"They are Indians without a doubt, Dick, but they don't appear to belong to the same tribe as those of Red Wolf and his gang who attacked our settlement."

"No, they don't belong to Red Wolf's lot, that's certain," said Dick, "for they are handsomer and better dressed, and take more care of themselves."

Yokee, who up to this time had maintained silence, now fell upon his knees before Lion Limb, and began to make the most dismal of noises.

"Oh, do not kill me!" he said; "do not kill me!"

"I have sworn not to do so," said Lion Limb; "but why this fright? Do you know who these people are?"

"Yes, I do; they are King Katamar's men; they are my friends, no doubt sent by King Katamar to look for his lost daughter among these islands, but if you tell them what I have done they will kill me," said Yokee.

"I'm glad all King Katamar's men then are not such sneaks as you are," said Dick, in disgust. "Come, get up, and make yourself known to them; Lion Limb will not forget his promise, your life is safe."

"Rise," said the young captain, "and make yourself known to them."

In an instant Yokee jumped to his feet, and looked over the rocks.

"What are they doing dancing about in such a way?" said Dick.

"Joe doesn't seem to mind it much," said Lion Limb; "he sits there smoking his pipe and grins."

"Look at him now," said Dick, "by Jove he is beginning to dance himself."

It seems that Mr. Pebbles, after seeing the Indians dance, was not satisfied, so he pulled up his trousers, and gave them the sailors' hornpipe in capital style.

"Why, the fellow must be drunk," said Lion Limb.

"Not much doubt about that, sir. See, he is lugging at a calabash there; but it contains something stronger than water, I imagine."

Such was the truth.

The Indians had brought with them several small contrivances which contained a rough spirit, which the Indians sometimes made and indulged in, and Mr. Joseph Pebbles had not been many minutes in their company before he made the pleasant discovery, and did not rest contented until he had drank at least half-a-pint or more.

At this moment Yokee raised a quick sharp cry, which caused the Indians on the beach to stop dancing, and look around with astonishment.

He repeated the signal.

It was answered by a terrific yell which made the rocks echo again, and in another moment they ran up towards the spot where Lion Limb was.

While he spoke the Indians arrived on the spot. They rushed towards Yokee, whom they instantly recognised, despite his disguise of European clothing, and then they raised a shout of triumph.

Yokee was lifted on their shoulders and borne down towards the beach, while numerous attendants laughed, and sang, and danced like madmen.

Lion Limb made signs to one or two who assisted him with his burden, and in less time than we can say it, both the Indians and Europeans were shaking hands and the very best of friends.

"What means this, Yokee?" asked Lion Limb "Why do they dance and kick up such a row, then?"

"I told them that Princess Marmi was safe, and they yelled with delight."

"I think they did; I shall be deaf for a month, after all this uproar."

"And what do they intend to do now?" asked Lion Limb.

"They have a great many canoes with them, and will take back all our people to Katamar Island, if you'll permit it."

"I have no objection."

"Nor I either; the Indian devils at the colony eat a devil of a lot, captain, and don't seem to like work much. Hard work don't agree with 'em, I think," said Dick. "The sooner we ship off the red-skinned varmint the better, I think."

"And do you wish to go with them, Yokee?"

"No, master," said the Indian, " my whole life is in your hands; do with me as you think proper."

But though he spoke thus, Yokee's voice trembled, which made Lion Limb feel certain that he *did* want to go.

"If you like, you can go home with them, Yokee."

"But, may I return, master?" he asked, humbly.

"Why ask that?"

"White men much better than us," was the reply. "Me go and come back, stay long time with you, then me teach my Indians to be like white men."

"Very good, and so you shall; then, we might as well try to civilize these savages, Dick."

Dick grunted out something about " a good rope's end, and plenty of flogging," but by this time the boat was launched, and, followed by the canoes of the Indians, Lion Limb sailed homewards again with a fair wind.

*   *   *   *   *

But what had happened at the colony during the absence of Lion Limb?

Harry Woodruff was left in command of the place, and, as a sensible fellow, he made every one work hard in tilling and sowing, and a thousand other things that were necessary, and everything was prospering around them.

He had taken a great liking to the lion skin cloak which his young leader usually wore, and, as it hung up in Lion Limb's cabin, Harry put it on, and seemed very proud.

"This skin wasn't got without a deadly fight," said he, "and Lion Limb deserves all the honour. They tell me that Red Wolf's men have a mortal terror of this, and run like demons when Lion Limb approaches. They call him the 'fire king,' 'lion-hunter,' and a thousand other names. Suppose, then, I wear it for a time, and see what they'll think of me. I'm bound to have an adventure of some sort before he returns home; no one will be the wiser."

With such thoughts, Harry started forth into the forest, armed with gun, pistol, hunting-knife and the like, and did not intend to return for a whole day.

He had not proceeded far, however, in his travels when he heard the voices of some savages not far off, who were conversing in very animated tones.

From what little Harry could understand, he became aware that the ugly villains were rejoicing greatly at something which had occurred to their king and leader, Red Wolf.

"He has got him;" said one.

"Who?" was the response.

"Why, Katamar."

The other Indian gave a yell of triumph.

"How did it happen?"

"I hear that old Katamar started forth alone on his journey in search of his daughter Marmi, whom the 'young fire-king' took from us; but, Red Wolf was too cunning for Katamar. His footsteps in the forest were closely followed, and, when least expected, Katamar was seized and bound, and taken captive."

"And what is his fate?"

"Red Wolf had him chained and placed in a loghouse which he had built after the pattern of the young white people's strong houses, and there he awaits his doom."

"Red Wolf has been drunk for several days, so overjoyed is he on account of the capture of his old enemy."

Harry heard thus much of the conversation, and when he advanced cautiously a few steps to hear more distinctly whatever else might be said, the two Indians had disappeared.

"Oh, if Lion Limb were here and heard all this," said Harry, "how he would rejoice; but then he isn't here, and something must be done, and done quickly to prevent old Katamar's death."

Fearlessly Harry Woodruff left his hiding-place, and as secretly as possible made his way towards the camps of Red Wolf's barbarians, which were situated in a very strong place, and almost defied the attempts of any one to storm or take it.

About midnight, however, Harry reached the savage settlement, and although it was broad moonlight, he crept along through bushes and brushwood until he came within sight of Red Wolf's great stronghold, the newly-made block-house, and hid under the shadow of a tree.

"This must be the plan," said Harry. "I am right in the midst of the savages, and perhaps this adventure may end in my own death; but I care not, with such a valiant leader as we have, we should not fear any danger, nor will I."

He clambered up to the open windows as softly as a cat, and inside the log-house he saw a tall Indian chained and unable to move.

This was the king, Katamar.

In a few moments afterwards, and without noise, Harry perceived that a second Indian crawled into the log-house, while Katamar to all appearance was sound asleep.

This was Red Wolf.

"Oh, what a monster," sighed Harry. "He has come to commit cool deliberate murder."

But Katamar was *not* asleep.

He had perceived the approach of Red Wolf, and in an instant sprang upon him.

He seized the intruder by the throat (See Cut). The struggle between them was something awful to behold.

"Die!" shouted Red Wolf, with his gleaming knife in hand.

A sudden report of a pistol was heard.

A groan followed on the instant—who was killed?

THE BOY KING

OF THE SOUTH SEA ISLANDS.

EMMA CLARENCE CARRIED OFF BY A GORILLA.

CHAPTER XLV.

IN WHICH ALLAN NORMAN ESCAPES.

HAD the devil himself, described as he often is, with his horns and cloven hoofs, suddenly confronted

Dr. Shorthorn and his visitors, they could not have been more paralyzed than they were at the sudden release of Allan.

They staggered back in terror and alarm.

The first thing which Allan did was to strike

No. 16.

down Jerry with a blow, which instantly broke two of his ribs.

His next thought was to escape.

Flourishing his iron bar, he rushed out of the chamber and dashed downstairs.

The back doors were open, and this facilitated Allan's escape.

Several of the keepers and servants met Allan, who shouted out,

"They are coming! They are coming! Look to yourselves or you will all be murdered!"

Fancying that all the lunatics had once more broken loose, the servants rushed helter skelter away in all directions, and like very wise people bolted the doors.

The females began to scream long before anyone else, although there was no real cause of alarm, and Allan seized the moment of confusion to dash forward into the garden, climb over the wall as best he could, and after half an hour's run found himself in the open fields.

Up to the present moment intense excitement had given him strength, but now he sank down upon the ground, near a hay-stack, and felt as weak as a cat.

In truth, Dr. Shorthorn and his assistants were in the habit of half starving their patients, and young Allan's allowance of food consisted of nothing else but bread and water.

He was pale, and thin, and weak, and as he threw himself upon the hay he almost prayed for death, so weary and tired of life was he.

How long he remained in this spot he had not the slightest notion, for he fell fast asleep almost immediately.

A shower of rain fell meanwhile, and it refreshed the slumberer.

"What shall I do now?" thought Allan, as he awoke and rubbed his eyes. "I have no money, nor friends, and am in rags. I know not where to go."

He looked at his clothes, and they were torn in all directions.

His hands were thin and white, and his shoes almost without soles.

He had but one friend near him, and that friend was part of the iron bar of his cell, which he still firmly clutched in his right hand.

"Where am I? How far have I run?" thought he. "It all seems like a dream."

He knew not, but the truth was that the poor lad in fright and horror of ever being incarcerated again in the asylum had so wrought upon his young mind that he had actually run over two miles, across hedge and ditch, before he stumbled and fell near the hay-rick.

"Never mind," thought the brave young Allan, "I have escaped, and that is one great blessing. I will make my way to town and seek out Jem Rawlings, if I can."

He went to a brook and washed himself, and was about to make his way to the nearest highway, when his quick ear caught the sounds of barking of dogs.

At first poor young Allan imagined that they might be the dogs of some sportsman.

Then he thought, as they came nearer and nearer, that they were animals that belonged to a neighbouring firm.

He listened attentively, and the sounds came nearer and nearer.

"Surely they do not belong to the asylum," he imagined. "What shall I do? Shall I fly?"

He knew not what to do.

The poor lad was so weak and feeble for the want of proper nourishment, that his limbs trembled under him.

"I shall be torn in pieces," he said.

And tears started to his eyes.

"What have I done that I should be thus hunted down like a murderer? I have never injured any one; I have never stolen anything; I am as innocent of all crimes as a baby. Oh! what a miserable life is mine!"

He threw himself again upon the hay, and he prayed in his simple humble way that a kind Providence would assist him, for all earthly aid seemed hopeless.

"Suppose I have killed Jerry Marks," he argued; "then they will have me up for murder; but then it was only in self defence. Yet who will believe me? Poor Norman," he sighed, "I wish I had been transported and been drowned with you in those far-off seas, then all my troubles would have been at an end."

Without father, without money, with no friends to guide or help him, Allan was alone in the world.

He was very young in years, but he had seen many severe trials, and why he should suffer all this misery he could not tell.

But now the sounds of the barking of dogs had died away.

"Thank Heaven!" he sighed; "I am safe once more. I will go back to London and seek a living somehow, and try to find out Jem."

While he thus mused and formed all sorts of good resolutions for the future, he was horrified to see three large dogs rush into the field, and run towards him with terrible yells.

A moment afterwards the animals were followed by Dr. Shorthorn, old Marks, and two keepers.

With a sudden pang at his heart, young Allan perceived all this, and jumped to his feet and faced the dogs.

"There he is! there he is!" shouted old Lawyer Marks.

"On to him, dogs, on to him!" shouted Dr. Shorthorn.

"We have got him safe, now," said the two keepers, almost breathless as they ran across the field.

The three dogs were now close upon Allan, who, with a sudden resolution to be free or die, rushed forward with the iron bar in his hand, and confronted the savage beasts.

With one blow he killed the first upon the spot.

A second flew at his throat.

But another blow broke the animal's ribs.

The third one retreated, and would have made his escape, but Allan pursued, and overtook him, and almost cut the brute in halves.

Turning on Dr. Shorthorn and the others with looks of fury,

"Come on!" said Allan.

His pursuers were amazed at his daring, and stood stock still.

Old Marks, however, saw something in Allan's eyes that he did not like, and ran away at the top of his speed.

Allan then advanced towards Dr. Shorthorn, and, brandishing the weapon, so frightened the doctor that he also ran away.

"Stop there, keepers, until I procure assistance," said he; "don't leave the young villain, or lose sight of him for one moment: he must not escape."

Allan, however, got behind the hay-stack again, and hid himself.

After consulting for a few moments, the two keepers resolved to out-wit Allan.

"You go round one way and I the other, we shall then trap the ferocious madman," said one.

This plan was agreed to.

Each keeper advanced cautiously and slowly round the hay-stack.

But, judge of their astonishment, when they discovered the lad could not be found.

Allan had escaped !

CHAPTER XLVI.

THE YOUNG HOUSELESS WANDERER.

"HILLOA, my covey," said a rough-looking fellow who met Allan on his way to London, "you seem werry hard up, and no mistake. Where have you come from ?"

"A long way, sir," said Allan, resting himself under a hedge.

"A long way, eh ? You seem to tremble, what's up ? Have you had the cholery or yellow janders, which ?"

"Neither."

"Well, you needn't answer a fellow in that sharp sort o' way, you know," said the other, with a dry grin, "for I daresay you don't like to be asked too many questions no more than other folks."

Now the person that Allan met deserves a few words of notice.

He was a strongly-built man of about thirty years, attired in corduroys and a velveteen jacket, he wore a rough hairy cap, very heavy boots, his hands were large, bony, and puffed from drinking.

One eye was black, and his nose was very much flattened, while his hair hung down at the side like a pair of corkscrews.

"I don't know what you mean," said Allan.

"Oh, you doesn't, eh ? Well, no matter, will you have a smoke ?" said he, offering the lad the use of a small black pipe.

"I never smoke, thank you," said Allan.

"What, not smoke," said the rough-looking man in astonishment ; "well, you *is* a innocent. What does you do then ? Get out o' gaol, and that sort o' thing ?"

"No, sir, I have never been in gaol but once, and then I was——"

"Innocent, in course ; ah ! so am I. I've been in quod many a time, and was always innocent ; as innocent as a baby. But then, you see, the beaks has got a grudge agin me ; they don't like Micky."

"And is that your name ?"

"Yes, Micky is my right name ; but, then, some folks, friends o' mine at Bow Street, always writes it down on a broad sheet of bran new paper, Michael Huggins, you know."

"Then, Huggins is your name ?"

"Yes, but I always drops the Huggins, and takes to be called Micky ; it sounds shorter and sweeter, you know."

"And what might your business be, Mr. Huggins ?" said Allan, innocently.

"Eh ? What ?"

"Your business."

"Oh, ah, just so, my young friend ; I don't mind telling you, you know, in confidence, but, I'm a very useful member of society — I'm a retired coster."

"Oh, I understand," said Allan, innocently. "So you've come out into the country for a little pleasure, I suppose ?"

"That's just it, young 'un, if you *must* know ; I don't mind telling you I've come out here to pick out a house."

"To live in ?"

"Yes, for a little while," said Mike Huggins, sucking his pipe and laughing.

For a moment Mike said nothing, but he looked hard, nay, very hard, at little Allan, and smoked his pipe with self-evident pleasure.

"He's quite a innocent," said Mike, as he looked at Allan again and again, and smoked his short pipe. "He'll jest do for me, he will."

After a long pause, Mike said,

"Ain't you very hungry ?"

"Yes, and thirsty also."

"I thought so. Well, suppose we move on and call at some public ? I've got a bob or two ; a drop of beer will do you no harm. Come this way ; follow me, young 'un."

"But why not go by the high road ?" said Allan.

"Oh, through the fields is best—what a innocent he is to be sure—come, follow me, young 'un ; I see a house yonder."

"But, why not go by the high road ?" said Allan. "We shall be taken up for trespassing."

"No fear o' that, young 'un," said Mr. Huggins ; " you be guided by me."

Hungry as he was, young Allan felt very desirous of having some food, and, as he had no money, he felt very thankful for the kind offer of his newly-found friend, and told him so.

In a few moments they arrived at a tavern, and Mr. Huggins straightway went into the tap-room, and called for bread and cheese and beer.

"There," said Mr. Huggins, "have a go in at that ; have a tightener, mind you, for I am going to introduce you to some of my friends when we get to London."

Huggins himself drank heartily of the beer ; but Allan's appetite had gone, and he ate very sparingly of the bread and cheese.

"What, done already, young 'un ?"

"Yes, thank you."

"Well, it won't take much to keep you, I see. Why, a sparrow would eat almost as much as you do."

After a pause, in which Mr. Huggins drained the pot, and filled it again, Allan said,

"Hadn't we better get on the road again ?"

"No, not yet awhile."

"Why not ?"

"Are you in any particular hurry, young 'un ? Are the beaks after you ?"

Allan scarcely understood the slang of Mr. Huggins ; but, although he at first felt very much inclined to tell him his whole story, he refrained from doing so.

"Well, you know," said Huggins, "I'm in no particular hurry myself, so, if you don't mind, we'll wait here until dark, and then all will go square. I've got a particular job to do here in this neighbourhood, and shall go out for a walk. Can you read ?"

"Yes."

"Well, that's more than I can, but I dare say they'll lend you a paper to look at until I come back. You stay here, mind."

"I will."

Feeling very thankful indeed to his newly found acquaintance for his kindness, Allan remained in the tap-room before the fire, but before long he went to sleep on a bench, and dreamed that he had seen a great many people of Mr. Huggins's stamp, but where he could not say, except in Newgate.

However, the sleep did him a great deal of good, and he waited impatiently for his friend's return.

But the business upon which Mike Huggins was bent was very difficult indeed.

He went across the fields by a foot-path, until he came in sight of a very large country house.

"The family is away," mused Mike, "and I don't think me and my pals would have much difficulty in getting in there; besides, there's any quantity of plate in the pantry, and the butler always spends his evenings out of the house."

This mental expression proves that the kind Mr. Huggins was a villain, blackguard, a thief, and a housebreaker.

He prowled about the grounds of the house for several hours, and having made all the observations he desired was about to return, when a horseman approached.

He was a well-dressed person, and handsomely mounted upon a fast-going, well-made horse.

Anyone would have taken him for one of the finest gentlemen in the land.

He had plenty of money; kept one or two race-horses, and was well known among betting men.

But for all that he was a rogue and vagabond, and ought to have been transported long before.

"Hullo, Mr. George," said Huggins; "is that you?"

"Yes, Mike; but we musn't be seen talking here."

"This is one of your jobs, then?"

"Yes."

"Ah, Mr. George you are a lucky fellow; just look at me, I have been lagged three times, and here are you galloping about like some lord."

Mr. George laughed; but saying that he would meet Mike in London that night, he went through the park gates, and rode up to the house.

"Well, of all the cheek I ever heard on, that beats all," said Mike; "here have I been dodging round the place for two whole days trying to hit upon a plan to get into the house, and here he goes straight up to it on horseback. Well, I never; I thought as how Mr. George had something to do with this job, although Portland Bill never let on. Well I never."

It is thus seen that Mr. Huggins was one of a gang who sometimes acted under the orders of this Mr. George, who was the head of all.

"If that's the game I shall go to town at once; why didn't Portland Bill tell me on it afore?"

Huggins went back through the fields to the public-house, but Mr. George rode fearlessly up to the house.

He dismounted, and seemed very much annoyed and surprised when told by the butler that my Lord Manfred was not at home, and away shooting in the highlands of Scotland.

Mr. George came to see one or two of his lordship's horses, who were reported for sale, and as he (Mr. George) was well known to Lord Manfred, and had been at Greenvale Hall before, the butler gave him refreshments, and showed him not only over the stables but the entire Hall.

This was all Mr. George wanted.

"I must get that bond from my lord somehow," said Mr. George, "for I owe him £10,000; he is away now, so the thing can be done very nicely. I see that Portland Bill has commenced operations already. Mike Huggins is a first class hand."

When he left the Hall, Mr. George rode straight to London, and towards evening Mr. Huggins and young Allan followed in the same direction, but Mike seemed loth to go by the high-road for fear of the mounted police.

"If I get collared they'll give me fifteen years next time," thought he.

By bye-roads and lanes Allan and Huggins walked, but Mike never passed a public-house without having a drop of gin or a pot of beer.

That and his pipe seemed to supply the place of food on all occasions.

"This cove here," he mused, "will do the trick nicely. I must get him into the Hall somehow, and then when night comes he can easily open a window; but suppose the young brat wont do it, or blows on us?" thought Mike, and he grinned so horribly that it almost frightened Allan.

"Oh, I'll soon manage that," he said, pulling out two crown pieces and marking them. "There, you put 'em in your pocket," said he, "and mind 'em for me. Don't you spend 'em."

Before Allan was aware of it, Huggins placed the two silver pieces in his pocket, and laughed louder than ever.

"What are you laughing at?" asked Allan, who now began to dislike his companion very much.

"Oh, nothing," said Huggins, laughing still more.

"There must be some reason," said Allan.

"Well, then, if you will know what I'm grinning about," said Huggins, sucking his pipe with even more vigour than usual, "I'll tell you."

"I wish you would," said Allan, who now began to feel very uneasy and timid.

"Well, can't a fellow laugh, then, young 'un?" said Mike. "What next, I wonder? Who could help laughing at such a young guy as you is? Why, you've not a boot nor shoe scarce to your trotters, you're out at elbows, got a dirty face, and look as lean as a grey-hound."

"Well, poverty is no crime," said Allan, proudly. "I wasn't always in such a plight as I am now. Poverty is no crime," he repeated.

"Ain't it, though?" said Mike, with a low whistle. "Where did you learn that 'ere sentiment from? from a tea-paper, I suppose, eh? ha, ha! Well I thinks that poverty is a very great crime, that's my opinion about it. You might as well be dead as without money."

"You might as well be dead as to get money dishonestly," said Allan, proudly.

"Honestly, eh?" said Mike; "do you know what the old Quaker told his son, young 'un?"

"No," said Allan.

"Well, he says—and a very wise cove he was, I thinks—he says, says he, 'My son, get money, honestly if you can, but anyhow get money,' and that's just what I thinks about it."

"Well, I don't, so there's the difference"

"Nonsense, gammon," said Mike. "You can preach like a good many more, but I dare say you'd have no objection to nicking a purse or two if you had half a chance."

"What is 'nicking?'" asked Allan.

"What! don't know what 'nicking' is? Well, of all the greenhorns I ever see, you are the worst."

"If you mean stealing," said Allan, "all I can say is that I would scorn to do anything so mean. I'd rather have my right hand cut off first."

"And what would you do then?"

"Why, go and beg first."

"Oh, begging is your game, eh? Well, it ain't a bad game no way, if you are only well up in your business; I knows plenty o' chaps as makes a rare old thing in the cadging line. I shall meet a good many to night were I'm going to."

"I suppose if they beg they are honest for all that," said Allan.

"Well, I don't know so much about that," said Mike; "I wouldn't trust none on 'em no further than I can see 'em. Now, there's the soldier, a chap as goes out a singing, he makes a pretty tidy thing on it, and has always got the price of a pot in his pocket, and a rare pair o' lungs he's got, and no mistake; if you can't hear him a mile, I'll eat my head."

"Do you know him then?"

"In course I do, and nearly all on 'em. And then there's old Whistling Barney, from morning till night, and up to twelve o'clock on Saturday nights, you'll see him with a stick in his hand, crawling along the quiet streets, whistling the same old dismal tune; what the name of it is no one knows nor himself either, but there he goes whistling up and down; and as to coppers, lor! I've seen him with both pockets filled long before dinner, and he wouldn't mind giving thirteen for a shilling. He used to go out with a woman with a child in her arms, and the fake told very well, but then she used to want too much gin, so the old man gave her a pair of black eyes and discharged her. He goes out alone now, and how it is he hasn't got the consumption years ago is a mystery. His whistling tunes give me the tooth-ache whenever I hear 'em."

"Then," said Mike, "there's the chap with the stumpy legs, who calls himself blind. Lor' bless you, young 'un, you should hear him in the markets on Saturday nights. He makes the streets ring again, and the more drops of gin he gets the noisier he is, until at last he bawls out so you'd think he was going to get up on his stumps and pitch into every one as didn't give him a penny; but I see him the other day with a new white hat, bran new clothes, and a gold watch chain, walking across the dials with a stick in his hand, but you wouldn't think it were one and the same party as regularly goes his rounds cadging. If he is blind, he gets about well enough, without any one to help him. Then," said Mike, sucking his pipe, "there's Chaunting Barneys; but that work is too hard when you can get the coppers without opening your mouth. But the women get along best in the cadging line," said Mike. "I know one or two on 'em as keeps their husbands without work; what do you think o' that? If they can only hire one or two nice-looking kids, they stand at the corner of a crowded street, and look as if they had swallowed something as didn't agree with 'em, and then the silly wives come along with odd pennies to spend, 'Poor creetur'! Give her a penny,' says she to the husband, and in that way they get many a good shilling during the night. I've known some women to pay as much as two bob a night for hiring a good-looking kid; so you see, young 'un, there's plenty o' fakes you can pick from without working, if you've a mind"

"They are impostors," said Allan, indignantly, "and should be given into custody."

"Well, you'd better not tell 'em so where we are going to-night."

"And where is that?"

"Why, some place to sleep. I dare say you wouldn't care about staying out and lying in the cold streets all night."

"No, I would not," said Allan; "but it is very kind of you."

"I knows it is, but we wont mention it now. You only do as I tells yer, and all will go right enough."

Now, from the conversation of his rough-looking companion, Allan began to shrewdly guess that he was a person of very unenviable character.

They were now approaching the suburbs of London, and although it was dark, young Allan noticed that a great many policemen looked very hard at Mr. Huggins.

"Did you notice the policeman that time?" said Allan.

"No. What did he do?"

"He looked so hard at you."

"Not at me, young 'un, he was squinting at you."

"No he wasn't."

"I'm sure he was; none on 'em knows me."

"Well, one or two pulled out their pocket books and put something down as you passed."

"They were sketching out your portrait, young 'un, that's all; they are very fond o' that game."

For some time they walked on in silence, and Micky Huggins, as if in deep thought, said half aloud,

"Looking at me! lor bless yer, they never see me afore."

And then he added, in an angry tone,

"They never will let honest people get a living."

Just as he spoke, some one said,

"Got a young pal, Mike?"

Mr. Huggins seemed to recognize the voice, for he stopped instantly.

"Ah, Mr. Green, that you?" said Huggins. "Long time since I've seen you."

"How long have you been out, Mike?"

"Oh, only about two months, Mr. Green."

"You'd better take care next time, Mike, or it will go very hard with you."

Mike did not stop to hear more, but was about to pass on, when Mr. Green, the policemen in plain clothes (for such he was) tapped young Allan on the shoulder.

"I want to speak to you, my lad," said he. "You can go on, Mike, I'm not talking to you. Is that your friend, my lad?"

"No, sir."

"When did you meet him?"

Allan was about to answer, when Mike retraced his steps.

"Go round the corner, my lad, and stay there till I come," said Green.

"I want to speak to you about that boy," said Mike to the policeman.

"Well, what of him? Why, where has the little brat gone to?" said Mr. Green, in well-feigned surprise; "why, he was here a moment ago."

"Ah, I thought he would give me the slip," said Mike; "and just to fancy he robbed me of ten bob."

"How was that?"

"I gave him the money to buy something for me, and instead of that he has hooked it, money and all. Who'd a thought the young wretch was so artful? But I dare say I shall meet him again before long."

"Where?" said Green, laughing.

"Why, in Newgate."

"Very likely, if he is a pupil of yours."

Mike made some remark and went off in a hurry, bent on finding Norman, who was hiding in a deep doorway and saw Mike pass.

Mr. Green, the detective, followed Mike a few yards, and, as he passed the door in which Allan was hiding, said—

"Go right through into the mews, my lad, I want to speak to you."

Allan obeyed, and was quickly joined by the detective.

"Tell me the truth, my lad;" said he, "you have come out of the country to-day? I can tell by the dust upon your clothes."

"Yes, sir, I have."

"How far?"

"About ten miles."

"But you didn't start very early, then; how is that?"

"That man met me, and said it would be cooler to walk in the evening."

"Do you know who your companion was?"

"He said his name was Mike Huggins."

"Yes, but that is only one of many names he goes by," said Green. "I have known him longer than you, my boy, and he is a rascal. He has been transported once or twice."

"Transported!" said Allan, surprised.

"Yes, and he would have made you as great a rogue as himself; he has been the cause of more than one poor boy being sent out of the country."

"Well, I thought he meant no good," said Allan. "I'm glad I met you."

"Did he call anywhere upon the road, my lad?"

"No."

"Did you hear him say where he had been to?"

"No; but I heard him ask the publican if a large house that stood away from the road wasn't Lord Manfred's."

"Lord Manfred's, eh?" said the officer, producing his pocket-book, and making a note therein. "Is it true that you robbed him of two crown-pieces?"

"No, sir; I have them here," said Allan. "He told me not to spend them but to keep them."

"Let me look at them," said the officer, who took the coins and minutely examined them.

"They are marked, I see."

"Are they, sir?"

"Yes, my lad."

"And why did he mark them?"

"To get you into trouble; nothing else, my boy. Did he say where he was living now?"

"No, sir."

"And now, my good boy, let me ask you a question. Where did *you* come from to meet such a fellow as that?"

The question confused young Allan, who trembled violently for a moment, and turned very red.

At last, with honest boldness, Allan told the whole truth to the officer, who seemed greatly surprised at what he heard.

"And so they confined you as a lunatic, eh?" said the officer, biting his lip. "These Marks, then, have a deep grudge against you?"

"Yes, sir."

"Well, never mind, I will be a true friend to you; you seem to be an honest lad, and are as sane as I am; there is some mystery about it that will be fathomed some day; but in the meantime come with me."

The officer took Allan to a comfortable lodging, and paid for it.

"Stay here," said he, "until I return; perhaps if your story is true, I can find out where this Jem Rawlings is that you speak so much of."

So saying, the officer left, and in about an hour afterwards he returned with Jem Rawlings.

Allan almost jumped with joy when he saw Jem enter the room, and he clasped his hand with a tight grip of friendship.

"Now," said the officer, "you have pleasant lodgings and plenty to eat and drink. There is only one thing I have to say: don't leave these premises until I give you leave; I shall be here again in the morning."

"What can all this mean, Allan?" asked Jem, when the officer had gone.

"I cannot tell, Jem; it is all a mystery as yet."

CHAPTER XLVII.

LAWYER MARKS RECEIVES AN OFFICIAL VISIT.

THE officer did not trouble himself to make any enquiries that night about Doctor Shorthorn or Lawyer Marks, for he had too much on his mind regarding another matter, namely, the visit of Mr. Michael Huggins to the country seat of Lord Manfred.

"Singular fellow that," thought the officer; "he is no sooner out of prison than he does all in his power to get in again. I know that he is in league with some others more clever than himself, but who they are has long puzzled the best of us. No matter, I dare say we shall fall foul of them one of these fine mornings: the judge at the Old Bailey will do the rest."

Straightway he went to Bow Street, and after making a few inquiries of his companions he made up his mind that Mr. Mike Huggins had some grand scheme in view at Lord Manfred's mansion, and it would not be out of place to wait and watch for the execution of it.

Next morning, however, he gave an early call at the offices of Lawyer Marks, and in incidental conversation ascertained the important fact that Mr. Jerry Marks was confined to his bed with a broken rib.

His long nose was also terribly swollen, and two teeth were knocked out.

"And so you have never heard anything more of this youth who escaped from the lunatic asylum?" said the officer.

"No; not a word."

"I wish we could," said Jerry; "I would willingly give £100 to have the young rascal captured and punished."

"Is this lad any relation of yours, Mr. Marks?"

"No, not the slightest."

"It is very kind of you to take so much interest in the lad, then."

"So it is; and yet see how we are repaid for it all."

"Ah!" sighed Jerry, "that only aggravates the assault."

"We gave chase to the young villain," said old Marks, "but were unable to capture him. Three dogs were also sent in pursuit but he killed them all, and would have killed me likewise, had I stayed a few moments longer."

"Ah, it is a sad affair!" said the officer, "and I take particular interest in the matter, for this affair at Dr. Shorthorn's asylum had been partly placed in my hands."

"Oh, indeed!" said the old man, pricking up his ears; "then in the hands of such a skilful officer as you are we may expect soon to hear of the young culprit's apprehension."

"Perhaps so, sir; but then you must aid us all you can."

"Nothing would give me greater satisfaction, I assure you, officer; but you detectives are such deep fellows, you don't require the assistance of poor people like us," said old Marks, who began to imagine the officer might want some money.

"Yes, some of us are deep enough, Mr. Marks, and often hear of startling things; for instance, every day of my life I see men who I am morally certain ought to be transported, and yet they hold up their heads higher than the best of Christians."

"You don't mean that?"

"I do, though."

"How very strange and wonderful!"

"Truth is stranger than fiction, Mr. Marks," said the officer, coldly, "and if it won't inconvenience you, would you please allow me one moment's conversation in *private?*"

"In private?" asked the old man in surprise.

"In private!" said Jerry, half choking with excitement.

"Yes, in private, sir, if you please."

"Why not before my son, officer?" said old Marks, getting very fidgetty.

"Because it concerns you more than any one else."

"Oh, certainly, if you so wish it, officer. Come in my back office."

Jerry was dying with curiosity, and as he lay on the sofa he stretched himself far over towards the partition door to hear what might be said.

"Now, officer, what is it you wish to ask me?"

"In confidence, you know."

"Solemn confidence, you know."

"You won't tell any one?"

"No."

"Not even your son?"

"No."

"He can't hear us, can he?"

"No, not at all. But what is it you wish to say?"

"I want to ask you only one question," said the officer, loud enough for Jerry to hear in the next room, for he felt certain he was listening attentively.

"Then what the devil *is* the question you wish to ask?" said old Marks, getting hot and red with expectation.

"Why this, Mr. Marks," said the officer, very coolly. "*How long has your son been called Allan Norman?*"

"The old Jew's lips trembled, and he turned very pale.

The only answer to the officer's question was a deep groan, and the sound of some heavy body falling in the front room.

"What was that?" said old Marks, startled, "what was that?"

"Let us go and see," said the officer, with an icy smile.

CHAPTER XLVIII.

THE GORILLA HUNT.

WHEN Lion Limb returned from the expedition to the Blue Rocks, and had landed his treasure with safety, he called together Katamar's Indians, and, in full council of the boys, not only treated them well, but feasted them in every possible way.

The night was celebrated with a supper and a dance. The next morning Lion Limb was astir early, and felt very anxious for the return of Harry Woodruff, of whom nothing had been heard.

"What can have become of him?" asked Lion Limb.

But no one was able to answer the question.

"Has he been murdered by Red Wolf's savages?" said one.

"No, no," said many; "if anything has happened you may be sure the gorillas have seized and carried him off."

"Gorillas?" said Lion Limb. "I can't believe there are any of those monsters on this island."

"I'm sure of it," said one. "I tracked their footprints the other day, and came upon two huge monsters up a tall cocoa-nut tree."

"I can scarcely believe it," said Lion Limb. "I have heard much of these animals, but accounts differ so very much one doesn't know what to believe or what to disbelieve."

"I've heard they go in companies and fight in regular order like soldiers."

"They can pull up young trees by the roots travellers say, and carry large heavy clubs with them."

"Well, no matter, lads, what they are, we must organise our expedition to go with these Indians and seek out Katamar, their king, who, they say, landed on this island in search of his daughter. I fear me the old man has fallen into the clutches of that devil Red Wolf. If we should be lucky enough to fall in with any gorillas we might tame them."

"I don't think any of us will be clever enough to do that."

"Ted Rawlings caught and tamed a young monkey," said Lion Limb.

"Yes, and Miss Emma has made a regular suit of regimentals for Jocko, cocked hat and all. You should have seen him when we were all out parading yesterday, it was a rare lark. Jocko had his uniform on, and armed with a stick he stood upon his hind legs, and went through the musket drill in fine style."

"You must mind and not let him play with fire-arms or steel weapons; he doesn't know the danger, but we do."

"He seems very partial to Miss Emma, and follows her about everywhere like a dog."

"I should not like to be in the place of anyone who attacked Miss Emma while Jocko was near, for he would tear them in pieces without a doubt."

"Then Jocko after all is of some use as well as ornament," said Lion Limb.

"But if there *are* any gorillas about, what would keep them off?" asked one. "What can attract them to her?"

"They have a great passion for carrying off young females, so I have heard," said Dick.

"Miss Emma and the others, then, must take care and not go too far into the forest alone."

Next morning all the young colonists were up early, and ready to start on their expedition in search of old Katamar.

Some carried provisions, others bottles of water.

All, however, were well armed, and Dick Hamilton led the way, followed by the friendly Indians.

Through the dense forest for many a weary mile they picked their way, always keeping a very sharp look out for any enemy.

Indians they could not discover anywhere, but monkeys in hundreds fled before them screeching loudly.

Wild hogs, panthers, wild cats, racoons, and a thousand other animals, disturbed in their shady retreat, growled, yelled, grunted, or screamed, while parrots, paroquets, cockatoos, and other birds, were heard everywhere.

All at once a shot was fired in front by Dick as a signal of warning.

In an instant every one fell flat to the ground, except Lion Limb, who hurried forward to see the cause of alarm.

"What did you see, Dick?"

"I don't know what it was, captain. It looked to me like two men coming this way; but they were so far off I was not certain."

"Were they Indians, Dick?"

"I can't say, captain, they might have been a couple of gorillas for all I know."

For some time all remained very quiet where they were in the high grass, until at last the signal was given to resume the march.

Again did Dick fire, and again the lads hid themselves as ordered.

But on this occasion Lion Limb was surprised to hear another shot fired, and from a quarter far beyond the range of Dick's gun.

Again and again it was repeated, each time more quickly than before.

"That can't be Red Wolf's savages, Dick?"

" No, captain, I don't think it is."

" Think you any of the buccaneers are having a row with Red Wolf ?"

" Not unlikely, captain "

For some time silence was maintained; when again and again the firing was repeated, approaching still nearer and nearer.

" Whoever they are, they are coming towards us, captain," said Dick.

At last a faint yell was heard.

" It is the savages, Dick. Be on your guard. Whoever they are fighting with have got the worst of it. Didn't you hear the rascals shooting ?"

" Yes, sir ; but hear that," said Dick, as six shots were fired in rapid succession.

" And hear that also, Dick ; it is a cheer."

" So it is, sir. I'll wager my life it is Harry Woodruff fighting with the Indians."

" Up ! men ! up !" said Lion Limb, " and follow me ! Let the Indians remain behind until called upon. Follow me ! It is Harry Woodruff !"

With a deafening cheer the young colonists jumped to their feet, and followed Lion Limb through the forest.

Their loud shouts were quickly answered by a second cheer from those contending with the Indians ; but judge of the astonishment of all when they suddenly came upon Harry Woodruff, who, standing over the wounded body of old Katamar, was fighting, single-handed, more than twenty of Red Wolf's men.

Harry himself was wounded.

" His hands and face were all bloody and begrimed with dirt, and he almost fell to the earth with weakness when he discovered who his deliverers were.

Giving the command over to Dick Hamilton, with orders to push Red Wolf's Indians as hard as possible, he went to Harry and his wounded companions and administered a few drops of brandy which revived them.

" Is Red Wolf among his men fighting yonder, Harry ?" asked Lion Limb.

" No. He is dead."

" Who killed him ?"

" Well, I tried to do so, and made sure I had, but I was much mistaken ; my shot missed its aim. Yet, when I went into the log-house, I discovered that Katamar here had wrenched the knife from Red Wolf's hands, and with one fatal blow laid him out as flat as a flounder. I then released him from the chains which bound him, and we made our escape. The savages gave chase, and I have been fighting them for the last fifteen miles."

While Harry was telling Lion Limb all the particulars of his visit to Red Wolf's camp (which we have explained in a previous chapter), Dick Hamilton and his men were driving the savages before them like so many sheep.

The Indians, however, when they discovered Katamar, their king, and found him wounded, yelled like demons, and, regardless of all warning, dashed into the forest and engaged the savages hand to hand.

They fought like very devils, without showing any mercy or quarter on either side.

Dick recalled his men, and allowed Katamar's Indians the honour of finishing it.

Screams and yells and screechings were heard on all sides, until it made one almost deaf to hear them.

" They are having a rare go in among themselves, captain," said Dick, laughing.

" Well, let them ; but we must return home at once. Harry Woodruff and Katamar both are wounded, so make up a litter and carry them home."

This was quickly done.

Two stretchers were made, one for each sufferer, which was carried on the shoulders of four men.

" Send some one back and draw off Katamar's Indians. You go, Joe Pebbles, they seem to like you the best."

" All right, captain," said Joe, in high glee ; " I suppose I can pick out one or two of the lads to go with me, in case of any accident ?"

" Yes, take three or four, Joe ; but mind, let's have none of your hanky-panky tricks, but return to camp as soon as possible."

" All right, sir," said Joe, who gave a sly wink to those he wished to follow him.

" Our captain couldn't have given me a pleasanter job," said Joe, when he left the company. " Won't we have a jolly lark with these Indians before we return ?"

And off Joseph went, as happy as a lord with his four lads, and soon disappeared in search of Katamar's Indians, who were then fighting and hard at it, too, with Red Wolf's savages, who were gradually retreating before them.

Joe soon came across several dead bodies, both of the Indians and savages.

In each case they were frightfully mutilated and disfigured.

" Don't these red devil's fight though," said Joe, pointing out the dead bodies to his companions; " they ain't giving or taking quarter on either side."

Meantime, however, Lion Limb and his party wended their way through the forest, carrying Katamar and Harry in litters, and their path was long, tedious, and difficult.

They had several miles to go before reaching their camps, and halted to refresh themselves.

While they were thus occupied some one was heard shouting loudly near them, and presently a messenger from the camp came up, running breathless with haste.

" What's the matter ?" asked Lion Limb.

" Miss Clarence is lost !"

" Lost !"

" Lost !"

" Lost !" exclaimed several, in horror at the news.

" What *do* you mean ?" said Lion Limb, angrily.

" The gorillas, captain ; it's all the gorillas."

" What, Miss Emma carried away by those monsters ?" said several in a breath, and pale with horror.

" Yes ; seized before our eyes, and carried off by a huge ugly beast."

" How did it happen ?"

" The lads in camp were going through their exercise, and Miss Emma was playing with Jocko, the monkey, under a shady place, when the terrible beast, which must have concealed himself, suddenly rose up out of the high grass, and before we could do anything from astonishment he carried her off.

" We all gave chase instantly, but were afraid to fire at the monster in case we should hit Miss Emma. One of the lads ran with all his might, sword in hand, and dealt the gorilla a blow which wounded him ; but the monster dropped the girl, tore off a thick branch in an instant, and struck the youth, who had stumbled over a log, and left him senseless.

" Still we gave chase to the brute ; but the foremost of all in the hot pursuit was Jocko the monkey (See Cut).

THE BOY KING
OF THE SOUTH SEA ISLANDS.

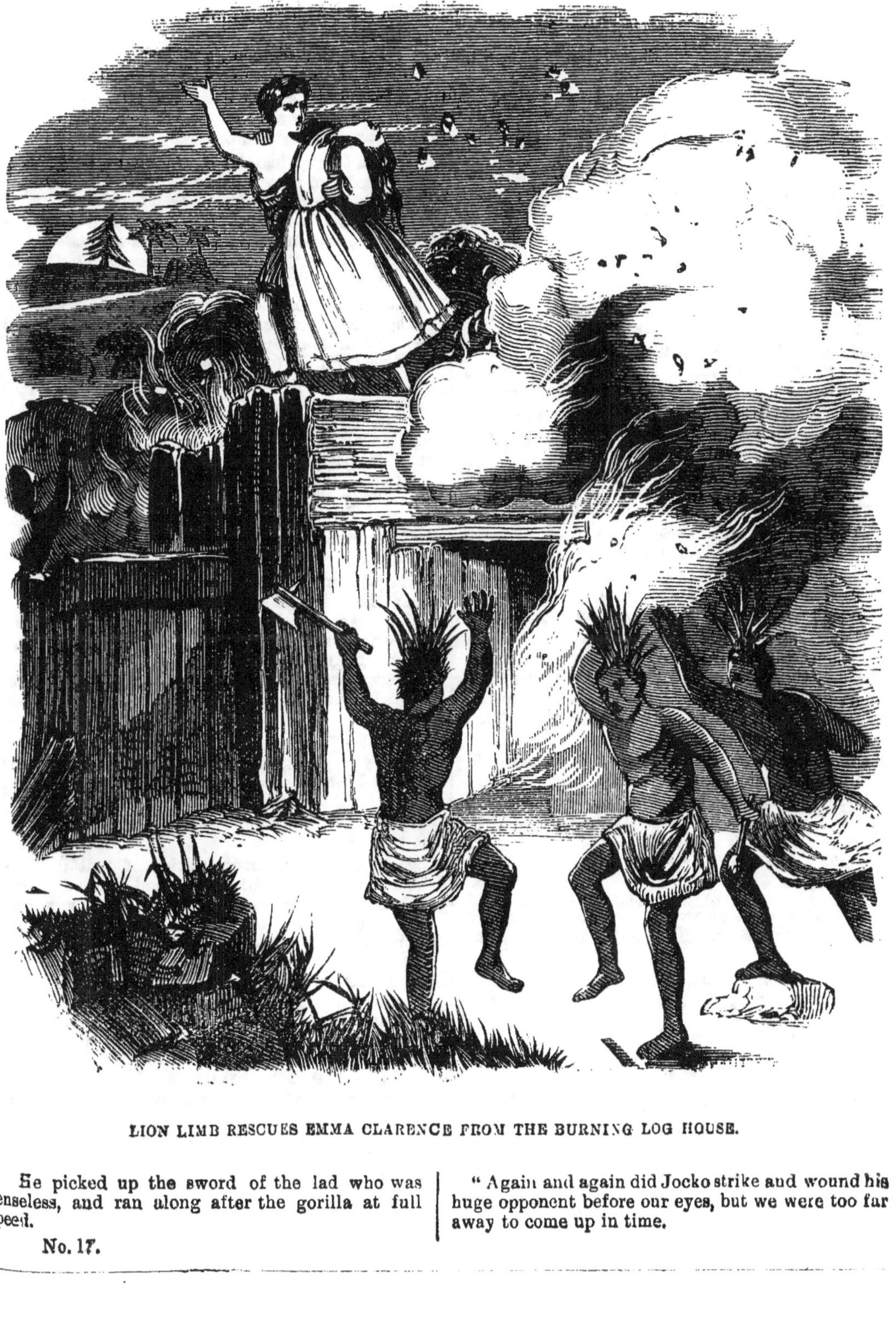

LION LIMB RESCUES EMMA CLARENCE FROM THE BURNING LOG HOUSE.

He picked up the sword of the lad who was senseless, and ran along after the gorilla at full speed.

No. 17.

"Again and again did Jocko strike and wound his huge opponent before our eyes, but we were too far away to come up in time.

"On each occasion the gorilla dropped Miss Clarence upon the ground, and with a terrible noise turned upon his active pursuer.

"Several times he seized a thick stick and made a smash at Jocko's head, but each time the monkey jumped away out of danger.

"But by the time we were close upon him the gorilla would seize the girl and start off again."

"Horrible," said Lion Limb.

"I left those pursuing the monster to come and warn you; if we go home to our camp in this direction," said the messenger, "we may meet the brute."

"What distant noise is that?" said Lion Limb, quickly, as he listened.

"It is the Indians fighting, I think, sir," said one.

"No, it ain't," said Dick, "the sound comes from a different direction."

"There it is again," said Lion Limb, flushed with excitement, "it comes nearer and nearer; it is our brave lads in pursuit."

"See, see yonder, see yonder captain!" said a dozen voices at once, pointing to a dark gigantic object rushing through the forest, but a good distance away.

"It is a wild boar!"

"It is a bull!"

"It is a gorilla!" said Dick, "for £100."

"It is a gorilla! There it is again—see it now—by heavens it is!—I see him—he is hard pressed—he has Emma Clarence in his arms!"

With a loud shout Lion Limb dashed into the dense thicket, sword in hand, followed by several.

Breathless they ran, as best they could, and came within full view of the monster, who had stopped.

Emma lay insensible on the ground.

The horrible gorilla, club in hand, knelt over her about to deal the fatal blow.

"Fire! Fire!" shouted several voices at once, who stood looking on in horror.

"Fire! or the monster will slay the poor girl."

It was all very well for them to shout fire, fire, in Lion Limb's ears, but it was a much more difficult thing to do successfully than any of them imagined.

For the ugly monster was leaning over the body of the unconscious girl, and, to fire at all, was most dangerous in the extreme; for to hit the gorilla might cause the death of Emma Clarence as well.

This Lion Limb saw at a glance.

Yet, there was little or no time to spare in reflection.

The ugly brute had his club raised over the girl's head, and next moment she might be a mangled corpse.

The gorilla was in a fearful state of rage and alarm.

He had been closely hunted on all sides, and several flesh wounds received in various parts of his huge body only rendered him all the more ferocious and deadly.

With a look of intense ferocity, which no words can fully describe, he gazed around him for a second.

His eyes rolled in a fearful manner.

His huge mouth was opened to its widest capacity, and his teeth shone like so many deadly fangs.

In a second Lion Limb placed his rifle over the branch of a tree, and took deliberate aim.

The excitement of those around him was now most intense.

He pulled the trigger.

The ball whizzed through the forest foliage, and struck the monster on the ear.

With a terrific roar it jumped up, and seemed to suffer the greatest agony.

But this only tended to increase his hate and vengeance.

He raised his club once again to deal the fatal blow.

Another shot, however, aimed with even greater precision than the first, struck his right arm, and the club fell useless to the ground.

A loud shout was now raised by the hunters on all sides.

But at that moment, and just as Lion Limb was about to fire a third shot, he lowered his rifle again.

In the distance he caught a glimpse of his faithful dog Dragon, who now came bounding through the forest, right upon the gorilla's track.

His mouth was all clotted with blood as if he had been already engaged in some former fray, and his eyes were fiery and bright.

With a sudden leap, he jumped upon the gorilla, and seized him by the throat.

The huge monster writhed in agony.

But he had been taken unawares, and the fangs of the dog were too deeply set in the gorilla's throat, and the monster, with all his great strength, was unable to shake off his enemy.

The fight did not last more than a minute.

The young hunter made sure that Dragon would be killed in the encounter, and they hastened forward accordingly to save him.

But when they arrived upon the spot all was over. The monster was dead.

Dragon had severed his windpipe, and there the gorilla lay in a pool of blood, a mangled and horrible-looking mass.

Dragon, however, stood by, over the still insensible body of his young mistress, Miss Emma Clarence; nor would he stir from her until Lion Limb approached and took up the insensible girl in his arms.

She was immediately conveyed to a small spring, where her temples were bathed, and her face and hands washed from the filth with which the gorilla had contaminated them.

She quickly recovered consciousness.

She was not wounded in any way, but she complained of bruises upon her body, received while in the giant-like embrace of the beast that had sought to abduct her.

She was placed in a hastily-formed litter, and conveyed away as quickly as possible to the camp; where rest, and every attention, would tend to restore her to her wonted self-possession and merriment.

Every one was rejoiced at this providential escape of Miss Clarence; but so enraged were the boys against the huge, dirty, and ugly monster, that they resolved one and all not to return to their camps again until they had killed a few of the beasts, if they could possibly find any.

Old Katamar, however, was not forgotten.

He and his faithful Indians wished to join the hunt, and display their bravery before the eyes of their friends, the young colonists, but this proposition Lion Limb would not for a moment listen to.

"No, no," said he to Harry Woodruff, who at that moment was near; "no one has a doubt of the bravery of old Katamar and his Indians, but this is not the moment to exhibit it. Conduct your friends to our camp, and make them as comfortable as possible in my absence; they require repose after their long and dangerous sea voyage in their frail canoes ; and as for you and Katamar," he added with a smile, "after your adventure with Red Wolf, sleep would do you more good than gorilla-hunting ; therefore conduct our Indian friends to the camps, give them plenty of the very best we have, and, in conversation, learn all you can about the many islands to the south-west ; we have not visited any of them as yet, but now that we have silenced the buccaneers and Red Wolf's fiends, for a time, at least, let us prepare our gallant schooner for a long voyage, for the islands must be explored at once ; some of them may be inhabited by Europeans for all we know, who have occasional intercourse with passing ships."

Harry Woodruff obeyed the commands of his young chief, and, marshalling the Indians in single file, marched them off towards the beach, leaving Lion Limb and his companions to continue their gorilla hunt.

Blowing his horn three times loudly, the young chief soon gathered around him his faithful followers, some of whom had wandered away a considerable distance in search of adventure.

He gave his orders as to the manner in which all should proceed, which were as follows—

Every man was to march ten yards apart from his companion, and, as far as possible, keep in line, and by no means to go wandering in advance of the others, so that an accidental shot might not prove fatal to any one.

Many of the lads desired much to have had the bold dog Dragon with them.

But that faithful animal was too fond of his young mistress, and would not, on any account, disobey the orders of Lion Limb, who, in a peremptory tone, had commanded him to follow and attend Miss Emma.

Jocko, the monkey, however, still lingered near Lion Limb, and, in order that he might enjoy the hunt, and not be obliged to return to the settlement with Harry Woodruff and the others, climbed up a tree, and there hid himself until the hunt should commence.

Having gorged himself with nuts, and various sorts of delicious fruits which he found in abundance all around him, Master Jocko descended from his hiding place, and cautiously creeping towards the dead body of the gorilla, he commenced dancing upon it, and thrusting his sword through and through the monster's still warm body.

Chattering, and full of antics, he at last attracted the attention of Lion Limb, who, until that moment, imagined Jocko had returned to the camps.

Jocko, to show his gallantry, now ran forward, and brandished his sword, all gory as it was, and, fastening on his cocked hat more firmly than before, jumped off in front, as much as to say " Follow me, I know where to find the gorillas."

In an instant he clambered up a tree and soon disappeared.

The hunters took no more notice of Jocko, but cautiously continued to advance, guns and rifles in hand.

They had thus walked for more than half an hour, when the forest began to get denser and darker, until at last the faintest rays of sunlight could scarcely be observed, and yet not a single shot had been fired by any one in the party.

At length, however, they came to a cocoa nut tree, and from the number of nuts that were on the ground and only half consumed, it was evident that some animal much larger than a common monkey or ape had been there gorging.

They stopped for a moment to consider, when Jocko suddenly appeared looking fierce and wild.

He pointed to huge footprints in the grass, and by all sorts of motions and grimaces indicated that gorillas had been disturbed while eating, and were not far off.

He again went away, and Lion Limb followed the track of the footprints with his rifle cocked ready for instant use.

More slowly and cautiously than ever each one advanced, but still they could see nothing.

At last, however, a shrill chattering from Jocko, who hurried back scratching his head and partly lame, told plainly that the monkey had seen much more than he cared to see again.

In a second afterwards deep grunts were heard not far off, and when least they expected it, six immense gorillas appeared, each with an immense club in his hand.

They were horrible beastly objects to behold, and as they stood scratching themselves and glaring upon the young hunters, it was more than sufficient to appal the hearts of the stoutest and bravest woodsman who ever dared venture into the depths of a primeval forest.

It had been the intention of Lion Limb and his young companions to capture some of these monsters if possible in order to find out their real habits and manners, for the reports of travellers had been so different that no one could say with certainty whether the gorilla was or was not the animal so often described as half man half monkey.

One explorer said that they lived on human flesh and delighted in carnage.

Another affirmed that they were timid and peaceful animals, who lived solely on fruits, herbs, and roots, and would fly at the approach of man.

Others again asserted most positively that they had been known to assemble in large numbers, attack the Indian and native settlements, carry off the women and roast their male prisoners alive.

With so many accounts before him, young Lion Limb knew not what to believe, so resolved to hunt and judge for himself.

" It would be a capital thing, though," he thought, "if we could tame one of these monsters and send him to England ; it would make the fortune of a showman to have him dressed up and go through his performance like a human being."

But although Lion Limb's intentions were at first merciful towards these grim brutes, they soon made him change his mind, for they at once began pelting him and his followers with stones, nuts and other missiles with so much accuracy and force of aim, that although they laughed, more than one of them had a narrow escape of being knocked over.

Perceiving that the hunters did not now advance, the gorillas began to make the forest ring again with their shouts, grunts, screams and other unearthly noises, until, at last, all the monkeys, apes and gorillas of the forest seemed joined against them.

" We must fire, lads," said Lion Limb, at last, "the forest is now swarmed with animals, and they are showering all sorts of things upon us. Look well before you, for the gorillas are now numerous, and can use their clubs with deadly effect."

With these orders the fight began.

In a few moments several of the monsters were wounded.

But instead of this frightening the rest, it only made them the more savage.

Their shouts and noises were most hideous, and almost deafening.

On all sides they came on, until at last Lion Limb began to imagine the brutes were bent upon surrounding his little band.

He, therefore, sounded his horn, and gradually the line of hunters began to close in upon the centre, and could either advance or retreat in a body.

"I never thought it would turn out this way, captain," said Dick; "why, the forest seems all alive with brutes just now, and the trees are swarming with monkeys of all sorts and sizes."

Jocko knew this as much as any one, and his strange attire seemed to cause a great sensation among the monkey tribes, who were trying all the tricks they could to get hold of Jocko.

But that cunning animal kept his eyes open on all sides, and remained close at the heels of Lion Limb, tucking in his tail very carefully, for fear of being taken prisoner by his wild, untamed brethren, who, hanging in all sorts of ways from limbs of trees, tried their very best to lay hands upon and secure the gorgeously-attired Jocko.

But the tamed monkey had no ambition to roam wild again, for he was too well cared for by every one at the settlement, which he very well knew; and as to reigning over all the monkey tribes as their king, he had not the slightest ambition.

"We must give the brutes a volley, sir," said Dick.

"Yes; but not yet. Don't you see them advancing all together? When I give the word let them have it."

In a few moments more the gorillas came closer and closer.

But a well-directed volley laid many of them low, and the others, appalled at the unlooked-for slaughter, jumped back a few paces, and then, with horrible noises, scampered away in all directions.

"I thought that would settle 'em," said Dick, laughing. "Let us give them another."

"No," said Lion Limb; "they have all disappeared. But load up your guns with small shot, and warm these swarms of monkeys who are chattering all around us in the trees."

The order was quickly obeyed.

But directly the weapons were levelled at them, the swarms of monkeys jumped from branch to branch in hundreds, and when the guns were fired dozens of them dropped in all directions.

For a moment Jocko was appalled at the destruction of his species, and chattered in great fear.

But when he saw the forest now completely cleared, where a moment before it was filled with animals, he jumped about, immensely relieved, and appeared more brave than ever.

"Shall we pursue these brutes any further, captain?"

"No; we cannot expect to *kill* them all."

"What shall we do with the dead ones?"

"Cut off their heads, and when we get back to the settlement, we will stick them on poles; so if any of the others come to trouble us or prowl about the camps, the heads will frighten them off through instinct."

It was not a bad device.

So when six or seven heads had been severed from the bodies of the dead monsters, and placed on the ends of stout ash branches, the young hunters retraced their steps towards their camps again, and were met and welcomed when near home by companions who had been compelled to stay and guard the camps.

The sounds of Lion Limb's well-known horn were returned by tremendous shouts by all the young colonists, but no one was more struck with astonishment than old Katamar, who looked with amazement at the ghastly gorilla heads, and shuddered.

He feared gorillas.

And well he might, as the succeeding chapters of this story will shortly show.

CHAPTER XLIX.

THE STORY OF THE BRAVE DOG DRAGON.

THE meeting of old Katamar and his long-lost daughter, Marmi, as might be expected, was most affectionate and tender.

The old man listened to all her narratives, and as she spoke of Lion Limb's great bravery and kindness, the old Indian's naturally savage nature was warmed, and he felt towards the young chieftain feelings not only of intense respect and admiration, but also of love.

The cooks, according to the orders they had received from Harry Woodruff, prepared and served up a first-rate supper, and when Lion Limb and his companions unexpectedly returned, and were in time to share in the festival repast, the Indians were delighted.

Old Katamar had never tasted before anything cooked by Europeans.

Soups, and fish, and venison, and roast beef, were things unknown to him.

But the savoury odours were not at all disagreeable to the old man, who, though he did not trouble himself with a knife and fork, demolished such a quantity of the roast beef that Dick Hamilton was heard to whisper to Hary Woodruff,

"Harry, the old fellow seems to have a rare appetite, don't he?"

"I believe you, my boy."

"I'd rather keep him a week than a fortnight, though. That makes the sixth lump of beef he's had."

The supper passed off merrily, and Lion Limb himself could not but laugh, as he sat for a full half-hour after his own supper, looking at his Indian guests, still stuffing themselves with all and everything they could lay hands upon.

"Captain," said Dick, winking at his young chief, "you may talk of eating, but of all the demons I ever saw, old Katamar and his chiefs beats 'em all."

"Oh, they are like camels, Dick," said Lion Limb, laughing. "They take in enough to last them for a week."

"Well, if old Katamar hasn't demolished six pounds of beef besides other tack, you can hang me for a butcher, that's all."

"We'd better get 'em away from our settlement as soon as possible," said Harry. "for we can't afford to keep such a lot of gluttons here very long or our stores will soon run short."

"In two days, Harry, we'll set sail, and then we can have a chance of seeing what sort of cooks old Katamar has."

But if the Indians enjoyed the supper, they were astounded at the drinks that followed, for when Harry and Dick made a bowl of punch, and gave some to Katamar and his friends to "wet their pipes," as they said, the old chief smoked pipe after pipe of tobacco, and soon was glad to lay down on the ground almost insensible.

Joe Pebbles played his fiddle, and amused a round dozen, who, outside, round the the camp fires, were dancing and kicking up their heels in great delight.

The grog, however, was making Harry Woodruff and Dick Hamilton very talkative, and for more than an hour they and some other sailors were narrating some very long yarns, so "tough," indeed, that very few of their hearers believed them at all.

When they had fully satisfied themselves, and nobody else, Lion Limb put down his pipe, and after trying the virtues of a new jorum of punch, thus began :—

"Well," said he, "you have all been amusing yourselves with stories of one thing and another, and, if you have no great objection, I myself will tell one about a certain member of our colony, which, I have no doubt, will prove interesting."

"A story from the captain," said Dick, in high glee. "Oh, let us have it by all means."

"About some member of our colony, eh?" said Harry. "Why, who can it be?"

"It isn't me, eh?" said Dick, laughing.

"No, it is not; but what I have to say is about our faithful dog Dragon."

"Oh, Dragon, eh?"

"Didn't he give it to the gorillas, though?" said one.

"I could never fancy that any dog could have performed such wonders as he has done since we have been here," said another.

"Well, then," said Lion Limb, "as you all, I know, love the dog, and are very well acquainted with his courage and devotion, I have thought proper to say a few words about him."

"But where did you get the history from?" said one.

"Well, Mr. Clarence, who, as you know, was captain of the 'Rattlesnake,' was extremely fond of Dragon, and in his leisure moments filled several very interesting sheets of note-paper, which, if you have no objection, I will read."

"Hear! hear!"

"All attention for the account of Dragon."

"Silence for every word."

"It was by mere accident that I discovered these few notes among the captain's papers," said Lion Limb, "and you will find that Dragon has not been a sailor all his life but a soldier also."

"A soldier?" said several.

"Why, Dragon is not very old."

"Quite old enough to have gone through many strange adventures in life for all that," said Lion Limb. laughing, as he commenced to read Captain Clarence's note-book thus :—

"My dog Dragon comes of an excellent family, and, as I have good reason for knowing, has knocked about the world a great deal before he came into my possession. Dragon, then, was born at no less a place than London.

"He escaped the many snares of dog-fanciers and thieves, and at the age of six months was given to a grocer who lived at Plymouth.

"But Dragon, strolling about the town one day not long after his arrival, he happened to come upon a company of soldiers, who, like myself in the navy, were just about to go to the Crimea and fight the Russians.

"The soldiers were in excellent spirits, and with their drums and fifes performed such excellent music that young Dragon was delighted, and whisked about in high glee.

"Dragon was immensely pleased with the martial and gallant appearance of the gentlemen in red coats.

"The drummers and fifers were equally as much pleased with the noble-looking dog as the animal was with them.

"When they commenced to play a lively jig young Dragon capered about so merrily that he attracted the attention of the officers, who made up their minds to have him, if possible, in order to please their men.

"Several of the drummers tried to catch him; but Dragon was too old a bird to be caught with chaff, and he ran away to his old shop, the grocer's.

"But the round-bellied old grocer, not so much admiring the dog's many comical antics as the soldiers had done, kicked the faithful dog, and, as Dragon didn't much admire this cruel treatment, he resolved to leave the regions of the chandler's shop and seek distinction in other regions.

"He growled savagely at old pot-belly, and scampered away through the town after the soldiers, who now started on their march.

"In less than an hour he overtook the gallant red-coats, who raised a shout of pleasure as Dragon marched at the head of their band in a very grave manner.

"The life of a soldier on service, taking all things together, is the finest in the world except that of a sailor.

"While he moves on, a roving adventurer, care, pain, and trouble, are vanished from his mind.

"Though he is at times on short commons, and often driven to his wit's end, he but seldom repines.

"Once fairly on the road, it is astonishing how the hours glide away.

"The formation of parade, or drill-marching, are now at an end, and every one indulges in that mode of perambulation which best suits him.

"When the commanding officer is not one of your strict disciplinarians, the regimental juniors congregate together in groups, some in front some in rear, while the men, though keeping their sections, trail in open ranks, filling the entire space of ground over which the route extends.

"At the head of the column is to be seen a host of senior officers, among whom the laugh and the joke prevails, and there many a long-minded veteran inflicts upon the ears of his patient auditors a narrative as endless as the road.

"Ever and anon the second major falls back, and, in order to show his consequence and zeal, especially if a general with his staff should chance to be passing, he calls out in a most important tone—

"'Gentlemen, get into your places. Keep on the flanks,' and other friendly admonitions.

"As soon as he is convinced of the approving looks of the great man with the long feather and epaulettes, that his vigilance has been duly noticed, he gallops off to his old station, and the gentlemen betake themselves to theirs, till another appearance of the chief, when the stray sheep are again called back to their flock.

"I know of nothing that these second majors have to do, unless it is to act the part of moveable pivots for dressing up the line—in which they are generally very fussy—or in whipping in the young officers whom they endeavour to keep in order.

"The surgeon, who is generally a very hearty fellow, with better things than boluses and pill-boxes in his panniers, together with the adjutant and his brethren of the staff, attract around them in the rear a batch of thoroughly pleasant men, who keep up such a volley of jest and drollery as frequently to beguile the weariness of the longest march.

"Thanks to their amusing powers, I, while away from my ship, acting with them by orders, have often found ourselves at the gate of the town, or at the camp ground, without being aware that we had travelled any distance.

"At intervals of one or two hours each day, the troops are halted for a few minutes' rest.

"Then all, as if by magic wand, are quickly squatted, and, havresack being called for, the whole of them, like hungry cormorants at their prey, are soon engaged in one scene of mastication.

"Some perform a solo on the shank-bone of a well-picked ham.

"Others display their talents on the drum-stick of a half-starved fowl, while the majority gnaw their way through the skinny junk of an old tough bullock.

"The vulture, and other birds of evil omen, are meanwhile hovering in mid air, ready to pounce upon the remnants of the feast when they are gone.

"At the well-known sound of pipe or bugle, the warriors are again on their legs, stretching them out with renewed vigour.

"Among the soldiers there is much drollery and mirth; nothing makes much difference with them, it matters not whether trumps turn up or not, whether the chance be a good battle or a good billet; they are still the same, and trudge along devoid of care.

"Give them their allowance and a little rest, and they require no more.

"Day after day I have listened to their jokes and stories, and been highly entertained by their originality and humour.

"For, I would here make a note to my narrative, to inform any one who may come into possession of these few sheets of note-paper, that I have often been ordered to leave my ship and act with soldiers instead of sailors during the Crimean war.

"Thus it happened that, although a sailor, I know much about soldiers, and thus bear my testimony to their bravery and worth, for I have been assigned duty with them for months together, and sometimes on very dangerous and arduous service.

"But to return to the anecdotes of my dog Dragon, and of what he did before he came into my possession.

"He was dirty; he was tolerably ugly, but there was an intelligence, a sparkle and brightness about Dragon's eye that could not be overlooked.

"'We have only one dog in the regiment,' said one of the men, 'and at any rate the dog looks as if he could forage for himself.'

"A sergeant having a pipe in his mouth nodded assent, and Dragon attached himself to the band.

"The dog was soon found to be possessed of considerable tact and talent.

"He already fetched and carried to admiration.

"Ere three weeks were over he could not only stand with as erect a back as any private in the regiment, but shoulder his musket, act sentinel, and keep time in the march.

"He was a gay soldier was Dragon, and of course lived from paw to mouth; but long ere they reached the Crimea, Dragon had contrived to cultivate a particular acquaintance with the mess-man of the company—a step which he had no cause to repent.

"He endured the fatigues of war with as good a grace as any veteran in the army, and they were soon at no great distance from the enemy.

"Dragon had by this time become quite familiar with the sound not only of drums but of musketry, and even to be inspired with new ardour as he approached the scene of action.

"The first occasion in which he distinguished himself was this: his regiment being encamped on the hills, a detachment of Russians were ordered to attempt a surprise and marched against them during the night.

"The weather was stormy, and the men had no notion that any Russians were so near them.

"Human suspicion, in short, was asleep, and the camp in danger

"But Dragon was on the alert; walking his rounds as usual, with his nose in the air, he soon detected the Russians.

"He gave the alarm, and these Russians turned tail immediately, a thing Englishmen never do.

"Next morning it was resolved nem. con., that Dragon had deserved well of his country.

"The Greeks would have voted him a statue, the Romans would have carried him in triumph to the Capitol; but Dragon was hailed with a more sensible sort of gratitude.

"He would not have walked three yards, poor fellow, to see himself cast in plaster; and he liked much better to stand on his own toes, than to be carried breast-high on the finest hand-barrow that ever came out of the hand of a carpenter.

"The colonel put his name on the roll.

"It was published in regimental orders that he should henceforth receive the ration of a full private per diem, and Dragon was the happiest of dogs.

"He was now cropped à la militaire, a collar with the name of his regiment was hung round his neck, and the barber had orders to clip him once a week.

"From this time Dragon was certainly a different animal; in fact, he became so proud that he could scarcely pass any of his canine brethren without lifting his nose on high.

"In the meantime a skirmish occurred, in which Dragon had a new opportunity of showing himself.

"It was here that he received his first wound; like all the rest of his company, Dragon was in front.

"He received a scratch of a bayonet in his left shoulder, and with difficulty reached the rear.

"The regimental surgeon dressed the wound which the Russians had inflicted.

"Dragon suffered himself to be treated medically, and remained in the same attitude during several days in the infirmary.

"He was not yet perfectly restored when the battle of Inkerman took place.

"Lame as he was, he could not keep away from so grand a scene.

"He marched, always keeping close to the banner, which he had learned to recognise among a hundred; and, like the fifer of the great Gustavas, who whistled all through the battle of Lutzen, Dragon never gave over barking until evening closed upon the combatants of Inkerman.

"The sight of the bayonets was the only thing that kept him from rushing personally upon the Russians.

"But his good fortune at last presented him with an occasion to do something.

"A certain ensign had a pointer with him, and this rash animal dared to show himself in advance of the ranks.

"To detect him, to jump upon him, and to seize him by the throat, all this was, on the part of Dragon, only a moment's work.

"The large pointer being strong, truly despised to flinch, and a fierce struggle ensued.

"A musket-ball interrupted them.

"The pointer fell dead on the spot, and Dragon, after a moment of bewilderment, put up his paw, and discovered that he had been hit in the ear.

"He was puzzled for a little while, but soon regained the lines of his regiment, and Victory having soon after shown herself a faithful goddess, Dragon ate his supper among his comrades with an air of satisfaction, that spoke plainer than words— 'When posterity talks of Inkerman, it will be said that the dog Dragon also was at the Soldier's battle.'

"I think it has already been observed that Dragon all that time owned no particular master, but considered himself as the dog of the whole regiment.

"In truth, he had almost an equal attachment for every one that wore the uniform, and a contempt for every one in plain clothes; and when he did not think himself strong enough to attack a stranger, he ran away from them.

"He had a quarrel with his company, who, being in garrison, thought fit to chain the dog to a sentry-box.

"He could not endure this, and took the first opportunity to escape to a body of Riflemen, who treated him with more respect.

"In the heat of the action he perceived the ensign who bore the colours of his regiment, surrounded by a detachment of the enemy.

"He flew to his rescue, barked like ten furies, did everything he could to encourage the young officer, but all in vain.

"The gentleman sank covered with a hundred wounds, but not before, feeling himself about to fall, he had wrapped his body in the folds of the standard.

"At that moment the cry of victory reached his ear; he echoed it with his last breath, and his generous soul took its flight to the abode of heroes.

"Three Russians had already bit the dust under the sword of the ensign, but five or six still remained about him, resolved not to quit it until they had obtained possession of the colours he had so nobly defended.

"Meanwhile, the brave dog Dragon had thrown himself on his dead comrade, and was on the point of being pierced with half-a-dozen bayonets, when the fortune of war came to his relief.

"A discharge of grape-shot swept the Russians into oblivion.

"The moment he perceived he was delivered from his assailants, he took the staff of the ensign's banner in his teeth, and endeavoured all he could to disengage it.

"But the poor ensign had griped it so tight in the moment of death, that it was impossible for the dog to get it out of his hands.

"The end of it was that Dragon tore the silk from the cane, and returned to the camp limping, bleeding, and laden with this glorious trophy.

"Such an action merited honours, nor were they denied.

"The old collar was taken away from him, and the colonel ordered a red ribbon to replace it with a little copper medal, on which were inscribed these words:—

"'He saved the colours of his regiment.'

"Meantime it was found necessary to dress the dog's wounds.

"He bore the operation without a murmur, and limped with the air of a hero.

"As it was very easy to know him by his collar and medal, orders were given that at whatever mess he should happen to present himself he should be welcomed, and thus he continued to follow the army.

"But one day a soldier, mistaking his dog, no doubt, hit him a chance blow with the flat side of his sabre.

"Dragon, piqued to the heart, deserted, abandoning his regiment.

"He attached himself to some dragoons, and followed them.

"He continued to be infinitely useful during the campaign.

"He was always first up and first dressed.

"He gave notice the moment anything struck him as being suspicious.

"He barked at the least noise, except during night watches, when he received a hint that secresy was desirable.

"At the affair of Kirtch, Dragon gave a signal proof of his zeal and skill by bringing home in safety to the camp the horse of a field-officer, who had had the misfortune to be wounded.

"How he had managed it no one could tell exactly, but he limped after him into the camp, and the moment he saw him in the hands of a soldier, he turned and flew back to the field, nor did he return until he had succeeded in attracting attention to the wounded officer, and thus saving his life.

"After this, by a strange circumstance, the good dog came into my own possession, and, as experience soon proved, the noble animal took to the sea as much as he had formerly taken to soldiering in the camps.

"I should never have come into possession of the animal, but for a strange chance which befel me, in which the good dog saved my life."

"What," said Dick, "did the dog save the life of Captain Clarence, then?"

"Oh, so it appears from the late captain's notes, which, if you are quiet, I will continue to read."

"Oh, by all means read it," said Harry; "it is one of the most extraordinary stories I ever heard."

"And true, you may depend, as such a gentleman as Captain Clarence would not have taken the trouble and time to write it down," said Lion Limb.

"We are all attention, captain, for the rest of the story," said one and all.

Lion Limb was just about to recommence, when a strange and unusual alarm was raised outside the log-house in which they sat.

Every one jumped to their feet in dismay.

CHAPTER L.

THE CAMP ON FIRE.

"SILENCE!" said Lion Limb; "you may be mistaken."

"No, captain, we are not," said Dick, in alarm; "I heard the sounds plain enough."

"And so did I."

"And I also."

"Listen; we may hear it again."

"There it is."

"There it is!" said one and another.

Lion Limb listened.

"Fire! fire! fire!" were the sounds which now fell upon his ear.

"Fire! fire! fire!" were the dreadful sounds repeated again and again.

"Turn out! turn out! Fire! fire! fire!" shouted the night watch.

Lion Limb leaped from his seat, and dashing open the log-house door, came out into the open camps, and there beheld one of the log cabins in full blaze.

The flames shot upward, and illuminated the whole camp.

"Follow me!" said Lion Limb; "it may only be one of our store-houses, and, so that no life is lost, I do not mind."

"It is worse than that, captain," said one of the lads who had just run up out of breath; "it is worse than that, it is Miss Emma's cabin."

"*Her* cabin?"

"Yes, captain, and it has been set on fire by a band of rascally Indians, who are running about our camps like madmen, stabbing and shooting all they meet."

"Follow me, then," said Lion Limb; "the greater the danger the greater prudence is required."

Hereupon, Lion Limb blew his horn thrice, and, in a few moments, his followers rushed out of their cabins in all directions, armed to the teeth.

The fire had not been burning more than ten minutes, yet it had taken firm hold of the building, and the flames and sparks shot upward in grandeur against the moonlit sky.

Giving his orders to Dick and Harry to march well together, and disperse the Indian savages who had intruded into their camps, he and some half dozen others rushed forward to the fire, and, in order to get close to it, were obliged to fight their way through a circle of savages, who were dancing in wild delight outside the stockade which surrounded the log-house.

Cutlass in one hand and a small hatchet in the other, brave Lion Limb clave his way through all who opposed him, and, jumping over the stockade, made his way towards the burning, blazing house.

"Don't enter—don't enter it!" shouted his companions, "you will be suffocated?"

"He will be burned alive!"

"Miss Emma is not there, or if so she is already dead."

"Beat back the black savages, and leave me to my fate!" shouted Lion Limb, as, hatchet in hand, he beat in the door, and rushed madly into the burning house.

"He is lost! he is lost!" shouted his young companions in dismay.

"The roof will fall in upon him!"

"They will be smothered together!"

"All hope is lost; he is buried in the flames!"

These, and such like, were the remarks of his young followers; but they had no time to stop and make conjectures as to the fate of their much-loved chief, for the savages returned to the combat, and beat back all who opposed them.

In all directions was fighting going on.

The Indians were intent on setting fire to every house and cabin.

But they were met boldly and bravely by the young settlers, who, under Dick, Harry, and Joe Pebbles, beat them in every encounter, and saved the dwellings and store-houses.

Blows were given and received on every side without mercy, but the Indian soldiers were routed at all points, and dozens of them scalped upon the spot by old Katamar and his men, who fought with the fury of demons.

On every side the young settlers were victorious; but, thinking that Lion Limb was safe as usual, and more than a match for all who opposed him, neither Dick, Harry, nor any one else, thought of rushing down to learn the result of the fire, but contented themselves with following up the savages and driving them off.

This neglect almost proved fatal to their young leader, for the few brave lads who had gone with him to the burning dwelling were unable to contend successfully against the multitude of savages who, regardless of their companions, danced and yelled round the burning house with most horrible glee, brandishing their weapons, and making night hideous with their demoniacal noises.

Lion Limb, however, was unconscious of what was passing around him.

The heat of the flames, and the volumes of black smoke which enveloped him when he first entered, almost prostrated the gallant youth.

But he had a great prize in view; he had to rescue Emma Clarence from the devouring elements, or to die in the attempt.

That the fair girl was in that log-house there could not be a doubt.

She had been placed there by her faithful Indian maid when she returned from the gorilla hunt.

Yokee, as usual, was in attendance, and slept just inside the door as a guard against all intruders.

The first thing which Lion Limb stumbled against when he entered the house was the prostrate body of Yokee.

He did not know how it had happened, but poor Yokee was insensible.

Several arrows were in his body.

His face was all cut and bleeding, and the flames had already burnt his clothes in part.

To drag the body out of the house and beyond the reach of the flames was the work of a second.

Then returning to the room Lion Limb began to grope about for the (as he now supposed) dead body of Emma Clarence.

Upon his hands and knees he crawled and felt in every corner.

But nowhere could he discover her.

His bodily sufferings were now very great.

He was badly burnt and almost suffocated with smoke.

"Had the savages borne the girl away in triumph?" he thought.

"Had Yokee, faithful to his promise, fallen under the hands of the savage assailants in defending his mistress?"

These and such like were the thoughts which filled the heart and mind of the gallant youth.

Now and then he could hear the shouts of the savages outside, and their yells and hideous noises only tended to give him greater courage.

And still he searched in vain.

"Can she have crawled up the rough staircase into the loft above?" he thought.

On the instant he mounted the rudely-made stairs.

They were crackling and all ablaze.

He had not got more than half-way up when they fell, and left him clinging to a rafter.

His position was perilous in the extreme.

Still deep intense love for Emma Clarence cheered him on, and he clung to the burning beam and got into the loft above.

The air was a little purer and he breathed more easily.

The blaze lighted up the loft, and to his intense horror he beheld Emma lying in the midst of blazing woodwork.

Whether she was dead or alive he knew not.

With a feeling of madness, and a mixture of stern joy at having thus at last discovered the object of his search, he clasped her in his arms.

She was in the last stage of suffocation.

She was totally insensible, yet her heart beat wildly.

With a shout of triumph Lion Limb clasped her tightly to his manly breast, and thrusting open the trap door he leaped upon the burning roof. (See Cut.)

THE BOY KING

OF THE SOUTH SEA ISLANDS.

THE GORILLA FIGHT.

CHAPTER LI.

JERRY MARKS IS PRESCRIBED CHANGE OF AIR

THE sudden thud on the floor of the front room in which Jerry Marks lay, and which for the time

being attracted the attention of the father and the detective, causing them to stop in the very middle of their most interesting conversation, is soon explained.

From the moment the stranger entered the house

and spoke to Lawyer Marks, Jerry made sure it was a detective.

When his father and the officer were conversing in undertones in the back room, Jerry stretched himself as far as possible on the sofa, and with his ear to the key-hole listened to every word.

But when he heard the officer say, in a suppressed and ironical tone, "How long has your son gone under the name of Allan Norman?" Jerry lost both heart and confidence.

He knew now that the secret of their easily acquired wealth was known to another at least besides himself and father.

His fears almost choked him.

He lost his balance, and, by falling from the sofa, re-opened the wound which he had received at the hands of Allan in their short but desperate encounter in the lunatic asylum, when and where, as it will be recollected, Allan defended himself with one of the bars of his iron cage.

The floor was blood-stained, and, to all appearance, Jerry lay in the agonies of death.

"Why, the youth is dying," said the humane officer; "he should be seen to at once."

"Yes, I fear he will never recover from that desperate wound," sighed the father.

"He should be seen to at once."

"So he should; but the surgeon who attends him lives some distance from here. I dare not leave him, or I would go," said the father, wringing his hands.

"He will die without something is done, and done quickly, Mr. Marks," said the officer.

"You don't know where Dr. Killum lives, do you?" asked the old man.

"Dr. Killum?" said the officer, in surprise.

"Yes, do you know him?"

"I know enough of him to be certain of this much," said the officer, in contempt, "that he is no doctor at all."

"Oh, I beg your pardon; he is a most skilful——"

"Skilful humbug!" said the officer. "He is nearly always drunk. How he gets his living has always been a mystery to me."

"You have been misinformed, sir," said old Marks, turning very red. "Dr. Killum has attended me for many years."

"On money matters, I suppose?"

"No, you are mistaken. He is a most clever person."

"Every one to their taste. But he shouldn't prescribe for a dog of mine!" was the contemptuous remark of the officer.

"At all events, he pleases me," said old Marks, "and I will not permit any other medical man to enter my house. If you would be so kind as to take a cab and bring him, I should feel extremely obliged."

"Oh, I have no objection, you know," said the officer; "your son needs advice, and as soon as possible. I will go for him if you wish it."

"Without official business of some sort detains you here."

"Oh, no, not in the least," said the officer. "I have no case against you or your son at present," said the officer, smiling. "I merely called to make a few inquiries about a certain lad, now under my protection, who calls himself Allan Norman. If you wish it, I will call upon Dr. Killum on my way home, and see you another time."

The officer left, and the instant he had gone Jerry raised his head and looked aghast at his father.

"Did you hear that?" said Jerry. "The young scoundrel is free, and we are to be hunted down like dogs, I suppose."

"No," said the old man, "there is no fear of that. Money will do everything. Did not the baron make over the right and title of Allan Norman to you?"

"Yes; but I forgot that."

"I did not. Let the law do its worst," said the old Jew; "it cannot harm us."

Jerry now seemed to recover greater strength.

"You are much better, my son."

"I am."

"Are you strong enough to bear moving?"

"Yes, anywhere out of the sight of police-officers," sighed Jerry.

"Then, I will call a cab at once."

"Do so; I am not dangerously wounded."

"He wants change of air," said the old man; "and I know that my friend, Dr. Killum, would so prescribe for him if I wished it."

In a few moments a cab was drawn up in the alley way at the back of the house, and Jerry was placed in it.

"Where to?" asked cabby, touching his hat.

The answer which the father made was not audible, but the cabman understood it well enough and drove off.

"There," said the old man, "he is gone; and now I will wait and see my friend, the doctor, and have a word or two with him. Poor lad, he has lost a great deal of blood through the wound inflicted by that young villain, the escaped lunatic. But I must discover this Allan Norman, if it costs me a thousand pounds. He must be got out of the way somehow, for he will always prove a thorn in my side."

The old lawyer sat in his arm-chair thinking and smiling, and playing with his skinny, bony hands, when a loud rat-tat at the door aroused him from his revery.

CHAPTER LII.

THE SECRET COUNCIL—"WOULD POISON DO IT?"

"THAT must be the doctor," said the old lawyer.

It was none other than the red, blear-eyed physician.

A single nod was exchanged between the two expert rascals, and then the old lawyer went to a cupboard, and produced a bottle of brandy.

The doctor tasted it very carefully, and feeling satisfied that it was not some subtle, poisonous compound, he helped himself freely to the liquid, and his nose became redder than ever.

"Why did you send that fellow for me?" asked Dr. Killum. "Couldn't you have sent somebody else?"

"It was by mere accident I met him, and he went off his own accord."

"Oh, did he? He has a fine pair of eyes," said the doctor, winking.

"You know him then?"

"I have seen him once or twice."

"Indeed, where?"

"Why, prowling about this house," said the doctor, winking in a mysterious manner.

The lawyer smiled, and said that his friend must surely be mistaken.

"For," said he, "what can a police officer want about my premises?"

"Oh, as to that, I might ask, what do they want about my premises? Yet I often see them squinting around the corners, honest as I am."

"Hem!" said the lawyer, smiling.

"But what do you want of me now?" said the doctor. "How is Jerry?"

"Jerry!" said the lawyer, very much annoyed at the doctor's freedom. "My son, Mr. Marks, is not very well."

"Oh, it is *Mr.* Marks, now, eh?" said the doctor, grinning. "Well, then, if it is not too bold a question, how is your dear son, Jeremiah Marks?"

"You are inclined to be insulting to-night, I fear, Dr. Killum."

"No, not at all; but as you seem to stand upon your dignity all at once, I might as well do the same."

"Well, the truth is, doctor," said the old lawyer, in his blandest manner, "I sent for you to see my son, for an unlooked-for accident re-opened the wound he has, but I have since sent him off to a friend's house."

"Dr. Shorthorn's?" said Mr. Killum, with a wicked smile.

"No, I have no occasion to do that. My son is not a lunatic, I think."

"Nor his father either, I think," the doctor rejoined, drily, "as I have already had occasion to know."

"I have always been straightforward and honest to you, Dr. Killum."

"Perhaps so, but not over generous, I think; but of that, no matter; to business. I know very well you did not send for me on your son's account."

"Oh, indeed; and what makes you think so?"

"Various and very many reasons. If the truth were known, you would not care if the cab were to be smashed, and Mr. Jeremiah killed upon the spot."

"You are joking, doctor. You have been drinking too much, I fear."

"Yes, too much of that abominable wine you sold me so very cheap last week. It is almost pure poison."

The lawyer laughed, or pretended to laugh, as he thought, "It would give me infinite pleasure to hear of your death, Dr. Killum, if you only knew it."

"But," he said, with a very grave air, "jokes aside, I wish to speak to you on business."

"What is the amount?"

"That depends upon the success of the undertaking."

"Do you want another certificate for some young friend of yours, about to reside with the lenient, merciful, and humane Dr. Shorthorn?"

"No, nothing of that, although Dr. Shorthorn, and his admirable establishment, has something to do with it."

"Admirable establishment, eh?" laughed Dr. Killium. "Admirable enough for *your* purposes, no doubt, but a perfect hell upon earth for many who have no occasion to be inmates of it."

"No occasion?"

"No, not half so much as you or I have, if the truth were only made known."

"That is a matter of opinion, doctor."

"No, it isn't; it's only a matter of money, Marks, if it comes to that, for what occasion had such a youth as Allan Norman to be confined there?"

"But he isn't."

"No!"

"No, not now."

"So much the better for the poor little wretch, then, that's all."

"So much the better, eh?"

"Yes; why not?"

"It very much concerns *me*, then, doctor."

"And well it might. Poor devil! I dare say you made a pretty penny out of the youth."

"And if I did, didn't you also?"

"No, not one thirtieth part of what fell to your lot."

For a moment not a word was exchanged between them.

The lawyer perceived that "his dear friend, Dr. Killum," was only half-drunk, and in one of his sentimental moods.

To render his dear friend more pliable and elastic for his own devilish designs, he plied the doctor with plenty of brandy and cigars.

In less than half-an-hour Mr. Killum forgot all about his sentimentality, and felt very much inclined to cock his feet on the mantel-piece, and indulge in a song or two.

"Are you short of money, doctor?" the shrewd villain of a lawyer began.

"Short! why, you know I'm short, I always *am* short. Why?"

"I have a little job on hand for you."

"I suppose you have; what is it?"

"About that boy who has escaped from Dr. Shorthorn's asylum."

"Well, what about him? Can't afford to let the poor wretch have his liberty? What harm has he ever done to you?"

"More than you imagine."

"Explain?"

"Well, the long and short of it is that while he is at liberty——"

"Your neck is in danger, I suppose?"

"No, not so much as that; but while he is free ——"

"You are in fear?"

"Yes, just so."

"Well, and how can I help you?"

"In many ways, my dear doctor."

"'Dear doctor,' eh?" thought Mr. Killum; "I know there is something cunning now; he never uses that word without a deep motive."

"Explain, then," said the doctor; "we are too deep in the mud together to get out now."

"Quite right," said the lawyer.

And then sitting back in his chair, the old villain began to play with his thin, skinny, bony, clammy hands, and thus went on—

"As you justly observe, my dear doctor, we are too deep in the mud to think of getting out now, and as I know or think I know where this youth is now concealed, I should like to—ah—you know, to get him, you see—ah——"

"Just so," said the doctor. "Pass over the brandy bottle; go on, I'm all attention."

"Well, what I meant was this, you see: I should not like to use any force or violence, but——"

"Oh, exactly," said Mr. Killum, looking the very picture of innocence, and elevating his eye-brows. "We couldn't for a moment think of using force or violence; it wouldn't do; as gentlemen it would be impossible. Fine brandy this, upon my word."

"There are many more ways of killing a cat than by hanging, you know."

"True, true; or a dog either; poison would do it, it is much better."

"So it is."

A long pause ensued between the two villains, and old Marks bit his lips and rubbed his hands so hard that he made the bones crack again.

"So it is," said the lawyer, in a soft voice, and as if to himself; "poison is much better, and no one would be any the wiser."

"But poisons of all sorts are remarkably dear, now-a-days, and very scarce indeed, very scarce."

"No matter what the price is; if it is necessary to kill the cat or dog that annoys us, we must buy the poison, cost what it will."

"Annoy us;" said the doctor, "I beg your pardon, Mr. Marks, neither dogs nor cats annoy me."

"You don't understand me, Mr. Killum," said old Marks.

"Oh, yes I do; but as to any animal annoying me, you know, that is out of the question, for I'm too poor to have any leavings or spare-bones on my table. You may have some troublesome animal in view, but I haven't."

"Well, to make short work of my story, I have an animal that annoys me, and I wish——"

"To kill it, I suppose?"

"I do," replied Lawyer Marks, in a hissing tone.

"And you would have me do the deed for you?"

"Yes, for a price."

"And what price, pray?"

"A good sum."

"Name it?"

"I wouldn't mind £500," the old lawyer replied; "as I am about to leave England, I don't mind being liberal."

"Leave England, eh?"

"Yes."

"And allow me to make the acquaintance of Calcraft alone, I suppose?" said the doctor, laughing. "You are cunning to the very marrow, Marks, but you have mistaken your man this time."

"Indeed; how so?"

"You may perhaps imagine I don't know anything about this youth and his aristocratic parentage."

"Aristocratic parentage? Why, you must be raving."

"You are a liar, Mr. Marks, allow me to say," said the doctor, in a calm, determined tone. "You are an old liar, sir," he repeated, "and are as well aware of all the facts; yes, better than I am. But you don't get me to kill this youth for any price."

The old lawyer was astonished at the anger of "dear Dr. Killum," and he shoved his chair back against the wall in fear.

"What has this poor boy done to you that you should seek to kill him like a dog?" said the doctor.

"Come, come, doctor, don't talk in that way; if your offended innocence can be soothed by more than £500, name your own sum then, and get the young vagabond out of the way in whatever manner you please. If he were only transported, now, and to go to the bottom of the sea like his twin brother, I should feel happy."

"Well, that is a milder way of putting the question than the other, you know; and now I come to reflect over it, I can see a hundred ways of keeping him silent and quiet without drugs or that sort of thing, if the price is suitable."

"Well, name your price, then."

"Halves!"

"Halves?" gasped the lawyer. "Why he has nothing; he is worth nothing—not one penny."

"All stuff!" said Killum. "I have known the lads longer than you have, and know more about them than you dream of, Marks."

"You do?"

"Yes, I do. What do you think of that?" said the doctor. "I wasn't always so low down in the world as I am now; but one thing and another (he might have said one professional crime after another) has reduced me, and now that I am lost to all self-respect, now that I am penniless and ragged, now that I am shunned by my professional brethren, and looked upon as the scum of the earth—although

I still hold my certificate in order to keep practising—Dr. Killum, as they call me, has fallen into the hands of scoundrel Jews. Why, sir," said the doctor, striking the table, and looking very red and fierce, "I know more of those Norman lads than their own mother. I brought them into the world! What do you think of that, Mr. Marks?"

"You brought them into the world?" said the lawyer, staggered.

"Yes, I did, Lawyer Marks! What do you think of that? I, Doctor Killum, was the medical man."

"Who was their mother? Where does she live?" asked the foxey old lawyer, eagerly trying to worm out a grand secret.

"That has nothing at all to do with you," was the calm reply. "Would you go and levy contributions on the poor unfortunate lady?"

"She is a woman of title."

"I know it."

"We could make money out of the secret," said Marks, in great glee.

"You might, but I would not. She paid me well, nay, more than well for all I did, and I have squandered it all on drink; but, wicked and depraved as I am, I will never kill the lad."

"Who'd a thought it?" the old Jew sighed. "I'd give a thousand pounds to find her out."

"And I would give ten times as much that you should not. You will never discover her without I tell you all."

"You think to puzzle me, doctor, but you cannot. I already know the father; and have had dealings with him."

"Mind you don't have too many dealings with him, then, that's all."

"What mean you?"

"If ever you get fairly into his hands, he will hang you!"

Dr. Killum spoke so coldly, and with so much meaning, that old Marks shivered again.

"Oh, if I had only known this fellow had been so deep, or had known so much as he does, I would never have entrusted any of my secrets in his keeping."

He did not speak for some moments, but bit his nails in annoyance, as he thought,

"Why, instead of this penniless scapegrace being my tool, as I have all along fondly imagined, I am his. What would I not give if he were lying dead at my feet?"

Mr. Marks, cunning and old as he was, had found out a secret, which, sooner or later, becomes palpable to all villains, whether great or small, namely, that with all their cleverness, secresy, subtlety, and double dealing, one knave is sure one day to meet with a greater and a cleverer rascal than himself.

It was this conviction passing through his mind that made old Marks tremble, and caused cold drops of perspiration to ooze out on his wrinkled brow.

"Yet, what hold has he on me?" thought the Jew. "He has participated in this affair of Allan Norman's, and if I ever do get into the felon's dock through it, he will stand beside me, I'll take very good care of that, clever as he is."

"And yet," ruminated the lawyer, "I have known him for years—yea, drunk and sober, for more than ten years—and yet I never found him out. Oh, what an ass I must have been; I should have known that no clever man, such as this Killum is, would drink himself to death daily, yes, hourly. I should have known, fool that I was, that he had some secret, some heavy secret weighing him down by inches. Still, it is well that I now know the very worst; it was all through that strong brandy I gave him, or I might never have wormed such important disclosures from him. He might have gone on for years in this secret way if not by accident I discovered all. But what if he should dare to call upon the baron and disclose everything? I care not; I will still keep him under my thumb, but as to giving him half of what I get to keep silence, that is all moonshine. Jews are not generally such ignorant fools as all that. I will manage this Dr. Killum, and if he dares to disobey me, I'll have the rascal transported; a false oath won't kill me, or I should have been dead long ago; lawyers live by lies, and so will I, as I have always done."

Silence was maintained by both of these worthies for so long a time, and each was so very busy with his own thoughts, that they heeded not the flight of time, and were only roused at last by the striking of a clock upon the mantel-piece.

"You seem to be buried in deep thought, doctor," said the old lawyer, with a forced smile.

"And so I was, but now that the brandy is all finished, I suppose I may go? You have no further business with me?"

"No, not to night, my dear friend; but I suppose you will stand by your bargain?"

"What, in getting that youth out of the way, I suppose?"

"Yes."

"On the terms I stated?"

"What, for halves?"

"Yes."

"Oh, come, come, you are getting exorbitant in your demands."

"I will not undertake the job for less."

"Well, then, consider the bargain settled. I *will* give halves. What do you think of that? Isn't that liberal enough?" said the Jew, rubbing his hands.

"Nothing but fair, I think"

"Then, when shall I hear from you again? I suppose in three or four days he will be out of harm's way?"

"Perhaps so; but I can't commence this difficult job without money, you know."

"What, want money now! Oh, impossible. I have'nt a penny by me."

"Then I cannot proceed, that's all."

"But you must."

"Then, you also must get money, and at this moment, for I am sadly in need of it."

"He's got the screw upon me," thought Marks, "and I must give him some to begin with."

Heaving a heavy sigh, the Jew fumbled very long in his pockets, and at last drew out one sovereign, and then another, until, with a few bank notes, more than one hundred pounds were placed before his insatiable friend.

But each coin, and each note that he took from his pockets, was accompanied with such a look of agony and vexation, one would almost have been led to believe that the old Israelite was having all his teeth extracted under the unskilful hands of some village blacksmith.

"There," said Marks, "the villain has gone at last; and if he is not as good as his word, I'll never rest until I get him transported."

He sat long in his arm-chair, thinking of many things, but was at last aroused by hearing some one laughing at him through the hole in his shutters.

He sprang to his feet as if a bomb-shell had fallen into the room.

"Who can that be?" he thought. "Surely I have not been watched or overheard?"

"Yes, yer hev, guv'ner," was the rough reply of some unknown person, who laughed again more hoarsely than before, and then suddenly disappeared.

CHAPTER LIII.

ALLAN FINDS A FRIEND IN INSPECTOR SHARP.

"WHAT a villain I have been," thought Doctor Killum, as he sauntered homewards to what he familiarly called his "Den," two small dirty parlors, which boasted of but little furniture, but a vast quantity of dirty bottles and such like. "What a villain I have been in my time," he repeated, and his heart sank within him at the thought of what he had done. "If it were not too late I would repent, and turn over a new leaf, as they call it. Some people say 'it is never too late to mend,' but in my case I fear it is."

He walked along musing for some time, and then said, half aloud,

"What has this boy done to me that I should try and destroy him? It is not his fault that he is helpless and friendless; no, no, it is *not* his fault—and I will not injure him, by Heaven I will not. Yet, what must I do? This Jew has got me fast in his clutches, and how can I get loose again? Heigho! I wish my hand had withered before I had done one wrong act in life, and then, perhaps, I should feel happy. Why don't I feel happy? Everyone around me laugh and smile. Why cannot I? I cannot laugh—I cannot look an honest man in the face. But I could once; yes, before drink, damnable drink, had rotted my heart and soul. Is there no turning back? Must I still go headlong in the stream, or buffet the waves, and be a new man again? Oh! that I could—if I could feel but honest once more, I'd give half that remains of my life. Yes, I'll try; I feel that I *can* turn back to the path of honesty again, and with the help of heaven I will."

These, and such like thoughts, rushed through the mind of the crime-stained man; but remorse, grim, gaunt remorse, stared him fully in the face, and, as he crossed one of the bridges, and looked down into the moon-lit waters, he felt half inclined to end all his earthly miseries by committing suicide.

We say he "thought" doing so.

Nay, more than this, overcome with dread at what he had already done, and fearful of the future, he seemed, for the moment, to abandon the good intentions that had possessed him but a little time before, and loosened his cravat.

"There is no hope for me," he said; "I am too abandoned and wicked, there cannot be any hope for a wretch like me."

He was about to spring upon the parapet of the bridge, and leap into the dismal tide below, when his sickly, glazy, frenzied eyes caught sight of some object which seemed to arrest him in his act of madness.

He looked again.

"I am not, I cannot be mistaken in that face," he said, turning sharply around; "it is young Allan Norman, or I must be blind!"

It *was* Allan Norman, who, with Jem Rawlings, were accompanied by the officer who had called on him that evening, and summoned him to the office of old Marks.

"I could not be mistaken in that face," thought the doctor; "but what has he to do with that detective? Who is that other youth, I wonder? My face must not be seen. I will follow, and watch them."

In a half-crazy frame of mind, and scarcely knowing what he did or why, the doctor followed the three persons, and kept a long distance away for fear of being recognised.

"So you know this old Jew lawyer, then," said the officer to Allan as they walked along, "and feel certain you could point out his offices?"

"Yes, with the greatest of ease," said Allan. "Are we going there now?"

"No, my lad, it is very late, and I should not have brought you out, only I have to introduce you to a friend of mine, who seems to know more about you than I do, and who feels great interest in your welfare. He wants to see you particularly to-night, and, if you do as he wishes you, all will go right."

"And who is this officer, then?"

"He is an inspector of detectives, such as I am, you know, and has great authority."

"What's his name?"

"I daresay you have often seen it if you read the papers. His name is Inspector Sharp."

"Sharp?"

"Yes, and a very sharp, keen gentlemen he is when you come to know him. This way."

Up one street and down another the lads went, led by Green, and at last they came to the corner of a dark, dirty court, which had an outlet into a mews, at the end of which flickered the faint rays of a broken lamp.

Here they were met by a very roughly-dressed man, who suddenly emerged from a door-way.

"That you, Green?" said the unknown. "Glad to see you up to time. Are these the lads you spoke of? Oh! of course they are, I know their features well," said he, smiling.

He had seen them before in the dock at the Old Bailey, when they were tried with their brothers for the mysterious murder of Alderman Inglis

"Yes, sir," said Green; "these are the boys, and very well-behaved, intelligent lads they are. Shall you want me, sir, to night?"

"No, you may go home. I don't think they'll start to-night," said the inspector; "but be ready, for at any time I may call on you. Do you think any one has been watching you here, Green?"

"Watching! No, sir. Why?"

"Because I see a shabby-genteel fellow lurking about yonder; he came up the street just when you did."

Mr. Green felt indignant that he should have been outwitted by any one, and went away at a sharp walk towards the "shabby-genteel" person, who, as quick as thought, perceived the detective's intention, and vanished like a shadow.

"Come along with me, my lads," said Inspector Sharp, in a kind tone; "you are under *my* care now, remember, and must do whatever I tell you."

So saying, he went down the dark, dingy court with the two lads, and, as he passed No. 10, he said, in a very low tone—

"You won't forget that house and its number, will you, my lads?"

"No, sir; why?"

"Ah, now you ask too much. Don't be so inquisitive; in a week or two you'll understand it as well as I do."

Allan was puzzled, and looked so.

But Jem Rawlings rather liked to walk about and talk to persons in high position; so he said, half aloud, "Wouldn't I like to be a first-rate detective though, eh, Allan, it must be jolly sport,—lots of money, riding about on railways and steamboats, and doing nothing but catch thieves."

The inspector smiled; but by this time they had left the court, and after telling the lads not to forget the name and number of the house in the court, he said, "And so you think it fine sport, my lads, to be a detective?"

"I do said Jem.

"And I do not," said Allan.

"Why not, is the work too dangerous for you?"

"No; not that. I wouldn't give a button for an Englishman or boy either, who would fear danger in the discharge of his public duty; but I think there is so much of the sneak and hypocrite in dodging people about, pretending to be friends, and then turning the very worst of enemies, that I don't think I should ever be a detective."

"Well; but suppose you were acting for your own benefit, what then. You wouldn't call it sneaking about, if an officer was looking after your stolen property, I suppose?"

"I mean no offence, sir; but if I was working for myself, it would be a very different thing."

"Well, then, you see you are working for the public at large, and the case which I have now in hand, Mr. Allan, concerns *you*."

"Me?"

"Yes, you, and nobody else, my lad; and, although you may dislike it, you *must* play the part of a hypocrite for a time, and a detective also. When *you* have done what I tell you to do, then *I* will step in and complete the case," said the detective, smiling.

"What case?" asked Allan in surprise. "Surely I am not accused of anything, am I?"

"No, but other people are, and it amounts to the same."

"It is a mystery to me, sir," said Allan; "heaven knows I have seen trouble enough for one of my age, without getting into more."

"I know you have, my lad; but I think it was a very lucky moment when you fell in on the road with Miky Huggins."

"Lucky? Why, Mr. Green said he was one of the greatest scoundrels in the world, and meant me harm."

"Quite true, my lad; but for all that I repeat it was a lucky moment that you met him, for now you are beginning to get out of all your troubles. Shortly I hope you will be a gentleman in pocket and appearance."

"And all through Mike Huggins the house-breaker?"

"Yes."

"Strange!"

"Very strange, I dare say; but when you have gone through this last trial and are well off, my young sir, don't forget that it was through the exertion of a detective that you won it all. You will not look upon them then as 'sneaks' and 'hypocrites,' as you were just now pleased to call them."

"I meant no offence personally, sir."

"I know you did not, my lad; but you spoke like thousands of people who, because they have no personal or direct interest in cases, look upon policemen generally as worthless, lazy drones."

The inspector was so good-tempered in all he said, and spoke in such a fatherly tone to the two friendless lads, that Allan and Jem began to like him very much.

This rising opinion was still more increased when the inspector took them to a coffee stall and treated them liberally to tea and well-buttered cakes.

Jem looked upon the officer, now that his appetite was appeased, as if he were not mortal; but for the life of him he could not imagine why he dressed so roughly and looked so ugly.

Taking out his watch the inspector compared it with the market clock, and feeling satisfied as to its accuracy, he said,—

"Couldn't you find your way back to the court again, I wonder?"

"What, Spider Alley, as you called it, sir? Of course we could."

"Then do so. Go down one by one, and sit in a

door passage, out of the light; pretend to be asleep, but keep a sharp eye on No. 10, and when you hear the clock strike four, leave,—come to me; I shall be at this coffee stall."

Allan and Jem, as directed, went to Spider Alley and secreted themselves in a house-passage opposite to No. 10.

"I don't like sneaking after anybody, Jem," whispered Allan, "but I'm working for the sake of justice now, you know."

And so he was.

And he was acting as a detective in his own cause also.

The cause of public justice should always be the cause of every honest man.

But Allan was as yet only a youth, and could hardly understand that.

He learned to think so shortly afterwards, however, as this story will show.

CHAPTER LIV.

THE YOUNG DETECTIVES.

"THIS is snug enough, I think," said young Jem Rawlings, as he sat crouched up in the passage, and looked upon the whole adventure as a capital joke.

"I don't though," said Allen, in disgust, "this court is a perfect fever den; the smell is enough to knock one down."

"Never mind, it ain't for long you know," said Jem; "everybody appears to be a-bed and fast asleep in this alley; they ain't afraid of robbers much, I imagine, or they would not leave their doors open. Oh, if they only knew what we was up to though, wouldn't it be a spree?"

"I don't know that; if they did know, or even guessed at it, Jem, I wouldn't give much for our lives; this place swarms with thieves, housebreakers, and the very worst sort of most desperate people."

And so it did.

Spider Alley had for years been under the eyes of the police, and many a good dozen of worthless rascals had lived and thrived there, and many a score had been sent out of the country for the country's good, also from the same locality.

Now and then drunken men and women, full of oaths and foul expressions, found their way into Spider Alley while they lay concealed in the passage.

More than one ragged and breathless youth was seen to run into and through it at breakneck speed, as if chased by some one he did not wish to know.

And, stranger than all, as Allan imagined, several well-dressed, nay, fashionably and stylishly attired females, went into various houses.

But all bore the imprint of vice and dissipation.

"Number 10 is very quiet," said Jem, getting restless. "I don't hear any one moving or talking."

"Perhaps not; but the inspector did not ask us to come down here for nothing, you may depend. Hush!" said Allan, "I hear some one approaching."

They held their breath, and in a few minutes a flashily-dressed woman came down the court and knocked twice at No. 10.

"What does that mean?" whispered Jem.

"Listen, and we shall find out."

A second time the woman knocked, but still no one answered her summons, although the two youths could plainly hear an upper window raised at No. 10, and some rough-headed individual say—

"Is that you, Meg?"

"Yes."

"All right, I'll be down in a second," and the window was closed to again, with a loud noise.

"I should know that voice," thought Allan.

But for the moment he could not remember when or where he had heard it before.

In a few moments a man in his shirt sleeves and stockings came to the door, smoking a short pipe.

Apparently he had been to bed, and was not over pleased at being aroused.

"Hillo, Meg, is that you? How are you? I thought you were never coming."

"Two knocks ain't for you, Mike," said the woman.

"I know it ain't, but Nick isn't at home; he's gone down in the country a little way."

"I've got a letter for him."

"I thought that party would be sure to come or send—where is it?"

"Here it is."

"Where did you see him?"

"Down the Haymarket."

"Did he say anything?"

"No; he only said this would do either for you or Nick."

"Nick is at work by this time, I think," said rough-head, who was no other than Mr. Michael Huggins. "Will Mr. George come to night?"

"He said he might; but this note will explain all."

"All right! Good night, Meg."

"Good night. If you can see anything that will suit me, Mike, I'll square it with you."

"Sound you are, Meg!" said Mike, who retreated into the doorway, and disappeared up stairs.

"That is Mike Huggins," said Allan, "and if he knew I was watching him he would murder me, Jem.'

"Oh, lor'," said Jem, in horror at the thought, "how must the detectives then feel, that's always at this game? It ain't quite so funny as I thought it would be, if Mr. Huggins is the sort of fellows they have to deal with. Why he looked as rough as a badger and no mistake."

"Suppose we were surprised in this passage," Jem.

"I don't think it very likely they would let us off without a good thrashing, at all events," said Allan, with a grin.

"But for all you know, your fortune in life depends upon our prudence here. The inspector said as much."

"So he did, and I hope it may turn out to be so," said Allan, "not only for my sake but for yours also, Jem."

"Well, I don't know," said Jem, "I can't see that it would make much difference to me, you know. The inspector did not hold out any hope of ever making me a gentleman; but I should dearly like to see you one, Allan."

"And if I were one, then you may depend upon it you should share all I had, let it be ever so much."

"I've no doubt of it, Allan; we've always been like brothers, ain't we?" said Jem.

"And so we will always be, I hope."

The two young friends were thus conversing in whispers, when they came to the bold resolve to leave their present hiding-place, and go into the passage of No. 10, and, if they could, overhear the conversation of Miky and his companions. if he had any.

Very cautiously they advanced and crossed the alley-way, and then one by one they crawled into the passage.

Miky had descended the stairs with two companions, and at that moment was hard at work in sharpening some carpenter's tools.

"I don't thank Mr. George for sending his note

at this time of night," said Mike ; "why didn't he come or send earlier ?"

"Oh, Gentleman George must be obeyed, you know, Miky," was the answer of one of the men inside, "it isn't our place to dictate to him."

"I know it ain't," said Mike, "I wish it was, and then you and I, and all the rest of us, would have a greater share of the booty than we do."

"Yes, it is rayther aggravating, ain't it," said a third, "just to think on it. Here we coves have all the hard and dirty work to do, and just when we could do the trick ourselves, in steps Gentleman George and his brother, and they takes the lion's share."

"It won't always be so though," said Mike. "You can take my word for it, that if Gentleman George and his brother ain't a little more liberal than they have been, some one or other will let the cat out of the bag, and then Mr. George will have to give up his racing and fine clothes for many a long year."

"Is it true he has got two racehorses, then ?"

"In course it is ; and how has he made 'em I wonder, if we didn't do it for him ?" said Mike.

"He is very clever, though, and no mistake."

"Oh, he's all there, you know," said Mike ; "he and his brother have been at it off and on for about fifteen years."

"Who got up this job, Mike ?"

"What, the one we are now on ?"

"Yes."

"Why, it seems that an old Jew lawyer that lends money sometimes to Gentleman George, was very much in want of certain papers which are known to be in Lord Manfred's mansion."

"The one you were a looking at t'other day ?"

"Jest so."

"How came you to know it ?"

"Why, didn't Mr. George tell me all about it, stupid ?"

"Well, all right ; go on."

"Well, Mr. George took the hint from the lawyer, and although no price has been fixed upon, the job, you can tell, will prove something handsome. ' But, then,' says Mr. George, ' while we are about it, we might as well get into the pantry and other places to clean the whole lot out.' "

"A very wise thought."

"That may be ; but you must know that it will prove very dangerous on this occasion."

"What makes you think so ?"

"Well, the detectives have been swarming around this neighbourhood for the last two weeks. I saw two or three to-night hanging about the alley, and you may depend they've got a notion that something is up among us."

"I should think so," said Allan, in a whisper to Jem.

"What are they up to, Allan ?" asked Jem.

"Why, I have peeped through the key-hole twice and I can't make it out "

"Let me have a peep."

"Oh, now I see," said Allan, in a whisper ; " they are sharpening and packing up a lot of carpenter's tools ; how beautiful and new and bright they are."

"Let's have a peep," said Jem.

"Why, they are packing them in a box. Hush !"

"I think they will do, mates," said Mike, looking at the box of tools in admiration. "They look as bright as silver, and I'll warrant there ain't an edge among 'em as wouldn't shave a man as clean as a whistle."

"Are you going to cart 'em, Mike ?"

"Cart 'em," said Mike, in a tone of contempt ;

"no, not if I know it ; they are going down by railroad, and when we wants 'em we can call, you see."

"That's a dodge you learnt from Gentleman George, Mike."

"Yes, and a good many more, I can tell you. It ain't a bad move, though, for you see if the 'slops' (policemen) do happen to lay hands on us they can't convict, for we've got no burglars' implements about us, and so they lets us go. I've been up several times on suspicion, but they couldn't prove nothing, and so I gets off with a warning. We does the same with the 'swag' (booty) ; we don't carry any about with us, no not so much as a penny piece worth ; we has it sent away in boxes or portmanteaus, like gents, and has it ' left till called for ' at any out-of-the-way station we please, and when all suspicion and that sort o' thing is over, we goes down and calls for the trunks and divide at leasure. Lor' bless yer', Gentleman George and his brother have made a fortune in a single night I've known 'em to."

Allan and Jem were intently listening outside the back parlour door, when some one approached them noiselessly, saying, in a stern voice :—

"Hillo ! what brings you here, eh ?"

So sudden was this short speech, and so startling to the lads, that they jumped up and dashed out of the passage, followed closely by a determined pursuer, full of oaths and blasphemy. It was Gentleman George !

CHAPTER LV.

THE GORILLA FIGHT.

WITH the flames crackling all around him as he held up the insensible body of Emma Clarence, the position of Lion Limb was perilous in the extreme.

He seemed to be deserted by his young companions, who were busily engaged in putting out fires and fighting the Indians in different parts of the camp.

Indians also still surrounded him, and were dancing like madmen round the burning log-house.

Escape seemed impossible.

The blazing beams were crackling and breaking under his feet.

There seemed to be no particle of hope for him and the fair maid, and the Indians knew it.

But least when they expected it, two bands of boys armed to the teeth, led on by Dick and Harry, burst in upon the scene ; and so furious was their assault, that the Indians were slaughtered without mercy on all sides.

To rescue Lion Limb was the first thought of Dick.

Ladders they had none.

But he resorted to a device.

Six lads leaned their heads against the log-house, and thus made a platform of their bodies.

Upon the backs of the six, four other lads jumped and did the same, and upon the backs of these four two boys clambered.

Having thus formed a sort of ladder with their bodies, Lion Limb and Emma were saved from the roof of the burning log-house.

It was well that Dick had been quick in his movements, for the instant that Lion Limb and Emma were saved, the roof fell in with a crash, and the flames burst out so furiously all around the log-house, that the brave youths who had been standing against the hitherto uninjured part, were very much scorched and blackened by the body of flames which so suddenly burst out upon them.

LION LIMB

THE BOY KING
OF THE SOUTH SEA ISLANDS.

THE FALL FROM THE ROCK—(See next Number.)

The hours passed, and the schooner was soon made ready for its intended voyage.

Harry Woodruff was left in charge of the camps, and everything prepared for the defence of the little colony should any of Red Wolf's savages feel bold enough to again attack it.

Lion Limb selected a picked crew from among his followers, and took Dick Hamilton with him as second in command.

Many presents were put on board for any friendly Indians they might meet with.

Emma Clarence was also of the party, and the

general bustle and haste of preparing for departure very much pleased her.

She begged hard that Joe Pebbles might also go, and bring his fiddle, to which request the young leader willingly assented.

Everything being arranged and in proper order for sailing, the prisoner Whetherby was conducted on board, and placed below, being safely guarded by two men.

"Weigh anchor, my merry, merry men," said Lion Limb, and in an instant a dozen jumped to the capstan bars, and worked away to the rollicking strains of Joe Pebbles' fiddle, which seemed to much lighten the heavy work.

Joe was in his glory.

One of the stewards on board had wetted Joe's whistle with a rather strong glass of grog previous to commencing, and Mr. Pebbles scratched away like a madman all sorts of jigs and reels, to the no small delight of old Katamar and his warriors, who danced and capered about like so many escaped lunatics.

Both the tide and winds were favourable for a rapid journey towards the Blue Rocks, and the gallant schooner danced across the white-crested waves at great speed, and soon came in sight of the headlands of Blue Rock Island, and within a mile or two of their chief rendezvous on the coast.

Lion Limb full well knew the importance of making the Indians and islanders generally feel friendly towards his own colony, and, as old King Katamar was a man of great importance in his own country, and, in order to impress the Indian with a true idea of what all true Englishmen are, and are able to do, he ordered the cooks to prepare a grand repast, which consisted of bacon, beef, and other things, not forgetting several wild ducks and geese, and other fowl, which abounded on the island.

This meal was some time in preparing, but long before it was ready the pleasant odours of boiled and roasted meats attracted the attention of all the Indians, who danced about the ship's galley like so many playful children.

In due time, however, the dinner was served on deck, and all partook of it most heartily. Old Katamar and his warriors gorged themselves, and never seemed tired of devouring the good things before them, making faces and gestures to the merry crew, telling them as well as they could how much the abundance of savoury food had pleased them.

When the things were cleared away, and the schooner was rapidly approaching the Blue Rocks, Lion Limb gave orders that every man should stand ready at his post, and await his commands.

Old Katamar and his warriors were drawn up on the larboard side of the deck, each with his rude weapon in hand.

On the main deck the crew had all assembled about the hatchway, which said hatchway was ornamented with several gratings, which had been prepared for the coming ceremony of flogging.

For some time all were whispering together, and the Indians, not then knowing what all this parade and preparation meant, looked on, and chattered away loudly.

Soon, however, a dead silence reigned on all sides.

Not a female, whether Indian or European, was allowed to be present, but were confined to the main cabin by Lion Limb's orders, who would not permit even the lowest female slave to witness what was to take place.

At length, when all things were ready, the young captain appeared on deck, and all the crew presented arms, and then, addressing King Katamar, he explained what was to take place, and why, for he felt very desirous that the Indians should fully comprehend the aim and reason for all that he did.

The Indians listened very attentively to all that was said to them, and so grave, solemn, and impressive was his manner, that the Indians, who at first had laughed at the idea of simply flogging a traitor and enemy, now looked grave and interested.

"Bring forth the prisoner," said Lion Limb, and, in a moment afterwards, Bill Whetherby appeared, looking more haggard and scornful than before.

He struggled hard to release himself from the firm grip of those who held and conducted him; he wriggled and writhed, but the more he did so, the more firmly and painfully did the chains which bound him lacerate his limbs.

It was as much as four men could do to drag the culprit from the lower hold on to the deck, and, so violently did he resist, that it was feared he would kill some one.

His oaths and imprecations were something most horrible and revolting to hear.

But by main strength the villain was dragged along to the place of punishment.

His jacket and shirt were quickly thrown over his shoulders, while two strong fellows lashed his elbows to the gratings so that he could not stir beyond an inch or two either way.

"Kill me, shoot me, hang me to the yard-arm, do anything you like, but do not flog," groaned Bill Whetherby.

But his entreaties were of no avail.

The schooner's sails were partly furled, and as they approached the headlands of the Blue Rocks, Lion Limb and all on board could see numbers of buccaneers who had clambered high upon the rocks to see what was about to take place.

"Cast anchor, Dick," said the captain; "we are now in shallow water, and in full view of the cut-throats yonder on the rocks; they can have a fair view of all that takes place, and we can defy them, for we are all out of harm's way."

Loud shouts from those on land now told plainly enough that they recognised the culprit lashed to the gratings, and with wild gestures the villanous-looking rascals stood looking on.

"Prepare the guns for a broadside," said Lion Limb, "for if the rascals dare fire upon us we will sweep them off the rocks with plenty of grape shot."

All this was done, and advancing towards the culprit, Lion Limb said:—"Those among you who have been whipped by Whetherby on board the old 'Rattlesnake, step forward."

Six youths instantly came forward.

"Let two of the strongest take this pair of cat-o'-nine tails and do your duty. Spare him not."

Two tall brawny youths took each a whip, and having taken off their own jackets and carefully measured their distance so as to be able to strike with full swing of their arm, they flung the tails of the cat round their heads, and with all their strength brought them down successively on the bare body of Whetherby.

The rascal gave a sudden jerk and almost tore the gratings away from their positions.

He cursed and swore and screamed aloud with agony as blow after blow descended upon him in slow and measured time.

Large welts as big as a man's finger were instantly raised on his back, spreading from his shoulder blades nearly to his loins.

As soon as they had given one blow they slowly and carefully ran their fingers through the cords to clear them and prevent the chance of a single lash being spired the culprit, and flinging them round and round their heads repeated their blows.

Each slashing sound upon the bare flesh was succeeded by shrieks and struggles to get free.

But still blow followed blow slowly and in measured time.

His back by this time was nearly covered with deep red gashes.

The skin was roughed up and curled in many parts as it does when a violent blow on the skin causes an extensive abrasion.

The effect of the cuts upon his back had rendered it a fearful sight, but when these were repeted with all the vigor of fresh and untiring arms, Bill Whetherby's body exhibited a dreadful spectacle.

The dark red of the wounds had assumed a livid purple, the flesh stood up in mangled ridges, and the blood trickled here and there like the breaking out of an old wound.

Each moment heavy lashes were descending on him, and his screams were loud and horrible to hear, as he gasped and begged for water.

The sentence was not yet completed and water was given to him.

His thirst was most intense.

Each lash caused a violent burning pain at his heart.

The villain Whetherby did not scoff and laugh now.

He who had been so eager and willing to whip others was now suffering himself; and there was not one who saw the ghastly sight but said that it served him right.

Katamar and his Indians were mute.

They who had laughed at the bare idea of flogging being severe chastisement, seemed amazed as they gazed at the gory scene before them.

The flesh from the nape of the neck to below the shoulder-blades was one deep purple mass, from which the blood oozed slowly.

At every stroke a low groan escaped him, and his whole frame quivered with a sort of convulsive twitch; his eyes were staring, bloodshot, and protruding from their sockets.

He was insensible.

The last ten lashes had almost killed him.

The cords about his arms were cut, and Bill Whetherby fell a senseless heap upon the deck.

A rough blanket was thrown over him—the flogging was over. It was a terrible sight to look at that huge-framed man lying insensible in his own blood.

Yet not one was found to pity him.

Each and all rejoiced that justice was meted out to him who had long oppressed and injured them.

"Carry him below," said Lion Limb, "and let some one attend him, for, from the activity of those on shore yonder, I fancy the buccaneers are on the move, and mean mischief. Be prepared to weigh anchor and set sail, my lads; we have given the buccaneers another taste of our quality, and should they attack us——"

He spoke not further.

"A sail, a sail!" roared the man aloft.

"What kind of craft is she?"

"A fast-sailing brigantine, captain."

"What colours?"

"The black flag."

"'Tis the buccaneers' craft; we must prepare instantly for battle. Go aloft, Dick, and see what you can make of the strange sail."

"Aye, aye, sir," said Dick, and up the rigging he went as nimbly as a monkey.

"What is she, Dick?"

"A brigantine, captain, low and rakish; she flies the pirates' colours; there's no mistaking her."

"How many guns?"

"Six guns, sir; and she sails before the wind as prettily as ever I saw any craft do."

"Quick, lads, quick; haul up the anchor, and let us get clear of these headlands, and be prepared to give her a warm reception," said Lion Limb, gaily. "I have often heard of the pirates' brigantine, and am glad she comes out to meet us boldly."

In a few moments the anchor was raised, and the "Rattlesnake" turning her head, went forth boldly and with a fair wind to encounter the "Scorpion," which from all that could be learned, was commanded by no less a person than Bloodhoof, who was now chief of the buccaneers of the Blue Rocks.

CHAPTER LIX.

THE FIGHT BETWEEN THE "RATTLESNAKE" AND "SCORPION."

IT was well that the crew of the "Rattlesnake" was so well drilled as it was, or otherwise the vessel would have been lost, for directly after the "Scorpion" had been sighted contrary winds sprang up, and prevented Lion Limb from approaching his enemy, and almost drove him upon a reef of treacherous rocks.

The pirate perceived the danger of the "Rattlesnake," and endeavoured to approach nearer and nearer to her, in order to add to her peril.

But just at the moment when every one on board thought that she must certainly be dashed to pieces, Lion Limb seized the helm, and with great skill steered his craft in beautiful style through a most dangerous channel, and ere many minutes had elapsed, the "Rattlesnake" was safe and in deep waters again.

Three hearty and lusty cheers were given by his crew for the great skill their young commander had displayed, and every heart was light again, and rejoiced at the almost miraculous escape which had befallen them.

The danger arose not so much from bad seamanship as an over anxious desire to get as near to the pirate as possible, for Dick, who at that time had been at the helm, not doubting for a moment that they were in deep water, steered the schooner close to the wind, in order to save time and bring on the battle between them as soon as possible.

But the wind changed now so much that despite all their skill neither the "Rattlesnake" nor "Scorpion" could approach each other or fire with effect.

For many hours these two vessels sailed around each other almost in a circle, and yet they were always beyond gunshot.

At length, when night came on, the wind abated, and gradually and slowly the antagonistic ships approached closer and closer.

Firing began when they were within pistol-shot of each other, but not a moment sooner.

Each commander seemed bent on "victory or death," and would not waste a single cartridge in any random or long-distance firing.

Each was working to get the weather gauge of his opponent, and it must be confessed that, though pirate as she was, the "Scorpion" was beautifully handled and guided by its captain, whether that person were Bloodhoof or any other.

About midnight they were nearly alongside of each other, and immediately exchanged broadsides.

The action then went on, supported on each side by incessant and destructive firing.

They fought on vigorously and obstinately for more than an hour, but the wind was so changeable that Lion Limb was not able to lay his vessel broadside on and board the pirates, as he wished to do, and oftentimes a few puffs of wind would cause the rivals to separate, and thus defer the conclusion of terrible duel.

For four whole hours the combat continued, and neither could claim the mastery.

The pause that ensued ushered in daylight, and each ship's crew in that interval was busy in repairing the damages of their respective vessels.

When the sun rose above the horizon, the action was renewed with even greater energy and fury than before.

Still, however, so equally were the vessels matched, that for the present neither could compel the other to yield.

The broad defiant flag of England floated still on board the gallant "Rattlesnake," and though it was shot through and through, and rent and torn, it was never for a moment lowered.

On the other hand, the pirate brigantine and its black flag with skull and crossbones thereon, seemed determined to fight to the very last, and although her hull was shot through in many places, and was leaking dreadfully, Bloodhoof, its captain, scorned to yield or fly.

It was a desperate battle.

The pirate was much larger, and carried more men and guns than the schooner.

Yet she had suffered much more both in loss of men and general damage, for the fire from the "Rattlesnake," though less quick than that of the pirate, was more deadly.

At daylight, then, the action was again renewed, and as the vessels approached each other nearer and nearer, the crews of each gave hearty cheers.

Broadside after broadside was delivered on each side.

Balls, grape, and rifle shot, shells, and rockets, were hurled at each other.

Still they seemed equally matched.

It was impossible to tell for which side victory would decide.

The daring attempts of the one were being constantly defeated by the valour of the other.

For more than ten hours was the battle raging between them.

The mainmast of the brigantine had been shot away.

The sails of the schooner were riddled like a sieve.

The pauses that ensued between the numerous actions of these obstinate and unflinching vessels were employed by both in constantly preparing for a renewal of the fight, and no sooner had the one cleared away its wreck than it again manœuvred and commenced the work of destruction.

Like two gladiators, who have fought themselves to a perfect standstill, and pause a moment to recover breath, the "Rattlesnake" and "Scorpion" luffed in the wind, and stood off and on, each crippled, though not subdued.

How long this action could be maintained by each was a mystery.

The firing on both sides began to be faint and irregular, and at long intervals.

Nearly all the ammunition on board the "Rattlesnake" was now expended.

Many were wounded, and not a few killed on either side.

The brigantine was almost a perfect wreck, and was riddled with shots.

She was fast settling down, and before night would sink despite the most strenuous exertions of Bloodhoof and his daring crew.

Whatever mortal men could do the captains and crews of both vessels did.

They were fighting for the mastery and dominion over the whole South Pacific.

But while the battle seemed yet undecided, a strange sail appeared in sight.

The buccaneers hailed its approach with rounds of cheers.

Those cheers sounded sadly on the ears of the schooner's crew.

It boded ill to Lion Limb.

He was crippled, but he scorned to fly in the face of his foes, even should there be two to one.

The moment was one of intense excitement to all on board.

Their very existence hung trembling in the balance.

As may be readily acknowledged, the position of the two ships was perilous in the extreme.

Both of them had fought very long and hard, and yet neither could claim the mastery.

Who or what the strange ship might be, which just then appeared on the horizon, neither could tell.

Each hoped that it might be a friend.

The pirates on board the "Scorpion," had at first hailed its appearance with joy, and shouted out boldly and defiantly.

If possible, these shouts were more alarming to Lion Limb's followers than all the previous perils of battle.

"It cannot be a friend, captain," said Dick, "and from the way those fellows are bawling, there cannot be a doubt but that it is some smuggler or pirate like themselves."

"Never mind, Dick," said Lion Limb, bravely. "Come what may I will never give up my ship to either or both of them. We will fight on to the bitter end, and if the worst befals us, why, then let us die and sink together like men."

These few words had a very great and visible effect on his crew.

They idolised their young commander now more than ever.

Three rousing cheers were called for and given by the crew, and though crippled in almost every part, her hull was sound, and all hands prepared to clear for action again.

"Can you make anything of her, Dick?" asked the young captain.

"Yes, sir. She sails very fast before the wind, and she is very rakish and low down in the water."

"Has she shown any colours yet?"

"No, sir. Not any that I have seen, but I have not the least doubt but that she is an enemy."

Hour after hour passed away, and the strange ship approached closer and closer.

She was armed with six long, heavy guns, and crowded with men.

All hope now seemed lost to those on board the "Rattlesnake."

The stranger was not more than half a mile away.

She opened one of her ports and instantly afterwards a cloud of sulphury smoke wreathed therefrom, and a heavy shot crashed through the rigging of the gallant little schooner.

The men on board the "Scorpion" hailed this first shot with rounds of applause.

"I fear the stranger is bent upon destroying us,

captain," said Dick, sorrowfully. "The odds are against us."

"Never mind. Cheer up the lads the best you can, and while our powder and shot remain, return gun for gun. Let us die gamely, if we are to die."

And gamely enough did the "Rattlesnake" fight her fresh antagonist for more than an hour, when the wind changed suddenly, and a heavy storm came on.

Black masses of clouds rolled over the sea far and wide, shutting out all sunlight from view.

The winds whistled and howled most fiercely, and vivid lightning flashes were quickly followed by loud thunder claps, which shook the schooner from stem to stern.

Yet the fight went on.

At intervals the stranger fired, and the fire was always returned by the schooner; but the gale was gradually increasing to a terrible hurricane, and ere long both vessels were driven far apart and beyond sight of each other.

The strange vessel, which was not at all disabled, ran before the gale in gallant style, and was soon lost to view.

But such was not the case with either the "Rattlesnake" or "Scorpion."

Both were sadly damaged, but the schooner's hull was yet sound, although her rudder had been carried away, and she was unmanageable.

The great fear of both vessels now was that they would be driven on to the Blue Rocks, and be dashed to pieces, and both commanders used their best endeavours to prevent this as far as possible.

After riding the gale for more than an hour, the wind greatly abated, and the sunlight again peeped through the deep, dense clouds.

The strange vessel had disappeared, but it struck terror to the hearts of many to see how close the schooner was to the treacherous reefs and shoals of the Blue Rocks, to which they were gradually but most surely drifting.

Lion Limb was now able to ascertain his situation, and knew that their fate depended upon the possible chance of weathering the Blue Rocks.

By the uncommon exertions of her fatigued and exhausted crew, in making all the sail they could set, the "Rattlesnake," at eleven o'clock, with six feet of water in her hold, passed about three-quarters of a mile to windward of the Blue Rocks, enabling her officers and men, after a day and night of incessant exertion, and many hours' fighting, at length to rest from their toil, and to thank Providence for their deliverance.

The fate of the strange ship was not so fortunate.

She struck the ground about ten minutes after she ceased firing.

Her crew displayed the most admirable discipline.

From half-past five until nine o'clock they were employed in making rafts, and not a man was lost, or attempted to leave the ship, except six, who stole away the cutter from the stern, and were drowned.

The captain and his officers remained by the ship until they had safely landed, first the wounded, and afterwards every man of the crew.

Of course, having landed on the Blue Rocks, they were treated well.

The "Scorpion" saw the land soon after the schooner hauled off, and, after hopeless attempts, first to avoid it, and afterwards to anchor, she struck the ground almost at the same moment as the stranger did.

The main-mast went overboard at the second shock.

The foremast and bowsprit had fallen a few minutes before, in her attempt to keep off the land.

When the danger was first seen the crew gave an alarm.

Presently the ship struck on a bank of sand, nearly opposite their own cavern residences.

Cries of dismay were now heard from every part.

Signals of distress were fired, and several guns hove overboard.

Many of the people were soon washed away by the waves, which broke incessantly over her.

At daylight the shore was seen covered with buccaneers and others.

But they could afford no assistance.

In the meantime the stern was beaten in by the sea, and no provisions or water could afterwards be obtained.

At low water an attempt was made to reach the shore; but two boats, which were brought alongside, drifted away, and were dashed to pieces on the rocks.

A small raft was constructed to carry a hawser to the shore, by the aid of which it was hoped that preparations might be completed for safely landing the crew.

A few having embarked on it, the rope was gradually slackened to allow it to drift to land.

But, some of these people being washed away, the rest became alarmed, cast off the hawser, and saved themselves.

After a second unsuccessful attempt with a raft, an officer attached a cord to his body, and tried to swim on shore.

But he was soon exhausted, and would have perished, but that he was hauled back to the ship.

On the second day, at low water, the captain, and eight others, launched a small boat, and landed safely.

Their success justly restored confidence to the rest on board, proving, as it did, how easily all might be saved, if proper means were adopted.

Perishing with cold, and thirst, and hunger—for the ship, her stern now broken away, no longer afforded shelter from the waves, and they had tasted nothing since the ship struck—the unhappy crew saw the third day arise upon their miseries.

Still the gale continued, and there was no prospect of relief from the shore.

It was now determined to construct a large raft, and to send away the surviving wounded in a boat which remained.

But, as soon as she was brought alongside, there was a general rush, and about twenty threw themselves into her.

Their weight carried down the boat.

Next moment an enormous wave broke upon them, and when the sea became smoother their corpses were seen floating all around.

An officer attempted to swim on shore.

He plunged into the sea, and was lost.

"Already scores had perished," says one among them, who was on board, a prisoner, "when the fourth night came with renewed terrors.

"Weak, distracted, and wanting everything, we envied the fate of those whose lifeless corpses no longer needed sustenance.

"The sense of hunger was already lost.

"But a parching thirst consumed our vitals.

"Recourse was had to wine and salt water, which only increased the want.

"Half a hogshead of vinegar floated up, and each had half a wine glass full.

"This gave a momentary relief, yet soon left us again in the same state of dreadful thirst.

"Almost at the last gasp, every one was dying with misery.

"The ship, which was now one-third shattered away from the stern, scarcely afforded a grasp to hold by to the exhausted and hopeless survivors.

"The fourth day brought with it a more serene sky, and the sea seemed to subside.

"But to behold, from fore and aft, the dying in all directions. was a sight too shocking for the feeling mind to endure.

"Almost lost to a sense of humanity, we no longer looked with pity on those who were the speedy fore-runners of our own fate.

"A consultation took place to sacrifice some one to be food for the remainder.

"The die was going to be cast, when the welcome sight of a sail boat renewed our hopes.

"A cutter speedily followed, and both anchored at a short distance from the wreck.

"They then sent the boats to us, and. by means of large rafts, about a hundred and fifty who attempted it were saved that evening.

"Twenty were left to endure another night's misery, when, dreadful to relate, above one-half were found dead next morning."

Such was the fate of the strange vessel and of the pirate, "Scorpion."

Both were total wrecks, and parts of them were scattered up and down the coast of the Blue Rocks for many miles.

There was an agreement between all the survivors that they should jointly own the island, which they did; and the gang of buccaneers, which had before been well nigh extinguished, suddenly grew into new life and strength, and were more powerful than ever, and each one among them would never rest until they had extirpated every one of Lion Limb's followers on their happy Island home.

CHAPTER LX.

THE RATTLESNAKE IS DRIVEN ON TO A STRANGE ISLAND.

BUT the winds which had driven their enemies to destruction on the Blue Rocks proved more favorable and kind to the disabled schooner and all on board.

The helm being gone, Dick and others endeavoured to replace a new one.

But they were unable to do so on account of the wildness of the weather.

They were drifting to and fro for many days and many anxious nights, and whither they knew not.

That they were gradually going towards the south-west could not be doubted; but rudderless, and without scarcely a sail to steady her, her brave crew could not manage or control her.

For eight days and eight nights the gallant shot-pierced schooner was at the mercy of the winds and waves, but on the 9th day they saw an island, and that night they discovered numerous fires burning on the hills which told them it was inhabited.

The current of the sea drove them into a pretty barbour, and at the dawn of the tenth day they were driven on the sandy beach and found themselves far from home, and far from King Katamar's island also.

The first thing to be done was to rescue the schooner from all further harm and to make preparations to resist any attack by the natives should they prove dangerous.

But in this they were agreeably disappointed.

Several of the natives came towards the strangers, and by signs and words they explained that there were white people on the mountains—people with the same clothes and arms and manners as they had.

To ascertain this fact more clearly and to solve the doubt, Lion Limb engaged one of the natives to guide him and two or three more to the "white men's settlement."

Leaving Dick in charge of the schooner and its crew, and telling old Katamar that he would soon return again, Lion Limb and his friends set out on their voyage of discovery, having engaged a half-civilized native to act as guide and to loan a mule which he possessed.

He was to deposit them and provisions for a couple of days at a certain spot on the mountain-side, which he professed to know intimately, where there was a camp of English wood-cutters.

Here they proposed to remain as long as meat and drink lasted, and then return on foot.

The plan was a simple one enough, but, unfortunately, its execution depended on the statement of the native.

For seven or eight hours they plodded onwards and upwards under the shade of the mighty cedars which clothed the mountains from base to summit, without coming upon a sign of camp or wood-cutters.

This seemed strange, and turning to their guide for an explanation, they perceived that his face, which in the morning had beamed with confidence and self-esteem, now wore a rather puzzled and dejected expression.

It was easy to see how matters stood, and after a little cross-examination, it came out that he had never been on the mountain before, and knew nothing whatever of the camp except by hearsay.

He swore stoutly, however, that it was somewhere in the neighbourhood; so stoutly, that had they not had the word of others for it, they would unquestionably have doubted its existence.

"When in doubt or difficulty take refreshment," is the maxim of a mountaineer.

It helps to remove irritation, makes you take a philosophical view of your position, and gives you time to think.

Thus fortified, they resolved to push on for the highest point of the mountain, which rose just above their heads, leaving the guide and his beast to follow at their own leisurely pace, and their look out for smoke ascending through the trees, or any other signs of human life.

If there was nothing of the sort to be seen, it was clear they must make up their minds for a bivouac, for to return was out of the question.

And nothing of the sort was to be seen.

There were fidgety mountain partridges running in and out of the brushwood below, and a pair of stately vultures wheeling in wide circles high over head

But these were the only signs of life within the visible horizon.

Right and left stretched the great cedar forest, filling up the glens with dense masses of dark green, forming broad shelves of foliage along the steep sides of the ravines, lying sparse and thin on the bleak summits where gnarled stems and bleached tree-skeletons showed how storms swept over them.

But everywhere all was grim, still, and silent.

And for stillness and silence, there is no place like a cedar forest.

On the sultriest, most breezeless day, there is always a stir and a whisper among the leaves of the oak and the needles of the pine.

But the cedar is a tree not susceptible of the gentler emotions.

He may writhe and groan under a storm, but he is far too rigid to yield to the blandishments of a zephyr.

On descending, they found that mule and guide had disappeared. Their first impression, of course, was that the miscreant had bolted with the provisions, and they felt rather in a fix.

A night under the greenwood tree is no very great evil in fine weather, but then it is as well to have some creature comforts beyond a lump of bread, a half empty dram flask, and some tobacco, which were all the stores they had.

On second thoughts, however, they felt it was absurd to fancy that even an Indian would think it worth his while to make off with such paltry plunder, especially when he was certain to be caught sooner or later.

A free expenditure of breath in shouting at last brought an answer from below; and they perceived the guide making for a kind of col or depression in the ridge, obviously with the intention of crossing over to the other side.

On rejoining him and asking what he was about, they found he was utterly opposed to camping in the woods.

It was not to be thought of, he argued, on account of the cold at night, and certain lawless natives who pervaded these mountains, not to speak of lions and panthers.

But on the other side there were honest and civil natives, who would gladly give us shelter and food.

Well, perhaps a tent was better than a tree if it rained, and perhaps the woods were not safe, though they more than suspected at the time, what they afterwards found to be the case, that his description of the dangers was largely embellished with the word "bosh."

The Indians whom they met the next day had never seen or heard lion or panther during their residence in the forest, and were of opinion that the natives who were about there were not a bit worse than any other natives.

As they crossed the col before mentioned, they had a wonderful scene before them.

As far as the eye could reach to the south and west, a vast plain lay spread out, a great yellow sea, into which the sun was sinking like a disk of burnished copper.

A strange reddish haze, as if the air was saturated with desert sand, hung all along the horizon.

Many miles away to the south was a long shining strip, which they knew must be a great lake.

Below them the mountain side went down steeply for some distance, and then broke off into a series of bluffs and buttresses, separated by deep grassy valleys.

Down one of these they travelled, and presently came on one of the honest civil natives, leading home his goats.

He was evidently puzzled at the guide's proposition about lodging in the tents of his tribe, but he raised no particular objection, and before long they came in sight of the encampment to which he belonged.

They had no means of ascertaining what were the statements made by the guide in introducing them to the notice of the authorities, but they had reason to believe that the tone he adopted was very much that of a popular instructor wishing to secure some provincial town-hall, and the interest of the mayor and corporation, for a lecture which he proposed to deliver to the inhabitants.

They did not mean to disparage the hospitality of the worthy hosts, and they had no doubt that had they been alone and unintroduced they would have been just as well treated.

But, as matters stood, it was quite plain that the guide put them on the footing of an "object of interest," rather than of a guest. It must be admitted there were certain temptations before him.

Europeans are very scarce in those parts of the world; and it is by no means unlikely this might have been the first time anything of the sort had ever been seen in that valley, and that at least one half of the natives had never before had an opportunity of examining closely a specimen of that variety of the human race.

As Lion Limb afterwards said, speaking of this journey,

"I considered myself to be a perfect stranger in the country, so I submitted, and was docile, and, I hope, instructive.

"But ever since I have had a fellow feeling for dwarfs, giants, Bosjesmans, Aztecs, fat boys, pig-faced ladies, and all other fellow-creatures who are exhibited on account of their strange appearance.

"I go to see them much oftener than before, and when I see the poor creature walking round and trying to look as if he did not mind it, I feel tempted to say, 'O Giant!—O Fat Boy!—there is one here who can sympathise with you: there is one here who knows the effect of fifty eyes staring at you "with a wild surmise"—who has experienced what it is to contemplate some two dozen faces, each saying, as plain as expression can say it, "Well, I don't wish to be personal, but you *are* a queer-looking object."'

"I should have liked to remain outside, for the scene had its picturesque points—the circle of low, black tents; the gaunt, wild-looking figures of the natives, stalking about, or sitting in clusters, and eyeing us curiously from under their hoods; the flocks coming trooping into camp for the night, and the great mountain range behind us growing black as the light faded from the sky.

"But my guide would not permit it.

"He evidently thought that I was making myself common and injuring him, and he insisted on retiring to one of the tents.

"At first I was on what may be called private view; at least, only a few of the elders of the camp were admitted, who examined with much interest my knife, watch, revolver, and especially a pocket compass, which I fear was explained to them as a Christian talisman by means of which a man might travel to Mecca without once asking the way; my guide all the time giving a popular sketch of European manners and customs—as I inferred from his frequent employment of the word 'English'—and using me as an illustration.

"The general public began to drop in afterwards.

"But there was no provision for admitting children at half price; perhaps they did not think me an improving spectacle, and the younger members of the community were driven to taking glimpses of the performance under the edge of the tent, which materially improved the ventilation.

"For some time I continued drawing crowded tents.

"But at last, owing no doubt to the fact that every one belonging to the camp had been in, the popular excitement seemed to be dying away, and then my spirited guide got up the startling novelty of supper.

"This made quite a sensation scene, especially when our rum bottles were produced, as they we e with some remarks, which were, I have no doubt, to the following effect—

"'And now, O children of the mountains (or whatever the name of the tribe was), this descendant of English jackasses, whom I have caught and brought here for your amusement at enormous expense, will drink the abominable beverage of the Christians—may the grave of its inventor be defiled. Although he is a drunkard by habit, his manners are mild and pleasing, and at the end of the performance he will shake hands with any lady or gentleman that desires it.'

"'But perhaps the most brilliant stroke of all was getting me to eat some of their food, which I was obliged to do, although loth, to avoid giving offence.

"In a well-regulated tent, where they have a professed cook, this, their favourite dish, I am told is far from unpalatable.

"It is wheaten flour, rolled by the hands into compact pellets about the size of duck-shot, then boiled, and served up with milk, butter, or grease of some sort.

"But the worthy people in whose tent we were, being simply country-folk, did not keep a cook, and the process and the result were not appetizing.

"The food looked and smelt just like a mess of brewer's grains seasoned with train oil, and was turned out into a huge wooden bowl, round which the family squatted.

"Not the women, of course; they had nothing to do with the dish, except preparing it.

"Wooden spoons were served out in the proportion of one to every six people, but I observed that the correct way of feeding was to plunge your hand into the mass, grasp a handful, give it a good squeeze to get rid of the extra grease, and cram it down your throat.

"One old fellow who sat next me, and was evidently a man accustomed to good society, always used his long grey beard in the light of a napkin after each handful.

"I had prospected a little digging of my own in an untouched part of the heap, and was making a great show of appetite; but this old gentleman thrust his venerable paw up to the wrist into the hole I had been feeding out of, and I had to give up, and explain that I found this food like pork pie, very filling at the price.

"A great deal of it, however, disappeared before the natives were filled.

"A night in a South Sea island tent by no means partakes of the peace and calm which are supposed to belong to pastoral life.

"The turning in of the last man, and the hanging up of the curtain across the tent door, seem to be the signals for a concert on the part of the animals of the tribe.

"The sheep and goats which have been driven at nightfall, begin to bleat perseveringly about the encampment, and the dogs, of which there are always three or four per tent, keep up an incessant barking in every note of the canine gamut, to let the world know that, however men may trust it, they do not mean to go to sleep while it is in its present dishonest state.

"Sometimes there will be a lull for a minute or so, but some unlucky jackal will whine in the distance, or a bark will come on the breeze from some far-off camp, and instantly dogs, and sheep, and goats, are off again; and so it goes on all night.

"Nor is this the only annoyance which the dogs give a stranger.

"If you lie down near the edge of the tent, as a European always will for the sake of air, you feel, in the night watches, something grubbing at your feet or your head, and become aware of a wolf-like countenance and a pair of wicked eyes glaring in at you.

"It is no use, even if you knew the native name for it, calling him 'poor fellow,' or 'good old doggy;' he is not to be coaxed, but treats you to a snarl, that says plainly, 'I can't bite you now, because it would make a row, and I should be kicked, but just come outside, and see if I don't consult my feelings in reference to the calf of your leg.'

"He has just one redeeming quality: he is an arrant coward, and holds a stone in great awe.

"No traveller ought ever approach an encampment without providing himself with half-a-dozen heavy stones, and, if he delivers a good family shot into the first pack that rushes at him, he may be let pass.

"He must take care, however, while he meets an attack in front, lest his flanks be turned by the supports coming up from behind the tents.

"We did not succeed in finding the wood-cutter's camp in the course of the next day's ramble, so returned.

"We made arrangements to go and seek these English settlers in some other part of the island; for that these natives had had dealings with them there could not be a doubt.

"Consequently, next morning, as the sun was sending his first rays over the wide plain, travellers might have been seen mounting the southern slopes of the highlands, one of whom, as they crossed the ridge that rose above the plain, looked back as though he cared not if he never saw that place again.

"The first half of the day's journey was neither interesting nor exciting.

"Hour after hour we continued to mount, wind along, and descend steep, bare, brown hill sides, all alike, and I began to think there was not much, after all, in the scenery of the island.

"My guide was unavailable for purposes of conversation, for he did not understand a word of English, and my native lingo was exhausted when I had asked what the first village was called; and as the sun got high in the heavens he began to beat upon us unpityingly.

"Then there arose a struggle between indolence and compassion.

"Indolence said, 'Get up and ride.'

"Compassion said, 'No, poor beast, he has enough to carry with your portmanteau and that able-bodied native.'

"But indolence ultimately had the best of it, and quieting my conscience by recollecting that I had many a time seen horses and mules twice as heavily laden, I mounted in front, while my native sat behind and chanted the dreariest ditty I ever heard.

"There is some chance of stimulating the horse into a temporary, spasmodic liveliness, and he occasionally varies his gait by a trip or a stumble.

"But the mule plods on from morning to night at the same unvarying, dawdling pace.

"You may belabour him, and rain kicks upon his ribs, and shout in true savage fashion, but you will get nothing beyond a grunt out of him.

THE BOY KING
OF THE SOUTH SEA ISLANDS.

THE FIGHT BETWEEN BLOODHOOF AND MUNGO.

" Every one knows the tendency which a sameness of motion, combined with a sameness of sound, has to set some old tune or rhyme vibrating through your brain.

No. 21.

"As I jogged along listening dreamily to the perpetual clank, clank, of the animal's hoofs, I found myself ringing changes and stringing rhymes which Joe Pebbles and I sang loudly, as follows :—

" ' As we ride, as we ride
On the lonely hill side,
With a howling native guide,
As we ride, as we ride.
Our patience sorely tried
In this sweltering moontide,
Parched and dried, boiled and fried,
As we ride, as we ride.

" ' As we ride, as we ride,
We take no sort of pride
In the steed that we bestride,
As we ride, as we ride.
He is spavined, he's wall-eyed,
If he died, hanged if I'd
Give sixpence for his hide,
As we ride, as we ride.

" ' As we ride, as we ride,
No saddle is supplied
His dorsal ridge to hide
As we ride, as we ride ;
And it threatens to divide
The wretch that sits astride,
And men galled and scarified
As we ride, as we ride.

" ' As we ride, as we ride,
We can't say we confide
In our shambling scrambling stride,
As we ride, as we ride ;
The path is far from wide,
There's a precipice beside
For a slide if he shied,
As we ride, as we ride.'

" As we rose higher and got more into the heart of the mountains, the air became sensibly cooler, and the scenery improved rapidly.

" We entered upon a region where the dwarf-palm and the ever-green oak grew thick, and where the trailers of the wild vine hung over the rocks.

" The slopes of the mountains became so steep, and the valleys so deep, that the path no longer went up hill and down dale, but wound round the rows or ran along the topmost ridges.

" So tortuous and eccentric are these ravines, that many a time we found ourselves working back to within almost a stone's-throw of the spot where we had been a good half hour before, but cut off from it by a mighty chasm, hundreds of feet deep.

" In fact, from any height that gave a bird's eye view, the country looked as if it had been honey-combed and channelled by some huge worm.

" On each summit and each of the headlands formed by the winding of these glens, there stands a quaint Indian village : the houses huddled close together, and holding on to one another to keep themselves from toppling over, like children on a style.

" And round each village, where the slope of the ground admits of it, are grove of figs and olive trees. Our halt for the first night was at a village called Karee.

" At first I meant to lodge with the leading man of the place and see native life ; but I soon found that my experiences of native life were likely to be more varied than I had anticipated.

" I know my host thought I suspected him of some design on my life or property, but I could not explain to him that, though I had every confidence in him, I felt there were inmates of his house who thirsted for my blood, and on whose account I preferred to sleep on the cool, hard floor.

" The next day's journey brought a valley that was walled in by a magnificent range of mountains.

" One tall conical hill in particular filled me with admiration, and I remarked to Joe Pebbles that it was a good-sized mountain.

" ' Dam-good' was the prompt and astounding reply of the native guide.

" ' Hallo !' thought I ; ' so the schoolmas'er is abroad, and our English language is appreciated even here.'

" But presently I found the poor fellow was equally innocent of English and profanity, and only meant to say, though he pronounced it rather strongly, that the native name of the mountain was ' Tamgoot.'

" The next day was spent in an attempt at ascending the Tamgoot, which was only partially successful, owing to a series of mistakes about the route and distance.

" The view from the summit seemed to me one of the most magnificent I had ever looked on from a mountain height.

" To the south lay a rugged but rich country through which we had travelled, scored with ravines and bristling with peaks, and separated from the mount-in on which I stood by a valley.

" To the north the eye ranged over a region even wilder and grander—a mad jumble of mountains and valleys, stretching away to the sea.

" There was not much spare time for studying the landscape, glorious as it was, for the young mule I had to carry my baggage had not been punctual, and we were at least two hours later than we ought to have been.

" Just at the top of the pass we overtook a native and his mule on their way to one of the villages on the north side, and when he heard we were bound on a visit to the English settlers on the island he held up his hands in astonishment, and expressed an opinion that it was not to be reached that night.

" I told my guide to ask him how many hours he reckoned it to the ' English,' and then transpired the astonishing fact that the natives knew nothing of the division of time into hours.

" To give my guide a new idea I showed him my watch, and tried to explain that a certain relation existed between the position of its hands and the position of the sun.

" But I am afraid the only idea he carried away was, that by some means I kept a portion of the solar system in my waistcoat pocket.

" In company we commenced the descent. And such a descent !

" It is a very steep incline, and all hands were told off to hold on to the tails of the mules, and act as human drags, to keep them from plunging into the basin, down the side of which we had to go.

" Arrived at the bottom, we had to mount again by a similar path, and so on, the only bits of level walking we enjoyed being along narrow ridges, or narrower shelves, worn into the substance of the mountain.

" How the fig and olive trees grow on such slopes it is hard to say.

" But grow they do, and bring forth fruit abundantly, for every native village we passed had its row of oil jars, each big enough to contain the whole forty thieves, and its rudely-constructed oil-press, standing in the middle like the stocks in an old English village ; and every villager we met had his jacket stuffed with dried figs, of which, with a jolly manner, he would generally thrust a handful into our hands.

" Except these, I had eaten nothing since a light

breakfast at five. but there was no time to stop and dine, so I had to perform a feat which, from its difficulty on a mountain path, I can recommend to Blondin as likely to be effective on the tight-rope, that of opening and eating rock oysters while walking at a brisk pace.

"So hour after hour we tramped onwards, until night came down upon us. and the oak thickets which had afforded us a friendly shade all day, became our worst enemies, and robbed us of the little light the stars gave.

"And then hour after hour, we groped along in the dark, sometimes running bolt against a village where we got a hint as to the road, sometimes dropping suddenly upon a ghostly band of natives who advised us to turn back and put up at their village.

"But I was determined to get to the 'English,' and enjoy a good supper and a good bed.

"At last the mule driver gave in; he could do no more.

"He was dead beat; and, besides, he did not know the way.

"I got him to mount the mule, and at the next village we secured a fresh guide.

"With him stalking on ahead, and looking, through the black night, like some benevolent spectre who had taken us in charge, we got on much better, though the 'English' still seemed wofully distant.

"Again and again I made my companion ask how far further we had to go, and again and again came a shake of the head.

"At last, far away, a clear-blown trumpet rang out through the night air, followed by the brassy roll of a drum.

"I never thought I should come to bless that vile sound.

"It was the 'English,' and we were approaching them fast.

"Half-an-hour afterwards we were within a quarter of a mile of the 'English,' and we halted until we sent a messenger with word who and what we were.

"Although it was night and very dark, I could see that the place was strongly fortified, and placed in such a position so as to defy all the attempts of the natives to capture it if ever they were silly enough to attempt it.

"Large log-houses were built on the hill sides and on tops, and from all I could discern there was a very numerous colony living there.

"That the native guide was right in calling them 'the English' could not be denied, for as well as I could make out I perceived a tattered flag floating in the wind, which seemed to be a well-worn and ragged 'Union Jack.'

"Joe Pebbles was mad with excitement, and wanted to go up and introduce himself at once, but I forbade it.

"We had not long to wait for an answer, for the messenger had not been absent more than ten minutes when we were all startled by the sounds of drums and the ringing notes of a bugle, which in turn were almost drowned by a succession of rousing English cheers.

"'Hurray!' said Joe; they are English and no mistake. 'But who'd a thought of ever finding any of our countrymen in such an out-of-the-way place as this.'

"'True,' I replied; 'and who would ever think of finding us at our settlement?'

"We had not time for many words, for a swarm of men, women, and children came running down the hillside with lighted torches and knots of pine wood blazing in their hands.

"Before we could say a word, we were surrounded by a crowd of sun-tanned, brawney men, who seized us, and nearly wrung our hands off in hearty welcome.

"They next carried us on their shoulders up the hillside, shouting, and cheering, and laughing, and before we could recover from surprise, we found ourselves at the gates of the little town, which were thrown wide open, and we entered the place like conquerors.

"They did not look very much like English people, although they spoke the language pretty well.

"But we soon found out what I had long suspected when I first heard of their existence on this island, namely, that they were part English and part half-breeds, with whom they had inter-married.

"When the gates were closed after us, we were taken to the house of the chief man in the place, whose name was Robert Martin, and feasted there to the very best they could afford.

"While Joe Pebbles was amusing a score or more in an adjoining room by playing his fiddle and singing songs to his noisy, boisterous, and applaud-ing audience.

"Old Bob Martin, who was called 'the Governor' of the place, soon explained who he was.

"His story was much like the one I had told to him regarding ourselves, namely, 'that many years before he and many more, both men and women, were journeying to Australia, but, bad weather coming on, and the ship being old and leaky, she was wrecked and went ashore on that island; and since that time they had never seen the face of any Europeans until we came.

"'The cargo of the ship consisted of all sorts of useful articles which were destined for the markets of New Zealand and Australia, and with these things they built themselves comfortable houses, and like true honest fellows as they were, they set to work to till the soil.

"'They one by one married native women when all the English girls were married, and their colony had not only prospered, but had become very numerous.'

"The natives it appeared, from old Martin's story, had given them much trouble, and many a battle had been fought between them to see who should be masters of the island.

"But the English and their fire-arms had proved too much for the natives, who, except the women, though conquered, would seldom or ever have any-thing to say or do with them.

"The natives, however, within the last few years had become gradually more civilized, and they had taken pattern by the English, and seemed much inclined to raise sheep and mules and such like, and raise small crops of grain.

"Some of them had even learned to speak a few words of English. But although the British settlers tried all they could to make them true and reliable friends, all their efforts had been unavailing.

"This is the reason why old Martin and the rest were obliged to select hills for their villages, and have them well fortified, for, from the first moment of their landing, they had all observed military rule; they raised fortifications and gates around them, since, on one occasion, the natives had taken them by surprise, and many a good man's life was lost through negligence or over confidence.

"Old Martin and the original number of forty souls who were saved from the wreck had been on the island over thirty years, and their offspring had increased so rapidly that little villages had been founded by them far and near in different parts of the island; but the chief place was the one they were in, and, out of honour to the old man, they had unanimously and always called that hill and its village Fort Martin.

"Such, in substance," said Lion Limb, "is the outline of the history of the place. They were visited once or twice by stray ships, who came there for wood and water, chiefly by American whalers, from whom they had uniformly received much kindness.

"The colonists, who, though far away from civilization, had prospered.

"Much land was under cultivation, and increasing in extent yearly.

"They could raise all sorts of crops; their wives and daughters made their clothes from the raw material, and several settlers, still having a taste for old English ale, had turned their hands to brewing, and could even manufacture a raw, rough article of whisky and other spirits.

"The laws in force among themselves were generally obeyed with willingness.

"Everybody had work of some kind to do, and what they wanted of each other was done by exchange, for such a thing as silver or gold or copper money was unknown among them.

"There was one thing, however, that they could not do, and that was ship-building

"They had tried, but always failed in producing anything that was sea-worthy, or that could be trusted in a storm.

"I was much interested in all that the old man told me, and he, on the other hand, was greatly surprised at all which we had been able to accomplish; and when I informed him of our frequent fights with the gorillas, Red Wolf's Indians, and the buccaneers, he and his friends were greatly astonished, for such persons as pirates and the like had not been seen or heard of in those parts.

"After conversing a long time with old Governor Martin and the chief men of the fort, I accepted an invitation to stay with one of the settlers, who seemed greatly attached to us, and who expressed a wish to sail with us, and render us all the assistance he could in repairing our vessel, which, I told him, was high and dry on the sandy beach.

"This man's name was Tom Johnson, and by trade he was a carpenter.

"I accepted his offer, and, although old Governor Martin and his native wife and children were clamorous for me to stay with them, I went to Morton's place in the village and resolved to stay there a day or two, and, meanwhile, learn all I could regarding the other little villages of English settlers who were living in the plains, so that in future we could have regular communication between the islands, and thus form an alliance defensive, and, if need be, offensive also, for, as I guessed, the buccaneers would never let us remain in peace, at least, not while Bloodhoof lived.

"They all listened to my proposals, and Governor Martin was in such a rage against Bloodhoof and his gang of sea-robbers that he swore he would go on a cruise with us, old as he was, and lend a hand in 'cleaning out,' as he called it, every living soul on the Blue Rocks.

"The houses, as I have said, were all strongly built of huge logs and rough mortar, made out of a limey and hard sandy soil, and so arranged round the hill-top as to present the appearance of a huge block house, against which the natives might fight for a year without any hopes of capture; and so wise was the old governor that he had large granaries and store-houses erected also, which were filled with all sorts of grain.

"One of the houses, Tom Johnson's, had sufficent self-assertion left to call itself an 'hotel,' trusting to its ability to make up two beds, and its possession of a bar and a hen-coop, to support the character.

"Here I took up my quarters, intending to remain no longer than was necessary to buy mules and lay in provisions for the expedition homewards again.

"But mules were scarce, and their owners disinclined to hire them out.

"So I stayed on day after day, living upon hens and the hope of a speedy return.

"The dreariness of the place was of itself a sufficient reason for being anxious to quit it, but I had yet another in the penitentiary for fowls just mentioned.

"Not that I objected to a poultry diet; the traveller in out-of-the-way places in such islands must take what he can get, and be thankful, even though he may find that 'fare is fowl' to a monotonous extent.

"The fact is, thanks to Tom Johnson, I found myself steadily eating my way through the occupants of the coop up to a certain elderly cock, whose figure promised a toughness such as I had never yet encountered, and I vowed to submit to almost any sort of food rather than regale on his accursed carcase.

"Like a prisoner, this old cock had been so long in confinement that he had become quite used to it, for death, as the natives put it, 'would not accept of him' by reason of his extreme unfitness for the table.

"Day by day he saw his plumper and worthier companions carried off.

"But the fact that they were taken, and he left, excited no thankful feeling in his obdurate breast.

"On the contrary, I think it made him arrogant and self conceited.

"He ascribed to his merits what was due simply to his age, and contemplated the future with the eye of a sceptic.

"Being a bird of advanced opinions, he had shaken off that prejudice of his race which makes crowing a ceremony connected with daybreak, and took a purely sensual view of the matter, crowing all through the night whenever the whim seized him, and treating it as a branch of the fine arts, in which he obviously considered himself a proficient.

"There was something, too, peculiarly aggravating about his crow.

"It was always delivered in two parts; the first addressed to the world in general; the second, a kind of self-satisfied, confidential clucking to himself and those in his immediate neighbourhood, as much as to say—

"'There! and now perhaps you'll furnish me with the name and address of any cock you know of that can turn out a crow like mine.'

"In short, while he was a nuisance by day, he was as bad as a troubled conscience by night, for the head of my bed was within three feet of his dungeon, and more than once I thought it would be almost as well to eat him and have done with him.

"I might escape with dyspepsia.

"But vengeance, though long delayed, came at last.

"Day by day I saw my fate approaching, until one night I found that not a single fowl remained between me and the old rooster, and I 'bitterly thought of the morrow' and the morrow's breakfast.

"But one night, some time after midnight, the house was roused up by the arrival of two travellers.

"With—to quote the words of the poet—feelings that can be more easily imagined than described, I heard the demand made as to what there was for supper, and the answer given that fowl was available, and shortly after, just outside my door, the shrieks and struggles of the expiring cock told me I was saved and avenged.

"The travellers, as it afterwards appeared, survived the night, for I met them next morning at breakfast, which was an inferior meal, but, they affirmed, far better than their supper, for, said they, 'the fowls of this place are as tough as iron.'

"I mention this old cock because it is to him that, to some extent, I owe a pleasant excursion, and something of an adventure.

"Weary of hearing him singing his own praises, and of the monotony of Fort Martin generally, I determined to go abroad in search of excitement.

"About ten miles to the south of the village there rises a noble mountain range.

'From an inspection with the telescope, and 'from information which I received,' it seemed probable that a day or two might be spent in exploring its wilds with much pleasure and advantage.

"I made a few hasty preparations, and, as I and Joe Pebbles were thought a great deal of at the Fort, old Governor Martin made up his mind to go with us, and visit one or two of the small settlements on the sea coast.

"The spot which I wished to visit was on the borders of a large and commodious bay, which I thought would be much nearer to Fort Martin, and better adapted for us to anchor in, should we think fit to visit the place again.

"Accordingly, I set out with Joe Pebbles, old Governor Martin, and two others.

"We were all well armed and provisioned for our trip, for old Martin said the natives were particularly strong on our route, and could never be brought under control like those on other parts of the island.

"We had two pack mules with us, and started forth for the settlement called Brown's Hole, and were accompanied for several miles on our journey by quite a throng of people, young and old, who issued from the village and fort to do us honour.

"Had we been conquerors, and returning from, or going on some great and all-important expedition, the people could not have made a greater fuss and noise about us.

"But the gentleman who attracted most attention was our old friend, Joe Pebbles.

"He, and his fiddle, seemed to have many attractions for every one ; so, to accommodate them, Joe was perched on one of the mules, and, half drunk as he was, he played so many lively jigs that he had all the boys, and girls, and half-breeds, dancing around us like so many madmen.

"Joe was always singing or playing his fiddle, and the half-breeds of the fort had been enticed several miles away on our journey before they could make up their minds to leave us.

"We travelled a long distance through a mountainous country on the first day, and at night lit fires and camped in the woods.

"Joe, however, had a great terror of snakes and wild animals, which were very numerous on our road, and, unknown to us, he was in the habit of climbing a tree and slinging his hammock there for the night.

"This practice almost cost Joe his life, for one morning we started earlier than usual, and not seeing Joe, or knowing what had become of him, yet still thinking that he might have gone on some short distance ahead of us, we went on our way as usual, without the slightest sign that we had been watched and followed by any of the natives.

"But we were much mistaken.

"They had, through spies, ascertained all about our numbers and movements, and, having got us far enough away from Fort Martin, they resolved to attack and rob us, for this tribe of natives feared and hated old Governor Martin, and had long secretly resolved to kill him.

"Thus it was, then, that although we had not the slightest suspicion of their movements or intentions, we had been more or less surrounded by the savage natives the night before, who had delayed to attempt their design upon us until morning.

"But we had started, as I have said, much earlier than usual on that particular morning, and Mr. Joe, having drank a little too much rum the night before, was sound asleep in his hammock high up in a thickly leaved tree.

"When he awoke, and looked around, he found us gone ; and, when on the point of descending from his high roost to hurry on and follow our trail, fancy his horror when he discovered that the place was swarming with half-naked savages !

"Some were tattooed and painted in all sorts of ways and colours.

"They were armed with bows, arrows, tomahawks, knives, war-clubs, and spike-headed poles, while poor Joe hadn't so much as a tooth-pick about him to defend himself.

"He had his fiddle, however—not that he took it to sleep with, although passionately fond of it, but he always felt anxious lest any accident should befal the old fiddle, and thus took great care of it on all occasions, both night or day, sleeping or waking.

"What to do he knew not.

"To stir out of the tree, and descend among the savages, would have been certain death ; and yet to stay there would have been madness.

"He resolved to keep as quiet as possible until the natives should have gone, and so closely did he hide, that they were on the point of leaving, when, by some accident, a small twig touched the fiddle-strings, and made a slight noise.

"Though the sound was very faint indeed, it arrested the attention of those beneath him.

"With a wild yell, they examined, and shook the tree so violently, that poor Joe was on the point of losing his balance, and tumbling headlong down, fiddle and all.

"Seeing that he was discovered, and had no hope of escape or rescue, he bethought him of the fact that 'music hath charms to soothe the savage breast,' and resolved to try the experiment in his own case.

"At first the savages began to pelt him with stones, and some were half-way up the tree when he instantly tuned his fiddle, and began to play jigs and reels as if for his very life.

"As if stupefied, the savages stood and listened for some time, and then began to grin, and laugh, and shout wildly, and at last, as if unable to restrain themselves any longer, they began to dance and caper round the tree as if they had been suddenly possessed by so many devils (See Cut in No. 19).

"The longer Joe played the more noisy and wild the savages became, until their shrieks, and shouts, and yells were almost deafening, as they clapped their hands and kicked up the dust with their heavy heels.

"Joe said afterwards that he was almost sick and sore with laughing at their wild antics.

"But he soon found out that playing the fiddle for a band of savages to dance to was anything but a joke, for they kept him hard at it. And whenever he dared to leave off, even to screw up a string occasionally, they yelled and shook their weapons in such a savage and threatening manner that he trembled for his very life.

"For two hours and more was poor Joe compelled to play as fast and furious as his fingers would allow him, and there he sat sweltering in the hot sun, scraping away, and so weak and tired that he was almost ready to faint and fall from the limb of the tree on which he sat, and which was swaying so much that he could scarcely keep his proper balance.

"How long poor Joe would have been compelled to fiddle for the dusky rascals is beyond conjecture had we not returned and liberated him, for when we had gone several miles on our journey without overtaking him as we expected to do, old Governor Martin resolved to return and seek for him.

"Any one who did not thoroughly know old Martin the Governor might have supposed it impossible that he could or would dare to face several native savages single-handed; but the old gentleman was a person who scarcely knew what fear was.

"He had been in trials and troubles nearly all his life, many, many years of which were actually passed in the very midst of barbarians and savages.

"And he had scarcely a limb on any part of his body which was not in some manner scarred or cut from the frequent battles and skirmishes in which he had taken part.

"His name itself was a tower of strength, and his voice was a terror to the ear of savage nations.

"Hence it was that they had christened him old 'Grey Bear,' or, as they more frequently called him, 'Bearfoot.'

"The old man's quick ear soon detected the wild shouts and yells of the Indians as we approached the spot where Joe was fiddling; and old Martin with a round oath swore that he was sure the savages had secured some prize or other, and we hastened on to the rescue ere it was too late.

"The Indians were upon the point of firing at Joe, and then compelling him to come down, when myself, old Martin, and others arrived upon the spot.

"Without much warning or ceremony old 'Bearfoot' rused into the thickest of the fray, and for more than half-an-hour the fight was hot and determined.

"Poor Joe was in a sad position, for several savages climbed up the tree, and thus Joseph was between two fires.

"The number of arrows and bullets that passed quite close to him tore down the foliage and broke off the timber of trees in every direction, and Joe at last slipping down through the hollow trunk of the tree in which he was got out of the way of the arrows and bullets.

"But instead of escaping from harm he was almost suffocated.

"For had we not chopped a hole into the trunk and let him out again he would have been buried alive.

"As it was, we rescued him from his peril, and dragged him forth into broad daylight again; and the poor fellow was as white as a ghost, and so weak he could scarcely stand.

"Three of the savages were killed, one or two more were desperately wounded; and such was the price we compelled them to pay for forcing Joe Pebbles to play his fiddle."

Thus spoke Lion Limb regarding his journey to Fort Martin, and the various doings of the newly-discovered colonists there.

In another chapter we will continue his adventures, and of what he did with Katamar and his Indians, and his various wanderings and narrow escapes in several islands adjoining.

CHAPTER LXI.

BLOODHOOF DEFENDS HIS TITLE WITH THE SWORD.

THE severe battle that had been fought between the "Rattlesnake" and "Scorpion" had been witnessed by many of the desperadoes on the Blue Rocks, and when they saw how gallantly the little schooner had resisted the fierce attacks of the well-armed brigantine, the buccaneers cursed and swore roundly, saying that Bloodhoof was no seaman at all, but a perfect lubber.

When, however, the storm had driven the brigantine ashore, and she became a total wreck, many of them swore to have the life of Bloodhoof, for the ill success of all his ventures.

When, therefore, their band was increased in number by the crew of the strange vessel, which was none other than an armed slaver, the question arose on every side who should be captain of the band, and in future command them.

Up to the present time Bloodhoof had been unfortunate in all his undertakings, and instead of doing any good he did harm to his band of savage cut-throats.

When, therefore, Mungo Brama, the captain of the slave vessel, had joined the buccaneers, nearly all the band were in favour of deposing Bloodhoof and choosing Mungo.

Now this Mungo had been long known to the buccaneers, and as a ferocious and bloodthirsty villain he perhaps had no equal.

He was half European and half African, by blood, and had for many years carried on the slave trade on the river Pongos, in Africa, whence he used to ship hundreds of slaves to Cuba, Brazil, and other places.

But through this traffic in human beings he became rich and haughty, and went so far as to seize vessels which might anchor in the Pongos, and imprison their crews, and sometimes put them to death.

How this once noted chief had fallen in his fortunes and been forced to fly from Africa, to seek a home with buccaneers in the South Sea Islands, is thus explained :—

In consequence of a letter from a British merchant, complaining of the piratical seizure of his vessel in the river Pongos, by Mungo Brama, the notorious slave dealer, a young midshipman and a boat's crew were sent up the river to demand her release.

The master of a Dutch slaver engaged in the slave trade by Mungo's orders, fell upon the boat's crew and murdered the midshipman and six of his people with every circumstance of the most revolting barbarity.

Two of the men who were saved, and subsequently made their escape, reported that with seven others, including the officers, they were dragged on shore, stripped, and exposed to a vertical sun for a considerable time; that after a consultation with Mungo, it was agreed that the Europeans should be put to death, but that these two being men of colour, should be sold for slaves; that the officer, seamen and marines were shot amidst the shouts of hundreds of persons; that the bodies of the sufferers were disinterred and carried away by wolves, having previously been mutilated by the inhuman tyrant, Mungo.

Such atrocities could not be suffered to pass unpunished, and accordingly a signal vengeance was inflicted on the savage perpetrators.

After some resistance, a steamer, carrying four guns, succeeded in setting fire to eight towns belonging to the miscreants.

All the property they contained, ivory, rice, rope, cotton, and other goods were wholly consumed.

The loss on the English side consisted of three men wounded, and one who died of fatigue.

The country was scoured far and wide, in hopes of capturing Mungo and his friends, but they escaped during the night in a fast vessel which was anchored up a river some fifty miles lower down the coast.

The English cruisers caught sight of the escaping slaver, and gave chase.

But although they did all that men could do to overhaul and capture Mungo, he gave them the slip and never appeared again until the moment when he suddenly came within view of the Blue Rocks, and took part in the engagement against the "Rattlesnake."

He was well known to all the smugglers, pirates, and buccaneers all over the globe, and had at times visited Nat the Don to buy or to dispose of plunder.

That the arrival of such a man among the buccaneers should be hailed with joy cannot be wondered at.

But the very name of Mungo was wormwood to Bloodhoof, who looked upon him as an intruder.

Mungo, on the other hand, treated Bloodhoof with contempt, and thus, in a very few days, there was much disunion among the rascals at the Blue Rocks, and each aspirant for the highest honours were lavish in dealing out rum, brandy, whisky, and tobacco to their respective partizans, and nought was thought of but carousing and feasting all day and all night, so that for more than a week after the wreck of their respective vessels, the whole gang did nought but lounge idly about, quarrelling with each other, and discussing the merits and demerits of Mungo and Bloodhoof.

If the latter ordered any man to do this, Mungo would advise just the contrary; and if Bloodhoof gave any one a certain amount of liquor or tobacco, Mungo would give the same man just twice as much out of his own private stores, which had been washed up from the sea.

These two black-looking desperate rivals rarely met each other, and when they did, but seldom spoke, and even then in such a harsh and insulting tone that an open rupture was looked for at any moment.

Every man on the island knew that at one time or other they would come to blows.

But this occurred sooner than any one expected, and in this peculiar manner.

One day at dinner, when all were assembled together, and conversation was both angry and very noisy on every hand, some one asked Bloodhoof to pass the wine, and not keep the bottle so long near his elbow.

"Don't ask him to pass the bottle," said Mungo, in a satirical tone of voice. "Don't ask Bloodhoof to pass the wine, for he looks so cross and sour that he'd turn it into vinegar."

A roar of laughter followed this expression, for all knew very well that Mungo was alluding to the loss of the "Scorpion" and other failures.

"Take this bottle," said Mungo to the person who asked.

And, suiting the action to the word, he knocked off the neck of a bottle, and passed it along.

For the present, then, the laugh was against Bloodhoof, who bit his lips in rage, but spoke not a word.

Some moments afterwards, however, Mungo, who was a famous glutton, said,

"Pass the bread."

And on the instant Bloodhoof thrust his cutlass into a large loaf, and handed it across to Mungo.

The African slaver turned deadly pale, and trembled with passion.

He seized the loaf, and throwing it back at Bloodhoof, drew his sword, saying,

"Follow me to the beach."

In an instant the greatest confusion and uproar reigned among the buccaneers.

"Follow me!" shouted Mungo, flourishing his cutlass.

Bloodhoof and his friends instantly obeyed and accepted the challenge.

In great haste all rushed forth from the cavern on to the beach.

But Mungo and Bloodhoof were so infuriated one against the other, that they crossed swords the instant they met.

A dead silence reigned on all around.

Every one knew it would be life or death to one if not to both of them.

Their eyes glared in deadly rage.

Their weapons clashed, and showers of sparks flew out.

It was a terrible moment.

Quickly blood flowed from both.

They breathed hard.

A few strokes more would decide who should be the pirate chief.

Their swords flashed again and again.

A groan was heard. (See Cut).

CHAPTER LXII.

THE TRAITOR'S LEAP FOR LIFE!

BUT although the Indian savages on Lion Island had been often defeated in their frequent battles with the young colony, they had never yet been entirely subdued.

So long as they were wise enough to refrain from hostilities and be content with that part of the island which they inhabited, young Lion Limb betrayed little desire or disposition to molest them.

"As long as they do not interfere with us," said the young leader, "I do not see any reason why we should entirely exterminate them. It is barbarous to make unnecessary slaughter of the savages, so long as they remain quiet and allow us to do the same. Besides," he often was wont to say, "our colony is not very numerous, and we may be able in time to civilize them and make them useful."

It was the idea and design of young Lion Limb to make friends of them instead of enemies.

"We can make use of them ; we can teach them to till and cultivate the soil, and thus make ourselves independent of hard, manual labour, to some degree. Only let them see that we wish to do them good and improve their condition, and we may depend upon it that selfish motives, if not feelings of friendship, will turn their hearts towards us ; and should we be attacked again by the buccaneers from the Blue Rocks, or from any other quarter that we know not of at present, Red Wolf's Indians will fight as bravely for us as they have hitherto done against us."

These ideas had long been adopted by most of his followers.

But even among his own band there were discontented fellows, who looked upon themselves as much better fitted to rule the island than Lion Limb, and in their hearts they resolved to wait and mature their plans, and when ready to rise in open rebellion against Lion Limb and his faithful band of followers.

One of these plotting, conniving spirits, had long looked with longing eyes upon the beautiful and rich valleys that surrounded them, and at last he became so lazy and indolent that he shirked and shunned all work that he was required to do, as far as he possibly could without bringing down upon himself the punishment which his rebellious spirit deserved.

This fellow was one of the original convicts who had escaped from the "Rattlesnake," and his name was Ike Rattlebon, or, "Rattlebones," as the boys always called him.

"Why should Lion Limb rule the roost over us ?" Rattlebones would often grumble. "He never takes me with him on board his schooner, and I'm a better man than he is ; older, stronger, and just as fit to command as Harry Woodruff or Dick Hamilton. Let half a chance turn up, and see if I don't let all of 'em know who and what I am, that's all."

It was the deep design of Rattlebones to secretly make friends of the Indians and enter into a league with them, after which, at some time when Lion Limb and other leaders were absent from the island, to lead on the savages to the camp and make himself master of everything.

On several occasions, Rattlebones had absented himself from the colony, and where he had got to no one could imagine or tell.

But the traitor had to deal with savages even more cunning than himself.

But, eaten up with envy of Lion Limb and his faithful followers, he made his plans, and, although he had more than once met and conferred with several native chiefs, he had not, as yet, fully made up his mind how to act or when.

But, at the appointed spot, he met with young Black Bear, Red Wolf's only son.

On the top of a cliff, which over-looked a swift, dark stream, and in sight of the tents and camp fires of the savages, who had been collected together to go on the secret expedition.

Black Bear and Rattlebones sat discussing the probable chances of success, and the traitor, greatly to Black Bear's delight, who was eager to avenge his father's wrongs, was rioting in anticipation of

his looked-for success, when strange sounds reached his startled ear.

The savage understood not the traitor's commotion.

He perceived that he turned suddenly deadly pale.

Fearful that, after all, the white man might and did mean dastardly treachery to himself and tribe, he seized Rattlebones by the throat, and a fearful struggle ensued.

Both were terror-stricken, and fearful of their lives.

But, at that moment, the sharp and ringing report of a rifle was heard.

Black Bear relinquished his hold.

The bullet had wounded both of them, when, with a loud curse, and eyes starting in horror at the well-known forms of distant men approaching, Rattlebones shouted—

"Never will I fall into their hands alive !"

And, with a shout of defiance, the traitor leaped from the high rock into the deep, dark waters beneath. (See Cut in last Number.)

Who fired that fatal shot ?

Who were the new-comers that startled the traitor so ?

It was a mystery then, but which we shall quickly explain in another place.

CHAPTER LXIII.

THE DUEL ENDS IN GENERAL STRIFE AND DISUNION AMONG THE BUCCANEERS.

THE sight of blood only excited and inflamed the two fierce duellists more and more.

They fought on fiercely and with demon-like ferocity.

Every one supposed that the tall, heavy, and black-looking slave captain, Mungo, would have proved too powerful for his opponent.

But what Bloodhoof lacked in height and weight he made up in superior activity and swordsmanship.

Mungo's rage was ungovernable.

He had never before met with any one who could stand so long before him.

A deep gash in his sword arm, and another across his temple, presented a gory, ghastly sight, and the blood flowed freely from both wounds.

Bloodhoof also had been cut in more than one place, and a rent in his thigh had almost disabled him.

With a bitter smile he gazed upon Mungo, as they both stood gasping for breath.

Their looks were more like those of demons than human beings.

But though at first most of the noisy and passionate audience were loud in their praise and applause of Mungo, the superior swordsmanship of Bloodhoof gained him many friends, who, as usual, always go with the winning side.

"Separate them," cried some.

"No, no ; let them fight on."

"We cannot have two chiefs."

"Hurrah for Mungo !"

"Three cheers for Bloodhoof !"

"Kill him, Mungo."

"Don't give him breathing time, Bloodhoof."

These and such like were the conflicting shouts and cries of all around.

Both Mungo and Bloodhoof were momentarily getting weaker and weaker from loss of blood.

They were staggering, bleeding, and could scarcely stand erect.

Their swords and arms were linked in deadly embrace.

THE BOY KING

OF THE SOUTH SEA ISLANDS.

REJOICINGS AT FORT MARTIN.

Partizans on both sides gathered around their favourite, shouting and cursing.

All was confusion, noise, and blasphemy.

Neither party wished to see their champion killed.

And yet it was only the mere question of a single successful blow or thrust which would decide it.

"Finish it with pistols!" shouted many.

"No, no; let them fairly have it out with swords," others replied.

But all the crowd around them became more noisy and passionate, and at last a general fight ensued.

Pistols, swords, knives and other deadly weapons were now freely used on all sides, and a fierce battle raged.

The followers of Bloodhoof carried him away from the ground.

Friends of Mungo acted in a similar manner with their hero.

Shouts of defiance and derision filled the air on every hand.

All was now an unearthly uproar.

The clashing of steel, the sounds of fire-arms, and the oaths of half-drunken, frenzied combatants were heard on every side.

Men fell, killed or wounded, each moment.

Soon the alarm sounded all over the Blue Rocks.

Many, who had been away and unaware of the deadly fray, now quickly armed themselves, and rushed madly to the scene of conflict.

Some of Mungo's men, who had been living near the two wrecks, endeavouring to construct as well as they could a light draught sloop from the hull of the "Scorpion," seized their heavy hammers, adzes, immense iron-headed mallets, and whatever else they could lay their hands on, and mingled in the crowd.

Each moment the conflict became more and more fierce and deadly.

Both Mungo and Bloodhoof, after having their wounds dressed and well bound up, broke loose from their friends, and, like giants refreshed, went forth to do battle again.

The sudden reappearance of the two rival chiefs in the midst of the fight was hailed with loud shouts by their respective followers.

Mungo at the first onset lost his cutlass.

It was knocked from his grasp by a pistol shot.

Nought remained of it but the hilt.

With fearful oaths he threw the fragment away, and wounding an opponent near him, he seized a mighty sledge hammer, and twirled it round his head as if it had been but a stick or sling.

On the instant he struck down one who confronted him.

The heavy hammer descended with unerring aim and frightful force upon another, whose skull was instantly smashed into pieces.

Mungo lost the hammer with the force of that fearful blow.

But before one of Bloodhoof's men could discharge a pistol at him, Mungo rushed upon him and buried a dagger in his throat.

Then recovering his hammer, he renewed the attack upon those nearest to him.

Fast and furious the combatants fought.

Now one party and then the other gave ground, or drove all before them.

Neither asked for quarter nor gave any.

It seemed to be an exterminating fight.

One after another were shot or knocked down senseless and bleeding on the sands with hammers, bars of iron, or cutlasses, weapons which proved more suitable for the fray than pistols or guns, which required loading, and occasioned loss of time.

Such a fight the oldest villain among them had never seen before.

But the combatants were now getting weary with the slaughter.

Many African negroes, or half-breeds, who formed part of Mungo's crew, were the first to show signs of cowardice.

As long as they outnumbered Bloodhoof's men, they fought on, inspirited by the shouts and example of the tall Mungo.

But when they perceived that many of the original mutineers, under Bloodhoof, were clever swordsmen, and well disciplined, as we know they had been on board the old "Rattlesnake," they found that buccaneers, with English blood and English arms, were more than a match for weak-legged, though brutal, African negroes.

It was in vain that Mungo shouted to his followers.

They would not stand.

The combat, for them, proved too long and dangerous to be very pleasant.

They preferred to fight under some cover, where there was plenty of ammunition, rather than in the open air with cold steel.

The English maxim of a fair field and no favour was not pleasant, when the numbers on both sides became more equal.

With one accord, then, they retreated towards some sheds and log-houses in a very hasty and scrambling manner, followed slowly by Mungo and a few others, who seemed at first disinclined to turn their backs upon the foe.

Stubbornly and sullenly as bears, Mungo, and a few faithful friends, retreated, fighting all the way they went.

Pell-mell did Mungo's men rush into the nearest cabins and log-houses, where they supplied themselves with powder and ball, and kept on firing from the cracks and windows.

The confusion among them now was something awful.

Bloodhoof, and his fellow mutineers, quickly followed at the heels of their retreating foes.

The carnage was terrific.

Numbers of the negroes threw down their weapons, and rushed forth from the houses in which they had taken refuge.

Those inside endeavoured to close and bar the door again.

But this Bloodhoof's men tried to prevent.

"Remember you are English," cried their leader; "remember you were man-of-wars men once. Never give in to those African devils and their mongrel friends!"

These words were answered with a sturdy cheer by Bloodhoof's men.

Shouts of defiance came from the houses.

The mutineers made a desperate rush at the doors.

Their strength was too much for those inside.

The doors were smashed in, and headlong plunged the mutineers inside.

Then a terrible struggle ensued.

Every inch of ground was fiercely disputed and fought for.

Every spot was slippery with blood.

Bodies of both parties thickly strewed the ground.

And yet the fight raged more fiercely than ever.

The mutineers gained ground fast upon their swarthy opponents.

They acted together and with some sort of order.

Nor did they shout and curse like the followers of the African chief.

The mutineers had been well drilled in the English manner, common to seamen, and cleaved their way in silence, but with deadly determination.

Indeed, the fearful power and impetuosity of the mutineers were not to be resisted.

The numbers who each moment fell before them

were enough to awe even Mungo and his swarthy brutes.

The house in which Mungo had taken refuge was assailed on all sides.

When sufficient of the building had been won to carry out Bloodhoof's design, he ordered his men to set fire to it in various parts at once, taking good care that all the outlets to the cellars and vaults below were well fastened, so that none could get down, and those who had already sought safety and shelter in such places should be compelled to remain and die there.

In a few moments the log-house, and several small buildings near it, were in a blaze, and flames issued from numerous places in the roof, lofts, and windows.

The sight was grand, but appalling.

The cries and shouts of those both within and without would have softened the hearts of any other men but Mungo's and Bloodhoof's gore-loving desperadoes.

But both gangs had been so long used to sights of carnage and desperate encounters both by sea and land, that they seemed to rollick and riot in such a spectacle as that then around them.

Mungo saw at a glance that the fortune of war was against him.

Yet he would not yield.

His own numbers and friends had been much more numerous than those of his opponents at first, but the steadiness and order of the mutineers, who, when fighting, never forget they had English blood in their veins, however great rascals they were, proved almost invincible wherever they went.

They kept close to one another, resolved to die together rather than have a half-bred African slaver chief to command them.

All were now fighting for their very lives, and to set at rest once and for all whether the mutineers and others should be the servants or the masters of the proud and arrogant new-comers.

Bloodhoof and his band stood without, ready to capture those who, finding their stronghold, as they deemed it, thus in the course of inevitable destruction, must rush from it and render themselves prisoners to save the lives they must else lose in the flames.

As the flames and smoke mounted, the wood crackled and burnt briskly and brightly.

Mungo's men, who had commenced posting themselves at the upper windows to fire upon the foe beneath, no sooner perceived their alarming position than, throwing away the muskets they were about dealing death with, they made a very hasty descent, and leaping through the flames delivered themselves prisoners to those who were waiting outside to receive them.

In a very little while the house was cleared of many of its living tenants, who were instantly seized and recommended to the particular care of many stout fellows, who frankly made them acquainted with their intention of cutting them down the moment they attempted departing without leave.

Bloodhoof watched the burning building with impatience, for he longed to return to the scene of action which he had previously quitted, where a desperate fight was still going on, and where he knew every man was of importance.

He was spared waiting very long, for a sudden and tremendous explosion took place unexpectedly, shaking the ground where they stood with its report, while the sheet of flame nearly deprived them of eyesight.

Another instant and huge fragments of rafters and beams came clattering about their ears, wounding many in their descent severely, and hurting a large number.

Several other small explosions followed in succession.

Showers of sparks flew up into the air, springing from broad masses of hot flame, which scorched as well as almost blinded those around.

Each explosion was like a tremendous discharge of artillery, roaring and crashing with violence, making the ground tremble where they stood, as though it were convulsed by an earthquake.

It was evident a very large quantity of gunpowder must have been on the premises in readiness to supply their wants, but it was thus disposed of without proving of the service for which it was intended.

The explosions followed each other so quickly as to bewilder, both by their magnitude and tremendous uproar, all present, and prevent any attempt to escape the falling fragments until the last crash took place, and then a hasty retreat was made to reach beyond the range of the burning masses which fell like a fiery shower upon all indiscriminately.

A comparative silence followed the terrific sound which had the moment previously stunned the ears of the bystanders, and a deep gloom, almost darkness, followed the dazzling brightness which the sheets of flame accompanying each ignition of the gunpowder had shed around.

A minute sufficed for Bloodhoof and his followers to penetrate the darkness and continue the attack upon such of Mungo's followers who still united together for the purpose of resistance.

The disastrous destruction of their houses and places of refuge, the capture of their chief, Mungo, who was more dead than alive when dragged from the flames, and the loss of many of their comrades, filled the rest with a dismay which assisted greatly to defeat them.

They were driven from every position until many flung down their arms and fled, to be hotly pursued.

The rest called for quarters and tendered their submission.

Bloodhoof gathered them together, saw that they were all deprived of their arms, marched them to a place of security, and leaving a small party to guard them, hurried at once back to the principal scene of action near the beach, which he had quitted with regret to pursue Mungo's party.

The roar of musketry, the din of weapons and the sound of shouts and cries told all that the battle was still raging fiercely.

Bloodhoof increased his speed as he drew nearer, and was soon again among his followers, who were busied in the strife.

He was speedily recognised, and an opening was made for him and the band accompanying him to pass on to the front, where the contest was at its fearful height.

Their presence was hailed with delight.

Cheers greeted them, and animated them to push forward into the part of the fray to do justice to the favourable feeling evinced towards them by their comrades.

When the balance is pretty equal it requires but a small thing thrown into the scale to turn it in favour of one party or the other.

And thus at a moment when the victory was doubtful at that particular spot; when, with all the sturdy courage, the unflinching bravery, the stern, deadly resistance they displayed, it appeared impossible for the few mutineers then there any longer to withstand Mungo's numerous followers in their incessant and terrific attacks, the appearance of Bloodhoof and his band, small as it was, turned the scale in favour of the opponents of the African chief's tyranny and slavery.

The volumes of smoke arising from the discharged fire-arms rendered it difficult to see very far.

But the flashes from the muskets and pistols, which still continued their devastating work, gave sufficient light for the African slaves to perceive their opponents had a reinforcement, though to what extent they were unable to judge.

They were not long either in discovering that the fresh comers attacked them with a vigour which in consequence of the work they had already performed they were unable to resist.

They, therefore, gave ground before them.

With a single glance, Bloodhoof detected this symptom of weakness.

In a voice, which was heard already above the tumult and din, he called on the mutineers to follow him, for victory was in their hands.

A simultaneous rush echoed his appeal.

Every man seemed to feel it was the last effort.

And a mighty one they made it.

Many kept near to Bloodhoof, and echoed his war cry, fought as he fought, and, with clear, loud tones, called in such terms to their own immediate followers, that they fought as if possessed by a spirit compelling them to bear down all before them.

The struggle at this spot was now dreadful.

The combatants on both sides fell fast.

But the fury with which the mutineers attacked their antagonists gave them but little time to note this.

The impetuosity which characterized the onslaught of the mutineers, drove them still further back, and Bloodhoof exerted himself to the utmost to increase the pressure upon them.

No chance was given Mungo's men to stand their ground.

Once made to move, they were compelled to continue their retreat ; in fact, it appeared as though it was the object of the mutineers to cut their way through the foe.

Step by step they beat them back, and, as Bloodhoof's men kept gaining ground, a fresh animation fired them.

They shouted, delivered their blows with double force, and rapidly they fired their muskets and pistols with new dexterity and swiftness.

Every inch they gained they called up fresh energy, and increased the speed of the foe, until a panic began to seize them in the rear, who found their companions pressing upon them, and compelling them also to give ground.

An effort was made by those who were the freshest, to get in front, and their endeavours added to the confusion.

Many, believing the victory was going against them, endeavoured, while yet safe, to make good their retreat ; some few, detecting their intention, strove to prevent them, thus assisting the disorder.

But, ere long, the valour of the English, under their determined leader, prevailed, and, with loud shouts, they utterly routed Mungo's followers and friends ; and, while the African slaver's men were scattered in all directions, pursued, and cut down by the mutineers, Bloodhoof placed his foot on the neck of the prostrate Mungo, and was, with almost endless cheers, proclaimed, by his blood-stained, frantic friends—

King and chief of the Blue Rocks for ever !

CHAPTER LXIV.

LION LIMB AND OLD GOVERNOR MARTIN FORM AN ALLIANCE BETWEEN THEIR RESPECTIVE COLONIES.

FOR several days Lion Limb and old Governor Martin travelled together to different parts of the island, and everywhere they were received with great demonstrations of joy.

Old Martin's colony, although they had been many many years inhabiting the place, were unable for want of a ship to go and visit other distant islands which were not many days' sail away.

Nor had they the slightest idea that any Europeans were so near to them.

For although at long intervals natives in canoes of strange build, and all sizes, landed at different spots, the terror with which old Martin's powder and shot, muskets and cannon had inspired them, always prevented much intercourse with the European settlers.

It was thought by old Martin that none of the islands contained any white or European people, or else the stray natives who were sometimes cast upon his coast would have known or heard something about such settlers.

Believing himself and friends to be the only English for thousands of miles around, he, like his young friend Lion Limb, hoisted his flag, and claimed the country for England.

But the fact that Lion Limb was king and master of an island also, and the knowledge that he commanded and owned a good fast-sailing schooner with guns and a well-trained crew beside, set old Martin's friends beside themselves with joy.

They all volunteered to render every assistance in their power to repair the damage done to the schooner in the late fight with the pirate vessels at the Blue Rocks, and to sail along with its young commander to explore all the islands, and land old King Katamar and his Indian warriors on their own soil.

Lion Limb and old Martin, with their friends and followers, assembled in council, and swore eternal friendship and amity between their respective colonies, and as they journeyed homewards again to Fort Martin, having made their tour of inspection, presents of every sort were thrust upon them, such as bear-skins, panther skins, flour, wool, honey, fruit, and a hundred other things which Lion Limb very well knew would be grateful to all on board the schooner.

For two days and two nights great rejoicings were kept up at Fort Martin.

Guns were fired ; feasts were given.

Dancing under the direction of Joe Pebbles was kept going on at all hours ; and Joe would have long before professed fatigue and disgust had it not been for the smiles of a pretty half-breed girl, who had won Joe's heart, and thus inspired him with fresh hopes and renewed vigour.

Fort Martin itself seemed for awhile to be turned into a fair, and when at last Lion Limb prepared to depart for his vessel again, more than twenty half-wild mules were laden by the good-hearted people of the fort with all sorts of gifts for his friends, and more than a score of the settlers set out with him to the coast.

It was as much as Lion Limb could do to prevail upon Joe to leave the place at all, for he had been so well treated and feasted. The men thought so much of him, and the almost miraculous as well as enchanting powers of his fiddle, and the charms of his many comic songs ; and the girls on the other hand were so delighted with his expertness and cleverness in dancing jigs, hornpipes, and the like, that Joe became bewildered and perplexed.

However, he at last consented very reluctantly to leave his many friends, both male and female, and with a plentiful supply of presents in the way of shells and beads, beaver skins, and tobacco, he kissed all the girls around him, and, mounting one of the mules, played several lively tunes, and then left the fort like some conqueror.

At night time great precautions were taken to guard against any surprise by the half-savage vindictive natives, through whose part of the wild and uncultivated country they were compelled to pass on their nearest way to the coast; and although on one or two occasions they had to halt and fight their way through many dangerous and difficult defiles in the mountains, they at last came in sight of the sea once again, and when the sun rose brightly over the heights of the mountains they raised a joyful shout as they descried in the distance their schooner high and dry upon the sands, and the smoke from the camp-fires of their friends. Old Governor Martin and his own people were enraptured with the view of this camp of Europeans, and their features beamed with joy.

They were yet too far away to make themselves heard by shouting; but, Lion Limb, nudging the old governor, said,

"They do not see any of us as yet; but, watch, and see how quickly I can make a movement among them."

"How?" said the old man.

"Why, this way."

And, suiting the action to the word, Lion Limb blew one or two shrill blasts on his horn, and the sounds being re-echoed again and again by the rocks and hills, reached the ears of his distant friends, who raised their heads, and, scanning all the landscape around, soon espied the dust caused by the train of mules winding down the mountain side, and, raising their caps, they waved them wildly and frequently, while at the same time faint sounds were heard, as if the echo of their shouts and cheers.

Abandoning their work about the temporary camp and the repairs they were doing to the schooner, several of the crew hastened forth to meet the train, which, in less than an hour, marched into the camps with an air of great pomp and show.

The surprise of all was very great indeed when Lion Limb explained to them the agreeable discovery he had made of Europeans like themselves being settled on the island, and old Governor Martin was the observed of all observers.

And now commenced a second course of feasting and dancing until Joe and his fiddle were almost worn out.

Lion Limb was much interested to hear all that had taken place since his departure.

Many things had been done during his absence.

The schooner was repaired roughly but stoutly, and was sea-worthy again.

The sails had been patched and re-patched in a hundred different places, and they were only waiting for the tide to launch her again when it pleased Lion Limb to give the order.

But what puzzled the young leader most was the news that a strange vessel had been seen hovering off the coast both night and day; but particularly at night-time, and that she looked very ugly and suspicious.

The vessel was reported to be a small one, rakishly built and rigged, and would occasionally approach very close to the land, and then sail away again without showing any colours.

"But did you not display ours, then?" asked Lion Limb.

"No, we were afraid to do so, for we imagined it might be a pirate for all we knew," was the answer.

Lion Limb could not at all understand the meaning or the object of this mysterious vessel; but fearing it might be a piratical craft from its description and suspicious movements, he made all haste in preparing the schooner for departure, for although he had now a plentiful store of provisions of every sort—thanks to his own foresight, and the kindness of the good folk at Fort Martin—he had not the chief thing that he wanted, namely, plenty of ammunition.

In truth there were not more than a dozen rounds of cannon cartridge in his magazine, and should he have the misfortune to fall foul of an enemy before his stores were replenished he felt certain that he should fall an easy prey to them.

With the care of so many human beings on his shoulders, both afloat and ashore, the young leader became very thoughtful and solemn.

He told his fears to no one, except old Governor Martin, who shook his head very gravely, and advised his young friend not to put to sea under such circumstances.

But such counsel was distasteful to the young and daring commander.

He gave immediate orders for all to go aboard, and stow away the stores, and, in addition to the mules, he sent a party of his men on a hunting expedition, who returned in less than two days with some wild goats, wild hogs, sheep, a few parrots, singing birds of different sorts and colour, and, in one word, brought back whatever they thought would prove useful or ornamental to themselves on the voyage home, or at their camps in the colony.

CHAPTER LXV.

THE CHASE.

HAVING made every necessary arrangement the schooner was launched again after some labour and trouble, when the midnight tide was at the flood, and with scarcely any sails set more than was sufficient to steady and steer, the schooner crept along the island coast like a shadow in order to elude any dangerous craft which might be on the look-out for them.

In this design the young leader was successful, for heavy fogs favoured him, and before the sun rose in the morning he had left Martin Island far behind him, and was sailing south-eastward in the direction where he supposed old Katamar's island to lie among a group some sixty or seventy miles away.

But all on board were rejoicing a little to soon.

When the sun had risen and dispelled the fog, all were surprised and alarmed to perceive a vessel with every stitch of canvas set, in full chase after them.

"Don't fear any of you; she is far enough away yet," said Lion Limb, coolly. "She sails well, and looks very much like a piratical craft; but we'll lead them a merry dance before we surrender to them."

Every bit of canvas that the schooner could bear was now crowded on her.

"Let her fly before the wind, sir?" asked Dick.

"Yes; we cannot keep on our regular course; so if we haven't good luck to give yonder craft the slip, we must defer landing Katamar and his Indians until a better opportunity occurs."

But the stranger all this time had been fast creeping on the schooner, and in less than two hours she was within cannon shot.

She hoisted English colours.

"Shall we show ours, sir?" asked one of the crew.

"No; I think it is all a trick on their part. She doesn't look much like an English vessel; it is only done to deceive us; don't notice her. Put the helm hard aport, Dick, and let her go straight before the wind."

Dick did so.

But at that same moment a small curl of white smoke rolled from the chaser's bow, and in a few seconds afterwards a round shot crossed the schooner's bows, and plunging into the sea, threw up a column of water.

"Rather close, sir," said the sailor; "shall we return the compliment? We have a few rounds of ammunition left."

"No; keep all we have until we come to close quarters; every single cartridge is worth more than its weight in gold."

Again and again the chaser fired; but the wind increasing each moment, and the sea becoming very rough, the shots fell short, but in most cases overshot the mark.

"We cannot get out of it, sir, I fear," said Dick; "she'll stick to us like a leech. How she carries so much sail puzzles me."

"She won't be able to do so much longer, I think," said Lion Limb; "we shall have a perfect gale of wind shortly. Her masts will snap like a couple of matches with so much canvas."

And, true to his prediction, this actually took place, for a sudden squall fairly struck the chaser with its full force, and, on the instant, the foremast snapped close to the cap.

A shout of joy was raised on board the schooner for this unexpected deliverance.

But the chasers, full of anger for their mishap, fired gun after gun, and, with such precision, that one carried away part of the schooner's bulwarks, another crashed through the windows of the aftercabin, but without injuring any one, and a third rent a great hole in the jib.

"Close shaving that, sir," said Dick.

"Yes, but don't fire; now the squall is over, carry all canvas again. Had the stranger followed our example she would not have had her fore-mast go by the board."

Perceiving that the schooner must now escape them, the chasers, whoever they were, fired furiously, but without doing any harm, for in less than half an hour the "Rattlesnake" had left the stranger far behind and was bowling along at a rapid rate, and had changed her course again, if possible to land old Katamar and his Indians.

This they did with great success during the day, for the old chief's sharp eyes soon detected his own island home among a group of ten or twelve others; but notwithstanding all his entreaties to stay for a time, Lion Limb would not do so, but wisely resolved to sail homewards as soon as possible, and not to trust himself on the high seas any longer without a fresh supply of powder and shot and landing the non-fighting part of those with him, promising to return and see the old Indian at the first opportunity.

The "Rattlesnake" set sail again, but Marmi lingered on the beach, nor did she leave the spot until long after the schooner was out of sight, and then she sat down with head buried in her hands and wept most bitterly.

She dearly loved, but was not loved in return.

CHAPTER LXVI.

THE ISLAND IS SURPRISED BY AN UNEXPECTED AND DISTINGUISHED ARRIVAL.

In less than twenty hours after landing King Katamar, Lion Limb and his crew were rejoiced to perceive on the far-off horizon the signal fires burning on the headlands of his own island, and ere morning broke they fired a signal gun which quickly aroused all in the colony, who lined the cliffs, and welcomed back the schooner and its gallant crew, which they had almost given up for lost.

As soon as the vessel was moored, and had safely anchored in the small and safe inlet which had been always selected for her, and which also was completely shut out from view from the sea, all disembarked, and repaired to their various quarters, there to recount the perils and adventures they had seen, each taking with him one or more of old Martin's men, and making them comfortable and happy.

Joe Pebbles was love-sick; and, more than that, now that there were no more hearty buxom girls to dance to his music, he hung up the fiddle and the bow, and resolved never to touch them again, if possible, at least, until he should visit Fort Martin and see his lady love again.

Poor Joe was sadly joked and laughed at by his companions for his love affair, and to seek a little rest and quiet from their good-natured jests, he betook himself to the sea-shore and the lonely woods, where, in company with the laughter-loving Ted Rawlings, he would again and again describe the wonders he had seen, and go into raptures continually about the belles and beauties of Fort Martin.

One morning, three days after the schooner's return to the island, some one reported that during the previous night they had espied a strange vessel with a broken foremast sail within gunshot of the signal-fires, but suddenly disappeared in the darkness again.

Lion Limb began to think that perhaps the pirates had tracked him, and intended to attack the settlement.

He gave orders, therfore, for every man to be near and ready at his particular post, in case of any sudden emergency.

Joe Pebbles was appointed to a distant post up the coast, and to stay there both night and day, until relieved by some other person; to signal at night by twisting burning brands, and in the day by means of a small red flag, should any suspicious craft come in view of the high rock on which he was stationed.

Right glad was Joe at thus having peace and quietness.

He kept watch very well for two days, but on the third night he fell fast asleep, and in the morning was suddenly and rudely aroused from his dreams of Fort Martin and its buxom lasses, by a hearty kick in the ribs, and a voice which said in a rough, cheery tone,

"Hello! Shipmate! What cheer? Who are you?"

"Eh? What?" said Joe, jumping to his feet, and thunderstruck at seeing an English sailor standing near him.

"Hello, shipmate! Who are you? What cheer, my hearty?" was the repeated salutation.

"Who am I?" thought Joe. "Now, who the devil is *he* I wonder? I mustn't let him know I'm one out of the convict ship that was wrecked, or I can't trust the consequences, so I'll put a bold face on it."

"Who am I?" said Joe, aloud, rubbing his ribs.

"Yes, who *are* you?"

"Why, I'm a gentleman, *I* am."

"The deuce you are, my hearty," said the jolly, rosy-faced tar, roaring with laughter. "A gentleman, eh? Well, then, where the devil did you get those patched and ragged clothes from? You've seen some sarvice somewhere, I know."

"I'll have you know, sir, I am king of this island," said Joe, proudly.

"King, eh? Well, I'll be hung, but that's rich, and no mistake. And how long may you have reigned over these 'ere parts?"

"What business is that of yours?" said Joe.

"You're an Englishman, at all events," said the tar, "and my name is Jack Ratline, that's what my name is, and I don't care who knows it."

"Jack Ratline, eh? and of the sloop of war, 'Skylark,' I think, judging by the ribbon on your cap," said Joe.

"Just so, mate; but who the devil told you it were a sloop?"

"I know all about it, my friend; but don't slap me on the back any more, it'll shake all the teeth out of my head."

"Yes, it *is* a sloop," said the jolly tar. "We came across a pirate in these waters, and gave chase, but carried too much canvas, so lost our foremast, and put in here to repair, and take in wood and water. But come, my lad, follow me; our sloop is anchored in a small bay hard by. I know the captain will be pleased to see a fellow countryman, who has been wrecked and living on this island more than—how many years did yer say?"

"Oh, I'm not particular as to date; but you can say forty years at the least."

"Forty?"

"Yes, more or less, and I have conquered all the savages hereabouts, and partly civilized them also."

"The devil you have," said the tar, looking at Joe in surprise. "And done it all yourself, eh?"

"Just so; all alone," said Joe, repressing a grin.

"And perhaps you can tell us something about the pirates who they say sail in these waters?"

"Oh, I've conquered them also," said Joe, calmly.

"What, conquered them also?" said the sailor, in surprise.

"Yes; but which of them are you looking out for?"

"Which? Why, you don't mean to say there are more than one?"

"Yes, I do. I know of two myself; I sank them both myself."

"You did?"

"Yes, *I* did," said Joe; "one was a brigantine."

"A brigantine! that's it; that's the very one we have been on the look out for."

"She's sunk!"

"And you did it?"

"Yes, me," said Joe, looking proudly about him.

"Then, hang me, if you mustn't come and see our skipper."

"No, I'll stay here; the king of this island is deserving of some honour, I think, and I'll stay here until the captain comes to me."

The jolly tar was so pleased at all he heard that he hurried away to inform his officers of the great discovery he had made.

Joe laughed heartily at the idea of how he had deceived the honest tar, and sat down to smoke his pipe until the captain's return, dreaming all the while that great honours would be shown him.

"They'll come ashore with fife and drums, and cocked hats, and all that, and bring any quantity of good things with them, and no mistake. I shall be in clover when they find out their mistake, and make the acquaintance of our young captain, I shall be missing for a day or two.

Thus thought Joe, and he grinned often, and smacked his lips at the bare thought of the good things he would soon receive in abundance.

CHAPTER LXVII.

MUNGO SUDDENLY BECOMES A GREAT MAN AGAIN —THE SECRET COUNCIL.

THE terrible fight which had taken place between the respective partizans of Bloodhoof and Mungo the African slave chief, ending, as it had done, in the subjugation of the latter, was celebrated by the victorious mutineers with great rejoicings.

Spirits of all kinds were lavished on every hand, and for three whole days and nights confusion and drunken riotings were the order of things among the rough and tattered inhabitants of the Blue Rocks.

A council of war was held to decide what should be done with Mungo.

As for his late friends, they were loud in their praises of Bloodhoof, and willingly swore allegiance to him.

As frequent fights and incessant bloody quarrels between themselves had greatly diminished their numbers of late, the council decided to accept the offer of faithful service tendered by Mungo's men.

But, as to Mungo himself, that was quite a different and far more difficult matter to decide.

If they killed him it would only sow the seeds of everlasting distrust and disunion among them all, and if they decided to allow him to remain at the Blue Rocks, Bloodhoof's supreme command would always be endangered.

Now, Bloodhoof knew very well that despite all their past quarrels, dissensions, and loss of life, he could make a friend of the African chief, who could do much good to the buccaneers on the Blue Rocks, although he might not chose or even be allowed to live and remain among them.

After several interviews it was decided to spare Mungo's life and make use of him for their general good.

"He has been forced to fly from Africa," argued Bloodhoof, "and a price is put upon his head as well as our own, therefore, he will not inform upon us, for it will not save his own neck from the rope, which is the thing he most fears."

"In the next place," argued another of the council, "ift he English cruisers really have destroyed several of his small towns and villages and burnt much of his property there, they have *not* destroyed his influence among the natives; if, therefore, we can by some means build a small craft for him out of the two wrecks on the coast, and let him depart to Africa again, the slave trade will soon make him as rich as ever; he can run two or three cargoes of prime fat negroes to Cuba or thereabouts, receive the money, and purchase for us lots of useful things in American ports, and thus pay us for his ransom."

"Yes; all this might be done," said another, very suspiciously, "if he *would*. But these Africans, you know, are the most cunning and deceitful wretches under the sun, and the half breeds are worse than all."

"But we can *compel* him to keep his promises with us," said Bloodhoof; "haven't we got several of his friends and relations in our hands?"

"He cares little for them, I think, if he can only manage to escape himself."

"But he *can't* make his escape from us," said Bloodhoof; "and I have a plan in view which will compel him to stick to his bargain, whatever we may think proper to insist upon."

"And what is that, Bloodhoof?" asked several, very eagerly.

"Why, this : we'll build some swift, light craft out of the two wrecks, and place on board two good guns in order to protect himself against any stray lubberly cruiser, and man the vessel with a crew of our best men, so that he *can't* do as he likes when he leaves us, but always be watched night and day."

"Capital," said one and all ; "the plan is the best that could be hit upon, but Mungo must not be made aware of it."

"No he shall not, you may depend ; but if he flinches from his engagements our chosen friends on board will put him into irons on the spot or blow his brains out."

"And what are the conditions you think of imposing on him ?"

"Why, these : the first cargo of niggers that he lands in Cuba and gets the money for must go to buy a clipping brig that can outsail anything that opposes us ; rifled cannon also we want. He must bring half-a-dozen on board, with plenty of rifles, pistols, and ammunition of all sorts, together with choice provisions, and plenty of brandy and rum ; in fact, he must load the vessel he brings for us with a general and full cargo of ' all sorts.' "

Bloodhoof's plans were listened to very attentively, and every one present in the secret council approved of them.

"But has he money enough to do all those things ?" asked one.

"If he has not, we have a good round sum in our hidden treasury. Nat the Don's sealed note to whoever might succeed him, should he not return from among the young convicts' settlement, has explained all that. We will put several boxes of gold and silver on board unknown to Mungo, and trust it in the hands of some one of our men we can depend upon," said Bloodhoof ; "and whatever Mungo is unable to purchase out of his niggers we can buy out of our own coin."

This plan also was assented to, and at the bright prospect of what good things were in store for them, each one of the council drank deeply, and were very noisy in their rejoicings.

"But, I know a better plan than any yet mentioned," said Lasco, a particular friend and admirer of Bloodhoof.

"Name it."

"What is it, Lasco ?" said one and another.

"Why," said Lasco, with a round oath, "if we have to man the craft we build until such times as we get one of our own, I don't see why we shouldn't enter into the slave trade with him."

"Well, now I come to think of it," said Bloodhoof, "I don't think it is a very bad idea, because, if he ran his cargoes and landed them near us for a time, he would throw the cruizers off the scent, for we could re-ship them without much trouble from one of the islands near by, and no one would suspect for a moment what our quiet little game was, for there's none of them cursed men-of-war that visits this latitude much."

"But the young convicts might get wind of it."

"We can easily prevent that. Why not shift our residence to some other island that is more fruitful than this, for the Blue Rocks has always proved unfortunate for us so far ?" said one.

"Has it ?" growled Bloodhoof, who thought that this remark was in some way directed at himself in particular. "Well, the best plan to improve it is for us to lay a trap for young Devil's Limb, as I call him, and if he is put out of the way we haven't much cause to fear the rest, for his whole colony will soon die out after he has gone. I have made up my mind to slay him, but I will do so by stratagem."

Nothing further was said regarding Lion Limb, on that particular occasion ; but it was resolved to seize some other island for their head-quarters, and to make the Blue Rocks in future only a sort of general store-house and rendezvous, and the council separated.

Mungo, who was confined in prison, expected every hour to be dragged forth and hung or burned alive.

But his astonishment was great indeed when his dry bread and water was changed for much better diet, and he himself allowed some liberty for exercise.

A few days thereafter many of the buccaneers were busily employed at all hours in constructing a vessel out of the wrecks, and as it gradually approached completion, Bloodhoof was summoned before the secret council, and informed of its determination to set him at liberty under certain conditions and promises.

Mungo was only too glad to escape with his life ; and, as might have been expected, he faithfully promised to fulfil any engagement that Bloodhoof and his band might think fit to impose upon him.

But in his own heart he resolved to keep no faith with any of them when once he could call himself free again.

Desires of revenge filled his heart, and although he smiled and appeared friendly and happy at the merciful disposition displayed towards him, he secretly resolved to take signal vengeance on all who had forsaken or thwarted him while at the Blue Rocks.

He was suffered also to pick his own crew—a boon that he never for a moment expected—and holding his own men in contempt for the shabby part they had played towards him, he resolved to choose most of his men out of the mutineers, if he could prevail upon them to serve under him.

For he argued " They are brave men and thorough seamen ; they will never surrender to any British ship for fear of their lives, and as they are desirous no doubt of cruizing about for a few months, to enjoy themselves, they will most willingly go with me, and be glad of the chance."

Mungo found no difficulty, owing to Bloodhoof's private advice to his men, in selecting a good round number of mutineers for his crew, and the remainder were made up of such others as had long been on the island in Nat the Don's time.

When, therefore, all was ready for Mungo's departure, and a good-sized, roughly-built vessel had been prepared for him, Bloodhoof took the mutineers aside, and fully explained to them what they had to do, and reminded them not for a moment to trust Mungo too much, and that if he did not fulfil his promises faithfully and to the letter, they must arrest Mungo, put him in irons, and navigate that vessel or any other which might be bought or exchanged, and bring it with a full cargo of necessaries to the Blue Rocks.

"For you know," said Bloodhoof, " British, American, French, and other men-of-war on the African coast only cruise in certain latitudes ; so if they give chase put up your helm straight for these islands, and if you do not throw them off the scent you will leave them so far behind that you'll have time to unship the niggers with us, and be off again long before any chasers can make their appearance in these waters.

But Bloodhoof little dreamed, in that hour of his triumph, of *the swift and signal vengeance that at that moment awaited him.*

THE BOY KING
OF THE SOUTH SEA ISLANDS.

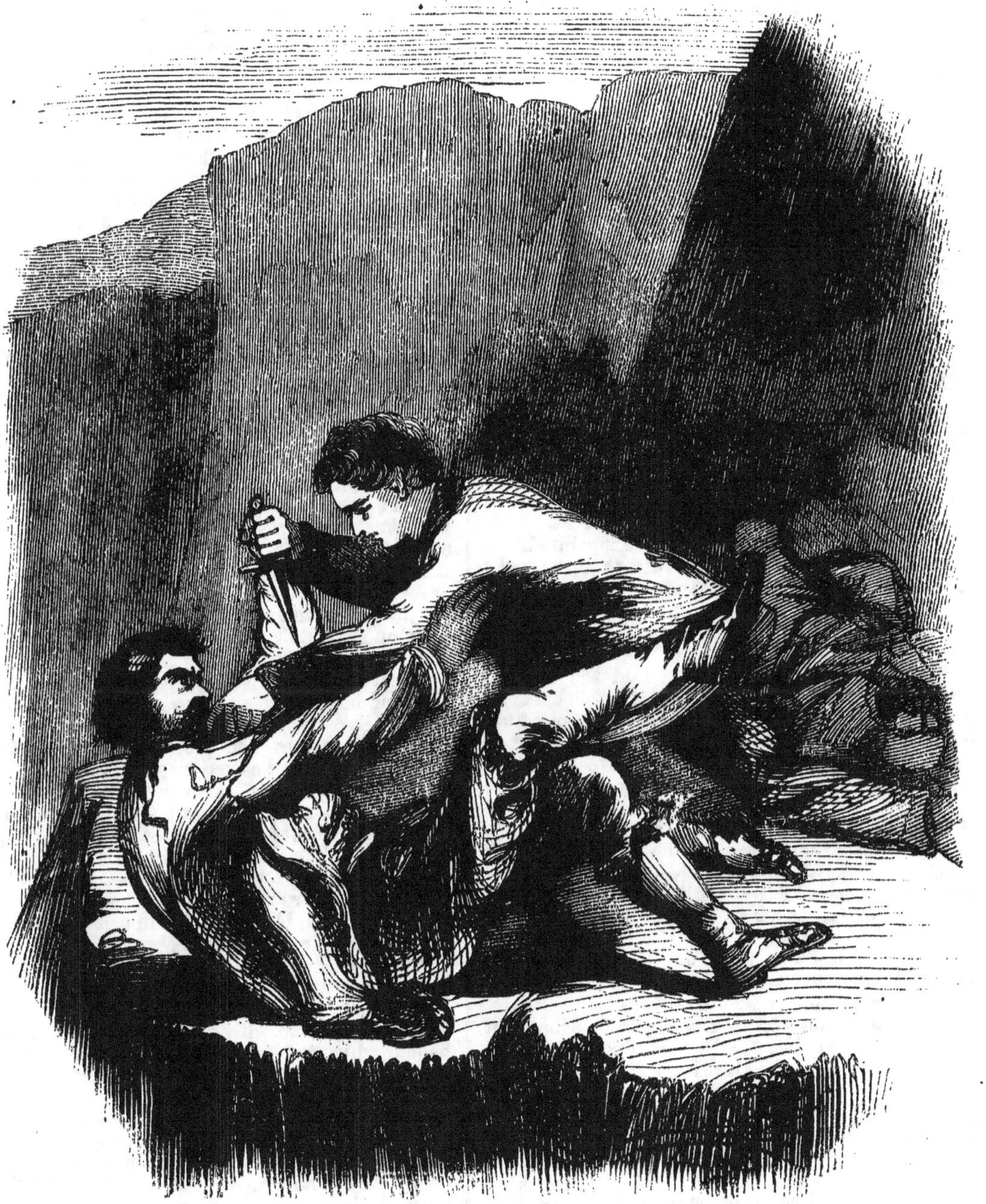

"SURRENDER OR DIE!" SHOUTED LION LIMB.

Such as we have described in our last Number was Bloodhoof's secret advice to those of the crew —and they were the majority—he could trust with the secret, and, with the consent of all, Lasco, an old buccaneer, was chosen among them

as their chief, to whom they should look up for advice or counsel in all things unknown to Mungo.

"And now, Lasco," said Bloodhoof, "all that remains to do is for us to go to the secret treasure-house, and carry some boxes of gold on board Mungo's craft, the 'Vulture,' unknown to him, and what you have to do with it I have already explained."

Bloodhoof and Lasco went forth together and determined to put the treasure on board the "Vulture" that same night.

"Come with me, Lasco," said the chief; "I have never yet visited the cave, but I dare say we can soon find its whereabouts from the description Nat the Don has left of it. It is filled with treasures of all sorts, and I will entrust you with the secret, but no one else."

Lasco, the grisly buccaneer, felt honoured at such a mark of confidence, and they went forth together towards the cave.

Mungo now was a great man again with the buccaneers, who expected wonders to result from his intended voyage.

But it was an unlucky day for Bloodhoof and for Lasco also, as we shall quickly see.

CHAPTER LXVIII.

INTERVIEW WITH BRITISH OFFICERS—LION LIMB'S MISSION TO THE BLUE ROCKS—HE ENCOUNTERS BLOODHOOF.

JOE PEBBLES sat upon a huge stone laughing and giggling to himself, and expecting all sorts of honours at the hands of the officers of the British war sloop "Skylark," when suddenly he was aroused from his reverie by the reappearance of old Ratline and an armed party of sailors, with the captain at their head.

Joe expected that they would present arms, and ask him to dinner on board at the very least.

But he was sadly mistaken and disappointed.

"Is this the fellow in the red shirt that you spoke of, Ratline?" asked the captain.

"Yes, your honour."

"And does he call himself king of the island?"

"Yes, your honour."

"Why, the rascal is a slaver," said the captain. "I distinctly saw him on board the schooner we gave chase to the other day, when we lost our foremast. Seize him! There are others of his party on the island, without a doubt; we'll have them all, now we have found out their hiding-place. Seize him, and bring him on board. Kick the rascal well if he resists."

In a moment, and before he could open his mouth to offer any explanation whatever, Joe found himself roughly handled by Ratline, and two others, who did not fail to shake him well, and to sound his ribs with their fists.

"If this is the way they are going to treat a king," thought Joe, "I'll soon let 'em know I ain't one," so he shouted out loudly,

"I'm not a king! I ain't anybody! Don't hit me! I'm nobody but Joe Pebbles, an Englishman. I never saw a slaver in all my life!"

"You lie!" said several of the men. "We saw you the other day. Didn't we chase you all the way from the Pongos river?"

"Pongos river!" said Joe. "Why, where's that?"

"Why, in Africa, to be sure. You are very innocent, I dare say; but we'll find out where Mungo is before long, if there's any virtue or persuasion in a cat-o'-nine-tails."

"Mungo, Pungo, Rungo! Who the devil is he?" said Joe. I never heard of him in my life. D—n

Mungo, but don't hustle a fellow along in that way. I'm nobody, I tell you, only an Englishman, and a poor devil at that."

"We'll soon see," said the captain. "Mungo and you wretches are not going to kill our people when you like, if you are English."

"Me kill anybody!" said Joe. "And am I going to be punished for this d——d unknown Mungo? That's what I call going against the laws and constitution altogether."

"I'll soon try your constitution for you, my fine fellow," said the captain. "Bring him along. Fifty or a hundred lashes will soon refresh his memory."

And without further ado Joe was dragged along, and ultimately came in sight of a small, secluded bay, in which the sloop of war "Skylark," was making good whatever repairs she required.

Those on board were greatly surprised at beholding a true Englishman living on an island where no European was supposed to exist, and at first every one was disposed to believe in the story that he really was one of the slaver's crew, until poor Joe, more dead than alive, told them that if they doubted his story, let them send messengers or a boat's crew, and then from the lips of his own young captain learn who and what they were.

"For suppose," said Joe, "that I should say we were for the most part convicts who had escaped from the old 'Rattlesnake,' they won't believe me, perhaps, and if they do, they may seize every one of us, make us leave the colony, and drag us to some penal settlement."

This reasoning was very creditable to him, but for some time no one would believe anything he said, until he promised to get men to assist in making good the repairs of the "Skylark," and that object being the chief in the captain's mind, he sent a boat's crew away down the other side of the coast to ascertain the truth or falsehood of all that Joe had told them.

With a small Union Jack flying at the stern of the jolly boat, and with a small sail up, they started early on the following morning, and ere long came in sight of the cliffs near to the colony.

"That's it," said Joe, with an air of pride; "see those log houses, and that flag on that tall flag-staff; —that's it."

But before they had proceeded much further a small puff of smoke curled away on top of the cliff, and a booming sound came over the water, which salute the boat with a small mountain gun in the bows duly returned with interest.

The colonists could now be soon running down to the beach, and by their gestures indicated how pleased they were at once more beholding the flag of Old England, if even it flew in a jolly boat.

"You see I told you no lie," said Joe.

"Yes, you did," said Ratline, "you said you were king here, but I'm sartin you ain't."

In a few moments the boat and its crew landed, and were received with every mark of respect and honour which the colonists could show; and what with the firing of cannon and muskets, and loud shouts, the reception was equally pleasing to the visitors as to their newly-found friends.

Hearing much firing going on in the distance, and fearing that something might have befallen his boat's crew, the captain of the "Skylark," and most of his officers and men, launched their boats, and quickly followed after.

Their surprise was very great indeed when they arrived at the colony, and beheld on every hand so many signs of comfort, peace, and prosperity.

Our young hero was the "lion" of the day, and

when he recounted all the trials and hardships which they had undergone, and how bravely they had fought against misfortune in all shapes, the officers of the "Skylark" were amazed and delighted at the good government and discipline which marked all things they had seen.

Old Martin also recounted to them his adventurous story, which was listened to with much interest.

Lion Limb gave them the exact latitude and longitude of Fort Martin and the whole island, which their visitors promised to land at when more convenient; and in the name of the British Crown the officer took formal possession of both islands, and gave Governor Martin and Lion Limb full powers on parchment to administer the laws, a right for the benefit of all, and offered a passage home at some future day to such as had any inclination to go to England.

He likewise said he would use his best endeavours to have the punishment to all who deserved it remitted, which he knew and felt certain would be readily granted by the government for their actions and bravery against the neigbouring buccaneers—those seas which he had never heard of before.

The chief thing which occupied the captain's mind, however, was the repairing of his sloop, and when he explained how he had lost his foremast in a gale, while chasing some pirate or slaver, Lion Limb laughed and told him all about it, apologizing for his conduct by saying that he also had been labouring under misapprehension, for he all along mistook the "Skylark" for some buccaneer, and being short of ammunition, resolved to fly before the wind, or otherwise he would have given them gun for gun.

In answer to the captain's inquiry about slavery in those parts, Lion Limb told him plainly that he did not believe there was any. The captain could scarcely believe this statement, but resolved at some other time to clear the Blue Rocks of the buccaneers, should the colonists themselves be unable to do so.

"All I want is power," said Lion Limb; "if I only had authority for what I do, I could accomplish almost anything; but men cannot fight well without they know they have the right on their side; give me a commission to show, and I'll guarantee to do wonders in these seas."

"Which I can and will with pleasure give," said the captain, "for I fully understand your valor and lofty notions. Come to me in my own cabin, both you and Governor Martin, I wish to speak to you of important matters; in fact of nothing else," said the captain, "than to ascertain the fate of the chief men among the mutineers. If any of them are still alive, it would be rendering great service to justice and our country both to have the villains tried and hung."

"When do you think of returning to these parts, captain?"

"Perhaps in three months."

"Before your return, then, I will have them all secured, and ready to be sent to England. I have one already in our prison, Bill Whetherby."

"We will not take the trouble to send them to England, my young friend; I will return with full powers to try and hang them on this very island."

Most of the day passed merrily and happily on every side, and many volunteered to go and assist the "Skylark" to repair her damage, and supply it with wood and water.

The next day all who could write were very busy in sending letters home to their friends, telling them of all that had happened, which letters the captain promised to forward by the first mail steamer he met with.

But in addition to these letters, Lion Limb delivered into the captain's hands several square boxes of bullion, old gold and silver coin, some pearls, diamonds, and other treasures, which were to be consigned to his brother, Allan Norman, who was to make use of it in buying up many things that the colony then needed, and send them by the first ship that was bound for their far-off regions.

In a few days the "Skylark" departed in all haste on some secret mission, which was not explained to Lion Limb or his friends. And our young hero determined to visit the Blue Rocks very secretly, and bring away whatever treasure he had left behind in his first visit.

With Dick Hamilton, Harry Woodruff, and a chosen boat's crew, he set sail by night, and the wind and darkness favouring him, our young hero landed, and with Harry and Dick left his boat in a secure and hidden creek, and set out towards the cave where they had on their first visit so mysteriously encountered Yokee.

The morning was misty and foggy.

The sun had not yet risen.

After proceeding some considerable distance they lost their way.

Climbing up a tall tree Lion Limb tried to ascertain their old track again, but could not.

"Stay you here, lads," said he; "keep quiet, and don't stir, I will go out alone, and if anything should happen which may require your prudence, I will sound my horn three times very faintly, so as not to arouse the attention of these blackguard buccaneers, and when you hear it come quickly."

Both Dick and Harry loudly protested against heir young captain going forth alone.

But he insisted upon doing so.

With a smile he girt on his good sword, looked well to his pistols, and went forth alone, and without a particle of fear.

On reaching the confines of the wood through part of which he had passed, and emerging in the open space, he advanced up an irregular ascent, rocky and wild in its aspect.

It was too high to be denominated a hill, and yet not sufficiently dignified in appearance or height to be termed a mountain.

A thick mist enveloped it, and our young hero had some difficulty in penetrating the gloom although his eyes were accustomed to discern objects in the most obscure atmosphere.

As he rose higher it grew less dense, and, on reaching a spot where a small wooden bridge crossed a deep chasm, he was surprised to perceive two figures approaching him.

A single glance convinced him that one of them must be Bloodhoof.

Lion Limb instantly stood motionless.

They advanced with quick steps, crossed the bridge, and, on advancing nearer to him, Lion Limb suddenly moved a few steps out of a thicket, and stood in the path of Bloodhoof, and prevented his proceeding further.

Bloodhoof started at this sudden appearance of Lion Limb on his island.

"What means this insolence, young villain?" growled the buccaneer chief, with haughty anger. "Stand out of my path!"

"I have important—nay, very important—business with you, Bloodhoof," said Lion Limb, proudly. "You must accompany me."

Bloodhoof eyed him for a moment with indignant surprise, and put out his hand to thrust him back.

But, though possessing considerable strength, he might as well have essayed to move a rock as force our young hero from his path.

The latter smiled in scorn, and, drawing from his breast a small scroll, he unrolled it, and held it before the eyes of Bloodhoof, saying,

"Behold the warrant for your arrest!"

At the sight of the English coat-of-arms emblazoned at each corner of the parchment, a cold shudder ran through the body of the villain.

But he speedily recovered this exhibition of weakness, and cast a hasty glance round him.

The spot was very lonely, and his companion Lasco a trusty scoundrel.

A moment served to make up his mind.

He snatched the scroll from Lion Limb's hand, perused it attentively, and then tried to tear it.

But, being written on parchment, the skin would not give.

He crumpled it in his hand, and threw it in our hero's face.

"It is a contemptible forgery!" he exclaimed, in a sneering tone. "And thus will I punish a young villain who dares for some vile purpose to assume the name and rank of an English officer without even wearing their garb to cover his shallow roguery."

At his side he wore a very long heavy sword, in the use of which, as we have already seen, he was particularly expert.

He drew it from its scabbard.

Unbuckling the latter, he cast it from him, that it might not impede his movements.

Lion Limb, who, in the furtive glance which Bloodhoof at first cast towards him and around, had detected his intention, was fully prepared and equal to it.

His own sword in a moment leapt from its scabbard.

"You short-sighted, shallow-pated hound!" cried Bloodhoof, "think you to catch a prize so easily. The price fixed on my head might be worth the hazard you are incurring; but it will take your whole tribe of convict robbers to capture me. Dog! you shall never return to your island home to tell the result of your experience. This hour is your last! Upon him, Lasco," said Bloodhoof, in tones of fierce anger. "Let the dry earth drink his vile blood!"

In addition to this command, Bloodhoof suddenly struck our hero a violent blow with his gloved hand upon his mouth, which was delivered with sufficient force to send him staggering back.

In an instant all the blood in Lion Limb's veins rushed like molten lead through their narrow channels to his brain.

A furious passion seized him.

With a shout of indignation and contempt, which sounded like a death knell, he sprung with the ferocity of a tiger upon Bloodhoof.

His weapon gleamed in the air, but was received on the huge sword of his antagonist, who returned it with a tremendous cut with his terrific weapon.

Lion Limb leaped lightly upon one side, or he must have perished beneath it, and encountered the sword of Lasco, Bloodhoof's follower.

"You are a meddling fool!" shouted our hero, with contempt, as he received the blows levelled at him by the retainer. "This for your pains."

With the rapidity of lightning, he disarmed Lasco at a blow, and the next instant his own flashing sword descended upon the cowardly villain's skull, braining him.

With a death shriek the wretched victim fell to the earth.

His dreadful groans were a fearful accompaniment to the desperate hand to hand struggle which now ensued between Lion Limb and Bloodhoof.

The former still smarted under the blow he had received, and employed his weapon with a fury which was ungovernable, but which, as yet, gave him no advantage.

Bloodhoof, as we have frequently seen, was very clever and dexterous with his sword, which he wielded with great ease and swiftness on every side.

But the nimbleness of Lion Limb up to this present moment had enabled him to avoid the tremendous and deadly blows which Bloodhoof intended for him, and after a struggle which, as yet, brought no injury to either, Lion Limb began to recover his usual self-possession, and fought more warily and more to the purpose.

He had barely recovered his wonted coolness, when Bloodhoof felt himself wounded in the shoulder.

And then quickly afterwards, in spite of his skill, a gash was inflicted on his hands, and the sword immediately after was torn from his grasp with a jerk, the effects of which he could easier perceive than understand the means by which it was accomplished.

Lion Limb sprung upon him.

With his left hand he seized him by the throat.

They had during their struggle gradually edged nearer a small but deep precipice and now were on the very brink of it.

With a strength which few youths but himself possessed, Lion Limb forced his burly antagonist to his knees, and bade him surrender.

Bloodhoof only answered by a bitter and savage oath.

"Surrender or die!" shouted our hero again.

"Never!" growled Bloodhoof. "I'll never surrender alive to a boy—a convict chief."

The struggle was fearful.

Lion Limb did not wish to kill the villain but desired to take him alive.

But what could he do?

"Surrender!" he again cried.

"Never! We shall both die together first," was the response of the buccaneer chief.

With his left hand, which was the only one he had at liberty, Bloodhoof drew a long dirk from his belt and aimed a deadly blow at Lion Limb.

This our hero succeeded in avoiding, and throwing his sword from him, seized Bloodhoof's wrist, which was again uplifted to slay him.

Superior nimbleness enabled Lion Limb to gain possession of the long dirk and drag Bloodhoof to the earth, and in an instant, producing a pair of handcuffs, he made his enemy helpless.

When he had thus secured his prisoner, Lion Limb sounded his horn three times very faintly, and in a short time Dick Hamilton and Harry Woodruff appeared from the place of concealment which Lion Limb had appointed for them.

Both Harry and Dick were greatly surprised at all that had so quickly taken place, and wondered how it was possible that a youth like their gallant leader was could have done so much in so short a time, and felt a little annoyed that they also had not been summoned from their hiding-place to take part in the unequal combat.

Lion Limb only smiled and said, "it was an honor he could not have divided with any one."

Bloodhoof with his revengeful, blood-shot eyes, scowled upon Harry and Dick, but spoke not.

The black-looking villain who had accompanied the buccaneer chief was found upon inspection to be quite dead.

The body, by our young hero's orders, was lifted from the ground and cast down the precipice and fell into a wild mountain torrent which ran swiftly at the bottom.

The body splashed in the dark tide below and for ever disappeared from human view.

Our young hero watched its disappearance with a look of cold contempt, and then turned to his prisoner, who sat upon the ground with downcast head convulsed by a raging passion he was too proud and stubborn to give vent to.

"Bind up his wounds and let us proceed homewards, again," said Lion Limb to Dick and Harry.

They did as they were told, and then Lion Limb addressed his prisoner thus :—

"Bloodhoof, you and your gang have always been enemies to us and our little colony, and now has come the hour of our triumph. We have seized you, not so much on account of what you have done to us islanders, but you have to answer a more weighty charge, namely, the destruction of the ship of war 'Rattlesnake' and the loss of many valuable lives, for, as you must be aware, not only did Captain Clarence refuse to leave his ship, but his officers also, and those who fell not under the brutal hands of your mutineers in the conflict that ensued on board were afterwards drowned ; this is the serious charge against you and others who still live, Bill Whetherby among the number."

"Bill Whetherby!" said Bloodhoof, half aloud, "Is he alive?"

"He is."

"Then he must have more lives than a cat, for I have heard all about your flogging him," said Bloodhoof.

"A ship of war called at our island not many days since," said Lion Limb, "and I explained much of all that took place on board the old 'Rattlesnake,' and I have the satisfaction of knowing that our Government has been pleased to pardon——"

"Pardon all of us?" growled Bloodhoof, brightening up.

"No ; not you mutineers, but the convicts and others who so gallantly defended the ship, and stood by its noble captain in the hour of trial."

Bloodhoof growled out a bitter oath as he heard this news.

Lion Limb continued,

"The vessel of war, 'Skylark,' did not visit these lonely islands with any idea of finding them inhabited, nor had the officers the remotest idea that the 'Rattlesnake' had been wrecked in these waters. They came on quite a different errand."

"And what was that, pray?" asked Bloodhoof, filled with curiosity.

"They had been cruizing off the Pongos river in Africa, looking after a noted slave-chieftain, by whose orders several English persons had been brutally murdered while in the execution of their duty."

"Humph!" said the prisoner, with a smile of triumph.

"The 'Skylark' burned seven or eight towns that belonged to this inhuman slave-dealer, and all his corn, cotton, ivory, and other valuables, but——"

"The slave-chief escaped, though, I suppose?"

"He did."

"I know he did," said Bloodhoof, bitterly.

"Do you know him, then?"

"I do."

"Are you aware that he was chased right across the ocean from Africa into these adjoining seas?"

"I am, and he commanded one of the finest, fastest-sailing crafts that ever touched the waters. She was a Baltimore clipper, that had been long in the Cuban slave trade, and had run many cargoes of niggers safely enough, and could show her heels to anything on the seas, in the sailing line. His name is Mungo."

"Mungo Brama?"

"Yes."

"Where is he now?"

"I don't know," said Bloodhoof, "and if I did I shouldn't split on him, you may depend on't."

"Is he a friend of yours, then?"

"No, quite on the other side—a villanous foe."

"Is he on your island?"

"No," said Bloodhoof, telling a lie. "He suffered severely in a gale lately, and anchored near us for awhile, but most likely he's back in Africa by this time. Not all the sailing ships in the world could ever catch him."

"Then that was the strange sail that fought against our schooner when we were engaged with you?"

"It was ; and a miracle you were not blown out of the water. You would have been, only the storm increased and separated all three of us ; but," added the hardened villain, "I should have rejoiced had your craft sunk to the bottom, and all hands with it."

Dick and Harry could scarcely control their rage at the coolness and effrontery of their enemy, but they raised him from the ground and helped him along through the woods, towards the spot where their sail-boat was moored, and they quickly put him on board, and having visited the treasure-cave, they made all haste away again from the Blue Rocks, greatly elated at the capture of their implacable enemy, and the spoil they had secured.

———

CHAPTER LXIX.

MUNGO'S CRUELTY TO GOVERNOR MARTIN'S WIFE.

THE sudden and mysterious disappearance of Bloodhoof from the Blue Rocks, and the evident sign of a deadly and bloody conflict which must have taken place near the ravine, as we have already described, with the unaccountable absence of Lasco, Bloodhoof's bosom friend, confirmed the buccaneers in their first idea that some of Lion Limb's men must have done the deed.

But whether their chief was still alive or dead sorely puzzled them, and they swore the most dreadful oaths that they would be avenged.

The uproar and commotion among them was something dreadful.

Mungo, in his heart, was delighted at the news, for it removed from his path a dangerous superior.

"Now," said he, "I am master here, and I will rule the Blue Rocks with a rod of iron."

A meeting was called immediately to decide upon what had best be done.

The discussion was a stormy one.

A hundred propositions were put before the meeting, but such was the clamour, jealousy, and discord that prevailed, that none of them were acted upon.

After discussing for more than an hour, Mungo rose, and begged leave to be heard.

At first the fierce men would not listen to anything he had to say.

The majority were for going to Lion Island immediately, and assailing the colony there, and laying it in waste with fire and sword.

"But how are you going to get there?" said Mungo. "We have but one small vessel, and that will not do; it's no use of talking about attacking and killing the young settlers before you are fully prepared."

"But we are prepared," said some angrily.

"We'll avenge Bloodhoof with our lives," shouted others.

"All right enough, my lads," said Mungo, with a sneer. "I know you liked Bloodhoof well enough, but you can't walk on the sea, can you?"

This last remark seemed to silence them all, for they knew that they were unable to leave the place without good craft to carry them, and as to setting out in mere row boats on such a hazardous expedition, the thing was impossible.

They therefore listened more attentively than before to what Mungo had to say, who rose again, and remarked—

"The only plan, and the wisest that I know, is this," said he, "if your temper and impatience will allow you to listen."

"What is it?"

"Let's have it!" shouted the noisy throng.

"Well, what I have got to say, is this," remarked Mungo; "you know, at least many of you have heard, that I have had years of travelling, and was on the best of terms with more than one of the chiefs of the Blue Rocks, long before the time of Nat the Don."

"We know it; what of that?"

"Well, a great many of you don't know, as I do, that there are other English settlers on some of the islands, not further than two days' sail from here, somewhere to the southward."

"Well, go on."

"These settlers are more numerous than Lion Limb's colony; and natives have told me long ago, that there is both plenty of gold and silver among them, for precious metals are abundant there."

"So much the better."

"But what do you intend to say or do?"

"Cut it short," said one and another.

"If you'll only listen," said Mungo, in an angry tone, "I'll soon tell you."

"What is it?"

"Out with it."

"Well, you all know that Bloodhoof, as the price of my life, made me promise to go to Africa, run a cargo or two of niggers, to buy a vessel and other things with the money, and make you all comfortable."

"We know it."

"Quite right too."

"Well, I didn't say it wasn't," said Mungo, getting red with anger, "but I know a shorter and a better way than to attempt all that in such a small leaky craft as the one you've given me. I can do all you want me to do in half the time."

"How?"

"Why, instead of risking our lives in crossing the Atlantic, and rounding the terrible Cape Horn, with its everlasting storms and dangers, I propose to sail down upon the settlements of these English, and force them to pay heavy ransoms for their lives; for, as I have said, the gold and silver ore which is reputed very abundant there, is of no earthly use to them or the natives either; then we can sail away to the South American ports, purchase a vessel, and whatever else you need, and return in half the time it would take us to get to Africa."

Murmurs of applause greeted Mungo's remarks, and he went on to explain at greater length the greater advantages of his own plan over that of Bloodhoof, who knew nothing of the English settlement and the golden ore which it possessed, but which natives had years before revealed to him.

"I shan't trouble myself about Lion's band yet," said Mungo. "Young Devil's Limb here won't trouble us again for some time yet, I know, for he and his followers seem only desirous of being let alone."

"But we shall trouble him though," growled many very savagely.

"Yes, with all my heart," said Mungo, "but not yet; let us prepare for it; wait until my return, and when we have a ship and guns as good as he has got, then Lion Limb shall know what we are made of, and have no mercy shown to him or his followers either."

That night and the following day Mungo and his friends were busily employed in preparing their new vessel, the "Vulture," for her intended cruise.

Contrary to Bloodhoof's orders, however, twice the number of men volunteered to go on the cruise, a circumstance that greatly pleased Mungo, who had reckoned rightly that the thoughts of money and plunder would soon gather around him as many friends as he had had enemies before.

Crowded in every part with its numerous crew, the "Vulture" set forth on its perilous voyage, and as the sun sank in the west, Mungo took the helm himself, and a fine breeze coming up, his craft soon disappeared from view, greatly to the joy and expectation of many rough-looking scoundrels, who, left behind, lined the tallest rocks to gaze on the craft in which their dearest hopes were embarked.

The wind carried the "Vulture" away through the waters at a terrific pace.

Once, a small vessel was perceived by them, following in their wake; but the "Vulture," though roughly put together, possessed extraordinary sailing qualities, and the strange vessel, whatever it was, soon disappeared and was seen no more.

The night turned very dark and stormy; but still onward the "Vulture" sped with almost unparalleled speed, and long before the break of day they espied the island and Fort Martin, the name of which they knew not.

Coasting along cautiously and steady, they came upon some villages in the distance, and resolved to anchor.

This they quickly did in a safe and convenient place, and leaving three or four men to mind their craft, Mungo and the rest landed.

They now divided themselves into four parties, and being well armed, marched silently towards the nearest village, but suddenly came upon a body of native islanders, half savage and nearly naked, who thus at night were prowling about the sheep-folds and villages, in hopes of living by plunder on the abundance provided by the industry and labour of their sober and hard-working rulers.

These natives at first supposed that they had been watched and surrounded by some of the settlers, and their fright and alarm was extreme, and they humbly craved for mercy in a jargon of broken English and their native tongue.

But when escape proved impossible, and they were hemmed in on all sides, and found that Mungo and his followers were the enemies of the English settlers there and had come on a plundering expedition, they were greatly rejoiced, and promised to follow Mungo anywhere.

From these natives the buccaneers learned that a great many of their leading people had gone away for a short time to visit a famous young white chief who had called at the island and had a fast-sailing schooner.

From their words and description there could not be a doubt but that this young white chief was none other than Lion Limb.

In answer to many questions the natives told Mungo all about Fort Martin, of its position, strength, and the number of its people.

It was too far inland for Mungo to think of marching there at present.

He resolved to attack and sack the villages nearest to him, and at once.

Promising the Indians all manner of rewards if they would follow him, Mungo led the way; and in half an hour the buccaneers and Indians assailed the place on all sides with fire and sword, to the great consternation of its peaceful inhabitants, three of whom alone were English, namely, Dame Margaret, the wife of Governor Martin, her only son, Roger, and an old negro named Snowdrop.

Roger and his mother had come into the village from Fort Martin, to reside there until her husband should return from Lion Island.

But at the moment of the attack Roger was away in the mountains, hunting among the streams for beavers and otters.

Snowdrop fought beside his old mistress for a long time, but perceiving the ferocious aspect of Mungo, poor Snowdrop took to his heels, and ran away for his dear life as fast as his legs would let him; nor did he stop nor stay until he found Roger and his young wife, to whom he related all that had happened at the settlement.

Roger was incensed at the idea that the buccaneers should have dared to descend upon the island settlements; but be started out that same hour, himself, Rachel, his wife, Snowdrop, and a half-breed named Zac.

Old Snowdrop was very loud and noisy in narrating what he had or had not done in the battle, and if any one would have believed him, Snowdrop would have passed off as a great warrior.

The old negro wished to appear well in the eyes and estimation of old Governor Martin's son, and so told scores of thumping lies.

But he could not satisfy him about the fate of his aged mother, whom he had left behind in the village, and who might for all he knew have fallen a victim to the rapacity and brutality of the stone-hearted and remorseless vagabonds from the Blue Rocks.

He would have flown to his mother's rescue on the wings of the wind, but that was impossible.

He followed the advice of old Snowdrop, who promised to lead him by a short cut to the village, by going along a lonely gorge, that led very close, in fact but 100 yards, to the settlement.

They travelled fast, but the paths were rocky and hard, and in many cases filled with mud.

Snowdrop had represented that this route through the gorge would prove both pleasant and safe.

But it was very far from pleasant, as Snowdrop afterwards confessed, for rats, hedgehogs, snakes, wild hogs, and other "varmint," as he called it, frequently detained them, and they had to fight their way through a whole pack of wolves, who had been prowling round sheep-folds and cattle pens.

Many a good round oath did Roger utter against the stupidity of Snowdrop, but he could not but laugh at the poor old negro, who, by going on first, had more than once fallen into mud holes and was very far from looking pleasant or beautiful.

The road had proved much longer than either old Snowdrop or Roger had expected; and towards morning and after the sun had risen, they found themselves still walking in the ravine, a sort of covered way full of hills and declivities, walled in by rows of tall trees, the boughs of which met in a thick arch over their heads.

By degrees they approached closer and closer to the little settlement, and found themselves enveloped in smoke and dazzled by the red reflection of distant burning buildings.

They heard in the distance clamours and noises that rang through the air, and at length on emerging from the ravine they suddenly became witness to a strange spectacle.

One of the companies of privates were camped upon the green and extensive turf of a wooded glade, in the midst of which rose, in the form of a half circle, long rows of sheep and cattle folds.

Afar off could be heard the neighing of horses, the lowing of oxen, and the barking of dogs, driven as they had been by fire from stables, stalls, and outhouses.

The green sward was enclosed on all sides by forest trees, except on one side, where houses still stood burning at the foot of steep hills.

In the midst lay mirrored a large pond or pool of water.

No one for a moment doubted but that the destruction visible on every hand had been the wanton sport of the pirates.

The buccaneers, however, and their savage Indian friends, were crouched upon the sward, laughing and drinking and enjoying the scene of destruction around them.

Cows, bulls, goats, sheep, dogs, and wild horses were galloping furiously about in all directions through the smoke and flames, goring each other and madly fighting.

These sights only seemed to whet the appetites of the blood-loving wretches who, regaling themselves with prime joints of beef and mutton, were laughing boisterously.

Some of the villains, half drunk and bent on every sort of mischief, ran and gave chase to horses and animals of every description, shooting them at will, or driving them headlong by droves into the large pond or lake, where they were drowned or bled to death amid the deafening yells of the savages on all sides.

Directly Roger came in view of the scene of destruction, where but a few hours before all had been peace and plenty, he turned deadly pale, and stood scanning the burning landscape in hopes of detecting, if possible, the figure of his aged mother, perhaps a captive among the brutal revellers; or, perhaps, could catch a glimpse of any of the half-breed villagers who had been driven from their homes, or slain, perhaps, in defending them.

But neither one nor the other could he see.

He strained his eyes more and more, and at last caught sight of some human object which was tied to a stake in the water, around which a score of Mungo's men were assembled, pelting with mud and stones.

"Inhuman wretches," gasped Roger, who resolved to creep through the brushwood and thus come close upon them without either of his friends being perceived.

"Nay, do not, I beg you, do not approach those inhuman monsters any nearer," said Rachel, young Roger's wife; "we are but four and they are many; let us fly before they perceive and fall upon us."

"No," said Roger, "that would be cowardice; let us go and rescue the prisoner, if even we die."

"It is not your mother, Roger," said Rachel, "do not go nearer. I know it is not old Margaret."

"It matters not," said Roger, "I can now plainly see that the victim is a woman, and whether it be my aged mother or not, it matters not, we must act as men, if even we die in the attempt to rescue her. Follow me."

Roger dashed into a low copse wood, followed by Rachel, Snowdrop, and Zac.

They were unperceived for some time, and the old negro, going before the rest, he soon came in full view of the brutal scene which the buccaneers were enacting at the edge of the lake.

Old Snowdrop nearly fainted as he recognised in the victim no less a person than Dame Margaret, Roger's mother.

She was up to her neck in the mirey pool.

Her brown woollen hood had fallen on her shoulders, and suffered her thin grey locks to float about wildly in the wind.

Her long, lean, and bony arms were cruelly fastened to a stake, but an iron resolution was revealed in her pale blue eyes, in the quivering of her nostrils, and thin pale lips.

Roger came up at that moment, and seemed transfixed to the earth when he beheld his own mother thus tortured.

He could not speak, but his lips trembled as he held back his wife from gazing on the harrowing scene.

"Well, old hag," said one of the buccaneers, in a drunken tone, "well, old hag, what do you think of us now, eh? Where are all your valorous islanders? Where is that son you were raving about just now?"

"Has the cold bath cooled you, old girl?" said another.

"If she won't tell us where old Martin has hidden all his gold and silver ore, we'll burn her alive."

"Listen to me, old hag," said Mungo; "if you only tell me where the gold and silver and pearls are, we will set you at liberty; but if not, you shall be pelted to death with stones."

"You are fiends, not men," old Margaret gasped; "you speak English, it is true, but you are worse than cannibals."

"Cease your babbling, old hag," said Mungo, with an oath; "keep your mouth closed and die where you are quietly; if not, I shall put a bullet through your head very quickly. Where is the treasure hidden, I say?"

"No, no," said several at once, "shooting is too good for the old sorceress; throw a rope round her neck and hang her up on the highest tree to serve as a scarce-crow to all who come this way."

"Nay, nay, let the old witch die where she is, and if anyone should ever have the boldness to come forward and avenge her, I will write my name on this rock here, so that all may hereafter know and fear me."

Roger, who had been as if it were spellbound, now suddenly dashed out from his place of concealment, pounced like a wolf on the nearest buccaneer, seized his sword, and before any one could recover from surprise, he stood face to face with Mungo, and sword in hand. "I have come, villain," said he, in trembling tones. "I know I am in the very midst of enemies, but I care not; death is better than dishonour."

Old Margaret had perceived her son, and fainted; but Mungo, who retreated a few steps, looked with contempt at the small stature of young Roger, and said sneeringly—

"Oh, you have come at last, eh, and challenge me?"

"I do," gasped Roger, bursting with fury.

"Kill him! kill him!" shouted Mungo's followers.

"Nay, don't touch him," said Mungo, in tones of contempt. "Leave him to me."

And then approaching one or two steps nearer to Roger, he said, "Would you mock me, fellow? I have not time to banter with such a scare-crow as you are; and yet it is but right I should teach you manners in a rough way."

Roger smiled with scorn, as he said, "Poor fool, you were brave enough just now when talking to a poor helpless old woman; but when you face a man, you lower your voice and retreat before him."

And then, in a sudden burst of anger, he said, "Fight, I say, or by the blue heavens above us, I will, before all your ruffian crew, drive you naked from this glade."

The tall African, with red hair, eagle nose, and powerful frame, heard Roger's words, and they acted on him as if he had received a heavy blow on the head.

He never dreamed of meeting with such an enemy; and, in spite of his herculean proportions compared with the slight lithe figure of Rogers, he in his heart wished to avoid a combat which would, if even successful, redound neither to his honour or glory, nor profit to himself or followers.

"It does not become the conqueror of this island to fight a prisoner," said Mungo, biting his lip with vexation and rage.

"I am got a prisoner," said Roger, "nor shall I be while I breathe, nor are you the conqueror of this island."

"Strike the rascal dead," said many angry voices. "Don't take much trouble in displaying your sword play. Chop off his head at once."

"He is not worthy of my steel," said Mungo.

"Then this for your valour, boasting savage," said Roger, and he tossed his beaver skin cap into Mungo's face.

In an instant the African sprang forward like a bull pierced by an arrow, and their swords instantly crossed for the encounter.

In a moment a ring was formed.

"Mungo will soon polish him off," said one.

"The vultures will have a rare feast to-day," laughed others.

But Roger heard not what they said.

He watched his tall opponent like a cat does a mouse, and seemed full of confidence.

The first stroke which Roger dealt at Mungo came within an inch of cutting his head into halves.

As it was, it seemed to stun him, and had it not been for an old steel cap which the savage African wore, he would have been felled to the earth like an ox.

Indignant at this, Mungo sought to repair the affront, and aimed a savage cut in return at Roger's head, but missed, and the blade coming in contact with a tree near which they stood foot to foot, it entered into the wood and snapped in pieces.

In an instant Roger leaped upon Mungo!

The latter with his right hand seized the deadly weapon which was thrust at his throat!

THE BOY KING
OF THE SOUTH·SEA ISLANDS.

MARGARET MARTIN IN THE HANDS OF THE BUCCANEERS.

As it was he was wounded in the arm, and his face was fearfully gashed, so that, mad with rage and shame, and almost blinded by the blood which streamed down his face over his clothes, he could no longer distinctly see his opponent, whose sword he clutched and held with the firmness of a vice.

"Part them! part them!" shouted the buccaneers who were greatly surprised and annoyed at th turn events had taken.

"Hold off! leave me to finish my battle!" shouted Roger.

The buccaneers now closed around the two com-

No. 24.

batants, and Roger would have been cut in twain; but at that moment Mungo fell heavily to the earth shouting,

"Hands off, men! hands off!"

They obeyed, and as Roger, panting and flushed, stood over him, Mungo gasped,

"Young man, you and your friends are free. You have fought well and valiantly; your life is granted without ransom. You have true English blood in your veins; you must be the very devil himself."

The buccaneers were at first disposed to treat what Mungo had promised like a jest; but directly he rose from the ground—the chief ordered old Margaret to be released, and sent her away, escorted by her gallant son, who, with Rachel his wife, left the spot with the air of conquerors.

Old Snowdrop the negro, and Zac the half-breed, had bolted from their hiding-place when the fight began, and ran like two escaped lunatics; but just when they began to think they were far away and perfectly safe they rushed right into the midst of a second band of Mungo's men, who were approaching their chief's camping place from a different direction.

Poor old Snowdrop tried to escape this second peril, but a shot was fired after him, and took off a bit of his ear.

Fancying that another shot might drill a hole through his head, he fell flat on his face, gasping and blowing like a stranded fish.

"Stop, Zac, stop, you tief, or you'll be dead afore you git haf de road to Fort Martin."

But Zac was not inclined to stop.

He ran along like a hare, and was perfectly blind as to where he was going to, until at last his thick head came into sudden contact with the stout limb of a tree, and he fell back all of a heap.

In a few moments both the runaways were made prisoners, and guarded by the buccaneers.

For a few moments neither of the prisoners were able to speak.

They had run so far, and so fast, that old Snowdrop's legs bent under him, and had they not kicked and cuffed the old darkie and thus knocked new life in him, there is no telling when he would have found the use of his tongue again.

The old negro puffed and blowed and rolled his eyes so wildly, first on one side and then on the other, and his teeth chattered so loudly, that one might have thought his jaws would have been rent asunder.

He and the half-breed, Zac, shivered and shook as if they had the ague, and notwithstanding much rough usage, they could not utter half-a-dozen words properly.

"What are you going to do with these two dogs?" asked one of the men to the leader of his party.

"Why shoot them if they ain't English."

"They are not English, then," said the first one, pulling out his pistol. "I'll soon find out what countrymen they are."

And putting the muzzle of his weapon to Snowdrop's head the darkie soon found the use of his tongue again, and roared out with a gasping voice,

"Yah! yah! massa, me English! D-d-don't shoot, please, massa, me true English, 'pon my word."

"How can he be English," said another, "he's a darkie?"

"No, massa, I'm English. D-d-don't shoot, please don't; I'm English, I tell you, massa; I'm d——d if I ain't, there!" said Snowdrop.

"Oh, yes, he's English," said one, "or he couldn't swear so well."

"Yes, me English, no mistake," said Snowdrop, wiping the perspiration from his brow. "Me true English; no mistake."

"Can you fight? Are you brave?"

"Me?" said Snowdrop, winking and blinking, and rolling his 'eyes. "Oh! yah! me brave as a bull, and fight like de berry debil," said Snowdrop, grinning. "Oh! yah! me berry brave; no mistake; real English me, massa!"

"Glad to hear it," said one. "We'll soon give you a chance to prove it. We are going to Fort Martin. Do you know it?"

"Oh, yes, me come from dar, massa."

"Well, then, you must show us the way. We shall there join three other bands of our men. If you are honest and brave, and all that, we'll spare your life, darkie; but if not you must pay a ransom for your life, and then be sold in slavery for ever."

Snowdrop tried to smile; but he couldn't.

"Next week we shall be masters of the whole island, darkie," said one.

"Yah! berry easy to take Fort Martin. De ole guv'nor's away now, and de grown men too."

"Glad to hear it."

"What are you gwine to do wid Zac dar? He no brave; him no English. He run away; him half-breed, massa."

"He must purchase his life with gold or silver, or else we'll make him food for the crows," said the leader.

Zac was even more dead than alive already, and he didn't at all seem to care what they did or said to him.

He knew very well that he'd have to fight for one party or another, and as he expected that some stray bullet would finish him shortly, he didn't seem to care, but took things very coolly, and was accordingly kicked and cuffed all the more by his captors, who placed a heavy burden on his back, greatly to the pleasure of old Snowdrop, who smiled.

But he soon had to laugh the wrong side of his mouth, for the buccaneers put an extra load on the old negro, which almost weighed him down to the ground; and old Snowdrop, now that they had turned him into a beast of burden, bitterly bewailed his fate, every yard he was compelled to travel.

CHAPTER LXX.

MUNGO AND HIS MEN ATTACK FORT MARTIN—MUNGO AND HIS PRISONERS—THEIR RANSOM IN GOLD, AND WHAT CAME OF IT.

A LONG, long journey it was, to Fort Martin, but the buccaneers, in four gangs, having learned that the old governor and a great many of his principal fighting men had gone with Lion Limb, rejoiced greatly at the pleasant news, and made up their minds not to leave the island until they had extorted all they could out of the panic-stricken people, both English and half-breeds.

The buccaneers travelled very fast in order to arrive at Fort Martin before the news of their descent upon the island should be made known to the peaceful inhabitants.

But bad news travels fast, they say, and although the invaders were on foot both night and day, they did not reach Fort Martin before very many unpleasant rumours had been circulated at the Fort.

At first the good people there were loth to believe the strange and thrilling reports.

They had never heard of buccaneers in the islands adjacent, or if they had they paid no heed to any such reports, for their peace and quiet had never before been disturbed.

Not one in ten would give any credit to the many rumours that were flying about, and accordingly they made no preparations for defence.

When least they expected it, however, their enemies were upon them,

For the four bands of buccaneers, advancing from different directions, arrived before Fort Martin in exceeding quick time, and joined their forces.

Old Snowdrop and Zac were sent before them with a guard to each; and the poor prisoners, in fear of their lives, went boldly up to the gates of the place, and reported that the persons approaching were not enemies, but friends, and some of Lion Limb's colonists, who had come there unexpectedly to visit and stay some time with them.

The thoughts of meeting the ever-green, ever-gay Joe Pebbles and his fiddle again, acted like a charm upon the joyful half-breeds, who opened the gates with loud expressions of gladness.

But directly this was done, up came the buccaneers, each band led by a ruthless officer, and sword in hand they dashed into the place, and soon the tumult within became alarming and general.

Old Snowdrop and Zac were only too happy to escape the scene of carnage, and were permitted to depart for the time being on solemnly promising to ransom themselves in three days hence, at the price of twenty ounces of pure gold for each and all who thought proper to accept the conditions.

Besides Snowdrop and Zac, some six others promised to ransom themselves on like conditions, and left the fort on a prowling expedition among the savage Indians in another part of the island, among whom there was reported to be a large amount of precious metal, in the shape of rings and ornaments of every description.

For two days and nights Zac, Snowdrop, and six others were among the Indians, collecting all the gold they could, by giving various articles in exchange; but the natives seemed very loth to part with their ornaments and trinkets; so that at the end of the second day, they determined to retrace their steps towards Fort Martin, throw themselves at the feet of their hard and conscienceless masters, and trust to their generosity and mercy.

After being almost starved for two days, these mean, dusty, and footsore wanderers lay in the woods all night and tried to sleep, but the thoughts of the ropes which awaited each, should they not gather the gold, kept them from sleep.

Next day, about eight in the morning, these eight wanderers on foot, unarmed, and in pitiable plight, were mournfully pursuing their way along the road which led to Fort Martin, when they espied through the foilage of rows of olive trees a small inn, which they walked up to and entered for the purpose of procuring some scant refreshment.

A wrinkled and sunburnt hag, who combined the functions of waiter and scullion, on seeing the tattered and deplorable condition of the new comers, and knowing nothing of what was or had taken place at the Fort, hesitated to bring the strangers any wine, as she very much doubted their capability of making any recompence.

Fortunately, the inn-keeper, who was a half-bred Englishman, recognizing in these eight poor devils some of his own countrymen, hastened to produce a large jar of native wine, which he deposited on the rudely made table around which the eight travellers were seated.

"I hope," said he, placing a ninth goblet by the side of the other eight, "that you will not refuse an English islander who was born here, the pleasure of emptying a jug or two with his fellow countrymen?"

"With all my heart," said Zac; "these are hard times for all of us, and we oughtn't to be over particular as to a shade or two of colour; eh, Snowdrop?"

"Ah," said the darkie, "you may well say dat, Massa Zac, me have seen 'em we has, and mighty ugly devils dey is."

"I understand you, lads," said the landlord; "I've heard all about what's going on up at the Fort; but I didn't tell the old woman, or she'd go into fits."

"They haven't given you a visit then yet?" said Zac.

"No, not yet; I'm in such an out-of-the-way place, that I sometimes think they'll never find me; but ain't you afraid, my friends, to go so near the camps of the invaders?"

"No, no, we ain't afraid of them, are we Snowdrop?" said Zac.

"No, not me," said the negro who, at the same time was shivering with fear. "What's de use ob being scared? If we run away, dey sure to find us."

"Make yourselves easy on our account, Mr. Host," said Zac; "we don't mean to give the vagabond buccaneers the trouble to run after us, do we Snowdrop?"

"No, not us," said the negro, who was drinking goblet after goblet of the raw wine to keep his courage up, "for ebery debil on us have sworn to enter Fort Martin dis very night."

"Into the Fort," said the host, "why, the cut-throat devils are masters of the place, and every one of you will be—"

"Hung, I suppose."

"Yes, of course you will."

"Me know it very well, landlord—we are going there on purpose."

"What, to be hung?"

"Just so."

"The devil!" said the landlord.

"It can't be helped, Mr. Landlord," said Zac. "We were all taken prisoners, and paroled on the promise that on the third day we should return and be hung directly, unless we found twenty ounces of gold each as a ransom."

"In that case," said the landlord, "I suppose many of you won't be in any particular hurry to take yourselves back again; for twenty ounces of gold for each of you is not very easy to find, although, at one time, as I can well remember, there used to be plenty of golden ore among the Indians; indeed, they used to make playthings of it for their children."

"What you say, is quite true, landlord," said Zac, with a deep-drawn sigh.

At the same time he detached a small bag from his girdle, and emptied the contents on the table.

"That's all the eight of us have been able to gather; and for that small quantity we have run the risk of our lives among the untamed natives, and have been compelled to part with nearly every blessed thing we had, except our shirts and trousers. I much doubt if there is over twenty ounces in all."

"Poor devils," said the host; "you must surely hang, my dear friends, for there are not scarcely twenty ounces, as I live."

"Well, even that amount is not to be despised. It is very nearly, if not quite sufficient to ransom one."

"There will then be only seven to be hung," said the landlord, sorrowfully. "Poor devils; who is the lucky one among you who is not going to be hung then?"

"I vote dat Massa Zac has it, for he has got a wife and two children—dis darkie hasn't no friends except de Crows."

"My wife is young and strong," said Zac, "and my two children can earn their own bread. Let the twenty ounces go to Snowdrop, he is the only true full-blooded Englishman among us."

"Yes, yes, well said," the others joined in, "well said, Zac, we are only half-breeds, but an Englishman's life is worth ten of ours, for they have dragged us out of cannabalism. Let old Snowdrop have the twenty ounces, we'll be content to die."

"Well den," said old Snowdrop, winking and blinking, "as you say I'm an Englishman, I accept de ounces; but, to show you what an Englishman is when his monkey is up, I'll tell you, Massa Landlord, what I'll do with it."

"What?"

"Why, take de ounces, and we'll eat it! Prepare a good feed for ebery one; let de fat ob de land come out ob de kitchen; bring in de best ob eberyting. We sing English songs, get drunk as fiddlers, and den let's hang all together."

"Bravo, Snowdrop, bravo," shouted the poor devils.

"We will have a good meal, spend all the gold, and let the cut-throat buccaneers go to the devil," said Zac.

"Yah, yah, dat's it, Massa Zac," said Snowdrop. "You talk like a real Englishman now. I'se too old to do much good now, so hanging won't hurt me much. I'll do bery well to hang up in a tree near a corn field, to scare de crows. Throw down de ounces, Massa Zac, we all good English here; let's have a jolly good feed, and drink confusion to our hangmen."

All the eight unfortunates, now heated with native wine, jumped to their feet, and drank success to the proposition.

All, except the landlord, seemed merry.

But he was dumb with astonishment.

At length, he said—

"No, no; you shall not spend the twenty ounces so, it is the life of one man. I cannot obey you; I will not do such a thing. Let me give you a piece of good advice."

"Be quick about it then," said Zac, "for our time is short."

"Well, then, eat, drink, and be merry; have the best I have, and in one word——"

"All right, what next?"

"Drink till you all fall fast asleep, [and then forget to go to the fort to night."

"That can't be, we've given our word; and if we lived to see all this out, and it should come to the ears of old Governor Martin, that we perjured ourselves——"

"Why, they are cut-throats and murderers."

"Never mind, we have given them our solemn word of honour, and must keep it—such has always been the teaching of old Martin."

"Poor old man, 'tis a pity he's away," said the landlord; "he saved my life once, and to him I owe everything I have in the world."

"That don't surprise us, host, for our old governor is capable of everything that is good and kind. It was an evil day that he and many of our people left the fort to go with that young hair-brained leader, Lion Limb."

After a short time, the worthy landlord prepared a substantial meal for his hungry guests, who greedily devoured it, and drank much of his wine.

"'Tis hard that you should all hang for a few ounces of gold," said the landlord, thoughtfully, "and as you all seem such jolly good fellows, I think I can manage to rake and scrape sufficient together to save your lives."

"What, all of us?"

"Yes, all of you."

"Are you mad? Is he dreaming?" said one and another, astonished.

"What, one hundred and sixty ounces of gold!"

"Yes, neither more nor less," said the landlord, smiling.

"Why, there isn't a man in the whole island that has so much," said Zac.

"No one, perhaps, except myself," said the landlord; "but what is the use of hoarding treasure in such a place as this island is? It came easily, and may go easily, for all I care."

"I begin to think the landlord am a good sort ob fellow arter all," said Snowdrop."

"How did you ever get so much, landlord?" said Zac.

"Very easily, my boys; the old governor gave me this piece of land, and taught me to brew and all that, and when the friendly Indian tribes used to go to the fort, they often camped close by here; they drank my beer and wine, and I helped myself to their gold ornaments, while they lay around drunk and insensible."

"Oh, he's a true Englishman," said Snowdrop, grinning.

"But old Governor Martin must know of it."

"It ain't likely I was ever going to tell him. I hid away the gold, in case there should ever be a row about it; and thought, perhaps, some day I might visit England I've heard so much about. Them times are all gone now though," sighed the landlord, "and the gold isn't of any use among us."

"It is now, though, eh, Snowdrop?"

"I believe, Massa Zac; we no hang dis time. Bring along de stuff, landlord."

The landlord disappeared, and quickly returned with two bags of gold, which he gave to Zac and Snowdrop.

The eight doomed men embraced and hugged the landlord by turns, and almost wrenched his hands off as they parted.

The worthy landlord also gave them plenty of food to last them on their journey to the fort, and they went on their way rejoicing.

When they approached the fort, and were only about a mile from it, they perceived approaching them, a tall, ugly-looking, ferocious, and well-armed man.

Zac and Snowdrop instantly recognised Mungo in the stranger, and they began to tremble in every limb.

"How de debil he get here!" said old Snowdrop; "he ought to be dead about dis time, considering what Massa Roger gave him."

"Let us be respectful," said Zac, "don't say anything—here he comes on his mule and looking ugly as sin."

When the eight trembling prisoners of war found themselves very near to Mungo, they saluted him very humbly, and almost bowed themselves to the ground.

Mungo was about to pass them with a scornful smile, when his quick eye caught sight of the two bags, which old Snowdrop and Zac vainly tried to hide under their tattered garments.

"Hello!" growled Mungo, with glistening eyes. "What mean those bags, trembling rascals? whither are you bound?"

"To de fort, kind gentle sar," mumbled Snow-drop.

"With those two bags?"

"Yah, massa."

"What do they contain?"

"Gold, massa."

"What for? How much?"

"One-hundred-and-sixty ounces, massa, to ran-som de lives of de seven white folks and myself."

Mungo's heart beat with joy at this good news, and he resolved to possess himself of the whole amount, and let the eight prisoners escape the halter as best they could.

"Why, you sneaking hounds, you are telling me lies, I know you are," said he savagely.

Then shrugging his shoulders with an air of in-credulity, he said—

"It is impossible that] such dirty, dusty, ugly, tattered devils as you are to have become possessed of such a sum by any honest means."

"We came by it honestly, sir," said Zac, pluck-ing up a spirit, "and it would surprise you to know that we became possessed of all the sum in less than five minutes."

"I can't believe your story; but how did all this happen, knaves?"

"We owe it all to a generous man, whose house you can see from here."

"Stuff and nonsense; you must think I am a fool to believe such lies as that. Say that you stole it, rascals, and, perhaps, killed the owner."

"But all of us can swear to what I say," Zac remarked.

"Liars, and fools, I shall hang every one of you. Don't talk to me. I know you birds of a feather flock together. You can't deceive me. My name is Mungo, recollect."

"We are all honest men, sir," said Zac; "poor, but unfortunate."

"Unfortunate, eh?" said Mungo, hoarsely; "very fortunate, I think, without your friend has palmed off on you worthless earth instead of nuggets; it may not be gold after all; he may have given it to get rid of such dirty, hungry vagabonds."

At the mere thought that, perhaps, after all, they had been hugging and tugging along only worthless pyrites instead of golden ore, made the eight un-fortunates turn deadly pale.

"If I thought he had so tricked us," said Zac, "I'd go back and give him a right good trouncing."

"And I too, Massa Zac," said Snowdrop, gloomily.

"Open the two bags, and let me examine them," said Mungo.

They did so with trembling hands.

Mungo examined the ore with greedy eyes.

"No, by Jupiter! it's right good stuff, and pure metal; but now I am convinced that you did not get it honestly," said he, "and shall keep the bags."

"You still believe us thieves and robbers, then?" said Zac.

"I do, slaves, of course I do; you are the truest picture of graceless vagabonds I ever saw in all my travels; at all events, now the bags are in my hands I shall not part with them until I know whether your story is really true or not."

"Shall we follow you, massa, to de cottage yonder?"

"No need to follow me at all. I shall go alone, and get you to the camp as soon as possible, and be hanged every one."

The eight poor devils looked at one another rue-fully, and knew not what to do or say.

"Could we not go with you, sir," said Zac, "and carry the bags, it would save you the time and trouble?"

"Oh! by the horns of Satan!" exclaimed Mungo, "I never felt stronger in my life than I do at this particular moment; so strong, indeed, my fine fellows, that I could not only carry half-a-dozen such bags as these, but strong enough also to break every bone in the carcasses of every one of you if you dare to whimper and follow me. Begone, villains, and hang."

So speaking, Mungo trotted away on his mule, bags and all, and quickly disappeared.

"It's all up wid us now, Massa Zac," said Snow-drop.

"So it is, Snowdrop; before to-morrow morning the vultures will make a good meal out of us." And disheartened, the unfortunate eight crawled along towards the fort.

———

CHAPTER LXXI.

OLD GOVERNOR MARTIN NARRATES HOW HE AND HIS FRIENDS LANDED ON THE ISLAND, AND FORMED THEIR COLONY—THRILLING ACCOUNT OF THE WRECK OF AN EMIGRANT SHIP.

As might have been supposed, there was no one in Lion Limb's colony who attracted more of Governor Martin's attention than Miss Emma Clarence; and, in their conversations beside the blazing log fire at night, the good old man often told to her many of his adventures.

"How came we to land in the island, my child?" said the old man, smiling. "Well, I can soon explain, if you will only favour me with your attention. My narrative is a thrilling one, but shall be put into as few words as possible.

"Well, then, you must know that ours was an emigrant ship, bound for the colonies. We had on board an assorted cargo, and a good many passengers, both male, female, and children, besides a stout and hardy crew. All went well with us until after we had rounded Cape Horn; and then our miseries began.

"We called at one of the islands for water and wood; and had proceeded on our voyage again, with light and merry hearts. But a storm set in, and though not violent, lasted for several days.

"I went to bed one night in a very moody state of mind; for although I did not tell any of the passengers of what I dreaded, for I knew the South Seas better than they did.

"But I had not slept long before I started up suddenly.

"The voice of the captain aroused me from my reverie. 'We shall have a greasy night I doubt,' said he, anxiously looking round towards the re-ceding land.

"I turned to gaze upon it.

"Masses of dense and marble-like clouds en-veloped it.

"The evening was waning, and although there was scarcely enough of wind to fill the sails, there was that uneasy motion of the waves, termed by seamen, 'a short sea,' and occasionally fitful squalls of wind swept past us, hurrying the vessel for an instant with the swiftness of a meteor, and then leaving her to plough her sluggish course, rolling and pitching as the short abrupt seas struck her, now forward and then aft.

"Everything, as the captain observed, seemed ominous of a squally night; nor was he deceived.

"I had continued on deck listlessly watching

the crew as they bustled about the ship and rigging, making all snug in anticipation of the gale; till at length the perfect stillness about me, broken only by the booming of the sea against the ship's sides, and the creaking of the masts and rigging, warned me of the lateness of the hour.

"I descended to my berth.

"It was then blowing a fresh breeze from the N.E.

"I suspect I had slept about three hours, when I awoke and found the ship lying down nearly on her beam ends, and by the rapid rush of waters past her sides, I knew that a heavy squall must have caught her.

"There was a great stir above, and the boatswain was turning up all hands.

"I rushed immediately on deck.

"The night was pitchy dark, and the wind had freshened to a hard gale.

"All the following day it increased.

"By night it blew a furious tempest, and the heavy sea increasing, literally rose mountains high.

"We had hitherto laid on our course, but the wind now hauled round to the eastward; to ease her, the captain sent down the top-gallant masts, mizen top-masts, and jib-boom, and kept as close to the wind as the violence of the weather would permit.

"But the sea canted her head off, so that she made more lee than headway, and the rigging was terribly strained with the work.

"About daybreak a tremendous storm tore the foresail in ribbons.

"We had now but a close-reefed main-topsail, and fore-trysail set, every hand refusing to go aloft to bend another sail to the fore-yard, so that we had little hope of keeping off the shore, near to which we imagined we must have driven.

"The gale too seemed to increase.

"The sky was one vast black cloud, and the rain fell so thick that we scarce could distinguish an object from the wheel to the mainmast.

"One pump had been constantly at work for the last three and twenty hours; but the water gained so fast upon her that we were obliged to rig the weather one, and even then we could scarcely keep it under.

"About noon, however, the rain ceased.

"The atmosphere cleared, and the wind lulled, and then our spirits revived.

"The captain now determined, if possible, to wear the ship.

"After a hard struggle we succeeded and found to our great joy that she made better weather on this tack, as the sea now headed her, and she had time to rise to one sea before another struck her.

"By four p.m. we had gained considerably on her.

"She had still some water between decks, but nothing to be alarmed at, and though we had battened down the hatches there was such a weight of water on deck from the continual seas she shipped that it was impossible to keep them perfectly tight.

"Our anxiety was in a great measure dispelled, and we sat down to the first comfortable meal we had enjoyed since leaving the island.

"The weather continued moderate for the whole of the two following days, and with a fair and leading breeze we rapidly sped on our way.

"It was now the fifth evening since our departure.

"The day had been sultry, and the captain and myself stood upon the poop conversing in high spirits.

"Suddenly it became very dark, and now distant thunder was audible from the south-west, dark clouds gathered in that quarter, and they waxed more and more dense till they almost covered the horizon, and seemed but just suspended over us.

"The wind which had hitherto been north-east, was now perfectly lulled.

"The captain started up in evident alarm, and hastily summoned his crew.

"In a moment the decks swarmed with men, and the bustle and activity succeeded the perfect stillness which had prevailed but an instant before.

"The sailors shouted as they clung aloft to the yards, and those on deck responded.

"Blocks and slackened cordage clattered, and the sails flapped and dashed heavily as they hung in the trails.

"Something serious was evidently anticipated.

"The captain had his eyes steadily fixed on the quarter whence the ominous appearances gathered, and every gaze seemed to strengthen his apprehension.

"He beckoned to the mate and muttered something to him in a low tone.

"The man turned deadly pale, and exclaimed, "'Good God! should it be so.'

"'Hush!' said the captain, 'say nothing, but bear a hand and make all snug before it reaches us.'

"I asked him if he apprehended very bad weather?

"His abrupt and morose answers increased in uneasiness, and I descended to the quarter deck.

"The boatswain was here seeing to the battening down of the hatchways, and to him I repeated my question.

"This fellow, a Swede, I believe, the most phlegmatic fellow in the world, just raised his huge body from his stooping position, and turning a plug of tobacco in his mouth, growled out,

"'I believe it vos a taam'd hurricane a brewing,' went coolly on with his work.

"I had seen the terrible effects of these convulsions of nature on shore, and was aware they were not less fatal on the ocean.

"My heart sickened, and I gave up all on board as lost.

"I leant over the star-board-quarter with my eyes fixed on the terrible south-west.

"Presently a cloud of a very extraordinary nature arose above the horizon.

"Its colour was a dark gloomy red, and it seemed palpable to the touch.

"It appeared almost to reach the surface of the ocean, and to approach towards us.

"I looked at the captain.

"He also had seen it, and the expression of his face was hopeless.

"'Captain,' I said, 'do you anticipate danger?'

"He made no reply, but mournfully shook his head, and continued his hurried walk athwart the break of the poop.

"The terrible phenomenon approached nearer and nearer, and we could now hear the shrill howling of the wind and the breaking and boiling of the sea.

"A few men yet lingered in the rigging.

"The captain shouted to them to make haste down again, and the sound of his voice too plainly evinced the state of his mind. It was sad and mournful.

"The crew were fully aware of their perilous position, and they had clustered together on the main-deck in silent and stupid bewilderment.

"At last it reached us.

"The maddened elements, with lightning and

rain, tempest and sea, seemed to have poured forth all their fury for our annihilation.

"The ship whirled round and round.

"Every timber and plank trembled.

"The masts and yards creaked and bent like twigs.

"One huge sea struck her fore and aft, for a space engulphing her beneath it.

"Then she rose trembling and quivering to the summit of a mountainous wave.

"Again, with the swiftness of an arrow, she plunged into the fearful hollow beneath.

"Thus, for a time, did she drive, totally ungovernable, at the mercy of the waves.

"Meanwhile, I had clung to the mizen-mast.

"My heart beat convulsively, and perfect consciousness forsook me.

"At length I felt the ship shooting as it were to the sky and again hurled back again.

"There was a fearful pause, followed by the mighty rushing of waters by the crash of timber; and a wild shriek of agony and despair arose even above the howlings of the tempest.

"The foremast and bowsprit both were gone, and had carried with them three unhappy wretches in their fall.

"At last the day beamed, and the hopeless state of our ship was but too plainly visible.

"The hurricane had indeed broken, but the wind, though it continued to one point, blew with the most fearful violence.

"We had no sail set, and we rolled, gunwale under, in the trough of the sea.

"At length several waves successively struck her and dashed over every part.

"The hatches were driven in, and the decks below were deluged in torrents, till at last the water burst upwards again, carrying everything before it from the waist to the forecastle.

"The ship now seemed rapidly settling down.

"The decks were knee-deep in water.

"Horror was in every face, despair in every bosom.

"Vainly did we stretch our eyes to catch, if possible, an approaching sail, but nothing could we see but water, water, water!

"The crew, as the only place of safety (for the decks were torn up), had collected on the quarter-deck, holding on by the staunchions and bulwarks to save themselves from the furious seas that almost momentarily broke over them.

"At length, one of the men suggested, as a means of delaying at least the catastrophe that seemed ineviatble, that the main and mizen masts should be cut away; but then, who would be hardy enough to put the suggestion into execution?

"Alas! every arm was unnerved, every heart paralysed.

"'A few minutes more,' uttered the captain.

"The ominous words seemed to fall from him almost unconsciously.

"'O God!' he exclaimed, vehemently; 'and is there no one among you who will make an effort to save her?'

"He seized a hatchet, and sprang over the side into the starboard main chains, exclaiming—

"'Let him that would preserve himself follow me!'

"Urged either by shame, or the hope of saving themselves, two or three obeyed the summons.

"The rigging was cut away—the masts, without any support, creaked and nodded.

"The ship, struck by a great sea, lurched fearfully—again right suddenly—and the masts were gone.

"It was noon, and since day-break, or a little after, had we been in a manner water-logged, clinging, or lashed to the wreck, the furious sea every moment washing over us.

"Near to me sat the wife of the Governor of Victoria, one arm clasped around her pale child, the other passed through a ring bolt.

"Her long hair matted together, hung wildly about her neck and over her features, and her white dress, heavy with water, clung to her spare, emaciated figure.

"The ship now became weaker and weaker, and the sea began to make greater inroads.

"From the mainmast forward she was already under water, and further aft but a few inches remained above the surface.

"We could hear the washing of the cargo in the hold—and now she began to break up forward.

"One boat yet remained little injured, a cutter, on the larboard quarter.

"She was lowered, and instantly twenty men crowded into her.

"The captain and a few more refused to leave the ship.

"'The boat is too crowded. I will trust in my Maker. But the unhappy women, save them if possible,' he said.

"One child was taken from the arms of its unconscious mother, and placed in the boat, and a generous fellow had lifted her in his arms; and was about to step into the boat, when a huge billow from the fore part of the ship came rushing furiously towards her, and bore her away on its summit from alongside.

"A receding wave dashed her impetuously back; against the ship's counter she struck.

"Then arose a shriek and a cry.

"There was a struggling in the raging sea—and all perished!

"The hapless mother had just enough of perception to be sensible of her child's fate, and she sprang with a thrilling cry, 'my George! my son! my child!' from the seaman's arms, into that wild sea; and, as if in mockery, it dashed and tossed her from billow to billow, for a space, and then closed over her for ever.

"And there we clung to the wreck—myself and the wretched remnant of the crew and passengers—in despair, watching the slow, gradual approach of the waters that were to be our grave.

"A man close beside me, exhausted, let go his grasp; and he floated, life not yet extinct, from side to side, and vainly stretched out his hands to regain his hold; his features were distorted with the agony of his mind. I could not look upon him —I closed my eyes, and, as I thought, in death.

"Of what followed I have but a confused recollection; I remembered something weighty falling across me.

"I opened my eyes—it was a mutilated corse! and the bloody, disfigured features were in cold contact with mine.

"And even in that awful moment I shuddered, and endeavoured in vain to rid myself of my loathsome burden.

"And now I heard a shout, and an exclamation of joy—'land! land!' but I had not strength to raise myself.

"Presently, I felt myself loosened from the lashings with which I had bound myself to the deck. I was lifted in the arms of some one—from hence all was blank.

"When I woke I found the wreck had drifted on some unknown island, and we were all mercifully saved from a watery grave."

CHAPTER LXXII.

TRAITORS AT WORK—MUNGO GAINS FULL POS-
SESSION OF FORT MARTIN—WALTER BANNON
RECEIVES THE PRICE OF HIS GUILT.

WHEN Mungo and his buccaneers fully discovered
that a great number of the islanders had left the
fort with old Governor Martin and Lion Limb, they
greatly rejoiced, for they made quite sure now of
subduing the entire island in a very little time.

But they met with a greater resistance in some
quarters than they ever imagined.

Finding that the village or town, though strongly
posted on a hill, must sooner or later fall into the
hands of their ruthless invaders, a council of war
was held by the citizens, and it was decided to erect
some strong earth-work and stockades on a neighbouring hillock, on which already stood a very large
rough, stone, straggling building of great age and
strength, and which overlooked Fort Martin.

This wise resolve was immediately acted upon.

Men, women, and even children, assisted with all
their strength, and, in a very few hours, a very
strong and commodious place was erected, into
which all who could, immediately retired, taking
with them whatever they had of food, ammunition
and fire-arms.

All this was so quickly accomplished that it took
Mungo and his party completely by surprise.

The chief cause why Mungo had not as yet subdued the place was the scarcity of powder and shot
among his followers, and the great distance it was
to his own craft on the sea-coast.

For several days, he and his band laid siege to
this large fortified hillock, but they were repulsed
with loss in every attempt they made to storm it,
sword in hand.

To add to the determination of the islanders,
news was now spread abroad among them that a
messenger in a small, fast, sailing-boat had gone
off several nights previously in hopes of finding
Lion Limb and his colonists, who were expected to
return with all speed, and put the buccaneers completely to the rout.

Mungo himself had heard this rumour, and it
filled him with alarm.

Lion Limb might suddenly come down upon the
island, and, if he succeeded in capturing their
piratical craft, the "Vulture," what was to become
of himself and followers far away from the coast?

He made tremendous efforts to subdue the newly-
built fort; but the gallant defenders were not to be
taken by surprise, for both night and day they
fought bravely on, still clinging to the fond hope
that Governor Martin and Lion Limb would soon
return, and force their fierce enemies to retreat in
dire disgrace and confusion.

Mungo and his men were now at a standstill, and
knew not what to do.

To retreat would cover them with shame; and
the islanders, emboldened and embittered more
than ever, would follow them through the country,
and cut off every man of them by ambuscade or
stratagem.

What to do Mungo knew not.

The chief object which he and his followers came
for, namely, gold and silver ore, they had not discovered in anything like the abundance they anticipated, for the inhabitants had hidden away
most of their treasures of every kind, and what
little Mungo and his men could get by force and
cruelty was not sufficient to satisfy the greedy demands of his followers.

But it was now whispered abroad by Mungo that

immense treasures had been carried into the newly
made fortification, and that if they could only capture the place their fortunes would be more than
made.

This announcement was received with great rejoicings by Mungo's followers, and they resolved to
make, at least, one more attack upon the place, and
tear down the remnant of an old English flag which
floated defiantly on the fort, both day and night.

Mungo was preparing his men for a grand night
attack and surprise on the fortification, when rank
treason displayed itself among the islanders, and a
whisper reached Mungo's ears that the officer in command of the islanders in the fort was treacherously
inclined, and willing to listen to terms.

Walter Bannon, a half-breed, was in chief command at the newly-erected fort, and, as we have
said, for several days he defied the besiegers, but,
becoming propped up with pride, he wished to be
proclaimed governor and king of the island in opposition to his brothers, and, when least expected,
Walter was seized and cast into one of the vaults
of the old stone mansion, where he was to remain
until the place should be entirely destroyed or the
buccaneers had been compelled to retreat.

In this deep vault, then, Walter Bannon lay
biting his lip in rage and vexation. Nor was escape,
he thought, possible.

But Walter had heard it said that at one time an
Indian of desperate character had been confined in
that very same vault, and that he effected his escape
therefrom by accidentally discovering a secret
passage.

Walter, not being of a disposition to give way
to despair while the least glimmer of hope presented
itself to his mind, seized eagerly upon this legendary
account, and, though not very sanguine in his expectations, determined, at all events, to attempt the
discovery of the reported outlet, well knowing that
the strongholds of the first settlers frequently
abounded with a multitude of secret and subterranean passages, for which any person except the
original proprietors would be puzzled to find a use.

Groping, therefore, his way, as well as he was
able, he proceeded slowly along, carefully examining
with his hands the walls of the vault, which, ere he
had gone very far, became sensibly larger, and he
was enabled to stand erect.

Still holding on his dark and dreary track, he
was, ere long, agreeably surprised to find himself
come in contact with a strong current of air.

He now became confident that he could not be
very distant from some opening.

Directing his steps towards the point whence a
draught of air appeared to issue, he soon found his
course considerably impeded by heaps of rubbish,
and large fragments of stone, which had evidently
been forced out of their proper place.

With a light heart, he cautiously removed the
huge masses which obstructed his way, and, in a
short time, had the happiness to find himself safe
on the north side of the rocky ruins.

Once more at liberty, he surveyed, as well as the
darkness of the night would permit, those parts of
the fortress which were near him.

Burning with a desire of being revenged on those
who had injured him, in an evil moment he formed
the dread design of betraying the place into the
hands of its blood-thirsty enemy — the ruthless
Mungo and his buccaneers.

And this resolution was no sooner formed than
he proceeded to carry it into execution.

But he little dreamed at that moment of the fate
which hung over him, or he would have paused
and trembled!

THE BOY KING

OF THE SOUTH SEA ISLANDS.

THE WILD MAN IN THE WOODS.

He was soon clear of the stockade and the granite ruins.

"It shall be so," said Walter Bannon ; "this very night will I deliver the place into the hands of Mungo the cruel buccaneer chief. Why should I not rule in the island as well as old Martin or others? I am as brave as they, and have as much right to honour and a proud position as any one else, and I'll have it, or I'll destroy every soul of them. They think me fit to command in the hour of danger, but will not raise me to dignities ; but what they won't grant I'll take. I'd rather serve the half-breed, Mungo, than old Martin, and if all comes to all I'll turn buccaneer myself. A roving life would suit me very well ; anything is better than living any longer on this island ; besides, am I not as worthy of old Martin's daughter as the rest who

lay claim to her hand? Of course I am ; and more than that, I think that Dora Martin even loves me and would willingly fly with me if I only made the offer to her. Fancy Walter Bannon a buccaneer chief, with a ship at his command, and plenty of men willing and ready to do his bidding ! Ha !" said Walter Bannon, to himself, "that is the thing for me. I will instantly make my way to Mungo's camp and there disclose my plans and intentions. Yet I will not appear craven-hearted or a willing slave ; if he is civil, I also will be so, if not, then we can best fall foul of each other and come to blows."

With such thoughts and designs, Walter Bannon, the renegade and scoundrel, smiled in triumph and scorn as he left the precincts of the place his own friends had so long and so ably defenced, and directed his steps from them.

The distance being but short, he soon arrived at the enemy's pickets, by whom, as he did not endeavour to conceal himself, he was of course seized.

Having thrown himself into their power, he merely demanded that he might be led into the presence of Mungo their chief, which demand the guards, after first blindfolding him, in order that he might not distinguish the disorder that prevailed around, proceeded instantly to obey.

When ushered into the tent, and permitted to make use of his eyes, he perceived Mungo sitting at a small table, gazing intently at some papers that lay thereon.

On the entrance of Walter, however, he raised his head, and, attentively surveying his appearance, in his usual harsh and abrupt manner addressed the following laconic question to him:

"Now, Mister, your business here?"

"I came to act and not to parley," replied Walter; "to offer to a foe what most he wishes—possession of our stronghold. If he accepts the offer, let him get ready instantly, and trust to the guidance of one who is willing to be his friend to-night, even at the expense of honour."

Mungo, who scarcely knew whether to look upon his prisoner as a madman, paused ere he made a reply.

However—as the chances, judging from the resistance which the garrison had already made, were so many against his being able to take the place by force of arm—he determined, as a last resource, to embrace the opportunity which thus afforded itself, be the consequences what they might.

"Be it so, then," was the answer of Mungo; "he whom you address is always ready. Lead on then. But hearken, knave; should you belie your promise, your life shall be the forfeit."

"Had I been the subject of fear," "replied Walter, "I should not now be in your tent. A truce, then, to your threatenings; yet think not I betray our just cause thus basely. Hear first the terms, Mungo — nay, frown not; I'll not be frightened from my purpose by the frowns of any man; and, unless my conditions are agreed to, not all your threats shall make me even now turn traitor.

"My life is in your hands and you may take it instantly, or to-morrow, but that is all you have in your power.

"I ask but for the life and freedom of the garrison, for every living soul—from the person of the governor's nephew, though he is my rival and foe, down to the meanest half-breed that treads along the walls.

"That the few females, one of whom is dearer to me than life, shall be secure from the gross insults of your brutal men. On these conditions only, I become your guide."

"Mungo will pledge his word," was the reply, "that life and freedom shall be given to all *at present* within the fortification; and as for the women, buccaneers or not, we are not the merciless followers that Bloodhoof once commanded. You need not be under any anxiety for the safety of the old women, at least. We came to fight with men, and not with women! Now are you satisfied?"

Walter replied in the affirmative, observing, as he concluded, that he "would trust for once to the honour of a buccaneer, if such a thing existed."

Mungo scowled, as it seemed as if his guide suspected his intentions.

But prudence bade him conceal his rage, and he merely remarked, as he took his pistols from the table, "that he might do so safely."

With a chosen body of men upon whose fidelity he could depend, Mungo committed himself to the guidance of Walter, whom, however, he kept close beside during the march, which, without occupying much of their time, brought them unseen to the opening from which the betrayer had escaped.

The men, having entered the breach, and being provided with the necessary implements, immediately commenced removing the earth from the spot pointed out to them by Walter Bannon, while Mungo and his guides kept watch without.

With such secrecy were their operations carried on in the dead of night, that no person within the place was in the least degree disturbed by them.

Once only, and that by mere chance, had they any occasion to be alarmed.

An officer, marching to relieve guard, perceiving from the hill-top some persons below, hailed them in the accustomed form.

"Who goes there?"

"Friends."

"To whom?"

"To Governor Martin, our chief."

The presence of mind exhibited by the traitor, Walter Bannon, who thus answered the challenge, extricated them from this danger,

For the officer, on hearing the password, not doubting but they were sent there by the governor's nephew, passed on his way, and left them to proceed with their undertaking without any further interruption.

The buccaneers, after having effected an opening in the ground above, were enabled, with very little trouble, by means of a temporary ladder, which they formed of their implements, to enter into the particular and strong party described to them by their guide.

Here they had time to rest, and room enough to prepare themselves for the attack which it was to be expected they would still have to undertake.

At the end of a long, dark passage, in which they now were, a narrow door was now the only barrier to be removed ere they effected the object they had so long wished for—an entrance into the heart of the fortress.

From its situation, as they could not hope to penetrate this, however trifling it appeared, as silently as they had done the first part of the passage, they proceeded by one sudden effort to force the door open, and by the rapidity of their subsequent movements to terrify the garrison from making any resistance.

Nor were they disappointed.

For the door, yielding to the first assault, they found themselves in possession of the fortress before many of its defenders were even aware of their approach.

When morning dawned the standard of the unfortunate defenders floated not as heretofore, above the fort, for those who had defended it so gallantly had either fallen sword in hand, or had departed to seek for shelter in some other place that was still enabled to keep on high a little longer the well-known ensign of their proud independence.

*　　*　　*　　*　　*　　*

One only of the former garrison remained.

And he, with beating heart and anxious eyes, had there already explored each hole and corner which the place contained, in search of the object of his every hope and fear, namely, Dora Martin.

But all in vain.

Still coping with the grim fiend, Despair, he was in the act of doing so for the third time when he was summoned by a sentinel, and, upon refusing to obey, he was instantly and roughly forced into the presence of Mungo.

Forgetting for an instant his treason and treachery, he stood before the tyrant Mungo with such a forbidding and knavish mien as greatly surprised all those around, and even Mungo himself seemed undecided how to act with the rascal.

At last he said—

"Now, then, base traitor, has not the promise which I made been kept? Hath maid, wife, or widow been violated? The lives and freedom of the garrison were likewise promised, and that promise I have faithfully kept. Remember, rascal, when my word was pledged *you* was not amongst them; therefore, I owe you nothing, since it was to gratify your own revenge, and not from love to me that you have betrayed your party. Had the service you have done us been done with other motives, I would have thanked you for it; as it is, I love the treason but I hate the traitor! Take, then, a traitor's just reward!"

Quick as thought the pistol of the tyrant left its belt.

It flashed!

CHAPTER LXXIII.

ALLAN NORMAN AND JEM RAWLINGS REFUSE DR. KILLAM'S OFFER.

THE last time that we spoke of Allan Norman he and Jem Rawlings were sleeping in a coffee-house, and were very much surprised indeed to discover that the companion of their room was none else than the notorious Dr. Killam.

As will be remembered, Dr. Killam had a long conversation with Allan Norman, in which he used the name of Jerry Marks very freely, and even went so far as to accuse him of having been the murderer of the old Alderman, and had also been the chief instrument in having poor Edgar and his companions transported.

Poor Allan was in a sad way when he heard the doctor speak so knowingly of the sad events in which he and others had been concerned.

The doctor wanted Allan and the faithful Jem to accompany him, but they would not.

"Would you rather trust yourselves in the hands of Inspector Sharp than mine, then?" said the doctor.

"Yes, I would," said Jem, rubbing his eyes. "I don't like your looks."

"No?"

"I do not."

"And why not, pray?"

"Because you look so dark and ugly," said Jem. "There's something about the look of the inspector's face that I admire more than yours."

"And what may that be?" asked the doctor, looking very angry.

"Why, in the first place," said Jem, "he's clean, and that's more than you are; in the next place, he has a fair, open countenance, and has a bright, clear eye, which possesses a pleasing expression of good-nature and cleverness, and——"

"What else?" said the doctor.

"Well, take him all in all, I would rather trust myself in his hands than in yours—your eyes are red and flaring; your face is thin, hollow-checked and sallow; and if you really want me to speak my mind," said the bold Jem, unabashed, "you look more like a rogue than an honest man; so that's flat."

The doctor seemed rather inclined to administer a slap on the head to Master Jem; but Allan frowned, and said,

"Look you here, sir, don't you dare lay a hand upon my friend; if you do, you will have to fight both of us."

"Oh, indeed," said the doctor, with a scowling look. "And do you suppose I should care much about that? If you do, you are very much mistaken. I'm a desperate man when any one insults or arouses my anger."

"Then," said Allan, "you should be very careful what you say to other people; but I repeat it, if you hit him you hit me." And as the handsome lad so spoke the blood mounted to his face, and his eyes flashed fire.

"But why do you dare doubt my word?" said the doctor.

"Dare! You speak very strongly before us lads; but let me tell you," said Allan, "if we are young, we know more of the world than you suppose; and why should we not distrust you? What proof have you given me that what you say is true? You come here unbidden; you follow and dog our footsteps; come stealthily to my bed-side and wish me to believe all you say about the murder, and place all the blame on the shoulders of Jerry Marks; for what object we don't know. Then why should we be bound to obey or believe you?"

The doctor seemed now very much surprised in turn, and for a moment looked very hard and intent upon the features of young Allan as he whispered half aloud,

"His features are the very image of his father's."

"But if you are a person of such very good intentions towards us both, as you now profess," continued Allen, "why did you not give all this information to the police long ago, and help to bring the real culprit to punishment, instead of allowing my poor brother and other innocent ones to suffer so grievously as they have already done?"

"It is never too late to mend," said the doctor, bitterly; "at one time I could not—I dared not—give information; but I am sadly altered, and I hope changed much for the better; I will do you much good, I tell you, if you will only let me."

"But you must give me good proofs of your intentions first," said Allan.

"What do you intend to do then?" asked Dr. Killam. "Will you come with me, or what?"

"We would rather stay where we are at present," said Jem. "You may be only a spy, for all we know, and us lads hate spies. I know I do."

"Then why don't you hate Inspector Sharp and his detectives?"

"Oh, that's a different matter entirely; they are the proper sort of spies, and we can't do without them."

"As for myself," said Allan, "I, like my companion, will stay here, and leave Mr. Sharp to unravel the whole mystery; he knows how to go about it better than you, or us either."

"You will not say anything of what has passed between us, of course?"

"Of course I shall," said Allan, boldly; "why not? 'tis nothing but right I should do so. Every word that I can remember of our conversation will be reported to him."

"Then if so you will ruin me."

"I care not for that," said Allan; "let justice have its course; many a person suffers through life for not speaking out the truth boldly."

"But if they hunt me down and make me desperate, what then, youngster?"

"That is a matter which concerns you, not me. I shall not mention any names, but simply state the facts as they have occurred."

"You must not—you shall not!" said the doctor, vehemently.

" You talk in a threatening manner," said Allan ; " I like not the tone of your voice."

" Nor I either," said Jem, bouncing out of bed, and seizing a poker, in case any quarrel should take place.

" I am not afraid of such a trifle as that," said Dr. Killum, contemptuously pointing to Jem's poker which that youth was twisting around his head in imitation of Irishmen with their shillelahs at Donnybrook Fair. " I carry something smaller and more useful," said he, producing a dirk, and with glistening eyes gazing on the astonished and open-mouthed Jem, who, in his night-clothes, retreated behind the bedstead.

" You are very clever, indeed," said Allan ; " but you ought to be thoroughly ashamed of yourself for exhibiting deadly weapons to two lads such as we are ; but to show you how careful we are of ourselves, look at this !" said he.

At the same time, Allan hastily thrust his hand under the pillow, and produced a small revolver already cocked and ready for use.

" What do you think of this, eh ?" said he. " I think we are even now. I found the weapon this very night in an old deserted alley-way, not far from the residence of the late alderman who was murdered."

" What !" gasped the doctor, in surprise, " let me look at it."

" Oh, no, thank you," said Allan, very coolly, " that is too much to ask ; but, as you see, it has long been lying in the place where I found it ; one of the chambers are empty."

" You—found—that—revolver—near—the—residence—of—old—Alderman—English !" gasped the doctor, turning deadly pale.

" I did."

" What ? That revolver is *mine!*"

" Your's ? It cannot be !"

" It is, I tell you. I have lost it for a long time, and can swear to it. It has an ivory handle."

" So it has," said Allan, " and the handle, as you perceive, is smeared with blood !"

With a frightful oath Dr. Killum dashed from the room, exclaiming, " It was stolen from me ; I did not do the deed ; it was stolen from me, it was stolen from me !"

" Hillo !" said Jem, who now jumped into bed again out of the cold, " what the deuce is all this, Allan ? You never told me anything about that revolver."

" No ; nor did I intend to do so even now ; it was a mere accident that compelled me to do so. I intended to tell the inspector all about it though, but have not as yet."

" Why, what object can you have ?"

" What object ?"

" Yes."

" Why, don't you remember that at the coroner's inquest is was proved that the old alderman must have struggled with the assassin, and his death hastened by a pistol-shot as well as several deep knife wounds ?"

" Yes, I do remember."

" Well, then, the truth appears to be to me that, after using the weapon, the murderer must have flung the revolver from him, and hastened away, for I am certain that this weapon must have had something to do with the barbarous murder."

" How can you prove it," said Jem, whose hair now begau to stand on end, for he looked about and pulled the bed-clothes tight about him, as if he expected to see the gory ghost of the old alderman peep in between the curtains.

" How can you pr·o·o·o·ve it, Allan ?" he repeated with chattering teeth, and in a solemn whisper.

" Prove it ?" why easily enough.

" The coroner has kept the bullet that was found in the old man's body, and I have no doubt that it will fit the barrel."

" But that man said Jerry Marks did the deed."

" And he could prove it," said Jem.

" So he did."

" But, then, afterwards he said the pistol was his. How can you make the two stories agree ?"

" I don't know, without he loaned the weapon to some one, or had it stolen from him, as he says."

" Its a mystery still then," said Jem, " and I suppose always will remain so."

" No, it won't, if I can help it. I'll unravel it in time. But let us go to sleep, Jem—I'm tired. Lock the door and blow out the light."

Jem, who would do anything Allan told him, crawled out of his warm bed, and blew out the light. He then locked the door, and was groping his way all shivering and shaking back to bed again, when loud raps were heard at the chamber door.

CHAPTER LXXIV.

ALLAN NORMAN AND JEM RAWLINGS MEET WITH A FRIEND IN INSPECTOR SHARP.

" WHO the devil can that be ?" growled Jem, who did not by any means relish the idea of keeping out any longer in the cold.

" It's some one who has mistaken his room, I think—don't answer."

Again the knocks were repeated.

" Don't answer, Allan. We don't want to be disturbed any more," said Jem.

" But we *must* answer : it won't do to have them knocking there all night. Who are you ; what do you want ?" he said, angrily.

" Open," was the surly answer.

" But we are in bed," said Jem. " Hang it ; find some other room."

" Open, I say ?"

" Go to the devil," said Jem. " Who are you? What is your business ?"

" Open, I say ?"

" I shan't. We'll see you in Jericho first," bawled Jem, who was now getting very angry and furious.

" Open, I say, in the name of the law ?" was the gruff response.

" In the name of what, did he say ?" grumbled Jem.

" Open to officers," said some one outside, this time more gruffly and surlily than ever.

At the word officer, Allan felt a cold tremor pass through his frame.

Young Jem yawned and commenced to pull his hair about in a frantic manner, as he moaned,

" Oh, lor ! oh, lor ! What next is to befall us, Allan ? Whatever have we done that we should be hunted about like this ? Let us escape. Let us open the window and get over the tiles. Anything is better than going to prison."

" No, no," said Allan. " Don't think of doing anything so rash as that ; you would break your neck."

" I don't care," said Jem ; " anything before going into prison."

So speaking, he jumped out of bed and ran to the window.

But the cold winds blew and chilled his ardour.

Beside the winds, however, there was something else which checked him.

By the dim light he perceived the ominous outline of a policeman, who was already on guard out there to prevent all escape, and he ran back to Allan and informed him of the terrible object he had seen.

"There is no hope for us, then, I see," Allan sighed; "we are fairly in the hands of the police again and escape is impossible. The worst of it is I don't know what we've done."

"That's just it," groaned Jem. "We arn't gone and done anything, have we?"

"Come, come, open the door?" said those outside. "Open the door, or we'll smash it in?"

"Open the door, Jem," said Allan. "Let's have no violence used here."

Jem opened the door, and in the instant a bull's-eye lantern-light was cast upon him, and in walked three officers.

"What's your business with us, gentlemen?" said Allan, boldly.

"Your name is Allan Norman, I think?" said the chief of the officers.

"It is."

"I thought so; I've seen you before somewhere."

"Yes, sergeant, in Newgate," said a policeman. "I know him well."

"You know no harm of me," said Allan, proudly.

"And your name," said the first speaker to Jem, "is Rawlings?"

"Y-e-e-s," said Jem. "James Rawlings is my name, England is my nation, London is my dwelling-place, and ——"

"Ah! never mind the rest," said the sergeant, coldly. "London won't be your dwelling-place long, or I am very much mistaken. Haven't you any relations abroad?"

"What me?"

"Yes, you."

"Not as I know on," said Jem.

"Yes you have; or had, rather."

"I had a brother once, but he is ——"

"In Botany Bay, I think."

"No he isn't, he's in some other and a better place than that," said Jem, colouring up.

"He was sent there, then."

"Yes; but he went to Heaven for all that," sighed Jem; "and I shouldn't regret it much if I were there also."

"What do you mean?' said the officer.

"Mean? I mean that he was drowned in H. M. ship 'Rattlesnake,' and a great many more with him; and so was Allan's brother, young Edgar Norman."

"Well, it is about that business we come now," said the sergeant.

"What business?" said Allan.

"About the old alderman's murder."

"We were not found guilty."

"That is very evident, or you wouldn't be here now, my lad; but you are in possession of certain proofs of the old man's murder, and we want them, and you also, to know how you came by them."

"I don't know what you mean."

"You have in your possession a certain ivory-handled revolver."

"How do you know?"

"That is my business, not yours."

"Who told you, then?"

"That remains a secret. It is sufficient that we know you have the property in question, so produce it at once."

"Let 'em find it, if they want it," growled Jem. "I wouldn't trouble myself about it if I were you, Allan?"

"Search the room, men," said the sergeant. "Bread and water diet may make these young rascals a little more civil."

"I wish it would make you a little more civil," said Jem. "Hang the pistol, I wish Allan had never found it; but he's always fond of poking about the old offices."

"I'll save you the trouble of searching for the revolver," said Allan; "here it is."

"Ah, this is the very thing," said the sergeant; "there always hung a mystery around that murder, but if we had had this revolver at first, things might have turned out different for your brother, Allan Norman.

"How is that?"

"This pistol was stolen many months ago from the mansion of Lord Manfred; who committed that robbery was never known; but Mike Higgins and others, were arrested on suspicion, and sentenced for several months as rogues and vagabonds. This pistol, and many other articles of the stolen property, were disposed of to a Jew, but were so well placed in hiding holes, that, until this hour, no one could trace them; if we can only find an owner for this revolver, or the person in whose possession it was last, then we shall be able to learn more about that foul and atrocious murder of the old alderman than we have ever known before."

"Then you don't hold us two in suspicion, then?" said Allan.

"No, not for the actual deed; but we must detain you in order to make certain necessary inquiries."

While Allan and Jem were listening to all that the officers had to say, meanwhile putting on their clothes, and feeling very sorrowful indeed at what had so unexpectedly happened to them, a very heavy and hasty footstep was heard upon the stairs, approaching the room in which they all were.

The landlord, however, and his vulgar talkative wife, together with two daughters, and a solitary servant, who looked fagged and worn, half starved, and pale, had in the interim entered the apartment, and there was a perfect Babel of tongues, as each and every one vented their spleen and angry denunciations against the two poor friendless youths.

"I told you not to let the young vagabonds sleep in my house," said the wife.

"I knew they were houseless and homeless thieves," said one of the daughters.

"They have the perfect look of pickpockets," chimed in the other.

"Sartingly mum, just as you say," remarked the servant, or "slavey," as she might very justly be termed. "I knew as how our beds were too good for the young ragamuffins; but muster wouldn't listen to what I said; in course not, he wouldn't."

"Hold your noise," said the old landlord, "none of you know what you are all talking about; these two boys are young gentlemen, I tell you."

"What!" said the wife; "are you dreaming?"

"No, I ain't."

"Father must be mistaken," said the two daughters.

"What do girls know about this 'ere world, I should like to know? You had both better go to bed, I think."

"I'm sure I'se disgusted with the young wagabones," said Miss Sarah, the servant, who, of course, always wished to be in harmony with her mistress and the two young ladies.

"You go down into the kitchen, Sarah," said the

master," or go to bed, whichever you chooses. I tell you all that these two boys are all right, and are perfect gentlemen; what do you think of that?"

"Gentlemen!" said the policemen and their sergeant in chorus.

"Yes, gents, what do you think of that?" said the landlord, "and no mistake about it."

"What makes you think so?" said the sergeant; "for, to my certain knowledge, the two young ras——"

"Ah, ha; stop there, Mr. Sergeant, if *you* please; but they ain't rogues and rascals as you suppose, and I know it. Do you think for a single moment I'd let two young pickpockets sleep in my house?"

"Oh, no; of course not," said the police officers, trying to suppress a grin. "Oh, of course not."

"Oh, I can see you all a larfing," said the coffeehouse keeper, very coolly; "you is all very clever in your own way, but you have made a very great mistake this time, I can tell you; for I had orders to supply these two young gents with whatever they liked to call for."

"Indeed! Who from?"

"Why, from one as is your superior officer."

"I don't understand," said the sergeant. "What is the name of my superior officer, pray?"

"I forget his name," said the landlord; "but he came to-night, and says he, 'If them 'ere two young gents wants anything as you have got in your house, let 'em have it, as far as grubbing goes;' and of course I shall."

"But what was the name of this individual?"

"Well, to tell you the plain truth, I forget now; but I think it was Inspector—Inspector, what, missus?" asked the landlord, addressing his wife.

"Oh! don't pretend to ask or bother me with any such questions," the stern and angry wife replied; "I don't think it were any inspector at all."

"Yes it were, I know it was," said the landlord; "for one night when I was drunk, I was taken up before him, and charged with 'salt and battery;' but what it all meant I forget now; all I knows, I knocked a man in the eye for insulting of me—it warn't much. I only cut his nose you know, and blackened his eye, cause as how he called me hard names; but, howsomever, I had satisfaction out of him, and was fined forty bob, or ten days' dance on the treadmill. So, therefore, I has good cause for knowing of that 'ere gent; but his name—what the deuce *was* his name?" said the querrulous landlord.

"Inspector Sharp," said the identical individual himself, walking into the room.

"The devil!" said the landlord, in surprise.

"Why, it is Mr. Sharp," said the officer, very much surprised.

"What is the matter here?" said the inspector, quickly and loudly.

The sergeant explained in brief terms.

"Oh! that is nothing," whispered the inspector, in answer.

And with a very polite manner he advanced and shook hands very cordially with young Allan, saying—

"Some person here informed the authorities respecting a certain ivory-handled revolver which you are said to have in your possession."

"'Tis perfectly true, sir," said Allan. "I found it."

"I don't doubt it for a single moment; but the officers attach more importance to the fact than it deserves. I know all about it."

"But sir, we were sent here to arrest these two youths," said the sergeant.

"I know you were; and I come on my own responsibility to release them—*they* have nothing to do with the revolver; and if the police in that particular district where the murder occurred had been a little more particular in their inquiries, and far more diligent in their search, the verdict against the brothers of these two poor friendless boys might have been much different."

"I do not understand you, sir," said the sergeant.

"What I mean to say, then, at this moment, is, that these two boys have no crime attached to them whatever; yet they must remain under the eye of the police, for some time to come, for through them I hope to unravel the whole mystery of the murder, and to arrest, as well as transport for life, the true rogues and rascals who were interested and had a hand in it."

Every one present seemed greatly surprised at the turn which things had now suddenly taken, and were most polite indeed to the two lads.

"I told you they were young gentlemen," said the landlord in triumph.

"What two nice-looking youths they are," whispered the daughters, quite loud enough to be heard.

"So they is, now I comes to have a good look at 'em," said the wife.

"They must be young lords, at the very least," sighed the servant, "for jest to think as how the inspector stands up for 'em. Lorks a daisy! what a change! They won't take to Sairy now."

"Come," said Inspector Sharp, to Allan, "I have been out all night. You must accompany me. Before this time to-morrow night we shall have discovered who this revolver belongs to, and many more important facts in the case. But are you afraid of danger, Allan?"

"Me? not a bit on it," said Jem, with a flushed face. "I'm as brave as a ——"

"I dare say you are; but I didn't ask," said the inspector, tartly, "are *you*, Allan?"

"Never, in a good and just cause."

"And such is just the cause we are now engaged in. Come, my lad, I know you feel anxious to have this mystery cleared up."

"I do, sir, with all my heart."

"Then, come with me. Have a bold heart. If, I say again, you are afraid of danger, do not come; stay where you are."

"I am *not* afraid of danger," said Allan, bravely.

"Then, follow me."

"I will."

They went forth; but no one knew, nor could they even imagine, what they were doomed to brave and endure the next night.

It was a trying ordeal, both to the police as well as young Allan, but what it was we shall quickly see.

CHAPTER LXXV.

THE WILD MAN OF THE WOODS AND HIS HIDDEN TREASURE.

HER Majesty's ship "Skylark," which our readers will remember called at Lion Island for wood, water, and to make good the damages, which she suffered in the severe gale while pursuing Lion Limb's "Rattlesnake" in mistake for the pirate's ship, "Vulture," carried away with her much treasure that belonged to Lion Limb and his young colonists, besides many letters which were destined for their friends in England.

Lion Limb and his young companions, as well as old Governor Martin and his islanders, were in hopes that many months would not pass ere Government or their friends would send out a vessel laden with supplies.

But the best hopes, wishes, and aspirations of the good are oftentimes frustrated by the dangers and many perils of the sea.

And so it was, as far as their anticipations went, with that gallant vessel.

For the "Skylark" and her officers were fully on their course to the nearest mail station on the mainland of the South American continent, when a succession of heavy gales occurred, and despite their own brave and manly exertions, [they were unable to battle successfully with the storm, and at last succumbed after many severe trials, and were drifting about on the broad ocean, a helpless, dismasted wreck.

For more than a week the "Skylark" and her crew knew not what hour, or at what moment the angry seas would for ever engulph them; when a friendly gale blew up, and drove them along at headlong speed towards a group of fertile and verdant isles, which geographers knew but little of, for the islands were unnamed and to all appearances uninhabited.

Any spot in the world, however, was preferable to the miserable state in which they then were; and when heaving billows bore them onwards, and drifted them heavily on to a long sandy beach, every one on board felt infinite relief at the good fortune so unexpectedly vouchsafed them, and they disembarked with feelings of joy and renewed hopes.

Directly they landed, the crew of the "Skylark" began to explore the adjacent beach; but the captain himself went out alone, gun in hand, for, by the aid of his powerful glass, he espied some strange, wild, shaggy-looking object, which appeared to be neither man nor animal, but a mixture of both.

That it was not a gorilla the captain felt certain, and hurrying along, he soon ascended a shelving rock, from the height of which he had a capital view for many miles around.

"What could have been that object I saw?" mused the captain of the "Skylark." "I never saw such a strange-looking object in all my life."

Yet, while he thought and gazed around, a loud coarse laugh resounded in his ears.

He quickly turned his head.

Judge of his surprise, when he beheld an aged man dressed in skins, standing within a few yards of him.

He was fierce looking, powerfully made, and his hair was long and matted.

From head to foot he looked a most ferocious and formidable person, and in his hand he held a long heavy club, which he twirled around his head with the greatest of ease.

"Who are you?" asked the captain, gun in hand.

"What's that to you?" was the gruff and savage answer.

"You are a man, I perceive," said the captain.

"Yes, and an Englishman also."

"I should judge so; you speak English well. How long have you been here?"

"Thirty years or more."

"How came you here?"

"Ah! thereby hangs a tale, laughed the wild man, in a bitter manner; "but come, if you mean well, approach, shake hands, and I will give you what information I can."

"Were you cast ashore, or wrecked here?"

"I was cast ashore here, but not by the waves," said the wild man.

"Explain, I cannot understand you."

"Our vessel was attacked by pirates, we lost nearly all our crew in the engagement. I was spared; they wished me to join their band, and I would not. To get rid of me and several more, they landed us on this island, and there left us to starve or to fall a sacrifice to the cruel natives. But we did neither; I am alive as you see; and, happy day as this is, I can show you a sealed box which the pirates buried not far from here."

"Indeed, what does it contain?"

"I know not that, but something of importance and value, for the box is made strongly of iron, and resists all my efforts to break it open."

"But, did you see them burying it?"

"I did, unknown to them. Come," said the wild man, "I will first show you the hiding place of this strong box; and then, if it so pleases you, I will go on board and make friends with the sailors yonder."

"With all my heart," said the captain; "we will carry this mysterious box on board, and examine it at our leisure."

So speaking, the wild man led the way until he came to a cluster of trees.

"There," said he, stopping and leaning on his club; "in that hole you will find that of which I speak."

The captain knelt down and began his search, and at last he discovered the strong box spoken of.

But, he turned pale as he gazed at the treasure, and for a moment was unnerved.

The wild man's eyes gleamed with fire as he slowly muttered, pointing to the iron box, "thereby hangs a tale."

What the wild man meant, and the causes of the captain turning pale, we shall quickly know in another chapter.

CHAPTER LXXVI.

LION LIMB RECEIVES INFORMATION OF THE DOINGS OF MUNGO, ON MARTIN ISLAND, AND SAILS TO THE RESCUE—ROGER, TO AVENGE HIS MOTHER, FORMS A BAND OF PARTISANS, WHO AVENGE THEIR WRONGS ON MUNGO'S MEN.

THE success which attended Mungo's efforts on Martin Island, almost turned the brain of that savage chief.

He sent his vessel back to the Blue Rocks at full speed to inform the buccaneers there of all he had accomplished, and urged them to send him supplies and reinforcements as quickly as possible, in order to keep a firm hold on all they then had.

When Mungo's vessel arrived at the Blue Rocks, and gave a glowing description of his great conquest, scores volunteered to go to the island and keep it for themselves for ever.

The buccaneers were intoxicated with success, and they sailed away for Martin Island in high glee and expectation of still greater conquests in neighbouring islands.

But Lion Limb had also heard of what was transpiring on Martin Island, and made all haste to go to the rescue of his friends there.

Old Governor Martin was astounded at the news.

But what made matters worse, was, that the simple sail-boat which had brought the information, had been blown about, and occupied fully two weeks in the passage.

This great delay was of much benefit to Mungo, who, with fire and sword, was laying waste the comfortable homesteads of the islanders far and near, for all who did not pledge themselves to support him he drove mercilessly away into the woods and wilds, there to perish of hunger.

Mungo managed to enlist hundreds of the uncivilized native islanders in his cruise ; but those who were civilized, and had known old Governor Martin and the white colony of Fort Martin, formed themselves into small bands, and fell upon small parties of the invaders as they passed to and fro to the coast with plunder and spoil.

Driven as the poor island settlers were nearly to despair, they knew not what to do or how to act.

It was indeed no difficult thing to rouse these exasperated people, whom a sense of their injuries kept in continual irritation.

Some of the fathers of families, who had obtained the means of supporting a miserable existence by the labour of their hands, prefered a peaceable state of slavery with their wives and children, under the buccaneers, to any separation of their fate.

But the younger part were all actuated by one spirit ; and in the course of a month, Roger, whose single-handed encounter with Mungo all will remember and admire, found that there were thirty men prepared to follow his fortunes in the work of retribution, and to share his fate.

Roger recovered from the state of mind into which his misfortunes had placed him.

But the effect which his mother's and sister's wrongs had produced upon his character was irremediable.

The wound was healed, but the scar which it left was indelible.

He was no longer the cheerful being he had been in his childhood ; the accomplished youth he had appeared when in the chase ; or the pleasing, the animated link in the chain of society which had entitled him to the smiles of the beauties of Fort Martin.

He was changed in every point.

The airy dreams of romance had given way to the gloomy imaginings of despair.

The smiling dress in which his fancy used to deck all the objects from which he derived pleasurable sensation—and, in spite of all his early disappointments, these had predominated over the more peaceful ones of his life—was now stripped off.

The thought of pleasure was banished from his mind.

The thought which approached nearest to it was the satisfaction he derived from the anticipation of wreaking his vengeance on the destroyers of his family.

Daily and hourly did he repeat the oath by which he bound himself to consider this the only occupation of his life.

Daily and hourly did he imagine aggravated scenes of horror, which he ardently hoped to realize in the progress of his revenge, for he and all believed now that no succour would or could come from Lion Limb, or elsewhere.

Something like a recurrence of the softer images of his mind would at times present themselves to his fancy in the form of the fair half-breed, his sweetheart.

But he dwelled not on the thought, and rather strove to chase it away, by painting the probable sufferings of his sister, in quest of whom all search had been fruitless.

She had not fallen a victim to their cruelty and thirst for blood, for her body was nowhere to be found.

Nor could she have fled from their barbarity, for whither would she have sought refuge but in Fort Martin, where she possessed so many friends ?

And if she had chosen any other place of security, would she not have returned during the period which had elapsed, or at least have informed her friends of her retreat ?

The little troop which Roger and old Snowdrop had engaged in their cause, and who now styled themselves a party of " guerillas," were, not without difficulty, secretly provided with the necessary arms, and were not only ready to commence their campaign, but impatient of delay.

Roger was anxious that the first blow they struck should be one which would make them feared by their enemies, who had been hitherto unaccustomed to be upon their guard against guerillas, near Fort Martin, where no organized party of them existed.

After some consideration, he decided upon executing a plan which had been suggested to him by the remembrance of the unhappy fate of an old friend.

The villains who had perpetrated atrocious acts had long left the neighbourhood ; but another detachment had been established, for the purpose of communication not far distant.

It consisted of twenty men, and occupied a solitary house, called the Midway House, between Fort Martin and the coast, for the communication between which places it was the relay.

It was by the annihilation of this detachment that Roger determined to make the existence of his guerillas at once known and feared.

Everthing was ready.

Roger, with the artful old negro Snowdrop, visited individually the persons who composed their little band, and informed them of the speedy commencement of their campaign.

" Meet me," said Roger, " to-morrow, an hour before sun-set, on the banks of the river, near the Indian village. The sun of to-morrow shall set for ever upon every living being in the Midway House. Let every man seek a different road to the place of rendezvous, and let them arrive there singly lest our meeting be observed, and our design frustrated."

Roger slept not that night.

The anxiety of his mind banished every thought of repose.

He felt that he was about to commence a career which would be the future one of his life ; in which he sought not glory, but just revenge for deepest injuries.

He felt that he was about to draw the sword to avenge his murdered relations and friends.

Delighted with the idea, he occupied his mind the greater part of the night in placing it in its most bloody forms, and in tracing the progress of his revenge till it should end in the extermination of all the brutal buccaneers.

He was upon the road to the Indian village, accompanied by the cunning old darkie, Snowdrop, shortly after dawn, although it would hardly require three hours to reach that place.

A friend was the only one not concerned in the secret who was entrusted with it ; and to him Roger confided such part of his small stock of treasure as he found it inconvenient to carry in his leathern girdle.

At parting he took an affectionate leave of him, for he thought not of returning alive.

THE BOY KING
OF THE SOUTH SEA ISLANDS.

THE UNEXPECTED VISIT AND DEMAND.

His labours once commenced, he meant to abjure a life of quiet, and to devote himself to all the hardships and privations that the danger with which he must be constantly surrounded would impose upon him.

He resumed the Spanish disguise, which had been the means of preserving him more than once, and he made external differences between himself and those who partook of his dangers.

The river where they met rolled its shallow and

interrupted course round the base of a high bill which intervened between its stream and a large Indian village.

It was on the side of this hill, as it shelved down to the river, that Roger first collected together his little troop, and here it was that they swore to prosecute an interminable war upon the ravagers of their country, and never to spare the life of a buccaneer whom it was in their power to destroy.

Here too they acknowledged Roger as their chief, and promised an entire obedience to his commands.

Thus was formed their bond of union, and they prepared to place the seal upon it by dipping their weapons in the blood of their enemies.

Roger determined not to give his enemies any time for preparation, but to fall upon them, if possible, entirely by surprise.

To ascertain the probability of a vigorous resistence from them, he went and procured a quantity of wild native tobacco, under the pretence of selling which, he intended to introduce himself into the Midway House, to be able to seize the favourable opportunity of attack.

To this end the guerillas crossed the river at different times, and concealed themselves in the wood with which the Midway House is surrounded; all, however, sufficiently near to it to be able to hear any signal that might be given from it.

Rodger and Snowdrop, with their tobacco, crossed the river higher up, and got upon the road which led them to the Midway House.

As they approached it they discovered several buccaneers sitting before the door smoking, whilst others were employed in cleaning their arms in a shed which adjoined the house, and where there were ten horses ready saddled and prepared for service, with the swords of their riders hanging at the pummels.

Roger judged from this that half the detachment of buccaneers at this place were kept on duty at one time.

The buccaneers accosted them.

"Hillo, what have you got there?"

"Tobacco to sell. Will you buy any?"

"Let's see it."

Roger produced his tobacco, which one of the buccaneers took from him; and calling to some of his companions, they began without ceremony to share its contents.

"If you take it," said Roger, "you must pay for it."

"The devil!" cried a surly fellow. "Be off at a trot; and thank your stars we don't take your horse from you."

Roger acted his part by grumbling and pursuing his road, but he had seen enough to know in what state he might expect to find the buccaneers.

As soon therefore as he had got out of sight of the house he struck off amongst the trees that bordered the road on either side, and, retracing his steps, was not long in rejoining his companions, who were in ambush in the rear of it.

It had been a fine day, but the evening sky had gradually become overcast, and the gathering clouds, by impeding the rays of the sun, seemed to hasten him to his bed, bringing earlier on the night, for the arrival of which Roger and his party so anxiously longed.

It came at last, and the conspiring clouds shut out every twinkling star, whose ray might have too soon betrayed the approach of the death-bearing guerillas.

They left their ambush, and gaining the road they arrived within a few yards of the house unperceived.

The buccaneers had retired within it to their supper; and apparently mirth proceeded at the banquet, for the rude noise of their loud laughter fell upon the ears of Roger and companions.

The open shed by the side of the house was still occupied as when Roger passed.

The horses of half the detachment were ranged under it, ready for mounting; their bridles only were wanting, and these were suspended from the pummels of their saddles on one side, whilst the weapons of the buccaneers hung on the other.

A solitary sentinel paced along this line of horses, and the clang of his empty sword sheath, as it drawled along the ground, responsive to his measured footsteps, was the only sound from without the house which mingled with the indications of mirth from within.

Having ascertained from this circumstance that their horses were guarded but by one man, Roger advanced to the shed with his band.

"Who goes there?" vociferated the sentinel.

The answer was a fatal one.

The sentinel fell, deprived of the power of repeating the question or giving the alarm.

The horses were quickly bridled and the sabres in the hands of the guerillas, who were before only armed with such weapons as could be concealed—pistols, knives, and daggers.

A sufficient number of the party remained with the horses to protect them, whilst others, headed by old Snowdrop, went round the house in search of the other stable, where they expected to find the remaining horses.

Roger led the rest of his men to the house.

The door was confined by a wooden latch, which was capable of being raised as well from the outside as from within.

Proceeding with caution, Roger gently pushed the door open, but was scarcely able to distinguish clearly the objects that presented themselves, from the quantity of smoke which filled the great and almost only room of the house, for the lofts above stairs hardly deserved to be so called.

This was a combination of the smoke which the strong wind prevented from ascending through the ill-contrived chimney, and that which had passed through the mouths of the buccaneers, who were regaling themselves with the tobacco of which they had robbed Roger.

The noise of their mirth had a little abated, or rather was drawn to one point by the attention of the whole to the song of one man, who was amusing his comrades and himself by singing a noisy ditty; and this temporary silence rendered more electric the shock which was produced by the pistol of Roger, with which he effectually and eternally silenced the voice of the singer.

The confusion that ensued is not to be described.

It must be left to the imagination to picture the bloody sacrifice, of which it was the prelude.

If any are revolted at the scene which presents itself to their minds, let it be remembered that the islanders were seeking redress by the law of retaliation, when no other law was respected, and that in the execution of its dictates of taking life for life, they were punishing, by a rapid and almost instantaneous death, those who were deliberately and wantonly inflicting torture, and committing murder under the most aggravating circumstances of cruelty.

Nor can it be said that they were punishing the innocent for the guilty; for the thirst for plunder, and the consequent indifference, or delight in the production of human misery was too general among the buccaneer invaders, for any of them to escape its influence: and Roger felt as the work of death was going on, that although no hand there perhaps had held the brand that fired Fort Martin, nor fixed the fatal knot that deprived his friends of life, yet that he was avenging the destruction of many another place, and the fate of many another friend.

The guerillas were not long in effecting their purpose.

The manner in which the invaders were surprised, and the confusion of mingled friends and enemies in the house, greatly assisted them.

Five or six who where in the stable with the unsaddled horses when Snowdrop's party attacked them, had opposed no resistance, but saved themselves by flight.

Of the rest of the buccaneers not one remained to tell the tale.

One of the guerillas had been killed, and two slightly wounded.

Those who fled would certainly alarm Mungo at Fort Martin, and a speedy retreat was necessary.

They possessed themselves of the horses and arms of their victims, and having taken all that was found of any value about their persons, they assembled round Roger to receive his orders.

"My friends," said he, "the work of retribution has been performed in a manner worthy of the cause which we have armed to defend, and of the vengeance which your wrongs require. We must now seek a safe retreat; we shall nowhere find so secure a one as in the woods and passes of the Red Hills. Thither let us repair. Let each man take his own road, taking care to avoid the neighbourhood or the stations of the enemy, where our arms would subject us to discovery and death."

The guerillas, exhilarated by their success, and delighted with their booty, divided themselves into small parties.

Those to whose lot the horses had fallen, retained their arms and military appearance; but the remainder, who were obliged to walk, kept their concealed weapons only, and assumed the appearance of common half-breeds.

They separated according to the directions which had been given them.

Roger and Snowdrop continued together. They struck off into a small path with which both were acquainted, and which led them over the mountain to an Indian village.

It was still dark when they crossed the bridge and entered the ruined streets of the poor village.

They passed by Xeres de la Frontera without entering the town; and, having halted for some time at Las Cabezas de San Juan, they arrived at nightfall at the Venta de la Alcantarilla.

The miserable accommodations which this inn or venta* afforded at the best of times were now rendered much worse by the frequent passage of the buccaneers, who, at each visit, took care to leave nothing in it which they could devour or conveniently carry away.

Roger and Snowdrop, therefore, contented themselves with some eggs for their supper, and made a cloak, stretched out before the fire, serve for their bed.

They had been journeying since the earliest dawn, and were tired.

"Why so sad, Master Roger?" asked the innkeeper. "All does not seem to be well with you. I dare be sworn now that the kiss of some little girl fashioned your mouth that way when you left her, and you're afraid to disturb it with a smile. Come, cheer up, man; the girls about here have as black eyes, and as brown skins as in any part of the island—aye, and as tender hearts, too. The half-breeds that you will find shall make you forget those you left behind. Our girls shall make you bring up your love as Francisco wanted to make old Antonio, the buccaneer, bring up his."

Roger inquired to what he alluded.

"What! did you never hear the story of the beautiful Anduessa, the flower of our valley?"

Roger replied in the negative.

"Stop till I light my pipe, and I'll tell it you then."

He speedily performed the operation of striking a light upon his linen, prepared in the manner of tinder, but white and spungy, with which every islander is commonly provided, and, having communicated the spark to his pipe, and returned the little box containing his apparatus into his pocket, he resumed his discourse.

"Anduessa was the most beautiful girl in Seville. There was an orchard before the house where she lived, and the young men used to go and sit there for hours together, but all the while watching for an opportunity of seeing her at the window.

"But it was all labour lost; for, although they saw her often enough, and used to make signs that she might take as kisses to herself, as the humour suited her, she always wilfully mistook the meaning, and crossed the love-making intention of the gallants, for she was betrothed to a brave and handsome youth, of a worthy family and character, and, being a very pattern of virtue herself, she never thought of swallowing the sugar plums that the gay young men threw at her.

"But there was a rascally old buccaneer, ill luck to him, one Antonio, who belonged to the band in this place, all a set of reprobates alike; ill-luck to 'em again, say I.

"This Antonio, as I told you, cast his eyes upon this paragon of perfection, and he must needs fall in love as well as all the rest of the world.

"At first he only stopped at the window when he saw her there, and joked her, which joking she received with all due humility, from one of his sinful calling.

"But this wouldn't do for the old buccaneer.

"By degrees he got into conversation with her, and spoke most pleasant words to her, which she took for so many steps ascended of the ladder of her safety.

"He wanted her to make him her betrothed.

"But her mother had already chosen a ram from the same flock, and as black a one as this for aught I know.

"As he used to come and see her at the house almost every evening, he began at last to be a little bolder, and to mix kisses with his words, too, which the simple girl took for friendship, not knowing that they carried the sting of the devil's own curse.

"As he got on so well he took heart, and, finding it so easy to take his own heart, he thought it might not be difficult to take hers; so one evening he mustered up courage, and asked her to let him come into the house the next day, after dinner time, and to meet him alone.

"The girl did not know what to think of this, but she did not like to let him come in till she had asked her father, and so she put him off till another day.

"But her father knew very well what to think of it, and he told her what sort of a wolf she had to do with dressed up in sheep's clothing.

"'But,' says he, 'we must lay a trap for him. You must pretend that you understand this old

* Ventas are solitary inns, erected at convenient distances from towns or villages, where travellers take rest. They are generally miserable sheds, which afford better accommodation for horse than for man, and, no doubt, are so named because Spaniards, at one time, were known to have lived on the island.

rascal, and you must let him come in. Only give me notice when he is to be with you.'

"The girl entered into the joke of it, and played her part so well that the worthy Antonio sucked his fingers with delight at having caught his bird.

"The next day was named, and Antonio took devilish good care that he would not be behind his hour.

"But the father was before his time, and, hid up in a closet in the room, was preparing the hour of retribution for the old villain.

"The girl put on all the airs she had learned that she thought would suit the occasion, and her father, quietly waiting until he could not be mistaken as to the intentions of Antonio, opened his closet door suddenly, and appeared like a ghost to the astonished child of the devil, holding a large bottle in one hand, and a drawn sword in the other.

"'Hillo! here we have you, Mr. Buccaneer. How will you get out of this scrape?' said he.

"'And now,' says he, 'you villain, you deserve a worse fate than what my mercy has designed for you; look at this bottle; it contains something to mortify that body of yours, and make you vomit forth the love that the devil has put into you. It is only a gentle mixture of ipecacuanha, tartar emetic, and other such pleasant ingredients; take your choice, either the contents of the bottle to the very gregs, or the blade of my sword to the very hilt, one or other must go into your stomach.'

"Only fancy the old buccaneer, begging and entreating for mercy, and the father swearing he would give him none, but quietly pouring out the comfortable cordial into a basin which he had provided for the occasion.

"But they say you may as well have to do with the devil as with his son; and if this buccaneer was not his son, and his eldest son too, he must have been the devil himself; for while the father was kindly preparing the potation for him, out he pulls two pistols, and holds one to each of their heads.

"'Now it's my turn,' says he; 'now my pretty cunning pair, if either of you stir a foot, one of these pistols prevents a second step. Most valorous knight-errant, have the goodness to present that goblet to the hands of your all-beautiful daughter; and do you, all charming one, take care not to drink more than half of its contents, that your magnanimous father may have the pleasure of drinking your health in the other.'

"It was of no use to talk, or to pray—the villain was inexorable, and, faith, made them drink up the whole of the nice stuff that the father had prepared for him, taking care that each should have his share.

"Then, keeping his pistols still pointed at them and retiring backwards to the door, 'I am sorry,' says he, 'that I cannot indulge myself in the pleasure of waiting to behold the salutary effects of the wholesome medicine you have taken; but, I have no doubt, they will be sufficiently rapid.'

"Then, leaving the room, swearing loudly, he double locked the door, and left the discomfited pair staring in each other's face.

"It was not long before the father found that his Indian apothecary was an honest man, and had sold him very effective physic.

"Both he and his daughter made a bolt to the window, as the key was still turning in the door, and, when they reached it, they began to feel very sick, as if the house had been a ship in the rolling sea.

"Antonio, as he passed by the window, deliberately gave them his bitter curse, and walked on.

"Anduessa and her father were obliged to confess themselves *sick* of joking with buccaneers, as they lay in their beds for a week afterwards."

The mirthful vein which this story excited in the travellers, Roger and Snowdrop, continued throughout the whole of the evening.

"But, are the buccaneers still very numerous about here?" asked Roger.

"Yes, but they have despoiled us of everything of value or use, and we are reduced to the very lowest state of poverty. It seems they have made up their minds to stay on the island for ever, and make all of us their slaves."

"That shall never be while *I* have life," said Roger, firmly. "But what means those large fires burning on yonder hills?" asked Roger, anxiously.

"Fires! I have never seen them before," said the astonished landlord. "There is some mystery in it. Perhaps they are signal fires of the buccaneers."

"No, it cannot be."

While they stood at the door of the rude venta or inn, a horseman galloped up in great haste, saying,

"Good news! good news! Lion Limb has landed on the island this very night!"

CHAPTER LXXVII.

THE ARRIVAL OF LION LIMB.

THE sudden intelligence that brave Lion Limb had arrived on the island with his gallant band, sent a tremor of joy through the veins of Roger and his black companion, Snowdrop.

For a moment they could scarely believe the news to be true.

Roger, in his eagerness and joy, seized the reins of the horse, and questioned the new-comer.

"Who are you?" said Roger.

"I am one of Lion Limb's men."

"Aye, that may or may not be true; but what is your name?"

"My name is Ted Rawlings," said the youth, attempting to smile; "perhaps you have heard of me before."

"I think I have; but, then, you know, I have no positive proof that you really are what you pretend to be."

"Oh, as to that," said Ted, coolly, "you shall not have to wait long for sufficient evidence that I am a friend, for in less than half-an-hour you will hear the guns of Lion Limb's 'Rattlesnake' thundering in the distance; for he swears by all that is good, he will sink the piratical 'Vulture' before he leaves the island, and scatter the buccaneers to the four winds of Heaven."

"Yes, but dat's more easy to say dan to do," remarked old Snowdrop, rolling his eyes; "dat dam Mungo hab as many libes as a cat."

"Trust to what our young captain promises, darkie, and all will go right," Ted Rawlings remarked, confidently.

"Don't you call me a darkie," Snowdrop answered quickly and pettishly; "don't you call me a 'darkie,' young 'un. I'se a coloured pusson."

"Well, then, a coloured pusson, if you like," said Ted, grinning, "it's all the same to me; I daresay you are a jolly good fellow enough, and brave as steel."

"Oh, yes, me brave, me berry brave, eh, Massa Roger; all de buccaneer debils are afeerd of me. I can lick 'em all—one by one."

"In what way?" asked Ted.

"In what way?" asked the darkie, in an indignant tone.

"I suppose in a foot race you can give Mungo's man a long, nay, a *very* long start."

"You shut your mouth, young 'un," said Snowdrop, very much annoyed at Ted's jokes.

"Stop that prattle," said Roger; "this is no time for foolish jokes. But, tell me, young 'un, how do you know that Lion Limb intends to do what you say?"

"When he arrived off the island, he landed four of us, the lightest lads in the colony; he mounted each of us on a fast native pony, and told us to scour the whole island, right and left, in order to arouse all the friendly natives and colonists, and then to repair as speedily as possible to Fort Martin and await the arrival of all his men, who are to advance on the place in four bodies, and thus take the robbers by surprise from all quarters at once."

"Not a bad plan," said Roger, "and it shows Lion Limb's forethought and wisdom."

"But, do he know whar de buccaneer's 'Vulture' am?" asked Snowdrop.

"Yes; as we approached the island Harry Woodruff mounted up to the truck of the main-mast, and, with a good glass, descried the black flag of the buccaneers waving from the foremast of the 'Vulture,' which was anchored in a small bay not more than twelve miles distant. Lion Limb would have sailed right down upon her, but, as I have already said, he landed several couriers, and then went out to sea again, with the intention of fighting her to the very death; but, just as he left the land, a rocket was seen to go up in the air, and, shortly afterwards, as I stood on a hillock, I perceived that the 'Vulture' had got some information of our arrival, and put out to sea."

"I am very sorry for it," said Roger; "for, if Lion Limb had had the good fortune to catch the cursed piratical craft in harbour, and at anchor, I doubt very much if he would have left a single plank of her hull entire and sound."

"Oh! you need have no fear," said Ted, "she can't escape us."

"I don't know that; you are over confident, my lad. I know more about those men under Mungo than you do."

"So we does," chimed in Snowdrop; "we know more about 'em dan ever Lion Limb. See what dangers we hab gone through."

"Well," said the landlord, who had been attentively listening to all that was said, "are you satisfied that this youth is a friend of yours or not?"

"Yes," answered Roger, "I am."

"Then the very best thing we can do for him is to lay before him some refreshments."

"The very thing I was about to propose myself," said Ted, who commenced to dismount. "What have you got?"

"Oh! something that will satisfy a hungry man. Weary travellers are not over particular or nice in their demands. If a bottle of good native wine, a new loaf, some beef, and a few grapes are at all acceptable, they are at your service."

"Many thanks. I could not have wished for better or more agreeable fare."

"Bless your stars, you weren't a buccaneer in disguise," said Snowdrop, who did not by any means relish Master Ted's boldness; "because we should hab skinned you like an eel."

"Very kind of you certainly," said Ted, grinning. "I shan't forget your politeness, Mr. Colonel Pusson."

"My name's Snowdrop, if you please."

"Well, Junius Brutus Snowdrop, I'm——"

Bang! bang! bang! resounded heavy reports of cannon among the rocks and hills.

"De Lor' hab mercy on us, what dat?" asked old Snowdrop, rolling his eyes, and trembling. "What's dat, Massa Roger?"

"That's young Lion Limb's cannon," said Roger, with a face flushed with pleasure.

"What am he doing, Massa Roger? it sounds as loud as de bery deb——"

Bang! bang! bang! were the sounds again repeated, quicker and louder than ever.

"It is our young captain giving the buccaneers an extra dose of pepper," said Ted.

"They must be a good distance away though," said Roger.

"Yes, the nearest point to the sea beach from here is eight miles at least," said the landlord; "but the wind blows this way, and we can consequently hear more distinctly."

For a few moments all intently listened to the sounds as they rolled through the air.

They became quicker and quicker each instant, but to the surprise of all, they grew more distant and faint, until at last but the echos of the faintest reports were audible.

"I can't make it out," said Roger.

"Nor I either," Ted remarked.

"Perhaps one vessel is chasing the other," the landlord ventured to say.

"Aye, that's it," said Ted; "The 'Rattlesnake' is chasing the 'Vulture,' you may be sure of that," said Ted.

"That may be," said Roger.

"True, sar, it may be," said Snowdrop, rolling his eyes in grave doubt.

"*May* be," Ted asked, indignantly; "I *know* it is."

"You doesn't know no more nor anybody else," said Snowdrop. "What *I* know, I knows; and what I knows is dis——'

"What?"

"Why, dat de 'Vulture' hab got a good many guns on board and rare ole clinkers dey is, and if Massa Limb——"

"Captain Lion Limb, if you please," said Ted.

"Well den, if Massa Captain of de Lion Limb hab got no guns as big as Mungo, why, den Massa Mungo play de bery debil with Massa Limb."

They again listened attentively for a repetition of the sounds of conflict, but the reports were so faint, far distant, and long between, that no one could form any conjecture as to how things were going on.

"It may be that the 'Rattlesnake' is chasing the 'Vulture,'" mused Roger, "but——"

"Yes, sir," said the landlord, in a half whisper; "but suppose the boot is on the other leg?"

"I don't understand you," said Roger.

"Suppose, sir, that the buccaneers have proved too much for Lion Limb, and that they are chasing the 'Rattlesnake.'"

Roger made no reply, but looked fixedly at the landlord for a moment in thoughtful silence.

At last he murmured, with a heavy heart,

"If it should prove to be so, I fear all our fondest hopes and expectations are for ever blasted. We are doomed to slavery; we shall all pass under the yoke of that detested and inhuman African—Mungo."

"Perhaps, be carried away in cargoes, and sold to the South American planters," sighed the landlord, "for Mungo has no mercy for those who oppose his wishes."

"I shall be a dead man ere that takes place," sighed Roger. "But before I die I'll make some of the vile rascals bite the dust."

"And I, too, sar," said Snowdrop. "Massa Mungo no hab dis coloured pusson in chains and sold to sugar planters in de Spanish settlements. No catchee no habee. I can lib on nothing for a month, and run like a deer, Massa Roger."

"Well," said the landlord, "if you are determined to have revenge on the buccaneers you can commence this very night, Master Roger."

"How?"

"Not more than five miles from here there is a large and extensive stone building, which we natives have a tradition was built two centuries ago by some adventurous visitors to our island. Whether they were Spaniards or of some partly civilised nation of the continent, I know not; but, at all events, they had good notions of architecture both as to soundness and beauty of design. There is a history connected with this old building, which at this moment is too long to relate; but suffice it to say, that a party of buccaneers have made the place their rendezvous and head-quarters. They nightly carouse there, and fatten on the immense spoil which their roving bands collect with fire and sword far and wide."

"Well, what do you propose?" asked Roger, impatiently.

"I propose that we visit the place to-night, and blow up the rascals."

"Blow them up? That is more easily said than done," Roger remarked. "I have never seen the place."

"But I have, and know it well."

"Indeed, how does that come to pass?"

"Why, the black-looking villains visited my poor venta, and robbed it of nearly all I possessed; and had I not had foresight and prudence, and hidden away much that I possessed, it is more than likely you would not have had a single bottle of wine to refresh you."

"I understand; they took all they could find," said Roger.

"No; they didn't *take* my property, but simply made an inventory of it. They left *me* to carry the things to them, do you see, the lazy villains. And many a long and weary journey I have had, I can assure you."

"So they made a pack-mule of you?"

"Yes; that's just it. I dared not disobey, for they left two rough cut-throats to watch me, with strict orders to shoot me if I dared to disobey."

"Very pleasant, indeed, I shouldn't wonder," Ted remarked.

"You hold your noise," said Snowdrop, angrily. "What do *you* know about tings about here? You hold your noise, I tell you."

"So, in your frequent journeys to and fro, you had grand opportunities for scanning all the ins and outs of this old building," said Roger.

"Yes, I had; and I observed that in one of the cellars they had a quantity of powder, and ——"

"But, suppose they had removed it; what then?"

"Why, we could set fire to the place for all that."

"How? The bare walls wouldn't ignite."

"The bare walls wouldn't catch light, I know," said the landlord; "but you don't think for a moment that these villains live so humbly as we do?"

"Do they not?"

"No, they have decorated their rooms with rolls of cloth and damask and silk, which they brought with them from the Blue Rocks, the proceeds of robbery, no doubt, and you would scarcely believe how luxuriously they live among themselves."

"Oh, de debils!" sighed Snowdrop, "and here am me, Massa Roger, almost in rags."

"If that be the case, then," said Roger, "I have no doubt we could easily set fire to the place, and burn out the rats."

"I should like them to get a good warming," said Ted, "and, if you don't mind, I'll make one of the party."

"Very well, then, let us start," said Roger.

"I will go first," said the landlord, "and take a small hamper of wine with me as an excuse."

"Are there none of our friends to be met with on the way?" asked Roger.

"Yes, I know more than a score of poor, houseless natives who are living in the woods and forests, and on my way I will arouse them all."

"But we don't know the way."

"I can easily point that out to you. I will light a small fire here and there to direct you."

"But the natives might mistake us for enemies in the darkness."

"I can soon prevent any such mistake as that."

"How?"

"Why, let us all have a pass-word."

"A good idea."

"What shall it be?"

"I propose 'Lion Limb,'" said Ted.

"A very good pass-word indeed," Roger remarked; "we couldn't adopt a better one."

"Then, it is agreed to?"

"It is."

"I will start at once, then, and pass the word to all who are friendly towards us."

"Do so."

"You may rely on my fidelity."

"We can go at once when we see your first signal fire. We will follow in your trail."

"Very well, then, I am off."

With a small hamper of choice wine which he had managed to conceal from the prying eyes of the buccaneers in their frequent visits, the landlord mounted a stout mule, and departed, leaving the venta and all it contained to the care of his friends, with strict injunctions to lock up and make fast the doors and stables when they should depart.

Roger and Snowdrop were excited beyond measure at the proposed expedition, and each one began to look well to his arms, so that all should be ready for instant use.

Now, Master Ted Rawlings didn't much relish the idea of encountering the buccaneers in their stronghold.

He would have much preferred staying behind, and making free with the wines and liquors which the venta possessed.

Both the eyes of Snowdrop were upon him, and, for the honour of Lion Limb and his followers, Ted resolved to pluck up courage, and do his best in the coming fight.

Perceiving that it was useless to complain of fatigue, he commenced to talk so very bravely of what he had done, and what he intended to do, so that at last old Snowdrop looked upon him as a prodigy of valour.

As long as the bottle of wine at his elbow lasted, Master Ted jabbered away, and the longer he talked the greater lies he told, until at last he got fairly tired of boasting, and began to yawn and get very sleepy.

The landlord had been gone about half-an-hour, when Snowdrop exclaimed—

"Dar it is, Massa Roger ; dar's the fire."

In the distance Roger perceived a small fire flickering on a hill-top, and giving the word to Ted and Snowdrop, they locked up the house, and went forth into the darkness on their perilous expedition, not forgetting to take with them a bottle of wine each to keep the cold out.

*　　*　　*　　*　　*

The buccaneers had made up their minds for a long, if not for a permament, stay on the island, and accordingly they made themselves remarkably cosy and comfortable in this dwelling, which even among the natives went under the name of the Casa de Moneda.

But Roger and his friends, full of hope, resolved to punish the invaders as we have seen.

The buccaneers, under Mungo himself, were at the Casa, and as they supped and caroused, they looked forward to a long life of pleasure and rapine, and plans were made for the morrow, on which another and more extensive plundering expedition should start forth from their head quarters at the Casa.

But there was a long dismal night before the arrival of that day, and to many of them it might never arrive.

Patriotism and revenge had determined that to some it should not ; and the intervention of a gloomy night afforded the means of putting that determination into execution.

With the blindness of security, the buccaneers repaired to their splendid apartments in the Casa de Moneda, and sought repose from the fatigues of their plunderings on the luxurious beds which were there ready for them.

But they were suddenly roused from the deep sleep, which the guilty can purchase only by excess of fatigue, by the alarm of fire !

And scarcely were their faculties awakened to a sense of their danger, when the columns of thick smoke which assailed them on all sides almost deprived them of the power of endeavouring to escape.

Unacquainted with the situation of all the rooms, and with the vast building of which they formed a part, some ran into the danger while attempting to fly from it.

Others threw themselves from the windows at the risk of losing their lives or disabling their limbs.

The wing of the building, in which were situated the apartments of Mungo's men, was discovered to be on fire in three different parts.

And in such a manner did the flames increase

that in the course of a short time that wing was but a shell of stone ; but by the exertions of some of the buccaneers who were employed in duties outside the place, they were prevented from spreading beyond the wing in which they had commenced.

The dining-room, the splendid apartments, and all the property of the ruffianly thieves had fallen a sacrifice.

Nor were there wanting several lives to complete the offering which this pyre had been lighted to make to an injured country.

Mungo himself escaped with no other personal injury than the fright which the sudden alarm had occasioned him.

Mixing almost in a state of nakedness amongst the crowd which had collected around the burning house, he eagerly asked,

"What fire is this ?"

"It is the fire of *patriotism,*" replied a native who was near him.

It was, indeed, the fire of Patriotism.

It was a spark of that fire of patriotism which had been lighted in many places—of that inextinguishable flame which from its houses had been communicated to the hearts of its inhabitants.

It was a brand which the invaders had fired that now was employed to consume themselves.

That brand had inflamed the bosoms of Roger and his guerillas, and it was by them that it was now made a weapon of retribution.

Secure in the retreats of the mountains, Roger had, as we have seen, inured his men to the fatigues of their new life, and organized them for the destruction of their enemies in every possible way.

By the interception of couriers, small parties of officers and buccaneers generally, and by daring attacks upon convoys of provisions and treasure, he had rendered himself feared throughout the whole island ; and the more, that the buccaneers in the Casa had hitherto remained unmolested by any native bands or organized party of guerillas.

The natives generally either had hitherto found no chief to form and connect them into a body, or they had been intimidated by the proclamation of the bloody tyrant Mungo, which decreed that all persons taken with arms in their hands, fighting for the cause of Governor Martin, should be considered as banditti and rebels, and treated accordingly.

The conflagration in the Casa de Moneda took place exactly three hours after the departure of the patriotic landlord from the venta.

But how it happened, or who had done it, remained a profound secret even to Roger himself, for he could not bring himself to believe that the destruction had been caused by a single man.

But, be that as it may, there was the conflagration before his eyes, and there were the half-naked villains rushing about, cursing, and swearing, and vowing vengeance on every inhabitant of the island.

Mungo himself was stamping and raving like a madman, and such was the terror he inspired into the hearts of all around him, that many of the poor natives, who acted in and about the Casa as servants or slaves, stood trembling, and knew not what to think or say.

One poor wretch had fallen dead with a single blow from Mungo's sword.

He was the one who had bravely said—

"The fire was the fire of patriotism."

Dearly, indeed, had he paid for his brave speech, and, as he lay weltering in his blood at the tyrant's feet, Mungo's eyes flashed deadly fire.

"I'd give one thousand ounces of gold to know how this happened," said the tyrant, bursting with rage, as he gazed and frowned on some few natives near him.

"We can soon ferret out the secret, Captain Mungo," said one of his men. "Seize a dozen of the islanders, and roast them alive. The torture will soon make them disclose the secret."

"So it will; the heat of the fire will make them open their mouths like an oyster on hot coals. Seize a few of the devils, and bind them hand and foot."

Some of his men were about to execute his orders, when a buccaneer, all haste and muddy, galloped up to the Casa, and, vaulting from his horse, pushed his way through the crowds around the burning place, and approached Mungo, who, in his shirt sleeves and cutlass in hand, stood gazing at the dire conflagration with looks of disappointment and rage.

"What news?"

"What news?"

"When did you start?"

"How about the 'Vulture?'"

"Is all safe?"

"Has anything important happened?"

These and a hundred similar questions were put to the new-comer, who, however, replied not, but looked anxious, pale and troubled.

"What news?" asked Mungo, gruffly.

"The very worst, captain."

"What mean you?"

"Captain Lion—"

"Ah! What of that young bastard? Tell me, is he dead?"

"No, captain; he lives still."

"Curses on him then!"

"He lives, captain, and has landed on this island this very night."

"What!"

"'Tis true."

"Can I believe my own ears?" said Mungo. "Landed!"

"Yes, Mungo."

"And in spite of all the precautions which I have made against him?"

"Yes, captain, 'tis perfectly true."

"And did not the 'Vulture' sink his craft? Did I not give strict orders that my signal-men on different parts of the island should warn me of his approach?"

"He escaped their notice, captain."

"I will hang every one of them. But the 'Vulture'—what of her?"

"As soon as she received news that Lion Limb was near the island, she put out to sea, and——"

"Sunk the 'Rattlesnake,' I suppose?"

"No, captain, the 'Rattlesnake' sailed down boldly towards our craft, and a fierce engagement immediately ensued, and I am sorry to report that——"

"Sorry to report!" gasped Mungo, turning pale. "Speak out, man. What do you mean? Speak quickly, I say, or, by my——"

"I am sorry to say, Captain Mungo, that the firing of the 'Rattlesnake' was so excellent, and so far superior to that of our men, that——"

"Impossible! I cannot; I will not believe it! death and fury! What! Are you mad? Their gunnery better than ours? you must be raving."

"Indeed, I am not, captain, I speak the plain and naked truth."

"It cannot be—a mere boy like that young bastard convict, Lion Limb, to instruct his men better than I have mine!"

"Whatever you may think, captain, what I say you may firmly rely on. I was standing on eminence and saw all that happened."

"How could you, the night was dark?"

"It might have been in this part of the island, captain; but on the sea shore, the clouds drifted at times, and the moonlight, peering on the water, gave me an excellent view."

"Well, and what happened then?"

"I saw that our men on board the 'Vulture' fired quickly and wildly; but the guns of the 'Rattlesnake' were worked slowly and coolly; our shot fell wide or short, or over shot; but their's rent our sails, split our main mast, hulled the 'Vulture' several times, until at last I began to think our ship would sink at every broadside."

"But it did not."

"No."

"Good news, then. Well, go on."

"From some cause I could not understand, the 'Rattlesnake' did not close with the 'Vulture,' but seemed to be crippled in her rudder, for when our craft made sail away the enemy followed, but seemed unable to keep her course."

"Excellent," said Mungo; "thank the fates for so much good luck. If the enemy has been injured in her rudder, the 'Vulture' is safe, and can escape."

"True, captain, and so thought the enemy; for after chasing for more than an hour, she tacked about, and came bowling along towards the shore again; and, I fear, before morning she will land her men and march on towards Fort Martin, and take us by surprise in all directions."

"Death and fury!" swore Mungo. "Let every man of us arm for the worst, then; for if that young Devil's Limb and his hungry followers fall upon us, I fear there will be many carcases for the buzzards to feed upon and pick."

But while Mungo and the courier were thus speaking, the fire still continued, and the buccaneers seemed to be suddenly seized with fear, and were undecided how to act or what to do.

"What means this laziness?" shouted Mungo, impatiently. "Don't you see the fire still blazing?"

"Yes, yes, captain; take care of yourself. The flames have penetrated to the stone vaults below, and it may catch the powder."

The man had scarcely spoken, when a loud report took place, and the building blew up in all directions.

Beams, stones, windows, casks, planks, furniture, and many unhappy human beings were hurled with terrific violence in all directions; and where before had been a lurid mass of flames rushing to the skies, nothing was seen but four bare smoking walls, and a mass of ruins, while just in front of the main door lay a helpless man with a burning torch in his hand.

He was senseless, and bleeding and blackened, and over him lay a heavy beam.

It was the heroic innkeeper!

But, before Mungo and his terrified men could recover from their astonishment and dismay, loud shouts were heard.

It was Roger and his faithful band rushing on to give battle to the tyrant Mungo.

"On, men, on! Don't give the villains breathing time; throw them into the smoking red-hot ruins! On, men, on! strike for your homes, your country, and all that's dear. Follow me. Victory or death! Your watchword, remember, is, 'Lion Limb!'"

All now was intense excitement and danger!

THE BOY KING

OF THE SOUTH SEA ISLANDS.

ENGAGEMENT BETWEEN THE "RATTLESNAKE" AND THE "VULTURE."

CHAPTER LXXVIII.

THE FAITHFUL INNKEEPER AND GUIDE FALLS INTO THE HANDS OF MUNGO.

THE sudden assault which the brave Roger and his few friends made upon the band of furious bucca-

neers as they stood outside the burning ruins of their once comfortable dwelling was unsuccessful.

Roger and his gallant guerillas were driven back by the furious bravery of Mungo's desperate followers, and it was just as much as Roger himself and young Ted Rawlings could do to escape with their lives.

Not heeding the terrible news that the invincible Lion Limb and his crew had landed on the coast, Mungo and his gang had determined at once to wreak their vengeance on those that still remained in their hands.

The brave innkeeper, with the torch still fast clutched in his hands, was the first victim seized.

He was faint and bleeding, and had been looked upon as dead; but the quick eye of Mungo soon espied him lying on the ground, and he was dragged forth, and heavily manacled.

"What shall we do with him?" shouted many.

"Shoot him!"

"Hang him by the heels until he dies!"

"No, let us try and get all the information we can out of him first," shouted many.

The more violent and drunken party, however, prevailed.

A court of three had been organized on the spot, and the victim, again surrounded by a rabble, was now brought before this august tribunal.

"Whom do you belong to?"

Such was the first question addressed to the prisoner.

"I belong," answered the innkeeper, with much solemnity, "to the God who made us all."

A reply so unusual was received by some with a stare, by others with a laugh, redoubled at the repartee by one of the judges.

"To God! Ah, I rather reckon you belong to the devil! Anyhow, he'll very soon have you."

To reiterated demands as to who he was, the innkeeper steadily replied that he was a free man, when the same witty judge raised a new laugh by requesting him to show his free papers.

The court, after hearing a witness or two, pronounced him guilty of murder.

After which he was asked, with a sort of mock solemnity, if he had anything to say why sentence of death should not be passed upon him.

"Go on," said the indignant culprit; "hang me, kill me, do your will! My wife was flogged to death before my eyes. As a free man, you have hunted me with bloodhounds, and shot at me with rifles, and placed a price upon my head. Long have I fooled you, and paid you back in your own coin. One by one, two by two, three by three, I defy, and would whip the whole of you; but the whole dozen, mounted and armed, with dogs to boot, were too much for one poor man, with nothing but his feet, his hands and his knife. They have not always been too much; but I am getting old. Better die now, while I have strength and courage to defy your worst, than fall into your hands a broken-down old man."

These words of defiance wrought up the assembled mob to a fury perfectly devilish.

"Hanging is too good for him!" some of them cried out.

And presently the awful cry was raised—

"Burn him! burn him!"

No sooner was the horrible idea suggested than volunteers were found to prepare to carry it into execution.

It was in vain that two or three of those who had been engaged in the capture of the innkeeper remonstrated against this horrible and illegal cruelty.

The same brutal Mungo who had dashed the water from the poor man's lips now stood forward as the leader and manager in this new atrocity.

"It was necessary," he said, "with the country agitated by incendiaries, some of them in communication with Lion Limb, now that they had him in their power, to make an example of him.

"The stories of his exploits, circulating among the natives, had done infinite damage, and might make many imitators.

"It was necessary, therefore, to counteract the impression by having his career terminated in a way to inspire awe and terror."

A pile of wood was soon collected, and the victim of Mungo's vengeance was placed in the midst of it.

The pile was then lighted, and the smoke and flames began to wreathe above his head.

But even yet unsubdued, he looked round on his shouting tormentors with a smile of contemptuous defiance.

Unable to endure the horrid spectacle, several natives attempted to rush from among the crowd, but found themselves watched and directly seized and, by order of the self-appointed master of the ceremonies of this horrible scene, conveyed close to the burning pile, as such on whom the spectacle of such an execution might make a salutary impression.

The old man recognised several — at least, he thought so — from amid the flames, and he lifted up his arm, as if to bid them farewell.

"Oh, the horrible agony of that moment! Had I myself been in the place of my friend, could I have suffered more? My heart-strings seemed to crack; the blood rushed in a torrent to my brain. Nature could not endure it. I dropped fainting and senseless to the ground."

So spoke a native afterwards who had seen all.

CHAPTER LXXIX.

THE ACTION BETWEEN THE "RATTLESNAKE" AND THE "VULTURE"—STRANGE CONDUCT OF DICK HAMILTON—WAS IT LOVE OR TREACHERY?— DISAPPEARANCE OF DICK—LION LIMB VISITS KING KATAMAR AND HIS ISLAND POSSESSIONS— THE ROUND OF FESTIVITIES AND GAMES THAT THEN ENSUED—THE OLD KING OFFERS HIS DAUGHTER, MARMI, AS A PRIZE TO THE BRAVEST —TWO STRANGERS ENTER FOR IT—THE SUDDEN DISCOVERY—THE HAPPY MARRIAGE OF ONE OF LION LIMB'S LIEUTENANTS.

BUT the reign of cruelty and riot which Mungo had maintained in the Island was soon brought to a conclusion.

When he and his followers had barbarously murdered the faithful half-breed who had set fire to the venta, Mungo rallied all his forces and took the shortest route to the sea-coast, for he feared Lion Limb and his gallant band, who were reported to be advancing in all directions against him.

He safely reached a secluded spot where he remained for two days, when by constant signalling with fires and rockets, he attracted the attention of the "Vulture," which, though somewhat disabled, was cruising off the island.

The vessel, in obedience to these well-known signals, approached the land, and Mungo with his men hastily embarked.

"No time is to be lost," said the brutal chief, "for I hear that Lion Limb and the 'Rattlesnake' are on the bright look-out for us both day and night; so, therefore, let all hands prepare for action, for we may be attacked at any moment. We fight this time, you must recollect, for 'life or death.'"

It was unnecessary for Mungo to remind his men of this, for all of them knew it, and prepared accordingly.

For two or three days they kept the "Vulture" well away from the land, but at night they kept closer and closer to the island to spy out the doings of Lion Limb.

The "Rattlesnake," however, was seldom in the same place two days together, but moved [about hither and thither in search of the "Vulture" and its numerous crew.

Nor was it very long ere Lion Limb had the satisfaction of discovering the enemies' hiding place in one of the many large and commodious inlets of the island.

"All right, my merry men," said Lion Limb, cheerily, "we have found them out at last, and to-morrow we will sail down unexpectedly upon them and give the rascals a right good thrashing."

"We are all agreeable, sir," said Harry Woodruff, "but there ain't one among us as isn't sorry we've lost gallant Dick Hamilton. I can't make it out, sir; why he left us so suddenly and quietly is a mystery to me."

"I dare say it is, Harry, and to many beside you, but not to me."

"Ain't it, captain?"

"No, Harry."

"Is it treason, treachery or desertion, then, captain?"

"It is a case of desertion, Harry, but not of treason or treachery, you may rely upon it."

"I can't see the drift of your remarks, captain," said Harry, scratching his head in doubt."

"The truth is this, Harry, Dick Hamilton is in love."

"In wh-a-a-at, sir," said Harry, in astonishment, "in love!"

"Yes, in love, Harry; I have seen and known it for a long time."

"In love with what, sir?"

"In love with a girl, to be sure, Harry."

"Well, hang me if I should ever have thought it. I always thought he loved you and me and his ship better than anything else."

"We are all mortal, Harry. For man to love is natural."

"True, sir, quite true; but I don't think any on us have had any time to think about the girls much. And where is the lass, sir, may I be bold enough to ask?"

"On one of these islands."

"But which?"

"We shall soon discover, Harry, after we have disposed of the buccaneers in the next engagement."

"You speak as if we are sure to beat them sir."

"Of course I do, Harry; if Englishmen can't thrash a lot of buccaneer cut-throats in a fair fight we had better haul down our flag and sail to the devil. So let all prepare; we shall sail down upon them unexpectedly to-morrow, Harry."

"But suppose they sail unexpectedly down on us, sir."

"No fear of that, Harry, I think."

"I don't know so much about that," grumbled Harry, to himself, as he moved away to the fore part of the ship. "Mungo is an active brute, so I hear, and a good seaman to boot. Never mind, come when it will, we are all ready for 'em. Our guns are double shotted, and we've plenty of grape in store—the magazine is stocked with all sorts of good things for the African slaver and his friends. I've owed 'em a turn this long time, ever since we had that affair with 'em at the Blue Rocks, and I'm bound to pay 'em back with interest, as sure as my name's Harry."

On the eve of the day that these remarks passed between Lion Limb and his trusty lieutenant, Harry Woodruff, orders were given to weigh anchor, and sail towards that particular part of the island coast where the "Vulture" was reported to be.

All things progressed pleasantly and favourably on board, until about midnight, and they were rapidly approaching the western part of the island, when the young captain, Lion Limb, came up from below, fully armed and ready for immediate action.

"We only have to round yonder rock which juts out into the channel, Harry, and then we shall have all plain and smooth sailing. Mungo and his men cannot be very far away, I imagine."

"True, sir; but the night is very foggy and thick. Do you know the channel well, sir?"

"Yes, I do, Harry; but it appears to me we are too far off the Point; we could go a point or two nearer."

"With all due respect to you, captain, I'd rather bear away a point or two more than we are; there are plenty of rocks and reefs hereabouts. Look at the breakers yonder."

"It's only the tide, I think, Harry, nothing more."

"But yonder light, sir, on the Point there, I never noticed it before."

"Nor I. I dare say, though, that some of the friendly natives, half-breeds or whites, have placed it there to give us warning of the shoals. You know that old Governor Martin and his friends have been landed, and no doubt caused that signal fire to be lit. Keep her closer up to the Point, Harry."

"I'd rather not, sir; the water looks foamy, lumpy and dangerous."

"No fear, my lad."

"Two heads are better than one."

In obedience to orders, Harry Woodruff took the helm, and relying upon his young captain's well-known ability as a navigator, he hummed a tune and rolled the quid of tobacco in his mouth in perfect satisfaction.

"I don't like the look of that fire, Harry," said Lion Limb, once or twice, as he walked the deck in doubt.

"After all, sir, it may not be a friendly signal."

"Keep your eyes open, Harry, don't let us get aground."

Scarcely were the words uttered, when a squall struck the vessel, and she was driven on to a sand bank with great violence.

In a moment every one on board were engaged in furling sail, and making strenuous endeavours to get the vessel off the treacherous bank, but without success.

"Keep a good look out, my men," said Lion Limb, "we may be attacked before we know it. The vessel is all right; the pumps are unnecessary; she is perfectly sound; there is no leakage; not a foot of water in the wells."

"The next tide will float her off, sir," said Harry. "'Tis lucky we didn't get on the rocks yonder."

For several hours the seamen were hard at work, but the vessel could not be stirred from its position; but as morning dawned, and the sunlight began to peep through the dense clouds and fog, an alarm was raised from all quarters.

"They are upon us!"

"The buccaneers are within range."

"Beat to quarters!" said Lion Limb, "the treacherous rascals shan't find us unprepared. Every man to his post, and obey orders silently."

Within a few minutes the "Vulture" was discerned through the mist a few hundred yards away, while six or seven boats, armed and ready for boarding, approached the "Rattlesnake" rapidly and from all sides.

"They are coming on boldly enough, sir," said Harry; "and if I don't mistake there is Mungo himself in the bows of the foremost boat."

"Give 'em three cheers, my lads," said Lion Limb, merrily, "and then let 'em have a few doses of grape shot."

The three cheers were heartily given, and as loudly and defiantly responded to by the bold buccaneers, who were now within pistol shot.

In an instant the action began and the noise was deafening.

Cannons, rifles, and pistols, boomed and cracked on every hand, and in less than five minutes the engagement was both fierce and sanguinary.

The "Vulture" being in deep water was thus enabled to move about, and for some time her shot flew thick and fast through the rigging of the "Rattlesnake."

But Harry Woodruff soon put a stop to this, for he directed a well-aimed shell at the enemy, which crashed through and through the hull of the enemy and caused fearful havoc above and below.

Mungo himself, however, boldly led the boats, and his followers attempted to board the "Rattlesnake," sword in hand.

Lion Limb, however, seemed to be everywhere where danger threatened most, and with bare head—for a shot had carried off his cap—he rushed forward to repel the enemy's daring and spirited attack.

Again and again did the buccaneers swarm on deck, but as often were they beaten back again, until, after two hours of hard and desperate fighting, they sullenly withdrew from the engagement with a loss of many in killed and wounded, amid the derisive cheers of the bold and brave tars under Lion Limb and his trusty officers.

"Beaten them again, sir," said Harry Woodruff, with a powder-blackened face, and several ugly scars, still fresh and bleeding; "we gave the villains more than they expected."

"True, Harry, but we have not conquered them yet, they will give us more trouble some other time."

"If we hadn't got on this sand bank, sir, we should have killed every mother's son of them."

"It can't be helped, Harry; but I doubt very much if they will dare to remain in these waters many days."

Lion Limb's idea was a correct one.

Mungo and his men did not remain near the island long; for, with the first fair wind that blew, they sailed away, and no one knew whither.

For more than a week, Lion Limb cruized round the island, but becoming satisfied that the fierce and brutal invaders had left, he rendered all the assistance that lay in his power to the islanders, and promising to quickly return again, he took on board such of his own men who were on shore, except Joe Pebbles, who made his way to Fort Martin with his fiddle, and then steered for the dominions of King Katamar, where he was well received, and with whom he had frequent interviews and secret conferences on divers matters that concerned the safety and prosperity of the islands round about.

And, strange to say, some tidings were here gleaned regarding Dick Hamilton, who was reported to have made his way to the island in a small sail boat.

From all that Lion Limb now heard, he felt certain that Dick had long been violently in love with Princess Marmi, old Katamar's daughter.

For several days all sorts of sports and pastimes were continued by the Indians, in honour of their friends and visitors, such as leaping, wrestling, running, horse-riding, tilting with spears and lances on horseback, in which sports the natives excelled, greatly to the astonishment of Lion Limb's followers, many of whom competed with the Indians and were defeated.

A rude circle or circus was formed, and surrounding it were vast numbers of natives, who, far and near, journeyed to witness the festive games.

Those of high birth occupied conspicuous places, while at the foot of two thrones, rudely constructed for the use of Katamar and Lion Limb, two natives stood with horns in hand ready to act as heralds.

There was one Indian wrestler of gigantic stature, who had thrown several Englishman, and was on the point of being proclaimed victor, no one any longer daring to cope with him, though the anxious Lion Limb had repeatedly offered a reward of considerable magnitude to any one who should throw him, but in vain.

The voice of the crier was uplifted for the last time, when a graceful figure, habited in a plain disguise that sat close to his shape, and displayed its symmetry, stepped forward from among the throng.

He was masked, and signified to the crier that he would contend only upon the condition of not being required to make himself known until he pleased, provided he was victorious.

Lion Limb being made acquainted with this, acquiesced, though with some reluctance.

None of the English present hoped a favourable event, when they contrasted the form of their unknown champion with the brawny vigour of his Indian adversary, or that of those he had already overcome.

But the field soon rung with their shout of joy and exultation.

A victory more speedily and easily achieved than any that had humbled them, now relieved them from the mortification under which they had seemed by no means easy.

They crowded round the conqueror, and it was not without much difficulty he could prevent the mask being torn from his face; and was at last able to escape from their rude kindness only by a notice that he would take a part in the ensuing sports.

In all those of which he in consequence did participate.

The foot race, the throwing of the javelin, archery, &c., he seemed to win without an effort.

But when he had knelt and received the prize for the sixth victory from the hands of Lion Limb, he suddenly disappeared, leaving the crowd disappointed at his escape, but delighted with the address he exhibited.

On the ensuing day, however, he was again on the field.

But the fervour of the moment was gone by, and he was suffered to remain unmolested.

The reader will doubtless have anticipated that this was no other than Dick Hamilton, the daring prowess of whose youth they will call to mind.

It was indeed no other.

And he now awaited a further opportunity of increasing the title to the favour which had been already strongly expressed towards him; after which, he having resolved to throw himself at the feet of Lion Limb, and having made himself known, demanded to be confronted with the persons who had calumniated him.

While he was thus arranging in his own mind

the manner in which he should proceed, the horns sounded, and a champion of either nation, fully armed, entered the lists to commence an Indian tournament, which was to be the chief business of the day.

The Indian champion was unhorsed at the first onset.

But the victor soon yielded his honours to a new antagonist.

For some time the alternation of success was pretty even.

But at length an Indian champion, of graceful stature and singular strength of skill, maintained the field, after having worsted six English successively.

The countenance of Lion Limb glowed with shame and indignation as he saw his men pushed from their seats.

While a seventh competitor was arming, he took from his finger a ring, which the crier was ordered to proclaim worth very much, and flung it to where the original prize, consisting of a sword, the hilt of which was inlaid with diamonds, was deposited.

It was of no avail.

The knight shared the fate of his predecessors.

The Indian champion brandished his lance, and wheeled his steed round the ring elated with victory, and desirous of showing that he was yet fresh and anxious to reap new laurels.

The wrath of the English waxed hotter.

Lion Limb seemed to labour with some thought that had struck him, and which, after a little time, he appeared to have matured, and found likely to answer his expectations.

He called the crier, and whispered something to him.

The man bowed, and went over to a part of the circle where a number of Indian women, richly clad, were seated, viewing the sports.

He seemed to deliver a message to one of them, whose place denoted the elevation of her rank, and she instantly rose, and giving him her hand he led her to Lion Limb.

As she proceeded to the throne, she was obliged to pass near where Dick stood, disguised as before.

Her vesture was enriched by a blaze of jewels, and the plume of the ostrich, rising from a coronet of pearl, shadowed her polished forehead and arched brow.

Lion Limb seated her beside him; and the herald proclaimed, that if the lady, the richest heiress of the nation, should find the mind and countenance of the victor, in the existing contest, as well worthy of approbation as his valour, she would bestow on him her hand, and in the event of his not pleasing her sufficiently to justify her acceptance of him as her spouse, Lion Limb and King Katamar would richly endow any other maiden whom he might select, and find less difficult of choice.

The first emotion of Dick, when he heard this extraordinary proclamation, was pity mingled with disgust for the weakness of the vain creature who would thus permit herself to be exhibited as the prize of brutal strength, or of a skill which he had learned to think infinitely less of than he was wont to do.

He looked at her.

Heavens! she was eminently lovely!

A thought now struck him what a pleasant vengeance it would be if he could win, and then reject her—what a torment to the beauty and the love of the fickle, but the dear, dear Marmi.

As he thought of the rich triumph he wished to obtain, he loved her more than ever.

But he was destitute of horse and arms.

While a thousand anxious thoughts and desires were agitating his mind, a person who stood by him said—

"This is all a trick."

"A trick!" said he, startled both by the words and by a confused remembrance of having somewhere seen the person who had uttered them, though he could not recollect where or when.

"A trick!" he repeated.

"Yes," said the other, who appeared to be a young Indian prince; "that is an old practitioner among us, who has been so successful; he is the favoured lover of Marmi; and Lion Limb having some time since proposed to her what he has just now done, to set her up as a prize, the Indian to whom he had before refused his consent to marry her bethought himself of this stratagem to obtain it. This I have had from the Indian himself, who is a friend of mine."

Dick now thought it would be a cruelty, which his own happiness had divested him of the wish to practise, if he were to intercept the object which the lovers had in view.

But again he reflected that he would have a right to resign his prize in favour of the vanquished.

And then, how sweet would it be to combine such an act of generosity with his vengeance—a vengeance which he could not think otherwise than fair.

He might enjoy at once the sweets of revenge, and that proud conscience of magnanimity for which others had been glad to abandon it.

But it was of little use to speculate upon a triumph he had not the means of achieving.

He was just turning to ask a question of the person who had spoken to him, when he observed the eye of Katamar directed first towards an Indian who was pressing forward to offer himself a candidate for the beautiful maid, and then, with an appearance of anxiety, towards himself.

He was standing at the edge of the circle, and as Lion Limb looked fixedly on him, he bowed respectfully.

The bow was returned by a gracious nod, and a smile of satisfaction; and the herald was immediately dispatched to him, with an inquiry whether he would enter for the prize.

He made known the obstacles that were opposed to his wish to do so.

Immediately orders were issued, to his infinite joy, that he should be accommodated immediately with a steed and weapon.

In a few minutes he was in the circle, and as he took his lance from the person appointed, he bowed gracefully to the assembly.

With a practised hand he pulled round the head of a beautiful barb that bore him, and was pawing the ground, as if proud of his gallant burthen.

Then, stretching his limbs, to give his arms pliancy, he revealed all the symmetry, flexibility, and elasticity of his frame.

The circle rang with the acclamations of those who had witnessed his activity and courage on the preceding day.

He now wheeled to his ground, and before the horns sounded the charge he cast his eye once more towards Marmi.

She had at length dispelled the smile that had so often grieved him.

An emotion of the deepest anxiety and terror sat upon her countenance.

Her mouth, half open, disclosed her ivory teeth, and her eye was intently fixed upon the combatants.

A slight emotion of wounded vanity stung the mind of Dick.

Another, then, had aroused a sensibility, which had been proof against all his efforts!

And yet she now witnessed his danger with every symptom of the most painful apprehension.

The reflection filled him with an anger which he had not time to subdue.

The last note of the war-kindling trump still vibrated on the air when his Indian adversary lay stretched upon the ground.

His fall had stunned him.

And as the bystanders, in order to give him air, speedily disengaged his head from its covering, Dick could not sufficiently wonder at the taste of his quondam mistress.

For her lover was, to all appearance, about fifty-five years of age, with a thin head of hair, already grey, and a countenance covered with scars, that accounted for the prowess he had exhibited, and in other respects so ill favoured, as to form a perfect contrast with the robust symmetry of his stature.

He had not leisure, however, to indulge his wonder at female caprice, for Lion Limb, who had descended to the foot of his throne, was urgent that he should come and receive his prize, and make known the gallant warrior who had so ably maintained the honour of his countrymen.

He approached, led by the herald, bowed gracefully, and, falling upon one knee, lifted his mask.

"Dick Hamilton!" said Lion Limb, starting.

"Dick Hamilton!" echoed a thousand voices.

The English side of the field was filled with murmurs and shouts of applause.

"I knew," said an old sailor, "it could be none other."

"I knew the graceful flexure of his arm, and the gleam of his eye through the mask," said a fair dame. "Did I not tell you it was himself?"

The women waved their handkerchiefs, and clapped their hands.

The assembly shouted, and threw their caps into the air, for he had been a prodigious favourite; and Lion Limb, after appearing to sustain a short conflict with his feelings, stretched forth his hand.

Dick pressed it respectfully.

"I have reason to think you have been injured," said Lion Limb; "but, were it otherwise, you have redeemed yourself; you are restored to your dignities, and it is with no slight satisfaction I now place in your hands the vast augmentation of the latter, which your valour has won."

As he spoke, he beckoned the Princess Marmi, who advanced, and, taking her hand, he placed it in that of Dick's.

Dick cast his eye towards her for a moment.

She was more beautiful than ever, and her countenance was animated by a smile of exultation and delight, blended with a slight confusion.

He joyed in her beauty, but it was because the public sacrifice it enabled him to make, enhanced by it.

He wondered at her pleasure; but that, he felt, in reality reduced the sacrifice to nothing.

What! to be satisfied to change from one lover to another in the twinkling of an eye, because a little skill in arms, perhaps chance, had favoured him!

Oh! monstrous levity.

Could she that was guilty of it belong to the royal blood?

"My liege," said he, as he rose, and threw an elegant sword over his shoulder, and placed the ring upon his finger, "with this I shall be ever ready to combat the boldest of your foes; and as this ring compasseth my finger, so shall a sense of your favour ever compass the heart of the wearer; but for the wealthy, the beautiful bride you offer me, (oh, why should she wear so beauteous a semblance?) I cannot accept her. It *cannot* be Marmi!" sighed Dick."

"Cannot accept her?" cried Lion Limb, with a mingled emotion of astonishment and anger. "Cannot accept her? How—why? Is she not beautiful? Is she not rich? Were you not formerly her lover?"

"She is beautiful, and she is rich, and I was her lover; but——"

"Oh, pooh, pooh!" said Lion Limb, interrupting him: "you will love the better as spouses; but, I had forgotten, in the hurry and surprise of the moment, to ask what were the feelings of the lady. Fair one, do you accept the conqueror? Do you love him?"

The countenance of the unknown assumed an expression of the most impassioned tenderness, as she said, "Yes, I accept him as the best boon my gracious friend can bestow; and, oh! to say how I love him (she pressed her hands to her bosom,) a thousand summers' suns would afford not space sufficient for that pleasant task!"

Lion Limb smiled, and again put her hand into that of the victor, who stood shaken by a variety of conflicting emotions, now looking towards where the women were seated, among whom an audible titter had arisen, and now at the unknown, but beautiful creature, from whose lips such words had issued in such a manner as he thought would have suited only one already a wife, or some amourous wanton.

And while his astonishment every moment increased, so did his disgust.

For besides that her boldness was so well calculated to beget it, he still thought that her return to him, from one whose danger a little before had so much distressed her, was merely the effect of the good fortune he had just enjoyed.

He kept his eye fixed on her for a moment, calculating which, her beauty or her worthlessness, was the greatest, while the eye of the bewitching creature seemed sportively to supplicate acceptance.

"I see," said Lion Limb, "your repugnance has soon vanished. It would be singular indeed if it did not, and it is singular enough that it should ever have existed."

These words recalled his scattered thoughts.

"My liege," said he, somewhat softened by the love that was evidently felt either for himself or his glory, which, after all, was his attribute, was a part of himself, "my liege, I regret much I cannot answer now the love of this all too lovely creature—I am engaged."

"Engaged, engaged, without my permission?" said Lion Limb.

"My liege——"

"Well, well—no matter, no matter," hastily rejoined Lion Limb; "it will be easy to get a divorce."

"No," said Dick, with emphasis, and looking towards heaven; "my vow was registerd above, and no human power can dissolve it. And, where it otherwise, the wealth of worlds could not purchase my consent to its dissolution."

"What!" cried Lion Limb, "do you dare to thwart my wishes for your welfare—to set my will at defiance? What! ho, guards! But no—I had forgotten; here my power is limited. Well, be it so; I withdraw the grace I so freely tendered."

"My liege, I can only regret that such is your determination; I cannot cast from my bosom the loved one that fills its every crevice. I came hither from a shed to you to seek for justice; it is refused me, and to that shed I must again retire. But the light of heaven enters it, and freedom is around it; and she whom I have sworn to love for ever could soften the horrors of a noisome dungeon and make that shed a heaven! As for the lady here, I know her not. I claim a victor's right, and, with her own consent, which I presume there will be no difficulty in obtaining, I shall deliver her to one, who, before I entered the field, impelled by my desire to regain your favour, had fairly won her—to my valiant adversary."

"What!" said old Katamar, who had left his own throne and advanced to that of his brother monarch, curious to learn what was going forward and to see the man who had with such ease unhorsed his champion, "what! the lady consent to become the spouse of Yokee, whom I knew I could find no one so likely to ensure a triumph over your English warriors! And, by my faith, sir, I must have leave to say that never was there so proud a wreath so easily won, for my island boasts not the man who would have entered the lists with the hardy and long-practised Yokee; but in what regards his marriage with the lady, I fear, if indeed her admiration of valour be so great that she would dispense with every other attribute that in our sex is wont to captivate the female heart—I fear me, I say, that such a laudable inclination, one that, if it should become prevalent among the fair, would fill the world with a bolder race of men than heretofore hath trod its surface, cannot be gratified."

While Katamar spoke, he kept his eye intently fixed on the rich prize, whom one of the combatants, as it appeared, was unwilling to accept; and Dick, who still held her hand, having pondered for a few moments on the motive that the person from whom he had derived his information could have had for deceiving him, now, without trusting himself to look upon the face of the victim, while in the act of sacrifice, led her close up to Lion Limb, saying,

"Here, then, my liege, I deliver up to you a treasure too costly to be deposited in the bosom of one who can, at your bidding, be reduced from rank to poverty and exile."

The boldness of this speech, which the vexation of recent disappointment had drawn forth, seemed to augment the anger of Lion Limb, and the daring individual who had uttered it was expecting some fresh burst of rage from him, when, to his infinite astonishment, the whole expression of his countenance suddenly changed to that of the most intemperate mirth, and putting his hands to his sides, he laughed till the platform on which he stood shook beneath him.

Dick was wholly unable to account for this sudden transition.

He first looked at him, then at Katamar.

But perceiving that the countenance of the latter indicated as much wonder as his own, and that he still kept his eye fixed on the fair lady, he suddenly turned round, and beheld a metamorphosis.

The plume and coronet, together with the braids of flaxen hair which they surmounted, had fallen from the head of the unknown maiden, and together with the diamond-spangled robe, which was extremely full, and fastened with loops, that could be loosed in a moment, lay at her feet.

Dark ringlets clustered around her alabaster brow, and the holiday garb of an Indian princess sat close to her shape.

Gracious Heavens! it was Marmi herself.

But Marmi, no longer the dark Marmi.

The whiteness and transparency of her skin, vied with that of the fairest of the fair, and the mantling crimson of her cheek was like the flower that drops from the bosom of the village maiden, and rests in the centre of the vase which her hands have filled from the distended udder of rich pastured kine, when she kneels beneath the hawthorn in the coolness and fragrance of the evening hour, and chaunts the unpremeditated lay of love.

Dick gazed in mute astonishment and perplexity.

"Deliver up, then, Dick, this treasure, that is too rich for your bosom!" said Lion Limb, hardly able to get out his words for laughing.

"Will you no longer love me," said the damsel, "because I have cast away my borrowed complexion?"

As as she spoke, she looked a look at him so full of all that love can boast of sweet, of tender and of sportive—oh! that look itself was worth a diadem.

Ah! poor Marmi, Dick loved you, but——

Some confused notion of this truth flashed suddenly on the mind of Dick.

It at first increased the ludicrous confusion in which he stood, his eye glancing from object to object, and his breath almost suspended with anxious doubt.

But that look of love overwhelmed every other emotion; it was the very, very eye of Marmi, he would doubt no longer, nor check the powerful impulse, till a tedious explanation had assured him.

He looked at his beautiful prize with kindling eye.

But again he hesitated, and examined her from head to foot.

The slight and graceful swelling of her shape was distinctly perceptible.

It dispelled every remnant of uncertainty, and he clasped her to his heart, more delighted with her than ever, notwithstanding the tricks he perceived she had assisted in playing on him, because he had found her to be the only women he had ever truly loved.

He then led her to Lion Limb, and both knelt before him.

The old Indian king, delighed with the issue of a plot which had been of his own devising, was again about to require the offered renunciation, but he could not get out the words for laughing.

And he took a hand of each, and threw it round the neck of the other, patted the cheek of his fond daughter, and bid her maintain the loyalty of her husband, reminding her that but for Lion Limb's trick, she would never have known whether he loved her or her position the best.

The whole party now came forward to greet the happy pair, who had just risen, after having kissed the hand of their sovereigns.

Dick, though he felt somewhat awkward, when he reflected on the credulity which had enabled them to impose on him, for he now perceived that, from whatever motive he had yet to learn (though circumstances forbid him to surmise that it could be other than a good one) they had imposed on him, met nevertheless the congratulations of each with the cordiality of one upon whom a long vista of happiness has suddenly opened.

"But where," said he, after he had for the second time respectfully pressed the lips of the beautiful Marmi; "where is the person who has led me to the felicity that promises to shine upon my future days? I feel that I am indebted for all that is in my grasp—where is Emma Clarence?"

"Here," said Lion Limb, proudly.

As the eagle of the mountain stoops from heaven upon the tired hare crouching in the fern, he rushed, regardless of the noble presence in which he stood, on her who united in her single person all that he had ever admired or loved in the mind or body of woman. She shunned not the stormy embrace, as heretofore in her dream, and when Lion Limb raised his head from her ruddy lips to gaze upon her, hers lay still upon his arm.

And in the witching smile that disclosed her ivory teeth, there was love, and joy, and triumph, heightened by the delicate flush of modesty.

A crowd of Dick's acquaintances, among whom were even some of those who had looked down upon him in his supposed disgrace, now crowded about him with importunate congratulations.

He was too happy to use the opportunity he enjoyed of retaliating neglect; but soon becoming weary of hypocrisy, which he could not but despise, as well as of the sports, which had recommenced by order of the king, he led his bride away from the crowd, to question her as to the wonders, in creating which it appeared that she had so considerable a share.

She persuaded him to postpone the gratification of his curiosity till night, when she could explain everything at leisure, and without fear of interruption; and then she led him through several rows of tents, disposed in the manner of a fair, till having reached a remote part of the field, she suddenly directed his attention to a cloud of horsemen who were hastily approaching.

"Are they friends, Marmi?" asked Dick, anxiously.

"I know not," was the whispered answer.

———

CHAPTER LXXX.

IN WHICH DETECTIVE SHARP SETS TO WORK IN EARNEST TO FIND OUT A GREAT SECRET.

HITHERTO we have followed the strange and ever-varying fortunes of Lion Limb in his island home, and have faithfully recounted the many strange adventures and extreme perils he encountered.

But it is time now that our many readers should take a glance of how things were progressing in England.

For it will be recollected that Lion Limb and his brother, Allan Norman, were children of mysterious parentage and birth, a secret which, as yet, has not been unravelled.

Inspector Sharp, the clever detective, knew, or at least felt certain he would soon find out and know, this great secret.

But for a time he knew not how to proceed.

"Who is the mother? Who is the father of these two handsome boys?" were questions which often passed through his mind, and he resolved to use his best endeavours to find out who they were.

But how was he to do so?

"The manners of the boys, as far as I have seen of them, betoken high birth," he often thought, "and it is a great pity they should be allowed to run wild through the world unfriended and a prey to the wiles and plots of such villains as old Marks and his cunning, ferret-eyed son, Jerry."

Now Jerry Marks had fully recovered from his sickness, and having plenty of money, he assumed the name of Captain Zacary, and spent his money very freely in all sorts of places; but balls, concert-balls, and theatres were his sole delight, and he spent money lavishly in these pleasures.

Inspector Sharp, in his wanderings about town, had come in contact with Jerry, but the cunning young Jew little thought that the "Captain" Sharp, he had so often met and who on all occasions had proved such a pleasant companion, was none other than a detective.

But such was the fact.

Mr. Sharp, in order to ferret out the secret of the murder, and the mystery of the birth of Edgar and Allan Norman, donned the name and style of a captain in the army, and so well did he play his part that Captain Zacary *alias* Jerry Marks was delighed with his newly-formed "military" friend, and spent much money in his company.

"It hasn't taken me long to find out Jerry," thought the officer, "but I must now endeavour to discover who and what the parents of these two unfortunate lads are."

"There is an opera ball masque to-night at Her Majesty's Theatre, I will go and keep my eyes open. Plenty of 'nobs' and 'swells' go there; if I keep my ears open I dare say I shall hear many things worthy of remembering, and at the same time have an eye on the tricky doings of this young Jew, Jerry."

To the ball masque, then, Captain Sharp went, but disguised himself in a long, loose dress or domino. To prevent observation or detection, he wore a black masque also, and on the hood of his domino he pinned a small knot of blue and yellow ribands; but why he did so, or select those particular coloured ribands, he could not tell. It was done without thought or premeditation; but as will be seen, these simple ribands were the cause of his discovering an important secret connected with the parentage of Lion Limb and his brother Allan.

When he arrived at the theatre the ball masque was in full swing.

A splendid orchestra performed delightful music, and hundred of dancers, both male and female, were twirling in the dreamy mazes of a delicious waltz.

Hundreds of others, some in plain attire and others in all manner of costumes, walked about, chatting gaily; dozens lounged in the boxes, looking on the brilliant assembly below, while here and there were many groups joking and laughing, and making fun of the dancers, many of whom were dressed as clowns, negroes, and other fantastic characters.

"Captain" Sharp had been moving about for some time knowing not how to amuse himself, when a gentleman remarked to his friend—

"Why, hang me, if that tall military-fellow (meaning the detective) hasn't got a bunch of the same coloured ribands as you, major."

"So he has; but that don't matter much, he doesn't know what 'Juliet' or 'Romeo' mean—those are the pass words."

"Don't be too sure of that," thought the detective. "I should like to have a lark, and if the lady, whoever she is, mistakes me for some other, why let her—it won't be *my* fault."

He sauntered about from place to place, and soon discovered "Captain Zacary," who thus early was half intoxicated, and very boisterous in his mirth, as he jumped about, attired in the costume of "Shylock," a character he well suited.

But as the detective moved to and fro, knowing not what to do to amuse himself, somebody said in mysterious tones——

THE BOY KING
OF THE SOUTH SEA ISLANDS.

JEM FOLLOWS HIS INSTRUCTIONS.—SEE NEXT NUMBER.

"Who is that tall domino, evidently masculine in its gender, which is on the look-out for adventure? That knot of yellow and blue ribands on his head is no doubt a signal of rallying and recognition."

"Oh," said an inquisitive woman, of gay manner and attire, "it is some serious *rendezvous*—I will prevent the meeting by following the steps of this mysterious personage."

Unfortunately for this malicious design, a crowd carried away with it Mr. Sharp, who wore the knot of yellow and blue ribands, and who rapidly disappeared.

Some moments afterwards, Mr. Sharp ascended the staircase which led to the second tier of boxes, and walked up and down the corridor for several minutes.

He was soon rejoined by a female domino who also wore a knot of yellow and blue ribands.

After a moment's examination and hesitation, the female approached him, and said in a low voice—

"Juliet."

"Romeo," replied the male domino.

These words exchanged, the lady hesitatingly took the arm of Mr. Sharp, who led her into the ante-room of one of the stage-boxes, greatly wondering where or how the adventure would end, but resolved to play his part to the best of his well-known ability, and see what came of it.

The female who had accompanied him was masked with extreme care.

Her hood so covered her, that it was impossible to see even her hair.

Her very full domino enveloped her figure, whilst large gloves and large shoes concealed her hands and feet, which otherwise are such certain evidences.

The lady appeared agitated.

The words which she several times tried to utter expired on her lips.

At last she said—

"I received the letter which you were so obliging as to write to me, requesting me to be here and masked, with a signal and words of recognition. Your letter appeared so serious, that, in spite of the uneasiness with which my health fills me, I am here at your bidding."

With a hand trembling from emotion, the domino unmasked herself with an effort.

"Lady Oxenford!" exclaimed Mr. Sharp, in extreme astonishment.

It was the identical person he had longed to see, and her likeness to Allan Norman was remarkable.

The detective could scarcely believe his eyes.

It was no illusion ; he was really in the presence of Lady Oxenford.

It would require the pencil of some great artist to depict the firmness, the decision of that queenly visage, as pale and as stern as a statue of antiquity —to describe that look, as piercing and as fascinating as that of the evil spirit of some legend.

It is but by invoking the resemblance of Cleopatra or Lady Macbeth, that an idea can be formed of the mixture of seductive loveliness and sombre majesty displayed in the countenance of the lady.

Lady Oxenford had removed her mask.

The hood of her domino projected a deep shadow on her forehead, whilst the rest of her face was strongly lighted up.

Her eyes seemed to glow even more brightly than before from out of the shadow that enshrouded the upper part of her features.

With the exception of this look, sparkling like a star in the dark sky, the physiognomy of the lady was utterly without expression.

She said in a firm and grave tone to Mr. Sharp—

"I confide, sir, the secret of this interview fearlessly to your honour."

"I will prove myself worthy of your confidence, madame."

"I know it, but I required this certainty ere I risked the step to which unwittingly you have forced me."

"I, madame?" said the officer, with amazement.

"It is your conduct alone that has driven me to seek this interview."

"For Heaven's sake, madame, explain yourself !"

"It is now about two months since, sir, that you prayed your aunt, Madame de Lormoy, one of my intimate friends, to present you to me.   I acceded with pleasure to this request.   Some days afterwards, you informed Madame de Lormoy, that you would not, on any account, be presented to me."

Mr. Sharp cast down his eyes, and thought " the devil I did," but he replied—

"It is true, madame."

"From that instant, sir, you have affected to fly every place where you fancied there existed the least possibility of encountering me."

"I cannot deny it, madame," replied Sharp, sorrowfully, but suffocating a rising laugh as he thought, "she's mistaken in the party."

The lady continued—

"Some time ago, not knowing that Madame le Roy had given me a seat in her box, you entered it ; at the end of a quarter of an hour you left it under a pretence too ridiculous to deceive any one."

"The deuce I did," thought the officer.   "Is she dreaming ?"

"Also, when Madame de Sèmur invited you and a small party to attend a lecture you were most anxious to hear, you accepted the invitation eagerly ; but no sooner had Madame de Sèmur mentioned that I was expected, than you declined being present."

"That is equally true, madame.   I'm fond of lectures, very," said Sharp.

"In a word, sir, you have manifested, I may say, affected, so decided a determination to avoid me, that it has been remarked by others as well as by myself."

"Madame, believe me that ——" coughed the good-looking officer.

"I hear the frankness of your character, your invariable politeness, praised everywhere ; you must then have cogent reasons for thus studiously avoiding me.   Let me assure you that your conduct would not occupy me for a moment, were it not for a circumstance with which I am bound to acquaint you."

"Madame, I am aware how strange—how rude, my conduct must appear to you ; yet I must tell you I am not ——"

She interrupted the officer with a bitter smile.

"Once for all, sir, let me assure you I am not here to upbraid you for thus shunning me ; I have reason to believe that your resolution to avoid me is dictated by motives so imperative, that to make them known would endanger the happiness, if not the life, of two persons."

As she spoke, the lady darted a searching glance at Sharp.

The latter coloured and replied—

"I assure you, madame, did you but know who I am you ——"

"I do know sir," interrupted the lady, "that there exists a secret between us.   You have discovered that secret between the day when you asked to be introduced to me and that fixed for the introduction ; from this moment arose your determination to avoid me.   You are a man of honour. Tell me if I am mistaken ; swear to me that you have had no motive for thus avoiding me—that chance, that caprice, alone, have occasioned this, and I will believe you ; and then, thank Heaven, the purpose of this interview will be accomplished !"

After some moments of hesitation Mr. Sharp seemed to make a violent effort, and said—

"Madame, I scorn falsehood, I think there does exist a secret of vital importance."

"I was not deceived," she cried, interrupting him ; "you do possess the secret which I believed known but to two persons, one I thought out of town, the other had good cause for secrecy, for his own honour was affected by it.   It was for this reason that I requested this appointment, as I could not see you at my own house, and I never meet you in society.   I care but little for the opinion you have formed of me after the revelation that has been made you.   Your studied aversion shows me that it is horrible. Be it so, Heaven is my judge. But enough of this. You are not aware, sir, perhaps, of the terrible importance of the secret that chance or treachery has placed in your hands. My son, Edgar Norman—is he not then dead? Is it really true that he did not perish, as was generally believed? For mercy's sake, sir, answer me. If that were the case, much would be explained to me."

"Edgar Norman! I never heard the name uttered, madame," said the detective, coolly telling a lie.

"It was the baron who told you, then?" cried the lady, involuntarily.

Mr. Sharp regarded her with increasing surprise; for the last few minutes he could not comprehend how to act or what to say.

"I scarcely know the baron, madame, and I am ignorant if he be now in London."

For the first time during this interview Lady Oxenford's real or assumed composure forsook her.

She rose hastily, and her pale face became crimson as she exclaimed—

"There is no one living except the baron who could have told you what passed years ago at Venice on the night of the 13th of April, 184—"

"Years ago, at Venice, the 13th of April, 184—?" repeated Mr. Sharp. "I assure you, madame, it is not that I allude to. Not a word more on that head. I would not, for the world, surprise your confidence. Again, madame, I assure you the reason that forces me to fly you has nought to do with the names or dates you have mentioned. This motive has not for a moment altered my sincere respect, my admiration, for your character. In avoiding you, madame, I fulfil a promise—a sacred duty," said Sharp, still telling lie upon lie.

"Oh, Heaven! what have I said?" cried Lady Oxenford, covering her face with her hands, and thinking of the half confession she had involuntarily made to Mr. Sharp. "No, no, this cannot be a snare to entrap me."

Then addressing the officer—

"I believe you, sir, by a strange fatality, by a singular chance, when I knew you had urgent reasons for shunning me, I fancied you were actuated by sad, too sad circumstances, in which I might seem to prejudiced eyes to have acted an unworthy part, that would, indeed, have entitled me to your aversion. Your word relieves my fears; I was deceived without doubt; nought concerning this melancholy adventure has transpired. Now, then, sir, the purpose of this meeting is attained. I came hither to relate to you what the probable consequences of indiscretion might be. Fortunately my fears were vain; I care little now. As for the cause, that is equally indifferent to you. Adieu, sir, you are a man of honour, and I doubt not of discretion;" and Lady Oxenford rose to quit the box.

Mr. Sharp took her hand respectfully.

"One word more, madame, I shall never, probably, be alone with you again; hear, at least, some portion of my secret."

Lady Oxenford, who had risen, resumed her seat, and listened to the officer in profound silence, who began to suit his own purposes; to relate some circumstances of her history and intrigues which had occurred while he had been watching her actions from a house adjoining that of her husband, Lord Oxenford.

"Upon your arrival in London," said Sharp to Lady Oxenford, "you were not aware, perhaps, that the adjoining house to yours belonged to a friend of mine."

"No, sir, I was not aware of it."

"Permit me to enter into some details, puerile, perhaps, but yet indispensable. In my friend's house, a small window, wholly concealed by the leaves of the ivy, looked into your garden; it was from that window that I first perceived you, madame, and without your suspecting it, for no one could imagine that any eye could penetrate the shady and retired walk which you frequented."

Lady Oxenford seemed to recall her recollections of the place and answered—

"I certainly recollect the wall covered with ivy, but I did not know there was a window there."

"Forgive my indiscretion, madame; I have bitterly suffered for it."

"Explain yourself, sir."

"Closely attending upon my sick friend, I rarely quitted the house; my only pleasure was to gaze daily from that window, and the hope of seeing you kept me whole hours there. At last you came; sometimes your steps were slow, sometimes rapid, and you frequently threw yourself as if in agony on a marble seat, or stood motionless with your head buried in your hands. Alas, how often, when after these reveries you raised your head, was your countenance bathed in tears."

At these words Lady Oxenford replied, austerely—

"We are not speaking, sir, of any moments of weakness you may have witnessed, but of a secret you are about to communicate."

Sharp regarded her with a sorrowful air, and continued—

"After some few days—forgive my presumption, madame—I fancied I had penetrated the cause of your grief."

"Your penetration seems very great, sir."

"I was then suffering from the same cause (at least as I think) as that which at that moment tormented you. This was the secret I believed I had discovered."

"Surely, sir, you are not speaking seriously? and yet any attempt at pleasantry would be most unseasonable."

"I speak most seriously, madame."

"And so then," said Lady Oxenford, with a contemptuous smile, "you imagine I am a prey to grief, and that you have discovered the cause of it?"

"There are symptoms which are infallible."

"The outward marks of every kind of sorrow are the same, sir."

"Ah, madame, there is but one mode of lamenting those we love."

"Is this mentioned in confidence? Is this an allusion to your own regrets or to mine?"

"Alas! I, madame, have no regrets; you have made me forget them all."

"I do not comprehend your meaning, sir; I expected you were about to tell me an important secret, and yet to the present moment ——"

"One other word, madame. A sentiment that I believed unalterable, a long-cherished remembrance, spite of myself, was gradually effaced from my heart. In vain did I blame my weakness; in vain did I foresee to what this love would expose me. The charm was too powerful. I yielded before it. I had but one thought, one desire, one pleasure—that of seeing you. From constantly contemplating your features, I fancied I could read in them, so often overclouded with sorrow and melancholy, that despair, sometimes mute, sometimes so expressive, which the absence or loss of those dear to us invariably occasions."

Lady Oxenford shuddered, but remained silent.

"Ah, madame, I repeat, I had suffered too much

myself not recognise the same sufferings in you by indescribable, yet manifest symptoms. With what eager curiosity did I strive to read your thoughts in your countenance. The part of the garden that you frequented most was separated from the rest by a gate, which you opened or shut at pleasure. You alone could enter into this secluded ally. I ventured on a folly; each day I dropped at the foot of the seat where you were accustomed to repose, a sort of memento of the reflections which, as I believed, had agitated you on the previous evening. How shall I describe my suspense when I saw you first open my letter? Never shall I forget the expression of surprise you manifested after you had read it. Forgive these foolish recollections of the past; but I did not think you were offended, for, instead of destroying the letter, you retained it. One day your agitation was so great, that you did not perceive the letter—you seemed a prey to the most violent anger and grief. My own experience told me that your sorrow was not occasioned by any fresh event. It seemed to me rather some unhappy occurrence had been recalled to you. It was under this belief that I again wrote to you, and on the morrow, whilst you perused my letter, you wept."

Lady Oxenford made an impatient gesture.

"Oh, madame, do not blame me for dwelling on these recollections. Thus encouraged by the anxiety with which you seemed to look for my letters, I wrote daily. Unhappily, my friend's illness assumed a threatening form; I never quitted his bedside for two nights. The crisis passed, he was out of danger. My first thought was then to hasten to my window. Soon after you entered the walk. I could scarcely believe my eyes when I saw you go quickly to the marble seat; there was no letter there. An exclamation of impatience escaped you."

Sharp glanced anxiously at Lady Oxenford.

Her eyes were cast down, her arms folded, her face was devoid of expression.

In thus speaking, in thus informing Lady Oxenford of the facts that he had discovered, Sharp cut off all hope of retreat.

"What can I say, madame?" replied he; "for two whole months I had the happiness of seeing you; every day when I learned you were on the point of quitting the house adjoining ours, oh, how sincere was my emotion! Perchance it was only then that I really felt how much I loved you and trembled for your fate."

At these last words, Lady Oxenford raised her head suddenly.

Her cheeks became deeply tinged, as she replied, with a satirical smile, "This strange confession, sir, is doubtless connected with the secret you are about to reveal to me."

"Yes, madame."

"I am all attention."

"Up to the period of your quitting the adjoining house to ours, I had often met you, and I found an indefinable charm in the mystery that enshrouded you. I was utterly unknown to *you*. I knew you so well. Unfortunately, a revelation was made to me, that, instead of seeking, I felt it my duty to avoid your society."

"Fool!" exclaimed Lady Oxenford, from her seat, her features convulsed by fear and grief.

This involuntary cry of the lady, was, in fact, an avowal that betrayed her fear of Sharp, hitherto so carefully concealed.

A look of joy irradiated Sharp's face; but that first transport past, he shuddered as he thought of the abyss of misery and sorrow which the involuntary exclamation of Lady Oxenford revealed.

Lady Oxenford was too much mistress of herself not to subdue instantly all traces of her transient emotion.

Hoping to deceive Sharp, she said, with an air of gaiety that quite confused him,—

"You must allow, sir, that my surprise was tolerably natural on hearing you declare my name was associated with unpleasant revelations. Only permit me to observe that you might have reckoned my marriage, for that is a final answer to all the world might slanderously whisper against me. And now let me speak of your letters which I have received because I could not help it, and which I read, and sometimes preserved, because a series of thoughts admirably worded, could not be called a correspondence. You have too much real merit, sir," continued the lady, "to be vain; I have, therefore, no dread of wounding your pride by telling you, that if I read these your productions with curiosity and sometimes with a strong emotion, it was partly because of the 'mystery' that enshrouded you, and partly because chance sometimes sent you thoughts so touching as to call forth my tears, for I am so unfortunate or rather fortunate, as to shed tears during the perusal of anything relating to lost or abandoned children."

"Ah, madame, your heart is yet tender, I see."

"I could wish, sir, that this interview, began under such gloomy auspices, should at least end gaily; for, after all, are we not at a masked ball at the opera? Besides, why should we part in sadness? I believed that you were acquainted with an annoying secret; it is not the case; I find my fears, then, were futile and are forgotten. I have the recollection of my position in the world to defend me from your declarations, as well as my utter indifference as to the revelation that has been made to you by some mischievous persons. Our position is perfectly clear, what more could any one desire? Farewell. I know that I need not recommend you to secresy on the subject of a step that would painfully compromise me and others," whispered Lady Oxenford. "For precaution's sake, I will leave the box first; you will have the kindness to wait here a short time."

As she spoke Lady Oxenford rose, replaced her mask, and opened the door of the box.

"Madame," exclaimed Sharp, "for Heaven's sake one word more."

Lady Oxenford made a gesture so proud, so dignified, that Sharp no longer endeavoured to prolong the interview.

Lady Oxenford opened the door and disappeared.

In a few minutes Sharp followed her example.

As he passed along the lobby he found a crowd so great that, whilst waiting to pass it, he had time to overhear these words—

"My stars, my lord," said a malicious domino, who had been sitting all the evening, "what a sensation you produce. What a scream the domino with a knot of blue and yellow ribands gave when she passed you!"

"I don't claim the merit," replied Lord Oxenford, gaily; "I am not responsible for the domino's screams."

He little dreamed it was his wife who passed.

"The domino could not have been more alarmed if she had seen the devil himself," said the gay lady.

Sharp listened with the greatest attention when he found that Lady Oxenford formed the subject of their conversation.

She wore, as our readers will recollect, a knot of

blue and yellow ribands, which she had not removed.

She hurried home as fast as a private cab could drive her, convulsed with fear and passion.

"He knows me," she sighed, as she flung herself into a chair and wept. "He knows my secret, and yet I know him not!"

CHAPTER LXXXI.

IN WHICH MYSTERIOUS LADY OXENFORD IS WATCHED.

THE house which Lord Oxenford occupied was situated in a pleasant street.

Utterly indifferent to the enjoyments or little comforts of a well-arranged home he had simply commanded the upholsterer who furnished them to see no expense spared.

And with this unrestricted permission before him the tradesman employed had done his best to produce the very *ideal* of a furnised house.

That is to say, he had given to the residence of Lord Oxenford the most chill, comfortless, and common-place aspect imaginable.

Nothing that marked a taste, pursuit, or personal convenience, was to be seen in the dreary mansion ; not a portrait, a picture—not a vestige of the fine arts embellished the spacious rooms.

The only one exempted from the vulgarity that predominated over the others was a small drawing-room specially appropriated to Lady Oxenford, and in which she passed entire days.

Spite of the advanced hour of the night, or rather morning, for it was now four o'clock, it is into this very chamber we are about to introduce the reader.

Although the continual absences of Lord Oxenford might well have accustomed his partner to them, yet she experienced little anxiety on his account, or ever retired to rest until assured of his return, for she led the life of a hypocrite to her husband and to all the world beside.

It was then four o'clock in the morning, and Lady Oxenford, seated in an arm-chair, her clasped hands reposing on her lap, was mechanically gazing on the expiring embers which flickered on the hearth.

A lamp placed on a small table beside her, on which lay a half-open book, shone full on the delicate features of the pensive wife, and cast a soft glow upon the glossy bands of her rich chestnut hair, which, braided so as merely to display the finely formed ear, with its roseate tip, was plaited in with the luxuriant masses, ornamenting the back of her small and classically shaped head.

The most striking characteristic of the countenance of Lady Oxenford was its look of sweetness ; and when she raised her large blue eyes, it was impossible to resist their influence.

Her somewhat serious mouth seemed rather intended to express the smile of affection and univeral benevolence than the noisy laugh of extreme gaiety, while the meditative attitude in which she sat displayed to advantage the graceful roundness of her white throat.

She now wore a dress of light grey silk, whose subdued shade harmonised admirably with the delicacy of her transparent complexion.

On one side of the fire-place stood a pianoforte loaded with music, and over the mantel-piece were suspended two portraits.

A considerable number of plain black frames, containing copper-plate engraving, were hung around the small chamber, the walls of which were covered with embossed red paper, that gave it an air of lightness and cheerfulness very different from the rest of the apartments.

And on the chimney-piece stood an old enamelled clock and two small blue and white candlesticks of Limoges enamel.

A tear which had long hung suspended from the thick lashes of her eyelid, fell on her cheek like a liquid pearl.

Her bosom heaved convulsively—a sudden tremor seized her frame, while a deep flush suffused her countenance, as again she sunk into her former gloomy abstraction.

Four o'clock struck, and aroused her from her reverie.

Absorbed in her deep and painful meditation, she had taken no note of the hours, and was surprised to find the night so completely gone.

At this moment a carriage stopped at the door, and she began to regret having sat up so late.

Her husband had peremptorily forbidden her ever awaiting his return.

The servants, also, by his orders, retired to rest whether their master were in or not.

He usually entered by a small side door, of which he alone had the key, but he was compelled to pass through her sitting-room in order to reach one of the two sleeping apartments which communicated with it.

At the sight of her husband, Lady Oxenford rose to meet him, endeavouring, by a forced smile, to deprecate the storm she dreaded and anticipated.

The contraction of my lord's features, indicated the evil passions which at that moment possessed him.

"How is this, madam ?" exclaimed he, as he entered. "Four o'clock in the morning, and you not yet retired to bed ! May I inquire the meaning of such strange conduct? Or is it that you may know at what hour I return home? Am I, or am I not, master of my own actions? Is your inquisitorial system to recommence the instant I set my foot in this place? Perhaps it may be as well, since we are upon the subject, to go into it at full length, in order that we may have no further occasion to revert to it during the whole of the winter."

So saying, he threw himself abruptly into the chair my lady had just quitted, while she remained standing by the piano, surprised at this abrupt torrent of reproach.

"You know," answered she, "your wishes are at all times mine. Only tell me what you wish me to do, and rest assured of my obedience."

"What folly is this ?" exclaimed he. "You really waste many fine words, madam, most unnecessarily. I am not arraigning your conduct as though you had committed a crime ; but of this be assured, I am not to be cheated as to the real motive that kept you from your bed to-night. All I require of you is simply to render my home agreeable to me, and to put on a smiling look of happiness, instead of perpetual melancholy and other affectations. If I thought fit to indulge my inclinations by marrying you, it was because, first, I was in love, and secondly——"

"To have a wife submissive to your commands ; I am perfectly sensible of that. You preferred me to a richer bride, because gratitude for the sacrifice you had made for me would necessarily render my duties still more binding and sacred."

"But what is the meaning of your continual sadness ?"

After a moment's hesitation, with downcast eyes, she replied—

"There may be among my actions some that render me sad, without my venturing to explain them."

"You are under a gross error, madam, if you suppose that we stand upon equal grounds as regards the indulgence of passion. Whether I am faithful to you or not, in no degree affects your consideration with society. But that I, who have sacrificed everything for you, should be exposed to your melancholy and sighs! I tell you," continued my lord, rising from his chair, his teeth clenched, and his hands compressed with rage, "that at the very supposition I can no longer command myself!" and, as though unable to master the boiling rage which shook his frame, and inflamed every feature, he commenced rapidly pacing the room.

While my lady scorned to reply, her husband had approached the window, and mechanically opened the curtains drawn before it.

He observed on the other side of the street, on the first floor of the house opposite his own, lights in the window corresponding to the one by which he stood.

And through the glass he could discern *the outline of a man attentively gazing from that window!*

It was now nearly five o'clock in the morning.

All was dark without, and the street was perfectly deserted.

What object of interest, then, could the individual opposite have in thus keeping watch, unless it were to reconnoitre the windows of his apartment, doubtless the only one throughout the house in which a light was burning at that unusual hour?

Turning quickly round towards his wife, and looking at her with angry glances and threatening countenance, he exclaimed,

"Madam, I insist upon knowing wherefore that light is burning in the opposite house."

Then suddenly interrupting himself, to give way to a suggestion equally ridiculous with his jealousy, he abruptly drew back the curtain, opened the window, and went out upon the balcony, where he took up his station with an air of proud defiance.

At this unexpected apparition, the curtains of the opposite windows were hastily closed.

The shadow disappeared, and almost immediately the light was extinguished.

Lady Oxenford, wholly ignorant of her husband's fury, and still less able to comprehend his fancy for throwing open the windows in the month of January, was advancing towards the balcony, when he turned sharply round, and, jerking the window-curtains back to their places, exclaimed,—

"So, madam, it is thus, then, you occupy your leisure hours while awaiting my return?"

"Indeed, sir, I understand not what you mean."

"You do not? Ah, false woman, tell me, why was the window of the first floor in the house facing this lighted up just now?"

"Just now! the window! in the opposite house!" she repeated, with increasing surprise.

"Oh, you feign astonishment admirably, madam, but it will not do. Just this minute, some person opposite was attentively watching your window, but disappeared the instant I showed myself."

"Very probably. I know nothing about it. But why do you tell me of so trifling a circumstance?" asked my lady, reddening.

"Why?"

"Yes, I ask you again, why?"

"Because, doubtless, there is a mutually good understanding between yourself and this person opposite, and that some disgraceful intrigue is carried on by means of *signal-lights* in your respective windows! I cease now to feel the smallest astonishment at your having kept watch to-night, instead of retiring to rest."

To this accusation my lady found it impossible to frame any reply, but clasping her hands, she raised her eyes in anger.

"All those tragedy airs are no answers to my question," cried he, more and more excited; "and I ask you again, madam, why that light burned in the window directly facing yours, and wherefore that man gazed so attentively over here?"

"How is it possible I can know?"

"Ah, madam, this is not replying, but meanly equivocating."

"But what other answer can I give?"

"Have a care! Have a care!" exclaimed my lord, almost foaming with rage. "Do not imagine me fool enough to be duped by your hypocrisy. I have seen what I state with my own eyes. I am not blind, whatever you may think. I insist upon knowing who lives opposite to us?"

"For Heaven's sake, how should I know?" she replied.

Interrupting his wife with increased fury, and violently striking his forehead, he exclaimed,

"I have it! Now, I remember, a post-chaise arrived and stopped before the opposite house. You are followed—perhaps, even watched. Oh, I am sure—quite, quite sure, some disgraceful mystery is attached to all these circumstances; but depend upon it, wretched creature! that I will discover it, and drag the infamous participators to the shame and ignominy they deserve."

And as thus he spoke, Lady Oxenford trembled and turned deadly pale.

"More than that, madam, I have very good reason for supposing that you are frequently visited unknown to me, by a certain baron. There is some mystery yet unrevealed."

"I am watched!" she gasped.

"You are!" said he, coldly and sternly.

"And wherefore should I be watched?" she asked, with a crimsoned cheek, as she boldly turned and confronted her husband.

"Watched—and wherefore should I be?" she repeated, again and again, mechanically, as she cast a fierce look at my Lord Oxenford.

"We are not always what we seem," said the old lord, sarcastically.

"That may apply to yourself, my lord, but when you give breath to false accusations regarding me, I cannot and will not bear with them."

"There is some secret connected with you, madam, that I have endeavoured to find out," said he, bitterly.

"And have tried in vain, I suppose?"

"Yes, in vain, as yet; but I may not always be so unsuccessful, mark me."

"And what do you suppose this secret then to be, my lord?" asked Lady Oxenford, tauntingly. "Is it that I have gone to the opera unknown to you, at times; that I have gone to balls and parties without your sanction?"

"No, nothing of that, madam; the matter is far more weighty than that. You ramble in your sleep, madam, and babble about children in such a manner that one would suppose you were or had been a mother yourself."

"Sir!" said my lady, indignantly, and as she spoke, a deep flush mantled her snowy brow, and with the air of injured majesty she swept from the room, indignantly, casting a fierce glance at the aged lord.

"I cannot believe that she is guilty of infidelity," sighed the good old man; "she is lovely, and yet there is a something in her manner I cannot comprehend. When she smiles on me it is with a sickly look, and yet when the Baron Templeton dines here she is all life and gaiety. How is that? Surely there is no secret or any intrigue between them. No, I cannot believe it, for the baron is the soul of honour; it was through him I was married to her, for he was the first to introduce me to her."

He sat for some moments in deep thought, and then murmured half aloud—

"She is a soft-hearted woman; any little romantic incident affects her sensibility wonderfully. I remember a long time ago, when two lads, brothers, were tried at Newgate for murder, she wept and sobbed for days, aye, weeks together; in fact, she has never appeared to be the same woman since, and the judge himself, Baron Templeton, seemed as much affected as any one else. Ah, he is a kind, good-hearted man; I dare say it *did* affect him to pass sentence on such promising, handsome boys as they were. Heigho!" sighed the old lord at last, rising from his seat, and walking about in deep thought, and distracted with all manner of jealous feelings.

At last he left the apartment, and finding that his lady had retired to rest, he went downstairs and opened the small side-door of his mansion already mentioned.

He remained standing there some time, and at last he was joined by a stranger, who walked up to my lord and bowed very respectfully.

"A raw morning, my lord," said the stranger, bowing again.

"Ah, so it is; I had forgotten my appointment with you. Let me see, your name is Sharp, is it not?"

"It is, my lord."

"I thought so; I recollect now; you sent me a note some few days ago about some property that was stolen at Manfred Hall."

"I did, my lord."

"And I promised to see you immediately after you had been to the ball masque."

"Quite true, my lord."

"I had forgotten it, but you did not, it seems."

"No, my lord, we detective officers are generally very punctual as to time and place."

"Come this way, Mr. Sharp, make as little noise as you can, for no one knows of your visit, nor do I want them to do so; the fact was I couldn't sleep, and had thought of taking a ramble round the houses."

"There are a good many persons moving about, sir," said Sharp, "and some very noisy ones, for there was a ball masque at the opera, as you know, my lord, and it is only just over."

"Ah, quite true, I had forgotten," said my lord, showing the way to his private library.

"And as to that great robbery which took place some time ago at Manfred Hall, my lord, I have to say that I found out much to-night that will interest you."

"Indeed."

"Yes, my lord, you wouldn't think it, but I saw some of the parties last night at the ball."

"Some of the very parties who did it at the ball masque?"

"Yes, my lord."

"You surprise me."

"Oh, they seem to have plenty of money, and do the thing very grandly, I can tell you. One of them keeps race-horses."

"A thief keep race-horses, Sharp?"

"Yes, sir; nothing less than four race-horses, my lord."

"And yet you know him to be a thief?"

"I do, my lord."

"Then why not apprehend the rascal?"

"Ah, there it is, you see, my lord. I know he *is* a thief and the most expert burglar in the world, but then he is *too* expert for us; he never gives us a chance to prove anything against him."

"So much the worse then."

"I have no doubt we shall capture him one of these fine days; in fact, I am laying a trap for him now."

"How is that?"

"His friends didn't do as well as they might have done in their last visit to Manfred Hall, and I have reasons for thinking they will go there again soon."

"Let us hope then, Mr. Sharp, that you may prove successful this time, and capture the rascals, for the robbery at Manfred Hall cost several of my friends very dearly."

"I know it, my lord; but I am on the search now for some of the goods, and have good reasons for supposing they are in the shop or warehouse of one Luke West, a very respectable 'receiver' in the New Cut."

"Be that as it may, Mr. Sharp, I am glad you called, for now I come to think of it you may be of great use to me in an important inquiry which I am determined to make regarding certain persons in a very high position in society."

"Indeed, my lord."

"Yes, Sharp, and I don't know any one, I think, who could aid me more effectually in this painful matter."

"Painful matter, my lord?"

"Yes, Sharp, painful, very painful to me, I assure you."

After a pause he continued, very slowly and in a whisper, thus—

"I can confide a secret with you, I think, Mr. Sharp?"

"You may, my lord."

"Do you know Baron Templeton?"

"The judge, my lord?"

"Yes, the judge; you look surprised."

"I do know him, my lord; that is, I have had several cases tried by him; but he has never sat upon the bench for these many months; he isn't the same looking man he was."

My lord smiled as he said—

"What was the last case he heard?"

"Well, let me see, my lord; ah, now I come to think of it, the last case was the murder of old Alderman English, by his young clerks, the Norman lads, and the brothers Rawlings. Why do you ask, my lord?"

"Oh, nothing of great importance. The baron, I hear, is very eccentric in his habits of late."

"So rumour has it, my lord, but I have seen no evidences of it, myself."

"Perhaps not; but it is very possible I may give you plenty of opportunities for proving it."

"How do you mean, my lord?" asked Mr. Sharp, for the first time observing the deep red colour which now suffused Lord Oxenford's face.

"The truth is, Mr. Sharp," said my lord, with a great effort, at the same time with a hesitating manner, whispering in a faint voice, "there is some mystery connected with the past life of my wife."

"Your wife! my lord?"

"Yes, my wife, Lady Oxenford, that I cannot clear up."

"Have you any doubts of her truth and honour, my lord?"

"At present, no, Mr. Sharp; but you will be surprised when I tell you that since Baron Templeton has ceased to sit upon the bench, my lady has been seized with an unaccountable melancholy, and in her dreams she starts and cries and sobs, frequently calling upon the baron's name and imploring him to save the boys."

"What boys, my lord?"

"Allan and Edgar Norman, the two brothers who were arraigned for the murder of the old alderman."

"I understand," said the officer, stroking his chin thoughtfully; "but the singular behaviour of Lady Oxenford, my lord, may arise merely from imagination; she has had no family yet, my lord, and, perhaps, is doatingly fond of children. She was present at the trial of the lads, perhaps."

"She was, and has never been the same woman since."

"And do you suppose for a moment, my lord, that my Lady Oxenford has anything to do with these lads?"

"I cannot tell, Sharp; that is the very thing I wish to discover."

"Does the baron visit your mansion often, my lord?"

"Sometimes; but of late, less frequently than before."

"Have you observed anything remarkable in his behaviour?"

"I have not; he is an old friend, at least I have always treated him as one; but as I have said, of late his behaviour has been somewhat eccentric; it will be your duty, Mr. Sharp, to ascertain the true relationship that exists between my lady and the baron. I *will* have my doubts cleared up, cost what it may; every expense you incur I will willingly pay."

"It will take a very long time, my lord, I think, and will cost a good sum of money, for such inquiries as these cannot, indeed, must not, be prosecuted in any hurry."

"Quite true, Mr. Sharp, quite true. I fully appreciate your caution; indecent hurry might spoil and thwart all our calculations; besides, you must remember, Mr. Sharp, I am not quite sure but that all my crude suspicions may be groundless after all. At all events here are a few pounds in notes," said my lord, handing him a sealed envelope. "Use them to the best advantage and let me hear from you when and where you please."

The officer left the house as noiselessly as he had entered it, and when in the open street he heaved a deep sigh.

"This is a pretty mess I have got into," he thought. "I am on the scent for one thing and before I know it am engaged on another job. What shall I do? I have no doubt but that the Norman lads are related in some way to Lady Oxenford; but is she the mother? Young Allan is very much like her in the face; and as to Edgar who was transported and shipwrecked in the convict ship, all the gaolers swore that he was the dead image of the judge who condemned him; and as there is such an intimacy between Baron Templeton and Lady Oxenford, it might turn out, nay, I am almost certain it will turn out, to be that the lads are their chance children. If it should be so, and the truth comes to light, what an exposure it will be for the fashionable world. Well, it is a difficult and very tangled matter as yet; but I daresay, with prudence, I can make it pleasant for all parties; at all events, I'll try."

And, filled with all manner of thoughts, Detective Sharp walked slowly to his home, for he was thoroughly wearied with his night's labour.

"I must separate Allan Norman from young Jem Rawlings," thought he. "I know of a situation that will suit him. Old Brown, the 'receiver,' in the New Cut has been in want of a shop lad for some time; young Jem will suit him, and be a spy for me at the same time."

CHAPTER LXXXII.

JEM RAWLINGS AT THE RECEIVER'S.

TRUE to his word, Inspector Sharp got Jem the situation of shop and errand boy to old Brown, but the "receiver" had no idea who Sharp was, for the detective had so changed his attire, and his voice and manner at the same time, that old Brown really thought he was nothing else but a professional house-breaker, and treated him as such.

"I suppose the lad is sharp, isn't he?" asked Brown; "and don't know much about our business?"

"As sharp as a needle, and as innocent as a dove," the officer replied, and, with this recommendation, Jem Rawlings was accepted for the situation.

"Look here, my lad," said the officer to Jem, before they went to old Brown's, "if you'll behave yourself I'll make a man of you. But you mustn't pretend to know anything or anybody that comes to the shop, but, when I meet you, tell me all you suspect, and I will act accordingly; for it is for your own interest, and that of your young friend, Allan Norman, that I wish to undermine old Brown, who, I have good reasons for supposing, has been in league with first-class burglars for several years."

"It will be all a lark if we find the old rascal out," said Jem, laughing. "Allan told me all about your plans, and advised me to be guided in all things by your advice."

"Mind," said the officer, "I have told old Brown you are a little hard of hearing and short-sighted, therefore you must pretend to be both."

"No fear of me, Mr. Sharp," said Jem, in high glee, and, without more ado, he went to old Brown's shop, and commenced his labours.

Old Brown's shop and warehouse were crowded with all sorts of things.

Clothes, cutlery, boxes, hardware, pots, pans, jewellery, watches; in fine, every imaginable article was there, stowed away or exposed for sale, and how he got so many things, and could afford to sell them for the low prices he did, puzzled everybody except Mr. Sharp and his brother officers, who had long had their eyes on Brown, without ever being able to detect or apprehend him.

For two or three days, Jem attended to his work faithfully and well, but he could not help remarking that a great many rough and suspicious-looking persons were in the habit of talking to his master in a secret and mysterious manner.

One night, while Jem was moving about goods in the shop, a stout, strongly-built fellow, in rough clothes and a hairy cap, entered, and nodded to old Brown.

"All right," said Brown, "talk away; there's nobody about. What's up now?"

"But that lad of yours?" said the stranger, winking suspiciously.

"Oh! no fear of him, George; he's half blind, and deaf."

"Sure?"

"Positive. He's one of the clumsiest young villains as ever lived, but very willing to learn. What do you want?"

"Several boxes and portmanteaus for that job we've got in hand."

THE BOY KING
OF THE SOUTH SEA ISLANDS.

THE DUEL BETWEEN ALLAN NORMAN AND "CAPTAIN ZACARY."

"Where? At Manfred Hall?"

"Yes; the chaps didn't half do their work last time, so I'm going down this time myself," said the rough-looking stranger.

"So Gentleman George is going to 'perform' this time, eh?" said old Brown, grinning, with his hands in his pockets.

"Yes, I'm obliged; racing has not paid me of late; my horses have always managed to come in last."

"Better luck next time, George," said old Brown, laughing. "How many trunks will you want?"

"About five or six. We shall leave them at the old places, remember."

"I shan't forget, George. When they are there let me know; I will quickly have them removed, and make it all right with you. Jemmy," said he to young Rawlings, "get up on that counter, and hand down those trunks up there, and see if you can't tumble down and break your neck by way of variety."

Young Jem clambered up on the counter to do as he was ordered, when on the instant his foot slipped, and he tumbled backwards head-over-heels knocking over and breaking things in his descent, including crockery and glass of all sorts. (See cut in Number 28).

Gentleman George, disguised as he was in his

strange and unfashionable attire, burst out laughing at Jem's mishap; but old Brown turned red with rage, and threatened to kick the boy unmercifully for the damage he had done.

"What a clumsy imp he is," said old Brown, clenching his fist.

"Never mind," George remarked, "he'd never do for *my* trade, that's certain; he'd alarm all Manfred Hall. Yet I should very much like to get a lad of his size; he'd prove very useful to me, if he wasn't so awkward and stupid."

"Take him, then, and try," said old Brown, "for I'm tired of him."

"Not yet; I'll think about it."

After a moment's pause, George said,

"Now I come to think of it, he could bring the trunks away for us, when the time comes."

"So he could," said Brown. "No one would suspect him, and they might me, you know, for I've been so long in the business."

"Come," said George, "put one of those trunks on your shoulders, my lad, and carry it to my cab; it stands round the corner of the next street."

"Yes," said Brown, "carry those trunks for the gentleman to his cab, and then you may go home for the night, and be here early in the morning."

Jem carried the trunks as ordered, and when the cab drove away, he sat upon the springs behind, and *resolved to see where Mr. George went to with them, and for what purpose!*

After all Jem wasn't the fool he was taken for, as we shall quickly see.

CHAPTER LXXXIII.

DETECTIVE SHARP AND THE FORTUNE-TELLER.

"So far, so good," said the inspector, Mr. Sharp, when he had got a situation for young Jem Rawlings. "So far, so good. Young Jem is provided for for some time, at least; and now I must also provide for Master Allan in some way. Poor lad, he is a prey to all sorts of plots and plans and schemes; and, although he is not yet aware of it, he is the rightful heir to a vast amount of property. But, then, how is he to get it? There is a deep and much tangled mystery surrounding the whole affair. Baron Templeton and my Lady Oxenford possess a secret of importance between them, but what it *is* as yet I cannot tell. If either of them were only inclined to speak out boldly and truly it would prevent a great deal of misery and unhappiness to all parties; but they *won't*. I must find it out the best way I can. And yet I don't want to expose any one if I can help it. But I care not what happens or who suffers, I must and *will* find this murder out; for the more I think over it the more certain I am that old Marks and his son are deeply concerned in that affair. But, yet, how am I to bring the guilt home to the rascals? Ah, there's the rub. I have not sufficient evidence as yet, and if they were to imagine for one moment who and what I am, and to suspect at all the deep game I am playing, Mr. Jerry, who swaggers about the town under the name of Captain Zacary, would give me the slip at once and for ever. Then, again," thought the intelligent officer, "I wished to break the news of what I know or suspect to Lady Oxenford, quietly and confidentially; but she is too proud and unbending, I cannot approach her. And then, again, the old lord her husband also has very rude suspicions about her past life and conduct, and employs *me* to find it out. What must I do? Shall I turn traitor to my Lady Oxenford?

No, I cannot please everybody," thought Mr. Sharp, "so, therefore, I shan't try. I shall do whatever I think is best for all parties, without making matters worse than they are, and then please myself."

This resolution of the officer was a very wise one; and although, as our readers will see, his task was a very difficult and annoying one, he resolved not to rest either night or day until he had sounded the very depths of the mystery which surrounded the birth and parentage of the boys Edgar and Allan Norman.

"I must, somehow, get another interview with her ladyship unknown to Lord Oxenford; but how I know not. I don't wish to injure her, yet I must speak very plainly and put her on her guard. She may be very greatly displeased and annoyed, perhaps, but in the end will thank me. The money which Lord Oxenford gives me for the purpose of proving, perhaps, her inconstancy, I will use for a better purpose. I must get an interview with her ladyship somehow, and must work my plans with *the servants*. Through some one of her favourite maids I will get to see the mistress."

How Mr. Sharp did this will require a little explanation.

There was an old gin-drinking woman that Sharp knew who got her living by telling fortunes; and, as female servants are very fond of consulting such "oracles," when they have "a day out," Sharp thought it was more than likely he could by private means induce some of the females in Lord Oxenford's household to try the fortune-telling powers of old Sally Graffles, who lived in Somer's Town.

For this purpose Sharp himself wrote several notes, in which he portrayed the great power of Mother Graffles, and these letters being thrown down the area of Lord Oxenford's house, got into the hands of the females of the household, each and all of whom, by constant watching, were well known to the officer.

Having done this, Mr. Sharp had an interview with old Mother Graffles, and said,

"I expect certain parties to call on you to have their fortunes told. When they come I will also call, and, unknown to your visitor, give you a certain paper, with the name, occupation, age, and other particulars of the stranger, which, being all true, will greatly puzzle and surprise the person, who consequently will have the greatest faith in your power of magic or fortune-telling. Do as I tell you and all will go well, and you will reap a rich harvest by it."

Old Sally, who had long known Inspector Sharp, very willingly promised to obey him in all things; and ere many days had passed Oxenford's maid left her ladyship's mansion, and turned her steps towards Somer's Town, and was followed by Sharp.

The officer got to old Sally's first, and, giving the name of the fast-approaching visitor, sat down behind a large screen in the parlor to listen to all that was said.

The lady's-maid arrived, was ushered into the presence of the renowned Sally Graffles, and sat trembling in expectation.

"You come to have your fortune told, young woman?" said Sally, who smelt strongly of four-penny gin.

"I do, ma'm."

"You know my price?"

"Yes; half-a-crown."

"Half-a-crown for half-a-dozen questions, miss; but *my* price is five shillings if you want your future fortune told. And if you want to have a description of your future husband, that's one shilling more; if you want to know the secrets of your master and mistress, that's two shillings extra; and if you want to enter the magic circle, and make me produce the living image of any one, or bring the dead from the depths below, that's half-a-crown extra again. And my rules is that if you want——"

"Never mind, Mrs. Graffles, never mind; but I should dearly like to find out certain things, and having heard of your great powers——"

"I am the very best in my line, my dear," said old Sally, very importantly. "You couldn't have come at a better time. I have been studying the stars for the last thirty years, and last night I had a vision about you which, if you knew all, my dear—which in course you can, if you pays the extras—why it would make the very hair on your head stand upright, like so many barber's poles, and fill your young heart with such a joy, my dear, that——"

"A vision about me?" said the lady's-maid.

"Yes, you, my dear; and if you only saw the handsome man which loves you—rich, and grand, and——"

"How much will you let me know all for, Mrs. Graffles?" asked the maid, anxiously.

"Let me see, let me see," said old Sally, thoughtfully. "You want me to unfold all?"

"Yes, everthing."

"Put on my astrologer's dress, with its Egyptian charms?"

"Yes."

"But that's a shilling extra again," said Sally, sucking her almost toothless gums in delight at the simpleton before her.

"Never mind; tell me how much it will all cost?" asked the maid. "I want to know everything."

"So you shall; and considering you are a poor girl, I'll bring the whole lot for a sovereign."

"A sovereign! Good heavens!"

"It ain't much, after all, my dear, for the ceremonies, and the time and expenditure."

"But your circular said half-a-crown, and no more. Besides, how am I to know but what you may tell me is all nonsense?" said the maid. "A sovereign! No, never. I don't mind half-a-crown."

For a moment old Sally looked at the girl with a cunning smile, and turned to a cupboard, where for a moment she consulted one of her most powerful oracles, namely, a bottle of gin, and then, turning to her visitor, she said, in a solemn, hiccuping tone, and with a half sleepy and moist look about the eyes,

"Jenny is your Christian name."

"It is," said the girl, surprised. "Who told you?"

"Parker is your other name."

"It is. But who, in the name of mercy, could have told you? I didn't."

"You are a lady's maid."

"I am."

"Am I to be trusted now?" asked old Sally, in triumph.

"You are, you are. You are a most wonderful woman, and I now fully believe that you really have dealings with the stars."

"Ah, young woman, speak not hastily in this room of wonders," interrupted old Sally. "My price for the whole, extras and all thrown in, is one sovereign, young woman; not a farthing less."

"Here it is, ma'm," said Jenny, trembling with astonishment, "here it is. I freely give it, for I feel certain you are a true astrologer."

Old Sally took the money, and left the front room for a few minutes; but soon returned, attired in a long robe, spangled all over with bits of silver and gilded tinsel, cut into the shape of moons, rising suns, stars without number, and all sorts of curious figures and characters, much like the unintelligible words, ciphers, and nonsense which one sees on the large red, white, blue, saffron, and blood-red-coloured bottles in chemists' windows.

Her hat was tall and conical, and, like her dress, was a mass of different colours, and decorated with bats and owls, dragons, serpents, and other strange devices, in gaudy colours and tinsellings.

In her hand she wielded a long cane, or wand, and her general appearance was so strange and hideous in the darkened room, that Jenny Parker trembled more than if she were about to undergo a serious and painful surgical operation.

With different coloured chalks she made a circle on the floor, and placing a chair in the centre, Jenny took her seat, and with many strange mutterings, and sighs, and groans, interspersed with various wavings of the magic wand, the grand revelations began.

"Now," said Sally, after again consulting her gin-bottle in the cupboard, and taking a long draught therefrom, "ask me what questions you like."

"You have told me my name and occupation, but with whom do I live?"

"Lady Oxenford," was the prompt reply. "Is her ladyship married?"

"She is; her husband is old and jealous."

"Her ladyship—is she grave or gay?"

"Very grave and sorrowful at times; some mystery hangs over her; her husband suspects her."

"So I have always thought."

"You are very fond of soldiers."

"Me?"

"Yes, you, my girl; the Life-guards are your idols. You were out walking with one two Sundays ago. He borrowed a crown from you which he will never repay, but he will not be your husband."

"I don't want him," said Jenny, pertly, "and whoever told you about that soldier——"

"No one tells me anything, my dear; I find out all by astrology, and in the vision which I saw last night, I saw you talking at the corner of your square with a person dressed in dark blue."

"Was he a fine-looking man?"

"Very."

"Had he whiskers?"

"Very large ones; they were brushed out round his face in the fiercest manner."

"He was an officer."

"Oh, without a doubt, my dear."

"In what regiment, ma'am?"

"In the regiment of night-police."

"You are making fun of me."

"No, I'm not, for you know it is true."

"Well, if it is, it hasn't anything to do with me; its cook's sweetheart—that's all."

"I know it; he often slips down the area on wet nights and has a good supper; be careful your master don't find it out, my dear."

For a moment Jenny Parker was puzzled what to ask, for all that old Sally Graffles had said was strictly true.

At last she said, "Do you think her ladyship has any admirers?"

"I am positive of it, and could call into this very

room the living image of the man who is dying to make her acquaintance."

"Do so, then."

"Ah! but that would be telling you her ladyship's fortune, and would be half a sovereign extra," replied old Sally, with an eye to business.

"But you can tell me where I might see him, perhaps, couldn't you?"

"I'll see," said Sally, and for the third time she consulted the "spirits"—in her gin bottle—and whispered a few words to Sharp behind the screen.

When she took her place again, she produced a dirty pack of cards, and after much shuffling, and going through a great many strange antics of throwing her arms about, she described the exact appearance of the gentleman who was supposed to be in love with Jenny's mistress, who at last consented to forego the pleasure of beholding her own future husband if Mrs. Graffles would only condescend to give her a single peep at the ardent lover of her mistress.

"I'll go and consult the oracle, and see if it is convenient to bring the gentleman forward."

"Why, I thought you always made them appear in a looking-glass?"

"Ah! common astrologers do; but I don't, my dear. I bring 'em forward bodily, you know; but it might frighten you."

"Oh! don't fear," said Jenny, boldly, "I shan't faint."

"Very well, just as you like, my dear; only promise me one thing."

"What is it?"

"Why this; if the gentleman you are about to see should send a note to you, will you meet him?"

"What for?"

"He will explain all about that; once you see him you will never forget his face; and more than all, you will perceive that this gentleman will hand me a note for you before your own eyes."

"What, now?"

"Yes, now, in this room, when I have finished my ceremonies and incantations," said old Sally, who began to wave her wand around her head, and mutter all sorts of unintelligible rubbish, when suddenly she struck the screen, and tumbling down with a sharp sound, the half-terrified girl screamed aloud and fainted, for she there beheld a living man!

Sharp having acted his part left the room, unobserved by Jenny Parker, who was lying on the floor, for a few moments, unconscious.

When she recovered, old Sally gave her a drop of gin and inquired whether she wanted to know or see anything see.

But the foolish girl was so terrified at what she thought was the magical power of Mrs. Graffles, and perhaps in fear that the old woman would next call forth into her presence the very devil himself, that she hastily departed, filled with astonishment and awe.

CHAPTER LXXXIV.

JENNY PARKER MEETS INSPECTOR SHARP— WHAT CAME OF THE INTERVIEW.

THE note which Sharp handed to old Sally, in the last act of the fortune-teller's drama, was duly given to Jenny Parker before she left old Sally, and as it begged for an interview with Jenny, the foolish girl was only too glad to accede to the request, and signified as much to old Sally.

Sharp, having consulted old Sally, was duly at the spot mentioned for the meeting in the note.

It was a fine, clear night.

The cold was sharp and biting, and the moon shone out in all the brilliancy of a frosty sky.

After waiting patiently some time, Sharp observed a cloaked and muffled figure leave the side door of Lord Oxenford's mansion.

Sharp hastened towards the young person, whispered something to her, and without another word he led her, trembling with curiosity, to a cab in waiting, into which they got.

"Thanks, many thanks, for your kindness," said Sharp; "and in the first place," said Sharp, endeavouring to slip a purse of gold into the hands of the maid, "take this, my good girl, for your trouble."

Jenny, however, indignantly rejected the offering, saying, in a tone of offended dignity, "You are evidently labouring under some mistake, sir."

"Nay," said Sharp, trying to force it upon her acceptance; "nay, accept it as a feeble mark of my profound esteem."

"Esteem!" responded Jenny, with an expression of ironical contempt so unmistakably displayed that Sharp, perceiving his error, returned the purse to his pocket, saying,

"I believe I have the pleasure of speaking to Lady Oxenford's favorite maid?"

"You are perfectly correct, sir."

"May I ask whether you have been in her service very long?"

"Yes, I have, very long."

"Doubtless for several years, then?"

"For six or seven years, sir."

"You thoroughly know her ways and habits, then?"

"I do."

"You will remember that in the note which came into your possession so mysteriously, and which you answered, I stated I had intelligence of the greatest importance to impart to your mistress, Lady Oxenford."

"So the note stated."

"Have you told her ladyship of this our interview?"

"I have not."

"No doubt," said Mr. Sharp, sarcastically, and with a smile, "you always maintain equal silence towards my Lord Oxenford in regard to the occasional visits which it is said the Baron Templeton pays her ladyship?"

"Sir," said Jenny, with a sudden flush on her face, "I seldom see or converse either with my lord or the baron."

"Now, let me ask," said Sharp, "what was the real motive you had in meeting me this evening? Was it simply to gratify your curiosity regarding me, or——"

"To ascertain what you had to communicate to my mistress, Lady Oxenford, and to apprise her of it should I deem it advisable."

"You are extremely young," said Sharp, with a quiet smile, "and I can scarcely judge how much you may or may not be in the confidence of her ladyship."

"The best way then, sir, for you to do, perhaps, is to solicit an interview with her ladyship direct."

"The very thing I was going to ask you to assist me in doing. Put me in the way of doing that privately, and I shall be under many obligations, I assure you."

"That permission must be granted by her ladyship personally, sir," said Jenny.

"But could you not do it? Any price you may put on the services rendered would be immediately paid."

"I can do nothing, sir, without the knowledge and consent of her ladyship."

"Could you not simply give her a letter from me?"

"Impossible."

"There is nothing in it that is at all objectionable. I have merely said that having matters of the deepest importance to communicate, I venture to implore the favour of being instructed how to convey a letter into her *own* hands, without fear of it being intercepted," said Sharp, in a whisper.

"Then, sir, your letter is useless for the present. I will repeat to her what you say, and if she thinks proper to grant your request, I will tell you. Now, what, sir, is your name and address?"

"My name is—eh—oh—ah! What did you say? Yes, yes, I now remember. My name is Captain Sharp. You will not forget."

"I shall remember the name, sir."

"Is that name quite unknown to you?"

"It is."

"Did you never hear it before?"

"No."

"Not even mentioned by my Lord Oxenford in ordinary conversation?"

"No, sir, I have never heard it before."

"Are you sure?"

"Positive, sir."

Now, Mr. Sharp had good reasons for supposing that she *had* heard his name before.

He could tell from the sudden glow on her cheeks that Captain Sharp was a name not totally unknown either to Jenny herself or her ladyship.

Irritated and annoyed by the reserve thus shown by the maid, Sharp, like an old soldier, determined to make a fresh mode of attack.

"My dear, dear girl," said he, "it is useless, I see, to attempt to conceal anything from you. 'Tis true I *have* most interesting communications to make to her ladyship, but," he added, with an insinuating tone of voice, and an almost tenderness of tone, "I have something almost equally important to say to you."

"To *me*, sir?"

"Yes, indeed, to *you*, my dear girl. I saw you the other day, as you drove out in the park for a morning airing, in company with her ladyship, and I——"

"Sir!"

"Pardon me, I must confess it. I saw you, I say, and I found you much, yes, very much, too charming and fascinating for my peace of mind."

"Sir, I really—that is—I must say that your cool imp——"

She did not finish the sentence.

She reddened very much, and stammered out something.

But Sharp's well-timed and oily speech appeared to have taken an effect upon her vanity, for she hung her head, and spoke not.

"She is infinitely more vulnerable on the side of vanity than by bribes," thought the wily Sharp. "I will try the effect of a little more flattery."

"Yes, my dear, dear girl," he continued, in very seductive tones, "from the first hour in which I saw you, my anxiety to obtain an interview has been doubled and redoubled, I can assure you. In the first I longed to tell you how deep and ineffaceable an impression you had made upon my heart; and, in the second place, to speak with you concerning those important matters which are for the ear of your mistress, Lady Oxenford."

"I fear, sir, you are jesting with me—nay, mocking me."

"No I am not, on my word, I am not. I might have found other means of effecting my communication with her ladyship, but I preferred addressing myself to you. Your expressive and handsome features pourtrayed so much intelligence, mingled with passions both ardent and generous, that I felt in speaking to you of the mistress you love and serve, and the ardent affection with which you have inspired me, you would not be wholly deaf to my suit, Miss Parker."

"You have my name glibly on your tongue, I find."

"I have; and many, many other things and names you may think me unacquainted with, I can assure you. Oh, how could it be otherwise, dearest one, when you have wholly engrossed my every thought? Believe me, your tender and long attachment to Lady Oxenford has but tended to increase the fervour of my regard for you."

"I must not listen to such language, sir," said Jenny, in a tone that betrayed deep emotion.

"Good," thought Sharp, "she sighs already; the game is won. Victory is mine—she is now my tool. Hark, how she sighs! She has swallowed my bait whole. This poor simpleton is like all her sex, and unable to resist a little well-timed flattery mixed with a few expressions of everlasting love and devotion. Why do you retire so far from me, my pretty one?" said Sharp to Jenny, in an endearing manner. "Let me hold your hand and support you. You tremble."

"No, sir, I do not; but I must stop this cab, and return home again. I know not whither you are leading me."

"Only for a mere ride, my dear."

"I must return at once; I have business with her ladyship."

"I cannot suffer you to depart yet; I have scarcely said a quarter of what I intended to say."

"Then let me beg that our conversation may be entirely confined to my mistress, Lady Oxenford, sir."

"I am most, nay, very desirous that it should; only for that purpose it is necessary that we should repose the greatest and most perfect confidence in each other. By that means, and by acting in strict concert, we may be enabled to prevent the most fearful calamities to her ladyship."

"Sir, I do not understand you, by fearful calamities. Why, what has she done, what could she do, to fear any?"

"Fear not, lovely Jenny. If you will aid me, these evils, however greatly they may threaten Lady Oxenford, may be dispelled. With such a friend and ally as yourself nothing would be impossible. And, upon reflection, it seems to me that if once you and I come to a right understanding on the subject, it will be better, just for the present, not to inform her ladyship of what we are endeavouring to effect."

"And wherefore, sir, should she be kept in ignorance of what so much concerns her to know?"

"She might not be enabled to impose sufficient command on herself, and her very apprehensions might endanger the success of the project I wish to work out for her good."

"But what can I do in the matter? Why is it so indispensable, sir, that you and I should become such fast friends and sworn confidants?"

"I will explain. But in the first place you must candidly answer the questions I shall put to you. Will you promise to do so?"

"Alas! I seem as though you exercised some spell or fascination over me. Although nearly a stranger to me, you seem to have inspired me with sufficient confidence in your word to do whatsoever you ask me."

"Because I speak the language of innocence and truth, that ever reaches the heart," said Sharp, proudly.

"Oh, no, no! I must not believe you. Your resolve and motive for speaking to a girl like me, must conceal some hidden and deep design."

"Let my extreme anxiety to obtain an interview with you for the sake of revealing the passion with which you have inspired me, and of carrying out my good intentions to serve and save your honored mistress, plead my excuse for having had recourse to the plan I have for accomplishing the two dearest wishes of my heart. Will you accept this excuse, dearest Jenny?" said Sharp, with enthusiasm.

"Perhaps I am wrong in doing so, after having made me grant you an interview. I ought, perhaps, to mistrust you."

"Why reproach yourself for what you have done, dear Jenny?" said Sharp, in an endearing manner. "This our interview is based upon the purest and most praiseworthy motives, and I am happy that I have met you; very happy, indeed."

"Are you quite so?" asked Jenny, blushing.

"How can I be otherwise when you are beside me, and your arm is locked in mine?"

"Let me beseech you to speak not of me but of my mistress, Lady Oxenford," said Jenny, confusedly. "It is more fitting you should speak of the business that brought you here."

"Then must I still talk of you, dear Jenny. But if that theme be forbidden me, let me indulge the dear delight of being near to you."

"No, sir; I must return home. Each moment that I stay convinces me you are deceiving me, and have designs I dream not of—I feel persuaded, something tells me that you are laying a trap to ensnare me or mistress."

"And suppose I had such a design?"

"Why, then, it would be base and wicked of me to endeavour to assist you in harming my mistress. Stop the cab. I must return at once."

"Come, come, Jenny, be calm; if you will not answer the questions I put to you regarding her ladyship; if you will not answer them—"

"Speak of my mistress, sir, if you like; but cease your flattery of me."

"We will, then. Tell me, is it not about a week since her ladyship went secretly to the masque ball?"

"It is; but could you have known it?"

"But you see I do."

"So it appears. I remember the night well. His lordship, I heard, returned home very late, and ever since there have been violent quarrels between them."

"And while she was at the opera you were all alone. Ah! would that I had known it, what happiness would it not have afforded me to have been permitted to share your solitude with you!"

"Speak, sir, of my mistress, not of me."

"Pardon me, Jenny, but let me ask in what state did your mistress appear to you when she returned from the masquerade?"

"She looked cold and stately, walked the room up and down for about an hour, and passed a restless night, and then suddenly arose, and wrote several letters."

"Did she post them?"

"No, they are in her private desk,—one that is full of secret drawers and springs, which had been especially designed for herself."

"Oh! indeed," said Sharp, pricking up his ears;

"but now I come to look at you closely, what splendid eyes you've got."

"Have I not told you to cease your flattery, sir?" said Jenny, blushing.

"And I suppose my lord never troubles himself about my lady's letters, does he?"

"Not much."

"Do you think he ever goes to this private desk?"

"I never saw him; he has too much confidence in her ladyship to give way to foolish jealousy."

"Has he though; what an excellent man, to be sure! What a lovely hand yours is, Jenny, and how white and small."

"Leave off these foolish compliments, sir, I beg."

"Pardon me, Jenny; but has her ladyship's manner changed much since that night?"

"Oh, very greatly; her agitation and nervousness increased daily. I attended her as usual, and with more than ordinary care. She would have no one near her but me, and often when we were alone she would bitterly weep. Oh! how bitter were her tears!"

"Where they, indeed?"

"Even I could scarce refrain from crying!"

"Did she seem angry at all?"

"Oh, no! on the contrary, she appeared broken hearted and very miserable, raising her clasped hands towards heaven as if to implore mercy, while tears flowed down her pallid cheeks. Sometimes she will call me to undress her, but as soon as I have done so, instead of retiring to bed, she sits down to her writing desk and begins to write in a sort of private memorandum book, which she carries in her breast. I have observed her sitting for hours writing them; and when all the household are fast asleep, her ladyship's lamp is still burning."

For a few moments Sharp did not speak.

He was in deep thought.

"I'd give anything to get possession of this book," thought the officer. "I have no doubt but that it contains a great deal of information that would be of immense value to me. But then how am I to get it? I dare not ask this girl to steal it for half an hour, for it would open her eyes too much. I must be patient, and wait. This girl is open to flattery, I see, and in a few more such meetings as this I have no doubt but she would do anything I desired of her; but for the present I dare not hint at my real designs for fear of a premature discovery."

After much conversation on indifferent topics, the cab returned to the place whence it had started, and, promising to meet the officer again, Jenny Parker alighted.

"You will not tell your mistress anything of what I have said?" Sharp remarked.

"Oh, of course not."

"May I rely on your word?"

"You may."

"You know, dear Jenny, that I am deeply in love with you."

"Yes, I think that you are so, but the future will prove all. Good-night, captain."

"Good-night; but be sure not to name anything that has passed between us to her ladyship."

"I will not."

But Jenny *did* tell her mistress, and that very night.

And as her ladyship sat up in bed, and listened to the narration of her faithful servant, she heaved a deep sigh, and thought,

"My secret is known to a stranger, yet not for all the world would I have it divulged to my Lord Oxenford. I will meet this unknown but inquisitive stranger, and if a woman's depth and cunning is not greater than his, then I am ruined. I tremble at the meeting, but I will confront him, and go in disguise. There is to be another masquerade this week. I will go in the dress of Jenny Parker, and worm out every secret this mysterious gentleman possesses."

Her ladyship rose from bed, and sitting down to her desk, began to write.

Jenny had gone to bed long before this, and Lady Oxenford was alone.

But as she wrote, the door opened quietly behind her, and looking haggard, pale, and revengeful, Lord Oxenford entered.

CHAPTER LXXXV.

THE REUNION AT COUNT BLANCO'S—THE USE OF FOILS.

POOR Allan Norman, now that his constant companion and friend, young Jem Rawlings, had been separated from him, felt lonely and sad.

Mr. Sharp frequently saw Allan, and on no occasion of their meeting did the officer fail to give him money, and quite sufficient to maintain him in the style of a young gentleman.

Whom this money came from puzzled Allan, and on one or two occasions he had courage enough to ask Inspector Sharp all about it.

But the officer would not gratify Allan's curiosity, for very good reasons, and told him to rest satisfied, and ask no unnecessary questions.

Allan knew that his prospects in life were in the hands of the restless officer, and therefore remained silent.

But as to what Sharp was or was not doing in his behalf, not a word was breathed by the officer.

Allan was now well clothed and very comfortably lodged, and passed his time in respectable pleasures.

While in the park one day, lolling away an hour in looking at the fashions and gay equipages that passed, a sudden shout of alarm was heard.

Allan quickly turned his head, and beheld approaching at a tremendous pace a pair of horses, tearing along, and dragging along behind them a mail phaeton, in which sat two affrighted ladies and a foreign gentleman, of tall, majestic appearance.

The rein had snapped asunder, and every one expected each moment to see the vehicle dashed against a post, and be shivered into a thousand pieces.

The foreign driver, Count Blanco, stood up in the carriage, pale from fear and alarm, but unable to arrest the progress of his horses in their wild and mad career.

No one attempted to stop the runaway horses; but Allan, perceiving the danger, ran after, and clambered up behind the vehicle with great agility, and getting in front, very coolly stepped upon the pole, and bestriding one of the animals, seized the fragment of the rein with such a firm grasp, that, after a few moments of determined tugging, the horses gradually slackened their pace, and amid the loud shouts of approving crowds, the two ladies and Count Blanco safely alighted.

This act of coolness and bravery took all by surprise, and many gentlemen on horseback rode up, shook Allan by the hand, and applauded his heroism.

Count Blanco was delighted with his almost miraculous escape, and the ladies, one of whom was

the count's young daughter, kissed Allan's hand in gratitude.

Allan visited the count's residence, and dined with him, where he met with several young officers, all of whom invited him to dine with them at their favourite club.

Allan accepted this invitation, and went to the club, where he supped and made merry for several hours with the greatest delight.

Count Blanco was also there, and never tired of introducing Allan to many friends, and recounting to them the gallant deed of which he was the hero.

There was one among those present who, however, seemed to be sitting on pins and needles during the repast.

Who he was Allan could not tell.

How such a vulgarly-spoken person could have introduced himself into such company, was a problem that young Allan could not solve.

He heard, however, several very ungracious remarks fall from the lips of this talkative individual.

And more than once did Allan feel the hot blood mounting to his temples.

This loquacious and very sarcastic personage was called Captain Zacary by those there assembled.

Many of the young gentlemen seemed to look up to him as their leader; and from the manner in which this Captain Zacary spoke of his great wealth and prospects, Allan seemed to think he must indeed be the son, if indeed not the only son, of some great banker or millionaire.

Allan sat and pondered, and ill at ease.

The Count Blanco was extremely attentive and polite to the young hero of the evening.

But there was a something about this Captain Zacary that Allan did not like.

This person never dared to look Allan fairly in the face, and, for some cause best known to himself, always averted his face when Allan looked in his direction.

After a time Allan began to think he had seen or had known somewhere this Captain Zacary.

When or where he could not recal.

The voice sometimes sounded familiar to Allan. But then he spoke in such a drawling tone, whether natural or assumed, that young Norman began to think he must be mistaken in the person.

However, when supper was over, Captain Zacary carefully avoided any introduction to Allan, and conversed mysteriously in whispers among several of his acquaintants, who seemed greatly surprised and annoyed at what he told them.

"Are you sure of this, Captain Zacary?" asked one, in a tone of indignation.

"I am quite sure."

"There cannot be a mistake, I hope?"

"On my honor, there is not."

"And do you mean to say that Count Blanco's young hero, then, is nothing more nor less than a half-convicted felon and murderer?"

"I do."

"This is a most serious charge."

"I know it is."

"But how can you prove it."

"Have I not seen them both, he and his brother, in the dock, and tried for their lives at Newgate?"

"You saw them?"

"Yes; and will swear to what I say at the point of my sword. I will defend the truth of what I say."

"Why did you not tell us of this before? He should never have sat down in our company had we known it."

"I dare say not. He ought to be kicked out immediately."

"Then why not inform Count Blanco?"

"Nay; I have enough to do to mind my own business. The count is old enough, and should have discretion in choosing his acquaintance."

"True. But see the service which this youth has rendered him to-day."

"Pooh, pooh; that is nothing."

"He risked his own life to save them."

"And so would a common crossing-sweeper for a small reward."

"Shall we inform the count of your words, Captain Zacary?"

"As you please."

"The consequences may prove fatal."

"How do you mean?"

"The youth is high spirited, and may fight."

"Fight!" said the captain, contemptuously. "Fight! Don't make me laugh. Why, he looks as timid as a mouse."

"And yet may prove as brave as a lion," said another one.

"I will go forth at once, and whisper what you have said, to the count, captain."

"As you please. I am willing."

The person who had been conversing with Captain Zacary now crossed the room, and began to whisper in Count Blanco's ear, apart.

"What!" said the count, in surprise, "you must be mistaken, sir—it cannot be."

"But Captain Zacary says he will swear to it."

"And, even then, I cannot credit it, sir."

"But would it not be advisable to sift the affair?"

"In what manner?"

"Interrogate the youth."

"Nay, I would not so insult him by any such rude suspicions and inquiries. Look at the youth, does he look or talk like such a one as Captain Zacary has described?"

"I know not that, count; but of this rest assured, your friends feel very uncomfortable in the presence of this youth."

"They did not appear so until Captain Zacary had poisoned their ears, sir."

"But what do you propose to do, count?"

"I will stake my life that what Zacary says is all fiction."

"I hope it may prove so, count."

"Well, think as you like, I shall not turn my back upon the youth; and should he need a friend I will prove one to him through all my life."

The count turned and touched the arm of Allan, who was leaning on the mantle-piece in great thought.

"Your name is Allan Norman, I think?"

"It is, count, and I am not ashamed to own it."

"You will excuse me asking any questions that may hurt your feelings, sir, but—"

"There is no questions, count, you could ask me that would hurt my feelings, I assure you."

"You do not recognize any one in this room that you know?"

"I do not."

"Are you sure?"

"Quite sure, count; but during the repast I thought I occasionally heard a voice that was, alas! too familiar to my ear."

"Oh, indeed; and who might have been the speaker?"

"The person yonder who is called Captain Zacary."

"Oh, indeed; the person, you say, who is 'called' Captain Zacary?"

"I use that word, count, for if his voice is really that of the person who has been the enemy of myself and brother through life, he is no captain at all, nor is his name Zacary."

"Indeed! You speak passionately, young man."

"I do, and have need to feel deeply, I can assure you, count, if you knew all."

"And what may the real name of your supposed acquaintance be?"

"Jerry Marks, a young villain who is luxuriating in ill-gotten wealth; a Jew's son, who is forced to assume disguises to keep him out of the clutches of the police."

"This is most serious to say; you may be mistaken in the person."

"It is possible, count; but if I am not, what I say is true, every word of it."

"The person yonder that you allude to is an officer."

"In what regiment?"

"I know not."

"An officer of what?"

"I know not that either."

"Then how do you know he is an officer?"

"Such has always been his title among those he associates with, that is all I know."

"It is very simple to assume titles, but not so easy to prove them, count; it is the fashion of the times, count, for worthless persons to assume honorable titles, so as, if possible, to hide their own deformities and wickedness."

The count and his friend spoke not, but Allan asked—

"Have you narrowly watched the face of this Captain Zacary?"

"I have not."

"He wears his hair in a particular manner; generally the left temple is nearly always covered," said the count.

"Then I am not mistaken," said Allan, smiling, "but if you have no objection I should like to be introduced to this Captain Zacary."

"By all means."

"But do so in a quiet manner, and don't let him suppose that you intend to introduce me."

"Why not?"

"Because it will only render our meeting all the more interesting," said Allan, clenching his fist with angry determination.

The count sidled up to Captain Zacary, and ere many minutes they approached the fire-place where Allan stood, with his face from them.

As he approached Allan a cold tremor passed through Captain Zacary.

He was about to turn abruptly away, when the count said suddenly, and with a quiet smile,

"Allow me to introduce to you, Captain Zacary, my young friend here; I believe you have not yet been introduced!"

Allan turned, and with an angry flush on his face, gazed long and steadfastly at his foe.

"Captain Zacary, Allan Norman—Allan Norman, Captain Zacary," said the count, bowing.

"You are much mistaken, Count Blanco, if you think I desire to form the acquaintance of such a——"

"Jerry Marks!" said Allan, passionately, and in a loud tone. "You are a scoundrel and a villain. Count, you are mistaken; this person is not a captain at all; he is an impostor, and before the whole company here assembled I brand him as a villain of the deepest dye; and in proof of what I say, I treat him like a dog!"

With these hasty words, uttered in a fierce tone, Allan raised his clenched fist, and with a powerful blow, felled Captain Zacary to the ground.

HOPEFUL LIMB

THE BOY KING
OF THE SOUTH SEA ISLANDS.

THE FUNERAL OF PRINCESS MARMI.

This action was so sudden, and the blow so well directed, that it occasioned immense surprise.

The room was instantly in an uproar.

"Turn him out!"

"'Tis a gross insult!"

"A duel is inevitable!"

"Nothing but blood can wipe out such an insult!"

Such were the confused and half-intelligible whisperings that buzzed among the crowd.

Some one raised the "Captain" from the floor, and he was bleeding profusely from the nose and mouth.

Allan expected that Jerry would have rushed upon him with some deadly weapon.

But the craven-hearted young villain dared not

encounter the steadfast gaze of his brave opponent.

"Who is he? What is this youth, captain?" asked many.

"A rascal, who but barely escaped the hangman a few months ago," said Jerry.

"Liar! villain!" shouted Allan. "On my life and honour, gentlemen, he is a scoundrel and imposter! He is a hook-nosed Jew, and a cowardly cur!"

"I suppose you wish satisfaction, captain?" asked one.

"I do," said Jerry, with trembling lips. "But a gentleman cannot fight without weapons."

"We have foils at hand, and sharp-pointed."

Jerry, when he heard the foils spoken of, smiled in a ghastly manner.

There was a triumphant look in his eyes now, for he had long practised with these weapons, and he knew, or suspected, that Allan knew nothing of them, at least, in a scientific manner.

"Satisfaction! satisfaction!" growled Jerry, who never for a moment dreamed that Allan would accept a duel. "Satisfaction! Blood alone will satisfy me for so gross an insult."

Allan smiled contemptuously.

"A duel cannot be brought off here, gentlemen," said the count; "we have no weapons at hand. Suppose we arrange a meeting for to-morrow morning at dawn?"

"No, now, now; I cannot, I will not, wait," said Jerry.

"Don't trouble yourself, villain!" said Allan. "I am ready and willing to meet you when, and where, and how you like—the sooner the better."

"But we have nothing at hand, except foils," said the count.

"Never mind, they will do," said Allan. "I'm not very particular."

"But you know nothing of fencing," said the count.

"But I know I have justice on my side, and Heaven will guide my arm in this encounter."

"Let me persuade you not to do so," said the count. "The captain is a practised hand, and very clever."

"I care not for that. He has no heart, or if he has, it is a corrupt and vile one. Give me a weapon, I am impatient to begin."

"Be it so, my brave boy, but I fear you will regret your impatience; and your want of skill will entail the most serious consequences. You may be killed."

"Never," said Allan, "I shall never fall before such a rascal as he is."

By this time Allan had thrown off his coat and waistcoat, and, tucking up his sleeves, stood ready for the fray.

Jerry, who had before been all smiles and confidence, now turned pale, as he cast a sidelong glance at his impatient and confident foe.

He also had divested himself of all superfluous attire, and, taking a foil, advanced to meet his enemy.

Those present stood around, anxious spectators of the scene, and all was breathless silence.

Their weapons crossed, and the long thin blades trembled and jarred together.

"I perceive he knows nothing of fencing," thought Jerry. "My victory will be an easy one."

And for a moment or two he made three or four passes in a very careless, showy manner, and smiled with self-conceit.

Allan, however, to the surprise of all, handled his weapon in an excellent manner, and very easily.

"I see you are wearing a false moustache, Jerry," said Allan, with a look of contempt. "That disguises your thick lips somewhat."

"'Tis false," said Jerry. "There is nothing false about me, as I will quickly prove."

And, stung with Allan's boldness and clearness, he made several rapid thrusts at young Norman's heart; but was foiled in every attempt.

In return Allan drew up to closer distance, and, after a feint or two, the point of his weapon struck Jerry on the lip, and stripped therefrom the false moustache he wore.

Jerry, perceiving this, was enraged beyond all bounds.

He grew purple in the face, and could not shut his ears to the suppressed laughter of his former friends.

He made desperate lunges at Allan, and their weapons became entwined like two snakes in mortal conflict.

Jerry now began to perceive that his foe was equal to himself in alertness and skill.

Indeed, he began to tremble with fear.

His looks became wild and haggard.

More than once had Allan's foil point grazed his breast, and caused his blood to run cold.

Allan, however, was all smiles and confidence.

He was as fresh and nimble as at the beginning of the combat.

Jerry, however, was getting weaker and weaker, and his limbs trembled.

At last Allan struck Jerry in the sword arm, and blood flowed.

"Part them! part them!" said the seconds. "Blood has been drawn. Honor is satisfied."

"No, no," said Allan. "I will not give up my weapon until that villain falls upon his knees, and confesses all his iniquity before those assembled here."

"You will never condescend to such a degradation?" said one to Jerry.

"No, never," replied Jerry, faintly.

But in his heart he would have confessed anything rather than meet Allan again.

But, in the presence of such company, he could not show the white feather of cowardice so prominently. So, therefore, hoping by some chance or lucky stroke to disable young Allan, he took his foil again.

The combat was now resumed even more fiercely than before.

The display of skill was very great.

Each combatant now felt and knew that a single stroke would decide the duel, and, perhaps, mortally.

For several moments they fought on most ferociously, and Jerry was blind with despair.

Allan, however, was cooler than Jerry, and parried every thrust very cleverly, and with ease, until at last, after fighting for more than fifteen minutes with great rapidity, a sharp cry was heard.

One of the combatants lay on the floor, bathed in blood.

CHAPTER LXXXVI.

LION LIMB WITNESSES AND DESCRIBES MANY EXCITING INDIAN SPORTS—COMBATS OF ANIMALS—THE SNAKE CHARMERS—THE LION AND BUFFALO FIGHT.

BUT the tournaments and such like games were not the only amusements which old King Katamar provided for the pleasure of his guests.

He was under so many obligations to Lion Limb

for what he had already done for him and his daughter, that he had long resolved when Lion Limb should visit the islands over which he ruled, to make such a display as should astonish the Europeans.

After they had partaken of a grand dinner, old Katamar invited his visitors to follow him to a strong enclosure not far away, which was made like a large circus, the sides being very high all round, and seats so elevated that all could have a good view of what was to take place.

Old Katamar had ransacked all of the neighbouring islands for clever persons to exhibit their feats before Lion Limb, and when all was prepared there entered the ring several natives, each with a small, flat-covered basket, and after bowing many times to old King Katamar and his powerful friends, they prepared to exhibit their various tricks, to the great surprise of all present.

"The first ones to perform, Lion Limb, will be our snake-charmers. They are very wonderful fellows, and as you may never have seen any exhibition of the kind in your own country, I daresay that this display will please and amuse you."

"Snake-charmers, eh?" said Harry Woodruff. "What sort of snakes do they perform with?"

"All sorts."

"Rattlesnakes, cobras, and them sort?"

"Yes; why not?" said old Katamar, smiling.

"I hope they will keep a respectful distance from me, then," said Harry, "for of all things in the world I hate reptiles the most."

"These jugglers of the South Sea Islands have long been celebrated; but the natives themselves imagine they must have intercourse with demons. It is even said that they are sometimes employed to kill persons secretly by poison or otherwise, and thus it is that the poor natives generally look upon these fellows with fear and trembling."

The charmers, as we have said, entered the arena, and placed their flat baskets on the ground, in which were snakes of various sorts and sizes in a state of deep sleep.

The charmers produced small reed pipes, and began to make the most hideous noises.

It was astonishing to observe how soon the baskets began to move, for the reptiles inside hearing the noise gradually lifted up the covering of the baskets, raised their heads, gradually erected themselves, waving their necks to and fro as if in a state of great delight.

The hooded snake is always a prominent performer in these tricks; another, the rock snake, is not venomous; but the bite of the hooded snake is nearly always fatal.

Some think that these charmers extract the poisonous fangs from the snakes; but this is not true, as they exhibit the reptiles with all their powers of mischief unimpaired.

It is the perfect knowledge of the animals that they exhibit which secures them from danger.

The rock snake is usually about sixteen feet long, of a sluggish nature, and suffers itself to be handled by the performer without making any effort to escape.

The man who exhibits it ties it round his neck like a lady's boa, and coils it into all sorts of fantastic figures, the reptile all the while remaining perfectly docile.

But to make extracts from Lion Limb's diary of these games, we will proceed to relate them in his own words.

Speaking of these Indian snake charmers, his diary reads:—

"This class of jugglers perform numberless tricks

with these reptiles, taking and handling the most deadly and venomous in their hands, and sporting with them like toys.

"They told King Katamar that they had extracted all the fangs from the animals; but this was only said to quiet a good many of my lads, who didn't like the idea of being perhaps bitten and devoured by those nasty creatures.

"Whenever any poisonous snakes are known to be in a certain locality, or among the villages of the settled tribes, these snake-charmers are sent to remove them, and they always undertake to get rid of the unpleasant visitor for a small amount of preserved meat, or such like.

"But these charmers are great thieves and rogues.

"They pretend to rid places of snakes, but they do not.

"One arrives on the spot with a snake concealed about him, and having made every one retire for a good distance, he shoves his own snake into a hole, and then begins to pipe away on his shrieking instrument, and the snake, well knowing its master, answers his music by coming out.

"The charmer then holds it aloft, and the simple natives believe that he has really caught one.

"If, on some other occasion, the natives are troubled with snakes about their cabins, the charmer is sent for again, and the same farce is performed a second time.

"Whenever these charmers are hard up and want a job, they endeavour to persuade the natives that their lodges or huts are infested with snakes; and in order to convince the owners of the truth of what they say, they secretly thrust two or three of their own snakes into various holes of the lodge or cabin.

"They then enter the place with loud words and many gestures, and begin to play on their pipes, until at last the terrified natives perceive snakes crawling about in all directions, which cause them to flee for their very lives.

"The charmers, however, seize the snakes, place them in their baskets, and are triumphant.

"In this manner these imposters will go to every cabin for miles around and practice the same deceits, and then live for weeks together very lazily and comfortably, and do nothing.

"Such were the sort of fellows which performed before us, and certainly some of their tricks were astonishing.

"But these snake-charmers and performers were quickly succeeded by a band of jugglers, and it must be confessed that some of their tricks of manual dexterity were really astonishing.

"These fellows possess an elasticity of body and flexibility of limb far exceeding anything ever seen in England.

"I will not enter in this diary full particulars of all they did, but simply mention one or two of their cunning juggles, and then a feat of physical activity which I have witnessed more than once.

"These jugglers come to your house or cabin in broad daylight and perform their tricks before your eyes.

"They have no cunningly planned tables or chairs, or bulky clothing, or anything of that sort; and the only things they carry are a few odds and ends in a basket, with which they perform.

"Almost naked, these conjurors stand before you; and such is their extreme cleverness, that one almost doubts his own eyes and understanding.

"One of their favourite tricks is to take the seeds of a mango, which they put into a small pot of earth, about the size of an ordinary flower pot.

"In a short time the earth is seen to heave, and after a few seconds the head of a plant peeps forth !

"To the astonishment of the beholder this plant rises higher and higher ; the buds swell—the leaves unfold—the blossom shows—the fruit forms, grows, and ripens, when it is plucked off by the conjuror, and presented to you, and always turns out to be an excellent mango, or whatever the fruit may be !

"The impression on the mind of the beholder is so vivid, and the whole effect so overpowering, that the person looking on actually fancies he sees the various operations of the growth as I have described.

"The deception is so clever and perfect, that the reality and truth of the thing never for a moment loses its hold on the imagination, although the palpable fact of the mango-tree being about the size of an ordinary English oak (although the mango-tree does not grow higher than a currant-bush) sufficiently attests the delusion ; however, it is altogether a remarkable delusion ; but it should be said that the beholder is never allowed to approach too near the juggler while he is performing.

"Another very common trick of these native jugglers, and which they performed before King Katamar, is to strew the ground several feet with growing flowers. The principal juggler spreads on the ground a long broad cloth, and having done this he groans or grunts out a sort of magic spell.

"The juggler after a few moments rises, lifts up the cloth, and the whole space which it had covered is overspread with flowers of all sorts peculiar to that climate.

"He again spreads the cloth, and after a few moments he lifts it up again, when lo ! there is not a flower of any sort to be seen.

"Upon the occasion spoken of, when the foregoing trick was done, a tall, strong bamboo, forty feet long, was fixed upright in the ground, and sufficiently firm to bear the weight of any man.

"About five feet from the top there was a transverse pole fastened to the upright bamboo with strong ends, the whole forming a lofty cross.

"When this was done, and all was ready, a short, active native, with compact limbs and rigid muscularity of frame, approached the cross, grasped the shaft, and using his hands and feet with equal dexterity, climbed to the cross bar, with the ease and agility of a Tom cat.

"Placing himself on his back on one of the ends of the transverse poles, he folded his arms, and lay so still that every muscle of his body appeared in a state of complete repose.

"In a moment afterwards he sprang upon his feet, without any apparent preparation or perceptible movement of his limbs.

"He then threw himself horizontally upon the point of the upright bamboo, and spun round with velocity quite distressing to behold ; one while turning on his back, and then upon his stomach, changing his position with a quickness and precision which defies all description.

"He then placed his head on the extremity of the pole, shook his legs in the air, and raised his arms with most distressing animation.

"While thus occupied, and every one expecting he would tumble down and break his neck, eight red balls were thrown up to him, which he caught and danced into the air one after another, throwing them in various directions above and around him, when suddenly he sprang upon his feet, standing upright and firm upon a surface of two or three

inches, and caught every ball, without allowing one to fall to the ground.

"Another fellow performed some most extraordinary feats upon the cross pole, having nothing but his arms to balance him, throwing a round twelve-pound stone over his head, catching it below his right shoulder, and, by mere muscular force, repelling it back again, as if it had been thrown by the hand.

"After suspending himself by the chin, by the legs and heels, he dropped from the transverse beam to the ground, a height of more than thirty feet, and bowed to the audience, as if not shaken at all.

"These native jugglers and the like were very clever, and their performances highly delighted the lads.

"But old King Katamar had provided something better than jugglers to amuse us.

"We were to have combats with wild beasts, and such like ; for there were various dens inside the circus, dug in the earth, and covered over with sand bags, which contained wild animals of different kinds, whose growls and cries had continued during the performance of the jugglers.

"I had never seen anything of this kind before, nor had our lads. Some looked forward to it with great interest and delight.

"The first contest was between a wild boar and three wild goats. But the next contest was of a far more fearful character, as I will explain.

"For several weeks the settlements of old Katamar had been overrun by herds of wild buffaloes, and so fierce were some of the bull kings of these intruders, that many of the hunters had been killed while chasing them.

"Old Katamar determined to capture some of these wild and fierce buffalo bulls, which after many days of hard labour he succeeded in doing.

"One of the animals who showed more ferocity than the rest was reserved for the show which we were now about to witness.

"We could plainly hear from time to time the bellowing of this terrible buffalo bull, and the fierce growlings of many other animals.

" 'You will now see,' said old Katamar, 'a terrible fight between a wild buffalo bull and a strong lion.'

" 'But the lion will be sure to conquer,' said I.

" 'You may think so, and it is very probable he will; but it is a matter of doubt as yet, for lions are not always victors in their fights with other animals, as I have often witnessed. The lion, I know, is the royal emblem of England. And now you shall have a chance of seeing what the king of beasts, as he is called, can do, against an inferior animal.'

"At a given signal, one of old Katamar's attendants went into the arena, and very carefully withdrew the heavy bar which fastened the buffalo's cage, and in a few moments the animal came forth, snorting, whisking his tail about, and pawing up the dust in the arena.

He gazed long and fiercely at the assembly, who, as I have said, were safely out of reach, and shook his head, and bellowed angrily.

"He walked about for a few moments, and then began to gallop round the arena at a slashing pace.

" 'It is a fine animal,' said Katamar, ' what a noble stride it has ; it would take a good horse to keep up with him—for they will gallop that way for hours and hours together.'

" 'Yes, but he will have no chance with the lion,' I said.

" ' You will see presently whether he has or not.'

" Katamar gave the signal for several persons to unfasten the lion's cage, which they did by standing on top of the strong cage and drawing the door upwards.

" They had no sooner done this, and clambered up the poles out of danger, when the lion bounded forth, and shook his mane.

" He was a splendid young animal, full of fire and life, and as he stood in the centre of the ring, with heaving sides, flashing eyes, and angry tail, treading the ground, he looked a perfect study.

" The buffalo bull by this time had laid himself down on the ground, and didn't seem to mind the presence of the lion, who moved about slowly, and loudly growling.

" The lion then jumped about and round playfully for a few moments, very much like a cat does before she springs upon a mouse.

" But perceiving that the buffalo bull did not stir the lion became very fierce and angry, and with a savage growl leaped upon the bull's neck, and held fast.

" In an instant, however, the buffalo rose to his feet, and lifting up the lion on its horns, tossed him clean over his head, and the lion fell upon the hard ground with a shock which would have broken the ribs of any other animal but himself.

" He quickly rose again, however, and it could then be plainly perceived that the buffalo had fearfully gored the lion's sides with its short strong horns, and deep, red gashes could be seen from which the blood flowed freely.

" The bull, however, was frightfully bitten about the neck and shoulders, and his gory sides told plainly the marks of the lion's claws.

" ' What think you of that ?' said Katamar to me.

" ' I should never have believed it, had I not seen it.'

" At that moment the lion again approached the buffalo, and gathering all its strength sprang upon the bull's neck a second time.

" But, at the moment of doing so, the buffalo lowered its head, and plunged one of its horns into the lion's neck.

" Then, lifting up its head again, he tossed the lion a second time far from him, and following up this act, gored his enemy several times, and then retired several yards, where it stood lashing its tail and tearing up the earth with its fore feet.

" The lion seemed stunned for a few minutes and lay all of a heap, but recovering itself again, he approached his bleeding foe with a mighty spring, and fastened for a third time upon the buffalo.

" With a desperate effort, the buffalo again tossed the lion far from him, and rushing upon him as he lay stunned upon the ground, began to gore him fiercely and desperately with its blood-stained horns.

" The contest between these two beasts was most exciting ; but the bull's fate would soon have been sealed, for he could scarcely stand from shear weakness, and the natives so much admired the buffalo's courage, that they shouted out loudly, ' Save him ! save him !'

" Old Katamar gave orders to several of his most expert hunters, who soon got into the ring, and in a moment dexterously threw several ropes, and safely secured both the lion and the buffalo by the legs, and then calling upon others, both animals, weak from loss of blood, and unable to extricate themselves, were dragged out of the circus and each placed in its own den or cage.

" I did not like to tell old Katamar that these and such like exhibitions were distasteful to me, for the old man and all his subjects were, in their own way, doing their very best to entertain and amuse us ; and for this reason, neither I nor any of our party complained or left our seats.

" The next performance was even more exciting than what had gone before.

" When the ring was clear, a small door was opened, and through it came into view a tall, wiry and handsome Indian, but not of Katamar's tribe.

" He was almost nude, and wore a small cloth about his loins.

" In his hands he carried a small, rudely-made weapon, very much like a sword.

" It was of steel.

" He turned to old Katamar, and smiled with confidence around him.

" ' What is he going to do ?' I asked.

" ' Fight for his life,' said old Katamar. ' He is one of my captives.'

" ' What, fight with wild beasts ?'

" ' Yes ; he's going to encounter a large-sized leopard, that has been kept without food for more than three days.'

" ' I cannot sit and see it,' I answered ; ' it is too cruel and barbarous.'

" Old Katamar smiled.

" ' Bring the captive to me,' he said.

" The tall, handsome Indian soon came before Katamar, who thus spoke to him.

" ' Are you afraid to encounter the savage leopard ?'

" ' No ; nor any beast that lives !' was the bold answer.

" ' Who asked you to run this danger ?'

" ' No one. I heard that the young king of the white faces was here, and that sports would take place in his honor. I volunteered to enter the circus, and perform before him.'

" ' I am very much obliged to you, King Katamar, and your subjects, for these games in our honor, but—'

" ' You are unaccustomed to such sights as these, Lion Limb,' Katamar replied to me ; ' but you see the man is not only fearless, but even vain and anxious to exhibit his prowess before you. Were he afraid and inexperienced, I would not have granted his request ; but if he succeeds in disabling or killing the fierce brute, he shall have his freedom. I will make him presents, and if he likes to leave us, I will restore him to his own country with all honor.'

" The indian captive's face beamed with joy as he listened to old Katamar's words, and, bowing very lowly to the king, to myself, and to all our lads, he returned to the circus, amid the loud applause of the many who were anxiously waiting to see his feats.

" He jumped and ran about to and fro for several moments, and turned sumersaults many times, to try the suppleness of his limbs ; and, having rubbed himself all over with oil, he gave a shout that he was ready.

" The leopard's cage was soon unfastened, and the animal sprang out into the arena.

" Perceiving the Indian standing some yards away with folded arms, and in an attitude of great composure and fearlessness, the brute stopped, licked its jaws, and sprang towards him.

" I and all the lads expected to see the Indian demolished in the instant.

" But, judge of our great surprise.

" When the fierce animal, with flashing eyes, got within six yards of the Indian, it instantly stopped, and gave a fierce growl, but moved not an inch further towards him.

"The Indian, with a stern, fixed look, stared at the savage brute.

"There seemed to be something in his eye which charmed or cowed the leopard, for it lay down on the ground and wagged its tail, but dared not look at the man before him.

"The Indian stamped his foot savagely, and, shouting loudly, advanced towards the brute, which, with a sudden bound, leaped away from the man, and lay down as humbly as a tame kitten.

"The applause of the audience was loud and long, as they watched the movements of the brave Indian, who slowly approached the leopard, which as slowly retreated from him.

"All round the miry dirt the advance and retreat took place, and each moment I expected to see the leopard spring upon the man, and devour him.

"But it did not.

"Never for a moment did the Indian take his eyes off those of the fierce and open-mouthed animal before him, but with bright and flashing orbs he looked sternly at his foe, and with folded arms seemed fearless of all and every danger.

"But a change soon took place in the actions of the man and brute.

"The Indian now slowly retreated, and this time, sword in hand, ready for any emergency.

"The leopard followed him.

"When the Indian had so retraced his steps some half dozen yards, the leopard made a sudden spring upon him.

"The Indian, however, seemed to expect this, and with great agility sprang a few feet to the right, and was safe.

"With a fierce growl, the leopard turned; but his eyes met those of the Indian who was close at hand.

"Again the brute seemed to be powerless, and did not stir.

"But the Indian retreating again the leopard sprang towards him.

"In an instant the man jumped out of reach to the left, and as the brute reached the ground. the Indian's weapon flashed and fell with a powerful stroke upon a hind leg of the beast, and broke it.

"With a terrific growl, and suffering intense pain, the beast rushed towards the man, dragging his leg dangling behind him; but the Indian. light footed and full of courage, jumped aside, and before any one could think of it he had delivered a stroke with his deadly weapon, which cleft the leopard's head, and with a last and savage growl the brute lay dead at his feet.

"The uproar and applause which followed this feat was deafening.

"Every one rose and shouted till they were tired, and the Indian was carried out of the ring in triumph by many admirers, and soon made his appearance before old Katamar, who, true to his promises, rewarded him with many things.

"The Indian was untouched, and appeared as cool and unconcerned as if he had only been playing with a cat instead of a wild fierce leopard, and begged to be allowed to enter the ring again to perform other feats.

"But this none of us would allow.

"While other things were going on in the circus for the amusement of the natives, old Katamar said to me, with a broad grin on his sunburnt face,

"'I and my people are under great obligations to that man who killed the leopard.'

"'In what way, may I ask?'

"'I will tell you. You and your people sow a great deal of grain in your settlements, I know.'

"'We do.'

"'And you are very much troubled with crows and other hungry birds who steal the grain.'

"'Yes, we are. Our harvests suffer very greatly from crows and such-like thieves.'

"'Well, then, I will tell you how to get rid of them,'

"'How?'"

"'Very simply. If you'll only do as our people have done.'

"'How is that?'

"'You know we have always cultivated a great deal of what you English call Indian corn?'

"'You have.'

"'But we could never drive the birds away, for when we used to sow, the crows and such like used to uproot the seed, or tender sprouts, and lay our corn patches in waste. We did not know what to do.'

"'And who told you how to proceed?'"

"'That tall, brave fellow who was here just now.'

"'And what did he say?'

"'He told us to erect tall poles in the fields, and to each pole fasten a monkey; but so that he could mount the poles with ease, and run about a few yards round it. These were to frighten off the crows.'

"'And did they?'

"'You shall hear. We had four monkeys so placed as he directed, and they were fed every day, with a plentiful supply of food; but sometimes when they were asleep, the crows came and stole their food, and as a consequence the animals were half-starved, and no one knew how or why. One morning, however,' said old Katamar, laughing, 'one of my monkeys, getting very savage and hungry beside, made up his mind to get rid of his tormentors, and did it in this way. We fed him as usual, and after eating as much as he wanted he lay down on the ground close to his food, and pretended to go to sleep. In due time thousands of crows and other birds flew about in all directions, and as usual came very near the monkey-pole, and helped themselves to all they could find.

"'The monkey, however, had one eye open, and, before the crows expected it, he suddenly seized two of them, and the rest flew away.

"'What did the monkey do with them?' I asked,

"'I will tell you.'

"'He killed them, of course?'

"'No, he did not. I dare say the loss of his food had very often made him savage, but for all that he didn't kill his enemies.'

"'What, then?'

"'Made good use of them,' said Katamar, laughing. 'With a bit of strong grass, he tied one by the leg to his pole, and commenced operations on the other.'

"'In doing what?' I asked, very much amused.

"'In turning a black crew into a red one.'

"'Into a red one?'

"'Yes.'

"'How was that?'

"'There was plenty of soft, red chalk near his pole, and after great labour, he managed to paint the crow all red, and having done this, he tied the painted one by the leg and commenced work upon the other.'

"'What did he do to the second one?'

"'The second one fought hard to get away, and pecked the monkey very often, and in tender places. The monkey did not forget all this, and when the first one was done with, he set to work and picked every feather off him, except its wings and tail !'

" ' What then, did he do ?' I asked, in wonder.

" ' He remained very quiet with his two birds until a very large flight of crows came about, and then having attracted their attention by fluttering his two captives, the crows swarmed around and around him, and then suddenly he let them go !'

" ' Did they fly ?'

" ' The painted one flew very well, but the plucked one fell to the ground and was killed by the others.'

" ' The red one, what became of it ?'

" ' It was chased for a long time by the others, but at last it got weak, and that, like the first, was killed by the others, to the great delight of the monkey and our people also, for strange as it may seem, our fields in that part of our village have never been troubled or disturbed, either by flights of crows or any other sort of birds since that time, and our crops are very good.'

" ' It is not a bad idea,' I said, laughing, ' and when I return to our own settlement I shall employ a few monkeys and try their power, but I doubt very much whether they will prove as successful as yours, King Katamar.' "

Thus far we have borrowed our account of the games from the diary of Lion Limb, but now we proceed in our more direct narrative of what afterwards took place.

CHAPTER LXXXVII.

THE FATE OF DICK HAMILTON AND THE PRINCESS MARMI.

KING KATAMAR had scarcely finished speaking when the whole assembly seemed suddenly terror-stricken, and arose from their seats in a frantic manner.

The place was discovered to be on fire in different directions, and the flames burst forth with great violence on all sides.

How this came to pass no one could tell; and to add to the horror of the scene, many of the wild animals managed to escape, and rushed into the arena with great ferocity.

King Katamar at once suspected treachery.

Nor was he mistaken.

He hastily rose from his seat, and calling upon all to follow him who were brave men, descended to the circus, and began to slay the wild beasts which were galloping about.

In this daring deed he was followed and imitated by Lion Limb and his brave boys, who, sword and pistol in hand, coolly advanced upon and slew whatever beast presented itself.

Lion Limb and others who had looked upon the coolness and courage of the Indian leopard-slayer a short time before, now enacted similar feats, and with as much, if not more, fearlessness than the Indian had done.

For they were not opposed to one animal only in any case.

On every hand and on every side of them were leopards, buffaloes, hyenas, and other brutes, galloping and jumping about in great wildness and terror.

Around them also, adding greater terror to the scene, was the plank and pole-built edifice in a blaze.

The crackling timber, the roar of flame, the shrieks and cries of the injured and affrighted filled the air, and the interior was filled with a dense smoke, which almost blinded every one then inside.

It was with the greatest difficulty, and after many heroic efforts, that the animals were slain, and the audience got safely away.

And when Lion Limb and his merry men rushed forth from the burning place, they were black and begrimed with smoke and dirt, and their swords all gory with the blood of slaughtered beasts.

Old Katamar and his braves were loud in their applause of the heroism displayed by the white faces, as they were generally termed, and so full of gratitude were they that they hugged and kissed Lion Limb and Harry Woodruff, and would have carried them away in triumph to their tents and houses.

" No, no !" said Lion Limb, looking very anxious and pale, "this fire is only the beginning of what has to follow !"

" What mean you, bold boy ?" said the old king.

" I mean this, Katamar; some villain or villains, enemies of yours, have done this, and we must all be on our guard against fresh calamities, which, I fear, may befall us."

" Where is Dick Hamilton and his newly-made bride, the Princess Marmi ?" he asked, suddenly.

No one could tell.

" They are safe, I hope," said the old king.

" I hope so, too ; but I fear they are not."

" Why so ?"

" They are nowhere to be found."

" But some of my people say that they saw the loving pair strolling together towards the deep forest, while our games were progressing."

" That may be all correct and true," said Lion Limb, " but several hours have passed since then, and again I say, I fear, nay, I am almost certain, that treachery has befallen them. Call forward the natives who saw them rambling together, and let me question them."

In a moment several Indians were summoned to the presence of their king and detailed all the circumstances of having seen the brave white face, Dick Hamilton, and the Princess Marmi, strolling slowly along.

" Was there any one near them ?"

" No."

" Are you sure of that ?"

" We are."

" Could you lead the way to the exact spot where you last saw the couple strolling ?"

" Yes, most easily, and with pleasure."

" Lead on, then," said Lion Limb, " I will follow you with a party of my men ; and so you, Harry Woodruff, stay with Katamar and the rest."

" But why not let me come also ?" asked Harry.

" No, Harry, you must not. Old Katamar and his braves are gallant enough, but if anything should happen in my absence ——"

" That is what I fear," said bold Harry. " Then, why not let me be near you ?"

" Nay, you must not have any fear for me, Harry. I will go forward with a few lads, so you remain behind with the rest, and if any new danger happens to old Katamar, you, and the other lads with you, will prove more than sufficient to stop it, and fight any number of rascally traitors who even now may be concealed in the neighbouring woods waiting for an opportunity to wreak their vengeance on our friends."

So speaking, Lion Limb, and a few of his men, led by the Indian guide, went in search of Dick Hamilton and the Princess Marmi.

Harry Woodruff, meanwhile, arranged his plans for stopping the further progress of the conflagration then raging, and in preparing to repel any sudden attack that might be made upon the place.

Old Katamar could not be kept back; and follow Lion Limb he would.

The thought that harm might have befallen his beloved daughter almost crazed the old man.

Harry Woodruff tried to restrain his impatience and curiosity, but in vain.

He leaped upon a fast pony, and soon overtook Lion Limb and the Indian guides.

For a considerable distance they walked along, and the tracks of the horses were clearly visible, until at last they came to a spot where the ground was much trampled, and gave evident signs that many heavy feet had been there.

Further on Lion Limb discovered the dead body of a strange and strongly-built Indian, and a few yards further, another was seen.

Both men dead.

Both had deep gashes in the head, as if from a sword wielded by a powerful arm; and, as Lion Limb saw the evidences of the bloody and deadly encounter which must have taken place, he sighed.

"Alas!" he whispered to one of his men, "I fear that both Dick and poor Marmi have fallen victims to some foul ambuscade."

"I fear so also, captain."

"But if they have," said the brave young captain, fiercely, "woe to those—woe to the tribe who have been the occasion of it."

He turned to look who was coming, for he heard in the distance the tramp of a horse, and perceived old Katamar galloping forward.

"Follow me, my men; get into the forest quickly, and unperceived; we don't want old Katamar here. If anything has happened to his daughter it will craze his brain."

Acting accordingly to this order, every one plunged in the deep forest, and gave the old king the slip.

He shouted loudly.

But no one answered.

Progressing forward, and still following the footprints in the deep grass, Lion Limb soon discovered the body of Dick Hamilton.

He was not dead, but bleeding greatly from various wounds, and his sword-blade was broken.

One part was still in his hand, and the fore part was embedded in a tree, at the foot of which he lay bleeding and moaning.

In an instant he was raised from the ground, and his wounds examined.

None of them were fatal cuts or gashes.

The Indians present soon bound them up, and Lion Limb administered a draught of liquor from a flask that he always carried, which had great effect on the system of poor Dick, who, after a time, slowly opened his eyes and recognised his deliverers.

"Marmi! Marmi!" he gasped, with a pale, bloodstained face, "Marmi! Marmi!"

And pointing his finger in the direction in which he thought she might be found, he fell into a swoon.

Leaving Dick in the careful hands of his friends, Lion Limb hurried forward in the direction indicated by Dick, and to his great horror, soon perceived the body of a girl lying under a tree, and quite close to a limpid stream, whose waters musically bubbled by.

It was Princess Marmi.

She was pale, and cold, and—dead.

"Dead!" gasped Lion Limb.

And, for once in his life, Lion Limb's heart melted within him.

He knelt down and kissed the body of the poor faithful, and beautiful girl, and he vowed that should he live, he would never rest until he had his vengeance on all who might have perpetrated such a heinous crime. As far as decency would allow, her body was examined for marks of violence, but not a scratch could be seen.

In turning her head, however, and looking more closely, Lion Limb suddenly exclaimed,

"Poison! poison!"

"Where? How?" asked many, eagerly.

"Where? Here. Look; see for yourselves."

And, in astonishment, the bystanders perceived a small blue mark in her neck, and around the spot was all swollen, and looked like a mixture of dark blue, green, and yellow.

"An adder's bite," said one.

"A rattle-snake's," said another.

"A centipede," remarked a third.

It was useless to attempt to apply any remedies for the poison, for the lovely maid was dead; and, upon further examination, it was decided unanimously that the unfortunate maid had fallen a victim to treachery and poison, but through whom or by what means no one could imagine.

Nor could the wisest present form any conjecture of how the victim had become the prey of the unknown and undiscovered villain.

"Shall we take her up, and carry her to the village, captain?"

"No; let her remain where she now lies," said Lion Limb, sorrowfully. "A few of you remain to guard the body. She shall have a funeral fitting her youth and station. Aye, equal to that of any queen on earth."

Giving these orders, Lion Limb turned away to where Dick Hamilton lay, and, to his great joy and surprise, when he got to the spot, Dick was much better, and able to recognize and speak to those around him.

"Is she dead?" asked Dick, with a trembling lip.

Lion Limb did not answer, but looked cold and very determined.

"Tell me, captain," said Dick, with a choking utterance, "is she dead or living?"

"Dead, Dick! Marmi is dead!" answered Lion Limb, slowly, and with a tone of great sorrow.

Dick turned paler than before.

He wished to say something but could not.

His lips were of ashy hue, and trembled.

All those around maintained a solemn silence, and after a time, Dick rallied again.

Lion Limb knelt by his side and asked in a whisper,

"Are you too weak to speak to me, Dick?"

"No, captain. You have always been my friend, and I——"

"You have always been a true, faithful, and gallant officer."

Dick's face was suddenly flushed with proud satisfaction as he heard these words from the lips of the gallant young leader he loved so well, and for a moment he was silent, but pressed the outstretched hand of his leader firmly.

"How did all this dreadful affair happen, Dick?"

"I can scarcely remember all," was the faint response.

"Can you tell us something that may lead to a discovery of this mystery?"

"I can!—listen, it will chill your young blood!"

THE BOY KING
OF THE SOUTH SEA ISLANDS.

THE SNAKE CHARMER'S GIBBET

After a painful pause, poor Dick said, "All I distinctly recollect was this,—myself and Marmi were strolling along, when we suddenly saw approaching a party of men on horseback. Their appearance greatly alarmed Marmi, who wished to return at once. I laughed at her fears.

"'They are snake charmers,' said Marmi, when they approached close enough to distinguish them. 'They are crafty and villanous persons. I fear and distrust them.'

"'Never have such foolish thoughts, I replied. 'They are on their way to perform before your father and all assembled in the circus; if they can perform any great feats before us, we will detain some of them and let the rest go on. I calmed her fears, and some of the snake charmers went on, while three remained with us and performed various tricks. I learned from them that they came from a far-off part of the island near the sea coast, and had not only seen but conversed with persons belonging to a strange vessel which had landed for wood and water there.

"From the description given of this craft I had no doubt but that it was the 'Vulture,' with Mungo and his buccaneers. I did not put many questions to them about it, but it struck me that they had informed Mungo of their intended visit to old Katamar, and that Mungo was perfectly aware that you were on the island.

"But while I spoke to one of them, the other two were performing before Marmi, and showing her some of their strange tricks.

"Suddenly Marmi screamed aloud, and turning my head, to my horror I perceived an adder had stung her in the neck.

"I dashed towards her to render assistance, but had not advanced many steps ere I was assailed on all sides by the three desperate villains, who for the first time displayed their hidden weapons.

"My sword was out in an instant, and I fought like a demon.

"Whether I killed more than one I know not now. I am certain, however, that one of them fell by my hands, but more than that I recollect nothing until you came."

"There are two bodies near here," said Lion Limb; "they are stone dead."

"But the third villain?"

"I fear he has escaped. We have tracked him for a considerable distance, but his horse was a swift one, and there are no hopes of our ever taking him. They also attempted to burn us all alive; but were mistaken."

"Are you sure that the snake-charmers were the authors of all this also?" asked Dick, faintly.

"There cannot be much doubt about it, for when we began to search for the rascals not one was to be found."

"If I live I will avenge her death," sighed Dick, and he looked as if all reason had bereft him.

His appearance was totally changed.

His hair was all matted and rough.

His eyes were bloodshot, and his face, all haggard and lank and pale, presented a vivid image of one, who, by some sudden calamity, had been deprived partly of reason.

This was what Lion Limb had supposed from the first moment he gazed upon him.

It was with much difficulty, and a great amount of coaxing, that Dick would allow himself to be removed from the spot, and he raved and swore, and kicked and plunged so dreadfully that it required six stout fellows to bear him away from the scene of blood.

But if Dick's passion and emotion were so great, let our readers judge of the display that took place when old Katamar and his subjects were made aware of the dreadful news.

The fond old father threw himself upon the dead body of his lovely daughter, and wept and bewailed in the wildest and most impassioned manner.

The screams, yells, oaths, and shouts of the Indian braves resounded on all sides, and many of them vowed never to eat, drink, or sleep until they had found out and immolated the wretches who had caused so much suffering and woe.

Men, women, and children flocked to the spot where poor Marmi lay, and sitting in groups around, they sang strange, wild, and weird ditties, and kept up blazing fires for several nights, and the sad news soon spread far and wide over the island.

That the wretches who had done this hellish deed had been paid to do so, and were instigated so to act by the bloodthirsty Munge and his myrmidoms there could not now be a doubt.

Lion Limb did all in his power to calm down the anger and wild fervour of the Indian braves; and to show them in what estimation he held the friendship and esteem of King Katamar, he resolved to join his forces to those of the Indians and go forth on an expedition to the distant sea coast, where the snake-charmers and other villains loved to dwell.

But first of all it was agreed that nothing should be done or attempted until Katamar and Lion Limb should give positive and final orders respecting it.

For three whole days the men were busily engaged in arming and equipping themselves for their distant expedition.

But the women and children were night and day performing funeral rites over the body of Marmi.

It was the custom of these Indians to burn the dead bodies of those they loved best; but after much persuasion, Lion Limb prevailed upon Katámar to forego this ancient custom, and as Marmi herself had often expressed a wish, "whether in life or death," to be near Emma Clarence, and the white faces at Lion Limb's island, it was resolved that the body should be buried there with all suitable honour and ceremony.

After three days' watching and wailing, the body was roughly embalmed, and the finest boat to be had was decorated and painted to convey poor Marmi down the stream, then to be transferred, on the sea coast, to the "Rattlesnake," which lay moored at the river's mouth, ready to receive her.

With plumes and other decorations the boat was embellished.

The body, prettily attired, and with a white chaplet on its head, in token of virginity, was placed on a small raised platform in the craft, and there all that remained of poor Marmi lay, within full view of both banks of the river, like a thing of marble beauty; while chiefs and braves, and women and children, lined both shores, gazing in sorrow on the helpless maiden, as the tide slowly bore her onwards to the sea. (See Cut in No. 30.)

CHAPTER LXXXVIII.

DICK HAMILTON'S REVENGE—THE NIGHT FIGHT IN THE WOODS.

THE body of poor Marmi had scarcely gone out of sight down the river, slowly, and in tow of a chosen crew, when Dick Hamilton, armed to the teeth, and looking like a maniac, rushed forth, and sounded the dread alarm of battle.

Lion Limb and others thought at first that this strange action was that of a madman.

They were all prepared to start to the coast on the morrow, but yet, in the gloom of evening, all were suddenly aroused, and rushed forth, why or wherefore they knew not.

Armed men dashed about from place to place, and every one seemed to have suddenly gone mad, when the distant report of rifles was heard in the woods adjoining.

There could not now be a doubt but that some foe was at hand, who had thought to take the village by surprise and storm.

With great presence of mind, Lion Limb kept his men well together; nor would he move until the enemy had more clearly betrayed their intention.

But, while he stood with his men ready to act at any moment, a heavy volley of musketry was heard near by, and the shots whistled around his head.

"Forward men, follow me!" he cried.

"Death or glory ! Spare none of them !" shouted wild Dick.

And dashing into the thicket, amid fire and smoke, Dick disappeared.

"Follow men, follow !" shouted Lion Limb, fiercely.

The savage energy of Dick Hamilton, and his burning desire to revenge the cruel death of Princess Marmi, brought on a terrible fight before the moment which Lion Limb had desired it.

But, to save the life of Dick, he followed hastily into the thickest of the fight, and soon, with the assistance of Harry, Lion Limb taught Mungo's followers and their snake-charmers that they could not take the brave young settlers by surprise.

Lion Limb at one time thought that old Katamar's braves would not be able to fight well in the woods and darkness.

And this, no doubt, was also the thought of the crafty Mungo.

But he soon found out his mistake, and had to pay very dearly for it also.

The rush of Katamar's braves, as they assailed their enemies, was something terrible, and, picking out the chief Indians among the snake-charmers, they killed them off quickly and with unerring aim.

Lion Limb and Harry Woodruff were delighted at the bravery of old Katamar himself, who, thirsting for revenge, dashed with Dick into the thickest of the fight, and used his weapon with deadly swiftness and precision.

In all directions the din of battle resounded through the deep, dense forests.

Arrows and shot flew thick and fast.

The sharp report of rifles and pistols mingled with the savage yells of the Indians.

Now and then the loud, stern voice of Mungo could be heard, urging on his men, and as often the cheering words of Lion Limb were audible, as from time to time he arranged and re-arranged his men in order of battle.

It was the darling desire of our young hero to meet the fierce Mungo face to face, but that crafty leader always shunned the encounter.

He had often boasted, it is true, when speaking to his followers, of what he could and would do to Lion Limb, if ever they should meet face to face.

But now that he had that chance he rather shunned than courted the presence of his enemy.

Many, many times did Lion Limb, Harry Woodruff and Dick imagine they had at last picked out the huge form of Mungo in the smoke of battle.

And as often had they cut their way towards the villain.

But Mungo's eyes were keen, and he always managed to escape the death which was intended for him.

For more than an hour the fight lasted, but at last, little by little, it became less loud and fierce.

For Mungo, finding that he could not prevail against our hero, drew away his men to the rear, and covered their retreat by a body of Indians, who in consequence had to stand the whole shock, while the buccaneers slunk away.

For Mungo, when the fight began, said to his Indians,

"You have asked to have the post of honour in battle, and I have granted it ; you shall go in front, and my men will support you ; but if any of you retreat, I will cut down every man of you."

The snake-charmers, therefore, were placed in a very difficult position.

They could not advance, and they dared not retreat, for death was equally certain in either case.

When, therefore, Mungo and his men had got safely away the Indians took flight also, while Lion Limb and his little army hotly pursued.

But the night was very unfavourable, and the ground was not known to them.

The woods abounded in pitfalls, swamps, and the like, on all sides.

Katamar and his braves knew the place very well, and pointed out several paths by which Lion Limb might pursue, but fearful of falling into some snare, he ordered his men to lay on their arms for the rest of the night, and promised to pursue again when the sun rose.

But an adventure took place which prevented this plan being carried out.

Among the prisoners captured was an Indian, who, around his neck, and on his arms, wore shells of different sizes and colours.

That the owner put great value upon these simple things could not be doubted, for he seemed very proud of them, and smiled with confidence and defiance when told he was to be hung.

Katamar soon explained this confidence and defiance.

"His life is charmed," said the old king.

"How, pray ?"

"Those shells and rings were given to him by a great sorcerer, who dwells not very far away in the midst of an old ruin. He has great power with all the islanders, and his fame has spread far and wide."

"He is consulted by the chiefs, I suppose, in all great events ?"

"He is, and hundreds stand in dread of him day and night."

"And do *you* believe in him ?" asked Lion Limb, laughing.

"I believe in him this much, that I think he is in league with bad spirits, and I would not pass a night among the old ruins not for all the islands in the seas."

Lion Limb and his followers laughed heartily at this.

"I dare say, now, if the truth was known, Mungo has had dealings with the sorcerer ?"

"Ask the captive," said Katamar, "and if he speaks the truth I will spare his life. Speak, captive ; is it so ?"

"It is ?"

"Did the sorcerer say that Mungo might go to battle ?"

"Yes, and more than that, he charmed us all, so that none should get killed."

"Well, all I can say is, that for once the sorcerer was a fool, at all events. The number of your dead proves how stupid you all are to believe in him."

"He has promised Mungo to secure your death," said the captive.

"Mine ?" asked Lion Limb, laughing.

"Yes, and also swears to call forth your spirit this very night in the ruins, in the presence of Mungo."

"The deuce he has !" said Harry. "If I though we could only catch a glimpse of the old sorcere and Mungo, I wouldn't mind going there this very night,"

"Nay, do not think of such a thing," said old Katamar, shaking his head.

"What say you, captain—shall we go ?"

"With all my heart," said Lion Limb, gaily.

"Do not go, I pray you ; the sorcerer is very powerful, and——"

"No matter," said our hero, laughing. "Come along, Harry ; we will return before morning."

And taking the captive as a guide, our hero

Harry, and Dick started for the ruins, to pry into the sorcerer's secrets and abode.

They were not very long in reaching a small, secluded, and thickly-wooded valley, in which the ruins were situated.

Carefully guided by the captive, they approached quite close, and hid themselves near the entrance of the ruins, and diligently listened for any sounds.

But none were heard.

But unexpectedly, and just as Harry had secured the captive to a tree, so that he might not escape, they were all startled.

CHAPTER LXXXIX.

MUNGO'S FRIEND THE INDIAN SORCERER — LION LIMB BOLDLY ENCOUNTERS HIM — GHASTLY CEREMONIES AND AUGURIES.

"SILENCE," said Lion Limb; "there are people passing in the wood where I was just now."

All looked, as he pointed. Concealing themselves behind the shrubs that had ornamented the entrance of the ruins, two figures were discovered stealing down towards the ruins; while they endeavoured to elude observation, cautiously keeping within the shades of the trees.

They had scarcely passed, when a third appeared, who, as he bore a lantern, was immediately recognised as the terrible old sorcerer.

He stopped for a few moments, and holding the lantern high, looked around him.

He spoke to himself, and as the wind blew towards the ruins they were enabled to catch his words.

"All hitherto proceeds well," said he. "Heaven grant that nothing may keep the bird from his cage.

"The night is favourable, everything conspires to seize his imagination, overcome his mind, and make him an easy prey.

"How mournfully the wind sighs through the heads of those tall cypress trees! The very appearance of that old, gloomy, deserted fabric, is sufficient to damp the courage of the bravest man!

"I could almost feel inclined myself to yield to terror, whenever I behold its mossy ruins at such an hour as this.

"Often it has been the scene of my triumph when I have trampled upon the spirit of the living, and fearlessly communed with the dead!

"But time presses.

"Ere this he will have been in anxious attendance."

As he spoke this he passed on.

Harry Woodruff now proposed that they should retire, and conceal themselves in the adjacent woods, till the sorcerer and his myrmidons, thinking that their victim had escaped their snares, should withdraw.

But Lion Limb, who found his curiosity wound up to such a pitch, determined to reconnoitre the operations of the enemy, and his companions could not be persuaded to leave him; although, if he were assailed, it was not probable that they could afford him assistance.

Harry said that since Lion Limb was determined, he thought the best way of ascertaining what was going forward would be to ascend a mound near by, where he had been stationed the night before, and where it was utterly impossible they could be discovered.

Harry thought he could easily find the way, and

as the entrance to it was at the farther end of the ruins from that towards which the sorcerer and his accomplices had passed, they would, if they made directly for it, be almost certain of escaping observation.

Each now felt that there was no time to lose, and while Lion Limb contemplated with pity and uneasiness the evidently diseased frame of his young friend, Dick Hamilton nodded acquiescence in the proposal.

The whole party soon made good their lodgement, and awaited in mute expectation the result.

A breeze had arisen, accompanied by driving rains, which sometimes sweeping the clouds that obscured the moon, allowed her disc to appear for a moment, as if to show more clearly the wildness and desolation of the scene.

Then darkness returned.

The winds sang loud amidst the fissures of the ruins and the high trees that waved without.

And now it paused, and now it rose again, and, as it rose, the wild plaints, as of spirits whose reign had been disturbed, rose to the ear of fancy in melancholy accompaniment.

"What a cheerless place!" said Harry.

"It's no wonder that we should find it so," said Lion Limb, "when the sorcerer himself seems to feel its influence."

Dick was about to express his denial of all temerity that had been thought of on his account, when a light appeared at the gate of the ruins.

Immediately after the sorcerer appeared with his lantern.

He was unaccompanied, and stepped cautiously forward, turning the light alternately on either side, and examining every recess.

At length he called Lion Limb by his name, in a low tone.

The echoes of his voice whispered along the walls.

He traversed the whole length of the ruins several times in this manner, and at length evident marks of impatience were discernible on his countenance, as the light which he held, falling occasionally athwart it, showed all its terrible lineaments, rendered more ferocious and repulsive by the chagrin under which he suffered.

He seemed to abandon all hope of finding Lion Limb.

He thought, and suddenly gave a loud whistle.

Immediately two men in the garb of savages rushed through the breach in the old wall from among the trees where they had been concealed, and advanced towards him.

A third man followed.

It was Mungo.

When they reached him he said—

"For this time you have missed your victims; we must choose some better opportunities. Fear not that I shall let him escape."

Mungo appeared extremely dissatisfied, and after a short pause, seizing the sorcerer by the collar, cried—

"My friend, this is child's play; I much doubt you have brought me upon a wrong scent, in order that the game might escape."

The sorcerer looked at him with a frown that seemed to overawe him, for he slowly relinquished his grasp.

Then with a smile, in which scorn, derision, and disappointment were blended, and in a voice that without effort seemed to possess a volume of sound equal to that of a dozen ordinary men—

"Worm," said the sorcerer, "thinkest thou that I directed my steps hither for the sake of the miserable reward proffered by you to tempt my avarice? Or thinkest thou a menace from such a reptile as thou art, Mungo, could stir in me any feeling but contempt? Slave! I am prompted to spurn thee; but no," added he, assuming a calmer tone, produced probably by the terror displayed by Mungo; "no; thou art no fit object for the wrath of me. Know that it was for purposes of my *own* I sought to deliver Lion Limb into your hands. My power," his form dilated as he spoke, "might preserve him. But I fear it may not be."

He sighed deeply, and, crossing his arms as he spoke, looked upon the ground.

He then turned to Mungo, who seemed more dead than alive, and said—

"You shall have your enemy, fear not; and before yon solitary star shall fade—ere that star shall sink—thou shalt here behold the spirit of him thou seekest torn from his body; my summons and awful powers may not be disobeyed. Tremble not, Mungo; wretched man, *thou* shalt take no harm. My power is as effectual to save as to destroy."

Having spoken thus, he passed through the breach, and soon returned, bearing in his hand a large bag, which having opened, he displayed an apparatus of magic.

He immediately proceeded to set the tapers in their sockets, and arrange them before Mungo.

While the sorcerer was thus occupied, Harry and Dick in a low voice besought Lion Limb to leave the place.

But he had no ears for them.

He perceived that the meditated incantation was to be directed against himself.

And his bosom was heaving with tumultuous self-interrogations as to the conduct he should adopt.

Should he wait till his spirit, wrested—as the sorcerer said it would be, from his body—should leave that body a prey to him and Mungo, or, rushing down, become the assailant in the contest, however unequal?

He embraced the latter resolution, and drawing his sabre, delayed putting it into execution only till he should have seen some portion of the sorcerer's proceeding, which a curiosity, inflamed almost to madness, induced him to believe could not immediately affect him.

The sorcerer, meanwhile, completed his preparations.

Describing a circle round where he stood, within which he placed Mungo and the two trembling savages as if for protection, he poured a vial of liquid in three several places, and then scattered a powder over each.

Each spot sent up a small flame that filled the building with a heavy and intolerable odour.

He then, with a wand which he took in pieces from the bag and fastened together by joints framed for the purpose, drew several strange figures upon the ground, then waved it aloft.

He immediately fell into a fixed attitude.

Harry and Dick gazed upon him with a wild expression of terror.

Their countenances were pale.

Their limbs almost shook beneath them, and they clung round Lion Limb to protect him from the old man's charms and spells.

Lion Limb alone was fearless, every emotion was sunk in that of curiosity.

And in the eagerness of his desire to miss no part of the coming spectacle, he advanced in full view of his enemies, bending over the top of the mound, so that they would have needed the aid of no sorcerer to discover him, had not their faculties been too completely bound up by fear to admit of

their using them for any other purpose than to contemplate the terrible being that stood before them, his spirit to all appearance wrapt into some other sphere of existence.

His countenance was turned towards the east, and had just exhibited signs of returning animation in a slight convulsion, when suddenly a blaze of light burst from it that filled the whole place with a light, clear, pure, and brilliant as the summer's noon when the east wind has chased the clouds, and the frame of man springs buoyant in the lightness of the tempered air.

The sorcerer worked in stronger and stronger convulsions.

At length he seemed to have completely recovered his suspended animation.

Dick and Harry, who conceived that the brilliant light was the effect of the sorcerer's power, expected every moment the tone of high command to issue from his lips, and were now for rushing down, and were again withheld by curiosity, when, to their astonishment, instead of any expression of authority, the sorcerer's countenance assumed every symptom of extreme terror and dejection.

He looked fixedly towards the east, from whence the light seemed to proceed.

A sudden weakness seized him.

He tottered, and at length sank on his knees, his eyes still fixed upon the light with a terror that had increased almost to frenzy.

"What means this?" asked Harry.

"I know not," said Lion Limb. "I never could believe in sorcerers or their magic powers at any time, but you may depend upon it from what I now see that heaven will punish the old villain and Mungo also."

Harry did not make any further observation at the moment, but stood beside poor Dick, whose senses at the moment seemed to leave him.

"See," said Lion Limb, "the great change which has come over the old man. He who smiled and frowned like an angry demon but a few moments ago is now apparently powerless and feeble; his intercourse with demons cannot hurt any of us."

"But look at the features of brutal Mungo and the two savages; they are ghastly pale, and their lips tremble violently."

"I see it all," said Lion Limb, with a smile of triumph; "it was through the direction of this wicked old wretch that the snake-charmers did so much mischief, and——"

"Poor Marmi," sighed Dick.

And clenching his weapon, the half-demented lover would have rushed down and slain the sorcerer, and Mungo also.

But Harry Woodruff restrained him.

"Silence, Dick," said Lion Limb, in a whisper; "do not move or lift a hand; we have not seen all yet. Something terrible, I am positive, will befall yon old villain."

"I will do anything for you, Lion Limb," said poor Dick; and all of them gazed intently on the scene below.

A pause ensued, during which even the most high-wrought expectation could not prevent Lion Limb from gazing on the astonishing scene that was passing before his eyes.

The light, the purity of which declared a source far different from any of the gross materials of man, spread wide through the atmosphere, insomuch that, the wind having become perfectly hushed, the song of birds, aroused by what seemed the light of day, was heard in the neighbouring trees, filling the silence.

The terror of the sorcerer, the savages, and Mungo,

with their faces on the earth, the emotions of his friends, which seemed now to have in them more of wonder and less of terror, all presented a scene that filled Lion Limb's bosom with a painful feeling of awe, with which the loveliness of that clear light and the sweetness of the birds' notes had blended admiration.

While he stood half entranced, awaiting the issue, a voice, loud as the thunder's roar, issued from the rocks!

"In thy impious daring, sorcerer," it said, "thou didst at first barter thy wretched soul for permission, as thou thought, to fulfil the decrees of Omnipotence, and thou wert suffered for a season to gratify thy miserable pride!

"When the guilty fall, it matters not whether Heaven's lightning blast, or a worm sting them.

"But with this thou wert not satisfied.

"Thou hast presumed, in the madness of thy arrogance, to war with Heaven, seeking to thwart its immutable resolves. Thy hour is come! wretch, it may not be averted! Perish! perish! perish!

"And thou, unhappy Mungo, seek not, in the restlessness of thy spirit, to explore those depths of fate which the Almighty in his mercy hath concealed from man."

The voice ceased.

Its subsiding murmur was like the far-off swell of ocean, when the whirlwind hath passed from its bosom.

A short interval of silence ensued, during which the light glowed with augmented splendour.

Again the birds' song was heard, and then the light gradually withdrew, till no vestige of it remained.

The spirit of the sorcerer seemed to revive in the absence of the voice, before which no sternness of mind could bear him up.

He raised his head, and supporting himself by the aid of the wand as he knelt, for he appeared too weak to stand—

"'Tis even so," said he; "the hand of Heaven may not be staid; we seek to shun the precipice, and when we think ourselves secure we awake as from a dream, and stand upon a brink.

"My doom is pronounced; I feel the death within me from which I had fondly hoped I was exempt. Oh! the fiend whom I have served works within me, and drags me to his footstool. Yet baffled, cheated, stricken to the dust, the spirit that taught me to aspire above mortal hope is yet unconquered within me; fear is yet a stranger to my spirit."

As he spoke a sudden revulsion of feeling seemed to belie his words.

He again stared wildly towards the rocks, from which a feeble, dismal, bluish light, which formed a strong contrast to the former, now streamed.

Again his countenance quivered and wrought with strong spasms—

"Hah!" he cried, "art thou too there, demon? Stay, stay, stay! thy reign is not yet begun."

He strove to rise, but was unable.

Then by a strenuous effort he seemed to recover a portion of his intrepidity, while a hideous grin of satisfaction struggled with the terrors that still distorted his features, and at length triumphed.

He was calm.

But his calmness was more terrible than any passion that shakes the frame of man.

The hand of death seemed to fasten on him, but moved not his spirit.

The livid hue of expiring mortality overspread his countenance, which again was all distorted.

But his eye confessed not the influence of pain; it still marked the fullest consciousness.

It was fixed and dreadfully stern.

At length he fell, but again raised himself, and again looked with the same expression towards the rocks; but he could do no more.

The weakness of the body rapidly augmented.

He again sunk to the ground.

His limbs writhed.

He struck his clenched hands against the ground. Then he was motionless.

A heavy groan, half stifled, marked to the last the inflexible stubbornness of his spirit, and proclaimed his dissolution.

The light that had issued from the rocks suddenly withdrew.

The tapers were extinguished with a hissing sound.

Dismal yells, as of exulting demons, filled the ruins.

When these were no longer heard, Lion Limb and his friends remained for some minutes silent, each rapt in their own thoughts.

At length—

"Has man," said he, "ever before witnessed any thing similar to this?—has ——"

"Hark!" said Harry, "the wondrous scene has not yet closed. List to those sounds! Oh, are they not divine?"

As he spoke, a strain of more than mortal melody swelled in the direction of the rocks.

All listened with a mixture of awe, wonder, and delight.

Again the strain arose, and the praises of the Deity were breathed upon the midnight air; so sweet, so solemn, so impressive as that strain, no sound had they ever heard.

And now it was confined to one clear voice of exquisite flexibility and modulation.

And oh, how soft, how tender, and yet how holy were its accents!

Then as it paused—

A full rich chorus burst upon the ear, filling the soul with a lofty enthusiasm.

This in its turn died gradually away, until but one note of thrilling sweetness lingered on the silence.

And now it was heard no longer; the ear still watched for its renewal, but no sound answered its expectation.

"Heavens, 'tis the Spirit of Marmi," gasped Dick suddenly, and with intense love and passion in his tone.

"Heaven," said Lion Limb, in a solemn tone, "giveth up no part of this fair skill to the rule of the evil one; if, in fulfilment of its purpose, it permits malign spirits to brood within these ruins, their reign is bounded, and the yell of the demon yields to the sweetness of angelic minstrelsy."

"I have heard," said Harry, "that strains, such as we have just listened to, are the voices of the dead."

The excitement of poor Dick was now intense.

Lion Limb and Harry held him back, or he would have rushed forward and disclosed their presence to Mungo and the two savages, who, silent and awe struck, were gazing on the dead body of the once famous Indian sorcerer.

This would have defeated the desires and plans of Lion Limb, who had resolved to confront Mungo single-handed.

But at that moment the sweet voice heard a moment before, resumed its lovely song, and, to the astonishment of both Lion Limb, Harry, and Dick, a fairy-like form was seen, as if floating in the air near, and within reach of them.

For a moment neither could speak, but gazed in wonder upon the fairy one, the features and form of which became, or seemed to become, more distinct and sharply defined each moment.

Her head was thrown back, and her eyes upraised to heaven.

Her long and luxuriant hair thrown carelessly over one shoulder, fell down her side in graceful angel-like negligence, leaving one side of her beautifully-formed neck exposed to view.

Her attitude floating in the ether, the rapt expression of her countenance and general loveliness, proclaimed her to be a spirit of the skies.

" 'Tis Marmi! 'tis Marmi!" said Dick, in great wildness and excitement.

He saw in the fairy form of his departed one only a saint who should be worshipped.

In a transport of love he rose to his feet, as if to clasp the lovely spirit to his own fond heart, but at that instant the spirit vanished!

The sudden cry of Dick, and the efforts of Lion Limb, with Harry, to restrain him, aroused Mungo and the savages, who up to that moment had not suspected they were observed.

Jumping to his feet, Mungo drew his sword and prepared for action, but the two savages were terror-stricken and fled in all haste away.

Mungo knew not what to do.

To stay was certain death.

And yet there stood not many yards away from him the face he hated more than any living man.

For a moment he knew not what to do, but a sudden fear seized him.

The spirit of Marmi rose up before his affrighted sight, and struck more terrors to his soul than the swords of all his enemies combined.

With a loud shout of terror and dismay at the unexpected apparition, he dashed from the ruins, and disappeared in the inky darkness, followed in hot haste by Lion Limb, Harry Woodruff and Dick.

CHAPTER XC.

ALLAN DENOUNCES AND DEFIES JERRY MARKS.

THE sudden cry of pain which arose between Allan and Captain Zacary, the two duellists, as spoken of in a former chapter, was occasioned by a sudden thrust which Allan administered to his foe.

It was not a deadly one, indeed, but Jerry Marks (alias Captain Zacary) felt certain from the way in which his antagonist fought, that he was bent on slaying him like a dog, before the eyes of his own friends.

Jerry had learnt fencing under one of the best masters in London, in order to be prepared for any emergency that might occur.

He was clever with the foils without a doubt.

But it requires more than "cleverness" to withstand the just and honest indignation of a stout-hearted youth or man.

When justice is on the one side, and wickedness combined with faintheartedness and cowardice on the other, it does not require much time to form an idea of which one will ultimately prove the victor.

And so it was in this case.

Allan knew no more about the skilful use of a foil than a cat does about a fiddle.

But he did not care for that.

He would have fought with anything, rather than ruin the chance of punishing the young villain before him.

Hence it was that, with a stout heart and a strong arm, he faced his foe fearlessly, and soon got an insight into the science of fencing.

And so quick was he, that he surprised all who witnessed the combat.

Jerry might have fought well, perhaps, against another person, but he could not resist the terrific onslaughts of Allan.

Young Allan's eyes glowed with fiery passion.

Every time that Jerry dared to look at him, his heart sunk within him.

He knew he was guilty of crimes, although those crimes were as yet unknown to the world.

When, therefore, he saw his own blood oozing from several ugly wounds, he quivered.

His heart beat wildly.

His eyes became glazy.

The legs under him trembled, and his breath became shorter and shorter.

Death stared him in the face!

Allan, the avenger, stood before him.

One last thrust in the thigh made Jerry reel.

He groaned aloud, and fell heavily to the floor.

In an instant he was surrounded by his seconds, and a few friends, who raised him up to a sitting attitude.

"Honour is satisfied," said his seconds. "The duel is at an end."

"And splendidly has young Allan fought," said the count, in raptures. "He is English to the backbone. Are you satisfied?" said he, approaching Allan, and shaking him cordially by the hand.

"Satisfied! no," said Allan, trembling with unsatisfied passion.

"But you *must* be," said another. "Blood has been drawn. Advance to your enemy and shake hands."

"Never."

"But such is the code."

"I care not for that; nothing but the villain's life will satisfy my just revenge."

"But that would be murder."

"He deserves death," said Allan. "He is the very incarnation of wickedness. He is a perfect devil."

So speaking, he advanced to Jerry, who was having his wounds bound up.

"Devil!" said he, "you have cheated me this time out of my revenge."

Jerry turned away his eyes, and gasped in trembling tones—

"He will murder me. Disarm him, I say; I see murder in his eyes."

"Coward!" Allan replied, in a hissing tone. "I would not murder such a cur in cold blood; but the day will come when I shall see my brother Edgar avenged. Rely on it, I shall never rest till I do."

"Sir, retire if you please," said one of the seconds. "My principal, Captain Zacary, is satisfied, and so ought you to be."

"Your principal—Captain Zacary—satisfied!" sneered Allan, in profound contempt, as he cast a fierce and angry glance at Jerry. "Satisfied, eh?"

"You must give up your weapon, sir, and not stand there in such a threatening attitude," another of Jerry's seconds remarked.

"Must, eh?"

"Yes, you must, sir."

"And who will force me, pray?"

And, as he spoke, he looked around on the company in triumph.

"Come, come, my gallant lad," said the count, in a pleasant, smiling manner, "give your weapon up to me. I ask it as a favour."

"Count, you are a gentleman, and I believe a friend."

"I *am* your friend, my brave boy, and will prove it."

"I am thankful for your good opinion, count; but ah! you know not the intense agony of heart, and the many long and acute sufferings I have undergone through the villany of yon prostrate man."

"I can see plainly enough that you are deadly enemies, my boy; and had I thought you would have met such an unworthy fellow in this gallant company, I would not have brought you hither."

"Nay, I am pleased that things have happened as they have. I have long desired to confront the scoundrel, but up to the present never had the chance."

"Another time you can satisfy your revenge."

"I hope so."

"Have you no legal redress? Why not apply to the law?"

"That process is too slow and uncertain; yet I have no doubt, and that very shortly, Captain Zacary, as he calls himself, will suffer heavily, justly, and by the law, for this long career of crimes and imposture. He will grace the gallows one of these days."

Allan repeated the last few words so slowly and solemnly, that the count stared.

"You do not mean that, I hope?"

"I hope I do, and feel certain of it."

So speaking he left the room, and as he walked home thought, "How glad Jem Rawlings would be if he only knew how I have served out Jerry."

With such thoughts, and his heart almost bursting with conflicting feelings, Allan slowly walked along, when to his astonishment he saw a cab drive past at a very quick pace, and a youth standing up behind it.

CHAPTER XCI.

THE ROBBERY AT MANFRED HALL—JEM RAWLINGS IN A NEW CHARACTER.

If the spirit of his brother Edgar had suddenly appeared before him, Allan could not have felt more surprise.

"Why, that is Jem Rawlings," he said, half aloud. "It *must* be Jem; I cannot be mistaken." And he shouted after the cab, "Jem Rawlings! Jem! Jem!"

But the cab rattled along over the stones, and the sounds of its wheels drowned the shouts of Allan.

He thought at first to call a cab and go in pursuit of his friend, and had turned round to do so, when he unexpectedly confronted a gentleman, who touched him on the arm.

"What! you out this time of night, Allan?"

"You know me?"

"I do."

"But I do not know you, sir. I have never seen you before in my life, that I know of."

"Oh, yes you have."

"I have not the slightest recollection of it."

"Can't you tell by the voice?"

"No, I cannot."

The gentleman laughed heartily.

"Oh! now I know you," said Allan, grasping his hand; "it is Mr. Sharp."

"The same; and what keeps you out so late, my lad? It is time you were in bed. You look a little excited—what's the matter?"

Allan in a few words explained all that had happened, and attempted to justify himself.

"I am sorry that this has occurred, Allan," said Mr. Sharp, thoughtfully.

"I am not."

"Perhaps not; but I am."

"And why so?"

"You have taken the law into your own hands, and that is a very serious matter."

"But was I to be insulted by a fellow that——"

"Stop! step! don't call him any harsh names; this Captain Zacary is a gentleman."

"A what!" said Allan, in disgust.

"A gentleman," said Mr. Sharp, smiling.

"A villain, a scoundrel, a mur——"

"Stop, my fiery young friend," said Sharp, taking him kindly by the hand; "he is a gentleman until he is proved to be otherwise."

"But you know, Mr. Sharp, that he is my enemy, and that he has done——"

"I *think* so, Allan; but thinking a thing and proving it in a court of law are two different things. Suppose, for instance, I had reason to think that you were a rogue, and could not prove it, what then?"

"It is a hard case for me, Mr. Sharp," said Allan, mournfully. "I have always been in troubles and trials."

"And so have all of us in some degree. And I suppose you have made up your mind to meet this Captain Zacary again, no doubt?"

"I have; and as soon as possible."

"Then don't."

"Why not?"

"Never mind that; you *must* not; if you do, you spoil and thwart all I am labouring for."

"And what is that?"

"To get all the rascals in one net together."

"But can you?"

"I hope so."

"But what necessity have you for separating me from my only friend Jem Rawlings?"

"I have very good reasons for it."

"If I am not much mistaken, I saw him to-night."

"I know you did."

"How do you know that?"

"He was behind a cab."

"So he was."

"I saw you standing and shouting after him; but I am better pleased than if I had £100 he did not hear you."

"I was going to get a cab, and give chase after him."

"That was what I imagined; and to prevent your doing so I stopped and talked to you."

"And what is he up to?"

"No harm, you may be sure. He is working very hard for your good, Allan."

"I can't see that at all."

"It is not necessary that you should; nor does young Jem know or even suspect it himself; but I know, and have been following and watching all his movements to-night; if he succeeds in accomplishing my designs, all things will progress favourably and successfully."

"But you don't mind telling me all about it, do you?"

"I might tell you a part of what I *know*," said Mr. Sharp, in a very emphatic manner, "but I won't breathe a word to you of what I *suspect*."

"And why not?"

"It might turn your head."

"Turn my head?" said Allan, smiling; "make me crazy, I suppose?"

"Yes; I think so."

"And what is it you *do* know?"

THE BOY KING
OF THE SOUTH SEA ISLANDS.

THE ARREST OF GENTLEMAN GEORGE.

"That a great robbery is about to be committed to-night."

"Where?"

"At Manfred Hall."

"And what has that to do with me?"

"A great deal; the robbers are employed, at least one of them, and for a very great price also, by old Lawyer Marks."

"The old villain!" sighed Allan, heavily, and with clenched fists. "To bring away a certain box

of deeds, which concerns you and your brother Norman—"

"But he is dead."

"Well, it concerns you; and your father and mother also."

"My father and mother!" sighed Allan. "We were orphans. My parents are not living."

"P-e-r-h-a-p-s not," mused Mr. Sharp.

Allan looked at him in astonishment.

"Perhaps not," he sighed.

"Perhaps not, and p-e-r-h-a-p-s they are."

" Oh, do not let me linger in this suspense and agony, Mr. Sharp," said Allan. " I always supposed they were dead. I will go myself to Manfred Hall and warn them."

" There you go again," said Sharp. " You won't let me manage this business in my own way ; as we say, you want to throw all the fat in the fire, and upset everything. Be satisfied with how things are progressing, and don't be in any hurry."

" Oh ! but my mother and father," said Allan. " I am dying to see them."

" But perhaps they don't want to see you, though ?"

" Oh, they could not be so inhuman as that, Mr. Sharp."

" Ah ! you don't know anything about it. This world is a very curious and wicked place. I don't mind saying," said Sharp, after a pause, " that there are some men who are living and moving in high society who ought to be transported, if they had their merits. For instance," he continued slowly, " I read once of a judge *who condemned his own sons.*"

" His own sons !"

" Yes ; and the mother was present in the court when it happened."

" I can't believe there is so much wickedness in the world, sir."

" But *I* do."

" This story of your's has nothing to do with my case, though ?"

" No. Oh, dear no ; nothing at all. I was only saying, you see, that this world is a very queer place, and lots of wickedness in it."

" But there is also a great deal of good in it also, I think," said Allan.

" Perhaps so," was the quiet reply.

And if the truth was known, Mr. Sharp himself was not one of the worst fellows in the world, and his heart was large and soft and good, if he *was* a detective officer.

But he didn't think so, which no doubt will make our readers like him all the more.

" And if you know," said Allan, after a pause, " that this robbery is about to take place at Manfred Hall, why not go and see about it ?"

" My plans are made, and my nets all perfect, Allan. They can't escape me. There is one gentleman I have been after a long time for many things, but he was always too clever for us. This time, however, he will not be sharp enough."

" And how do you intend to act ?"

" If any number of policemen had been set down there, these gentlemen would have got wind of it, for gentleman George and his pals are old birds you can't catch with chaff. They have had watchers all around the mansion for weeks ; but I have got one, who is also sharp, and very fond of prying into secrets, *he* will ferret out the whole affair, and quietly inform me of everything."

" Who is he ?"

" A boy."

" His name, I suppose, can't be revealed ?"

" Oh, yes. I don't mind letting you know."

" Who is he, then ?"

" Your friend, young Jem Rawlings."

" Never !" said Allan, in great surprise. " I never thought he was wise enough to do such a thing as that."

" He may not be very wise, perhaps, but he's brim full of cunning."

" I can't believe it," said Allan.

" I hope you do not doubt my word ?"

" No, I don't mean that, Mr. Sharp ; what I thought was, that such an exploit would be impossible for Jem to accomplish."

" Well, if you like, I'll give you proof of what I say."

" When ?"

" To-night !"

" But how are you to prove it ?"

" I will show you the lad himself."

" Safe and unhurt !"

" Yes ; safe, unhurt, and as merry as a cricket over it "

" I should very much like to see him."

" But you must not make yourself known though."

" I will not."

" At what hour will you see him ?"

" Let me see," said Sharp, pulling out a large silver watch, and looking at it under the lamp-post. " In about two hours ; come with me, we will have a cab, and take a drive together."

Calling a hansom cab, Sharp and Allan got into it, and drove rapidly eastward.

When they had gone some distance the cab stopped, and they got out.

" Stay here, cabby, until we return ; you ain't afraid of your money, are you ?"

" Not a bit of it, sir. *I* know you well enough," cabby replied, with a knowing wink.

Mr. Sharp turned the corner of a street, and stopped opposite a lawyer's office.

" Why, *I* know that house," said Allan, " it's old lawyer Marks."

" So it is."

" And there are lights in the front parlour."

" Two candles in the window," said Sharp, grinning. " All right, the old fellow is up, ready, and watching ; but I'll soon spoil his little game, I know what those two candles are for, well enough."

Allan did not ask him why nor wherefore, for at that moment a constable appeared in the street.

Sharp went up to him and made himself known.

" Seen anything suspicious about to-night ?"

" No, sir."

" There's a nice little game on foot ; I know all about it."

" Indeed ! Where ?"

" No matter. Do you see those two lights in yonder window ?"

" Yes, it is the office of old lawyer Marks ; it is nothing unusual for lights to burn there all night. They are up, busy in copying deeds, perhaps."

" To-night they are not," said Sharp ; " let two or more men watch that house to-night, they need not hide themselves ; if any cab calls there, stop it, and arrest those inside."

Having given these directions, Sharp and Allan re-entered their cab, and drove around the neighbourhood frequently, but very often passed the office of old Marks, and Sharp could see that already three policemen were on the watch.

After about an hour's riding about, Sharp espied a four-wheel cab coming along at a very sharp pace, but as it approached the street in which Marks lived, it went more slowly.

" That's them for a sovereign," said Sharp, in great glee.

But for some cause the four-wheeler stopped at the end of the street, a man jumped out, and having passed Marks' door more than once, and seen the policemen on duty, returned to his four-wheeler and drove off.

" I thought so," said Sharp, with a quiet chuckle, as he looked out of his hansom, and cautiously observed the movements of those in the street, " I thought they wouldn't call or stop at old Marks' after they had taken a squint at those stationed there."

"Where to now, sir?" asked cabby, through the hole in the roof.

"Do you see yonder four-wheeler, going along at the devil's own rate?"

"I do, sir; why!"

"Do you think you can follow it?"

"Follow it," said the hansom driver, in a tone of astonishment, "follow it?"

"Yes."

"Why, in course I can. Do you think my old 'oss ain't better than his?"

"I don't mean that; can you follow it without being observed, I mean?"

"I think so, sir; and now I comes to think on it, I haven't much doubt I knows that 'ere wehicle."

"Oh, indeed!"

"Yes, sir; it comes from Simpson's yard, I'll be sworn, and I could pick it out from a hundred, and not make any mistake."

"In that case, drive on, and if we should miss it, you might enable us to find it out again."

"All right, sir."

"But be sure they don't observe you, for I think they have some very queerish people inside."

"All right, sir; I understand you."

And the hansom driver whipped up his horse and went in pursuit of the four-wheeler.

But, from all appearances, it looked as if the hansom had been observed following the four-wheeler, for those inside the latter, from time to time, put their heads out of window, and urged their driver on to greater efforts.

Mr. Sharp's keen eyes had observed this, and he told the hansom driver not to go so fast.

This order was observed.

But although the hansom remained a considerable distance behind, the four-wheeler managed to slip away out of view.

Mr. Sharp was greatly annoyed, and to tell the truth he raved and swore very much.

The hansom was now driven round the houses at a furious rate in hopes of overtaking the other conveyance, and the horse was whipped unmercifully by the red-faced jarvey.

But all his efforts were in vain.

The four-wheeler, as if by magic, had disappeared, and the poor horse in the hansom was all afoam.

"What had we better do now, sir?" asked the driver. "Shall I take you to the station?"

"No; drive to Simpson's yard, we may be in time to find out the cabman and his number."

To this yard, or very near it, they were conducted in very quick time.

The driver got off his box and disappeared down the mews.

He had not been gone very long ere he returned, his face glowing.

"I've found it, sir," said cabby, in great glee. "I thought I knew that 'ere wehicle the first moment I clapped eyes on it."

"But did you find out where the parties went to?"

"Yes, sir."

"How many of them were there?"

"Three persons, sir."

"Did they all go to the same place then?"

"No, sir; two of 'em were dropped at two public-houses, as I knows on; but the third party, the gentleman came ——"

"What of him?" said Sharp, quickly, and anxiously.

"What, the party as had the trunk and the tin box?"

"Oh! he had a trunk and a tin box, eh?"

"Yes, sir; so the other driver said."

"Well, what of him?"

"Oh! he was a big swell, and stopped at his hotel."

"Hotel, eh?" said Sharp, laughing. "Well, some fellows have plenty of cheek, and no mistake."

"He treated all hands very well, sir; t'other driver said he was awful liberal with his money."

"His money, eh!" said Sharp. "Somebody else's money would have been nearer the truth. However, did the other driver know the hotel where he stopped at?"

"Yes, sir."

"Where was it?"

"In Leicester Square."

"And the name?"

"Hotel Garibaldi."

"All right, then; drive on to Leicester Square. I thought he lived somewhere about there."

Again did the cab rattle away, and soon did they arrive at the place desired.

Mr. Sharp alighted, but did not go to the hotel.

He went to the police-station near at hand, and when he came out again, two gentlemanly-looking policemen in plain clothes accompanied him.

They bade Mr. Sharp good-night, and took their stations at convenient distances from the hotel, so as to be within full view of all who entered or left the place.

"I suppose you've done with me for to-night, sir?" said cabby, touching his hat.

"No, I'm not quite."

"My old 'oss, sir, is nearly done up. You've had him a precious long time to-night."

"Can't help it; you must come with me all my rounds to-night, for I shall want you as a witness one of these days in this important case."

"I hope you'll pay me well then, sir," said cabby, with a grin, "for witnesses are awfully bad paid in general."

"I'll make that all right with you," said Sharp. "I don't mind a pound or two over this job."

"Thank'ee, sir," said cabby, mounting his box again, and tucking a thick rug around his legs. "Where to this time, sir?"

"The Minories."

"Where?"

"The Minories."

"Why, we've just come from there, sir!"

"Do as I bid you, and drive as fast as the horse can go. I want to see some one before they go to bed."

Obeying orders, off the cab rattled again at a good pace, and pulled up at a coffee shop.

"Allan," said Sharp, "you can go in and wait till I return. If I should bring any one with me, be engaged in reading the newspaper, or pretend to be asleep; but by no means must you speak or make yourself known."

"I will not."

"And must I stay here, too?" asked the cabman.

"Of course."

"Why, you'll keep me out all night, and my old woman ——"

"Never mind your old woman," said Sharp; "have something to eat and drink, I'll soon return."

Cabby took the hint, and Sharp went through the streets until he reached the shop of the well-known receiver, where Jem Rawlings worked.

Hiding himself in a doorway, he waited for the appearance of some one.

In a short time Jem appeared, and walked along very weakly and languidly.

He appeared perfectly fatigued, and was mud-stained and exhausted.

He sat down on the door-step of his master's shop, and in a short time would have fallen off to sleep.

But Mr. Sharp approached, and suddenly tapping the lad lightly on the shoulder, said—

"What! is that you, Jem?"

The lad seemed perfectly surprised when he recognised the inspector, but a few kind words soon quieted his apprehensions.

"And so you have been out on an adventure to-night, eh, Jem?"

"How did you come to know that, sir?"

"I followed you."

"You don't mean that?"

"I do though, and more than that, I know who you were following."

Jem looked and felt astonished.

"Come, come, tell me all, Jem. I know you were excited by curiosity; but how did you succeed?"

"I failed, sir."

"Failed! eh?"

"Yes."

"But how?"

"I don't want to tell you here, out in the open street, sir; somebody might be listening."

"True; then come with me, Jem."

And they entered the coffee shop together.

No one was there but Allan, and as soon as he perceived Jem enter, he pretended to be asleep, and was not observed.

"And so you failed, eh, Jem?" said Sharp.

"Yes, sir."

"How?"

"I followed behind the cab, until they got near to Manfred Hall, when their conveyance stopped, and I jumped off."

"Three men were in the cab?"

"Yes, sir."

"When they got out, what did they do?"

"Each one took an opposite direction, and I lost sight of them."

"And the cab?"

"That drew up in the lane out of sight."

"But didn't you try to enter the park also?"

"I did, sir; but directly I had got over the gate, a ruffianly fellow rushed at me, and would have knocked my brains out."

"What then?"

"I ran away and hid myself, and while I was doing so, I found a scarf and a gold pin."

"Where is it?"

"Here, sir, in my pocket."

"Let me see it."

Jem produced the pin and scarf.

Mr. Sharp looked at it for a moment and smiled.

"Well, what happened then, Jem?"

"I remained hid for more than an hour near the cab, when I heard a shrill whistle."

"What happened?"

"The cab moved away, and I followed, without being observed."

"Did the cabman do anything?"

"No; he only opened the door, and two men appeared, carrying a trunk, which they placed—"

"Outside?"

"No; inside."

"Where was the third?"

"He soon appeared also, sir, and carried in his hand a tin box."

"What size and color?"

"Such as lawyers use, sir."

"I thought so."

"After they got in, they began to laugh very loud and seemed to be much rejoiced at what they had done."

"And what do you suppose they had been doing, then?"

"Robbing, sir."

"Robbing the Hall, you mean?"

"I do."

"You are right, my lad."

After a pause, Sharp asked,

"Did you not hear any noise at the Hall, barking of dogs, or anything of that sort?"

"I heard the barking of a dog or two, but it soon ceased."

"And did you ride behind the cab as before?"

"Yes, sir. I jumped up behind and rode back to London; but when I got a good way, a policeman saw me, called out, 'whip behind,' and as the cab stopped, I was compelled to leave."

"And after that you lost sight of them?"

"Yes."

"Do you know a man they call Gentleman George?"

"Yes, sir. I know his voice well, and have seen him once at my master's shop."

"You are sure he was one of the three men?"

"Yes, I am positive. He was the best dressed of the three, and seemed the merriest."

"I am glad you took notice of all these particulars, my boy," said Sharp, "it shows you are cute, and may make a bright man."

"Thank you, Mr. Sharp."

"Here's a sovereign for you, Jem."

"Thank you, sir; you are very kind, indeed you are."

"I will be kinder still, if you do what I ask you."

"I will, sir."

"Then come with me, have a little sleep, and to-morrow morning at ten or eleven o'clock take this pin and ring to the Garibaldi Hotel, Leicester Square, and ask to see Mr. Nelson."

"But they don't belong to Mr. Nelson, sir."

"I know they do not if there was any real person living there of that name, but Mr. Nelson and Gentleman George are one and the same person, my lad."

"But perhaps he might hurt me."

"No fear of that; I will take care of you, you may depend."

Acting upon the advice of the inspector, Jemmy went to bed, Allan and Mr. Sharp went home in a cab, and when they had arrived at their journey's end, cabby was well paid, and went homewards very tired, but, at the same time, very well rewarded for his time and trouble.

*　　　*　　　*　　　*

When next morning dawned, Jem kept his appointment with Inspector Sharp.

He dressed himself up in his best, and, in order not to be recognized as the person who worked at the receiver's, the inspector disguised him so completely, that Jem hardly knew himself.

"Now," said Sharp, "you look more manly than ever, and not even Allan Norman would know you at this moment."

Jem went to the hotel, and waited in the hall at the foot of the staircase.

Mr. Nelson, the servant said, could not be seen by any one.

He was at one time writing.

When asked for again he was at breakfast.

But in no case, as ordered, would Jem deliver his message to any one but Mr. Nelson himself.

At last Mr. Nelson condescended to appear, and he came down the staircase in his dressing-gown.

"Well, young man, and what may be your business?"

Jem was approaching him to make a reply, when two policemen rushed in.

Mr. Nelson was arrested.

CHAPTER XCII.

MEETING OF LORD AND LADY OXENFORD, ALLAN, AND HIS GRANDFATHER.

It must not be supposed, however, by the reader, that Baron Templeton was not aware of the mistrust and jealously of Lord Oxenford, for Lady Oxenford had fully informed him privately of everything that had taken place, as also anything that might occur.

The baron was greatly annoyed and agitated, but he was unable to extricate her ladyship from the spies which his lordship had employed to watch her.

Lady Oxenford was the only daughter of an old painter, who, through reverse of fortune, had been greatly reduced in life.

Baron Templeton had been in the habit of visiting the famous old artist (who was still alive), and during his visits, Lord Oxenford also formed the old man's acquaintance, and his offer of marriage was not, by the baron's advice, refused by the daughter, and Lord Oxenford was so enraptured with the grace and beauty of his bride, that he allowed the old artist a respectable yearly allowance on which to live.

Lady Oxenford usually passed every Thursday morning with her father, who still dwelt near to the residence of the Baron Templeton.

Since his daughter's return to London, the old artist had not once seen her.

But, informed of her arrival, he awaited her coming on Thursday morning.

Full of joy at the prospect of embracing his beloved child, the old man, according to usual custom, bestowed all possible care to give an air of festivity to his humble abode, which consisted of a small sitting-room and two chambers, up three pairs of stairs.

From the windows of these small apartments a view might be obtained of the river Thames, while, in the horizon, the tops of tall trees were discernible, and, further still, appeared the lofty dome of St. Paul's.

The chamber formerly occupied by his daughter was almost worshipped by the artist, who had not permitted the least change to be made in any of its arrangements.

The little painted bedstead, with its white cotton curtains, the old walnut-tree chest of drawers, which had formerly belonged to her mother, the small, rickety pianoforte, on which his daughter had acquired her musical proficiency, were all there as she left them.

And there, too, safe under a glass frame, were the wreaths of victory gained by the youthful aspirant during the course of her studies at school.

The father could not be less than seventy years of age.

His tall figure, bent beneath the pressure of his years, his bald head, white beard, which he had ceased for many years to touch with a razor, added considerably to the stern severity of his features.

His eyelids were nearly always half closed, and proved but too painfully how much his sight had suffered from his incessant labour.

The infirmity, added to a slight nervous tremor which had settled upon him after a long and severe illness, had compelled him to relinquish his occupation of painting, and, sorely against his will, to accept a pension from Lord Oxenford.

The chamber of the old man, which had formerly been his studio, was scrupulously neat and clean.

Beneath the window stood his work-table, with the implements of his now abandoned profession laid in exact order, as though for immediate use.

A small iron bedstead, a table, four chairs of walnut-tree wood, composed the almost anchorite-simplicity of the fittings-up of the apartment.

Over the recess, where stood his bed, hung an ancient sword of honour.

Above the sword was a framed copy of the celebrated appeal made by Cromwell to the people.

The old man religiously preserved this curious specimen of that terrible period, which, however blood-stained, was still not wholly without glory.

Honest though unpolished—just and conscientious—the only fault to be found with the old man was his somewhat overstrained notions as to the moral distinctions which, in his opinion, existed between the rich and the poor.

And, if he carried the pride of poverty too far, he might fairly be excused on the score of his noble and unaffected disinterestedness.

After thirty years of incessant application, hard labour, and economy, the old man had succeeded in amassing the sum of £25,000, which he destined for the future provision of his daughter.

The bankruptcy of the lawyer in whose hands he had placed the money deprived him of the dear gratification of seeing his child independent, and left him no help but to redouble his exertions, in order to bestow on his daughter, then quite young, some profession by which she might honestly earn her bread.

From this slight sketch the reader may form some notion of the intense eagerness with which the old man awaited his beloved daughter.

At length his watchful ears were gladdened with the sound of a vehicle stopping.

Then a quick, light, and well-known step sounded up the staircase.

A few seconds more, and his daughter, rushing into the room, threw herself into her father's arms, who, tenderly embracing her, cried, in tones of deep emotion,—

"At length, then, my child, I embrace you once again."

"Dear, dear father!" replied Lady Oxenford, weeping tears of joy.

The tender parent himself disencumbered his child of her bonnet and cloak, which he carefully placed on his bed.

Then, seating her in an arm-chair beside the fire, he took her chilled hands in his.

"Poor dear!" said he, "you are quite frozen,—there, try and warm yourself."

"Ah, dear father, you spoil me, as you ever did."

Without replying to her remark, the old man gazed with intense delight on the sweet face before him, then murmured—

"Once more, once more, after six long weary months of absence."

"Dearest father, the time, then, has seemed to you very long."

"But you have been quite happy, my child, have you not?"

"Oh, yes—quite—quite," and she sighed.

"Perfectly happy?"

"Yes, indeed, as much so as ever."

"And the thought of your felicity has armed me

with courage to endure your absence. And your husband is still kind, good, and devoted to you?"

"Certainly, my dear father," and she sighed again.

"And, during the time you have been away, no doubt the constant enjoyment of each other's society has been far more congenial to your mutual tastes than your mode of life in London."

"Yes, father."

"And you still rejoice in being his wife?"

"I do, indeed. But, dearest father, why these questions?" she asked, lowering her eyes.

"Lord Oxenford, in fact, is precisely what you thought him when he assured me that he would wed none other than you?"

"Assuredly he is," answered the daughter, more and more surprised at the close questioning pursued by her father, but which will sufficiently show how scrupulously she had concealed her unhappiness from her father, but said—

"Indeed, father, he has not changed since then."

"Heaven be praised! then, I confess I am deceived."

"Deceived, dear father! and in what respect?"

"Can you guess wherefore this year I have awaited your return to London with so much more impatience than in previous years?"

"No, dear father, indeed I cannot."

"And you know not either why my joy at welcoming you to-day exceeds that I have hitherto experienced?"

"Father, I beseech you, explain to me the purport of all these strange inquiries; you know not how they pain me—but, gracious Heaven, you weep—father, dearest father, what mean these tears?"

"Can you not guess? can you not perceive that they flow from joy—oh, yes, heartfelt, overwhelming joy?"

"Oh, so much the better."

"My child, the trial has been a severe one."

"What trial do you speak of?"

"It cost me so much, old and infirm as I am, to pass my days alone; I, who from the hour of your birth had never passed a morning or evening without embracing you—you who absorbed the love that was once shared between you and your mother, think what a painful thing it must be for me only to see you for a few hours each week, and to lose sight of you for months together."

"Dearest father, be assured that I suffered equally with yourself."

"That is not all; the time you passed here, while your husband was in Italy, rendered our separation still more painful; it was like losing you a second time."

"But, my dear father——"

"I know what you are going to say—when you were first married, my lord offered me a small suite of rooms in his house, and you subsequently reiterated the proposition, which I, however, constantly refused to accept."

"Alas! yes."

"Because, my daughter, I doubted this Lord Oxenford, and the duration of his at first so violent love. I could not have remained a passive spectator of your unhappiness; my very anxiety might have disturbed your domestic comfort; for these reasons, then, I imposed a severe restraint on my inclinations.

"No," said I, "I will wait; my daughter has never deceived me, and if, after years of marriage, she still proclaims herself happy, I shall then feel satisfied as to the future, and be equally persuaded of the goodness of Lord Oxenford's nature; that moment has arrived. I find your husband worthy

of you, and this very day will I say to him, 'I have doubted you, I have proved myself wrong, and I am here to solicit your pardon.'

"What are you saying, father?" exclaimed Bertha.

"I say, my beloved child, that my years upon this earth are too few to be passed at a distance from you. No, no, henceforward I will enjoy the happiness permitted me by Providence, and henceforward your husband, yourself, and your old father, shall live in indissoluble union."

Lady Oxenford's only reply was to throw herself, weeping, on the neck of the old man, who, mistaking both the movement and the tears which accompanied it, tenderly pressed his daughter in his arms, saying,

"Why, you little simpleton, if joy thus agitates and overcomes you, what effect would grief have? To tell you the truth," added the father, smiling, "though I affect all this resolution, I am as much delighted and moved as yourself at the thoughts of our never again being parted from each other;" and with these words he passed his trembling hand across his humid eyes.

The situation of Lady Oxenford was most cruel.

Not content with filling up the measure of her own injuries, Lord Oxenford had just taunted her with the trifling pittance granted by him to her father, and now, at this moment, was her father deceived by the generous deception of his daughter.

Until then, his daughter had contrived to conceal her bitter sorrows, and to attribute her dejection of spirits to her regret at living away from him.

But the cruel contrast presented by the hopes and expectations of her father, made her bitterly weep, and forced her father to exclaim, in a severe tone,

"Daughter, you have deceived me—you are *not* happy!"

Recalled to a sense of her duty by these words, she shuddered at her own imprudence, and bitterly, though too late, regretted the emotion she had been unable to restrain or conceal.

But, as she strove for words to reassure her parent, the door was suddenly opened.

"Gracious heavens!" cried Lady Oxenford, in extreme terror, "my husband!"

And Lord Oxenford, without knocking, or any other announcement, abruptly entered the apartment of the old man.

The unexpected appearance of my lord was followed by an unbroken silence of several instants, neither of the three actors in the scene uttering a single word.

His wife's heart sank within her, as at the first glance she read the hard-hearted mockery impressed on the features of the husband.

The stern countenance of her father, which, until then, had relaxed into an expression of gentleness and kindness, suddenly assumed a look of proud energy.

Drawing up his tall figure, and placing his daughter behind him, as if for protection, he advanced a few steps towards Lord Oxenford, saying briefly—

"What is your pleasure here, my lord?"

"My pleasure is to know whether or not your daughter has told me the truth in saying she was coming to pass her morning with you; and, having my own reasons for doubting the veracity of her statement, I have thought fit to come hither to substantiate the fact."

"My lord!" murmured her ladyship, in a tone of reproach.

"I desire, my lord, that you will not presume to

accuse a child of mine of falsehood," retorted the old man.

"I do not consider myself responsible to you, sir, or any other, person, for my actions," said my lord. "And, if I suspect my wife of uttering that which is not true, it is because——"

"If she has spoken untruly," cried the father, fiercely interrupting his son-in-law, "it has been to *me*, not you."

"In what manner?" inquired the latter, regarding his wife with astonishment.

"I beseech you!—and you too, dear father?"

"She spoke falsely but now," exclaimed the old man, in a loud, stern voice, "when she assured me she was happy."

"Ah, now I understand," replied my lord, coldly. "She came hither amid hypocritical tears and sighs to dwell upon her domestic felicity—a clever idea! I give her much credit for it."

"My lord," cried the old man, "four years ago, when my daughter was lying at the point of death in this very chamber, I told you I would rather lose her then than see her perish one day through the wretchedness you would occasion her. I spoke truly. You will be her death!"

"Father!" said her ladyship, "I must not allow you to remain under so fatal an error; and, at whatever sacrifice, I will speak the truth, nor warrant by my silence those reproaches I pledge myself are undeserved by my husband. 'Tis true I concealed from you some of those trifling disagreements from which the happiest unions are not exempt; but you were so delighted to learn, that in all essential points I was perfectly happy, that I was unwilling to dispel the illusion which could do no person any harm, but which I trusted would be the means of still more attaching you to him. You judge too severely."

"My child! I can make allowances for your weakness, which renders it the more imperative in me to evince a necessary degree of severity."

"Severity!" cried my lord, with a burst of sardonic laughter—"severity! Upon my word I like the word vastly. It seems, then, that I am here to be lectured by you into a right understanding of my duties. May I ask if you are aware to whom you are speaking!"

"Too, too well! To the destroyer of my child."

"You use strong language, my good sir."

"Daughter!" said the old man, with stern manner, "take this man from my sight!"

"Come, come, my lord, I pray—I beseech you! Adieu, father, till Thursday next. Pardon me for quitting you so abruptly now—possibly I may come and see you again to-morrow," she added, anxious at all risks to terminate so painful a discussion as the present.

"Since, sir, you have taken upon you to dispense advice," interrupted my lord, "perhaps you might judiciously recommend your daughter not to adopt the unwise plan of treating her husband with coldness and contempt, after having justly awakened his jealousy."

"Daughter!" said the old man; "what am I to understand by these words?"

"My lord!"

"Be assured madam, whomsoever else you may impose on, I am not the dupe of your affected delicacy—your over-strained scruples. You are carrying on some base, some disgraceful intrigue; but rely upon it, I will detect it!"

"For mercy's sake talk not thus in my father's presence! Adieu, father, adieu."

After a momentary silence, the old man approached his daughter, and gazing steadfastly on her, said, in a deep solemn voice—

"Daughter, do you merit this charge?"

"No," she answered, with a deep blush, and flashing eyes.

"I believe you, my child. And now, my lord, listen to me; for four years have I been deceived by the belief that my daughter was happy. I now know the truth; my daughter has no other support than myself, a poor, old, and infirm man; but still there is strength enough left me to bid you beware."

"Oh, then, to advice and lectures succeed threats and menaces? What next, sir?"

"At least, henceforward, we plainly understand our relative situations; and, first, from this hour I reject the pecuniary aid I accepted at your hands, solely at the solicitations of my daughter."

"You find it more convenient to be ungrateful?"

"Ungrateful! for having sacrificed my own notions to spare your pride?"

"Father, I conjure you——"

"Thus, then, my lord," continued the old man, "we meet upon equal grounds, as man and man; as such you shall account to me for the misery heaped on my gentle, my unoffending child; I give you a fortnight to repair the wrongs you have done her."

"Really, a fortnight; can you make it no more?"

"And if, at the end of that period, you do not conduct yourself as honour and justice require, towards her ——"

"Well, sir, and what then?"

"You shall see."

"Come, madam," said my lord, taking his wife by the arm.

"Farewell, father; I pray you calm yourself; I will soon come again."

"That is, if I think proper to permit you," said my lord, with bitter irony.

"Make yourself easy, my child; your father will watch over and protect you," cried the old man, weeping bitterly.

Her ladyship followed her husband out, and the old man was left alone.

* * * *

A few days after the meeting we have just recorded, as the hour of six o'clock sounded forth from the church of St. Paul's, a fog, rendered more intense by the proximity of the Thames, spread itself over the banks of the river.

An individual, wrapped in a cloak, was slowly pacing along the banks, stopping occasionally to observe the rapid current of the Thames, now swollen by the rains of winter.

The wild and lonely spot was buried in gloom and silence, while the rapidly increasing mist entirely concealed the opposite banks of the river, and, half veiling the dilapidated walls of the Abbey, communicated to them an almost grand and sublime aspect.

The lofty walls, partly destroyed, with the occasional gaps left by the places which had once contained the arched windows, casting their dark time-coloured masses in bold relief against the grey sky, imparted almost the appearance of vast and imposing ruins.

The person we have mentioned seemed to find a melancholy pleasure in contemplating this solitary spot, as, with head bent forwards on his breast, he continued to walk up and down, pausing, from time to time, to listen to the rush of waters, or to follow, with fixed gaze, the rapid flow of the current, as it pursued its boiling course.

It was Allan Norman.

His reveries were suddenly interrupted by the sound of approaching steps.

He looked up and beheld advancing towards him a man of more than the usual height, with a long white beard, and who, although walking with a firm step, kept occasionally sounding the road with his stick, as though to satisfy himself as to the safety of the path he trod.

The fog had by this time become very dense, and the old man (in whom the reader will doubtless have recognised the old artist), whose sight was feeble and uncertain, instead of following the proper direction, had considerably deviated to the right, and advanced close upon the personage in the mantle ere he was aware of his vicinity, while the latter, by a natural impulse, drew aside to allow the new-comer to pass.

But scarcely had the old man reached the bank, than he lost his balance, slipped, and disappeared in the river, throwing out his arms and crying aloud for help.

All this occurred in much less time than is required to narrate it.

To strip himself of his cloak, plunge into the Thames, and save from death the unfortunate being who had just been precipitated into its depths, was the first thought of young Allan, for, as we have said, he it was who in the cold and solitude of a winter's evening took his lone walk.

Weak and feeble, though possessed of a highly nervous frame, Allan felt, in the violent excitement of the moment, sufficient strength and energy to enable him, after the most incredible efforts, to grasp the sinking form of the old man.

The current was running so strong, that during the few seconds it took to effect the unhoped-for preservation of the old artist, the two persons immersed were swept a considerable distance, and conveyed, most fortunately, to a level and accessible part of the shore, for Allan was exhausted.

Preserving his habitual coolness amid the danger which threatened him, the old man, instead (as is too frequently the case in such untoward circumstances) of paralysing the efforts of his preserver, facilitated the attempts to save him by every means in his power.

When Allan and the old man were safely landed, the old artist had in a manner to change places and become the preserver of him whose courageous act had saved himself from death.

For to the strength and feverish excitement which had hitherto sustained Allan succeeded the most perfect prostration.

He sank utterly insensible at the feet of the old man, ere the latter could pour forth the praises and blessings with which his heart was filled.

Night was fast approaching, and the deepening shades of twilight increased the effect of the thick fog which kept all objects wrapped in its dusky veil.

In vain did the old artist shout aloud for help.

His voice was lost amid the mingled roaring of the wind and waters.

And had the weather been more propitious, it was a rare circumstance for any foot-passenger to pass those lonely banks after night-fall.

Allan shook with convulsive tremors, and it was but too evident that his slight and fragile frame must have been endowed with an almost superhuman courage to dare a peril its physical powers were so unequal to struggle against.

Still vigorous, and more than ordinarily robust for his age, the old man raised Allan in his arms, as he would have done a child, and, carefully choosing his way, reached one of the landing-places.

The old man found himself exactly opposite his own house.

Aided by his servant, the old man conveyed Allan into an apartment, and, spite of his veneration for the chamber of his daughter, he placed him there before an excellent fire.

As Allan regained his senses, he gazed around him with extreme astonishment.

" My preserver !" exclaimed the artist, while large tears of gratitude trickled down his furrowed cheeks ; " you have saved my life at the imminent hazard of your own, how shall I ever find words adequately to speak my thanks ?"

" Where am I ?" inquired Allan, striving to collect his ideas ; " and who are you that speak to me ?"

" Try to compose yoursef, I pray, sir, while I relate to you what has happened. A short time since, deceived by the fog and my own imperfect sight, I got out of my right road, and found myself, without being aware of it, on an embankment of the river, and ere I could recover myself, I fell from the summit of the path into the river, when, listening only to the generous devotion of your noble heart ——"

" Ah, now I remember all," said Allan ; " and I also recollect, that if my first thought was to endeavour to snatch you from the peril which menaced you, my second was to fear, lest my good intentions should prove fatal to you. I am so extremely weak, that you were probably obliged to defend yourself from my ill-managed efforts to preserve you, and even to save me yourself after my awkward endeavours to rescue you from danger," added Allan, with a smile full of sweetness.

" No, no, sir, I cannot have you undervalue your noble conduct in this way ; like all brave and generous natures, you found sufficient power to back your efforts to preserve me from a certain death. Delivered from danger by you, it then became my turn to succour your feebleness, for it is very evident you have far more courage than strength. I therefore brought you hither ; and you are now under the humble roof of one who owes his life to you, and who is well known in the neighbourhood."

Just as Allan was about, in his turn, to declare his name and station, the chamber-door opened.

At the sound, the old man turned suddenly round, and saw his daughter, who, pale and bathed in tears, her features distorted with grief, threw herself into his arms, exclaiming—

" Father ! dearest father ! will you not receive your child who has no shelter ?"

The abrupt entrance of Lady Oxenford, and the precipitation with which she threw herself into her father's arms as he turned towards her, had so entirely concealed Allan from her, that she was not aware of there being a third person in the apartment.

" He has driven me from him ; sent me from his roof," murmured Lady Oxenford, in a voice half stifled with sobs, as she still kept her arms tightly twined round the neck of her father.

" My child," said the old man, in a low voice, " we are not alone."

A feeling of inexpressible joy shot through the frame of Allan at the sight of Lady Oxenford.

As the old man pronounced the words, " We are not alone," his daughter, sinking with confusion, was hastening to the door, but the old artist caught her by the hand, and, pointing to Allan, said—

" My child, behold and bless the preserver of your parent !"

THE BOY KING

OF THE SOUTH SEA ISLANDS.

LADY OXENFORD IS WATCHED.

"What mean you, dearest father?" said her ladyship trembling, and averting her face.

"A little while ago I lost myself in the fog, and, mistaking my road, fell into the river."

"Gracious heaven!" exclaimed her ladyship, again throwing herself into her father's arms, and pressing him passionately to her heart, then gazed in his face with mute anxiety.

"This gentleman was accidentally on the bank at the time," continued the old man, "and generously saved my life, but his strength being entirely exhausted, I brought him hither."

"Ah! sir," cried her ladyship, trembling with agitation, turning her expressive looks on Allan, "you have restored me my father at the very

moment when I stand most in need of his tenderness and protection; and we, alas! can do nothing for you in return. But God will recompense you, and repay a debt far beyond our poor powers to discharge."

"Be assured, madame, that I am already more than paid in the happiness of finding I have been instrumental in preserving a father to his child."

"But, at least, permit us to know to whom we are so largely indebted," said the old man.

"Yes, teach us what name to remember in the prayers we shall daily put up to heaven to invoke the blessing of the Almighty on your head," added her ladyship, looking wildly on him.

"My name is Allan Norman," said Allan, blushing, and with some hesitation.

Attributing this embarrassment to the extreme modesty of his preserver, the old artist continued—

"But where can I present my grateful thanks to him who has prevented my child from being fatherless?"

Again a deep flush suffused the cheeks of Allan; after a short pause he replied—

"With your permission, my good sir, I will afford myself the gratification of calling occasionally to inquire after you, and thus receive the reward of what you are pleased to call my good actions."

"Nay, sir," said the old man, "'tis not for me to insist, be it as you will. I can easily guess the feeling that makes you conceal you dwelling, and it may even be your real name, from us, but I honour and respect your reserve; only be generous enough to come and see me sometimes, since you will not permit the gratification of offering up my grateful thanks at your own door. Promise me that you will come, and spare me even the appearance of ingratitude towards you."

"I do faithfully promise it, my worthy friend," said Allan; "but I feel quite recovered now; could you do me the favour to cause some conveyance to be sent for, by which I could return home? I will not longer trespass on your hospitality."

Allan cast one long glance on Lady Oxenford, and left the room.

On the instant all her ladyship's strength of mind gave way.

She uttered an agonizing cry, and fell to the floor, murmuring with sobs and tears—

"Oh! heavens, forgive me, forgive me; 'tis he! 'tis he!"

CHAPTER XCIII.

BARON TEMPLETON, AND HIS MYSTERIOUS ABODE.

THE sudden departure of young Allan from the abode of the old artist, whose life he had saved at the imminent peril of his own, filled Lady Oxenford with inexpressible grief.

As we have said in a previous chapter, she uttered a sudden exclamation, and swooned.

"'Tis he!" she said, "'tis he! alive, not dead! Oh, heavens! how proud and handsome he is!"

When fully recovered, she hastily embraced the old man, and with streaming eyes, dashed from the apartment, entered the dark streets, and was lost to view.

Before her old father could recover from his surprise, Lady Oxenford was far away.

But whither did she flee?

To the mysterious abode of the still more mysterious and eccentric Baron Templeton.

Reader, let us also go there, and visit the man who had condemned Lion Limb.

*   *   *   *   *

An immense chamber, occupying the whole of one wing in the Spanish hotel, formed the entire dwelling-place of the Judge, a personage concerning whom so many strange conjectures and varied rumours were afloat.

And well might the aspect of the long gallery or chamber he inhabited, and which we are about to describe, warrant the many charges of whimsical originality.

The moment chosen for introducing the reader to this strange abode of the mysterious Judge, is about the hour when the pale light of a winter's day began to dissipate the mists of the morning.

Let the reader picture to himself a room nearly one hundred feet in length, with a ceiling crossed by large projecting beams, once painted and gilded, as well as the spaces between them.

By a caprice of the Judge all the windows had been closed up, except one high, long and narrow Gothic casement, placed at the extremity of the gallery, and filled with panes of painted glass.

The light thus admitted through this narrow opening produced a singular effect by struggling against the blaze of six wax-lights, burning in an ancient brazen candelabrum suspended from one of the joists by a silken cord, close to the window itself.

Thanks to this method of lighting the place, that portion of that vast gallery was, day and night, supplied with a clear, soft light, while the remainder of the spacious chamber was lost in obscurity.

Nothing could be more singular than the gradual shading off of the light, which, at first entering all the more brilliantly, as the rays were in a manner filtered through the high window with its variegated panes, decreased insensibly, until it wholly disappeared in the distant recesses of the chamber.

The different objects it encountered on its passage, sharing in the effect of the diminishing brightness, assumed all manner of wild and fantastic forms.

For instance, as the expiring light struggled towards the end of the gallery, its fading beams, striking against the designs wrought upon various suits of Damascus steel armour, seemed to send forth a shower of bright, scintillating sparks.

Almost beside the only small door which gave admittance into this gallery, and in one of its gloomiest corners, might be discerned a white mass resembling a human form!

This was a skeleton attired in the most whimsical manner!

On its head it wore a crown.

One hand leaned upon a beautifully ornamented sword, of the time of the Revolution!

The other held a seven-stringed ivory lute, the base of which was supported on the knee.

By a fanciful caprice, a wreath of roses (a great rarity at that time of year) of surpassing beauty and exquisite perfume, surmounted this lute. A mantle of white cloth, studded with mystic letters, interwoven and embroidered in gold, hung in majestic folds over the hollow chest of the skeleton, and, falling in long-flowing drapery, allowed no part of its figure to be seen, with the exception of the lower part of the thigh and the whole of the right foot.

This foot, remarkable for its smallness, was clad, as though in mockery, in a white satin shoe, whose silken sandals floated in long-streaming bows on the leg-bone, white and polished as ivory.

But if the eye of the spectator, becoming sufficiently accustomed to darkness, should thoroughly investigate the more minute parts of this singular object, he might be able to discern beneath the silken sandals and slipper of satin various dark-coloured spots, easily recognised as those formed by blood.

This strange and awful memento of mortality was placed upon a pedestal of ebony, exquisitely ornamented with bas-reliefs and inlayings of silver and ivory.

By one of those striking contrasts which abounded throughout the whole of this strange apartment, the ornamental part of the pedestal by no means assimilated with the bony object it supported.

On the contrary, the perfection of art seemed expended on this masterpiece of carving and sculpture.

Nevertheless, the pure and exquisite style of the ornaments, charming as they were, bore reference to the gloomy object whose base they decorated.

The figure of the skeleton, leaning one hand on a naked sword, and with the other supporting a lute, its head bearing a crown, and its foot a woman's shoe, was to be seen amidst all the varied and artistical combinations of design.

Thus cupids, supported by fabulous birds, resembling the eagle in the head and wings, and the syren in the capacious folds of their tail, were introduced as bearing the hideous skeleton in their tiny arms.

In another part was represented a group of nymphs, whose chastely elegant attitudes would have reflected no discredit on the sculptors of Greece itself, sporting beneath the walls of the richest and most splendid salons, while busying themselves in preparing the toilette of the grizzly phantom ; one graceful creature holding the sword, another the lyre, and a third presenting the crown.

In a corner of this exquisite specimen of skill, two nymphs, gracefully designed, were represented as holding between them the sandals of the shoe, while a little Cupid, nestled in this Cinderalla's slipper, was employing it as a swing.

During these fanciful preparations, the skeleton, reclining on a Grecian couch, and half hidden by its flowing draperies, looked on, smiling with a ghastly smile at the sportive dances of the nymphs, whilst with its bony fingers it grasped a bouquet of roses presented by a group of lovely children.

A small tripod of silver gilt, most elaborately wrought, was placed at the base of this pedestal, for the double purpose of serving as a lamp, and, likewise, a burner of perfumes.

If the remainder of the furniture of this spacious gallery was less remarkable for its mixture of gloomy and sportive ideas, it was not less worthy of notice from its singular combination.

Some of the articles meriting close attention from their extreme rarity, the others claiming observation from the extraordinary mutilation they had undergone.

A painting, placed in one of the divisions of the gallery, where but a dim, religious light stole in, represented a female of exquisite beauty, and by the freshess of the colouring, the half-concealed light, the perfect grace of the design, and softness of touch, it was easy to recognise a masterly hand.

But, alas ! instead of the liquid, clear, expressive eye, to which the artist had doubtless almost communicated life, two sharp, fine stilettos, or sharp, glittering blades of steel, shot forth from the sockets whence the eyes had been ruthlessly, barbarously torn !

Could this fearful mutilation have been a mournful, yet ferocious jest, upon the ancient maxim that *the eyes of beauty dart forth mortal arrows ?*

It was impossible to view this outrage to a work of art, in itself a master-piece, without considerable indignation.

But this sentiment was quickly forgotten in the admiration excited by a small white monument close adjoining, the ornaments of which were borrowed from the Pagan and Christian mythology.

Indeed, various copies or engravings of the most celebrated cartoons of Raphael, placed side by side with fragments from the Parthenon, selected with perfect taste and correctness of judgment, gave evident proofs of an intimate acquaintance with, and a passion for, the fine arts, wholly irreconcilable with the barbarous mutilation of which we have before made mention.

But, in proportion as the enlightened part of the gallery was approached, so did the objects in this so singularly selected abode of the baron change their character.

The nearer they drew to the light, the greater was their splendour.

For instance, near the window was to be seen a rare collection of Indian and Eastern arms.

Sabres of silver encrusted with coral.

Poniards, whose hilts were studded with precious stones, were sheathed in scabbards of crimson velvet, richly wrought in gold.

The blue steel of Damascus bent beneath its golden case, glittering with emeralds and rubies.

Indian bucklers, bearing bas-reliefs of silver gilt, sparkled with the dazzling constellations of bright gems they presented, forming one bright, glowing, luminous mass, to which the light admitted by the painted window added still more glowing and varied hues.

Language would fail in describing the splendidly curious articles of gold, enamel, and carving, piled in gorgeous confusion upon the mother-of-pearl shelves, placed immediately in the close vicinity of the window.

The flood of light let down by the many-coloured window, and reflected back by the dazzling objects on which it fell in rainbow hues, resembled a cascade of sparkling brilliancy, to which the sun lent every shade.

This comparison seemed so much the more striking, as, immediately beneath the window, and occupying the arched space under it, stood a large organ.

Two figures, three feet high, of angels, sculptured in ivory, supported the keyboard of the instrument, which was also of ivory.

The rest of the body of the organ, whose summit reached the window itself, was composed of Gothic panels of finest ivory, carved with the fineness and delicacy of lace, without in any way detracting from the sonorous depth of the instrument.

Four light and graceful figures, adorned with golden crowns and ornamented with precious stones, separated the panels and supported a frieze of solid stones, represented a garland of flowers, fruit, and leaves, the cherries being formed of cornelian, the plums of amethyst, the apricots of topaz, blue-bells of lapis, with leaves of malachite and hyacinths of aqua marines,—shone with all the brilliancy and natural look of the fruits and flowers so skilfully imitated.

This organ, ten feet high and five wide, occupied the entire space beneath the long painted window, let into one end of the gallery !

The space which remained at each side of the window was filled up to the ceiling with the innumerable rich and gorgeous articles we have elsewhere described.

Seated before this ivory organ was the baron !
He wore a long tunic of black woollen, loosely

confined round the waist, a sort of black velvet cap but half concealed his hair, portions of which, escaping, fell in long, light locks upon his shoulders, which were somewhat bent.

His long, loose sleeves were thrown back almost to the elbows during the rapid passage of his long, thin fingers over the keys of the instrument, displaying hands and arms white and polished as marble, but unnaturally small and wasted.

The finger-nails, even though well shaped, hard, and polished as agate, possessed not that roseate tint so sure a harbinger of good health, but were surrounded by a pale, blue circlet.

The head of the baron, slightly thrown back, proved that his eyes were cast upwards towards the ceiling.

After having paused for some time, the baron recommenced playing, but in an extremely low key.

Whether it were the superior excellence of the mighty organ, or the skilful hand that touched it, it is certain that never did sounds so full, so soft, yet so sonorous, breathe forth in notes of melancholy sweetness, amounting almost to passionate expression.

It would be wholly impossible to trace the source of those feelings which found vent in passages at once so thrilling, yet soul-saddening, now plaintive as a sigh, yet sweet and touching as the smile bestowed by the mother on her infant.

Then breaking forth again in strains harmonious, vague, unfinished, capricious as the thought which, flitting through the mazes of a saddened imagination, suddenly glows with the pure, rapturous whispering of hope, whose finger points from troubled clouds to the clear, serene azure of summer skies.

The hardest heart must have owned the influence of those delicious sounds descending in gentle melody like a flood of happy tears.

In the solemn stillness of the night, the rich full sounds of the organ pealed forth in grander majesty, and ascended unto heaven itself, even as the incense of the heart.

There was one particular strain which occurred frequently and at regular intervals during these inspired performances.

To convey a notion of the ideas which were called up by this enchanting passage, played on the highest and most glassy notes of the instrument, it will be requisite to evoke youthful, smiling, and joyous images, such as these.

Like each pearly drop as it hangs on the soft green moss, or the roseate colours of an early spring morning.

All that is soft and gently soothing in the mild silver beams of the moon, as during a delicious summer's night she plays amid the dark shadows of the thick woods, whose wavy branches keep time to the delicious warbling of the nightingale.

All the happiness, pure joy, and innocent hope, poured forth by the innocent maiden of sixteen summers, as, in the fulness of her youthful delight, she warbles her pleasure at seeing the rising sun gild the summit of the trees at the moment when flowers unfold their leaves and expand their perfumed blossoms.

But no words can adequately describe the poetical images evoked by that sweet and gentle melody which, stealing in at intervals, appeared to cast a bright and serene charm over the gloomy style of the compositions performed by the baron.

The descriptions of pieces chosen by the baron savoured, indeed, of his own peculiar character.

They breathed, indeed, ideality fancies, not altogether that which conjured up so many graceful fantasies, but rather the gloomy whisperings which invoked the pale shade of the departed.

Sadness was so far peculiar to the baron, that, although perfectly resigned to his sorrow, he harboured neither anger nor bitterness of spirit.

His greatest delight seemed to be in modulating the exquisite music we have alluded to.

To it he clung with the fondness and tenacity we are apt to feel for some dear object of our early recollections.

The sharp, shrill, and prolonged sound of a bell made the baron start as though painfully aroused from his reverie.

At the harsh sound of the bell he suddenly discontinued his strain.

The last vibrations of the organ died away in the vast gallery like an expiring sigh.

He bent his head with deep dejection on his bosom, while his thin white hands, quitting the keys of the organ, fell listlessly on his lap.

His slight fragile form stooped languidly forward, the feverish strength which had hitherto sustained him fled, and left him weak and powerless.

The first dawn of morning, mingling with the light of the wax candles burning in the Gothic chandelier, formed a sort of artificial glare, gloomy as that of tapers burning in daytime around the bed of death!

This unnatural light fell direct on the forehead and cheekbones of the baron, who still sat with his head drooping on his breast.

While through his long downcast eye-lashes might be observed the fixed eye-ball lose the clear lustre of its limpid blue, and become motion less and rigid.

His fingers, too, were stiffened by the intensity of the cold, for the fire had long since been extinct in the vast chimney.

Again the bell rang forth its shrill summons, but this time the call was more imperative and repeated twice.

The baron seemed to start from a lethargic slumber.

He rose as though by a powerful and painful effort, and proceeded to the other end of the gallery, the only entrance to which was by a low and thick door, heavily barred with iron!

With an air of mistrust and suspicion, the baron half opened a small wicket formed in the door, then asked, in a feeble voice,

"Is that my valet, Antonio?"

"Yes, 'tis I, baron."

"You are quite sure 'tis you, Antonio?" repeated the baron.

"Why, in the name of all that's good who should it be if not old Antonio? Open the door—you shall see me from head to foot."

"No, no, not to-day."

"Come, come, you are low-spirited, my lord, I know it. But take this box."

The baron stretched forth his hand and eagerly took a small mahogany casket bound with steel, which was passed to him through the wicket.

"Good-night, or rather, good-day, Antonio."

"Adieu, my lord," said the valet, in a melancholy tone, and withdrew.

With these few hasty words, the wicket was again quickly closed by the baron.

Not far from the door was a bed composed of two thick and silky bear-skins, spread over a large divan.

On this couch the baron seated himself, placing the box on a small, curiously wrought ebony table, on which lay a pair of loaded pistols!

Taking a key, which was also on this table, he

opened the casket, which contained merely a small loaf just fresh from the oven, and some winter fruits.

The baron regarded these eatables, worthy of an anchorite, with a species of mistrust, as though his suspicions struggled with his appetite.

However, he broke the loaf in half, and after closely examining it, he lifted it to his lips, but suddenly changing his intention, he threw it from him in terror; then, concealing his face in his hands, Baron Templeton threw himself back on his bed, and wept bitterly.

At that instant, the bell rang again three times quickly and in succession!

The baron started.

His face turned deadly pale, and his lips quivered in agitation.

"'Tis she!" he muttered; "something strange has happened or she would not call; it is Lady Oxenford!"

In a few moments afterwards, the secret door already described was opened.

Lady Oxenford, pale, and haggard-looking, advanced into the apartment.

When the baron saw her, he walked hurriedly forward and embraced her.

CHAPTER XCIV.

SECRET INTERVIEW BETWEEN LADY OXENFORD AND BARON TEMPLETON.

As Lady Oxenford saw the baron approach, she flew towards him, and wrapping her arms around him, she laid her head on his bosom, saying,—

"Now, then, I may freely indulge my joy that I still again behold you, dear, dear baron; the very idea of losing you seems horrible for my brain to bear."

"Calm yourself, my child," said the baron, with a mournful smile.

"Now," said Lady Oxenford, bursting into tears, "you are all I have in the world."

The baron tenderly pressed her hand within his own, and then said, in a tone of bitterness,—

"What fresh sorrows have you to relate, my poor girl?"

"He hates and suspects me as ever," she replied, weeping bitterly; "my lord hates me, and finds me a burden to him!"

"Oh, my predictions!" cried the baron, mournfully.

"Have pity on me!"

"Alas! I meant it not reproachfully; it was but an involuntary cry of bitter triumph at finding how truly I foretold all this. My love for you did not mislead me as to the consequences of your marriage. But what fresh grievance have you met with?"

"You are aware that after our arrival in London, my lord's temper became daily more soured. Up to that period he had observed some restraint, he had even expressed regret at having acted so harshly towards me. The very next day fresh miseries broke out for me."

"And yet you concealed them from me! Wherefore did you not tell me?"

"I feared so much to grieve you; but now my strength is exhausted, I can bear no more. Oh, if you only knew—if you but knew!"

"Take courage—take courage, explain yourself without fear; let me know all."

"Indeed, I will. Well, after the night of my being at the masquerade, my lord, who had hitherto been irritable and violent, became gloomy, sullen, and unkind. I scarcely ever saw him. He was out all day, and only returned late at night, or rather morning. At meal-time, he was silent and abstracted. Two or three times he left the dinner-table ere the cloth was withdrawn, and went to shut himself up in his own room. If I questioned him upon the vexations he appeared to have, he coldly replied that it did not concern *me*, and frowned so angrily, that I durst not mention the subject again. This morning, however, seeing him look more cheerful than usual, I ventured to remark,—

"'You seem better to-day, my lord, than you have been lately;' that is all I said, indeed it is. I did not utter another syllable—on my honour, I said no more than that."

"Well, but go on."

"Immediately his features became overcast, and he exclaimed in a bitter tone,

"'What is the use of my being better? What have I to hope for? If I could only look forward to anything better than the wretched life I lead! but *I see you for ever before my eyes like a chain, to which I am eternally bound.*

"'Oh, accursed was the day in which I was weak enough to make you my wife, and to fall, like a fool, into the snare you and the baron laid for me.'"

The baron repressed a movement of rage, but said in a firm voice,

"And then——"

"This reproach, so cruel and unexpected, took from me all power of reply. My lord rose violently from his chair, exclaiming,

"'Oh, what a bitter lot is mine! oh, my liberty—my liberty!'"

"Oh, patience! grant me patience!" cried the baron, in a voice of forced calmness.

"Seeing him go on thus," resumed Lady Oxenford, I exclaimed,

"'My lord, do you wish to leave me? If I am a burden to you, say so!'

"'Yes,' cried he, furiously—'yes, you are a nuisance, and a burden I am tired of enduring. I tell you, I hate and *detest* you! you have constrained me to entangle myself in a marriage as absurd as inimical to my happiness, and never will I forgive you for it.'

"'But,' said I, 'what have I done! and with what do you reproach me?'

"'Oh, with nothing,' said he, 'you are too good a manager for that; you dare not betray me, because you know that, if you were, *I would kill both yourself and your paramour*; it is not *virtue* which makes you respect your duty as a wife, but *fear*.'

"And with these words, he dashed out of the room.

"Poor and broken-hearted, I come to pour my sorrows into the bosom of my only friend, and to say," added she, sobbing as though her heart would break, "that she has none to love her, or pity, or protect her, but you."

"There could be no other result," said the baron; "his selfish heart, and haughty, obstinate spirit, were sure to make you pay dearly—oh, how dearly—one day or other, for the sacrifices he had imposed on himself in order to obtain your hand, for which he would then have paid any price. However, things cannot go on in this manner; you must see the propriety of my interfering to prevent this man from torturing the heart of one who has behaved like an angel towards him: he shall not trample you under foot as the mere plaything of his whim and caprice!"

"But what will you do? How can you alter my lord's conduct?"

"Oh, make yourself perfectly easy, I will compel a change on his part; I have still sufficient strength and energy left," said the baron, sternly.

"For mercy's sake let us have no violent scenes!"

"Fear not; I shall oppose, not violence, but firmness to his tyranny and oppression; besides, I have reason on my side, and I will stand up to defend your cause. You see how quiet and composed I am. But, in the first place, we must quit this roof; fortunately I have lived so frugally, that I have managed to lay by a considerable sum, and——"

"Oh! never, never!"

"Well, then, what must you do? how contrive to live?"

"Listen, baron. Since the painful scene which occurred some days since, I have reflected much and deeply on my situation, and I think I have found a good way to improve it, if you will only assist me."

"Speak, speak!"

"Alas! I am poor; but, thank God, I still possess talents which formerly helped to support me; since my marriage it has been my only solace amid the many sorrows by which I have been surrounded, and now in this my day of trouble it will and shall be my resource."

"What do you mean?" asked the baron.

"I am left at liberty to devote every Thursday morning, what is there to hinder me from receiving music pupils as I used to do before I knew you? I can attend to them; I will beg of some of my old pupils to procure me fresh ones; and to prevent my husband's pride from taking the alarm, I will give my lessons under my maiden name, and in this manner I shall be able to escape want."

He interrupted her by tenderly pressing her in his arms.

"No, no," said he, "I cannot suffer you to add the fatigues of study and instruction to your other cares."

"Oh, but, on the contrary, the occupation will be to me the most delicious consolation. You consent?" cried Lady Oxenford, with inexpressible pride.

"No; this fresh mark of the elevation of your soul imposes on me more than ever the duty of insisting upon your husband treating you with proper respect, as well as evincing towards you the attention and care you require; and, as certainly as my name is Templeton, I will not only demand, but obtain it!"

"Oh, that I should ever have been born to endure the shame, agony, and painful existence which has fallen to my lot," sighed Lady Oxenford.

"Nay, be calm," said the baron.

"I cannot if I would, baron. My heart is breaking; one sin has begotten a whole brood, and day and night I am haunted! haunted! haunted!"

And with a sudden outburst of passion, she called feebly on the name of her lost son, Edgar Norman, and sank to the ground.

The baron trembled like a guilty thing—shook like an aspen leaf.

He had condemned his own son!

He was dead!

"Oh, if worlds could bring him back again, I would freely give them," he faintly sighed.

And in a few hurried questions and answers,

Lady Oxenford briefly explained to the baron the rescue of her father from a watery grave, and the unexpected meeting with young Allan.

The baron was very pale.

He listened to the words of the broken-hearted woman, and her hot, scalding tears of sorrow and repentance fell upon his ice-cold hands.

"The secret is not yet known," he hoarsely whispered.

"I fear it is, baron; I fear it is. My steps are watched; the footsteps of eavesdroppers and spies have been traced in the garden. I cannot move but all my actions are narrowly scanned and accounted for."

"Fear not," said the baron; "meet me to-night in your garden at the hour of twelve. I have resolved on instant action. Let Lord Oxenford learn to fear me. In the garden to-night at twelve—remember. Meet me there."

"I will. Do not fail to come."

"I will not."

CHAPTER XCV.

THE SPY—LION LIMB'S GALLANTRY GETS HIM INTO GREAT TROUBLES—THE RIVAL BEAUTIES —THE QUEEN OF THE PEARL ISLANDS AND EMMA CLARENCE—LOVE AND JEALOUSY—REVENGE.

THE following evening, after Lion Limb's encounter with the magician, while the rays of the setting sun yet tinged with gold the settlements of Katamar, a strange horseman was seen galloping at full speed in the direction of the main gate.

His horse, covered with foam, panted and bent his knees under him at every step.

As for him, his dusty surcoat of goatskin, his sandals of string dangling over large spurs of wood, his torn hose, the alteration in his features, distorted with fatigue, all proclaimed that he had just performed, without halting, a long and perilous journey.

When he perceived the summit of the gate tower, a massive battlemented construction three stories high, the foot of which was bathed by the river, a sigh of joy escaped him, and he murmured—

"Oh! I shall arrive in time."

Nevertheless, the nearer he advanced towards the town, the greater was his surprise at seeing the inhabitants of the country proceeding in the same direction as himself, with an expression of curiosity and gaiety, and not with the signs of uneasiness and fear.

Soon after, he heard a flourish of trumpets burst forth, and saw numerous tents stretching out in a line, whilst Indian horsemen in light armour amused themselves with hurling their javelins, and picking them up again at full gallop of their horses, over the necks of which they bent lightly.

The gate was guarded by Telumites, so named from the iron with which their head and shoulders were covered, according to the Indian custom, and these soldiers were gravely contemplating the exercises of the others, whose warlike sports seemed to indicate great mental security, and to form part of the programme of some coming battle, perhaps.

While the stranger was casting looks of astonishment upon this scene, the richly harnessed and caparisoned horse on which he was mounted stumbled against the root of a laurel tree.

And as if he had only awaited this moment to succumb to the fatigue that overpowered him, the animal snorted loudly, gave a plaintive neigh, and then made one strong effort to recover himself.

But his strength was completely exhausted.

His legs gave way.

He sank trembling on the ground.

The horseman rose, muttering curses, and prepared to continue his route on foot.

Unluckily, this accident had drawn upon him the notice of the guards, and all were greatly surprised to see a man so meanly attired mounted upon a palfrey of such high breeding, and magnificently caparisoned.

"God is great!" cried one of the guards, advancing towards the poor animal, which lay extended on the ground.

"Can this be the horse of our lord, King Katamar, which escaped miraculously from its stables this morning?"

"It is he!" replied one of his companions. "I recognize him by the white star in the middle of his forehead."

"Aid me, brothers," replied the first. "Let us not suffer this fellow in rags to escape. It is probably the magician who worked the miracle."

An expression of veritable despair overshadowed the stranger's countenance on hearing those ill-omened words.

And spite of his fatigue, his swollen and bleeding feet, he attempted to fly, which still further excited the suspicions of those who were pursuing him.

The two Indian horsemen had soon overtaken him.

He made no attempt at resistance, but striving to appear calm, he demanded why they opposed his passage.

"Would you play the innocent?" asked the first. "Can you deny that this poor animal is one of the twenty horses that our master, King Katamar, intends for a present to the noble Lion Limb?"

"It is very possible," coolly replied the stranger, "but I know nothing about it."

"Come, do not play the fool. Confess that you have stolen the horse."

"No, I have not stolen it. I met it straying in the open country on the road; and as I was exhausted with fatigue, I got upon its back, but only with the idea of bringing it back and restoring it to its master, as soon as I should meet with him."

"Ha, ha! A very excellent and honest intention; but I fancy its master will not be much obliged to you for restoring it to him in such a pitiable condition."

"Since the king is here, I demand to appear before him as soon as possible," said the stranger, with visible agitation.

"You are a little hot-blooded, friend," quietly observed the Indian; "but it strikes me that you will appear quite soon enough before our king. If you had brought this valuable horse carefully back to the stables, you would have obtained a rich recompense; but for having so brutally half-killed it under you, you must expect to make acquaintance with the sticks of the black slaves who guard the doors of the beautiful Aixa, King Katamar's niece."

"Aixa!"

"Yes, the Queen of the Pearl Islands," emphatically replied the Indian.

"Oh! I am the bearer of news which will make both Katamar and his niece forget the loss of a horse quickly enough."

"News?" said the Indian, in an accent of curiosity.

"Bah!" replied the other. "A tale like that he has told us on the subject of the horse, perhaps."

"This news," continued the stranger, "I ought to communicate without delay to your king. I must see him within this hour. Conduct me."

"Impossible! All are out of doors to celebrate the entry of a body of auxiliary troops that Lion Limb marches to the aid of his ally, King Katamar."

"It is somewhat late," murmured the stranger, with an ironical smile; "but take care," he added, aloud, "if you do not listen to me, you will answer with your heads for this blind obstinacy."

The Indians looked at each other as if to consult.

"I implore you," he cried, striving to restrain his rage, "bind me like a thief, tie me like a murderer to the tail of your horses, but conduct me to Katamar! It is in order to speak to his niece Aixa, that I have fled here. It concerns the safety of you all!"

And as these last words were received with an incredulous laugh,

"Madmen!" he exclaimed. "If I were what you think, a vile robber on the highway, is it likely I should have been such an idiot as to ride to the very gates to throw myself into your hands?"

This observation seemed to strike the guards.

And as, at the same moment, the flourish of trumpets announced the arrival of the king, who was going to review the ranks of his horsemen, the Indian confided the care of the supposed horse-stealer to his companion, and went to inform King Katamar of this incident.

The king lent serious attention to the brief recital of the slave, and ordered the prisoner to be conducted to the palace, in the train of the brilliant procession that accompanied him.

He passed his troops rapidly in review, and re-entered the town endeavouring to dissimulate the traces of a vague uneasiness.

The procession wended its way towards the palace.

On approaching this beautiful palace, the prisoner had need to congratulate himself on the chance which had caused him to be arrested on his way.

For but for that, the entrance to the palace would have been rigorously denied him, and he could never have succeeded in reaching without password, and even without message, the presence of the favourite, Aixa.

A double row of footmen lined the battlemented walls that formed the enclosure of the palace.

The procession stopped before a high square tower, in which was situated the principal entrance, known under the name of the Judgment Gate, because the ancient Indians had the custom of rendering justice, according to the custom of the East, beneath this gigantic porch, formed by an arch cut in the form of a horse-shoe, which rose nearly half the height of the tower.

On the foundation stone of the exterior archway, the prisoner remarked a gigantic hand.

On the corresponding stone in the interior, figured an enormous key, emblem of the Indian faith, which had shone on all the Indian standards since the time when they were sole masters of all the islands.

With a wave of the hand the king dismissed his escort with the exception of a few keepers of the gate of the palace, who were armed with heavy axes.

Then dismounting from his horse, while a black slave respectfully held the reins, enriched with precious stones, he prepared to listen with a calm and solemn air to the complaint of the guard who had arrested the stranger, and to the justification of the latter.

"Powerful lord," said the guard, leading his prisoner before the monarch, "I laid hands upon this man because he was mounted upon a horse which had disappeared this morning from your stables, and because, after having killed him under him, he would have fled at our approach."

"It is well," said Katamar. "I have heard the accusation, I would now hear the defence of the accused. Speak without fear, stranger, but seek not to deceive me. I am just towards all, like my faithful ally, Lion Limb."

And caressing with his hand the silken waves of beard, he fixed upon the prisoner his large black and brilliant eyes.

"Noble king," replied the latter, with an accent of rough frankness, "I am not a stranger."

"What matter! It is the will of Heaven that justice be administered alike to all. I listen to you. Perhaps you will be able to give me some proof that you did not steal this horse."

"How could I have stolen it this morning from the stables of the palace, since I have just arrived from Lion Limb's settlement?"

"Indeed!" said Katamar, with a gesture of curiosity.

"And if I have killed this poor animal, whose value I can pay, in spite of the rags that cover me," continued the stranger, "it is because I bring news so important that I wished to be the first to communicate them to you, and the noble Aixa, your beautiful niece."

"*You* see my niece!" said the king, disdainfully.

"I must; I can only speak before her."

"Come, then," replied Katamar. "My hand shall be lavish towards a faithful messenger; but if you conceal treason beneath this loyal appearance of devotion, daybreak shall behold your head nailed to the Gate of Judgment."

And, detaching his cloak of dazzling whiteness, he threw it over the shoulders of the stranger, and ordered him to follow him.

Notwithstanding his preoccupation, the unknown could not repress a feeling of surprise and admiration on beholding the interior of that marvellous palace into which so few had ever had the privilege of penetrating.

They traversed first a court, all paved with white marble, in the midst of which a large reservoir, four feet deep, bordered with a hedge of rose-trees, myrtles, and laurels, displayed its limpid waters.

This court was surrounded by light arcades, formed of sculptures, fine as lace, and supported by columns of marble.

They afterwards entered vast saloons, where the eye of the unknown was dazzled by ceilings of cedar and larch, by stuccoed cupolas painted in azure, green, and red, like stalactitic vaults, by heart-shaped arcades, arabesque panels, gilded cornices, and clusters of ornaments affixed to the glittering walls.

More than once during this journey Katamar let fall a sigh.

It was his ancestors who had built this magnificent palace, which now served as a fortress.

They at length reached a court, or, rather, a little interior garden, the soil of which was composed of a yellow sand saturated with water, and of incredible fertility.

The luxuriant vine sprouted from the crevices of the wall, and wound its capricious tendrils round the branches of orange-trees.

The red flowers of the pomegranate mingled with the thorny leaves of the aloe and the cactus.

The white flowers of the jasmine blossomed by the side of the shining laurels.

It was a perfectly tropical vegetation.

Pillars of marble supported a gallery which served for communication with the apartments of the women.

The steps of the staircase leading to the gallery were all of rich stone work.

Katamar was directing his steps towards this staircase, when a slave, whose white turban served to bring out in strong relief his ebony face, issued from the door of the bath, which was of cedar wood, sculptured in the form of lozenges, and bending the knee before the king, said—

"Dread lord, the Princess Aixa has just left her bath, and is reposing in the hall."

Katamar stood undecided for a moment, then Having again attentively regarded the calm and haughty countenance of the Unknown, he made sign to the slave to open the door of the bath.

The slave silently obeyed.

At the entrance the Unknown remarked a slab of white marble pierced by small holes, through which the smoke of perfumes burnt under the floor issued.

He entered boldly with the king this sacred place, which his presence profaned, and the beauties of which it had never been given to any one but the masters of the palace, their wives and slaves, to admire.

The bath-room was decorated at the lower part with squares of mosaic and filagree work of polished marble of divers colours, and of a variety as prodigious as that of the shells of the ocean.

The upper part of the apartment was covered with a beautiful stucco on which was inscribed texts and inscriptions in verse.

The middle of the apartment was occupied by a marble basin ornamented with an elegant vase, from which sprung a fountain of water.

Alcoves let into the wall were furnished with divans, covered with cloth of gold.

At fifteen feet from the ground were suspended, seemingly in air, the stands and balconies appropriated to the singers and musicians. The air around was impregnated with the perfume of aromatic essences.

As for the baths themselves, large receptacles of white marble cut out of a single block were placed in lateral grots, the low roofs of which admitted only a soft and pleasing twilight.

The Unknown could not, in spite of his habitual boldness, repress a sensation of fear and embarrassment when the door of the apartment closed behind him.

The niece of Katamar was lying upon a divan of gold brocade, enveloped in a tunic of fine white muslin, and gauze veils.

She did not deign to turn her head, and gently closed her eyes, whilst a slave softly waved over her brow a gold and silver embroidered fan of ivory.

But when she heard the heavy step which contrasted so strongly with the light and agile gait of her woman, she uttered a cry of surprise, and rising suddenly with a start,

"Is it you, my uncle," said she to Katamar, "who have permitted a stranger to follow you here?"

"Calm yourself, Aixa," replied the king, "this man has come to reveal secrets to us which should be known to none other. Now, this palace, perhaps, is the only place where we have reasons to fear the ears of a spy."

THE BOY KING
OF THE SOUTH SEA ISLANDS.

THE VISITOR TO THE OLD INN.

" What secrets have we to learn from a vagabond who, doubtless, reckons on our credulity to replenish his empty purse?" replied the princess, in an imperious tone.

The Unknown coldly contemplated her.

Aixa was beautiful, but hers was a severe and original style of beauty. It was purely of the southern type in its somewhat harsh exaggeration.

She had long, almond-shaped eyes, which looked from under their thick and curling lashes as if formed of mother-of-pearl and jet.

Her forehead was high, smooth, and polished.

The somewhat sharp contour of her chin, her teeth of dazzling whiteness, but some of which

were rather pointed, her thin and almost aquilien nose, all combined to impart a strange expression to her physiognomy.

Her lips, whose carmine was bright as that of the flowers of the pomegranate tree, contrasted well with the rich olive of her complexion, which would have ravished a poet of modern times.

Her feet and hands were extremely small and delicate, but it was easy to see through the transparent folds of her veil that her arms and shoulders had not yet acquired that splendour of form which constitutes the luxury of beauty among the Indian people.

Aixa advanced towards the unknown, almost irritated at his silence and audacious bearing.

"Speak!" said she, laconically, "and do not lie!"

"Noble lady," replied he, "I bring you news of Lion Limb, whom I know you love."

"If you speak truly, welcome, and blessed be the dust upon your feet! Well! is he conqueror? Has he driven back that horde of adventurers that fancied itself an army? Has he defeated that bastard Mungo?"

"No."

"You are deceiving me; it is impossible!"

"Alas! madam, I have beheld eight of the most respectable men of Lion Limb's city suspend to the points of their lances the keys of their eight gates, and come from a distance of four leagues to meet Mungo, and lay them humbly at his feet."

"And the faithful citizens, have they followed the example of these traitors?"

"They have received Mungo with the loudest acclamations of joy, and proclaimed him king."

"King!" repeated Aixa. "Oh! he is not that yet."

"He has caused himself to be crowned king," said the unknown, calmly.

"A folly that will cost him dear," replied Katamar, "if, indeed, this story be not a tissue of falsehoods, if you are not trifling with my surprise and my sorrow; but Lion Limb——"

"Has taken refuge at Fort Martin, I hear."

"Ah! I understand. The walls of that place are too tough for the teeth of these hungry adventurers, and the citadel is well fortified. You say that Lion Limb has taken refuge at Fort Martin. Taken refuge! yes, as the eagle takes refuge in its eyrie, the better to watch for the propitious moment when it may swoop upon its prey. There he will summon his partisans around him; there he will await the auxiliaries of you, uncle, his faithful ally; is it not so, my uncle?"

And speaking, she grew animated as a warrior who hears the sound of the trumpet, and gives the signal for the combat.

The Unknown admired this ardent, passionate, half-savage nature. He replied—

"Alas! I am forced to undeceive you, noble Aixa. The bastard Mungo has sailed there, I hear."

"And Lion Limb has, perhaps, opened the gates to him with his own hand!" said she, ironically.

"He fled because he found himself abandoned; he lost in a battle, I hear, or rather in a skirmish, on the borders of a forest, his last partizans."

"Calumny!" exclaimed Aixa, with flashing eye and trembling lips.

"Let this man be arrested, my uncle. He is a traitor, who has only come to spread trouble and alarm. By his account Lion Limb has all at once become a coward, vanquished without a blow.

"Order our slaves to chastise this wretch, and he will soon confess that all his tales are nothing but treachery and deceit."

"Patience, my niece," said Katamar, calmly. "The truth will not be long in making itself known. Certainly the events related by this man are strange, but they are not impossible. The swords which should defend Lion Limb may have turned against him. What interest had this man whom you accuse with so much vehemence in coming to announce to us these dismal tidings? If he were sent by Mungo he would not have demanded permission to speak to us privately. He would have publicly proclaimed the disasters of my unfortunate ally through the streets."

"Your niece has accused me with a woman's impetuosity," said the Unknown. "You, Katamar, you speak like a man whose brow has long supported the weight of the royal crown. I did not come to spread a false and puerile rumour. I came hither, at the risk of my life, to forewarn you of the danger, and to summon you to the aid of Lion Limb."

"Heaven protect us still," said Aixa, eagerly; "since he has permitted us to assemble so promptly five thousand braves."

"Five thousand!" exclaimed the Unknown, affecting a joyful surprise. "Oh, that will be the saving of Lion Limb; it will be the kernel of an army, at whose head he will not again run the risk of being made prisoner by a band of savages, as happened to him in the course of only yesterday."

"Prisoner! Lion Limb fallen into the hands of savages," said Aixa, with an expression of deep anxiety; "and you relate this to us as coldly as if it were a matter of a pedlar set upon by village rogues."

"Thanks to heaven, however, and to the efforts of his friends, Lion Limb, I hear, has extricated himself from this wasp's nest, together with the fair prisoner, for whose sake he so madly staked his liberty."

"The fair prisoner!" exclaimed the favourite, whose eyes flashed fire. "What mean you?"

"You know that Lion Limb is generous and chivalrous. Well, he wished to rescue a victim from Mungo, and he has succeeded, but not without difficulty and without danger."

Aixa fixed upon the Unknown a menacing look.

"Who is this woman?" she demanded, in a sharp, hissing tone.

The Unknown perceived that he had struck the right chord.

"This woman is the beloved daughter of Captain Clarence."

"Ah! English!" exclaimed the favourite, with disdain, while her countenance, which had so suddenly changed, regained an expression of serenity.

"But if I had not to-day obtained the favour and privilege of beholding the noble heiress of Katamar," rejoined the Unknown, "I should be obliged to proclaim that Emma Clarence is the loveliest daughter of mortals born."

Aixa gave a start.

"She is called Emma, this beauty?" she replied; "and Lion Limb has looked upon her, spoken with her, remained long with her?"

"It is to him that she owes life and liberty. For her sake he was nearly drowned in the river; for her sake he was for some hours the prisoner of savages."

"It is strange!" murmured Aixa. "A king forget the interests of his crown to save a low-born maid, whose existence was of no importance to any one! And you say that she is beautiful! Oh! really, I should be curious to admire this extraordinary beauty!"

"You will see her shortly," replied the Unknown, with an ironical smile, "for Lion Limb may bring her here."

"Here! He would not dare conduct her to my presence, in this very palace! Oh! I will never suffer it. If he ventured to forget that I am of royal race; if he feared not to offer us so outrageous an insult, you, uncle, would aid me to avenge myself! We would abandon this ingrate, for whom we are sacrificing the sum of our treasures, the blood of our most valiant warriors. As long as I am at the palace, no other woman must enter it save as a slave devoted to my caprices and my will. If this English maid be beautiful, am I then become hideous all at once? Am I not also young? Is it at this moment that I am to be forced to quit the palace, to avoid finding myself face to face with an unworthy rival? * * * * * Come, bird of ill-omen, answer me. Think you that Lion Limb really loves this girl?"

"I am ignorant," calmly replied the Unknown. "I have related to you all that I know, and all that I have seen. To reach your presence, I have braved all sorts of fatigues and dangers. I have nothing more to tell you."

"But what motive has led to your acting thus?" impetuously demanded the beautiful Aixa; "is it cupidity that has rendered you so zealous in my service? Would you be rewarded with heaps of gold, or are you only actuated by motives of hatred and vengeance?"

"You would know the truth, madam?" sorrowfully replied the Unknown. "Why should I conceal it from you? I love the girl; that is all my secret. I love her, and it seems to me that I would prefer to see her dead at my feet, than see her become the wife or the favourite of another man, were it even King Katamar himself. Do you believe now in my fidelity? Who else would have exposed himself, for the mere temptation of a reward, to the dangers, sufferings, and insults which I have undergone to obtain admission to your presence? My life is in your hands as a pledge of my words, and if I have deceived you, noble Aixa, it will be easy to punish me."

He had not cast down his eyes before the piercing looks of the favourite, and, satisfied with this scrutiny, she replied,—

"You speak boldly, stranger, but I believe in your sincerity, and I thank you. My uncle," she added, "it must not be that the man who has rendered me this signal service should remain at the palace, liable to be recognised."

"He can remain in the tents, Aixa," said Katamar, "and if we have need of him, he can come immediately."

"It is well," said the proud beauty. "Go, loyal servitor, await my uncle in the garden of the interior court; he will rejoin you directly."

The Unknown bowed respectfully, and withdrew, satified with having implanted in the heart of the favourite suspicions and seeds of hatred.

In the meanwhile, Aixa was left alone with King Katamar, and she then gave free vent to her jealousy and resentment.

"Well, king!" said she. "You have heard! You see the incomprehensible inconstancy of this Lion Limb, whom I love, of whom you, one of the descendants of kings, are only the humble vassal, and by whom I, your niece, am despised! Oh! I am a strange Queen of the Pearl Islands—the toy of caprices. To-day a queen, to-morrow, perhaps, degraded below the women who serve me. Is this, then, the fate to which you destine me, my uncle?"

"Child," replied King Katamar, sorrowfully, "think you because I remain calm during the storm, because I confine my thoughts to myself, instead of suffering them to escape in vain words, that I am, therefore, a coward, and weak-minded, deprived of all power of calculation and prudence? Be patient, and you will be strong."

"Patient! Oh, I have been patient long. When you recognised the sovereignty of Lion Limb, and ordered me to appear with uncovered face before that Christian, that infidel! when you saw him,

with joy declare himself dazzled by my beauty, you required that I should consent to smile upon him, I obeyed, not without anguish and remorse. You thought that I should be able to exercise ascendancy over him. I feigned to forget my family and my name, to think only of him."

"Well, have you not beheld at your feet, gentle and submissive as a child, this youth, who is called so terrible?" said Katamar.

"Yes, and in my humiliation it has been the supreme joy of my heart to see our conqueror, this redoubted Christian, subject his will to the caprices of an Indian maid.

"But how short and fragile has been this empire! How rapidly have my dreams faded away!

"Like you, I hoped that Lion Limb would consent to espouse me, and perhaps secretly abjure the Christian faith, for the sake of securing in you a more faithful ally.

"But all these hopes have been but dreams.

"When I thought I had subdued that heart so haughty and suspicious; when, relying with weak credulity on the appearances of love which he lavished on me, I spoke to him of marriage, he replied by a smile, which was an insult.

"When I spoke to him of abjuration, his countenance crimsoned with formidable anger.

"The slave became again the master!

"It was in a changed and severe voice that he ordered me never to revert to a like subject; adding, that he would pardon me this first outrage, but that he would never tolerate a second. This, my uncle, is what we have gained by the sacrifice which I have made."

"But you have done well to show yourself patient, Aixa," said Katamar. "Misfortune humiliates and casts down the hearts of the proudest. Better days are arising for the children of the islands, thanks to the intestine wars of the Christians. Henceforth it is not for us to supplicate Lion Limb to accept our alliance, as the means of saving us from complete ruin; it is we who accord it to him, as the condition on which the safety of his crown depends. We shall have the right to impose our claims on Lion Limb, and, if he would not have his sceptre shiver in his hands, he will accept them."

"And yet, in this hour of distress, he dares defy me. He dares to bring this miserable English girl into the palace."

"What matters her entering the palace, Aixa, if she must quit it in disgrace directly after? To bind our alliance to Lion Limb, I shall require his secret abjuration, and he will obey. I shall require him to give up to me four islands, and he will give them up. As for this English girl, he will soon forget her. Oh! the hour is arrived for the children of the islands to reconquer what they have lost!"

"And yet," interrupted the Queen of the Pearl Islands, with an air of doubt and incredulity, "if he should not consent to sacrifice, like the apostate Julian, his religion and his country to his revenge?"

"If he should push pride and obstinacy so far as to reject my alliance at the price I set upon it," replied King Katamar, "I would treat with Mungo, and the ambitious buccaneer would welcome my advances with joy."

"We understand each other, uncle; and now I can await Lion Limb with a brow more calm and a heart less disturbed."

Katamar embraced his niece, the young and haughty queen, and withdrew to seek repose beneath the brilliant-coloured tent which his slaves had erected for him in the midst of their camp, near the gate.

The next morning he advanced to meet Lion

Limb, according to information he had received from the Unknown, at the head of two hundred horsemen, and encountered him a few leagues from the town, in company with the beautiful Emma, and escorted only by a few followers.

As to Lion Limb, his bearing was neither downcast nor drooping. Strong in his right, he was calm and haughty. He seemed to forget everything to gaze upon Emma, who had but recently arrived, and whose face was mysteriously concealed under a large brown woollen hood.

When Lion Limb perceived King Katamar and his brilliant squadrons, he made no display of vulgar joy.

He waited till his powerful vassal and ally had dismounted from his horse to render him homage, and then bestowing a satisfied look upon the horsemen, he exclaimed,—

"We rest to-day, noble gentlemen; but if it pleases God, we will shortly issue from these gates to give battle to the bastard Mungo, and his gang, who, I hear, are still laying waste these islands. Allow me to introduce to you, King Katamar, Emma Clarence; she has just arrived from my own settlement, which, I am told, has suffered in my absence from the robbers of the Blue Rock.

King Katamar did not permit himself to hazard the smallest reflection on the subject of the young girl to whom Lion Limb was acting as squire in the same way as if she had been a queen.

When they had dismounted from their horses in the courtyard, Emma said to old Katamar, with a sort of surprise,—

"Queen Aixa has not come to meet me!"

"She awaits you, no doubt," replied the king, "for she desires to see you without witnesses."

At these words, pronounced with significant coldness, Emma stopped, confused and trembling.

But Lion Limb took her by the hand, and leading her forward with gentle violence—

"Come, Emma," said he, "you are no longer a child; fear nothing, I will go with you, trust in me. I will present you to the young Queen Aixa, for I wish to place you under her protection."

They all ascended the steps leading to a little terrace at the top of one of the towers of the palace, a charming retreat, supported by slender columns built upon arches, which seemed suspended over an abyss of azure.

Aixa awaited Lion Limb there with disdainful coldness.

He entered hastily, whilst Emma, intimidated, stopped on the threshold, and advancing towards Aixa—

"I do not return as a conqueror bringing trophies," said Lion Limb, with an expression full of bitterness. "You will have to console an unfortunate victim of treason, whose sword has shivered in his hands before he could make use of it."

"In the chances of war there is nothing but fortune and misfortune," she calmly replied. "But have you returned alone?"

"Oh! I do not yet despair of future good fortune. One, at least, of my allies has remained faithful—your uncle, the generous Katamar. He has not waited for my summons to come to my aid . . . . Thanks to you and to him."

"Is it, then, still on me that you depend, Lion Limb, to raise your courage? Is it still from my eyes you would draw that heroic strength that will either lead to triumph, or conduct you to a glorious end?"

"What mean those strange doubts, Aixa?"

"I will explain them by a single question."

And extending her hand to the threshold where Emma stood trembling in her brown woollen hood, terrified at the severe aspect, and imperious voice of the young queen.

"Who is this woman, Lion Limb?" she demanded.

"This girl," replied Lion Limb, turning pale, while still endeavouring to force a smile, for he felt at what the young queen's suspicions were aiming, "is a lady whom I am going to confide to you, Aixa; she is the daughter of my old captain, a poor child whom I saved from the waves, and whom you will love, will you not?"

"Whom I shall love," abruptly interrupted the beauty, "because you have staked your life and liberty for her."

"Should she, then, have been left to perish?" replied Lion Limb, restraining himself with difficulty.

"But the daughter of your old captain is English," said Aixa, scornfully. "Of what importance to you is the life and honour of a child of the sea? She cannot be my companion; she cannot even dwell in the palace without profaning it."

"Are you, then, a Christian of ancient blood, that you speak with so much arrogance?" said Lion Limb, in a low and angry tone. "I could scarcely understand such harsh language, such haughty sentiments, in the mouth of a noble queen like you, Aixa! Ah! I thought you more merciful."

"And, to love this English maid, you will not require either that she should abjure her faith, will you, Lion Limb?" replied Aixa, with gloomy irony. "But do not, I entreat you, humiliate me by such mean comparisons. Have you forgotten who I am? The daughter of a royal race, you could love me without shame. My love has never been a humiliation to you. Thanks to me, my uncle will defend you, like his own son, against all your enemies. He will spend his last follower for you; but it is on conditions that you, on your side, do not seek to break down by unworthy means, and humble her who has so devotedly loved you," said Aixa, faintly.

"But, really, I do not understand you, Aixa. You speak foolishly. How can I seek to humble you by asking you to grant an asylum and protection to a poor young girl?"

"What need has she of my protection, since she has yours?" angrily demanded the young queen. "Why does she not return to England? Upon what pretext, under what title should she remain at the palace? What means this caprice? Does it signify that I have fallen, and that another woman aspires to achieve the proud title of wife? Be frank, Lion Limb."

"Speak lower, Aixa; calm this causeless anger," said Lion Limb, who feared that this stormy debate should reach the ears of Emma. "I have sworn to watch over this maiden. Besides, in entrusting her to your care, I give the best proof that your suspicions are unfounded."

"What would you have, Lion Limb?" said the young queen, with a sardonic accent. "I love you, and I mistrust the pertinacity with which you endeavour to prove that I am in the wrong; I mistrust this sudden outburst of generosity that you testify for this girl, whose beauty is so much vaunted. I doubt, if she were ill-favoured and ugly, whether it would seem to you so very natural to forget the sacred interests of your crown for a pre-occupation unworthy of you."

"But I swear to you, Aixa," replied Lion Limb, "that you alone have invested my demand with this singular importance."

"So be it. I am willing to believe it, Lion Limb. I was deceived. This Emma is as a stranger to you. Do you wish that I should consent to keep her at the palace? The thing is easy. Let her augment the number of women destined to my service. She shall never quit me. Oh! I promise to watch over her with the solicitude of a sister. She shall fan my forehead. She shall bring my slippers. Do you accept of this? Am I free to dispose of this girl according to my will? Am I to thank you for so rare and precious a present?"

And an insulting laugh accompanied these words of reproach, and her eyes flashed deadly fire.

"There seems no means of making you listen to reason," said Lion Limb. "Can you speak so contemptuously of the daughter of my former captain?"

"How fond you are of his memory since you have begun to admire the beauty of his daughter. What do you say? In exchange for Emma, I promise you to have your coffers filled by my uncle until the defeat of your enemies one and all."

"And will Katamar be able also to prevent the whole of my men from revolting against me?" said Lion Limb, indignantly.

"It is not that fear that hinders you from complying with my wish. You seek in vain to deceive me, Lion Limb. This girl—you love her! *Well, then, woe be to her!*" and as she spoke, her voice hissed in deadly anger!

CHAPTER XCVI.

IN WHICH THE YOUNG QUEEN OF THE PEARL ISLANDS TRIUMPHS.

"THIS is the mere madness of jealously, Aixa. Your anger blinds you!" said Lion Limb, hotly.

"And yours makes you descend so low as to insult a woman! Oh! no, I am not blind. I read too well in your eyes, in your strange embarrassment, in your very irritation, you love this girl more than you ever loved before.

"For her you tremble. You entreat and threaten me by turns; you endeavour to wound me.

"You pretended to love me once, but only with that passion which the southern sun lights up so easily in the veins of the young.

"You liked me because it was something to boast of to have the niece of a king for your favourite.

"But this one," added the young queen, furiously, "you love her as we love but once in our lives, tenderly, doubtingly, distrustingly. To her you sacrifice your pride, to her you would sacrifice the very violence of your passion.

"Your love for her makes you timid.

"Oh! women understand well all the phases of love, and I am sure I am not mistaken.

"The more disinterested is your love, the more real and lasting will it be.

"You found in me a woman who equalled you in pride and energy. You prefer her, a humble girl whom you raise to your own rank, and of whom you would willingly make a queen.

"But have a care, Lion Limb; Aixa is between you, and she will not suffer herself to be ignominiously driven forth!"

"Aixa," said the king, severely, "I will say to you in my turn, 'Be frank!'"

"Lion Limb," exclaimed the favourite, "suffer me only to interrogate this young girl."

Lion Limb seemed powerless to reply.

Aixa advanced towards the threshold, and signed to Emma to approach.

Subjugated by her imperious air, Emma obeyed.

"You know that your companion, Lion Limb, is the king of these islands?" demanded the queen.

"Yes," softly replied Emma.

"He has promised you an asylum in this palace? He has doubtless told you that, after having saved you at the peril of his life, he would continue to protect you? He has told you that his own island did not offer you a sufficiently safe shelter, and you hesitated not to follow him?"

"No, madam; for he who had so nobly devoted himself for a poor girl would be incapable of deceiving me."

"But perhaps you do not know who *I* am, and by what title I have taken upon myself to interrogate you?" continued the favourite, whom the gentleness of Emma served but to irritate.

"No; but since Lion Limb confides me to you, it must be because he knows you to be good and generous, and my gratitude will be shared between you and him."

In place of being disarmed by these expressions of humble confidence, Aixa replied in an accent of cutting irony—

"Oh! Lion Limb forgot to mention me! I understand! Well, then, you must hear the truth from *my* lips. I am called Aixa, the favourite niece of King Katamar, Lion Limb's most faithful ally.

"It has been somewhat bold of you to enter this palace where I still reign! *I* love Lion Limb, and I desire not that he should love any other woman but *me*. It is for him, therefore, to choose between us!"

Terrified by this unexpected provocation, Emma Clarence trembled from head to foot.

Then stepping a few paces back, she raised her supplicating eyes to Lion Limb, saying as she did so—

"Have you brought me to this palace to allow me to be insulted? What have I done to merit such cruel outrages?"

"What have you done!" exclaimed the young queen, seeing Lion Limb indignantly rush towards the daughter of his old captain; "why, at this very moment, your insolence betrays you. You forget your feigned resignation to appeal to the wrath of Lion Limb, whose aid you invoke against me.

"You ask what you have done," she continued, approaching Emma; "you love Lion Limb—there lies your crime. Attempt not to deny it. Your lips would refuse the falsehood."

And snatching away Emma's veil, with a sudden gesture—

"Yes, you are fair, fairer than I could have believed," said she, regarding her with eager curiosity. "*Hope not, therefore, that I shall pardon you!* You have crossed my path, and *I shall crush you like a worm beneath my feet!* Your beauty will not avail, for in your pale and disturbed countenance, and heartrending sobs, I read the story of your love."

Lion Limb, choking with surprise and anger, had at first been unable to interrupt her, but at length seizing her roughly by the arm, and separating her from Emma Clarence,

"Aixa!" he exclaimed, "your conduct is infamous; I asked of you an asylum and protection for the daughter of my old captain, and you have mercilessly striven to crush beneath the weight of your hatred and pride this girl who cannot defend herself. Oh, do not abuse my patience further."

"So be it," said the young queen; "make no further attempt at concealment, Lion Limb. Confess openly that you love this girl, and defend her as we defend those whom we love. Fear not that I shall dispute your heart with the daughter of the old captain. I yield to this noble and triumphant beauty. You, at least, my uncle, will not abandon me. Together we will quit this island to return to my own, and we will leave the bright eyes of Emma to defend Lion Limb."

"Aixa!" murmured Lion Limb, with a bitter smile, "this is then your respect for me."

At the moment when the queen and Katamar were directing their steps towards the door, a messenger appeared at the threshold.

"My lord," said he to Lion Limb, "the banners of Mungo are already floating on the plain."

"Let all the gates be closed, the drawbridges raised, and let every man capable of bearing arms hurry to the ramparts!" proudly replied Lion Limb, striving to dissimulate his anxiety.

Emma Clarence trembled violently at the first announcement of the enemy's approach.

But her resolution was soon taken on seeing the alteration on Lion Limb's countenance, who could not lose, without deep regret and mortification, his last ally.

Emma advanced towards Aixa, and humbly knelt before her to bar her passage.

"Let me pass," said the young queen, in a harsh voice.

"Trample me beneath your feet, but hear me!" said Emma, in an accent of bitter entreaty. "I humble myself before you. I will do all you order. Dispose of me as you will. I will not rise until you have pardoned me. Those who told you that Lion Limb loved me have deceived you. I am ready to go away. If terror had not prevented my speaking, I should have told you so at first. How should a king love a poor girl? Kings have too much ambition in their hearts to descend so. Oh! I implore you, madam, do not abandon him; do not see him delivered up to his enemies!"

"Look, now, how you love him, unfortunate, since you humble yourself to me on his behalf," said the proud young queen, in derision.

"No, I love him not," said Emma, in a plaintive voice, and embracing the knees of Aixa, without daring to cast a look upon Lion Limb, in whose heart a fierce combat was waging, and whose impassioned looks were fixed upon her kneeling form. "He saved me because he has a brave and generous heart, and not because he loved me. And as for me, does it prove that I love him because I am grateful for so signal a service?"

"Well," replied Aixa, in a low voice, "rise, then. If Lion Limb suffers you to depart, if he seek not to detain you, I will remain at the palace, and my uncle will fight for him!"

Emma rose.

"My lord and king," said she, addressing Lion Limb, "at the moment of a terrible struggle my place is not here. I will return to some calm abode, where, far away from the tumult of arms, I may pray for the success of your cause."

Lion Limb hesitated for an instant whether he should detain her at the palace, at the risk of losing the support of Katamar.

But he heard the flourish of cymbals in the court, and his thoughts reverted to Mungo.

Aixa, who was observing him, signed to Emma to withdraw.

When the cymbals had ceased sounding, Lion Limb, without casting a look upon Aixa, without addressing a single word to her, descended, accompanied by King Katamar, and when they had gained the court, he only broke silence to say to his Indian ally—

"Let us go and visit the ramparts; I have dearly bought the right to defend your domain."

"Alas!" sighed Emma, when she had retired from the gorgeous apartment, "I was never worthy to be beloved by such a noble youth as Lion Limb, and at this moment would I willingly die, for— *I have lost him for ever!*"

CHAPTER XCVII.

THE MIDNIGHT MEETING—THE OLD NURSE— MR. SHARP PAYS THE NURSE AN UNEXPECTED VISIT.

THICK grey clouds, driven hurriedly along by the sharp north wind, floated rapidly across the face of the heavens,

And, as the moon sunk in the horizon, she covered the fantastic edges of the broken clouds with a bright silvery glow, whilst above numerous bright stars glittered and sparkled in the dark azure of the firmament.

The irregular mass of Oxenford House, with its gable ends, high chimneys with their whimsical supporters, stood out in bold relief against the clear transparency of the midnight sky, while an alley of evergreen pines raised their pointed and sombre-looking heads above the garden-walls.

The waters of the Thames, swollen by the rains of winter, dashed heavily on the shore, and by their mournful murmurs seemed replying to the prolonged whistling of the northerly breeze.

Save the rush of troubled waters, and the loud swelling wind, all was silent in this part of London.

Midnight had just sounded from the distant cathedral clock, when a carriage stopped at the door of Oxenford House.

A person wearing a large slouched hat, and wrapped in a cloak, descended from the carriage, and opened a small side-door of the garden.

Immediately afterwards, Lady Oxenford entered the garden.

Her ladyship, with a rapid step, traversed the long alley of pines which led to one of the wings of the mansion.

From time to time, the clear moonbeams, struggling through the thick branches of the trees, chequered the ground with patches of light, and displayed the singular effect produced by the figure of her ladyship, as she flitted along in her dark, floating drapery, beneath the alternations of light and darkness.

The extreme ceremony always kept up in such princely dwellings, the exactions of full dress and etiquette, with the immense number of servants of all ranks, perpetually hurrying to and fro on their respective duties, left the occupant of these mansions so little at liberty during the day, that they were generally reduced to the necessity of availing themselves of nocturnal expeditions to effect any important business.

Thus, then, there will not appear anything inconsistent with the custom of the period we are treating of in her ladyship's pausing as she reached the left wing of the mansion, opening a small door concealed amongst a clump of trees, and lightly ascending a narrow, winding staircase, which quickly brought her to a large ante-room, leading to her sleeping apartment.

Scarcely had she entered than she threw herself into an easy chair, as though exhausted with fatigue.

During this time, the individual who had followed her, carefully bolted and secured the door conducting to the secret staircase, then, throwing off the large hat and cloak, discovered a female form.

It was not Baron Templeton.

It was his messenger, the old nurse, Dorothy Dale.

Her ladyship, meanwhile, after a momentary languor and apparent depression of spirits, tore off her hood, then, abruptly rising, unfastened the girdle of her dress, which she threw on the ground, and trampled upon with rage.

Beneath the outer garment so rudely treated, her ladyship wore a black robe, with short sleeves, thus revealing arms, shoulders, and bust, worthy of the classic beauty of a Diana.

Her countenance, so proud, while conversing with the baron, was now agitated by a whirlwind of the most stormy passions.

Her eyes glittered like dark diamonds.

Standing erect before the large glass which surmounted the chimney-piece, she appeared as desirous of crushing the marble mantel-piece with the convulsive pressure of her clenched hands.

Wholly absorbed by the stormy passions which raged within her, she heeded not her old companion.

And a more singular old person could not be seen.

A deep brown, resembling the hue of bronze, tinged her colourless cheek.

Her thick grey hair was cut short, curled, and parted on the forehead, after the fashion of many of the male sex, who in the present day wear their hair of an almost feminine length.

Her old but regular features, had an undaunted and almost masculine expression.

And when she unclosed her thin lips, she displayed a set of teeth, white enough, indeed, but standing at wide distances from each other.

This singular old female was nearly as tall as Lady Oxenford, but old and decrepid. She wore a dress of black silk, with a small handkerchief of the same material tied around her throat, and an old-fashioned cap.

Dressed in a large flapped hat, and wrapped in a cloak, the female we are describing might easily pass for one of the opposite sex.

Perceiving the deep reverie into which Lady Oxenford had fallen, she said,—

"Child, it is very late, you must go to bed."

"I have seen him!" exclaimed her ladyship, impetuously. "He may be my ruin!" continued she, turning with flashing eyes towards the old nurse.

"Whom have you seen, child?" inquired the old woman, terrified at the wildness and desperation of Lady Oxenford's manner.

"Allan Norman!"

"What! impossible, my lady!" said the old woman, in astonishment.

"'Tis too true; and the baron also I saw last night."

"I know it, my lady; and he sent me here to keep his appointment in order to comfort you, but I don't think it possible you could have seen the *other*," remarked the old nurse.

"I tell you I saw him; and, oh, it was he too surely! and as surely does the presence of this youth portend some fresh misfortune to me, for I am watched by a detective day and night."

"I do not know this man who you say is watching you, child, or why you hate him so inveterately; but I, too, hate him with my bitterest scorn, because you have already told me that he occasions you great sorrow."

As old Dorothy pronounced the words, "I know not why you hate him so inveterately," she could not repress a slight shudder, which, however, passed unnoticed by Lady Oxenford.

"You ask me wherefore I hold him in such detestation?" cried her ladyship, almost wildly.

"I said so but from curiosity, child. But, if you hate, you would also be avenged."

"Avenged! Oh, yes, I would have vengeance great and startling as the ill he would do me."

"If I can serve you, speak."

"You!"

"Command, and I obey. Old Dorothy is yours—yours in all things; her life depends on yours—her breath is as your breath—she sees with but your eyes—she has no will but yours."

Without replying, Lady Oxenford extended her beautiful hand to old Dorothy, who raised it to her old lips with an expression of respect and devotion; then, suddenly springing up, she exclaimed,—

"Gracious Heaven, child! your hand is cold as death!—you shiver, too! You must go to bed—indeed you must—you are very ill."

"I am not; listen to me. I know not what occasions within me the foreboding that young Allan is the certain precursor of great perils and dangers to myself. Your services may, probably, be more needful to me than ever,—you do not know all, nurse, or how I became such a miserable woman, or, as they would call it, an unnatural mother. Listen to my sorrowful tale, and tell me if you have still some pity to bestow on me; but do not wonder why I hate Lord Oxenford, for, but yesterday I learned the truth of the terrible tale I am about to unfold.

"You know not of it, Dorothy, but years since, before my marriage, I left to go to Florence with my Aunt Vasari, and Gianetta, our waiting-maid."

"I remember it well. Your maid, Gianetta, whispered as much."

"That Gianetta was very inquisitive, indiscreet, and faithless. I fear I kept her in my service too long.

"At the end of six months," resumed her ladyship, "I returned to Paris.

"My Aunt Vasari," continued her ladyship, "went to Florence to attend to a lawsuit she had there. She went out every day, being able, as she thought, to influence her judges. In the evening we went out for a walk, and there I frequently met a Frenchman named M. Brevannes. He was very soon my constant shadow; his pursuit of me became incessant and troublesome, and from that time my indifference was changed to aversion."

"Was he a man likely to cause such a sentiment?"

"Why do you ask?" inquired her ladyship, scrutinising the old woman's features; then adding, "Yes, you may have heard of my cousin, Raphael, the son of my father's brother?"

Dorothy imperceptibly contracted her eyebrows, and replied in a short manner—

"Yes; each time he returned from sea he went to pass his leisure at Paris. Isn't he in the East? Have you had any news of him lately?"

"He is dead," said Lady Oxenford, with desperate calmness.

"Raphael dead!" exclaimed Dorothy, with feigned astonishment.

"Charles Brevannes killed him."

"And your aunt is ignorant of this?" asked Dorothy.

"Listen—the hour is come to disclose everything to you. I had been, as you know, brought up with Raphael. When a child, I loved him as a brother; as a young girl, as my betrothed husband; or, rather, these two sentiments united themselves into one."

"Is it possible—is Raphael dead? And when and where did this happen?"

"Listen. I was to have been married to him. You may now comprehend why M. Brevannes inspired me with so much aversion."

"I understand."

"His pursuit of me redoubled. Informed of our residence in Florence, he, by dint of perseverance and encouragement, contrived to form a connection with those persons who would be of so much service to my aunt in her process, and obtained such influence with them, that he was very soon in a position to be of the greatest possible use to us.

"His way thus cleared, he one day boldly announced himself at my aunt's, under the plea of lodging in the same hotel.

"Our reception of him was very chilling, but the man very soon proved himself so insinuating, such a flatterer, and so clearly showed my aunt how greatly he could aid the progress of her suit, that she begged him to visit us as frequently as he pleased.

"As he left the room, he cast at me a very significant look. He had only done this in order to be able to approach me.

"I told my aunt all my suspicions, and her reply was that I was crazy; that it was requisite we should avail ourselves of M. Brevannes' kind offices, since he could be so advantageous to us.

"You know my aunt had been very handsome, and at this time she was only forty years of age.

"M. Brevannes saw one day that she took in earnest some little gallantries which he addressed to her in jest.

"He increased his attentions, so that, in a very short time, she could really not do without him.

"He accompanied us everywhere, walking, or to the theatre. I remarked to my aunt that he was young and rich, and that this intimacy might compromise me.

"She then told me, with as much joy as pride, that I was quite wrong to alarm myself. She was a widow and free; M. Brevannes had avowed his love for her, adding that he only took so deep an interest in our law-suit because it gave him an opportunity of being so constantly near her.

"He saw us every day, often sent minstrels under our windows, and continually presented us with similar bouquets, in order (as he told my aunt) that my self-love might not be wounded.

"One day, finding me alone, he made me a declaration of love, considering as a merit in my eyes the ability with which he had deceived my aunt."

"And was your aunt informed of this avowal of Charles Brevannes?"

"That very evening he was told all."

"Then he was unmasked?"

"You do not comprehend the weakness and vanity of women!"

"What! she would not believe you?"

"Yes, at first; and that same evening our door was closed against M. Brevannes. He guessed the fact, and wrote a long letter to my aunt. The very next day he was received even more kindly than usual.

"Unhappy woman! she was mad!"

"Matters resumed their usual course. Charles Brevannes did not utter one other word of love to me, but he passed whole days with us. On the 13th of April my aunt said to me, after breakfast, that the noise of the court-yard of the hotel disturbed her so much, that she would, from that evening, change apartments with me. My room looked into the street, and had a balcony. What I have to add is fearful. That day we had been out for a long drive in the carriage, accompanied by M. Brevannes. On our return we sat together until very late in the evening, my aunt appearing very much preoccupied. At length he retired, and I went to bed."

Her ladyship turned horribly pale, shuddered, and then continued, in a broken voice—

"The next morning, I wished to go, as usual, to wish my aunt good morning, when Gianetta, with an embarrassed air, told me that madame could not see me.

"At the moment I was returning towards my own apartment, a stranger inquired for me, and a dark, pale man, handed me a letter, without uttering a syllable. I knew not why, but a tremor ran through my veins. I opened the letter—it enclosed a ring which I had given to Raphael."

"And the letter, child, the letter?"

"Was from Raphael, who was dying."

"From Raphael?"

"Yes, and contained these words which seemed to be written in characters of blood:—

"'I have been here for two days. I know all. This very night I saw Brevannes descending from your balcony, after which you closed the window. I fought with him instantly, as we both agreed. I sought death, and he has given it to me. Be thou accursed! My sight is——'

"And nothing more," added Madam, with agonising expression, "nothing but some letters."

"What a mystery!" said old Dorothy, clasping her hands. "Who, then, could have appeared at your chamber window?"

"Have I not told you that my aunt had occupied the chamber that very evening which I had before slept in? No doubt Charles Brevannes had obtained a rendezvous from her in order to serve his wicked designs; you will see how. She is my height—dark as I am; and thus was Raphael fatally deceived."

"Oh! how horrible!"

"After I had read this letter I was almost mad. I believed I was in a dream. I learned the rest but yesterday. Raphael, on his return from a voyage to Constantinople, had reached Venice. He only passed a day in that city, but, misled by some abominable calumny which had reached thither, he left that city suddenly with his valet, to whom he said,—

"'They tell me that my cousin has betrayed me shamefully; if that be true, I will kill my rival or he shall kill me.'"

"But who could thus have slandered you?"

"How do I know?"

"That is very strange."

"The attentions of M. Brevannes, explained by shameful scandal, had compromised me most fatally. I passed as his mistress, and, when Raphael inquired concerning me, I was accused by one common voice. However, determined not to be misled by appearances, he had gone straight to M. Brevannes, and told him of his love for me, and that we were betrothed, that young girls being frequently giddy and coquettish, without being culpable, and that the world was slanderous,—and then entreating M. Brevannes, in the name of honour, not to conceal the truth, and, whatever it was, he would believe it."

"And Charles Brevannes?"

"Far from being touched by this language, he treated Raphael with scorn, and said to him,—

"'Since you have watched your cousin for two days, you must know which is her chamber.'"

"'I know it; for, without being perceived by her, this very morning I saw her in the balcony.'"

"'Well, be this night at three o'clock in front of that balcony, and you shall have my reply.'

"You know the rest."

"Brevannes then said insolently to Raphael, 'Are you satisfied?'"

"In his rage, Raphael struck him in the face."

"A duel was to ensue at break of day."

THE BOY KING
OF THE SOUTH SEA ISLANDS.

MUNGO CAPTURES THE SPY.

"And the duel?" asked Dorothy, with a quivering lip.

"Ended fatally," said Lady Oxenford; "Raphael received his death wound, and all through the hate and vengeance of Brevannes."

For some time neither spoke.

Lady Oxenford wept.

Old Dorothy looked very solemnly at the fire, and at last asked rather timidly, "And who was the instigator of all this fearful detail of deceit and blood?"

"My husband, Lord Oxenford," replied her ladyship, reddening up to the temples.

"You cannot mean what you say, your ladyship?"

"I do, though."

"But what motive could he have had, then?"

"Jealousy. Deep and bitter enmity."

"Perhaps love also, your ladyship."

"*Love!* LOVE!" said Lady Oxenford, scornfully, "breathe not the word."

After a pause, she added slowly and calmly, "I tell you that M. Brevannes was only a *tool* in the hands of his lordship."

"Indeed."

"Lord Oxenford had professed marriage to me before the sad occurrence of which I speak, and had been rejected by me. He then formed the design to ruin me if possible through the exertions of this Brevannes, but did not succeed. For more than two years after this, his lordship followed me and persecuted me with his constant protestations; and *having met with a misfortune of which you may be aware*," said her ladyship, "I at last consented to marry him, and have ever since been miserable beyond all expression."

"And his lordship, you say, was the occasion of Raphael's death?"

"I do. But yesterday I found his private desk unlocked. Woman like, I was prompted by great curiosity, and then discovered the whole of the correspondence which had passed between him and the wretch, Brevannes; but revenge will come sooner or later," said her ladyship, sternly; and waving her hand, old Dorothy left the apartment and trudged off home, filled with all manner of strange thoughts.

"I fear me," said old Dorothy, "that as blood has already been shed, it will not be the last; for if Lord Oxenford knew all—ah, dear me, these big grand people in the world are terribly tried and in a thousand ways that we poor folk know nothing about."

* * * * *

Old Dorothy had not been very long home before she paid her attentions to a gin bottle and went to bed, where she had horrible dreams about duels, kidnapping, murders, robbers, and a thousand other terrible things, so that next morning she awoke with a violent headache (no doubt the effects of mixing gin with beer), and remained at home all day.

When evening came, old Dorothy cleared up her little parlour in Barbican, where she resided, and was about to commence to do a little knitting, when a knock was heard at the door.

The door was opened, and Mr. Sharp entered with a bow.

Dorothy of course did not know the inspector, who was disguised, nor had she any idea of what he wanted.

Mr. Sharp took a chair, and after making a few remarks about the weather and other ordinary topics, he said,

"You will excuse me, Dorothy, but I wish to be a friend to you."

"To me, sir?"

"Yes, you."

"How, might I ask? to do any odd jobs, to go out cleaning, or anything of that sort?"

"No, Mrs. Dale, nothing of the sort."

"What then, sir?"

"Suppose I send out for some beer, and we'll talk the matter over together."

"I seldom or never drinks beer," said Dorothy, "I always prefer a drop o' gin."

"Well, then, we'll have a drop of both," said Sharp; "the gin for you and the porter for me."

"With all my heart, sir, and thank you kindly."

A little girl in the house was sent for the beer and spirits, and after Dorothy had had a couple of glasses, she become very talkative and seemed to enjoy Mr. Sharp's company very much.

"So you mean to say you know me, eh, Mr. Jones?" (the name Sharp chose to go by.)

"Of course I do, for these many years past."

"Deary me; how wonderful to be sure. Why, I haven't lived here very long."

"I know you have not."

"And how do *you* know, pray?" asked Dorothy, whose curiosity was aroused.

"Know? Ah! well, you see I *do* know, Mrs. Dale," said Sharp, smiling. "You lived a few months ago in a small cottage at Ealing."

"Lor' bless the man, so I did; but how did *you* know that?"

"How did I get to know that you passed several hours last night at Oxenford House?"

"At Oxenford House! Me! why you must be mistaken, sir."

"I am not. And more than that you had a long chat with her ladyship."

"Well, and so I did; but who told you? You ain't a detective officer, are you?"

"*Me* a detective officer! Nonsense," said Sharp, "do I look like one?"

"Well, no; leastways I don't think you are."

"I am glad you think so."

"You know I don't much like them sneaking, prying, tale-telling detectives, you know. Not that *I* care about them, you know."

"Oh! of course not, Dorothy; you are right. All *honest* people trouble themselves but little about detectives. It is only rogues and vagabonds who *do* care about them."

"Jest so, Mr. Jones; and, if you don't mind, I'll jest trouble you to pour out another glass of gin, for my poor stomach *does* ache so; it's the rheumatiz, I think."

Sharp poured out the gin as desired, and Dorothy, having swallowed it, the officer said—

"You have an excellent memory, Mrs. Dale?"

"Well, yes, pretty tidy."

"Could you recal now any event that happened seventeen or eighteen years ago?"

"Why, yes; let me see, the winter seventeen years ago was a very hard one."

"So it was."

"The way I remember it was, because I remember when Mr. English, the good, kind-hearted, old merchant was elected alderman of Eastcheap."

"Exactly. I suppose you knew the old gentleman, then?"

"Oh! yes; I used to do odd jobs in charing at his house and offices."

"Did you though?"

"Yes; and a very good, kind, charitable old man he were. The poor had always a good friend in him. He never sent anyone away hungry if he could help it."

"He had no family?"

"No; but he dearly loved children, though."

"Did he, indeed?"

"Yes."

"How do you know?"

"Know! why, of course I knew. Who had a better right to know than I had?"

The gin was now beginning to work on old Dorothy, and her tongue ran wildly, the two very things Mr. Sharp much desired.

"Oh, I didn't wish to contradict you, Mrs. Dale."

"Then don't."

"But you said old Alderman English was very fond of children, and you had good reason to know it."

"And so I have. But what right have *you* to

ask me so many questions about the old alderman's affairs? I don't know you, sir."

"No, perhaps not; but if you answer all my questions I will make it worth your while."

"How do you mean? The old man is dead."

"Yes; but he left a will."

"A will! did he though?"

"Yes; and you, I fancy, was mentioned in it."

"Mercy on me! you don't say so."

"I do, though; but I am not quite certain. He left some money for two boys that he adopted."

"Two boys! Did you hear their names?"

"No; if I did, I forget them."

"Was it anything like Norman?"

"Yes."

"Allan and Edgar Norman?"

"Yes; you are right."

"Poor children," said old Dorothy, turning very red.

And to drown her rising feelings she drank more gin.

"And so he left money to 'em, eh?"

"Yes; so I have heard."

"I remember the lads well, and fine bonny children they were. I remember 'em both well. They used to take to me like a mother."

"Oh, indeed."

"Yes; the poor creatures were left at the alderman's in a basket one snowy night. The old gentleman took them in, and behaved like a Christian to the poor mites."

"It was rather a mysterious affair," said Sharp.

"Yes, and so it were."

"You never could learn anything about them, I suppose?"

"No; at least, the alderman never could; but I did though."

"Oh, indeed."

"Yes; but I didn't tell the old alderman, for I thought it would be a pity to take the two babes away from such a nice home."

"Perhaps it would."

"I did hear, though," said Dorothy, taking another drop of gin, "that they were the children of a young lady who was going to marry a lord; and she put 'em out to nurse with an old charwoman. But the old woman got tired of 'em, and placed them at the alderman's door, and years after made the mother believe they were dead."

"You seem to know all about it."

"I do; leastways, more than most people."

"And what did the old alderman do with them?"

"He engaged me to look after 'em, which I did at ten shillings a week, and my board and lodging, for more than six years."

And I dare say now that the wicked old nurse who had placed them at the alderman's door still continued to draw money regularly from the mother?"

"Yes, I hear she did; but she never saw the mother or the father either for years, but received her money through the post, and thus made a good thing of it."

"How much did the mother allow for the support of the children?"

"One pound a week, so I've heard."

"I shouldn't wonder, now," said Sharp, looking fixedly at old Dorothy, "if the old nurse didn't save her money and buy a house or two with it."

"What do you mean, Mr. Jones?" said Mrs. Dale, looking very nervous.

"I mean that she might have bought a nice cottage at Ealing, and a house or two in Barbican."

"Really, Mr. Jones, you put me all into a fluster, that you do."

"Why so?"

"You look so hard at me."

"Do I?"

"Yes, in truth you do. You begin to look more like a detective every minute."

"I am one, Mrs. Dale."

"You? Gracious goodness! if I didn't think so. Get out of my house immediately. What business have you here? Begone, sir! I say I'll not speak another word. You are only pumping me, that's all; and I'm as innocent as the day is long, that I am. I don't know anything about the two brats, nor never did. Drat the gin! it was that which made me open my mouth—dash it!"

And old Dorothy began to cough and weep and sigh and moan in a dreadful way.

"Come, come, Mrs. Dale, don't take on so. I hope there is no harm done."

"No; but there may be. You didn't come here to give me half a pint of Old Tom for nothing, you sneaking hypocrite! Get out of my house, I say, or I'll raise the whole neighbourhood, that I will."

"If you are not very quiet, old gal," said Sharp, curtly, "I'll call in an officer and march you off to the station house, mind that. I have had my eye on you a long time, Dorothy."

Mr. Sharp's manner was so cool and determined that it quite sobered old Dorothy, who wiped her eyes, and asked—

"What do you want of me, then?"

"Tell me the whole truth about these boys, then, and answer all the questions I shall put to you truthfully and candidly. No lies, mind; or it will be the worse for you."

Old Dorothy tried to compose herself, but could not.

She seemed to be sitting on thorns and thistles.

Sometimes she sighed and sobbed, and then, to speak the plain truth, she would rave and swear in a frantic manner.

She felt she had got into the clutches of a man who was very powerful, and she doubted much if, after all she might disclose to him, he would use his influence in her behalf.

At last, when she was calm and collected, and had taken a large glass of gin to screw her courage up to the sticking point, she crossed her old withered arms, and looked grimly at her interrogator, who said, producing his note book and pencil—

"You were the party who placed those children at the alderman's; don't deny it."

Dorothy nodded revengefully, and her old cap frills shook menacingly at the officer.

"And you received money regularly both from the old alderman and the parents of the children?"

"Well; and if I did, they knew nothing about it; and a good thing I did. Who wouldn't? They were rich and I was very poor. I think I acted very wisely. It helped me to give my only son an education, and fit him out for sea."

"And much good that did either you or him. He turned a rogue and vagabond, and was lost."

"So he was, but that's no matter. It has nothing to do with you I hope?"

"It only shows, Dorothy, that ill-gotten wealth nearly always sows the seeds of evil instead of good."

"You are very wise I daresay, Mr. Jones."

"My name is Sharp—Inspector Sharp, Mrs. Dale. Disguises of any sort are useless now between you and me."

Old Dorothy bit her lips in anger, and screwed up her mouth in mental pain.

If she could have done so, Mrs. Dale would very willingly have strangled Mr. Sharp.

"You know the mother of these boys, Mrs. Dale?"

"Do I? Oh! indeed, you are very clever, I dare-say; but who told you so?"

"I know all about it."

"If so, then why question me?"

"That's *my* business."

"If you say I do, of course I do."

"She is the present Lady Oxenford."

"Well, yes, so she is."

"And the father——"

"I never saw."

"Are you sure?"

"I am, on my oath."

"Have you any notion or idea of who or what he is?"

"Not the slightest."

"But you were present at the birth of these two boys."

"No I wasn't."

"Yes you were. Tell no lies!" said Sharp, sternly.

"How do *you* know?"

"You have no right to ask. They were born in this very house—in this very room. You were only a lodger then, now you are the landlady."

"I am; what you say is right."

"And who was the doctor?"

"I don't know."

"Yes you do. Didn't you engage him! Wasn't he paid a very large sum, which you divided between you? Didn't he turn to drink and become a profligate?"

"I don't know."

"You do know. What was his name?"

"Well, suppose it don't matter now; the doctor is dead long ago, so I hear."

"But his name?"

"Dr. Killum, if you *must* know."

"I thought so; but you are mistaken, Dorothy, the doctor is *not* dead."

"You don't mean that."

"I do though; and I could lay my hand on him any time, if I wanted him."

"I don't see what reason you can have for asking so many questions about two brats of illegitimate children," said Dorothy, in a sneering manner.

"They are *not* illegitimate, Mrs. Dale."

"How can you prove it?"

"I can do so at any moment I think proper; but that matter as to when or how rests with me."

"Are they entitled to anything then?"

"Yes, a great deal. They are lawfully heirs to title and great possessions, but as yet the whole matter is shrouded in mystery; but you will be one of the principal witnesses in the case when it is called up in the court, and, therefore, I would advise you to say nothing until you are called upon to do so. If you should be so unwise as to go babbling about this matter—if you dare whisper a word of what I have said to you to Lady Oxenford—it will go badly with you; instead of rewards, you may expect nothing better than punishment."

So speaking, Mr. Sharp left Dorothy, who felt more dead than alive, and directly he had gone, she burst out into a wild flood of tears and fierce imprecations.

CHAPTER XCVIII.

THE QUEEN OF THE PEARL ISLANDS RESOLVES TO KILL EMMA CLARENCE—THE INDIGNATION OF HARRY WOODRUFF, WHO DISCOVERS ALL.

WHILE Lion Limb and his followers went forth, in all their strength, to give battle to Mungo in the plain, Aixa, the proud, haughty young queen of the Pearl Islands—who was staying at the house of old Canbool, King Katamar's treasurer—sat brooding over various plans for the destruction of Emma Clarence.

She thought of many devilish schemes, but, at last, beckoned to old Canbool, and whispered in his ear.

The old man turned pale, but, bowing, promised to obey the young queen's commands, and retired.

He soon found Emma, and entered into conversation with her about Lion Limb.

"I fear not King Lion Limb, for he has a loyal heart," said Emma; "he will never abuse his power over a poor girl who loves him, but who would prefer death to shame. I envy not the title of favourite, and the proud Aixa does wrong to fear me."

"Well said," cried the treasurer. "May the blessing of Heaven, and that of thy father, descend upon thee!"

Then rising, he opened the door which led to an interior gallery.

He there saw servants, who had laid a table there, and were covering it with dishes, on which smoked a quarter of lamb, chick-peas, an olla podrida, baskets piled with pomegranates and oranges, silver-necked bottles of wine, and porous earthen jars containing snow-water fresh and cold as ice.

"Wherefore this royal feast?" demanded the astounded treasurer of his servants.

"It is the repast ordered for the English captain, Harry Woodruff," replied the servants.

"Moses preserve us! There is enough upon this table to ruin any honest house. But, however great a glutton this captain may be, he can never consume such a considerable supply of provisions. Let us see; hand over a few fragments of this feast. My frame is exhausted with fatigue, and I should not be sorry to know if the cheer we are offering to this brave cut-throat be worthy of him!"

The servant hastened to obey, and the treasurer pressed Emma to share his repast.

But the latter contented herself with peeling a pomegranate out of complaisance, whilst the old man made astonishing havoc in the viands accumulated for the use of Harry Woodruff.

All at once he seemed listening to some distant sound, and exclaimed—

"I fancy I heard some one knocking at the gates. Run and see. Can it be the English captain already?"

And while an old servant hastened to descend, he added—

"Look out a moment, Emma, from the top of the gallery, and see if I am not mistaken."

The young girl, whose heart beat violently, flew towards the gallery.

She had no sooner disappeared, than the old treasurer drew from the pocket of his long robe a flask containing a red liquor, and hastily poured a few drops into a goblet filled with wine, destined for Emma.

Emma shortly returned, and said—

"You were mistaken, sir."

"Probably. But how pale you are, child! You

scem unwell. If you would not appear like a poor victim stricken with fear, drink a mouthful of this generous wine, which warms and rejoices the heart."

"If you wish it," said Emma, "I will."

And she mechanically raised the cup to her lips; while, thinking that she was soon again to see Lion Limb, an involuntary joy took possession of her soul.

She listened with feverish agitation for the sound of the footsteps of Harry.

Confused pictures intermingled in her brain.

Her eyes closed in spite of herself, and her senses grew benumbed with a strange torpor.

She seemed to behold in a dream Lion Limb repulsing Aixa.

The old man observed her with anxiety.

Suddenly she let her head fall on her breast, as if overpowered by an unnatural slumber.

Then she strove to struggle against the unknown power that assailed her, and her trembling lips murmured—

"Have pity on me! Whence comes this lassitude? My heart freezes. My eyes grow dim."

She stretched out her arms towards the old man.

She strove to rise, but almost immediately fell back, exhausted and fainting.

"Oh! my God! I am struck with a mortal coldness. Am I then going to die? To die without seeing him once more—to die without one last prayer to Heaven? It is Aixa who would prevent me from seeing Lion Limb again. Father! father! I die! Aixa—oh! cruel——!"

And after having thus struggled vainly against this implacable slumber, she lay extended, cold and pale, upon the divan.

"Good!" said the old treasurer, bending over Emma, with a strange mixture of uneasiness and joy. "My narcotic has produced all the effect I intended. This sleep, the image of death, should last twelve hours. I have time, then, to prepare everything to save Emma from the dishonour that awaited her at the palace, and for the death that would perhaps be reserved for her by the hand of her rival, Aixa. Now to complete my work."

He then began to utter piercing cries, enough to alarm the whole neighbourhood; and when the old servants came hurrying in, all trembling with fear, they found their master tearing his beard, beating his breast, rending his garments, and uttering lamentable groans over the body of Emma Clarence.

All stood terrified in the presence of this sudden and unlooked-for misfortune; one, a poor Indian woman, could find neither tears nor sobs to express her grief, on contemplating the sweet and lovely Emma, cold, inanimate, dead! She fell on her knees and kissed her cold hands, while a convulsive shudder shook her frame.

Absorbed and stupefied by her grief and consternation, she heard not the cries and hubbub of the neighbours, who were knocking at the gate fit to burst it in.

"Open the door," said the old treasurer, in a faint voice.

The Indian woman rose as if moved by a mechanical spring, and although her legs tottered under her, went and opened the door to the friends of the treasurer, who rushed hastily into the house; and who, according to the custom, sought only to console their neighbour by adding to his lamentations their own cries and frantic howlings.

Meantime, the hour appointed for his meeting with Aixa, Harry Woodruff, and others was approaching. He ordered his servants to array the dead in her winding-sheet; and when the Indian woman had executed this order with mechanical obedience, he, assisted by his neighbours, bore the body of Emma down into the vault of his house, and placed it on a funeral bier which stood ready prepared for its tenant, with the face turned towards the east.

He then re-ascended with his friends, who, by look and gesture, silently bade him adieu, and finding himself alone,—for the faithful Indian woman had remained below to keep watch to the last moment over Emma Clarence—he seated himself cross-legged on the threshold of the vestibule, after having sprinkled with ashes his head, his beard, and his rent garments, despair imprinted on his countenance, and his eyes red, as if with weeping.

Night was come.

A torch, fixed to one of the pillars of the vestibule, threw a flickering and funereal light upon the door, which stood wide open, and in front of which a watchman was installed to invite the passers-by to cast upon the threshold a handful of ashes taken from the urn which he held in his hand.

Four personages, carefully enveloped in heavy cloaks, met at the same time at the door of the old treasurer.

At the sight of the old man, a dismal presentiment struck the heart of the foremost among them, and, taking a step backwards, Harry Woodruff said,—

"What, then, has happened in this house?"

"The hand of the Lord has stricken it," said the old man, in a mournful voice. "Death has been busy here."

"Who, then, is dead here?" demanded Harry, in a tone of the deepest anguish.

And rushing into the doorway—

"But this old man weeping and lamenting is Katamar's treasurer," he added.

Then, shaking him by the arm, with haggard eyes, clenched teeth, and heaving breast, he demanded—

"For whom are you weeping, old man?"

The treasurer made no reply.

He regarded Harry fixedly in the face, as if he did not recognise him, and an inarticulate groan escaped his lips.

"Which of us two has lost his senses?" continued Harry, violently. "Answer! I left your dwelling calm and peaceable, and I return this evening to find it a house of mourning. You spoke of death. But that is an imposture, is it not?"

"It is Emma Clarence who is dead," interrupted the old man in an undertone.

Harry started, and thought he felt madness flash like lightning through his brain.

The pang of grief that shot through his heart caused his hair to stand on end, and his limbs were bathed in a cold sweat.

A burst of convulsive laughter broke from him, and his eyes remained wildly staring, as if the shadow of Emma rose up before him.

He pressed his hand upon his heart as though to still its wild and almost audible throbbings, which caused him pain as acute as the entrance of cold steel into the flesh.

The other personages had advanced as far as the vestibule, and, surrounding the treasurer, they threw back their ample hoods upon their shoulders. The old treasurer recognised Aixa.

When Harry, whose lips trembled violently, had succeeded in somewhat controlling his anguish, he continued,

"But it is impossible that Emma Clarence should be dead! Do not trifle with me! I saw her scarcely a few hours since; she was beautiful, serene, almost smiling. Death could not have seized upon her so suddenly. Ah! you are deceiving us. If it were a crime!—But who could have chosen for a victim that innocent girl? Who could help loving her? Who has she ever harmed? She knew but how to succour the weak and the unfortunate! Oh! if a cowardly vengeance has pursued and overtaken poor Emma, I will have ample justice. But no, I am mad! She is not dead! I would see her!"

And, his countenance distorted by doubt and suffering, he made signs to the old man.

"Calm yourself, friend," said he.

"It is a trial sent by the Lord," added Aixa.

But Harry stood motionless, and smiled disdainfully.

"What matter to me all things else, if Emma be dead?" he replied. "My life, my strength, my ambition, we have lost all in losing her."

And he leaned half fainting against a pillar.

Then, encountering the dark and spiteful glance of the favourite, Aixa, he recollected her rivalry with young Emma, and a terrible suspicion entered his mind.

"Oh! I shall still have strength to avenge her," he exclaimed. "Emma, if it be true that I must never see thee more, I promise thee that thy enemy shall not long rejoice at thy death."

But, as he was advancing threateningly towards Aixa, who fearlessly awaited his approach, the old man said in a trembling voice—

"Accuse no one! It was I who told Emma that King Katamar required that she should be conducted to the palace. Dishonour awaited her there. She preferred to die."

"So that she has fallen a victim to the tyranny of Katamar?" said Harry. "It is upon him alone that vengeance should fall."

Aixa laughed.

"You know it as well as I do," she added, with a venomous smile; "she loved Lion Limb, this beautiful and chaste Emma."

"Do not insult her," interrupted Harry.

"May my words prove a consolation to you, captain," pursued the favourite, "but, I do not believe in the death of Emma."

"You do not believe in it?" exclaimed the treasurer.

"I shall not believe in it," continued Aixa, "until I have contemplated the dead and closed eyes of Emma, until I have touched her icy forehead, until I have assured myself that no sigh will evermore issue from her pale lips. This proof I even demand. Be frank, and you will confess that you have concealed her to remove her from all these dangers to avoid confiding her either to Harry or to Aixa. This, I am very certain, is the whole truth."

"Oh! if you have deceived me thus, if you have trifled thus with my misery and my despair, I will never forgive you," said Harry. "Dead or alive, I would see her once more," impetuously exclaimed Harry. "Who knows if I shall not again hear that sweet voice that was wont to vibrate through my heart! But, if even I must only behold again those charming features, to engrave them for a last time on my memory, it will be a mournful pleasure for me."

"So, you will not respect her repose even in death?" said Aixa.

"If caprice is the cause of this death," said Harry, with savage excitement, "it is over the body of his victim that I will extract an answer from Katamar, and wreak vengeance on him who

has caused the death before the hour appointed by God, of the fairest and best beloved of the daughters of our land."

"Come, then," replied the old treasurer.

And he proceeded towards the vault.

Harry had hardly descended the first steps of the staircase leading to the vault, when he perceived the funeral platform on which reposed Emma, arrayed in her winding-sheet.

His limbs tottered beneath the weight of his body; he regarded with mournful and fearful avidity that countenance, pale, cold, inanimate as marble, and in which he vainly sought to surprise a furtive movement, a stray spark of existence.

"Emma! Emma!" he repeated in a voice of despair, fondly hoping that at this ardent invocation she would rise up alive upon the platform, and tear away her shroud.

But not a breath stirred her clay-cold lips.

Her eyelids remained closed.

A sinister silence was the sole reply to the wild appeal of Harry Woodruff.

"So much youth, so much beauty, all blighted by the caprice of the king," said Harry, sententiously; "whilst the Lord might perhaps have accorded long years of happiness to this fair child had she not fallen in the way of the tyrant."

While they were descending into the vault, Aixa, still mistrustful, had drawn aside with a daring hand, the winding-sheet of Emma.

She had touched her forehead, her eyes, and her lips, but not a contraction, not the faintest murmur of a breath had revealed the slightest sign of her rival's existence.

During all these solemn moments of contemplating the lovely dead, Aixa had never ceased to examine, with the most mistrustful attention, the marble countenance of the dead.

At this moment, however, the old treasurer fancied he beheld an almost imperceptible movement in the folds of the winding-sheet which covered the bosom of the dead.

He felt his heart beat wildly with fear and excitement, and drawing away Aixa, who now no longer doubted the truth of her rival's death, he remounted the steps of the vault.

Aixa's heart beat loudly in triumph.

But as she passed him, Harry Woodruff smothered a fearful oath of vengeance.

CHAPTER XCIX.

LION LIMB'S DESPAIR—THE PLOT.

As soon as Aixa returned to the palace, she repaired to her own splendid apartments, and after disengaging herself of her cloak, she seated herself on a pile of cushions, and ordered her servant maids and slaves to adorn her as in those days of festival and triumph when she was wont to appear resplendent with beauty and pride.

She assumed a calm, and almost smiling countenance, but it was easy to perceive by the flashing of her dark eyes, and the heaving of her breast, that a storm was raging within her.

"Pour out some more perfume," she said, in an impatient tone. "Mingle diamonds and pearls in my hair, in order that I may appear beautiful before him for whom my whole soul pines."

Her eyes shone with a sinister light, her olive cheek assumed a tint of livid paleness, whilst with her white and pointed teeth she bit her lips till the blood came.

"I am disdained by him," she murmured, "when

for the accomplishment of my ends, I have yielded to the wildest and maddest desires. I have lowered myself in the eyes of all the Indian tribes. I have despised noble chiefs who sought my hand, and yet he smiles not on me. Yet my time will come; I will wait patiently; I may subdue the hand of this youth yet; I will not despair; yet terrible will be my revenge, if he turns coldly upon me, for I have swallowed all pride and bowed down before him, and why, I know not, his presence fascinates me; in one word, I *love* him.

"And now," continued Aixa, becoming more angry still, "by an implacable fatality, this alliance of which I fondly dreamed—those mad dreams of ambition—are all crumbled into nothing by the bright eyes of that wretched English girl, Emma Clarence. But happy; ah! thrice happy me, vengeance is in my power."

Then taking from the hands of a female slave a small mirror of polished steel, she regarded herself in its shining surface with singular attention.

By degrees the muscles of her face, contracted by feelings of resentment and disdain, relaxed.

A smile played upon her vermilion lips, and her half-closed eyes assumed an indefinable languor.

"Before announcing to him the death of this accursed girl," said she, rising, "I must for the last time try my power over this Lion Limb. If he loves me—if the thought of the girl, Emma, has not driven me from his mind, like some vain passing shadow—I will use all my powers, in this and other islands, to deliver into his hand his implacable enemy, the brutal Mungo, and his ferocious band. But if he remains cold and deaf to my entreaties, if he turns aside his eyes from mine, if he presses not my hand in his, as he did before this war broke out, then woe to him, for these buccaneers shall be the instrument, in my hands, to seek and obtain revenge."

Quitting her apartment, calm and smiling, she descended into the luxurious, spacious court, where, as she anticipated, she found Lion Limb, reposing after the fatigues of the day.

He was sitting in a very thoughtful mood, his head leaning on his hand.

Aixa softly approached him, passed her taper fingers through his hair, and gently drawing his head back imprinted a kiss on his pale forehead.

Lion Limb started at the touch and uttered an exclamation of surprise, as if his dreams had given place to reality; but his looks no sooner encountered those of Aixa, than his features resumed their expression of deep melancholy.

"Ah! is it you, Aixa?" he said, carelessly, and falling back into his former position.

The haughty Queen of the Pearl Islands feigned not to remark the significant attitude of Lion Limb, and kneeling on a cushion at his feet, she placed her clasped hands upon his knees, and fixing on him her large eyes of mother of pearl and jet, she looked at him for some time without speaking.

"You are ill, Lion Limb," she said, at length.

"No; I am only thinking, Aixa," he replied.

"You would seek to hide your grief from me, but I can easily discover it. You are neither cast down nor discouraged, for you rely on your firmness and stubborn courage; but you are learning to despise men, to put no more faith in their oaths, to expect no more from their gratitude."

"It is true, Aixa; but reassure yourself, my situation is not yet desperate that I should think of fearing the mongrel Mungo or his desperate followers."

"I would not shrink from any danger to accompany you," said Aixa.

The brow of Lion Limb darkened.

"And what renders me very happy," said Aixa, "I think Emma Clarence will no more trouble or pester you."

Lion Limb let fall an expression of impatience, and rose abruptly.

Aixa then drew herself up before him, fixed and rigid as a statue, and seizing his arm, exclaimed,

"Stay, Lion Limb! Confess to me before you go that you still love this pretty English girl."

"Why do you question me thus?" said Lion Limb, feeling much annoyed. "Am I, then, standing before a judge?"

"Lion-Limb, if I did not love you I should take no heed of your coldness," said Aixa, in haughty and sardonic accents.

"Have I not been asked this foolish question more than a hundred times?" said Lion Limb, coldly.

"But can I trust your word more than that of any other man?"

"You may. I have always been true to my word, and if I were to send for this girl this moment——"

"She would not come, I tell you," Aixa replied, with a smile of triumph.

"Would not!"

"I have said it—she would not."

"Notwithstanding my orders?"

"Notwithstanding your orders," replied the revengeful queen, while a strange and threatening smile played upon her lips.

"If I were to tell you," pursued Aixa, clasping her hands like a suppliant, "that if you persist in enforcing such an order for her reappearance, I should die of grief. You would not—could not be so cruel as to order it. I should regard the entrance of Emma into this palace as my own condemnation."

"One would almost fancy that you had gone mad, Aixa. Your demands of late are simply impossible."

"Ah, no, Lion Limb, it is you who demand the impossible," said Aixa, with a sudden burst of wild laughter that made our hero shudder.

Rising with a sudden start, she exclaimed,

"You are ignorant of what has taken place this day in Katamar's treasurer's house?"

"What mean you?" said Lion Limb, struck with a vague terror.

"That Emma Clarence, who loved you—that you loved also—*is dead!* She died cursing your name —ha! ha!—think of that!"

And she hurriedly took a few steps towards the door in a wild manner.

"Dead! dead!" repeated Lion Limb, as if dreaming, and rushing madly forward towards Aixa, to retain her.

"Do not deceive me," said he. "Do not thus rend my heart; do not add to my sorrow."

"Your sorrow, Lion Limb," said Aixa, haughtily, "at one time would have caused me pain, but now it gives me joy. But yesterday, I would have given my life for one of your smiles; to-day I would give ten lives, if I had them, for one of your tears."

Violently disengaging herself from Lion Limb, who stood pale and stupefied, Aixa bounded from the apartment, radiant and triumphant!

For a few moments Lion Limb remained plunged in the most horrible perplexity.

He knew not what to think or say.

Misfortunes of various kinds had fallen upon him of late, through whom or by whom he knew not.

Yet he was not at all discouraged.

His heart was bold and brave, and equal to any danger.

Yet he could not but sigh deeply as he thought of the cruel, nay barbarous fate which might have befallen Emma Clarence.

Had old Katamar's treasurer then really poisoned Emma, or, rather, had not the haughty, proud queen, Aixa, deceived him by the grossest falsehood?

Should he send one of his lieutenants, with a company of his brave lads, to the house of old Canbool, the treasurer, or what had best be done?

Lion Limb, after some reflection, determined to entrust the secret of this important mission to five of his own men, and for this purpose summoned them, young Ted Rawlings among the number.

"My brave lads," said Lion Limb, "the times are very critical. We are surrounded by enemies and spies in all directions, and at this moment I have need of devoted followers to execute a difficult and perilous undertaking. I have faith and reliance on all of you."

"We feel honoured, captain," said all the five with one voice.

"Do you think you could introduce yourselves to-night, in that particular part of the town where old Canbool, the treasurer, lives?"

"Yes, we will answer for it," said several, "for without the least noise we can make a breach in the wall, and let ourselves in."

"You know, then, the abode of the old treasurer?"

"No, we do not, but will soon discover it, captain."

"I have heard," said Lion Limb, with emotion, "that Emma Clarence is dead. Whether she died from natural causes I know not; but whether dead or alive, you must carry her off from the old treasurer's abode—where I know she now is—and bring her here."

Not a word escaped the lips of the five determined and heroic adventurers, but they bowed their heads in obedience.

"How long will you require for this expedition?" said Lion Limb.

"If we are discovered carrying off the maid from old Canbool's house, whether dead or alive, we shall be a long time before we return, captain; it is even possible that we shall not return at all," said Ted Rawlings.

The other four laughed at young Ted's fears.

"You can, and will do this?" asked Lion Limb.

"We can, and *will*, captain," was the bluff reply.

And they left the apartment.

The enterprise which these five devoted lads had undertaken was much more difficult and hazardous than they had supposed.

Emma Clarence, as we have previously seen, was shut up in a vault, whose sole issue was defended by a stout oaken door, furnished with bars of iron.

As for the residence of old Canbool, the treasurer, it was guarded by four warriors, in the secret service of the young Queen Aixa, who, full of suspicion, did not, and would not trust the truth and fidelity even of old Canbool.

The five adventurers, however, swore to accomplish Lion Limb's orders, and were careful first of all to dress themselves as Indian chiefs of Katamar's household.

They then, when night had come, penetrated into that quarter of the town where the old treasurer lived, but as yet knew not his residence.

Accident, however, discovered this, for while they were hiding near a large dwelling, the door opened, and old Canbool came forth with a bundle of keys at his girdle, and followed by a faithful slave.

The idea then occurred to the leader of the party, who was none other than mad Dick Hamilton, to follow the old treasurer, and if possible obtain possession of his keys, and particularly that of the treasury, for he well knew that Lion Limb stood much in need of money to carry on the war against Mungo and his swarm of hirelings.

They also thought it possible that among these keys might be the one of the vault in which Emma was confined.

They followed old Canbool, and at length he and his trusty slave stopped before the gates of an enclosure, which was surrounded by a high wall.

Old Canbool entered, and, before the five conspirators could follow him, the gate closed again.

The five brave fellows were much annoyed at this, but Dick whispered—

"We must get in here, and see what old Canboo is about, somehow or other; let us make a ladder of our bodies."

Dick instantly placed himself against the wall, a second leaped upon his shoulders, and had nothing more to do than to hold out his arms, and assist young Ted to mount upon him.

This young Ted Rawlings did very willingly, and in a few seconds was perched on the wall.

"Well," asked Dick, in a low tone, "can you see anything of old Canbool and his slave?"

"The moon is struggling to appear through the black clouds," said Ted, "and I cannot discover anything as yet."

"Then jump into the enclosure without noise, and find out what they are about, Ted."

"You often said I was as nimble as a squirrel," said Ted, "but the wall is old and rotten, Captain Dick; there are many stones loose. I will kick a few of them down, and then make stepping-stones of them, for if I fall, I should be discovered, and, perhaps, murdered, you know, which is not a pleasant subject to think about."

Ted quickly loosened some heavy stones, which fell among the rank weeds and high grass at the bottom of the wall.

"Wait for me," said Ted; "if I need assistance I will whistle."

Crawling like a serpent among the grass, young Ted proceeded to the spot where old Canbool and his slave stood conversing before an open grave.

On his way Ted felt great fear, and his hair stood on end. But he was only a few feet away from old Canbool, who said to his slave—

"Did you hear anything?"

Old Canbool and the slave looked suspiciously around.

Young Ted stopped, and squatted behind a large stone, and not a murmur, not an undulation among the grass, announced the presence of a living being so near them.

"Come, master," said the slave, "I have heard that this Christian girl must be buried in a grave according to the English fashion; must I go and arouse some grave-diggers, then?"

"Hush," said old Canbool; "listen to me. If I have brought you here, it is not to dig graves, but to confide to you a grand secret, the revelation of which would be my ruin and death!"

"I have never betrayed my master yet," said the slave; "speak on, I am all attention."

Young Ted cocked his ears, and redoubled his vigilance to find out their secret.

"It is not to this place I would have the English girl transported," said old Canbool, "but to *your* house."

Prize § **H H** § Ticket.

THE BOY KING
OF THE SOUTH SEA ISLANDS.

TED'S BUFFALO RIDE—(SEE NEXT NUMBER).

"How is that, my master?" asked the slave, in wonder.

"I will explain all that at another time," said old Canbool; "but obey my orders. Go and employ

four slaves, blindfold them, and introduce them to my dwelling by the garden gate, of which here is the key. Let them wait there till I am informed of it. If I am not at home, however, but at the palace with King Katamar, or his niece, Aixa, you will find the key of the vault—wherein lies this pretty English maiden—in an old jar behind the garden gate, where I have hidden it. You will observe the same precautions with these four slaves while they are carrying the body to your house, and you will not by any means remove the light bandages from their eyes until they have left, and are far away from your abode."

"I will do so, master, said the faithful slave, bowing; "there is some mystery in this matter which I will not now dare to inquire into. I will obey to the letter."

The old treasurer and his slave then parted.

Young Ted wound his way through the long grass like a swimmer through the waves, and soon rejoined his companions, who were impatiently awaiting him.

Ted told them all that he had heard, and on the instant Dick resolved to track and follow old Canbool's confidential servant and thwart his designs.

The slave soon engaged four Indians; he covered their eyes so tightly, and in such a manner, that the bandages seemed to stop their ears as well, and ordered them on pain of losing their reward not to breathe a single word on their way.

Canbool's slave started at the head of his four men who held him by his robe; but when they had gone some distance, they were met by four other blind-folded men led on by young Ted, and Master Rawlings, suddenly giving a loud shriek, so frightened the opposite party, that they refused to go forward until Canbool's slave, Karnack, went some distance before them to explore the way.

Karnack had not gone many yards in the dark before mad Dick and his companions followed close on his heels.

Dick slightly pushed Karnack, who, not dreaming of any trickery, was only too glad to see that his four men had recovered from their fright, and so extended his robe to Dick and the others who boldly followed him.

Young Ted meanwhile approached the four real slaves, who stood trembling in the dark, placed in the hands of the foremost a corner of his cloak, and in this manner led them in a totally different direction to that which they should have taken.

It highly amused young Ted, who, for more than an hour, made them execute the most extravagant evolutions.

While Ted was engaged in leading the four slaves round and round a circle like horses in a mill, Dick and the others, led on by the unsuspecting Karnack, arrived at the garden gate of old Canbool's residence.

Here Karnack left them for a moment to go and seek the old treasurer.

That moment was precious to Dick and his men.

"Off with your bandages, lads," said he, "and follow me."

Dick soon found the key of the vault which was hidden in a jar as before described, and they entered the residence of old Canbool.

They were not many seconds in discovering a stone staircase numbering forty steps, and which all thought must of a certainty lead to the vault.

They descended cautiously and silently.

On arriving at the foot of the staircase, they found themselves stopped by a massive door.

But the key which Dick had secured really belonged to this door, and they quickly entered the vault, where, according to old Canbool's instructions, his faithful slave, Karnack, should have discovered the body of Emma Clarence.

Dick boldly advanced towards the bier, where the white shroud of the young girl showed itself in strong relief from out of the darkness of the vault.

But, just as Dick was about to place his hand upon the body, he thought he heard a faint sigh!

A sort of gentle murmur was heard without a doubt, and he shrunk back terrified.

"What is the matter, captain?" asked one, in a whisper.

"The dead has spoken," said another, horror-stricken.

"If she has spoken," said Dick, "it is because she is not dead; and, besides, you heard the order of Lion Limb, dead or alive, we must transport the body to him. But, let us not lose any time."

One of them timidly laid his finger on the forehead of Emma.

"You are right, Captain Dick," said he; "she is not dead; her forehead has not the icy coldness of death."

Dick bent over her face, and added,

"A breath warm and light as that of a sleeping child escapes her lips."

"Let us be quick, then," said one. "If she should awaken, she might, perhaps, be frightened at finding herself in this vault wrapped in a winding-sheet; she might shriek. Old Canbool's savage guards might hear her, and we should be lost."

"Right," said Dick, with mad energy.

And, taking her in his long, sinewy arms, Dick lifted her from the bier as carefully as he would a child.

All were anxious to get out of the vault and the house as soon as possible, and they lost no time in doing so.

They all left the garden with the same ease that they had entered it, although the place was well watched, and, having replaced the key of the vault in the jar where they had found it, they hurried away, and soon met young Ted, who was still exercising his four blindfolded men.

By a sign Dick gave Ted to understand that it was time to take them to old Canbool's dwelling.

Ted obeyed.

He took them to the house, and bade them rest and hide under some trees until they were wanted, and then rejoined Dick and his bravo party, who were about to depart, when they distinctly heard old Canbool speaking to Karnack.

"So," said he, "my orders have been punctually executed?"

"They have, master."

"These four men are ignorant of where they are, and whither they are going?"

"I am sure of it."

"Are you also sure they have have left no mark on my house, on the garden gate, for instance, in the hopes of finding it again on the morrow?" demanded the suspicious old man.

"All such attempts have been impossible, master."

"That is well, Karnack. While I go to get the key do you descend with them to the vault."

When they had reached the bottom of the staircase, they waited for Canbool, who soon appeared with a small iron lamp in his hand, softly opened the door, and entered first into the vault.

But, as his eyes caught sight of the empty bier, a cold sweat bathed his face, his head swam, his limbs tottered, and he leaned against the wall to save himself from falling.

He at first imagined that Emma, having perhaps recovered her consciousness, and burst asunder the shroud, had heard his footsteps upon the stairs, and had taken refuge in some obscure corner of the vault.

But when, after searching everywhere, he felt certain that the maiden had disappeared altogether, he experienced so violent a shock of agony, that, forgetting all prudence, he uttered such a cry of despair, so wild and shrill, that it scarcely seemed to proceed from the mouth of a human being.

The four hired slaves hearing his terrible lamentations, tore off their bandages, and, in spite of all the efforts of Karnack, were about to fly in horror, when Canbool's savage guards appeared at the top of the stairway, attracted by the old treasurer's despairing cry.

"Where is she? where is she?" moaned old Canbool.

And he listened again and again, as if expecting to hear some response to his question.

"You well know the girl was dead and cannot hear you," said one.

"Who told *you* so?" said Canbool, rushing frantically upon him.

And, shaking him violently by the arm, the old man fixed upon him his gleaming eyes, and seemed turned crazy.

"Where is she, where is she, I ask all of you?" he said, foaming with passion. "She is not dead, fools that you are! She was only sleeping—only sleeping, I say. And, oh! I wanted to remove her from Lion Limb, from Katamar's envy, and Aixa's deadly hate; but, it is now too late."

And, exhausted by the violence of his disappointment, rage, and vexation, old Canbool, the treasurer, fell heavily forward, like one thunderstruck, upon the stone floor of the vault, in presence of his startled guards and attendants.

CHAPTER C.

THE REVELATION.

NOT long after their departure from the old treasurer's house, Dick, Ted, and the others arrived at the palace of King Katamar, and, by a secret way, conveyed the body of Emma Clarence into a private apartment, and placed her upon a divan.

Then mad Dick related to Lion Limb, with the brief and heroic simplicity natural to him, every incident of their expedition.

Lion Limb did not content himself with thanking his noble and brave companions in arms, but embraced each and all warmly.

They then withdrew, and Lion Limb was left alone with the inanimate body.

There was something peculiarly mournful and touching in this interview between the lovers, one of whom was wrapped in a winding sheet.

"And is it thus that I again behold thee, Emma," he murmured, "thou who hast ever been to me so devoted and faithful?"

After a few moments of hesitation he ventured to approach the body.

"How lovely she is still!" he said. "Death has not dared to touch her beauty; but how cruel is the thought that that soft and pleading look will never more be fixed on me! That I shall never more hear that silvery voice! Happy, a thousand times happy, he whom she loved.

"That happy being was myself, and yet I suffered her to leave my presence for a single moment! They thought I would or had sacrificed her to that haughty and vindictive woman, Aixa, who loved me only because she knew I was king of all the islands. Like the silly child who breaks his toy, I let her escape and destroyed my own happiness. Oh! if I could restore her to life, and by a kiss upon her cold lips reanimate and revive her heart!"

He bent over her in a transport of passion, then started back as if afraid of his own wild delirium.

"Whence comes this sudden terror?" he exclaimed, laying his hand upon his wildly throbbing heart. "Is it, then, a profanation, or a sacrilege to believe that her soul still lives in that clay-cold tenement? No; though dead she will hear me; she will know that I love her; she will bear with her to the tomb the confession of my love."

He bent forward boldly, and his trembling lips touched the beautiful cheeks of the marble-like girl.

Was it an illusion?

There was nothing of the icy coldness of death in that touch.

Lion Limb started back, and looked upon her with glaring eyes.

"Oh, that Heaven might work a miracle!" he exclaimed. "Would that the Almighty powers might raise her to life again! and then this world, which now to me seems a desert, would be changed into Paradise."

In a frenzy of passion he seized her hands.

They became moist in his own.

Lion Limb fell on his knees beside her.

"Thanks; heaven be thanked," he exclaimed, joyfully. "I have found my guardian angel again. My life is not yet doomed to despair. I can struggle still. Emma will sustain my courage as she has always done. She will calm my royal annoyances and tortures. On her faithful breast I can repose with confidence."

While Lion Limb thus gave vent to his pent-up feelings, Emma Clarence heaved a gentle sigh like one oppressed with an indefinable weight; her eyes partially unclosed themselves and cast vague inquiring glances around.

Lion Limb, with wild joy, watched the happy awakening in a sort of grateful ecstasy.

"Is it a dream?" murmured Emma. "I no longer recognize the vault. Oh, how long and painful has my slumber been."

She raised herself half up on the cushions, not seeing Lion Limb, and passed her hand painfully across her brow.

"But no; I remember. I was in a vault like one dead. I could neither call nor murmur, but I heard. Oh, what terrible words I heard! Oh, if it is yet time to warn Lion Limb! But how to reach——"

"Lion Limb is beside you, Emma," said our hero, softly, showing himself as he spoke.

"You here! you still alive!" said Emma, intoxicated with joy, and shaking off the torpor which still hung over her. "Oh, may kind heaven be praised for this, for I never hoped to see you any more, Edgar."

"Fear nothing for me, Emma," Lion Limb replied. "I am beset on all sides by enemies I know, but I fear them not. I am safe here in Katamar's Palace.

"Ah, you think yourself in safety here, do you?" said Emma, with a bitter smile. "Beware, Edgar, beware! Oh, my dreams! But they were only dreams. Do not smile, do not smile; yet sometimes we dream something more than dreams."

She then pressed both hands to her brow, as if to evoke some confused and painful recollection.

"But how came I here?" she asked suddenly.

"The report of your death was brought to me, and I would not believe it," said Lion Limb; "but knowing you were surrounded by traitors and wild Indian fanatics capable of endeavouring to revenge themselves on me through you; anxious and restless I became hourly more wretched than ever through your absence; eager to behold you once again, I resolved to find you out and possess your presence whether dead or alive."

"Oh, I recollect all now," said Emma, with a look of terror; "the vault wherein I lay upon a funeral bier, was at one time filled with the boldest knaves and villains. My eyelids were closed. I could not move them; yet I saw in a dream all that passed before me. Among these bold villains who were plotting to kill and exterminate you and all your band was *a woman!* By my side she stood and frequently laid her hand upon my heart as if to question its beatings. I seemed to feel my heart wither under her murderous touch.

She then endeavoured to make a fresh effort of memory to recall all the details of the scene.

"Oh Heavens!" said she, "I know not how long my slumber has lasted. The conspirators were to act on the morrow, and the morrow was Sunday."

"Thus it is to-day the plot is to burst forth," said Lion Limb, frowning.

"To-day!" exclaimed Emma. "Oh, you may think me foolish, and wandering in my thoughts, but do not press Katamar, or his treasurer, for means to carry out your plans."

"You love me, Emma," said Lion Limb, fondly.

"Alas! how can I hide from you that I love you," replied Emma, trembling. "Why are we not free to wander beneath the sun, and beneath the leafy shade, without fear of enemies?"

At this moment a knock was heard at the door of the apartment.

Lion Limb opened it himself, when a slave appeared, and said, "My lord, king of all the islands, Canbool, the treasurer, wishes to speak with you."

At the mention of Canbool's name Emma started.

"He accompanies," said the slave, "four very large chests of gold and silver ore, which you levied on the island for the expenses of the war."

"The old treasurer, then, is welcome," said Lion Limb. "Admit him to the palace immediately, him and his chests."

When the slave had disappeared, Emma Clarence threw herself at the feet of Lion Limb, and uttered a piercing cry.

"Let not Canbool enter, Lion Limb," she exclaimed; "it is the signal for your ruin—perhaps death!"

"What means these mysterious words?" asked Lion Limb, in great surprise.

Emma stood regarding Lion Limb with an air of stupefaction.

A thousand confused thoughts chased each other through her burning brain.

It seemed to her, for a moment, as if her reason were about to give way.

At length a sudden light broke in upon her mind.

"In truth, Lion Limb, now I see all. You laughed at my silly dream, but in that dream there was mention of chests and armed men. Oh, I remember it all now, and I will explain. But before I begin, promise me the life of old Canbool."

"That miserable old wretch!" said Lion Limb, in disgust.

"But he might have killed me, Edgar."

"True, so he might. Well, then, go on; not a hair of Canbool's head shall suffer."

"Well, then, you must know, that when it became known that you had demanded treasure from the people, the conspirators resolved not to give it, but call in the aid of Mungo, and make friends with him. But the woman of whom I spoke advised differently. 'Give him the money,' said she, with a scornful laugh, 'that is, place in each chest two brave men, let them be then introduced to the palace; at a given signal they will get out, secure Lion Limb a prisoner, and then we can deliver him up to Mungo, or do as we like.'"

"And who was this wretched woman?" asked Lion Limb.

"This woman, who was thus rejoicing at my death, and plotting plans against you, you already know."

"Queen Aixa!" said Lion Limb; "is it she?"

Emma did not answer.

Lion Limb went to a small apartment near by, and spoke to a young man, who acted as private messenger, and such like.

"I have told you all now," said Lion Limb to him. "Let old Canbool be conducted into the armoury, whither I will cause these coffers to be placed. You can come there after you have made your plans, and settle accounts with these villains, but first of all tell Queen Aixa I wish to speak to her," said Lion Limb, biting his lip. "Let us see if I cannot wring some avowal of all this villany from her."

Taking Emma's hand he led her behind some tall tapestry, that concealed the door of the armoury, and told her not to show herself until he should invoke her name as a crushing testimony against the fiendish queen.

Young Aixa was not long in appearing.

Lion Limb received her with a calm and smiling visage.

"I am as obedient to your orders as the meanest of slaves, my lord," she said, drily, and with sarcasm. "You sent for me—I came immediately."

"It was not an order but a prayer," said Lion Limb. "I have wrongs to repair towards you, Aixa, and I will not commit fresh ones. I know your proud and indomitable nature; your generous and loyal heart, Aixa. Misfortune has come upon me; many friends are abandoning me; but you I know are not among that number."

"Ah! how truly you read my heart," said Aixa, with a strange smile.

Lion Limb did not allow himself to be deceived by this feigned burst of sincerity.

He remarked that she had approached the half-opened window, whence she could plainly see old Canbool and his large chests in the yard below, and keeping at a respectful distance, many of Lion Limb's men, who were trying to examine the chests more minutely than the old treasurer liked.

"You are admiring, no doubt," observed Lion Limb, "the zeal which good old Canbool has displayed in collecting the treasure I needed."

"Yes; and because the old treasurer is one of your warmest friends," said Aixa, indifferently.

"You would, then, advise me to have full confidence in the old man, Aixa?"

"Yes; unless you would mistrust yourself, Lion Limb," said Aixa, coldly. "Since the death of Marmi, King Katamar has been almost useless in state affairs, and Canbool does all and everything—he is a worthy man and incapable of dishonour."

"Nobleness of nature excites your sympathy and admiration," said Lion Limb, with a smile; "but women do not know so much of this world as men do. For you must know that this excellent—I might say super-excellent—old Canbool, whom it pleases you to adorn with so many virtues, has this very night fulfilled your predictions concerning him."

"What predictions?" asked Aixa, with an air of very vague anxiety.

"Have you already forgotten it, Aixa?" said Lion Limb, very drily. "Your memory, then, must be even more treacherous than your heart."

"Sir! what mean you?"

"I mean, Aixa, that this worthy Canbool, of whom you speak, has committed a crime very common in these days."

"I do not understand you."

"He has sold his master, that's all."

"Impossible!" said Aixa, her complexion assuming a livid tint.

"Impossible, Aixa; that is as much as to say that I am, then, a liar. Yet you of all persons ought to know the truth of what I say."

"How so—how mean you, Lion Limb?"

"Why, it is said that every malice, jealously, and other wild passions have instigated you to form a plot against my life; and I have it on good authority, that you even went so far as to make a speech to the conspirators."

"I—I, sir! It is an infamous falsehood," said she, in a shrill voice.

"And I hear that your speech met with great success, and that on your proposition they even went so far as ——"

"But you did not, you could not believe any such slanderous reports, I hope?"

"Why not? What is the use of denying it? You see I know all. Must I repeat to you your own words and phrases? You have displayed a talent at the house of old Canbool that I never thought you possessed, Aixa."

"A truce to sarcasms, sir," furiously exclaimed the young queen, her eyes flashing, and her face distorted with passion. "Where is he who has thus dared to accuse me falsely? Let him come forward and supplant his falsehoods against the woman he has wronged."

"You would insist on having a witness, then, fair Aixa?" said Lion Limb. "Well, then, if such is your wish, I can comply with it."

Advancing to the tapestry, which he suddenly drew aside, he said—

"Behold your accuser, and contradict her if you dare."

"Emma!" exclaimed Aixa, thunderstruck at this apparition.

She recoiled with terror from Emma, who stood motionless as a statue.

"Emma Clarence, whose testimony you did not fear, for you thought her dead," said Emma, in a grave voice; "Emma, who has risen from her funeral bier to save Lion Limb from the deadly snare you laid for him."

"Ah, ha!" said Aixa, in a bitter, scoffing tone of deadly irony; "then you played the part of a dead person that you might the better perform the part

of spy, eh? I understand, ha, ha! Cleverly done, indeed, very cleverly done."

"'Tis false, proud woman," Emma sorrowfully replied; "would that all which has happened within the past few hours really were a dream; but you know well, nay, too well, Queen Aixa, that what I say is *not* falsehood. It is now *your* turn to blush."

"Do not believe this whining girl," turning fiercely towards Lion Limb. "She accuses me because she hates me, and she hates me because she knows that I love you, and that I am jealous."

"*You* love him?" said Emma, with a melancholy smile of scorn; "you do not. Your heart is filled with poisonous hate."

Aixa broke forth in a loud laugh of derision as she exclaimed—

"Did you send for me here, Lion Limb, to hear this foolish girl's expressions of love? You ought, indeed, to be highly flattered with the affection of such a *thing* as she is, one not worthy to tie my shoes."

"A queen betrayed me, Aixa," said Lion Limb, "and a poor girl saves me."

"But the girl lies; she is deceiving you," said Aixa, furiously, and with flashing eyes.

"Punishment will follow close upon the treason," said Lion Limb, sternly.

"Punishment!" said Emma; "oh do not think of punishing Aixa. She is a queen, and even loved you once. Do not be harsh towards a foolish woman who, in haste and jealousy, has done wrong."

"I will have none of your prattling pity," exclaimed Aixa, exasperated at seeing Emma show herself so superior in heart to herself. "I know not how to abase myself, and ask pardon like a cowardly slave who trembles under his master's whip. I brave your punishment, Lion Limb, and will still preserve my hate."

"You have a proud and strong heart, Aixa," said Lion Limb, sternly. "You who are a queen, when you pass from place to place every one makes way for you, and bow respectfully, and yet, perhaps, if they knew you as you are, instead of making way for you and humbly saluting you, they would tear off your flowing veil, that only seems to hide a heart of hypocrisy and guile."

"You insult a woman, Lion Limb," said Aixa, mad with rage.

"I judge according to your merits, noble lady; and now follow me, for I have still another accomplice to confound."

"Whither would you lead me?" demanded the young queen, arrogantly.

"To old Canbool, your accomplice."

And leading Emma by the hand, Lion Limb went towards the armoury, followed by Queen Aixa, whose hands were clenched in rage.

CHAPTER CI.

LION LIMB FALLS INTO A TRAP, AND IS SURROUNDED BY ASSASSINS.

THE armoury into which old Canbool had the large chest conveyed, contained all sorts of old Indian weapons, trophies, and even rude suits of armour, some made of metal, and other complete suits formed out of the invulnerable hide of the rhinoceros.

These latter suits were six in number, of various sizes, and stood around the room full life size, and with weapons in the hands of the "dummies," to which the ball-proof hide was fitted.

As soon, then, as the slaves had borne the large chests into the armoury, old Canbool dismissed them, and examined every hole and corner with the most scrupulous attention.

Having satisfied himself that he was really alone, old Canbool undid the hoops and locks with which the chests were bound, and very gently raised the lids, in order to see if his accomplices, notwithstanding the air holes which had been contrived in the carving, were still alive and well.

"By all that's lucky," said one of those inside, "it was quite time to open the cage, for I was nearly suffocated."

Each one profiting by the example of the first, with their heads raised the lids of the chests in which they were confined, in order to breathe freely.

Meanwhile, old Canbool, with outstretched neck, and ears well cocked, stood sentinel at the door.

He soon heard footsteps, and when he perceived Emma Clarence, with Lion Limb, turned deadly pale.

He hurriedly fastened down the chests once more, and awaited Lion Limb.

He had scarcely secured the last fastening, when Lion Limb appeared at the door.

Lion Limb cast a rapid glance around the armoury, and seeing no one but old Canbool there, wondered why Dick Hamilton, Ted Rawlings, and others, were not there according to his own particular orders.

For a moment he stood irresolute at the door, but soon carried away by his adventurous disposition he boldly entered the armoury.

Old Canbool would then have approached to whisper to Aixa, but Lion Limb stopped him, saying,

"Thanks, old treasurer, for your promptitude in bringing this gold and silver ore."

Old Canbool bowed humbly, but trembled.

"But what," said Lion Limb, after a pause, "do these chests contain beside ore, I wonder?"

Old Canbool trembled in every limb, when Emma whispered to him,

"He knows all!"

Old Canbool's nose became purple.

"He knows nothing," said Aixa, contemptuously. "Get to work, quickly, I say."

Old Canbool, swayed by the fascinating manner of Queen Aixa, felt all his energies revive.

A dark cloud passed over his brow and then he replied to Lion Limb.

"King, the moment has indeed arrived for settling all our accounts and paying off old scores. You will soon know what these coffers contain."

Then, walking with a firm but hasty step towards the door of the armoury, he bolted it silently, locked it, and carefully put the key in his pocket.

"What mean you, Canbool?" hastily demanded Lion Limb, surprised at the old man's conduct.

"Nothing is more annoying than for one to be disturbed when settling accounts," said old Canbool, very drily.

"And you would prudently secure yourself against troublesome visitors, then?" said Lion Limb, thinking of Dick and the others, whom he expected would soon arrive.

"You have guessed rightly, my lord."

"But I who have not the slightest motive for mistrust, desire that the door be opened, and left open. So give me the key."

Old Canbool jumped behind the huge chest for protection, the fastenings of which he undid hastily.

"Restore to me the key, rebellious old fool!" said Lion Limb, making a rush at the treasurer.

"And I forbid you, Canbool!" said a voice, as if from the bowels of the earth.

At the same instant the lids of the chests were lifted up, and eight men, like eight phantoms, rose up terrible and threatening.

Emma, terror-stricken, threw herself before Lion Limb.

Aixa, her eyes sparkling like those of a tigress, sprang with joy to the side of old Canbool.

"Well played!" said she; "the wolf is caught in our trap."

Lion Limb, betrayed by the old treasurer and deserted by Dick and his companions, and with Emma only by his side, resolved to defend himself to the last extremity.

An extreme pallor reigned on his noble brow, but his eyes were calm and cool, his hand sure, and his heart beat freely.

At the same time he did not deceive himself as to the probable result of the desperate struggle in which he was about to engage.

He desired only, while making the sacrifice of his life, to die as a valiant soldier, with his face towards the enemy.

"To work! to work!" exclaimed old Canbool; "give him no time to think."

"One moment," said a desperado, advancing towards Lion Limb. "I wish to speak to our prisoner."

"Prisoner! no, not yet," said Lion Limb, fiercely.

"Will you surrender?"

"No—never."

"We don't want to kill you."

"Perhaps not, villains, but it is your desire to secure me alive and then hand me over, bound in chains, to my worst enemy, Mungo the Buccaneer."

"It is."

"Then ten thousand deaths first!" said Lion Limb. "Come on, rascals, one and all! I am ready."

"Patience," said old Canbool; "patience, Lion Limb; you will lose nothing by it."

And at the same time the old treasurer took from one of the chests several cords, all of which terminated in a running knot.

Lion Limb beheld all these preparations without betraying the slightest emotion.

But Emma, more and more frightened at this frightful scene, flung herself on her knees before the conspirators, and with tearful eyes, begged them to spare Lion Limb.

The desperadoes treated Emma's appeal with contempt, and they heaped upon Lion Limb and all his band volleys of vile oaths.

But Lion Limb bore it all with dignity and calmness.

The only arms he had at the moment was a long dagger.

This he drew, and retreating to a corner, so that he might have all his assailants face to face with him, he gazed upon his foes with fiery indignation.

He would listen to no proposition to surrender, but valiantly defied them to do their worst.

Meanwhile, Queen Aixa sought an opportunity to give vent to her rage, hatred, and vengeance before the conspirators struck the fatal blow.

Thrusting Emma Clarence aside, she leant her body forward, less like a woman than a lioness about to spring upon Lion Limb, and spoke thus in a hissing tone.

"Since you love this girl," said she, pointing to Emma, "it is right, before these men carry you away or slay you—for I know not what they intend to do with you—it is right, I say, that I should open the sealed book of my heart to you, Lion Limb, whose pages you have never been able to read. Well, then, hear me before you die. I *never* loved you—never, mark me, never. You thought, perhaps, that I was enamoured of your blue eyes and curly hair that you inherit from your ancestors, the Saxons. Poor fool! that which I loved in you, Lion Limb, was your power, your crown, your dominion over all our isles ; but since all these are now slipping from your grasp—since you have preferred a mere miserable English girl to me, Katamar's niece, and Queen of the Pearl Islands, be thou doomed and accursed !"

Lion Limb met this last insult with a smile of disdain, for his look at that moment had encountered the upturned gaze of Emma Clarence, which seemed to say,

"I, at least, love you for yourself alone, Lion Limb."

"By all our native gods and goddesses," said old Canbool, making a grimace, which testified the contempt with which all these brawlings inspired him, "how long, brave campanions, are you going to howl around this fellow, like half-starved wolves ? You all howl and grind your teeth, but you do not bite."

The truth was Lion Limb looked more cool and formidable than they liked.

"All these fellows are afraid," said Aixa, jeeringly, and with a loud scornful laugh. "Cowards never do much work."

These words produced a magical effect on the conspirators.

They now brandished their swords and daggers, and danced about and before Lion Limb.

But they did not dare to approach too close to him.

Old Canbool, notwithstanding, did not care to be the first man to endanger his skin, and waited to see what the others could or would do, and how they would sustain the first shock against a captain so renowned for skill and bravery as Lion Limb.

"Accursed cowards ! Dare you raise your hand against your king ?" said Lion Limb.

And he boldly marched forward to confront them all.

The conspirators recoiled before him, terror-stricken.

"You are not our king," said one, "and never shall be."

"We shall soon see about that, my dusky lads," cried a voice, at the sound of which Lion Limb started, while swords flashed around him !

CHAPTER CII.

EMMA CLARENCE SAVES LION LIMB'S LIFE.

It was the voice of Dick Hamilton.

The conspirators turned their heads in alarm, and saw four suits of rhinoceros armour move with a loud clatter, leap from their stands on to the marble floor, and rush into the midst of them, as if they had suddenly been endowed with life by some magical power.

There was an instant disorder and wild surprise.

"Treason ! treason !" shouted all the villains in a wild chorus, running wildly about in hopes of finding some outlet to escape.

But they forgot that old Canbool had the door key in his pocket.

Dick and his companions soon singled out their opponents, and fought fiercely with them.

Young Ted Rawlings, though hampered in his movements by the rhinoceros armour, did wonders.

Armed with a chain, at the extremity of which was suspended an iron ball bristling with sharp points, he made it fly round him with great dexterity.

With this implement he drove old Canbool and another into one corner of the hall, laughing boisterously all the time.

Old Canbool and Karnack followed, with terrified looks, the evolutions of this iron ball, and, crouching in their corner, uttered cries of grief and despair.

There was one ruffian, however, who dared to encounter Lion Limb ; but each time that the former attempted to spring upon his prey, he felt the sharp point of Lion Limb's dagger pricking him in the breast, and forced him to draw back.

Anger and disappointment made the villian's hand to tremble.

Lion Limb, being well skilled in arms, resolved to have done with an enemy whom he regarded as unworthy of him, and marching straight upon his foe, was about to deal a death blow, when a sudden cry of pain from Dick startled him.

It appears that Dick had made two prisoners, and was in the act of binding them with cords, when one of the rascals leaped upon, and wounded him.

Forgetting his own danger, and only thinking of Dick, Lion Limb was about to rush to the assistance of his friend.

But a villain had watched Lion Limb's movements.

He thought to deliver a death blow from behind, and advanced for that purpose with upraised weapon.

It would have been all over with Lion Limb, had not Emma Clarence, with one of those heroic impulses with which love inspires woman, flung herself between Lion Limb and the impending blow !

The villain's weapon inflicted a frightful gash in the shoulder of the brave girl.

The blood gushed forth.

Emma closed her eyes, sank down upon her knees, and fell at the feet of Lion Limb without uttering a single word of complaint.

Lion Limb had that instant turned round, and he heard that she was dead.

Losing all self-possession, and listening only to the promptings of despair, he rushed with wild, blood-shot eyes upon the villain who had done the deed.

Horror-struck at the sight of Emma bleeding before him, and beholding in her the adored being for whom he would have willingly given his own life ten times over, stretched apparently lifeless on the blood-stained floor, he seemed to feel the powers of a giant.

"Emma Clarence slain !" he exclaimed, with the fixity of regard of a madman. "Emma slain ; but by Heaven she shall be amply avenged. I am about to die !"

And with these words he dashed into the midst of the deadly fray.

Young Ted Rawlings, who had all this time been torturing old Canbool and Karnack, suspended for a moment the punishment he took delight in administering to the luckless treasurer and his slave, and broke out into wild laughter.

The next moment, singling out the villain who had struck down Emma Clarence, he twisted his spiked ball about with unerring aim, and cleaved the rascal's skull in two.

Had not this happened the villain might have escaped, for seeing what he had done, and finding that Lion Limb was singling him out from among all the rest, he flew to a window, and would have jumped down.

Queen Aixa, who, from a pedestal stood and gazed coldly on this scene of blood, excited her friends to still greater efforts.

But gradually they were overcome one by one, and bound with cords.

When she saw Emma struck down, however, and bleeding on the floor, her eyes flashed fire in joy.

The colour mounted to her cheeks until they became all crimson.

"Now I can die in peace," she sighed. "That wretched girl is dead, and been deservedly slain."

But when she saw Lion Limb bend over the wounded and motionless girl, and staunch and bind up her wounds, Aixa became pale as death again, and she cast fierce and bitter glances on all around her.

"Alive still!" she hissed. "Then she triumphs. Lion Limb also triumphs, and I—what am I? A despised slave! But that shall never be. Death—a thousand deaths is preferable to that. I will swallow poison, and die like my poor friends here stretched upon the gory floor.

She was about to drink the contents of a small phial, which contained a deadly poison.

But her hand was quickly arrested by Lion Limb.

Aixa, gloomy and silent, witnessed the scene of tumult as motionless as a statue.

She awaited the issue of the event with that haughty calm and stoical appearance of indifference which belief in fatality inspires in the faithful followers of Indian rites.

Turning to those who had remained faithful to him—

"Thanks to you, Emma," said Lion Limb, "to you who so generously risked your life to save mine! Thanks to you, my gallant brothers, who have defended me with so much boldness and courage! As for you, princess," he added, addressing Aixa, "as for you, renegades, I am about to pronounce your sentence. Let us begin with you, Canbool, who are the least culpable in my eyes, for you are but an enemy, while the others are traitors?"

"You are too good, my lord," replied the treasurer. "I am, on the contrary, a great culprit, unworthy of pardon. For the which reason banish me, I pray you, from your august presence; have me put outside the walls, with strict orders never to return. It is no more than I deserve."

"I will follow your advice, and you shall be hung, Canbool."

"Hung!" repeated Canbool, stupefied and heaving a profound sigh.

"You, noble lady," said Lion Limb, addressing Aixa, "I banish you. In an hour you will quit the palace with your women."

Aixa let fall upon Lion Limb and Emma a look of intense hate, cold and venomous as that of a viper; but she made no reply, and preserved a contemptuous silence.

"As for you, Karnack, and you others," continued Lion Limb, "if within twelve hours, independently of the tax which I have levied upon you, you have not filled one of these coffers with gold in payment of your ransom, you shall be hung from gibbets which you may see from this spot!"

"But you will give us our liberty on parole?" asked Karnack.

"On parole! Come, you are joking. Karnack, you will go alone to accomplish this mission, and you shall answer for the rest—body for body."

They broke out into dismal groanings.

CHAPTER CIII.
AIXA'S REVENGE.

AIXA was banished.

She left the city, and as she did so, vowed to effect the destruction of Lion Limb, and to aid the cause of Mungo.

Mungo, who had been very busy at no great distance from the walls, with his numerous bands of outlaws, knew that Lion Limb was pressed hard to supply food for his men, and therefore kept up a strong guard to prevent any of the natives from carrying flour, and other provisions into the city.

One of these messengers he caught himself, but Mungo did not recognise in the handsome fellow his old enemy, Harry Woodruff.

Harry had attired himself in a Spanish costume, and thought he might avoid detection in his disguise, for besides purchasing provisions, he had volunteered to go out and spy all the preparations of Mungo and his buccaneers; but in an evil moment he met a ferocious horseman, who was Mungo himself. (See Cut.)

Harry was made prisoner and bound with cords, but his captors never dreamt it was the famous Harry Woodruff.

How he lived, and what he did while under the keeping of the buccaneers, we shall presently see, and his exciting adventures require further notice, which in its proper place will be recounted.

Bill Whetherby, also, had escaped from captivity under Lion Limb, through treachery, and having rejoined Mungo, he was bitter in his hatred, and thirsted for the blood of Lion Limb.

To Whetherby, Mungo gave secret orders, and Bill resolved that no provisions should be allowed to get into Katamar's city, and for that purpose he kept vigilant watch both day and night.

Early and late did Bill Whetherby watch and nourish his hopes of speedy vengeance.

The sun was so powerful that Bill was compelled to stretch himself beneath the shadow of a gigantic tree to repose a little.

He was just beginning, at the end of a few minutes, to fall asleep, when, hearing a slight noise, he re-opened his eyes, and saw a gentle movement in the branches of a neighbouring fig-tree.

There soon appeared a man, whose shoulders bent beneath the weight of an enormous sack of flour, and who cast anxious glances around.

This man, dressed in white like a miller, descended a hollow path, at the extremity of which four soldiers awaited him.

Thanks to the shrubs and plants with which the ground was thickly covered, Bill was able to advance without noise, and distinctly behold these latter, in whom he recognised four friends of Lion Limb.

LION LIMB

THE BOY KING
OF THE SOUTH SEA ISLANDS.

LION LIMB'S MEN CAPTURING CATTLE.

These brave young men instantly set to work to move a heavy stone covered with moss, which concealed the entrance to an old aqueduct, and placed upon the back of one of the mules which were in the subterranean passage the sack of flour which the miller had just brought to them.

"The devil!" said Bill to himself, "while we are blockading the town on one side, these cunning foxes are victualling it from the other."

And, crawling on his hands and knees, notwithstanding the weight of his arms, he drew so near as to be able to catch the meaning of the words which the men were exchanging among themselves.

In order not to be taken unawares, and to be able to defend himself if necessary, he seated himself on a little mound, with his feet in a ditch, leaning his back against a solitary palm tree, and with his hand on the hilt of his sword.

"Which of you have the keys of the gate?" demanded one.

"I," replied another.

"Shall we enter by the palace or by the town?" said the miller.

"By the town," replied the first, "for the enemy must not know that we are bringing in these provisions."

"The motive is no business of mine," replied the miller. I have received the price of my flour, and whether the money comes from the devil or from Lion Limb——"

"It is Emma, the daughter of the old sea captain, beloved by Lion Limb," said one, "who has secretly sold her jewels to buy all the corn and all the provisions that we can contrive to introduce into our famished town."

At this moment, a sunbeam, falling full upon the armour of Bill Whetherby, revealed to the friends the presence of a stranger.

"We are betrayed!" they together exclaimed.

Bill, finding himself discovered, feigned to be asleep, and commenced snoring in a formidable manner.

They approached him.

"Bill Whetherby!" they exclaimed.

"Oh," said one, grasping the handle of his sword, "the capture of this captain would be the ruin of the bastard, Mungo, and the fortune of Lion Limb."

"Death, then, to him!" added the others.

"Death!" repeated one, regarding his dagger with a sinister look; "but he is alone, and sleeping."

"You are right," said a third; "but I know a means of forcing this ruffian to surrender at discretion."

"What means?" eagerly demanded one.

"Yes," thought Bill, "let us hear the means. I am curious to know."

"By counting twenty paces from the entrance of the aqueduct to the left, I have remarked," continued one, "an excavation produced by the filtration of the waters. I will undertake to transform, in a few minutes, this hole into a ditch deep enough for a man not to be able to get out of it without the aid of a ladder or a pair of wings. The ditch once dug, we will cover it over with leaves and branches of trees, will strew the whole over with a few shovelsful of earth, and we will draw the villain into this snare."

"To work, to work!" exclaimed the others.

They returned to the aqueduct, whilst the miller hastened to cut and gather up the branches, and one lay in wait a few paces from the sleeping ruffian with bow and arrow ready to take aim at him in the event of his waking before the ambuscade was ready.

For certain, Whetherby had never been exposed to more imminent danger; nevertheless his heart beat no faster than usual.

The friends, at the end of a quarter of an hour, made signs to the miller to come and rejoin them.

They then drove from out the subterranean passage one of the mules well loaded, the conduct of which they confided to the miller.

When this man was close to Bill, whom he feigned not to see, he made the animal return towards the entrance of the aqueduct, urging it forward with loud cries, and striking heavy blows upon the sacks with his thick stick.

Bill, judging rightly that the moment for awaking had arrived, rose suddenly, and sprang forward as if to stop the miller; the latter, according to the orders he had received from the others, uttered loud cries of alarm, and fled, driving the mule before him into the aqueduct, whither Bill followed him with his drawn sword.

When he had counted fifteen steps in walking under the arcades of granite he stopped, letting the conductor of the mule go forward; then he fixed his piercing eyes upon the wall, and, in spite of the darkness, he distinguished standing in front of the spot where the ditch was to be opened the four friends, who seemed paralyzed in their flight by terror, and who, clasping their hands, were uttering loud cries for mercy.

"Oh, the villanous traitors!" murmured Bill.

Then, replacing his sword in its scabbard, to encourage them to quit their position—

"Come out of that, rascals!" he exclaimed, "and tell me where you are conveying that corn and that flour."

"Have pity on us," replied one, in a whining tone, "and you shall know the whole truth."

"What is your name?" demanded Bill.

"I am a poor devil, beneath your anger, who only seeks to earn his bread."

"Well, my lads," said Bill, who longed to see them set their snare in operation, "I pardon you on one condition. You were transporting these provisions to the town, were you not, by this road?"

And he extended his hand in that direction.

"Yes, my lord," replied the others.

"Well, then, since you have yourselves just changed the direction of your road, you will continue to retrace your steps, and conduct your mules to the camp of Mungo, my master."

"To the camp of Mungo? Never!" they exclaimed.

"Oh, if needs be," said Bill, with a laugh, "I will serve you as an escort. If the worst comes to the worst, I will carry you there myself, you and your baggage."

But the scene had changed.

The four supplicants uttered a howl of fury in reply to the provocation of Bill, and now stood in threatening attitudes before him.

"Surrender!" they cried.

"Surrender to rogues like you!" disdainfully replied Bill. "What do you take me for? My trade is to make prisoners, and not to be a prisoner myself."

The four young men rushed furiously upon him all at once.

Assailed by a shock so violent and sudden, deprived of his sword, which had been broken at the commencement of the struggle, Bill was stunned for a moment and almost driven backwards.

He forgot the ditch that opened two steps behind him.

But the others had not forgotten it, and already gave utterance to a shout of triumph.

All at once Bill's foot, which he had planted firmly on the ground to recover his strength and breath, felt the earth trembling and giving way beneath it.

He found himself suddenly on the extreme verge of the ditch; but this critical situation, instead of lessening his courage, only served to strengthen it.

Collecting all his force with one mighty effort, at the very moment when the four friends thought to drag him into the invisible gulf, he gave them so terrible a shake, as they clung to him all at once, that they were forced to let go their hold, and rolled to the ground behind him, while the bold ruffian leaped like a tiger, in spite of the weight of his armour, right over the head of one.

The scaffolding of branches, leaves, and earth gave way beneath the weight, and precipitated them headlong into the ditch.

"It is now your turn to surrender, villains!" cried Bill.

"Do you speak to us of surrendering?"

"Boasters, like all Indians!" cried Bill, shrugging his shoulders, with the intention of goading their fury to madness.

As they advanced upon him he made believe to draw back, and continued to do so until he had got near to the mule laden with the sacks of flour.

At this juncture, the friends, certain of triumphing over their unarmed enemy, were preparing to take advantage of his desperate position, and to strike without mercy if he still refused to surrender.

It seemed as if nothing short of a miracle or some unforseen event could save Whetherby from certain death; when, all at once, he drew himself up to his full height, and grasping in his robust hands with square wrists an enormous sack of flour, he used it with such powerful effect, and hurled such vigorous blows upon them, that they strove in vain to resist and use their weapons.

Blinded and half-smothered with the flour, as the sack descended with a rapid succession of blows that allowed them time neither to reflect nor breathe, half maddened by the mocking laugh of Bill, they backed, in their turn, to the very edge of the ditch, where the others lay rolling and tossing like infuriated bulls.

"I must have some talk with you," said Bill, to the chief man. "I heard just now that it is you who have the keys of the gate that forms the outlet of this aqueduct on the side of the town."

"I have them," replied the chief, in a smothered voice.

"I must have them."

"Never! I will never betray Lion Limb in so cowardly a manner!"

"I must have them, I tell you; and if you do not give them me with a good grace, I will take them by force!"

"Stay!" exclaimed the man, seeing that Bill was preparing to put his threat into execution. "I will give them up to you, but God is my witness that I only yield to violence."

And he with difficulty drew from the pockets of his breeches two large keys attached to each other by means of a silver ring.

"Here are the precious keys," he exclaimed, showing them to Whetherby; "but you shall never have them!" he added, flinging them into the ditch.

But Bill had foreseen this movement, and forcibly compressed the man's hand at the same moment; so that the keys fell on the edge of the pit.

Meanwhile the miller, on whose clothes Bill was reckoning to effect his entrance into the town as quietly as possible, had quitted the aqueduct and taken flight across the fields, looking frequently behind him to make sure that he was not pursued.

This precaution, though good in principle, proved bad in practice, for the poor man fell plump into the midst of Mungo's men, who, seated in a circle, were awaiting the return of Whetherby.

A cry of mingled terror and anger escaped simultaneously from every mouth.

Fear so enlarges objects that they took this lean and trembling miller, whose countenance was whiter than his apparel, for Lion Limb.

"Ah, traitor, robber!" they exclaimed, rising simultaneously.

But they were not long in recognizing their mistake on hearing the miller entreat them in a supplicating voice to have pity on him.

"Whence come you?"

"Who are you?"

"Where are you going?" were questions poured in upon him from all sides at once.

"Alas! worthy sirs, such as you see me, I am flying from the terrible Bill Whetherby, whom I have left fighting with four soldiers."

"Whetherby?" exclaimed they, astounded. "Where is he?"

"In the old aqueduct, where I used to carry my sacks of flour."

"Well, then, act as guide to us," said one; "and woe be to you if we arrive too late!"

They then all, under the guidance of the miller, rushed hastily off in the direction of the aqueduct.

Bill was beginning to be greatly embarrassed with his prisoners, for he dared not set out in pursuit of the miller from the fear that in his absence the others would contrive to extricate themselves from the ditch by making a ladder of each other.

Thus the arrival of his men caused Bill a joyful surprise.

"Here we are, captain!" cried one, as soon as he had entered the aqueduct.

"Ah, is it you, my brave fellows?" said Bill. "You are welcome."

"We bring you back a prisoner," added one.

"What, the intrepid miller?" said Bill. "Well, we will procure him some companions. There are in this ditch four determined fellows. Get them out of this hole, where they are yelling like wild cats. They are prisoners that I will give to you, and you can draw a heavy ransom from them, for they are friends of the tyrant, Lion Limb."

"Thanks, captain. What are your next orders?"

"Undress this honest miller, and take off my cloak. It is an exchange that I wish to make with him. I condemn him as a punishment for having supplied provisions to a besieged city to march to the camp in the heat of the day."

And in the twinkling of an eye the miller was divested of his linen suit, in which Bill attired himself.

"Now," continued Bill, "conduct these five men to a hostelry; drink and eat gaily with your prisoners, without quarrelling, and without ceasing to watch over them."

Bill Whetherby had formed the bold project of utilizing the discovery of the secret entrance to the aqueduct by introducing himself disguised as a miller, into the city to learn, from personal observation, if the besieged could hold out still longer.

From time to time he stopped, for he thought he distinguished, with his eagle glance, floating forms afar off; but each time he thought it must be an hallucination, and he was in the act of laughing at his error, when he suddenly arrived at a sort of cross way, where the vaulted gallery of the aqueduct divided itself into three arteries.

He instantly stopped, greatly perplexed, but, after a few moments' hesitation, he resolved to trust to the instinct of the mules, who had continued their road by the middle gallery.

He proceeded on his way, and was about to overtake them, when he heard a heavy noise behind him, the sound of footsteps resounding on the ground, which was paved with bricks; and, just as he was turning round, a hand was laid upon his shoulder.

It was a woman, habited in a long white mantle, who had just sprang from out of the gallery that overhung the aqueduct.

Bill regarded her with surprise, whilst the young woman, her countenance animated with a radiant expression, exclaimed—

"These sacks of corn and flour cannot escape us, for I also was watching them on their way."

"Alas! have pity on me, good lady," replied Bill, greatly surprised at this sudden apparition, and persisting in playing the character he had undertaken; "you would not maltreat a poor miller, who has no other object than to gain an honest livelihood."

"You, a miller!" said the young woman, with a laugh. "The frock does not make the friar, merry jester. You are Bill Whetherby, and you shall not pass without hearing me."

"Ah, lady of darkness," exclaimed Bill, greatly chagrined at this unforseen incident, "to recognize me in this obscurity, and in spite of the costume in which I have disguised myself, you must be either a sorceress of the first water, or one of the best paid spies of the tyrant, Lion Limb."

"I am not a spy, but none other than a disgraced queen," replied Aixa.

"You, so renowned for your marvellous beauty?" said Bill, adroitly, with a courteous bow.

Aixa could not restrain a smile; she proceeded—

"Driven from the palace and banished, I have vowed an implacable hatred to Lion Limb, and I shall faithfully keep my word. We may, therefore, you see, speak quite freely."

"Well, madam, my object is simply to enter the besieged city by the aid of this sorry attire. But am I, then, so badly disguised that I cannot take a step without the risk of being discovered?"

"Take courage; my sorcery is very easy of explanation. I witnessed from a distance the encounter you sustained against the four soldiers, and I heard your name pronounced by them with hatred and fury, by your own troopers with joy and transport. Let us return to your projects. You have surrounded the town in order to intercept the arrival of provisions, but you had forgotten this aqueduct. Now that you have discovered it, you will content yourself no longer with so little. You wish to enter by this subterranean passage. You will ask me, and with reason, why I, who am so much the enemy of Lion Limb, did not reveal to you this outlet? Because my vengeance, sir, is not so easily satisfied as that of Mungo. His arises from ambition, mine from hate. I would have Lion Limb, who has despised me; Emma Clarence, who has humiliated me; the people of the town, who have insulted me, suffer prolonged tortures by my means. I have taken a terrible oath which has rendered me your accomplice. I have sworn to reduce to famine this city, which is odious to me, and I have succeeded. My emissaries are scattered all over the country, and all the corn, all the flour which had escaped the researches of the purveyors of your army and which Lion Limb had thought to purchase at its weight in gold, I have contrived to buy up from them. All these provisions are buried in caves under the ruined arches of the aqueduct, and these caverns I can at any moment inundate at need."

"By Satan," exclaimed Bill, "I should be sorry to give you cause of complaint against me, madam! I should tremble for my skin. Mungo will owe you a royal recompense, madam," said Bill, astonished at so much resolution and audacity in a young and beautiful woman.

CHAPTER CIV.

THE ADVENTURES OF TED RAWLINGS AMONG THE BUCCANEERS.

FROM all that we have related regarding the trials and sufferings of Lion Limb and his band of devoted followers, it will be admitted that unless something fortunate should happen to them, Mungo and his restless desperadoes would either kill them off one by one, or starve them into submission if possible.

It was for want of proper provisions and a regular supply that Lion Limb could not or did not take the field against his grim adversary, Mungo.

Mungo, as we have seen, had many friends among the subjects of Katamar.

And, as we know, there was no one who more ardently desired the downfall of Lion Limb than the revengeful young queen, Aixa.

Whenever Lion Limb made up his mind, which he sometimes did, to sally forth and give battle to Mungo, it was always necessary to leave a strong force behind him, or otherwise he would have had no town or place to fall back upon.

And Mungo also was too artful to venture forth in open battle with Lion Limb, for he knew the desperate bravery of the English youth and his men.

It was Mungo's desire to starve out the young settlers, if it could be done.

This idea was now strongly recommended by Queen Aixa, who used all her power and influence to swell the number of Mungo's followers.

Young Ted Rawlings, however, was resolved to attempt something bold and hazardous.

"Captain Lion Limb," said Ted, "what had we better do? We can't starve ourselves to death."

"I know that, Ted; I have sent out scouts to bring provisions into the city."

"But perhaps they may never return."

"Why do you think so?"

"We are surrounded by enemies, captain, and two out of every three who have gone out to get loads of provisions have never returned."

"Well, what would you have me do?"

"Fight, captain, fight."

"But the mongrel Mungo won't fight, Ted."

"So it seems."

"Every time we go forth to give him battle, the villain changes his ground, and goes far away."

"I wonder if they know how we are situated at Fort Martin, captain?"

"If they did, Ted, I don't think they would be able to render us much assistance."

"Perhaps not, sir; but they have an abundance of provisions."

"So they have."

"Then I propose to sail over to the island, and——"

"You, Ted!"

"Yes, me, captain; why not?"

"The dangers are many."

"I care not for that. Haven't you exposed yourself to thousands of dangers for our sakes? and besides that, captain," said Ted, "our lads couldn't afford to let you go, for we must have a leader."

"And do you seriously think of doing this, Ted?"

"I do so, captain; and if you can only manage to keep the devils out of the town for a few days, I shall return from Fort Martin not only with plenty of provisions, but with men also."

"But, how do you intend to go?"

"Go? Why, in a sail boat."

"But the distance is great."

"I know it is, but I care not for that."

"You don't know which way to sail."

"The devil I don't!"

"What, without a compass?"

"Yes, without a compass; I want no compasses, sir."

"Why, Ted, you must be mad."

"I was never more sane in my life, captain," said Ted, laughing.

"How can you find your way to Fort Martin, I ask, if you don't know which way to sail?"

"But I do know which way to sail, captain."

"How is that?"

"You know that high mountain on the sea coast near where we ran ashore in coming to this island?"

"I do. We called it Mount Hamilton, Ted."

"So we did, sir."

"Well, what about this mountain?"

"I ascended it once or twice, and at sunrise and sunset I could just see afar off a speck on the ocean, which, I am certain, is Martin Island."

"No doubt you did."

"Well, having seen it so, I can steer my way clear enough, and, if they don't come to our assistance like brave men when I have explained everything to them, why, then, Captain Lion Limb, I only wish the sea may swallow up their island altogether."

"It is a perilous undertaking, Ted."

"I know it is, captain; but, I am all the more pleased on that account. Some of the men used to say I wasn't brave and all that, and that I was in the habit of showing the 'white feather,' as they called it; but I'll show 'em all that I'm as brave as any one."

"You will never return, Ted, if you once set out, I fear."

"Don't say that, sir," said Ted, laughing. "I'm like cork, and shall always float. Good-bye, captain; I'm off!"

"Here, here, stop that mad youth," cried Lion Limb, in great haste. "Stop him, I say! he is crazy to undertake such a wild mission."

But, for all that, Ted did *not* stay.

He rushed away, full of hope and confidence, and when Lion Limb inquired for him several hours afterwards it was ascertained beyond a doubt that young Ted Rawlings had kept his word, for he was nowhere to be found.

*　　　*　　　*　　　*

In the darkness young Ted started out alone and unsuspected.

His road to the coast lay through that part of the country where Mungo and his men were encamped.

Ted's trials, difficulties, and dangers were many indeed.

Yet he had made up his mind to encounter even death itself to do honour to his beloved Captain Lion Limb.

More than once did Ted nearly fall into the hands of those who were prowling about and guarding the roads.

He was challenged two or three times, but he managed to elude all the cunning and vigilance of Mungo's men, and even contrived to enter their camps at night, when he heard a great deal that would have been pleasant for Lion Limb's ears.

It appeared from all that Ted could hear that Mungo had captured one of Lion Limb's men.

But who it was neither Tom nor the buccaneer chief then knew.

As he had been so far successful in not being discovered, Ted's heart became bolder and bolder.

"I'll see who it is they have captured, if I die for it," thought Ted.

And, on his hands and knees, he crawled in the inky darkness towards Mungo's tent.

Mungo and his chief men were feasting and carousing in very grand style.

They seemed to be living on the very fat of the land, while Lion Limb and his brave followers were almost starving.

"Why don't you march up to our men, and give battle to that brat called Lion Limb?" asked one.

"Why, you see," said Mungo, "we know this Lion Limb of old, and, although none of us care about him much——"

"No, no; just so," said the buccaneers, in chorus.

"We don't want to give ourselves more trouble about him than we can help," said Mungo, tossing off his glass. "In fact, we intend to starve them out like rats."

"An excellent plan, too."

"But we are getting more friends every day," continued Mungo; "and some powerful ones you may depend."

"That's what we want."

"There's the young queen, Aixa, Katamar's niece, she's the mortal enemy of Lion Limb."

"So I have heard; but for what cause?" asked one.

"How should *I* know," growled Mungo.

"Well, it is whispered that at one time she *loved* this Lion Limb."

"W-h-a-t!" muttered several at once, in tones of disgust.

"Love such a whelp as Lion Limb!" said Mungo, elevating his shaggy eyebrows. "Now, if she had loved *me*——"

"Aye, if Queen Aixa had only loved *him*," here chorused a dozen at once, "she would have shown good taste."

"So *I* think. Thank'ee, my lads, for your good opinions," said Mungo, drinking his own health.

"But, as I was about to observe," said Mungo; "Queen Aixa is Lion Limb's deadliest enemy, and nothing will satisfy her but the young brat's death."

"Then I fear she will have to wait a long time," sighed Ted, as he listened in his hiding-place.

"We shall soon starve him out," said one; "and that's better than all the fighting."

"So *I* think," another observed. "There's no use in shedding blood; at least, none of ours, when we can do all we want to do without it."

"Here, here; that's just what *I* say," observed Mungo, "and, to prove that we are none of us very far wrong, I hear that some of our men have captured a spy; but, although I have seen and questioned him, none of us can make anything out on him."

"I wonder who it can be," thought Ted, sighing.

"He seems a gallant sort of fellow, though," continued Mungo; "and he's dressed up in the Spanish fashion."

"Yes, but that was to disguise himself, you may depend," said one.

"Sure it was."

"But suppose all of us have a squint at this captive."

"I've no objection in the world," said Mungo, "and, if you can make anything more out of him than *I* have, why then you are all clever indeed."

"Never fear, but we'll make him open his mouth," said several, laughing in a rough and boisterous manner.

"Never fear, you will, my lads; but you mustn't use too much force. I don't want to have him killed just yet awhile."

"Is there any news from old Katamar's capital?" asked one.

"Yes; and before we have this stranger brought in, I will just whisper to you in all confidence that some of the news is very bad."

"Very bad, Mungo?"

"Aye, very bad; our old friends, Karnack and Canbool, have been discovered in their plans to assist us, and, as you may well suppose, they have suffered for it."

"Well, then, let us pay it back on this fellow we have captured, that's all; it will only be tit for tat, Mungo."

"No, I don't want this fellow killed as yet, I tell you, for we must first hear from Bill Whetherby. If he falls into Lion Limb's hands and is executed, why, then, let this fellow suffer also."

"There is not much fear of Bill Whetherby ever being caught again."

"I don't know so much about that; he has entered their city."

"Entered their city!"

"Yes; dressed and disguised as a miller; and if he don't find out all the plans of Lion Limb, and kill him besides, it will be surprising to me."

"It's all up with Lion Limb, then, if Bill Whetherby gets into the city," said several, laughing, and striking the tables in joy.

"Well, now that I have told you so much, let us call in the captive, and examine him."

"Yes, bring him in, bring him in."

In a short time Harry Woodruff was brought in bound with cords.

Ted turned deadly pale as he peeped from his hiding-place, and discovered that the captive was none other than brave Harry.

The buccaneers looked hard at the prisoner as he entered the tent, and were, perhaps, surprised and annoyed at his bold and defiant attitude and look.

They expected, perhaps, to see a poor, skinny, trembling knave, who would cower like a cur before their gaze.

But they were all very much mistaken if such, indeed, had been their thoughts.

"Who and what are you?" asked one of the half-tipsy buccaneers, in a quick, surly tone.

"Not so fast, not so fast," said Mungo, hiccupping; "I am captain here, I think, at present; let me ask the prisoner, not you."

After clearing his throat with a long draught of wine, and coughing several times very importantly.

"Who the devil are you?" said Mungo; "answer quickly, I say, or it may go the worse with you."

"I am, if you wish to know," said Harry, firmly, "one of Lion Limb's best friends, and——"

"His best friend, eh? Mark that, my comrades, and don't forget it, mind."

"Hang him at once, then," said the buccaneers.

"What else are you, then?" asked Mungo.

"Your enemy," said Harry, calmly.

"My what!" gasped Mungo, purple with anger.

"I have said it once; your enemy," Harry repeated.

"Oh! shoot him on the instant," growled the fierce-looking assembly.

And several pulled out their pistols to carry out this idea, but Mungo calmed them.

"Stop, my lads, I haven't done with him yet."

"How many men has Lion Limb got?" asked one.

"I refuse to say."

"He is almost starving, of course," said another.

"No he isn't," Harry replied, proudly; "he has plenty of provisions of all sorts."

"That's false sworn, Mungo; he and his men are in great want; I know that fact beyond a doubt."

Harry had told a lie, but he looked firm, and wished to deceive Mungo, if possible.

"For," thought he, "all's fair in war."

"That's a lie, of course it is," chimed in the buccaneers, "we all know that; the young villain is on his last legs; we have got him caged at last."

"Don't be too sure of that," said Harry. "You will have to fight hard, yes, very hard, before you subdue Lion Limb and his followers."

"Yes; but we don't intend to fight," said Mungo, laughing; "we mean to starve him out like a rat in a hole."

"A thing you will never be able to do, I tell you," said Harry; "and if it were to come to pass, it would be very cowardly so to act. Why don't you fight him fair?"

"Cowardly you call it, eh?" growled Mungo; "I think you had better mind what sort of words you use, young man, or you might get punished on the spot, mark me."

"Yes, and very severely handled, too, I can tell him," said another.

"I fear you not," said Harry. "If I am your prisoner you can only kill me."

"Only kill you, eh? Well, come, that's impudent if you like," said Mungo, with a hoarse laugh; "but tell me, young man, and tell me truly, what does this Lion Limb think of me now?"

"He looks upon you as a ruffian, and——"

"A rough 'un, eh? well, come, come, that ain't bad at all, is it, captain?" said several at once, laughing. "Lion Limb looks upon you as a rough 'un, and a rough 'un you are, and no mistake. Bravo! that's just what we think, every man on us."

"I didn't say rough 'un," said Harry, interrupting them in their mirth.

"Then what did you say?"

"Ruffian."

"Oh!" "Ah!" "Yes!" "Just so!" said one and another; "then that's a horse of another colour entirely."

"And if I fell into Lion Limb's hands, what would he do with me?" asked Mungo.

"Hang you in very quick time," said Harry.

"Just how I shall serve him, when famine reduces him down to a skeleton," said Mungo, with a grim laugh.

"Well, you seem a bold fellow," remarked one; "if we were to spare your life now, would you join us?"

"Join you!" said Harry, with a red flush of anger on his face. "No, never!"

"And why not, pray?" asked Mungo.

"You are not the sort of men I like to mix with. You are not gentlemen."

"Not gentlemen, eh? What else, then, I should like to know?"

"Why, thieves and cut-throats every man of you."

Mungo, who was getting savage at Harry's coolness and courage, was about to fire at his prisoner; but by some accident his seat tipped over, knocked over the table, lights, glasses and the like, and all was a sudden state of darkness.

This accident had been caused by young Ted.

No sooner were the lights out than Ted approached Harry, and whispered in his ear.

Woodruff was amazed.

"Here; I have a knife," whispered Ted, "and can cut your cord. Don't move; there it is; now go on your hands and knees, and crawl after me; before the rascals can get other lights we shall be beyond reach."

Harry, once released, seized a sword and pistol which had fallen on the floor, and followed Ted Rawlings.

They crawled from the tent unobserved, and found several horses already saddled, that belonged to the drunken buccaneers.

They instantly vaulted into the saddle, and before Mungo and his friends could imagine what had become of their prisoner, Harry and Young Ted were galloping towards the sea coast at a terrific rate.

"Which way are you going, Ted? This isn't the road to Lion Limb."

"I know it isn't, Harry," said Ted, laughing, "but didn't I do the trick for you well?"

"Yes, yes, I know that; but where are you galloping to? This is the road to the sea."

"I know it, and the sooner we put a dozen miles between us and Mungo the better, I think," said Ted. "He meant shooting you, but as he rose from his seat I tipped it over, upset the table and everything. Spur up, Harry, spur up! I think we are pursued."

"So do I. Don't you hear them shouting yonder?"

"Yes; but they won't think of pursuing this way, they will imagine we have gone post haste to Lion Limb, which is a thing farthest from my thoughts, Harry."

"Then where are you bound for, Ted?"

"For Martin Island."

"And alone?"

"No, not now. Such was my intention at first, but now I have secured you you will come also, I hope."

And thereupon, as they galloped along towards the sea, Ted told Harry of his bold intention, and Harry promised to go with them, and arouse all the friends of Lion Limb far and near.

"Well done, Ted," said Harry, as they rode along. "You *are* plucky."

CHAPTER CV.

ARRIVAL OF HARRY AND TED AT MARTIN ISLAND —DISCOVERY OF JOE PEBBLES—THE ISLANDERS FORM THEMSELVES INTO BANDS OF SOLDIERS TO GO AND FIGHT FOR LION LIMB.

AFTER many trials by sea, Harry Woodruff and Ted Rawlings arrived safely at Martin Island, having placed their horses before sailing in a small and well-grassed valley.

Nothing particular happened to them, until when within a mile of Fort Martin, the two travellers stopped suddenly at the door of a cottage, and, it being night, they were unobserved.

"I hear a fiddle," said Ted.

"And some one is singing inside. Listen! Who is it?"

"Listen! It is Joe Pebbles, by Jove! singing a song (which song ran thus):—

THE ISLAND SETTLER.

The English lord may possess his flocks,
  And boast his fields of grain,
My home is 'mid the mountain rocks,
  The desert my domain.
I plant no herbs or pleasant fruits,
  Nor toil for savoury cheer;
The desert yields me juicy roots,
  And herds of bounding deer.
The crested adder honoureth me,
  And yields at my command,
His poison bag, like the honey bee,
  When I seize him on the sand.
Yes, even the locusts' wasting swarm,
  Which mighty nations dread,
To me brings joy in place of harm,
  For of them I make my bread.
Countless springboks are my flocks,
  Spread o'er the bounding plain,
The buffalo bends to my yoke,
  And the wild horse to my rein;
My arms are the quivering spear,
  My rein the tough bow string,
My bridle curb is a slender barb,
  Yet it quells the forest king.
Then am I lord of the desert land,
  And I will not leave my bounds,
To crouch beneath no lordling's hand,
  And kennel with his hounds.
To be a hound and watch the flocks,
  For a cruel master's gain,
No! the swart serpent of the rocks
  His den doth yet retain,
And none who dares his sting provoke,
  Shall find its poison vain.

"Why, that must be. I can't be mistaken in that voice," said Harry.

"It is Joe, I tell you," Ted said, laughing; "don't you hear his old fiddle?"

"Let's go in at once, then."

"No, not yet," said Ted; "hearken to him; he's spinning some yarn to the half-dozen half-breeds in the house; let's listen to what he says."

"Well; but we won't waste much time."

"No; listen."

And, as Ted spoke in a whisper, they both attentively placed their ears to the door.

"Ah, my fine fellows," said Joe, "none of you have the least notion of what I was when I was in England."

"Massa Pebbles be a great man in England, I hear 'em say."

"I believe you," said Joe; "and very rich, too. Oh! I had lots of money, and lots of servants, and lots of houses, and lots of everything else."

"Massa Pebbles must have been very happy," one remarked.

"Happy! I believe you; happy as the day was long; and wanted for nothing."

"Then why did Massa Pebbles leave all dem good tings behind to come so far among the Indians?"

"Ah, that's a settler," whispered Harry, to Ted outside. "What a string of lies he's telling these poor devils."

"Never mind; let us listen a little longer."

"Why did I leave Old England?" said Joe, scratching his head, and looking very much puzzled at the question. "Why I left for the good of——"

"Your country, perhaps," said one.

"No I didn't. What! do you mean to insult me?" said Joe, in an angry tone. "I tell you I left for the good of my health—for the good of my health, mind; that's all."

"Oh, we understand, Massa Pebbles, now."

"You see, the Captain of the 'Rattlesnake' was a twenty-fifth cousin of mine, and loved me very much indeed, and was going to leave me all his money, and, as a particular favour, asked me to go a voyage with him to take Lion Limb and a good many other convicts to distant settlements; but I wasn't a convict myself; I was a true lord, bless you, in England."

"Hearken to the fellow's lies," said Harry.

"And did you know much about this Lion Limb and Harry Woodruffe, and Dick Hamilton?" asked one of the half-breeds.

"Oh, yes; knew all their history. None of 'em are much to talk about. *I* was the party the settlers should have elected for king among 'em; if it had so happened, I shouldn't have been here, but roaming the seas in search of the cut-throat pirates."

At this moment Harry and Ted resolved upon playing a trick.

They suddenly opened the door, and, walking straight up to Joe, placed a hand upon his shoulder, saying—

"We arrest you as a deserter, Joe Pebbles."

"The devil you do! And who are you two mud-stained travellers, I should like to know? Don't you know who and what I am?"

"We know quite enough about you, Joe, and hold warrants for your apprehension from Lion Limb."

"Oh, Jupiter! I *am* in a fix," sighed Joe.

"I dare say you know who we are, Joe," said Ted.

"No, I don't."

"Our names are Harry Woodruff and Ted Rawlings," said the former, with a broad grin.

"The devil!" said Joe, in surprise. "Now who

the deuce ever thought of seeing you again. How are you?"

"We are very well."

"I am married, you know," said Joe. "There's my wife," said he, pointing to a tall and buxom half-breed, who was sitting by the fire, smoking and rolling her eyes.

"I fear you will have to tear yourself away from her for some time, Joe."

"How's that?"

"Why, we come to summon every man and boy capable of bearing arms to the assistance of Lion Limb."

"What, is he in such danger, then?"

"He is; and stands in need of immediate assistance."

And thus, while Joe and his wife were laying supper for the two travellers, Harry explained briefly the actual state of things between Lion Limb, the buccaneers under Mungo, and the disaffected islanders.

Directly Joe comprehended the danger in which Lion Limb really was, he went to the door, blew three blasts on a horn, and very soon appeared several active half-breeds.

"These are some of my herdsmen," said Joe, proudly. "I am a great man in the island now, and have much authority."

Giving to each of these his servants certain instructions, they all vaulted upon horses, and galloped away in different directions at headlong speed.

"What does that mean, Joe?" said Harry.

"It means that those riders will soon spread the news of your arrival, and inform the authorities at Fort Martin."

"But we might as well go to the fort ourselves."

"There is not the slightest occasion," said Joe; "for, since the buccaneers were among us here, we have altered in our manners and customs very much for the best."

"What do you mean, Joe?"

"I mean that every man jack of us are trained like soldiers, and, in less than two hours, we can assemble over two thousand strong and hardy men at the fort."

"You astonish me," said Harry.

"You see since I have been here," said Joe, "I have taught the people a thing or two, for it is, perhaps, more owing to me than anybody else in the island, that we have got two gun-boats, and an immense gun-raft ready for use. Besides all these things, we have large stores of provisions housed away, and should any rascally buccaneer band dare to insult or invade us any more, they will find us this time more than a match for them."

While Harry and Ted were enjoying their supper, the only hearty meal they had had since leaving Mungo's quarters, Joe Pebbles took up his fiddle again, and played several lively tunes, between which he would relate all that had happened to him and the islanders since Lion Limb's last visit.

While these three old companions were thus chatting, a loud booming noise was heard afar off.

"Ah! there it is," said Joe.

"What?" asked Harry.

"Why, the signal-gun," Joe replied.

"For what?"

"To summon all our men to arms."

"What, so soon?"

"Yes, this very hour; and besides that gun warned our gun-boats to prepare also; before morning you will find over two thousand men under arms, and ready to march."

This was perfectly true, as will afterwards appear.

For, during the night, men were passing and repassing towards the fort, some on foot, and some on horseback, and, when they least expected it, old Governor Martin and his council rode down to Joe's house, and had an interview with Harry.

Harry explained everything to them.

"Well, if such is the case, my brave lads," said old Governor Martin, "the very best thing for you to do is to set sail towards the island once more, and give warning to Lion Limb and his gallant band that we are about to set sail to his assistance, and not to lose courage, or give an inch of ground."

"Then if they go I shall go with them," said Joe.

"Well, do so," said old Governor Martin, "and your presence will give an assurance to Lion Limb that we intend to act on the part of friends."

"Right," said Joe, jumping up; "and now, old woman" (addressing his wife) "prepare something for our journey on the instant; no time must be lost; we must get down to the coast, and get out to sea with the tide."

"Some time to-morrow we shall set sail with our fine body of troops," said the old governor, "so I advise you to make all possible haste."

Harry, Joe, and Ted did not need a second admonition, for in less than half-an-hour all three of them were on their way to the coast where Harry had made fast his boat in a creek.

Several half-breeds accompanied them with mules, each laden with provisions and necessaries, and when they reached Harry's boat, they well loaded it, and, hoisting sail, put out to sea with a fair wind.

"You must have been plucky," said Joe, "to set out on such a journey without a compass or anything."

"Oh, the sun by day and the stars by night directed us," said Harry, "and if I had not been rescued from Mungo's grasp, as I have before explained, young Ted here was going to hazard the voyage alone."

"Bravo!" said Joe; "I'll get him a wife one of these fine days for that, the fattest and blackest among the Indians."

"Thank you for nothing," said Ted; "none but an English girl will suit me. No offence to you, Joseph," Ted answered, dryly, "although I was not a lord in England."

"None of your chaff, young 'un," said Joe; "we'll change the subject; and now we are on our way with a fair wind, I'll tell you what we'll do."

"What?"

"Why, have a drop of this liquor here first," said Joe, opening a bottle of rum.

"And after that, Joe?"

"After that, my lads, we'll do this. Lion Limb you say is very hard up for provisions?"

"Yes."

"And yet there are plenty on the island?"

"Yes; but none of us can get at them."

"Perhaps not; but I can," said Joe, winking knowingly.

"What sort of provisions are they?"

"The very best sort—buffalo meat—and this is the way I'm going to do, my lads. Directly we land, we'll go in search of a buffalo herd, and drive them gently across the country towards Lion Limb, and when they perceive them so near that Mungo can't interfere, they'll come out and slaughter as many as they like."

"Buffaloes, eh?" said Ted; "what sort o' things are they?"

"Didn't yer ever see any on 'em, Ted?"

"No, not one."

THE BOY KING
OF THE SOUTH SEA ISLANDS.

AMBUSH FOR THE INDIANS.

"Not in the travelling shows of old England?"

"No, never."

"Nor you, Harry?"

"I have heard of them, that's all, but never had the pleasure of encountering any as yet," Harry replied.

"You calls it pleasure, eh? does yer," said Joe, winking; "well, if you knew as much about them as I do, Harry, you'd say it was anything but pleasant."

"Are there many on Martin Island, Joe?"

"Many! Aye, my lads, droves of thousands and thousands; and fine eating they make, and no mistake. If it hadn't a been for the buffaloes, all the folks in Martin Island would have died from starvation, for when the brute Mungo and his hyenas left the island, they destroyed all the flocks and herds they came across, and burnt all the grain in the store-houses. This being the case, every one was obliged to go out hunting for something to eat."

"Yes; they make capital food," said Harry; "I have read a good deal about them."

"Then tell us about 'em, Harry," said Ted; "I should much like to hear, for since we shall go

hunting them when we get on shore it might be as well to know something of their ways and habits."

"Never fear," said Joe; "the buffaloes will teach you all about it soon enough."

"The buffalo," said Harry, as he held the tiller, and the boat sped merrily on, "is a wandering race, the motives for their restlessness being either disturbance by hunters, or change of pasturage. After a fire has cleared the plains and prairies of the old dry herbage, the delicate and tender grass that then springs up is a most grateful food for the wandering buffalo herds.

"Fierce and terrible are the fights among the bulls at certain seasons, and it is very dangerous for any man to approach them."

"The buffalo is generally shy, and flies away from man, unless he is wounded, and then he will turn on the hunter with the greatest fury," said Joe.

"If the hunter is going to use a rifle he generally goes against the wind, for the sense of smelling is so sharp in the buffalo that he will otherwise get scent of him, and hastily retire," Harry observed; "and if the hunter only gets within shooting distance, he is careful so to take his aim that the beast may drop at once, and not be irritated by an ineffectual wound."

"But the way we islanders hunt the buffalo is this," said Joe. "A great number of men assemble, then divide, and form an immense square. Each band of men set fire to the grass of the savannah where the beasts are feeding. When the frightened buffalos perceive the fire approaching on all sides, they retire in confusion to the centre of the square, when the band close in upon them, and kill them as they are huddled together in heaps, without hazard; we have often killed a thousand this way in one hunt."

"No wonder all you islanders look so fat and well, then," said Ted, "if you can get such a plentiful supply of meat as that."

"Another way we have of capturing them is this," said Joe. "A buffalo pound is a fenced circular space of about 100 yards across, the entrance is a huge moveable gate, to prevent the animal getting out when once in.

"For about a mile on each side of the road leading to the pound, stakes are driven into the ground, at nearly equal distances, of about thirty or fifty yards apart.

"These stakes are dressed up to resemble natives, and to deter the buffalo from attempting to break out at either side.

"Within sixty yards from the pound, branches of trees are placed between these stakes to screen a body of natives, who lie down behind them to await the approach of the buffalo.

"The principal art in this sort of chase is shown by the horsemen, who have to manœuvre round the herd in the plains, so as to urge them to enter the roadway, which is about a quarter of a mile broad.

"When this has been accomplished, they raise loud shouts, and, pressing close upon the animals, so terrify them that they rush heedlessly forward towards the snare.

"When they have advanced so far as the men who are lying in ambush, the natives rise and increase the noise by violent shouting and firing of weapons.

"The affrighted buffaloes, now having no mode of escape, rush right into the pound, when they are quickly despatched with all manner of weapons.

"There is usually a tree in the centre of each pound, on which the uncivilized part of the hunters hang strips of buffalo flesh and pieces of cloth, as offerings to the Great Master of Life, and occasionally a native is placed in the tree, to sing to the Great Manitou as the buffaloes are advancing, and must keep his station until the whole herd have entered and been killed."

"You speak in such praise of the buffaloes, that I long to have a good hunt," said Ted; "if we are successful, Lion Limb shall not starve."

"Never fear," said Joe, "you shall have plenty of hunting when we get on shore once more."

"Another mode of catching and killing them," said Harry, "is practised by the natives, such as hunting them down on horseback."

"Yes," said Joe; "a good native hunter, when on horseback, dashes at a herd, and singles out the very best he can find, which he endeavours to separate from the rest. If he succeeds, he endeavours to keep it from the main body by a dexterous management of his horse, though going at full speed. Whenever he can get sufficiently near to let fly a good shot, he fires, and seldom fails in bringing the animal down, though of course when in full gallop, he cannot rest his gun against the shoulder and take such a deadly aim as if on foot and not moving.

"When hunting them, the rider is in great danger of being thrown from his horse, particularly from the rage of the buffalo, which, when closely pressed, often turn suddenly, and rushing furiously at the horse, frequently succeeds in wounding it or upsetting the rider.

"When the experienced hunter, however, perceives such an intention on the part of the buffalo, he suddenly stops, wheels about, and goes off in another direction."

"Don't the wolves prey upon the buffaloes? I have heard so," said Harry.

"Yes, they do," Joe replied; "but when a herd of buffaloes scent the approach of a pack of ravenous wolves, they place themselves in the form of a circle, the weakest keep in the middle, and the strongest are ranged on the outside, presenting to the hungry wolves a front bristling with horns! Should the herd be taken by surprise, however, and take to flight, numbers of them are sure to fall a prey to the wolves.

"Packs of wolves very often hang on the skirts of buffalo herds, and prey upon the sick or straggling young ones; but they very seldom attempt to attack the full-grown animal.

"In proof of this," continued Joe, "I have often seen wolves, in twos and threes, ramble among a whole herd, without exciting the bulls in the least.

"Hunters sometimes put a wolf-skin over them, and thus approach a small drove of buffaloes without creating alarm, and when they are sufficiently near kill as many as they desire."

"It must be exciting sport," said Ted, "and the sooner we meet with a herd of buffaloes the better."

"Old King Katamar had a few tame buffaloes, once," said Harry, "as I have been told, and they were trained to gallop and run races, like horses."

"What became of them?"

"They escaped, and are now, no doubt, among their wild companions again."

*   *   *   *   *   *

Thus, on their journey homewards, Joe beguiled the time in telling stories; but ere long they landed on Katamar's island, and safely anchored their trusty sail boat in a little harbour which was screened from view.

The provisions and other things were landed, and Joe raised a pole on a high bluff, to which a long streamer was fastened, to serve as a signal to Governor Martin and the rest, who were every day expected to land at that spot.

Ted was sent out to find the two horses which had been left behind.

But, instead of two, he found *three* horses in the small valley before described.

How the third got there he could not imagine.

Joe told him that one stray horse would invariably find out another, and such had been the fact in this case.

Harry and Joe and Ted went forth on the instant, and, by a dexterous use of the lasso, soon secured the three animals and brought them into their small temporary camp.

"Now," said Joe, "from what I have seen to-day, there are thousands of buffalo tracks about the place, and the best thing we can do is to find out a herd, and steadily drive it towards the city. When Lion Limb finds them close, he will lose no time in helping himself."

"But it is many miles to Katamar's city," said Joe.

"How many?"

"At least thirty miles."

"Just three hours' gallop for a buffalo," said Joe.

"I shouldn't like to ride one at that pace," said

Ted. "But suppose we go out and hunt them, at all events. We can kill a great number, and when Governor Martin lands, he and his men will find plenty to do in cutting them up and making them fit for food."

"Come, then, let us go at once," said Harry.

The horses were made ready, and young Ted was delighted at the prospect of a hunt.

"Oh, if Lion Limb only knew how successful we had been," said he, "and how near assistance was at hand, it would make him leap with joy."

Joe could not help but laugh at the mad antics which Ted gave way to on the plain ; but ere long they descried in the distance a large herd of buffaloes.

Ted scampered off towards the herd at breakneck speed, and soon distanced both Harry and Joe.

When the two latter were yet a considerable distance away, Ted plunged right among the herd and shot down several.

He was filled with delight, and shouted and capered about on his horse like a wild youth.

But his folly cost him most dear.

When least expected, the herd driven in by Harry and Joe completely surrounded poor Ted.

He was right in the midst of the angry buffalo herd.

Escape was impossible.

Both he and his horse were wedged in and pushed along.

Ted shouted and fired off his pistols right and left, but it was of no avail.

Onward, onward pressed the ferocious beasts all around him.

His horse was squeezed and crushed, and in wildness he reared, and plunged, and struggled.

Behind, and on each side of the wounded animal, buffalo bulls were goading him to death.

At last he sank helpless, and was instantly trampled to death by a thousand hoofs.

Ted Rawlings, however, was safe.

He had felt his good steed quivering under him some time before he fell, and in despair he seized a buffalo bull by the hump and was dragged out of the saddle in an instant.

Knowing not what to do, Ted clambered on the animal's back, and was quickly astride.

The affrighted bull, thinking that some animal had clambered upon it, bellowed aloud, and plunged headlong through the herd at a frightful speed.

Whither he went Ted could not guess.

All he knew was that he was seized with great fear, and held on to the animal tighter than ever.

Each time that he dared to look back, he saw a long, dark, buffalo line behind him, and clouds of dust.

Ted's hair now began to stand on end with fright.

Onward he rode, at increasing speed, and onward came the herd after him. [See out in No. 36.]

Harry and Joe had long disappeared.

Nothing could be seen of them.

"I am doomed to die," thought Ted ; "but my only safety is to hold on till the last."

And "hold on" he did.

Never did human being ever have such a desperate ride.

And never did human being clutch an animal more firmly than Ted did the buffalo's hump.

Whither the herd were travelling he knew not, nor had he the slightest idea.

For several hours the mad race continued, but still there was not the slightest sign of any stopping.

At last Ted, to his great dismay, perceived some distance ahead of him several camp fires and tents.

"Oh, misery !" he sighed, "this bull is plunging right in Mungo's camp. Shall I slip off, or what ?"

But to slip off would be of no avail, for he would have been instantly trampled to death.

Thinking thus, he placed a revolver in his breast, and urged on the bull to still greater speed, by pricking his flanks with his knife.

At one time the bull on which he was riding had been going much too quick for Ted's taste, but now that it began to slacken speed, the rider was in fear of falling into the hands of some of Mungo's men, and accordingly he spurred up the flagging animal with great energy.

Onward it went again with increased speed, followed by the herd.

As they approached the camps of the buccaneer's men, many shots were fired at the hero by Mungo's men.

But this did not stop the progress of the red-eyed animals.

Into the camps they plunged like an avalanche, and it being night took most of Mungo's sleeping men by surprise.

In all sorts of attire they rushed forth from their tents, weapons in hand.

But as well might they have fired and shouted and swore at the sea as to stop the sweeping rush of so many wild animals.

Carts, waggons, tents, and pots and pans, men, women, and children, buccaneers and natives, all, one and all, turned or fled before the mighty army of buffaloes, who galloped along more furious than ever, overturning everything and everybody that opposed them.

Ned was almost half dead with fear.

Yet he maintained his hold to the last, until at last he became insensible.

Mungo's camps were left far behind, and to his great surprise when morning broke Ted discovered himself lying on the grass, surrounded by some of Lion Limb's trusty friends. The buffalo herd had disappeared, but more than a thousand dead carcases were on the ground, and men busily engaged in dressing, cutting, and conveying them into the city, not more than half a mile distant.

"Where am I," said Ted, when he awoke as if from slumber.

"Come, and I will explain," said Lion Limb ; "you have rendered me good service, and you shall be well rewarded."

"But what brings me here ; it seems to me all like a vision ?"

"Yet it is not : come, rise, and go with me, I will explain at leisure."

CHAPTER CVI.

LION LIMB'S AMBUSH FOR THE INDIANS—THE FALSE MILLER.

LION LIMB had only just spoken, when in the distance he espied a numerous herd of wild cattle approaching.

Lion Limb knew not what to make of this second surprise.

But this time it was not a buffalo herd, but an immense number of bulls and cows.

Lion Limb and his friends around did not attempt to stop the progress of these now comers.

Of all things, this second herd was most pleasing to them.

On they came, galloping and kicking up the dust.

Nor did any one attempt to arrest their progress.

"Let them come on," said Lion Limb, "we stand much in need of a plentiful supply of wholesome meat."

In a dense drove the animals came along, and when they had approached the town, they stopped in their mad career.

"Who is that yonder that I see driving in this herd?" asked Lion Limb.

Several looked very anxiously in the distance, but no one could make out who the two horsemen were.

"They are some of Mungo's men, perhaps," said one.

"I don't think they would be bold enough to approach so close to us," another replied.

"How are they dressed?" asked Lion Limb.

"There were such heavy clouds of dust in the distance that no one could tell."

They had not long to wait, however, to find out who the two new comers were.

For in a few moments afterwards, Harry Woodruff galloped in, driving before him a lot of snorting cattle.

"That you, Harry?" said Lion Limb, in a loud voice.

"Yes, it's me, captain," said Harry, cheerily.

"And your companion yonder, Harry, who is he?"

"Who do you think, captain?"

"I can't tell."

"Then I can; but first of all, captain, let me ask have you seen anything of that wild young devil Ted Rawlings?"

"Yes, he is safe among us again," said Lion Limb; "but he looks more dead than alive; but who is that fellow yonder?"

"Joe Pebbles, captain."

"You are joking, Harry!"

"I was never more serious in all my life."

"Why, who the devil ever expected to see *him* alive again?"

"*I* didn't for one; but yet there is no mistake about it. Yonder fellow, that you see dashing about, and hear yelling at that drove of bullocks, is no other than our old fiddle-playing comrade, Joe Pebbles. We found him at Fort Martin."

"At Fort Martin, eh?"

"Yes; he's married now, and a great man among the islanders there; has a large tract of country to himself, and immense flocks and herds of all sorts."

"And do you mean to say you have been to Fort Martin already?"

"I have, captain; but had it not been for young Ted Rawlings, I should have been hung or shot by Mungo and his men."

"Indeed!"

"It is true."

"And how came that to pass, then?"

"I was out foraging for you, when I fell across one of your greatest enemies."

"Indeed! Who, pray?"

"Why, Bill Whetherby."

"You must be mistaken!"

"I am not, captain; any one who has ever seen Bill once, cannot mistake his face a second time."

"But he was a prisoner among our people at the settlement, and——"

"Yes; but he managed to escape, and has joined Mungo's gang again."

Lion Limb said nothing, but bit his lip in annoyance.

"Things are going against us, Harry, of late," he said, with a bitter smile.

"Yes, but better times are in store, captain, you may be sure."

"I have no doubt of it, Harry, and ere many days we shall be ourselves again."

"I am certain of it."

"And how did he capture you?"

Harry briefly told him all the particulars, which we have in a previous number explained.

"But as Whetherby is not in Mungo's camp, I fear he is intent on some devilish plan to ruin all of us, captain."

"No doubt."

"He swears that he'll never rest until he has your life."

"Which I hope may never be," said Lion Limb, laughing.

"He shall never take you alive, captain."

"I am certain of that, Harry."

"If I am not much mistaken, he is already in your city, and plotting with the natives."

"Are you sure of this?"

"I think as much."

"Then we must take instant measures to have him ferreted out."

"Leave that to me, captain. I shouldn't want a more pleasant job."

"Then I leave him in your hands."

"Never fear, he will not be very long at large, captain; I owe him a grudge."

"And what of old Governor Martin and his friends?"

"They are now on their way hither, with plenty of men and provisions."

"This is good news. But how can they brave the sea?"

"Since you were there, and thanks to your instruction, they have built two large gun-boats, and a very large flat boat, all of which are well manned and seaworthy."

"And when do you expect they will arrive?"

"Within two days."

"Then our prospects are better than ever?"

"Mungo and his band of desperadoes will soon find that out, captain," said Harry.

"I suppose they treated you, while in their camp, with great cruelty, Harry?"

"They did, captain; but I escaped with my life, thanks to young Ted, and we are bent now upon having revenge on the rascals."

"And do you really mean to say," Lion Limb observed, in wonder, "that young Ted was going to make the perilous voyage to Martin Island alone in a sail boat?"

"He was; but, as luck would have it, he fell across and liberated me, and we both set out together."

While they were thus speaking, Joe Pebbles galloped up, and was received with much pleasure by his old captain, Lion Limb.

"You haven't brought your fiddle, Joe," said Lion Limb, laughing.

"No, but I brought something better and more useful, Captain Lion Limb," said Joe, presenting two revolvers and a good sword.

"But what made you leave us at all, Joe?" asked Lion Limb, with a good-tempered grin.

"Well, you see," said Joe, "when you took us to the fort I saw somebody."

"Oh! I understand," said Lion Limb, laughing.

"A woman of course, sir," said Harry, grinning.

"Aye, true, and a beauty, too," said Joe.

"So you are married, then, Joe?"

"And done for," Harry observed.

"Yes; but not done for, Harry," Joe replied. "I am the happiest fellow on the island."

"Your fiddle captivated the lady, I suppose, Joe," said Lion Limb.

"Oh, no, it was his beautiful face, and delightful voice," Harry remarked.

"Why you don't mean to say you have turned music master, Joe?"

"Yes; I have in a small way, captain."

"And he sings like a nightingale," Harry remarked; "Ted and I heard him singing a splendid song the night we arrived, and that's how we found out who it was."

"You have much changed, Joe," said Lion Limb.

"For the better, I hope, captain."

"Oh, yes, much for the best," Harry remarked; "see how brown and fat and awkward he is getting."

"I don't know so much about being awkward, I can dance with any one living," said Joe.

"And give lessons," said Lion Limb.

"Oh, yes, I have a lot of the natives at my place once a week, and we have a dance; all the folks from Fort Martin give me a call, both great and small, and of all sorts and sizes and color. I'm not at all particular."

"And how do they pay you?"

"Oh, I do it mostly for fun, you know, captain. But in the season I receive all sorts of presents; sometimes a cow or two, or half-a-dozen sheep; young cattle of all kinds are not objected to."

"Then you are rich?"

"Rich as a Jew in all things except money, and that I don't stand in need of."

"Well, then, I am glad to see you, Joe; give me your hand," said Lion Limb; "I forgive you for deserting us."

"I didn't do so because I didn't like you, Captain Lion Limb," said Joe; "but when a lady is in the case——"

"I understand you mean to say, then, that the bravest and the best of soldiers can be tempted to leave their colors when a beauty is in the way?"

"Yes, but not to fight for an enemy, Captain Lion Limb," said Joe; "and to prove how much I always liked you I left the island the instant I heard you were pressed by foes."

"I know you did, Joe."

"And to show that I mean right, sir, I will fight in your cause now that I have come, as hard and as long as any man breathing," said Joe.

"I firmly believe it," said Lion Limb, shaking Joe again by the hand; "but how came it that young Ted got separated from you?"

Joe and Harry explained to him.

"But how is it, then, you are so close upon his heels?"

"Well, you see, captain, we followed the buffalo herd, and when we found the wild animals had charged through Mungo's camps and trodden them all under foot, Joe and I visited their cattle folds. At last the bulls and cows that they had gathered from all parts of the island, and——"

"And thinking they would be of more service to you Captain Lion Limb," interrupted Joe, "we drove them before us, and here they are all safe and sound, scattered about the plains ready for the butcher's knife, wherever you please to slaughter them."

"Well done, both Harry and Joe," said Lion Limb, laughing; "but I have my fears that the Indian friends of Mungo will soon pay us a visit and try to recover them, for they cannot stand hunger long no more than we."

"Never mind the cursed Indians, Captain Lion Limb," said Joe, "we'll soon settle 'em if they dare come to molest us."

"But they are such treacherous devils," said Harry.

"So they are, but I have lived long enough among them now to know all their ways," said Joe.

"And don't you think they'll come down upon us then, Joe?" said Harry.

"I am certain they will," Joe replied, "but what of that?"

"It matters a great deal," said Lion Limb, "we must be prepared for the villains."

"And so we will be, sir," said Joe; "only leave it to me, Captain Lion Limb, and all things will go well."

"How do you mean?" Harry asked.

"I mean this, Captain Lion Limb, the Indian devils won't trouble us much in the daytime; night is the time for them."

"And that proves my words to be correct then," said Lion Limb, "we must make preparations to receive them."

"Leave it to me, sir, if you please," said Joe, "I know how to serve the red rascals."

"And how do you suppose they will act?" said Harry.

"They will send out two or three spies in the daytime. We must have all our horses tied up to stakes as if they were at grass. When they have satisfied themselves how the land lies with us, they will go back and report that all of us are lazy and asleep."

"Well, what then?"

"They will be sure to gather a strong band and come again at night."

"Well."

"Our horses can be clustered in a grand pasturage, and when the Indian devils come, we will send them back with fleas in their ears," said Joe, "and perhaps bullets instead."

"I don't understand you, Joe," said Harry.

"You are getting very dull in your old age, Harry," said Joe.

"Then explain yourself."

"I will. Can't we be on the horses, and can't we so lay down upon them that they can't perceive us at a distance?"

"I see, I see," said Harry.

"Then that proves you haven't got mud in your eyes," said Joe, laughing; "and when the Indian rascals get near enough to discover us, it will then be too late for them to save their skins." [See Cut.]

"It is an excellent plan," said Lion Limb.

"I am glad you think so, captain."

"I have hunted and fought with them many a time, but such an idea never occurred to me before," said Lion Limb.

"I will make one of the party," said Harry.

"And I another," Lion Limb remarked. I should like to pay the rascals out; for I came to this island to render Katamar a service, but his people think we caused Marmi's death, and are turning against us."

"Ted Rawlings and Dick will be sure to be there," said Harry.

"How many men shall we want, Joe?" Lion Limb asked.

"About twenty, captain; but every one must have a good horse and plenty of powder and ball."

"Never fear, every man shall be well armed," Lion Limb said; "we have plenty of ammunition, but very little food until this morning."

"Then it is agreed on, Captain Lion Limb," said Joe.

"It is; and I leave the whole management of this affair in your hands. When you want me, I will be ready."

Lion Limb was about to leave the spot, when a messenger came running up in great haste, and almost breathless.

CHAPTER CVII.
THE UNEXPECTED ATTACK.

"WHAT news—what news?" asked Lion Limb, in a quick tone.

"The very worst of news, Captain Lion Limb."

"What is it, then? Speak, quickly I say! tell us what you know!"

For some few minutes the messenger could not speak, for he was pale, and seemed very much exhausted.

At last he said—

"I have come from the camp of Mungo; great confusion and scarcity is there, but Mungo himself seems joyful, and swears that in less than four-and-twenty hours he will conquer you and all your band, for he has a scheme on foot to take you all by surprise."

"And do you call this news?" said Lion Limb, laughing. "Nay, my good man, calm your fears, Mungo will never enter our city."

Lion Limb could not help laughing at what the pale-faced messenger told him, but dismissed him kindly; when, at the same moment, a second messenger came up, and reported that a friendly miller from a great distance had brought many sacks of flour into the city, but who he was no one could tell. He called himself Bertrand.

"Then, let some one go and look after this kind-hearted miller," said Lion Limb, "and thank him in my name. I cannot enter the city yet, for I have much to do here outside, and prepare for any attack that may be made."

When one of Lion Limb's men entered the city, he found the half-famished people full of joy at the unexpected arrival of so much excellent flour.

The people were surrounding the unknown native miller, who conducted ten mules heavily laden with flour.

Nothing was heard on all sides but the cry,

"It is food! it is corn that has arrived to us!"

Bertrand was surrounded, hemmed in, almost smothered by this famished crowd; the boldest of them were already endeavouring to get possession of the sacks.

But Bertrand held them at a respectful distance by the aid of an enormous cudgel.

"All this is for you," he cried, whirling his formidable weapon; "but no pillage. It must not be 'luck to the strong and bad luck to the weak!' for weak or strong, young or old, each one of you is hungry, and each one must have his share!"

"Yes, yes," replied the crowd.

The most robust of those that surrounded him then aided him to unload his mules and untie the sacks, while cries of "Your name! your name?" resounded on all sides.

"My name is obscure, and matters little to you," he replied. "I am but the agent of those who pay me. Honour to whom honour is due! This corn, this flour has been purchased for you. I only want to see King Lion Limb."

Lion Limb lost no time in profiting by the favourable change that had taken place in the popular mind, but mounted his horse, and wishing to get to the bottom of the mystery, as soon as he returned to the palace he ordered Ted to repair to the distributor of corn and invite him to come and dine with his king.

Ted obeyed, and transmitted to the miller the wishes of Lion Limb.

Bertrand at first knit his heavy eyebrows, for he did not feel more than half secure in his disguise.

But after a moment's hesitation, he foresaw a result which surpassed his most sanguine anticipations.

In short, his real object in venturing so rashly within the city had been to examine what means of defence the inhabitants had at their disposal; to reconnoitre the weak walls; and, above all, to sound the minds of the besieged; but he had never seriously hoped to gain admittance into the palace, nor to have a private interview with Lion Limb.

He resolved, however, to see the end of the adventure, and to enter the lion's den.

He replied to Ted with a sort of rustic simplicity, that as soon as the division of the corn and flour was over, he would repair to the palace; so much the more willingly, too, because from his childhood he had longed to see the interior of the palace, of which wonders were related in his village.

Ted told him that he would wait his good pleasure, the king having charged him to accompany the worthy miller, and not to quit him for an instant.

As soon as Bertrand had emptied his last sack, he doubled it in four and placed it, in the form of a saddle, on the back of one of his mules.

On seeing him preparing to depart, a few of his partisans manifested a desire to carry him in triumph, but the stranger humbly entreated them to spare him an ovation of which he felt himself unworthy, and to content themselves with assisting him to bestride his modest steed.

When he was comfortably perched upon his mule, he bade them adieu, and took the road to the palace, preceded by Ted Rawlings.

The archers, who were keeping guard, no sooner saw this man covered with flour from head to foot come ambling towards them in so grotesque a manner upon a mule, then they received him with shouts of laughter.

The animal, terrified at the noise, became restive, and reared and plunged so violently with his rider, that the poor miller, who, to judge from appearances, was very inexperienced in the art of equitation, had only time to link his two arms round the neck of his steed to save himself from falling off.

At each fresh prank of the mule, the miller, in spite of the precaution he had taken, was visibly losing his equilibrium; and at length one shock, more violent than the last, separated the animal and the rider, by throwing the latter somewhat roughly on the ground, amid the noisy laughter of the archers.

As the miller had, however, only suffered himself to be thrown off with the intention of misleading these individuals, he quietly suffered these latter to assist him to arise, although he had not hurt himself very much.

Then, having thanked them for their assistance, while pretending to limp from the consequences of his fall, he followed his guide within the portals of the palace.

While he was crossing the suites of apartments that preceded the hall where Lion Limb awaited him, he never ceased staring with astonishment at those marvels of art with the ingenuous surprise of a villager transported into fairy-land.

He appeared to be still under the influence of his surprise and admiration when Ted introduced him into the chamber, where he found two personages, whom he recognized at a glance.

They were Lion Limb and young Emma Clarence, who were seated beside each other on chairs with straight and carved backs, before an empty table.

Bertrand stopped at the threshold, twirling his broad-leaved beaver between his thumbs with an embarrassed air, and waiting till Lion Limb should order him to enter.

"You have had a rough job to-day, good miller," said Lion Limb, signing to him to approach, "and I should be glad to know the name of the brave fellow who so opportunely rendered me such a service."

"My name is Bertrand, my lord," replied the false miller, humbly.

At the sound of his somewhat rough voice, Emma suddenly looked up, and regarded Bertrand with singular attention. He felt a cold shudder run down his back, and experienced something like regret that he had ever set foot within the palace.

"Well, you may boast of having arrived just in time to dissipate the storm which was beginning to growl furiously round my palace," said Lion Limb.

"Oh! as the shepherds say, 'A little rain puts down a high wind,' my lord," said the miller, with a horse-laugh.

"And to teach those madmen," continued Lion Limb, "that they owe gratitude to Emma Clarence whom they had dared to pursue with their maledictions. But let us try to forget these horrible scenes," said Lion Limb, as Emma hid her face in her hands. "After so much fatigue and trouble you must have need of rest and refreshment."

"Of refreshment above all, my lord, for I am as dry as a stray dog in the middle of the day," replied the miller, with a candour that made the king smile.

"Come and seat yourself, then, at this table, and you shall share our frugal repast."

When the eyes of the false miller rested upon the bare table, which had just been decorated with some wooden platters, like those used by beggars, two or three jars filled with water, and some leathern bottles, he could not refrain from making a significant grimace. He came forward, nevertheless, and seated himself, saying—

"Long life to our master, Lion Limb."

"You do not seem to utter that wish very heartily, miller?" observed Lion Limb.

"Because God does not seem at present greatly disposed to grant it," replied the miller.

"How so?" demanded Lion Limb, surprised.

"Because no one can live long without eating. But, perhaps, this is a fast-day?"

"It is a day of want," replied Lion Limb, sorrowfully, "for the king as well as for his subjects."

"This miller seems rather difficult to please," said Ted, in a sour tone.

"I offer you meagre cheer, it is true, poor miller," said Lion Limb; "and I dare say you would sooner be at your own table, in your mill?"

"To speak freely, your palace is very fine, my lord," replied Bertrand, "and my mill is not worth much; but the meal-tub is always full, and I do not eat off wooden platters."

"It seems that your mill is well provisioned, miller?" Ted ironically observed.

"How many times have I been led to envy the fate of kings!" rejoined the false miller, "because they have no occasion to work for their living; because they dine off gold and silver plate; because they drink the finest wines; and because the most exquisite productions of the earth are reserved for their mouths! Well, then, to-day I no longer envy your fate, and would not change mine for yours, my lord."

"And to see plates of gold change into wooden platters, is it not?" said Lion Limb, with a bitter smile. "Alas! if my present poverty causes me suffering, it is not for myself, but for my beloved Emma. Poor child!"

"Oh! the young lady is as good as she is beautiful," said the false miller, looking at Emma, who blushed and hung down her head. "She is worthy, it must be owned, of the love of a king; nevertheless, my lord, if I were like you, starving and besieged, I should take little heed of the black eyes of the most beautiful girl in the world."

"My worthy miller," continued Lion Limb, "a king cannot be expected to hold the sentiments of a miller."

"That may be," replied the miller, "but, noble or simple, if you are not the strongest, you must always finish by yielding."

"Listen, miller," said Lion Limb, "if you had a sister, and one of your relations or your neighbours came to carry her off, to insult her before your face, to put her to an untimely death—what would you do?"

"Do?" exclaimed Bertrand, somewhat forgetting his part of a miller. "I should not ask counsel; I should fall upon the scoundrels with my trusty cudgel."

Lion Limb, taking a measure of wine, he poured some out for Bertrand in one of the unlucky wooden bowls.

"I have still another question to put to you, miller," said Lion Limb. "How comes it that my friends did not return at the same time as you; they went out foraging?"

"My lord," replied Bertrand, "the poor fellows have fallen victims to their zeal."

"How?" asked Lion Limb.

"Just as they were about to enter the city they encountered Mungo."

"Mungo!" exclaimed Lion Limb.

"Unfortunately he was asleep, which inspired them with the idea to surprise and take him prisoner."

"An excellent idea!" exclaimed Lion Limb.

"A deplorable idea, my lord," said the miller, "for the upshot was, that they were taken by him. I have only one piece of advice to give you: when you catch him, hold him fast," added the miller, dryly.

Emma smiled; and laying her white hand on the arm of the false miller, regarded him fixedly—

"You think, then, it is very difficult to make Mungo prisoner? You think he is a man to escape from all the prisons in the world, and that neither locks nor bolts have the power to hold him? I am not of that opinion, and if I had a piece of advice to give him, it would be not to suffer himself to be taken, or he will find out his mistake!"

"Oh! he would be a prize worth taking!" cried the miller, who dropped his eyes before the strange and persistent regard of Emma.

"And do you think," asked Lion Limb, "that Mungo knows to what extremity this city is reduced?"

"He knows it as well as I do," replied the imperturbable miller. "He knows that the inhabitants cannot endure the famine much longer, and that they will deliver you up, if you persist in sustaining the siege."

"Make peace with Mungo! submit to his conditions! Never! never!" exclaimed Lion Limb, with violent irritation.

Ted bent towards him and whispered—

"Mistrust the advice of this man. He is a spy. Detain him at the palace, if you would not have him sell the secret of our misery and our desperate situation to the enemy."

But Lion Limb replied, with an expression of unspeakable dignity—

"Loyal or traitor, this man is my guest!"

"But," said Emma, "look at his broad shoulders, his bow legs, and his back, which looks as if it had always bent under a heavy load. Is his the figure of a spy? No: this man is a true miller; his gait, as well as his words, bespeak it."

"Should you ever see Mungo again," resumed Lion Limb, "you will tell him that we can hold out much longer than he thinks for, and that behind the overthrown walls of the palace, he will find, like a fresh rampart, the breasts of my faithful followers."

"I will tell him every word," said the miller, "if I ever see him, as faithfully as if you had spoken to him yourself."

"And now," said Lion Limb, "all ruined and besieged though he may be, a king cannot suffer to go unrewarded so great a service as you have rendered me. You must choose the guerdon that pleases you best among the three sole gifts I have to offer."

At the same moment, the miller saw Ted approach, leading a magnificent horse by the bridle.

"There," said Lion Limb, "is a barb that will advantageously replace your mule, and with which it will be more easy for you to escape pursuit, should any offer itself."

"What! you would give me this noble animal?" exclaimed the miller, examining with wonder-struck eyes this splendid horse. "How he paws and snorts, and pricks his ears, as if he already heard the trumpet call to battle! He is a true child of the desert, light as the wind! Oh! a man mounted on so gallant a charger would have no need of spur! So brave a steed would be half the victory in a pitched battle!"

Ted, who had followed the king, said—

"Well, what think you now? This miller seems to understand horses as well as a man of high lineage."

"Patience, good lad," said Lion Limb, himself astonished at the enthusiasm of the false miller, and feeling his suspicions revive.

"So then, honest miller," he added, aloud, "you accept this horse as your guerdon?"

"Alas, no!" replied the cunning miller, shrugging his shoulders; "I love to see a fine horse; but not to use one. What should I do with such a one as this? He would embarrass me, and I should be forced to sell him. At the end of a week he would be broken-winded with carrying sacks of flour. I would rather have my mule, who is slow-footed but sure. He is not so handsome to look at, but he can carry a heavy burden for a longer time without wincing."

"You are right, and you will make a fortune at your trade," said Lion Limb, with a smile. "But accept, at least, to defend yourself, my trusty sword."

And he detached from his belt his glaive, often reddened with the blood of his enemies.

The false miller seized it in his huge palms, and made it bend like a reed.

"It is an admirable blade," he exclaimed. "How light it is in the hand! It must be easy to cut and cleave with this sword. You cannot feel it at your side. Yes, my lord, a weapon of this temper is a brave companion."

"The miller betrays himself!" whispered Ted. "See! His eyes gleam like buring coals at sight of your sword. His nostrils dilate, as if he were preparing to fall upon the enemy!"

"Take it, then, and you will be able to face Mungo bravely," said Lion Limb.

"Oh! I should not hesitate to make choice of this fine blade, if I were a warrior," replied the miller; "but you see, if I were armed, the buccaneers would attack me. If, on the contrary, I go peaceably on my way, like a poor inoffensive devil who has neither purse at his belt nor rapier in his hand, they will let me pass, with, at the most, a few blows. Besides, as I do not know how to handle swords," he added, flourishing it round his head like a cudgel, "I should have it taken from me, and perhaps my skull cleft with it into the bargain."

Lion Limb turned towards Ted Rawlings.

"Well," said he, "do you think this poor miller a knave in disguise?"

Ted shook his head with a doubtful air, and made no reply.

"The jaw-bone of Samson's ass would be almost as useful to him as my trusty sword," continued Lion Limb. "Well," he added, extending to the miller a leathern pouch, which Ted had just brought him, "accept, at least, in memory of our interview, this handful of gold."

The false miller knit his shaggy eyebrows; but this first movement had the duration of a flash of lightning, and instantly assuming an air of vulgar joy—

"With all my heart," said he.

Lion Limb, reassured by this expansion of vulgar contentment, said,

"You had better go now, miller, and I will pray for your speedy return with a fresh supply of provision; but I desire that you keep the horse and the sword, as well as the pouch of gold."

Meantime, the horse was impatiently pawing the ground, and Ted found difficulty in holding him.

It was a magnificent and fiery animal, who had never yet suffered any one to mount him, and the archers were preparing to indulge in a laugh at the expense of the awkward novice, who was surveying his steed with an expression of fear that was sufficiently comic.

"And are you sure there is no danger, my boy?" he inquired of Ted.

"White Star is as gentle as a lamb," replied Ted.

"Oh! he is called White Star."

"Yes, from that white spot in the middle of his forehead; but you have nothing to fear. His impatience proceeds from his not having been out of the stable for several days."

Lion Limb himself could not help smiling at the grotesque contortions of the poor miller, who could not persuade himself to get into the saddle.

At length, however, amidst peals of laughter from the crowd, he mounted the fiery animal, who plunged and reared bolt upright with his rider.

"I would rather have a mule, an ass, an ox, or even a camel, than this unmanageable brute," cried the miller, clinging to the horse's mane.

"Take care!" said Lion Limb. "The most difficult part is over, since he has suffered you to mount without flinging you ten paces off. You must not give way to his ill-temper. If you were now to attempt to dismount, he would, perhaps, play you an ill trick, and break your leg with a kick."

"But what would you advise me to do, my lord? You are a good horseman; aid me with your advice."

"Nothing more easy, my good miller. I should hold the reins with a firm hand instead of clinging to the horse's mane. I should dress his flanks vigorously between my two knees, instead of letting my legs hang down on each side like empty sacks, and I should render the animal as docile as your mule."

THE BOY KING
OF THE SOUTH SEA ISLANDS.

AN UNWELCOME VISITOR.

"So be it done according to your will; for, my lord, when I ask advice, it is with the intention of following it."

Bertrand punctually executed all that had been prescribed for him, and the barb, feeling that he was exhausting himself in useless efforts, and that he had found his master, ceased to rear and plunge,

to the great astonishment of the archers and of Lion Limb.

In this struggle the miller had dropped the bag of gold and the paper which was to serve as a safe conduct to carry him past the gates of the city.

Ted picked them both up, and returned them to him, but the miller only took the paper.

"Keep the purse, my boy, and distribute the contents among the archers," said he. "These brave soldiers have more need of it than I."

"What does that mean?" demanded Lion Limb, surprised at this sudden fit of generosity.

"Every one recognises, as he best can, the services that have been rendered him," replied the miller. "It only remains for me to take my leave of you, my lord, and to thank you for your kind reception of me, for the guerdon you have bestowed on me, and for your last piece of advice."

"I think you were not much in need of it," said Lion Limb, "and that you are a better horseman than you wish it to appear."

In effect a vague suspicion had just crossed Lion Limb's mind, and he turned to consult with Ted Rawlings.

"Oh!" replied the miller, "a docile pupil profits by the first lesson. If you followed those I gave you just now, you would find it none the worst for you."

"I begin to believe that, like a clever miller, you have more than one kind of flour in your sack; and who knows if you have not come here to fulfil some secret mission?"

"I know not what you mean, my lord," replied the false miller, with a smile. "I have no other mission than that which I have accomplished."

But he, deeming it advisable not to run the risk of prolonging this interview, exclaimed—

"I have delayed too long already: I can wait no longer."

Then, profiting by the disorder of those who surrounded him, he resolutely set spurs to the sides of his impatient steed, threatening with his cudgel any one who should attempt to oppose his flight, and set off at full gallop.

Ted was the only one who was not taken off his guard, and whilst the archers were running hastily to their horses, whilst Lion Limb, uneasy at this abrupt departure, was issuing orders which were scarcely heard in the midst of the general confusion, Ted sprang on the crupper of White Star with the agility of an ape, and was galloping away in company with the miller, without the latter being aware of it.

Bertrand had hardly passed the gate, when Harry Woodruff perceived him at a distance, and shouted,

"Stop! stop! it is Bill Whetherby."

"Whetherby!" exclaimed the archers, terrified with surprise, "stop the mastiff."

"The mastiff, whose fangs you could not manage to draw," replied Bertrand, turning towards them with incredible coolness.

"Your bows! your cross-bows!" cried Lion Limb.

"White Star goes swifter than arrows and bolts," cried Bertrand, whilst the arrows whistled over his head, "pursue at your peril!"

CHAPTER CVIII.

THREE VILLAINS MEET—THE DISCLOSURE—THE ERRAND OF JENNY SPARKS—THE DOCTOR TRIUMPHS.

DR. KILLUM, a character which has been one of prominence in this eventful story, after finding out that his own pistol had been found by young Allan —a weapon which without doubt had caused the death of old Alderman English—began to quake with fear.

He knew not what to do.

"If they once find out that *my* name is, or has been, in any way connected with the murder," thought the doctor, "the police will hunt me down like a cutthroat.

"What had I better do?" he thought, as he left the apartment of Allan Norman and Jem Rawlings. "Self-preservation is the first law of nature, and I don't see the reason why *I* should suffer."

And acting up to this idea, Doctor Killum, as we have seen, gave information to the police that very night.

But when Inspector Sharp found out that the person whom Doctor Killum accused was none other than his young friend Allan, he took no notice of it, but rather, as we have already seen, befriended young Allan, and placed him beyond all want.

Doctor Killum, however, was in a state of great excitement.

Wherever he went he thought that detectives were following him.

To keep his courage up, he went into nearly every public-house he passed, and partook freely of strong drinks.

Becoming almost intoxicated, he could scarcely walk, and although he had but a crown piece in his pocket, he resolved to take a cab and drive home.

Before doing so, however, he thought he would have a "parting drop," and therefore, visited the Haymarket, and when just on the point of entering one of the blazing, gas-lit houses there, a female spoke to him.

"Ah, Doctor Killum, is that you?" said the unknown.

The doctor was much surprised to hear his own name pronounced so patly by one he did not know, but he turned quickly, and said,

"You know me, then?"

"I do. Your name is Doctor Killum."

"And yours?"

"Jenny Sparks, the poor homeless, houseless outcast."

"Jenny Sparks," said Doctor Killum, "I don't remember ever to have heard your name before."

"Yet I know you well, for all that."

"I very much doubt it, my girl."

"But I have certain proof that I am not mistaken, doctor."

"Indeed."

"Quite certain that I am not mistaken."

"Then if you know me what do you want? Any medicine or advice?"

"No, neither medicine nor advice, doctor. In fact I shouldn't like to accept either," said Jenny, laughing.

"Oh, indeed! You are very complimentary, I see."

"But I'll tell you what *I* do want," said Jenny.

"And what is that, pray?"

"Eighteen pence to get a lodging to-night,"

"You are a beggar, I see. Go; don't trouble me, my girl, I don't know you from Adam, and if you persist in asking alms of me I shall be obliged to call a policeman and give you in charge."

"Call a policeman and give *me* in charge!" said Jenny, laughing. "You must be joking, surely."

"No, I am not."

"But I know you are."

"I am not, I say. You must not molest gentlemen in this way."

"Ah, doctor, your fine airs have no effect on me," said Jenny; "and, as to calling a policeman, you know a thing or two better than to do that."

"How say you?"

"Officers are the last persons in the world you

desire to see at this moment, doctor. I know that very well."

Doctor Killum felt amazed at what he considered to be the girl's impudence, and was about to walk away when Jenny touched his arm and said in a whisper—

"Do you know old Marks, the lawyer, doctor?"

Mr. Killum started at mention of that name.

But he said boldly—

"Well, and what if I do?"

"I know you do, doctor."

"Well, what of that?"

"You know his son also, Jerry, I think?"

"Well, and so I do; but I cannot understand the meaning of all your words."

"How long is it since you last saw young Allan Norman?"

"Allan Norman! I don't know any such person, girl."

"Yes you do, and Lady Oxenford, also."

"H-u-s-h!" said the doctor. "What do you mean? Come this way into some quiet bar-room. I should like to have a talk with you."

"And so you shall; but let me tell you, doctor," said Jenny, "you are acting the part of a villain to young Allan."

"How do you know that? Who told you such monstrous lies?"

"They are not lies, and I can prove every word I say, Dr. Killum," Jenny answered. "Why don't you show up old Marks and make a clean breast of all you know?"

"I have nothing at all to do with Lawyer Marks."

"Yes you have. You have had dealings with him for years. You know that Jerry is not entitled to the name and property either of Allan or young Edgar Norman, who was transported and drowned. And yet I see this Jerry Marks, 'Captain Zacary,' as he call himself, spending money freely every night and carrying himself as if he were a lord of the land."

"You don't mean that, my girl?" said the doctor, in a whisper, when they had both entered the private bar of a quiet public-house.

"I do mean it; and, as I said before, it is a great shame you do not open your mouth, and explain all. Why should those two pretty lads be done out of their property, when you could rectify all things?"

"And what has it to do with you?"

"I know it has nothing at all to do with me," said Jenny; "but, if I were a man, and a doctor like you are, I should feel delight in rendering justice to every one I could."

"Would you? I daresay you would," said the doctor; "but I am not a lawyer, you know."

"But Baron Templeton is," said Jenny.

"Baron Templeton!" said Dr. Killum, in surprise. "And do you know him also?"

"I do."

"Then you are a police spy."

"I am not, doctor," said Jenny, indignantly, "but what I know I have learned by accident, and, if I can render any service to young Allan Norman, I will do so with the greatest of pleasure."

"And why do you take so much interest in this youth then; are you in love with him?"

"In love!" said Jenny, with a mocking laugh. "No; he would not, he could not fall in love with such a girl as I am; yet on many a cold night Allan has passed me by with a good word, and given me a half-crown, when your lords and dukes wouldn't give a poor girl a penny. Us girls about town often know and hear more about private family matters than even lawyers do. What I am, and what I am not, will come out in time, doctor."

Mr. Killum was astonished to hear this unknown girl talking so glibly about his own affairs, and, for a few moments, could scarcely speak a word.

"A fine mess old Marks will get you into before long, doctor, unless you act right in this matter."

"What do you mean, girl?"

"I mean that old Marks will get you into such another scrape as he did Gentleman George a few weeks ago, and some others beside."

"Gentleman George! I never heard of him."

"But I have. He is safe in prison now, and all through the old lawyer."

"Why, what has this Gentleman George to do with old Marks?"

"This. Jerry is taking the part of Allan Norman, and spending Allan's money as fast as he can; and the father wished to get some documents from the house of a certain Lord Manfred, at Manfred Hall, which has something to do with a private will made by Baron Templeton and Lady Oxenford, in regard to their chance children, Allan and Edgar Norman. Marks promised Gentleman George £500 at least, if he could steal them, in order that he might make his own son Jerry, or 'Captain Zacary' as he is called, succeed to the baron's whole estate."

"You surprise me, girl."

"And it will surprise you still more to learn that this old Marks has resolved to get you transported as soon as he has made all his own plans perfect."

"Very kind of the old lawyer, certainly," said the doctor, with a grim smile; "I will be even with him, however."

"How?"

"That's my business, girl."

"I don't know so much about that, Dr. Killum," said Jenny, with a flush on her face; "you had better make a friend than an enemy of me."

"Indeed; and why so, pray? What have you to do with me and my concerns?"

"I could give you in charge in five minutes, if I liked."

"On what charge, pray?"

"On the charge of conspiring against and concealing the birth of the two boys, Allan and Edgar."

"You seem to know a great deal about my affairs."

"I do; but if you will take my advice, go to old Marks at once; he is not aware that you know all about his interview with Baron Templeton, in which Jerry was made heir to his property, and, with this knowledge in your possession, you can work wonders."

"So I can, so I can," mused the doctor. "I am now sorry I ever had anything to do with the lads at all; and, as to old Marks, I should like to see him dangling on a gibbet."

"And so he may one of these days, if he goes on much further in his career of villany and crime."

Dr. Killum, to speak the truth, was thunderstruck at the cool, calm manner of his poorly-clad companion.

"If I ask her name, business, or residence, she will not tell me," thought the doctor; "she evidently knows more about these boys than she cares to speak of now, but I will pump her still further."

"Do you know where Jerry Marks——"

"Captain Zacary is his public name, Dr. ——"

"Well, yes, so I have heard. Do you know the residence of this young scapegrace, Jenny?"

"I do; but it will not be necessary to go to his lodgings. You can see him in the Haymarket any night."

"To-night, think you?"

"Yes; this very night."

"And do you know the abode of his old father, the lawyer?"

"I do well."

"If we could only get father and son together now, the scene would be a grand one and no mistake; for they hate each other most deadly, I hear."

"So they do; but if I had the money I would take a cab, and drive over to the old lawyer."

"I only have a crown," said the doctor; "but here, take four-and-sixpence of it, hire a hansom and bring him over. I will write a note immediately; don't lose any time."

"Well, write your note, and while you are doing so, I will just peep into Kemp's supper and oyster rooms, and see if this Captain Zacary has been there yet; he calls and sups usually every night," said Jenny.

Jenny went out into the street, and she had not gone more than a score yards when some one touched her on the shoulder.

It was Inspector Sharp in plain clothes.

"All right, my good girl," said he. "Don't tremble and be afraid of me; you know I'm a friend of yours."

And without saying another word, the inspector dropped a sovereign into her hand, and disappeared down a quiet and dark street like a shadow.

For a moment Jenny did not know what to make of this strange transaction, and before she could recover from her natural surprise, the inspector was out of sight.

Jenny, however, felt glad that fortune had thrown a pound in her way, and went to Kemp's Supper Rooms, and passing in, discovered "Captain Zacary," as usual, enjoying himself there, in the company of several very "fast," and stylishly attired people.

Having satisfied herself that he would be some time there, she immediately returned to Doctor Killum, who had borrowed a pen and ink, and in the fly-leaf of his pocket-book had written the following note:—

"Haymarket.

"MY DEAR MARKS,—I have just come to town, and am commissioned by a friend to pay to you the sum of £100, which has long been due. You must come at once. Call at the 'Blue Boar,' and in the parlour you will find me. More particulars when you arrive.

"Yours truly,
"ANNERSLEY."

"There, take that," said Doctor Killum, "and leave it at his house, but do not wait for him. Watch, however, and see that he comes. When he calls a cab, do you drive back to the 'Blue Boar' as fast as possible, and apprise me of his coming."

Jenny did as she was told, and as fortune would have it, old Marks was at home.

He received the note from the hand of his servant, and having read it, thought very seriously as to whom the party might be.

The thoughts of receiving £100, however, which had long been due to him, banished all fears, and in a few moments he called a cab, and drove off to the Haymarket.

Jenny, however, who had watched him, ordered her cabman to drive on with all speed, and arrived at the "Blue Boar" some time before Marks, and told Doctor Killum all that had passed.

"Very well, my girl, you may leave me for a time, and stay in the public bar, and when I want you I will come out and tell you what to do."

Dr. Killum asked, as a particular favour, to be allowed to use a small private parlour at the "Blue Boar," and told the potman (at the same time promising him a half-crown) to introduce any stranger who might call and inquire for a gentleman of the name of Annersley.

In due time old Marks arrived, and entered the parlour.

As he did so Dr. Killum locked the door.

"What, is that you, doctor?" said the lawyer, in great surprise. "I expected to meet a Mr. Annersley."

"I know you did; but for the present moment I am the Mr. Annersley."

"Oh, indeed; and what may be your business, pray? I am awfully pushed for time."

"I can't help that, Marks, I have matters of very great moment to speak of."

"Well, and what are they?"

"You have shunned me of late, Marks."

"I know I have; our business together has long been settled."

"So you think, perhaps."

"No, I don't think anything at all about it; I am sure of it."

"But I am not, by a very great deal, Marks," said the doctor, very slowly and calmly.

"I suppose you want to extort more money out of me, eh?"

"No, I don't; but I sadly stand in need of some assistance."

"You won't get any more from me, then."

"We shall see," said Killum, with a grim smile. "I know all about your goings on."

"Pooh, pooh! You cannot frighten me, you know."

"Yes, I can, Marks; I can make every bone in your body ache with fear."

"You are trying to frighten me."

"No, I am not. Listen to me."

"I am doing so."

"You have imposed upon Baron Templeton, Marks, and your son is supposed to be the real Allan Norman."

"You seem to know all about it."

"I do; and he passes under the name of 'Captain Zacary' at present, and sports about with plenty of money in his pockets."

"And if he does that does not matter to you, I think."

"But I could soon put a stop to his fine game, Marks."

"You dare not utter a word."

"You had better not force me to do so; for the police are on your track—you and Gentleman George ——"

"Gentleman George!" said Marks, in surprise. "I have nothing to do with such a man."

"Oh, but you have; George has confessed it."

"He is a liar and a villain, then," said Marks, colouring up to the very temples.

"He is safe in goal, however, and Inspector Sharp has got the case in hand."

"Inspector Sharp ——"

"Yes. Oh! you need not think I am playing the fool with you; he has been watching your house for several months."

"And yours also, perhaps."

"No, not mine, for I have none now."

"So much the better; you never deserved to have any."

"Nor you either, Marks; but I'll tell you what I am going to do."

"What?"

"Why, unless you and your son come to some terms with me, I shall go and divulge all I know to the inspector; my evidence would clear up the whole mystery."

"But what good would that do?"

"I could prove that your son is *not* rightful heir to the property, but an impostor."

"You could not, for the baron himself swears that he is."

"Yes, that declaration was caused through threats and fear; but I, who brought both of the lads into the world, could tell the name of the street, the hour, the day, and besides other circumstances, could prove what I say by the peculiar marks on the body of both the lads."

"And had they any peculiar birth marks, then?"

"They had."

"What were they?"

"I shan't tell you."

"You never mentioned anything of this before."

"I know it; but when the time comes I will."

"But Edgar Norman, you know, went down to the bottom of the sea on board the 'Rattlesnake;' it would be no harm to say what peculiar mark he had."

"I know that; on his right arm was distinctly visible the perfect likeness of a lion's paw and part of the limb, and on the body of Allan Norman there was——"

"What?"

"I forgot myself; I was about to divulge the secret, but I will not; for it is the character and name of Allan that your son is now assuming, and you might endeavour, by artificial means, to counterfeit it."

The old lawyer smiled grimly, for the doctor had clearly divined his thoughts and intentions.

At last he said—

"You seem to think that you know a great deal of my own and son's affairs, Dr. Killum; but if you were to take your oath no jury would ever believe you, for your past life has been one of infamy and iniquity."

"Perhaps so, but I never *killed* any one," was the calm reply.

"Killed!"

"Aye, killed, Marks; you need not look so strange."

"You confuse and puzzle me."

"If the halter of the common hangman was round your neck, it would confuse and puzzle you a little more, I think."

"You are a base impostor, Dr. Killum."

"I am *not*, but you are one; every farthing you own has been obtained by knavery."

For some few moments neither party spoke, but looked at each other with hatred and distrust.

Jenny had been listening to all this conversation outside, by putting her ear to the keyhole.

"Now is the time to bring in 'Captain Zacary,'" she thought, and immediately went to Kemp's, and sent in word that that young gentleman was wanted immediately at the "Blue Boar," by one Colonel Annersley.

Jerry went thither immediately, but judge of his great annoyance and surprise when he found himself in the presence of Dr. Killum and his own father.

Jerry was mortified beyond all expression.

He cursed and swore like a drunken trooper, and made all manner of threats against both his father and Dr. Killum, and a perfect volley of oaths were insufficient to satisfy him at the bare mention of Allan Norman's name.

"It's no use of your cursing and swearing in that way," said the doctor, very calmly.

"And who are you, pray, to correct me?" he answered, in a scoffing, contemptuous manner.

"I may be found a friend, and you might make me an enemy."

"I care not a jot for you," said Jerry, striding about, and flourishing his gold-topped cane.

"I dare say not."

"No, nor for my father either. You are both a couple of swindlers when a gentleman——"

"A what!" said Dr. Killum, laughing.

"A gentleman, I said."

"And a captain in the army, also, I suppose."

"What, do you mean to insult me, Dr. Killum?" said Jerry, in a great rage.

"It would take a great deal to do that, my boy."

"You must not provoke me much more, or else——"

"You might *kill* me, I suppose," was the doctor's rejoinder.

Jerry sat down in deep thought.

The doctor's words had calmed him.

At length he said impatiently—

"I can't stop here gossiping any longer. What is it you want of me, money or what?"

"No, not money, Jerry," said the doctor. "I want to know what conclusion you and your father have arrived at in regard to Allan Norman and his property, which you now enjoy."

"Is the man mad?" said Jerry, striding about the room.

"No, I am not; but I would tell you, Jerry Marks, that the murder of old Alderman English is not yet settled, and——"

"What have I to do with that; it was Edgar Norman, Allan Norman, and the two boys, Rawlings, who did it; everybody knows that."

"Everybody does *not* know it, Jerry," said Dr. Killum, "fresh evidence has been brought to light within the past week or two, which entirely alters the aspect of the whole affair, and if I liked to speak——"

"Well, and what if you did?"

"I could *hang* you."

"Hang me!"

"Yes; you and your father also."

"Oh, the doctor is mad!" said the old lawyer; "clearly mad."

"I must be going home."

"Not yet."

"Oh, listen to all he has got to say first," remarked Jerry, in a scoffing tone.

"A certain weapon has been found, Jerry Marks," observed the doctor, "which weapon is now in the hands of Inspector Sharp."

"Hang Sharp," said Jerry, "I meet him everywhere I go to."

"Which shows he has strong suspicions against some one that you know."

"But this weapon; what was it?"

"A revolver."

"Indeed; was it *yours*, then?" asked Jerry, carelessly.

"It was."

"Then you are the probable person?"

"I am not; for, on the night of the murder, and for a whole week after and before it, I was in Liverpool, confined to bed by illness, which I have dozens of witnesses to prove, and as *you* know very well."

"*I* know," said Jerry, with a curling lip.

"Yes, you; and no one is more certain of that fact than your father also; for you, Jerry, visited my room while I was away, and, instead of borrowing my books to read, for which I left the key in your charge, you borrowed something else."

"Borrowed something else, instead," mused Jerry, as if dreaming.

"Yes; you borrowed my ivory-handled revolver, Jerry, and this weapon was found very near the spot where the murder was committed. You see what I mean."

"I understand what you are trying to insinuate."

"And suppose I were to divulge this secret against you?"

"I care not," said Jerry, "the murder was not committed with fire-arms."

"You seem to know all about it, then."

"No, I don't; but it was proved on the trial that the alderman's life had been taken away with a knife."

"The main part of the murder was so done; but if you will brush up your memory, you will recollect that a bullet wound was found in his breast; and into the knife part of the business, I dare say," coolly remarked Dr. Killum, "your father knows as much about that as any one."

"Me, rascal," said the lawyer, getting purple in the face.

"Yes, you. You need not stare at one another; I have found out all about it."

"I know nothing about a knife," said old Marks.

"You do."

"Oh, the man is dreaming."

"I am not. What became of that large bowie knife which Jerry had once?"

"I threw it away; it was not lawful to carry such weapons," said Jerry.

"You did not; your father tried to destroy or hide it, but you, Jerry, watched him and found it out again, and it still exists."

"Indeed!"

"Yes."

"Where?"

"In my possession. What think you both of that?"

Old Marks looked hard at Jerry, whose lips were blue and trembling.

"And where did you find it, pray?" asked Jerry.

"In my office."

"In your office?" said the old lawyer.

"Yes; and your beautiful son placed it there."

"Liar!" said Jerry.

"Fool that you are to tell me so; did I not unexpectedly arrive in town eight days after the murder, and you, not being aware of my presence in the room, opened the doors with the keys I loaned you, and placed the bowie knife behind a row of old dusty bottles."

A ghastly smile flitted across the features of Jerry.

His father turned deadly pale, and hung his head.

Dr. Killum's countenance was radiant with a triumphant smile, as he said—

"You see you are in my power, both father and son."

CHAPTER CIX.

IN WHICH THE DETECTIVE PROVES A GOOD GENERAL.

IN a moment afterwards, Dr. Killum left the room, and went into the street.

He knew not why he did so; but could not help himself, as it were, for he seemed seized on a sudden with an impulse to do something, and to go somewhere; but for what reason he couldn't explain.

The first person he met was Jenny, and saying a few hasty words to her, went up the street, and, as he expressed it, "fell across" Mr. Sharp.

"Ah! Mr. Inspector, I am delighted to see you," said Killum.

"And so am I, doctor. What I want to know of you is, why did you give such strange information about that revolver which was found, and make such base insinuations against the lad Allan Norman, and then disappear?"

"I beg ten thousand pardons."

"But begging pardon a thousand times would not have done any good if I had not the whole history of that murder at my finger ends, and knew that Allan was innocent."

"I am extremely sorry for it, and will make ample amends to the lad."

"And so you ought; but how?"

"I have come into much information within a few hours, and will make a full explanation to a distinguished lady that I know."

"I have nothing at all to do with that. All I am engaged upon is ferreting out all the persons who were engaged in the murder of old Alderman English, for the more I study that case, I feel sure there were at least half-a-dozen persons engaged in it."

"You don't say so?"

"I do. But let me ask what can a poor, broken-down, seedy doctor like you want to have to say with a lady of distinguished position?"

"A great deal. But you don't know her?"

"Perhaps not, but don't be too sure."

"I am certain that you do not know her."

"And I am equally as certain that I do, Doctor Killum. You refer, perhaps, to Lady Oxenford?"

"The devil!" exclaimed Dr. Killum, in surprise. "Who told you?"

"I know more about her than you suppose, doctor; and, although I have nothing much to say about the affair, I think she ought to provide for her two boys."

"Her two boys? Then, you know all about it, Mr. Sharp."

"I do."

Dr. Killum looked staggered, as he said—

"I never told you."

"I know you didn't. But it don't take us detectives long to discover things."

"I am going to see Lady Oxenford to-night."

"You cannot see her to-night, doctor."

"Why not? I have only to send up my name, and she would admit me immediately."

"No doubt she would, but she is not at home."

"Indeed!"

"She is at the opera house; or, at least, is supposed to be there."

"I see—I see; she is engaged elsewhere; perhaps at her old father's."

"No, she is not. She has an appointment with me."

"You?"

"Yes, me. Don't look so astonished, doctor."

"You surprise me, Mr. Sharp. Surely her ladyship has not been doing anything wrong."

"No."

"Then what can she want with you?"

"That is my business. Don't seek to know everything at present; but, if you wish to serve these lads, go back, and keep company with old Marks and his son, until I return, which will be within an hour. I shall have to make use of you then."

Mr. Sharp called a cab, and drove away in the direction of Grosvenor Square.

The cab stopped at the door of a very respectable coffee house, and he alighted.

As if everything were known to him, he walked into a private room, and there saw an elegantly-dressed lady, with a heavy veil over her face.

Mr. Sharp bowed profoundly, and whispered, "Lady Oxenford, I believe?"

A nod was the only reply.

"You received a note which I sent, my lady?"

"I did," was the calm, cool reply; "and its language was so strange that I came here to know the meaning of it."

"I am sorry if it gave any offence, your ladyship."

"No, but proceed at once; and tell me what are the 'imperative reasons' which you have for seeing me."

"Your honor is at stake, my lady."

"Indeed!" was the indifferent reply. "And who are you, pray, that dares to interfere with my honor, or to defend it?"

"I am but an insignificant individual, I know, my lady, yet I have it in my power to render you much good service."

"And your name, sir?"

"William Sharp, or, as I am styled, Inspector Sharp, of the detective force."

"A policeman, I understand?"

"Yes, your ladyship."

"Or a common spy?"

"As you wish, my lady; but I beg you will not use such expressions to me, your ladyship, or at least defer the use of them until I explain my errand."

"Then do so at once."

"I will, and as delicately as I can, your ladyship, if you will only answer me a few questions."

"What are they, pray?"

"You have been married to Lord Oxenford many years, but have had no family?"

"I have not."

"But you have children living, for all that?"

Lady Oxenford started as if stung by an adder.

"S-i-r!" she said, sternly.

"Nay, I beg that you will be candid with me, for unless you are so, it is useless of me to waste words. I came here to you on important service."

"Well, sir, and suppose, for instance, that I have had children, what of that; the world does not know of it."

"The world does not, my lady, and it is to prevent the world knowing it, that I came here to-night."

For a moment there was a pause.

"You, of course, know that my Lord Oxenford has placed a watch over you?"

"I have good reason for supposing it."

"*I* am the person who was requested to do so, your ladyship."

"And have fulfilled my lord's instructions, I suppose?"

"Only when I thought proper; but it is just right to say, my lady, that I am fully aware of your private visits to Baron Templeton and elsewhere, and am also aware of Dorothy Dale's visit to you. I was employed in quite a different matter, my lady, when your husband requested me to watch you."

"And what was it, may I ask?"

"You will not be offended with me, I hope?"

"No."

"Then in a few words, I may say, your ladyship, that your two sons, Allan and Edgar, who were tried for——"

"Name it not; do not breathe it," sighed Lady Oxenford, "they were innocent."

"So it now appears; and it was to track and have punished the right parties that I was engaged when certain little bits of information came to my knowledge which made me sure the two boys were yours."

Another pause ensued.

"One of the villains is now assuming the name of Allan Norman, and I understand this has been done with the consent of Baron Templeton, who has been forced into such an unmanly act to save himself and you from exposure."

"But it could not be prevented; the baron has explained the whole circumstance to me."

"But in *my* hands, your ladyship, all the mischief can be undone again and the exposure prevented."

"In what manner?"

"Both father and son are complicated in the murder of old Alderman English, and at five minutes' notice I could arrest both of them; but it is absolutely necessary that you and the baron should do something for the lad, Allan Norman, at first."

"He is a brave youth," sighed my lady.

"And a handsome one also," said Sharp.

"And do you suppose that Lord Oxenford knows of the existence of these boys?"

"He does, my lady, but has no positive reasons for knowing that you are the mother of them."

"Heaven be thanked for that."

"Nor do I see the good that could be done by informing him of it. He has left the task of watching you to me; and as he has lived in happy ignorance hitherto, why, let him so continue for all I shall tell him."

"You wish, then, to be a true friend to me, Mr. Sharp?"

"I do, my lady, and I have proved it all along. Whether the lads are or are not illegitimate, has nothing at all to do with the murder case, and requires no further attention from me. Let you and the baron provide for Allan, and there let the matter drop."

"But it is hard for a mother not to recognize or be recognized by her children, Mr. Sharp," said Lady Oxenford, weeping. "For many years I have acted the part of a hypocrite; but I cannot do so any longer."

"I can fully appreciate your feelings, my lady, for I am a family man myself," said Sharp. "But if you think you could keep the secret still, I don't see any reason why young Allan should not be near you, and in your family."

"How do you mean? To live with us?"

"Yes, my lady."

"But how could that be brought about?"

"Your husband, Lord Oxenford, needs a private secretary."

"So he does."

"I can recommend Allan to him."

"Besides, he saved my father's life, and that is also known to his lordship."

"Which will be another recommendation in the lad's favor."

"So it will."

"But before he accepts this situation, my lady, I will, with your consent, make him aware of who and what you are. And when my lord is out riding in the park, he can call on you."

"I have a better plan than that, Mr. Sharp. Do you introduce him to me in my opera-box to-morrow night. I shall be there alone, for Lord Oxenford has pressing engagements elsewhere. I cannot sufficiently thank or reward you, Mr. Sharp, for your kindness and good feeling," said my lady, extending her hand.

"No thanks, my lady. I am a detective officer it's true, but I am not devoid of good or honourable feelings. It always gives me much more pleasure to speak well than ill of any one, and to do all the good I can that falls in my routine of duty."

"I am certain of it. You have an honest face."

"And heart also, my lady; but I should have told you that, although you have been watched, and will be for some time to come, the persons so employed are under my direction, and, of course, will never know of the confidence existing between us."

"I am glad you put me on your guard; I shall now know how to act."

"And I would remind you, my lady, that although Lord Oxenford has given me large sums to expend during this course of watching, I have used it mainly on young Allan, who has of late been leading the life of a gentleman. I could not have put his lordship's money to a better use, I think."

"You could not; and the more I hear you say about this matter, the more I am convinced that your heart is made of gold, and that your talents are deserving of a higher sphere."

"Many thanks, your ladyship; but let me ask, have you seen or heard of a certain Dr. Kil'um?"

"I have," said my lady, slightly colouring; "I have never seen him, however, for many, many long years."

"But you have relieved his wants."

"I have, and liberally; perhaps I have paid him for his services too well."

"Very likely, indeed, my lady; but you see, the family secret is known to him, and to Dorothy Dale also."

"It is, alas!"

"Well, then, this doctor threatens to pay you a visit."

"At my house?"

"Yes, my lady."

"But I cannot permit him."

"He is more frequently drunk than sober, and if he should call in such a state, and my lord to inquire his business, all would be over; for a few pounds he would divulge all he knew."

"This, then, must be prevented."

"Yes, and at once. Leave it in my hands, Lady Oxenford," said Mr. Sharp, rising; "and now that we have full confidence in each other, I well know how to act and what to do for the best."

"In case you should need any money, Mr. Sharp, I beg that you will accept ——"

"No, thank you, my lady; his lordship's money is not all expended yet. Good night."

Lady Oxenford shook the detective by the hand, and she passed through a side-door in a by street, and was soon lost to view.

Sharp jumped into his hansom and soon returned to the Haymarket.

He went straight to the "Blue Boar," and standing against the door of the private parlour, he could distinctly hear an angry altercation still going on with the three worthies therein, and loudest in oath was Dr. Killum, who was vowing vengeance against old Marks and Jerry.

All three had been drinking rather heavily while Sharp was away, and were becoming very noisy indeed.

"I don't want to go in," thought Sharp, "and yet I want to get Killum out."

He went to look for and soon found Jenny, who was at hand.

"Jenny, go in and tell old Killum he is wanted outside."

Jenny did so.

"Ah! Mr. Sharp, back again, eh?" said Killum, "I have been giving the old lawyer a bit of my mind, you know."

"And I have come to give you a bit of mine," said Sharp, drily.

"How do you mean?"

"I mean that at this moment, and in this very street, there are no less than three sheriff's officers after you for debt."

"The deuce they are."

"No mistake about it; and, as a friend, I would advise you to leave London this very night."

"Leave London?"

"Yes, and England too."

"But I can't. I wish I could."

"Why, what prevents you?"

"I have not a single sovereign in the world. But if I could only get to see Lady Oxenford once more——"

"I know what you mean, doctor, but you have bothered Lady Oxenford too often already. I think she has paid you a hundred times over for what you have done. But I'll tell you what I will do."

"What?"

"Why, lend you £50 to go away with, and £50 more to start you in the colonies somewhere."

"Done!" said Doctor Killum. "Nothing would suit me better, you know. Give me the money."

"Not yet. Don't be so fast. If I were to give it to you now you would go and get drunk with it, and in the morning not have a single penny perhaps."

"Very likely. But I should like to have my revenge out of those two rascals in there."

"And so you shall."

"How?"

"If we need your evidence at any time we will write over and let you know."

"Very well; then it's a bargain."

"But you must start the first thing in the morning, and you will be in time to catch the New York packet that sails from Liverpool to-morrow."

"I am satisfied; but you must let me have a word to say to them before I leave."

"Very well, do so; but be quick; the sheriff's officers I tell you are in the neighbourhood."

"I will be quick, you may be sure."

Dr. Killum entered the parlour again, and a very long conversation took place between the three rascals.

"You wouldn't go if we gave you the money," said old Marks.

"Try me, that's all," said Killum.

"One hundred pounds each is a large sum," said Jerry.

"But it isn't much, considering what you have," said the doctor; "besides, consider what fine evidence I could give against both of you."

Jerry was disgusted, and so was his father also. It was like taking away their heart's blood.

But still the doctor got the sum he asked for, and swearing a terrible oath that he would leave England for ever next day, left the room, full of joy.

Dr. Killum found Sharp outside waiting for him, and they both went in a cab to a coffee shop near Euston Square station; but the doctor never mentioned what money he got from Marks.

Killum was provided with a bed for the night, and Sharp promised to call early in the morning, and see him off by the express train.

THE BOY KING
OF THE SOUTH SEA ISLANDS.

PUNISHMENT OF THE SPY.

CHAPTER CX.

MARKS IS SUDDENLY SURPRISED.

THE cab with Mr. Sharp returned to the Haymarket, and once again the officer visited the "Blue Boar."

"I think I have sufficient evidence against the two villains on more charges than one to warrant their immediate arrest. But how shall I proceed? If I accuse old Marks with imposing on Baron Temp'eton, that would rake up the affair of the two boys, which must not be; but since the old villain and his son have had extensive dealings in their time with Gentleman George and his gang of burglars and swell mobsmen, I shall have no diffi-

No. 40.

culty in getting them transported, for some of the gang will be sure to split on one another when the time comes."

Sharp, therefore, felt in his pockets, and found that he had two pairs of handcuffs ready for use.

He next whispered to two constables, in plain clothes, who were passing at the time.

They, in turn, gave the "office" to two others, and all four loitered around the tavern, ready to be called in when the proper moment arrived.

Sharp entered the parlour, and called for brandy-and-water.

He was so disguised that neither father nor son could recognise him.

For some time silence was maintained on both sides, until, at last, one remark brought on another, and conversation became very lively between the three.

Several topics were discussed, and at last they spoke of the arrest of Gentleman George and others of his gang.

"Yes, it was a very clever capture," said old Marks, "and we ought to thank the police for ridding society of such bad characters."

"But it is said that the police are on the track of others of the gang—men, so I hear, in respectable positions in society."

"No doubt there are plenty of wolves in sheep's clothing moving about London," said Jerry; "and I should, for one, rejoice to see them all discovered and punished."

"They say that this Gentleman George has made a confession," said Sharp, coolly.

"A what?" gasped old Marks.

"A confession."

"About what?" asked Jerry, hurriedly.

"The robbery at Lord Manfred's place."

The old lawyer turned very pale.

"It seems the robbers' aim was to get possession of certain legal papers in the mansion, which were of great value to a certain lawyer."

"And has the villain disclosed as much?" asked old Marks.

"He has."

"But how do *you* know that?"

"A friend of mine told me so, a doctor of the name of Killum."

"And do *you* know this Dr. Killum?"

"I do—a most respectable——"

"A most disreputable liar," said Jerry.

"And impostor, too," said the father.

"Then you know him also?" said Sharp.

"I should think we did, rather," said Jerry, with an oath; "he is a professional beggar and——"

"Well, *I* never found him so; but on the contrary, reposed so much confidence in him that this very night I loaned him one hundred pounds."

"You did?"

"Yes?"

"Then all I can say is," said Marks, "that you'll never get your money back again, for he's going to leave England to-morrow, and has swindled us out of £100 also this very night."

Sharp bit his lip and made no reply.

"If he does leave England, though," he thought, "the price is not too great."

"But if you knew him to be such a rogue, why did you let him have it?" said Sharp. "You must have had some motive."

"So we had," said Jerry. "We wanted to get rid of his hateful presence, that's all. If ever I see his ugly face again I'll kill him."

"But hanging follows murder," said Sharp, very coldly.

"I know it does," said Jerry, doggedly; "but I care not for that."

"Do you know," asked Sharp, after a few moments silence, "any one of the name of Marks?"

"Yes, I do."

"So do I," answered father and son.

"One is a lawyer?"

"He is."

"And the other?"

"A gentleman."

"Of a certain sort," said Sharp.

"What of them?" asked the lawyer. "If it is the Lawyer Marks that I mean, he is a most respectable gentleman, and a bright ornament of the legal profession."

"So I have heard also," Jerry remarked.

"It's wonderful how accounts vary now," said the officer. "I have heard, on the very best authority, that this old Marks is one of the most cunning, selfish, wicked, designing old villains that ever stepped in shoe leather."

"That is evidently a case of defamation of character," said the lawyer, "and the parties ought to be prosecuted according to law. I should like to know who spread such a report of my old friend Marks."

"The police are the authors of it."

"But what has this old Marks done to merit such an infamous reputation?" said the lawyer.

"He has cheated the widow and orphan, set fire to his premises more than once, to get the insurance, has swindled his creditors more than once by going through the bankruptcy court, and last of all has been a well-known receiver of stolen goods, and the companion of notorious thieves."

"Gracious goodness! what a character!" gasped the lawyer. "I never heard such a one in all my life."

"And that is not half of it yet," said Sharp.

"Why, he could not possibly be worse."

"Yes he could; he might go so far as to conceal murder, if, indeed, he did not have a hand in it."

"Murder!"

"Aye; cold-blooded, deliberate murder," said Sharp, with an angry look.

"If that be his character, then," said Jerry, smoking his cigar, and endeavouring to appear very much unconcerned, "the sooner such a villain is arrested, the better. What say you?" he remarked, addressing his father.

"I fully coincide in your remark," old Marks replied, and large drops of perspiration oozed from his brow, as, with trembling hand, he helped himself to the remains of his brandy-and-water, and called for more.

"Make it nice and hot and strong, waiter," said old Marks, smacking his lips, and looking very suspiciously across the room at Mr. Sharp, who, with a long pipe, was puffing away very unconcernedly.

"I will take another ' go ' also," said Jerry, to the waiter.

"And don't fail to make it nice and hot and strong," said Sharp, with a quiet smile. "Very strong, mind, waiter."

"What is it to *you* how I order my liquor?" said old Marks, tartly to Sharp.

"We didn't ask for *your* suggestions," said Jerry.

"I know you didn't; but I thought I would render you an act of kindness, that's all, as it is your ' parting' glass."

And as he uttered the word "parting," he used so much emphasis that both the old man and his son looked upon each other with fear and suspicion.

"What do you mean by ' parting glass?'" asked old Marks.

"We are going to have more after this," said Jerry.

"That depends greatly how you behave yourselves," said Sharp.

"Sir," said Jerry, indignantly, "recollect you are not joking, but talking to two gentlemen."

"I know all about that," said Sharp, very blandly.

"The fellow must be drunk," said old Marks. "I never heard such impudence in the whole course of my life. Depends upon *you*, indeed, what next?"

"The handcuffs will come next," said Sharp. "So drink up your brandy-and-water as quickly as possible—it is the last you will indulge in for some time—and come with *me*."

"You?"

"Yes, me."

"And who the devil are you?" said Jerry.

"A detective officer, and——"

"Hang me if I didn't think so from the first," said the old lawyer.

"He shall never take me alive," Jerry swore, roundly.

"Won't I?" said Sharp, producing his two pairs of handcuffs. "If you use violence it will go all the harder for you."

"Knock him down with that pot," said old Marks.

"I have something better than that," said Jerry, pulling out a revolver.

But before he could use it, the door was thrown open, and four policemen in plain clothes dashed in, and a blow from one of them "floored" Jerry on the instant.

Before father or son could recover full consciousness, they were handcuffed safely and conducted out of the parlour.

"On what charge am I arrested?" asked old Marks, spluttering with rage and passion.

"You will have all that explained at the station," said Sharp. "Bring 'em along, my men."

"Oh, for Heaven's sake! let us have a cab," said Jerry, who feared to be recognised by his numerous acquaintances in the Haymarket.

"No need of that," said Sharp. "Bring 'em along; we have not far to go."

And through the Haymarket both father and son were conducted, amid a crowd of people.

"What's the matter?" asked one.

"They are pickpockets," was the answer.

"No; they have been robbing a gentleman of his watch and money," said a third.

"They are well-dressed," said a fourth.

"All swell mobsmen," was the rejoinder.

"Why, that's Captain Zacary," said one or two swells who had just come out of Kemp's supper room.

"So it is."

"Why, what's the row?"

"Got into a fight, captain?"

"Oh, he has been thrashing some policeman," said others.

"Let's go and bail him out; he has got lots of money, and we know him well."

So spoke scores of inquisitive persons who followed the police to the station-house, jabbering and talking, and retailing a half-dozen rumours about the sudden arrest.

But, when Mr. Sharp had spoken to the inspector-orderly at the station, and whispered certain things in that functionary's ear, they were conducted to separate cells, and all bail refused.

"What am I accused of?" said old Marks. "I am as innocent of all crime as a babe unborn," he roared. "Send for a lawyer on the instant; I will not sleep in such a filthy den as this; it is only fit for cattle. I can give and get bail for any amount. Call the inspector this instant; this is an insult to any Englishman in the land."

Jerry was equally noisy, and stamped and raved like a madman, and beat at the cell doors, calling to his father and making all sorts of hideous howls.

"It is all through you, you wicked vagabond," shouted the father to Jerry, "I always said you would bring me to the gallows."

"Hold your tongue, you prattling old fool," was the son's impudent answer.

"You know you did it," shouted the old lawyer, frantically; "I knew it would come home to you."

"I wish you were dead," said Jerry, "and if I were in the same cell I would strangle you."

"It is all through Dr. Killum," raved the father, "I always knew he would turn police spy."

"Silence there No. 24 and 15," said the gaoler, rapping at their cell doors, "you won't let any one sleep."

"Put the old 'un into a straight waistcoat," said one prisoner, "I never heard such howling in all my experience, and I've been lagged a score o' times."

"What's the figure, young 'un," said another; "have you been 'nabbed' for snatching at some old gent's valuables?"

"You'll have your bread and water stopped, both on ye, if you get going on in that way; *I* know all about such a crib as this," remarked a professional street beggar, who had been "up" more than a dozen times.

The truth was that both father and son had been placed in a cell which contained a companion.

But such a noise was maintained, that the companion of old Marks, who was a burly costermonger, charged with fighting in the public streets, threatened to punch the old lawyer's head unless he made "less row," and illustrated his meaning in a very forcible manner, by giving old Marks such a hearty knock in the ribs, that for a moment or two it deprived him of all power of utterance.

But when the legal gentleman contrived to regain his breath again, he gave vent to such a volley of oaths and shouts, that the gaoler's attention was attracted to the spot and restored order.

Jerry also found his companion to be a drunken fellow, who had been amusing himself by rolling in the mud, and was arrested about the "small hours."

This individual insisted on shaking hands with and hugging "Captain Zacary" to such an extent that Jerry's fine and stylish attire was all soiled, and he was afraid to resist the lovingness of his companion for fear of further violence.

During the night, several persons visited both father and son, and offered to bail them out to any amount. One lawyer offered to go security in the amount of £2,000 for the appearance of old Marks in the morning, but the superintendent refused all such offers, saying that the charges against the two prisoners were of too great and grievous a nature to think of accepting bail at all.

"They have got us at last, I fear," thought Jerry, very despondingly. "If it were not for the fear of dying, I would strangle myself.

Jerry was an arrant cur and coward.

We have seen and shown this from the beginning of our eventful story.

When fortune was on his side, Jerry could laugh and jeer and make fun of police officers and prison cells, but now that he was fairly and safely in the hands of justice, he trembled violently and gave up all hope as lost.

His father, who in his time had sent many an innocent man to prison on the slightest, and oftentimes groundless, reasons, felt his own situation most acutely.

The cell was damp, and cold, and dirty; and nought to lie upon but a hard bench, or, at least, what little of it was not appropriated for his own use by the burly and snoring costermonger.

"I'd give every penny I am worth to be out of this scrape," thought the lawyer. "But I have reasons for thinking that my legal friends, with the aid of all-powerful money, may get me acquitted; for there is only circumstantial evidence of a very slight character against me."

During the night, the prisoners were greatly surprised to receive a visit from two persons that they very well knew—namely, Allan Norman and Jem Rawlings.

Their visit was occasioned by the obstinacy of the prisoners in not giving their proper names and addresses, and Allan and Jem were, therefore, called in to identify them, as being really and truly nothing else but Jerry Marks and his father.

Allan confronted the two rogues with an eye flashing with the fire of vengeance.

"You are here, at last, I see," said Allan; "you have been riding longer than I expected you would, and I am glad you are about to suffer for your past crimes."

Jem almost jumped with joy.

"What, the old ragamuffin and his son—both on 'em!" said he. "Oh, here's a jolly lark! Won't they get a 'lifer' neither. Oh, no, nothing less, I think, Allan!"

"Ah! if our poor brothers were only alive to see this triumph," said Allan, "I would give almost anything."

"And so would I," said Jem; "but it ain't no manner o' use to grumble, Allan; so the two villains 'll swing or get transported, I don't care."

The prisoners, when they saw Allan and Jem, raved and swore fearfully, and their glaring eyes looked deadly hatred against the two long-persecuted but blameless lads.

Morning came, and the other "cases" having been disposed of, Mr. Box, the magistrate, called up Marks and his son.

"What is the charge, Mr. Sharp?" asked the magistrate; "the one I mean which you intend to proceed upon first?"

"With being abettors before and after the fact, in robbing at Manfred Hall."

"I am innocent of such a charge," shouted old Marks, in the dock.

"And so am I," said Jerry.

"Silence, prisoners; you will have full opportunities for proving that, if you are so. What evidence have you to produce?" said Mr. Box.

"The voluntary confession of one whom I produce—'Gentleman George,' as he is called."

When this witness stepped into the box, old Marks shook with rage, and if looks could have killed the witness, Marks would have surely done so.

"I have made a statement to the police——" said Gentleman George.

"With a promise of pardon, I suppose? Ha, ha! listen to the informer," growled old Marks.

"Silence, prisoner!"

"I have had no promise of pardon," said Gentleman George, "and expect none, for I am more guilty, perhaps, than any one; but as I am told I can render an act of justice to a poor lad who has been basely persecuted both by Marks and his son,

I come forward to do so, and to serve the ends of justice."

"Well, what do you know?" asked the solicitor for the prosecution.

"I know both Marks and his son for many years. Marks, himself, was once legal adviser to a Widow and Orphan Club, and he confessed to me, often, that he swindled the club out of hundreds of pounds."

"But that has nothing to do with the case. Speak of the burglaries at Manfred Hall. Who planned them?"

"Old Marks did so, as I can prove by producing many letters written to me about it, from old Marks himself."

The letters were produced and read in court.

"Old Marks, the lawyer, promised me a large sum if I succeeded in bringing to him certain legal documents that related to the birth and parentage of two illegitimate boys, and having got possession of one document in the first robbery, he imposed upon a certain legal nobleman, and got much money out of him."

"Did you carry away any other property?"

"Yes; plate to a considerable amount."

"Where did you take it?"

"By arrangement with old Marks, we took it in small quantities to his own private residence."

"What became of it, then?"

"Marks melted it down himself, for he has a small furnace and ladles for that purpose on his premises."

"And then."

"The pure metal was sold by Marks to a silver-smith in Petticoat Lane, or somewhere near by, and the proceeds were divided among us."

"But the other property, what became of it?"

"It was sent to a well-known receiver, and I have heard that through the exertions of a lad named Jem Rawlings, and Mr. Sharp, several articles have been recovered, and are to be produced in evidence."

"The receiver, your honour, is also in custody," said Inspector Sharp.

"Have you anything further to say, witness?"

"Nothing, your honor, only this: I was first led into crime by the acts of the old man Marks, and have for several years defied all the police to convict me, and I now convict myself by this open confession. I repeat that my only motive in giving evidence is to have the chief leader and adviser of the gang convicted as well as myself, for it will be remembered by the court, and his honor may, perhaps, not forget it, that in all the scrapes I have ever got into, Marks has always been my counsel in defence, and got me off."

His honor said that he distinctly remembered having seen the witness before him, and in each case was defended by Mr. Marks.

"All that the witness has said is a string of black falsehoods," shouted Marks.

"Silence, prisoner," said the burly usher, in a gruff voice.

Gentleman George having given his evidence, Mr. Sharp was next called, and very closely cross-examined by the counsel of old Marks.

Sharp, in very brief terms, detailed the particulars of the robberies at Manfred Hall, and spoke in very high terms of the conduct of Allan and Jem in assisting him to ferret out the gang of scientific thieves.

He had been in possession of many important facts against all the prisoners concerned in the burglaries at Manfred Hall; but although he had not any direct evidence against the two prisoners until the day before, and then only through the vo'untary statement of Gentleman George. he had long suspected old Marks and Jerry Marks, *alias* Allan Norman, *alias* Captain Zacary.

He had proceeded with other officers to the residence of old Marks, and found a great many articles, the proceeds of other burglaries; and the furnace, ladles, smelting pots, and other apparatus described by the witness, Gentleman George, were discovered in first class order.

He had also been to the receiver's, where young Jem Rawlings had served under his instructions as shop-boy, and after a short resistence on the part of the receiver, he and young Rawlings brought to light many and sundry valuables, which had been hidden away in various parts of the shop, cellar, and house.

The history of the last robbery, at Manfred Hall, was again detailed, and Jem Rawlings was called upon to prove how he had heard the burglary planned, when, and by whom.

Jem's story made the whole court roar with laughter, as he described the many disguises which Mr. Sharp had put on and practised for the apprehension of the thieves, and when he explained about following the cab ferreting out the whole affair, his honor warmly commended him for his talent and perseverence.

During the whole time, however, of hearing the evidence against them, the prisoners were making noisy remarks and calling the witnesses names, nor could all the endeavours of his own counsel restrain old Marks.

"You wish to have all the prisoners remanded for trial on the same charge, Mr. Sharp?" said the magistrate.

"Yes, your honor; when next they appear, I have no doubt that much more evidence can be produced."

"But I submit that there has been no evidence to warrant the detention of young Marks," said Jerry's counsel; "and therefore I ask that he be discharged."

"Your honor," said Mr. Sharp, "there is more direct evidence against young Marks than even his father."

"How so?" asked Jerry's lawyer; "none has been produced."

"This diamond ring and watch, which were taken from his person, form part of the two burglaries, your honor, and both articles have been shown to and identified by Lord Manfred this morning."

Lord Manfred appeared, and swore to the truth of this statement, adding that he had also seen and identified many other articles as belonging to him.

Jerry's spirits now fell to the freezing point, and he could scarcely stand.

"My client can prove that he bought the articles," said Jerry's lawyer.

"Are his witnesses here?"

"They are not."

"Can they be produced at the next hearing?"

"Perhaps so, your honor."

"They are in prison, sir," said Sharp. "One of the articles fell to the share of Huggins, who received £5 for the ring from the young prisoner, who well knew it had been stolen. The watch was given to him by Gentleman George, and on the inside case can be seen the cipher and crest of Lord Manfred, which has been but imperfectly erased."

Jerry looked daggers at Sharp, and bit his lip.

"What is the value of the ring and watch?"

"My lord says that the brilliants alone are worth £200, and the watch, which was made per order, he

gave 80 guineas for. This is all the evidence I wish to lay before your honor on the present occasion," said Sharp.

"Then I remand the prisoners for a fortnight, to enable the police to make enquiries concerning other missing articles."

Bail was refused.

Old Marks, Jerry, and the receiver went to their cells again, and as they pa-sed through the court-room, the round chubby face of Jem Rawlings met them with a broad good-humoured grin.

"We have landed you at last," said Jem to Jerry. "What do you think of prison life now, Captain Zacary, ha! ha! Our turn has come at last, you see. Honesty is the best policy after all. Thieves and rogues can never thrive."

Old Marks was gasping for breath, and when he reached his cell, he almost fainted from excitement and fatigue.

"Call Mr. Sharp here, I want him immediately," said he, in a faint whisper to the goaler; "but don't let my son, Jerry, know it—for Heaven's sake don't let him know it."

In a few moments Inspector Sharp gave orders to have old Marks removed into a far distant cell, so that Jerry could not hear them talking together.

"What do you want, Mr. Marks?" asked Sharp.

"Oh! what a cool villain that Gentleman George is; if I get transported it will be all through him; but all he has said is lies."

"Well, then, you must disprove his statements at your trial."

"Oh, I could a tale unfold!" said old Marks, with a deep sigh.

"I would advise you to say nothing at all, because it may be used against you."

"That son of mine, Jerry, has brought me to ruin and infamy."

"Vices never bring forth good fruits, Mr. Marks."

"So it seems; but don't you think I could turn Queen's evidence now?"

"And save yourself?"

"Yes."

"No, you must have no such hopes as that; we have more evidence than enough already."

"But what I should tell you would be *truth*, you know."

"I suppose so; informers always say that, you know. When rascals are caught, we always find them willing enough to turn evidence against each other."

"But you don't know half what I do."

"Nor do I wish to know."

"You seem to think, then, that the evidence will transport us?"

"I certainly do."

"For how long?"

"For life, I think."

"*For life*," sighed old Marks, and then he shed tears, and tore his hair in a frightful way. "You have been to my house and searched everywhere?"

"I have, and at your offices also."

"At my bank books, and all, I suppose?"

"Everything."

"Then, all my money is lost for ever?"

"Yes, if you are convicted."

"But suppose I escape?"

"If you do on one charge, I have twenty others against you, Marks," said Sharp, coolly, "so therefore I advise you to make up your mind for a whole lifetime in prison."

"Why, that is worse than hanging."

"I never tried one or the other," said Sharp, "so therefore can't say."

"You are as cold as ice, Sharp," said old Marks, in disgust.

"I am long accustomed to hearing prisoners' tales of injured innocence."

"And where do you think they will send us all if we are convicted?"

"Can't say, but to some lonely island, far away from all land, where you will have plenty of nice hard work in cutting down forests, blasting rocks, breaking stones, and making roads, with a ball and chain to your leg."

"Very pleasant prospect indeed; but I am very sickly, you know, and hard work never agreed with me."

"Oh, they'll make you like it; and if it don't agree with you, they'll try the cat o' nine tails on your back, put you into solitary confinement, feed you on dry bread and water, and luxuries of that sort; that's the way we've got for 'em now."

Old Marks, finding it would avail him nothing to make "a clean breast" of it, declined to unfold the tale he had hinted at, and having refreshed himself with some food which his solicitor sent him, strictly protested his innocence of all and everything with which he was charged, and laughed and cried by turns like a lunatic.

"It always ends the same way," thought Sharp, "roguery never thrives; they all get picked up and punished one by one, sooner or later; they fall like ripe apples into our hands. The honest man is a prince among his fellows; but where *is* there one?"

Inspector Sharp was one!

CHAPTER CXI.

THE GREAT FIGHT BEGINS.

THE escape of the miller, or Bill Whetherby, in disguise, was a sad disappointment to young Ted Rawlings.

"He would have given his right hand," he afterwards said, "to have captured that bold ruffian."

But Bill escaped, and the information he gave to Mungo, stirred up that chief to still greater efforts than before.

"If they are starving, Bill," said Mungo, "we shall not have long to wait before they surrender."

"Surrender," said Aixa, in a desponding tone, "if you are going to wait until they do that, you will have to stay a very long time, I can assure you, for Lion Limb is not one of those who will give in."

"You seem to look upon Lion Limb as some great prodigy, then," said Mungo.

"I do," said Aixa, sighing; "but I would willingly die to see him and that English girl captives in your hands, for the triumph would be grand."

"And suppose I do deliver them both captives into your hands, Aixa, what would you give?"

"Anything you might ask. I am queen of the Pearl islands; those, my dominions, should be yours with pleasure."

"I don't want them," said Mungo, "but there is one condition that I would make with you."

"Name it."

"You must become my bride."

Aixa, for a moment, looked very much confused and annoyed.

She had loved Lion Limb, for he was brave, young, and handsome.

But the contrast with Mungo was very great, and even Aixa shuddered at the idea of becoming the wife of such a gaunt, tall, ugly wretch as Mungo.

But she attempted to smile, and promised to become the wife of Mungo, should he succeed in conquering Lion Limb and his brave followers.

"'Tis well, then," said Mungo; the bargain is made fairly between us, and in less than three days Lion Limb and Emma Clarence shall be placed in your power."

Aixa was delighted at the prospect, but she little dreamed what changes three days would bring forth.

For that very night, while Mungo and his men were rioting and filled with wine, terrible news arrived in their camp.

"What?" said Mungo, jumping up, alarmed "it cannot be true!"

"It *is* true, though, captain," said his messenger.

"Old Martin and his islanders landed, and advancing against us?"

"Yes, sir."

"They have brought ships with them, also?"

"They have; and well armed ones, too; I saw them with my own eyes."

"But how could Lion Limb have communicated with that far distant island? Have I not swept the seas, and ordered my men to prevent any boat leaving this island?"

"True, captain; but some of Lion Limb's men have escaped in a small sail boat and told their story, and even now, old Governor Martin and a strong band of well-trained and well-armed followers are marching towards you at a very fast pace."

"When will they be in sight, think you?"

"From the rate they were travelling at I should judge they will come in sight to-morrow some time."

"I must prevent their joining their forces with those of Lion Limb's," said Mungo, in a rage; "it will be two battles instead of one, that's all. I will beat old Governor Martin first, and then return and fall upon Lion Limb."

"It is easy to say, sir," said the messenger; "but old Martin's men are filled with hope and very impatient for battle."

"Let us call in all our forces, then, and march against old Martin at once."

In less than half an hour after this conversation, Mungo assembled his forces and prepared to march against and encounter old Governor Martin.

The greatest confusion reigned in Mungo's camp.

Horses, mules, oxen, and other draught animals were quickly collected.

His Indians were filled with excitement.

"Never mind the waggons," said Mungo, "we shall not need them; we shall only be absent about thirty hours."

"We had better leave a strong guard behind to protect our property, captain," said more than one.

"We have plenty of valuable plunder stored away, captain," said others.

"Yes, we don't want to lose all our hard earnings," chorused others.

"Well, then, leave a small body of Indians behind."

"What good would the Indians be if Lion Limb attacks them?" asked one.

"There is no fear of that," said Mungo. "Lion Limb is half-starved, and his followers also. What can *he* do against my well-fed followers? Do as I tell you; *I* am your chief, and know what is best."

Mungo's orders were accordingly attended to.

A small company of Indians were left behind to mind the baggage.

Mungo, Bill Whetherby, and the other leaders of the buccaneers, started out with their followers in the middle of the night.

They marched very quickly, and the Indians, with Mungo, were very eager for the combat, for it was told to them that those they were about to face had brought great riches with them and all sorts of valuables.

But Lion Limb was also prepared for anything that might happen.

He knew that the islanders were marching to his assistance; and Mungo had not left his camp more than ten minutes, when a spy arrived and told Lion Limb everything that had occurred.

"Has he withdrawn all his forces from around us?" said Lion Limb, with a radiant smile.

"He has."

"But how am I to know this for certain?"

"You may rely on the news being correct, sir," said Ted Rawlings. "I have been riding round, and can't see a single one of the enemy."

"Then pass the word to my men; we also will start out at once."

In less than an hour, and in the darkness, Lion Limb and his chosen band sallied forth, and marched with all haste towards Mungo's camp.

Lion Limb made such excellent arrangements, that he surrounded Mungo's camps, and took all the Indian guards prisoners before they were aware of it.

One of them, it is true, mounted his horse, and endeavoured to fly to Mungo, and tell him the news; but he was hotly pursued by young Ted Rawlings, and knocked off his horse.

"So you thought to warn Mungo, did you?" said Ted; "but I was too quick for you, you see. It would have spoiled all our plans if that blackguard had got to hear the news, so take that—and that—and that also."

At the same time he dealt the unfortunate Indian a series of hard kicks which knocked all the breath out of him, and then bound him hand and foot with cords.

Meanwhile, Lion Limb, after securing all that was of use in the camp, had them packed in waggons, which were immediately sent back to the city.

The rest of the things, such as old tents, and the like, were thrown into a heap and burned.

But the greatest discovery of all was yet to be made.

In a secret hiding-place was found much gold, silver, pearls, and the like, and when just in the act of taking poison, and making away with herself, Queen Aixa was captured.

She was brought before Lion Limb, who thus spoke to her.

"When I spared your life, Queen Aixa, it was with the understanding that you would leave this island, and return to your own possessions."

"It was," said Aixa, doggedly.

"But I now find you in the camp of my worst enemies, and in league with them."

"That is true."

"Since, therefore, no dependence can be placed upon your word, Queen Aixa, I must punish you."

"Kill me, if you like."

"No, I will not do that; but you shall be made a prisoner, and I leave you entirely in the hands of Emma Clarence; whatever she says I will do with you."

"That would be worse than death itself," Aixa murmured with a deep-drawn sigh; "I can never be the slave of the pale-faced English girl."

"But you must and shall," said Lion Limb, in a very stern tone of voice.

And Queen Aixa was escorted to the waggons, which were on the road to the city.

"Now," said Lion Limb, "since all our preparations are completed, let us march again. Let each of my men look well to his own company, and obey my orders."

Silently they left Mungo's camp, and followed the track of the bold buccaneers, sending out scouts in front.

"If old Governor Martin only knew that we were in Mungo's rear," said Lion Limb, "this battle approaching would crush all our enemies."

"I'll gallop forth and inform him, Captain Lion Limb," said Ted, boldly.

"It is a dangerous job."

"I know it is; but no harm will befall me. I am bullet proof."

"But do you know the exact spot where the islanders are encamped?"

"I do."

"Then go, Ted, gallop with all speed."

Before another word could be uttered, young Ted disappeared.

He kept well out of the way of Mungo's men, and after a long and dangerous ride, he came in sight of old Martin's camps.

The islanders had received some information about Mungo, and were drawn up in battle array.

Ted galloped in, escorted by some friends who recognised him, and he quickly told the old governor all that had happened.

Martin was delighted.

"But Mungo wasn't going to catch me asleep. You see," he said, "all my men are ready for action."

"Then you were aware of Mungo marching against you?"

"I was, but did not know that Lion Limb was in his rear."

"What plan of action have you agreed upon?" asked Ted.

"When the morning dawns, I shall fall upon and attack Mungo with great fury, and then let Lion Limb attack in the rear. We shall make a clean sweep of them this time, I think."

Having received old Martin's instructions, Ted mounted a fresh horse and galloped back to Lion Limb.

When he arrived, it was the grey dawn of morning, but he found that his young chief had made all preparations for the battle.

But when it was fully daylight, the greatest confusion was visible among Mungo's men.

Mungo was astonished to discover that he was opposed by Lion Limb in the rear.

He raved and swore like a madman.

"How are the islanders?" he asked of Bill Whetherby.

"They are very numerous, and preparing to march down upon us."

"How far off are they?"

"About half a mile, or more."

"And Lion Limb, where is he?"

"Three-quarters of a mile away."

"And his followers?"

"Not very numerous."

"Then I tell you we must turn our backs on these islanders, and beat Lion Limb, and thus secure our retreat.

Mungo then, on the instant, changed his order of battle, and turned his forces completely round.

"March on Lion Limb at once!" he said, "and do it quickly, or we are all lost."

But Lion Limb, from afar off, saw what Mungo was doing, and placed his followers in a strong position between two streams, so that Mungo could not see round him.

Old Governor Martin, also, had watched Mungo's new plans, and he hurried on his men at a rapid pace.

Mungo, for the first time in his life, felt very much afraid of his own safety.

To escape now was impossible.

Instead of his men marching in an orderly manner, they became very wild and confused.

The Indians, perceiving how they were placed, would have deserted and run away.

Old Charley, however, shot several of them on the spot, and this frightened the rest.

They were now fast approaching Lion Limb, and, to add to Mungo's mortification, he now learned for the first time that his camps had been captured.

Mungo called the leaders of his men around him and held a council of war.

His position was getting more perilous each moment.

He raved and swore and galloped about like a madman.

"We must fight for our lives," said he.

"There has been treachery at work," said Bill Whetherby. "Let our motto be victory or death."

"True, lad," said Mungo, "it has come to that at last, and no mistake."

At that instant the sounds of distant and very heavy firing was heard near the sea coast.

"What can that be?" asked Mungo, pale with rage and fear.

"I think it is the islanders attacking our craft," said Bill, "and if they destroy them we are lost altogether."

"Do you think our Indians will fight well?" asked Mungo. "We have more men than they have even now."

"I hope they may stand firm." said Bill; "but I very much doubt it."

While they were thus speaking, Mungo's men approached the advanced guard of Lion Limb, and the first shot was fired.

Almost at the same instant, a heavy sound caught Mungo's ear.

A shell came whistling right among his men.

"That is from the islanders in our rear," said Bill.

And the fight commenced with great fury.

CHAPTER CXII.

EMILY CLARANCE AND THE FAMISHED POPULACE.

BUT while Lion Limb was away fighting, let us for a moment look back at what Emma Clarance did in the city.

When she ascertained, beyond a doubt, that Lion Limb and old Governor Martin were about to join forces, she ordered her maids to attend her, and resolved to go forth and welcome the worthy allies and conquerors.

In the market-place, which Emma was obliged to cross, were a crowd of women and children covered with rags and tatters.

They were all pressing with eager looks round a large waggon drawn by oxen, which contained enormous sacks of corn and flour, and which had just entered the town, thanks to the courage and address of its conductors.

But the price of these provisions was so high that none of the famished wretches who crowded round it could afford to purchase any.

The crowd was visibly increasing meanwhile; men began to join it armed with clubs and sticks, and while the women shrieked and gesticulated, they threatened to strip the waggon of its contents which for them but renewed the tortures of hunger, when just at that moment the procession of Emma appeared in sight.

At sight of all this luxury and splendour which Emma so displayed, the famished multitude quitted the waggon to crowd round the litter, in spite of the shouts and menaces of the guards.

"See now! how this daughter of the English has sown pearls in her hair!" exclaimed a woman with wan and hollow cheeks, pressing a miserable child to her withered bosom.

"And what a bodice! all studded with rubies, like the sky glittering with stars!" added another.

"It is not surprising," said a third, shaking his fist at Emma; "Lion Limb has sold the people's bread to buy ornaments for his favourite."

"It would serve him right if the people should in their turn sell the ornaments of the favourite to buy bread for their children, who are crying with hunger," said the first, looking sorrowfully down upon her poor starved offspring.

The popular storm grew louder.

Emma signed to her guard to order her escort to stop, and leaning boldly out of her litter—

"Good people," said she, in a loud and firm tone, "I do not owe these ornaments which excite your anger to the generosity of Lion Limb. When I entered the palace, I had more jewels than I carry away with me. What is missing has been lavished in alms. And yet the people pursue me with their imprecations, because I have been the favourite of Lion Limb. Yes, it is for having to protect you against the rapacity of the buccaneers, who enrich themselves by your toil, your privations, your poverty."

The most profound silence reigned in the market-place.

It would have been impossible for the guards to urge forward their horses in the midst of this compact crowd.

Every look was fixed, ardent, and curious upon the favourite, every heart hung upon her lips.

Emma felt the feverish breath of this suffering mob upon her brow.

"Poor children! poor women!" she continued, with an expression of pity, "I feel regret, for the famine threatens to be long and severe; but neither my prayers or my offerings will be wanting. To-day I will share with you the little that remains to me. Buy these sacks of flour, which contain a day's life for you, and think sometimes kindly of Emma Clarence."

She then ordered her slaves to scatter some handfuls of small silver and coin among the hungry crowd, and while men, women, and children, dispersed themselves in the greatest disorder, to take advantage of this unexpected windfall, the procession was enabled to proceed on its way without further interruption.

She even arrived as far as the gate, accompanied by the benedictions of a few unfortunates who followed her litter, in the hope of a fresh shower of money.

But the gate had no sooner closed upon her, than her features assumed a singular expression of sorrow, and extending her hand in the direction of the ramparts, she exclaimed, "I will soon return."

She then summoned to the side of her litter the chief of her slaves.

"You will return," said she, "and take with you my women and my baggage. As for me, I shall remain here with fifty devoted followers."

"On what expedition do you mean to employ them, noble lady?"

"I would here await the return of Lion Limb."

LION LIMB

THE BOY KING
OF THE SOUTH SEA ISLANDS.

THE DISCOVERY OF THE MURDERED MAN.—See No. 43.

No. 41.

In the meantime, Emma, though weak and suffering, had parted, without a pang of regret, with all her jewels for the purchase of provisions for the famishing population.

When she heard the maledictions which the furious people hurled against her, she experienced neither fear nor anger; she smiled sorrowfully, as she murmured—

"Poor creatures! they do not know what I have done for them."

But the popular tempest grew louder and louder.

All these wretches who were perishing of hunger, and whom the remains of attachment to Lion Limb, whether from fidelity or fear, prevented from demanding the surrender of the town, sought a pretext for their ills, and were rendered credulous, suspicious, and cruel by so much suffering.

The secret partisans of Mungo were actively engaged in fomenting this disposition to revolt.

And no sooner had the cry, "Death to Emma! death to the English girl!" been shouted by the crowd, than it would have seemed as if an electric spark ran through the vast assemblage, so universally was the cry re-echoed on all sides.

"She has bewitched the king, this accursed girl!" said one, whose half-starved infant was trying in vain to draw some nourishment from nature's dried-up fount; "she rejoices to see so many honest Indians dying of want of bread, while she is sleeping or singing in the gardens of the palace, or taking her bath."

"It is she who encourages Lion Limb to hold out," added a little man, whose hand had been wounded on the ramparts by a stray arrow, and who, from the period of this glorious scratch, strutted heroically out of reach of danger. "What is the use of this obstinacy? The soldiers of Mungo will enter. That is all."

"And to think that my oven is empty," put in a baker, "when Providence bestowed such a rich harvest upon us this year! but it is said that the treasurer had the wheat burnt in sheaves to raise the price. And we have endured all this," he continued; "we have allowed ourselves to be led to death, like sheep to the slaughter-house, without taking our revenge. But if we have to pull down the palace with our teeth and nails, the white girl must be given up to us! And when we have got her, I promise you to burn her alive in my oven in the place of the bread of which we are in want."

"Death to her! death to her!" shrieked the exasperated multitude; and the crowd, bellowing and surging like the waves of the sea, surrounded the walls of the palace.

A chosen guard had, within the last hour, joined Emma. As long as the famished populace, roaring like famished wolves round the battlemented walls, had confined themselves to shouts, threats, and murmurs, she had contented herself; but when she beheld some of the most determined commence to attack the gates of the palace with pickaxes and spades, while some carried resinous torches flaming in their hands, she could no longer restrain her rage, and exclaimed,

"They demand justice; well, it shall be rendered them!"

"These poor creatures are suffering," she said. "What do they want with me? I know not. I love you, that is all my crime. Alas! their sufferings are but too real; they are becoming intolerable. When they see me trusting and confiding in the midst of them, they will not think me, perhaps, so great a criminal. I shall find words to touch their hearts."

"Credulous child!" said one of the guards, "why, these people are furious, an army of tigers! Think you they will listen to you? No. They hate you, and will rejoice to insult and torture you, because that would be worth a promised indulgence to them; the cowards, because you are a defenceless girl; the old and ugly, because you are young and beautiful. We must, therefore, face the storm, and disperse this brutal mob by force."

The captain of the guard tore himself from the grasp of Emma, and proceeded towards the door.

"Oh! I tremble for you," said Emma. "Do not quit the place. Venture not into the midst of this mutinous populace."

"They will think I am afraid," replied the captain. "Remain here, and you will soon see the storm disperse."

He rapidly ordered the guard to open the gates. He then advanced boldly, alone, and with stern brow, beneath the Judgment Gate.

The howling and infuriated multitude seemed calmed as if by enchantment. There was a moment of profound silence.

"Are you, then, traitors, to surround the palace, with imprecations and cries of death?" exclaimed he, in an angry voice.

A tanner, seeing that no one dared to reply, resolved to make a bold stroke, and approached the captain of the guard.

"My lord," said he, "we are no traitors; we have courage against lances and arrows, swords and javelins, but we have no courage against hunger, which causes our weapons to drop from our hands."

"Do you think, then," he replied, in a stern voice, "that your king does not suffer hunger also?"

"We love our king," replied the tanner; "our only grudge is against those who gave him bad counsel."

"Who, then, do you accuse?" demanded he, with fictitious calmness.

"The English girl!" boldly replied the mob-orator. "It is she who blinds his judgment—who closes his ears and heart to the complaints of his faithful subjects; it is she who induced you to banish Aixa, and through whom you are deprived of the assistance of the Indians, by whose aid we could have repulsed the armies of Mungo."

"Fools!" he said; "those who have imposed upon you with such idle tales, are liars and traitors!"

Suddenly a piercing cry was heard from the midst of the crowd. The cobbler's wife, with dishevelled hair, fixed and haggard eyes, clasping in her arms the clay-cold inanimate form of her child, rushed towards him, holding up to him her helpless offspring.

"And is this innocent, who has just drawn its last breath, a traitor, too?" she exclaimed, in a tone of anguish. "What harm has it ever done that it should die? I am a widow. His father died fighting for Lion Limb upon the ramparts; happy for him he did not live to see his child perish with hunger!"

There arose an explosion of confused clamour which made the captain of the guard tremble in spite of his courage.

For against these lamentations, against this revolt of supplicating hands, this sedition of countenances hollowed by famine, it was impossible to dream of employing violence.

The crowd surrounded him like an impregnable wall, and he soon found himself their prisoner.

He preserved a disdainful silence, knowing well that they should tear the heart out of his breast before the condemnation of his well-beloved king should escape his lips.

But the constraint which he was forced to impose on his naturally violent and irascible disposition became so painful, that he felt his reason about to give way, when all at once a sudden movement in the compact crowd that surrounded him caused him to raise his eyes, and he saw approaching a number of stretchers, on which were heaped several corpses, scarcely covered with a shroud, and whose distorted, elongated, and lean countenances bore witness to the frightful convulsions they had undergone.

It was the convoy of three noble families, whose houses had remained closed since two days.

The doors had been forced by the guards, and nothing was found within but corpses.

These haughty grandees, with the stoicism of pride, had preferred to die rather than to beg their bread.

The crowd regarded, with sinister looks of alarm, this mournful procession. The captain of the guard, deeply moved, raised his cap as the citizens passed before him, and said aloud—

"Poor people! to what martyrdom have you been condemned!"

"Why do you pity them?" said one; "a few more days, a few more hours, and we shall be all like those corpses; for after the famine comes the plague!"

The silence was so profound that these audacious words were heard by every one in that vast multitude.

The captain fixed upon the speaker a look full of anger.

"If it depended upon you," said he, "the famine would soon cease, I suppose; for you would hasten to open the gates of the city to Mungo, and deliver up your king to him?"

CHAPTER CXIII.

LADY OXENFORD OWNS HER SON.

"WELL," said Jem Rawlings, when he had heard the case, and returned from the court, jubilant and very happy, "I never heard of such rascality in all my life. What do you say, Allan?"

Allan was very thoughtful and pale.

The examination of old Marks, Jerry, and the confession of Gentleman George, to use his own words, had "fairly staggered him."

"What do I think of it?" mused Allan.

"Yes, ain't it jolly though?" said Jem. "I think it is awful jolly when you come to think of it, don't you?"

"No," said Allan, moodily.

"And why not, pray? You are never satisfied."

"All this villany has been brought to light too late."

"What do you mean?"

"Mean!"

"Yes."

"Why, I mean that if these rascals had only been brought into court before, poor Edgar might have lived."

"So he might," said Jem; "and my brother Ted also."

"But it is too late now, poor fellows."

"So it is."

"They were drowned, you know."

"I know it."

"Well I didn't, because I didn't know it at all till you read about the shipwreck of the 'Rattlesnake' in the papers. I'm not much of a scholar,

you know, Allan. What little I knew about reading and writing I have almost forgotten, for I have had no practice of late; but I understand the newspapers had very long articles about it."

"So they did, and the short notes which were washed ashore in the bottles gave but little account about it."

"Oh! don't mention it," said Jem, shuddering; "the thoughts of a great shipwreck, and all the crew going down at once, give me the horrors."

"And so it would to anyone else with a feeling heart."

"But do you know," said Jem, "I have had such _queer_ dreams lately."

"Oh! you are always dreaming about some nonsense or other, and you kick in bed at night as if you were in the clutches of some demon or other."

"I know I do, but I can't help it," said Jem. "But don't you believe in dreams, though?"

"No, I don't."

"Well, _I_ do."

"And what good do you get from them?"

"Not much, I know; but, if I didn't dream that old Marks and Jerry were arrested, you may hang me; and so they are, you see."

"Yes, thanks to Mr. Sharp."

"But look you here," said Jem. "You may laugh as much as you like, but I have been dreaming this last month about my brother and yours."

"But they are drowned, I tell you."

"I don't believe it."

"No! why not?"

"I can't tell, but I feel certain they are _not_ drowned."

"Why so?"

"Because I've been dreaming about 'em so."

"And what did you dream, pray?"

"Well, I thought they escaped on a raft, and got on to an island, they and a good many more, and commenced to work and live together like Robinson Crusoe."

"Nonsense."

"I did though."

"You are crazy, Jem."

"No I ain't," said Jem, firmly convinced; "we shall hear about 'em before long."

"I wish I could only think so."

"Wouldn't it be jolly though if my dreams were to come true?"

"Yes, almost too jolly."

Jem Rawlings and Allan spoke thus together for some time, when the former said,

"Do you know, Allan, I think that Mr. Inspector Sharp likes you very much."

"Do you?"

"Yes, I am sure of it."

"I think so also."

"And I can't get it out of my mind but what you are the son of some great and rich nobleman also."

"What stuff, Jem; what makes you think so?"

"I can't tell, Allan, but you and me are so different in looks and ways and all that, that I can't help thinking so."

"But why?"

"Well, I can't say exactly, but there is a something about your looks and manners so different to me. When you have new clothes on you looks a perfect young nob; but it don't much matter how _I_ am dressed, I never looks much the better for it."

After a moment's pause, Jem said,

"But if it should come true one of these days that you _are_ a great man, Allan——"

"Well, and what then?"

"You'll have plenty of money to spend you know."

"And what of that?"

"You will go into fine society, among lords and ladies, perhaps."

"And if I do?'

"You'll have young gentlemen to talk to and make companions of, and then——"

"Well, and what then?"

"You'll, perhaps, forget poor Jem," said the youth, in a faltering tone.

"Forget you, Jem?"

"Aye, forget me."

"You wrong me."

"No I don't."

"But I tell you you do, Jem. Why should I forget you?"

"I don't know, but I always find those who've got much money never think of the poor devils who has none."

"Don't talk such nonsense, Jem."

"It ain't nonsense, Allan," said Jem, with a downcast eye; "see if you don't forget me when you get a great man; but I will never forget you, Allan."

"Nor I either, Jem. Are we not sworn friends?"

"Yes, and haven't we been in all sorts of scrapes and ups and downs together?"

"To be sure we have; and it shall never be said, Jem, that I acted the rogue to you."

"I believe every word you say, Allan; but I often fancy we shall part some day, never to meet any more."

"Don't give way to such foolish feelings, Jem," said Allan. "Are you not my brother?"

"I have always acted towards you like one."

"I know you have."

"And would give my last shilling to help you any time, Allan."

"I am certain of it; but look, here comes Inspector Sharp. He is beckoning to us."

"Let him come over, then, and speak to us here. I am awful thirsty; let's go into this gin-shop and have a drop of beer."

Allan nodded to the inspector, who came over, with a light step and a smiling countenance.

"You have got them, at last, sir," said Allan.

"I think so; but the job is not yet finished."

"I hope you will hang 'em," said Jem.

"It is not a hanging matter, at present, my lad."

"I think it is."

"But I don't."

"Why, old Marks and his son are the right parties who killed poor old master."

"How do you know?"

"I am certain of it."

"But can you prove it?"

"No, I can't prove it exactly," said Jem; "but—"

"There must be no 'buts' or 'ifs' about it, my lad. I also feel certain that they had something to do with it; but I can't prove it, or I would."

"More's the pity," said Allan.

"So say I; but, if I can't fasten the murder on them, I can get them all transported for burglary and other offences," said Sharp, warmly; "and, more than that, I promise you that they shall be transported."

"Serve them right!" said Allan.

"Ah, but I should like to see them swing at Newgate," said Jem; "they deserve it. I wouldn't mind lending old Calcraft a hand to hang 'em."

Mr. Sharp smiled, and, taking Allan aside, said, "I have a few words to say to you."

"And to me too?" said Jem.

"No, not at present."

"I thought not. He always treats Allan like a gentleman, and me like a shoeblack. Never mind, though; Allan will tell me all, I know."

Mr. Sharp and Allan left the bar and went into a private room.

When they were seated, the inspector said, in a quiet way, "Allan Norman, I have something very important to tell you—very important indeed."

"What can it be, sir? You look very solemn over it."

"Do I? Well, it is nothing that can hurt you what I have to say."

"What is it?"

"You don't know your mother?"

"No, nor ever did."

"Or father either?"

"I never thought either of them were living, sir."

"But they are, though."

"Indeed!"

"Yes, and very grand people they are, Allan."

"I'm very glad to hear it," said Allan. "I should dearly like to make acquaintance with my mother."

"And so you shall."

"When?"

"That depends."

"Upon what?"

"Your own discretion."

"Oh, you may rely upon that, sir."

"I don't know that, Allan. When a poor youth like you suddenly discovers that your parents are people of title, rank, wealth, and such like, it is enough to turn his head. I think it would turn mine, at all events."

"But I may see them, sir."

'But suppose they don't want to see you, Allan, what then?'

"They must be very hard-hearted, then. Please tell me their names."

"It is not Norman, Allan."

"I suppose not. I don't remember to have seen any noble person of that name. What is it, then, sir?"

"I could tell you; but you might, I say, prove indiscreet, and wish to make their acquaintance before it is desirable you should; but this much I will promise you."

"What, sir?"

"Under certain conditions I will introduce you to your mother, Lady——"

"Lady what?" said Allan, eagerly.

"Ah, yes, I see; you almost got it out of me, Allan," said the detective, laughing; "but I stopped my mouth in time."

"When will you do this, sir?"

"To night."

"To night?"

"Yes."

"I am delighted."

"No doubt you will be; but promise me, Allan, one thing; do not stay with the lady more than half an hour, and I will watch, so that your interview be not disturbed by any one."

"But why should you watch me? Is there any thing very wicked in a mother speaking to her son?"

"No; but you must consult your mother's happiness as well as your own."

"It will be and is my chief object, sir."

"I have no doubt; but you must recollect your mother's husband is not your father."

"I understand," said Allan, moodily; "but my father is alive."

"He is."

"And his name?"

"That I shall never tell you, Allan, for if I were

to do so you might hate instead of loving him," said Sharp, with a flushed face.

"And where will this delightful interview take place, sir?"

"At the opera."

"A private room would be much better, I think, sir."

"Your mother's wish must be obeyed, sir."

"I understand you."

"And now I must request another thing, Allan?"

"Name it, sir."

"You must tell Jem Rawlings nothing of this."

"Why not?"

"That does not matter to you. You must not tell him anything at present, I repeat."

"Then I will not."

"Meet me to-night, then, at Bow Street station," said Sharp, "and be dressed in your very best."

Allan was so much excited that he could scarcely speak, and he was longing to see his mother and find out who and what she might be.

"She is a Lady somebody," thought Allan. "I wonder if she is ugly or handsome; at all events, I will dress in my very best, and dazzle her."

Allan was a little vain of his fine clothes and the glitter of his gold chain and watch.

And, it must be admitted, when he had finished his toilet he was not by any means a "bad-looking" youth, but, on the contrary, a handsome fellow.

Jem Rawlings could not make out what all these preparations on the part of Allan meant, and, in order to "pump" him, put a great many questions, which Allan did not answer.

"Ah, very well, I see how it is," said poor Jem, with a sigh; "you want to get rid of me already, I see, Allan; well, never mind. I'll go out and get a new situation as pot-boy, or anything, I don't care what it is. You are much too fine for me now."

Jem would not listen to anything Allan had to say in explanation, but rushed out of the apartment, to prevent Allan from seeing two large tears which were dripping from the faithful fellow's eyes.

"Jem, Jem," shouted Allan, after him, "come back; I want to speak to you."

But Jem left the house feeling very sad and despondent, and as he walked down the silent, dark streets he cried like a child.

"If it had been me who was rich," said he, half aloud, "I wouldn't have treated Allan so coldly; and just to think that his brother, Edgar, was drowned with Ted, and I have always been a faithful 'pal' to Allan. Ah, never mind; I wish I had a died in the workhouse, that's all; everybody can see I'm a charity brat. I can see that in Mr. Sharpe's face every time he speaks to me, hang him. I wish I was as good-looking as Allan; but I'm pock-marked, and got a pug nose. Never mind, I'll go and have sixpennorth at the gaff, and see what that'll do for me; and I think an eel pie or two would do me a world o' good."

Poor Jem went into a pie-shop, and indulged himself with "three twopennys," and while so engaged Allan kept his appointment with Mr. Sharp.

*   *   *   *   *

When Sharp came out of the office at Bow Street Allan scarcely knew him, so finely was the inspector attired.

White cravat and superfine black cloth became the officer remarkably well indeed, and he looked a very handsome man.

"You had better stay here a few moments, Allan, until I return," said Sharp, who went across the road to the opera at Covent Garden.

He perceived one or two plain-clothes policemen on duty at the box door entrance, and he beckoned to one.

"Have you seen my lord, Norris?"

"No, sir."

"Sure?"

"Quite so, sir. My lord has gone down to the House of Commons to-night; I saw him enter."

"Then the coast is clear?"

"It is, sir; besides, my lord always goes to his club after leaving the House, and, I am sure, will not visit the opera to-night."

"Has her ladyship arrived?"

"She has, sir."

"And how does she look?"

"As grandly as ever, sir, but——"

"But what, Norris?"

"She appeared to be very much troubled about something, sir, and looked deadly pale."

"No one accompanied her?"

"No, sir."

"Then all is right."

Having thus convinced himself that the coast was clear, Mr. Sharp returned and found Allan.

"Are you all right, my lad?"

"Yes, sir."

"Not excited, I hope?"

"Not in the least, sir," said Allan, boldly.

But he was, though, for all that.

"Come this way, then; step out boldly, Allan, as if you were worth twenty thousand a year, or else the attendants might form rude suspicions regarding our errand."

Allan did as he was bidden, and they entered the opera house.

What a delightful place it seemed to young Allan.

All was gold, painting, splendid music, and the very pink of fashion.

But Mr. Sharp hurried up the grand staircase, and, whispering to an attendant, they were ushered into the private room attached to the rear of Lady Oxenford's opera box.

Mr. Sharp went forward into the private box itself, spoke a few words to her ladyship, re-entered the room, and left it as noiseless as a shadow.

Allan seemed bewildered, and knew not what to think or say.

He gazed on the pictures and sumptuous furniture of this retiring room, and when he turned his head, he was amazed to see standing near to him a handsome lady beautifully attired.

Tears were in her eyes.

Her feet tottered almost from under her.

Her mouth moved, but not a sound was heard.

She tried, but could not speak.

At last she staggered forward, and suddenly throwing her arms round Allan's neck, sobbed.

"My boy! my child!—my child!" and sank helpless upon a sofa.

Allan's nerves were quivering through him.

He could not speak, nor did he attempt to resist the warm embrace of the lady, nor the scores of warm kisses and scalding tears which fell upon his cheek.

He felt, he knew instinctively that she was his mother, and his heart melted with tenderness.

Heedless of the opera and the soft swell of delicious music that from time to time fell upon her ear, Lady Oxenford pressed the hand of Allan, her son, and gazed upon his handsome face with pride.

Hours passed quickly, and still both mother and son sat side by side, smiles gave place to tears, and

Allan narrated in brief terms all his trials and sufferings.

"Mr. Sharp has explained everything to you, Allan?" said the mother, tenderly.

"He has, Lady Oxenford," Allan replied.

"Nay, do not call me 'lady' when we meet thus alone. I am your true mother and wish to be called such, my poor child. For years I believed you to be dead, and was pining to the grave with sorrow; but now that I know you live, I am happy, nay, supremely happy."

"But," said Lady Oxenford, after a short pause, "if we should meet in public, Allan, you understand, follow the advice of *my* friend and of *your* friend, Inspector Sharp."

"Your friend, mother?"

"Yes, child, *my* friend," Lady Oxenford replied, blushing deeply; "he has proved himself to be so, and I will always honor him as such. He has saved me from exposure and ignominy."

For three hours and more Allan remained conversing with his mother, until, at length, Mr. Sharp returned again.

"Madam," he said, politely bowing, "I hope I have not come too soon."

"Indeed, you have, sir," said her ladyship, smiling. "The time has passed so rapidly, I have not said half that I intend to say to Allan."

"I hope you are not disappointed in him, your ladyship."

"On the contrary, I am delighted, sir." And, shaking Mr. Sharp by the hand, she kissed Allan again and again, and her ladyship was again left alone.

"How handsome she is!" said Allan, when he had returned to the street. "I never thought I had such a pretty woman for a mother."

"And are you not delighted to see her?"

"I am brimfull of joy, Mr. Sharp."

"And so you ought to be, for you are a lucky young dog, in many ways."

Sharp had a glass of ale with Allan, and then advised him to go home.

"Don't go prowling about the streets, but in all things act and behave like a gentleman, for you have discovered that you are one. Good night; I will see you to-morrow, for I have something very important to say to you."

* * * * *

Allan went home, wondering at the strange events which had happened of late.

But Inspector Sharp put on an overcoat, and took a quiet walk to a supper-room, where he indulged in oysters and steak.

At about twelve o'clock he sallied forth towards the Unicorn Club, and inquired for Lord Oxenford.

"He has just returned from the House of Commons," said one of the footmen, "and, I KNOW, does not wish to be disturbed; so you had better call another time."

"Oh, you *know* it, eh? Well, then, you know nothing," said Sharp. "Take up this card; I will wait for an answer."

Lord Oxenford *was* engaged, but directly he had glanced at Sharp's card he said,

"Show him up immediately. I wish to see him on important business."

The footman was very much surprised that Lord Oxenford should display so much politeness; but he showed the way for Mr. Sharp, and looked very much annoyed.

"He has the very cut of a policeman in disguise," said the footman. "I dare say he is employed to watch us poor over worked and half-starved footmen."

"Jeames" didn't look very much like an over-worked, half-starved servant, for he was fat and sleek and had a pair of calves of tremendous proportions.

"Ah, Sharp," said my lord, when they were face to face in a private room, "I am very glad to see you. I have been to the House of Commons to-night."

"And I to the opera, my lord," said Sharp, smiling.

"And what success have you met with? Have you entrapped my lady yet?"

"No, my lord, nor did I ever expect to do so."

"Indeed, why not?"

"She is as chaste as the sun," said Sharp, coolly; "her character is beyond all suspicion."

"I am glad to hear you say so," remarked my lord, biting his lips, "but all of us have suspicions at times."

"So we have, my lord, but you may rely upon it that my lady is blameless, or I should have discovered something ere this."

"Very likely, Mr. Sharp, very likely; but her manners are sometimes very strange."

"And so it is with the best of us, my lord; the more we have the more inclined we are to have groundless suspicions."

"And you believe my lady is reproachless?"

"As your wife, sir, I am certain of it," said Sharp, very solemnly. "I have dodged her heels a long time both day and night, but have discovered nothing worthy of mention; but my lord——"

"But what, Sharp?"

"If you desire still to have her watched in all her movements; watched, I mean, like a cat does a mouse, in the house particularly, I have an excellent plan to propose."

"Name it."

"You need a private secretary."

"I do."

"I can recommend an excellent young man; a youth, in fact, of blameless morals, good manners, and address, and a very excellent scholar, who, I know, would do my bidding and yours also, but not in anything wrong, for his morals are beyond all reproach."

"A most excellent character you give him, Sharp."

"He deserves it, my lord."

"And who is he?"

"A youth named Allan Norman, my lord; an orphan."

"Allan Norman! Allan Norman," said my lord, musingly; "I think I have heard the name, Sharp, somewhere, but where or how I cannot recollect."

"It is not an ordinary name, my lord."

"I know it is not, and it is for the simple reason that I began to think where I might have heard it."

Sharp began to think, perhaps, that his lordship might have heard the name in connection with the affair of the murder of Alderman English.

But he said not a word.

"Unless he finds it out, *I* shan't say anything," thought the discreet Mr. Sharp.

My lord walked up and down the room several times, as if in deep thought.

At last he said—

"Well, Sharp, let me see this youth; you may introduce him to me at once, for I have not the slightest doubt that the youth is fully worthy of your introduction."

Mr. Sharp retired, much pleased with his interview.

"I *could* make words, and create a great disturbance if I liked," he thought, "but what is the use of it? I am a married man myself, and in the language of Shakspeare, 'what the eye doth not see the heart doth not grieve.' His lordship knows nothing about the early failings of his wife, nor perhaps does she know anything about *his* early sins. Very well, then, so far so good. I dare say my lord married the painter's daughter for her handsome looks and splendid manners, and I have no doubt, also, but Lady Oxenford married my lord for his title and money.

"Oh, it is trick and tie both ways," thought Sharp; "and if the truth was known, there are more sins to be placed to the account of his lordship than Lady Oxenford; let them, therefore, live in ignorance of each other's faults and failings, it will all come to the same thing one of these days.

"Why, lor bless me," thought Sharp, as he walked towards Allan's lodgings, "who is there who has not done some wrong in their lifetime? Why, no one. They say there is a death's head in every house, and his lordship can't expect to be without his trials and sufferings no more than anybody else, for if my old woman," he mused, "knew only half the rascality which *I* have been guilty of in my time, there would be the devil to pay; but what's the use of making words when one can avoid it?"

Mr. Sharp, in truth, was a man of the world and a person wise in his generation.

He had been "knocked about" considerably in his time, and now as he grew older he grew also wiser, and never made a fuss or any unnecessary noise when either could be conveniently avoided.

"I have children of my own," thought Sharp," and, as far as I am concerned, it shall never be said that I made mischief if I could help it."

A wise man was Sharp.

A good, nay, a *really* good man was Sharp, and that he was fully and amply rewarded for his goodness and charity, will appear in the sequel of our truthful story.

Oh, that thousands of others who had and have more ample opportunities for doing good for their fellow beings, would think as correctly of human nature as Mr. Sharp, the unpretending but vigilant and active detective.

In token of his success, however, Sharp had a glass of brandy and water on his way to Allan's lodgings; more than that, he indulged in a four-penny cigar, and when he told his "old woman" by the way of the upshot of his adventures, his good wife clapped her hands for joy and kissed her husband right heartily.

"You ain't a bad sort, husband," said his wife; "I always thought you wanted to make folks happy."

"And why not, wife?" said Sharp; "it is better to make people happy than uncomfortable, and when it costs you the same price, why not do the best for everybody?"

"Poor woman," said the wife, "and what is her name?" referring to Lady Oxenford.

"Ah, that is another question, my dear girl. I can't mention names you know."

"Not to me?"

"No, not to your wife."

"And why not?"

"A detective must not open his mouth even to his wife, on some occasions."

"Well, but you may say whether the poor lady is p'eased to find out her son. I know I should be."

"*You*," said Sharp, laughing. "Why *you* would go mad if you found a lost child."

"I know I should, and so did the big lady, also, or she isn't any true mother."

"Ah, wife," said Sharp, "you don't know as much

about the world as I do. These big people, as you ca'l them, consider it very vulgar —very vulgar, indeed, to betray their true feelings as *we* poor people do ; in fact, it is part of their education from early youth to disguise their feelings on all occasions, and especially when any disgrace may be attached to it."

"Out upon them, then," said the good wife. "Is it wrong to acknowledge, and kiss, and caress your own children?"

"Ah, wife," said Sharp, "you are but a child yourself, in the way of the world. Why, gentlefolk won't even laugh like us; they suppress all indications of surprise, astonishment, love, and such like, for it is considered very vulgar to give way to any such natural indications of human feeling. Their education teaches them to act and move, and so behave themselves, as if they were so many blocks of stone cut from the quarry."

"Then Heaven grant I may never be so, if I am without education and fine breed," said the wife. "I shall laugh and cry, and sing and dance as much as I please, and whenever the humour takes me, and if it don't suit the grand people of fashion, why then, let the grand people of fashion do as they like, and live and move like wax-work figures for all me. Out upon them! Men, women, and all."

Sharp could not but smile at the enthusiasm of his spouse.

She was a good and an excellent woman, with a family of six children, but she loved them all more dearly than she prized her own life; and, happily for herself, she knew nothing and could not long for "grand folks," as she called those above her; but enjoyed herself in her own way, and reared her family in the most exemplary manner, and to the great delight of Mr. Sharp himself, who thought "the whole world of his old woman," as he was wont to say.

* * * * * *

Sharp, however, went to see young Allan, but on his way was tapped on the shoulder by a brother officer, who knew him well.

"What's the matter?" said Sharp. "Don't stop me, I'm in a great hurry."

"Oh! but I will stop you," was the laughing reply. "Come in here and have a drop, I have some great news to tell you."

"Then tell me here, in the street; I am in a great hurry, I tell you."

"Great hurry or not, you must come in with me, I repeat."

"And why so—why not tell me here?"

"I don't want to let the whole street know about it."

"What is it, then?"

"You have had a case on hand for a long time in which a youth, named Allan Norman, is concerned."

"Who told you?"

"Oh! I know all about it."

"Well, what have you to say about it?"

"Much, and more than you will believe."

"Let's have it, then, for I'm in a hurry," said Sharp.

"You know that I'm engaged at the admiralty?"

"Yes, I know that; well, what then?"

"There has been an important arrival in England to you."

"Indeed!"

"Yes."

"How do you mean?"

"A ship, which was given up for lost, has turned up at last."

"Well, and what of that? It has nothing at all to do with me."

"Yes, it has."

"How? What is the name of the vessel?"

"The 'Skylark.'"

"The 'Skylark;' I have nothing at all to do with any vessel of that name," said Sharp, annoyed at thus being interrupted.

"Oh! yes, you have," was the laughing reply.

"I tell you I have not," said Sharp, very red.

"But I tell you, you have."

"How? when? where?"

"You have heard of the 'Rattlesnake' that was lost?"

"The ship that went down with the young convicts?"

"Yes."

"I have heard of it."

"Well, it didn't go down. What do you think of that?"

"I can't believe it."

"But it is true, I tell you."

"Oh! nonsense!"

"It is not nonsense. The 'Rattlesnake' was wrecked if you like; but never was totally lost."

"But the crew and the young convicts were."

"They were not; at least, most part of them were saved."

Sharp listened, and became very red.

He remembered that Edgar Norman or young Lion Limb, was one of those who went out in the "Rattlesnake," and, as he listened to it, became more and more amazed.

"And what vessel brought all this strange news to England?"

"The 'Skylark,' a vessel that was given up as lost many, many long months ago."

"And the 'Skylark' has come safely into port you say?"

"She has. She has been away for a very long time; but after all returns safe and sound."

"And she brought the news about the 'Rattlesnake?'"

"She did."

"And what were the full particulars of the wreck?"

"That I can't say; but while on duty at the Admiralty to-day, I heard it whispered about that most of the young convicts were saved."

"Was there such a youth as Edgar Norman mentioned?" asked Sharp.

"I don't remember such a name as Edgar Norman; but I heard the name of young Lion Limb mentioned very often."

"Lion Limb! Lion Limb!" said Sharp, in deep thought.

"Yes; the captain of the 'Skylark' has brought home most glowing accounts of that brave youth, whoever he may be."

"Indeed!"

"Oh! yes; the captain says he has subdued the natives on one of the South Pacific Islands, made himself king, and is playing the very devil among the natives."

"I know him," said Sharp.

"You do?"

"Yes."

"And who is he?"

"His real name is Edgar Norman; but he goes by the name of Lion Limb, because he was born with the mark of a lion's paw upon his arm."

"The devil! you don't say so."

"I do though, and I was just going to see his brother Allan Norman when you interrupted me on my way."

"It is most singular."

"It is; but have you heard what the government are going to do?"

"No."

"Surely they won't send out a vessel and re-capture these poor convict youths."

"I hope not, for they have fully earned their freedom."

"I think so too."

"I heard, by mere chance, that a vessel was going out to visit the South Pacific Islands, for there are one or two of them inhabited by buccaneers, against whom they say young Lion Limb is constantly fighting."

Sharp seemed for a moment bewildered with the news.

So very strange and startling events had happened of late that he could scarcely make himself believe that what he heard was true.

However, he said nothing, but went on his way towards the lodgings of young Allan, thinking as he walked,

"There seems to be some strange fatality connected with these two boys, Edgar and Allan Norman. How events will ultimately change or turn, I can't say, but it seems that fortune is in their favour, and that's everything. If it turns out to be true, however, that young Lion Limb is really living, it will alter matters very much indeed. If he were only in England at the present moment, I could manage to hang old Marks and his son, instead of transporting them, for I believe that young Lion Limb could rake and scrape together more evidence against them than I should ever dream of. However, it won't be right or proper at the present moment to inform young Allan of what the Captain of the 'Skylark' reports at the Admiralty if the Government thinks proper to keep the whole matter a profound secret at present. It is evident there must be good reasons for doing so also, therefore I shall not drop a single word to young Allan."

Mr. Sharp, with such ideas in his head, went to see young Allan, and told him that he had got a fine situation for him as private secretary to my Lord Oxenford.

Allan was delighted to think he was sufficiently well fitted to occupy such a position, and rejoiced beyond expression at the bare idea of seeing his own mother occasionally during the day.

"Yes, that is all right enough," said Sharp, "but you must not let his lordship imagine that you know her ladyship."

"No, not at all, Mr. Sharp."

"On the other hand, you must act as if you had never seen her in your whole life."

"I understand, sir."

"And if his lordship tells you anything about watching her, you give your consent; but, mark me, say nothing until you consult with me."

"I will not, sir."

"Very good then. To-morrow morning we must purchase for you a new suit of clothes, and I will give you a letter of introduction to his lordship."

"Thanks, Mr. Sharp, many thanks," said Allan, and he felt delighted at the prospect of going into the service of my Lord Oxenford.

"And shall I live in the house, Mr. Sharp?"

"Of course you will, but you must keep a very still tongue in your head, and have nothing to say to the rest of the servants in the household."

"Trust to me for that," said Allan.

"But more than that, you must not pretend to know me. You understand; so, therefore, if you should ever see me talking to his lordship, you must not appear to take any notice."

THE BOY KING
OF THE SOUTH SEA ISLANDS.

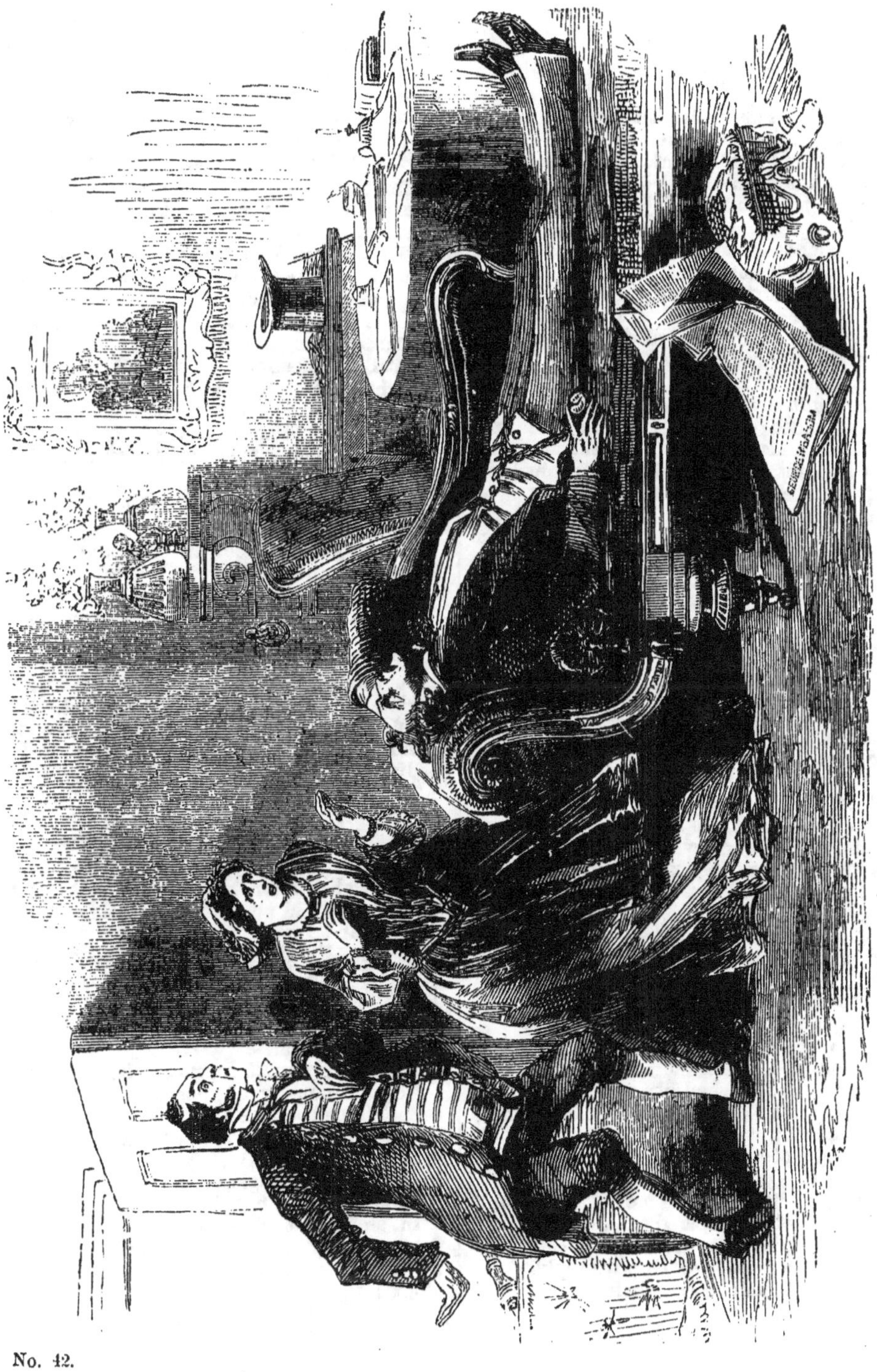

AN ALARM.--*See No. 43.*

"I will not; but will my salary be—"

"That matters but very little. You won't want for a good salary while Lady Oxenford lives, you may be sure."

Allan now began to look into the true character of Mr. Sharp, and he came to the wise conclusion that all detectives were not so black as some people paint them, and that some times they proved to be the best of men, and from no other motive than to do good and save their fellow man.

For what had Allan or Jem Rawlings done to merit so much care or anxiety on the part of Mr. Sharp?

Nothing.

Could not the active and intelligent detective have caused much misery in the fashionable world had he thought fit?

Yes; but he did not.

There was no occasion for it.

Some people might say, "Oh, he was well paid for it," and all such like.

But Mr. Sharp was *not* well paid for it.

He did good for its own sake, and what money he received from my Lord Oxenford, he laid out to the best advantage upon the two friendless boys, Allan Norman and Jem Rawlings, and felt more satisfaction in so doing than if he had been paid thousands of pounds for his senseless labours.

When morning came, Allan accompanied the inspector, and was furnished not only with a bran new suit of clothes, a watch, chain, and some pocket money, but also provided with a letter of introduction to his lordship, which spoke in the very highest terms of the young secretary.

It must be confessed that Allan felt very shaky, and trembled much when he went to Oxenford House; but when his lordship had spoken a few kind words to him, he felt all right again, and acted firmly and calmly during the interview.

"So *you* are the youth, eh?" said my lord, reading Sharp's letter. "Well, your introduction is a most excellent one indeed, and if you know yourself worthy, I will act kindly and liberally towards you."

"Thanks, my lord," said Allan, and his heart was bursting with feelings of great gratitude; but he could not express his thanks sufficiently in words.

My lord was much taken with the appearance of young Allan, and looked at the youth so long and fixedly, that Allan became much confused, and blushed deeply.

"You will not have much to do at present," said lord Oxenford, smiling, "except to copy or write a few letters occasionally from my dictation. Your time will almost be your own. It depends upon yourself, however, whether you stay here or not. If you become obedient and trustworthy, I may make great things of you; if you do not, however, we shall part in a minute's notice."

Lord Oxenford left the room, and Allan sat reading a book.

In a short time, however, his lordship returned, and with him came Lady Oxenford.

Allan felt very much confused at this sudden and unexpected visit of his mother, her ladyship; but he spoke not, and blushed like scarlet.

"This is the youth I spoke of," said his lordship.

"Oh! indeed!" was his wife's cold reply; although it must be confessed that her own heart beat wildly, and her face was all crimson.

"Yes; he was introduced to me by a friend," said his lordship, who whispered aside to his wife, "He is very handsome is he not?"

"Yes—rather," was Lady Oxenford's reply.

"He has magnificent eyes and hair."

Her ladyship smiled in a very faint and pallid manner.

"You do not agree with me, then?"

"Oh, yes I do, my lord. *I* think he is *very* good-looking," was her ladyship's reply.

"They tell me he is as trustworthy and honest as he is good-looking, wife."

"I am happy to hear it, my lord. Good looks without a good heart are worth nothing."

"Ah! wife," said my lord, when leaving the room, "if I had a son like him——"

"And what then?" said her ladyship, coldly.

"We have no children, wife."

"Such is the will of Providence."

"But if I had such a son——"

"If *we* had such a son, you mean, my lord."

"Just so—such was my thought. I would give all I am worth in the world."

For a moment afterwards not a word was spoke.

Lady Oxenford by turns changed from pale to red.

She smiled, and endeavoured to appear very gay; but her lips changed colour, her heart beat wildly, her limbs trembled, and she felt very faint.

Her own son was in her own house, under a false name, and yet she could not own or discover the fact.

When my lord had gone out, however, Lady Oxenford walked back to the private library with silent steps, and peeped in.

There was Allan, seated at a desk, with his back turned towards the door.

Yet Lady Oxenford could see his handsome and thoughtful face reflected in a mirror, and while she stood at the door irresolute and knowing not whether to go in or retrace her footsteps, tears—hot scalding, briny tears—gushed from her eyes, and she sobbed.

The feelings of a mother could not any longer be repressed.

She closed the door silently, and crept up to Allan unseen.

Falling on her knees she clasped her son, and placing her head on his knees, wept and sobbed aloud.

Poor Allan wept also.

But he could not understand the wild passion working in his mother's breast, and, therefore, he simply placed his arm round her neck, and in mute admiration kissed the tearful and upturned face of Lady Oxenford.

"My son! my own son!" she sighed.

"Mother, dear mother," said Allan, and in a moment both loving hearts were locked in a fond embrace.

"How glad I am, Allan, once more to see and to know you! I am your poor mother, half broken-hearted and forsaken. I have nought to live for save you. Forgive me, boy, for having been cruel and neglectful for these many years; but, if you only knew the pangs of agony which I have suffered on your account, you would pardon me."

Allan spoke not.

His mother's mind seemed to be rambling.

Nor did the poor lady herself know what she said.

She clasped young Allan more tightly and lovingly than ever, and both were heedless of a loud knock at the library door.

The knock was again repeated.

Lady Oxenford heard it.

In an instant she sprang to her feet, dried her eyes, and walked rapidly towards a distant table, and began to turn over the leaves of a costly bound album.

"Come in," she faintly answered to the third knock, but never turned her head.

A footman entered, and announced the visit of Baron Templeton.

"Baron Templeton!" said her ladyship, turning ashy pale.

But the footman had retired, nor did he notice her ladyship's tremor of surprise.

Before Lady Oxenford could utter a single word, Baron Templeton entered the room.

He bowed, and closed the door; but when he gazed on Allan's face, he looked like one who had been suddenly thunderstruck.

Allan rose from his seat, and knew not what to do.

He looked first at Lady Oxenford, and then at the new arrival, and changed color frequently.

If he had not been told who the gentleman was, he perfectly knew him.

Knew him! how could he help it?

"That is the judge who tried us for murder," thought poor Allan.

And as he remembered those fearful days of trial, his heart sank within him.

His heart sank, truly, but not from *fear*.

For why should the long-persecuted youth fear any man?

Had he done any legal wrong?

No!

His heart was pure and simple, and he had never known what crime was; and as to the murder of the old alderman, he knew no more about it than the babe just born.

With a feeling of mind which completely drowned in his soul every other sentiment or emotion, Allan rose from his seat, as we have said, and faced the baron with a firm look.

The baron himself was much disconcerted by the brave demeanour of the young secretary; but, without saying a word to him, he advanced towards Lady Oxenford, and sank into an easy chair.

"Do you know that person—that youth at yonder desk, Lady Oxenford?" he said.

"I do, baron; "and you also, I think," was my lady's calm reply.

"How comes he here?"

"By the merest chance imaginable."

"And does my Lord Oxenford know of his paternity?"

"He does not."

"Nor suspects?"

"I think not."

"'Tis well he does not; but some strange fatality hangs over me, and an unearthly feeling tells me that this youth will be the cause of much misery to me."

"How, baron?" said Lady Oxenford, with an air of pride and offended dignity. "What has the youth done to you? Is it nothing that you had the heart to condemn his brother? Would you now hunt down to the very death the only one who is left to me?"

The baron grimly smiled.

"Have you no feelings left, baron? Is it not enough that you once brought me to shame and misery? Would you still follow me through life, and blight every prospect of happiness?"

The baron said not a word; but for a moment looked steadfastly at my lady.

At length he replied,

"Lady Oxenford, I have no such paltry things as 'feelings.' I have no heart, and therefore cannot discuss human matters with you."

"But you have a soul, Baron Templeton?"

"Perhaps so," was the reply.

"Then, if you have a soul, at least have pity on me and mine. If you do not come to do good to the youth, at least do no harm."

Allan had heard the last words of Lady Oxenford, and was about to retire from the library, when the baron said,

"Young man, stay—approach!"

Allan did so.

"Do you know me, young man?" said the baron.

"Alas, sir, I have good reasons for doing so," was Allan's answer. "You were once a judge."

"True, my lad; and you were once a criminal in the dock?"

"Not a criminal, my lord," said Allan; "but one falsely accused of crime."

"That might be; but do you not know what I am towards you?"

"I do not, my lord."

"You have not the slightest suspicion?"

"I have not, sir."

"I am much pleased to hear it," said the baron, in a gruff voice. "You are an orphan, I am told?"

"I was, sir, until Providence discovered for me the author of my being—my mother."

"And you know that, then?"

"I do, my lord."

"And your father, also?"

"I do not, my lord, nor do I wish to know," said Allan; "for if I have a father living, and he is such an unnatural being as to disown and not protect me, why, then, let him live and die like the brute that he is and must be."

Allan said these few words with such emphasis and force, that Baron Templeton was astonished.

He smiled in a sickly manner, however, and motioned the young secretary to leave the apartment.

"Don't go, Allan," said my lady, turning deadly pale and rising.

"But *I* bid him begone," said the baron, sternly, at the same time almost forcing Lady Oxenford into her seat again.

Allan saw this movement, and in an instant was at the side of Lady Oxenford.

"Sir," said Allan, "I am but a servitor here in Lord Oxenford's establishment, but I cannot, and will not, allow any stranger to force my mistress in anything against her will.

"And, sir," he continued, with a flushed face, "I am surprised that you, who are a stranger here, should dare to assume so much familiarity."

"Dare!" said the baron, turning pale, "what does the youth mean by such impertinent language?"

"I mean this, sir, that if you dare again to seize her ladyship by the wrists, as you have done before, I shall take it upon myself to eject you from the house."

And as he spoke, Lady Oxenford felt proud of the son she had so bravely acknowledged, and looked with contempt on Baron Templeton, whose pale and cadaverous face indicated a man of guilt.

"He knows me not," thought the baron, "and shall never do so. If Lady Oxenford dares to disclose the secret, as far as *I* am concerned, she shall repent it all the days of her life."

He felt so much astonished at Allan's manner and words, that he left Oxenford House like one who is dreaming.

When he had gone, Lady Oxenford kissed Allan very tenderly, but said—

"Had you known the person you were speaking to, my son, you would have governed your temper better."

"But I could not sit still and see you insulted, Lady Oxenford."

"You must not give way to your feelings in such

a manner again, Allan, or my Lord Oxenford will discover our relationship—you must learn to be more discreet."

"Who or what then, my lady mother, is Baron Templeton to you or me?"

"Nothing," said Lady Oxenford, biting her lips; "he has been the cause of much sorrow and suffering to your mother, but why or how you must not now know. But I must not stay longer here, I hear Lord Oxenford coming up stairs."

And in great haste she left the library by one door just as his lordship entered by another.

"Well, Allan," said my lord, rather gaily, "I have been thinking of you all the morning."

"Indeed, my lord."

"Yes, in truth; and the more I see you, the more I am impressed with you and like you."

"Many thanks, my lord."

"I am going for a ride, Allan, will you accompany me?"

"With the greatest pleasure in the world, my lord."

"I am going to my lawyer's on very important business. I am, in truth, going to make my will, for I have of late made very important discoveries, that prompt the occasion of it."

My lord had been drinking to some extent, and was very chatty.

Had he been perfectly sober it is not likely he would have spoken thus freely to one who had been so short a time in his service.

"I hope, my lord, your discoveries may prove to be only fancies and not realities," said Allan.

"Real or not, Allan, you must come for a ride with me."

"Certainly, my lord."

And Lord Oxenford, accompanied by Allan, drove from the mansion.

Lady Oxenford saw them depart from the drawing-room windows, and when she saw how much pleased her husband was with his new secretary she was delighted, and shed tears of joy.

"Oh, if my son should only win the love of Lord Oxenford, how happy would I be."

Lord Oxenford, from some cause, had taken a violent liking to young Allan, but why he could not tell.

As we know from the beginning of this veracious history, my Lord Oxenford had no children, and was greatly annoyed and vexed at the disappointment, for one of his greatest and most ambitious dreams was to have his name and title represented in the land by a worthy offspring.

The want of a son and heir had caused much sorrow in the family, and especially to my lord, whose temper began to grow more sour every day, and he vented his spleen frequently on those who were blameless.

To the lawyer, therefore, Lord Oxenford drove through the city, and left Allan outside in the drag.

My lord's ordinary legal adviser was in his dusty office, and he bowed and scraped with an air of great humility.

"I come," said my lord, quickly, "on very important business, Clark."

"Indeed, my lord, state it. I am always most happy to render every assistance to my noble clients."

"Well, Clark," said my lord, "I have a great secret to confide to you. Is the door locked?"

"It is shut, my lord; but no one can hear us; the doors are double and padded."

"'Tis well, then; listen, Clark. I have killed a man."

"My lord, you are joking."

"No; I am speaking sober truth. I have killed a man, but not murdered him."

"Oh, I understand; you have fought a duel, and——"

"Yes; but a long time ago. It was through love and jealousy, Clark; it was a cousin of my wife's, a handsome young sailor who loved her, and was engaged to marry her."

"And does your wife know of this?"

"She does not, I think, for I was then known under another name, and the affair took place in France."

"Then the law of England cannot touch you, my lord."

"But my heart and conscience are already touched, and that is worse than death itself, Clark. I have lived through long years of misery on account of that fearful duel; but I am determined to make some amends for my past crimes."

"In what manner, my lord?"

"You know I am childless, Clark."

"I do, my lord."

"And having no son and heir, my name and station will be lost to the world."

"Just so, my good lord."

"I have a project in my head, and that is, Clark, to make my will."

"You have made one already, my lord; I have it in safe keeping."

"I know it, Clark, but you must destroy that and make another."

"I will do so, my lord."

"And, mark me, I wish to leave everything to one person."

"And might I ask who that person is, my lord?"

"I will not mention his name at present, but you can leave a blank space for his name, and I will fill it up at leisure."

"Your orders shall be obeyed, my lord."

"And to day, mind, Clark."

"I will, my lord."

"But, Clark, cannot a person petition to have his name and title transferred to one not of kin?"

"Yes, my lord, but it requires great interest at Court, and I could not advise your lordship to do better than consult the learned Baron Templeton, with whom you are acquainted."

Lord Oxenford frowned at the bare mention of the baron's name.

"I do not like him, Clark, though he is a visitor. He is a hard, cold, deep-designing man."

"But an excellent legal adviser, my lord, and possesses great interest at Court."

"Then I will speak to him, Clark. Good morning."

And mounting his "drag," Lord Oxenford drove away to the residence of Baron Templeton, and found him at home.

The baron was much surprised at the visit, but he did not indicate as much by his features.

Lord Oxenford stated his business in a few words, and the baron remarked,

"I don't think you will encounter any difficulty in transferring your title, my lord, for you have been a great politician in your time, and have much influence with the present Prime Minister; but might I ask the name of the person you desire to succeed you in the title, my lord?"

"I have no objection to name it as an inviolable secret, however."

"You may rely upon it, Lord Oxenford, I shall never divulge it."

"Well then, baron, having no children of my own, I have fallen violently in love with a youth, and he is so handsome and clever that I am resolved, if he proves worthy of it, to leave him all I possess."

"And his name is ——"

"Allan Norman, baron."

The baron's lips trembled, and his cheeks were of ashy paleness.

"You seem ill, baron," said my lord, looking in alarm at the baron's pallid countenance.

"No, my lord; have no apprehension, I am perfectly well, but sometimes I have sudden attacks like these; they arise, my doctor says, from rheumatism and biliousness."

After a few moments the baron fully recovered, and said, calmly,

"Who and what is this fortunate youth, Allan Norman?"

"My private secretary."

"Indeed; and have you fully resolved to do all this for him?"

"Yes; and since I have come to this resolution, my heart is glad, and I don't feel like the same man, so rejoiced am I, for when I speak to the youth or go near him, I seem attached to him by some hidden chain of attraction. Therefore, baron," said my lord, rising to depart, "you would render me eternally obliged if you were to think of this matter for me, and use your best endeavours for the desired object."

"I will."

Lord Oxenford departed.

"What an extraordinary change has come over Lord Oxenford," thought the baron, "and to think of making one of my own son's his successor. Oh! villain that I have been towards them all my life! While I have tried to shut them out from the world, fortune thrusts them forward in the path of honour; but if Lord Oxenford only knew the secret of Allan's birth, and my villany to the mother, of her abduction and forcible seduction, we should be at dagger's points; but he must not know it. Lady Oxenford dare not reveal the facts for her own sake. I must write to her at once."

CHAPTER CXIV.

MR. MARKS AND HIS SON TAKE A TRIP ON THE OCEAN.

THE news brought to England by the "Skylark" greatly surprised the Lords of the Admiralty; but the public were not made acquainted with it for many reasons.

The government desired to keep the matter a profound secret for some time, and the "Skylark" was again put into commission, and refitted for another voyage to the South Pacific.

The seamen were paid off their wages, and allowed a month on shore at home, and ordered to be again in readiness to go on board at the expiration of their leave.

What the government had in view nobody knew; but the captain of the "Skylark," when the vessel was cleaned and refitted, received orders to prepare accommodation for three or four dozen convicts who were to be sent abroad.

But while the vessel is undergoing repairs, and making ready for the South Pacific again, let us take a peep at Mr. Marks and the other prisoners.

As we know, through the exertions of Inspector Sharp, Marks and the other prisoners were remanded; but finding it inexpedient to ask for another remand, old Marks and the rest were transported for different terms of years.

Great was the groaning and howling in the cell of old Marks.

He almost went raving mad, and kicked about like a half-tamed savage.

He cursed himself and everybody until he was tired.

But Jerry was calm and determined.

As he left the dock after hearing his sentence, he whispered to Inspector Sharp,

"You have got me at last, *but I will have revenge, Sharp*. And let you be in England or not, I will find you out. *Remember my words.*"

Sharp only laughed at the threat; but, as we shall see, Jerry's words were not all idle boast.

"A nice batch these fellows will make for some penal settlement," thought Sharp, as he looked at them in their respective cells.

Gentleman George, Mikey Huggins, old Marks, and Jerry, together with some dozen others, were close-cropped and shaven, and looked very grand indeed in their fashionable prison attire; but they had no idea that government were going to send them abroad so soon.

"Well, old Marks, and how are you?" said Sharp to him one day in the cells. "I hear you are going to be sent across the water."

"Any place is better than this," growled the old lawyer. "You don't know, I suppose, where we are going to be sent to?"

"Yes I do, though."

"Where, then, Australia?"

"No."

"To Botany Bay, Van Dieman's Land, or any of those places?"

"No."

"Where, then?"

"They are going to send you to a new place."

"And where is that, pray?"

"To a newly-discovered Island in the South Pacific."

"And what will they make us do there?"

"Why, work, very hard, to be sure."

"Oh, I know that, but what at?"

"Why, blasting rocks, making roads, chopping down forests, and all such fun as that."

"Fun do you call it," growled old Marks, "I don't call it fun."

"Oh, you'll soon get used to it."

"Shall I though," thought the old lawyer, "hard work never did agree with me. Have they any hospitals out there?"

"No—why?"

"Because I might be sick."

"Oh, they'll give you lots of physic, as much as you can eat or drink."

"And who is the governor of this Island?"

"A very firm gentleman, so I hear."

"What's his name?"

"That you will find out soon enough."

"I hope he's a kind fellow."

"Oh, you may be sure of that. You know him well enough."

"I do?"

"Yes; and if I'm not much mistaken, he loves you about as much as you love him," said Sharp, with a dry laugh.

"You are joking, Mr. Sharp."

"Indeed I'm not. I thought you'd like to know where you were going to, and what sort of a governor you were to have."

"Thank you, Mr. Sharp; but do you think they'll send Jerry along also?"

"You mean Captain Zacary, don't you?" said Sharp, with a good-humoured grin.

"Oh, that be hanged," said old Marks, with an

oath of disgust, "Captain Zacary and his pranks have ruined all of us. Why don't you call him Jerry and have no nonsense about it?"

"Well, well, I don't want to torment you any longer, but I will say this much that you and Jerry, and Gentleman George, Mikey Huggins, and other choice rogues, are to be sent across the water immediately, and placed under the direction of Governor Martin, who has colonized and governed the place."

"You said I knew the governor, Mr. Sharp?"

"So I did."

"I never heard of old Governor Martin in my life. Who is he?"

"A fine, brave gentleman, so I hear; he has got lots of stone-breaking and wood-chopping for you to do out there, and if you don't suit him, he'll put you on another Island."

"Then I shan't suit him you may be sure; I'd rather live among savage Indians than break stones or chop down forests, for my hands are awfully soft and tender."

"They'll get hard enough by and bye, particularly if you get to work under Governor Lion Limb."

"Governor Lion Limb, who's he?"

"A young gentleman who has been appointed governor-in-chief of all the newly-discovered Islands, and has been entrusted with the first command out there in all military and naval matters."

"Lion Limb is a queer name for a governor."

"So it is; but that's not his real name."

"If his nation is anything like his name," said old Marks, "he must be a fine, noble, generous, and brave fellow."

"So he is. I hear all that; but his real name is—"

"What," said old Marks, looking up, with a peculiar look of doubt and interest.

"Edgar Norman," said Sharp, softly.

Had a mill-stone fallen on the back of old Marks, he could not have looked more surprised and staggered than he did at the bare mention of that name.

"Edgar Norman!" he said, aghast.

"I did."

"You are only joking?"

"I am not."

"Why, he was transported and drowned!"

"He was sent abroad through your son's false swearing; but though the vessel was wrecked, Edgar and some others were saved."

"And is he governor of the island?"

"Yes, the chief man of all the islands out there. He has fought his way up from nothing—has cultivated the soil and subdued the Indians—and in reward for all this, government has honored him with rank and title."

"Wonders will never cease. I must be dreaming," said Marks, "all this cannot be."

"Every word of it is truth."

"And who brought this startling news to England?"

"The ship of war, 'Skylark;' but Edgar Norman does not yet know of his promotion and pardon," said Sharp. "They are going to send out some guns, and a new vessel of war for the young colony, and a thousand other things."

"I would rather go anywhere than meet Edgar Norman," said the old man. "What will Jerry think of all this when he hears it?"

"It is a just punishment of heaven upon you both, Marks," said Sharp; "you know the poor lad had nothing at all to do with the murder of the poor old, good-natured old man."

"I know nothing about it."

"Yes you do. You cannot look me in the face and deny it, Marks; but you see, all your devilish schemes have come to nought, and the very lad you tried your hardest to hang has proved himself to be a credit to his name and country."

"I wish I could have five minutes talk with Lord Templeton before I leave England," sighed Marks.

"What good could he do you?"

"He might procure me a pardon."

"He could not, and would not if he could, Marks. He is only too much pleased to hear of your fate, I can assure you."

"Is he, though," said the old man, grinning fiendishly; "but what would he say if I exposed him?"

"Expose him—how?"

"Oh, you don't know everything in the world, Mr. Sharp, if you are a restless detective and thief-taker. Dr. Killum will come to see me before I go, and—"

"He cannot."

"Oh! but he can, and will."

"He is not in London, Marks."

"How do you know?"

"He has left for parts unknown."

"How could that be, he hadn't any money to pay his passage abroad?"

"Yes he had, for I gave it to him."

"You did, eh?" sighed the disappointed and revengeful old rogue. "Then it seems you do know all about it, Sharp."

"I do; and Baron Templeton also."

"And Lady Oxenford also?"

"Yes."

"But I have letters which belonged to her ladyship, which my son found the day he was confined in that college on the wild heath, and if they were brought to light, they would get me pardoned rather than be disgraced themselves."

Sharp laughed.

"I have got those letters, Marks," said the officer, "and at a proper time will give them up to Lady Oxenford myself."

It must be confessed that poor old Marks was in a sad way when he found that all his plans and schemes had been forestalled by the clever detective.

He knew not what to say, or how to look at Mr. Sharp, but he preserved his good temper as much as possible, and tried to be resigned to his fate.

"You have played your game with us very cleverly, Sharp," said old Marks, at last, "but it strikes me you must have had some traitor too in pay, or you would not, in fact, you could not, have arranged matters so nicely."

"Perhaps I had."

"And I think I can guess who it was."

"Who?"

"Jenny."

"Jenny who?"

"Oh, you know," said Marks, "she was once a servant of mine."

"And you treated her very badly, I hear?"

"No, I didn't, but Jerry did."

"And now you see she has had her revenge, and at the same time done good in the right cause."

"And what did you give her?"

"Nothing."

"Oh, that's all gammon," said old Marks.

"I got her a good situation, that is all; but I have not much time to waste on such matters of conversation, Marks; my reasons for seeing you this morning was to ask three or four important questions, which I hope you'll answer."

"What are they?"

"I have searched your house and offices, but cannot find some papers of importance."

"About the birth of Edgar and Allan Norman?"

"Just so."

"Well, then, you shall never have them; I have hidden them away."

"They are not destroyed, then?"

"They are not."

"Then why not give them up, they are now of no use to you, you know, or to Jerry either?"

"I know it; but I tell you that those documents shall never come to light while I live, and so, Sharp, there's an end of it."

"But we may be able to find them, after all?"

"You will have to be very clever then," said old Marks, with a wicked grin.

"If you don't disclose the hiding-place, it will be all the worse for you, Marks."

"How?"

"Why, if I let young Lion Limb know about it, when you get out to those far distant Islands, he will *force* you to disclose all you know."

"No he won't; I will *die* first; I *will* have revenge on him somehow or other, for I thought the rat was at the bottom of the sea, long ere this."

"I can't make anything of him," thought Sharp. "he has hidden away a large amount of money and valuables of all sorts, which belong to Baron Templeton, Lady Oxenford, and Lord Manfred, but he will not reveal anything about them."

He, therefore left old Marks, wishing him " a pleasant journey to the South Pacific Islands," and then for the last time visited Jerry.

Jerry's features and manners had wonderfully changed since his conviction, and he looked at Sharp with the gaze of an angry demon.

"Well, and what do you want now?" said Jerry, in a very surly manner.

"I came to tell you that your days in England are very few."

"Well?"

"If you can make any amends to those you have long injured, Jerry, do so before you go."

"How do you mean?"

"You have been living on the fat of the land for a long time, and, as I feel certain, must have plenty of money hid away like your father."

"I know I have; but let it rot where I have hidden it, or remain concealed until my return to England."

"I fear you will never return here, Jerry."

"Won't I though," said Jerry, with a sardonic grin. "You will see if I don't. And if I do——"

"Aye, if," said Sharp, "And what then?"

"You for one will have to regret my coming back, for I have sworn to have revenge on you, Sharp."

"Nonsense, lad; that is exactly what every culprit says when he's convicted. Many have said the same to me before you; but nothing has come of it. I have sent many a one abroad; but they have never come back; all their threats proved idle wind."

"But mine will not, Sharp," said Jerry, with a clenched fist. "I live now only for revenge, Sharp, and if it be thirty years hence I will not forget you."

Sharp laughed, and then told him where the government thought of sending them.

When the name of Edgar Norman was mentioned, and it was proved to his satisfaction that Lion Limb was the governor of that distant island, he looked like one amazed.

For some time he could not believe his own ears,

yet at last the mournful conviction dawned upon his mind that what the officer said might be true, and his heart sank within him.

"This is worse than all," thought Jerry. "Oh! how I always hated that Edgar Norman; and yet to think that he still lives, that he is honoured in the land, and that I should be under him, and be a servant!"

These and such like thoughts were worse than wormwood to Jerry, who bit his nails in potent anger, and stamped about like a maniac.

For several days thereafter Jerry was very dull and despondent.

He who before had been defiant, was now very humble—very humble indeed.

He felt the finger of Providence lay heavily upon him, and he sighed in agony.

"This comes of a wicked life," he thought. "I was always told and taught that the crooked way is always the shortest, and I have found it to be so. Well, no matter, I have had a short life and a merry one, as they say on town, and now have many long dreary years to think over my follies and to repent."

In a few days after this conversation between Sharp and Jerry, all the prisoners were removed to Plymouth, where they went on board the "Skylark," which was nearly ready for sea.

In all there were no less than a hundred convicts sent on board, and the vessel was thoroughly fitted out with every necessary and requirement.

In truth, a second vessel was also going on the same voyage, and was laden with a thousand things the government thought the young colonists, settled there, would require.

But before the vessel set sail, a distinguished visitor arrived on board.

It was none else than Dr. Killum!

He had left England for the United States, but he only remained a week there, and returned disgusted with that country.

Hearing that two ships were outward bound for some newly discovered islands, and hearing also that young Edgar Norman was still living, and chief man out there, he volunteered to go out there as a surgeon and physician, an offer which the captain of the "Skylark" accepted.

Sharp did not know of his presence on board, but old Marks soon did so.

"Ah!" thought he, "Heaven is kind to me, at last. Dr. Killum has been appointed medical superintendent over me, and I *know* he *will* be friendly and kind towards me, and Jerry also; therefore, I will sham to be ill, and then he will prescribe good food, and, perhaps, a small quantity of rum."

But Dr. Killum did not.

"Have you seen the convicts, Mr. Killum?" asked the captain, one day.

"Yes, captain; I *have* seen them."

"And what do you think of them? Are they all comfortable below?"

"Yes, sir; much too comfortable I think."

"We have several who complain of being sick already."

"Oh, indeed!"

"Yes, old Marks and his son, the late notorious 'Captain Zacary,' have been unwell ever since you came on board."

"Ah, yes; but you must not mind what they say; you know, captain, both of them are slightly touched in the brain."

"You don't mean that?"

"It's truth, upon my word; why, old Marks had

the impudence to say he knew me, this morning; what do you think of such impertinence?"

"Oh! we will soon cure him of babbling—the old fool—if that is his worse complaint."

"I never saw the low fellow in my whole life before."

"I fully believe you."

"I have not left America, the land of my birth, more than three weeks, you know; and it was only for the fun of adventure that I volunteered to go out to the South Pacific."

"I know it; and all I can say, doctor, is that all of our officers prize you highly; you can sing a good song, make and drink an excellent bowl of punch, tell a good story, and can play an excellent game of w——— accomplishments which are beyond all price, on a long voyage, you know."

"Send for this old Marks, then," said Dr. Killum, "I should like to see him; but do you be present at the interview, captain; it will prove all a capital joke—you'll see."

"I will."

The word was passed for old Marks, who soon entered the cabin, looking very forlorn and haggard in his convict suit, and very thin and shaky also.

"Well, and what is the matter with you, sir?" said Dr. Killum, in a very important style.

"Ah! doctor," began old Marks, in a drawling tone, "*you* know what's the matter."

"Do I, indeed?"

"Of course you do."

"You hear him, captain," said the doctor, triumphantly; "he will know *you* next."

"Ah! you may laugh as much as you like, doctor," whined old Marks; "but I could a tale unfold."

"Oh! the fellow is wrong in his head, evidently. Doctor, if *I* were you, I would order him to wear a straight waistcoat."

The features of old Marks turned blue at the bare mention of a straight waistcoat, and he thought of the pain and sufferings which young Allan must have undergone when in the private lunatic asylum.

"No, not yet," said the doctor. "I think he has had too much food to eat lately, captain, his diet must be reduced."

"Reduced!" gasped Marks. "Why I am almost a living skeleton already. Look at me."

"He certainly don't look very fat," laughed the captain.

"So much the better," said Killum. "It is always a good plan to keep convicts on a low diet, for if they get too fat they might become proud and unruly; for the present I will prescribe this old fellow a black draught every morning, it will do him good, and then, captain, he must be worked very hard."

Old Mark's eyes shot fire when he heard these instructions.

He could not help himself, however, for Dr. Killum prepared a strong black draught for him on the spot, which old Marks was forced to swallow.

"He'll soon get well under my treatment," said Killum.

And Marks went to his proper quarters, and was put to some nice hard work immediately.

"That Dr. Killum is a perfect demon," thought the old man.

"Well, and how did you get on, father?" asked Jerry. "Didn't the new doctor prescribe good things for you? I have never had a good look at him yet."

"Well, your turn will soon come, Jerry," sighed the old man. "He is a perfect devil."

Jerry, thinking that he also might sham sickness, and get off from hard work on board, also requested to see the doctor.

Killum sent for him.

Jerry was astonished.

He could not believe his own eyes; but when the doctor began to speak to him, he fully recognised him.

Dr. Killum grinned when Jerry came before him.

"You are Captain Zacary, I believe?" said the man of physic.

"No; my name is Jerry Marks," was the blunt and angry reply; "and your name is Dr. Killum."

"It is; and what's the matter with you?"

"My back is very sore in carrying heavy loads, doctor, and my hands are too tender for hard work."

"I dare say they are; but they will get used to it, after a time, my fine fellow; and when we arrive on the islands we are going to, I have no doubt that wood chopping, and such like amusements, under the direction of your old friend, Edgar Norman, will prove highly pleasant to you. You look rather sulky, I see, but that may arise from the bile, therefore, take these six pills, and go to work again; let me hear no more complaining, or I shall be compelled to prescribe bread and water only for four days in the week."

Jerry's heart sank within him.

Whichever way he went he found enemies ready and willing to torment him.

His life to him now was a perfect curse, and he wished himself dead every hour in the day.

But there was no hope for that.

He was now beginning to suffer the penalties and punishments for his many crimes, as he had once enjoyed the privileges of illgotten wealth.

But he cherished all sorts of mad resolves for vengeance.

Should he foment rebellion among the convicts, and sieze the ship?

To murder the captain and his officers was a plan that he frequently thought of during the dark still hours of night.

"I must wait," thought Jerry. "We are yet in England; but when we are far out on the broad ocean, I will 'sound' all the convicts, and see what can be done, for I would rather die a hundred deaths than fall alive into the hands of my old enemy, Edgar Norman.

"How he will triumph over me," he thought, "and kick and cuff me about. Oh! it is the bitterest fate any mortal was ever doomed to endure."

His father also suddenly became very reserved and thoughtful.

Wherever he went to and fro about the ship, his old eyes were busy in taking notes and forming plans.

But *his* ideas were different from those of his son.

To raise a mutiny on board was furthest from the father's thoughts.

"It cannot be done," he sighed. "The officers and crew are too numerous."

But another fiendish idea took possession of his heart.

His eyes sparkled with a deadly fire, and he clenched his fists in dread resolve.

"Yes," he thought, "I *can* do that, and *will*, but not now."

What was his resolve?

We shall see quickly.

THE BOY KING
OF THE SOUTH SEA ISLANDS.

AN ATTEMPT DEFEATED.

For that same day, having occasion to go for medicine for a sick convict, he noted the places wherein were kept the most deadly of all the drugs.

"'Tis well," he thought, "I will yet be free, and when once again my feet are unshackled, I will return to England, unearth my hidden treasures, and the world will know me not."

In a few days, old Marks made himself very useful with the cooks, and he proved himself so expert in manufacturing all manner of choice French dishes, that the officers were delighted, and the captain had serious thoughts of employing the old man in his own cook-house or galley.

But this proposition Dr. Killum resisted.

His reasons, however, he stated to none, but every

No. 43.

time he saw old Marks, he watched him with suspicion and fear, that caused him to tremble.

"There is a deadly vengeance beaming in the lawyer's eye," he mused, "but it cannot be that he entertains the dreadful thoughts that come to my mind, for that cannot be."

Old Marks soon found out who the person was that kept him from among the ship's cooks, and his heart grew harder and harder.

"The doctor, my enemy, may suspect me, but I will play the simple fool, and disarm all suspicions. My time will come, and sooner than he expects. Come night, the officers and crew will go to sleep, never to rise again, for I am desperate and resolved I will poison them, one and all."

CHAPTER CXV.

THE BATTLE BETWEEN GOVERNOR MARTIN, MUNGO,
AND LION LIMB — THE FLAG OF TRUCE—THE
MESSENGER AND SPIES.

THE onslaught of the islanders, under the command
of old Governor Martin, and the onset in front of
Mungo by Lion Limb and his band, was of the
fiercest description.

The Indians, who before had been taught by
Mungo and Bill Whetherby to look with indifference
upon Lion Limb's men, now altered their mind
altogether.

They did not care to be surrounded or taken in
front and rear.

Therefore, at the first opportunity, and when the
fighting became rather hot, they slunk away by twos
and threes as best they could.

Some pretended to fall dead, and were thus left
behind out of further danger; and when they perceived a good chance they, like the others, crawled
away as best they could, at the same time thanking
their stars that they had escaped with their lives.

Mungo and the buccaneers, now finding that
their Indian friends could not be relied on, fired
on the deserters as much as they did on those
opposed to them.

The fighting now became desperate indeed.

Mungo and Bill Whetherby got very pale, but
they determined to face death and fight till the
very last.

But they were losing men each instant.

Governor Martin, who was gradually approaching
very near to the rear of Mungo's line, saw how
quickly the buccaneers were losing men and
becoming weaker and weaker.

"It is a pity to see so many English men die
like dogs," he thought, and called to his side one of
his faithful guides.

"Do you see yonder line of battle?" said he.

"I do, governor," said the Indian guide.

"And do you perceive anyone on a prancing
horse in the thickest of the fight?"

"I do, Governor Martin."

"Well, that brave fellow is my friend, Captain
Lion Limb."

"What would you have me do then, governor?"

"I want you to ride round, and when you reach
Lion Limb (which I hope you may do in safety),
ask him whether I shall ask the villains to surrender."

"I will, governor."

And off the guide started at a rapid pace, and
after much hard riding, he safely reached Lion
Limb.

Lion Limb smiled when he heard the message of
the guide.

"Tell Governor Martin he may do as he thinks
proper, but from what I know of them, do not suppose that Mungo or any of them will surrender;
but if he thinks otherwise, I am willing to suspend
the conflict. How are the islanders under the
brave old governor getting on in Mungo's rear?"

"They are gradually and slowly advancing.
Mungo's men cannot stand aginst us, and nearly all
his Indians have deserted him."

"So I perceive; Indians on these islands never
fight well, in fact, they cannot be relied upon at
all, except they are always led on by a well-known
and victorious commander."

"So it seems, Captain Lion Limb; as I came
through the woods, I saw hundreds of Indians run
away."

"I suppose they have eaten up all Mungo's provisions, and now, finding they have a little fighting
to do in payment, all of them think better of it and
take to their heels."

"So it seems, captain," said the guide, laughing.

"You may return to Governor Martin," said Lion
Limb, "and faithfully report all you see."

"I will."

"You may tell him that we are gradually driving
the buccaneers towards the sea coast, and that
very few of my white followers are hurt at present."

"Very well, sir."

"Also tell him that wild Dick Hamilton, Harry
Woodruff, and all the young leaders, are performing
prodigies of valour; but also say from me, that if
he thinks proper, he can send in a flag of truce to
Mungo, but whoever he sends in with it, let him be
a bold, brave man, for Mungo is very cruel and
treacherous."

"I will, Captain Lion Limb."

"When I see the white flag going towards
Mungo, I shall cease fighting, until the result is
known; tell Governor Martin such are my orders."

"I will, captain."

The guide galloped back, quicker than he came,
to Governor Martin's camp, and reported what
Captain Lion Limb had said.

"He thinks, then, that Mungo is determined to
die, rather than surrender, guide?"

"So he said, governor."

"Well, he knows Mungo best, and has had more
to do with the dastardly buccaneers than I ever
had; nevertheless, I will give them one more chance
for their lives. I would not mind if they were the
lying and treacherous Indians we were fighting
against, but most of the buccaneers fighting yonder
are English born."

Old Martin called for one of his most trusty men,
who, like the governor himself, wore an old-
fashioned military suit on state occasions—one of
many such suits which they had, on one occasion,
found in a wreck off the coast.

"Here Ray," said the old governor, "Captain
Lion Limb and myself have made our minds not to
kill off all the buccaneers like so many dogs, but
will give them a chance of surrendering; take this
white flag and gallop yonder, to where you see
those black figures cutting about in the white
smoke. The tallest is Mungo, the chief, the other
is the demon, Bill Whetherby."

Ray, who felt proud of his ancient military suit,
took the flag, and felt joyful at the idea of being
the messenger of peace.

Directly he left the side of old Governor Martin,
firing and fighting ceased in all directions.

"Hullo! what does this mean?" said Mungo,
when he perceived Ray galloping towards him.

"It is a flag of truce," said Whetherby.

"So it seems; but what can be its meaning?"

"The islanders, under old Martin, may want to
make peace."

"I very much doubt it; but if such be the
case——"

"If it is the case," said Bill, "make peace with
them on the instant; but not with Lion Limb."

"No fear of me doing that," said Mungo, gruffly;
"but here comes the messenger. What an old-
fashioned suit he wears."

"Yes," said Bill, "that is the military sort of
suit our great grandfathers used to wear in England."

"How did they get them?" asked Mungo.

"Old Martin discovered three or four dozen such
suits in an old, very old, wreck on his part of the
coast. He wears one himself on all great occasions,

and a pigtail also, and topboots. Oh! he's quite an old buck when he likes, I hear."

By this time Ray the messenger galloped up.

"Well," said Mungo, "where do you come from?"

"Governor Martin."

"Does he surrender to us?"

"No; such a thing is furthest from his thoughts."

"What, then, does he want to make peace with us, and withdraw from the fight?"

"No, not that either."

"Well, what else can he want, then? Why stop us in the middle of the fight?"

"He wishes to stop the further flow of blood, Mungo."

"Very kind of him, indeed. Well, and how does he intend to do it?"

"He has consulted with Capt. Lion Limb, and—"

"Well, and what does that young usurper say?"

"He quite agrees with what Governor Martin intends, and I come here with the consent of both commands."

"For what purpose, then?"

"To beg of you to spare your men's lives, and surrender."

"And do what?" roared Mungo, in a terrible rage.

"To surrender, Mungo, nothing more nor less," said the gallant Ray, quite calmly.

"I think you came to insult us," said Mungo.

"Such a thought was never in my mind. Governor Martin said that all, or at least most, of the buccaneers were English, and he did not like to shed English blood."

"English blood, eh?" said Mungo, with a trembling lip; "but *I* am not English! I am half African; they call me Mungo the Bastard, if you would know, my young man, and I defy both old Martin and young Lion Limb!"

Mungo, in his rage, would have said more; but Bill Whetherby took him on one side and whispered for a moment.

"'Tis well," said Mungo, "I will do as you say. I will send him back with a message in order to gain time."

"That's it exactly, Mungo," said Bill. "We can collect all our men together, and fight our way then right down to our ships on the coast, for it must be confessed that we can place not the least reliance upon the dastardly natives with us; and we have lost a great many men already."

Mungo bit his lips, but for a moment said nothing.

Before the engagement began, he had never dreamed that old Governor Martin would have joined Lion Limb.

"If I could only make Lion Limb and Governor Martin jealous of each other, and divide their forces," he thought, "I could then very easily fall upon each in turn and destroy them."

Turning to Ray, he said,

"You seem to be a bold brave fellow, whoever you are."

Ray bowed.

"Was you not afraid to meet me?" asked Mungo.

"No," said Ray, "I was not.

Mungo grinned hideously.

"Where did you get that fantastic and old-fashioned English suit of clothes?"

"Governor Martin found a few such like suits in the remains of an old wreck, and he bestowed one on each of his most trustworthy men."

"And you are one of them, I suppose?"

"I am."

"And have seen a great deal of hard service and fighting in your time, I have no doubt?"

"I have."

"Where?"

"On our island."

"Against whom?"

"Against the Indians, natives, and also against your own buccaneers, Mungo, when you were driven from our island; you may, perhaps, recollect that event?"

"I do," said Mungo, scowling.

After a moment's thought, he said,

"Governor Martin wishes me to surrender, but he has not stated the precise terms."

"I understand no other terms than unconditional surrender," said Ray.

"You may be mistaken, young man; go back to Governor Martin and say Mungo never surrenders, but if Governor Martin wishes to make a league with us, we are ready, provided he promises to break his alliance with Lion Limb."

"Which he will never do," said Ray.

"You know nothing of the matter," said Mungo, "go and deliver my message."

"I will, but I am certain it will be to no purpose."

"Go, I say," said Mungo, in a terrible tone of anger.

Ray mounted his horse and departed.

"Now," said Bill Whetherby, "do you send a messenger to Lion Limb as I told you, and we shall be able to make these two friends the bitterest of enemies."

"Right," said Mungo, "I will."

And while Mungo was instructing his messenger to Lion Limb, Bill Whetherby was arranging the buccaneers for a hasty retreat, if necessary.

Mungo's messenger, under the flag of truce, safely reached the camp of Lion Limb.

The arrival of a messenger from Mungo, it must be confessed, greatly surprised Lion Limb.

He had never heard of such a proceeding on the part of Mungo or the buccaneers before.

"What is your errand?" asked Lion Limb of the messenger.

"I come from Mungo."

"I know you do; but what is your message to me?"

"Mungo, my master, sent me, Captain Lion Limb, to compliment you on your bravery, and although he is at present opposed to you in fair and open combat, he thinks it proper to acquaint you with the plot against your honor and life."

"My honor and life?"

"Aye, sir! Nothing less, I assure you," said the messenger."

"What means Mungo?" said Lion Limb.

"He means this, Captain Lion Limb, old Governor Martin has sent a messenger asking my master, Mungo, to make an alliance with him."

"With Governor Martin?"

"Yes."

"I cannot believe it."

"It is true, sir."

"What object can he have?"

"Old Martin is jealous of you, and wants to destroy both you and your followers; but Mungo, my master, who has much respect for you, though an avowed enemy, sent me to inform you of the whole truth, and offer his assistance, if you will accept it, to fall upon old Governor Martin and destroy both him and his islanders."

"And me afterwards, I suppose," smiled Lion Limb.

"Such a thought is furthest from my master,

Mungo's, mind," said the messenger, bowing meekly. " I heard him say, before I came here, he would rather be your slave than old Governor Martin's friend."

" Very complimentary, indeed," said Lion Limb, turning aside. " What think you of this message, Harry Woodruff ?" Lion Limb asked.

" What do I think ?"

" Yes."

" What can I think," said Harry, with a bitter smile. " This is only a trick of Mungo's to make you and old Martin enemies, nothing more."

" But it has been frequently told to me that old King Katamar has been negociating with old Martin to drive me from this island."

" Which old Martin would never consent to do," said Harry, gruffly.

" At all events we might not do wrong in inviting Mungo into our camp," said Lion Limb.

" Certainly not ; but he will not come, you may be sure."

" We will try it, at all events."

Turning to the messenger, he said,

" Give my compliments to your master, Mungo, and say from me that I feel deeply honored by his message, for its importance is beyond all estimate. In token of how highly I prize the information sent to me, say that I desire to see Mungo here in my camp, under a flag of truce, where we can talk over matters at leisure."

" I will," said the messenger, who instantly departed.

" He will never come," said Harry.

" If he does not, it will be a sure sign that what he has said is false," said Lion Limb.

" What shall we do ?" asked Harry. " Shall we commence the fight again ?"

" Not yet ; for you perceive the flag of truce flying in both old Martin's and Mungo's camp."

The messenger, who had been sent to Lion Limb, had not arrived in Mungo's camp many minutes, ere Ray appeared from the lines of old Martin.

" Your message, this time, young sir ?" said Mungo to Ray.

" Governor Martin says, Mungo, that the only object he had in proposing your surrender, was to spare the effusion of more blood ; if you agree, the surrender must be without conditions."

" An unconditional surrender ?"

" Yes."

" Old Martin must be mad."

" He said that Lion Limb and himself would afterwards determine what the proper conditions should be."

" Oh, indeed !" said Mungo, grimly.

Ray smiled at the anger and annoyance of the buccaneer chief, which Mungo's sharp black eyes did not fail to obtain.

" Did old Martin say anything else ?" asked Bill Whetherby.

" Yes ; and said that he and Lion Limb had the greatest confidence in each other, and that nothing that Mungo might say should ever shake it."

" But why do you smile ?" asked Mungo of Ray.

" In truth, Mungo, I smile because I know that, at last, you are caught in the tail, and that you must either surrender at discretion, or be cut down to your last man."

" Which you hope and desire, I suppose," said Mungo.

" I do," said Ray, gaily.

" Let my vengeance go with you," said Mungo, suddenly drawing a dagger, and throwing the weapon with an unerring aim, it struck almost up to the hilt in Ray's throat, who fell flat to the earth on his back, mortally wounded, and almost instantly expired from suffocation.

" There," said Mungo, " so may it be with all and every one of my enemies."

The act was so sudden, that even Bill Whetherby was surprised.

Everbody knew that Mungo could throw knives and daggers a great distance with an accurate aim, but they never imagined he was so skilful as to sever the jugular vein at one gash.

" Now," said Mungo to his own messenger, " do you go and tell Lion Limb all you have seen in my camp."

" Tell him that we have killed old Martin's messenger for his villany," said Bill Whetherby, " as a token of our obedience to Lion Limb."

" Ah, that's it," said Mungo ; " tell all the lies you can, and make the most of what you have seen and heard ; if we can but escape from between the forces of old Martin and Lion Limb, and get back to our vessel, all will be well."

The messenger returned again to Lion Limb, and in a very plausible tale, said it was impossible at that moment to visit Lion Limb's camp in person, as several of his officers were against the proposed alliance ; but to show Lion Limb how sincere Mungo was in his professions of friendship, he had killed, on the spot, a messenger from the camp of old Governor Martin, who had come to him with the intelligence that he was on his way to stab Lion Limb."

" Do not believe one word he says," Harry Woodruff observed. " No doubt Mungo has murdered old Martin's messenger, but not for the cause he asserts."

" What shall we do with Mungo's messenger' then ?" asked Lion Limb.

" Hang him, of course, in retaliation," said Harry, gruffly.

" I will question him first," said Lion Limb. Turning to the messenger, he said—

" Do you believe that what Mungo says in regard to me is true ?"

" I do firmly believe it."

" And you saw him slay old Martin's messenger ?"

" I did, and for only the reasons I have before explained."

" What would you advise me to do, then ?" asked Lion Limb.

" I should say the best thing you could do would be to join your forces with those of my master, Mungo, and fall upon the old hypocrite, Martin."

" But we ought to arrange upon some plan of action to do that."

" Nothing is easier," said the messenger. " Come with me to the camp of Mungo ; he will be very glad to receive you, and explain all things to your perfect satisfaction."

" I dare say he would," said Harry Woodruff, laughing right out, " and perhaps to a little more than our satisfaction."

" What do you mean ?" said the messenger, with an air of offended pride. " Do you think for one moment that my master, Mungo, would do anything wrong ?"

" Oh, no, not in the least," said Harry.

" He is the very soul of honour," said Lion Limb, with a smile.

Mungo's messenger did not much like the look of Lion Limb's smile, and endeavoured step by step to reach his horse.

" They have sounded the purport of my mission," thought Mungo's man. " I am standing on dangerous ground, and will depart ere it is too late."

But while he cautiously, and, as he thought, unperceived, slipped backwards towards his horse, Harry Woodruff clapped him on the shoulders, saying roughly—

"You are my prisoner."

"I a prisoner! Why?"

"For many reasons."

"State them."

"You are a spy."

"No, I am not; but simply a messenger under a flag of truce."

"More of a spy than messenger, I take it," said Lion Limb.

"What do you intend to do with me, then?"

"Make you confess your villany, or——"

"Or what?"

"Hang you."

"I have no villanies to confess."

"Yes, you have; and unless you disclose to us the true motives why Mungo sent you hither, why, then, you must die like a dog."

"Be it so, then," said the messenger, "Mungo's men never disclose the secrets of their master."

"Don't they, though," said Harry, "if you were left to my tender mercies I would put you to a slow torture over a hot fire, and that would soon make you open your mouth, my fine, bold fellow."

"If you kill me it will be a dishonour to your name and reputation," said the messenger, "for I came under a flag of truce."

"And who broke it first?" said Lion Limb, angrily.

"Did you not kill old Governor Martin's messenger?" said Harry. "Now we understand the drift of Mungo's plans, and will defeat them."

"Prepare to die, young man. You must confess all you know, else a gallows will be your fate," said Lion Limb; "there is little mercy for spies such as you."

"Bring him this way," said Harry. "His horse is not a bad-looking animal, and I claim it for my own use. Bring the prisoner this way; unless the rascal makes a clean breast of all he knows, he shall swing on the limb of a high tree in less than fifteen minutes."

The messenger was instantly seized and disarmed by several ferocious fellows, and dragged towards a tall oak tree that was in full view of Mungo's camp, and there tied hand and foot ready for execution.

"You had better confess," said Harry. "We don't want to kill you in cold blood, although you deserve it for being a spy and a liar."

"I have nothing to say to you," said the messenger. "All I have to communicate must be to Lion Limb himself."

"Be it so, then. Do you want to see our young captain, then?"

"I do."

A youth was sent for Captain Lion Limb, who soon appeared on the spot.

"What does the prisoner want, Harry?"

"He wishes to make a communication of great importance to you in hopes of saving his life."

"I have promised him his life if he fully confesses all," said Lion Limb, approaching the prisoner.

Mungo's messenger hung his head as Lion Limb advanced.

"What have you to say?" asked Lion Limb.

"Much," was the whispered answer.

"Then, speak."

"I will; but do not want any ear in the world to know what I have to reveal save yourself."

"Indeed! is it of such vast importance, then?"

"It is."

"And about what?"

"You and your position here and in England, about your brother Allan and young Jem Rawlings."

Lion Limb seemed amazed at the bare mention of his brother's name.

Despite the endeavours of the crafty Mungo to sow the seeds of discord between old Martin and his fast friend Lion Limb, he was unable to do so.

The non return of old Martin's faithful messenger, young Ray, awoke rude suspicions in the old man's breast immediately.

He felt certain that treachery had been at work.

For the instant, therefore, he pulled down the flag of truce which had been hitherto flying, and resolved to take ample vengeance.

"Before you renew the attack, Governor Martin," said one well-wisher, and a faithful adviser withal, "let some one go and ascertain the fate of Ray; he may not be dead after all."

"With all my heart," said the kind-hearted old man. "I am not one of those who would take any unfair advantage of an enemy."

A second messenger was therefore sent to Mungo; but when he arrived in the presence of that well-known sanguinary chief, and saw bloodmarks here and there, he felt sure that poor Ray had fallen a victim to the African's revenge.

"I know your errand," said Mungo, laughing with scorn at the messenger.

"In that case, then, it is unnecessary for me to speak."

"Ray is dead."

"Dead!"

"Aye; and yonder he lies," said Mungo, pointing to the spot where the bold young man lay stiff and dead upon the grass, with the dagger still sticking in his throat.

The messenger knew not how to withhold or restrain his rage.

He was endeavouring to conceal his rage and vexation as best he could; but at last broke out into a violent passion, and upbraided Mungo in a bold and defiant manner.

"Monster!" he said, "have you no human feelings remaining in your remorseless breat? What! kill one who came to you as messenger of peace and mercy!"

"Peace and mercy!" quoth Mungo, with a bitter laugh. "If you are wise you will restrain your impetuous tongue; if not, depart. I would not kill a second messenger without potent reasons."

"I defy you," said old Martin's friend, Gilroy, vaulting upon his horse, and brandishing his sword. "You will repent this day's work, Mungo, and should we meet in battle, mind, recollect you cannot expect mercy or quarter from any of your foes."

"Out upon the impudent varlet!" said Mungo, with a fierce oath. "Stop him! I say, stop him!"

But Gilroy spurred up his steed to a maddening gallop, and soon left Mungo's camp far behind him.

In a few minutes thereafter, the battle began against all sides, and raged with great fury.

But Mungo, during the interval of the truce, had drawn his men together, and, when least expected, retreated towards the coast, hotly pursued by Lion Limb and old Governor Martin, the followers of each captain burning to take signal vengeance upon the buccaneers for their treachery and villany.

But when, after several hours of hard fighting, Mungo had got beyond the reach of harm, and escaped through the forests, where neither Lion Limb nor old Martin cared to follow, the victorious wings of Lion Limb and old Martin's followers joined together, and rent the air with their shouts.

The meeting between Lion Limb and old Martin was of the most enthusiastic description.

The old man embraced Lion Limb again and again.

"Another such fight as this, governor," said Lion Limb, "and all the buccaneers will be cut into pieces."

"True, my brave lad, very true; but my poor Ray," said the old man, in a sorrowful tone, "they have barbarously murdered him. I would have sooner lost my right hand than the gallant Ray."

Lion Limb made every arrangement for hunting Mungo, but old Martin went forth to seek the body of Ray, and when he discovered him, stiff and cold, with the dagger still sticking in his throat, he lifted up his hands in anguish over the poor fallen boy, and vowed never to rest day nor night until he and his followers had taken ample revenge for the dastardly deed. (*See Cut, No.* 41.)

Leaving Lion Limb preparing to pursue Mungo, let us again return to England and narrate what transpired in regard to Allan and young Jem.

CHAPTER CXVI.

BARON TEMPLETON IS HUMBLED TO THE DUST BY MR. SHARP.

BARON TEMPLETON, when Lord Oxenford left him' sat in a deep reverie, and did not move off his seat' but sat as if he were fastened to his chair.

"Lord Oxenford adopt young Allan," he sighed, "whoever could have dreamed of such a thing. It is a miracle, indeed.

"Some one must have been at work in the lad's favour," he thought, "and worked very hard for him. I wonder who it is."

While he sat a servant entered.

"I will see no one this morning," said the baron to the footman, "don't annoy me, I am not well."

"But there is a gentleman below stairs who says he *must* see you."

"Tell him I can't; let him leave his name, that will be all sufficient; some other time he may call."

The servant left the room, but soon returned.

"Well, what now," said the baron, "don't you see I am prepared for a promenade, and don't want to be annoyed with visitors?"

"But this party as is down in the hall, my lord, says as how he won't go without seeing you; and more than that, he *will* see you."

"Indeed," said the baron, "he is a bold fellow who says that."

"You may be sure he is, my lord; he seems to have plenty of brass in his face, and no mistake."

"Is he a gentleman or ——"

"Oh, yes, my lord, he seems to be all the gentleman, and no mistake."

"His name is——"

"Sharp, my lord."

"Sharp, Sharp; I don't know any one of that name. Is the stranger a naval or military looking person?"

"A captain in the army at least, my lord, for he stands as straight as a lamp-post, and twirls his stick about at a fine rate, and brought it down very close to my nose once."

"Sharp, Sharp," mused the baron, still unsatisfied; "well, ask him his business with me."

"I did, my lord, and he told me to mind my own business, and if I didn't he would make me."

"Show him up," said the baron.

And the fat footman soon opened the door again and ushered in Mr. Sharp.

The officer bowed to the baron.

"Your business with me, sir?" said the Judge, sternly.

But Sharp saw the footman lingering near the door to listen, and said, in a very blunt manner,

"Do you wish that menial to hear our conversation, my lord?" pointing to the fat footman.

The word "menial" sank into the very heart of Jeames, who vanished in an instant.

"Your name is Sharp, I believe?"

"It is, my lord."

"You are in the army, I believe?"

"No, my lord."

"Yet I know your face somewhere," said his lordship, scrutinizing the features of the visitor.

"Oh, no doubt, my lord, you have very often."

"But where? at the clubs or at the levees?"

"Neither, my lord," said Sharp, blushing up to the temples, "but I daresay you may have seen me more than once at the Old Bailey."

"At the Old Bailey!" said my lord, frowning.

"Yes, my lord, it is a long time now since you sat upon the bench there."

"It is; but what *are* you?"

"I am called Inspector Sharp, your lordship, and a detective."

The countenance of the baron changed immediately.

"And what business can a detective have with *me*?" he said, very sternly.

"Well, my lord, I have a great deal to say to you, and on the most important business; if you think I am unworthy of your notice, so let it be. I will retire and will not call again."

Sharp was about to take up his hat and retire in disgust at the cool effrontery of the baron's manner, when the Judge said,

"Stay, I command you."

Sharp sat down again.

"Your business with me, sir," said the baron, "and in as few words as possible. I am going out."

"I came then, my lord, regarding the last trial in which you gave sentence at the Old Bailey."

"Let me see; what trial was that? I almost forget."

"Regarding the murder of old Alderman English, in which several youths, named Norman and Rawlings, were——"

"Yes, yes, yes," said his lordship, hurriedly, the crimson mounting to his forehead; "I remember, Sharp."

"I dare say you do, my lord," said Sharp, with a bitter tone.

And he thought, "If the cool, placid villain there don't remember, he ought to do, considering the two lads were his own sons."

"Well, what about the lads?" said the baron, hurriedly, "I haven't much time to bestow upon this subject; the one I sentenced was afterwards drowned, I believe."

"It was so supposed, my lord."

"And is it not true?"

"It is not."

"Good heavens, you surprise me, Sharp," said the baron, turning pale and trembling much.

"Not drowned!" he said, a second time.

"No, my lord, he is not only alive but honoured by all who know him. Of course you are aware that his brother Allan is in the employ of Lord Oxenford, as private secretary to his lordship?"

"Aware! how should *I* be aware of all these

changes and accidents, sir? You speak like one armed with assurance, if not authority."

"I am both armed with one and the other. I have no lack of assurance, my lord, for I have abundance of authority," said Sharp.

The officer's warm heart was thoroughly disgusted at the cool effrontery and hypocrisy of the judge.

But the judge sat down, and his teeth chattered as he looked at Sharp.

"I am sitting here in torture," he thought; "this detective's eyes seem to sink into my very soul. I must get rid of him."

"What is the meaning of your visit?" said the baron, in a pettish tone. "What have I to do with the lads of whom you speak?"

"A great deal, my lord; the lads are your sons."

"Ha!"

"Nay, my lord, turn not pale."

"My sons! and you, a detective, have the impudence to come and——"

"Beard the lion in his den," said Sharp, tartly.

For a moment both were silent.

At last the baron said—

"You, then, know all?"

"I do, my lord."

"And want some recompense for your silence, I suppose?"

"No, my lord; for once you are mistaken. I want no recompense for silence, for if by speaking aloud the truth in open court to-morrow I could do the two lads any service, I would gladly and willingly do so."

"To my shame, I suppose?"

"Shame, my lord. You know not what that is."

"Sir."

"Nay; I come not to insult you, my lord, but to do good."

"What do you want then?"

"I want you to let the youth, Allan, alone. I know that my Lord Oxenford loves the boy, and wishes to do him good, and, more than that, intends, if possible, to adopt him, and make him succeed to the property after my lord's death."

"How could you know all this?"

"I have ways and means of finding out things that you know not of," said Sharp; "but you know I am right."

After a pause, Sharp approached Baron Templeton, and said in a quiet, firm tone, "Look you here, my lord; I command you to no longer persecute either these two lads or Lady Oxenford; if you do——"

"I am master of my own actions, sir, and how dare a common detective——"

"My lord, I know what I am doing; but if you do not do as I wish you in this matter, why, then, all I can say is, I will have revenge, and *transport you for life!*"

"What!" gasped Baron Templeton, starting to his feet, "can I believe my own ears?"

"You may, my lord," said Sharp. "I have the proof of something in my pocket this instant, which, if I, my lord, were to speak, would cause you to be transported."

And as he spoke he touched the baron on the shoulder in a very significant manner, saying, "*You* know what I mean, my lord."

The baron *did* know what Sharp meant, although no one else did, and as he looked at Sharp with wild, staring eyes, he fell upon the sofa, gasping.

"Sharp, I am in your power, and am a willing slave in all that you may desire."

The baron seemed thunderstruck at the words of Sharp, and fell upon the sofa more dead than alive,

disarranging his watch, and as Sharp left the room, he met the footman, to whom he said—

"You had better call the housekeeper; my lord has been taken unwell very suddenly; see to him at once."

The footman and the housekeeper went instantly to the baron's apartment; but, on entering the room, they were greatly surprised to find their master looking pale and weak, lying upon the sofa, and groaning with agony of mind and body. (*See Cut, No. 42.*)

"I don't think that my lord will be so proud and austere towards me any more," said Sharp, as he left the house.

"I went there with the best intentions to inform the baron of the exact state of affairs in regard to his two sons, but received nothing more than freezing politeness and foolish pride.

"If any one had done only half to my sons, which I have endeavoured, and very successfully done for the baron's children, I should feel myself indebted to them for ever. Never mind; he is a cold, flinty-hearted man; I care not for *his* good will, for I feel certain his end will not be a natural one. He will be shot, stabbed, poisoned or something like that; but as for poor Lady Oxenford," said Sharp, "I like that woman, and no mistake. She would give me the Bank of England, if she could, poor lady, and how delighted she seems to be now that young Allan lives in the same house.

"But what will she think when I tell her all I know about her favorite son. Edgar, and his doings in the South Pacific islands?"

Straightway Sharp went to Lord Oxenford's mansion.

His lordship was not at home; but Lady Oxenford received him with much politeness.

"Oh, Mr. Sharp," said her ladyship, "ten thousand, nay, millions of thanks for your kindness."

"And young Allan, your ladyship, how does he get along with my lord?"

"Oh, Mr. Sharp, you never could imagine how my lord has changed for the best. He loves that boy."

"But he does not know the secret, my lady?"

"He does not; but he loves him, because he says the youth so much resembles *me*, you know, and takes out his young secretary riding and driving, all of which, as you may well imagine, make me supremely happy, Mr. Sharp," said Lady Oxenford, with a flush of pride.

"My lord, I suppose, is not expected home for some time, your ladyship?"

"He is not. He will not return for several hours."

"I am glad of that, my lady, for I wished to inform you of a very pleasing, but at the same time a very startling piece of news."

"Indeed, Mr. Sharp. Pleasing news, you say?"

"I did, my lady."

"And what does it relate to, may I ask?"

"It relates to your ladyship, especially; but I hope you will not give way to any loud demonstration of joy."

"What *can* you mean, Mr. Sharp?"

"I mean, your ladyship, that Edgar Norman, your favorite son, is alive and well. He was *not* drowned, it was a false report. He is a great man among the South Pacific islands, and has of late been intrusted with the naval and military command of those newly discovered islands by order of government."

The fond and happy mother was astonished at the news.

She was almost overpowered with joy, and wept and laughed by turns.

"Oh, let me tell Allan, Mr. Sharp," said Lady Oxenford, in rapture. "My two sons alive! Oh, thank heaven for so much kindness, and a thousand, nay, a million thanks to you, Mr. Sharp, who have ever proved such a true friend to me."

"No thanks, my lady; the doing of good brings its own reward. You must not tell young Allan of this my lady. Leave it to me, I will break the news better than you. Call in your son, my lady."

And Allan appeared, looking more handsome and gentlemanly than ever.

"I have great news for you Allan," said Sharp.

"Indeed sir; I am indebted to you for ever for your kindness already."

"Edgar is alive, Allan."

"Edgar, sir!"

"Yes, your brother, and a great man also in the Southern Seas."

Poor Allan turned pale, and would have fainted at the sudden and startling announcement, but Lady Oxenford approached an caressed him.

"It is quite true, my dear son. Mr. Sharp has just told me all about it."

"But I have also to say something else, my lady, that is even more startling."

"Indeed; what is it?"

"Lord Oxenford has paid a visit to the Baron Templeton."

"I know; Allan told me, Mr. Sharp."

"But he did not tell you the purport of that visit, your ladyship."

"No he could not; that as yet is a mystery."

"But not to me."

"Indeed, then you know the subject of their business."

"I do, my lady; it was this."

And in a few softly-whispered words Sharp told my lady (without Allan hearing it) that Lord Oxenford had serious thoughts of leaving his property to young Allan, should he grow up worthy of such distinction."

Poor Lady Oxenford was bewildered with the dazzling prospects and position of her two sons; and knowing not what to think or say, she sat down in a luxurious easy chair, and wept from pure joy; one hand clasping Allan affectionately about the neck, and the other held respectfully by Sharp.

"Well, it is a pleasure to do good," thought the officer. "I'm sure I feel as happy as if I were left a thousand pounds. How this poor woman loves her children to be sure. Her happiness now seems to be complete, and will remain long so if Baron Templeton's hate for Lord Oxenford does not prompt him to divulge the secret.

"But if the baron does," thought Sharp, as he went home, "he will find a deadly and an active enemy in me. He never dreams of the misery of which he has been the cause. Nor does he, perhaps, think for a moment that I could drag him down from his high seat of honour, and sink him to the hulks or abroad for life. But, simple detective as I am, I have got more power over him than he imagines. If he dares to disobey me I will make him repent it all the days he has to live."

What secret, then, had Sharp discovered concerning Baron Templeton that was of such vast importance?

We shall see that shortly.

But certain it is the baron stood in holy awe of Sharp, and trembled in every limb at the bare mention of the detective's name.

What was his crime?

What were his hidden deeds?

The baron shuddered at the idea of being publicly denounced and brought to trial by Sharp.

CHAPTER CXVII.

JEM RAWLINGS IN SEARCH OF HIS FATHER.

BUT it must not be supposed for an instant that because we have not before mentioned the fact, that either Mr. Sharp or young Allan forgot or neglected Jem Rawlings.

"All lads are not lord's sons," thought Jem, when first Mr. Sharp told him the news; "so I can't expect to be so well off and provided for as Allan, you know. Young Allan was always a gentlemanly sort of fellow; now, wasn't he?"

Sharp said he though so.

"And so do I, you know; but, Sharp, me and my brother Ted were always pals with Edgar and Allan, you know, and more like brothers than anything else."

But when Mr. Sharp, in a few words, told young Jem the important news that his brother Ted was alive, and was with Edgar, on one of the South Pacific islands, young Jem jumped off his seat like a mad lad.

"W-h a-t!" said he, with gaping mouth and staring eyes, "Ted and Edgar still alive? Oh, what a jolly lark!"

"Yes, and I am also told that they have lots of gold-dust ready to send to England."

"Oh! Mr. Sharp, you don't mean to say so! And they are so rich as all that, eh? I wish they'd come home as soon as possible, then, for I should like to get a little of their money, don't you know. I will have a fine house, and do no work when Ted returns with his bags of gold. And won't I enjoy myself? Oh, no, not in the least—you may be sure of that, Mr. Sharp."

"Well, you don't have to work now, do you, Jem?"

"No; thanks to Allan's kindness; but I should like to find out who my mother and father were, you know, Mr. Sharp. Wouldn't it be jolly, though, if you could discover them, and find them out to be a lord and lady, like Lady Oxenford and Baron Templeton?"

"It would, Jem; but you must not mention those names too often, you know."

"I will not, Mr. Sharp; but, do you know, I think I saw my father to-day, Mr. Sharp."

"Indeed! how could you tell him? You never saw him."

"I know that; but something told me it was my father, you know, and I could not drive it out of my head."

"And where did you see this man, Jem?"

"In the Strand, sir; and I followed him such a long way, until, at last, he went into a large hotel, and as he mounted the steps and told the groom to take the horse to the stable, he gave me such a look."

"Did he, indeed?"

"Yes, Mr. Sharp; and he called me on one side and, says he, 'Do you know me, my lad?' and I said 'No.'"

"'But,' he says, 'I think I have seen your face somewhere or other. Where do you live?'

"I told him, you may be sure; but when I told him I never had no father or mother, he got red in the face, and looked after me such a long way."

Sharp remained in deep thought for some time, but spoke not a word.

THE BOY KING

OF THE SOUTH SEA ISLANDS.

BROUGHT TO BAY.

At that moment a loud rap was heard at the door, and Jem left Sharp alone.

"Well, I never," said Jem, as he ran up into his modest room again, "if that ain't the same gentleman as I saw this morning. He's come to see me and is on the stairs, below."

Sharp whispered a few hasty words to Jem, and then concealed himself under Jem's bed.

The stranger entered, and took a seat without the least ceremony.

"You gave me the correct address, I see, my lad," he said.

"Yes, sir; I always tell the truth."

"I am very glad to hear you say so. Your name is James Rawlings, I believe?"

"It is, sir," said Jem; "and your name is—"

"No matter what my name is," said the unknown gentleman, very tartly, at the same time looking very fixedly at Jem's open countenance.

"He's a rum chap," thought Jem, "he gives me a sovereign, and calls on me, and takes a seat, and stares at me, and then won't tell me his name."

"You are very much like your mother," said the stranger, in a good-natured tone of voice.

"The deuce I am," said Jem; "I can't say much about that, for I don't recollect her."

"Don't you, indeed?"

"No, I don't, sir; but, do you?"

"I?"

"Yes, sir; you said I was very much like her, and you couldn't tell that without you had seen her."

The gentleman blushed, but said something about having made a mistake; but Jem could not help noticing how often the stranger changed colour, and sighed.

"What is the earliest thing you *can* remember, my lad," asked the stranger.

"But why do you ask me so many questions?" said Jem, feeling very hot and uncomfortable.

"In order that I may do you some good, nothing more."

"Well, then," said Jem, "the first thing I can recollect was being in the workhouse school, and getting plenty of cane for lunch."

"And after that?"

"I was sent with my brother Ned to Alderman English's to be errand boy; and a nice kind old gent he were, and no mistake."

"You can read and write, I suppose?"

"I should think I could, and well. There ain't many lads as can do that better than me. My brother Ned though was a perfect demon for doing long sums. I never could abear fractions though."

"And where is your brother then, my lad?"

"He is travelling in foreign parts for the good of his health," said Jem, very impudently.

"Oh, indeed; then he is well off."

"Oh, yes, remarkable well up," said Jem. "I'm told he's got gold in bags full."

"But *you* are not particularly well off my lad."

"No, not much to boast on. But, then, you see, sir, Ned and me differ so much; he was always more clever than me, and a bit of a gentleman, besides being a trifle better looking also."

"Travelling for the good of his health, eh?"

"Yes, sir," said Jem, very proudly.

"And when do you expect his return to England?"

"I can't say, sir, exactly."

"But you hear from him sometimes?"

"Yes, but not often; he's now residing in the South Pacific, sir; and doing the grand among the natives there. I shouldn't wonder if he were to bring home with him half-a-dozen Indian wives."

"I should very much like to see your brother Edward," said the stranger.

"Anything you have to leave for him you can trust to me, sir, I can assure you," said Jem.

"I may be able to do a great deal of good for both of you, if you were to know me truly."

"I'm most happy to hear it," said Jem; "and I hope you'll begin to do it for me at once, for I'm not very grandly provided for, as you were kind enough to observe a few moments ago."

"I believe I can find out your parents, my lad; what do you think of that?"

"I should be delighted to see them. Are they rich or poor?"

"What does that matter? if they were ever so poor they would be your parents all the same, would they not?"

"True, sir."

"And you would love them exactly the same, would you not?"

"Yes, sir, I hope so; but I think I should love them a little better, you know, sir, if they were only rich people, you know."

The stranger could not but smile at Jem's honesty, and promising to call again very soon, he left a five pound note behind him, and departed.

"What a funny-looking chap he was," said Jem to Mr. Sharp; "he *did* look at me, and so hard, too. He seems to have lots of money, though, don't he, Mr. Sharp?"

"He has plenty of money, as you say, Jem, and I know him well."

"Do you, though?"

"Yes."

"And what is his name?"

"I can't recollect it just now, but he keeps a great many race horses, and is a single man; that is, he is unmarried."

"What object can he have in view to come here and talk about finding my father and mother?" said Jem. "Why didn't he tell me, at once, and let *me* ferret them out, if they are still alive?"

"I will do that for you, Jem."

"You, Mr. Sharp?"

"Yes, I will, if you will let me."

"Let you, eh? Well, that's good, and no mistake. Why you are the greatest friend I ever had in my whole life, Mr. Sharp, and if you could only find out my father and mother, and find 'em to be rich and grand people, how nice it would be, wouldn't it? And I'd make you a present of such a devil of a lot of money, and you would be rich and independent for the rest of your life; and if it should turn out that I am a lord, or a duke, or a marquis, or anything of that sort, why——"

"There, don't be a fool, Jem; I don't think anything so grand is in store for you as all that; but we'll see what can be done in the matter, and do the best we can. I'll follow this gentleman, and make his acquaintance at once."

"Do, Mr. Sharp, and pray don't lose sight of the old fellow for a moment."

"Oh! if it should turn out that I am a count or something grand, won't I cut a dash and spend the money abroad," thought Jem, and he threw himself upon his bed, and indulged in all sorts of wild dreams.

CHAPTER CXVIII.

THE PERIL OF EMMA CLARENCE—KING KATAMAR IS SEIZED BY CONSPIRATORS.

IT cannot be denied that the position of young Emma Clarence, during Lion Limb's absence from the city, was very dangerous indeed.

The people had been suffering very much from want, on account of the war, and they attributed all their present miseries to the presence of the white people among them.

Emma Clarence, however, had firm faith in Lion Limb's fortunate star, and knew very well that a long time could not elapse ere he returned victorious to the city again.

Despite the grumblings of the people, therefore, and open threats of violence, Emma went abroad among the poor, and, with her own hands, distributed food and clothing among the most needy.

When least expected, however, a conspiracy broke out against her, headed by some relations of Queen Aixa; and they met, in secret council, to resolve upon some plan to rid old Katamar of the presence of the whites.

Old Katamar himself was present at the meeting, which took place at the house of one of the chief men.

"We have suffered naught but misery and privation since this Lion Limb came among us, and are determined to rid ourselves of him," said one.

"If we kill him, all the other leaders will join you, King Katamar," said a second; "but if they do not, each one of us will select his victim, and secretly slay him."

Old Katamar shook his head and said, gravely, "Chiefs, beware of what you do."

"Wherefore, oh king, are we not resolved; are we not brave?"

"That you may be, but remember Lion Limb is also brave, and his resolution is as tough as iron."

"And even that can be bent and broken," said one, in a sneering tone.

"You cannot do so with him, I fear," said the old king, "I know him better than you."

"And do you oppose our plans?"

"I do not either oppose or assist them, but remember what our wise men have said often and often, long ago."

"And what was that, pray?"

"This young English stranger is fated to rule over us all."

"I don't believe the predictions of our wise men, then."

"Nor I."

"Nor I either," said one and another, in an angry manner.

"Did you not lose Marmi through their devilish acts; Marmi, the dearly beloved of your soul?"

"Not through them," said Katamar, "it was all the hellish work of the snake charmer."

"Did not Yokee fall a victim to their revenge?"

"No, it was through his own fault he died."

"Did not Queen Aixa do all that a young queen should do to stop their greed and ambition?"

"Aixa was a snake in the grass," said old Katamar, "and she has got her reward."

"If these white people had never come among us, we should have been happy," said several.

"I brought them here as friends," said Katamar; "they have behaved themselves wise and well, I think, and if misfortunes have fallen upon us of late, it is not so much their fault as that of the bloodthirsty Mungo, who seeks to rule both us and Lion Limb. Mungo is a barbarous villain; wherever he goes his track is marked with innocent blood, and it is to save us from his iron and abominable rule, that Lion Limb is now fighting."

"It is not."

"He wants to rule and govern us like slaves, or why did Lion Limb leave his own island?"

"To bring to us the works of civilization and peace. Could we plough, or sow, or reap, as now we can, until he taught us how?"

Murmurs were audible among the conspirators.

"Could we march and fight then as well as now, until he taught us?"

"Yes."

"Of course we could."

"No, it is false; Lion Limb endeavoured to instruct us in all things that were good or useful, but it is not because calamities have fallen upon us that we should lay all the blame on him. As long as the buccaneers, with Mungo at their head, have power to do mischief on sea or land, so long may we stand in fear of becoming slaves for ever."

"Then if this Lion Limb wished to cement a closer union with us, why did he not do so by giving us direct and honest proof by marrying Queen Aixa?"

"Quite true," said another, "after you, King Katamar, there is not a more powerful person on these islands than she is."

"She is more beautiful than the English girl," said one.

"Yes, and taller."

"And can ride and swim and hunt better than the pale-faced Emma Clarence," said one and another.

"If Lion Limb chooses to set his heart upon a girl of his own country, he is the best judge as to its propriety," said old Katamar, rising; "all of us would do the same."

"You are going, then, King Katamar?"

"I am."

"We invited you to this meeting, to inform you of our good intentions towards you."

"And of your secret resolves against Lion Limb, also, I suppose?"

"We did. And do you not approve of our motives?"

"I do not. Lion Limb has proved a true friend to us all, and I will not be the man to assist in any plot against him."

"Ha! ha!" said the conspirators, rising in a body. "You are an enemy to our schemes, then?"

"I am."

"And perhaps will warn this Lion Limb of his danger?"

"I shall act the part of a true friend to him."

"And disclose our plot?"

"Yes."

"Seize him! seize him!" shouted several of the chiefs in an angry manner, brandishing their weapons.

"He must not go forth hence alive."

"Gag him!"

"Cut his throat!"

"He is an enemy to us and not fit to be king."

"Down with Katamar!"

"Long live Aixa, queen of the Pearl Islands."

"Hold!" said old Katamar, in a voice that astonished the nerves of all. "How dare you lay hands on your king?"

For a moment there was an ominous pause, when old King Katamar advanced in the midst of the conspirators, and said, slowly and calmly,

"If my life would give peace and plenty to our island home, I would sacrifice it upon the spot; but, then, whom would you have to succeed me?"

"Queen Aixa," said many.

"Long live the queen of the Pearl Island!" was the echo of all.

"And what is she, indeed!" said Katamar, contemptuously "It is always our custom to have a king, not a woman to rule."

"But we'll have Queen Aixa, for she is the sworn enemy of our deadliest foe, Lion Limb."

"And you wish me to resign, then?" said Katamar.

"We do, we do."

"Know, then, that Katamar, though old and feeble, is a king yet, and will never surrender his rights."

"Seize him!"

"Secure him!"

"The first man that approaches, dies," said the old man, brandishing his sword.

"On to him, I say!" shouted a leader of the party. "He is old and silly."

But, true to his word, the first man that approached his king, was struck to the earth by old Katamar, and lay weltering in his blood.

Next instant, however, old Katamar was seized and borne away to a strong and heavily barred cell near by, and there confined.

Having done this, they went into the city again in a body, and paraded the streets, calling upon the people to rise in rebellion, and drive from among them the white faces who were ruling them.

In a short time the whole city was in dire commotion.

Bands of armed men, and women also, congregated at the public buildings, and shouted out loudly against Lion Limb and his followers.

Others sang songs, which aroused the worst passions of the people.

"To the palace."

"Death to Lion Limb!"

" Death to Emma Clarence !"

" Long live King Katamar."

" Down with Katamar."

" Long live Queen Aixa."

These, and such like, were the cries that resounded on all sides about the palace, and Emma Clarence, hearing them, became alarmed.

There were but few faithful attendants around her, and she trembled for their safety as much as her own.

" What had we better do?" asked Emma.

" Bar and barricade all the gates and doors," said one.

" Oh ! would that Lion Limb would come speedily !" sighed Emma. " They will tear us all in pieces."

As they stood at a lofty window, looking out into the neighbouring streets, a strange and startling sight caught Emma's eyes.

A vast concourse of people were marching in procession, singing and shouting in a lusty manner.

In the midst of them, and borne on a sort of throne, sat Queen Aixa, looking thin, haggard, and pale.

When the procession reached the gates of the palace, Queen Aixa waved her hand, and addressed the crowd around her.

She told them how she had fled to Mungo's camp, and been taken prisoner there by Lion Limb, who had sent her back to the city to become the servant and slave of Emma Clarence, the pale-faced English girl.

Loud groans greeted this part of the speech, and weapons were brandished on all sides in a very threatening manner.

But when Queen Aixa explained how she had been rescued by the populace from Lion Limb's escort, and was proclaimed queen loudly on all sides, the shouts and cries of the people became deafening.

" What shall we do ?" shouted the surging multitude.

" Do !" said Aixa, with flashing eyes. " Do you not see this palace ? And know you not that it contains in safe keeping one whom I mortally detest ?"

" Yes, we do !"

" Then at once, and now, all of you assail it. Leave not one stone standing upon another ; but bring to me, safe and untouched, Emma Clarence. I will have her tortured in the public square before all my people. "

" But if Lion Limb should return ?" said one.

" I have little fear of that," said Aixa. " He can never conquer Mungo, for the buccaneers and our Indians outnumber the men of Lion Limb as five to one."

This news seemed to electrify all who heard it.

At once, then, and according to her orders, parties of men with crowbars and axes began hammering away at the palace gates ; but so well were they guarded by Emma's few valiant defenders, that dozens of the Indians were killed or wounded.

All such modes of attack seemed hopeless to Queen Aixa, who called away her followers from the gates, and ordered a different plan of action.

" Burn them out !" said the savage queen. " Collect all the wood and stubble that you can ; throw it against the gates, and woodwork. The smoke and fire will soon cause the inmates to yield."

With loud shouts the frantic citizens gathered together all the combustible matter they could, and flung it in huge heaps against the gates and prominent woodwork of the palace.

Aixa herself applied the torch to it, and soon the smoke and flames arose on high.

But the wind which before had been blowing towards the palace, now suddenly changed, and with great violence blew right in a contrary direction.

Aixa said nothing ; but bit her lips in anger and vexation.

" Even the winds," she said, " fight for them. How is it that all and everything tends to the favour and success of these victorious whites ?"

Nothing daunted, but even more aggravated than before, Aixa mounted a pony of great spirit and speed, and galloped far and near among the citizens.

" Gather all the burnable stuff you can, bring it immediately to the palace, and surround the building with it."

This was done with great alacrity by the people, and in a few hours the palace was completely surrounded with huge heaps of wood, straw, stubble, and other inflammable materials.

Emma, from above, in a high story of the palace, perceived all these preparations and considered that now nought could save her.

" We shall be suffocated with smoke," she said, " the furious people are bent upon killing us ; see on all sides how they are swarming like bees, and gathering faggots of all sizes. Oh, would that Lion Limb were here, or that we knew the worst, for I fear that he and his followers are all killed, and that no hopes now remain for us.

" Cheer up, my lady," said one, " we have seen trials before."

" True, we have, and many, but none that seemed more certain to end in death than this."

" I have firm hopes in Lion Limb," said another.

" If any danger had happened to him, some of his followers would have long since warned us of it."

" Have you a man still in the tower watching the plains outside the walls ?"

" We have, my lady ; we have kept watch and watch both night and day for more than eighty hours."

" And still no sign of Lion Limb's return ?"

" No, my lady ; all that the watchers have been able to make out was a rolling mass of smoke, and great clouds of dust rising and falling, yesterday."

" And what caused all these signs then ?"

" A battle, of course, my lady."

" Then perhaps Lion Limb is killed and his followers all routed, or he would have sent messengers to say to the contrary."

At this moment, and while Queen Aixa and her people were as busy as ants around the palace walls, the look-out man on the palace towers came down and reported what he had seen of late.

" What is it ?" asked Emma Clarence, all impatience, " have you brought good news? Is Lion Limb returning ?"

" I cannot tell that, my lady ; but all the morning with this telescope I have observed a distant battle progressing, but which side is successful I cannot say."

" What were the general appearances, then ?"

" It seemed as if two bodies of men were pursuing a third, and dealing out slaughter to the fleeing body, which was all haste on its way towards the sea coast."

" Those that were fleeing, how numerous were they ?"

" Not so great in numbers as those pursuing."

" Then I fear," said Emma Clarence, " that all is lost."

"How, my lady?"

"It is well known that Lion Limb's followers were far less in number than those of Mungo," said Emma, "and no doubt the buccaneers and their swarms of Indian followers have divided into two bodies, and proved too powerful for Lion Limb, who for safety is retreating in all haste to the sea coast and its rocky defences."

This reasoning could not be contradicted by any one there present, for they were, of course, unaware of old Martin's joining his forces to those of Lion Limb.

Emma Clarence sat as if in despair.

Her features were like marble and tears streamed from her eyes.

At this moment loud and terrible shouts assailed her ears.

Queen Aixa at that moment had applied the torch to the vast bulk of rubbish collected outside.

The smoke now slowly rose on all sides, and curled aloft round the palace towers.

Its density was almost smothering.

"We cannot resist the fire," said one.

"What had we better do?"

"I don't know, but if the young lady's white guards have made up their minds to die by her side, I don't see why her Indian friends should."

"I didn't bargain to be burnt alive," said one.

"Nor I either," growled another.

"Have you not been well paid?" asked Emma of the discontents.

"We have, my lady."

"You never wore such good garments before."

"No, that's true enough."

"Neither were any of you ever fed and provided for so well."

"We confess all, my lady, but——"

"But what?"

"We didn't agree to be burnt up like chips, you know."

"But you were engaged to protect me."

"So we were, my lady, and so we would, as long as possible ; but we don't agree to be burnt alive, you know."

"Do you hear the complainings of these men?" said Emma to one of Lion Limb's men.

"I do, my lady ; and they are cowards, every one. You, and all of us, have stinted ourselves, so that these natives should not want and complain, and now that they are threatened with a little extra danger, they show the white feather."

"What had I better do?" asked Emma.

"Do, my lady," said the youth, Roderick, "why, give us leave to show these cowards what Lion Limb's men think of them."

"How do you mean, Roderick?"

"Why pitch them from the battlements into the flames below."

"No, that must not be," said Emma. "Give them their choice to go or stay ; but as for myself," said Emma, "I have resolved what to do."

"And that is, my lady——"

"To die, rather than surrender, Roderick."

"Spoken like a true Englishwoman, my lady, and long life to you—such a woman deserves to be a queen."

"But it is not because I have resolved so to do myself, that I would wish *you*, Roderick, and your friends to follow my example."

"And do you think, my lady, that we are so weakminded and chicken-hearted as to show the white flag for ourselves? Oh! no, the followers of Lion Limb have braved too many dangers, and faced death too often to fear it now. We, like you, have resolved to die and perish in the flames rather than haul down the good old English flag that waves from the tower."

"How many native guards are there in this tower, Roderick?"

"Over fifty, my lady."

"And are they all discontented?"

"They are, every man-jack of them, and if it were not that we whites are too powerful and better armed than they are, they would endeavour to overpower us, and deliver the place up to our enemies."

"Then what do you advise, Roderick?"

"That we descend the tower with a dozen of them at a time, disarm them, show a white flag to our assailants, and let the natives go."

"Do so, then."

"I will, my lady."

Roderick and his companions gathered the natives together, and disarmed them.

One of the gates of the tower was opened, and a white flag was waved.

At the sight of this Queen Aixa and her friends were jubilant.

"The fire must have begun to reach them," said one.

"They don't care to be suffocated or roasted alive," another remarked.

"Oh! won't Queen Aixa make an example of that English girl," said a woman to her neighbour.

"What will be her punishment, I wonder?"

"Oh! as Queen Aixa hates her so much, no doubt the English girl will be cast among the wild animals, and be made sport of for the people."

"Or else impaled," said the other.

In truth, Queen Aixa herself, when she perceived the white flag flying, made sure that Emma Clarence and the white guards had surrendered, and was planning in her own mind some scheme for publicly disgracing Emma, and afterwards putting her to dreadful tortures and death.

But when it was ascertained beyond a doubt that it was *not* Emma Clarence, or any of Lion Limb's men who were desirous of making sure of their lives by surrender, but a band of renegades, her rage was beyond all control.

"Bring the prisoners to me," she said, in a voice tremulous from rage ; "bring them to my presence, I say, on the instant."

The prisoners were accordingly brought before her, to whom she spoke in this wise—

"Dastards, that you are! did the fumes of the smoke and the heat of crackling flames drive you from your hiding place, like rats?"

These words alarmed the poor prisoners who stood trembling before her.

"May it please your goodness, Queen Aixa, to hear us?" said one, in a faint and suppliant voice.

"Hear you, traitors! and for what reasons should I listen to you, knaves that you are?"

"We are good citizens, and faithful to King Katamar, Queen Aixa."

"And for that reason you are my enemies, slaves!"

The prisoner could not understand the great change that had taken place, but he said very meekly :—

"Then, in truth, good queen, if King Katamar is *your* enemy, he is also ours."

"Silence! fools that you are."

"We were sent into the palace by the king's orders, good queen."

"And leave it at the English girl's command, I suppose?"

"No, in truth, we left it of our own free will."

"Then the white faces have resolved to die ?" said Queen Aixa.

"They have, good queen ; and it was only to save ourselves from certain destruction that we turned against the white people."

"But you shall not escape your just deserts, for all that," said Aixa. "Do not think I or my faithful followers can or will allow ourselves to be imposed upon by your cringing and whining. No ! you shall suffer for your treachery upon the spot, and before the eyes of your former mistress—the white-faced girl."

"Ho, there !" said Aixa, "seize these men; guards, surround them, and if they attempt to stir one yard, kill them on the spot !"

"Do not kill them as yet, good Queen Aixa," said one of her councillors, "these fellows may know much of what is going on and being done by Lion Limb."

"True," said Aixa, "I had forgotten that ; let the chief man among them approach, I will question him."

The one who had been the chief speaker now came forward, trembling in every limb.

"Answer the questions I shall put to you, knave," said Aixa ; "your life may depend upon your truth !"

"Oh ! a thousand thanks, most merciful queen," said the Indian, cringing and bowing ; "only grant me my precious life, and——"

"Your precious life, eh ? What do you mean ?"

"I only mean, good queen, that it is precious ; very, very, very precious to me, if not to anybody else."

"Then answer me. How many whites are there in the towers of the palace ?"

"Not more than a dozen."

"Not more than that ?" said Aixa, in surprise.

"Not one more, believe, good queen."

"And so a dozen men defy all our Indian forces ?"

"Aye, in good truth, they do, Queen Aixa ; and they have bolted and barred themselves in so strongly, that I don't think the very devil himself could get them out, or kill them, so desperate and determined are they."

"Who commands them ?"

"Emma Clarence, good queen."

"I did not think she was so brave," mused Aixa, half aloud, with a curling lip.

"Oh ! yes, she is, good queen."

"But who commands under her, then ?"

"There is one they call Roderick, a perfect fire-eater."

"Young or old ?"

"Young, very young indeed, only a full grown boy, as one might say."

"Is he vigilant ?"

"Yes, uncomfortably so ; he is always walking about from place to place like a noiseless shadow ; and he never seems to have or to require any sleep like we common mortals. I know that, to my cost."

"How ; what do you mean ?"

"I mean, good queen, that if this Roderick ever caught any of us guards dozing on our posts, we get more kicks and cuffs than was at all pleasant I can assure you."

"Serve you right," said Aixa, "and if Katamar or Mungo had so trained their soldiers Lion Limb would not now have the proud title of king of all the islands."

After a pause she asked—

"Is the palace well stored with food ?"

"It is not."

"How many days could they defend themselves, think you ?"

"I can form no idea, good Queen Aixa, for those white people don't eat near as much as we Indians, and I have no doubt they can exist a long time on what they have got already in the tower."

"But Katamar built a subterranean passage to that tower ; are the white defenders aware of that fact ?"

"I think not."

"But are you not sure ?"

"I am not. I never heard them even hint at such a thing."

"Then it may be well for us to find out the outlet, or they might escape me after all."

Not being able to get any information from the prisoners, Queen Aixa ordered that they should be publicly scourged in sight of those defending the palace tower.

This was done ; and the shouts and cries of the victims rent the air.

They begged for mercy.

But there was no mercy in Aixa's breast.

The only thing she thought or cared about was to wreak her vengeance on Emma Clarence, and all who might aid or sympathize with her.

"Bring more wood, pile up the fires," she said, jestingly, "we will soon compel these English dogs, to surrender."

At this time the tower of the palace had caught fire in several places, and the smoke was most dense and almost suffocating.

Roderick was here, there and everywhere.

He was just as cheerful as though nothing had happened or could happen to dampen his spirits.

Emma Clarence and every living soul had resolved to die, rather than fall into the remorseless hands of Aixa or her frantic followers.

Had Emma or Roderick known anything of the secret subterranean passage spoken of by Aixa, they would have availed themselves of it, for there was scarcely enough air to breathe.

In many places the towers were crackling, and, the wind blowing hard, there could not be a practicable doubt in the minds of any one but that death or surrender must be the one or other alternative.

The look-out on the tower could not see distinctly enough to report anything he might perceive, and the brave garrison had now almost given up all hope.

Yet it must not be supposed for a moment that either Roderick or his companions remained idle.

Not by any means.

The arms of the Indians were now of great use to the little garrison.

"Save your powder and shot, my lads," said Roderick, "the Indian cowards have left their bows behind, and hundreds of well-feathered arrows. Let us use them, then, each man take good aim, and he that hits Queen Aixa yonder, as she sits on her pony cheering on the fanatics, shall be commander of all the rest."

"Well said, Roderick," several replied.

And forthwith the little garrison made good use of the bows and arrows taken from the Indians.

They did not fire away fast and furious, but took deliberate aim.

"Here goes for a shot at Queen Aixa," said Roderick, drawing his bow.

At the same instant, he took deliberate aim ; the arrow flew threw the air, and lodged in the pummel of Aixa's saddle.

The queen was much surprised and annoyed.

She was not, by any means, pleased at the "close shave," as Roderick called it, and, therefore, moved to a spot that was more protected.

She was excessively angry at the danger she had run, and directed her howling followers to keep up a shower of arrows on all the windows.

This they did, but without effecting any harm.

Roderick was in his glory, and never ceased firing while he had a single arrow to shoot.

"I'll die game, lads," said he; "give us some more arrows some of you. I have knocked over a dozen or two of the Indian devils already."

And so he had.

But those he commanded had also done much execution, until, at last, the excited multitude below outside were only too glad to get away from the immediate vicinity of the palace towers; and, therefore, the fires were unattended, and doomed to expire for want of sufficient fuel.

Those parts of the tower which had already caught the flames were the especial object of Roderick's attention.

He, and others, cut away most of the burning timber, which fell with a crash on the heads of those below; and, although flames were burning here and there, there was no immediate danger from the fire so much as from dense volumes of smoke.

"They haven't done such a great amount of harm after all," thought Roderick, "the towers are safe yet awhile; and if we could only get some assistance—"

"Fly to your arms and defend yourselves, men," said one, rushing up stairs. "The enemy, by some means, have got into the palace and are upon us."

The excitement, at that moment, was intense.

CHAPTER CXIX.

THE DOOMED CITY.

RODERICK called together his men on the instant, and divided them into small parties.

"Do you," he said, "defend yonder stairs; and let no one approach."

To another small party he said—

"Follow me! It must be some of Queen Aixa's cut-throats approaching; we will defend these stairs to the very last. Let no man flinch on peril of his life.

Emma Clarence seemed to be suddenly aroused.

The girl, who a few moments before had been pale and sad and melancholy, now felt the flush of pride upon her cheek.

"And shall I," she said, "remain an idle witness of this encounter when you are fighting in my cause?"

"Nay, lady, be calm and quiet," said Roderick. "It is not meet that one so fair should stain her hands in blood."

"Nay, say not so," Emma replied; "if I can but save the life of one of you. Why, then, shall I not arm myself and fight like the rest?"

"But you must not put yourself into danger, lady."

"Nay, but I will, Roderick," was Emma's calm reply. "I *will* fight with the rest, and fall like a true English girl."

So saying, Emma Clarence armed herself with two pistols and a light sword, and took her station at the head of the stairs.

"Who comes there?" asked Roderick, in a stern tone, as he listened to the approach of distant footsteps.

"Friends!" was the hoarse reply.

"Friends to whom?"

"To those in possession of the tower."

"That is not plain enough, whoever you are," said Roderick, cocking a pistol.

"Speak in plainer terms," said another of the defenders, "or we fire."

"Who are you, then?" said the voice below.

"English."

"So are we."

"But do you belong to Mungo's gang, or——"

"Out upon the butcher, Mungo!" said the voice, still advancing.

"Who are you, then, for the last time?" said Roderick.

"One of Lion Limb's men."

"Impossible!"

"Nay, it isn't; but quite the contrary."

"How many are there of you?"

"Only a dozen or two just in this spot; but let us come up and I will explain."

"Only admit one at a time," said Emma; "for after all they may be impostors."

"Just so," said Roderick; "but they can't catch old birds with chaff, you know."

"Come up, you who lead the party," said one of the defenders.

And after a few moments of grumbling and delay, the rough head of one of Lion Limb's men appeared.

When he had entered the apartment, he looked around in astonishment at the scene of dirt and wreck which was visible on all sides.

"Why, I should hardly have known you," said he, "if it were not for your pretty speech, Miss Emma."

And on the instant the defenders knew that he was one of Lion Limb's men.

"Let the other lads come up," said he, "they are well nigh dead beat, for they have been fighting and marching for two days and nights."

"And is Lion Limb successful?" asked Emma.

"Yes, as he always is, my lady."

"And not hurt?"

"Not seriously; but——"

"But what?"

"He has got an ugly scratch or two, and so have the majority of us."

"And Mungo," asked Roderick, "what of him?"

"He was deserted by the Indians directly they found out that old Martin and his islanders had joined us."

"And what has become of Mungo, then?"

"He was chased very hard by Lion Limb and old Martin towards the sea coast; but Lion Limb, fearing for your safety, Miss, left off the pursuit, and entrusted it to old Martin."

"Then Lion Limb is near at hand?"

"Yes; in fact, he is in the city."

"You do not mean that!" said Roderick, slapping his thighs in high glee.

"I do though; but you must not expect to see him for many hours yet, for he has enough to do in fighting against the rebellious rioters and quelling the disturbances caused by Queen Aixa."

"But how did you get admittance into the tower?"

"We had to fight for it."

"Yes; but where? We did not hear of any fighting."

"No, for a very good reason."

"And what was that, pray?"

"We were fighting underground."

"Underground?" said all, in great surprise.

"Yes."

"You astonish us," said Roderick.

"That may be so. And it astonished me also, I can assure you, at the time."

"Explain yourself?" said Emma.

"I will, my lady. When Lion Limb and his followers saw large clouds of smoke around the towers of the palace, he guessed immediately what had happened."

"But we didn't see Lion Limb approaching," said Emma, "although we kept a good look-out."

"You could not perceive our approach for two very good reasons."

"On account of the dense smoke by which we were surrounded, and almost suffocated," said Roderick.

"That was one reason, but the real cause was that you knew not which way to look."

"How was that?"

"You see yonder wood, a good half mile away?"

"We do," said Emma.

"Well, we halted in that wood, for Lion Limb said that in the trees and shrubbery was concealed the entrance to a cave, which cave was nought else but the mouth of a subterranean passage, which led to the palace."

"You surprise us," said the defenders.

"I never heard of such a passage existing before," said Emma.

"Nor did many others, my lady."

"Well, and you of course followed Lion Limb's directions, and arrived safely here?"

"Not exactly, my lady, there were others who knew of this subterranean passage as well as Lion Limb."

"Queen Aixa, perhaps?"

"Yes, Queen Aixa must have known it, for old Katamar knew it; and as we groped our way along in the dark and narrow windings of that passage, we had to encounter great danger, for Queen Aixa had sent men in advance of us to get into and seize the palace in the same way."

"Then you had to fight your way?"

"We had, and desperately also."

"How many were there opposed to your small band?"

"We slew at least a dozen, and many others fled."

"The contest must have been desperate indeed," said Miss Emma.

"It was, indeed, my lady, for life or death depended upon it; we knew that you were beseiged on all sides, and that if we faltered in our onslaught Aixa's men would mercilessly slay us. For this and other reasons our men fought like demons, and we made our way over the dead bodies of our foes."

Such a sudden and unexpected deliverance filled the heart of Emma Clarence and her friends with joy.

But they were clamorous in their exclamations of delight, and desired to see Lion Limb above all things.

From the windows of the palace tower, however, Emma could perceive a great commotion in progress among the citizens.

A great fight was going on among the citizens. Some shouted loudly,

"Long live Katama!"

Others, on the other hand, screamed wildly for Queen Aixa.

But a strong and unmistakable English shout was heard again and again, which completely drowned all the others, however loud they might be.

"Hurrah for Lion Limb!"

"Lion Limb for ever!"

"Down with Queen Aixa!"

"Death to Mungo!"

"Long life to old Martin and his men!"

Such were the cries of the English band as they dashed among the rioters and beat them back with the blunt edges of their swords, and so dispersed them, and cleared the streets once again.

It must be confessed that the people were thunderstruck at the sudden re-appearance of Lion Limb among them.

They had never expected to see him alive again.

Had not Queen Aixa sworn to them that he had been killed by Mungo, and all the English band slain or scattered?

Yes; but these reports were not true, as the Indians found out too late.

When, therefore, Lion Limb had restored something like order among the citizens, he seized several of the ringleaders of the rebellion and questioned them.

"Tell me," said Lion Limb, in a very angry manner, "what has become of Queen Aixa?"

"We know not," was the sullen answer.

"But a short time ago she was leading on the mob against me and my friends, but now she has disappeared like a shadow, and cannot be found anywhere; tell me, then, for you know where she is; tell me, I say, upon your peril?"

"We know not," was the sullen answer repeated.

"What has become of old King Katamar, then?" asked Lion Limb. "Surely you have not slain him?"

"We know not, valiant warrior, what has become either of Queen Aixa or Katamar."

"You simply call him now, Katamar; why not King Katamar?"

"Because he is no longer our king; he has been deposed, and Queen Aixa reigns instead."

"Villain, they have killed my old friend, without a doubt, but I will make them suffer for it yet!"

"Hark, ye," said Lion Limb, sternly, and with a face flushed with anger, "during my absence from the city much mischief has been done to myself and friends; I know that old Katamar would not desert me, and you, I am sure, have done him injustice, injury, and perhaps dishonour."

"We know nothing of him, great Lion Limb."

"Liars!" said Lion Limb, in a great rage, "do not stand there and unblushingly confront me with base falsehoods, but listen to these my last words. You must go hence, leaving hostages for your good behaviour, and without you conduct hither into my presence, before sunset, King Katamar and Queen Aixa, your heads shall be given to the headsman without delay!"

So speaking, Lion Limb ordered several of the chief men to remain as hostages; but the others left his presence vowing deadly vengeance and shaking with rage.

Lion Limb then ordered guards to patrol the city in various parts, to secure any who might be plundering, or filled with vengeance against the weak and inoffensive.

For during the riot which had taken place, gangs of desperate plunderers roamed the city, and did all manner of mischief.

Many of these scoundrels were instantly arrested by Lion Limb's desire, and whipped publicly in the market place.

This proceeding had wonderful effect upon the great mass of the people, who returned to their homes and bolted their doors.

LION LIMB

THE BOY KING
OF THE SOUTH SEA ISLANDS.

IN DANGER.

The city now being quiet, Lion Limb camped his followers in the principal squares, and repaired to the palace, where he met and tenderly embraced Emma, who, with tears in her eyes, fell upon his neck, and kissed him as her betrothed.

But there was much to be done on every side, Lion Limb knew very well; and, therefore, he lost no time in preparing many things that were absolutely necessary.

Messengers were now hourly arriving from old Governor Martin, who was still pursuing Mungo to his ships.

The news they brought was sometimes good, and sometimes otherwise.

No. 45.

"How far has the brave old governor driven them now?" asked Lion Limb.

"I should think ten miles or more," Captain Lion Limb.

"Do they stand and fight, or run?"

"They fight hard and desperately enough sometimes, captain, when the nature of the ground gives them any sort of shelter."

"So I supposed they would."

"Had you remained with us, captain, we should have completely surrounded the villains by this time, and taken all of them prisoners."

"I doubt now, though," answered Lion Limb, "whether old Martin will be able to do that alone, for when the buccaneers reach the rocks and gullies and shelving shingle, they will make a desperate resistance."

"Old Governor Martin expects that, captain, and has sent round a messenger to his own vessels to make sail at once, and bear down on the pirates of the Blue Rocks.

"If the attack by sea does not take place in a few days, I myself will go down to the shore, and take part in it; but as you see, and will explain to old Martin when you return, I have so much to do to repress rebellion here, that I cannot spare half an hour to write to him."

But while Lion Limb was speaking to old Martin's messenger, a terrific explosion was heard near by.

The palace and its tall towers shook again.

"What can be the meaning of this?" thought Lion Limb. "Surely they have not undermined the palace."

As he looked out at one of the windows, the air was filled with dust and fragments of building materials, such as beams and stones, flying through the air in all directions.

People were flying hither and thither, out of the way of danger, and the greatest alarm was exhibited by all, both Indians and whites.

But scarcely had one explosion ceased than another followed, and much more terrible than the first.

"It is an earthquake!" said Lion Limb, in great alarm.

He gave orders to all near by to quit the palace on the instant.

"Leave it, I say, and run into the open square; if another shock takes place the palace will smother us in its ruins."

The greatest confusion now raged on all sides, and it was just as much as Lion Limb could do to keep his men together.

"This is a curse fallen upon us!" cried the Indians, "because me have allowed the Palefaces to rule over us; seize your arms, citizens, and take vengeance upon them."

These cries were repeated frequently and loudly; and people ran frantically to and fro.

But, at that moment, a dead calm seemed to fall upon all surrounding nature.

It even affected animals as well as men; but when least expected a third noise, even louder and longer than the preceding one.

The earth trembled—houses tottered and fell—and, suddenly, a horrible noise was heard underfoot, and next instant the street yawned wide open and swallowed up half-a-dozen houses, inhabitants and all!

The terror of all was great.

The clouds became dull, heavy, and black.

Thunder rolled, and lightning flashed.

All portended a terrible disaster which would fall upon Lion Limb, equally with the rest; a disaster that could not be for many moments delayed.

CHAPTER CXX.

THE UNEXPECTED ARRIVAL OF AN ENGLISH MAN-OF-WAR—BOTELLO, THE MAGICIAN, FIRST DISCOVERS IT—THE SHIP IS SEIZED BY MUNGO—THE WONDERS WHICH MUNGO SEES—HIS REVENGE AND VENGEANCE.

BUT while Lion Limb in the city was endeavouring to fight down the rebels under Queen Aixa, there was an old and faithful follower in his train, who was silent and sulky, and would not for many days go forth at all, but sat in his lonely chamber, communing with the stars, and filled with divination and magic.

This was Botello, the magician.

He was a true native, and his pretended power had always exercised great influence on old Katamar previous to Lion Limb's arrival, but since then he had been discarded by most, if not all, of his former patrons.

"Why sit there, Botello?" asked one. "Why not take part in the stirring events taking place all around us?"

"I fear Mungo, the African chief of the buccaneers," said the old magician.

"Fear him, and why pray? Has he not been defeated by Lion Limb?"

"True, but yet I fear him; he is still on our island shore, and strongly entrenched."

"But Governor Martin and his followers are on his track."

"What of that? Is there not a strange vessel of war approaching our coast, a vessel big and strong and fleet? Who can tell that it does not bring men and munitions of war for Mungo?"

"You are dreaming, Botello."

"I am not; but you shall know within a week whether what I say is truth or not."

"It may be for Lion Limb after all."

"Then why should it cast anchor near to where Mungo's camps are placed?"

"Nonsense, Botello, you are dreaming, I say; if any such ship had been seen off our coast we should have long since learned all particulars from some of old Governor Martin's scouts. Botello, thou art but a silly dreamer!"

*   *   *   *   *

Yet four days after this conversation Botello left the city unawares, and travelled through unknown paths towards the encampments of Mungo, and hid himself in the forest.

Morning, noon, and night he watched the distant ocean in hopes of discovering some indications of the approach of the strange vessel which had haunted him in his dreams.

But still the vessel came not.

On the sixth day of his watching, however, and very early in the morning, Botello was delighted to discover a strange and handsome vessel not far off the land.

He immediately launched his trusty canoe, and put off to communicate with the strange craft. (*See Cut.*)

The distance was considerable, and ere Botello had travelled many yards, he was surprised to see several men put off from the ship in a small boat and approach the land.

One of them seemed to be quite a youth, and was dressed in the garb of an officer.

The others were evidently common seamen.

They had not reached land, however, before the boat struck upon a rock and was capsized.

What became of the men Botello knew not, but he waited and watched.

During the day several other boats went to look for their lost companions, but not finding them, they returned to their ships, which immediately set sail to some safer harbour in another part of the island.

"It was an English ship," thought Botello, "for their colours are the same as those of Lion Limb and old Governor Martin. I wonder though if those persons are really drowned, or whether they have fallen into the hands of the cruel buccaneers, who must be somewhere hereabouts encamped in one or other of the Indian villages."

He made up his mind not to rest or be satisfied until he had really discovered the fate of the strange white men, and that this might be effected properly he dragged his canoe upon the shore and wandered through the forests towards a distant village where he thought Mungo was.

Towards night he approached the village cautiously, and made his observations.

Every approach to it seemed to be guarded well, and banks of earth were thrown up here and there, to strengthen the position.

The village had formerly owned allegiance to King Katamar, but Mungo subdued it and seemed loth to leave it.

Zempoala, for such was its name, had been founded by an ancient Indian prince of that name, and from him Queen Aixa claimed descent.

It was laid out with a few streets, the houses were for the most part made of stone, and were decorated with gardens and the like.

An ancient Indian palace, with towers and huge wooden gates, was in the centre of the main square, and served as a sort of citadel for Mungo, who amused himself every night with dancing and feasting among the riotous natives.

All this Botello found out, if, indeed, he knew it not before, and the magician crept closer and closer to the main square, where carousing and rioting were at their height as usual, for Mungo and his men seemed not to fear an approach from old Governor Martin, for a dangerous and well-guarded river, called the River of Canoes, lay between the two armies.

But Mungo little dreamed that while Botello was absent, Lion Limb had joined old Martin.

Botello, having made all his observations, was about to depart when he was suddenly seized, blindfolded, and gagged.

He was a prisoner!

*   *   *   *   *

Midshipman Amador surveyed the prisoner, though somewhat indifferently.

He was, in figure and age, very much such a man as Baltasar, but in other respects very dissimilar.

His face was wan, and even cadaverous; but this might have been the effect of the blows he had received from the dying soldier, as was made probable by the presence of several spots of blood encrusted over his visage.

His cheeks were broad, and the bones prominent; his eyes very hollow, and expressive of a wild solemnity, mingled with cunning; his beard long and bushy, and only slightly grizzled, and a rugged moustache hung over his lips so as almost to conceal them.

His apparel of black cloth,—none of the freshest, the principal garment of which was a long loose doublet, under which was buckled an iron breastplate—his only armour; for, instead of a morion, he wore a cloth hat of capacious brim, stuck round with the feathers of divers birds, as well as several medals of the saints, rudely executed in silver.

Besides these fantastic decorations, he had suspended to his neck several instruments of the Cabala—a pentacle of silver, and charms and talismans written over with mystical characters, as well as a little leathern pouch filled with various dried herbs and roots.

This mystagogue, an agent of no little importance among many of the scenes of the Conquest, was led into the presence of the general, and approached him without betraying any signs of fear or embarrassment; nor, on the other hand, did he manifest anything like audacity or presumption; but, lifting his eyes to the visage of the Biscayan, he gazed upon him with a silent and grave earnestness, that seemed somewhat to disconcert the leader.

"Sirrah sorcerer," said he, "since the devil has deserted you at last, call up what spirits you can muster, and find me why I shall not hang you for a spy, early in the morning."

The sorcerer muttered in the gibberish of his art, with a voice of sepulchral hollowness, and with a countenance gleaming with indignation and enthusiasm,

"I defy the devil, and am the servant of his enemy; and in the land of devils, of Apollyon in the air, Beelzebub on the earth, and Satan in men's hearts, I forswear and defy, contemn and denounce them; and I pray for and foresee the day when they shall tumble from the high places!"

"All this thou mayst do, and all this thou mayst foresee," said Mungo; "but nevertheless thy wisdom will be more apparent to employ itself a little in the investigation of thine own fate, which, I promise thee, is approaching to a crisis."

"I have read it in the stars, I have seen it in the smoke of waters, and of blessed herbs, and I have heard it from the lips of dead men and the tongues of dreams," cried the professor of the occult sciences, with much emphasis. "But what is the fate of Botello, the swordsman, to that of the leaders of men, the conquerors of kings and great nations? I have read mine own destinies; but why shouldst thou trifle the time to know them, when I can show thee the higher mysteries of thine own?"

"Cans't thou do it? By my faith then, I will have thee speak them very soon," said Mungo. "But first let me know what wert thou doing when thou wert found prowling this morning so near to my camp?"

"Gathering the herbs for the suffumigation which shall tell me in what part of the world thou shalt lay thy bones," said the magician, solemnly. "The moon, in the house Alchil, showed me many things, but not all; a thick smoke came over the crystal, and I saw not what I wanted; I slept with a skull on my bosom, but it breathed nothing but clouds. Wherefore I knew, it should be only when the wolf spoke to the vulture, and the vulture to the red star, that the angel should unlock the lips of destiny, and lead me whither I longed to follow."

"I am ever bound to thee," said Mungo, with a manner in which an attempt at mockery was mingled with a natural touch of superstition, "for the extreme interest thou seemest to cherish in my fate; and again I say to thee, I will immediately converse with thee on that subject. But at present, I warn thee, it will be but wisdom to confine thy rhapsodies within the limits of answers to such interrogatories as I shall propose thee. Where lies thy master, the outcast and arch-rebel, my enemy, Lion Limb?"

"My master is in heaven!" said Botello, with a devout and lofty earnestness, "and there is no outcast and rebel but he that dwelleth in the pit, under the foot of Michael; and he is the enemy?"

"Sirrah! I speak to thee of the knave Lion Limb," cried Mungo, angrily. "When wert thou last at his side? and where?"

"At midnight, on the river, where he has rested, as thou knowest, for a night and a day."

"Ah!" said he, fiercely; "within a league of my head-quarters, whither my clemency has suffered him to come.'

"Whither God and his good star have drawn him," said the magician.

"And whence I will drive him to the rocks of the mountains, or the mangroves of the beach, ere thou art cured of thy wounds!"

"Lo! my wounds are healed!" said Botello; "the hand that inflicted them is stiff and cold; and yet my captain, whose fate I have seen and spoken, even from the glory of noon to the long and sorrowful shadows of the evening, marshals his band within the sound of thy matin bell; and woe be to his foeman, when he is nearer or further."

"Prattling fool," said Mungo, "if thou hadst looked to the bright moon to-night, thou wouldst have seen how soon the cotton-trees of the river should be strung with thy leader and companions, and with thyself, as a liar and an impostor, in their midst!"

"I looked," said the magician, tranquilly, "and saw what will be seen, but not by all. There was thunder in the temple, and peace by the river, and more wailing than comes from the lips."

The angry impetuosity with which Mungo was about to continue the conference was interrupted by the impatience of the young middy.

He had listened with much disgust to the idle demands and bravadoes of Mungo.

The interest with which he discovered how short a distance separated him from Lion Limb was increased by an irresistible excitement.

Rising, therefore, abruptly, he said,

"Mungo, I have to beg your pardon, if, in my own impatience to be satisfied in a matter which I have much at heart, I am somewhat blind to the importance of this present controversy. If you will do me the favour to examine the letters of the admiral on the Pacific station, which I carry, you will discover that it is not so much my purpose to lay claim to your hospitable entertainment, the proffer of which I acknowledge with much gratitude, as to request your permission to pass through the lines of your army, to join Lion Limb. Understanding, therefore, from the words of this lunatic, or enchanter, whichever he may be, that I am within the short distance of a league from him, I see not wherefore I should not proceed to join him forthwith, instead of wasting the night in slumber. I must, therefore, crave of you to grant me, to the camp of Lion Limb, a guide, to whom I will, with my life and honour, guarantee a safe return—or such instructions concerning my route as will enable me to proceed alone—that is to say, with my attendant."

The effect of this interruption and unexpected demand, on the countenances of all, was remarkable enough.

The buccaneers present stared with amazement, and even a sort of dismay.

As for Mungo himself, nothing could be more unfeigned than his surprise; nothing more unquestionable than the displeasure which instantly began to darken his visage.

He rose, thrust his hand into his belt, as if to give his fingers something to gripe, and drawing himself to his full height, said, haughtily and severely,

"When I invited you to share the shelter of this temple, I did not think I received a friend of the traitor Lion Limb or any of his people; nor did I dream an adherent of this outlaw would dare to beard me at my head-quarters with so rash and audacious a request."

"You have then to learn," said Midshipman Amador, "that if I boast not to be the friend of Lion Limb, whom you call a traitor, I avouch myself to be very much the creature of mine own will; and that if I cannot be termed the adherent of an outlaw, I am at least an English officer, bent on the prosecution of my designs, and making requests more as the ceremonies of courtesy than the tribute of humility. I will claim nothing more of you than you feel inclined to grant; and allowing, therefore, that you invited me to your lodgings under a mistaken apprehension of my character, I will straightway release you from the obligation, only previously desiring of you to reconsider your expressions, wherein, as I think, was an inuendo highly unjust and offensive."

"Now, by Heaven!" exclaimed Mungo, with all the irascibility of his race, and the arrogant pride of his station, "I have happened upon a strange day, when a vagabond esquire, wandering through my jurisdiction, asks my permission to throw himself into the arms of my enemy; and when I admonish him a little of his rashness, rebukes me with insult and defiance."

"A very strange day indeed," muttered a voice among the buccaneers, in which Amador, had he not been too much occupied with other considerations, might have recognised the tones of Botello.

"Mungo," said he, with an eye of fire, "I have given you all the respect which you had a right to demand."

"Is this another madman?" cried the infuriated Mungo, snatching up a sword from the table, and advancing upon the middy.

Amador, confronting Mungo, and waving his hand with dignity,

"Unless thou force me by thine own violence, I cannot draw my sword upon thee on thine own floor. Nevertheless, I fling this glove at thy feet, in token that if thou art as valiant as thou art ill-bred, as ready to repair as inflict an injury, I will claim of thee, as soon as may suit thy convenience, to meet me with weapons, and to answer thy manifold indignities."

"The devil!" cried Mungo, foaming with rage and stamping furiously on the floor. "What, ho! swords and pikemen! shall I strike this braggart with my own hands? Arrest him."

"The blood of him that stays me be on his own head!" said Amador, drawing his word and striding to the entrance. "I will remember thee when I see thee in a fitter place."

The arm of Mungo had been arrested; and in the confusion of the moment, though the door of the tower was instantly beset by a dozen gaping attendants, Amador would doubtless have passed through them without detention, notwithstanding the furious commands of Mungo.

But at the moment when, as he waved his sword menacingly, the hesitating statellites seemed parting before him, one stepped nimbly behind, and suddenly seized his outstretched arm, and calling to the guards at the same time, in an instant Amador was disarmed and a prisoner.

His rage was for a moment unspeakable; but it did not render him incapable of observing the faithful boldness of the young tar, his companion.

The only answer of Mungo was a scowl and a wave of the hand.

He was seized, and before he could follow the example of Amador, and draw his sabre, it was snatched from his inexperienced hand.

All this passed in a moment; and before the young tar could give utterance to the indignation which choked him, he was dragged away.

The fire had smouldered away; but in the light of the moon, which shed a far lovelier radiance, Amador, as he was hurried to the steps, saw, in place of the gay revellers, a few sentries striding in front of the towers, and among the artillery which frowned on either edge of the platform.

Nevertheless, if his rage had left him inquisitive, he was not allowed time to indulge his observations.

He was hurried down the steps, carried a few paces further, and instantly immured in the stone dwelling of some native chief, which, by the substitution of a door of plank for the cotton curtain, and other simple contrivances, had been easily converted into a prison.

In the meanwhile, the rage of Mungo, burned with fury.

"I will attack them to-morrow !" said he.

"Your excellency is heated by anger," said one, temperately, "or you would observe you have a follower of the rebel for a listener."

"Ay, Botello !" cried he, with a laugh of scorn. "He will carry my counsels to Lion Limb when the cony carries food to the serpent, and the sick ox to the carrion crow. Hark, sirrah—thou hast read the fate of thy master : will I attack him to-morrow ?"

"Thou wilt not," said Botello, with an unmoved countenance.

"Hah !" cried Mungo, "art thou so sure of this that thou wilt pledge thy head on the prophecy ? Thou shalt live to be hanged at sunset, with thy old comrades for spectators."

"Heaven has written another history for to-morrow," said Botello, gravely ; "and I have read that as closely as the page of to-day ; but what is for myself, is, and no man may know it. The fate in store for the vain pride and the quick anger may, in part, be spoken."

"Sirrah," said Mungo, "remember that though the vain pride might overlook one so contemptible as thyself, the quick anger is not yet allayed ; and if thou wilt not have me beat thee in the morning, proceed forthwith to discourse of our destinies."

"Blows shall be struck," said the magician, earnestly ; "but whether upon my own head or another's, whether in this temple or another place, whether in the morning or the evening, I am not permitted to divulge. Repent of thy sins, and pray ; for wrath cometh, and sorrow is behind ! By the spirits that live in the stars, by the elves that dwell in stones and shrubs, by the virtues that are caged in matter where the ignorant man findeth naught but ignorance, having been made acquainted with many things appertaining to thy fate, but not all. If thou wilt, I will speak thee the things I am permitted."

"Speak, then," cried he ; "for whether thy knowledge be truth or lies, whether it come from the revelations of angels or the diabolical instructions of fiends, I will listen without fear."

"*Adondi Melech !* under the heaven and above the abyss studied I mine art ; and there is nothing in it that is not blessed," said Botello, with a solemn enthusiasm, that made a deep impression upon all.

"Give me a staff, that I may draw the curtain from this loop," he continued.

The sword of one was instantly extended, the curtain removed, and the moon, climbing the blue hills, looked down into the apartment.

They stared at the astrologer and magician—for Botello was both—some with an unconcealed awe, and others, Mungo among the rest, with an endeavour at looks of contempt not in good character with the interest they betrayed in all his proceedings.

He raised his eyes to the beautiful luminary, enough to create by her mystic splendour the elements of superstition in the bosom of a rhapsodist —mumbled certain inexplicable words, and then said aloud, with a mournful emphasis—"Woe to him that sits in the high place, when the moon shines from the house Allatha ! But the time has not come : and I dare not speak the hour of its visitation."

"And what shall it advantage me to know my peril, if I have got such knowledge as may enable me to prevent it ?" demanded Mungo, with a frown.

"And what would it benefit thee to know the time of thy peril," said the stranger, "when God has not given thee power to avert it ? What is written must be fulfilled ; what is declared must be accomplished. Listen !—the queen of night is in the eighteenth mansion, and under that influence discord is sown in the hearts of men, sedition comes to the earth, and conspiracy hatches under the green leaf."

Mungo turned quickly upon his officers, and surveyed them with an eye of suspicion.

They looked blankly one upon another, until one laughing in a forced and unnatural manner, cried,

"Why should we listen to this madman if we are so affected by his ravings ? General, you will straightway look upon us all as traitors !"

"There have been villains about us before," muttered Mungo, "but I will not take the moon's word for it ; and the more especially that I must receive it through this man's interpretation."

"It is the influence, too, that is good for the friendless captive," continued the magician ; "and many a heart that beats under bonds to-night, will leap in freedom to-morrow."

"Every way this is bad for us," said one, banteringly. "I would advise your excellency to lay chains on him."

"And dost thou think this gibberish will move me to any such precaution ?" cried Mungo, with a compelled smile. "Thou canst not believe I listen to it for aught but diversion. Continue thy mummeries, Botello," he went on, "and when thou art done with the moon, of which I am heartily tired, I will look for thee to introduce me to some essence that speaks a clearer language."

"What wouldst thou have ?" cried the astrologer ; "what plainer language wouldst thou have spoken ? In the house Allatha is written the defection of friends, the dethronement of princes, the fall of citadels in a siege."

"Villain and caitiff ! dost thou dare to insinuate that this citadel is in a state of siege ?" cried Mungo, with a ferocious frown.

"I speak of the things that are to come," said Botello. "What more than this wilt thou have ?"

"It will, doubtless, be well," interrupted one significantly, "to evacuate this place in the morning. By encamping in the fields we can certainly avoid the danger of a besieged citadel."

"Dost thou gibe me ?" said Mungo, with a brow on which jealousy struggled with rage.

"What sayest thou, Botello? It is whispered thou canst raise devils, and force them to speak with thee!"

"Aye!" said Botello, with a ghastly grin, staring Mungo in the face, until the latter faltered before him. "Wilt thou adventure then so far? Canst thou, whose eyes tremble at the gaze of a living creature, think to look upon the face of a devil?"

"If thou canst raise him," said Mungo, stoutly, "do so, and quickly. It will be much satisfaction to my curiosity to look upon one of the accursed."

"They are about us in the air—they are at our elbows and ears," said Botello; "and it needs but a spell to be spoken to bring them before us. But woe to him that hath thought a sin to-day, when the evil one looks on him!"

"Mungo," cried one, with a most expressive and contagious alarm, "if it be your inclination to raise the devil, you must indulge it alone. For my part, I confess there have been, this day, certain thoughts about my bosom, which have unfitted me for such an interview; and—I care not who knows it—my valour has in it so little of the fire of faith, I would sooner, at any moment, speak with ten men than one devil. I wish you a good evening."

"Tarry; stay!" cried Mungo, losing much of his own dread in the contemplation of the apprehension of others. "Why, you are such a knot of sinners as I dreamed not I had about me! Faith, I am ashamed of you, for I thought thy shrewdness would have seen, in this knave's attempt to frighten us from the exhibition, an excellent evidence of his inability to make it."

"I could show thee more than thou couldst see," said Botello, "and I know more things will come to thee than thou shalt see. I know, with all thy vaunting, thou wouldst perish in the gaze of an angel of hell; for thy heart would be the heart of a boy, and it flutters already, even at the thought of the spectacle. I will show thee an essence thou mayest look upon without alarm."

"Do so," said Mungo, sternly; "and remember, while saying what may be necessary by way of explanation, that thou speakest to the chief and governor of these lands, who will whip thy head from thy neck in spite of all the devils if thou discoursest not with more becoming reverence."

"My fate is written!" cried Botello, with neither indignation nor alarm.

Drawing calmly from his bosom an implement of his art, he advanced to the light, and displayed it freely.

It was, or seemed to be, an antique jewel of rock-crystal, not bigger than a pigeon's head, set in the centre of the triangular disk of gold, on which last were engraved many unknown characters and figures.

Crossing himself twice or thrice, the enchanter swung it, by a little silver chain to which it was pendant, in the full blaze of the lamp; so that either of the persons present might have handled it, had any been so disposed.

"This," said the magician—"a gem more precious to the wise than the adamant of the East, but in the hands of the unfaithful more pernicious than the tooth of a viper—is the prison house of an essence that was once powerful among the spirits of night. Kalidon-Sadabath! the night is thy season, the midnight thy time of power! The lord of men calls thee from thy prison-house, the armed man calls thee with the sword! Lo! he wakes from his slumber, and will image out the destiny of the seeker."

The buccaneers, starting, gazed behind them with fear, as if expecting to behold some mighty fiend rising shadowy from the floor; but no intelligence more lofty or more ignoble than themselves was visible in the sanctuary.

They bent their eyes upon the crystal, and beheld some with surprise and others with deep awe, a little drop as of some black liquid, glittering in the very centre of the jewel.

The haughty crowd who would have rushed with cries of joy upon an army of Indians, shrank away with murmurs of hesitation, when Botello extended the talisman towards them.

But they mistook the gesture of the magician; his arm was outstretched more to display the wonder than to part with it.

He surveyed it himself a moment with much satisfaction; then turning to Mungo, he said—"Lay thy hand upon the cross of thy sword, say a prayer over in thy heart, and thou shalt be protected from the mischief of this inquisition, while I tell thee what I behold in the face of Kalidon-Sadabath."

"With your favour," cried Mungo, suddenly, and boldly snatching the enchanted crystal from the hands of Botello, "I will choose rather to see his visage myself, than trust to your interpretations; and as for the protection, I can con over a pater-noster while I am looking: though, why it needs to bestow so much piety upon this juggler's gewgaw, is more than I can understand."

"Say at least the prayer," cried Botello, earnestly, "for neither enchanted crystal nor consecrated gold can hold the strong spirit from the wicked and self-sufficient."

"I have much trust in myself," said the Mungo, coolly, greatly assured and inspired by the harmless appearance of the little mystery. "Nevertheless, I will follow your counsel, in the matter of the prayer,—the more readily that it will keep my mind from wandering to more important affairs; and because, in part, I am somewhat burdened with the sin of neglecting such duties, when there is more occasion for them."

He drew the lamp to him, grasped the crystal firmly in his hand, and bending over it so closely that his warm breath sullied its lustre, regarded it with a fixed attention.

All noted the proceedings with interest; they gazed now at the jewel almost concealed in his grasp, and now at Mungo, as his lips muttered over the inaudible prayer.

Suddenly, and before he had half accomplished the task, they observed his brow knit, and his lip fall.

His eye dilated with a stare of terror, a deadly paleness came over his visage, and starting up, and loosing the talisman from his grasp, he exclaimed wildly,

"By Heaven, there is a living creature in the stone!"

The sorcerer caught the magical implement as it fell from the hands of Mungo; and throwing himself upon his knees, exclaimed,

"Forget not the prayer, and be content to hear what is revealed by the imp of the crystal. Kalidon-Sadabath! He flingeth abroad his arms, and is in wrath and trouble."

"It is true," said Mungo, looking to his officers in perturbation. "While I looked into the shining stone, the black drop increased in size, and grew into the similitude of a being, whose arms were tossed out as if in agony, while spots of fire gathered round his visage."

"Say the prayer, if thou wilt not die miserably before the time that is otherwise ordained!" cried Botello, with a stern voice, that was remarkable enough, to be addressed by one of his station to the proud and powerful commander. "Once, twice—Ay! is there no more to be reckoned by thee, Sadabath? Once, twice—Yea, as the star sayeth, so sayest thou—Once, twice."

"What sayest thou?" said Mungo, ceasing the prayer he had resumed, to question the oraculous adept.

"To thy prayer! Listen, and ask not. Aye! thou speakest in mystery. I turn thee to the north, which thou knewest not, and the south, where thou hadst thy dwelling—to the east, which thou abhorrest, and to the west, where was thy dark chamber; to the heaven, whose light thou lovest not,—to the pit under the earth, where thou wast a wanderer, — and to man's heart, which was pleasanter to thee than the bonds of the crystal. In the name of the Seven that are of power under the earth, and of the Seven that are mighty above, I call to thee, Kalidon-Sadabath, the bright star that is quenched. In shadows, in fire and smoke—in thunder and with spears—with blows and with bloodshed thou speakest, and I hear thee!"

"I hear nothing, save thy accursed croaking, worse than that of the crows," cried Mungo, hotly. "If thy devil have no more intelligible gabble, cast him out, and call another."

"He speaks not but by images and phantasms pictured on the crystal. Now, listen, for thy story cometh. I see a great house on fire——"

"Ay, I shall perish then in a conflagration?" said he, hastily. "I have ever had a horror of burning houses."

"The smoke eddies, the flame roars, and one sitteth blindfold under the eaves, with the flakes and cinders falling about him, which he sees not."

"If thou meanest that I shall rest in that stupid state, under such peril, thy devil Sadabath is a liar, and I defy him!"

"And he that takes thee by the hand," cried Botello, without regarding the interruptions, "thy friend."

"Aye, answer me that question," said Mungo, "for if I am to be led out of the fire by a foeman, I will straightway forswear my friends, and give my heart to the magnanimous."

"Thou doest him obeisance!" cried the magician, with extraordinary emphasis.

"Villain!" exclaimed Mungo.

"Thou placest thy neck upon the earth, and he tramples it."

"Liar and traitor!" roared Mungo, spurning the magician with his foot, and, in his fury, snatching up a weapon to dispatch him.

"Why should'st thou stain thy hand with the blood of the dotard?" cried one, interposing for a second time between the intemperate commander and the object of his anger. "He is a madman, incapable of understanding what he says; and were he even sane, and speaking the truth, your commands to have him entertain you with his mummeries, should have ensured him against your anger."

"Very true," said Mungo, with a scowl. "I was a fool to strike him. Trample on my neck! thou grizzly and cheating villain! Go! begone! Thy devil, though he cannot tell thee what awaits thee in the morning, may show thee what thou deservest."

"I deserved not to be spurned," said Botello, tranquilly, after having gathered up his enchanted crystal, and raised himself to his feet; "and the dishonour will not fall on the side that was bruised, but on the limb that was raised against it."

Mungo waved his hand angrily and impatiently, and Botello was led away, followed by most of the buccaneers.

When Midshipman Amador found himself alone in the prison with Fabueno, with no other prospect before him than that of remaining therein till it might please the stars to throw open the doors, the rage that was too philosophic to quarrel with stone walls, gradually subsided into a tranquil indignation. Nay, so much command of himself did he regain, that hearing his companion bewailing his fate in a manner somewhat immoderate, as if regarding his incarceration as the prelude to a more dismal destiny, he opened his lips to give him comfort.

The apartment was spacious but low; a narrow casement opened on one side, at the distance of six feet from the floor, and admitted the moonbeams. The door through which they had entered was strongly barricaded on the outside. A passage leading to the interior was similarly secured, and equally impassable was the casement. A thick grating defended it, and shut out all hopes of escape.

"We can do nothing, unless assisted from without," said Amador. "At all events, I would we could mount to those iron stanchions, and take note of what is passing on the outside."

"Iron!" cried Amador, "a thought strikes me. I know well that in these lands, iron has almost the value of gold, and is too scarce to be wasted on the defences of a temporary dungeon, where it might be stolen, too, at the first opportunity, by the Indians."

"Dost thou mean to say that these bars are of wood, sir?"

"Indeed I think so; and if I had but a knife or a dagger, and the means of climbing into the window, I would warrant to be at liberty before morning. Here is a poniard, of which the villains forgot to divest me," said Amador. "Strike it against the stanchions—if they be of wood, we have much hope of freeing ourselves."

His companion did as he was directed. He raised himself on tiptoe, and the sharp weapon buried itself in the flimsy barrier.

"If I had but something to stand on," he cried, eagerly, "how soon might we not be free."

"There is neither stool nor chair in this vile den," said Amador; "but I will not shame to give thee the support of my shoulder, and the more readily, that I think thy slight frame would be incapable of supporting my own greater weight. Pause not," he continued, "if thy foot be near my neck, I shall know it is not the foot of an enemy. I will kneel to take thee on my back, as the Saracen camel does to his master. Stretch thyself to thy full height, so as to cut through the top of the bars; after which, without further carving, thou canst easily wrench them from their places."

"Why dost thou falter?" demanded Amador.

"Sir," replied the secretary, in a low voice, "there is a guard at a little distance."

"May Heaven strike me with pains and death," cried Amador, with an abrupt ardour, that nearly tumbled the secretary from his station, "if I do not covet the blood of Mungo, that false and cowardly traitor, who, after hiding his wrath under the cloak of magnanimity and religion, was the first to seize upon me, and that from behind."

"What is to be done, sir? He will discover me; and even if I can remove the grating, there will be no possibility to descend without observation."

"Cut through the wood as silently as thou canst," said Amador. "And then when the window is open, I will myself spring to the earth, and so occupy the dastard's notice, that thou escape without peril. Cut on, and fear not."

The secretary obeyed; but had not yet divided a single stake, when, suddenly, a voice was heard exclaiming furiously,

"To your bows, ye vagabonds! Quick and hotly! Drive your shafts through and through! Shoot!"

"Descend," said Amador.

But before his young companion could follow his counsel, there came four crossbow-shafts rattling violently into the window.

"Have the knaves struck thee?" demanded Amador, as he raised the groaning youth in his arms."

"Aye, sir," replied the youth, faintly.

"Be of better heart," said Amador, leading him to where the moonlight shone brightest on the floor. "Art thou struck in the body? If thou diest, be certain I will avenge thee. Where art thou hurt?"

"I know not," he replied, piteously; "but I know I shall die? Oh! heaven! this is a pang more bitter than death! Must I die?"

"Be comforted," said Amador, cheeringly, "the arrow has only pierced thy arm. I will snap it asunder and withdraw it. Fear not, there is no peril in such hurt, and I will bear witness thou hast won it most honourably."

"Will I not die, then?" he said, with joy. "Pho! it was the first time I was ever hurt, and I judged of the wound only by the agony. Pho! indeed, 'tis but a scratch."

"Thou bearest it valiantly," said Amador, binding his scarf round the wound. "If thou thinkest thou hast strength to support me for a minute or two, I will clamber to the window myself, and remove the bars, without fearing the arrows of these varlets can do me much harm through my armour."

"They are not above three score yards distant, and I feel a little faint. I know not, moreover, how I could escape, even if your honour should be so lucky as to reach the ground."

"I should not have forsaken thee," said Amador, giving over, with a sigh, all hope of escape. "There is nothing more to be done. The foul fiend seize the knave that struck thee, and the dastard that commanded the shot! I would to heaven I had beaten him soundly. How feelest thou now? If thou canst sleep it will be well."

"I have no more pain; but feel a sort of exhaustion, which will doubtless be relieved by rest."

"Sleep, then," said Amador, "and have a care that thy wounded member be not oppressed by the weight of thy body. I will myself presently follow thy example. If aught should occur to disturb thee, even though it should be but the pain of thy hurt, scruple not to arouse me."

*   *   *   *   *

Amador was roused from his slumbers by a cause at first incomprehensible.

The moonlight had vanished from the prison, and deep obscurity had succeeded.

But in the little light remaining, he saw, as he started up, the figures of several men, one of whom had been tugging at his shoulder, and now whispered to him, as he instinctively grasped at his dagger—

"Peace! I am a friend, and I give you liberty."

"I will thank thee for the gift, when I am sure I enjoy it," said the middy, already on his feet; "I remember thy voice—thou art one of the followers of the knave Mungo.

"I am one who laments, without extenuating,

the folly of the general," said the voice. "But tarry not to question. Hasten—thy horse is ready."

"They wait for thee, Amador. Delay not: the door is open. The magician will guide thee. Commend me to Lion Limb."

"By Heaven! I should think I dream!" said Amador. "Stay, I thank thee for thy honourable and most noble benevolence; and, in addition, would tax thy charity in favour of a certain——"

"Be silent, and follow me."

The moon was sinking behind the vast and majestic peaks of the interior.

A deep shadow lay over the dungeon; and only on the top of the principal tower trembled a lingering ray; and Amador could distinctly hear the foot-fall of a sentinel as he strode to and fro over the terrace. He looked to that quarter, whence, as he judged, had come the shafts which had so nearly robbed him of his fellow-prisoner. The crossbowmen slept on their post, in the mild and quiet air.

"Give me thy hand, Martin," said Amador, drawing his pionard again from the sheath. "I will shield thee from the dogs this time. And now that I snuff the breath of freedom, I think it will need a craftier knave's trick than that of Mungo to deprive me of it a second time."

Following the magician, as he stole cautiously along, the brothers in misfortune crept on with a stealthy pace under the shadows, till they advanced with greater assurance and rapidity.

The grey glimpses of morning had not yet visited the east when they betook themselves to the covert of a clump of trees, under which, in the figures that were there visible, Amador recognised with joy his friend.

"Rejoice in silence," said Botello, interrupting his raptures; "for there is an ear at no great distance very ready to hear thee. Mount and be ready. —You can look to your equipments a little, while I see if heaven will not confirm the fate of visions; for I dreamed I should ride back to Lion Limb on a good roan charger to-day."

The magician disappeared, and Amador, scarcely suppressing his ardour, when he found that not only his attendants and horses, but even the well-fleshed sword wrested from him in the evening, was in readiness to be restored to him, grasped it with exultation, and sprang into the saddle.

Then passing towards Martin, and finding that his arm caused him much pain in the act of mounting, he assisted him to ascend with his own hand. From whom also he learned, in a few words, somewhat of the secret of their liberation.

Less than an hour after Amador had fallen asleep, and while Martin was still kept awake by the pain of his wound, the door of the prison was opened, and Botello thrust in, who confronted him with a mystic, but still an unequivocal assurance of freedom before sunrise; and commanded him not to wake the middy, but to follow his example—he would need invigorating from slumber to support the toils of the coming day.

The sound of hoofs was heard approaching; and Botello, as they discovered by his voice, rode up to the trees.

"The dream was true; the imp that speaks to slumber was not a liar!" he cried, exultingly. "We leave the gaoler afoot; and Kalidon-Sadabath shall swing on a galloping horse. God is over all, by night and by day, afoot and on horse, in battle and in flight. Whip and spur, guide and cheer! and rocks and thorns spread over the path of pursuers!"

As Amador anticipated, the shout of the lunatic, for such he began to esteem Botello, was carried even to the head-quarters of Mungo.

THE BOY KING
OF THE SOUTH SEA ISLANDS.

A SURPRISE.

An arquebuse was discharged, and, as the fugitives began their flight, the flourish of a trumpet in one quarter, and the roll of a drum in another, convinced them that the alarm had been given, and was spreading from post to post in a manner that might prove exceedingly inconvenient.

The middy pressed to the side of Botello—an achievement of some little difficulty, for he perceived his guide was well mounted. "Magico," he cried, as he galloped in company with him, "dost thou know thou couldst not have fallen upon a better plan to oppose our flight, and perhaps reduce us again to bonds, than by the indulgence of this same untimely and obstreperous shouting?"

"Trust in God, and fear not!" replied the magician. "This day shalt thou look upon the face

of Lion Limb; and though the enemy follow us, yet shall his pursuit be vain and unlucky."

"I will allow that such may be the termination," said Amador; "yet, notwithstanding, can I perceive no advantage in being pursued, but much that is to be deprecated, inasmuch as we shall exhaust that strength of our horses in our hurry, which might have been reserved for a more honourable contingency."

"Your valour will by and bye perceive there is more wisdom than looks to the moment," said Botello, coolly, without slacking his pace; "and, provided you can keep your followers from swerving from the path, and that inexperienced youth from falling out of his saddle, I will, with my head, answer for your safety."

At the dawn of day, the middy became convinced he had ridden more than the distance which, he supposed, separated the camps of the rival generals; and wondering at the absence of all signs of life in the forest through which he was passing, he again betook himself to Botello.

The magician had halted on the brow of an eminence, where, though the dense wood, as well as the obscurity of the hour, greatly contracted the sphere of vision, he looked back as if striving to detect the figures of pursuers among the thick shadows.

"We are pursued, enchanter; and yet, I perceive neither tent nor outpost of thy friends, to give us refuge from our enemies," said Amador.

"Let them come," cried Botello, tranquilly; "it is worse for the stag when the pack is scattered; but better for the kite when the pheasants have broke the covey."

"There may be much wisdom in thy tropes, as well as thine actions," said the novice; "yet am I slow to discover it in either. Whether we are to be considered the stag or the hounds, the hawk or the pheasants, entirely passes my comprehension; but sure am I that, in either case, our safety may be considered quite as metaphorical as thy speech. I understood from thee, last night, and I remember it very well, that the river whereon Lion Limb was encamped was but a league from Zempoala; yet I am persuaded we have galloped twice that distance."

"He travels no straight road who creeps through the country of a feoman," said Botello, resuming his journey, though at a more moderate gait than before; "and Amador should be content, if he can avoid the many scouts and vedettes that infest the path, by riding thrice the two leagues he has compassed already."

"My horse is strong, and, it seems to me, his spirit revives at every new step he takes through these forests," said the middy; "yet even for his sake, were there no other reason, would I be fain to pick the shortest road that leads to the camp of Lion Limb. I am greatly concerned about my young friend, who, as thou hast doubtless learned, was last night shot through the arm with an arrow, by those knaves who kept watch at the window of the prison; and therefore, for his sake, am I desirous to find a resting-place as soon as possible. If I should give thee my counsel (a thing I am loath to do, as thou seemest experienced in all the intricacies of this woody wilderness, in which I am a stranger), it would be, to forsake all those crooked and endless by-ways without delay, and strike upon the shortest path, without consideration of any small party of scouts we might meet. For, even excluding the wounded, we are here together four strong men, armed, and well mounted, who, fighting our way to freedom, would doubtless be an overmatch for twice the number of enemies."

"The youth must learn the science of a soldier," said Botello, "and suffering is the first letter of its alphabet. Happy will he be, if, in the life he covets, he encounter no more agony than he shall endure to day. When we have time to rest, I will anoint his arm with a salve more powerful than the unguents of a physician. What I do, and whither I guide, are best, as you will acknowledge when the journey is over. Why should your honour desire to exchange blows with poor scouts? I shall win better thanks of the King Lion Limb."

To the surprise, and much also to the dissatisfaction of Amador, the noon-day sun still found him struggling with his companions among the rocks and forests.

It seemed to him, from a review of his journey, that he had been doubling and turning for the whole morning like a boy at blindman's-buff within a circle of a few leagues; and though he could not, upon the closest inspection, detect a single tree or brook which he remembered to have passed before, he shrewdly suspected it was Botello's intention to make him well acquainted with the forest before dismissing him from its depths.

It was, however, vain to wonder, and equally fruitless to complain.

For the whole morning, at different intervals, he was assured, sometimes from hearing their shouts in the thicket, and sometimes from beholding them from a hill-top crossing an opposing eminence, that his pursuers were close at his heels: of which fact, and the necessity it presented to move with becoming caution, the enchanter took advantage in the construction of his answers to every remonstrance.

At length, perhaps two hours after noon, the travellers approached a hill, whence, as Botello assured them, they might look down upon the River of Canoes.

This was the more agreeable intelligence, since the day was intolerably hot, and they almost longed for the bursting of a tempest which had been brooding in the welkin for the last half-hour, the drenching of which, as they thought, would be far more sufferable than the combustion of sunshine.

They reached the hill, and from its bushy and stony side looked down upon the valley, where the river, or more properly speaking, the rivulet, went foaming and fretting over its rugged channel.

At a short distance, and almost at the bottom of the hill, he was struck with the unexpected apparition of the army of Mungo, drawn out in order of battle, as if awaiting the approach of a foe, and commanding the passage of the river.

He rubbed his eyes with astonishment; but there was no delusion in the view.

"Sir," said Botello, in a low voice, as if reading his thoughts, "you marvel to see this army, which we left sleeping, arrived at the river before us; but you forget Zempoala lies only a league from the river."

"Let us descend and cross to the other side," said Amador, impatiently. "I see the very spot where sits the knave Mungo on his horse; and if the valiant Lion Limb have it in intention, as I do not doubt, to give him battle, I should sharply regret to watch the conflict from this hill side."

"I told Mungo himself," said the magician, with a sort of triumph, "he should not join battle with Lion Limb to day; and he shall not! When the time comes, Amador may join in the combat, if he will. Be content, sir, we cannot stir from this hill without being observed, and captured or slain. The thunder roars, the bolt glitters in the heaven, the storm that levels the tall ceibas will open us a path presently, even through that angry army."

Almost while he spoke, and before he could add words to the disinclination with which he regarded so untimely a delay, there burst such a thunderbolt over his head, as made every other horse in the party cower to the earth as if stricken by its violence.

This was immediately followed by a succession of separate explosions, and of multisonous volleys, less resembling the furious roar of the ordnance of a great army than of the artillery of volcanoes; and it became immediately necessary for each man to dismount, and allay, as he could, the frantic terrors of his charger.

In the midst of this sublime prelude, the rushing of a mighty wind was added to the orchestre of the elements; and in an instant, the face of day, the black vapours above and the varied valley below, were hidden in a cloud of dust, sand, and leaves, stripped in a moment from the plains and the forest, and in an instant also the army of Mungo disappeared.

Presently, also, came another sound, heard even above the peal of the thunder and the rush of the wind; the roar of a great rain, booming along like a moving cataract, was mingled with the harsh music of nature; and Amador looked anxiously round for some place of shelter.

Happily there was a spot hard by, where certain tall and massive rocks lay so wedged together, as to present most of the characteristics of a chamber, except that there was wanting the fourth side as well as the roof; unless, indeed, the outstretched branches of the great trees that grew among these fragments, might have been considered a suitable canopy.

Into this nook the party, guided by Botello, penetrated forthwith; and here they found themselves, in a great measure, sheltered from the rain.

Drops of rain still occasionally fell from the heavens, or were whirled by the passing gusts from the boughs; the clouds still careered menacingly in the atmosphere: and though the sunbeams ever and anon burst through their rent sides, and glimmered with splendour on the shivered tops and lacerated roots of many a fallen tree, it was still doubtful at what moment the capricious elements might resume their conflict.

The river, that was before a brook, now rolled along a turbid torrent, and seemed every moment to augment in volume and fury, as its short-lived tributaries poured down their foaming treasures from the hills.

"The boy to his bed, and the fool to his fireside!" cried the enchanter, with a sudden exultation, pointing down the hill, to the valley deprived of its late visitors.

The valley was silent and solitary.

"I said the tempest should open for us a path!" continued Botello: "and lo! the spirit which was given to me does not lie!"

"I must confess," quoth Amador, with surprise, "you have in this instance, as in several others, verified your prediction. What juggler's trick is this? Where is the hound, Mungo?"

"Galloping back to Zempoala, to amuse himself with the dancers on the pyramid," said Botello, with a grin of saturnine delight.

"He came, and his heart failed him in the tempest; he loves better, and so does his people, the comfort of the temple, than the strife of these tropical elements. Woe be to him who would contend with a strong man, when he hides his head from the shower! He shall vapour in the morning, but tremble when the enemy comes to him in dreams!"

"And I am to understand, then," said Amador, with a voice of high scorn and displeasure, "that these effeminate hinds, after drawing out their forces in the face of an enemy, have taken to their heels, like village girls in a summer festival, at the dashing of rain?"

"It is even so," said Botello: "they are now hiding themselves in their quarters; while those veterans who awaited them beyond the river, stand yet to their arms, and blush even to look for the shelter of a tree."

"Let us descend, then, and join them without delay, for I believe those men of Lion Limb are true soldiers, and I long to make their acquaintance," said the middy.

"It is needful we do so, and that quickly," said the astrologer; "for this river, though by midnight it shall again be shrunk to a fairy brook, will, in an hour, be impassable."

It required not many moments to convey the party to the banks of the stream; but when they had reached it, it was apparent it could not be forded without peril.

Its channel was wild and rocky; fallen and shivered trees fringed its borders with a bristling net-work, over and among which the current raved with a noisy turbulence.

Amador instinctively urged his steed full towards the threatening branches, he raised his head and perceived a man on a dun horse riding into the water, above the rocks hard by the tree, as if to convince him of the practicability of the passage, and the shallowness of the water.

This unknown auxiliary stretched forth his hand, and Amador instantly found himself in safety, and ascending the bank of the river.

Not till his charge was on dry land, did the stranger relax his hand, and then perhaps the sooner, that Amador seized it with a most cordial grip, and while he held it, said, fervently,

"I swear to thee! I believe thou hast saved me from a great danger, if thou hast not absolutely preserved my life; for which good deed, besides giving thee my most unfeigned present thanks, I avow myself, till the day of my death, enslaved under the necessity to requite thee with any honorable risk thou canst hereafter impose."

While Amador spoke, he perused the countenance and surveyed the figure of his deliverer.

He was a man in the prime and midway of life, tall and long-limbed, but with a breadth of shoulders and development of muscle that proved him, as did the grasp with which he assisted the war-horse from the flood, to possess great bodily strength.

His face was handsome and manly, though with rather delicate features, and a very lofty and capacious forehead shone among thin black locks.

His beard was black and thin like his hair, and Amador plainly perceived through it the scar of a sword-cut between the chin and mouth.

Such was the valiant man, who replied to Amador's courtesies with a frank and open countenance, and a laugh of good humour, as if entirely unconscious of any discomfort from his reeking condition, or any merit in the service he had rendered.

"I accept thy offers of friendship," he said, "and very heartily, senor. But I vow to thee, when I helped thee out of the stream, I thought I should have had to give thee battle the next moment, as a sworn friend of Mungo."

"How little justice there was in that suspicion," said Amador, "you will know when I tell you, that at this moment, next to the satisfaction of finding some opportunity to requite your true service, I know of no greater pleasure than a fair opportunity to cross swords with this ill-mannered, dishonourable and unworthy person, seeking my way, with my followers, under guidance of a certain conjuror called Botello, to the camp of the valiant Lion Limb: and I rejoice in this rencontre the more, because I am persuaded you are yourself a true friend of that much respected commander."

"Ay, by my conscience, you may say so!" cried the blithe cavalier; "and I would to Heaven he had many more friends that love him so well as myself. But come. you are hard by his head-quarters. Yet, under favour, let us, before seeking them, say a word to Botello, who, with your people, I perceive, has crossed the river."

"How now, Botello?" he cried, as he rode in among the party; "what news from Mungo? and what conjuration wert thou enacting, while he was scampering away before the bad weather?"

"Nothing but good," said Botello, baring his head, and bending it to the saddle.

The stranger was surprised to see this mark of homage in the enchanter, whom he had found, though neither rude nor presumptuous, not over-burthened with servility.

Looking round to the others, he discovered that they all kept their eyes upon his companion with looks of the deepest respect.

At the same moment, and as the truth entered his mind, he caught the eye of his deliverer, and perceived at once, in this stately though unarmed, cavalier, the person of the renowned Lion Limb himself.

For a moment it seemed as if he were disposed to meet the disclosure with a grave and lofty deportment suitable to his rank; but as Amador raised his hand with a gesture of reverence, a smile crept over his visage, which was instantly succeeded by a good-humoured and familiar laugh.

"Thou seest," he cried, "we will be masking at times, even without much regard either for our enemies or the weather. But trust me, you are welcome; and doubtless not only to myself, but to these worthier gentlemen, my friends."

All bowed with great respect, and Lion Limb himself, half raising his drooping cap, said—"Whether he come to honour me with the aid of his good sword or not, I am most glad to see him."

The sun was declining when the travellers made their way to the camp of Lion Limb.

The river of Canoes ran through a fertile valley; but this was of no great extent, and towards its upper termination, the scene of the events of the day, it was arid and broken with rocks.

Immediately beyond the river, in a place made strong by rocks and bushes, impenetrable to cavalry, and affording the safest covert to his crossbowmen, the wary rival of Mungo had pitched his quarters.

Temporary huts of boughs and fresh-woven mats were seen withering among the green shadows, and from these ascended the smoke of fires, at which the soldiers were dressing their evening meal. But in advance of this primitive encampment, dripping with rain like their commanders, yet standing to their arms with a patient and grave constancy, as if still in readiness for an enemy, Amador beheld the forces of Lion Limb and old Martin.

They had a weather-beaten and veteran appearance; nevertheless, they looked like disciplined and experienced soldiers. Amador observed that few of them had fire-arms: the crossbow, the sword, and the lance with its long double head of bright copper, were almost their only arms; but they handled them as if well acquainted with their value.

Behind this advanced guard, under the shelter of the rocks and bushes, he remarked several officers, a few of them mounted, as well as divers groups of Indian menials.

CHAPTER CXXI.

THE NIGHT MARCH—THE ATTACK.

THE sun had not yet set, when the rays, stealing through the vapours that gathered among the distant peaks, beheld Lion Limb and his little army crossing the River of Canoes. A quarter-league above the stream was more shallow than at that spot where it had been the fate of Amador to ford it; the flood had also in a measure subsided; and while the mounted individuals passed it with ease, the waters came not above the breasts of the foot-men.

Amador rode along, chafing with discontent at the thought that he should share no part in the brave deeds of the coming night.

The rivulet was crossed, and the hardy despe-radoes who were now marching with spears to attack a foe of five times their own number, forti-fied with cannon on an eminence, gathered about their leader as he sat on his horse on the bank, as if expecting his final instructions and encouragement. He surveyed them not only with gravity but with complacency, and smiling as if in derision of their weakness—for they did not number much over two hundred and fifty men—he said, with inimitable dryness—

"My good friends and companions, you are now about to fight a battle, the issue of which will very much depend on your own conduct; and I have to inform you that if you are vanquished, there is not a man of you that shall not hang at some corner of Zempoala to-morrow."

"Let us on!" cried all, with a shout of exultation —"we will conquer."

"Nay," cried Lion Limb, with a mock discretion, "rush not too eagerly on danger. Let us wait a day for those brown varlets, the Indian soldiers, yet will they doubtless make that triumph the more certain."

"We will win it ourselves," cried the excited desperadoes.

"Ye will have hotter work than ye think," said Lion Limb; "and surely I swear you, if ye force me to conduct you to Zempoala, I will not come from it alive, unless as its master."

"Let it be proclaimed death to any one that turns his back," cried a hundred voices.

"Ay, then, ye mad, valiant rogues, ye shall have your wish," cried Lion Limb, yielding to an excite-ment he had not easily suppressed, rising in his stirrups, and looking round him with that fiery en-thusiasm which was the true secret of his greatness, and which left him not for a moment even in the darkest and most perilous hour of his enterprise. "We will march to Zempoala and show this dog of a Mungo what it is to oppose the arms of brave Englishmen."

A few words explained the order of attack, and the duties of the several leaders, of whom young Harry Woodruff was appointed to the most honour-able and dangerous task—to seize the artillery and thus give passage for the assault of the towers, while Lion Limb himself should stand by with a chosen body of reserve, to witness the valour of his captains, and give assistance where it was needed.

Hard by the town of Zempoala ran a little brook, coursing through agreeable meadows, and here and there skirted by green forests. In a wood that overshadowed this current, but at the distance of a quarter league from it, lay concealed the forces of Lion Limb, waiting patiently for the time when the followers of Mungo, satiated with the sports of their tawny neighbours, should additionally recompense the exploits of the day with the oblivion of slumber. They had watched with contempt, and with joy (for they perceived in such spectacle a symptom of the infatuated security of their enemies), the great fire that lighted the diversions of the evening, blazing until it began to die away, as did many of the sounds of revelry, that, in the still hour of the night, were borne to their ears.

But it was not until their spies brought word that the last brand was flinging its decaying lustre over the eaves of the towers that they were bidden to arise, cross the stream, and array for battle.

In deep silence—for they knew there were sentinels on the path—they reached and forded the rivulet: trooper and footman passed over, and were ranked under their several leaders, and all seemed in readiness for the assault.

But though the moon frequently displayed her resplendent visage through loop-holes in the scudding clouds, the many clumps of trees that dotted over the meadows in the environs of Zempoala, so confounded the vision, that they had reached the very suburbs, without yet obtaining a view.

Indeed it had so happened, that not being provided with a guide acquainted with the various approaches to the town, they fell upon one entirely different from that trodden by Mungo. Not doubting, they pushed boldly on through a deserted street, echoing loudly to the clatter of their steps; nor did they discover their error until, to their great surprise, they found themselves issuing upon the great square, in full view of the temple.

They paused an instant. No tumult of shouts or fire-arms, but a deep silence brooded over the city as with wings; in fact, no sound broke the solemn tranquillity of midnight, save one which was the evidence and representative of peace.

The faint twangling of a lute, mingling with the sweet tones of a youthful voice, came from the chief tower; to hear which Mungo's sentinels had doubtless stolen from their posts among the cannon, which were now seen frowning in solitude on the verge of the platform.

The clattering of a horseman riding furiously up a neighbouring street, roused all from reverie—"Arma! Arma! A las Armas!" burst from the lips of the flying sentry.

In a moment of time this faithful watchman was seen dashing across the square; and as he flung himself from his steed, and rushed up the steps of the pyramid, still shouting the alarm at the top of his voice, there was heard another sound following at his heels, in which the practised ear detected the tramp of footmen, pursuing with the speed of death.

In a moment, also, ceased the lute and the voice of the singer; torches flashed suddenly from the doors of the towers; and as their light shot over the open square, there was seen a hurried mass of men running in confusion over the area.

But the same flash that revealed this spectacle, disclosed also the wild figures and hostile visages of the men of Lion Limb, rushing to the assault, and sending forth a shout that made the whole town ring and tremble to its foundations.

The shouts of the assailants, as they rushed up the steps, were met by the roar of a cannon discharged by a skilful hand, illuminating tree and tower with a hideous glare, and flinging death and havoc among their ranks.

But the foot of desperation was on the earth of the temple; and before another piece of artillery could answer to the hollow thunder of the hills, the spear was drinking the blood of the cannoneers.

At this moment there rose from the platform, above the shouts and yells of the combatants, a shriek as though of a woman struck by the spear of some ferocious dastard.

"We will sack these towers without the loss of a life. What ho! yield thee, Mungo," exclaimed Lion Limb, with a voice heard above the din; "yield thee up a prisoner, or thine own cannon shall bury thee under the temple!"

"On!" cried fifty eager men, as they rushed by their leader, and drove the followers of Mungo into the sanctuary. They vanished; but the pikes and muskets bristling checked the audacity of the besiegers at the door; and the voice of Bill Whetherby was heard exclaiming from behind—

"Clear for the cannon, and stand aside!" when suddenly a firebrand, dashed by some unseen hand to the roof, lodged among the palm leaves, and in a moment the whole superstructure was in flames.

"Spare your powder, and stand by for the rats!" cried Ted Rawlings, for it was he who had achieved this cunning and well-timed exploit.

"A hundred crowns to the knave of the firebrand!" cried Lion Limb, exultingly; "and three thousand paid in gold to him who lays the first hand on Mungo!—Burn, fire! smother, smoke! the night is ours!"

Loud was the shout with which the besiegers responded to the cry; and the disordered and unavailing shots from the other towers were lost in the uproar of voices.

"Leave shouting, and bring up the cannon! What ho, ye rogues of the towers! will ye have quarter and friendship, or flames and cannon-balls! Point the ordnance against the flank towers! Bury the knaves that resist us longer. Fire!"

But this measure was unnecessary. It was at this instant that the besieged, as much much bewildered by the surprise as discomfited by the fury of the attack, disheartened, looked from the loops of their strongholds, and their hearts were turned to water, and their assurance of victory humbled to the hope of capitulation.

The morn, which by this time was breaking over the sea, was ushered in with a thousand sounds of triumph.

The drums of the vanquished rolled in concert with the trumpets of the victors.

In truth, saving to the wounded and broken-spirited Mungo and some few who had remained faithful to him, the change of others from rivalry to subjection, was a circumstance more of gratulation than regret; as was proved by the ready alacrity with which they betook themselves to the audience of their conqueror, Lion Limb.

In the gilded and feather-broidered chair in which he had first seen the person of the unlucky Mungo, Amador now perceived the figure of the conqueror, Lion Limb, a rich mantle of an orange hue thrown over his shoulders, his head bare, but his heel resting on a certain footstool or ball of variegated feathers, and altogether preserving an appearance of singular but superb state.

His valiant and well-beloved officers stood ranked on either side, and on either side, also, his resolute followers were displayed, as if performing the duties of a body-guard.

In this situation of pride, he prepared to receive the congratulations or the griefs of his enemies.

And, as if to add still further to the imposing magnificence of the ceremony, at that moment, as a wild roar of drums, mingling with the wilder shouts of human beings, burst over the city, a great multitude of native warriors marching in regular and alternate files of spearmen and archers, and glittering with feathers and brilliant garments, strode upon the square, and dividing upon either side, halted with their warlike and most romantic array.

The spectacle was surprising to those who had

not before looked upon an Indian army, among whom Amador was one.

He regarded the picturesque barbarians with much admiration; though his eye soon wandered from them to dwell upon the leader, and the ceremonious part he was then enacting.

He sat in his chair like a monarch, and, at times, he arose.

It did not become Amador, though he surveyed these proceedings, to interrupt them.

Being thus a witness of the degree of friendliness which characterised the receptions, as well as the many petitions which the comers made to be accredited and enrolled among Lion Limb's true friends and followers, he began to lose somewhat of the wonder with which he had regarded the suddenness and facility of the victory.

It was apparent that most of the officers of Mungo had long made up their minds to devote themselves to the service of his enemy; and when they had paid their compliments, they dropped among his officers as if joining old friends and comrades.

It gave the middy pleasure when, at the conclusion of these ceremonies, he beheld the Biscayan led forward in chains (for he was heavily ironed), to salute his rival.

His casque was off.

A bandage covered his eye.

His face was very pale.

And he strode forward with an uncertain gait, as if feeble from the loss of blood, or agitated by shame and despair.

Nevertheless, he spoke with a firm and manly voice, when he found himself confronted with his vanquisher, Lion Limb.

"Thou mayest congratulate thyself, Lion Limb," said the fallen chief. "Thy star has the ascendant, thy fate is superior; and so much do I admire my own misfortune, that I could compliment thee upon it, did I not know it was wrought less by the valour of my enemies than the perfidy of my friends."

"Thou doest thyself, as well as all others, a great wrong to say so," said Lion Limb, gravely; "and it would better become thee magnanimously to confess thou art beaten by thy own fault, rather than to follow the example of little-minded men, and lay the blame upon others."

"I confess that I am beaten," said the captive; "and that the shame of my defeat will last longer than my grave. But I aver, and I maintain in thy teeth, though I am but a captive in thy hands, that this victory is altogether so miraculous, it could not have happened unless by the corruption of my people."

"To Heaven and my good soldiers, it is all owing," said Lion Limb, composedly: "and so little miraculous do I myself esteem it, after having twice or thrice beaten valiant men, that I vow to thee on my conscience, I cannot do other than consider this triumph as altogether the least of my achievements in these islands."

"It must be so, since you say it," responded Mungo, his breast heaving under those sarcasm, with a bitter and suffocating pang; "yet it matters not. Let the glory be ever so little, the shame is not the less notorious; and though thou scornest thy reward of fame, I will not fly from mine own recompence of contempt. What more is expected of me? I cannot, like the rest, kiss thy hand, and take upon me the oaths of service. I am thy prisoner."

"Had I been thine," said Lion Limb, gravely, "thou wouldst have fulfilled thy word, and *hanged* me, wouldst thou not?"

"What matters it?" replied Mungo, with a firm voice. "Doubtless I should have been as good as my word: for which reason I will anticipate thy excuses, and assure thee, out of mine own mouth, thou wilt but retaliate fairly, to dismiss me to the same fate."

"Thou canst not understand the moderation thou hast not practised," said Lion Limb, rising, and speaking with dignity. "The foolish rage that provoked thee to set a price upon my head I remember not; the madness that proclaimed these true and most loyal men for rebels and traitors, must be passed by: but as in doing this thou art worthy to suffer the death of a rebellious subject, for such thou hast acted. Nevertheless, I will do thee a grace thou wouldst not accord to me; I will conceive that, however traitorous have been thy actions, thou mayest have been mistaken: in which thought I give thee thy life."

The conqueror waved his hand, and Mungo was led away—to terminate, in after years, a life of mischance by a death of misery.

"What will my noble and thrice honoured friend, Amador?" cried Lion Limb, as he perceived the neophyte approaching him. "We should be good friends; for I owe thee much, and we have been in peril together."

"Twice, I thank you," said Amador, "you have done me the office of a true friend; for which I will not trifle the time to thank you, inasmuch as my arm is henceforth unshackled, and I can write my gratitude better with it than with my tongue."

*　　*　　*　　*　　*

To those, like Amador and friends, who had not yet witnessed with their own eyes the peculiar wonders of the interior, the approach to Katamar's city was full of surprise and interest. As the sun sank, the hills on which lay the city, and the pyramids and towers that crowned them, sent their long shadows over the plain to the feet of the cavaliers, and in the gloom, they beheld a vast multitude—the armies of the four tribes which composed the nation, under their several banners, glittering with feathers, and marching in regular divisions to the sound of wild music, as well as a host of women and children waving knots of flowers, and uttering cries of welcome—advancing to do them honour. Amador forgot the valiant appearance of the warriors, while gazing on the superior splendour of the armed native bands of old Governor Martin. These warlike people, in imitation of their Christian rulers, had learned to divide their confused throngs into squadrons and companies, ranked under separate leaders, and now approached in what seemed well-ordered columns.

Bunches of red and white feathers waved among their long locks, and ornamented their wickered shields.

The short tunic of coarse white cloth, left their muscular and well sculptured limbs free for action; and as they strode along, brandishing their swords of obsidian, a heavy bludgeon, armed on either side with blades of volcanic glass, or whirling in their slings those missiles of hardened copper armed with sharp horns, which were capable of piercing the toughest armour—and ever and anon mingling their fierce cries with the savage sound of drum and flute, they made a show not more remarkable than glorious.

At the end of each division, under his peculiar standard (the image of some bird of prey, or wild beast, very gorgeously decorated), marched each chieftain, with the great plume of distinction rising full two feet above his head, and nodding with a more than barbarous magnificence.

Thus apparelled and thus displayed, they advanced to the head of the Christian army, and dividing on either side, so as to surround them with a guard of honour, each individual, from the naked slinger to the feather-crowned chief, did homage to the Christian general, by touching the earth with his hand, and then kissing the humbled member.

While at the same moment a number of priests with black robes, and hair trailing almost to the ground, waved certain pots of incense before him, —a mark of distinction which they afterwards extended to the cavaliers that surrounded him. The religious ire of Amador was inflamed, when it became his turn to receive this fragrant compliment; and looking down fiercely upon the innocent censer-bearer and somewhat forgetting that English was not the language of the realm, he cried—"What dost thou mean, to smoke me in this idolatrous manner?"

"Sir," said Harry Woodruff, who sat at his side, "be not offended at this mark of reverence, which the customs of the country cause to be rendered to every man of dignity, and which is a harmless compliment. Thou wilt presently see them smoke their own generals and senatorial lawgivers, the last of whom thou mayst see yonder approaching us in a group—those old men with the feather fans in their hands."

As Harry Woodruff predicted, the priests were no sooner done smoking their Christian visitors, than they turned to do similar reverence to their own dignitaries; and Amador's concern was soon changed to admiration, to behold with what lofty state these noble savages received the tribute due to their rank.

"This fellow with the red plume, and the sword that seems heavy enough for a giant's battle-axe," he cried—"the knave over whom they hold a great white bird like an ostrich—he must needs be a king! He bends to Lion Limb, like an emperor doing courtesy to some brother monarch."

"That," said Harry, "is Xicotencal, of the tribe of the White-Bird, the most famous general of the Tlascalans, and, in fact, the captain-in-chief of all their armies.

"He is not less valiant than famous, and not less arrogant than valiant; and at this moment, I think he would rather be knocking his bludgeon over our heads, out of pure love of war, than kissing his fingers in friendship.

"This is the man who commanded the armies which fought us on our first approach; and truly I may say, he fought us so well, that had he not been commanded by the senators, who are the civil rulers, to make peace with us, there is much suspicion we should have seen heaven quickly. For, after having supplied us with food, as scorning to be assisted in his victory by famine, which was somewhat pressing with us, he fell upon us to win it in person; and I must confess, as will be recorded in history, he quite broke and confounded, and would have utterly destroyed us, had it not been for a providential mutiny in his camp in the very midst of his triumph; whereby we had time to rally and take advantage of his distresses.

"The same good fortune might have been his, another time, without so inconvenient an interruption. But it seems the senators only made war on us, to prove whether or not we were valiant men, and worthy to be received as their allies, according to our wish; which being now proved to their satisfaction, they ordered the war to be ended, and welcomed us as friends.

"There never were more valiant men than these soldiers of Tlascala."

"Of a surety," said Amador, "I begin to think

I was somewhat mistaken as to the courage of these barbarians."

"Thou seest the second chief—he of the green penacho, with whom Lion Limb confers so very courteously? That is Talmeccahua, chief of the tribe Tizatlan, a very young warrior, but second in fame only to Xicotencal; and being more docile and friendly, he is much a favourite with our general, and doubtless will be selected to accompany us to the great city.

"Of those reverend old senators I could also give you an account; but we who are soldiers, care not for lawgivers. It is enough to assure you that they are the rulers of Tlascala.

"Thou seest, they kiss their hands to us, as we enter their city.

"For my part, I think them rogues to love us, their truest enemies, better than their domestic rivals, the people of Tenochtitlan. Woe betide them who help us to conquer their foes, when their foes are conquered!"

As Harry spoke, Amador found himself entering the city of Tlascala.

Twilight had darkened over the hills, and in the obscurity (for the moon had not yet risen) he perceived long masses of houses, not very lofty, but strong, on the terraced roofs of which stood many human beings, chiefly women and children, who waved a multitude of torches, and, as they sung what Harry told him were songs of welcome, threw flowers down upon their guests.

Flambeaux was also carried before them in the streets; and with this sort of pomp they were ushered to a great building with extensive courts, sufficient to lodge the whole army, which was assigned them for their quarters.

Great crowds issued from this city to witness the approach of the English.

But although they bore the same features, and the same decorations, though perhaps of a better material, with the Tlascalans, it was observed by Amador, that they displayed no joy or triumph.

In place of these, their countenances expressed a dull curiosity.

And though they kissed the earth and flung the incense, as usual, in their manner of salutation, they seemed impelled to these ceremonies more by fear than affection.

He remarked also, with some surprise, that when they came to extend their compliments to Lion Limb's men, from their chief down to the meanest warrior, requitted them only with frowns.

All these peculiarities were explained.

"In ancient days," said Harry, "they were a nation, like old Martin's islanders, and united with them in a fraternal league against their common enemies, the buccaneers.

In the course of time, however, the people of the city were gained over by the bribes or promises of the pirates; and entering into a secret treaty, they obeyed its provisions so well, as to throw off the mask on the occasion of a great battle, wherein they perfidiously turned against their friends, and, aided by the perfidious buccaneers, defeated them with great slaughter; and, from that day, old Martin's islanders have not ceased to regard them with the most deep and unrelenting hatred."

"The hatred is just; and I marvel they do not fall upon these base knaves forthwith!" said Amador.

"Concerning the gloomy indifference of these people," continued Harry, "as now manifested, it needs only to inform you how we discovered, or, rather (for I will not afflict you with the details), how we punished a similar treachery, wherein they meditated our own destruction, more than half a year ago, when we entered their town.

"Having discovered their plot to destroy us, we met them with a perfidious craft which might have been rendered excusable by their own, had we, like them, been demi-barbarians; but which, as we are really civilized and Christian men, I cannot help esteeming both dishonest and atrocious.

"We assembled their nobles and priests in the court of the building we occupied; and having closed the gates, and charged them once or twice with their guilt, we fell upon them; and some of them having escaped and roused the citizens, we carried the war into the streets, and up the temples; and so well did we prosper that day, and the day that followed (for we fought them during two entire days), that we slaughtered full 600 of them, and that without losing the life of a single Englishman.

"It was a bloody and most awful spectacle," said Harry, with feeling. "We drove the wretches to the pyramids, especially to that which holds the altar of their chief god—the god of the air; and here it was melancholy to see the desperation with which they died; for having refused quarter, they declined to receive it, when pity moved us to grant it.

"About the court of this pyramid there were many wooden buildings, as well as tabernacles of the like materials among the towers, on the top. These we fired; and thus attacked them with arms and flames.

"What ruin the fire failed to inflict on the temple, they accomplished with their own hands; for having a superstitious belief, that the moment a sacrilegious hand should tear away the foundations of their great temple, floods should burst out from the earth to whelm the impious violator, they began to raze it with their own hands, willing, in their madness, to perish by the wrath of their god, so that their enemies should perish with them.

"I cannot express to you the horrible howls with which they beheld the fragments fall from the walls of the pyramid, without calling up the watery earthquake; then, indeed, with these howls they ran to the summit, and crazily pitched themselves from the dizzy top—as if, in their despair, thinking that even their gods had deserted them!"

"It was an awful chastisement, and, I fear me, more awful than just," said Amador.

Many evidences of the horrors of that dreadful day were yet revealed as Amador entered into the city.

The marks of fire were left on various houses of stone, and here and there were vacuities, covered with blackened wrecks, where, doubtless, had stood more humble and combustible fabrics.

The countenance of Lion Limb was observed to be darkened by a frown, as he rode through this well-remembered scene. It was just as he halted at the portals of a large court-yard, wherein stood the palace he had chosen for his quarters, that two Indians, of an appearance superior to any Amador had yet seen, and followed by a train of attendants bearing heavy burdens, suddenly passed from the crowd and approached him.

"Sir," said Harry, in a low voice, to his friend, "observe these new ambassadors, they are of the noblest blood of the city; the elder, he that hath the gold grains hanging to his nostrils, in token that he belongs to the order of princes, is one of the lords of the four quarters—the quarter wherein is our garrison. His name will be to you unpronounceable. The youth that bears himself so loftily is no less than a nephew of the king himself; and

the scarlet fillet around his hair denotes that he has arrived at the dignity of what we should call a chief commander—a military rank that not even the king can claim, without having performed great actions in the field.

As the ambassadors approached, Amador had leisure to observe them.

Both were of good stature and countenance.

Their loins were girt with tunics of white cotton cloth, studded and bordered with bunches of feathers, and hanging as low as the knee.

Over the shoulders of both were hung large mantles of many brilliant colours, curiously interwoven, their ends so knotted together in front as to fall down in graceful folds, half concealing the swarthy chest.

Their sandals were secured with scarlet thongs, crossed and gartered to the calf.

Their raven locks, which were of great length, were knotted together in a most fantastic manner, with ribands, from the points of which, on the head of the elder, depended many little ornaments that seemed jewels of gold and precious stones.

While from the fillets that braided the hair of the younger, besides an abundance of the same ornaments, there were many tufts of crimson cotton-down, swinging to and fro in the wind.

In addition to these badges of military distinction (for every tuft thus worn was the reward and evidence of some valiant exploit) this young prince—he seemed not above twenty-five years old—wore, as he had been noticed by Harry, the red fillet of the House of Darts—an order not so much of nobility as of knighthood, entitling its possessor to the command of an army.

His bearing was, indeed, lofty, but not disdainful; and though, when making his obeisance, he neither stooped so low nor kissed his hand with so much humility as his companion, this seemed to proceed more from a consciousness of his own rank, than from any disrespect to Lion Limb.

"What will these dogs with me now?" cried Lion Limb, at whose feet—for he had dismounted—the attendants had thrown their burthens, and were proceeding to display their contents. "Doth Katamar think to appease me for the blood of my brothers, and pay for English lives with robes of cotton and trinkets of gold? What say the hounds?"

"They say," responded Harry, to his angry general, "that the king welcomes you back again to his dominions, to give him reparation for the slaughter of his people."

"Hah!" exclaimed the leader, fiercely. "Doth he beard me with complaint, when I look for penitence and supplication?"

"In token of his love, and of his assured persuasion that you now return to punish the murderers of his subjects, and then to withdraw the followers from his city for ever," said Harry, "He sends you these garments to protect the bodies of new friends from the snows as well as——"

"The slave!" cried Lion Limb, spurning the pack that lay at his foot, and scattering its gaudy textures over the earth, "if he give me no mail to protect my friends from the knives of his assassins, I will trample even upon his false heart, as I do upon his worthless tribute!"

"Shall I translate your answer word for word?" said Harry, tranquilly.

But Lion Limb had already turned away, as if to humble the ambassadors with the strongest evidence of contempt, and to prove the extremity of his displeasure.

THE BOY KING
OF THE SOUTH SEA ISLANDS.

A LOVING SALUTE.

And it needed no interpretation of words to convince the savages of the futileness of their ministry. The chief bowed again to the earth, and again kissed his hand, as if in humble resignation, while the retreating figure of Lion Limb vanished under the low door of his dwelling.

But the younger envoy, instead of imitating him, drew himself proudly up, and looked after the general, with a composure that changed, as Amador thought, to a smile.

But if such a mark of satisfaction—for it bore more the character of elation than contempt—did illuminate the bronzed visage of the prince, it remained not there for an instant.

He cast a quiet and grave eye upon the curious cavaliers who surrounded him, and then beckoning his attendants from their packs, he strode, with his companion, composedly away.

"In my mind," said Amador, following him with his eye, and rather soliloquising than addressing

No. 47.

himself to any of the neighbouring cavaliers, "there is dignity and contempt in the smile of that heathen prince."

"Truly he is a very proper-looking and well-demeanoured knave," said one. "But the general has some deep policy at the bottom of all this anger."

"By my faith, I think so, now for the first time!" exclaimed Amador: "for although unable to see the drift of such a stratagem, I cannot believe that Lion Limb would adopt such a course, without a very discreet and politic object."

CHAPTER CXXII.

LION LIMB BENT ON WHOLESALE CONQUEST—HIS MARCH THROUGH THE ISLAND.

LION LIMB'S army was prepared, at the dawn of the following day, to resume its march.

But the events of this march were varied by

nothing but the change of prospect, and the wonder of those by whom the valley was seen for the first time.

Amador, after having satiated his appetite with views of lakes and gardens, surveyed the villages and towns of hewn stone that rose, almost at every moment, among them.

A neck of land separates the lakes of Chalco and Xochimilco; and the retreat of the waters has left their banks deformed with fens and morasses, wherein the wild-duck screams among waving reeds and bulrushes.

Originally, these basins were united in one long and lovely sheet of water, divided, indeed, yet only by a causeway built by the hands of man, which is now lost in the before-mentioned neck, together with its sluices and bridges, as well as a beautiful little city, that lay midway between the two shores.

Here was enjoyed the spectacle of innumerable canoes, paddled, with corn and merchandize, from distant towns, or parting with a freight of flowers from the floating gardens.

But this was a spectacle disclosed by other cities of greater magnitude and beauty; and when, from the streets of the city, the army issued at once upon the broad and straight dyke that stretched for more than two leagues in length, a noble highway, through the salt floods of Tezcuco; when Amador beheld islands rocking like anchored ships in the water, the face of the lake thronged with little piraguas, and the air alive with snowy gulls; when he perceived the banks of this great sheet, as far as they could be seen, lined with villages and towns; and especially when he traced, far away in the distance, in the line of the causeway, such a multitude of high towers and shadowy pyramids looming over the waters, as denoted the presence of a city, he was seized with a species of awe.

He rode at the head of the army, in a post of distinction, by the side of Lion Limb, and felt moved to express some of the strange ideas which haunted him.

But looking on the general attentively, he perceived about his whole countenance and figure an expression of singular gloom mingled with such unusual haughtiness, as quickly indisposed him to conversation.

The feelings that struggled in the bosom of the conqueror were, at this instant, akin to those of the destroyer, as he sat upon "the Assyrian mount," overlooking the walls of Paradise, almost lamenting, and yet excusing to himself, the ruin he was about to bring upon that heavenly scene.

Perhaps "horror and doubt" for a moment distracted his thoughts; for no one knew better than he the uncertain chances and tremendous perils of the enterprise, or mused with more fear upon the probable and most sanguinary resistance of his victims, as foreboded by the tumults that followed after the late massacre.

But when he cast his eye backward on the causeway, and beheld the long train of foot and horse following at his beck; the many cannons, which, as they were dragged along, opened their brazen throats towards the city; and rows of spears and arquebuses bristling, and the banners flapping over the heads of his people, and behind them the feathered tufts of his Tlascalans; and heard the music of his trumpets swell from the dyke to the lake, form the lake to the shores, and die away, with pleasant echoes, among the hills; when he surveyed and listened to these things, and contrasted with them the imperfect weapons and naked bodies of his adversaries—the feebleness of their princes—

the general disorganisation of the people—and counted the guerdon of wealth and immortal renown that should wait upon success, he stifled at once his apprehensions.

There were many things in Lion Limb, which, notwithstanding the gratitude and the desires of Midshipman Amador, prevented the latter from bestowing upon him so much affection as he gave to one or two of his followers.

The spirit of the leader was wholly, and, for his station necessarily, crafty; and this very quality raised up a wall between him and one who knew no concealment.

While the general gave himself up to his proud and gloomy imaginings Amador again cast his eyes over the lake. It seemed to him that notwithstanding the triumphant blasts of the trumpet, the neighing of horses, and the multitudinous tread of the foot-soldiers, as well as the presence of so many canoes on the water, there was an air of sadness and solitude pervading the whole spectacle.

The new soldiers were perhaps impressed with an awe like his own at the strange prospect; the veterans were, doubtless, revolving in their minds some of the darker contingencies over which their commander was brooding.

Their steps rang heavily on the stone mole; and as the breeze curled up the surface of the lake into light billows, and tossed them against the causeway, Amador fancied they approached and dashed at his feet, with a certain sullen and hostile voice of warning.

He thought it remarkable, also, that, among the throngs of canoes, there rose no shouts of welcome. The little vessels forming a fleet on either side of the dyke, were paddled along, at the distance of two or three hundred yards, so as to keep pace with the army.

The motion of the rowers, and the gleaming of their white garments, might have given animation, as well as picturesqueness, to the scene, but for the death-like silence that was preserved among them.

The novelty of everything about Amador gave vigour to his imagination.

He thought these paddling hordes resembled the flight of ravens that track the steps of a wounded beast in the desert—or a shoal of those ravenous monsters that scent a pestilence on the deep, and swim by the side of the floating hospital, waiting for their prey.

"What they mean, I know not," mused Amador. "After what Harry Woodruff has told me, I shall be loath to slay any of them; but if they desire to make a dinner of me, I swear I will carve their brown bodies into all sorts of dishes, before I submit my limbs to the imprisonment of their most damnable maws! And yet, poor infidels! methinks they have some cause to look upon us with fear, if not with wrath; I would, however, that they might shout a little, were it only to make me feel more like a man awake; for, at present, it seems to me, that I am dreaming all these things which I am looking at."

The wish of Amador was not obeyed; many a suspicious glance was cast, both by soldier and officer, to the dumb myriads paddling on their flanks; for it could not be denied, though no one dared to give utterance to such a suggestion, that were these countless barbarians provided with arms, as was perhaps the case, and could they but conceive the simple expedient of landing both in front and rear, and thus cut off their invaders from the city and the shore, and attack them at the same time, with good heart, in this insulated and very disadvantageous position, there was no knowing how obscure might be the story of their fate.

But this suspicion was also proved to be ground-less.

No sort of annoyance was practised; none, indeed, was meditated.

The thousands that burthened the canoes, had issued from their canals to indulge a stupid curiosity, or, perhaps, under an impulse which they did not understand, to display to their enemies the long banquet of slaughter which fate was preparing for them.

The army reached, at last, a point where another causeway, of equal breadth, and seemingly of equal length, coming from the south-west, from the city Cojohuacan, ruled by a king (the brother and feudatory of Katamar), terminated in the dyke of Iztapulapan.

At the point of junction was a sort of military work, consisting of a bastion, a strong wall, and two towers, guarding the approach to the imperial city.

It was known by the name of Holoc, and was made famous by becoming the head quarters of Lion Limb, during the time of the siege.

It stood at the distance of only half a league from the city; and from hence could be plainly seen, not only the huge pyramids, with their remarkable towers rising aloft, but the low stone fabrics whereon, among the flowers (for every roof was a terrace, and every terrace a garden) stood the gloomy citizens, watching the approach of the Christian army.

At this point of Holoc, at a signal of the general, every drum was struck with a lusty hand, every trumpet filled with a furious blast, and the Christians and Tlascalans, shouting together, while two or three falconets were at the same time discharged, there rose such a sudden and mighty din as startled the infidels in their canoes, and conveyed to the remotest quarters of Tenochtitlan, the intelligence of the advance of its masters.

Scarcely had the echoes of this uproar died away when the army resumed its march.

They repeated their shouts loudly and blithely, for they now perceived, by the waving of banners and the glittering of spears, that friends were coming forth to meet them.

Two or three mounted cavaliers were seen to separate themselves from this little distant band, and gallop forwards, while the causeway rung to the sound of their hoofs.

Amador, being in advance, was able, as they rushed forward with loud halloos, to observe their persons, as well as the reception they obtained.

His eye was attracted to him who seemed to be their leader, and who, he already knew, was Dick Hamilton.

He rode immediately up, and stretching out his hand, said gaily, and, indeed, affectionately,

"Long life to Lion Limb! I welcome thee!"

Lion Limb took the hand of Dick, and eyeing him steadfastly and sternly, while his old companions gathered around, said, with a most pointed asperity,

"My friend! thou has done me, as well as thy friends, a most grievous wrong; for, by the indulgence of thy hot wrath and indiscretion, thou hast, as I may say, dashed the possession of this island out of our hands, and much blood will be shed, and many Christian lives sacrificed, in a war that might have been spared us, before we can remedy the consequences of thy rashness.

A deep gloom, that darkened to a scowl, instantly gathered over the handsome visage of Dick.

Snatching his hand roughly away, he drew himself up, and perhaps with defiance!

But it was no part of the policy of Lion Limb to carry his anger further than might operate warningly on the officer and on those around; for which reason offering his hand again, as if not noticing the discontent of his lieutenant, he said, with an appearance of sincerity:—

"I have often thought how thou mightest have been spared the necessity of slaying these perfidious and plotting hounds; and it seems to me, even now, if thou couldst, by shutting thyself in thy quarters and avoiding a contest, have submitted to the foolish imputations some might have cast on thee, of acting from fear rather than from prudence, this killing might have been avoided."

CHAPTER CXXIII.

THE LAST GREAT BATTLE—THE INDIANS FIGHT WITH GREAT BRAVERY—THE RESULT.

THE appearance of the vast and remarkable city so occupied the mind of the middy, that, as he rode staring along, he gave but few thoughts, and fewer words, to his companions.

It was sunset, and in the increasing obscurity he gazed, as if on a scene of magic, on streets often having canals in the midst, covered alike with bridges and empty canoes; on stone houses, low, indeed, but of a strong and imposing structure, over the terraces of which waved shrubs and flowers; and on high turrets, which, at every vista, disclosed their distant pinnacles.

But he remarked also, and it was mentioned by those at his side as a bad omen, that neither the streets, the canals, nor the house-tops, presented the appearance of citizens coming forth to gaze upon them.

A few Indians were now and then seen skulking at a distance in the streets, raising their heads from a half-concealed canoe, or peering from a terrace among the shrubs.

He would have thought the city uninhabited, but that he knew it contained as many living creatures hidden among its retreats as some of the proudest capitals of Christendom.

Even the great square, the centre of life, was deserted.

The principal pyramid, a huge and mountainous mass, consecrated to the most sanguinary of deities, though its sanctuaries were lighted by ever-blazing urns, and though the town of temples circumscribed by the great Wall of Serpents which surrounded this Olympus, sent up the glare of many a devotional torch, yet did it seem, nevertheless, to be inhabited by beings as inanimate as those monstrous reptiles which writhed in stone along the internal wall.

In this light, and in that which still played in the west, Amador marvelled at the structure of the pyramid, and cursed it as he marvelled.

It consisted of five enormous platforms, faced with hewn stone, and mounted by steps so singularly planned, that, upon climbing the first story, it was necessary to walk entirely round the mass before arriving at the staircase which conducted to the second.

The reader may conceive of the vast size of this Pagan temple, by being apprised, that to ascend it, the votaries were compelled, in their perambulations, to walk a distance of full ten furlongs, as well as to climb a hundred and fourteen different steps.

He may also comprehend the manner in which

the stairways were contrived, by knowing that the first, ascending latterly from the corner, was just as broad as the first platform was wider than the second; leaving thus a sheer and continuous wall from the ground to the top of the second terrace, from the bottom of the second to the top of the third, and so on, in like manner, to the top.

But the pyramid, crowned with altars and censers, the innumerable temples erected in honour of nameless deities, strange and most hideous, were not the only objects which excited the abhorrence of the middy.

Without the wall, and a few paces in advance of the great gate which it covered as a curtain, rose a rampart of earth or stone, oblong and pyramidal, but truncated, twenty-five fathoms in length at the base, and perhaps thirty feet in height.

At either end of this tumulus, was a tower of goodly altitude, built, as it seemed at a distance, and in the dim light, of some singularly rude and uncouth material.

And between them, occupying the whole remaining space of the terrace, was a sort of framework or cage, of slender poles, on all of which were strung thickly together, certain little globes, the character of which Amador could not penetrate, until fully abreast of them.

Then, indeed, he perceived, with horror, that these globes were the skulls of human beings, the trophies of ages of superstition; and beheld in like manner, that the towers which crowned the Golgotha, were constructed of the same dreadful materials, cemented together with lime.

The malediction which he invoked upon the builders of the ghastly temple, was unheard; for the spectacle froze his blood and paralysed his tongue.

It was not yet dark, when, having left these haunts of idolatry, Amador found himself entering into the court-yard of a vast, and yet not of a very lofty, building—the palace, wherein, with drums beating, and trumpets answering joyously to the salute of their friends, stood those individuals of the garrison who had remained to watch over their prisoners and treasures.

The weary and the curious, thronging together impatiently at the gate, mingling with the garrison and some two thousand faithful Indians, who had been left by Lion Limb as their allies, and who now rushed forward to salute the viceroy of their gods, as some had denominated Lion Limb, made such a scene of confusion, that, for a moment, the middy was unable to ride into the yard.

In that moment, and while struggling both to appease the unquiet of his horse, and to drive away the feathered herd that obstructed him, his arm was touched, and looking down, he beheld his slave, Jacinto, at his side, greatly agitated, and seemingly striving to disengage himself from the throng.

"Give me thy hand," cried Amador, "and I will pull thee out of this rabble to the back of my horse."

But the slave, though he seized upon the hand of his patron, and covered it with kisses, held back, greatly to the surprise of Amador, who was made sensible that hot tears were falling with the kisses.

"I swear to thee, my boy, that I will discover thy father for thee, if it be possible for man to find him," said the middy, diving at once, as he thought, to the cause of this emotion.

But before he had well done speaking, the press thickening around him, drew the boy from his side.

And when he had, a moment after, disengaged himself, Jacinto was no longer to be seen.

Not doubting, however, that he was entangled in the mass, and would immediately appear, he called out to him to follow; and riding slowly up to Lion Limb, he had his whole attention immediately absorbed by the spectacle of the Indian king.

Issuing from the door of the palace, surrounded by the nobles, both male and female, of his own household who stood by him—the latter, at least—with countenances of the deepest veneration—he advanced a step to do honour to the dismounting general, Lion Limb.

In the light of many torches, held by the people about him, Amador, as he flung himself from his horse, could plainly perceive the person and habiliments of the Pagan king.

He was of good stature, clad in white robes, over which was a huge mangle of crimson, studded with emeralds and drops of gold, knotted on his breast, or rather on his shoulder, so as to fall, when he raised his arm, in careless but very graceful folds.

His legs were buskined with gilded leather; his head covered with the crown (a sort of mitre of plate-gold, graved and chased with certain idolatrous devices), from beneath which fell to his shoulders long and thick locks of the blackest hair.

He did not yet seem to have passed beyond the autumn of life.

His countenance, though of the darkest hue known among his people, was good, somewhat long and hollow, but the features well sculptured; and a gentle melancholy, a characteristic expression of his race, deepened, perhaps, in gloom, by a sense of his degradation, gave it a something that interested the beholder.

In the abruptness with which he was introduced to the regal barbarian, Amador had no leisure to take notice of his attendants, all princely in rank, and two or three of them the kings of neighbouring cities.

He only observed that their decorations were far from being costly and ostentatious—a circumstance which, he did not then know, marked the greatness of their respect.

In the absurd grandeur which attached to the person of their monarch, no distinction of inferior ranks was allowed to be traced, during the time of an audience.

In his majestic presence, a vassal king wore the coarse garments of a slave.

So important was esteemed the observance of this courtly etiquette, that, at the first visit made him, in the palace, by the young colonists, the renowned Lion Lion and his proud officers did not refuse to throw off their shoes, and cover their armour with such humble apparel as was offered them.

But those days were passed; the king of kings was himself the vassal of a king's vassal.

Yet, notwithstanding this, it had been, up to this time, the policy of Lion Limb to soften the captivity and engage the affections of the monarch, by such marks of reverence as might still allow him to dream he possessed the grandeur, along with the state, of a king.

Before this day, Lion Limb had never been known to pass his prisoner, without removing his cap or helmet.

Indeed, such had been so long the habit, that all, as they now dismounted, fell to doffing their caps without delay, until the action of their leader taught them a new and unexpected mode of salutation.

The weak spirit of the Indian king had yielded to the arts of the English.

Forgetting the insults of past days, the loss of his empire, and the shame of his imprisonment, he had already conceived a species of affection for his conqueror.

Lion Limb had no sooner, therefore, leaped from his horse, than the emperor, with outstretched arms, and with his sadness yielding to a smile, advanced to meet him.

"King!" said Lion Limb, "dost thou starve and murder my people, and then offer me the hand of friendship? Away with thee! I defy thee, and thou shalt see that I can punish!"

Thus saying, and thrusting the king rudely aside, he stepped into the palace.

A cry of lamentation, at this insult (it needed no interpretation) to their king, burst from the lips of all the Indians.

Many of them, therefore, indignant and grieved at the insult, had their sympathies strongly excited, when they beheld the monarch roll his eyes upon them with a haggard smile, in which pride was struggling vainly with a bitter sense of humiliation.

Several others rushed forwards to atone, by caresses, for the insult.

But it was too late; the king threw his mantle over his head, and without the utterance of any complaint, passed, with his attendants, into his apartments.

His countenance was never more, from that day, seen to wear a smile.

Don Amador de Leste was greatly amazed, and running to the gate, beheld, in the midst of a confused mass of men, rushing to and fro, and calling out as if to secure an assassin, one of Lion Limb's men lying, to all appearance, dead, in the arms of his friends.

Without a moment thinking of the unknown perils among which he was rushing, he ran rapidly in the direction of the cries, and straightway beheld, a little in advance of a great crowd of people, a group, consisting of four or five persons, several of them women, in strange attire, who, shrieking with terror, while at their feet rolled three or four on the ground in close and murderous combat.

The cries of one of these prostrate figures bespoke him to be English.

And while one sinewy Pagan seemed to hold him upon the earth, another stood with his uplifted weapon, in the very act of dispatching him.

At this moment Amador rushed forwards, and shouting, struck the menacing savage a blow that sent him yelling away, and seized upon the other by the shoulder to stab him.

Suddenly, the English youth rose to his feet, with a leap that tumbled the infidel to the earth, and showed him to be already dead, crying aloud, "Fly, or we are all dead men!—Arm! Arm! to the rescue!"

Thus shouting, and seizing upon one of the women, while Amador snatched the arm of the other (for he perceived they were like to be cut off by the approaching crowd), the old sorcerer, with his rescuers, ran towards the palace.

His cries had reached the quarters, and presently they were surrounded by a hundred soldiers bearing lights, in the glare of which Amador had scarce time to note the countenance of any one before he was locked in the arms of Harry Woodruff.

"Stop not to prate and be happy, for the storm comes!" exclaimed Harry.

"To the palace, all of ye! and to the cannon! for were you five hundred men, there are wolves enow at your heels to devour you."

Thus admonished, and perceiving, in fact, that a ...ough silent multitude was approaching, all

were fain to fly, and in an instant they were crowding into the gates of the court-yard.

"This comes of insulting the king!" cried a voice, as Lion Limb, shouting out to clear the gates, was seen himself assisting to draw a piece of artillery to the opening.

"I see nought—I hear nothing," cried the general, affecting not to remark this reproach (which was indeed just, for it was this over-refinement of policy, spread with wonderful celerity throughout the city, which dashed the last scale from the eyes of the Indians, convinced them that their monarch was indeed a slave, and let loose the long-imprisoned current of fury). "I see nought, I hear nought; and my brave lads have been flying from shadows!"

"Say not so; the town is alive," cried the magician. "The hounds set on me, as I was bringing, at your excellency's command, these princesses; and it was only through the mercy of God, my good star, an Indian that I killed for a buckler, and the help of this true middy (whose fate, out of gratitude, I will reveal to him to-morrow), that we were not all killed by the way: for small reverence did the false traitors show to the maidens."

"Clear the way, then. Discharge me the piece, cannonier!" said Lion Limb, "and we will see what our foes look like, so near to midnight."

The match was applied.

The palace shook to the roar.

The blaze, illumining the street to a great distance, disclosed it, to the surprise of all, entirely deserted.

"I will aver upon mine oath," said Amador, "that the street was but now full of people, but where they have hidden, or whither they have fled, wholly passes my comprehension."

"Hidden, surely, in their beds," cried the general, loudly and cheerfully, for he perceived the crowds about him were panic-struck. "They set on the old magician, doubtless, because they thought he was taking away the princesses with violence; and convinced of their error, they have now gone to their rest—a mark of wisdom in which I would advise all here to follow their example."

Thus cheered by their leader, the soldiers began to disperse, and Amador, musing painfully on the mysterious fate of the young Dane, was accosted by Lion Limb, who, drawing him aside, said—"It has been told me, senor, that your boy has made his escape."

"His escape!" echoed the middy, in surprise. "He did indeed vanish away from me, and I know not how, though much do I fear, in a manner that it shocks me to think on. I was about to ask of you, as the boy is a true Christian, as well as a most faithful servant, for such counsel and assistance as might enable me, this night, to rescue him out of the hands of the cannibals; for it would be a sin on the souls of us all, should we suffer him to come to harm."

"And are you so well persuaded of his faith, as to believe him incapable of treachery?" demanded Lion Limb, earnestly; "though forgettest, he has a father concealed among those infidels."

"Ay! by my faith!" cried Amador, joyously; "I thought not of that before. And yet, and yet—"

Here his countenance fell.

"How should he be so mad as to leave us in this strange and huge city, without any hope of discovering the villain, Bill Whetherby?"

"I can resolve thee that," said Lion Limb, "for it is avouched to me that he saw this wretch (whom may Heaven return to me for punishment, for he is a most subtle, daring, and dangerous traitor), this very knave Whetherby, at thy horse's heels; but he could not believe 'twas he."

"Ay! now I see it," said Amador; "and I remember that he wept, as he held my hand, as if grieving to desert me. But, methinks 'twill be well to seek him out and reclaim him. Will you allow me the services of any score or two of men, who, for love or gold, may be induced to follow me in my search?"

"I will answer thee in thine own words," said Lion Limb, "where wouldst thou look in this strange and huge city, with any hope of discovering him? And I will tell thee, what I conceal from my people (for thou art a soldier, and, therefore, as discreet as fearless), that I would not, this night, dispatch a hundred men a mile from the palace, without looking to have half of them slain outright by the rebels that are around us."

"And dost thou think," said Amador, "that these besotted, naked madmen, would dare to assail so many?"

"You will see, by my conscience!" cried Limb Limb, with a grim and anxious smile. "Sleep with arms at thy side, and forget not thy buckler, for I have known an arrow pierce through a good gorget; and they say the Indians can shoot as well. Let not any noise arouse thee, unless it be that of a trumpet. I would have thee sleep well, my friend, for I know not how soon I may need thy strong arm and encouraging countenance."

Thus darkly and imperfectly apprising the middy of his fears (for now, indeed, a demon had roused a thousand apprehensions in his breast), the general departed, and Amador disconsolately pursued his way to his chamber.

When Don Amador returned to the chamber, he threw himself softly on a cot of mats, covered with robes of fine cotton, over which was a little canopy—such being the beds of the better orders.

The crowded state of the palace (for it is recorded, that the number of allies, who remained in the garrison, now swelled the army of Lion Limb to nearly nine thousand men), left him no other choice; and he felt that his presence was perhaps necessary, in the unhappy condition of his knight.

He was mindful to lie with his weapons ready to be grasped at the first alarm.

He remembered also the hint that had been given him, not to be surprised at such tumults, when he heard a sound, continued throughout the greater part of the night, as of heavy instruments knocking against the court-yard wall, convincing him as well of the military vigilance and preparations, as of the fears of his general.

In addition to this disturbance, he was often startled by moans and wild expressions. But, above all, he was troubled with thoughts of Jacinto; and often, as the angel of sleep began to flutter over his eyelids, she was driven away, by some sudden and painfully intense conception of the great peril which must surround the friendless lad, now that the events of the evening proved him to be in the midst, and doubtless in the power, of an enraged multitude, to whom every stranger was an enemy.

Often, too, as he was sinking into slumber, the first voice of dreams would cry to him in the tones of Jacinto, or the silent enchanter would bring before his eyes the spectacle of the boy, confined in the cage of victims, or dragged away by the hands of ferocious priests, to the place of sacrifice.

These distractions kept him tossing about in great restlessness, for a long time; and it was not until the sounds of the workmen in the yard were no longer heard, and until a deep silence pervaded the palace, that he was able to drown his torments in sleep.

He was roused from slumber by a painful dream, and fancying it must be now approaching the time of dawn, he stepped noiselessly away, and gathering his sword and a few pieces of armour in his hands, left the apartment.

From the door of the palace, he could see, dimly—for it was not yet morning—that vast numbers were lying asleep in the court-yard among the horses, while many sentinels were stalking about in silent watchfulness.

He was now able, likewise, to understand the cause of the heavy knocking, which had annoyed him.

The gates were closed.

But in three rude embrasures, which had been broken in the wall by the workmen, frowned as many pieces of ordnance, commanding the street by which he had approached the palace.

Entering this again, and attracted by the distant murmur of voices, he discovered a staircase at the end of a passage, ascending which, he immediately found himself on the terraced roof of the building.

And now he could perceive the exposed condition of the royal citadel, as well as the preparations made to sustain it, in the event of a siege.

The palace itself extended over a great piece of ground, in the form of a square, the walled sides of which were continuous, but the centre divided by rows of structures, that crossed each other, into many little courts.

The buildings were all low, consisting, indeed, of but one floor, except that, in the centre, were several chambers on the roofs of others, that were called turrets or observatories.

The terraces were so covered with flowers and shrubs, that they seemed a garden.

This mass of houses was surrounded on all sides by a spacious court, confined by a wall, six or eight feet high, running entirely round the whole.

The palace, with its outer court, did not yet occupy all of the great square upon which it stood.

It was a short bowshot from the battlements to the houses, which lined the four sides of the square.

Opposite to each side or front of the fabric was a great street, along which the eye, in full daylight, could traverse, till arrested by the surrounding lake.

Directly opposite, likewise, to each of these streets, as Amador soon discovered, the careful general had caused to be broken as many embrasures as he had seen on the quarter of the principal entrance.

And now there were no less than twelve pieces of artillery (with those who served them sleeping in cloaks hard by), looking with formidable preparation down the yawning and silent approaches.

The middy had not yet given a moment to these observations, when he perceived on the top of one of the turrets, a group, who, being relieved against the only streak of dawn that tinged the eastern skies, were plainly seen, gesticulating with great earnestness, as if engaged in important debate.

He approached this turret, and, mounting the ladder that ascended it, was assisted to the roof by the hand of Lion Limb.

"I give you good cheer, and much praise for your early rising, Amador," cried the general, with an easy courtesy and pleasant voice, which did not, however, conceal that he was really affected by anxiety and even alarm: "for this, besides convincing me that no one is more ready than thyself for a valiant bout with an enemy, will give thee an opportunity to note in what way these Pagans advance to assault—a matter of which I am myself ignorant, though assured that nothing can be more warlike to look upon."

"I vow that there are no such besotted, mad, dare-devils in all the world beside, [as [you shall quickly see," said Ted Rawlings; "and I swear to you, in addition, my friends, I did sometimes think of a morning, the very devils that dwell in the pit were let loose upon me. But fear not: with my poor five-score, and the seven thousand Indians, who should not be counted against more than one hundred Christians, I felt no prick of dismay, except when I thought of starvation; and with the force that now aids us, 'twill be but a boy's pastime to kill ten thousand of the bold lunatics each day before breakfast."

To this valiant speech, which was characteristic of Ted—as notorious for boasting as for bravery—Amador replied, complacently—"To my mind, nothing could be stronger than this citadel against such enemies as we may have, especially since the placing of those cannon opposite to the great streets—a precaution which should be commended. Nevertheless, it does not appear to me that we are in any immediate peril of an assault; the infidels are not yet arisen."

"Cast thine eye down yonder street!" said Lion Limb, with a low voice, "keep it fixed intently, for two or three moments, on the shadows, and tell me what thou seest among them. And, while thou art so doing, do not shame to hold thy buckler a little over thy face; for, now and then, methinks, I have seen on yonder house-tops something unlike to rose-buds, glancing among the bushes."

"By my faith," said Amador, hastily, "it does seem to me, that there are men stirring afar in the street—nay, a great number of them, and doubtless clad in white—ay, I perceive them now! But I thought 'twas a dim mist, creeping up from the lake."

"If thou wilt look to the other three streets," said Lion Limb, knitting his brows and scowling around him, "thou wilt see other such vapours gathering about us. Thus do they surround stags in the woods! but sometimes hunters have found more wolves than deer among their quarry; and by my conscience, so will the Indians find their prey, this day, when they come a-hunting against us!—Hah! did I not warn thee well?" cried the general, as an arrow, shot from a distant terrace, and by some unseen hand, struck against the guarding shield with such violence as to shiver its stone head into a thousand fragments. "'Ware such cupids; for, when they miss the heart, they are content to rankle among the ribs. What say ye now? The knaves are coming nearer! Such big rain-drops do not long fall one by one, but show how soon the flood will follow. Cover yourselves! for by my conscience, that was another, though it fell short. I see the house it comes from; and I will reward the messenger shortly with such a cannon shot as shall leave him houseless. How now, trumpeter! thou art nodding! Wake me thy bugle, and let the sleepers look on the white clouds!"

A trumpeter, who stood ready at the base of the turret, instantly wound a loud blast on his instrument.

It was answered immediately by others from every part of the court and building.

As if by magic, the dead silence of the palace was straightway exchanged for the loud din and confusion of a thousand rising and springing to their arms. During this tumult, Lion Limb descended from the turret.

Amador, fascinated by the spectacle (for now, the light of dawn, increasing every moment, fully convinced the most sceptical, that countless barbarians were thronging in the streets, and advancing against the palace), remained for a time on the terrace in company with others, surveying their approach, and kindling into ardour.

The four streets were blocked up with their dusky bodies, for they seemed nearly naked.

Answering the drums and bugles of the English with the hollow sound of their huge tabours, and the roaring yells of great conches, and adding to these the uproar of their voices, and, what greatly amazed the middy, the shrill and piercing din of loud whistling, they pressed onwards, not fast indeed, but fearlessly, until they began to pour like a flood upon the open square.

Nevertheless, and notwithstanding their very menacing appearance, not a bow was yet bent, nor a stone or dart discharged against the English; and they were arraying, or rather grouping themselves (for they seemed to preserve no peculiar order) about the square, as if rather to support some peaceable demand with a show of strength, than to make an absolute attack, when the middy beheld Lion Limb spring upon a cannon, and thence to the top of the wall, and wave his hand towards them with an air of imposing dignity.

The vast herds stilled their cries, and immediately Aixa, guarded by two soldiers who held shields before her, was seen to ascend and stand by the side of her master.

"Ask these hounds," cried the general, with a voice that seemed meant by its loudness to strike the infidels with awe, "wherefore they leave their beds, and come, like howling wolves, to disturb me in my dwelling? What is their desire? and wherefore have they not come with baskets of corn, rather than with slings and arrows?"

The clear voice of Aixa was instantly heard addressing the multitude; and was followed by a shout such as may come from thrice a thousand score men, wherein, and among other inexplicable sounds, Amador heard words repeated with accents in which entreaty seem mingled with fury.

He could not discover the meaning of these cries. But he could conjecture their signification by the reply of Lion Limb.

"Tell the traitors," he exclaimed, sternly, "that their princes have avowed themselves the vassals of my master, the great monarch of England; that their lord and king is my prisoner, and will therefore remain in my dwelling. Tell them also, he charges them to disperse, throw by their arms, and return laden with corn and meat. And add, moreover, that if they do not immediately obey this command, the thunders which God has given me to punish them, shall be let loose upon them, and scatter their corses and their city into the air. Tell them this, and plainly; and hark'ee, cannoniers! stand fast to your linstocks!"

No sooner was this threatening answer made known to the barbarians, than they uttered a yell so loud and universal that the palace and the earth under it seemed to shake with the din.

Immediately every quarter of the edifice was covered with arrows, stones, and other missiles, shot off with extraordinary violence and fury.

Amador prepared to descend, but paused an instant to observe the effect of artillery, for he heard the strong tones of the general shouting,

"Now cannoniers! to your duty, and show yourselves men."

The very island trembled, when twelve cannon discharged nearly at the same moment, opened their fiery throats, and, aimed full among the multitude, poured innumerable death into their ranks.

The island trembled, but not so the naked barbarians.

If the screams of a thousand wretches, mangled by that explosion, rose on the morning air, they were speedily drowned by the war-cries of survivors.

And before the smoke had cleared away, the bloody gaps were filled, and the infuriated multitudes were rushing with savage intrepidity full upon the mouths of the artillery.

Amador hesitated no longer.

He ran down the staircase, paused a moment, and snatching up and rapidly donning the remaining pieces of his armour, immediately found himself in the courtyard, among the combatants.

The middy had been informed by a friend, as a proof of the degree of civilisation reached by the Indians, that their armies were formed with method, and as regularly divided and commanded as those of Christendom—each tribe displaying a peculiar banner, representing the arms of each tribe, separated into squadrons and companies, led by subalterns of precisely ascertained rank and power.

He perceived none of these marks of discipline among the assailants.

And, while properly appreciating their devoted courage, was obliged to consider them no better than a furious and confused mob.

He was right: the real warriors had not yet appeared, and these wild creatures, who came ungeneralled and unadvised to the attack, were no more than the common citizens, fired by the distresses of their king, and rushing to his aid, without any bond of connexion or government, save the unanimity of their fury.

The violence with which they leaped to the attack, carried them to the gates of the court, and to the mouths of the artillery, where they fell under the spears, or were scattered like chaff at each murderous discharge of the cannon.

Added to this, the Tlascalans, animated by their ancient hatred, and the presence of him whom they esteemed almost a god, clambered upon the wall, and with their clubs and lances did bloody execution on the multitudes below.

The Tlascalans were, indeed, almost the only persons of the garrison who suffered much loss; for the young colonists, fenced behind the wall, or the battlements of the terrace, discharged their crossbows and muskets, and handled their long spears in comparative safety.

The din of yells and screams, mingled with the crash and the sharp clang of steel, was in itself infernal; while the peals of artillery, served with such skill and constancy, that every half-minute there was one or other discharged from some quarter of the palace, leaving at each discharge a long avenue of death among the crowds, converted what might have seemed a scene of elysium into a spectacle of hell.

No man could reckon, no man could imagine, the slaughter made by the besieged army among their foes in the short space of half an hour.

But the sun rose, and still found the infatuated barbarians rushing—now with shouts of defiance, and now with mournful cries, as if calling upon their imprisoned king—to add yet another and another layer to the bloody ridges growing in the paths of the cannon-shot.

All this time the captive monarch, unseen by his people, though quickly detected by the sharp eye of Lion Limb, sat in one of the turrets, witnessing the devoted love of his people, and feeling, with sharp pangs, that he had not deserved it.

No smile lit the countenance of the king, and to the demand of Dick Hamilton he replied with dignity, yet with a bitter sorrow—"The Invincible" (so they called Lion Limb, not because they esteemed him a divinity, but a great prince, this being the title of one of the classes of nobility) "has made me a slave; my subjects are his. Let the king govern his people."

So saying, and immediately descending from the roof, he shut himself in his apartments, and resolutely refused to admit another messenger to his presence.

"And the dog denies me, then!" cried Lion Limb, when this answer was repeated to him. "He says the truth: he is my slave; his people are mine; and I will straightway convince them of their subjection. To horse, to horse, brave men," he shouted aloud. "Let it not be said we wasted powder on miserable naked Indians, when we have swords to strike them on the neck, and horses' hoofs to tread them to the earth!"

No one was more ready to obey this call than Amador.

He had stood upon the wall, occasionally striking down some furious assailant with his spear, but oftener cheering others with his voice, and yet remaining more as a spectator than a combatant, disdaining to strike, except when personally attacked, until his blood was heated by the spectacle.

"Mount now, friends, and perhaps we shall find my poor Jacinto among these outrageous infidels. Get to horse, for to-day we shall see what it is to be a soldier!"

His horse stood, in his mail, like the steed of a true knight, champing the bit, and whinnying, for he longed to be in the midst of the combat; and loud was the sound of his neighing, when he felt the weight of his master, and turned his fierce eyes towards the gate.

Before the soldiers, forming three abreast (as many as could at once pass through the gates), loosed their sabres in the scabbards, and couching their spears, had yet received the signal to dash upon the opposing herds, their came from the great pyramid, which was seen rearing its mountainous mass above the houses of the square, the sound as of a horn, sad and solemn, but of so mighty a tone, that it swelled distinctly over all the din of the battle, and sent a boding fear to the heart of Christians.

They knew, or they thought it the sacred bugle which sounded only during the festivals of that ferocious deity, or on the occasion of a great battle, when it was supposed their god, himself, spoke to his children, and bade them die bravely.

There was not one present who had not heard that the effect of this consecrated trumpet, so sparingly used, was to nerve even the vanquished with new spirit, and those fighting with additional rage; and that the meanest Indian, however overpowered, thought not of retreat, when thus cheered by his god.

The surprise of all was therefore great, when, at the first blast, the Indians ceased their cries, and stood as if turned into statues; and they were still more amazed, when, as the brazed instrument again poured its lugubrious roar over the city, the barbarians, responding with a mournful shriek, turned their backs upon the besieged, and instantly began to fly.

THE BOY KING
OF THE SOUTH SEA ISLANDS.

THE LOVERS.

A third blast was sounded, and nothing was seen upon the great square, or the four streets, save heaps of carcasses, and piles of human beings, writhing in the death-agony.

"Here is diabolical magic!" cried Lion Limb, joyfully. "There are more signals made by that accursed horn than we have heard of; and it seems to me, their high priest may be sometimes a coward! Nevertheless, we will look a little into the mystery; for I perceive shining cloaks, as well as the priestly gowns, on the temple, which we will make claim to: for doubtless some traitor is under one of them. Take thou thy party, Dick, and

scour me the streets that lie eastward. We meet at the temple! For ourselves, we are fifty horse, and three hundred foot, all good men; for in this work we shall need no Tlascalans. Let us go; only, 'tis my counsel and command, that we keep together, with our eyes wide open, lest we should have company not so much to our liking."

The colonists cheered, as they rode from the gates—and, with delight, urged their horses over the piles of dead, or smote some straggler with the spear—an amusement in which they were occasionally imitated by the foot soldiers, who followed at their heels.

The same solitude which had covered the city the preceding evening, now seemed again to invest it.

Corses were here and there strewn in the street, as of fugitives dying in their flight.

And once a wounded man was seen staggering blindly along, as if wholly insensible to the approach of his foes.

The sight of this solitary wretch did more to disarm the fury of Amador, than did the spectacle of thousands lying dead on the square; and certain grievous reflections, such as sometimes assailed him after a battle, were beginning to intrude upon his mind, when a horseman, darting forward with a loud cry, and couching his lance, as if at a worthier enemy, thrust the wounded barbarian through the body, and killed him on the spot.

A few rewarded this feat of dexterity with a loud cheer; but there were many, who, like the middy, met the triumphant looks of the champion with glances of infinite disgust and frowning disdain.

As the party approached the neighbourhood of the great temple, they began to perceive in the streets groups of men, who, being altogether unarmed, commonly fled at the first sight of the English; though sometimes they stood aside, with submissive and dejected countenances, as if awaiting any punishment the Tuctli might choose to inflict upon them.

But Lion Limb, reading in this humility the proofs of penitence, or willing to suppose that these men had not shared in the hostilities of the day, commanded his followers not to attack them.

And thus restrained, they rode slowly and cautiously onwards, their fury gradually abating, and the fears which had been excited by the late assault, giving place to hope, that it indicated no general spirit, and no deep-laid plan, of insurrection.

The groups of Indians increased both in numbers and frequency, as the colonists proceeded, but still they betrayed no disposition to make use of the arms which were sometimes seen in their hands.

And the colonists, regulating their own conduct by that of the barbarians, rode onwards with so pacific an air, that a stranger, arriving at that moment in the city, might have deemed them associated together on the most friendly terms, and proceeding in company, to take part in some general festivity.

Nevertheless, the same stranger would have quickly observed, that these friends, besides keeping as far separated as the streets would allow, and even, where that was possible, removing from each other's presence entirely, eyed each other, at times, with looks of jealousy, which became more marked as the Indians grew more numerous.

In truth, the feelings which had so quickly passed from rage to tranquillity, were now in danger of another revulsion.

And many an eye was riveted on the countenance of the general, as if to read a confirmation of the common anxiety, as, ever and anon, it turned from the prospect of multitudes in front, to the spectacle of crowds gathering at a distance on the rear.

"All that is needful," whispered, rather than spoke, Lion Limb, though his words were caught by every ear, "is to trust in our sharp spears. There is, doubtless, some idolatrous rite about to be enacted in the temple, which draws these varlets thitherward; and the gratitude with which they remember our exploits of this morning, will account for their present hang-dog looks. If they mean any treachery, such as a decoy and ambuscade, why, by my conscience, we must e'en allow them their humour, and punish them when 'tis made manifest. I counsel my friends to be of good heart, for I think the dogs have had fighting enough to-day. Nevertheless, I will not quarrel with any man, who keeps his hands in readiness, and puts his eyes and ears to their proper uses."

As if to set them an example, he now began to look about him with redoubled vigilance.

And it was remarked that he passed no house, without eyeing its terrace keenly and stedfastly, as if dreading more to discover an enemy in such places than in the street.

This was, in fact, a situation from which an enemy might annoy the Indians with the greatest advantage, and at the least risk.

The houses of this quarter were evidently inhabited by the rich, perhaps by the nobles.

They were of solid stone, spacious, and frequently of two doors, lofty, and their terraces crowned with battlements and turrets.

Each stood separated from its neighbour by a little garden or alley, and sometimes by a narrow canal, which crossed the great street, and was furnished with a strong wooden bridge, of such width that five horsemen could pass it at a time.

Often, too, the dwelling of some man in power stood so far back as to allow the canal to be carried quite round it, without infringing upon the streets; but more frequently it was fronted only with a little bed of flowers.

The stones of which such structures were composed were often sculptured into rude reliefs, representing huge serpents, which twined in a fantastic and frightful manner about the windows and doors, as if to protect them from the invasion of robbers.

Indeed, these were almost the only defences; for the green bulrush lying across the threshold could deter none from entering; and perhaps none but a barbarian would have seen, in the string of cacaoberries, or of little vessels of earthenware, hanging at the door, the bell to announce his visitation.

A curtain commonly hung flapping at the entrance; but neither plank nor bar gave security to the sanctity of the interior.

Notwithstanding the fears of the general, he beheld no Indians lurking among the terraces, or peering from the windows, but his anxiety was not the less goading for that reason.

For having now drawn nigh to the great square, it seemed to him that he had, at last, thrust himself into that part of the city, where all the multitudes were assembled to meet him—and whether for purposes of pacification or vengeance he dared not inquire.

The appearance of things, as the party issued upon the square, and faced the House of Skulls, was indeed menacing.

That enormous pyramid, which Amador had surveyed with awe, in the gloom of evening, was now concealed under a more impressive veil.

It was invested and darkened by a cloud of human beings, which surged over its vast summit, and rolled along its huge sides like a living storm.

The great court that surrounded it was also filled with barbarians; for though the Wall of Serpents, with its monstrous battlements and gloomy towers, concealed them from the eye, there came such a hum of voices from behind as could not have been produced alone, even by the myriads that covered the temple.

In addition to these, the great square itself was alive with Indians, and the sudden sight of them brought a thrill of alarm into the heart of the bravest.

The people thus, as it were, hunted by their invaders, even to their sanctuaries, turned upon them with frowns, yet parted away from before them in deep silence.

Nevertheless, at this spectacle the colonists came to an immediate stand, in doubt whether to entangle themselves further or to take counsel of their fears, and retreat without delay to their quarters.

While they stood yet hesitating, and in some confusion, suddenly, and with a tone that pierced to their inmost souls, there came a horrid shriek from the top of the pyramid, and fifty voices exclaimed,

"A sacrifice! a human sacrifice! and under the cross that we raised on the temple!"

"The place is defiled by the inhuman rites!" cried Lion Limb, furiously, his apprehensions vanishing at once before his fanaticism. "Set on, and avenge! Couch your lances, draw your swords, and if any resist, slay!"

So saying, he drew his sword, spurred his steed, and rushed towards the temple.

The half-naked herds fled, yelling, away, opening him a free path to the walls; and had that fearful cry been repeated, there is no doubt he would have led his followers even within, though at the risk of irretrievable and universal destruction.

Before, however, he had yet reached the wall, he had time for reflection; and, though greatly excited, he could no longer conceal from himself the consequences of provoking the Pagans at their very temple, and during the worship of their god.

He was, at this moment, well befriended, and numerously, indeed.

But at a distance from the garrison, without musketry, surrounded by enemies whom the eye could not number, and who had not feared to assail him, even when fortified in a situation almost impregnable, and assisted by three times his present force, as well as several thousand bold Tlascalans.

And in addition to all these advantages, there came neither sound of trumpet nor such distant commotion among the Indians as might admonish him of the approach of Dick.

He checked his horse, and waving to his followers to halt, again cast his eyes around on the multitude, as if to determine in what manner to begin his retreat, for he felt that this measure could be no longer delayed.

The Indians gazed upon him with angry visages, but still in silence.

Not an arm was yet raised; and they seemed prepared to give him passage which ever way he might choose to direct his course.

While hesitating an instant, Lion Limb perceived a stir among the crowds, close under the Wall of Serpents, accompanied by a low but general murmur of voices; and immediately the eyes of the Pagans were turned from him, as if to catch a view of some sight still more attractive and important.

His first thought was, that these movements indicated the sudden presence of Dick and his party —a conceit that was, however, immediately put to flight by the events which ensued.

The murmurs of the multitude were soon stilled, and the Pagans that covered the pyramid were seen to cast their eyes earnestly down to the square, as the sound of many flutes, and other soft wind instruments, rose on the air, and crept, not unmusically, along the Wall of Serpents, and thence to the ears of the English.

Before these had yet time to express their wonder at the presence of such peaceful music, amidst a scene of war and sacrifice, the crowds slowly parted asunder, and they plainly beheld (for the Indians had opened a wide vista to the principal gate) a procession, seemingly of little children, clad in white garments, waving pots of incense, conducted by priests, in gowns of black and flame colour, and headed by musicians and men bearing little flags, issue from the throng, and bend their steps towards the savage portal.

In the centre of the train, on a sort of litter very rich and gorgeous, borne on men's shoulders, and sheltered by a royal canopy of green and crimson feathers, stood a figure, which might have been some maiden princess arrayed for the festival, or, as she seemed to one or two of the more superstitious colonists, some fiendish goddess, conjured up the diabolical arts of the priests, to add the inspiration of her presence to the wild fury of her adorers.

She stood erect, her body concealed in long flowing vestments of white, on which were embroidered serpents of some green material.

In her hand she held a rod, imitative of the same reptile.

On her forehead was a coronet of feathers, surrounding what seemed a knot of little snakes, writhing round a star, or sun, of burnished gold.

As this fair apparition was carried through their ranks, between the great wall and the House of Skulls, the Indians were seen to throw themselves reverently on the earth, as if to a divinity.

Those that stood most remote, no sooner beheld her, than they bowed their heads with the deepest humility.

Meanwhile the Indians gazed on with both admiration and wonder, until the train had reached the open portal, at which place, and just as she was about to be concealed from them for ever, the divinity, priestess, or princess, whichever she was, turned her body slowly round, and revealed to them a face of a paler hue than any they had yet seen in the new world, and, as they afterwards affirmed, of the most incomparable and ravishing beauty.

At this sight all uttered exclamations of surprise, which were carried to the ears of the vision, but Amador, fetching a cry that thrilled through the hearts of all, broke from the ranks, as if beset by some sudden demon, and dashed madly towards the apparition.

Before the English could recover from their astonishment, the members of the procession—deity, priests, censer-bearers, and musicians—with loud screams vanished under the portals; and the infidels, starting up in a rage that could be suppressed no longer, rushed upon the middy to avenge, in his blood, the insult he had offered to their deity.

"Quick, to rescue!" cried Lion Limb, "for the young man is mad."

There seemed grounds for this imputation.

But besides the inexplicable folly of his first act, Amador appeared now, for a moment, to be lost in such a maze that the blows of the heavy clubs were rained upon his armour, and several furious hands had clutched not only upon his spear, but upon himself, to drag him from the saddle, before he bethought him to draw his sword and defend his life.

But his sword was at last drawn, his fit dispelled.

And before his countrymen had yet reached him, he was dealing such blows around him, and so urging his courageous steed upon the assailants, as quickly to put himself out of the danger of immediate death.

The passions of the multitude, restrained for a

moment by their superstition or their rulers, were now fully and unappeasably roused; and with yells that came at once from the pyramid, from the temple yard, from the great square, and the neighbouring streets, they rushed upon the English, surrounding them, and displaying such ferocious determinations, as left them but small hopes of escape.

"England for ever! honour and fame!" cried Ted, spearing a barbarian at each word. "What do you think of my Indians now, true friends?"

His cheer was lost in the roar of screams.

Nothing but the voice of Lion Limb, well known to be as clear and powerful in battle as the trumpet which he invoked, was heard pealing above the din.

"Now show yourselves Englishmen and soldiers, and strike! Ho! trumpeter, thy flourish, and find me where lag my lazy friends."

As he spoke he fought.

So violent had been the attack of the infidels, that they were mingled among, and fighting hand to hand with, the English, a confused and sanguinary chaos.

Scarcely, indeed, had the trumpeter time to wind his instrument before it was struck out of his hand by a brawny savage, and the same blow which robbed him of it, left the arm that held it a shattered and useless member.

The blast, however, had sounded.

Almost instantaneously, it was answered by a bugle, afar, indeed, and blown hurriedly, as if the musician were in as much jeopardy as his fellow, but still full of joy and good cheer to the combatants.

"Close and turn! Footmen to your square!" cried Lion Limb. "And, valiant lads, charge now as though ye fought against devils, with angels for your lookers-on!"

"To the temple! to the temple!" cried Amador, with a voice rivalling the general's in loudness, and turning in a frenzy towards the pyramid, down whose sides the infidels were seen rushing with frantic speed.

But the head of his horse was seized by two friendly followers, and while Amador glared fiercely on the other side, the tranquil voice of Harry was heard.

"Separate from our friends, we are dead men!" he said.

"Close and turn, I bid ye!" cried Lion Limb, furiously. "Heed not the wolves that are fast to your sides. Charge on the herds! charge on the herds! and overthrow with the weight of your hoofs. Charge, I bid ye; and care not though ye should find your lances striking against the breast of friends. Charge on the herds! charge on the herds!"

So saying, he set an example, followed by his men, and as the fifty horsemen spurred violently upon the mob, shouting and cheering, the multitude quailed before them, though only to gather again on their flanks with renewed desperation.

"Will ye desert us that are a-foot?" cried voices from behind, with dolorous cries.

"Ho, Dick! art thou sleeping?"

"Heaven be thanked! 'tis the voice of the general!" cried Dick, in the distance.

His voice came from the surge of battle like the cheer of a sailor who recks not for the tempest. It filled with joy all.

"Good heart now, brave hearts," shouted Lion Limb, "for Dick answers me. Rein round, and charge me back the infantry."

Backwards galloped the fifty, strewing the earth

with trampled Pagans; and footmen shouted with delight, as they again beheld their leader.

But the relief and the joy were only momentary.

"Fight ye, and slay! Be firm; wall yourselves with spears, and presently ye shall be lookers-on! Sweep the square again. Goad flanks! couch spears! and this time let me see the red face of my lieutenant, Dick Hamilton!"

Turning and shouting with a louder cheer (for the experience of the two first charges had warned the Indians of their destructive efficacy, and they now recoiled with a more visible alarm), the English again rushed through their foes with a whirlwind; and, brushing them aside, as the meteor brushing the fogs of evening, they dashed onwards, until their shouts were loudly re-echoed, and they found themselves confronted with Dick and his party.

The greetings of the friends were brief and few, for the same myriads, attacking with the same frenzied desperation, invested them with a danger that did not seem to diminish.

"Bring thy foot in front," cried Lion Limb, "and, while they follow me, charge thou behind them. Be quick and be brave. March fast, ye idle spearmen; and stare not, for these are not devils, but men. At them again! We fight for immortal honour!"

The valiant band again turned at the voice of their leader, and again they swept the corse-encumbered square, rushing to the relief of their own infantry.

Following the counsel he had given to Dick, the wary general passed by his foot-soldiers, and bidding them march boldly forwards, and join themselves with the infantry, he charged the infidels from their rear with a fury they could not resist.

Then rushing backwards with equal resolution, discovered the foot-soldiers in the position in which it had been his aim to place them.

The united infantry, fully seven hundred in number, were now protected, both in front and rear, by a band of cavalry; their flanks looking, on one side, to the temple, and, on the other, to a great street that opened opposite.

Arranging them, at a word, in two lines, standing back to back, and seconding himself, the manœuvre which he dictated to Dick, the general swept instantly to that flank which bordered on the Wall of Serpents.

Thus arranged, the little army presented the figure of a hollow square, the chief sides of which were made by double rows of spearmen, and the smaller by bands of horsemen.

Thus arranged, they fought with greater resolution and success; for, parting at once from a centre, the infantry drove the assailants from before them on two sides, while the cavalry carried death and horror to the others; until, at a given signal, all again fell back to their position, and presented a wall altogether inexpugnable to the weak though untiring savages.

It was the persuasion of Lion Limb, that, in this advantageous position, he could, in a short time, so punish his enemies, as to teach them the folly of contending with him, and perhaps end the war in a day.

But, for a full hour, he repeated his charges.

Now pinning his foes against the wall, or the steps of the House of Skulls.

Now falling back to breathe; and, at each charge, adding to the number of the dead, until their corpses literally obstructed his path, and left it nearly impassable.

At every charge, too, his men waxed more

weary, and struck more faintly, while the horses obeyed the spur and voice with diminishing vigour.

And it seemed that they must soon be left, unable, from sheer fatigue, to continue the work of slaughter.

The Pagans perished in crowds at each charge, and at each volley of bow-shots.

But neither their spirit nor their numbers seemed to decrease.

Their yells were as loud, their countenances as bold, their assaults as violent, as at first; and the English beheld the rising sun high in the heavens without any termination to their labours or their sufferings.

Christians already lay dead on the square, or had been dragged, perhaps while yet breathing, to be sacrificed on the pyramid.

This was a suspicion that shocked the souls of many; for, twice or thrice they heard, among the crowds who still stood on the lofty terrace, shooting arrows down on the square, such shouts of triumphant delight as, they thought, could be caused by nothing but the immolation of a victim.

Grief and rage lay heavily on the heart of Lion Limb.

But though the apprehension, that if much longer overworn by combat, his followers might be left even unable to fly, added its sting to the others, shame deterred him, for a time, from giving the mortifying order.

Harassed, and even wounded (for a defective link in his mail had yielded to an arrow-head, and the stone was buried in his shoulder), he nevertheless preserved a good countenance; cheered his people with the assurance of victory; fought on, exposing himself like the meanest of his soldiers.

And several times, at the imminent risk of his life, he rescued certain foot-soldiers from the consequences of their fool-hardiness.

There was among the infantry a man of great courage and strength, by the name of Lezcano, whose only weapon was a huge, two-handed sword, the valiant use of which had gained him among his companions the title of "Two-hands."

No spearman advanced to the charge with more readiness than did this fellow with his gigantic weapon, and none retreated with more constant reluctance.

Indeed, he commonly fell back so leisurely as to draw three or four foes upon him at once.

And it seemed to be his pleasure to meet these in such a way as should call for the praises of his companions.

His daring, that day, would have left him with the additional name of the bravest of the brave, had it been tempered with a little discretion.

But inflamed by the encomiums of his comrades, not less by the complimentary rebukes of his captain, his rashness knew no bounds.

Twice or thrice he thrust himself into situations of peril, from which he was rescued with great difficulty.

He had been saved once by Lion Limb.

It was his fate, a second time, to draw the notice of the general; who, falling back on the infantry, beheld him beset by a dozen foes, surrounded, and using his sword furiously, yet, as it seemed, in vain, for he was unhelmed.

"What ho, Amador!" cried Lion Limb, who was at his side. "Let us resce the madman!"

In an instant of time, the two had reached the group, and raised their voices in encouragement, while each struck down a savage.

At that moment, and while Lezcano elevated his

scimitar, to ward off the blow of a maquahuitl, the massive blade, shivered as if by a thunder-bolt, fell on the earth.

But, before it reached it, the sharp glass of the Indian sword had entered his brain.

The cavaliers struck fast and hard on either hand.

The barbarians fled.

But Lezcano, the Two-handed, lay rolling his eyes to heaven, his head cloven to the mouth.

"If we slay a thousand foes for every Christian man that dies, yet shall we be vanquished!" said Lion Limb, turning an eye of despair on his companion, and speaking the feelings he had concealed from all others.

Indeed, he seemed to rejoice that destiny had given him one follower, to whom he might unbosom himself, without the apprehensions of creating alarm.

He hesitated not to relieve himself of his grief to Amador, for he knew him to be inaccessible to fear.

"Be of good heart, my friend. I have drawn thee into a den of devils. We must retreat, or die."

"I will advance or retreat, as thou wilt," said Amador, with a visage in which Lion Limb now, for the first time, beheld an expression wild and ghastly.

"It matters nothing—here or at the palace! But it's my duty to assure thee of mine own persuasion: retreat may bring us relief—there is no victory for us to day."

"God help thee! art thou wounded?" cried Lion Limb.

"A little hurt," said the middy, tranquilly, "some one not yet being perfected in the use of the spear, thrust this weapon into my back, while aiming at the throat of a cacique. But that is not it. I have, this day, seen a sight, which convinces me we are among magicians and devils; and persuades me, along with certain other recent occurrences, that the time of some of us is reckoned. Therefore I say to thee, I will advance with thee or retreat, as thou thinkest best. To me it matters not; but my counsel is to fly. We may save others."

"It is needful," replied Lion Limb, mournfully.

He gave his orders to certain officers.

The retreat was commenced in the order in which they had fought—that is to say, the infantry, drawing their lines closer together, and facing to the flank, began to march down the street, preceded by Dick, charging the opponents from the front, while Lion Limb and his band, at intervals, rushing back upon the pursuers, kept the triumphant barbarians from the rear.

* * * *

The distance between the great temple and the palace was by no means great, though Lion Limb, for the purpose of prying into many streets, had led his followers against it by a long and circuitous course—a plan which had been followed by Dick, though in another direction.

Indeed, they were not so far separated but that a strong bowman or a good slinger might, from the top of the pyramid, drive his missile upon the roof of the garrison, to the great injury of the besieged, as was afterwards fully made manifest.

The distance, therefore, to be won by the retreating English, was small.

But it took them hours to accomplish it.

It seemed as if the infidels, fearing lest their foes might escape out of their hands, if they slackened their efforts for a moment, were resolved to effect their destruction at any cost, while they were still at a distance from succour.

They pressed ferociously and rapidly on the fugitives.

They gained their front, and thus encompassed them with a compact mass of human beings, against which the English charged, as against a stone wall, slaying and trampling, indeed, but without penetrating it for more than a few yards.

Each step gained by the van was literally carved by the cavalry, as out of a rock.

While the utmost exertions of Lion Limb could do nothing more than preserve his rear band in the attitude of a dike, slowly moving before the shocks of a flood, which it could not repel.

In addition to these alarming circumstances, there were others now developed, of a not less serious aspect.

The canals that, in two or three places, intersected the street, were swarming with canoes, from which the savages discharged their arrows with fatal aim, or sprang, at once, upon the footmen, striking with spears, and were driven back only by the most strenuous efforts.

They had destroyed the bridges.

The canals could only be passed by renewing them with such planks as the infantry could tear from the adjoining houses, and hastily throw over the water, a work of no less suffering than time and labour.

Besides all this, the annoyance which Lion Limb had first dreaded, was now practised by the crafty barbarians.

The terraces were covered with armed men, who besides discharging their darts and arrows down upon the exposed soldiers, tore away, with levers, the stones from the battlements, and hurled them full upon the heads of their enemies.

The sound of drums and conches, the fierce yells, the whistling, the dying screams, the loud and hurried prayers, the neighing of horses—and now and then the shriek of some beast mangled by a rough spear—the rattling of arrow-heads, the clang of clubs upon iron bucklers, the heavy fall of a huge stone crushing a footman to the earth, the plunging of some wounded wretch strangling in a ditch, and the roar of cannon at the palace, showing that the battle was universal—these together now made up such a chorus of hellish sounds, as Amador confessed to himself he had never heard before.

But to these dismal tumults others were speedily added, when Lion Limb, with a fury that increased with his despair, commanded the footmen to fire every house, whose top afforded footing to the ferocious foes—a command that was obeyed with good will, and with dreadful effect.

For though from the nature of its materials, and the isolated condition of each structure, it was not possible to produce a general conflagration, yet the great quantity of cotton robes, of dry mats, and of resinous woods about each house, left it so combustible, that the application of a torch to the door curtains, or the casting of a firebrand into the interior, instantly enveloped it in flames.

Among these, when they burst through the roofs of light rafters, and the thatching of dried reeds, the Pagan warriors perished miserably, or flinging themselves desperately down, were either dashed to pieces, or transfixed by lances.

But the same agent which so dreadfully paralysed the efforts of the Indian, brought suffering scarcely less disastrous to the Christian ranks.

They were stifled with smoke.

They were scorched by the flames of the burning houses.

And, ever and anon, some frantic barbarian, perishing among the fires of his dwelling, and seeking to inflict a horrid vengeance, grasped, even in his death-gasp, a flaming rafter in his arms, and sprang down with it upon his foes, maiming and scorching where he did not kill.

Thus fighting, and thus resisted, weary and despairing, their bodies covered with blood, their garments sometimes burning, the English at last gained the square that surrounded the palace.

Fighting their way through the herds that invested it (for, almost at the same moment that they had been attacked at the temple, the quarters were again assailed), and shouting to the cannoniers, lest they should fire on them, they placed their feet in the court-yard, and thanked God for this respite to their sufferings.

It was a respite from death, for behind the stone wall they were comparatively secure; but not a respite from labour.

The Indians abated not a jot of their ardour.

The same herds that covered the square at dawn, were again yelling at the gates.

And with the same unconquerable fury.

The soldiers, already fainting with fatigue, with famine, and thirst (for they had taken no refreshment since the preceding evening), were fain to purchase, painfully, a temporary safety, by standing to the walls, and keeping the savages at bay, as they could.

The artillery thundered.

The crossbows twanged.

The arquebuses added their destructive volleys to the other warlike noises.

But the Indians, disregarding these sounds, as well as the havoc made among their ranks, rushed, in repeated assaults, against the walls, and sometimes with such violence, that they drove the besieged from the gate, and entered pell-mell with them into the court-yard.

Then, indeed, ensued a scene of murder.

For the Christians, flying again to the portal, cut off the retreat of such desperadoes, and slew them within the walls, without loss, and almost at their leisure.

On such occasions, no one showed more spirit in attacking, or more fury in slaying, than young Ted.

The suit of goodly armour, and his rapid proficiency in the practice of arms, had inflamed his vanity.

He burned to approve himself worthy the companionship of cavaliers.

The native conscientiousness which filled him with horror at the sight of the first blood shed, the first life destroyed, by his hand, had vanished as a dream.

For it is the excellence of war, that, while developing our true nature, and remaining itself as the link which binds man to his original state of barbarism, it preserves him the delights of a savage, without entirely depriving him of the pleasures of civilisation.

The right of shedding blood mankind enjoy in common with brutes.

Doubtless a conformable philosophy will not frown on the privilege, so long as the loss of it would contract our circle of enjoyments.

There is something poetical in the diabolism of a fiend, and as much that is splendid in the ferocity of a tiger.

And though these two qualities be the chief elements of heroism, they bring with them such accompaniments of splendour and sentiment, that he would rob the world of half its glory, as well as much of its poetry, who should destroy the race of the great, and leave mankind to the dull innocence of peace.

There are more millions of human beings the victims of war, rotting under the earth, than now moves on its surface.

The pain of wounds had also produced a new effect in the bosom of Ted.

Instead of cooling his courage, it now inflamed his rage, and helped to make him valiant.

The mild and feeling lad was quite transformed into a ruffian.

So great had become his love of slaughter, and so unscrupulous his manner of gratifying it, that once or twice Amador noticed him, and would have censured him sharply.

But his attention was immediately absorbed by the necessity of self-defence.

The cavaliers had dismounted, and the middy fought at the gates on foot.

In the midst of an assault, in which the defenders had been driven back, but which disgrace they were now repairing, he beheld Ted struggling with a wounded savage, who grasped his knees and hands, but in entreaty, not hostility.

And greatly was Amador shocked when he beheld Ted disengage his arm, and with a shout of triumph plunge his steel into the throat of the supplicating barbarian.

"Art thou a devil, Ted?" cried the middy, indignantly. "That was a knave's and a coward's blow! Thou shalt follow me no longer."

While he spoke, and left himself unguarded, a gigantic Pagan, taking advantage of his indiscretion, leaped suddenly upon him, and struck him such a blow as, but for the strength of his casque, would have killed him outright.

As it was, the shock so stunned him, as to leave him for a moment incapable of defence.

In that moment the savage, uttering a loud yell, sprang forward to repeat the blow, or to drag him off a prisoner, when Ted, fired with the opportunity of proving his valour, rushed between them, and with a lucky blow on the naked neck, instantly dispatched him.

"A valiant stroke!" said Amador, losing somewhat of his heat, as he recovered his wits. "But it does not entirely wipe out the shame of the other. Moderate thy wrath, curb thy fury, and remember that cruelty is the mark of a dastard. Strike no more foes that cry for mercy?"

As his anger had been changed into approbation, so now were his censures abruptly ended by exclamations of surprise.

For at that instant, Ted, grasping his arm with one hand, and with the other pointing a little to one side, turned upon him a countenance full of alarm.

He looked around, and beheld with amazement Dick, entirely unarmed, except with sword and buckler, mingled with the combatants, shouting a feeble war cry, striking faintly, and, indeed, preserved less by his courage than by his appearance, from the bludgeons of the infidels.

His locks (for he was entirely bare-headed) fell over his hollow and bloodless cheeks, whereon glittered, black and hideous, a single gout of gore.

His face was like the face of the dead.

And the savages recoiled from before him, as if from a spirit rousing from Mictlan, the world of gloom, to call them down to his dark dwelling.

In a moment the middy was at his side.

He seemed as if, at the point of death, raised from his couch by the clamours of the contest, and urged into it by the instinct of long habit, or by the goadings of madness.

He submitted patiently, and without words, to the gentle violence of the middy, and was straightway carried to his apartment.

After much search and persuasion, a surgeon was found, and induced to visit Dick.

He dispatched his questions almost in a word, for he was a fighting bachelor, and burned with impatience to return to the contest.

He mingled hastily a draught, which he affirmed to be of wondrous efficacy in composing disordered minds to sleep.

Gave a few simple directions, and excusing his haste in the urgency of his other occupations, both military and chirurgical, he immediately departed.

The history of the remainder of the day (it was now noon) is a weary tale of blood.

Wounds could not check, nor slaughter subdue, the animosity of the besiegers.

The English, tired even of killing, hoped no longer for victory over men who seemed to fight with no object but to die, and who rushed up as readily to the mouth of a cannon, whose vent was already blazing under the linstock, as to the spears that bristled with fatal opposition at the gates.

But night came at last, and with it a hope to end the sufferings that were already intolerable.

The hope was vain.

The barbarians, apparently incapable of fatigue, or perhaps yielding their places to fresh combatants, continued the assault even with increasing vigour and boldness.

They rushed against the court-wall with heavy beams—rude battering-rams—with which they thought to shake it to its foundations, and thus deprive the Christians of their greatest safeguard.

In certain spots they succeeded.

The soldiers cursed the day of their birth, as the ruins fell crashing to the ground, and then saw themselves reduced to the alternative of filling the breaches with their bodies, or remaining to perish where they stood.

It is true, that in this kind of defence, as well as under other urgent difficulties, they received good and manly aid from their numerous allies, the Tlascalans, who fought, during the whole day, with a spirit and cheerfulness that put many a repining Englishman to shame.

But these, though battling equally for their lives, were incapable of withstanding long the unexampled violence of the assaults.

It was soon found that the naked bodies of the Tlascalans offered but slight impediment to the frenzied Indians.

The English, in the expedient used to drive the citizens from their house-tops, had taught them a mode of warfare which they were not slow to adopt.

The palace was of a solid structure, and seemed to bid defiance to flames.

But the same cedars that finished the interior of meaner houses, formed its floors and ceilings.

Every chamber was covered with mats, and most of them were hung with the most inflammable kind of tapestry.

In addition to this, the five thousand Tlascalans, who had been left with Dick, and who slept in the court-yard, besides strewing the earth with rushes —their humble couches—had constructed along the walls of the palace itself, many rude arbours, or rather kennels, of reeds from the lake, to shelter them from the vicissitudes of the rainy season, which had already in part set in.

And, to crown all, the cavaliers, whose horses, as they well knew, were each worth a thousand Tlascalans, had caused stalls to be constructed for them, wherein they were better protected from the weather than their fellow-animals, the allies.

With these arrangements, the Indians were well acquainted.

No sooner, therefore, had they succeeded in beating down several breaches in the wall, and found that they could sometimes drive the beseiged from them, than they made trial of the expedient.

They rushed together against the walls in a general assault, waving firebrands and torches, which those who forced their way through the breaches applied to the stalls and arbours, or scattered over the beds of the Tlascalans.

The dying incendiary, pierced with a dozen spears, ended his life with a laugh of joy, as he beheld the flames burst ruddily up to his brand.

The misery of the English was now complete.

They were parched with thirst.

The sweet fountains gushed only over the square of the temple.

A well, dug, furnished a meagre supply of water, and that so brackish, that even the brutes turned from it in disgust, till forced to drink by pangs that would allow them to be fastidious no longer.

The nearest canal, conducting the briny waters of Tezenco, was shut out by ramparts of savages.

The English, with one universal voice, sent up a cry of despair, as they beheld the flames run over the court, the stalls, the kennels, and up the palace walls, and knew not how to extinguish them.

The cry was answered from without with such yells of exultation as froze their blood.

In the glare of the sudden conflagration, they saw the barbarians rushing again to the attack, darting through the breaches, and leaping over the walls!

In this strait, beset at once by two foes, equally irresistible, equally pitiless, they struck about them blindly and despairingly, cursing their fate, their folly, and the leader who had seduced them from their island homes, to die a death so ignoble and so dreadful.

For a moment, the spirit of the general sunk, and turning to Amador, whose fate it was again to be at his side, he said, with a ghastly countenance, rendered hideous by the infernal glare,

"We die the death of foxes in a hole, very noble friend! Commend thy soul to God, and choose thy death; for we have no water to quench this hell!"

"God help all!" said Amador, with a desperate calmness. "The flames are hot; but the grave is cold."

"The grave is cold!" shouted Lion Limb, with the voice of a madman. "Live in my heart for ever! Cold grave, moist earth! What ho! mad English!" he continued, shouting aloud, and running as he spoke, round the palace. "Earth quenches flames, like water! Swords and hands to the task; and he works best who delves as at the grave of his foeman!"

If there was obscurity in the words of the general it was dispelled by his actions.

Dashing the rushes aside, he loosened the damp soil with his sabre, and flung the clods lustily on the nearest flames.

Loud and joyous were the shouts of his people, as hope dawned upon them with the happy idea.

In a moment the hands of many thousand men were tearing up the earth of the court, and casting it on the flames, while the savages, confidently expecting the result of their stratagem, intermitted their efforts for a while, leaving the gates and breaches nearly unguarded.

It is probable that even this poor resource, in the hands of so great a multitude of men, toiling with the zeal of desperation, might have sufficed to quell the flames.

But, as if Heaven had at last taken pity on their sufferings, and vouchsafed a miracle for their relief, there came, almost at the same moment, the pattering of rain-drops, which were quickly followed by a heavenly deluge; and, as the flames vanished under it, the English fell upon their knees, and, with devout ardour, offered up thanks to the Providence that had so marvellously preserved them.

They sprang from their knees, with bolder hearts, as the Indians again advanced to the assault.

But this was the last attack.

As if satisfied with the toils of the day, or commanded by some unknown ruler, the barbarians, uttering a mournful scream, suddenly departed.

They were heard during the night.

And in the morning, when the waning moon shone dimly through the rack, were seen stirring about the square, but in no great numbers.

And as they did not attempt any annoyance, but seemed engaged in dragging away the dead, Lion Limb forbade his sentinels to molest them.

The guards were set, and the over-worn soldiers retired, at last, to throw their wounded bodies on their pallets.

But throughout the whole night the noises of men repairing the breaches, and constructing certain military engines, assured those who were too sore or too fearful to sleep, that the leader they had cursed was sacrificing a second night to the duties of his station.

While these occurrences were transpiring, Amador had rambled through the streets, and following, very naturally, the only path with which he was acquainted, soon found himself issuing from that gate by which he had entered from Tlascalan.

The domination of the English had interrupted many of the civil as well as the religious regulations of the Indians; and with their freedom departed that necessity and habit of vigilance which had formerly thronged their portals with watchmen.

No Indian guards, therefore, were found at the gate.

The precautions of Lion Limb had not carried his sentinels to this neglected and seemingly secure quarter.

The middy passed into the fields, and was seduced to prolong his walk by the beauty of the night, and by the many pensive thoughts to which it gave birth.

How many times his reflections carried him back to the land of his nativity need not be here related; nor, if he gave many sighs to the strange sorrow and stranger destiny of his friends, is it fitting such emotions should be recorded.

He wandered about, lost in his musings, until made sensible, by the elevation of the moon, that he had trespassed upon the hour of midnight.

Roused by this discovery from his reveries, he returned upon his path, and had arrived within view of the gate, when he was arrested by the sudden appearance of four men, running towards him at a rapid rate, and presenting to his vision the figures of Indian warriors.

No sooner had these fugitives approached near enough to perceive an armed man intercepting the road than they paused, uttering many quick, and, to him, incomprehensible exclamations.

But though he understood not their language, he was admonished by their actions of the necessity of drawing his sword and defending himself from attack.

THE BOY KING

OF THE SOUTH SEA ISLANDS.

For the foremost, hesitating no longer than to give instructions to his followers, instantly advanced upon him, flourishing a heavy axe of stone.

Somewhat surprised at the audacity of this naked barbarian, but in nowise daunted at the number of his supporters, the middy lifted up his trusty sword, fully resolved to teach him such a lesson as would cause him to remember his temerity for ever.

No. 49.

But almost at the same moment his wrath vanished, for he perceived, in this assailant, Bill Whetherby.

"Sir!" said he, elevating his voice, but forgetting his want of an interpreter, "drop thy sword, and pass by in peace, for I am loth to strike thee."

But the valiant youth, misconceiving or disregarding both words and gestures, only approached with the more determination, and swung his weapon over his head, as if in the act of smiting, when one present exclaimed eagerly—

"Thou art safe."

Bill lowered his weapon, and merely surveying the middy with an earnest look, passed by him on his course, and was followed by the two others.

Meanwhile, Amador, regarding Bill, said—" I know not—notwithstanding this present service, for which I thank thee—not so much because thou hast stepped between me and danger (for it must be apparent to thee I could with great ease have defended myself from such feeble assailants), but because thou hast freed me from the necessity of hurting this poor prince ;—I say, notwithstanding all this, Bill, I know not whether I should not now be bound to detain thee, for it is not unknown to me that thou art at this moment a deserter and traitor."

"Sir," said Bill, withdrawing a step, as if fearing lest the middy would be as good as his word, "my treason is against my misfortunes, and I desert only from injustice ; and if my noble lord knows thus much, he knows also that to detain me would be to give me to the gallows."

"I am not certain," said Amador, "that my intercession would not save thy life, unless thou hast been guilty of more crimes thrn I have heard."

"Guilty of nothing but misfortune," said Whetherby, earnestly "guilty of nothing but the crimes of others, and of griefs, which are reckoned against me for sins."

"Guilty," said the middy, gravely, "of treating in secret with these barbarians, who are esteemed the enemies of thy Christian friends ; and guilty of seducing into the same crime thy countrymen, one of whom, I am persuaded, did but now pass me with the Indians, and one of whom, also, hath charged thee with tempting him."

"Sir," said Bill, hurriedly, " I cannot now defend myself from these charges, for I hear my enemies in pursuit."

"And guilty," added Amador, with severity, "as I think, of deserting thine own flesh and blood— thy poor and friendless boy."

Bill flung himself at the feet of the middy, saying wildly,

"My flesh and blood ! and friendless, indeed ! unless thou wilt continue to protect him. For the love of heaven ! for the sake of the mother who bore you, be kind and true to my boy ! Swear thou wilt protect him from malice and wrong !"

"Dost thou confess thou wert about to steal him from his protector ? Now, by heavens ! this is but an infidel's gratitude ?"

"Sir !" said Bill, "you reproached me for forsaking him ; and now you censure me for striving not to forsake him ! But the sin is mine, not Jacinto's. I commanded him to follow me ; and he would have obeyed me, had he not found thy friend swooning among the ruins. He tarried to give him succour, and thus was lost ; for the soldiers came upon him."

"Is this so, indeed ? My friend left swooning ? Thou wert but a knave not to tell me this before !"

"Go not, till thou hast promised to requite his humanity with the truest protection," said Bill.

"Surely he shall have that without claiming it."

"Ay, but promise me, swear it to me !" cried Bill, eagerly. "The colonists will call him mine accomplice."

"They will do the boy no wrong," said Amador ;

"and I know not why thou shouldst ask me the superfluity of an oath."

"I am a father, and my child is in a danger of which thou knowest not ! For the love of God, give me thy vows thou wilt not suffer my child to be wronged !"

"I promise thee this ; but acquaint me with this new and unknown peril. If it be the danger of an accusation of witchcraft, I can resolve thee, that that is not regarded by the general."

"My pursuers are nigh at hand," cried Bill, 'and I must fly ! A great danger besets Jacinto, and thou canst preserve him. Swear to me, thou wilt not wrong him, and suffer me to depart."

"Wrong him ?" said the middy. "Thou art beside thyself. Yet, as it does appear to me, that the soldiers are approaching us I will give thee this very unreasonable solace. I swear to thee, very devoutly, that, while heaven leaves me my sword and arm, and the power to protect, no one shall, in any way, or by any injustice, harm or wrong the boy Jacinto."

"I will remember thy promise, and thee !" cried the buccaneer, seizing his hand and kissing it.

"Tarry, Bill. Reflect ; thou rushest on many dangers. Return, and I will intercede for thy pardon."

But Whetherby, running with great speed after his companions, was almost already out of sight ; and Amador, musing, again turned his face towards the town.

"If I meet any of Lion Limb's men," he soliloquized, " I must, in honour, acquaint them with the path of Bill ; whereby he may be captured. I am resolute. I cannot, by utterly concealing my knowledge of this event, maintain the character of a just and honest man ; yet it appears to me, my duty only compels me to carry my information to the general. This will I do, and by avoiding the pursuers, preserve the obligations of humanity to the fugitive, without any forfeit of mine honour."

Thus pondering, and walking a little from the path, until the pursuers had passed him, he returned to the quarters.

CHAPTER CXXIV.

BILL WHETHERBY ABDUCTS EMMA CLARENCE, AND TAKES HER CAPTIVE TO KING BRAJOS—THE BRAVE YOUNG VALENTINE—THE FIGHT—THE UNKNOWN KNIGHT DEFENDS EMMA—THE MYSTERIOUS VISIT TO HER CHAMBER AT MIDNIGHT.

How the strange mischance happened, it remains to be seen in another chapter ; but certain it is that Bill Whetherby had an object in his sudden flight from the gallant middy, Amador.

He, and a secret band, had planned the capture of the beautiful Emma Clarence, and had effected his purpose.

He was then hurrying away, with the speed of the wind, to carry Emma away to the court of a barbarian king, on a distant part of the island, who had promised Whetherby both wealth and honour as the reward of his boldness and audacity.

Bill now well knew that the fortunes of Mungo were almost blasted, and it was to secure his own life that he had resolved on so bold a deed as the abduction of Emma, during the excitement and noise of the troubles and battles in which her lover, Lion Limb, was engaged.

Hence, but a very few hours had elapsed since his conversation with the middy, Amador, when Bill fled with his fair captive, Emma, and a faithful half-breed maid called Matilda.

Bill was proud of his deed, base as it was, and, having galloped very hard for many weary miles, he and his captives were met by a gallant cavalcade, sent out by King Brajos to escort them to his palace.

The cavalcade having reached the folding doors of the hall, the king alighted from his saddle, to salute Matilda, who awaited in a covered corridor to welcome his arrival.

Then severally presenting the gay cavaliers, companions of his visit, they dismissed their richly-caparisoned horses to the grooms, and repaired to the banquet-gallery, wherein an ample repast awaited to refresh them.

"How fares the lovely Emma?" inquired the king, addressing Matilda; "I trust, ere long, with all respect and friendship, to meet her."

"Pardon me, my lord; she is little accustomed to general society, and is yet too young to make her public appearance."

"But it must never be told," proceeded the rormer, "that King Brajos suffered a young and noble lady, during his presence at the palace, to femain a solitary captive in her chamber; beshrew me now, but the circumstance would be sufficient to hasten the departure of my friends."

"To Emma, such a seclusion is no sacrifice; she is accustomed to retirement; however, as the king so earnestly desires to meet the orphan child——"

"It shall be so," continued Brajos, filling up the pause.

Matilda bowed, and rising from table, begged permission to withdraw.

The gay manners of the king and his guests little accorded with the melancholy emotions which prevailed in her bosom.

There was a certain boldness, approaching to absolute command, in Brajos, which displeased her.

But it might be the effect of travel, and constant intercourse with the world.

His dark, glaring eye rather chilled the bosom of innocence with an unaccountable dread, than subdued it to esteem and love.

His light converse, ill according with the dignity of his rank and years, more excited contempt than veneration.

By no means delighted at the intelligence of her maid, Emma began to prepare herself for entering the hall at dinner, with an unwilling heart.

She loved solitude, and would have preferred a wild ramble among the hills with Lion Limb, to the proudest banquet of affluence.

"Bless me, lady," said the maid, as she assisted Emma to attire, "are you not quite delighted with the grand company in the hall? Oh, my lady, they look so noble, and so gallant too, with their feathers and their swords! There's one, my lady, much handsomer than the rest, with dark eyes; and would you believe it, absolutely he declares he is already desperately in love with me."

"I have read, Tilly, of some, who are in the habit of declaring a passion for every maiden they encounter," said Emma.

"True, very true," answered the maid, in an under and displeased tone of voice; "but this one sighs so tenderly, and utters such sweet things! and you know my lady, 'tis a dreadful thing to remain single for ever; what's to become of one, when one gets old and neglected, without a defender, or a friend to drive away the buccaneers?"

"We are told, Tilly, that there is no life more honourable than a state of virtuous union; and where congenial hearts and circumstances conspire to render it such, it is, I doubt not, commendable."

"Well, now," cried the maid, in ecstacy, "these are the very words of my poor own heart, as I uttered them to the weird gipsy woman in the glen."

Emma smiled.—"Well," said she, "I believe my raiment is properly adjusted."

The maid retreated a few paces to gaze upon Emma. At length—

"Oh," said she, "that I could be such a lady, to wear silks and satins! I'd flaunt with these high people; I'd laugh with the handsome, and sneer at the ugly; methinks, lady, already do I hear their drawn swords rattling to attain my fair hand."

"You are considerably changed, since even the sound of a distant bugle terrified you so much," exclaimed Emma, laughing.

"Oh, I thought that was the dreadful Mungo," cried Tilly, as Emma descended in order to go to the banquet.

On entering the hall, the guests, who already awaited their appearance, arose by way of courtesy, and a mingled tone of admiration, at Emma's beauty, ran through the apartment.

She was attired in deep mourning, which served to heighten her charms, and add additional effect to the pensive sweetness of her expressive countenance.

Brajos fixed his eyes upon her, and as he took her trembling hand, felt a sudden warmth gliding to his heart.

He had attended many native courts, where princesses had been renowned for beauty, but never had he witnessed such exquisite loveliness till now.

Emma felt truly uneasy in his attentions.

His looks chilled her with unconquerable dread.

And as her eyes averted to two knights, who appeared the confidants of the king, a heavy sadness weighed upon her heart.

For notwithstanding the rich apparel that attired them, the savage fierceness and bold confidence which they assumed, alarmed her sensitive mind.

Scarcely had the repast concluded, ere, pleading sudden indisposition, accompanied by Matilda, and contrary to the earnest entreaties of King Brajos, she withdrew.

Till grey twilight had veiled the castle, Lady Emma and her maid amused themselves in conversing on the manners and appearance of the king's guests.

Their sentiments were mutual on the occasion.

But the maid, fearful of terrifying her mistress, concealed the dark suspicions which her bosom harboured, by drawing happy conclusions to Emma's fertile suggestions.

At length, in order to drive away painful reflection, Matilda requested her to take the guitar, and accompany with its mellow chords some artless ballad.

But scarcely had her fingers wandered over the instrument, ere the loud and tumultuous sound of mirth echoed from the hall.

Terrified, Emma clung to her maid for protection, as the voices of two persons, warm in anger, assailed their fearfully attentive ears; and in an instant after, some one tapped lightly for admission at the door of the apartment.

"Who knocks?" inquired Lady Emma, struggling with her emotion.

"A friend, my lady," replied a faint voice.

Matilda instantly drew aside the bolt, as an Indian girl made her appearance in the chamber, and hastily closing the door, exclaimed, in a voice of terror—

"Oh, my lady, you will surely be murdered!"

"Murdered!" faltered Matilda and Emma, in a breath.

"Yes, my lady; the king has been disputing with one of the company, till at last they drew their swords, and fell desperately on each other; 'tis all on your account, Lady Emma."

"Mine!" shuddered Emma.

"Yes, my lady, for the king saying that you were uncommonly beautiful, and that he felt half resolved to marry you, one exclaimed,

"'Marry, indeed! a pretty resolution for King Brajos.'

"At these words the king appeared angry, when the former, speaking something to him in an under tone, he became furious; and the guest, deeply wounded, was conveyed to his couch as I left the hall."

"Merciful Heaven!" cried Emma, bursting into tears, "what will become of us, friendless, unprotected, as we are?"

"Ah!" continued the Indian girl, "Whetherby says this is nothing, in comparison to some of the king's deeds when in anger, to which he has been a frequent and unwilling witness."

"Help, help!" exclaimed Matilda, observing Emma fainting.

Opening the balcony for the admission of air, how great was her surprise at beholding the king and his company on horseback, winding through the valley by moonlight.

A thousand wild conjectures now flashed, with additional force, across Matilda's mind; and the distress which Emma evinced, added so materially to her alarm, that she was under the necessity of retiring to her couch.

Speedily forgetting the fears which had recently invaded her bosom, she hung, with genial tenderness of affection, over the pillow of her mistress.

And administering cheering restoratives with her own hand, endeavoured, at the same period, to inspire her with fortitude and implicit reliance on the benign and invisible aid, which is ever extended, in the hour of peril, to preserve the innocent sufferer from the triumphs of guilt.

It was the design of King Brajos, during his residence at the castle, to hold a solemn tournament, and to which he intended to invite all the neighbouring chiefs.

King Brajos, whose ever active, designing mind might well serve as a contrast to the cold and insipid turn of Whetherby, with latent emotions of contempt, laughed at the recital of Emma's abduction.

The following day was passed in the chase and revelry; till Brajos, at a late hour, withdrew, in order to be in readiness for the guests expected early the following morning at the castle.

Shortly after his departure, Whetherby informed an English captain, named Valentine, of his design of being present at the tournament.

"At which," added Bill, "you have now an opportunity of signalizing yourself in arms, agreeable to the frequent wish you have professed."

With the earliest streak of dawn, Valentine left his couch, and hastening to the armoury, selected a suit of blue and silver mail, on the helmet of which appeared a lamb, surmounted by a rich plume of white feathers; his shield of azure, studded with bossy stars, encircling the appropriate, but rude motto, in dead gold—

> "Heavene, I truste,
> Wille aide the juste."

Valentine's heart glowed with love and enthusiasm, as he equipped himself for the encounter.

"Yes," said he, internally, "I shall again behold Queen Emma, and perhaps, victor in the combat, kneel at her feet, and receive from her, too, the reward appropriated to the conqueror, rendered inestimable by the hands which bestows it."

His youthful breast was pregnant with these emotions, and he attended the summons of the trumpet.

The inner court of the castle, hung with sumptuous tapestry, was already thronged with numberless spectators, assembled to witness the tournament.

Near the folding doors of the hall, beneath an extensive awning of embroidered silk, and attended by a concourse of ladies, Emma, at the earnest entreaties of the king, had consented to behold the combat.

And, attired in virgin white, on a couch of rose-coloured satin, overhung with a plume, and canopy of spangled drapery, holding on her fair arm a richly-jewelled scarf, to be bestowed on the victor of the day, Emma sat, queen of the admiring throng.

At the accustomed signal, several knights entering, fought with one of unusual bravery and strength, who, in defiance of every effort to the contrary, seemed likely to win the prize, for which, observing his uncommon skill, few cared to dispute.

But as he still proudly paced the ring, and commanded the herald in haughty tones to proclaim again his challenge, young Valentine, mounted on a steed of snowy whiteness, whose ample trappings corresponded with the armour of its rider, made his appearance.

After a combat of unusual length, he succeeded in throwing his adversary to the ground, who retired in confusion.

The challenge was again thrice sounded.

But no one answering to the summons, the youth, amid the shouts of the multitude, lifting up his beaver, cast himself at Emma's feet, in order to receive the scarf.

Overjoyed at the sight of young Valentine, who had been a captive for a long time, with trembling hands she hastily threw over his shoulder the sparkling reward of his valour, and raising him with a smile of joy, congratulated him warmly on his success.

King Brajos, who had been a silent observer of Emma's countenance, mad with jealousy, now rushed into the lists.

"No," cried he, "for the honour of true knighthood, I shall not permit the triumph of a total stranger, but await to dispute the prize."

Valentine, at these words, imprinting a respectful kiss on Emma's fair hand, conducted her again to the canopy, and drawing his sword, rushed towards the king.

The blast of a horn now echoed through the castle gates, and a knight, in gold armour, mounted on a black charger, and accompanied by a long train of warlike attendants, clad in forest-green, galloped furiously into the court.

At the unexpected appearance of this martial band, a mingled tone of wonder and applause prevailed through the multitude, as the knight in gold armour resigned his charger to a page, and drawing his sword, approached the king.

"Wretch!" he exclaimed, in an indignant tone, "how long will you continue to shed the blood of innocence?"

At these words Brajos would fain have retired among the company.

But striking him with his weapon,

"Come," cried the knight, "thou proud and

guilty king, and dispute this prize with one as well skilled as yourself, and who neither fears your anger nor revenge."

Bursting with passion, Brajos now fiercely parried the skilful blows of his assailant.

But his furious efforts availed not.

Easily discomfitted, disgraced, and confounded, he abruptly retired, amid the loud derisions and repeated shouts of the assembly.

"Now, then," said the stranger, gracefully receiving the scarf from Emma, which Valentine had resigned, "the prize is *mine*, and I restore it to the person that I understand to be its rightful owner."

And, presenting it to the youth, he lightly vaulted to his saddle, and waving his hand with dignity, accompanied by his attendants, left the arena.

No sooner had he withdrawn, than a cry of alarm prevailed, and the people forming groups, inquired the name of this mysterious warrior, when suddenly "Lion Limb !" responded from lip to lip.

Women fainted.

The guests, in wild confusion, hurried to their homes.

As Bill Whetherby, her gaoler, did not present himself, it never occurred to Emma's mind that he was present at the tournament, till looking from the balcony during the evening, she beheld him in conversation with Brajos.

A sudden dizziness overcame her senses, and a dreadful conviction of the result of their secret communion pressed fearfully upon her heart.

She now meditated on the strange conduct of the king, and the words of the unknown knight forcibly returned to her recollection.

Labouring under gloomy and distracted thoughts till a late hour, Emma retired.

But not to rest.

The conference of Brajos with Whetherby, to whom he was almost a stranger, continued wildly to harass her nervous apprehensions, and she wept.

The clock was proclaiming the solemn period of midnight, as Emma, dejected and oppressed, with an unusual presentiment of something dreadful about to occur, still sat despondingly upon her couch, as the calmness of night became suddenly interrupted by the approach of horses in the valley.

Supposing it to be the king returned, she silently opened the lattice ; but the night being unusually dark and stormy, it was in vain she endeavoured to distinguish the surrounding objects, while the wind, howling mournfully through the battlements, and the warder's heavy tread receding along the ramparts, as it died away round some distant angle of the pile, added fresh solemnity to the sullen hour, by leaving an awful silence on the timidly-attentive ear.

Closing the casement, Emma cast her eyes fearfully across the chamber, as the apparent sound of some one breathing therein arrested her attention.

Horror-struck, for a moment irresolute and half doubting it to be the effect of the night breeze, as it whispered through the adjoining galleries, she took the lamp and examined the tapestry, but discovering no cause for her fears, became composed.

Approaching the bed, previous to retiring to rest, the lamp suddenly flashed and expired.

However, as the faint flickering moonlight fell upon the floor, casting thereon, in grotesque forms, the network of the lattice, and affording sufficient lustre to discover familiar objects, Emma silently sank on her knees, when the same sound again struck her terrified imagination.

Gazing around, she observed the door slowly and cautiously unclosed by a mailed hand, in which a drawn dagger reflected the opposite light.

Terrified at a circumstance so singular, Emma screamed aloud, as Whetherby rushed in the apartment, and throwing a heavy mantle over her features, forcibly conveyed her through the gallery.

Almost fainting, our heroine soon felt the chill night-air keenly on her confined hands, and perceived, by the motion of some rude native carriage, into which her remorseless persecutor had placed her, that she was rapidly descending the mountain.

At length, reviving from the intense heat of the drapery that enveloped her, Emma perceived herself extended in a covered litter, in a strange country, supported by the arm of Whetherby.

"Father of Mercy," sobbed she, raising her eyes, filled with tears, to heaven, "save me from the dark designs of evil-minded men."

"Silence !" answered Bill, in a savage tone of voice, which terrified her.

"Oh, tell me. Have I injured or offended you, that, like an unlucky criminal, you convey me to some lone solitude, wherein, perhaps — dreadful thought !—my devoted blood must pay the forfeit of its unconscious offences—my cold corse, a prey to the merciless vulture, slumber in an unknown, unhallowed tomb !"

With a sullen frown, Whetherby answered not to her inquiries, but descending from the litter, closed the curtains, leaving Emma a prey to sorrow and apprehension.

CHAPTER CXXV.

EMMA A CAPTIVE—DEATH OF VALENTINE—BENDETTA AND THE VILLAIN.

AFTER a journey of considerable length, Emma was permitted to descend.

But judge of her terror, on being conducted to a miserable cabin, filled with armed men, whose fiend-like appearance chilled her heart, as, unmindful of her agonizing and convulsed sighs, they began to carouse at a table, on which were arranged refreshments by a hag in human shape, whose ragged elf-locks, rude, unsightly garments, and pitiless aspect, bespoke her abandoned to that wretchedness, which, from long habit, becomes familiar, and deadens alike the throb of selfish and disinterested feeling.

"Bendetta," cried one of the men, in a tone of mockery, to the old woman, "sing us a song. What, no reply ? How now, thou shrivelled beldame ! is this your gratitude ?"

At the same time throwing the dregs of his cup into her face, the rest broke forth with loud and vulgar bursts of laughter.

"Cowards !" answered Bendetta, firmly approaching the ruffians, "call ye yourselves men ? Ye excel fiends in infamy !—Lion Limb would not have acted thus."

"Lion Limb," answered one of them, with a sneer, "seems, of late, to be highly estimated in your regards ; we should be glad to learn what *you* know about him ?"

"That whatever may be his profession," replied Bendetta, "he is too noble to trample on the sufferings of a female."

"Peace !" cried Whetherby, in a voice of thunder, smiting the table with his hand, "or we shall cool the warmth of your anger in the lake."

Emma shuddered.

But Bendetta, fearless of their threats, still continued,

"Yes, yes," exclaimed she, "that indeed would become ye; for in torturing the defenceless only, ye excel."

"Out, out, old hag!" vociferated one, rudely grasping her arm.

"Unhand her," interrupted another; "you know well enough she is superannuated; had we not better convey Valentine's body from the litter into the next apartment?"

They now lifted up the tapestry extended over the carriage in which Emma had been conveyed, and how indescribable were her feelings, at perceiving that the seat on which she had been sitting during her melancholy journey, was formed by the lifeless body of Valentine, who had expired of wounds given by King Brajos.

"It was too bad to give you no better companion, lady," said one, laughing at Emma's pale cheek. "But by this hour you must lack something to revive your drooping spirits," at the same time presenting a cup of wine, of which Emma, oppressed with fatigue, partook sparingly.

"Whose bloody work is this?" cried Bendetta, looking sorrowfully on the murdered body of young Valentine.

"This is the king's work," answered one.

"Then, has he, in one unlucky moment, undone more than his whole existence can amend?"

"Silence, woman!"

"Whetherby, I will not be silent; there is no other in your vile, unprincipled society, deserving the appellation of man, since poor Valentine is slain!"

She now gazed piteously upon the corse, as a solitary tear, gliding over her hollow cheek, fell upon the inanimate hand which she held in her own.

Emma's heart, at this sight, began to relent of the harsh opinion it had formed, from the uncouth appearance of Bendetta's person, as silently she continued to witness the emotions of her unrestrained grief.

"Bendetta's mad!" ejaculated Bill, in a tone of savage contempt.

"Would to Heaven that I were mad, since—curse on the pernicious influence of gilt—all that could render recollection valuable has flown! In obscurity my husband was happy, till King Brajos seduced him from the path of virtue, with promises of affluence, and persuaded him to commit crimes, for which he paid with a broken heart. Alas! he never cared to smile on me again, after the murder of——"

"Wretch!" thundered the ruffians, in a breath, the nearest placing his hand over Bendetta's lips, and dragging her from the cottage.

"Come, come," said one, "let us put Valentine into the next room with our charge, and then out and dig his grave in the forest."

They now conveyed the body into an adjoining chamber, and conducting Emma into it, secured the rude door, and withdrew.

Too pious to tremble at the presence of the insensible dead, Emma falling upon her knees, instantly recommended herself to the protection of Heaven.

While she thus continued to raise her soul to the Great Creator of all things, the ghastly features of Valentine met her eye.

His countenance, overcast with a livid hue, yet appeared distorted by the last struggle; and the hands, firmly clenched in each other, seemed as if,

in the latest throb, it had entertained some faint hope of benign forgiveness.

She earnestly prayed for the repose of his soul, when throwing over the corse a cloak, which hung in the apartment, she retired to a rugged couch, in an adjacent recess, and resigned herself to reflection.

A feeble ray of light only fell from an iron grating, far above her reach, over which some envious ivy mantling, withheld the more cheering sunbeam, which else had illumined her desolate solitude.

The walls of the hut, consisting of rugged fragments of stone, wildly heaped together, divested of covering, appeared green with dampness.

A heavy iron chain, suspended therefrom, betrayed but too evidently the horrible purpose to which this dungeon-like place was appropriated.

The ruffians now returning, she ventured to inquire for Bendetta.

But dragging forth the body of Valentine, they paid no attention to her words.

After they had for some time withdrawn, overcome by fatigue and sorrow, she insensibly sank into the arms of slumber, during which she imagined, in the feverish visions of fancy, that the bleeding form of her young defender stood before her.

A melancholy smile played on his pallid features as, extending his hands, he suddenly disappeared in a golden cloud.

She then thought a multitude of people assembled round a scaffold, on which Valentine, the pale image of despair, awaited to receive the fatal stroke of the red uplifted axe.

The latter delusion of her nervous imagination so shocked Emma's frame, that, starting from her dream, she burst into tears, as Whetherby, opening the door, desired her again to enter the litter, in order to proceed on their journey.

In the course of a few hours they again paused at a solitary mansion belonging to King Brajos.

An elderly woman, who seemed the only inhabitant of the pile, met them at the porch.

"Well, Mistress Barbara," cried Whetherby, "we have brought you a visitor."

"Welcome, welcome all!" replied the dame. "How fares the king, your master?"

"That will he prove in person to-morrow; in the meantime, you must provide for this young lady, with whom he is deeply in love, Barbara."

The litter, at the conclusion of this discourse, was again unclosed, and Emma assisted to enter the cot.

"Good lack! how you tremble, lady," exclaimed Barbara.

"Alas! I am sick at heart."

"Oh! what, love-sick, I suppose?"

A blush of scorn crimsoned Emma's countenance, and deigning no reply to this contemptible allusion, she begged to be conducted to some retired apartment, wherein she might indulge her gloomy meditations, uninterrupted by the intrusion of strangers.

On the night of Emma's departure from the castle, Matilda, the maid, oppressed with horrid dreams and inquietude, imagined that the groans of some person in the gallery died upon her ear.

But after a little reflection, attributing the cause to the agitated state of her oppressed mind, she, with fruitless efforts, endeavoured to bury her apprehensions in sleep, till the Indian girl informed her that Emma had already risen from her pillow, and wandered forth alone.

"*Alone!*" faltered Tilly, "my mistress wandered

forth *alone*, at such a period? Good Heaven! you alarm—you terrify me. Whither should she wander at so early an hour?"

"I know not; the dew yet trembles on the grass in the valley."

"Fly, fly, and conduct her to me."

The Indian girl instantly departed in search of Emma, while Matilda, resorting to the balcony, gazed towards the hills, indulging the fond hope of again beholding her.

But at length perceiving the girl alone, with no traces of the fugitive, she hurried into the hall, and encountering the king, inquired if he had seen her mistress.

"Queen Emma?" answered Brajos, somewhat confounded. "Is she not in her own chamber?"

Matilda made no reply, but hastening from apartment to apartment, called on the name of Emma, till the hour of noon convinced her that some mysterious occurrence must have transpired to prevent the appearance of her mistress.

The groans which she had heard in the gallery at midnight, now rushed to her mind.

In a state bordering on frenzy, she again sought an interview with Brajos, in order to unfold the nature of her fears.

"Foolish, but constant and faithful maid," exclaimed the king; "I am persuaded Queen Emma still wanders near; let us therefore seek her among those rocks, in the solitude of which, I am told, she much delighted; the vassals are already dispatched in different tracks, and probably, by this time, have discovered the place of her concealment."

Filled with hope, Matilda readily prepared to accompany him, and as they continued to ramble through the most intricate and inaccessible parts of the mountains, suddenly starting at the sight of several armed men, who, crouching in the underwood, endeavoured to elude observation.

"Good Heavens!" cried she, "do you perceive those strangers?"

"Yes," answered Brajos, laughing, applying his hunting-horn to his lips; "they came to escort you to Bill Whetherby, who loves you, and pitying your friendless state, would fain shelter you under his own protection."

"Ah, wretch!" exclaimed the frantic maid, "I am now fully sensible of your perfidy; my poor lady, she too is in your power. But, mark me—mark me, Brajos—the curse of God is on thee, and may Heaven act with thee, most diabolical of men! Nor till your dark heart turn from treacherous, impious deeds, shall that all-sufficient Power, which hears my humble voice, cease to oppress thee."

As Matilda thus spoke, assuming almost a supernatural form, she raised her eyes and hands to heaven, while the bitterness of her anguish, mingling with the earnestness of her curse, cast a ray of wild melancholy over her features, which imparted a chilling awe to the heart of King Brajos.

For awhile, Matilda remained, as it were, torpid, till awakened to a full sense of her misery by the rude grasp of the ruffians, about to convey her away, under circumstances still more agonizing than those which had formerly attended her to that detested pile.

Loudly did she shriek for assistance, when Valentine, who lingered near his favourite solitude, rushed to the spot, and drawing his sword, was driving off the assailants, as Brajos, with the malice of a demon, suddenly seized Matilda's arm, and unsheathing his dagger, plunged it into her bosom.

Senseless, she sank from the dizzy verge of the cliff, as snatching the horn suspended to his girdle, Brajos repeated several shrill blasts, in order to summon his minions to renew the attack, and following Valentine down the steep, the youth, overpowered by numbers, was necessitated to become the king's captive, who commanded him, in defiance of threats and resistance, to be dragged to the castle, and imprisoned in one of its dungeons.

Alone, and in total darkness, Valentine, perfectly at a loss to comprehend the meaning of these transactions, endeavoured, but in vain, to discover a clue to the designs of Brajos; his meditations, however, like the wanderings of some benighted traveller, through the inextricable mazes of a trackless labyrinth, terminated in uncertain conjecture and visionary ideas.

On the ensuing morning, his meditations were interrupted by the entrance of his gaoler, who desired him to follow into the state apartment.

Valentine now entering the chamber, judge of his consternation at beholding it filled with strangers; while Brajos, exalted on a covered seat, at the upper end, appeared in all the solemnity of judges, on a formal trial.

Brajos, after a pause, addressing himself to the astonished Valentine, exclaimed—"Unhappy youth! from what horrible motive, at years so tender, you may have been induced to commit an act, at which humanity shudders, and human nature revolts, is best known to the latent workings of your own breast. Vain has been our search for the corse of that unfortunate maid, yesterday precipitated by you from the cliffs—Queen Emma's attendant."

"Ah!" cried Valentine, "that God, in whose infinite disposal of events I confide, will bear witness for my innocence."

"Boy," interrupted Brajos, "how was it, that, contrary to my frequent mandates, you were yesterday wandering near the castle?"

"Sir," continued Valentine, proudly, "have I ever, by a single action of my life, evinced a sympton of thus readily steeping my hands in the blood of a fellowing creature? The callous heart of the assassin, and the remorseless grasp of infamy, are not momentarily steeled to evil; how then would it have been possible for me, a friendless, outcast boy, at once to have plunged into vice, atrocious and unparalleled, at committal of which the most daring ruffian might have shuddered?"

"Peace!" interrupted Brajos, abruptly; "were not mine own eyes witness to your baseness, and also those of my long-tried, faithful attendants, who are ready, on the most solemn oath, to attest thy guilt?"

"Unmanly, designing dastard," cried Valentine, snatching a sword, "has then Queen Emma too fallen into thy fell coil? But yes, proud king, the injured, friendless Valentine demands her at your hands, or thus, in defiance of the world, friends, kindred, foes, wreak on your head vengeance."

At the conclusion of this sentence, frantic with despair and anguish, he rushed towards Brajos, who, pale with dismay, was sinking at his feet, as the attendants wrested the weapon from the desperate hand which overhung him.

"Assassin!" exclaimed the king, sternly bending his eye on the frenzied youth.

Valentine endeavoured to speak, but the king, in a voice of imperative thunder, commanded the guards to drag him to the dungeon, till his fate should be decided upon.

*   *   *   *   *   *

On recovering from a state of torpor, into which the bitterness of oppression had thrown him, Valentine glanced with wild inquiry across the extent of his murky dungeon, through which a feeble ray of light, shedding its niggard influence, increased, rather than diminished, the horrors of surrounding gloom.

Taking the lamp, he proceeded more narrowly to examine the limits of his prison, and discovered in its extremity, that from the result of many years, an immense body of the cavern, labouring under the weight of some part of the castle, which it supported, had fallen in, forming an opening sufficient to admit an entrance into the adjoining vault.

Filled with hope, he continued to explore the dark cell, till it led him into a sepulchre, which, for many generations, had received the ashes of the dead.

Holding his lamp to the earth, Valentine beheld, with emotions of awe, that he stood near the bodies of many slain captives like himself.

"And will heaven," sighed he, "permit such impious actions to escape the reward they merit ? Ah, no !"

"Ah, no !" responded a hollow voice.

Valentine, starting for a moment, listened to hear if it continued.

But recollecting, in such a place it could only be the effect of some echo, he prepared to retire, lest his absence should be discovered.

Scarcely had he reached his dungeon, ere the lamp, with a sudden convulsion, expired.

In the mean time, King Brajos was proudly seated at the gay banquet, surrounded by the base ministers of his guilty pleasures.

The loud and horrid burst of obscene mirth, the voluptuous strain of the minstrel, and the copious draught of the high-foaming goblet, alternately conspired to erase the remembrance of his crimes.

Valentine had been repeatedly dragged into the presence of his inhuman persecutor, whose attendants had now discovered the mangled body of Matilda, which now reposed in the great hall, so disfigured with wounds, that it was impossible even to recognise the features.

"Gaze on, thou monster !" cried the king, addressing Valentine, as conducted in chains to the bier, he sadly and silently fixed his eyes on the mutilated corse. "Gaze on, impious, iron-hearted assassin ! does not the appearance of this poor victim, thus disfigured, thus lifeless, smite thy abominable conscience ? Oh, piteous sight! my heart bleeds thereat."

Here, affecting to dash a tear from his cheek, he silently turned away.

"Conduct me to my dungeon," answered Valentine, contemptuously. "Permit me not to witness such sacrilegious mockery. Torture me no longer, tyrant, with existence, but direct thy creatures to plunge their remorseless daggers into my bosom ; yet, ere I die, if thou wilt but unfold me the fate of my queen——"

"*Thy* queen ?"

"Yes, Queen Emma ! Go, then, mistaken one ; for a little space, exult in the success of your treacherous designs. Well I know, since a declaration of my innocence must eventually condemn *thee*, I have no hope of existence. But the after-hope, Brajos, and the after-reckoning, shall amply reward. I am prepared—calmly prepared to die. There sits on high an everlasting King ! He, from his great mansion, beholds thee, and me—my innocence—thy guilt—farewell !"

"Hold !" interrupted the king, his features black with ire. "Know this, insolent vaunter, that your queen yet lives—lives to become mine ! From her lips shall thy sentence of mortal anguish be pronounced : a state of bondage and servility shall gall thine arrogant heart ; and as I press the damask cheek of the lovelorn Emma, thine eye of jealous hate shall note my rapture ; then, slave, then shall be mine hour of triumph—my banquet of revenge !"

With these words, accompanied by a look of fiend-like indignation, Rajos commanded Valentine to be conducted from his presence.

But as he passed out of the hall, some one thrust a dagger in his heart, and thus the brave youth, one of Lion Limb's most faithful followers, died, defending his queen and country.

But swift came revenge for this foul deed.

CHAPTER CXXVI.

MUNGO'S CAPTIVITY—THE REASONS WHY HE BECAME A BUCCANEER—HIS REMARKABLE AND ROMANTIC STORY.

SINCE the last great fight between Mungo and Lion Limb, the former bold villain was chained and held in custody by the order of Lion Limb, until the English vessel, which was off the island, should arrive and decide the half-breed's fate.

Frequently, he desired to speak to those about him, and at last, being rather attached to young Ted Rawlings, who visited him, he said, one day—

"The history of my life has hitherto been a great mystery, and I am called all manner of names by those who know me not, but if you will listen, bold youth, I will recount part of my eventful life."

Young Ted did not object, and then the chief thus began :—

MUNGO'S STORY OF HIMSELF.

My father, Baron Fitzalan, was a nobleman of high estate, and renowned in the annals of his country, both by the towering height of ancestry, and the illustrious fame of his own warlike deeds.

My mother, who I have understood possessed all the requisites of a great and noble mind, died in giving birth to me, and from which unhappy circumstance, I may date the period of my misfortunes ; since my father, who was passionately attached to his wife, might, at her gentle instigation, have been content to look with less severity on the errors of his only son.

From the decease of my mother, I shall pass over a lapse of twenty summers, spent in the insensible felicity of childhood, and the follies of youth ; at the termination of which, I was suddenly summoned from my travels, in order to solicit the fair hand of a rich and powerful heiress, whose lands lay contiguous to those of Fitzalan Castle.

I confess the respect which I entertained for the author of my existence was very distant from inspiring me with a desire to comply with the peculiar nature of his commands, since, instead of readily acquiescing to them, I unhesitatingly refused even to behold the lady his kindness had selected to render me happy.

This incensed the baron to such a violent degree, that he not only threatened to disinherit, but to cast me off for ever.

In a few days after he again sent for me.

But judge of my surprise, when in opposition to the rules of all common order, I found him attended, not merely by the guardian, but by the Lady Isabella herself, who, unconscious of the deception imposed upon her, had been requested by Lord Fitzalan to enter his mansion, under pretences of a nature totally foreign to the actual design.

That Isabella had charms, it would be impossible to deny, but the thwarting spirit of youth had so steeled my breast against them, that it was not probable the stratagem, to effect which the baron had been at such considerable pains, would in the least tend to accelerate our union.

NOTICE.—This Tale will shortly be concluded.

THE BOY KING
OF THE SOUTH SEA ISLANDS.

A PLEASANT ABODE.

On the departure of his guests, the baron eagerly demanded my opinion of Isabella.

With some degree of consternation, I replied, that my inclinations were not so much indulged as those around me, who, at least, had the felicity of selecting partners for themselves.

"Surely, my lord," exclaimed I, "it is a subject of no mean consideration. Is it possible for me to state how far the inclinations and sentiments of the Lady Isabella may coincide with mine—would it not be rash to bestow my hand where my heart could not accompany it? Would it be honourable?"

For some time my father continued silently listening to my remonstrances; at length, his stern eye flashing fire, and haughtily rising from his seat,

"Boy," cried he, "wilt thou presume to dictate? Thou—but why do I debase myself, by stooping to

your absurd propensities—is it not sufficient for me to dictate? You know on what conditions alone I can harken to your conversation, or consent to shelter you beneath these walls."

He was now preparing to quit the apartment, but grasping his robe,

"Stay, my lord," I cried, "let us not part thus ; however religiously I might be inclined to observe your rigid mandate, a solemn and imprudent vow, made in the impulse of passion, never to wed, till I had witnessed twenty-three summers, prevents me."

"Where made, and to what object?" interrupted the baron, with a look of mistrustful scorn.

"The spot is sacred, the object lost, and the vow inviolable," replied I.

"Far be it from me," continued he, in a subdued

tone, "to inquire into the nature of your extravagant secrets; it is sufficient for me, if, at the termination of that period, you will be willing to comply with my wishes."

Thus foiled with the result of my own stratagem, I had no other resource but agreement.

However, as there were yet three summers to look forward, I hoped, ere the expiration of that time, some particular incident might take place, either to alter the resolutions of my father, or render the Lady Isabella deaf to his proposals.

I shall not dwell upon each particular occurrence, but merely state, that after some little hesitation, Fitzalan's overtures to Isabella, through the representation of her guardian, so far prevailed, that she consented to give me her hand.

I must confess that it occasioned me some disagreeable sensations to impose on the amiable qualities of this young lady, since to have loved her would have been no difficult task, but for the recollection of the apparent force exercised over my inclinations.

However, as I had not completed my travels, in obedience to the baron's commands, I again prepared to quit the mansion of my birth, and even Isabella, with a degree of regret.

Some time had elapsed, and the vessel in which I had embarked was swiftly conveying me to other climes, when a midnight storm suddenly arose.

So dark, so terrible were the elements, that as the torches' glare played across the features of the mariners, I could perceive them pale with emotions of horror and despair.

Oh! then did I repent my own rashness, for which I had fallen to destruction, and inwardly repine at the overbearing spirit that induced me to resign my home, and the yielding hand of Isabella!

But, alas! my reflections were of short duration.

A sudden wave breaking in upon the vessel, bore me, with inveterate force, along the world of sea.

At first, overwhelmed with the unexpected blow, I was fast sinking into eternity.

A momentary gleam of reason awoke me to a sense of danger, and excited my exertions to the first law of nature, self-preservation.

Long and fearful was the struggle.

At length, totally exhausted, I sunk fainting on a bed of rocks, towards which alone, the hand of Providence, in that awful night, must have conveyed me.

For some time, my benumbed faculties disdained to perform their accustomed offices; at last, offering up a prayer to Heaven, I anxiously gazed around for my companions in adversity.

Shall I, can I, ever forget that heart-rending scene?

A wildness so dismal, so solemn, overcast the face of creation, that the red thunderbolt and blue glimmering lightning, as they rent the low pitchy clouds, served, by their transient light, to reflect additional hideousness on the writhing waters, which, towering into mountainous forms, tossed their foamy heads to the skies, and seemed, in savage roars, to mock the yelling tempest as it burst upon their presumption.

The labouring vessel, by a light yet flickering in one of her cabins, might frequently be traced, now lifted high in air, now buried in the liquid deep, till a flash, which came like the crash of worlds, involved at once her feeble efforts, as the perishing cries of her crew (madly clinging to the sinking masts for life) filled up the momentary calm with more distracting sounds than the stormy roarings of offended nature!

What my emotions were at such a forlorn moment, can only be conceived by persons in similar distress.

I felt that I had acted the part of a disobedient, ungrateful child, and that the fatal result had fallen on mine own devoted head, while the acute remorse of my mind, and the miseries of my situation, were rendered doubly poignant by the conviction that they were merited.

These melancholy reflections, however, were subdued by fatigue.

In spite of the impending perils which overhung me, I unconsciously reclined on my cold flinty couch to repose; and so calm, so exquisite was the slumber, that day had thrown her golden mantle over the wide expanse of heaven ere I awoke.

Ah! how changed was the wizard scene!

Smooth as a mirror slept the silent deep.

Not even a passing zephyr presumed to kiss its subdued bosom.

All around seemed one broad sheet of sky-reflecting water.

The craggy island, on which I was cast, appeared the only earthly spec on the face of creation, and I its lone tenant.

At first, a prey to agonising despair, I half-resolved, with impious ingratitude, to plunge again into the treacherous waters, and seal for ever my woes in the chilling arms of death.

But the love of existence, which seldom deserts even the most abject, and the piercing calls of hunger, induced me to venture into the island.

No trace of human being, no voice, save the echo of mine own amid the rocks, offered me consolation.

Thus an outcast from my fellow-creatures, I learnt the life of a hermit, with no better repast than the wild fruits of the wilderness—no habitation but the samphire-hanging cliffs.

Long was the time, which, without admitting even the consolations of hope, glided over my solitary reign, with no better enjoyment than the sadly-pleasing pictures of memory, or the painful anxiousness of watching, from some beetling eminence, the distantly-rising surge, to which, full oft, as the sea-bird cowered, mine aching sight would turn, in the fond hope of its being some friendly adventuring bark, to snatch me from the sorrows of exile.

But as the delusive spray sank to its natural level, lamenting the hardness of my destiny, I have frequently sought relief in hopeless tears.

One morning, earlier than usual, having taken my accustomed station on the summit of the rocks, with indescribable joy I discovered the form of a vessel, from the sides of which several dark figures descending into an open boat, made for the island.

Transported at once again beholding the resemblance of a human being, hastily running towards the strangers as they landed, I threw myself at their feet, and implored their compassion.

At first, surprised by the wildness of my manners and attire, they recoiled as I approached.

But observing the supplicating attitude in which I still remained, at last they addressed me in a language totally foreign.

It was by signs, therefore, I expressed to them my desire of entering their bark, to which, after some little survey of the island, they consented to convey me.

It was the galley of a pirate.

The chief welcomed me on board, with unusual marks of condescension, and kindly attentive to my story (from his acquaintance with the language, being fully able to comprehend it), promised, by every means in his power, to aid me in recovering my country.

But, alas! that unpropitious fate which hovered over, was not yet satiated with my sufferings.

A very short space beheld the vessel wherein I sailed, surrendered to an enemy.

Its wretched crew, including myself and the corsair, were sold as slaves in the public market-place of Zanzibar.

The aged merchant, into whose services I had fallen, expressed himself so highly satisfied with my assiduity, that though I endeavoured to inspire him with hopes of infinite gain for my ransom, he would never consent to the proposal.

Yet, in the course of two years, he materially exalted me from my earliest employment, which was to cultivate the gardens, or with a number of unfortunate companions, attend his person to the bazaars.

Calling me one morning to his sofa,

"Mungo," said he, which was the title given me by himself, "since it is my design shortly to unite myself with the beautiful Zelinda, I shall, on that occasion, bestow great privileges on such of my slaves as have, by their attention and fidelity, deserved them.

"I need not add that you, from your integrity and diligence, will be foremost to receive both my favour and confidence."

At these words I was ready to fall at his feet, and solicit for that alone which could have made me happy—leave to return, once again, to that dear, that not-forgotten home, for which I deeply sighed.

Observing the sudden paleness of my cheek, Hasrac, my master, inquired into the cause.

At a loss how to reply, lest the apparent ingratitude of my inclinations should eventually destroy the few hopes that sometimes fluctuated in my breast.

"My lord," said I, "it is ever the duty of a slave to rejoice at the happiness of his master; but when that happiness comes with kindness to himself, the double ecstacy is insupportable."

"Virtuous Mungo!" exclaimed Hasrac, "thy sensitive nature has not escaped unheeded. Be ready, in a few hours, to attend me to the dwelling of Zelinda, whose fair hand I am desirous should bestow on thee a reward equal to such uncommon merits."

He now withdrew from the apartment, leaving me a prey to my own melancholy ruminations till the appointed time, when, entering his palanquin, in all the pomp of magnificence, he repared to the habitation of Zelinda.

His turban, of the finest muslin, figured with silver, was fastened in front with a star of blazing jewels, which, in corresponding manner, ornamented in clusters his embroidered and perfumed robes.

For me, a vest and drawers of rose-colour, constituted my attire, my task being to support the ample train of Hasrac, as he entered the harem to salute his mistress.

But scarcely had mine eyes beheld the sylph-like form of Zelinda, than, dropping the garment from my nerveless arm, I remained motionless beneath the united influence of love and admiration.

She was reclining on a couch of scarlet and gold, surrounded by her domestics, whose beauty, though unusual, served but to heighten the effect of her own charms.

Her raiment, of snowy whiteness, studded with pearls, added to the symmetry of her lovely person, inspired the captivated soul with an idea of being in the presence of some celestial being.

So sweet, so tender too, were her accents, they fell upon mine ear like the melodious breathings of a love-toned lute.

But while, lost in ecstatic transport, I incautiously continued to gaze, Hasrac, suddenly frowning, awoke my bewildered mind to a sense of shame and duty.

The interview, being merely formal, was not of long duration.

Hasrac hastened to his own princely abode, fraught with every anticipation of coming joy, while I, the victim of love and wretchedness, sought alone my lowly pallet, to weep and sigh unseen.

The beauty of Zelinda had made so deep an impression on my heart, that fruitless were all efforts to banish her recollection.

In the bitterness of my woe, I deplored that Isabella had not been Zelinda.

My spirits became gradually dejected.

I, of late, the most cheerful among my companions, was now the most melancholy, and loved solitude in preference to their mirth or conversation.

My songs no longer enlivened their labours, or heightened the festivity of their holidays.

Under various pretences, I loved to linger in the most unfrequented solitudes of the gardens, which were only divided from another, surrounding the palace of Zelinda's father, by a wall of unusual height.

One evening, as I sat beneath the friendly shade of a cedar, the voice of some female softly uttering my name, startled me from the gloomy ruminations in which I was enveloped, and gazing wildly around, what was my surprise on beholding a matron, one of Zelinda's attendants, narrowly investigating my features.

"Mungo!" exclaimed she, at length, "how is it that you avoid the society of your companions, to wander like some forlorn creature through these secluded windings?"

"Alas! madam," replied I, "however I may seem, I am not alone; there is a form deeply fixed in my heart, with which I converse and reason."

"Is it the form of her you love?" inquired the attendant.

"Even so," sighed I.

"Surely, then," continued my interrogator, "the mistress of your affections must esteem herself fortunate in so fond and faithful a lover."

"She, alas! madam, is unconscious of my presumption."

"What if Zelinda were inclined to return thy passion?"

"Zelinda, lady?"

"Be not surprised, Mungo, at my knowledge of your secret, when even the very trees are witness to your rashness."

She pointed to the cedar beneath which I had been reclining, and the name of Zelinda, engraved upon the bark, awoke me to a fearful sense of the imprudent abstraction which accompanied mine own actions.

"Blush not, Mungo," said she, seeing my embarrassment; "but at the hour of midnight, if possible, escape unnoticed from your chamber, and meet me on this spot, when I shall conduct you to Zelinda, whose love, perhaps, is only to be equalled by your own."

So saying, she suddenly retired into a bower of myrtle, leaving me a prey to a thousand hopes, fears, and wild conjecures.

Ah! how anxiously did I watch the lingering hours till the time appointed.

Methought those around me seemed inclined to converse till daybreak.

While inwardly condemning the various subjects of their discourse, I listened painfully for its termination.

At last, as all was still, I secretly deserted my pallet, and hastened towards the cedar tree in the extremity of Hasrac's gardens.

My nocturnal guide was already in attendance, and, as I approached, angrily exclaimed against my suffering her to remain so long.

I assured her of my anxiety, and the cause which, so repugnant to my inclinations, detained me.

She now motioned me to follow, and after gliding through a variety of secret walks, we arrived at the harem, wherein Zelinda, oppressed with fear, awaited the return of her governess, Mandane.

I instantly threw myself at the feet of my mistress, who, raising me up with tender condescension, welcomed me to her presence.

"Angel of light!" sighed I, "how can thy slave repay such benign goodness?"

"By continuing to love me, Mungo," she replied.

In an ecstacy of delicious transport, I called heaven to witness the purity of my vows.

And so soft, so sweet was the mutual exchange of our love, that like the magic influence of a rapturous dream, it seemed but a momentary heavenly delusion, ere the governess entered to apprize us of the blue-eyed appearance of dawn, which must rend us asunder, or betray us with its envious light.

After some little reflection, I tore myself from the object of my adoration, and hurrying back to my apartment unseen, sank into joyous slumbers, wherein the preceding adventure of the night was again depicted to my love-sick imagination.

From this era our interviews became frequent; till one fatal night, while I hung fondly on the witching charms of Zelinda, the governess, pale and almost breathless, rushed into the apartment, and, in trembling articulation, proclaimed the approach of Hassan, who having received secret information of my being there, was coming, attended by his guards, to punish or destroy me.

Zelinda, almost fainting, cast her eyes upon mine, and fearfully gazed around for some means of escape; but it was already too late.

The angry voice of her father echoed in the adjoining chamber.

Terror-struck, I endeavoured to screen myself behind a lattice-work, covered with fragrant shrubs, when the governess, suddenly grasping the skirt of my raiment, forcibly drew me back, exclaiming at the same time, in haughty accents—

"Ah! stay, thou perfidious traitor, thou shalt not profane the sanctity of my lord's harem, while I, his vigilant, eternal vassal, have sufficient strength to struggle against thy presumption!"

She now made the place re-echo with her cries for assistance; and suddenly turning to Hassan (who had entered time enough to witness the proceeding), swooned at his feet.

Speechless, I gazed upon the weeping Zelinda, at a loss to comprehend the treacherous conduct of her attendant, till, loading me with heavy chains, the guards, in obedience to the furious mandate of their chief, prepared to drag me to confinement; at which, recovering from her state of apparent inanity—

"Allah be praised!" faltered the governess, "I have preserved, by my exertions, the credit of the sacred trust reposed in me, from the attempts of this young libertine. Last night, my lord," continued she, addressing herself to Hassan, "while I was reading in the Alcoran deeds of the faithful, such as Allah loves, raising mine eyes from the sacred volume, I beheld this stranger wandering in the lonely paths of the harem; but deeming him merely some new attendant on your pleasure, I suddenly forgot him; judge then, how great must have been my alarm, on beholding this maniac rush into the presence of myself and Zelinda, while we were yet engaged in our nightly devotions.

"Whether, my lord, he fled from your pursuit, I know not, since, in the visible terror of his mind, he endeavoured to hide himself behind those roses, as, forgetful of the weakness of this arm, I endeavoured to detain him, till the loudness of my cries might summon assistance."

Hassan, with an air of credulity, gazed earnestly on the governess.

At length—

"Faithful creature!" he cried, "why should I doubt the truth of these assertions, since long-tried service has proved the integrity of all thy former actions! As for thee, unhappy wretch, son of some abject Christian, whatever cause might impel this insult I reck not; confinement, and haply death, must reward thee."

I was now dragged from the presence of all I held dear on earth, to a lone dungeon in the remotest turret of the mansion.

On my departure, as another has since informed me, the governess, throwing herself at Hassan's feet, wept aloud.

"Oh, my lord," sobbed she, "if I have not acted in conjunction with your wishes, let me die—let me sink beneath the force of your sabre."

"Arise," replied he, throwing her some pieces of gold, "and with my Zelinda be happy, nor dread again the interruptions of this arrogant slave, of whose entrance into the harem I was apprised by an attendant, that observed his approach from the garden of Hasrac."

So saying, he departed, after embracing his daughter, and recommending her to repose.

"Oh, thou perfidious and deceitful woman!" said Zelinda, scornfully rejecting the offered hand of her attendant, "thinkest thou I can ever give my hand to Hasrac, whose secret reward has thus secured thee to his service? No. The captive, that yesterday you artfully professed to be the handsomest and most amiable, possesses my fondest love. Guide me, ye invisible powers who overrule the destiny of Mungo, to the gloomy chamber wherein he sighs beneath the weight of his chains, that I may console and speak peace to his wounded heart; that, in spite of surrounding obstacles, I may convince him of my unabating passion, and live or die with him."

"Stay, rash girl," cried the governess; "dry those tears of sorrow, I beseech thee. Thinks then Zelinda so hardly of my affection, as to suppose me capable of being the thing I seem? Leave the fate of Mungo to me. Wouldst thou be content to quit thy native land?"

"I would do any thing to preserve the life of my love, and avoid the arms of Hasrac."

"Zelinda," resumed the governess, "I am myself a Christian. For many years the ardent wish of returning to my friends has been uppermost in this bosom ; a merchant, in whose fidelity we can rely, has offered, for a trifling sum, to afford me any conveyance towards the land of mine and Mungo's birth. My husband, returning from a long and perilous voyage, was captured by a corsair. It is useless now for me to enumerate the peculiar circumstances which placed me in the service of your father, and separated me for ever from one I tenderly loved, and of whose fate I am still ignorant. An opportunity now offers for effecting my escape ; I shall therefore, dearest Zelinda, lose no time in endeavouring to save Mungo, that both thy lover and thyself may render me happy by becoming voluntary partners of my long-meditated flight."

Zelinda sank delighted on the bosom of the faithful attendant, and, thanking her warmly for the judicious part she had sustained, urged her to lose no time in endeavouring to effect my release from the sorrows of rigid captivity.—"I will fly with thee and Mungo," she cried, "to the utmost verge of the globe; let us hasten, therefore, to those plains which I have so frequently heard him describe with rapture."

I was lamenting my hard and calamitous life, on the cold flinty pavement of my dungeon, in an agony of despair, as the sound of secret footsteps suddenly assailed my ear.

A transitory gleam of dismay rushed upon my soul.

Gazing fearfully around, I expected some midnight instrument of Hassan or Hasrac's vengeance, to approach and plunge into my defenceless brea the knife of untold murder.

I listened.

All was still as the awful pause of n precedes the thundering burst of a vo

"They come," thought I, "to miseries which I have so often wi

My heart chilled at the id which misfortune had of lat no longer taught me to defy

I now beheld the grim approaches, and shrunk from his gelid touch.

Resolved, however, out a struggle, at the prison door, I dart far as the ring to would admit, tow

Merciful heav opposing my s limits of my madness came

With furic rend asunde

Then, o obedience already b

"Fath and fell

Haply still it see whose app

The pale sipate the

I heard mine ear, a hand, whicl mine own.

Light, heav disordered sen

which tenderly overhung me, the venomous glance of a basilisk could not have driven with more inveterate force the ice back to my inanimating heart.

It was the governess of Zelinda, and hastily snatching my arm from her support,

"Woman," I exclaimed, "is not the measure of thy rancour complete, but thou comest thus, like the handmaid of Lucifer, sighs in thy bosom, tears in thine eyes, to torture me again, even after the quiet slumber of the grave had placed, methought, its leaden seal upon me ?"

"Oh, talk not thus wildly, poor captive," answered she, with a look of compassion which almost disarmed my resentment ; "I come to bring thee comfort."

"Comfort !" I ejaculated—"sorceress ! such comfort as thou broughtest me to the cedar tree in the garden of Hasrac ? Hence with thy spangled net, deluder, hence ! let me not hear of my Zelinda's marriage ; leave me to die alone and bro hearted, and I'll not curse thee, wo guilt."

"Reproach me not, ti this ring—'tis H with me ; the blushir

"

journey by land, and meet the vessel at another point, from which the captain intended to prolong the voyage.

Fain would I terminate my sad story, in the short-lived enjoyment which we experienced in this delightful land, as, wandering through the forest, mead, and dale, we contemplated the serene beauties of an Italian summer sky, or beheld, through distant openings in the foliage, the elevation of some proud castello, and witnessed, with emotions of awe and admiration, the cloud-sourced cataract, bursting above our heads.

But my narrative, as it lingers towards a close, opens again the wounds of unforgotten misfortune.

Let me, therefore, dwell briefly upon the period of my arrival at the castle of Fitzalan.

My father was still living; but, on receiving the unpleasing intelligence of my marriage with Zelinda, refused to see me, and denied that welcome which, as his son, I had a right to expect.

The aged steward alone beheld my reception with ~~~~ at the intercession of this worthy man, ~~~ my father a trifling sum, with ~~~ happy in the enjoyment of ~~~ ttage, near the dwel- ~~~ escaped from ~~~ at, and

CHAPTER CXXVII.

LION LIMB GOES IN SEARCH OF EMMA.

THE last shades of twilight were stealing behind the distant hills, as Lion Limb, in disguise, approached the outer gates of the castle of King Brajos.

A vassal presently appeared with an invitation from the king, desiring Lion Limb to enter the banquet gallery.

Feigning the infirmities of age, Lion Limb slowly following his conductor, now entered the presence of his enemy.

Surrounded by the ministers of his guilt and pleasure, the king for a time listened to the story of the supposed stranger.

At length abruptly interrupting him, he inquired if, in his solitary rambles, he had not encountered Queen Emma in disguise.

Lion Limb inquired—"Has my lord the king then any remaining animosity against those that have voluntarily abandoned his protection? or such as, taught by the first law of nature, prefer the wild range of the forest to the sorrows of confinement?"

"Stranger!" exclaimed Brajos, sternly, "from whence proceeds this cautious inquiry?"

"From the cause," resumed Lion Limb, solemnly, "which ever forbids me to aggravate the sufferings of others; and haply, by confessing that I had witnessed the wanderings of the persons you mention, ~~~ night unconsciously heap on their heads the ven- ~~~ of offended power."

~~~ evident, then, that you entertain at least ~~~ ledge of a secret I wish to acquire," con- ~~~ "the place in which my enemies ~~~ lves; be brief—at once unfold it; ~~~ shall amply repay thy service."

~~~ teach me to forget, even did I ~~~ require, that I had voluntarily ~~~ se that had never offended

~~~ ratagem, to increase thy ~~~ ess, since to name a re- ~~~ but to receive it; if ~~~ shall bring thee to

~~~ indignation the ~~~ the overtures of ~~~ tily, rising from

~~~ ruptly grasping ~~~ uiries, but at ~~~ sect in death

~~~ suddenly ~~~ his sword, ~~~ but thus, ~~~ o defend

~~~ furiously ~~~ ned, and ~~~ dants. ~~~ confusion, ~~~ opposers,

~~~ asioned by ~~~ his opposer ~~~ his revenge, ~~~ mmediately ~~~ prepared to ~~~ no aware of ~~~ g himself be-

neath the underwood of the forest, from which he not only perceived the vigilance of his pursuers, but heard the rancorous threats of King Brajos, as he passed near the spot, and his design to place sentinels at the various cottages for many leagues around, with immense rewards for his head—not as that of the disguised bard, but of the notorious Lion Limb.

Thus dreading detection, Lion Limb deserted not his concealment till nightfall.

The rustling of the leaves, and the moaning of the sapless branches, as they complained to the chill breeze, filled him with apprehension.

At a loss what steps to pursue, or in what isolated place to conceal his head, he beheld, with emotions of anguish, the glimmer of a distant lamp, as it darted forth a friendly invitation to some benighted peasant.

" Alas !" sighed he, " for me the hand of affection places no cheering beacon in the lattice—no anxious heart comes to the opened door to welcome my return. Thou art forbidden even to approach the hospitable shelter of poverty, and driven to seek refuge with the ravenous wolf."

Thus sad, he continued to wander through the most unfrequented parts of the forest till midnight, directed only by the light of the stars, as they hung, in countless numbers, in the blue ether, when, exhausted with fatigue, he sunk upon the earth, and resigned himself to sleep.

In his troubled dreams, a hundred wild phantoms danced before his feverish imagination.

He thought of Emma, attired in shining apparel, wearing on her brow a golden coronet, whose nameless lustre dimmed the eye of mortality.

She arose before him in a vision, and enclosing his form in clouds of purple mist, conducted him to spheres of never-ceasing transport.

On awaking from such illusion, which gladly he would have enjoyed for ever, the broad light of day was beaming upon Lion Limb.

Ascending a neighbouring cliff, in order to take a survey of the country, he witnessed, with indescribable emotions, the distant landscapes.

He proceeded towards the castle again, and descending through the private opening to the cavern, gazed around, as if for the salutation of those features which long acquaintance had rendered familiar to his mind.

All was still—all deserted—as the gloomy sepulchre of death.

Each object conspired to fill his breast with disagreeable reflections, and impelled by the piercing calls of hunger, he determined to venture towards the valley, and apply at the cottage of Bendetta for food.

But so enfeebled was his nature, that the hour of evening had arrived, ere he could reach the cabin.

Sorrow and absence had so changed his features, at first Bendetta was at a loss to remember him.

At length, rendered sensible that it was no other than her well-known guest, she hospitably spread before him the choicest viands her means afforded.

*　*　*　*　*　*

To this same cot, humble as it was, King Brajos and his attendants repaired the next day.

An hour or two later Bill Whetherby and his fair captive Emma arrived at the same place, and recounted all that had happened to the king, who, deep in thought, resolved to speak to Emma at once and declare his passion.

Lion Limb secreted himself, unknown to any one save the owner of the cot, and awaited a favorable moment to confront King Brajos again.

But he knew not that Emma was so near to him,

or he could not have restrained his impatience or passion for one single moment.

King Brajos, inflamed by passion, thrust himself into the presence of Emma at once and said—

" I have long felt a regard for you as the object not only of my compassion but of my protection : be not surprised, then, if my esteem has ripened into love ; but hear me, thus at your feet, declare the sincerity of my passion."

At these words, sinking on one knee, he continued—" My hand and my heart, beautiful Emma, are both equally devoted to your service ; deign then to make me truly happy by accepting them."

" Rise, my lord," interrupted Emma, deeply blushing ; does it become King Brajos to kneel before the object of his pity, with proposals that her misfortunes teach her not to hear ?"

" How ! am I then deemed unworthy your esteem ? Is my love——"

" Name it not again, my lord ; you distress me beyond measure—permit me, I beseech, I implore you, instantly to quit this place."

" Heaven forbid such charms should be hidden in obscurity," said Brajos, gently taking her hand ; " it will not be consistent with my reputation to permit it—would not the world report that the fair and lovely Emma fled unwillingly from my protection ?"

" Unhand me, my lord," replied Emma, indignantly ; " by what authority do you oppose my inclinations ? I insist on leaving immediately !"

" Hold !" cried he, detaining her ; " can you then quit for ever, one whose only offence is the declaration of an unfortunate passion ?"

" Torture me no longer with your passion, my lord ; Emma's heart is not at her own disposal."

" Then," answered the king, bending his angry brow, " *force* must make thee mine."

" Sir," returned Emma, " though you exercise unheard-of cruelty, death is still mine to accept. Shall the hand of innocence be united to that of guilt, and not partake its infamy ? Though the thorn and the rose flourish together, virtue and vice may not mingle. Wed with thee ! Never—I pronounce it, never."

" Weak girl ! I have said my will, and is it not enough for thee implicitly to obey ?"

" Oh ! unjust, designing man ! till I knew thee I was happy. Can I forget moments of felicity, and love the being that changed my happy calm to one dark storm of woe ? Can I prize the ungenerous hand which thwarts my last sad consolation ?"

" Sweet reasoner !" cried Brajos, clasping her in his arms, and rudely kissing her lips.

" Wretch !" shuddered she, struggling, " was it not sufficient for thee to blast every earthly joy I possessed, but that I must submit to this ! By the spirits of my virtuous ancestors, I swear never to be thine ! Sooner shall the spray of ocean beat at heaven's gate—sooner shall the hills crouch to hail thee !"

" Proud fool ! like thy haughty kindred," thundered the king, flinging her from him, " art thou so stubborn ? Like them, too, shalt thou feel my vengeance, till thy high soul shrink to subjection."

" I bend to thee ! Never ! Thou desolator of the domestic hearth—thou secret and abominable assassin, never."

Stung with rage, he placed his hand upon his sword.

" Strike !" she cried ; " strike deeply ! 'tis not death I fear."

At these words he furiously raised his poinard to her bosom, as a peal of thunder shook the vaulted roof of the apartment.

"Proceed," continued Emma; "'tis but the voice of Heaven, which murmurs at thy impiety."

"Sorceress!" vociferated he, mad with rage, and was preparing to strike, but the form of Valentine, clad in awful majesty, seemed suddenly frowning upon him.

Dismayed by the dreadful interposition, he abruptly let fall his sword, and staggered to a chair for support.

"Didst thou see *that?*" inquired he, after a pause, fearfully gazing around.

"See what!"

"The offended ghost of——Oh!"

"I saw nothing; but if the hand of Providence hath interposed to check the dark purpose of your mind, I rejoice. Oh, beware! the hour comes, and comes quickly, in which you must render up an account to Heaven of your secret offences; and dreadful, I fear, truly dreadful, is the punishment that awaits you."

So saying, she left the room, while he, absorbed in gloomy reflection, possessed neither the wish nor the power to detain her.

On entering her own apartment, she discovered a female slave busily employed in twisting a ladder of ropes.

Almost fainting, Emma sank on the couch, and motioning her attendant to secure the door, desired to learn the nature of her employment.

Presenting at the same time a cup of water—

"See, my lady," exclaimed she, "by means of this ladder, we may succeed in escaping at midnight."

Joy beamed in Emma's expressive countenance at the intelligence of the girl's stratagem, and readily assisting in the undertaking, the hope of liberty gave new life to her drooping spirits.

In the course of the day she cautiously repaired to her chamber, and securing such gold and jewels as might prove serviceable to their wanderings, quickly returned.

Emma now began to consider what means would be best for them to pursue, in case their plan of escape should prove successful.

It was at length, however, decided, that they should disguise themselves in two suits of male apparel.

At midnight, therefore, attiring themselves in their disguise, they prepared to descend from the chamber.

The night, being unusually dark, befriended their designs; and easily reaching the ground they slowly and fearfully approached the gate, when a sentinel called out—

"Who goes there?"

Trembling with dread, they returned no reply to the interrogation, but silently unbolting the gate, hastened away.

When King Brajos was made acquainted with the flight of Emma, his rage became boundless.

And with promises of large rewards he dispatched spies to all parts of the country, in the hope of discovering her retreat.

For some time his attempts proved abortive.

At last the retirement which she had found was made known to him.

It was in the castle of a petty chief.

The sun had sunk behind the distant hills, when Emma, who had been wandering to and fro on the battlements, prepared to retire, as the night was unusually cold, when the gleam of warlike implements, gliding through the underwood of the valley, excited her attention.

Naturally concluding these comers were the followers of Brajos, Emma prepared for any attempt which they might intend to make.

And repairing to the donjon, in order to observe their motions, discovered Brajos, by the light of the moon, giving directions to his attendants, who were busily launching a small bark on the moat around the castle, in which it was evident they meant to stem the current.

Emma, now causing the alarm-bell to be rung, in order to summon the vassals to her assistance, drew a sword for the encounter.

And, locking the door, placed the key in her own bosom.

When, witnessing the approach of the friendly chief, who, heavily armed, was conducting the vassals to the battlements, she instantly retired, and related to him the cause.

At which instant, gazing from the turrets, he beheld that the enemy had already succeeded in beating down part of the outer wall, through which they rapidly forced they way into the inner court.

At a sign from Emma, a volley of arrows was now discharged upon them, which so disconcerted their movements, that, in spite of King Brajos's offers and menaces, they were almost ready to fly.

Noticing their confusion, Emma and the chief waved their swords, while the vassals, setting up a shout of defiance, followed their heroic leaders into the court, where commencing a furious assault upon the invaders, they shortly succeeded in putting not only Brajos but his whole train to flight across the drawbridge, which had recently been let down to facilitate their designs.

At this moment, one, pale with terror, rushed towards Emma, and pointing to the aperture through which the band had entered, fainted.

"Never mind, fear not," said Emma, boldly.

"But they are many, my lady, and we are few."

"How many!"

"Some hundreds, as you see."

"Is King Brajos among them?"

"He is."

"Then let some of the archers on the wall pick him off."

"That they are now trying to do."

While the battle in the court continued, another one came and reported the appearance of a new band of horsemen in the distance.

"How are they attired?

"In mail?"

"And their banners?"

"They are new and strange to us."

"What colour?"

"Red."

"Red?"

"Yes, my lady."

"And do they come hither hastily?"

"Yes, as men who would come to deliver you."

"Heaven then, be thanked," said Emma, for my heart tells me they are friends and not enemies."

"Ah!" said one, "King Brajos and his men also note the approach of the strangers, and they are wavering."

"So I see," said Emma, calmly; but if the new comers are really friends, King Brajos and his minions will not escape so easily as they fondly imagine."

While she spoke the band of horsemen approached still nearer and nearer, and to her great surprise and joy Emma discovered in the foremost the well known form and manly bearing of Lion Limb, dressed in the same glittering armour that he wore on the day of the memorable tournament when as an unknown knight he had entered the lists, glittering in gold and in gallant array, and dashed to the earth all who dared to oppose him.

NOTICE.—This Tale will shortly be concluded.

THE BOY KING

OF THE SOUTH SEA ISLANDS.

THE QUARREL IN THE STREET.   THE FRENCHMAN GOT MORE THAN HE
BARGAINED FOR.

CHAPTER CXXVIII.

ALLAN NORMAN SECRETLY MARRIES AND RUNS
AWAY WITH JULIA, THE NIECE AND HEIRESS OF
BARON TEMPLETON—THE SUDDEN APPEARANCE
OF ONE OF THE BARON'S OLD ACCOMPLICES IN
CRIME—THE BLACK CHAMBER AT HOLLY HALL
—THE DEATH OF THE BARON, AND CAPTURE OF
THE VILLAIN REUBEN.

BARON TEMPLETON rose from his library chair,
and, with slippered feet, slowly paced the room.

As we have pveviously remarked in this veracious
history, he was a tall, aged person, and, at one
period of his life, might have been justly termed a
handsome gentleman.

For even at that moment, his long, curly hair,
silvered with the snows of many winters, he was erect
in bearing, austere and reserved in manner, slow of
speech, and with a restless eye—all of which combined to form the outward character of a man whom
the world called opulent and proud.

At the first glance a superficial observer would
have pronounced the baron to be a gentleman of
most *distingué* habits and manners.

But a certain habitual and almost indescribable
twitching about the mouth, added to a dry sarcastic
chuckle, and deep dark flashes of cunning in his
eye, at once stamped him as a man of most dangerous depth, whose presence might prove anything
but agreeable and comfortable in the company of
unsuspecting youth and innocence.

With a letter in his hand, which time after time
he looked at and savagely crumpled up, and then
reglanced at, the baron, slowly and in deep study,
paced the room with almost noiseless steps.

After thinking for a moment, and in mental
pain smoothing his wrinkled brow, he loudly rang
the bell, and a servant instantly obeyed the summons.

He entered the room without the slightest noise,
and shadow-like.

"Williams," he said, in a calm, dry manner,
"when did this letter arrive?"

"At sunset, baron."

"And saw you not the messenger's face?"

"I did not, sir; he passed the Lodge at a hard
gallop, and was so muffled up to protect himself
from the storm, that I did not see his features distinctly."

"But could you recognize him again?"

"I very much doubt it, baron; I saw nothing
distinctly of him except his two eyes, fiercely glaring under the slouching hat he wore."

"How looked he, then?" asked the baron, biting
his nether lip.

"Like a person, sir, who seemed afraid to be recognised by anyone, and even distrusted his own
shadow."

"Something between a lunatic and a robber, I
suppose?" said the baron, smiling grimly.

"Precisely so, sir."

"Well, well, it is of no consequence, Williams;
I know the person very well—that is to say, I have
been slightly acquainted with him for the last few
years. He is in necessitous circumstances, and
usually comes to borrow from me two or three
hundred pounds in the depth of winter. Hitherto
I have obliged this person, but on the present
occasion I cannot—in fact, will not, Williams;
therefore, should he call again, as perhaps he may
this very night, give him lodgings and entertainment,
but I myself am supposed to be in town on pressing
business, you know, Williams, and not expected to
return to Holly Grange for several days."

Old Williams, the butler, bowed and was about to
retire when his master said, slowly,

"This eccentric individual is dangerous at times,
I have heard, Williams; they tell me that he is
possessed with some mania, and rambles in his sleep;
therefore, for our own safety as much as his own,
place him in some secure place. There is always a
bed ready for use, I think, in the Black Chamber,
put him there."

"In the Black Chamber, baron?" said the old
butler, starting back with surprise. "In the Black
Chamber?" he said, with trembling lips.

"Yes. Why not?" answered the baron, with an
angry frown. "What makes you turn pale and
stand there aghast? Surely *you* do not believe in the
ghost and hobgoblin stories told about the place, do
you?"

"Well, no, baron; that is, yes—no; but, really,
sir," stuttered the servant, trying to smile, and
knowing not what to think or say, "really, sir, there
are and have been so many curious stories afloas
regarding that Black Chamber, that we servants past
and repass it on tiptoe in dead silence, and the
mournful sounds which sometimes issue from the
cracks and crevices fill me with a holy horror and
dread of the apartment."

The baron looked gravely at his old servant,
and upbraided him right soundly and sarcastically
for his groundless fears.

"But, sir, the river is high, the flood-gates have
nearly burst asunder, the marshes for miles around
are partially overflown, and the angry waters,
lashed into fury by fierce north winds, rise and
surge against the north-end walls of the Hall,
and its spray and seething foam dash upon the
very window-sills of the Black Chamber. Hence,
methinks, no traveller will call to-night."

"Is the night, then, so very violent and
stormy?" asked the baron in an indifferent tone.

"It is, sir. Snows have fallen, followed by a
quick succession of heavy deluging rain-storms,
so that, as I have said, sir, the roads are all but
impassable, and the very foundations of the Grange
are threatened by the river and the floods."

"Then he may not come," mused the baron.
"Yet should he do so, Williams, fulfil to the very
letter whatever orders I have given you."

The old butler left the presence of his master,
and shook his head very ominously again and
again as he murmured, solemnly—

"Ah! the world don't know or suspect half
what *I* do, or Holly Hall would not stand very
long."

The baron resumed his walk, and as he moved to
and fro in the light and cheerful apartment, buried
in deep and conflicting thoughts, he drew aside
the damask window curtains, and shading his eyes
from the brilliance of the lamplight, he gazed upon
the wintry storm without, revelling and rioting in
wild majesty and grandeur.

For miles, as far as the eye could reach, the whole
landscape was one vast bleak and uninviting
waste.

Sleet and snow and hail were driven to and
fro, and twisted in fantastic forms amid the howling
blast.

The rivers, streamlets, ponds and dykes were
swollen, and each moment threatened to overflow
their banks, and sweep before them in dire inun-
dation the ivy-covered and castellated ruins of
Holly Hall.

Church bells in village steeples rocked to and
fro on their old oak beams, and clanged out dis-
cordantly in the whisting winds.

The elements were in deadly strife, and vivid,

constant, lurid lightning flashed with blinding brilliancy, and cleft in twain huge masses of inky, leaden clouds, which ceaselessly rolled on, enveloping all in impenetrable darkness, while ever and anon sudden and staggering peals of thunder shook the very earth.

"It is, indeed, awfully grand," thought the baron. "I never remember to have seen a more frightful storm since—since that fatal Christmas Eve when——"

As he spoke sulphurous lightning suddenly flashed before his eyes, and crashing peals of thunder burst right over the mansion, and shook the old Hall to its very foundation.

For a moment the baron stood as if he had been struck and paralysed by the electric shaft.

For a few seconds he was blind to every object around him, and then staggered from sheer weakness.

He fell back in his chair powerless and immovable.

Sudden lulls and ominous pauses in the storm were again broken by repeated rain squalls, quick and successive flashes of lightning, and repetitions of deafening volleys from Heaven's own artillery, until at last the old man retreated from the window, and, like a guilty thing, slunk away into a dark and distant chamber, terror-stricken and with palpitating heart.

But, even then the plaintive sounds of moaning winds fell upon his troubled ear as if mysteriously sighing,

" 'Tis twenty years ago, baron! 'tis twenty years ago!"

Seized with pale remorse, he wandered thoughtlessly from place to place in the pitch darkness.

His brow was damp, his hair hung long and lank upon his shoulders; his teeth chattered, and his limbs trembled under him.

"Yes," he mused, as if communing with unseen spirits, who tracked his listless footsteps along the broad corridors and galleries, "yes, 'tis twenty years ago this very night, twenty years ago; and never since that hapless hour has my heart known peace. Friends have vanished, I am alone, cheerless, and comfortless, and my niece—my darling one—far away, and, perhaps, cold in death. The whole world shuns me; my very shadow, like a funeral pall, ominously trails after me; and why all this? Why did I ever dye my hands in human blood? No, no, I did not—I could not; it was not I, it was the villain Whetherby, since transported, and another called Reuben Martin, still at large, who slew my elder brother, Claude, to make me lord of the manor, and master of Holly Hall. Martin stole away his infant son from the arms of a frantic wife—and that child! Has ruthless Reuben slain the young innocent also? Oh, no, no; it cannot be. He would not—he could not be so cruel; and yet I feel his blood upon my very soul. Would that I had never been born ere I had seen that fatal Christmas Eve twenty years ago."

Filled with remorse and horror at life's retrospect, the baron armed himself with a rapier, but as he unsheathed it a deadly resolve flashed across his mind.

He smiled demonically, and with a savage leer, he whispered,

"If he comes, Reuben shall never see the morning's sunlight. I have sworn it! The secret of the Black Chamber can never be divulged!"

The storm without had now abated.

And winds and rain had ceased.

The bright moon once more peeped through dense volumes of storm-laden clouds, and ere long lit up with silvery radiance immense masses of rugged, distant rocks, through which mighty floods of roaring waters were dashing in foaming fury onwards to the sea.

The roads and gulleys, far and near, were overflown and impassable.

Yet, as the old man, from his chamber, peered out upon the distant scene, he perceived, not far away, two objects on horseback, who fearlessly rode down the mountain side, and boldly essayed to cross the swollen torrent at its base.

The wooden bridge had been shivered by the lightning and washed away, yet onward rode the riders at a fearful pace, and as they came nearer and nearer towards the Hall, the old baron, with a powerful glass, clearly perceived one of them to be a young female, and her companion no less than a young handsome man.

"Who can they be, to venture out so rashly, on such a night as this?" thought the old baron. "He seems to be supporting the female in her saddle, and has passed his right arm round her waist. 'Tis wonderful their horses are not washed away by the flood, and yet they seem to know the road hither perfectly."

Yet as he still gazed, filled with intense curiosity, he suddenly started in surprise and alarm, for quick and distant reports of fire-arms were heard, and the riders' horses were seen to kick and plunge, and madly rear, and then to fall helplessly in the flood and carried away, riders and all.

How long the old man stood mute and overpowered with conflicting emotions he knew not; but as if transfixed to the spot, he sighed,

"Never since that fatal hour, has ever a Christmas Eve passed without bringing with it some curse to me; and yet, Reuben, the instrument of all my ills and woes, comes not. For once he has broken faith on this memorable night—but why? Could he have divined my intentions? No. The secret of the Black Chamber is only known to me. For one whole year, both night and day, have I worked to accomplish my design.

Yet even as he spoke the hall bell rang, though the baron heard it not.

A stranger, muffled up and cloaked, sought shelter for the night.

The hall door was opened by old Williams, for the rest of the domestics were all long abed, and as he did so a sudden gust of wind blew the oaken door heavily against the butler's nose, who fell flat upon the ground.

At the same instant a heavy hand was laid on him.

The old domestic was terror-stricken, and dared not move a limb, yet he gasped in a pitiful, tremulous tone,

"In mercy spare an old man's life!"

The stranger instantly blew out the light.

They were in total darkness.

"Where is your master, sirrah?" said the unknown, in a hoarse whisper. "Tell me truly and I will spare you, for I come not for plunder but for vengeance."

And as the visitor uttered the terrible word "vengeance," his tone of voice hissed like that of an angry serpent.

"Is your master at home?"

"No," sighed the old butler.

"He doesn't wish his absence to be known, I suppose?"

"He does not."

"Has he given you any instructions regarding the call of strangers?"

"He has spoken to me of one visitor whom he

expected to call, and left instructions as to how I should act, which is that I am without more ado to give him entertainment and lodging."

"Very, very kind of him, indeed," said the unknown; "and where is this stranger to sleep, pray?"

"Sleep! sleep," said the old butler, in a choking voice, "why, he is to sleep in the —— Oh, pray don't choke me. I am almost gasping for breath."

"Speak, then, quickly; where is this stranger to sleep?"

"In a room, of course," sighed old Williams, who thought that every person had heard and had a horror of the Black Chamber.

"Cease your jokes, fool," said the stranger, administering a hearty kick in the ribs to old Williams; "cease your jokes, fool; I didn't suppose he would have to sleep in a stable. What particular room has been placed apart for the accommodation of this stranger?"

"The B-l-l-ack Oh-h-hamber," stuttered the old butler.

"Your answer has saved your life, fool," said the stranger.

"Now get up, and if you attempt to escape in the darkness I shall be under the painful necessity of tickling your ribs with this bit of steel."

And so speaking, he exhibited a long knife before the astonished eyes of Williams, the faint glimmer of which was visible in the darkness.

The old butler groaned and meekly curled himself up on the hall mats as humbly as a cur terrier, and promised in the very mildest of whispers to do all that would be required of him.

"Then, as you are so obliging, my fat friend, I'll trouble you to change clothes with me at once."

"Change clothes!" gasped the rotund butler, in horror; "why, your things are too small for me."

"No matter; commence at once, I say."

"But you are dripping, soaking wet."

"One of the very best and most urgent reasons, my fat friend, why I should change garments at once."

"But I shall catch my death of cold," groaned the butler.

"Catch what you like, my fine fellow; but if you rather prefer to make your exit out of this wicked world at once instead of doing my bidding, all well and good; so off with your clothes, I say, or die."

Tread on a worm, and it will turn, 'tis said; and so it was with the old butler; he turned with an intention to run away and alarm the household, but on the instant a heavy hand seized him by the nape of the neck, and a series of vigorous thumps with the stranger's right fist beat such a tattoo on the butler's ribs that his carcase sounded as hollow as a drum.

At last, a final hit in the stomach knocked out what little breath remained in the butler's body, and he collapsed at once.

Rolled up as he was like a ball for some time, the obese butler was subjected to very rough treatment; yet he dared not make the slightest noise on the peril of his life.

He was red, and very indignant, as may be readily supposed.

But every time he dared to speak beyond a whisper, he received an additional thump or kick, until at last he was black and blue, and sore in every limb.

The process of disrobing was a very trying one to fat old Williams.

The hall was large and cold, and the freezing winds chilled him to the very marrow.

In due succession several articles of the servant's attire were taken and put on.

There old Williams stood, shivering, and with chattering teeth, endeavouring to introduce his limbs into the small and soaking garments of his strange visitor.

After much thrusting and squirming, the old butler thrust his corpulent figure into the saturated clothes.

When he attempted to fasten them, the buttons popped off in an irregular volley, and sundry seams gave way in all directions, so that when his toilet was fully completed, his figure and general appearance was very unprepossessing and tattered.

During the exchange of garments, Williams was remarkably quiet.

Except a few very angry words, uttered in a smothered tone, he said nothing.

But at last he plucked up courage, and muttered,

"You'll excuse me asking a single question, I know; but who the devil are you?"

The answer was a warm slap on the nose from the stranger's heavy fist, which sent the old butler staggering against the dining-room door, and occasioned several additional and by no means ornamental rents in his nether garments.

"Follow me," said the stranger.

And straightway upstairs he went, and, as if excellently acquainted with every internal arrangement of the Hall, he boldly walked along the first corridor, and entered the cosy library of the baron, followed a few feet behind by the miserable and inconsolable-looking butler, who dragged his weary limbs along as if they were made of lead.

"Hullo!" said the stranger when he perceived the fire still brightly burning in the grate; "hullo, my fine fellow, this doesn't look as if the baron were away. How dare you tell me such audacious lies, eh?"

Perceiving now for the first time that the visitor's countenance was clothed with a black mask, and trembling in every joint lest he might recommence to amuse himself with kicking and thumping, as he had already done down in the entrance hall, old Williams fell upon his knees to beg pardon for his untruthfulness, and in doing so all the wet clothes were suddenly rent from top to bottom, and there he stood with his coat and trousers dangling beside him in long dank ribbons.

Even the stranger could scarcely refrain from laughing at the butler's deplorable plight as he stood shivering and shaking as if attacked by the ague or delirium tremens.

"Now, varlet, listen to me," the stranger began, as he walked to a small sideboard, and liberally helped himself to several potations of cognac, and smacked his lips thereat with unctuous satisfaction. "Now, varlet, listen to me, and answer my questions without lying, if you can."

"There ain't a truthfuller man as walks than I am, kind sir," old Williams whined; "but if you'd be so werry kind as to give me the least taste in the world of spirits, it would do me an amazing amount of good."

"Silence, rogue. Your red nose, with its bountiful crop of bilberry blossoms, testifies to the honesty of your dealings with the baron's wine cellar; but tell me how long have you been in service here at the Hall?"

"Over twenty years," grumbled old Williams.

"You are telling me another lie."

"Upon my word——"

"Your word is good for nothing; you have *not* been here over twenty years, for the baron did not come into possession of the property at so early a date; I know all about it. But answer me, how came the baron entitled to the Hall and its surrounding domains?"

"If you know all about it, why do you ask me?" growled Williams, who by no means relished the idea of standing shivering far away from the fire, while the masked man was taking things so pleasantly.

"If you dare answer me again in that flippant manner, rascal, I'll horsewhip you."

"Well, then," grumbled the butler, "I heard his elder brother Claude suddenly died, and——"

"That's a third lie," interposed the stranger; "he was murdered. Go on."

"What a great pity it is you weren't murdered also," thought Williams.

But he dared not give expression to the sentiment, for the stranger's eyes flashed through his black mask like two coals of fire.

"What else do I know? Why, nothing," said Williams.

"Sir Claude had a son, was it not so?"

"I've heard as much."

"And what became of him, pray?"

"Murdered also, I suppose."

"That's a lie; he was not. He was stolen from his mother's arms, kept in ignorance of his birthright, subsequently sent adrift on the wide world, and then lost sight of."

"I wish I could lose sight of you for five minutes," murmured old Williams, half aloud. "I shall shake myself all to pieces with shivering thus."

"What is that you are muttering, you ungrateful rascal?" said the stranger, angrily.

"Ungrateful, eh? What for?"

"What for? Did I not tell you I came not here for plunder, but for vengeance?"

"Not on me, kind sir," whined old Williams, very dolefully, and suppliantly.

"That depends. If you do my bidding all will be well, if not, you may commence to say your prayers at once. You know not who, nor what I am, trembling knave."

The stranger was about to speak still further, when his quick ear detected the sound of footsteps on the gravel walk beneath the window.

He hastily peeped through the curtains, and, as if stupefied, he gasped—

"Heavens! this must not be; my plans must be instantly changed. I thought he was killed and drowned."

"Who? Sir Claude?"

"No, his son, fool."

"Is it his ghost, then, dancing on the gravel in the moonlight outside? Oh! in mercy spare us. Good ghost vanish!"

On the instant the terrified butler fell upon his knees, and commenced to mumble something very rapidly and incoherently, until his devotions were suddenly stopped by the stranger, who, walking rapidly and wildly up and down the room, bade him rise instantly and follow.

Cautiously and noiselessly they descended the stairs, into the entrance hall, lamp in hand.

"Now, if you dare disobey me," said the man in the mask, "I will murder you. Come in here."

Entering a parlour, the stranger quickly bound old Williams, hand and foot, with several strong bell-ropes.

"Be silent, and all will be well; make the least noise, and I will scalp you. Hush—hush!"

At that moment the hall bell rang, and the stranger, pulling off his mask, and with all the manners of a well-conducted servant, opened the door.

A travel-stained, gallant young gentleman stepped forward, and pulled off his cloak.

"Most welcome to Holly Hall, Allan Norman," said the improvised footman.

"You know me, then?" said the stranger, in surprise, and with a faint smile, and a very fatigued and languid manner.

"Yes, I know you very well, and have orders from the Baron Templeton to entertain you in the most handsome manner, but he has had a sudden attack of the gout, and cannot see any one."

"Baron Templeton! Holly Hall!" said young Norman, perplexed. "Really, I am sorely puzzled. I have heard of these names and places, but never for a moment dreamed that this was Holly Hall, or that the baron would receive me so handsomely. My young and newly-married wife, his niece, Julia, was always under the impression that the baron would spurn all her friendly advances, and disavow relationship. Indeed, I should not have called even now, but for a very sad accident that has befallen my young bride?"

"Oh! indeed," said the would-be butler, with a sardonic grin.

"You see, Julia and myself being in this part of the country were riding out in the afternoon but were caught in the storm; we stayed for several hours in a peasant's cottage, and had resumed our journey when we were suddenly fired at by some unknown and disguised villain. The wounded animals fell in the flood, and we were carried along helplessly in the waters, but providentially both of us escaped an untimely grave, and, save a severe shaking, I personally am none the worse for the perilous adventure.

"My young wife, Julia, is even now but a few hundred yards behind me carried on a litter by four stout fellows, and, not knowing it, yet trusting to English generosity and hospitality, I came hither as to the first house to ask shelter until a carriage and horses shall have arrived in the morning."

"I can assure you, sir, that the baron has heard every particular of your recent marriage and sad mishap, from some labourers on his estate, and immediately gave orders that should you call you were to be treated with all the respect and consideration due to your rank, relationship, and comfort."

"Thanks, many—nay, a thousand thanks for so much kindness."

"Will you not partake of some refreshment, sir? A collation is prepared in an adjoining apartment."

"No, thanks; I am too much fatigued, and will immediately retire. Here comes my young wife, who, as you see, is well nigh unconscious. Please show the way to some chamber at once; all she requires is rest and quiet."

The self-made butler, lamp in hand, led the way.

"Come, Julia," said young Allan, "let me bear you in my arms."

And, with the greatest ease, he passed his arms around her slender waist, and carried her upstairs towards the Black Chamber.

They entered the room, and, bowing most profoundly, the villain placed the lamp on a marble table, and left the apartment hastily with a sardonic smile of triumph on his curling lip.

"'Tis done!" he sighed.

The door was closed, and, at that instant, as the heavy lock clicked, a small bell was heard to tinkle in some distant room.

In that same room the baron lay tossing in troubled sleep.

But the ominous tinkling of the bell near his pillow, instantly aroused him.

"'Tis well!" he said, with eyes sparkling in pleasure. "Reuben has arrived. Williams has done my bidding. He has entered the Black Chamber. In less than three hours he will trouble me no more!"

Hastily putting on his attire, and filled with intense excitement, he left his room and hurried to the library, yet, as he moved along the gallery, he nervously looked to the right and to the left, as if he feared his own shadow.

But he perceived not a figure glide along and enter the library far in advance of him.

Seating himself in an arm-chair, the baron drew a small table to his side, and, helping himself to brandy and cigars, was soon lost in reverie which he vainly endeavoured to banish or drown with repeated draughts of liquor.

"Oh!" said he, with a chuckle. "Reuben never dreamed of such a Christmas Eve as this is."

But Reuben Martin, at that moment, noiselessly emerged from behind a large screen, and unperceived, stood behind the baron's chair.

For some time thus he stood statue-like and triumphant.

The baron's gaze had long been fixed on the fire, but as he raised his face to the mantle mirror, their eyes met.

The baron turned deadly pale.

His eyes distended.

And, with a gaping mouth he gazed at Reuben's scowling visage, as if he had suddenly encountered some dread and formidable apparition.

With a sudden bound he leaped from his chair, and stood horror-stricken.

"Merciful heavens! Can it be possible!"

"Nay, call not on heaven, baron," said Reuben, in a solemn tone. "You would have murdered me!"

"Is it Reuben Martin?" gasped the baron, still disbelieving his own senses.

"It is not his ghost as yet, although you would have had it so," answered Reuben, in a scoffing tone. "You would have me do your bidding in all things first, and then murder me afterwards, eh? You are tired of my annual calls at Christmas Eve, but _I_ am not. Remember your bargain long ago. If you die first the property comes to me."

"I remember the compact distinctly," sighed the baron, "and I suppose you now call for your yearly money? I have it here ready in notes, locked up. Take them and begone, your presence drives me mad, Reuben Martin!"

Reuben took the proffered notes, and placing them in a breast-pocket, said,

"I came not for money, baron, but as this probably is my final visit to Holly Hall it may prove useful; but I came here for vengeance," said Reuben, solemnly, "and I have already accomplished my wishes in part. The secret of the Black Chamber has already done my work. I will quickly finish what remains."

"What mean you?" said the baron, in a state of alarm.

"Listen, and I will explain. You have already by deed transferred your whole property to your niece Julia, but money, which can do anything, has revealed this your base design against me."

"Julia is far away, with friends and relations."

"She is at this moment lying helpless in her husband's arms."

"What, married?"

"Yes, eloped with a penniless fellow, a devil's brat, that bullets will not kill, or mine would have surely done so."

"Julia married!—eloped with a penniless fellow," said the baron, amazed. "Have you heard his name?"

"I have. Tis Allan Norman!"

"Allan Norman? Stop!" gasped the baron, and a moment afterwards he whispered, "is all this mere fiction to annoy or frighten me, Reuben?"

"Truth."

"Can you prove it?"

"Every word, and when I choose I can give you living proof—no, no, not living proof, I meant to say _dead_ proof, baron."

"What mean you by that devilish grin, Reuben?"

"I mean that both Julia and her young husband, Allan Norman, are dead."

"Who killed them, villain?"

"You did."

"I?"

"Yes you."

"How? when? where?" gasped the frantic old man, tearing his hair in agony.

"Open the Black Chamber and see for yourself; the trap which was set for me by your cunning and treachery has already done its work."

"Nay, nay, this cannot be true, Reuben. Let us haste away, and unlock the door, it may not be too late; they may yet live to forgive us."

"I want them to die," said Reuben, "for then Holly Hall is mine; nor shall you stir from this apartment until you have given up the title deeds to me."

"What!"

"You need not start, baron, you know I am a man of desperate resolves. The deeds, I say; I come prepared to enforce my claims."

And as he spoke he placed a pistol at the baron's head.

"The deeds or die!" he hoarsely whispered.

"Take them, villain, and take my life as well," groaned the baron, with downcast head; "and this is Christmas Eve again."

"Yes, I do not forget it. The very chamber where Sir Claude suddenly died, is again tenanted by the dead," said Reuben, who took the bundle of title-deeds from an escretoire, and placed them in his bosom.

"Come," said he, "we must again visit the Black Chamber, and dispose of the bodies before morning."

"I cannot—I will not!"

"But you _must_ assist me in this, and I will spare the miserable life I had resolved to rob you of. Come, follow me."

The baron left the room, and led the way to the Black Chamber, but he trembled so violently that he could not handle the key which unlocked a secret door of the dread apartment.

"Here, give the key to me, drivelling fool!" said Reuben, scoffingly, and he opened the door.

But as he did so, a sabre suddenly descended on him.

He fell to the ground, and young Allan Norman rushed forth into the corridor carrying Julia in his arms.

"Villains! Monsters!" said he, "you would have buried us alive; but Heaven be praised! we have been miraculously saved!"

The baron fell upon the stone floor.

Fright, surprise, and intense excitement crazed his brain.

He was seized with an apopletic fit and died murmuring,

"'Tis my own son, Allan Norman; Heaven forgive my many crimes."

Reuben lay weltering in his own blood, and when the alarmed and frightened household gathered together, the Black Chamber was examined, and it was discovered that the bedstead, whole and entire, had disappeared through the flooring into a deep well-like vault, in which could be plainly seen, what afterwards proved to be skeleton remains, and thus was the Black Chamber at Holly Hall discovered, and the last villain in our story (Reuben Martin) captured and consigned to jail for his long life of wickedness and crime.

CHAPTER CXXIX.

MUNGO'S RIGHT-HAND MAN, KENARD, TELLS WHY AND HOW HE JOINED THE ROBBERS AND BUCCANEERS.

"WELL, Captain Mungo," said another prisoner, when Mungo had concluded the account he had given of himself, "you are our chief, or rather were, until this Lion Limb took us all prisoners; but if you don't mind, and that young man there ——"

"Ted Rawlings, you mean?" growled Mungo.

"Aye; he has listened to your tale patiently enough, and if he has a mind to listen to another, why I'm his man; for, you see, we shall all be dead men soon, I think, and my statement will serve as a good 'last dying speech and confession' like."

"Well said, Kenard," grumbled Mungo, "you have always been my right-hand man, so let us hear your yarn."

"I would have had my say before, but the young man never asked me; but why, I don't know."

"Because," replied Ted, "I am ever unwilling to harrow up the mind, by a bitter recollection of events, which may have placed a man in an unfortunate station of life, so far below the order of his merits, and so opposite to the natural bent of his inclinations."

Kenard, smiling at this reply, assured him that it was very possible to form wrong notions, even of the integrity of our nearest friends; and without hesitation proceeded to the narration of his own adventures, thus :—

"Misfortune, at a very early period, marked me for her own.

"My father, a man of no inconsiderable property, dying when I was very young, left his affairs in a state of so much embarrassment, that my mother though accustomed to a state of affluence, was under the necessity of quitting the home in which she had passed the greater part of her life, and to take shelter in a rude cabin, on the sea coast, with scarcely the means of existence.

"My earliest employment was to attend the nets of a neighbouring fisherman—for which a trifling reward was daily given to my mother.

"However, as my years increased, too proud to submit to a state of subordination, I procured a boat of my own, and by exposing the productions of my aquatic exertions for sale, became, at least, able to support a life of honesty and independence.

"At this era I date the actual happiness of my existence.

"No apprehensions for the morrow, no cares for the past, clouded my days of peace.

"I arose cheerfully with the first dawn of Heaven, and as merrily proceeded to my labour; the great God of Nature was the Deity of my adoration—and the rude hymn of the mariner, my prayer of thankfulness.

"One evening, being more unsuccessful than usual, I tarried so late on the waters, that the dark gloom of night had already soared above the horizon and the sudden clouds which accompanied it, frowning awfully prophetic of a dreadful sea storm, induced me to lose no time in reaching the shore.

"Ere I could effect this, the vivid lightnings darting over the broad expanse of ocean, scattered my humble bark in numberless fragments to the furious and remorseless elements,

"Benumbed and weary, with the utmost difficulty I at length succeeded in swimming to the strand.

"But, alas! were I to state that my grateful heart offered up a tributary prayer for preservation, it would be only adding falsehood to ingratitude.

"On that night I beheld the total overthrow of my ambition, in the boat which had perished in the storm; and the idea of returning home with the sorrowful intelligence, deeply wounded my bleeding heart.

"With emotions far different from those I had been accustomed to feel, I beheld the distant glimmer of the lamp in the cottage lattice, and received the fond welcome of my parent, with the torturing anguish of an aching breast.

"In vain were her tender inquiries after my health and the reason of my visible distress.

"I was for a time only enabled to convince her with tears of the loss we had sustained.

"Observing, however, my silent grief greatly affected her, I communicated the cause.

"But judge of my surprise, when, instead of sharing in the agony which I endured, she reproached me with the weakness of my fortitude.

"'Ah! Kennard,' exclaimed she, 'is it thus you sink beneath adversity? Is this the aspiring spirit you boast of? Repine not, my son, but let us rather exalt our voices to Heaven, which, in its infinite mercy, spared thy life.

"'Oh! how different would the effect have been, had I beheld thee inanimately cold, and prostrated before me, or heard, with a mother's pangs, that the only consolation which my widowed heart possessed, was for ever buried in the deep!'

"I flew to my aged parent, I hung upon her bosom, imprinted a kiss upon her cheek, and bathed it with tears of filial affection.

"Her matron fortitude inspired me with new vigour, while her religious admonition awoke me to a sense of my own unworthiness.

"On the following morning I repaired to the habitation of my old employer, with an account of my loss.

"His extreme poverty prevented him from affording that necessary aid to our wants which the goodness of his heart prompted.

"At a loss, therefore, how to act, my mother at length resolved to make application for the loan of a trifling sum to a brother of her father, called Bardolph the miser, whom for many years she had not beheld, on account of her calamity and lowly state.

"As we approached his residence, a thousand wild hopes and chimeras filled our breasts.

"Bardolph was far advanced in years, and ourselves the only relatives he possessed.

"The pride of my mother had prevented her making any appeal to him on the death of her husband, of which, for my sake, she had deeply repented, since Bardolph, added to considerable power, possessed immense riches, although with those riches he did not conspire to promote the happiness of others, nor the comfort of himself.

" On reaching his dwelling, I was forcibly impressed with the wretched and desolate appearance it possessed.

" The antiquated and decayed furniture, sparingly arranged in the apartments, on which the hoary dust had for years bid defiance to the hand of industry, proclaimed the niggard soul of its owner, who, seated on a tattered couch, in a gloomy and comfortless chamber, with unbending features and jealous eye, glanced sternly on our entrance.

" Pale care, famine, and haggard fear were imprinted on his hollow cheek and tall meagre frame —the latter scantily attired in coarse raiment.

" With some degree of hesitation, my mother pronounced the object of our unexpected visit.

" Bardolph's features crimsoned at the appeal, and hastily closing down the lid of a huge coffer, the contents of which, it seemed, he had been recently examining, he eagerly thrust the key into his bosom, and at the same time, gazing fearfully around, betrayed a visible suspicion of the integrity of our designs.

" 'Alice,' said he, at length addressing my mother, ' I am poor, very poor ! and for aught I know, may need, in my latter days, enough to supply the cravings of expiring nature ; return, therefore, to those charitable friends, whose liberality assisted you at the dawn of widowhood, when the rich acres of his father went to supply the clamorous creditors of thy extravagant lord.'

" The noble soul of my parent was deeply wounded by this sarcastic and unfeeling reply, and rising—' Know, abject wretch,' she exclaimed, ' that I despise not only you, but myself, for this degradation. Let us hence, my son ; the animals of the forest will offer us more commiseration, and that hand which bountifully scattered manna in the wilderness, will as benignly be extended to us.'

" Her reproach availed but little on the heart of the miser, and with a visible expression of internal satisfaction, he beheld our departure from his inhospitable mansion.

" Finding our application to such as possessed the most undoubted right to relieve us of no avail, I once again exerted myself in the service of others, under the resolution of preserving a trifle from my weekly earnings, towards reinstating myself in comparative independence.

" But, alas ! calamity had taken shelter, as it seemed, in our cabin, and, with pangs of indescribable anguish, did I witness the decline of that best and most indulgent of parents, with whom, from infancy, I had shared so many sufferings.

" Ah ! how vain were my hopes, while I gazed upon the hectic flush of her cheek, and conceived the delusive garment of contagion to be the rosy down of returning health !

" My nights were devoted to watching by her pillow—my days into misery, that I could not attend it.

" With what fear did I quit my home at sunrise, lest I should behold her no more !—with what anxious dread return, lest those fears should be realized !

" One evening, as I sat near her lowly pallet, and administered such comfort as our humble means afforded, my mother, in feeble accents, spoke to me of Bardolph.

" ' Teach me to curse him !' I exclaimed, in the bitterness of recollection.

" 'Ah, no, my child !' sighed she ; ' let us not add guilt to our poverty, and forfeit the ecstatic hope of becoming happy hereafter. Perhaps even Bardolph, did he know the nature of our present adversity, might yet relent, and stretch forth his hand to assist us.'

" These words were sufficient to inspire my resolves, and, accordingly, on the following morning, instead of proceeding to my usual avocations, I lost no time in returning to the miser.

" As formerly, I found him deeply occupied, and throwing myself at his feet, with tears I supplicated his charity, in behalf of my unoffending parent.

" But with a stern and angry countenance, he commanded me to quit his presence, if I wished to escape punishment for such unwarrantable intrusions.

" Mad with despair, I fastened my hands on the scanty foldings of his raiment, and raising my eyes in piteous supplication, implored him, for the sake of his eternal soul, to have compassion on my woes, and spare from his abundant store, some little assistance towards the relief of a dying mother.

" Endeavouring to elude my grasp, he hastily proceeded to the door, and called aloud for help.

" Panic-struck, I instantly comprehended that he meant to accuse me of some unlawful design, and hastily gliding past him, fled for safety.

" Twilight had long since thrown her sober vest over the bosom of nature, ere I arrived within sight of the home which contained all that was dear to me on earth.

" With a heart heavy and sad, I entered the first apartment of the cottage, silently and cautiously, lest I should disturb my mother, who rested in an adjoining chamber.

" A lamp glimmered on the hearth, and the charitable matron, who kindly proffered assistance, had withdrawn to the duties of her own family till morning.

" All was still.

" I listened—so tranquil were the slumbers of my mother, not a breath, not a sigh was heard, and I devoutly sank on my knees.

" Here rising from the earth, I resolved to steal softly into my mother's apartment, in order to bless and gaze upon her, ere I retired to my own.

" Having placed the lamp carefully on the table, I gently divided the curtains.

" But how shall I describe the icy chill which rushed to my heart, as a faint gleam of light, falling upon those features whereon I had so often gazed with filial affection, betrayed them pale, distended, and lifeless !

" Agonizing recollection !

" The best of mothers, during the fatal absence of her only child, had paid the last sad tribute of nature, without the aid of his duteous hand to close her dying eyes.

" Overwhelmed with horror and affliction, I sank senseless to the earth, nor did a single gleam of memory return, till, at the sullen sound of the funeral bell, something like a sense of irremediable misery flashed across my distempered intellect, and I discovered myself hanging unconsciously over the grave of my lost parent.

" Then fell the weight of calamity, like the crush of earth upon me ; and my poor, lacerated, bruised heart, which had exhausted its bleeding tide, became seared and savage.

" With the first dawn of reason, I hurried back to the cottage, that the dreadful conviction might again be fully proved to my rational ideas.

" Alas ! it was all too true.

" Wildly did I wander from chamber to chamber.

" Each alike was deserted and gloomy, the furniture having been seized by the order of certain creditors, during my insanity, for debts contracted in the illness of my mother.

NOTICE.—*This Tale will shortly be concluded.*

THE BOY KING

OF THE SOUTH SEA ISLANDS.

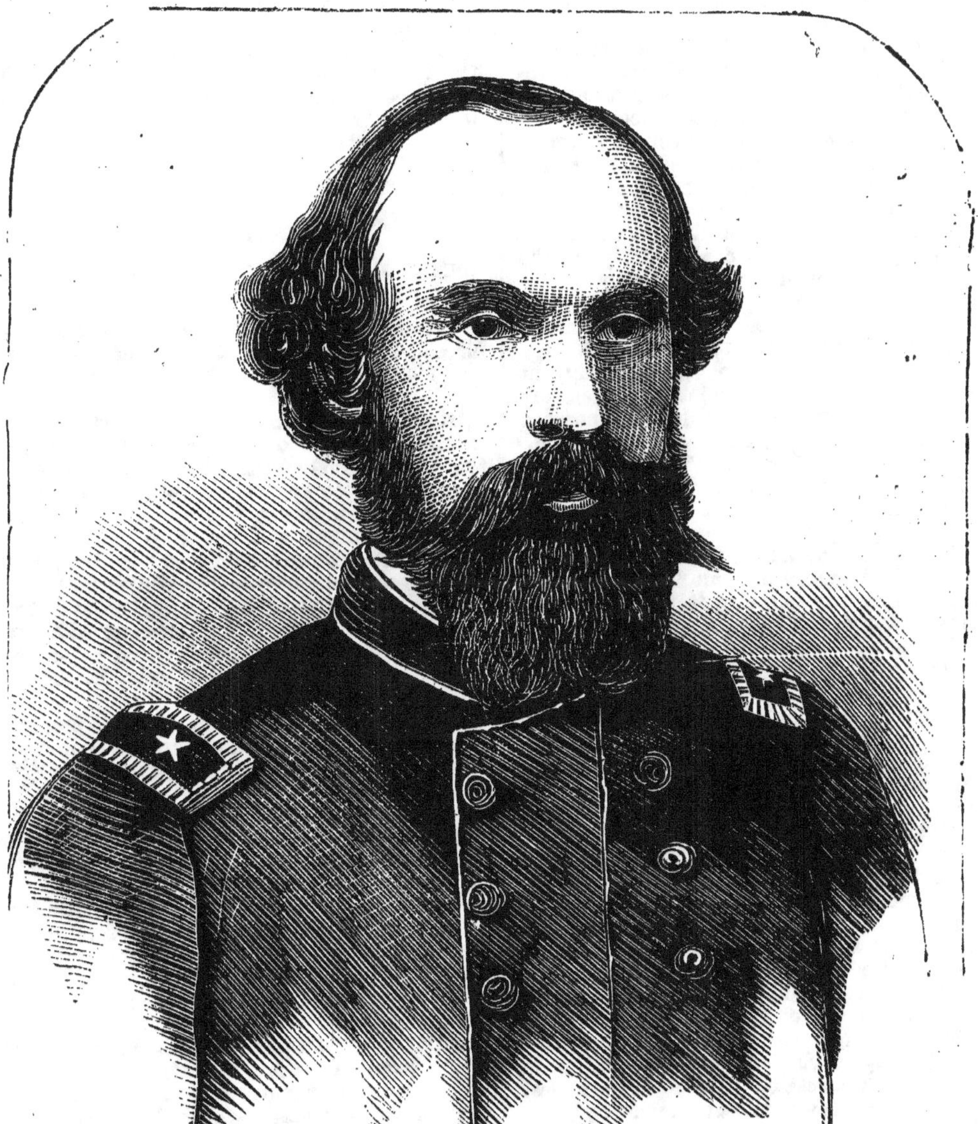

THE COUNT DE SARIVIER.

"Forlorn and alone, I cast my eyes around the desolate apartments, for some traces to remind me at least that I *had been* happy, when a small dagger, formerly belonging to my father, hanging in the lattice arch, excited my attention.

"It seemed this instrument had either, from its peculiar situation, or being of little value, totally escaped the despoiler's observation.

"In the visionary and nervous emotion of my distress, I readily imagined the singular preservation of this weapon was intended to promote some peculiar purpose.

"And reaching forth my hand to secure it, the remembrance of Bardolph's cruelty came with redoubled freshness into my mind.

"But for his uncharitable and unconscious nature, my mother, perhaps, at that moment had been living, in health, and happy, nor had perished, as was too evidently the case, for lack of proper assistance.

"While these reflections crowded forcibly to my scarcely-recovered senses, a dreadful thought came across me.

"Rushing from the cabin, I heeded not the cries of affrighted children, as they fled from my approach, nor the pitying sigh of the matron that blessed my crazed wanderings, but once again repairing to the house of Bardolph, resolved never to quit it. till his blood had been offered as an atonement to the offended spirit of my mother.

"The haggard picture of woe, I again entered his apartment, my heart fiercely burning for vengeance —my firm, unshrinking hand still grasping the dagger intended for his heart.

"But how was I surprised, on discovering the object of my search extended almost lifeless on the earth, and already weltering in his blood.

"Raising him in my arms, so great, so poignant were his agonies, that the poniard fell from my nerveless hand, and my heart, of late so incensed against him, bled for the visible pangs he endured.

"'Oh, Kenard!' sighed he, 'much wronged, much offended boy, forgive me! too late do I repent of the injustice I have shown to thee and Alice, for which I am amply punished.'

"He now proceeded, with difficulty, to inform me that robbers had broken into his habitation, and, not content with the treasures it contained, had planted their swords in his breast, under the idea of his confessing the name of some secret place, wherein they suspected great part of his gold to be concealed.

"The only servant he possessed had escaped during the disorder which prevailed, and the dread of his speedy return, with sufficient hands to arrest them, had prevented their further researches.

"Something dreadful seemed to weigh heavy on Bardolph's mind.

"He essayed in vain to unbosom himself.

"The cold perspiration of death stood trembling on his wan cheek, and the convulsion of expiring nature quivered on his lip, as, firmly grasping my feverish hand, he suddenly fell back, with a horrible groan, and expired.

"At a loss in what manner to proceed, I was contemplating the features of the dead, as the sound of approaching footsteps excited my attention, and observing the dagger which I had brought still upon the floor, I hastily concealed it in my bosom, lest the sight of it should awake unfavourable suspicions against me.

"The domestic of Bardolph now made his appearance, attended by the lord and servants of a neighbouring castle, who observing the wretchedness of my apparel, and the haggard hollowness of my cheek, rendered pale by sickness and long suffering, readily concluded the murderer of Bardolph stood before them.

"Seizing me accordingly, the dagger fell from my raiment, stained with blood, with which also my hands were embrued, in endeavouring to assist in his last moments the unlucky Bardolph.

"My confusion was construed into guilt, my supplication to confession.

"The recollection which the domestic entertained of my last unwelcome visit, with the reception I had received from his master, confirmed the few doubts remaining in my favour.

"I was unfeelingly dragged to a miserable confinement, and sentenced to linger out the remains of my days therein.

"After some months, passed in darkness and sorrow, the attack of a feudal chief restored me to liberty; when, flying to the sea coast, I entered a foreign-bound vessel, which conveyed me to unknown shores; and having travelled from kingdom to kingdom, subject to numberless adventures and misfortunes, fate gave me to Mungo's gallant band; their fellowship relieved my sufferings—their bounty my wants; cast off by the world, I have ever since resided amongst them, and hope, as I have lived, to die with their chieftain."

CHAPTER CXXX.

YOUNG JULIA'S TRIALS AND SUFFERINGS—HER ARTLESS NARRATIVE TO ALLAN NORMAN.

THE tragical events which had so suddenly taken place at Holly Hall filled the mind of Allan Norman and his young bride with feelings of horror.

Allan, by chance, during his office as private secretary, had often met Julia, and they had mutually fallen in love with each other, but in order that their mutual affection should not be thwarted they had agreed upon a runaway match and marriage unknown to any one, and then it was that, by some strange accident, they were forced to call and seek shelter for the night at Holly Hall.

On more than one occasion while waiting at the hall for the return of Reuben Martin and the settlement of the baron's will, Allan observed his young bride to be in deep melancholy, and in answer to his many tender inquiries respecting it, she at last said—

"I am the victim, and have been the property of one of those monsters who disgrace a civilized state —a being who traffics in the younger part of my hapless sex!

"He deprived me of the first blessings of life— such, alas! they appear to me—the tenderness of parents, the endearments of relatives, and the certain knowledge of my origin!

"This is all I can relate of my infantine years; but I believe I have a confused recollection of having passed them in a place resembling in some degree a hall, and even this Holly Hall reminded me, I thought, of my first residence.

"Many things on my arrival here appeared familiar to my remembrance; which I can no otherwise account for than by their affinity to those objects on which my eyes first opened, and on which they might, perhaps, have dwelt for rather more than three years.

"I have an idea of having seen in the Hall many ladies dressed with splendour, whom my heart, or perhaps my pride only, prompts me to suppose my near connections.

"One of these I particularly recollect to have engaged my affections and fondness.

"I loved her, indeed, so much, that I cannot even now forget my sensations of delight on receiving the caresses she lavished on me.

"I believe she was very handsome.

"But this may probably be only an idea attached to her extreme kindness to me, which induced me to think very favourably of her appearance.

"I remember likewise a gentleman who was past the middle age, whose mien inspired me with mingled reverence and affection.

"This man I called my father, and I think I used to admire the decorations he wore.

"I was admired and cherished by every one.

"I was confided at length to the care of an old woman, who was either my nurse or governess.

"And she treated me unkindly when my supposed parents and friends left the Hall, I think to undertake some long journey.

"Shortly after their departure, this woman awaked me in the middle of the night, dressed me hastily, and accompanied me in a carriage to a considerable distance; for we did not reach the place she was anxious to arrive at until the next evening.

"At this place, which I thought very dirty and forlorn, compared with the residence I had hitherto supposed my home, I beheld a woman, who caressed me excessively, and was extravagant in her commendations of my person and aspect.

"She remarked that I was very tall for the age that was given me.

"And I have since learned that I was then six years and three months.

"But notwithstanding the favourable sentiments and apparent kindness of the stranger, I was prevented from replying to the testimonies she gave me of her goodwill, by the deformity of her features and her figure, which terrified and disgusted me.

"Yet she ceased not in her efforts to conciliate my confidence and regard.

"And having presented me with cakes and sweatmeats, she at length put me to bed in her own apartment, where the fatigue of my journey soon closed my eyes in slumber, from which I awoke to find myself abandoned by my former protector, whose ill humour I now forgot in my eagerness to regain the cares and the society of some one to whom I was accustomed.

"But my new guardian continued to behave so kindly to me, that I was soon appeased for the loss of my cross nurse.

"After I had breakfasted, the stranger took me to a carriage, which we both entered, and I was very successfully amused by her until we again stopped at a large town, where I am certain I beheld the sea.

"Here we remained three or four days.

"And the invariable good-nature and complacency of my companion had by that time completely attached me to her.

"Again I was removed in the night.

"But I happened to be so extremely overpowered with sleep, that I know not how I was conveyed to the coach in which I found myself in the morning, and on the knees of a woman, whose aspect did not at first sight displease me like that of my last protector.

"I observed that I was now associated with four girls nearly of my own age, and another woman, who had a gentle voice and a mild countenance.

"After having surveyed them all with extreme surprise, I enquired why I was taken from my late friend; and I was instantly informed that I should see her again the following day.

"The two women were very attentive to my companions and myself, and we soon became acquainted and pleased with each other.

"In a day and a half we reached our destination, which was a very spacious and handsome villa, so situated as to delight the eye, and preserve health.

"Here we were received by a lady, whose beauty and gentle sweetness of deportment instantly captivated my young heart.

"The next morning we were all habited alike, and our dresses were remarkable for their simplicity and neatness, and the entire liberty of motion they allowed.

"We were then all sent to play in a large garden behind the house, but our sports were superintended by the handsome lady.

"In a few days our little community was much increased.

"We soon assembled together twenty in number, not one of us knowing from whence we came, or who were our present protectors.

"Nor could we indeed feel any concern upon the subject, as we were most impartially and kindly treated.

"Every day was marked with new satisfactions and pleasures—every bosom expanded with content and happiness; and the perfidious woman, who caressed and nurtured us only to plunge us into misery and destruction, was idolized by us all!

"Yet when I reflect upon the modesty of her appearance, the serious, the gentle grace of her aspect, and the virtuous precepts that dwelt upon her lips, I know not what to think, and experience a contrariety of sentiments and opinions which harrass and perplex me.

"When we were of an age to comprehend our situation, we were told that we were children of distinction, whose parents and friends wished us to be well reared and instructed; we were, therefore, confided to the care and protection of Monsieur and Madame Desprez, to whom the villa belonged: this circumstance we were at the same time desired to preserve a secret, as our safety depended upon discretion.

"Some of us—I was of this number—enquired the appellation of our parents.

"But our curiosity on this point was gently repressed, nor could I ever learn the name of my family: we were all, however, so happy with Madame Desprez, that it was our wish to pass our lives with her.

"I did not experience the same degree of affection and attachment for her husband, for he was sometimes grave to austerity.

"But his disposition, so little suited to our years and gaiety, did not much incommode us, for he inhabited a distant wing of the house during the day, and we only beheld him occasionally.

"These people gave to each of us an education such as girls of the highest rank seldom obtain.

"Our manners and our morals were very strictly watched over, and their system appears to me to have been equally founded on virtue, wisdom, and experience.

"Eight of our youthful society were removed from the house of Monsieur Desprez at ten and twelve years old.

"They were the least handsome, and the least intelligent and good-humoured of our party.

"But we still regretted them, though they evidently became more unpleasing every day, and the promise which their infancy had given of beauty was not fulfilled.

"My eleven companions, who still remained at this epoch, were by far the most lovely girls I have ever beheld.

"Some in this number possessed, with every grace of adolescence, the understanding and acquirements of a much more matured age.

"One after the other, our society diminished.

"The wretches who governed us informed those who yet dwelt under their treacherous roof that the girls who departed were required by their parents and friends, and that they were almost every one married on their return home.

"Camille, my only friend, at length was taken from me, and I alone remained in the almost deserted mansion.

"I wept with bitterness the loss of my friend and favoured companion, who promised, however, to alleviate the concern I felt by writing.

"But I feared she would forget me in the happiness of being received and cherished by a family who must, I thought, idolize her.

"Many of our hapless society had repeatedly given the same promise, and each in turn had broken it.

"At this juncture Monsieur Desprez appeared to lose all the austerity I had formerly observed in this character.

"But he became thoughtful and melancholy, and when I sometimes endeavoured to enliven his gloom, it considerably increased.

"His wife, who had ever distinguished me from my companions by a superior tenderness and consideration, was now cold, embarrassed, and reserved, and regarded me sometimes with a sort of distant displeasure I could not divine the occasion of.

"I was uneasy and disconcerted at a deportment so new from her to me, and redoubled those testimonies of affection and deference my heart involuntarily paid her—affection, alas! how ill-bestowed.

"But my efforts to dispel her secret disgust were wholly vain, and when I threw myself at her feet, and conjured her to tell me how I could have offended her, she rose in silence, and bursting into tears, withdrew.

"My situation now became terrible to me.

"I ardently longed for the moment when my friends should send for me, as those of my young associates, I believed, had already done.

"That moment, so long wished for, at length arrived.

"Madame Desprez, who had resumed some portion of her former regard and friendship, embraced me affectionately at parting, and said she should ever think of me with maternal solicitude and fondness.

"But she did not advert to any future intercourse.

"Now I can well ascertain the reason of this reserve, which I then thought strange.

"Monsieur Desprez was indisposed, and could not bid me adieu; but he sent me by his wife some handsome trinkets and ornaments, and he had required that my wardrobe should be very well furnished.

"He had accompanied every one of my associates and friends in their journey; but I was attended by the elder sister of Madame Desprez, who was the very plain and deformed person into whose hands my nurse had given me.

"I was now again consigned to her care; and,

attended by a valet, we traversed many leagues—more than a hundred I believe.

"On the sixth day from my leaving the house of her brother-in-law, we arrived at a very pretty habitation, where this woman informed me I was to be united to a gentleman, whose principal study would be my happiness.

"This intelligence surprised me; and from that moment I experienced a vague and indefinite sensation of terror and alarm, which I could not exactly determine the object of.

"'Where are my parents and relations?' demanded I, with a trembling voice.

"'They will meet you at this place, I believe,' replied the wretch.

"'Until they arrive, then, you will not leave me?' returned I.

"We were now met by some domestics, who conducted us to a saloon superbly decorated, and with a palpitating heart I expected the appearance of some person to welcome us.

"But no one appearing immediately, I turned to my wicked companion, and demanded to whom the house belonged.

"'To a friend of yours,' replied she, 'I will prepare him to see you.'

"And without allowing me time to prevent her, she left the apartment; and I found myself alone, bewildered, apprehensive of I knew not what, and almost regretting that I had quitted the dwelling of Madame Desprez.

"I believed, however, that her sister would return to me, and anxiously counted the moments as they passed, in expectation of seeing her re-enter.

"But she came not.

"I think I must have awaited her more than an hour—though possibly my impatience might have made me suppose so—when a carriage drove with uncommon rapidity up the avenue that led to the house, and having stopped at the already opened door, I beheld a young man spring from it, whose appearance was rather prepossessing.

"Who he could be, or what was his motive for a precipitation so remarkable in every feature and every motion, I had not leisure to reflect upon; for he entered the saloon the next moment.

"'Welcome, my Julia, welcome to this retreat!' exclaimed he, 'which I shall from this happy hour regard as a paradise!'

"I was so much confounded at this address and at his abrupt entrance, that I stood silent and motionless, whilst he advanced towards me, and kissing my hands alternately, lamented the imperious necessity which had compelled him to delay his return, and occasioned him to be absent on my first arrival.

"'To whom does this place belong?' demanded I, retreating from him with extreme inquietude. 'Who are you, and where are the parents, the relations I was told I should meet?'

"I now recollect that he appeared embarrassed at this inquiry.

"But at the moment my own spirits were too much agitated to judge with any precision, the motives of the frequent transitions in his countenance and manner I could not but observe.

"After hesitating a few seconds, he replied,

"'Have you not met a friend? Be assured of it. One who——'

"'But what affinity is there between us?' I resumed, in an earnest accent: 'what tie of relationship or family interest——'

"'Suppose I should be your brother, my charming Julia?' interrupted he.

"'My brother!' I exclaimed: 'are you indeed

my brother ? Oh, how sweet to my estranged ear does this word sound ! Where is my mother ? Shall I not soon behold her ? Is she not very handsome ?—and my father, too, is he still in existence ? If he be the same my infant recollection portrays to me, he must be old. Do you resemble him—do you resemble my mother ?'

" ' Should you love me better for the resemblance ?' asked he ; ' but tell me, do you love me already ?'

" ' How is it possible that, after an estrangement I have so impatiently endured,' returned I, ' I can meet any one of my family, and not experience an increase of that interest and affection which, alienated as I have been from my cradle, my heart has ever felt ? Inform me then, my brother, where is this father—where the mother on whom my imagination has ever so fondly dwelt ?'

" ' I cannot immediately reply to your enquiry,' returned he, in an accent I thought cold and unkind ; ' at some future season you will perhaps learn all you wish to know : in the interim, you will not, I hope, be sorry to hear that you are to inhabit this little mansion, where I will fly to enjoy every moment I can snatch from the importunate duties of my situation, which must sometimes tear me from you. I see in that lovely aspect,' he added, ' other questions and enquiries arising ; but I must now seek the good woman who brought you hither ; what do I not owe her for a service so inestimable !''

" He then withdrew, and I endeavoured in his absence to recall my recollection, and calm the perturbation of my mind ; but I had not in any degree succeeded when he returned, though his conference with the vile sister of Madame Desprez was not a short one.

" I immediately enquired for this woman, and was extremely surprised to hear that she had just quitted the house.

" ' Is she gone ?' exclaimed I ; ' gone, without bidding me adieu—without carrying to Madame Desprez a single acknowledgment from me ?'

" ' Your acknowledgments, my Julia,' returned my pretended brother, ' will be better dispensed with than mine on this occasion ; and believe me, I have offered mine with as much avidity as they will be received. But let us not talk of these Desprezs, we will dismiss them and the whole world from our recollection, and live only for each other !'

" Far from being delighted with this uncommon, fraternal affection, I felt embarrassed and ill at ease.

" Though I did not withdraw my hand from his, I experienced not the satisfaction or security the presence of a brother should inspire.

" As he concluded the last sentence, he embraced me ; and though I did not wish to reject those endearments our affinity might authorize, yet his repeated kisses at length alarmed me, and I pushed him from me almost involuntarily.

" ' You do not then love me, Julia ?'' exclaimed he, in an accent half reproachful, and half tender.

" ' I think I could love you,' replied I, hesitating, ' only ——'

" ' What would you say—what is this barrier which you will not define ?' demanded he.

" ' I know not of any barrier,' I replied.

" ' Nor I !' he exclaimed, in an animated voice ; ' I find you the most lovely creature Nature ever formed !—I know that to every external grace you unite a superior understanding, and the most captivating talents. I am satisfied of the purity of your soul, for that ingenuous embarrassment cannot

be counterfeited ; and all these varied perfections ensure me a happiness unalterable, if I can but obtain your heart.'

" ' What mean you ?' I ejaculated, trembling with a suspicion, which almost deprived me of sensation.

" ' To-morrow I will explain myself,' he replied, ' my Julia will perhaps in the interim further charm my soul with those strains of divine melody which she only can create !'

" He then brought from the adjoining room a superb harp.

" But I was so dreadfully shocked with the horrid surmise that had assailed me, that I pleaded the fatigue of my journey, and begged that he would suffer me to retire to my apartment—a request to which he unwillingly complied.

" A young woman appeared in obedience to his summons for the attendance of my *femme de chambre*, who conducted me to an elegant dressing-room, where every luxury which art and refinement could produce, awaited me. I experienced an earnest desire to learn if I was considered by the domestics as the sister of their master.

" And for the first time I recollected that even the appellation of my self-entitled brother was unknown to me. I discovered it, however, by the unintended communication of my new attendant, who replied to my enquiry, whether she had long inhabited the villa, that she had only been hired the preceding week, by a Madame Dumargue, to whom she happened to be known, and who had been commissioned by the Comte de Sarivier to procure a *femme de chambre* to attend a lady under his protection.

" ' Did you not understand,' said I, ' that I am the count's sister ?'

" ' No, madam,' replied she with a suppressed smile ; ' at least, I do not quite recollect,' she added hastily, ' whether Madame Dumargue mentioned it or not.'

" The manner of this woman, notwithstanding the obsequiousness she endeavoured to display, mortified and shocked me.

" Unable to endure her presence, in addition to my own alarming apprehensions, I dismissed her to reflect at my leisure on the degraded light in which I must inevitably be considered by every individual of the household, since the count had not thought it necessary to communicate to them the only circumstance that could give a colouring of decency to my residence in his habitation.

" Every succeeding moment, every recollected look and sentence during our conference, but increased my suspicions.

" Having fastened my door, I sunk into a chair, and endeavoured in vain to compose and calm my mind, that I might form a better judgment of my situation, and of the justice of the fears that assailed me.

" In little more than an hour the count himself tapped at my door, and requested me to return to the saloon, and take some supper.

" ' Your woman informs me,' added he, ' you refused to take any refreshment, and that she believes you are not yet retired to your repose.'

" I replied that I intended immediately to do so, and that my extreme fatigue prevented me from rejoining him until the next morning.

" ' But why not open your dressing-room door ?' exclaimed he. ' I wish to speak to you for a few moments, and it is impossible to converse thus.'

" ' We will meet early in the morning,' I replied, unwilling that he should discover by my swollen eyes that I had been weeping bitterly. ' Good night, my brother !''

"He returned my complimentary adieu in a peevish accent, I thought, and then retired.

"That I might not appear to have deceived him by pretending a weariness I did not really feel, I then undressed myself, and laid my aching head upon the pillow.

"But sleep forsook me for the first time.

"I counted the passing hours until the day almost dawned, and then a restless slumber, into which I sunk, was attended by a dream so horrible that I awoke in terror, and shortly after arose.

"Again I revolved with earnest precision all that had passed since my entrance into the house of the count, and my doubts were almost removed for a certainty that terrified me.

"The unexpected and hasty disappearance of the sister of Madame Desprez—the manner and the language of my pretended brother—the recollected sneer on the countenance of the attendant he had given me, who regarded me not as his sister—and the sentence that had escaped the count, in which he avowed his hope of gaining my heart, all this overwhelmed me with consternation, and predicted the future colour of my fate.

"At length when I heard the household in motion, I rang, and my attendant appeared, who expressed great mortification that I had not summoned her to assist at my toilet.

"I informed her that I had been accustomed to dress myself without the aid of another; and I then enquired if the count were up.

"She replied that he was already in the breakfast saloon; and I begged she would conduct me to it.

"He started on beholding me, and hastily demanded what had agitated and disturbed my mind.

"'You are pale and unrefreshed,' added he, 'and that expressive countenance informs me that you are ill at ease: yet in this mansion, where every individual it contains is ambitious only of serving and obeying you—where you meet a man who would consecrate with transport every moment of his life to render your's happy—'

"'Cease, I conjure you,' interrupted I, in impatient disgust, 'cease this strain, and reply to my enquiries! Why, of all my unknown family, am I only received by a brother? Ah! tell me—tell me who and what I am, and why I was given up so suddenly by Monsieur and Madame Desprez? You cannot be ignorant of the events that induced my family to seclude me from them all so entirely, nor why it was forbidden that I should even learn the appellation and the rank by which my parents are distinguished! Ah! little can they conceive the impatience with which my heart has often throbbed to behold the beloved authors of my being, and to be taken to the bosom of a mother! Can they partake an affection, an inquietude that fills my soul, and yet leave me one unnecessary moment in a situation so cruel? If, indeed, you are my brother, relieve my anxiety—explain why I have been so long insulated, and why, at length, when I was taught to expect a happiness I have ever panted to obtain, I am still thus enveloped in ignorance, and kept from the paternal mansion?'

"The count regarded me with silent attention some minutes after I had ceased, and appeared to meditate upon the reply I eagerly expected.

"'I will not conceal from you,' said he, at length, 'all it imports you to know of your situation; nor can I indeed any longer suffer you to continue in an error which deprives me of the power of explaining how complete and entire your ascendancy over my heart is become. I am *not* your brother!'

"Notwithstanding my strong suspicion of this, I started from my seat as he spoke, and would have fled I knew not whither; but the count caught my hand, and placing me again on a chair, soothed my perturbation by assurances of paying to my wishes and commands every deference I could expect, were I in the house and protection of a parent.

"It was a considerable time, however, ere I became in any degree calm; and the first use I made of returning recollection was to enquire with earnest anxiety what fatality had so strangely associated the count in my destiny.

"'An accidental circumstance,' he replied, 'obliged me to be for some time in the neighbourhood of the place where you have resided from infancy. Desprez, with whom I became acquainted, afforded me several opportunities of seeing you, unknown to yourself, and I have listened for hours to the harmonious voice which alone would have charmed me, even had it not proceeded from the loveliest mouth in the world! Could I behold you, Julia, and not adore you? Ah! no! I was impatient until I obtained a treasure so inestimable; and by repeated proofs of the most ardent attachment, challenge the grateful affection of a heart, which to possess might create envy in the bosom of the greatest potentate on earth!'

"At this exclamation I clasped my hands in renewed agony, and deplored my adverse fate, and the credulity which had aggravated it.

"'Let me leave this house!' I exclaimed. 'How can I remain here? Send me to some neighbouring house, and from thence I will write to the treacherous Desprez, and require him to inform me who my parents are. If you experience for me the attachment you possess, you will assist my endeavours to discover the authors of my existence: if I am happy enough to succeed, they must be consulted in the disposal of me; but you will ensure their gratitude and esteem by a conduct so benevolent and just.'

"'You compel me, my lovely friend,' replied he, 'to utter what will not be pleasing to your ear! Desprez himself is unacquainted with your origin, except that, from the circumstances attending the incident that threw you into his hands, he is convinced your parents were far from being elevated, or even opulent. This man educated you on speculation; and since I must avow it, he has succeeded, by means of the passion your beauty alone inspired, to the utmost extent of his avaricious views; but I detest the thought of claims which are not founded in your favourable opinion, and ——'

"I now comprehended that the infamous Desprez had sold me, and that the count considered me as his property; and, uttering an exclamation of agony as the idea assailed me, I sunk back in the chair, and lost every sense of my misery.

"When I recovered, the count dismissed the women he had called, and conjured me not to suffer the discovery he had been unwillingly impelled to make, to affect me further.

"'My whole fortune is at your disposal,' said he; 'and the only wish I shall henceforth form, will be to merit the returning tenderness I sigh for. Let me endeavour to win your esteem and love—this is the only concession I ask. If I am so unfortunate as to fail, I promise in six months to conduct you to any place you may fix upon. An employment I have in the royal household will not allow me to be perpetually here; but you will not deny me the happiness of flying to you every moment I can escape from the insipidity of a court. This place is your own, and every domestic will obey you assiduously, except you should require to leave the house; and that I must forbid them to accede to.'

"Having vainly awaited the reply I was unable

to give, he now quitted me, and sent the young woman he had given me as an attendant, to offer her services. She led me, at my request, to my apartment, where I desired to be left alone; and after an officious display of attachment and concern, she attended to the intimation.

"It is impossible to conceive the anguish I now experienced.

"Every dream of happiness I had formed was suddenly dissipated.

"It seemed to me that I had fallen into an abyss of wretchedness from which no human being was sufficiently interested in my welfare to withdraw me, whilst the only two people who had given me their attention and cares, and in whom my earliest regard was placed, became in my eyes ruthless and unprincipled monsters.

"Yet when I reflected upon the manner in which I had been educated, the examples of virtue which had been perpetually offered to my contemplation, and the precepts which had enforced them—when I reviewed the conduct of Madame Desprez, and the scrupulous attention which she had ever given to the preservation of that native and innate delicacy and modesty which are the greatest charm of youth, I could not conceive that they had doomed me to infamy; but supposed, at length, that they intended me to be the wife of the count, who had received me from them to become my husband.

"'It must be so,' I exclaimed; 'Madame Desprez could not have given me up with any other motive; it is surely impossible for the most perfect hypocrite to counterfeit the humanity, the gentleness, and the virtuous serenity her countenance and manners perpetually indicated!

"'The turbulence of vice and the struggles of conscience must in some degree be manifested on the aspect.

"'This sentiment is her own; and when she uttered it, I well remember to have remarked the complacent harmony her features exhibited.

"'Well, then, I have mistaken the intentions of the count, who means to marry me; and I now recollect the sister of Madame Desprez told me so.

"'He is generous; he appears to possess a large fortune, and will raise me to a rank which must flatter those sensations of pride and elevation I cannot conquer.

"'But I love him not; I may, however, become attached to him, were it only from gratitude; for will he not be my support and my defender?

"'He will supply to me the absence of parents, relations, and friends. Why do I then hesitate? Any further deliberation is useless, since I must finally accede to his expectations. Such is my fate, and I cannot evade it!'

"I now felt more calm and composed; and having taken a few turns in my apartment, I compelled myself to descend once more to the saloon, where a domestic, who observed me as I passed to it, instantly brought some chocolate.

"I was really in want of sustenance, as I had neither breakfasted nor supped the preceding evening.

"I found my spirits more on their usual level after my repast; and supposing the count to have gone out, I applied myself for amusement, and as a resource against my too busy reflections, to the harp which I found in the apartment I had been first introduced into.

"All the music given to me by Monsieur Desprez was already ranged on a stand; and I discovered that a greater quantity, to which I was a stranger, was placed by the side of it, apparently for my use.

"I employed, I believe, several hours in an occu-pation in which I had always experienced great delight, and it soothed the yet unsubdued inquietudes of my soul.

"At intervals, indeed, I found my forehead resting against the instrument, and my hands clasped over it; but I checked these inauspicious musings, and when they would recur too often, I rose and walked in a garden, on to which the opened windows gave entrance.

"The heat, however, soon forced me to return to the house, and again I resumed the harp.

"In another hour the door of the saloon opened, and the count entered.

"He flew towards me with an aspect of pleasure, exclaiming—

"'Oh, my Julia, with what transport do I return to you! Your woman tells me you are more composed; and finding you thus, I must hope that you have dismissed the ill-founded inquietudes of this morning. I was grieved to be compelled to leave you ere I could essay to dissipate them; but I was under the necessity of attending the royal levee, and I trembled to find you at my return still unhappy or uneasy!'

"He led me to a chair, for we were standing, and placed himself by my side.

"'I am penetrated to the soul, my lovely friend,' said he, after a pause of a moment, 'with your innocent candour, and that amiable *naiveté* so seldom to be found; and I never felt so sensibly as at this moment the misery of being enchained by public opinion! You are the most interesting, the most beautiful creature I ever encountered, and worthy the serious attachment of a monarch. The condescension you have this moment testified, flatters me with the hope that I am not unpleasing to you. What further can I desire? My fortune is already ample, and will further increase at the death of an uncle, who, on losing a beloved daughter designed in infancy to become my wife, secured to me all his possessions when he declared me his sole heir. It is not then from sordid motives that I hesitate to marry you. I might deceive you, Julia, by professing that I intended at some future period to give you my name and my hand, and then avail myself of the specious pretext, to obtain what you may perhaps refuse to the most ardent love; but my idea of honour and rectitude forbids me to act thus; and were I to be deprived of the happiness which yet, however, I must hope for, I will not owe it to a falsehood.'

"'I thank you for the frankness of your communication,' said I, 'and I entreat that you will excuse my ignorance of the principles and opinions of a world to which I am so new, which induced you presumptuously to suppose that it was possible I could ever become your wife.

"'To your proposal of a union, I shall reply with as little reserve as you have yourself employed in making it. From the suggestions of reason, therefore, I reject it; and I abhor it likewise from the suggestions of that virtue I believe to be innate in my heart, and which has been assiduously cultivated, for what purpose I know not. Six months, or six years hence, my sentiments must remain the same. I require, then, my immediate liberty at your hands, because you cannot have bought it without my concurrence; and from the professions of honour you have just made, I expect that you suffer me instantly to remove from a place which, with every luxury that adorns it, is become to me a loathsome prison.'

"'You would not express yourself thus cruelly,' exclaimed the count, 'if you knew how much I adore you.'

" ' Spare yourself these protestations,' I replied, 'which from this hour I shall disbelieve, and which I will no longer listen to !'

" I rose to leave the room, and he made an effort to detain me ; but my increasing dislike of him gave me resolution and strength, and I darted from him to take a present refuge in my apartment, where I locked myself in.

" Having barricaded both the doors, I refused to open them to the united entreaties of the count and the attendant he had given me, who exerted all her eloquence to be admitted.

" The count conjured me, if I would not descend to dinner, to have it served for myself alone, in my dressing-room.

" But I abhorred the idea of being subjected for a moment to the horror of again beholding him, and resolved to die with hunger, rather than hazard an interview.

" I heard him walking with an agitated step up and down the corridor, until the twilight appeared.

" At intervals he renewed, with as little success, his entreaties that I would return to the saloon, and hear what he wished to say.

" At length he retired, and night came on ere I had wholly resolved upon my projected plan.

" I had remarked that the garden was separated from the open fields only by a wall not very high, and that at a particular part of it was affixed an iron grating, by which I believed I could climb over it without much difficulty.

" My windows were not very distant from the ground, and a treillage that supported a pomegranate tree immediately beneath them, would facilitate my descent.

" Upon these favourable circumstances I grounded a project to escape the usurped power of the count, and throw myself, unprotected, unassisted, upon a world I knew so little of.

" When, after listening attentively, I concluded that every one of the household, as well as the master of it, were retired to rest, I opened one of my windows with silent precaution, and fastened the outward Venetian blind to the wall.

" To this I clung with all my strength, whilst I stepped from the balcony to the treillage, a part of which gave way beneath my weight, but I recovered myself with a little exertion ; and at the expence of the tree, which was broken in many places by my efforts to sustain myself as I descended, I reached the ground in safety.

" I then flew towards the grating ; and having passed the wall without injuring myself further than receiving a few scratches on my hands, I found myself in a large, unenclosed field, which led to a great road.

" I had in my purse some money, which I had received from Madame Desprez at different times.

" For at her house we were not suffered to be without money, that at a future period the sudden and unaccustomed possession of it might not render us either prodigal or avaricious.

" With this small sum I flattered myself I might support my existence, until I found some kind of employment which would become a permanent resource.

" I walked forward without knowing whither my adventurous steps would lead, yet I soon discovered that I must be very near a large town, because I distinctly beheld a number of buildings, which appeared like houses, and the roofs of others of a greater height, which I supposed to be churches and public edifices.

" Towards these I hastened, and at length found myself in a considerable street, called the *Faubourg Saint Martin.*

" I walked for some time without encountering a single being, and at length perceived a group of men advancing, who appeared by the faint light of the moon, which was now going down, to be firemen in uniform.

" I was terrified, and turned down another street which just then presented itself, to avoid meeting them.

" But one of the party having bid the others good night, followed me.

" I endeavoured to run forward ; and the inequalities of the pavement on which I had never been accustomed to walk, soon occasioned me to stumble, and I fell.

" The man raising me up with great humanity, exclaimed—

" ' Good God, madam ! how came you here alone, and at this hour ?   Where are you going ?'

" ' I know not !' replied I, bursting into tears.

" ' You seem very young,' resumed he, 'and I don't think you are used to be in the streets at midnight ; the military patrole will soon pass, and you will be sent to prison—do you know that ?'

" ' Oh heavens !' I ejaculated, 'protect and succour me !'

" ' Come home with me,' said he, apparently affected with my distress ; 'my wife is a good woman, and will take care of you till morning.   If I am of service to you, I shall not be sorry at having been called up to-night, though the fire went out so soon, that none of us will get much by our job ; but that is so much the better for the master of the house, who saves his furniture and effects by it : and though I am a fireman, I don't want people to be ruined to bring grist to my mill.'

" There was a tone of honesty so apparent in this man, that I accepted his hospitable proposition, to which indeed I was as well disposed by my terror of the night-guard, as by the extreme hunger I now experienced.

" For not having taken anything but a cup of chocolate since I had been under the roof of the count, the anxiety and perturbation of my mind did not prevent me from feeling severely a want of sustenance, to which I had never before been exposed.

" I followed the good-natured fireman, therefore, very thankfully, and he conducted me to a house at the distance of a few streets, where we ascended a common staircase excessively dirty and narrow ; and he opened, with a key which he drew from his pocket, the slip-lock of a door, by which we entered a chamber tolerably spacious and very clean.

" His wife was in bed ; and Gregoire, her husband, drawing back the curtain, abruptly informed her that he had brought her home a young lady, who had not any other place to put her head into.

" ' Look at her,' added he, 'and you will agree with me that it would have been a pity if any misfortune had happened to her !'

" The good woman, far from being displeased at this address, assented to the humane sentiment it testified ; and instantly rising, whilst the husband busied himself in rekindling a fire, she assured me in reply to my acknowledgments, that she was only anxious that she could not accommodate me in the manner she was certain I had been used to.

" ' But I have a little closet here,' added she, opening the door of it, 'where my sister sleeps when she comes to see us.   The bed is not a bad one, and I will get it ready in half an hour.'

NOTICE.—This Tale will shortly be concluded.

THE BOY KING

OF THE SOUTH SEA ISLANDS.

"Those who are acquainted with the dispositions of the lower order of people at Paris, will not experience any incredulity at this instance of goodness and hospitality; in the same degree that people of distinction, and even tradesmen, entrench themselves in suspicion and reserve towards a stranger who demands compassion and succour, artizans and workmen are zealous to assist and serve them.

"I was ashamed of the trouble I was the occasion of giving this worthy couple; yet when they enquired if I had already supped, extreme hunger compelled me to acknowledge that I had not.

No. 53.

"'I have but indifferent fare to offer you,' said the wife, 'and at this hour of the night it will be impossible to get anything out of doors; but if you can make shift for the present with a couple of eggs, and a bit of bread and cheese, to-morrow you shall be better served.'

"I eagerly swallowed what she so kindly placed before me; and then retiring to the closet, threw myself on the bed.

"Fatigue and weariness soon overpowered the reflections that would arise upon my situation, and I fell into a profound sleep.

"The poor people were very kind to me, and they would not suffer me even to soil my hands with work of any kind.

"I frequently took walks abroad, attired in humble costume, so as not to be recognised by any one, the good fireman's wife being my constant companion.

"I generally contrived, in these excursions, to shade my face from observation.

"But one day, when the weather was very close and oppressive, and the walks were almost deserted, my companion and myself sat under the trees to rest ourselves, and I threw back the black silk hood I wore, to breathe more freely.

"In a few minutes a woman passed me, whose features struck my recollection, and she likwise regarded me with marks of recognition.

"'Good God! is it you, ma'am?' exclaimed she, turning back suddenly.

"I now discovered her to be the woman the count had given me as an attendant; and in my first emotion of terror, was on the point of flying from her without replying, but was retained by the superior apprehension of separating myself from my friend, and losing myself in a place nearly two miles distant from our home.

"The woman perceived my alarm, and the sudden intention it had produced.

"'Do not run away,' said she, seating herself very familiarly by my side, and taking hold of my gown —'I am so pleased to meet with you, and I suffered so much, as we all did indeed at your giving us the slip, that you owe me the satisfaction of chatting a bit with you.'

"I was for a moment surprised at the different tone this woman had adopted since her last interview with me; but casting my eyes on my humble adjustment, to which her's was elegant and superb, I soon discovered the reason of it.

"As I saw that my companion regarded her with an air of suspicion and displeasure, I would not appear to shun any explanation her conversation might give of this prefatory sentence.

"I sat still, therefore, though I replied coldly to her address, and was resolved to evade, by every means in my power, suffering her to discover my present habitation.

"'Well, you threw us all into fine confusion!' continued she; 'Monsieur le Comte walked in the corridor till he was fairly tired; so finding that you were obstinate, he came away at last, but he would not have any supper, because you fasted, I suppose.

"'His valet told me he went to bed in a very ill humour; and he really believed, by what he said, that he meant to marry you privately, since you refused to listen to him on any other terms, for your scorn of him only made him the more in love.

"'He said out aloud, once or twice—

"'"If I could but be certain that she was attached to me, I would overcome every obstacle of pride and prejudice, and listen only to the dictates of my heart!"

"'As the valet said afterwards, it was a pity you had run away, for it was impossible any woman could resist such a fine sentiment; and I really think the rogue intends to use it himself upon occasion. However, when the count got up the next morning, he wrote you a letter; what it was about I don't exactly know, but he desired me to carry it to you, and to entreat you in his name to take care of your health, which would be hurt for want of food.

"'He told me to say, too, that you might come down stairs without any apprehension of meeting him, if that was your reason for shutting yourself up, for that he would not appear before you until you wished it, and sent him word so. He only asked you in return to receive his letters, and answer them.'

"'"Well," said his valet, Gamard, to me, "if this don't melt her flinty heart, nothing will."

"'But when I rapped at your dressing-room door, and listened if you were stirring, behold I received not a word of answer, and did not hear you even breathe, though the bedchamber door was wide open, which I saw by peeping through the keyhole; and what was more suspicious still, the bed had not been lain upon.

"'So I ran back to the count in a fright, and told him what I had seen, and he flew like lightning to your apartment to listen too; but all was still as death; and having called to you several times to conjure you to relieve his agonizing inquietude, he ran to the garden, and examining your windows, could see nothing of you still; but the broken treillage, and the tree torn down in places under the open window, made him turn as pale as death.

"'So up he goes, at all events, to see how matters were.

"'I am sure he was not a minute climbing up, though he trembled like a leaf. Well, as you may suppose, he looked in every nook and corner in vain —you were not to be found, though the outward doors were well fastened.

"'Again he returned to the garden, flying about like wildfire, and asking the gardeners if they had not seen you.

"'And when they all declared they had not, he came back to the house like a madman, calling everybody to him, and asking for you.

"'But as nobody knew what had become of you, he went into a rage, threatened us one minute to turn us all away, and the next entreated that we would find you, and restore you to him, because he could not live without you.

"'Well, three or four of the men were sent on horseback to scour the country, and the count galloped to Paris, to enquire of the police if a handsome young woman had been met by the patroles in the night, alone and well dressed; but they all told him you could not have been there, for they had seen nothing of you.

"'So, after searching about for six or seven leagues round Paris, he set off to the house of your friends, where they say he had you from.

"'But there again he was disappointed of finding you, for he thought, perhaps, not knowing anybody else, you might have returned to them.

"'But on reaching the place, he found the habitation shut up, and was told by the people in the neighbourhood, that the gentleman and lady who had lived there, had sold the house not above a fortnight back, and that they had set off for a long journey, it was believed towards Calais.

"'Monsieur Le Comte, on hearing this, took the road thither, and travelling night and day, reached it half dead with fatigue; and poor Gamard, who accompanied him, was laid up.

"'But after all this trouble and toil, no such people as the Desprez had been there.

"'So they came back to Paris very glum, you may be sure, and the count had a fever. He is now at Versailles, but the moment he hears you are found, you may expect to see him; and if you are not so cross as you have been, who knows what may happen!'

"' You would do well not to recall me to the recollection of the count,' replied I, terrified at this intimation, ' for I will not remain another hour in Paris, if I find myself exposed to his solicitations!'

"She only smiled at this menace, and I plainly perceived that he would not long be ignorant of the unfortunate encounter that had taken place.

"She now endeavoured to insinuate herself into the good opinion and confidence of my friend, who received her advances, however, with the most repulsive reserve.

"At length, finding all her efforts to conciliate her confidence wholly unavailing, she quitted us.

"I then lamented to my companion and protectress my evil fortune in having been recognised by this woman, and informed her that the count, of whom she spoke, was the person whose house I had quitted, to find a shelter in her little dwelling.

"' I guessed so by what she said,' replied the good woman; 'and her story gives me such an opinion of you, that I will hazard my life sooner than you should be taken away from me! Come, let us get home—at the worst, she can only tell him that you are in Paris; and if by chance he should find out where you are, my husband and I will not let him enter our door—so be easy on that head!'

"Whilst she spoke, a postchaise drew up, and with it a guard of soldiers.

"I turned towards Madame, and with an imploring eye, conjured her to save me, for I knew that I was again in the hands of enemies.

"I clasped my hands in increasing agony, and turned my supplications to Heaven; but they were instantly interrupted by the officer of the guard, who brutally informed me that he could not waste his time, and I must enter the chaise immediately, or I would be forced into it.

"' What have I done to be treated thus like a criminal?' I asked, the tears streaming down my cheeks; 'for what heedless or misrepresented action?—Oh, Madame, can you indeed leave me with such unconcern, in a situation so cruel! Will you at least inform your——'

"Two of the guard, in obedience to the signal of their commander, seized me, and, spite of the shrieks which terror extorted from me, placed me in the vehicle, into which the officer followed, and it drove away very rapidly, escorted by the four soldiers.

"After the first affright had in a degree subsided, I endeavoured to collect myself, and suppress any useless indication of those feelings which I plainly perceived only excited ridicule or anger in the callous wretches to whom I was consigned.

"After a long silence, in which I repeatedly, and still vainly dried my flowing eyes, I at length found courage to entreat my gloomy companion to inform me why I was thus torn from the place that served me for a home, and from the benevolent being who considered me with the affection of a parent.

"But I merely received an answer that commanded me to cease an importunity that must be useless, and resign myself to my destiny.

"From this moment I was wholly silent, and my unfeeling adviser soon after sunk into a slumber.

"Night came on, and still we journeyed with equal rapidity.

"One of my undesired attendants rode forward to every post, and when the chaise appeared, the horses were changed in two minutes.

"At length the morning dawned; and glancing a fearful regard out of the window of the chaise, I beheld my guards on each side of it, armed with sabres and pistols; and instantly withdrawing my eyes in terror I conjured of Heaven to protect me.

"In little more than an hour the carriage stopped before a large and gloomy fortress.

"The chains of a *pont-levis* rattled in my ears. I started.

"The sentinels saluted the officer who accompanied me, and the chaise passed on.

"' Where am I!' I exclaimed, with a pallid aspect, ' Oh, why am I brought hither?'

"No reply was made to this enquiry, and I was the next moment taken from the carriage, and led into the *Chateau Trompette*.

"The Governor happened to be absent; and the order that deprived me of liberty, and designated my prison, was presented to his Lieutenant, a morose and unfeeling man, who scarcely regarding me, mentioned the particular apartment he desired I should occupy; and without beholding a single being of my own sex, I was conducted to it.

"It was a single chamber, in which the light of the sun, in its meridian brightness, could scarcely penetrate.

"The walls of stone, uncovered and unadorned, except by melancholy inscriptions cut into them by their former occupiers, struck my chilled soul with horror.

"And from the comfortless and dirty bed I turned in disgust. Yet in this desolate place I was compelled to exist, on that bed to repose many a weary day, and many a long and almost endless night.

"Every alleviation of my chagrin, inquietude, and *ennui*, was rigidly refused me.

"I could not obtain either paper, pens, or books, and beheld only the inflexible aspect of the gaoler, or the austere visage of some strange visitor. I was in a dungeon and all through the count's implacable villany!"

CHAPTER CXXXI.

JULIA CONTINUES HER EXCITING NARRATION AND EXPLAINS HER DELIVERANCE FROM THE GLOOMY CASTLE AND ITS RUDE INMATES.

AFTER a long pause, during which Julia seemed to be very much affected by the remembrance of her exciting trials and captivity, she thus resumed:—

How long I may have been doomed to linger in my lonely prison without hopes of deliverance it is difficult to conjecture, had not a strange accident occurred to the villanous comte who seemed resolved on my destruction.

Hearing that I was in the Castle Trompette, and wishing once more to try his villanous arts and plans upon me, he resolved upon setting off at once to visit me, and force me if possible to be his wife, or perhaps something worse and more degrading.

With these ideas, Monsieur le Comte stepped into the chaise he had ordered, and, indulging a very satisfactory reverie, was driven at a round pace, which corresponded with his impatience to arrive at his destination.

The postillion lashed, sung and swore.

The unhappy animals he drove groaned and trotted.

The comte rubbed his hands with anticipated delight in the contemplation of the success that awaited him.

Suddenly casting his eyes on the road he was passing he perceived that the off wheel of the chaise was much too near the edge of a precipice which skirted it for several hundred paces.

Calling vehemently to the driver, he bade him be more careful.

"What is the matter, monsieur?" asked the man, with all the nonchalance of intoxication.

"The matter!" repeated the comte; "why, you profane sot, do you not see the precipice? Mind what you are about, man! For the love of Heaven and your own soul, take care how you turn that angle! Here; stop, stop, I say, and let me out!"

"Jupiter! here's a pother!" exclaimed the fellow; "why, monsieur, I have driven this road these ten years, and never had such a thing asked of me before! Nobody is afraid when Pierre Martin drives them. Monsieur, I can't think of it; I should be dishonoured for ever, and never look up again!"

So saying, he lashed his horses into a quicker pace.

And to demonstrate his sense of security he began a favourite ditty, which the agonized comte cursed very heartily, as well as the obstinate singer. Having again vainly clamoured to be let out, he watched the course of the wheels with the eager attention of a man who felt himself on the brink of perdition.

Perdition and eternity were very synonymous terms with Monsieur le Comte.

When the driver had nearly approached the angle in the road, of which he had been warned, he interrupted his song, and, turning his head towards the trembling comte assured him that there were not two more tractable and sure-footed creatures in the whole province than the beasts that drew him.

But, alas! ere this comforting intelligence had well passed his lips, the horses, chaise, and monsieur suddenly vanished, leaving the inebriated postillion suspended to the branch of a large pine, which caught him out of his jack-boots, and arrested his descent into the chasm, whither the carriage was now rolling, with a noise and clatter that completely dissipated the fumes of the brandy he had drunk.

At length it rested on a large jutting crag, having made three or four tremendous somersaults, by which one horse was almost killed, and the other was severely wounded.

The luckless comte, who still retained his senses, was unable to extricate himself from the shattered vehicle, although he foresaw that the least motion of the surviving horse must precipitate him to unavoidable destruction.

He endeavoured to call for assistance.

But his agonies were so acute, that he could only groan out an ejaculation it was impossible for any one to understand.

When the postillion had in a degree recovered his scattered recollection, he perceived the danger to which the comte was exposed.

And as an equal danger threatened the animal he had still hopes of saving, he instantly descended to the relief of both, by the aid of the branches of trees and the inequalities of the rock.

But when he reached the wounded and maimed party, as he was impelled by affection for his horses, and attention to his own interest, to afford them the first succour he could bestow, he examined into their situation, after having disengaged them from the harness, before he drew the comte from beneath the ruins of the chaise.

Animated by this insolent neglect into a power of uttering his rage and indignation, the comte began a string of anathemas and denunciations, which terrified the delinquent, and proved that the person who poured them forth was neither very patient nor very resigned to the dispensations of Providence.

The man would now have transferred his cares to the comte, had not the shaft-horse at this unlucky moment breathed his last, whilst a torrent of blood spouted from his mouth and nostrils.

At this deplorable sight, the man made every surrounding cliff reverberate with his outcries and lamentations, which effectually drowned the sinking voice of the comte, who gave up the point without much contention, and resumed his groans.

At length the postillion found leisure to assist him.

And having, rather more roughly than the comte thought necessary, dragged him from the broken chaise, he spread his coat over the cushion, at the request of the sufferer, and laid him upon them.

The comte had no use of his left arm and his right leg, which were indeed both broken.

On his head he had received a very dangerous contusion, besides numberless other wounds and bruises which overspread his whole body.

When the increased agony, which the motion had given him, was a little subsided—

"You see," exclaimed he, "you see the effects, you obstinate scoundrel, of disregarding my cautions!"

"Ah, monsieur," replied the fellow, blubbering, "those poor beasts have as much right to reproach me as you have! There is one of them has already given up the ghost, and the other is not much better off—and what to do with you all, or how to get you all up the rock, I can't tell! If you will have patience, monsieur, whilst I go to the next town for help, I will give you the last drop of brandy I have left, to keep up your spirits."

He then produced a little flask, which the comte, who felt faint and sick, did not object to empty.

The postillion then hastened away in search of a farrier and a surgeon.

Fortunately when he had walked a few paces, he was overtaken by one of his comrades, who was conducting two post-horses to the town he wanted to reach.

He mounted one of them, and galloped thither, bewailing the whole way the injury he had done himself and his beasts, throwing in at intervals, however, an apostrophe of indignation at the meddling and silly injunctions and exclamations of the comte, without which he might have performed the journey without any mischance—so at least he asserted to his comrade.

In two hours he returned to the fatal spot, followed by people bearing cords and mattresses, and attended by a surgeon for the unlucky comte, and a farrier for the wounded horse.

It was with great difficulty the comte could be

extricated from his undesirable situation, and carried to the nearest cottage.

He suffered so severely whilst this necessary task was being accomplished, that he thought it impossible he could long survive—an opinion which that of the surgeon corroborated.

"Send to Salignac!" exclaimed the comte, in a mingled agony of mind and body—"send to Salignac, and conjure Monsieur Dupan of the Chateau to have the charity to come hither; inform him of the cruel accident that has befallen me, and that I cannot die in peace unless I see him!"

This request was immediately complied with.

But the messenger had not been dispatched half an hour, ere the comte impatiently demanded why he thus lingered, although he was reminded that Salignac was nearly four leagues distant.

When his fractured limbs had been set, and his contusions dressed, he eagerly required a clergyman; and the pastor of the place being called to him, he made an avowal of his cruel persecution of me.

"It is necessary that you make a formal declaration of the injustice you have committed towards this young woman," said the priest, "and that you send to liberate her; without these proofs of the sincerity of your repentance, I cannot conscientiously give you the requisite absolution."

The comte, who had death so immediately before his eyes, was very willing to do both the one and the other; and lest Monsieur Dupan should not arrive in time to receive the instructions he meant to give him, he consented to commit his confession to the pen of a notary, and that it should be witnessed by the surgeon and the priest.

The comte closed this necessary acknowledgment by an earnest entreaty that I would forgive him, and intercede with Heaven for mercy and pardon on him.

After fulfilling this important duty, his mind became more tranquil, and in two hours the good Dupan entered his chamber, prepared to hear something important and extraordinary by the importunity of the unhappy comte, which the messenger had represented to hasten him.

At the earnest intercession of the wretched sufferer, he remained with him until the next morning, and was present when his contusions were again examined, from which the surgeon apprehended a mortification to be inevitable.

The good Dupan then bidding him adieu, procured a copy of the declaration properly attested; and impatient to make a proper use of it, he proceeded towards Versailles without returning to Salignac.

When Monsieur Dupan arrived at Versailles, he went immediately to the residence of the favourite secretary; and presenting to him the confession of the comte, whose misadventure he related, he requested an order for my release.

The secretary, shocked at the injustice and cruelty of the comte, and a little alarmed likewise at the publicity given to the circumstance by the declaration of the discomforted nobleman, sent instantly to the commandant of the castle.

"As for the young English woman," continued the secretary, "at your request I undertake to procure, in a few days, or order to be dispatched to the Governor of the Chateau Trompette for her unconditional release."

My deliverance from prison followed in a very few days, and I had resolved to bring the comte to justice in open court, but the tidings of his miserable death soon reached me, and I was persuaded to forego any publication of the trials I had undergone by many English nobles and gentlemen who had heard of them with surprise and dismay.

I was not long in discovering that my uncle, Baron Templeton, was in England, but from what I heard of his temper and habits I cannot say that I was in any hurry to cross the channel and place myself under his protection, although I had been informed again and again by many friends that he had made a will making me his sole heir.

My best friend in France was the lovely Lady Oxenford, that you, my husband, so much resemble in form and feature.

"It was at Lord Oxenford's house, as you will remember, that I first saw and learned to love you. You know the rest; her ladyship perceived our mutual attachment and did not attempt to thwart it, so——"

"So we ran away and got privately married, did we not?"

"We did."

"And are you not happy?"

"Perfectly happy," said Julia, blushing; "but my poor uncle?"

"Is dead," said young Allan; "and the villain, Reuben Martin, who now turns out to be a ticket-of-leave man——"

"A returned convict, Allan?"

"Yes; he has broken away from the officers and is still at large, where, perhaps, under an assumed name, he will still continue in his career of villany until he falls to the hangman's lot."

"But is not Lady Oxenford some relation of yours, Allan?" asked young Julia; "I have often thought so."

"She is," said Allan.

"And what relation, dear?"

"My own mother."

"Impossible!"

"'Tis true; but breathe not the secret to any one."

"And does Lord Oxenford know this?"

"He does not, nor must he know it."

"I have heard it said that my lord feels so much attached to you that he intends leaving you most part of his wealth."

"It is perfectly true. He has made a will to that effect, which was placed in the baron's hands, so that you see, dear Julia, heaven, after many trials, has rewarded our long life of trials, and now we may look forward to happiness and love, unclouded by sorrow or pain."

"But your poor brother, Edgar, who was drowned. Oh! if he were only alive, now," sighed Julia, "how he would rejoice at our marriage."

"Yes; but alas! he is dead!"

CHAPTER CXXXII.

STARTLING NEWS FROM LION LIMB AND HIS BRAVE YOUNG COMRADES.

"Dead! dead! Who is dead?" said a stranger, coming into the room.

It was Inspector Sharp.

Allan was greatly pleased and surprised, as he shook the officer by the hand.

" You did not expect to see *me* here, I think, Mr. Allan ?" said Sharp, bowing to Julia.

" No, in truth, I did not."

" I was sent to look after you."

" By whom ?"

" By the orders of Lord Oxenford and his lady ; but you need not look alarmed ; as you are married, the affair is all over, you know, and I am ordered to say that you may both return and live with his lordship, as his own son and daughter, and let all the past be buried in oblivion."

" His lordship has been very kind to me," said Allan, " and I know not how to repay him."

" Act as you have always done, Allan, and you will please not only man, but heaven also, for honesty is always the best policy, as you know, from the career of old Marks, Jerry, and others, who have been enemies to you through life."

" And now," said Sharp, after a pause, " I have something of importance to say, but you must not give way to any inordinate wonder or surprise."

" What is it ?" asked Allan.

" Edgar, your brother——"

" Yes, yes ! what of him, I beg ?"

" He lives !"

" What !"

" And is a great man, also," said Sharp, smiling.

" Where is he ?"

" On his way to England by this time, no doubt."

" But how did you gain all this startling news ?"

" From the Government offices."

" Indeed !"

" Yes, Edgar Norman, or young Lion Limb, as they call him in the South Sea Islands, has greatly distinguished himself, and Government have conferred honour and distinction upon him and his brave companions."

" And is there any one that I know with him ?"

" Yes, there is a youth named Ted Rawlings."

" I know him well," said Allan, with a flushed face.

" And there is Miss Emma Clarence, the daughter of the captain of the ' Rattlesnake.' "

" I saw her on board before she started on the voyage. Any one else ?"

" Yes, there is one gallant leader among them, who is called Harry Woodruff."

" I don't know him."

" Another called Dick Hamilton, who was for some time insane, but he is all right again."

" I don't know either of them. But how did you receive all this startling information. ?"

" Well, you see, when the ship which took out old Marks, Jerry, his son, Gentleman George, Mikey Huggins, and many other convicts, around all the islands on which your brother and others were cast ashore, they landed a young middy called Amador, who, with two sailors, were to travel some distance inland and return with all the information the young middy could gather about the young English colonists that were there.

" A storm arose, however, and drove the ship out to sea, and left Middy Armador and the two young sailors alone on the island.

" The middy was not long before he made many strange and startling discoveries, and found out that Lion Limb, your brother, was king of all the islands, and at that moment, assisted by old Governor Martin and his band, was making war against a desperate band of buccaneers under Mungo, their chief.

" For a long time your brother waged this war against Mungo and his villains, as also, and at the same time, against the rebellious kings and princes of the island.

" When least expected, however, Amador's ship hove in sight again, but in another part of the island, and just at the moment when your brother had concluded his war, and subjugated the buccaneers and fierce native tribes.

" The ship anchored, and when Lion Limb had visited it and concluded a long and interesting interview, the captain and crew saluted him with cheers and the booming of cannon ; for on each and all of the islands young Lion Limb had planted the British flag, and claimed them for the English crown."

" Your words seem to me like some pleasant and startling dream," sighed Allan.

" Your brother is now immensely wealthy," continued Sharp, " for he has sent over to England a very large quantity of gold dust and quartz, besides a collection of diamonds, pearls, and precious stones, worth an immense sum. Besides these things, he has also brought with him much ivory, precious stuffs, and spices, which altogether are worth tens of thousands."

" But when, then, will my brother return ?" remarked Allan, impatiently.

" That is not yet known, for certain," said Sharp, smiling. " He has much to do on the island before he can leave there, for he is governor now under the crown."

" What a strange meeting it must have been between all his enemies on that foreign shore."

" Yes," said Sharp, " I have seen an officer who was present when the convicts landed, and paraded on the shore before your brother. He says that Jerry Marks looked as pale as a sheet, and trembled like a leaf."

" And his father, old Marks ?"

" He and his son attempted to poison the officers and crew on their voyage out, but the discovery was made in time by Dr. Killum. Both father and son were tried for that crime on board, and received three dozen lashes."

" They will live villains to the very last," sighed Allan, " they seem to delight in iniquity of all kinds."

" Yes, truly ; but their rascality did not end well—the attempt to poison. They endeavoured to foment mutiny among the crew, but this also was discovered, and some of the convicts who assisted the captain and crew have been granted a pardon, and will shortly return to England again as ticket of leave men. Marks and his son were again most severely punished for their crimes, and have been condemned to heavy irons ever since, and sentenced to penal servitude for life, without the slightest prospect before them except an existence of misery and hard labour."

" But did not Emma Clarence, the captain's daughter, return in the ship that has just arrived ?"

" Well—no," said Sharp, smiling.

" Why not ?"

" You would not have her leave her husband, would you ?"

" Is she married, then ?"

" Yes."

" To whom ?"

" To your brother Edgar."

" Impossible !"

" Not at all ; and besides that, Edgar inherits all the property left by Captain Clarence, and so he is doubly a rich man, you see, and is possessed of immense wealth."

" Jem Rawlings will almost go mad when he hears that his brother Ted is still alive."

" Oh, he knows all about it already."

"Indeed! How so?"

"*I* told him. I met him in London yesterday, swelling about and living on the money you kindly allow him, and when he was informed of all that I have spoken of to you the young fellow wept for joy."

"But is he not in business then?"

"No, not yet; he says he is happy enough as he is, and if you will only 'stick to him,' as he calls it, he will be the 'jolliest fellow' in all the world."

"But there is another person who would be delighted to hear all you have said, Mr. Sharp," said Allan, very calmly.

"I know there is, but the news must not be broken to her yet."

"Why not?"

"She is in deep affliction."

"On what account, pray?"

"When you left France together his lordship was seized with a paralytic stroke, and should he be so afflicted again he must without a doubt lose his life."

"What a number of strange and startling things have come to pass within these last few days," said Allan, thoughtfully.

"True," replied Mr. Sharp, calmly, "but I hope and trust that no new trials are in store for you, Allan, or your brother, for truly I never knew or even heard of two youths who have had to buffet the world as you and your brother have been compelled to do; but, as I always told you, there was a Providence above us who would never desert the innocent or allow the guilty to triumph for long together."

"So you have always spoken, Mr. Sharp, and to you, next to Heaven, I owe all that I now possess; but yet I would give half of all which by fortune falls to me, could I but find out who the villain or villains were who really and truly murdered my first good friend in life, old Alderman English."

"I have not much doubt about that matter myself," said Sharp; "but yet I can't *prove* it."

"You think, then, as I do, perhaps?"

"Yes; if there is any one living who did that odious act, that one is——"

"Jerry Marks."

"Yes; I have no moral doubt about it; but I fear the villain will never acknowledge the deed until the hour of death."

"But now, Mr. Sharp, allow me to ask you one favour?"

"What is it?"

"You have, from the beginning, been a true friend to me, and I should wish to reward you in some substantial manner for all you have done."

"Don't name it, Allan," said Sharp, shaking his head.

"But I insist on it."

"I am sufficiently rewarded already, I can assure you."

"But you are poor."

"Not so much as you may suppose," said Sharp, smiling.

"I don't understand you."

"Well, the truth is, Allan, I am about to retire from the police force in a few weeks, and am promised a handsome pension as a reward for long and faithful services."

"I am exceedingly glad to hear it."

"Besides that income, I have received very large rewards at times for what I have done, and Lord and Lady Oxenford have not forgotten me, I can assure you, for they have settled £300 a year upon me for life."

"I never knew of that before; but it pleases me much to hear it."

"But what gives *me* the greatest satisfaction is, Allan, that during the whole time I have been engaged in your case and those of others, I have always endeavoured to make those around me happy, and have never attempted to use family secrets to the annoyance of others, or for my own personal gains. You understand me, Allan, I think?"

"I do," said Allan, nodding.

"There are certain secrets which, I think, ought to be buried with the dead," said Sharp, slowly and calmly.

"I understand to what you allude—the baron, I suppose?"

"I do."

"Let his secret lie undisturbed with his ashes, Allan; there are but three persons in the world who know it—myself, Lady Oxenford, and you."

Lady Julia had left the apartment a long time before, and while Allan and Sharp were there talking, a messenger arrived at the hall, post haste from London, with a letter for Allan.

"A letter for me!" said Allan, opening the missive; "who can it be from, I wonder?"

"I think I know the writing," said Sharp, smiling. "Allow me to open it, your hand shakes so much."

"Do so," said Allan, colouring to the temples and looking much excited.

"This letter is from your brother, Allan."

"What, from Edgar!"

"Yes."

"When will he return to England?"

"He is in England already," said Sharp, smiling.

"But you said that——"

"I know I did; but that was to prepare your mind by degrees, for the whole truth. In fact, I knew he was in England, and it was by his desire I came down here."

"Read the letter," said Allan, hastily, "I am all impatience to hear the wonderful news."

"I will. All attention," said Sharp, as he began to read the letter, which ran thus:—

"Clarendon Hotel, London.

"DEAR BROTHER,—By the time this letter reaches you, Mr. Sharp will have informed you of much that has taken place since I left England.

"I thought at first of seeking you myself, but after two days spent in making enquiries, I found out that fortune had smiled upon you, and that you had run away with a beautiful girl from Paris. Accident threw me in the way of Mr. Sharp, who, it appears, had already traced you to Holly Hall, and from him I learned all that you had suffered since last we met; and to him, on the other hand, I related all the adventures which myself and companions had gone through on the islands of the South Pacific.

"It was my intention of remaining on these islands for some longer time, but the Government, in recognition of my services, conferred rank and honours upon me, and desired my presence in England at once; so therefore, after the newly-arrived convicts had been cared for, and a host of buccaneers had been shipped for trial, we set sail, and had a safe and prosperous voyage homewards to Old England once more.

"Of course you knew that old Marks and Jerry were among the convicts, and for what they were sent out; but a most singular affair took place just at the moment I was going on board. One of the newly-arrived convicts was reported to be dying from the effects of poison, and wished to see me.

"It was Jerry Marks.

"He had taken a deadly draught, and was in great agony. He was too weak to speak much, but put a note into my hand.

"This note I read before several witnesses.

"It was a full and true confession of his having murdered the old Alderman, and of his attempting to swear our lives away.

"I will leave this painful subject, and speak of one more cheering.

"Young Ted Rawlings has returned with me. Harry Woodruff and Dick Hamilton, two of my officers, also, but as yet you do not know them; neither, perhaps, have you ever heard of Mr. Joe Pebbles, who plays the violin like Paganini; but, in due time, I will introduce them and others to you.

"I am married, as you have, perhaps, been already informed, to Emma Clarence; and all I can say is, that she is, what she has always been to me, a guardian angel.

"We have brought home much gold dust and other precious things.

"Among our passengers are several petty kings and chiefs of the numerous islands which I have conquered and claimed for the British crown. They come to bow their knee before our throne, and a fine lot of fellows they are in their gold tissue trappings, paints and feathers. They will be all the rage in London, no doubt, for a few months to come, and as they seem particularly attached to young Midshipman Amador, no doubt he will escort them about everywhere and anywhere.

"Besides these princely people, we have brought over, as I said before, certain fierce buccaneers, who have, for many years, been ravaging the South Seas. As they have been guilty of great enormities and atrocities, their trial will be short and their punishment great.

"The chiefs of these rascals are Mungo, an African half-breed (as they call him), and Bill Whetherby, one of the crew that mutinied against Captain Clarence.

"We have besides several among us whom I have liberated on ticket of leave, and I hope when they arrive in England that they will take good advantage of their tickets and become reformed men, although I much doubt whether some of them will or not, for even among convicts there are good and bad classes. Should these ticket of leave men, however, change their names when they land, which in nine cases out of ten they do, the police will not be long in looking after them and ferreting out the various pranks and games they may be up to.

"I shall watch the progress of two or three (whose names I will not now disclose) with great curiosity, for special reasons I cannot and will not explain.

"Dear Brother, you must excuse this hurried letter; but, believe me, directly I finish my business with the Government I will run down to see you.

"Before I close, however, I must tell you an important piece of news!

"I have just heard that your great friend, Lord Oxenford, is dead.

"He died suddenly last night on his way from France.

"You may rely on this news being correct, for I had it from the lips of Lady Oxenford, whom, through Mr. Sharp's exertions, I find is no other than our mother!

"What a startling discovery was this for me!

"What a sweet lady she is, and how she kissed and embraced me!

"I cannot say more, Brother, my heart is too full for utterance.

"Health, wealth, fame and fortune are ours after long years of struggling, and, before all men, we stand innocent of that crime for which we have been so long condemned.

"Vice and virtue have met with their due reward, and so may it always be is the hope of

"Your Brother,
"EDGAR."

CHAPTER THE LAST.

A PARTING WORD.

THOSE who have followed our heroes through their eventful history—who have seen them rise from poverty to opulence, and watched them through their many startling adventures both with friend and foe—will, no doubt, rejoice with us to see so signal an example of virtue and worth triumphing over vice and worthliness.

From the beginning they have closely followed the careers of the brothers Allan and Edgar Norman, and their almost foster-brethren Ted and Jem Rawlings, at home and abroad, and now that this eventful and veritable history is drawing to a close, there remains but little more to relate.

After the inquest upon the body of Baron Templeton, Allan, and his beautiful young bride, continued to reside at Holly Hall, where they were frequently visited by the noblest in surrounding counties, who had heard of the strange pranks which fortune once played upon the handsome owner, and were delighted to do him all possible honour.

From all directions came congratulations and best wishes; for when the name of Lion Limb was mentioned, surrounded as that name now was with all possible honour, Allan and his fair bride were inundated with visitors, both great and small, to hear from his own mouth some additional particulars of the startling adventures which the Boy King of the South Sea Islands had undergone.

This Allan found himself unable to do; but in less than a month after his arrival in England, Lion Limb himself visited Holly Hall, and after great festivities and rejoicings, he placed upon paper a sketch of his career, which we have already used in the fifty-two numbers comprising this wonderful tale.

It is needless to say here that the conversations of so great a traveller were listened to with rapt attention, for that may be most readily believed; but many of his friends were at first inclined to turn an incredulous ear to his vivid descriptions, had he not been corroborated in his statements by many of his followers, who were also temporarily domiciled at Holly Hall.

The final proof of the truth of Lion Limb's history was given by the buccaneers themselves, upon their trial for murders on the high seas, and the confessions of Mungo and Bill Whetherby, before their execution, filled the public mind at once with wonder and horror—horror at the unblushing statements of the buccaneers, and wonder that a band of youths, such as the young colonists were, should have been able to accomplish so much for society and civilization.

THE BOY KING

OF THE SOUTH SEA ISLANDS.

JULIA RELATING HER HISTORY TO ALLAN NORMAN.

The bones of Mungo and Bill Whetherby, with many of their gang, are now but so much dust, buried deep in prison graves; but it is but right to state now that the Government were not slow to lavish wealth and honour upon all who, like young Lion Limb, had held high, through weal, through woe, the honour and dignity of his native land.

Governor Martin, though very old and grey, refused to stay long in England.

He loved his old island home so well; its associations, climate, and other endearing ties, had such a firm hold on him, that he was anxious to return to the far-off Pacific, and as Lion Limb had no intention of journeying again abroad for a few years, at least, old Martin was installed Governor-General of all these islands, which our young hero, as we have already seen, so nobly conquered, and, for the most part, civilized.

Among the most lively guests at Holly Hall, we would name young Ted Rawlings and his brother, Jem, who, with Joe Pebbles, and his indispensible fiddle, made more noisy merriment than any half dozen persons there assembled, for they were singing all the day long.